Books by Barbara Delinsky

Looking for Peyton Place
The Summer I Dared
Flirting with Pete
An Accidental Woman
The Woman Next Door
The Vineyard
Lake News
Coast Road
Three Wishes
A Woman's Place
Shades of Grace
Together Alone
For My Daughters
Suddenly
More Than Friends
The Passions of Chelsea Kane
A Woman Betrayed

BARBARA DELINSKY

COAST ROAD
THREE WISHES

POCKET BOOKS
New York   London   Toronto   Sydney

POCKET BOOKS, a division of Simon & Schuster, Inc.
1230 Avenue of the Americas, New York, NY 10020

ISBN: 1-4165-0745-0

First Pocket Books trade paperback edition January 2005

10 9 8 7 6 5 4 3

POCKET and colophon are registered trademarks of
Simon & Schuster, Inc.

Manufactured in the United States of America

For information regarding special discounts for bulk purchases,
please contact Simon & Schuster Special Sales at 1-800-456-6798
or business@simonandschuster.com

These titles were previously published individually by Simon & Schuster, Inc.

COAST ROAD

acknowledgments

Coast Road was born of three things I admire—the Big Sur coast, people with artistic ability, and men who rise to the occasion. My own instinct as a woman, plus an annual trip to Big Sur, helped with research into those things, but there were other elements of the book that required outside expertise.

I wish to thank Nancy Weinberg, nurse-educator of the Critical Care Unit at the Newton Wellesley Hospital, for the generous sharing of her time, knowledge, and imagination. Likewise, and not for the first time, my thanks to Margot Chamberlin for advice on the nuts and bolts of being an architect. For their help framing Rachel's pieces, I thank Renata, Rob, Chris, and Steve, of the Renjeau Gallery. For her assistance, her ear, and great color, I thank Barbie Goldberg.

As with any large project, some things inevitably hit the cutting-room floor. Although none of the 1950s trivia that Elaine Raco Chase sent made it into this book, I am grateful for her tireless efforts. Nor did anything of Pukaskwa make it into *Coast Road*, despite the generous contributions of Margaret Carney, writer, naturalist, and *acknowledgments*

friend; and Bob Reside, Park Warden, Pukaskwa National Park. I was deeply impressed with the beauty and isolation of Ontario, north of Lake Superior, and imagine that it will appear in a future book.

My book group. Ah, my book group. How long have I talked about writing its story? The full focus that I had initially intended went the way of 1950s trivia and Ontario, but what remains is true. No, no, guys. Don't look for yourselves in any of my characters. I promised I wouldn't, and I didn't. I do believe, though, that you will identify with the deeper meaning of the group, as do I.

Again and still, I thank my agent, Amy Berkower, who has worked nearly as hard on this book as I have. I am also grateful to her partner, Al Zuckerman, for his gracious input, and her assistant, Jodi Reamer, for being there every single time I call. I thank my editor, Laurie Bernstein, for making me one of the pins she juggles.

As always, for their enthusiasm, support, and patience, I thank my family—my husband, Steve; my son and daughter-in-law, Eric and Jodi; and the twins, Andrew and Jeremy. Those twinges Jack feels when he thinks of family? Autobiographical all the way!

prologue

WHEN THE PHONE rang, Rachel Keats was painting sea otters. She was working in oils and had finally gotten the right mix of black for the eyes. There was no way she was stopping to pick up the phone. She had warned Samantha about that.

"Hi! You've reached Rachel, Samantha, and Hope. We're otherwise occupied. Please leave your name and number, and we'll call you back. Thanks."

Through a series of beeps, she applied a smudge of oil with a round brush. Then came a deep male voice that was too old to be calling for Samantha. Rachel would have pictured a gorgeous guy to go with the voice, but he'd said his name too fast. This man wasn't gorgeous. He was a ticket agent, a friend of a friend, more sleaze than style, but apparently good at his job. "I have in my hand three tickets for tonight's Garth Brooks concert," he said. "San Jose. Gooooood seats. I need to hear from you in five minutes or I'm moving down my list—" Rachel made a lunging grab for the phone. "I want them!"

"Heeeey, Rachel. How's my favorite artist?"

"Painting. You need a credit card number, right? Hold on a second." She put the phone down, ran through the house to the kitchen, and snatched up her wallet. She was breathless reading off the number, breathless returning to the studio. She swallowed hard, looked at the canvas on the easel and six others nearby waiting to be finished, thought of everything else she had to do in the next three weeks, and decided that she was crazy. She didn't have time to go to a concert.

But the girls would be absolutely, positively *blown away!*

She threw the window open and leaned out into clear, woodsy air.

"Samantha! Hope!" They were out there somewhere. She yelled again.

Answering yells came from a distance, then closer.

"Hurry!" she yelled back.

Minutes later, they came running through the woods, Samantha looking every bit as young as Hope for once, both with blond hair flying and cheeks pink. Rachel shouted the news to them even before they reached her window. The look on their faces was more than worth the prospect of an all-nighter or two.

"Are you serious?" Hope asked. Her eyes were wide, her freckles vibrant, her smile filled with teeth that were still too large for her face. She was thirteen and entirely prepubescent.

Rachel grinned and nodded.

"Awesome!" breathed Samantha. At fifteen she was a head taller than Hope and gently curved. Blond hair and all, she was Rachel at that age.

"Tonight?" Hope asked.

"Tonight."

"Good seats?" Samantha asked.

"Great seats."

Hope pressed her hands together in excitement. "Are we doing the whole thing—you know, what we talked about?"

Rachel didn't have the time for it. She didn't have the money. But if her paintings were a hit, the money would come, and as for time, life was too short. "The whole thing," she said, because it would be good for Samantha to get away from the phone and Hope to get away from her cat and, yes, maybe even good for Rachel to get away from her oils.

"Omigod, I have to call Lydia!" Samantha cried.

"What you have to do," Rachel corrected her, "is anything that needs to be done for school. We leave in an hour." She was *definitely* crazy. Forget *her* work. The girls had tons of their own, but . . . but this was *Garth.*

She returned to her studio for the hour and accomplished as little as she feared her daughters had. Then they piled into her sport utility vehicle and headed north. Having done her research during the someday-we-will stage, she knew just where to go. The store she wanted was on the way to San Jose. It was still open when they got there, and had a perfect selection. Thirty minutes and an obscene amount of money later, they emerged wearing cowboy boots under their jeans, cowboy hats over their hair, and smiles the size of Texas.

Thirty minutes after that, with the smell of McDonald's burgers and fries filling the car, they were flying high toward San Jose.

Nothing they saw when they got there brought them down. There were crowds and crowds of fans, light shows and smoke, sets that rose from nowhere to produce the man himself, who sang hit after hit without a break, longer-than-ever versions of each, and how could Rachel not be into it, with Hope and Samantha dancing beside her? If she was conservative through the first song or two, any self-consciousness was gone by the third. She was on her feet dancing, clapping high, singing. She cheered with Samantha and Hope when familiar chords announced a favorite song, and shouted appreciatively with them at song's end. The three of them sang their hearts out until the very last encore was done, and then left the arena arm in arm, three friends who just happened to be related.

It was a special evening. Rachel didn't regret a minute of it, not even when Samantha said, "Did you see that girl right in front of us? The tall one with the French braid? Did you see the tattoo on her arm? The rose? If I wanted something like that, what would you say?"

"No," Rachel said as she drove south through the dark.

"Even a tiny one? A little star on my ankle?"

"No."

"But it's *way cool.*"

"No."

"Why *not?*"

"Because she was older than you. When you're twenty-five—"

"She wasn't that old."

"Okay, when you're twenty-two, you can think about a tattoo. Not now."

"It has nothing to do with age. It has to do with style."

"Uh-huh," said Rachel, confident on this one, "a style that makes a statement that you may not want to make at twenty-two, if you set your heart on a particular person or thing that doesn't appreciate that kind of statement."

"Since when are you worried about conformity?"

"Since my fifteen-year-old daughter is heading straight for the real world."

"Tattoos are hot. All the kids have them."

"Not Lydia. Not Shelly. Not the ones I see getting off the school bus."

Samantha crossed her arms and sank lower in her seat, glowering for sure under the brim of her hat. Hope was curled up in the back, sound asleep. Her hat had fallen to the side.

Rachel put in a CD and drove through the dark humming along with the songs they had heard that night. She loved her hat, loved her boots, loved her girls. If she had to fall behind in her work, it was for a good cause.

She wasn't as convinced of it the next morning, when the girls woke up late and cranky. They picked at breakfast on the run and even then nearly missed the bus. Rachel was wildly relieved when they made it, and wildly apprehensive when, moments later, she stood in her studio and mentally outlined the next three weeks.

She worked feverishly through the day, breaking only to meet the girls at the bus stop and have a snack with them, her lunch. Samantha was still on her tattoo kick, so they reran the argument, verbatim at times, before the girl went off to her room in a huff. Hope hung around longer, holding her cat. Finally she, too, disappeared.

Rachel spent another hour in the studio. Half convinced that the otters were done, she stopped and put dinner in the oven. When she returned to the studio, it was to fill another sort of need. But the otters caught her eye again. She gave herself another hour.

Now that the hour was gone, things were flowing. It was always the way.

One minute more, she told herself for the umpteenth time. With alternating glances at field sketch and photograph, she used the fine edge of her palette knife to add texture to the oil on her canvas. The sea otters were playing in kelp. Her challenge was capturing the wetness of their fur. She had started with raw umber and cobalt blue, and had found it too dark. Using raw umber with ultramarine blue was perfect.

"The buzzer rang, Mom," Hope called from the door.

"Thanks, honey," Rachel murmured, adding several last strokes. "Will you take the casserole out and turn off the gas?"

"I already did." Hope was at her side now, studying the canvas. "I thought you were done."

"Something wasn't right." She stood back for a longer view and was satisfied. "Better." Still eyeing the canvas, she set her palette aside, reached for a solvent cloth, and wiped her hands. "I'll clean up and be right there." She looked at Hope. "Did Samantha set the table?"

"I did."

"She's on the phone again?"

"Still," Hope said so dryly that Rachel had to chuckle.

She hooked her baby's neck with an elbow and gave a squeeze. "Five minutes," she said and sent her off.

As promised, five minutes later Rachel was in the

kitchen doling out lasagna and salad. Twenty minutes after that, digesting her meal along with a blow-by-blow of the late-breaking news that Samantha had received from her friends, Rachel gave out cleanup assignments. Fifteen minutes after that, having showered herself free of paint smells and put on fresh clothes, she ran a brush through her hair. Then she paused and looked wildly around for the book she had read the weekend before.

She searched the chaos of her bedroom without success. Thinking she might have already set it out, she returned to the kitchen and looked around. "Is my book in here?"

The girls were doing the dishes, Samantha washing, Hope drying. "I'd look," Samantha said with little grace, "but you told me not to do anything until these were done."

Rachel shifted a pile of mail, mostly clothing catalogues addressed to the self-same woman-child. "I was referring to the telephone," she said, checking in and around cookbooks. She doubled over to search the seats of the chairs pushed in at the table. "I remember having it in my hand," she murmured to herself when that search, too, proved fruitless.

"You're not organized," Samantha charged. Rachel regularly preached the merits of organization.

"Oh, I am," she mused, but distractedly. She went into the living room and began searching there. "I just have a lot on my plate right now."

That was putting it mildly. With her show three weeks away and closing in fast, she was feeling the crunch. Okay. She had finally hit gold with the sea otters. But there was still the background to do for that one and six

7

others, and eighteen in all to frame—which would have been fine if she had nothing but work to do in the next three weeks. But there was a dress to buy with Samantha for her first prom, an end-of-the-year picnic to run for Hope's seventh-grade class, dentist's and doctor's appointments for both girls, a birthday party to throw for Ben Wolfe, who owned the art gallery and was a some-time date, and a share-your-career day to spend with three fifth-graders she didn't know.

She had splurged last night. She shouldn't be going anywhere tonight.

But last night had been for the girls and their mother. Book club was just for her. She loved the women, loved the books. Even if it added pressure to an already hectic work schedule, she wasn't missing a meeting.

Hope materialized at her shoulder. "I think it's in your studio."

Closing her eyes, Rachel conjured up the studio, which lay at a far end of her rambling house. She had left it for the day, then returned for an unexpected little while. And before returning? Yes, she'd had the book in her hand. She had carried it there and set it down.

"Thanks, sweetheart." She cupped Hope's chin. "Are you okay?"

The child looked forlorn.

"Guinevere will be fine," Rachel said softly. "She ate, didn't she?"

Hope nodded.

"See there? That's a good sign." She kissed Hope's forehead. "I'd better get the book. I'm running late."

"Want me to get it?" Hope asked.

But Rachel remembered what she had been drawing

before the otters had recaptured her eye. She wanted to make sure that that drawing was put safely away.

"Thanks, sweetheart, but I'll do it." When Hope looked reluctant to let her go, she begged, "Help Sam. Please," and set off.

The book was where she had left it, on a corner of the large worktable. Hope had arrived while she was at the easel. The drawing—a charcoal sketch—still lay on the desk by the window.

Rachel lifted it now and carefully slipped it into a slim portfolio. As she did, her mind's eye re-created the image her sliver of charcoal had made, that of a man sprawled in a tangle of sheets. Even handling the heavy paper, she felt his trim hips, the slope of his spine, and widening above it, dorsal muscle, triceps, deltoid. Had it not been for the hair, it might have been an innocent exercise in drawing the human form. The hair, though, was dark and just a little too long on the neck. The identity was unmistakable; this figure had a name. Better the girls shouldn't see.

Taking care to tuck that last portfolio behind the desk, she retrieved the book and hurried back through the house. She gave the girls quick kisses, promised to be home by eleven, and went out to her car.

chapter one

WHEN JACK MCGILL'S phone rang at two in the morning, the sound cut sharply into the muted world of a soupy San Francisco night. He had been lying in bed since twelve, unable to sleep. His mind was too filled, too troubled. The sudden sound jolted already jittery nerves.

In the time that it took him to grab for the phone, a dozen jarring thoughts came and went. "Yes?"

"Is this Jack McGill?" asked a voice he didn't know. It was female and strained.

"Yes."

"I'm Katherine Evans, one of Rachel's friends. There's been an accident. She's at the hospital in Monterey. I think you should come."

Jack sat up. "What kind of accident?"

"Her car was hit and went off the road."

His stomach knotted. "What road? Were the girls with her?"

"Highway One, and, no, she was alone." Relief. The girls were safe, at least. "She was near Rocky Point, on her way to Carmel. A car rammed her from behind. The impact pushed her across the road and over the side."

His feet hit the floor. The knot in his stomach tightened.

"She's alive," the friend went on. "Only a few broken bones, but she hasn't woken up. The doctors are worried about her brain."

"Worried how?"

"Bruising, swelling."

He pushed a hand through his hair. The disquieting thoughts about work that had kept him awake were gone, replaced by a whole different swarm. "The girls—"

"—are still home. Rachel was on her way to book group. When nine o'clock came and she hadn't shown up, I called the house. Samantha said she'd left at seven, so I called the state police. They told me there'd been an accident, and ID'd her car. They were still trying to get her out of it at that point and didn't know how she was, so I called her neighbor, Duncan Bligh. He went down to sit with the girls. I called them a little while ago to say she's okay, but I didn't tell them about the head injury, and I didn't know whether to tell Duncan to drive them up here to the hospital. That's not my decision to make."

No. It was Jack's. Divorce or no divorce, he was the girls' father. Clamping the phone between shoulder and jaw, he reached for his jeans. "I'm on my way. I'll call Samantha and Hope from the car."

"Rachel's in Emergency now. Check in there."

"Right. Thanks." He hung up realizing that he couldn't remember her name, this friend of Rachel's, but it was the least of his worries, the very least. "Unbelievable," he muttered as he zipped his jeans and reached for a shirt. Things were bad at the office and bad in the field. He was living an architect's nightmare, needed in both places come morning, and then there was Jill. Tonight was the charity dinner that she had been working on for so long. He had deliberately planned business trips around this date, knowing how much it meant to her. His tux was pressed and waiting. She was expecting him at five. Five—and he hadn't slept a wink. And he was heading south to God only knew what, for God only knew how long.

But Rachel was hurt. *You're not married to her anymore,* his alter ego said, but he didn't miss a beat stuffing his shirt into his jeans and his feet into loafers. *You don't owe her a thing, man. She was the one who walked out.*

But she was hurt, and he had been called, and depending on what he found in Monterey, there would be arrangements to make for the girls. They would have to be told how she was, for starters. They were too old to be sent to bed with empty reassurances, too young to face this possible nightmare alone. Rachel was their caretaker, companion, confidant. The three were thick as thieves.

The doctors are worried about her brain, the friend had said. Well, of course, they would worry until things checked out.

He tossed cold water on his face and brushed his teeth. Minutes later he entered his studio—and in a moment's dismay wondered why he still called it that. It had become more a place of business than of art. What few drawings he had done were buried under proposals, spec sheets, contracts, and correspondence—the refuse of an insane number of construction projects in various stages. The place reeked of pressure.

Using the slate gray of dawn that filtered through the

skylights, he crammed his briefcase with his laptop and as many vital papers as would fit, and his portfolio with multiple versions of the Montana design. Tucking both under an arm, he strode down the darkened hall to the kitchen. He didn't need a light. The place was stream-lined and minimal. Grabbing his keys from the granite island and a blazer from the coat tree by the door, he set the alarm and went down to the garage below. Within minutes, he was backing out the BMW and speeding down Filbert. His headlights cut a pale gray swath in the smoky night, lighting little of Russian Hill. Other than the occasional street corner lump that could as easily be a homeless person sleeping as trash waiting for pickup, San Francisco was one big foggy cocoon.

Pressing numbers by feel on his car phone, he called information. He was heading south on Van Ness by the time he got through to the hospital in Monterey. "This is Jack McGill. My wife, Rachel Keats, was brought in a little while ago. I'm on my way there. Can you give me an update?"

"Hold on, please." Several nerve-wracking minutes later, he connected with a nurse in the emergency room. "Mr. McGill? She's in surgery. That's about all we know at this point."

"Is she conscious?"

"She wasn't when they took her upstairs."

The doctors are worried about her brain. "What's the surgery for?"

"Would you hold on a minute?"

"I'd rather not—" The sudden silence at the other end said he had no choice. He'd had no choice when Rachel had moved out six years ago, either. She had said she was going, had packed up the girls and their belongings while he was away on business. He had come home to an echoing house, feeling as thwarted and helpless then as he felt now. Then, armored in anger, he had sold the house and moved to one that didn't echo. But now, there was no such out. Her face came to him with every shift of the fog, an urban Rorschach in which her features were beautiful one minute, bruised the next. His nervous heart was beating up a storm.

He pushed the car faster.

"Mr. McGill?" came a male voice, choppy over the speaker but audible. "I'm Dr. Couley. I treated your wife when she arrived."

"What's the surgery for?" he shouted, gripping the steering wheel.

"To set her left leg. Compound fractures, both femur and tibia. They'll be inserting pins—"

"I was told there were head injuries," he cut in. A person didn't die from a broken leg. "Has she regained consciousness?"

"No. There's some cranial swelling. We don't yet know what direction it'll take."

"I want a specialist called."

"Our man is on his way. When will you be here?"

"I'm just leaving San Francisco."

"Two hours, then?"

"Less," Jack said and, slowing but barely, sailed through a red light. "Here's my cell number." He rattled it off. "Call me if there's any change, will you?" When the doctor agreed, Jack punched out another set of numbers. He wasn't as quick to press *send* this time, though. He didn't know what to say to the girls. They weren't babies anymore. And teenagers today were a different breed from the ones he had known. Add the fact that he no longer lived with them, and that they were *girls,* and he was at a *triple* disadvantage.

But this time he couldn't pass the buck. There was no one else to take it.

Katherine. That was the friend's name. Katherine.

Rachel had never mentioned her, but then, Rachel never mentioned anything that didn't deal directly with the girls. The girls had spoken of her, though. He thought he remembered that.

They definitely had mentioned Duncan Bligh, and more than once. He was the rancher who shared Rachel's canyon. The sloping meadow where his herd grazed lay above her redwood forest. Both meadow and forest were part of the Santa Lucias, rising east of the Big Sur coast.

Jack had a bad feeling about Duncan. He didn't like the affectionate way the girls described his cabin, his beard, or his sheep. He didn't like the way they grinned when he asked if Rachel was dating him. Oh sure, he knew they were trying to make him jealous. The problem was that he could see Rachel with a man like that. Mountain men had a kind of rugged appeal. Not that Jack was a slouch. He was tall. He was fit. He could hammer a nail with the best of the carpenters who built what he designed, but he didn't chop down the trees from which the two-by-fours came, and he didn't shear sheep or shoot deer.

Did he want to talk to Duncan Bligh in the middle of the night? No. Nor, though, could he let his daughters think that the rancher was the only man around.

He pressed *send.*

The first ring was barely done when there came a fast and furious "Hello?"

He lifted the phone. "Hi, Sam. It's Dad. Are you guys okay?"

"How's Mom?"

"She's okay." He kept his voice light. "I'm on my way to the hospital. I just talked with the doctor. They've taken her into surgery. It sounds like she smashed up her leg pretty good."

"Katherine said it was her ribs, too."

"It may be, but the leg is the thing that needs setting. Refresh my memory, Sam. Who is Katherine?"

"Mom's best friend," Samantha said impatiently. "I gave her your number."

"You could have called me yourself."

She grew defensive. "I didn't know if you were around, and if you weren't, you'd have had to book a flight and wait at the airport, and then if you missed a connection, you'd have taken forever to get here. Besides, Katherine says Mom has good doctors, so what can *you* do?"

"I can *be* there," he said, but the words were no sooner out than he imagined her retort. So he added a fast "Let's not argue, Samantha. This isn't the time."

"Are you telling me the truth? Is Mom really okay?"

"That's the truth as I heard it. Is your sister sleeping?"

"She was until the phone rang. We knew it had to be about Mom. *My* friends wouldn't call in the middle of the night," she said with such vehemence that Jack suspected they had done it more than once. "Dad, we want to go to the hospital, but Duncan won't take us."

"Is he there now?"

"He's asleep on the chair. Asleep at a time like this. Can you *believe* it? Wait, I'll put him on. Tell him to drive us up." She shouted away from the phone, and even then it hurt Jack's ears, "Duncan! Pick up the phone! It's my father!"

"*Samantha!*" Jack called to get her back.

Her reply was muffled. "No, Mom is *not* dead, but that cat will be if you don't let her go. You're holding her too tight, Hope. You'll *hurt* her." She returned to Jack. "Here. Hope wants to talk."

"Daddy?" The voice was a fragile wisp.

Jack's heart shifted. "Hi, Hope. How're you doin', sweetie?"

"Scared."

"I figured that, but your mom's doing fine right now. I'm on my way to the hospital. I'll know more when I get there."

"Come *here,*" begged the small voice.

"I will," he said, melting at the idea that at least one of his girls needed him. "But the hospital's on the way, so I'll stop there first. Then I'll have more to report when I see you."

"Tell Mom—" She stopped.

"What, sweetie?"

Samantha came on. "She's crying again. Here's Duncan."

"Duncan Bligh here." The voice was curt. "What's the word?"

Jack wanted Hope back. But it wasn't his night. "The word is that I don't know much. I'll be at the hospital within the hour. Don't drive them up."

"I wasn't about to."

There was a muted protest in the background, then an aggrieved Samantha returned. "Daddy, it's *sick* sitting around here while she's there."

"It's the middle of the night."

"Like we can *sleep* with her there? She's our *mother*. What if she *asks* for us?"

"She's in surgery, Samantha. Even if you were at the hospital, you wouldn't be able to see her. Look, if you want to do something, help your sister. She sounds upset."

"And I'm not?"

Jack could hear the tight panic that was taking her voice a step beyond brash. But Samantha wasn't Hope. Two years apart in age, they were light-years apart in personality. Samantha was fifteen going on thirty, a little know-it-all who didn't take kindly to being treated like a child. Thirteen-year-old Hope was sensitive and silent. Samantha would ask the questions. Hope would see every nuance of the answers.

"I'm sure you're upset, too," he said, "but you're older than she is. Maybe if you help her, she'll help you. Give each other strength, y'know?"

"I keep thinking about Highway One, Dad. Some of those places, if you go over the side, you fall hundreds of feet straight down, right onto *rocks*. Was that what happened to Mom?"

"I don't know the details of the accident."

"She might have fallen into water, but that'd be nearly as bad. Like, what if she was stuck underwater in the car—"

"Sam, she didn't drown."

"You don't know that. You don't know whether the only thing that's keeping her alive is a bunch of machines."

"Samantha." She was nearly as creative as Rachel, without the maturity to channel it. "Your mother has a broken leg."

"But you don't know what *else*," she cried. "Call the troopers. They'll tell you what happened."

"Maybe later. The doctor has my cell number. I want to leave the line open in case he tries to call. And I want you to go to bed. It doesn't do anyone any good if you start imagining what *might* have happened. Imagination's always worse. So calm down. I'm in control of things here. And don't sit up waiting for the phone to ring, because I'm not calling you again until after the sun comes up."

"I'm not going to school."

"We'll discuss that later. Right now, the one thing you can do to help your mother most is to reassure your sister. And get some sleep. Both of you."

"Yeah, right," she muttered.

JACK CONCENTRATED on driving. The fog had stayed in the city, leaving the highway dark and straight. He pressed his middle in the hope that the warmth of his hand would ease the knot there, but his palm was cold and the knot stayed tight. Nerves did that to him every time. Lately, it seemed the knot was there more often than not.

He willed the phone to ring with the news that Rachel had awoken from surgery and was just fine. But the phone remained still, the interior of the car silent save the drone of the engine. He tried to distract himself with thoughts of all he had been agonizing over in bed less than two hours before—contract disputes, building delays, personnel losses—but he couldn't connect with those problems. They were distant, back in the city fog.

He would have calls to make, come morning. There were meetings to reschedule.

Or if Rachel woke up, he might be back in the office by noon.

That was likely, the more he thought about it. Rachel was the strongest, healthiest woman he knew—strongest, healthiest, most independent and self-sufficient. She didn't need him. Never had. Six years ago, she had reached a fork in the road of her life and gone off in a different direction from him. Her choice. Her life. Fine.

So why was he heading south? Why was he postponing even one meeting to run to her bedside? She had left him. She had taken ten years of marriage and crumpled it up, like a sketch on yellow trace that was so far off the mark it was worthless.

Why *was* he heading south?

He was heading south because her friend had called him. And because it was his job as a father to help out with the girls. And because he was terrified that Rachel might die. His life with her had been better than anything before or since. He was heading south because he felt that he still owed her for that.

THE VERY FIRST time Jack had laid eyes on Rachel, he decided that she wasn't his type. Oh, he liked blond hair, and she had endless waves of that, but he usually went for model types. Rachel Keats didn't fit that bill. She looked too pure. No long eyelashes, no glossy mouth, no flagrant sexuality, just dozens of freckles scattered over a nose and cheeks that were vaguely sunburned, and eyes that were focused intently on the most boring professor Jack had ever heard.

The subject was rococo and neoclassic art. The professor, renowned in his field, was the man whose grant was paying for Jack's architectural degree. In exchange for that, Jack graded exams and papers and helped with research and correspondence to do with the textbook for which the grant had been given.

Jack was only marginally interested in rococo and neoclassic art and even less interested in moving from Manhattan to Tucson, but the slot had been the only one open that offered a full ride plus a stipend. Being penniless, Jack needed both.

The job wasn't taxing. The professor in question had been delivering the same lectures, from the same printed lesson plan, for twenty-plus years. Since Jack read the lectures beforehand, his presence in the lecture hall was more for the sake of fetching water or a forgotten book or paper for the professor than anything educational for himself. He sat far off to the professor's side, where he could be easily accessed. It was a perfect spot from which to view the fifty-some-odd students who attended a given class, out of three times that many enrolled in the course.

Rachel Keats attended every class, listened raptly, took notes. Jack told himself that his eye sought her out for the simple constancy of her presence. It didn't explain, though, why he noted that she went from class to lunch at the smallest campus café, where she sat alone, or that she drove an old red VW bug and put a sunshade on the dash that was surely hand-painted, since he had never in his life seen as large or vividly colored a *bug* sitting behind the wheel of a car as her sunscreen hilariously depicted.

She was an art major. She lived in an apartment complex not far from his. She was a loner by all accounts and, if the easygoing expression she wore meant anything, was content.

Not only wasn't she his type, but he was dating someone who was. Celeste was tall and leggy, loaded up top and sweet down below, asked precious few questions and made precious few demands, liked the sex enough that he could do what he wanted when he wanted in between. She cooked and cleaned his bathroom, but he hadn't been able to con her into doing his laundry. That was why he found himself in the laundromat on a Tuesday night when Rachel came through the door.

Those waves of blond hair were gathered up in a turquoise ribbon that clashed with her purple tank top, but her shorts and sandals were white and as fresh as the blush that stained those sun-stained cheeks when she saw him there.

In the extra-long heartbeat that she spent at the door, he could have sworn she was debating turning and leaving. Not wanting her to do that, he said, "Hey! How're you doing?"

She smiled. "Great." The blush remained. She sucked in her lips, raised her brows, and seeming self-conscious, hugged an overstuffed laundry bag as she looked down the row of washers for raised lids. "Ah," she said, spotting two side by side. She smiled at him again and headed toward them.

Jack's heart was pounding. He didn't know why. All she'd done was smile. There hadn't been anything remotely sexual in it. She wasn't his type *at all*. But he slid off the dryer he'd been sitting on, and following her, he leaned up against the machine that backed on one of those she had chosen.

"Rococo and neoclassic art?" he prompted. He didn't want her to think this was a blind pickup, because it wasn't a pickup at all. She *wasn't* his type. He assumed that was why she intrigued him. It was safe. No risk. Just an innocuous hello.

She acknowledged the connection with a simple "Uh-huh." She was blushing still, pushing dirty laundry from the mouth of her laundry bag into the mouth of the washer.

He watched her for a minute, then said, "Mine's in the dryer."

It was probably the dumbest line he'd ever handed a woman. But he couldn't tell her that she was pushing reds and whites together into her machine. He couldn't ask if the reds were shirts, bras, or briefs. He couldn't even look directly at those things, because she would have been mortified. Besides, he couldn't take his eyes from hers. They were hazel with gold flecks, and more gentle than any he had seen.

"You're Obermeyer's TA," she said as she filled the second machine with things that went way beyond red. Her current outfit was conservative by comparison. "Are you training to teach?"

"No. I'm in architecture."

She smiled. "Really?"

"Really," he said, smiling back. She really was a sweet thing, smiling like that. The sweetness remained even when she suddenly opened her mouth and looked around—left, right, down, back.

Jack returned to his own possessions and offered her his box of soap powder.

He was rewarded with another blush and a soft-murmured "Thanks." When she had both machines filled with soap, fed with quarters, and started, she asked, "What kind of things do you want to build?"

The question usually came from his parents and was filled with scorn. But Rachel Keats seemed genuinely interested.

"Homes, for starters," he said. "I come from a two-bit town, one little box after another. I used to pass those little boxes on the way to school and spend my class time doodling them into something finer. Those doodles didn't help my math grade much."

"No. I wouldn't think it." She shot a glance at the text that lay open on his dryer. "Is the book on home designs?"

"Not yet. Right now we're into arches. Do you know how many different kinds of arches there are? There are flat arches, round arches, triangular arches, pointed arches. There are hand arches, back arches, groin arches. There are depressed arches. There are diminished arches. There are horseshoe arches."

She was laughing, the sound as gentle as her eyes. "I don't think I want to know what some of those are." She paused for the briefest time, said almost shyly, "I was a doodler, too."

He liked the shyness. It made him feel safe. "Where?"

"Chicago, then Atlanta, then New York. My childhood was mobile. My dad takes old businesses and turns them around. We move when he sells. How about you?"

"Oregon. You won't have heard of the town. It doesn't make it onto maps. What did you doodle?"

"Oh, people, birds, animals, fish, anything that moves.

I like doing what a camera does, capturing an instant."

"Are you still doodling?" he asked in response to her use of the present tense.

She lifted a shoulder, shy, maybe modest. "I like to think it's more. I'm hoping to paint for a living."

"With or without a day job?" Jack asked. The average artist barely earned enough to eat. Unless Rachel was significantly better than average, she would have a tough time paying the bills.

She wrapped her arms around her middle. Quietly, almost sadly, she said, "I'm lucky. Those businesses keep selling. My mom heads one of them now. They think I'm crazy to be here doing this. Art isn't business. They want me back in the city wearing designer dresses with a designer handbag and imported boots." She took a fresh breath. "Do you have siblings?"

"Five brothers and a sister," he said, though it had nothing to do with anything. He rarely talked about family. The people he was with rarely asked.

Not only had Rachel asked, but those wonderful eyes of hers lit up with his answer. "Six? That's great. I don't have *any*."

"That's why you think it's great. There were seven of us born in ten years, living with two parents in a three-bedroom house. I was the lucky one. Summers, I got the porch."

"What are the others doing now? Are they all over the country? Are any of them out here?"

"They're back home. I'm the only one who made it out."

Her eyes grew. "Really? Why you? *How?*"

"Scholarship. Work-study. Desperation. I had to leave. I don't get along with my family."

"Why not?" she asked in such an innocent way that he actually answered.

"They're negative. Always criticizing to cover up for what they lack, but the only thing they really lack is ambition. My dad coulda done anything he wanted—he's a bright guy—only, he got stuck in a potato processing plant and never got out. My brothers are going to be just like him, different jobs, same wasted potential. I went to college, which makes what they're doing seem smaller. They'll never forgive me for that."

"I'm so sorry."

He smiled. "Not your fault."

"Then you don't go home much?"

"No. And you? Back to New York?"

She crinkled her nose. "I'm not a city person. When I'm there, I'm stuck doing all the things I hate."

"Don't you have friends there?"

"A few. We talk. I've never had to go around with a crowd. How about you? Got a roommate?"

"Not on your life. I had enough of those growing up to never want another one, at least not of the same sex. What's your favorite thing in Tucson?"

"The desert. What's yours?"

"The Santa Catalinas."

Again those eyes lit, gold more than hazel. "Do you hike?" When he nodded, she said, "Me, too. When do you have time? Are you taking a full course load? How many hours a week do you have to give to Obermeyer?"

Jack answered her questions and asked more of his own. When she answered those without seeming to mind, he asked more again, and she asked her share right back. She wasn't judgmental, just curious. She seemed as interested in where he'd been, what he'd done, what he liked and didn't like as he was in her answers. They talked nonstop until Rachel's clothes were clean, dry, and folded. When, arms loaded, they finally left the laundromat, he knew three times as much about her as he knew about Celeste.

Taking that as a message of some sort, he broke up with Celeste the next day, called Rachel, and met her for pizza. They picked right up where they had left off at the laundromat.

Jack was fascinated. He had never been a talker. He didn't like baring his thoughts and ideas, held them close to the vest, but there was something about Rachel that felt . . . safe, there it was again. She was gentle. She was interested. She was smart. Being as much of a loner as he was, she seemed just as startled as he to be opening up to a virtual stranger, but they gave each other permission. He trusted her instinctively. She seemed to trust him the same way right back.

As simply as that, they became inseparable. They ate together, studied together, sketched together. They went to movies. They hiked. They huddled before class and staked out their favorite campus benches, but it was a full week before they made love.

In theory, a week was no time at all. In practice, in an age of free sex with two people deeply attracted to each other, it was an eternity, and they were definitely attracted to each other. No doubt about that. Jack was hit pretty fast by the lure of an artist's slender fingers and graceful arms. He didn't miss the way her shorts curved around her butt or the enticing flash of midriff when she leaned a certain way. The breasts under her tank tops were small but exquisitely formed. At least, that was the picture he pieced together from the shadow of shapes and the occasional nob of a nipple. The fact that he didn't know for sure kept him looking.

Was she attracted to him? Well, there was that nipple, tightest when he was closest. There was the way she leaned into him, so subtle, when they went to a campus concert, and the way her breath caught when he came close to whisper something in her ear. All that, even without her eyes, which turned warm to hot at all the appropriate times. Oh, yes, she wanted him. He could have taken her two days after the laundromat.

He didn't because he was afraid. He had never had a relationship like this with a woman before. Physical, yes. But not emotional, not psychological, not heart-to-heart. Rachel made him feel comfortable enough to say what he thought and felt. Not knowing how sex would mix with that, he avoided taking her to his apartment or going to her apartment, avoided even kissing her.

A week of that was *more* than an eternity. He'd had it with avoidance by the time she invited him over for dinner, and apparently she had, too. He was barely inside the door when that first kiss came. It was a scorcher, purity in flames, hotter and hotter as they slid along the wall to her room and fell on the bed. There was a mad scramble to get clothes off and be close and inside—and it was heaven for Jack, the deepest, most overwhelming lovemaking he had ever in his life dreamed could take place.

When it was done, she sat on the bed with pencil and paper and drew him, and what emerged said it all. With her hands, her mind, her heart she made him into something finer than he had ever been before. She was his angel, and he was in love.

chapter two

THE SURGICAL WAITING ROOM was on the second floor at the end of a very long hall. Dropping into a seat there, Jack folded his arms on his chest and focused on the door. His eyes were tired. Fear alone kept them open.

It was a full five minutes before he realized that he wasn't alone. A woman was watching him from the end of a nearby sofa. She looked wary, but she didn't blink when he stared.

"Are *you* Katherine?" he finally asked, and saw the ghost of a crooked smile.

"Why the surprise?"

He would have liked to be diplomatic, but he was too tired, too tense. "Because you don't look like my wife's type," he said, staring still. Rachel was all natural—hair, face, nails. This woman was groomed, from dark lashes to painted nails to hair that was a dozen different shades of beige and moussed into fashionably long curls.

"It's *ex-wife*," Katherine said, "and looks can deceive. So, you're Jack?"

He barely had time to nod when the door opened and

a doctor emerged. His scrubs were wrinkled. Short, brownish gray hair stuck up in damp spikes.

Jack was on his feet and approaching before the door had swung shut. "Jack McGill," he said, extending a hand. "How is she?"

The doctor met his grip. "Steve Bauer, and she's in the Recovery Room. The surgery went well. Her vital signs are good. She's breathing on her own. But she still hasn't regained consciousness."

"Coma," Jack said. The word had been hovering in the periphery of the night, riding shotgun with him down from San Francisco. He needed the doctor to deny it.

To his dismay, Steve Bauer nodded. "She doesn't respond to stimuli—light, pain, noise." He touched the left side of his face, temple to jaw. "She was badly bruised here. There's external swelling. Her lack of response suggests that there's internal swelling, too. We're monitoring for intracranial pressure. A mild increase can be treated medically. There's nothing at this point to suggest that we'll need to relieve it surgically."

Jack pushed his hands through his hair. His head was buzzing. He tried to clear out the noise by clearing his throat. "Coma. Okay. How bad is that?"

"Well, I'd rather she be awake."

That wasn't what Jack meant. "Will she die?"

"I hope not."

"How do we prevent it?"

"We don't. She does. When tissues are injured, they swell. The more they swell, the more oxygen they need to heal. Unfortunately, the brain is different from other organs, because it's encased in the skull. When brain tissues swell, the skull prevents the expansion they need, and pressure builds. That causes a slowing of the blood flow, and since blood carries oxygen, a slowing of the blood flow means less oxygen to the brain. Less oxygen means slower healing. Her body determines how slow."

Jack understood. But he needed to know more. "Worst-case scenario?"

"Pressure builds high enough to completely cut the flow of blood, and hence oxygen to the brain, and the person dies. That's why we'll be monitoring your wife. If we see the pressure when it first starts to build, we stand a better chance of relieving it."

"When? What's the time frame here?"

"We've done a head scan, but nothing shows positive. We'll watch her closely. The next forty-eight hours will be telling. The good news is that what swelling there is now is minimal."

"But you said she doesn't respond. Assuming the swelling doesn't get worse, when will she?"

The doctor caught the dampness on his brow with a forearm. "That's what I can't tell you. I wish I could, but it's different with every case."

"Will there be permanent damage?" Jack asked. He needed it all on the table.

"I don't know."

"Does the chance of permanent damage increase the longer she's comatose?"

"Not if the swelling doesn't worsen."

"Is there anything you can do to get the swelling down?"

"She's on a drip to reduce it. But overmedicating has its problems, too."

"Then we just let her *lie* there?"

"No," the doctor replied patiently. "We let her lie

there and heal. The body is a miraculous thing, Mr. McGill. It works on its own while we wait."

"What can we do to help?" Katherine asked from close behind Jack. Startled by her voice, Jack turned, but her eyes didn't leave the doctor's.

"Not a whole lot," Bauer replied, but he looked torn. "Ask nurses specializing in coma, and they'll say you should talk to her. They say comatose patients hear things and can sometimes repeat those things with frightening accuracy when they wake up."

"Do you believe that?" Jack asked.

"It doesn't jibe with medical science." He lowered his voice a notch. "My colleagues pooh-pooh it. Me, I don't see that talking to her does any harm."

"What do we say?"

"Anything positive. If she does hear, you want her to hear good stuff. The more optimistic you are, the more optimistic she'll be. Tell her she's doing well. Be upbeat."

"What about the girls?" Jack asked. "We have two daughters. They're thirteen and fifteen. They're already asking questions. Maybe I should keep them away. There's no point in frightening them if there's a chance she'll be waking up later or even tomorrow. Should I say she's still out of it from the anesthesia, and keep them home?"

"No. Bring them. Their voices may help her focus."

"How does she look?" he asked. "Will they be frightened?"

"The side of her face is swollen and scraped. It's starting to turn colors. One of her hands was cut up by the glass—"

"Badly?" Jack cut in, because that introduced a whole *new* worry.

Apparently agreeing, Katherine added, "She's an artist. Left-handed."

"Well, this was her left hand," Bauer said, "but nothing crucial was cut. There won't be any lasting damage there. Her leg is casted and elevated, and we've taped her ribs to prevent damage if she becomes agitated, but that's it."

"Agitated," Jack repeated, wondering just how much more there *was*. "As in seizures?"

"Sometimes. Sometimes just agitated. We call it 'posturing.' Odd physical movements. Then again, she may be perfectly quiet right through waking up. That's what'll scare your daughters most. They'll be as upset by her silence as by anything physical they see."

Jack tried to ingest it all, but it was hard. The picture the doctor had painted was the antithesis of the active woman Rachel had always been. "When can I see her?"

"Once we make sure she's stable, we'll transfer her to Intensive Care—no," he explained when Jack's eyes widened, "that doesn't mean she's critical, just that we want her closely watched." He glanced at the clock on the wall. It was four-ten. "Give us an hour."

JACK and Katherine weren't alone in the cafeteria. A handful of medical personnel were scattered at tables, some eating an early breakfast, others nursing coffee. Voices were muted. The occasional clink of flatwear on china rose above them.

Jack had paid for one coffee, one tea, and one thickly coated sticky bun. The coffee was his. The rest was Katherine's. Her polished fingernails glittered under the overhead fluorescents as she pulled the warm bun apart.

Jack watched her for a distracted minute, then studied his coffee. He needed the caffeine. He was feeling tired all over. But he couldn't eat, not waiting this way. Rachel dead was unthinkable; Rachel brain-damaged came in a close second.

Taking a healthy drink of coffee, he set the cup down and checked his watch. Then he stretched up and back in an attempt to unkink his stomach. He checked his watch again, but the time hadn't changed.

"I can't picture her here," he said, absently looking at the others in the cafeteria. "She hates hospitals. When the girls were born, she was in and out. If she'd been a farmhand, she'd have given birth in the fields."

Katherine nodded. "I believe it. Rachel's one of the free spirits of the group."

The group. Jack had trouble seeing Rachel in any group. During the years of their marriage, she had been a rabid nonjoiner—and that in a city where the slightest cause spawned a gathering. She had rejected it all, had rejected *him,* had packed up her bags and moved three hours south to Big Sur, apparently to do some of the very things she had refused to do under his roof.

Stung by that thought, he muttered a snide "Must be some group."

Katherine stopped chewing for an instant, then swallowed. "What do you mean, 'some group'?"

"For you to be here, what, all night?"

She returned a piece of the sticky bun to her plate and carefully wiped her hands on a napkin. "Rachel's my friend. It didn't seem right that she should be in the operating room with no one waiting to learn if she lived or died."

"They were only setting her leg. Besides, I'm here now. You can leave."

She looked at him for a minute. With a small, quick head shake, she gathered her cup and plate and picked herself up. In a voice just confident enough to drive home her point without announcing it to the world, she said, "You're an insensitive shit, Jack. No wonder she divorced you."

By the time she had relocated to the far side of the room, Jack knew she was only partly right. He was insensitive *and* ungrateful. Topping that off with rude, he could begin to see why the two women were friends. If he had used that tone on Rachel, she would have walked away from him, too.

Taking his coffee, he went after her. "You're right," he said quietly. "I was being insensitive. You're her friend, and you've been here for hours, and I thank you for that. I'm feeling tired, helpless, and scared. I guess I took it out on you."

She stared at him a minute longer, then turned back to her roll.

"May I sit?" he asked, suddenly wanting it badly. "Misery-loves-company kind of thing? Any friend of Rachel's is a friend of mine?"

It seemed an eternity of pending refusal before she gestured toward the table's free chair. She sipped her tea while he settled, then put the cup down. Staring at it, she said a quiet "For the record, you are not my friend. Rachel is. She's earned that right. I don't take people to heart readily, and you're starting at a deficit. You're not the only one around here who's tired and helpless and scared."

He could see it then, threads of fatigue behind the neat facade. He hadn't meant to make things worse. He was glad for Rachel, having a close friend like this. No doubt Katherine knew more about who Rachel was today than he did.

He looked at his watch. It was only four-thirty. They had time to kill. He was curious. "Rachel never told me she was in a book group."

"Maybe that's because you're divorced," Katherine reminded him, then relented and said more gently, "She helped form the group. We organized five years ago."

"How often do you meet?"

"Once a month. There are seven of us."

"Who are the others?"

"Local women. One is a travel agent, one sculpts, one owns a bakery, two golf. They were all here earlier. Needless to say, we weren't talking books."

No, Jack realized. They weren't talking books. They were talking about an accident that shouldn't have happened. Turning to that for lack of anything else to attack, he said, "Who hit her? Was the guy *drunk?* Did the cops get him, at least?"

"It wasn't a guy. It was a gal, and she wasn't drunk. She was senile. Eighty-some years old, with no business being on any road, least of all that one. The cops got her, all right. She's in the morgue."

Jack's breath caught. *In the morgue.* The fact of death changed things. It made reality suddenly more real, made Rachel's situation feel more grave.

He let out a long, low groan. His anger went with it.

"She was someone's mother, someone's grandmother," Katherine said.

"I'm sure." He sank back in his seat. "Christ."

"I do agree with you there."

~ ~ ~

THEY actually agreed on another thing—that Jack should be the one to see Rachel first—and he was grateful. Entering a predawn, dim, starkly sterile room whose railed bed held the pale shadow of the woman whose personality had always been brightly colored felt bad enough in private. Having his own uncertainties on public display would have made it worse. Not that there was total privacy. The fourth wall of the room was a sliding glass door. A curtain that might have covered the glass was pushed back so that medical personnel could see Rachel.

Quietly, he approached the bed. His mind registered one machine against the wall and multiple IV poles beside the bed, plus Rachel's elevated leg, which, casted, was three times the size of her normally slim one. But his eyes found her face fast, and held it. The doctor had warned him well. Even in the low light coming from behind her, he could see that around a raw scrape, the left side was swollen and starting to purple. The color was jarring against the rest of her. Her eyes were closed, her lips pale, her skin ashen, her freckles out of place. Even her hair, which was shoulder length, naturally blond and thick, looked uncharacteristically meek.

He reached for the hand nearest him, the right one, free of sutures and tubes. Her fingers were limp, her skin cool. Carefully, he folded his own around it.

"Rachel?" he called softly. "It's me. Jack."

She slept on.

"Rachel? Can you hear me?" He swallowed. "Rachel?"

His knees were shaking. He leaned against the bed

rail. "Come on, angel. Time to wake up. It isn't any fun talking if you don't talk back." He squeezed her hand. "Your friend Katherine said I was a shit. You used to say it, too. Say it now, and I won't even mind."

She didn't move.

"Not even a blink?" He opened his hand. "How about moving a finger to let me know you can hear? Want to try? Or are you going to keep us all guessing about what you hear and what you don't?"

She showed no sign of having heard him.

Nothing new there, he thought. She had gone right ahead and done her own thing for years, certainly for the six they had been apart. So, did she hear him? Or was she deliberately ignoring him? He didn't know what to say next.

Lifting her hand to his mouth, he kissed it and held it to his chest. With the slightest shift, it covered his heart, flesh on cotton, but close.

"Feel that?" The beat was heavy and fast. "It's been that way since I got the call. Samantha and Hope are scared, too. I talked with them, though. They'll be fine." When that sounded dismissive, he said, "I'll call them again in a little while." That didn't sound right, either, so he said, "I'll drive down once I leave here. They'll believe me better if I tell them you're okay in person. Duncan's there now. So, what's the scoop? Is he just the baby-sitter, or what?"

He wondered if she was laughing inside. "I'm serious. I don't know the guy. Do you two date?"

She said nothing.

"Sam informed me that she wasn't going to school. She'll go." He thought aloud: "Or maybe I'll just drive them back up here to visit. It won't kill them to miss one day of school." But they were approaching June fast. "When do finals start?" Rachel didn't answer. "No sweat. I'll ask."

He rapped her hand against his chest. "Wake up, Rachel." She slept on.

He brought her hand to his mouth again. Her skin was as soft as ever, but it lacked a distinct scent, which wasn't like Rachel at all. If she didn't smell of whatever medium she was working with, she smelled of lilies. He had started her on that, way back when he hadn't had enough money and had resorted to stealing lilies of the valley from the shady side of his landlord's house. For their second wedding anniversary, he had found perfume like it. No, not perfume. Toilet water. Perfume would have been too strong for Rachel. Even when he started earning money, he avoided perfume. Light and floral. That fit Rachel.

Light and floral was worlds away from her antiseptic smell now.

Not that she would still be wearing the same toilet water. She would have switched. Wouldn't have wanted the memories, though more than a few were good.

"Wake up, Rachel," he begged, suddenly frightened. He had lived without her for six years, but all that time he had known where she was. Now he didn't. Not really. It was as unsettling a thought as he'd had of late. "I need to know how you're feeling," he warned in a slightly frantic singsong. "I need to know what to tell the girls. I need you to talk to me."

When she remained silent, he grew angry. "Damn it, what *happened?* You're the safest driver I know. You used to save me from accidents all the time—'Maniac on the left,' you'd say, or, 'Jerk on your tail.' Didn't you *see* a car behind you?"

But she might not have. She had been driving north on a road that wound in and around, from the lip of one canyon to the lip of another. She would have been squeezed on the east by cliffs, and on the west by a single lane of oncoming traffic, then a guardrail and a harrowing drop. Once she rounded a sharp curve, she wouldn't see the car behind her until it, too, rounded the curve. If it did that at high speed, she wouldn't see it until seconds before the collision. And then, where could she go?

Feeling the panic she may well have felt, he whispered an urgent "Okay, okay. Not your fault. I know that. I'm sorry I suggested it. It's just . . . frustrating." Frustrating that he couldn't rouse her. Frustrating that the doctors couldn't, either. Frustrating, too, that the offending party was dead and beyond punishment, but he *sure* couldn't say that to Rachel, not if there was a chance she could hear. She was a softhearted woman—hardheaded but softhearted. She would be crushed to learn that someone had died. If she needed to hear upbeat things, that wasn't the news to tell.

And what was? *You'll be pleased to know that my firm's falling apart.* But Rachel wasn't vindictive. So, that wouldn't do it. Nor would *I've lost the touch; nothing I design is right anymore.* Rachel had no taste for self-pity. Nor was she one for jealousy, which meant that he couldn't tell her about Jill. Besides, what would he say? Jill was nearly as softhearted as Rachel. She was nearly as pretty and nearly as bright. She was nowhere near as spirited, or as talented, or as unique. She would always pale by comparison.

What was the point of telling Rachel that? She had left him. They were divorced.

Feeling useless and suddenly more tired than he would

have thought possible, he said, "Your friend Katherine is here. She was the one who called me. She's been here since they brought you in. She wants to see you, too. I'm going to talk to the doctor. Then I'll go get the girls. We'll be back in a couple of hours, okay?" He watched her eyelids for even the slightest movement. "Okay?" Nothing.

Discouraged, he returned her hand to the stiff hospital sheet. Leaning down, he kissed her forehead. "I'll be back."

DAWN was breaking to the east of Monterey when he left the hospital. Once he was past Carmel, the hills rose to stave it off. Inevitably, though, the sky began to lighten. By the time he reached the Santa Lucias and Highway 1 began to wind, a morning fog had risen from the water and was bathing the pavement with a shifting mist.

Jack kept his headlights on and his eyes peeled, but neither was necessary. He couldn't have missed the accident site. Traffic was alternating along one lane while a pair of wreckers worked in the other. One mangled car had already been raised, but it wasn't Rachel's sturdy four-by-four. A mauled section of guardrail lay nearby.

Feeling sick to his stomach but needing answers, he pulled up behind the wreckers and climbed out. The air was cool, moist, and thick in ways that should have muted the brutality of the scene, but what little the shifting fog hid, Jack's imagination supplied.

Rachel's car lay against boulders a distance below. Its top and sides were dented and scraped. Water shot up from the rocks not ten feet away, but the car itself looked dry.

"Better move on, sir. If one stops, others do. Before we know it, we have a jam."

Jack pushed shaky hands into his pockets. "My wife was in that car. Looks like it went head over tail. It's a miracle she's alive."

"She's all right, then?" the trooper asked in a more giving tone. "We never know, once they leave the scene."

"She's alive."

"For what it's worth, she was driving within the speed limit."

Jack looked back at the road he had just climbed. It wound up from a basin lined left and right with cypress, dark and spectral in the fog. "Too bad. If she'd been going faster, she might have been down there when she was hit. Then she'd have gone off onto evener ground."

"She might have gone head-on into trees or traffic. There were a number of cars traveling south. Be grateful for small favors."

Jack tried, but Rachel hadn't asked to be hit. She hadn't done anything to deserve it. He didn't need to be told that she was driving safely—or that she had been wearing a seat belt. If not, she'd have been dead down there on the rocks.

The workers were struggling to hitch cables to her car and haul it up.

"When'll those guys be done?" he asked the trooper. "I'll be bringing our daughters back this way, and I'd rather they not see this."

"Couple of hours, I guess. Can you wait that long?"

He hadn't planned to, but he could. If he found the girls asleep, it might actually work out fine. He could use the time to figure out the most sensitive way to break the news.

chapter three

JACK DIDIN'T SEE MUCH of the rest of the drive. Fog continued to float across the road, lifting and lowering across the rugged terrain, allowing now and again for a glimpse of sea stacks in gray water on his right or the ghost of chaparral against rocks on his left, but an ashen pall lay as thick in his mind as in his eye. The world around him seemed dense, a heavy weight on shoulders that were tired and tense. It was twenty-four hours since he had last slept. Life had been a nightmare. And now he had to face the girls.

Part of him still pictured his daughters as the towheaded little monkeys who had adored him before things fell apart. They were more blond now than towheaded, more adolescent than little, more female than monkey. Yet the same old something twisted deep in his chest whenever their names came up.

They weren't babies. Hugs alone wouldn't be enough. But hugs hadn't done it for a while. They were more cautious than adoring with him now, strangers in many respects.

Thinking about that as he drove through the fog, he had a sudden, brutal sense of the limits of his relationship with his daughters. Taking them to a movie, or to watch a wedding in Chinatown, or to breakfast in Sausalito at Fred's was one thing. Filling in for Rachel, dealing with heavy-duty stuff, was quite another. He faced a trial by fire.

Thirty minutes south of the accident scene, Rachel's canyon rose from the sea. Its road was marked by an oak grove and a bank of mailboxes nine deep. Only one of the nine was painted, the fourth from the left. This year it was fire-engine red, Hope's choice. Last year it had been Rachel's butter yellow; the year before that, Samantha's purple.

He turned off the highway, downshifted, and began the climb. The road was unpaved, narrow, and steep. It hugged the hillside and wound steadily upward, broken only by driveways that careened down and around into private homes. The higher he drove, the thinner the fog. Oak yielded to sycamore and madrone, which mixed farther on up with cedar. Redwood had replaced that by the time he reached Rachel's.

Her home was a cabin of weathered cedar shingles. It meandered over a small space of the hillside, up a bit here, down a bit there. Pulling in on a rough gravel drive, he climbed from the car, and for a minute he stood there unable to move, breathing in something different, drawn to it. Fresh air, he decided, snapping to with an effort. He stretched and rubbed his face with his hands. He needed a shave, a shower, and some sleep. What he got when depended on what he found inside.

Wide wood planks that the elements had blanched led to the front door. His loafers echoed in the silence, but he didn't need to rap on the door. It opened before he reached it. The man filling its frame was far older than Jack had expected—mid-sixties, he guessed, from the pure white of his hair and beard and his weathered skin—but neither detracted from his presence. He was a large man, taller than Jack's own six-two by several inches, but that wasn't what kept Jack from putting out a hand. It was the forbidding look that met his.

"The girls are asleep," Duncan Bligh said in the same hard voice he had used on the phone. That it was lower now did nothing to soften it. "How is she?"

"Comatose," Jack replied, low also. He didn't want the girls waking up and hearing him. "Her condition isn't critical. Her body is working okay. The bang on the head is the problem."

"Prognosis?"

He shrugged and hitched his chin toward the inside of the cabin. "They calmed down, I take it?"

"No." Duncan pushed beefy arms into a flannel vest. "They just wore themselves out." He strode past Jack, muttering, "I got work to do."

Jack raised a hand in thanks and good-bye, but Duncan had already rounded the house and was striding up the forested hillside. "Nice meeting you, too, pal," he muttered. Going inside, he quietly shut the door and leaned against it to get his bearings.

It was the first time that he had been this far. Most often, when he picked up the girls for a visit, they met at a McDonald's just north of San Jose. In the instances when he drove all the way down, the three of them were usually waiting for him at the bank of mailboxes. He could count on one hand the number of times he had been to the cabin, and then, only to the door.

From there he'd had glimpses of color. Now the glimpse became a blur of natural wood, furniture that was green and lilac, purple planters, wild colors framed on the wall. The living room opened into a kitchen, but the back wall of both rooms was a window on the forest. The view here was simpler, more gentle to his eye. Pale shafts of sun broke through the redwoods, a bar code of rays slanting toward the forest floor.

Soundlessly mounting several steps to the left of the living room, he went down a hall and peered into the first room. Between the guy posters on the wall and a general sense of chaos, it had Samantha's name written all over it. The bed was mussed but empty.

Up several more steps and on down the hall, another door was ajar. This room had watercolors on the wall and a softer feel entirely. Both girls were asleep in Hope's double bed, two heads of blond hair as wild as their mother's. Hope was in a ball, Samantha was sprawled. In a gulley between them was a puff of orange fur that had to be the cat.

When none of the three showed signs of waking, Jack returned to the main room and sank into the sofa. Slipping lower, he rested his head against its back. His eyes closed, his body begging for sleep, but his mind kept going. Within minutes he was back on his feet and lifting the kitchen phone.

He called the hospital first and, speaking quietly with the ICU nurse, learned that Rachel's condition hadn't changed.

Next he called his partner at home. In response to a breathless greeting, he said, "Working out?"

"Treadmill," David Sung gasped, and Jack pictured him in the dining room that had been filled with exercise equipment after David's last wife had taken off with the Chippendale table and chairs.

"Sorry to interrupt," he said, "but I have a problem. Rachel was in a car crash last night. I'm down here with the girls."

"Down where? In Big Sur?" The beat on the treadmill slowed. "Not Big Sur. Ess *Eff*. We have a big meeting here in two hours. What kinda car crash?"

"A bad one." Jack kept his voice low and an eye on the far end of the living room so that he would know if one of the girls appeared. "She's in a coma."

"Jesus."

"I stopped at the hospital on my way down, but I need to bring the girls back there. We'll have to cancel the meeting."

"A coma," David repeated, still breathless. "Bad?"

"Any coma's bad."

"You know what I mean. Is she on life support?"

"No. But I can't get to that meeting."

There was a pause, then the blowing out of air and an exasperated "We can't cancel. We've already rescheduled twice." Another pause, another exhalation. "You're not ready for the presentation, are you?"

"Oh, I'm ready," Jack said, and it all rushed back, what had kept him tossing and turning before Katherine had called, "but they won't like what I have this time any more than they did last time."

He had been hired to design a luxury resort in Montana. The client wanted something with reflective surfaces that would disappear under that big open sky, but Jack had been to Montana. Glass and steel were all wrong. Even stone was pushing it. He wanted wood.

When his first design was rejected, he incorporated

granite with the wood. When that was rejected also, he had tried fieldstone and torn it up, glass and torn it up, steel and torn it up. He had gone back to wood and made the design more dramatic, but even *he* wasn't wild about it. The best rendition was the very first.

Only, that was beside the point. "Look," he told David. "I need your backup here. That's what this partnership is about. I can't be there. This is a family emergency."

"There's one hitch. You're divorced."

"Not from my kids."

"Okay. I get that. I do get it, Jack, but these guys have been waiting, and there's many millions at stake. If I tell them you can't be there because you have to be with your kids, they won't buy it."

"My wife's life hangs in the balance, and they won't buy it? Fuck *them.*"

"Do that, and they'll take their business elsewhere."

Jack ran a hand around the back of his neck. The muscles there were wire tight. "Let them."

"Y'know, pal, I'd have said the same thing a little while back, but right now I'm worried about Sung and McGill. This is a major project for the firm. Two others went with our associates who went out on their own last month."

"We still have more than we can handle."

"But this is a good one," David coaxed. "We've been doing educational institutions for years, but resorts are hot and lucrative. We're talking jumping to a new level. We can't let a project like this go by default."

"Then *you* take it over."

"Hell, I'd have done that weeks ago, only they want you. They want you, and you've lost your edge."

Jack was suddenly so weary that his bones ached. "I can't handle this now. Tell them . . . whatever, but I can't be at that meeting. I'll call in when I know more." He hung up the phone, knowing that his partner would be swearing and not wanting to hear it. Dealing with Rachel's accident, dealing with his daughters—trying *not* to think about the future—was all he could handle just then.

But Rachel and the girls were all sleeping. Stretching out on the sofa, with one arm over his eyes and one on his stomach, he followed suit.

HOPE came awake as she always did, slowly growing aware, getting a feel for morning before she opened her eyes, listening and thinking before she moved a muscle. She felt bits of sun, weak but warm. She listened to the soft sound of Guinevere's breathing close behind her neck. She began to think—and her eyes flew open.

Swinging her head around, cheek into cat fur, she saw her sister sleeping beside her, and it was suddenly real, what had happened last night. Samantha hadn't slept with her in years. She would have thought it beneath her, if things had been less scary.

Guinevere tipped back her head and gave her a nudge.

She nuzzled the cat for a minute, gathering courage. Moving the mattress as little as possible, she sat up and carefully drew the tabby into her arms. Silently, she backed off the bed and started for the door. Stopping suddenly, she returned, pushed her feet into her cowboy boots, and tiptoed from the room.

The sight of her father in the living room brought

instant relief. She had wanted him there so badly. Samantha had said he wouldn't come—that he hadn't *been* there when they needed him for *ages;* that he was too busy with *work*. But Hope had sensed he would come. She did that sometimes—sensed things—and it wasn't necessarily wanting that brought it. She had sensed that something was wrong long before Katherine had called looking for Rachel, had felt an unease when her mother left. She had thought it was about Guinevere. The vet had warned that the end would be silent and swift, and Hope was prepared. She had been the one to insist that Guinevere die at home, with her. But she wanted her mother to be there when it happened.

It wasn't until Samantha had said into the phone, "Hi, Katherine," that Hope connected the eerie feeling inside with her mom's well-being, and then it was like the bottom had dropped out of her world. She had felt the same thing when they moved to Big Sur without her father—shaky, like she was suddenly standing on only one leg.

Lowering herself to the rug not far from her father, she folded her legs and gently settled Guinevere in her T-shirted lap. The tabby looked up at her, purring softly. Hope imagined that Guinevere felt the same reassurance seeing her as she felt seeing her father.

Only, he didn't look very well, she decided. His hair was messy and his beard prickly. The shadows under his eyes said that he hadn't slept much, which made her nervous.

But he was sleeping now. That said something. If Rachel was dead, he would have woken them right up— wouldn't he have? If she was dead, he would have come sooner—wouldn't he have?

But Hope didn't know how long he *had* been there. She had tried to stay awake, had tried to do what her mother did when she was feeling lonely or down, which was work. But she could only recheck her homework so many times, and the book she was reading hadn't held her thoughts. So she had fallen asleep.

She hated the thought that her mother might have died while she slept. If that had happened, she would feel guilty for the rest of her life.

She was debating waking her father when his eyeballs began darting around behind his lids. Seconds later, his whole body tensed and he jerked awake. He stared at the ceiling, sat quickly up, pressed the heels of his hands to his eyes. He was in the process of pushing them into his hair when he spotted her.

He sounded shaky. "You should have woken me up."

"I figured that if you could sleep, Mom's okay," she said, holding her breath, watching him for the slightest sign of denial.

"She's okay," he said. "She needs to do a lot of mending, but she's okay."

"Did you talk with her?"

"No. She was sleeping. But I think she knew I was there."

"She isn't dead?"

"She isn't dead."

"You're sure?"

He seemed about to speak, then stopped, and her heart stopped right along with it. She drew herself straighter and didn't look away. She was thirteen. If her mother was dead, she wanted to know. She could handle the truth.

Something crossed his face then, and she knew she

had made her point. His voice was different, more reassuring. "No, Hope, she isn't dead. I would never lie to you about that. Deal?"

She nodded, breathing again. "When can we go?"

"Later this morning." He looked at the cat. "So this is the thing that showed up at the front door one day all bitten and bruised?"

Hope fingered the tabby's ear. "The bites healed."

"Gwendolyn, is it?"

"Guinevere. Did you learn anything about Mom's accident? Sam said she didn't know how anyone could survive driving off a cliff."

"Your mother didn't drive off the cliff. She was hit by someone else, and she did survive, so Sam was wrong."

"Is her leg in a cast?"

"Uh-huh."

"Will it heal?"

"Sure. Broken legs always heal."

Hope hated to contradict him, but she knew better than he did on this. "Not always. Things can go wrong. There can be permanent damage. That'd be awful for Mom. She'd have trouble with the hills."

Those hills meant the world to Rachel. She loved hiking them with Hope and Samantha. Hope had one favorite spot. Samantha had another. But Rachel? Rachel had *dozens*. Like the eucalyptus grove. Rachel said that a person didn't have to be sick to be healed by the smell of eucalyptus. Hope couldn't count the number of hours she had sat in that grove with her mother, smelling that smell, listening to the distant bleat of Duncan's sheep, thinking about things that needed healing. Hope usually thought about Guinevere. And about Jack. She wondered if Rachel did.

"Your mom's leg will heal," Jack said now. "Trust me on that."

Hope wanted to but wasn't sure she could. He had missed every one of her birthdays for the last eight years, and only six of those had come after the divorce. He had promised he would be there those first two times, then had been out of town, away, somewhere else. It didn't matter that he called and apologized and celebrated with her later. He had broken a promise.

Samantha said he cared more about buildings than kids. Samantha said that Rachel was *ten* times more trustworthy than Jack.

Only, Rachel wasn't there.

"This comes from the doctor," Jack insisted. "Her leg will heal."

Hope lowered her head, smoothed Guinevere's ruff, and was starting to silently repeat the words in a precious mantra when Samantha's voice came from the door.

"WHEN DID YOU get here?" she asked Jack.

He looked up and, for a minute, muddled by fatigue and nerves, thought he saw Rachel. It was partly the hair—blond but no longer as fine as Hope's, now as wavy and textured as Rachel's when they had met. It was partly the figure, more defined even in the six weeks since he had seen her last. Beneath a T-shirt similar to the one that swam on Hope, Samantha stood confident and as subtly curved as her mother. But it was the voice that clinched it, the echo of caution, even hurt, that he had heard in Rachel on their last night together—and suddenly he was back in their bedroom that night, sorting

53

through the closet for ties to pack while Rachel spoke from the door.

He could see her clear as day, with her tousled blond hair and gentle curves. She had just left the studio they shared on the top floor of their pink Mediterranean-style home in the Marina, and was wearing an old pair of slim jeans and one of his shirts. The once-white shirt was spattered with a dozen different colors, not the least of which was the aquamarine she had repainted their bedroom walls with several months before. Her face was pale and held the kind of disappointment that put him on the defensive in a flash.

"I thought you weren't going," she said.

"So did I, but I had to change plans." He pushed ties around on the rack, looking for ones to go with the suits he had laid out.

"We've had so little time. I was hoping you'd be here for a while."

He didn't turn, didn't want to see her pallor. "So was I."

"Couldn't you just . . . just . . . say no?"

"That's not the way it works," he answered, more sharply than necessary, but she sounded so reasonable and he felt so guilty, and he was tired; it had been that kind of week. "I've been hired to design a convention center. A big convention center. The basic design may be done, but that's the easy part. The hard part is fleshing it out for function and fit, and to do that, I have to feel the city more." He tossed down a tie and turned to her, pleading. "Think of your own work. You make preliminary sketches, but so does every other artist. Okay. Your skill sets you apart. But so do the choices you make on depth, attitude, medium, and you can't make those choices without spending time in the field. Well, neither can I."

She kept her voice low, but she didn't back down. "I limit my travel to one week twice a year, because I have responsibilities here. You're gone twice a month—three times, if you go to Providence tomorrow."

"This is my *work,* Rachel."

She looked close to tears. "It doesn't have to be."

"It does, if I want to succeed."

She folded her arms on her chest—he remembered that, remembered feeling annoyed, because she was such a slim thing, shutting him out with that gesture, and still barely raising her voice, which made what she said even stronger. "That leaves me alone here."

Only in a manner of speaking, he knew. "You have the girls. You could have friends if you wanted to do things besides paint. You could be out every night, if you wanted."

"But I don't. I never have, never once, not when we met, not now. I hate dressing up, I hate small talk, I hate standing around on spikey heels munching on pretty little caviar snacks."

"Not even for a good cause?" Charity fund-raisers were an integral part of social life in the Bay Area, particularly for someone like Jack. He needed to see and be seen. It was good for business.

Sadly, she said, "I can't paint here."

And painting was her world, which made him even *more* defensive and annoyed. "Every artist gets blocks."

"It's more than that." Those folded arms hugged her middle. "I'm dried up, creatively dead. I can't see color here. I can't feel subjects the way I used to. I don't need a shrink to tell me the problem. Art imitates life. I'm not happy here. I'm not satisfied. I don't feel complete. You and I are apart more than we're together."

"Then travel with me," he urged, shifting the responsibility to her.

She rolled her eyes. "We've been through this."

"Right. You won't leave the girls. You do it for your work, but not for mine. How do you think that makes me feel? Like a second banana, is how it makes me feel."

"Jack, they're *babies*."

"They're seven and nine. They can live without you for a handful of days here and there."

"Handfuls of days add up. And maybe it's me. Maybe I can't live without them. It's different for mothers. Very different."

They had been through that before, too. He tossed more ties on the bed.

"Look at those," Rachel cried. "*Look* at those. They're so *conservative*. We were going to be different. We were going to do our *own* thing, not get caught up in the rat race."

"We've done our own thing. You freelance, I have my own firm."

She pressed her lips together. After a minute, she bowed her head.

"What?" he asked.

The eyes she raised were hollow, her voice low. "I won't be here when you get back."

"You said that last time."

"This time's for real."

He sighed. "Come on, Rachel. Try to understand."

"*You* try to understand," she cried, then quieted again. "If I have to be alone, there are other places I'd rather be. I'm moving to Big Sur." Softly, she asked, "Come with me?"

"Are you serious?"

"Very."

He was frightened. More, he was *furious*. She *knew* he couldn't move to Big Sur. Big Sur was *three hours* from San Francisco.

"I've done fifteen years here for you," she said, softly still. "Now it's your turn to live somewhere else for me."

"Rachel." Didn't she *get* it? "My firm is *here*."

"You travel all the time. You don't do much more than visit the city anyway. You can commute from Big Sur."

"That makes no sense."

She was hugging her middle again, seeming in pain. "I'm going. I need you to come with me."

Frustrated that she didn't understand the pressure he felt, exasperated that she couldn't give a little, angry that everything about her should suggest that . . . *pain,* he cried, "How can I do that, if I'm on my way to Providence?"

"*Dad!*" Samantha's shout brought him back to the present. "How *is* she?"

He ran a hand over his face and took a steadying breath. When he was firmly back in the present, he told her about the leg, the ribs, and the hand. Then he reached out and touched Hope's hair, wanting desperately to ease the blow but not knowing how. "The thing is that her head took a bad hit. She's still unconscious."

Hope's eyes flew to his. "Sleeping?" she asked on an indrawn breath.

"In a manner. Only, nothing we do wakes her up. The doctors call it a coma."

"Coma!" Samantha cried.

"No," Jack hurried to say, "it's not as bad as it sounds." He gave them a shortened version of the doctor's explanation, then improvised on a hopeful note.

"Coma is what the brain does when it needs to focus all its energy on healing. Once enough of the healing's done, the person wakes up."

"Not always," Samantha challenged. "Sometimes people are comatose for years. Sometimes *coma* is just another word for *vegetable*."

"Not the case here," Jack insisted. "Your mother will wake up."

"How do you know?"

He didn't, but the alternative was unthinkable. "The doctor had no reason to think she won't. Listen," he began, looking down to include Hope, but she was bent over her cat, shoulders hunched and quivering. He slid to the floor and put an arm around her. "We have to be optimistic. That's the most important thing. We have to go in there and *tell* your mom that she's going to get better. If we tell her enough, she will."

Samantha made a sound. He looked up in time to see her roll her eyes, but those eyes were tear-lidded when they met his.

"Do you have a better suggestion?" he asked.

Mutely, she shook her head.

"Okay. Then this is what I think we should do. I think we should have breakfast and drive up to Monterey."

Hope said something he didn't hear. He put his ear down. "Hmm?"

"Maybe I sh-should stay h-here." She hugged the cat to her chest.

"Don't you want to see your mom?"

"Yes, b-but—"

"She's scared," Samantha said with disgust. "Well, so am I, Hope, but if we sit home, we'll never know whether she really *is* alive."

"She's alive," Jack said.

Hope raised a tear-streaked face to her sister. "What if Guinevere dies while I'm gone?"

"She won't. The vet said she had time."

"Not much."

"Hope, she's not dying today."

"Am I missing something here?" Jack asked, looking from one to the other.

"Guinevere has a tumor," Samantha explained. "The vet wanted to put her to sleep, but Hope wouldn't let him."

So the cat was terminally ill. Jack was wondering what else could go wrong when Hope looked up through her tears and said, "She's not in pain. If she was, I'd let the vet do it. But I love Guinevere, and she knows it. I want her to keep knowing it a little longer. What's wrong with that?"

"Nothing," Jack said.

Samantha disagreed. "Priorities," she told her sister. "Mom's always talking about them. The thing is that Guinevere isn't dying today. If the accident hadn't happened, you'd have left her home and gone to school. So if you leave her home now, she won't know whether you're going to school or to visit Mom. But Mom will."

Jack was thinking that she had put it well, and that maybe there was hope for his elder daughter yet, when she turned to him in distaste and said, "You're gonna shave and stuff before we go, aren't you, Dad? You look gross."

"Thank you," he said. Patting Hope's shoulder, he pushed up from the floor and, needing fortification after—what?—an hour of sleep, went to put on a pot of coffee.

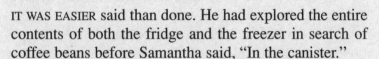

IT WAS EASIER said than done. He had explored the entire contents of both the fridge and the freezer in search of coffee beans before Samantha said, "In the canister."

He looked up. Both sisters were at the kitchen door, Hope a bit behind but watching as closely as Samantha. He tried to sound authoritative. "She always kept the beans in the fridge."

"Not anymore," Samantha replied, not loudly but with even greater authority. Rachel always did the same thing.

Knowing better than to question that tone, he pushed the fridge door shut. Rachel's canisters were brightly painted ceramic vegetables, all in a line on the counter. He opened a tomato and found sugar, opened a cabbage and found macaroni, opened an eggplant and found little nibbles of something he couldn't identify.

"Cat treats," Hope coached. "Try the cuke."

"The cuke has to hold spaghetti," he said and opened a fat yellow pepper to reveal flour. The cuke was the only thing left. "This isn't Rachel," he argued, feeling a little dumb as he measured spoonfuls of beans into a coffee mill. "A cuke is made for spaghetti. It's common sense. That's its shape."

"Mom says you have to break out of the mold sometimes," Samantha said. "When are we leaving?"

"As soon as I have coffee and a shower."

"How long is that?"

The kitchen clock—another ceramic thing that was no doubt also cast by Rachel's hand—was a beaver with whiskers that said it was seven-forty. "Twenty minutes." He arched a brow at Samantha. "Can you handle that?"

"You don't have to be snide. I was just asking. *We*

have to shower and dress, too, y'know, and if I'm not going to school, I need someone to take notes and get papers and give messages for me, so I have calls to make." She left, pulling her sister along with her.

Jack had calls to make, too, but they would have to wait. He had a feeling it was going to be a long day.

chapter four

HAD JACK KNOWN of any other road to take back to Monterey, he would have, but there wasn't a one. Samantha sat in the passenger's seat, hair wet from the shower, mouth clamped shut, eyes riveted to the road. Hope was stuffed in what passed for the BMW's backseat, staring out between the front buckets, her knuckles white on butter-soft black leather by her sister's shoulder, her cowboy boots planted on either side of the hump.

Jack knew what they were thinking. He was thinking it, too, hoping—*praying*—that Caltrans had finished its cleanup and left. Not knowing what else to do, he turned on the radio to create a distraction, and it did, for a minute.

"Just what we want to hear," Samantha remarked in response to an NPR report on starvation and death in another little African state. Between nervous glances at the road, she pressed another button, then another, then another. "Do you ever listen to *music?*"

"What was that a second ago?" Jack asked.

Samantha was working the manual controls. "Geek

chords, and we won't be able to get anything good here, the reception stinks." She flicked off the radio, clutched the hand loop above her door, and fixed alert eyes on the road.

Jack slowed the car to take the first of a series of turns. "What do you normally listen to?"

"CDs," Samantha snapped.

Hope shot her a timid glance. "Mom listens to news."

"Not when one of us is lying half dead in a hospital room."

"Your mother isn't half dead," Jack told Samantha.

"She's in a coma. What would you call that? People in comas die just as easily as not. Lydia had an uncle who was in a coma for months until they finally took him off the machines, and then he was dead in five minutes."

"Your mother's situation is entirely different. She isn't even on life support. The only machines in the room are ones to monitor her vital signs so they'll know if anything changes. She's—"

"*Look!*" Samantha pointed. "That's where it happened. See where the guardrail's gone, and all the mess of the dirt on the road where there isn't supposed to be dirt? That *is* where it happened, isn't it?" she charged, swiveling to watch as they passed the spot. "Slow down. I want to see."

Jack kept driving. "There's nothing to see. The car's been towed. It's probably already in the shop."

Both girls were looking out the back window. "Katherine said she was hit," Samantha said. "What happened to the other driver?"

"I don't know," Jack lied.

She flopped forward again. "You do, but you're not saying. I can tell by your voice. *Mom* would want us to know."

Jack doubted that very strongly, but it was beside the point. Annoyed at being pitted against Rachel, he said, "Right now, your mother would want you to say good things or nothing at all."

"That's what *you*'d say, not what she'd say. She'd want us to say what we think, and what I think is that this accident was more serious than you're saying, which means we're all in big trouble. What if she doesn't wake up?"

"She'll wake up."

"I'm not going to live in San Francisco. My friends are all here. I'm not moving."

"Good *God,* you have your mother dead and buried," Jack charged.

"Daddy?" came a frightened cry from behind.

He found Hope's face in the rearview mirror. "She's not dying, Hope. She'll be okay. I told you that, and I mean it. She was in an accident barely twelve hours ago. This is the worst of it. From here on it's about getting better. Let's take it one step at a time. For all we know, by the time we get to the hospital, your mother will be awake and asking for breakfast."

RACHEL wasn't asking for anything. She was as unresponsive when they arrived as she had been when Jack had seen her earlier. The tightness in his middle was back, the shock of seeing her this way, the fear that in the next breath she would be gone.

"She's sleeping," Hope whispered, and for a minute he thought she might be right. Aside from the bruise, Rachel looked almost normal. She might well have emerged from the coma and fallen into an innocent sleep.

The doctor might have tried to call him in the car and been unable to get through. Car phones were iffy that way.

He approached the bed, hoping, hoping. He rubbed her cheek. When she didn't respond, he gave her hand a squeeze. "Rachel?"

"Don't *bother* her," Hope cried in a fearful tone.

Samantha said nothing. Her eyes were wide, her face pale.

Backing to the open half of the sliding glass door, Jack stood with the girls while they adjusted to the scene, and he readjusted to Rachel's not having changed. When he had his disappointment in check, he said a quiet "See? No respirators, no life supports. She broke her leg. There's the cast. She cut her hand, so that's bandaged, and the bruises on her face are where she banged it against the car. Remember when you got a tennis ball in the eye, Sam? Black, blue, and purple for a week, then green, then yellow, then back to normal. But it took a while."

Samantha nodded. Her eyes didn't leave Rachel.

"The IV poles have medicine and food," he went on for lack of anything better to say. "The TV screen behind her registers things like heart, pulse, and oxygen. There's a person at the nurses' station who sees all that and knows if there's any change. They can also watch your mom through the glass. That's why she's here, instead of in a regular room."

Hope moved closer to his side.

"See the top readout?" he tried. "The heartbeat, that little green up-and-down line? See how regular it is?" He felt Hope nod against his arm. "Want to go let her know you're here?" The nod became a quick head shake. "Samantha?"

65

Without defenses, Samantha looked as young and frightened as Hope. "Can she hear us?"

"The doctor says so. It seems to me that if she can, she'd like to know you guys are here."

"What do we say?"

"Whatever you want."

"Are *you* going to talk to her?"

He knew a challenge when he heard it. Leaving them again, he approached the bed. Taking Rachel's hand, he leaned over and kissed her forehead. He stayed close, with an elbow braced on the bed rail. "Hi, angel. How're you doing? See, I said I'd be back, and here I am. Got the girls with me. They're over by the door. They're feeling a little intimidated by the machines and all."

"I am not intimidated," Samantha said and was suddenly beside him. "Hi, Mom." He heard her swallow, saw her fingers close around the bed rail. "It's me. Sam. God, look at your face. What did you *do?*" From the corner of her mouth closest to Jack, she whispered, "This is dumb. She *can't* hear."

"Do you know that for sure?"

"No."

"Then don't assume it." He looked around for Hope, who was still at the door. When he invited her over with the hitch of his head, she shrank back.

"What are they doing to wake her up?" Samantha asked.

"See that drip?" He pointed to one of the bags that may or may not have been the one the doctor meant. "That keeps the swelling in her head down, so that blood and oxygen can flow and heal the injured tissues."

"Why can't they just give her a shot or something to wake her up?"

"It doesn't work that way."

"Did you ask?"

"No."

"Did you ask for a *specialist?*"

He gave her a stare. "That was the first thing I did. Give me a little credit, huh?" To Rachel, lightly, he said, "Where did this one get her mouth?"

"Like you were perfect?" Samantha asked, not lightly at all.

Jack preferred his daughter when she was too frightened to be a smartmouth. He didn't know whether it was her age, or whether he just brought out the worst in her. In any case, he didn't want things going further downhill, not within earshot of Rachel.

"Tell you what," he said. "I'm going to leave you here to talk with your mother. Don't be bashful. Tell her how awful I am. Tell her that she'd better wake up, because you're *not* moving to the city. Tell her that I don't know *anything*. Get it all off your chest. I have some calls to make." He turned to find that Katherine had arrived and was standing with an arm around Hope. "Hey. Katherine. I'll be down the hall." As he passed, he told Hope, "Right down the hall. I won't be long."

He felt like a deserter leaving the room, but what was the point of staying? Samantha had nothing good to say with him there, Hope wouldn't budge from the door, and Rachel wasn't helping, not one bit.

"Is Dr. Bauer around?" he asked at the nurses' station.

"Tuesday mornings, he teaches in the city," said the nurse monitoring the screens.

"Are you Mr. McGill?" asked a woman who was doing paperwork nearby. She wore a silk blouse under her lab coat, and pearl earrings. They were large. Power pearls. Jack suspected they were supposed to make her look older than the barely thirty that he guessed she was.

"Yes. I'm Jack McGill."

She put down her pen, extended a hand, and said, "I'm Kara. Dr. Kara Bates. I'm in neurology, second under Dr. Bauer. He checked your wife before he left. She's holding her own."

"But not awake yet. He mentioned cranial pressure. What's happening there?"

"It's the same."

"Then the drip isn't helping?"

"It may be, since she isn't getting worse. We'll have to wait a little longer to see improvement."

"And there's *nothing* else we can do in the meantime?" he asked, hearing Samantha in the words; but hell, he was scared, too.

"Not yet. Are those your girls?" Kara Bates asked with a glance toward the room.

On the other side of the glass, Katherine had coaxed Hope to Rachel's bedside. Though Samantha was nearly as tall as Katherine and a head taller than Hope, both girls looked very blond, very young, very frightened.

"I'm not sure I should have brought them. They might have been better off at home. I keep telling them this is temporary, but it's hard for them to see. I don't know what to say to make it better."

"Let me give it a try," Kara said.

Willing to forgive her the pretense of power pearls if she succeeded, Jack walked her back to the room, but he waited at the door while she went inside. Gently, she told the girls much of what Steve Bauer had told him earlier. They listened. Their eyes went from Rachel's face to Kara's and back. They nodded when Kara asked if they understood, and didn't balk when she told them what they could and should do. By the time she was done, Hope was standing at Rachel's side under her own power and Samantha was holding her mother's hand—and suddenly Jack felt angry that two strangers, two women who were no relation at all to his daughters, had been able to reach them when he couldn't.

His family wasn't supposed to be like that. *His* family was supposed to be cohesive and communicative. It was supposed to be everything his childhood family hadn't been.

Turning against a sense of failure, he strode down the hall to the phone.

FIGHTING mental static, he made two calls. Both were to San Francisco.

"Sung and McGill," said Christina Cianni. She had been with Jack since the firm's inception, back then as receptionist, general assistant, overall gofer. The ten years she had on Jack didn't show. Her hair was a rich mahogany, her olive skin smooth as ever, her smile ready, her manner calming. Sitting at the front desk in those early years, she had conveyed an aura of success long before they had any. Now she manned the front phone only when the regular receptionist was on break. She divided the rest of her time between keeping the books and doing PR. The most precious of her traits was her undying loyalty to Jack.

"Hi," he said in relief when her voice cut through the static in his head. She was an anchor in his suddenly topsy-turvy world.

"Jack! I'm so sorry to hear about Rachel! How is she?"

"Comatose. Her injuries wouldn't be all that serious if it weren't for the one to the head. But that's a tough one. I don't know what's going to happen."

"I can't begin to picture it. I'm so, so sorry. How are the girls?"

"Scared."

"Do you think she'd be better off at a hospital up here?"

"Not yet. This team seems on top of things, and if they are, there's no point moving her. But I want an expert to tell me for sure. Can you get me the name of the best neurologist in the city?"

"Done," she said with blessed confidence.

"What's happening there?"

There was a pause, then a pregnant "You don't want to know."

"We lost Montana?"

"Worse. We didn't. They rescheduled for next Tuesday."

He was tired enough to laugh. Only Tina understood him enough to put it that way. She had seen him through years of increasing success when the adrenaline was rushing and wild dreams were coming true. But something had happened to the joy. Lately, it was harder to come by. Lately, there was less actual designing, less creative satisfaction, and more business meetings, one after another after another after another.

"I should be flattered," he said. "What about Napa?" He had designed a restaurant there and was scheduled to meet with the owner, an electrician, a plumber, and a kitchen consultant.

"Next Wednesday."

"Good. I want shop drawings before then. And San Jose?" He was supposed to have a preliminary meeting with the owners of a computer company that had outgrown its space and wanted to build.

"Wednesday, also. David was pushing for this Friday. He wants to get them hooked. Lucky they couldn't make it. You're supposed to be in Austin on Friday." After the space of a breath, she asked, "Think you'll make it?"

Jack closed his eyes and massaged tired lids. Standing there at the phone, he felt shrouded in fog. "God knows. She could wake up later today. Or tomorrow. Or Thursday. Or next week. This is bizarre."

"Are you staying down there with the girls?"

"Well, I don't have clothes. But, yeah, I guess I am. Just for a night or two, until we know more of what's going on. Rachel will wake up. She's too healthy not to, but even then, her leg is smashed up, so she won't be doing much driving, which means I'll have to do something about the girls." He pushed a hand through his hair. "Austin on Friday may be tight, but leave it for now. Clear my appointment book for tomorrow. I'll take it a day at a time."

"David won't be happy."

"No. I don't suppose he will." But Jack couldn't worry about David. There were now more urgent players in his life.

The second call he made was to one of those. His "Hey" was gentler, but the sense of wallowing in fog remained.

"Jack!" It came through with the delighted smile that he thrived on. Jill always liked hearing from him, liked being with him, and it showed. What man wouldn't value that?

"It's early," she said, still smiling audibly. "I didn't think you'd be calling so soon. Is your meeting done?"

"Never took place. I have a problem, Jill. Rachel's been in a car accident. She's in Intensive Care. I'm here with the girls."

There was a pause, then, minus the smile, a cautious "In Big Sur?"

"In Monterey. She's in a coma." He passed on the basics of the case. "She could wake up in five minutes, five days, five weeks—or never. The doctors have no way of knowing, and the girls are terrified. I can't leave them alone right now."

The pause that followed was long enough for him to hear the static in his mind loud and clear. Finally, Jill said, "You won't make it to the ball." Her disappointment was as obvious as her delight had been. She wore her feelings on her sleeve. Usually that was a plus. He preferred it when her feelings were positive.

"Not unless she wakes up within the next few hours. I'm sorry, Jill. I really am. I know what you've put into tonight, but you're not the only one I'm doing this to. I canceled three meetings today and just told Tina to do the same for tomorrow. I stand there looking at Rachel, thinking there has to be something that someone can do to bring her out of this, but no one has any answers. So it's a stinking, lousy waiting game."

"You can't be there all the time. Isn't there someone who can stay with the girls tonight?"

Duncan Bligh could, he supposed. Maybe even Katherine Evans. But Jack remembered the scene he had just witnessed and felt again the same annoyance— annoyance, defensiveness, pride. It had become a matter of principle.

"The girls are my responsibility. They're still young. They don't understand why this has happened. Not that I do. But I can't leave them, Jill. Not today. The situation is too shaky. I mean, I don't know what in the hell to say to them, how to make things better, but I can't just drive off. Trust me. This is not what I want to be doing right now."

"I'm the cochair of this," Jill said. What she didn't say, because she wasn't a shrew, but what Jack heard, was that she didn't want to be without a date.

"You told me you'd be running around most of the time."

"But I wanted you there." It wasn't whiney—mere statement of fact, which only increased his sense of guilt.

"I know." He pushed a hand through his hair, torn between what he knew Jill wanted and what he wanted to give her but couldn't. "I know. But I've slept a total of one hour in the last twenty-four. I drove down here with my laptop and scads of papers—no change of clothes, no comb, no razor. If I try driving back to the city, I'll either nod off at the wheel or in the middle of your lovely black-tie dinner. Either way, it wouldn't be pretty. I feel really bad, Jill. If I could be in two places at once, I would."

"She isn't your wife anymore."

This, too, was softly spoken, another simple statement of fact. What Jack heard was something entirely different. What he heard was, *I've dated you for two years, Jack. I've met your business partner, been at your business dinners, spent weekends with you here and in Tahoe—I've even met your daughters. Doesn't that say something? Haven't I finally come to mean more to you than your ex-wife?*

David had said something similar. Jack answered her

now in kind. "She may be my ex-wife, but there's nothing ex about the girls. They're still my daughters." No fog in his mind when it came to that. "They're only thirteen and fifteen. Their mother is in a coma from which she could either wake up or die, and the next day or two are crucial. How can I leave them alone here, so that I can go back to the city to party?" He caught sight of Katherine heading his way. "Hey, I gotta go. I'm really sorry, Jill. I'll call you later, okay?" He hung up the phone and drew himself up. Katherine looked like she might have gotten a little sleep, certainly had freshened up. Her pantsuit was linen and stylishly creased, her makeup immaculate, her long curls just so. Her expression was all business.

"Are the girls still with Rachel?" he asked.

"They are." She tucked a hand in her pants pocket. "Are you heading back to the city?"

"No. I just cancelled everything so that I can be here."

She looked startled by that. Then someone called her name. She swung her head around and paused for a second before breaking into a grin. "How goes it, Darlene?"

Darlene didn't miss a step. All big white teeth in a dark, dark face, she gave Katherine a thumbs-up in passing and was gone.

Jack pushed off from the phone booth. When Katherine fell into step beside him, he said, "You didn't think I'd stay?"

"I didn't know what to think. All I know about you is what I've heard from Rachel. And it sounded like you were better at leaving than staying put. She felt abandoned."

That quickly, he stopped. Katherine did the same. "Abandoned?" he echoed. "I didn't walk away from this marriage. Rachel did. She was the one who packed up and left the city."

Katherine looked about to say something, then pressed her lips together and simply nodded.

"Go ahead," he invited. "Say what you want." He was just tired enough, just frustrated enough, just worried enough to pick a fight.

She thought for a minute. When she spoke, her tone was innocuous, but there was challenge in her eyes. "I was going to say, the way Rachel sees it, you'd already left. Her moving on was just in response. San Francisco stifled her. She couldn't paint there. She was frustrated, and bored."

"If she was bored, it was her own fault. There were dozens of things she could have done and didn't." He told himself to walk on. This wasn't the time or place. But Katherine Evans had scratched a festering scab. He stood his ground. "She blamed *me* because she was bored?"

Katherine gave a small shrug. "The only person she wanted to do things with in the city was you, but you weren't around."

"No, I wasn't." *Definitely* not the time or place, but hell, this friend of Rachel's had accused him of abandonment, and beyond keeping his voice low, he couldn't let the charge go unanswered. "I was working my tail off to build a successful practice, so that I could keep us housed and fed and, P.S., let her paint without worrying about earning money. She wouldn't take money from her parents. I wanted to give her everything I thought she deserved." *Enough!* a voice inside him said, but the rest of him didn't listen. "What in the hell did I ask of her? To dress up and go out once or twice a week? Was that so much? God only knew she did it enough as a kid. She was *raised* dressing up. She could do the party thing with her eyes closed. Besides, she knew it was business. If you're trying to build a name, you have to be seen."

"She knew that," Katherine conceded. "The traveling bothered her more. To hear her tell, you were on the road more often than not."

Jack turned away, swearing under his breath, then turned back in the very next beat. "Rachel told you all that? Funny, she didn't tell me about you. Who the hell are you, to be coming between my wife and me?"

"It's *ex-wife*," Katherine said, seeming bewildered, "and you asked. Who I am is Rachel's *friend*. I love her and the girls. They're like family. I don't want them hurt."

"And I do? Wrrrrrong." This time when he set off, he kept going.

IF SIMPLY to spite Katherine Evans, Jack stuck to his daughters like glue. He stayed with them at Rachel's bedside for a time, took them to breakfast in the cafeteria, returned with them to sit with Rachel again, took them to lunch. In between, he spoke with a neurologist from the city, who agreed to see Rachel the next day.

Of the medical personnel who came and went from Rachel's room, the nurse heading the case was the most encouraging. Her name was Cindy Winston. She wore white leggings, a long blouse to hide plumpness, and thick glasses, but there was a quiet to her, an endearing shyness. She spoke slowly and softly and seemed kind as could be. If Kara Bates was a teacher, Cindy Winston was a friend. The girls hung on her every word.

"Keep talking," she told them. "Tell her what you've been doing." She looked at Rachel. "Tell her jokes. Tell her you're sad. Or angry. Or scared." She looked at the girls again. "You can laugh, or cry. Those are all normal things. She'll understand them."

"What if we run out of things to say?" Samantha asked.

Cindy studied her own hand. "Then touch her. That's important. See me?" Though she was addressing the girls, Jack looked. She was massaging Rachel's shoulder, had been doing it the whole time she was talking. "Your mother feels. Touching is a way to connect." She demonstrated with measured movements. "Don't be afraid to lift her hand. Or bend her knee. Or brush her hair. Or move her fingers or toes." She let that sink in, then asked, "Does she have a favorite scent?"

Hope's eyes lit. "Lily of the valley."

"You could bring some in."

"And it'll help?"

"It can't hurt."

UNFORTUNATELY, Cindy Winston's comfort was short-term and specific. More generally, more *urgently,* Jack wanted to know when Rachel was going to wake up, but no one was saying.

He drank so much coffee to stay awake that by late afternoon he was starting to shake. When Katherine arrived with several friends, he barely heard the introductions. As soon as they were done, he ushered the girls to the car.

They had barely hit the road when, in a big, bold voice, Samantha said, "So what do we do?"

"Do?" It was too general, and he was too tired. How to answer?

"If Mom dies."

"She's not going to die."

"Then if she lies there for a while. Who's taking care of us?"

"Me."

"Where?" The word was thick with distrust. He remembered what she had said earlier about not living in San Francisco. This wasn't the time to challenge her, not about a quandary so far down the road, not to mention an improbable one. Rachel would wake up. There might even be a message on the machine saying that she already had, by the time they got home.

"Big Sur." The logical short-run choice. He wasn't thinking about work, couldn't think about work. "If there's no change by tomorrow, I'll drive up for clothes while you guys are in school."

Sam was horrified. "We can't go to school."

"You can't not go. It's the end of the year. Aren't exams coming up?"

"Yes, but—"

"I'll pick you up at school." Since the school in Big Sur went only to sixth grade, the girls were bused to Carmel. From Carmel to the hospital in Monterey was a ten-minute drive. "You can spend the rest of the day at the hospital."

"Like I can *really* concentrate on classes?"

"I really think you should try. I really think your mother would want you to. I really think we have to try to maintain a sense of normalcy."

"*Nothing* is normal."

It was a truth so bluntly stated that he wanted to strangle her. "Look, your mom's apt to wake up anytime now. This won't go on forever."

"How do you know?" came Hope's small voice from behind.

He caught her eye in the rearview mirror. "Because it *won't*. Your mother is young and healthy. She'll heal. She'll wake up."

"You don't know it for sure," Samantha argued.

"No. But what's the alternative? Would you rather assume she's going to die?"

"No! I just don't know what's happening! There's a mess of things we're supposed to be doing, doctor and dentist—"

"My picnic—"

"My prom, for which I have *no dress*. Mom was taking me shopping this week, but if she's in the hospital, who'll do it?"

"Me," Jack said.

She sagged into the seat and looked out the window. "Yeah. Right. You don't have time. You never have time."

"I'll make time."

"Like you made time for my gymnastics meets?"

Her gymnastics meets. She hadn't done gymnastics in years, not since well before the divorce. There had been a time when he attended every meet. Then work had come in the way and he had missed more and more. She had been young. He wouldn't have thought she remembered. He was shaken that she did, and with such venom.

"This is different," was all he could say. Then, angered at being put on the defensive when there were two sides to every story, he held up a hand. "Y'know, what's happened to your mother is kind of hard on me, too. I'm past the point of being tired right now. What I'd like is a little silence."

"Did you call Grandma?"

He let out a defeated breath. Incredibly, he hadn't thought about Victoria Keats. But then, not incredibly at all. Victoria sent lavish gifts but rarely visited in the flesh. Since the gifts were largely unwanted and went unused, her presence in their lives was minimal. There were phone calls, but they were often more trying than not.

"Nope," he said as gently as he could. "Haven't called Grandma. Think I'll wait. If your mom wakes up soon, there won't be much need." He was taking the coward's way out, but what the hell, he had enough else to deal with without that.

He felt Hope even before she spoke, a tiny, timid warmth by his shoulder. "What'll we do for dinner?" she asked.

Jack thought of black tie and tails, beef Wellington, elegant dancing at the Fairmont with Jill, who adored him—and the same static he had heard earlier rang in his ears again. Dinner, shopping, doctor, dentist, picnic—with a glint of panic, he wondered if he was up for the task Rachel had set him.

What were they doing for dinner? "Something," he answered gruffly. "Now, shh. Let me rest."

"Are you going to fall asleep at the wheel?" Samantha asked, but the question was more frightened than snide.

"Tell you what," he said, "it's your job to make sure I don't. Watch my face. If my eyes close, hit me. Okay?"

THE REST of the ride was accomplished in silence. Jack was aware that the sky was clear, that a low western sun skipped over the ocean to gild the hills, that it was spring and not winter. But he was too tired to absorb details, too numb to see color.

The spot where the accident had happened came and went without comment. They reached the oak grove and the bank of mailboxes, left the highway, and were quickly immersed in the canyon's growth, trees thickening as they climbed. The instant they pulled up at the cabin, Hope said something about seeing Guinevere and raced from the car. Samantha followed, squawking about urgent phone calls.

Jack straightened and closed the car door, then stood rooted to the spot much as he had been earlier that day. Something about the air held him captive, something about the late afternoon shade, the grandeur of the redwoods, the silence, the smell.

The smell. That was it. It was clean, strangely sweet, unique. He inhaled, exhaled.

And the silence. Listening to it, he realized that the static in his head had cleared. He stood a bit longer, savoring the novelty.

Then, having gotten a second wind, he went in to see about dinner.

chapter five

HOPE WOKE UP with a stomachache. Curling into a ball, she had barely pulled the comforter over her head and begun to wish that Rachel was there when she heard a plaintive meow. She threw the comforter back and was up in an instant. Guinevere was crouched on the wood floor, eyeing her beseechingly. Not far from her was a middle-of-the-night accident.

"Ooooh, baby, it's okay, it's okay," Hope cooed, gently lifting the cat and cuddling her. "That's no problem, no problem at all. I can clean it up right away. You're such a good girl." With exquisite care, she placed the cat in her bed and ran to clean up the mess before Samantha or, worse, her father could see.

SAMANTHA woke up with a crick in her neck. It wasn't until she clamped the phone to her ear with a shoulder and winced that she knew its cause. *Repetitive tongue disorder,* her mother called it. But what could she do?

She'd had to call Shelly about math, John about science, Amanda about Spanish, and by the time that was done, Brendan was calling to talk about nothing in the annoying way he had of thinking she was interested in just the sound of his voice. And then there was Lydia. What time had they hung up? Twelve-thirty? One?

"ICU, please," she told the receptionist. When a nurse came on, Samantha identified herself with the confidence her mother said would get her answers. It was an act. She felt no confidence at all deep inside, in the place that feared Rachel might have died during the night. "How's my mom?"

"She's doing just fine."

Samantha's hopes soared. "She woke up?"

"No. Not yet."

So what is "just fine" supposed to mean? Samantha thought. "Thank you," she said with more disappointment than grace, and hung up the phone. Gnawing on her cheek, she wrapped tight arms around her knees and rocked on her bottom. So this was her punishment, this being left alone with her father. It was Rachel proving the point she had been trying to make the afternoon before, that though Samantha might complain that her mother wouldn't let her get a tattoo, she had no idea how lucky she was.

Samantha thought about that argument. If it hadn't taken place, Rachel wouldn't have been distracted. She would have put her book-group book down in the kitchen, instead of carrying it to the studio. If she hadn't gone back there for it, she would have been on the road two minutes sooner, and if she had done that, she wouldn't have been hit. So was the accident Samantha's fault?

It wasn't fair. She studied as hard as she could and still got B's instead of A's. She couldn't play the flute like Lydia or sing like Shelly. She had been best at gymnastics, then she had *grown*. So now her looks were her strength—and what good did it do? Rachel fought her at every turn. The coolest kids were piercing third holes in their ears and getting ankle tattoos. The *coolest* kids were wearing mascara and tight tops to school. Lydia wasn't, but she wasn't *cool*. Poor, sweet, dorky Lydia— who was getting cold feet; Samantha knew it.

She also knew that if *Rachel* hadn't liked her prom plans, Jack was going to like them even less.

JACK woke up with a hard-on. He didn't bother to think back on what he'd been dreaming. No need. Rachel was everywhere—in the rowdy billow of fabric topping the windows, the velour robe hooked on the door, the nubby shawl draped on the rocking chair, the dried flowers in a vase that was plump, green, and—so help him—fertile. She was in the overflowing basket of clothes waiting to be washed, the haphazard pile of books and magazines that sat on the floor beside a huge hand-sculpted piece of clay with multiple arms holding baseball hats and a cowboy hat that went with the boots below. The chaos was vintage Rachel, but hell, he could keep his eyes *closed* and see her. The scent of lilies permeated the sheets.

Throwing grogginess aside, he grabbed the phone. When he heard a click and no dial tone, he pressed the button several times, wondering what else could possibly go wrong. Mercifully, the dial tone came.

It was only a minute before he learned, with relief, that Rachel was still alive; with fear, that she was still comatose; and with unexpected pride, that Samantha had had the wherewithal to call the hospital on her own.

He wasn't used to feeling emotions so early in the day, much less three such hefty ones. At least his erection was gone. He didn't want to have to analyze that.

Pushing the covers aside, he went to the window, hooked an elbow on the frame, and peered out. Morning fog filled the canyon, but it was different from the fog that filled his courtyard in the city. This one was softer, gentler. It was flannel gray and fuzzy green, and for a minute, not understanding what lured him, he just stood there and watched. Nothing moved. Nothing changed. He saw trees, moss, and fog. His eyes lapsed into a sleepy stare.

"Daddy?"

He looked over his shoulder at the door. Hope's face was all that showed through a narrow wedge of space.

"I don't feel good, Daddy. My stomach hurts."

Just that quickly, so did Jack's. He straightened. "Hurts, as in pain?" If it was appendicitis, he would pull his hair out.

"No. Not pain."

"Ache?"

"I guess."

He went to the door and touched her cheek. "You don't feel feverish. Think it was something you ate?"

"I don't know. But if I go to school and start feeling sick, they'll have to call *you,* and if you're in the city, you can't come, so maybe I should just stay in bed."

She didn't look sick to him. She didn't feel sick to him. The freckles she had inherited from Rachel lay soft on creamy skin. "Don't you want to see your mother?"

Her eyes widened. "If I sleep this morning, I can go when Sam goes, can't I?"

She seemed genuine enough about that. So it had to be the cat. "Where's Guinevere?"

Bingo. He saw instant worry. "In bed. I don't think she feels good, either. If I stay here with her, the *two* of us will feel better."

Jack rubbed the back of his neck. What to say? "Well, that sounds fine. Except what if one of you isn't feeling great tomorrow, either? Or the day after that?" The cat was dying. Dying didn't get better in a day or two. "Between your mother and Guinevere, you could miss the rest of the school year. I don't think either of them would want you doing that."

"But if I go to school and then go see Mom, Guinevere will be here alone for a whole, long day."

"Didn't Sam say she'd sleep most of the time?"

A meek nod.

"Well?"

A hard swallow. "She's my cat. I can't leave her all alone. Not . . . not now. I love her."

He pushed a hand through his hair, but the gesture seemed inadequate even to him. So he put an arm around her shoulders. They felt small and frail under a T-shirt that reached her knees and was nearly as wide. Bare bits of skinny leg showed between where the T-shirt ended and her cowboy boots began. "I know you love her, Hope." He tried to think of a solution. If children were buildings, he could redraw the background. He was creative when it came to architecture, not parenting. "You'll be with her all weekend."

She didn't say anything, just looked up at him with fear on her face and the beginning of tears in her eyes, neither of which made him feel great.

He had a thought. "What would your mom say?"

Hope gave a one-shouldered shrug.

"Would she let you stay home from school?"

"No. But she'd be here to check on Guinevere."

And he wouldn't. It went without saying. He was dropping the girls at school in Carmel, heading north to Monterey and the hospital, driving north again to San Francisco, back down to get the girls at school, up to the hospital again. Big Sur was forty-five minutes south of Carmel. It didn't make sense to add ninety minutes, round trip, to all that other driving, just for the sake of the cat.

"I can't leave her alone, Daddy," Hope begged. "Not all day. Not when she's so sick. Would you leave Mommy lying there all alone, all day long?"

"Mommy's different. There are doctors and nurses—" He realized he had fallen into a trap when she began nodding.

Sighing, he gave in. But he really didn't want Hope missing school—okay, largely because he *really* didn't want to have to drive down to get her midday. There had to be another way. "What about Duncan?" If the man was so all-fired devoted, he could do this. "Think he'd check on her?"

Hope looked skeptical. "He's gone a lot, too. But he comes home for lunch." She brightened marginally. "I could ask."

DUNCAN had a counteroffer that Hope liked even better, though Jack had no idea why. He didn't understand why Guinevere would be better off spending the day at Duncan's than at her own house.

"He has faith," was all Hope said when Jack asked,

and he didn't push. He had been hearing about Duncan's faith for years. The girls mentioned it in the same breath with the man's name, so often that Jack had actually asked Rachel whether Duncan belonged to a cult. Big Sur had its share of free spirits, aging hippies, sun worshipers, he was told. Rachel had laughed roundly.

So Duncan was religious. Fine. What mattered more to Jack was that in the rush to get dressed and carry the cat, litter, and food to the small ranch three minutes up the road, Hope forgot about her stomachache.

Jack waited by the car while she got the cat settled. When Duncan came out, he said, "Thanks. This means a lot to her."

"How's her mother?"

"The same. I'm heading there now."

"Better call Ben."

"Who's Ben?" he asked, but before Duncan could answer, Hope had taken the big man's hand and was looking up at him with reverence.

It was some picture—beautiful Hope, with sunny blond hair, hazel-gold eyes, and now, finally, just a touch of color under her freckles, and Duncan, who approached homely with his big white beard, long ears, and leathery hands.

"I'll come for her later," Hope was saying.

The big man nodded, gave her hand a squeeze, and nudged her toward Jack.

WHEN JACK arrived at the hospital, Rachel was freshly bathed, lying on crisp white sheets, smelling as antiseptic as she had the day before. He had brought a tube of cream from her bathroom and began rubbing it onto those stretches of her skin that were bare.

"Better," he said when the scent of lilies rose. "More you. I'm flattered. I'd have thought you would switch." He touched lotion to her cheeks, working carefully around the bruise. "Black-and-blue here," he told her. "If they didn't know better, they'd be wondering who hit you. Good thing I was in San Francisco." Not that he had ever raised a hand to Rachel—*or* to either of the kids. For, whatever other faults he had, that wasn't one. As the son of an avid disciplinarian, he had seen enough raised hands to last him a lifetime. "I'll bet you have a headache."

She didn't respond. Her hand lay limp, her arm dead weight. He studied her eyes for a sign of movement behind the lids. When there was none, he checked the monitor screen. Her heartbeat was undulating evenly. She was definitely alive. He wondered if she found his worry amusing.

He told her about getting the cat to Duncan's, about waiting ten minutes for Samantha to finish blowing her hair stick straight, about dropping the girls at school with minutes to spare. He told her his plans for the day. He told her that she was messing up his life in a major way, and when she didn't respond even to that, he left the room in a fit of frustration.

He found Kara Bates in the hall. The pearl earrings had been replaced by onyx squares, powerful in their own right on ivory lobes, a foil for black hair knotted stylishly in back. So, she wanted to be taken seriously? He could give her that chance.

"Shouldn't Rachel be reacting to something by now?" he demanded. "It's been a day and a half."

Kara stuck a thumb over her shoulder. "It's been a

month and a half for the family in there. These things take time, Mr. McGill. Your wife isn't getting worse. Her stats are stable. There's been no drop in oxygen saturation, no rise in arterial pressure. We have to assume that something's working the right way in there."

"Easy for you to say."

"No," she said crisply. "Not easy at all. I want to *do,* not to wait. This isn't easy for any of us."

"I have a neurologist coming from the city. He said he'd be by today."

She reached behind the desk and produced a business card. "He was already here. He suggests that you call him midafternoon."

"Did he see her file?"

"Her file, her, everything. He says he agrees with our diagnosis. He doesn't feel that anything else should be done right now."

Jack ran a hand through his hair. Another hope thwarted. "If you were to make a guess as to when she'll wake up—"

"I can't do that."

If she wanted to play in the majors, she had to do better. "Try."

She simply shook her head. "I'd like to give you hope, but I just—don't—know. Head injuries are like that. The best I can do is to say that Rachel is a good candidate for recovery."

That was only part of what Jack wanted to hear.

HE SHOULD have felt better driving north toward San Francisco. This was his city, his turf. It was where his

home was, where his business was. He had seen remarkable success here, had felt the headiness of landing plum
jobs and the satisfaction of seeing his designs built. He
was known here, respected here. He had a potential significant other here.

But his middle grew tighter the closer he got and was
joined by an odd grogginess. It was like his mind was a
leg that had fallen asleep. Tingly. Dense.

He stopped at his house first, hoping to get his bearings there, but the place felt cold. Frequent traveler that
he was, he tossed a duffel on the bed, quickly filled it with
clothes, packed up razor, shaving cream, hairbrush—seeing little of it, barely thinking. In the studio, he stuffed a
briefcase with papers from the fax, a portfolio with plans
in varying stages of completion. He didn't bother to look
out at the courtyard. Nothing to see—it was foggy again.
He spent a total of ten seconds flipping through yesterday's mail before tossing it aside, then started out the
door, stopped short, and returned. Standing in the front
hall, whose walls had been rag-painted a charcoal gray
that he had thought handsome at the time, he called Jill.

"How'd it go?" he asked as soon as she said hello.

"Jack! Where are you?" The enthusiasm in the simple
question invited more.

"My place, but not for long. A quick stop at the office,
then I'm headed back. I told the girls I'd pick them up at
school. Rachel is still comatose. How was last night?"

"It was fine. Successful."

"I knew it would be. You do things like that so well."
She was a warm, generous hostess, whether entertaining
at home, at a restaurant, or in a ballroom. They had met
as fellow guests at someone else's party two years
before, and he had been immediately impressed. She was

poised and intelligent, knew how to ask questions, could discuss politics with the best of them, but—important, here—knew when not to. "How much did you raise?"

"We're still tallying the last of the raffle receipts, but it looks like we topped a quarter of a million."

"That's great, Jill. Good for you. You must be thrilled." He *was* pleased for her, even if his voice didn't show the inflection. She had worked hard. She deserved good results.

"I missed you," she said.

I missed you, too, he should have been able to say. But he was too preoccupied with Rachel's condition to have thought much about Jill. "You deserve better than a guy who ducks out at the last minute, even though his reasons are good. Was it very awkward?" He was inviting her to yell at him, all the while knowing she wouldn't.

"No. You were right. I was running around. You'd have been stranded. Will I see you, Jack?"

"Not enough time, Jill."

"Not even for a *minute?* Just a quick run in on the way to the office?"

"I can't."

"When will you be back again?"

She had asked that question often during the past two years. Jack traveled constantly. Any woman he dated knew that. Jill was the first who had accepted it graciously. And why not? She had her own life, her own causes, her own friends, and was a mature, giving individual. He loved those things about her. He especially loved the fact that she made him feel wanted. He would always need that. But she didn't nag—and she wasn't nagging now, though the question sounded different this time. He could have sworn he sensed fear. It was the same fear that he had sensed a time or two before, when she alluded to a future together.

Usually he skirted the issue by blaming his work. "You don't want to be tied to a man married to work," he would tease. Or he would say, "Let me get through this patch, and we'll talk again," or even, "My life isn't my own, Jill, not with so many big projects going on."

This time he simply said, "I'll be back as soon as I can. Pray for Rachel?"

Knowing that, bless her, she would probably do just that, he drove to the office, but the minute he pulled into the space that he paid dearly for each month, he had the urge to back right out and leave. There were problems here, too many to label or count—none to do with economic survival, though that was what he had spent a lifetime fearing. More to do with *him*. He felt confused. The grogginess in his head became a buzz. He wanted to run, escape, *flee*.

But this was his firm. As a name partner, he had a responsibility to the twenty-some-odd people that he and David employed.

Taking the stairs two at a time, he crossed through the brick-walled foyer with only a passing nod at the receptionist. He strode down the hall, looking at none of the open cubicles lest his eye be caught, and didn't stop until he reached Tina Cianni's glass-enclosed office.

She was on the phone. Eyes widening, she hung up within seconds. "What are you doing here, Jack? You're supposed to be in Monterey." More cautiously, she said, "How is she?"

"Alive. But still comatose."

Tina released a breath. "Well, the alive part is good. How are the girls?"

"Hanging in there. What's doing?"

She paused, gave him a warning look. "You don't want to know."

Again? "Is it worse than a coma?"

"David would say it is," she said dryly. "Michael Flynn was supposed to have revised plans done for Buffalo last night. Calls are coming in fast and furious. Every day those windows don't go in is costing John Perry a pretty penny."

Jack knew that all too well. The last time he had worked with this particular developer—on a series of housing clusters—heavy snows had brought work to a standstill at three crucial points. Each day of delay meant another day carrying the construction mortgage with interest. This time the project was an art gallery with adjoining studios, a project closer to Jack's heart than most, and the windows had come in wrong. The contractor swore he had ordered the right ones. Whether he had or not was moot. Reordering and waiting for delivery could set them back two months.

As designing partner, Jack had done the original work. He had revised the plan to incorporate the windows as delivered. Michael Flynn, as his project manager, was supposed to see that what Jack designed was built, which meant making blueprints of Jack's revisions, getting them to Buffalo, and following them there posthaste.

"Where is Michael?"

"Home. He ran out of here at three yesterday to take his two-year-old to the doctor. She was having a massive poison ivy attack, and his wife panicked. He was rear-ended on the way home, then tripped and fell down a flight of stairs with the child in his arms. It's a miracle neither of them was killed. The little girl is fine. Michael thinks he broke his ankle. It's swollen. He's going for X rays."

The buzz in Jack's head grew louder. "Where's everyone else?"

"They're working, but it's slow. When Michael ran out, he implied that he was nearly done, but he wasn't. Alex and Brynna are on it."

Jack took a tired breath. He should have been irate. His name would be the one tarnished if Buffalo was upset. His reputation was the one at stake.

But he felt numb. "What else?"

"Boca. Regulations and committees. Back to the drawing board."

The project in Boca was a combined office building and shopping mall. He had already revised the design not once, not twice, but *three* times to satisfy the quirks of one vocal member of one crucial committee. With preliminary approval of that revised design, he had put two draftsmen to the task of producing working drawings. He had already compromised to the limit, not to mention swallowed wasted hours for which he had to pay his draftsmen without reimbursement. Was the money worth it?

Tina was right. He didn't want to be there.

"Shall I cancel you out for tomorrow?" she asked.

"Yeah."

"You look done in. Did you sleep?"

"Some." Dropping his head back, he eyed the ceiling. He couldn't focus on Buffalo, couldn't focus on Boca. But he was the leader of the firm, and morale was low.

So he walked down the hall and stopped at one cubicle after another, making his presence felt in the barest way—a question here, a suggestion there—wading through the static in his head for relevance. He was singly responsible for three-quarters of the design work the firm did. It was good work, increasingly important work. *Metropolitan Home* had photographed his museum in Omaha; *Architectural Digest* was doing a piece on his library in Memphis. He was getting invitations to bid on some of the most exciting projects—that, and repeat clients. Every architect dreamed of tying himself to a conglomerate with ongoing projects, and the dream was coming true for Sung and McGill. Still, Jack felt detached, felt angry to be in the office.

Mercifully, David was on-site in Seattle. Jack wasn't up for explaining himself. How could he explain what he didn't understand?

His own office was in a far corner of the suite. Like his studio at home, it harbored more business than art. Oh, there were pictures on the wall, lots of black-and-white under glass, elegant renderings of his favorite projects, reprints of magazine pieces—and for a minute, looking at them, he felt that old glory and the glow. There had been nothing, absolutely nothing, like the high of seeing his first design turned into a home. And there were other highs—the high of designing something bigger, more complex, more expensive; the high of winning an award or being solicited for work by a client so powerful that Jack was stunned. He felt pride. Yes, he did. But it was distant.

He needed a break. Maybe that was it. He had been working nonstop for too long. He and Rachel used to take vacations, trekking through remote areas of Canada or South America, always with pads and pencils, often with the girls. Since the divorce, he hadn't taken more than an occasional long weekend to himself, and then always for something more lazy and posh. Jill wasn't a trekker. She was a skier, so they did that together. But it didn't clear his head the way vacations with Rachel had.

Maybe he was burning out. There had to be an explanation for the revulsion he felt.

Then again, the revulsion could be from fatigue. Or worry. Any normal person would feel shell-shocked given the recent turn of events. Any normal person would feel the need to decide what was most urgent and focus solely on that.

Rachel called it prioritizing. This time, at least, she was right.

Pocketing a pile of telephone messages, he returned to the front desk and told Tina to cancel Austin.

Then he headed south to Monterey.

FOR A PETITE woman, Rachel had incredibly elegant arms and legs. Jack had always attributed that elegance to a grace of movement, but he saw it now even as she lay inert. He rubbed lotion over her hand—flexing it from fingertip to knuckle to wrist as he had seen the nurses do—then smoothed it along her forearm to her elbow. Her upper arms had no fat, just the gentle muscle of an active woman. He had always admired that in her. She wasn't one to play the weaker sex, was as quick to lift what needed to be carried as to ask for help.

Admirable. Humbling. Hard to be the stronger sex when she just took it upon herself to do things. He remembered being furious with her, way back in Tucson, when they had moved in together. They had been dating for three months, had decided that paying two rents was foolish, and had chosen his place over hers for its size and its sun. On the appointed day, he had raced to her apartment straight from school to start moving, only to find nine-tenths of the furniture already gone. And there she was in his place, sweaty, dirty, grinning from ear to ear as she pointed out where everything was and how well it fit. His fury didn't last long. She was too excited, too proud, to eager to make life easier for him. Lord, he had loved her for that strength.

Strength. Independence. Self-reliance. Stubbornness.

"Hi." Katherine's voice brought him back. She was another strong one, here to see her friend even when her friend's husband—*ex*-husband—kept taking his frustrations out on her.

"Hi," he said, determined to be kind. "How's it going?"

"It'd be better if Rachel woke up. Still sleeping?"

"Still sleeping. I bore her."

Katherine actually smiled. "She said you weren't always boring. She said you were fun at the beginning." The smile faded. "She looks the same. Isn't there *any* change medically?"

"None. I was hoping she'd be awake by now." That was one major source of worry. He sought Katherine's thoughts on another. "Think I should call her mother?"

The sudden caution on Katherine's face said she knew something about Victoria Keats.

"What do you say, Rachel?" Jack asked dryly. "Should I call your mom?"

He half expected Rachel to jump up and cry, *No! no! no!* The fact that she didn't do so much as blink said a lot about the depth of her sleep. She and her mother didn't get along. As far as Rachel was concerned, Victoria combined the worst of new wealth and of corporate America.

She was more materially than personally involved with life, even when it came to her only child. He doubted Rachel would want the woman near her—unless, perhaps, she was dying.

"I'll wait a little longer," he told Katherine. "She's bound to wake up soon. My man from San Francisco examined her and agreed with Bauer's plan. So we all wait." He grunted. "This isn't how I like to operate."

Katherine took a hairbrush from the bed stand. "No, I don't guess that it is. Men like action. This brush is hers. Did you bring it?"

"Yes, and you're only part right. Men like *progress*. They don't care how it's achieved, as long as it is. So maybe it's happening." He studied Rachel's face, studied the pale lashes lying in a perfect crescent beneath her eyes, a whisper of freckles, scrapes and an ugly bruise, a slack mouth.

Katherine began brushing Rachel's hair. Her fingernails flashed as she worked. "Are the girls in school?"

Jack could have sworn those fingernails had been brown the day before. Today they were red.

"Yup. In school." Moving the sheet aside, he warmed lotion in his hands and began rubbing it onto Rachel's uncasted leg. "I didn't think Rachel would want them missing another day. Besides, I had to drive to the city and didn't want them here alone the whole time. I'll pick them up in an hour. They'll see her then." He eyed the monitor. "This is hard for them."

Katherine slipped an arm under Rachel's head, gently raised it, and began brushing the hair in back. "I have a hunch this is only part of it."

He paused. Carefully, he flexed Rachel's knee. "What do you mean?"

"I have a hunch that your being here raises other issues."

"The divorce? Uh, I don't think so. They're worried about their mother. They're worried about a school picnic and a prom. They're worried about who's cooking dinner tonight. They're not thinking about the divorce. The divorce is old news."

"They're thinking about it," Katherine insisted, all pretense of hunches gone. "I'd wager Samantha's *obsessed* with it. She's resenting authority anyway. Most teenagers do. It's the age. She's been pushing her limits with Rachel, and now suddenly you're in the picture, taking over after being out of her daily life for so long. She's probably thinking that you don't have the right to tell her what to do."

"Did she say that?"

"No. But I'd guess she's wondering why you're here." She raised her brows and said in a mild singsong, "I've wondered it myself." She gently returned Rachel's head to the pillow and began brushing the hair in front.

Jack stared at her for an astounded minute, looked down at Rachel, then back. "My wife is in a coma. Where else would I be?"

"She's your ex-wife. You keep forgetting that. Is it an unconscious slip?"

"Rachel and I share more than a decade together and two children. It's only natural that I'm here. Don't make more of it than it is."

"It *is* more, if you still love her."

He did not. "We've been divorced for six years. I barely know who she is now and what she's done all that time. How can I love a woman I don't know?"

"Men cling to memories, sometimes. You wouldn't be the first."

"You're amazing." He didn't mean it as a compliment.

She stopped her brushing and smiled. "Is this another fight? I love fighting my friends' battles when they can't do it for themselves, and Rachel can't, that's for sure." The smile waned as she looked at Rachel. "At least if she's listening, she'll like knowing we discuss the girls. They've always been her first priority."

"Yup, and right now they're mine."

"Do you know about the cat?"

"How not to? We had to cart the damn thing up to Duncan's this morning. Hope wouldn't hear of leaving it alone all day long."

"She loves that cat," Katherine said, sad now as she studied Rachel. "The thought of it dying before was bad enough. Now it's even worse. She's apt to be feeling abandoned by everyone and everything she loves." Her eyes met his. "So there's another way in which the divorce comes into play. She felt abandoned by you. She won't abandon that cat. That's one of the reasons she absolutely refused to let the vet put the poor thing to sleep."

"Because of the divorce?" He thought that was pushing it a little.

"Know what I think?"

He couldn't wait to hear.

"I think you're here to make up for all you didn't do back then."

"I'm here because the girls need me."

"And Rachel?"

"Old times' sake."

Katherine smiled. "It's guilt."

"Guilt? Fear of abandonment? Christ, you have us all figured out. What are you? A shrink?"

"Close." She set the brush on the bed stand. "I'm a hairdresser."

Of all the things he thought she might have said, that wasn't one. "You're kidding."

"Why would I kid you?"

"You don't look like a hairdresser."

She laughed. "Like I didn't look like a friend of Rachel's?"

"A *hairdresser.*" He couldn't believe it. "The last time my wife stepped foot in a hair salon was on the day of our wedding. She swore she'd never do it again."

Katherine gave him a tiny shrug. "Apparently, she saw the error of her ways."

chapter six

JACK MCGILL reminded Katherine of her ex-husband. Roy had the same arrogance, the same myopia. To this day he thought the divorce was about her being unable to fill his needs, which was a joke. The guy's needs had been basic—food, clothes, sex. Any fool would have sufficed.

Unable to fill his needs? Not quite. *Unwilling* was more like it. He had refused to acknowledge *her* needs, which had been just fine for years. She had a career. She had friends. She found loyalty, sensitivity, intellectual stimulation elsewhere. But the one time she had needed him, he hadn't been there for her. After that, being his personal maid had grown old fast.

She had been his first wife. He was currently divorcing his third in five years. She found a certain validation in that. He was a slick one, Roy was. Slick, shallow, self-centered.

Don't judge a book by its cover. She had learned that the hard way, with Roy. She had been snowed by the package, hadn't seen the mettle—or lack thereof—

beneath. Roy. Then Byron. Different men, same pain.

Arms folded, eyes down, she tried to put it aside as she took the elevator to the coffee shop, but the setting didn't help. She didn't like hospitals in general and this one in particular. But she did know her way around. Heading straight for the tea bags, she grabbed an Earl Grey, filled a Styrofoam cup with hot water and paid, took a seat at one of the small tables, and wondered how long Jack McGill would hang around if Rachel's coma went on.

She was dunking the tea bag with more vehemence than was truly necessary when a voice said, "Excuse me? Haven't we met before?"

She looked up. The man regarding her with curiosity wore a blazer, shirt and tie, and jeans. His hair looked damp. It was more pepper than salt, thick, and well cut. Katherine noticed things like that. It went with her line of work. She also noticed that he was good looking. But then, so was she. And he'd just handed her the oldest line in the book.

Her expression said as much.

He was unfazed. "I think it was yesterday morning. Early, early morning." He extended a hand. "Steve Bauer."

Ah. Now she saw it. Rachel's neurologist. On her own, she never would have recognized him out of scrubs and cleaned up.

It was still the oldest line in the book, but she offered her hand. "Katherine Evans. I'm Rachel Keats's friend. Have you seen her today?"

"Early. I've been in surgery ever since." He glanced at the coffee machine. "I need caffeine." Holding up a finger, he left.

Katherine didn't like being told to stay put. Roy used

to do that—to point out his instructions, like she couldn't understand without a diagram—and while Steve Bauer hadn't exactly *pointed,* his finger had spoken.

Her first instinct was to get up and leave. For Rachel's sake, she didn't.

"Better," he said between sips from a steaming cup when he returned and slid into a seat. "Have you been with Rachel?"

"Yes. She seems the same. Isn't there anything more that can be done?"

"Not yet. The fact is she's not getting worse. That's good."

Katherine felt a stab of annoyance. She was growing impatient, worrying about Rachel. "You people all say that, but I have to tell you, it doesn't do anything for me. A coma seems one step removed from death. I don't want her taking that final step."

"I know." He sat back in the chair.

She waited for him to reassure her, but he didn't. So she waited for him to tell her how frustrating his job was, how difficult, how heart-wrenching. When he didn't do that either, she said, "How do you stand it?"

"Stand what? The waiting? It's standard protocol for head injuries. Do you live nearby?"

"Not terribly," she said, realizing where *his* mind was.

"You look familiar."

"You saw me yesterday."

"You looked familiar then, too." He seemed genuinely puzzled. "Maybe I'm wrong. Sometimes when you see a face that sticks in your mind, you start thinking you remember it from further back. You've never worked here?"

"No." To show him how far off he was—maybe even

shock him, the way she had shocked Jack McGill—she said, "I'm a hairdresser."

The ploy backfired. He looked intrigued. "Are you now? In Monterey?"

She shook her head.

"You have spectacular hair."

She shot a beseeching glance skyward.

"I'm serious," he said.

"That's what worries me. I'm sitting here upset because my best friend is in your hospital in a coma and there's nothing you or your staff can do to help her, and you're noticing my *hair?*"

Smile fading, he backed off. "It was an innocent comment."

"It was inappropriate."

"No. What would be inappropriate is if I discussed the medical details of your friend's case with you or, worse, made empty promises about her recovery. In lieu of that, I made an observation. You do have spectacular hair. Nice nails, too. How do you keep them like that if you're washing people's hair all day long?"

She stared at him. "Rubber gloves."

"Is it your own shop?"

It was, but she wasn't saying so. She didn't know why doctors felt they could ask all the questions. It was one step removed from their wanting to be called "Doctor," while calling their patients by first name. "Where do *you* live?" she asked, doubting he would answer.

But he did. "Pacific Grove."

Oh my. Pacific Grove was posh. Another doctor feeling the brunt of managed care? Not quite.

"I bought a little house there seven years ago," he said. "It's right down the street from the water."

"Do you have family?"

"One ex-wife. Plus two sons and a daughter, all grown and moved out."

That surprised her. Despite the graying hair, his skin was smooth. She would have put him in his mid-forties. "How old are you?"

"Fifty-three."

And genetically sound, apparently. Lucky him.

"How old are you?" he asked back.

Feeling suddenly off balance, she sighed and rose with her tea. "Old enough to know I'd better be getting back to my friend. I don't have long. Bye."

THERE WERE ten teenagers waiting for Jack when he pulled up at the school. Hope opened the door first and scrambled into the tiny backseat. "How's Mom?"

It was a gut-wrenching question. He kept his answer as light as he could. "Pretty good. Still asleep."

Samantha slipped into the passenger's seat, pointing at the others crowding on the curb at the open door. "These are my friends—Joshua, Adam, Shelly, Heather, Brendan, Amanda, Seth, and you know Lydia. They want to know how Mom is. Did she wake up?"

He had raised a hand in general greeting. "Not yet. But she's okay."

"Is she getting better?" asked the girl leaning in closest to Samantha. He guessed it was Lydia, whom he did know, but only by name. Not that it would have mattered if he had met her before. She was a carbon copy of the other girls—snug T-shirt, slim jeans, long hair swishing with every move. Actually, Lydia wasn't exactly like the others. She still wore braces, still looked more sweet than sophisticated. Her hair wasn't as straight, shiny, and neat. She had natural waves. So did the other girls. Now that he looked, Samantha's was the straightest. She was the most sophisticated-looking of the bunch.

He wasn't sure if that was good or bad.

"The doctors say she's healing," he answered.

"Can we visit?" asked another girl. He had *no* idea which name from the list was hers.

"Maybe in another day or two."

A boy face materialized among the girls, looking even younger. "I'm Brendan. My mom says to tell you she's totally on top of plans for the prom, so you shouldn't worry about a thing. She talked with Samantha's mom on Monday, and everything's set."

Samantha pushed her friends back. "We have to go." She slammed the door.

"What's set?" Jack asked.

"Prom plans. Let's leave. I want to see Mom."

He put the car in gear and pulled away from the school. "What prom is this?"

"The one I need a dress for. I told you about it."

She might have, but he'd had a lot on his mind. "What prom? You're only fifteen."

From behind him came a pleading explanation, clearly meant to ward off a fight, "Ninth and tenth have a prom."

"When?"

"A week from Saturday," Samantha said. "I need to buy a dress this weekend. You said you'd take me if Mom isn't better. She should have woken up by now. This isn't good."

"It isn't?" asked Hope, no longer making peace, simply scared.

"It's fine," Jack said. "The doctors are pleased with her progress."

"What progress?" Samantha asked.

"Vital signs. All good." He didn't know what else to say. Rachel was only supposed to be in a coma for a day or two. He had thought she would have woken up by now. The wait was unsettling.

"Daddy?" from the backseat.

"What, Hope?"

"What're we going to do about my picnic? Mommy was supposed to run it, but if she has a broken leg, she won't be able to drive, and it means going back and forth to school and calling other moms and picking stuff up and all that."

Jack felt a little like he was holding an armload of bricks, staggering with the addition of one, then another and another. He could handle buying a dress for the prom. All that meant was standing in a store, saying yes or no, and producing a credit card. Running a picnic was something else. It sounded pretty time-consuming to him—not to mention out of his realm—and he still had his own work to do. He could ignore that all he wanted for a day or two or three. But it was there, hanging heavy and hard in the back of his mind. It, too, was longing for Rachel to wake up.

He figured he could fill the car with two-liter bottles of soda and get them to a designated spot, maybe even buy a couple of dozen subs. But run the whole thing? There had to be another parent who could do it.

"I'll call your teacher tonight. Do you have the number?"

"Mommy does. And tell her about Career Day. Mommy can't do that."

"What about her show?" Samantha asked.

"What show?"

"Mom's supposed to have a show at P. Emmet's. It's a gallery here in Carmel."

"I know where P. Emmet's is." He wasn't *that* far removed from the art scene. The charming little side streets of Carmel had gallery after gallery. P. Emmet's was one of the best. He was impressed.

"The opening is two weeks from Sunday. What if she isn't awake by then?"

"She'll be awake," he decided. The list of things Rachel was missing was getting too long. He was just a stand-in, muddling along.

"But what if she *isn't?* Or what if she doesn't wake up until a week before? The paintings aren't done. She was kind of freaking out about that. I think you need to talk with Ben."

"Ben?"

"Ben Wolfe. He manages the gallery. He's the one who set up the show for Mom. They've been dating," she added—smugly, he thought. "Well, you are divorced. You didn't expect that she'd sit around doing nothing, did you? You date. What does Jill say about your being down here?"

"Jill understands that I have responsibilities," he said. At least, he assumed that she understood. He owed her another call. He owed her lots of other calls.

"Ben sells more of Mom's work than any of the other galleries do. He's giving her a solo show."

He whistled, doubly impressed.

"What if her paintings aren't done?" Samantha asked. "This is the only solo slot he has for months. She really wanted it. What do we do?" He felt another weight hit the load he held. His shoulders ached. The bricks in his arms were starting to teeter. "I'll talk with Ben," he said and tucked the thought away, back behind a growing need for Rachel to wake up, and fast.

THE THOUGHT didn't stay tucked away for long. Ben Wolfe was at the hospital when Jack and the girls arrived. He had auburn hair and wire-rimmed glasses, an average-looking man with regard to height, weight, and presence, certainly not one to catch the eye when he entered a room—certainly not the offbeat personality Jack would have guessed Rachel would go for. And she had thought *Jack* was conservative? Ben Wolfe was the epitome of it, but it worked for him. Between his crisp white shirt, neatly tucked into tailored gray slacks, and the reputation of the gallery, Jack guessed he had to be capable enough.

The woman with him was something else. Everything about her screamed rebel, from the pink streaks in her hair to the half dozen earrings she wore in one lobe to her layered tank tops and skinny skirt. She was clearly an artist. Jack guessed she hadn't hit thirty yet. He had her pegged as the sculptress in Rachel's book group even before they were introduced.

Ben Wolfe. Charlene Avalon. Jack nodded his way through the introductions but quickly focused on Rachel. Her face was peaceful, pale, and still. The tiny kick in his belly told him she hadn't moved since he had seen her last.

He touched her cheek. Then he took her hand. Holding it made him feel better, as though he had every right in the world to be there.

The girls were beside him, staring at Rachel, unsure.

To Hope, at his elbow, he said, "Want to tell her what you did in school today?"

"I flunked a math test," Samantha announced before Hope could speak.

"*Did* you?" Jack asked in alarm, because her performance in school was suddenly his concern.

Hope was shaking her head, saying in her timid little voice, "She just said that to see if Mommy hears. Hi, Mommy. It's me, Hope. I'm still wearing my lucky boots."

"That is so dumb," Samantha said.

"It is not. They make me think about Sunday night. I'm wearing them until she wakes up." To Rachel, she said, "Guinevere is at Duncan's. I hope she's okay." She raised frightened eyes to Jack. "Did you call to check?"

He should have thought of it, but hadn't. "I figured Duncan would be out with his sheep." He checked his watch. "We'll try him in a bit."

"Charlie knows Duncan. She visits him a lot."

"He has a shed filled with rusty old stuff," Charlene said. She was at the foot of the bed, her eyes not leaving Rachel for long. "He lets me take what I want for my work."

"You work in metal?"

"Clay until I met Duncan. Rachel introduced us."

Duncan and Charlie? If Duncan was too old for Rachel, he was *definitely* too old for Charlie. "How did you meet Rachel?"

"Through Eliza."

"Eliza?"

"You met her yesterday," Samantha told him, and while he didn't remember meeting any Eliza, he knew better than to argue. There had been friends in and out.

112

He hadn't paid them much heed. "She owns a bakery in town," Samantha added. "It's French."

"How did your mother meet her?"

"At the *bakery*," Hope said with innocent delight. "It's the kind of place that makes sandwiches, too. When we first moved here, we tried eating at lots of different places, but we kept going back there because Eliza made special stuff for Sam and me, and then she and Mommy used to sit talking while we helped in the kitchen."

"You'd hate it," Samantha said, flipping her hair back. "There's always a line. You'd have to wait right along with everyone else."

So Jack hated waiting in restaurants. Was that so bad? He hated waiting, period. *You know that, Rachel, don't you? Some tiny part of you must be enjoying this.* "You didn't really help in the kitchen, did you?" he asked. He was sure it would have been against state regulations.

"Well, we didn't *cook*," Samantha conceded, "but we did other stuff, like fold napkins and decorate the chalkboard. Eliza's cool."

Jack asked Charlie, "How did you meet Eliza?"

"I used to work for her. I still do sometimes. Mostly I just stop in to visit. We're friends."

"And she's in this book group?"

Charlie nodded, returning worried eyes to Rachel. "We never expected this on Monday night." She clutched the earring that dangled lowest, a feathery thing. "She won't like that cast. It'll slow her down." She looked at Jack. "Ben and I were wondering what to do about the show. You do know there's one planned?"

"Of course," Jack said as though he had known about it all along. "The opening's in two weeks. I'm guessing she'll be awake long before then."

"Still, the cast's a problem."

The cast wasn't the only problem. There was also the bandaged hand. Granted, the better part of artistic talent was in the mind, but the body was the mind's major tool.

Jack caught Ben Wolfe's eye. "Can we talk a minute?" Drawing Samantha into his place beside Rachel, he went into the hall. When Ben joined him there, he asked, "Any chance of delaying the show?"

Ben shook his head. "I've been trying, but nothing's working. I've called everyone else who's scheduled to show, and none of them can be ready this fast. Since summer's a busy tourist season, our inventory is at a high, which means we don't have space to do more than one show at a time. They're scheduled back-to-back from now through September."

"How many of Rachel's pieces are ready?"

Ben nudged his glasses higher. "I'm not sure. She promised me eighteen. Only five or six may be done, and none are framed yet."

Jack wondered how that had happened. In all the years of Rachel picking him up at the airport, she had never been late. Granted, there had been close calls. More than once, she had come straight from work, disheveled and reeking of paint thinner, or covered with paste from some project she had been doing with the girls, but grinning, always grinning, and definitely on time. She prided herself on being where she was supposed to be when she was supposed to be there.

"It's not her fault," Ben rushed on. "She was doing us a favor, actually. Another artist was supposed to have this slot and chose London instead. Rachel's been selling so well that it seemed the logical choice. She likes to do the framing herself, but if push comes to shove, we can do it in the shop." He slipped a hand in his pocket, glanced back at the room, and lowered his voice. "What's the story? Is this long-term?"

"Beats me. Can you do a smaller show?"

"Yes. I'd hate to, if enough of the work is there. Maybe if I drive down and take a look at what she has, I'd get a better feel for where we stand."

Jack was surprised the man hadn't already done that. If Ben and Rachel were seriously dating, he would have spent time in her studio. Jack always had. Rachel's art was an intimate part of her, foreplay of a sort. Making love among oils had always been way up there among his list of turn-ons. That had started back in Tucson, in sweltering heat, when the smell of the oil would have been overpowering had it not been diluted by sweat and sex. At least, that was what they had told themselves. Granted, they had ceiling fans to dissipate the heat, but it didn't hurt the desire. Nor had the arrival of children. The studio door had a lock. They used it often and well.

"No need for you to do that," Jack said now. Ben Wolfe was too tepid for Rachel. He would never challenge her spirit, would never want to wallow in sweat and sex and oils. He was too neat, too pale. Nothing he did in bed would match what Jack had done.

Feeling dominant, he said, "I'll take a look. Got a business card?" Minutes later, he had one in his hand. "I'll let you know what I find."

WHAT JACK found were photographs. He came across them that evening—after cleaning up the remnants of pizza, calling Hope's teacher to beg for help with the picnic, spending two hours at his laptop and another grappling with design problems faxed to him from Boca—when, too tired to face Rachel's studio, he settled for searching her drawers. Cindy Winston had suggested that she might be more comfortable in familiar clothes; certainly the girls would be more comfortable seeing her in them. Given the obstacle of the cast, a nightgown made sense.

Propriety wasn't an issue. Rachel's nightgowns were prim affairs. She had always been into warm flannel things, claiming that San Francisco nights were too damp to go without when she was alone in a too-big bed. Her double bed in Big Sur was small compared to the king they had shared, and it was covered by the kind of thick goose-down comforter that he had never allowed her to buy lest he roast, and even then, her drawer was filled with neck-to-ankle gowns.

He had to hand it to her, though. They were vivid. He chose a purple one, a turquoise one, and a chartreuse one, and was debating about one that was poppy red, pushing it aside to see what was left, when he found the frames. They were facedown, seven frames covering the entire bottom of the drawer, familiar to him even after all this time, even from behind.

He turned over the largest first. It was in the kind of elaborate gold frame that only Rachel's mother would buy and that Rachel had always kept to remind her of that. Inside, extravagantly double-matted, was the formal picture taken at their wedding, of bride and groom standing dead center, flanked by two sets of happy parents. Jack and Rachel had both hated this picture. They had seen it as the perpetuation of a myth—bride and groom looking all done up and unlike themselves, with smiling parents who rarely smiled in real life.

Their engagement picture was better, but what a fight they'd had over that. It was totally casual, totally them—and totally unlike what Rachel's mother had wanted for the newspapers, but they had held out. He touched it now, the simple wood frame onto which Rachel had shellacked bright foils and decorative paper. Seventeen years younger, their faces were vibrant, defiant, happy as only the innocent could be. Rachel hadn't changed much, he decided. When he had seen her six weeks before, she had looked every bit as vibrant, defiant, and freckled. And he? Not much change in height, weight. His hair—*pecan, as in the nut,* Rachel used to say—had gone from tan to weathered, and he had crow's-feet at the corners of his eyes. The face he saw in the mirror each morning was broader, more mature, with a distinct worry line between the brows, an occupational hazard.

And the other pictures? Saving the smallest for last, he turned over four of him, taken by Rachel at various times, in various places. He had been happy. That showed in each print. He assumed she had kept these four for the sole purpose of leaving them lying face-down, buried deep.

But there was one more. It was his favorite. Feeling a catch deep inside, he turned it up. He hadn't missed it at first, had been so consumed by anger after Rachel's departure that he had only wanted things around him that were new. In time he went searching through the cartons in his attic. So. She'd had it all along.

Framed in a rustic stone frame, the photo was one that Rachel had snapped a year before the divorce. It showed the girls and him tumbling together in the tiny yard behind their Pacific Heights home, with Rachel behind the lens but so clearly involved in the scene that she might have been its subject. A tangle of arms and legs there might be, but three pairs of eyes, three smiles, three laughing faces were looking straight at Rachel with varying amounts of daring and love.

Jack had always treasured that picture. In the days that followed Rachel's taking it, when he felt increasingly distanced from her, it had said that—bottom line—things were all right.

Then Rachel had left, and the whole thing had seemed even more a myth than the pomp and circumstance of their wedding.

Setting the little stone frame carefully back in the drawer, he followed it with the four pictures of him and the engagement picture, but when it came to putting the wedding picture in place, he couldn't. That one didn't fit. It was the bad apple in the bunch. He couldn't help but think it contaminated the others.

Bent on burying it alone and as far from the others as possible, he opened the very bottom drawer—and felt a hard knocking in his chest. After a long minute, he moved his hand over a collage of fine lace, silk, cotton damask, even gingham, and was suddenly back in time to early evening in a warm Tucson apartment more than sixteen years before.

The apartment was larger than his old place. Since he had his degree and a new job, they could afford it. They had moved in the week before.

Jack returned from work to find Rachel in the spare bedroom that was supposed to have been a studio. With the wedding barely a week off, it had become a repository for daily deliveries. The latest gifts, still boxed, were nearly lost in a sea of empty cartons, torn paper, and discarded ribbon.

Rachel was a golden figure sitting at a long table in the midst of the mess. Her hair was in a thick ponytail; her freckles were bright; her face, arms, and throat were tanned amber above a lemon yellow tank top. She was working at a sewing machine, so intent with the whirring start and stop, the shift of levers and turn of fabric, that she didn't see him at first. The surface of the table was covered with pieces of fabric, predominantly whites and ivories, a few pale green or blue.

He couldn't imagine what she was doing. Victoria had refused to let her make her wedding gown, and she had already made curtains for the rest of the apartment. Curious, he came closer.

She looked up and broke into a smile, then held up her arms and tipped her head back for a kiss when he came over her from behind.

"What are you making?" he asked, thinking that she was adorable upside down.

"A shower quilt."

"For rainy days?"

"Not rain showers. Wedding showers."

He took a better look at the fabrics then, from what was in the machine to what was already sewn to the pieces in line. "Oh my God. Isn't that lace from the tablecloth your mom's Irish connection sent?"

"Not sent," Rachel said, clearly delighted. "Brought. To my shower."

The shower had been in New York the month before. Knowing how lavish it would be, Rachel had attended only under duress. Her greatest joy was in returning home empty-handed after instructing her mother to keep the gifts for herself. Not only had Victoria sent every last one to Tucson, but, to add insult to injury, Jack and

Rachel had then had to move the whole lot of them from their old apartment to this one.

A shower quilt. Jack's eye returned to the pieces of fabric with greater insight. Among them, he saw now, were bits from peignoir sets, satin sheets, table linen, aprons.

"She insisted I needed them," Rachel said, still looking up at him backward. "Do I ever wear silk nighties? No! Do I use fancy tablecloths? *No!* Do I want to sleep on sheets that have to be *ironed?* No, no, no. A quilt is far more practical."

"Do you know how expensive these things are?" Jack asked, but distractedly. Even all these years later, what he remembered first about that moment was the view into Rachel's tank top.

"I know exactly how expensive they are. Mom told me. That's why I'm so pleased to have put them to good use rather than let it all sit in boxes and drawers unused."

When Jack tore his eyes from her breasts long enough to look again at what she'd done, he had to agree. There was skilled hand stitching as well as machine stitching, in the kind of creative arrangement of fabric that only someone with Rachel's eye could achieve—and several different levels of poetic justice. Not only was there the sheer cost of the materials, and the fact that Rachel wouldn't be using these things as Victoria wanted, but there was the fact that Victoria *hated* it when Rachel sewed. She had taught Rachel to sew, herself, but she believed that they had outgrown the need to make their own clothes when Rachel's father came into his first money, a decade before.

"She'll die when she sees this," he warned.

Rachel shook her head, more serious now. "She won't

ever see it. She's not coming out here, Jack. This isn't where she wants me to be living, so she'll ignore the fact that I live here."

"And that hurts."

"Not as much as it used to." The smile returned. "Not since I found you."

She often said things like that, little things that made him feel loved, and she was right. It did help ease the hurt. He kissed her long and deep, and might have gone on forever if he hadn't worried about her neck, bent back this way. Ending the kiss, he framed her head for support. "For that, I'll help with shower thank-you notes."

"No need. They're all done." Her smile grew wry. "My conscience drew the line. I couldn't take a scissors to these things until I'd done that." She raised both brows. "But you can do some of the notes from *my* wedding list."

"I already am," he protested. Their initial deal had been for each to write notes for gifts coming from his or her own side. Then Keats gifts began outnumbering McGill gifts twelve to one, and he had taken pity on her. Spotting several unopened cartons, stacked and rising from the maelstrom, he sighed. "More today. Are you sure you know what's where?"

She lowered her arms and looked around. "Exactly. These are in piles."

"I don't see any piles."

"You're not looking at them the right way. Everything here"—her hand slashed the center of the room and swung left—"is duly acknowledged. Everything here"—her hand went the other way—"needs notes. *And* among these on the right"—she started pointing clockwise—"we have silver, gold, glass, fabric, and unclassified, as in *disgusting.*"

Jack saw something emerging from the disgusting pile and agreed. It was either an ornate lamp, a humongous candlestick, or something he had yet to make acquaintance with.

Rachel's arms came up again. She tipped his head forward to meet hers tipping back. Her throat was delicate and sleek, he thought. Stroking it, he felt her voice.

"Invite half the world," she said, "half the world sends gifts. Does half the world care what we want? No. We registered for plenty of stuff that we wanted, but half the world knows better. Do we want these things, Jack? No. Are they *us?* No! So not only do we write gracious thank-you notes to half the world, but we have to find a place to *put* this stuff."

Jack wasn't putting it anywhere. "Make that, find a place to *dump* this stuff."

"I wanted it all done before we left. I wanted this to be *our* place when we got back. So, why am I sewing a quilt instead of attacking this mess?" He knew precisely why she was doing it.

"The answer," she said, grinning, "is that since we're leaving for New York the day after tomorrow and I don't have a chance in *hell* of getting everything acknowledged and cleaned up and put away or dumped, I might as well have some fun."

At the slightest urging of her fingers, he lowered his head and kissed her again.

Her voice was more mellow when he let her up for air. "Whose wedding is this, Jack?"

"Ours. Ours. We agreed on that. What happens on the outside isn't what we'll be thinking and feeling on the inside. You love me, don't you?"

"I do, I do."

"Madly and passionately."

"Quite."

"Then look at it this way. We're doing our own thing about where and how we live, so we can cut your mother some slack here. But this does it. Evens the score. Our good deed is done. No more compromise. No more guilt."

"No more guilt."

"No more guilt."

"Okay."

HAD IT BEEN up to Rachel, they would have eloped. Looking back now, Jack wondered if it would have made a difference, perhaps gotten them off on a better foot.

But Victoria Keats had had her heart set on giving her only child the dream wedding she had never had herself, and Eunice McGill, of a no-name town a forlorn hour's drive from Eugene, Oregon, in her delight to be able to throw one son's success in her stern husband's face with impunity, had gone right along.

Both women were widows now. Eunice never called Jack. She waited for Jack to call her, then criticized him for not calling sooner. Victoria did call from time to time under the guise of being worried about Rachel, but if she was, it was one small, back-burner worry in a corporate executive's life. What she wanted was a reconciliation. Marriages didn't fall apart in her family. Her friends could be on their second or third, but her daughter's marriage was sound. Jack had a feeling she hadn't told any of those friends about the divorce.

Corporate headquarters were in Manhattan. Victoria

wouldn't have them anywhere else. Nor would she think of living anywhere but on the Upper East Side. She loved the ambiance, the glitz, the cost. Jack didn't know her number offhand, but he knew it would be in Rachel's book.

Jack closed the drawer on the shower quilt. One by one, he put nightgowns over the facedown pictures in the upper drawer and closed it. Opening the one directly beneath it, he slid the wedding picture in under a pile of sweaters. When that drawer, too, was closed, he stretched kinked muscles in his lower back and ran a hand through his hair. He needed a haircut. He had always worn it on the long side, but this was pushing it.

It would have to wait.

He glanced at the time. It would be late in New York. But Rachel had been comatose for forty-eight hours, and faults and all, Victoria was her mother. In good conscience, he couldn't wait any longer.

Sinking down on Rachel's bed, he lifted the phone. "Two minutes," he told Sam, "then I need the line." He hung up before she could tell him to use the cell phone, and started timing off the face of his watch.

chapter seven

WHEN JACK ARRIVED at the hospital the next morning, Rachel was lying on her side with her back to the door. His heart began to pound. *Awake!* He crept forward, cautiously rounding the bed, wondering what those curious hazel eyes of hers would be focused on and what the rest of her face would do when those eyes saw him there. After all, she was the one who had moved out and initiated the divorce. She might not be at all happy that he had come.

But her eyes were closed.

He stole closer. "Rachel?" he whispered, watching her lids for a flicker.

Kara Bates turned into the room. "We've started rotating her. Two straight days on her back is enough. We've also put a pressure mattress under her sheet. It adds a measure of mobility."

Jack swallowed down a throatful of emotion. Disappointment was there, along with fear—because what the doctor was saying suggested that with Rachel still comatose after forty-eight hours, they were looking farther down the road.

"Is there any change at all?" he asked, studying the monitor.

"Not up there. I think her face looks better, though. Not as purple."

Jack agreed. "But if the swelling is going down out here, why isn't it going down inside?"

"The swelling inside is encased," Kara said, cupping her hands a skull's width apart, "so the healing is slower. I was trying to explain that to Rachel's mother, but she wasn't buying."

"Victoria called here?"

"Several times."

Jack should have known. He had left a message on her machine asking that she call him at Rachel's, which she did at five in the morning, all excited, thinking they had reconciled. She was nearly as disappointed to hear that they hadn't as she was upset about the accident. She was in Paris on business, hence the early call. She grilled him for twenty minutes. When she asked if she should come, he discouraged it. He was hoping Rachel would wake up that day.

"She's an insistent woman," the doctor said.

"She's an *insufferable* woman," Jack muttered, then added a cautious "You didn't tell her to fly over, did you?"

"I told her she was stable. The rest is up to you," she said, peering into the small overnight bag on the bed. "What did you bring?"

"Nightgowns. Rachel likes color."

"I was starting to guess that," Kara remarked, arching a brow at the windowsill. It was crammed with flowers. "Those made it past the ICU police *only* because Rachel's problem isn't infectious or pulmonary."

A vague part of Jack had known the arrangements were there. For the first time now, he really looked. There were five arrangements, vases and baskets filled with flowers whose names he didn't know but whose colors he did. They were Rachel's colors—deep blue, vivid reds, rich greens, brilliant yellows. She liked basic and bright. Each arrangement had a card.

We need you, Rachel, heal fast, wrote Dinah and Jan. *To our favorite room parent, with wishes for a speedy recovery,* wrote Hope's seventh-grade class. There was a bouquet of hot-red flowers from Nellie, Tom, and Bev, a tall blue arrangement from the Liebermans, and a vase of yellow roses whose card read, *With love, Ben.*

"She has lots of friends," Kara observed.

"Apparently," said Jack, vaguely miffed. There was actually a sixth arrangement. It was from David. Stuck to the side and behind, it was much larger and less personal than the others.

Kara went on. "We've been getting calls at the desk asking if visiting is permitted. I wanted to talk with you about that. Medically, there's no reason why she can't have visitors."

"In Intensive Care?"

"We're a small hospital. Flowers—visitors—we can be flexible. Hearing familiar voices can help, and Rachel isn't in danger of infection. If she was a heart or a stroke patient, we might worry about someone doing something to upset her. Since that worry doesn't apply with coma patients, we restrict guests only when the family requests it."

Jack could do without Ben Wolfe and his love bouquet. But, okay. He and Rachel were divorced. He dated other women. He had slept with other women. Rachel was free to do the same. To live her own life. If friends had come to be a part of it, he had to give those friends a chance to help wake her up.

It was in his own best interest. He had to get back to San Francisco. Clients needed attention, his associates needed direction, design revisions were overdue. Jill had been a good sport, but she was growing impatient. The whole of the life that waited in the city was starting to make him nervous. If friends visited Rachel, he would at least be free to return to the office. He had been hoping to get a few hours there again today while the girls were in school, but he didn't want to leave Rachel alone.

"Let them come," he told the doctor.

KATHERINE swept in moments later. Her eyes widened, her mouth formed a hopeful *O* when she saw Rachel on her side. Jack shook his head.

She swore softly and came to the bed. "I was hoping . . ."

"So was I."

She leaned down and talked softly to Rachel for a minute, then straightened and sighed. It was another minute before she looked at him. "I wasn't sure you'd still be here."

"Oh, I'm here," he said, but he wasn't in the mood for sparring. He was wondering about those flowers, wondering about the friends Rachel appeared to have made since she had left him. In San Francisco, she had been a loner—independent in that regard, focused solely on her art, the kids, and him. "Who are Dinah and Jan?"

"Dinah Monroe and Jan O'Neal. They're in our book group. You met them yesterday."

He had met lots of people yesterday. One face blended into the next. "Who are Nellie, Tom, and Bev?"

"Bridge friends."

He had to have heard wrong. "Bridge? As in the *game?*"

"Cards. That's right."

He tried to picture it but couldn't. "That's a kicker."

"Why?"

"The *last* thing Rachel would have done in the city was play bridge. It stood for everything her mother used to do while she was waiting to get rich and busy. So what's Rachel doing playing it here?"

Katherine scrubbed the back of Rachel's hand. "Should I tell him?" she asked, looking amused. "The poor guy is mystified, absolutely mystified. Where's his imagination?"

"It's there," Jack assured her. "I'd never be where I am today if I didn't have it. There are people who say I have too *much.*"

"What people?"

"Clients who want a house exactly like one that their neighbor's brother has in Grosse Point, or a library to match a charming little one in upstate New York. I argue with them. I mean, hell, why are they hiring me? Any draftsperson can copy someone else's work. I don't want to give them what's already done."

"But you do," she said with a little too much certainty for his comfort.

"Is that what Rachel said?"

"Not exactly. What she said was that you'd gotten so far into big money that you'd lost your artistic integrity."

He felt offended—by Rachel for thinking it and speaking it, by Katherine for repeating it. "That's not true. And how would she know, anyway? She doesn't know what I'm doing now."

Quietly, smoothly, Katherine listed the six largest projects he had designed since the divorce.

Jack had mixed feelings about several of those. His initial designs, the ones landing him each job, had been exciting. Not so after developers, contractors and consultants, financiers, regulatory boards, and politicians had chipped away at the plans. That was what happened, the bigger the money. You weren't your own boss anymore. So maybe Rachel was right. Maybe he had lost his artistic integrity.

If so, he wasn't discussing it with Rachel's friend. "What does my artistic integrity have to do with playing bridge?"

Katherine smiled. "Spoken that way, not much. The subject was actually imagination. I've often wondered why men have so much trouble understanding how women's minds work. You're right. Rachel hated what bridge stood for in her mother's life, but she had been taught to play, and soon after she moved down here, she met Bev, a bridge player who does the most incredible stuff with acrylics on rattlesnake skin, and somehow playing with her didn't sound so bad."

Acrylics on snakeskin. It was a novel use of a medium. Rachel would have appreciated that. "Did she meet Nellie and Tom through Bev?"

"No. She and Bev advertised in the local paper to complete the foursome. Tom owns the paper. Nellie answered the ad."

"Is Nellie an artist?" It would make sense. Charlie. Bev. Nellie.

"Nope. She's a Carmelite."

"A *nun?*"

"A secular member of the order, but devout."

"Okay." Rachel had never been terribly religious. But, hey. His parents had been devout. "And the Liebermans?"

Katherine smiled with genuine warmth. "Faye and Bill. Faye's in our book group. She's one of the golfers. Jan is the other, and a young mother, to boot. She'll be by later."

Jack was trying to picture Rachel in a group with golfers, but all he could see was the adamant way she had always shaken her head when Victoria suggested they take up the game. "You're not going to tell me that Rachel plays golf now."

Katherine laughed. "No. I doubt either of us would go that far."

"Then how do you come to have golfers in your group?"

"Golfers read," she said, giving Rachel's hand a conspiratorial squeeze.

"Obviously. But what's the connection? If you don't golf, how do you know golfers?"

"They come to my shop. I've been doing Faye's hair for years, and we like talking books. Jan has her nails done every Thursday. She heard us talking once and joined in. When Rachel and I decided to form the group, they were both logical choices."

"What about Dinah?"

"A travel agent in town. We've all used her one time or another."

There was one connection left to make. "And you and Rachel? How did you meet?"

"In the gynecologist's waiting room," Katherine said. With a glance at her watch and a look of concern, she leaned over Rachel's shoulder. "I have a nine o'clock, so I can't stay long. I want to talk to you, Rachel. I miss that." She made a little scrubbing motion on Rachel's back, a casual movement, but the concern remained. "It's Thursday. You've been sleeping since Monday. How about cracking an eye open for me?"

Jack watched Rachel's eyes. The lids were inert.

"Looks like Jack's brought in some of your nightgowns," Katherine said. "I've cleared an hour midafternoon to come by and do your hair." She asked Jack, "Shall I get the girls at school and bring them here?"

Jack was feeling possessive again. "I'll do it."

The corner of her mouth twitched. "I don't think he trusts me," she told Rachel.

"The girls are my responsibility."

She straightened, suddenly sober. "Then can I make a suggestion? Buy a new car. Rachel's is totaled, so she's going to need another anyway, and you can't keep driving around with Hope stuck in that itty-bitty thing you call a backseat. If you want to risk your own life in a car that size, that's your choice, but I don't think you should take chances with the girls."

Jack was startled by the intrusion. "Is this your business?"

"You bet. Rachel can't say it, so I'll say it for her."

"Good morning!" Steve Bauer said, crossing the threshold and approaching the bed.

Katherine pushed off. "Bye," she said in a lighter voice, with an open-hand wave to no one in particular.

The doctor watched her exit. "Don't leave on my account."

But she was already out the door before Jack could wonder why the sudden rush.

JACK needed to work. His laptop was full of messages each time he booted it up. There were more on Rachel's answering machine, and papers piling up by her fax. He had driven north from Big Sur that morning intending, in logical geographical order, to drop the girls at school in Carmel, visit Rachel in Monterey, and continue up to San Francisco. Now that he was with Rachel, the urgency had left.

Bracing his elbows on the bed rail, he studied her face. Even with the vision of fading purple on the left side, he thought it a beautiful face. Always had. He used to tell her so all the time. They were art students then, sitting hip to hip in life drawing class, which he had taken solely to be with Rachel, since it had little to do with architecture. He had used whatever clout he had as a graduate student to wangle credit for it, but it was far from a gut course for him. He had to struggle far more than Rachel to reproduce, in the most minute detail, the face of the model.

"She's the beauty," Rachel used to whisper, pink-cheeked and pleased, if adamant. "Widespread eyes, strong cheekbones, clear skin, no freckles."

But Jack had always loved Rachel's freckles. His father, who had a negative take on almost everything, condemned them as the excess of spirit in a highly spirited person. Rachel had always been highly spirited, all right. Jack took pride in that. When he first met her, freckles had danced unchecked over the bridge of her nose to her cheeks. She was twenty-one then. After the children were born, the freckles faded, then faded more when she entered her thirties.

They were more noticeable now than they had been in

years. His father, God rest his soul, would have declared with disdain that a highly spirited person could be restrained for only so long. So, had marriage restrained Rachel?

The sun might be bringing them out. She was spending more time outdoors, said her work. He had seen several recent pieces in a SOMA gallery. She painted wildlife in its natural habitat.

Or did the freckles show more because her face was so pale?

He ran his thumb over the smooth, unbruised cheek. "Something's agreeing with you here. You're painting again. And you have friends." Suddenly that annoyed him. "What was the problem, Rachel? You could have had a *slew* of friends in the city. If you wanted them, why didn't you? You went off and did what you wanted in just about everything else. Why not that?" He felt the full weight of a confusion that had been hovering just out of reach. "And those pictures in your drawer—why are they there? I'd have thought you'd have cut them up and made them into a papier-mâché statement. That would have been poetic. Kind of like the shower quilt. Are the pictures facedown because you can't bear to see them? Or because you're angry? What do *you* have to be angry about? Looks to me like you're doing better without me than with me."

Sadness lurked under his anger. "What happened to us, Rachel? I never did understand. Never did figure it out." He paused. "Can you hear me? Do you know I'm here?"

Her skin smelled of lilies from the lotion he had spread. It taunted him with memories of a love that was supposed to have lasted forever. "I think you hear. I think you know. I think you're lying in there waiting and watching and wondering what's going to happen. Is this payback time for the traveling I did? You want me to spend more time with the girls? Well, I gotta tell you, I'm spending time with them, and we're doing just fine, so if you thought we'd fall apart, you were wrong. I love my daughters. I always did. Believe you me, when you packed them up and took them away from me, it was *hard*." Pushing up, he stared at her, then paced to the window, muttering under his breath, "Damn hard. Empty house. No noise. No smiles." He paced back to the bed. "You knew how I felt growing up, and how much I needed what we had. I *relied* on having family waiting when I got home from work. You took that away."

He put his face in close and spoke softly, under his breath. "Fine. It's over. We're divorced. You got that done nice and fast and clean, thank you. But this coma is something else. One day or two, okay. But three days? Wake up, Rachel. I'm doing the best I can, but the girls need *you*. I'm just filling in. You're the main attraction in their lives; always were." After a minute, he said, "And I have to *work*. People are depending on me for their livelihood. I'm being *paid* to make certain things happen, and I can't do it from down here. How long are you planning to let this go on?"

She didn't blink, didn't flinch, didn't answer.

Okay, he wanted to say—because if she wasn't cooperating, why the hell should he?—*that's it. I'm going back to the city. At least there I can accomplish something. At least there I'm appreciated. Ciao. Sayonara. See ya later.*

He didn't know how long he stood scowling at her. But the scowl slowly faded, and in time, he pulled up a chair and sat down.

～ ～ ～

KATHERINE'S one o'clock arrived twenty minutes late. She would have told the woman she had time only for a quick wash and blow dry, but the woman was a regular customer, flying out that night for a weekend wedding in Denver. So Katherine gave her the cut she needed and was late taking her one-forty-five, then had to deal with a minor uproar when a woman whose highlights had been done by Katherine's newest colorist stormed in with hair that even Katherine had to admit was alarmingly red. In the process of mixing the correct color, she splattered dye on her blouse, so she had to take a fresh one from the small collection she deliberately kept there, and with the bathroom door closed and her back to the mirror, she quickly changed.

She didn't reach the hospital until four. Looking nowhere but straight ahead, she made a beeline for Rachel's room. She felt a letdown the instant she reached it and saw that Rachel was still comatose.

Hope was reading a book on the bed, inside the rail, legs folded, boots on the floor. Jack stood facing the window with one hand on his hip and the other tossing a cell phone in his hand. The tray table beside him was covered with papers.

She gave Hope a hug. "How's your Mom?"

The child turned a longing look on Rachel. "Okay."

Katherine held her tighter. "What're you reading?"

Keeping her finger in her place, she closed the cover so that Katherine could see the title. It was an aged hardcover, John Hersey's *A Bell for Adano*.

"Is this from a school list, or a Mom list?"

Hope lifted a shoulder. "A Mom list."

"Do you like it?"

"Uh-huh. Mom said she did. Look." She opened to the inside cover, where Rachel's name was written in the precise hand of a schoolgirl who hadn't yet found her individualism. The date was below it.

"Wow," Katherine said. "Twenty-seven years ago."

"She was my age then. I think that's kinda neat."

"Me, too."

Jack turned around. "How're you doing?" he asked, but headed off before she could answer. "I'll be back."

Katherine watched him go, then turned questioning eyes on Hope.

"They wouldn't let him use the cell phone in here," Hope explained. "It messes up the monitors."

"Ah. He seems distracted."

"It's work. Look." She pointed at a flower arrangement on the sill. It was the newest, tallest, most lavish one there. "From Grandma."

Katherine might have guessed it. She also guessed it wouldn't be the last of Victoria's gifts. "That was sweet of her."

"Uh-huh." Hope refocused on Rachel, looking so sad this time that Katherine ached for her. "Do you think she knows I'm here?"

"Definitely."

"Really?"

"Really."

Hope considered that, then said, "Sam's down the hall."

"I know. I passed her on my way in." She had been tucked up in a phone booth with an algebra book in her lap, a pencil in her hand, and a huge wad of gum in her mouth. The sudden cessation of talk and the too-wide grin she gave Katherine suggested that she wasn't doing math.

"She was in here with Mom for a long time," Hope said in quick defense of her sister, "but she wanted to use Dad's phone, and he had to make his own calls. She'll be back. I called Duncan's. Guinevere's sleeping. She's been doing that a lot."

"What is it they say—that cats sleep eighteen hours a day?"

"She's been doing it more. Sometimes I think she isn't really sleeping, just doesn't have the energy to move. Like she's in a coma. Like Mom's."

"Uh-uh-uh," Katherine scolded gently. "Not like Mom's. Guinevere has a tumor. Your mom does not."

"Then why doesn't she wake up? How can she hear me and know that I'm here, without waking up to let me know? Doesn't she want to?"

"More than anything, I'd bet," Katherine said. "She's probably trying her best and annoyed that she can't . . . can't break out of whatever it is that's holding her there. We have to be patient. We have to let her know we'll be here until she does wake up."

Hope glanced cautiously back toward the hall, then whispered an urgent "Sam is scaring me."

Katherine leaned closer and whispered back, "Scaring you how?" She imagined Sam was talking gloom and doom about Rachel, trying to act old and wise, trying to get a rise out of Jack. But it wasn't that.

"The prom," Hope whispered. "I think they're planning something. I can't say anything to Daddy, because he'll get angry at her and then she'll get angry at me. And it's not like I *know* anything. I just *feel* it." She hunched her shoulders, which made the rest of her look even smaller. "She'll kill me if she knows I told you this. But I don't want anything *else* to happen."

"Tell you what," Katherine suggested. "How about I drop a few hints to your dad? No one needs to know you said anything. I'd only be doing what your mom would be doing."

"Mom would be talking to the other mothers. But Sam knows Daddy won't do that. *That's* what scares me most."

Katherine figured it would scare Rachel, too. "I can handle this," she said for the benefit of mother and daughter both. "Trust me?" she asked Hope, just as Jack returned. When Hope gave her a wide-eyed nod, she smiled and pulled a $5 bill from her pocket. "I'm desperate for tea. Would you run down and get me an Earl Grey? Maybe your dad would like coffee?"

Jack asked Hope for anything strong and black. Katherine waited until she had left before eyeing the work on the table. "Rachel said you were a workaholic."

"Not always. What you see here is my conscience. I'm holding people up because I'm not doing what I've committed to do. Except for picking up the girls, I've been here all day."

Katherine hadn't expected that. "I thought you were driving up to the city."

He tossed the phone on the table. "So did I. I changed my mind."

"Why?"

"Beats me." He pushed his hands through his hair. It looked like he'd done it more than once. Katherine had to admit that he seemed tired, and felt a trace of sympathy. He had a lot more on his mind this week than last week. She hated to add to it but had no choice. "Hope seems worried, but I think she'll be okay. How's Sam?"

"Actually," he said, sounding surprised, "she was pretty sweet this afternoon."

"That could mean trouble."

"Yeah, well, I'm not looking a gift horse in the mouth."

"Maybe you should," she said, only half teasing. "Teenaged girls are wily. I know. I've been there. Is she all set for the prom?"

"We're shopping for a dress this weekend."

"Want me to take her?"

"No. I'll do it. It should be an interesting experience."

Katherine would have gladly gone along. She had shopped with the girls before. Apparently, though, Jack was taking that responsibility he had mentioned earlier very seriously. Fine. Then she felt less guilty worrying him. "Is she still going to the prom with Brendan?"

"In a manner of speaking," Jack said, but he looked puzzled. "I can't get a feel for how paired up this is. In my day, you had a specific date, but Sam's pretty vague about who's with who. There are ten of them going in the limo from Lydia's house. The girls are spending the night there after the prom." He hmphed. "I think that's what did it."

"Did what?"

"Changed her mood. She tossed the spending-the-night thing at me when she was leaving the car this morning, fully expecting I'd refuse, but I don't see anything wrong with it. It sounds to me like a big sleepover. They've been doing sleepovers for years."

"Are you sure it's only girls?"

That gave him pause, but it passed. "She says it is. She says Lydia's parents will be there."

"I think," Katherine tried, making a show of debating it herself, "that Rachel might want you to give them a call."

Jack's jaw went harder. "If I did that, it would suggest I didn't trust my daughter."

"This isn't about trust. It's about checking in and being involved."

"I take it you've been through this. How old did you say your kids were?"

Katherine didn't have kids, and it hit home. There had been a time when having a child had meant the world to her. Then she had been advised to wait a bit. Then Roy had left. And Byron had come and gone. And suddenly she was forty-two.

"Low blow," Jack surprised her by saying. "Sorry, but I'm going through a tough time here. I've never parented a teenager before, not for more than a weekend, and *not* for things like this, but I'm trying my best to do what's right, and it isn't easy. Samantha and I don't exactly have a love fest going on down there in Big Sur. She doesn't like what I bring in for dinner, doesn't like the coffee I brew. She doesn't like my talking on 'her' phone, or sleeping in Rachel's bed or using Rachel's shower, or driving her to school. As far as she's concerned, I'm a major inconvenience in her life—like I was the one who caused the accident, like I'm enjoying all this, like I should sleep on the sofa night after night. She's given me lip about almost everything I've done— but maybe, just maybe we've turned a corner. She actually smiled at me when I picked her up at school." Pleading, he paused for a breath. "Let me enjoy it for a little bit, huh?"

JACK thought about enjoying it a bit as he drove down the coast. It wasn't the first time he had used those words in response to the antics of Samantha McGill. The first time was fifteen years before, when she was five months old and vehemently opposed to sleeping through the night. They had been living in San Francisco a full month, Samantha in a room that Rachel had painted the same hot pink and navy as her room in Tucson, so she didn't have the excuse of a strange place. She had been fed cereal at six, along with Rachel's milk then and again at eleven. It was now two in the morning, and she wanted more.

The battle had been going on for two weeks, and they were exhausted. Jack was working a new job, pulling sweatshop hours as junior architect in a San Francisco firm. Rachel was pulling similar ones caring for the baby, doing the last of the unpacking, sewing drapes, and painting furniture and walls. They had both been dead to the world when Samantha's wails blasted in from the next room.

Rachel moaned and took cover under Jack's arm.

Jack pressed the pillow to his ear. "She can't be hungry," he mumbled.

Rachel mumbled back, "She isn't. Go back to sleep."

But the wailing went on.

Rachel slipped out of bed and, wrapped in his largest red flannel shirt, went off to the baby's room. The crying stopped. She returned to bed and curled up against him again. They had barely settled, spooned together, when the crying resumed.

Jack pulled the blanket over their heads. That muted the sound, but it went on. Still under the covers, he turned to face Rachel. "She's not hungry," he whispered into the warm, sleepy dark that would have been purple had a light been on. "Think she's sick?"

"Not sick," Rachel mumbled. "Angry. Pediatrician said to let her cry."

They let her cry. After five minutes, the wailing was more persistent. Jack threw the blanket back and started to get up.

"Don't you dare bring her here," Rachel cried.

Jack wasn't about to. He wasn't touching that baby. He had changed a diaper earlier. One per evening was his limit. "I want to make sure she isn't stuck between the slats and the bumper."

"She wasn't before," Rachel murmured, but she was right behind him, tiptoeing from their room to Samantha's with her fingers hooked on the waist of his shorts. When he stopped at the baby's door, Rachel settled against his back with her cheek to his skin.

In the fragmental glow of a tiny night-light, he saw a pale crib, polka-dot bumpers, a mobile with Rachel's felt creatures cut and pasted in every color imaginable, and beneath it, his angry daughter.

The wails were higher pitched now, but he backed away. "She's kicking her arms and legs, the little pest."

They returned to bed and lay entwined for a minute, listening to a fury of cries, before Rachel snaked free. "She's working herself into a frenzy," she said and disappeared into the night.

Seconds later, the crying stopped. Two minutes later, Rachel climbed back into bed. They held their breaths, listening, holding each other, on edge. "That did it, that did it," Jack whispered hopefully.

Samantha screamed.

Rachel laughed. "Whoa."

"Whose idea was it to have this baby?"

"Not mine," she said, laughing again.

"Not *mine*."

The crying escalated.

"Let her cry," Jack whispered.

Rachel snuggled closer. "She'll wear herself out."

"Just a matter of time."

But they were wide awake. When wails became screams, Rachel announced full-voice, "I can't sleep with that noise."

"*You*."

Rolling away, she pushed out of bed and closed all but inches of their door. Back in bed, she pulled him under the covers again to dull the sound coming through the walls. "Kiss me," she said. "Drown it out."

"This is a sexy moment? With that *racket* going on?"

"Kissing's what started it, isn't it? So fight fire with fire."

Jack had to admit it made sense. If the first kiss he gave her lacked passion, he put more into the second. By the third, he was hearing less beyond the bed. His mind was filling with the sweet sounds of Rachel, the warmth of her mouth, the swell of her breasts, the gentle curve of her belly. He had dispensed with her shirt and was fully erect when she said with an audible smile, "It's working."

"Oh, boy," his voice was hoarse, "is it ever."

She laughed brightly. "Samantha, not you."

Sure enough, the noise from the other room was slowing to the sounds of a tired baby on the verge of sleep. But was Jack tired? Not on your life! "That's nice," he practically purred. "Might as well enjoy it a bit." Lacing his fingers with Rachel's on the pillow, he came over her, found just the right spot between her open thighs, and thrust in.

AN AMBER SUN hung low on the horizon when they arrived back in Big Sur. Samantha headed for the house. Hope headed for Duncan's. Not knowing quite where he should head, Jack remained standing by the car. He took several deep breaths. Curious about what it was in the air that he found so appealing, he wandered off the gravel drive, through alternating patches of redwood sorrel and dark, packed earth, to a fallen tree. Purple flowers were budding around the lowest of the dead branches. He sat down midway along the trunk.

Looking straight up, he found the tops of the redwoods, where the foliage was the fullest, and watched for movement. It was a cool, dry, quiet May night. The air smelled of thick textured bark, of patches of moss, of sweet cedar from the lower canyon. At a sound on the forest floor, he spotted a ragged bird hopping among the brush. It was a Steller's jay, its feathers a motley slate blue and gray.

"You won't find much here, bud," he murmured. The forest floor was too heavily shaded to allow for food. Berries and bugs would be more plentiful beneath the live oaks and madrones.

Still the jay foraged, hopping downhill, then up. Jack watched for a bit. It was a mindless interlude that ended before he was quite ready. At the sound of footsteps in the undergrowth, he turned. Hope was coming toward him cradling the tabby. Her face was so serious that for a minute he feared the cat had died. But its eyes opened and its paws and tail shifted the smallest bit when Hope sat down on his tree.

"She didn't eat today. Nothing."

Jack didn't know how to console her. Rather than say something dumb and meaningless, he slid along the branch until they were arm to arm. She was petting the cat, running her small hand over its fur, from nose to ears, over neck, back, and rump, all the way to its tail. She repeated the motion again and again, a hypnotic stroking. In the silence of the forest, Jack heard the cat's purr.

"She likes that," he murmured.

Hope nodded. She kept up the petting. The purring went on.

After a bit, curious, Jack stuck in one stroke between Hope's. The cat's fur was surprisingly soft, surprisingly warm. He tried it again, half expecting that the cat would raise her head and express her objection to a stranger's touch. But Guinevere didn't. Without moving her chin from the crook of Hope's elbow, she simply looked up at him with total trust.

It nearly did him in.

chapter eight

BY FRIDAY MORNING, when there was still no change in Rachel's condition, Jack requested a consultation with his man in the city, William Breen. Jack had every confidence that the man was the best. Not only had Tina come up with his name, but Victoria Keats had faxed him the very same one.

The conference took place by phone in Steve Bauer's office. Besides Bauer, there were Kara Bates, Cindy Winston, and Jack.

The latest stats were sent to Breen's computer. Bauer orally reviewed them. Kara gave interpretations based on her observation of the patient. Cindy described Rachel's lack of response during bathing, turning, and range-of-motion exercises.

Jack kept thinking that the millions poured into research each year would surely have produced some procedure, some medication to help Rachel, but in the end, Breen said, "I wish I could say there's something else to try, but we wouldn't be doing anything different if she were in San Francisco. Her case is typical. She continues to hold her own. This is only the fourth day."

Jack hadn't expected the coma to last *two* days, and said as much.

"Mm, that would have been nice," the doctor responded, "but head injuries don't always do what's nice. Her GCS score is holding steady."

"Yeah," Jack remarked. "At rock bottom." He had learned about the Glasgow coma scale. Since Rachel showed no eye opening, no verbal response, and no motor response, she had the lowest possible score.

"But the data says she's not getting worse."

"Will she?" Jack asked. "Is there a chance she'll take a sudden turn?" He still felt a clinch in his stomach every time the phone rang, every time he arrived at the hospital after being out of contact for even a brief time.

"She could," said the doctor. "But if that were to happen, your team will know immediately and be able to act. With comas, it's a waiting game. I'm sorry, Mr. McGill. I know that isn't what you want to hear, but it's a little like defusing a bomb. Hurry the process, and it's apt to explode."

ON HIS way back to Rachel's room, Jack placed a call to Victoria. She had wanted an expert involved in the case; he wanted her to know it had been done. He also wanted to thank her for the flowers and to give her an update on Rachel's condition, discouraging as it was.

He had to settle for leaving a message in New York. Victoria was still abroad.

WHEN BEN WOLFE arrived, Jack was sitting by Rachel's hip, feeling useless. After trading bland observations about her hair, which spilled nicely from the topknot Katherine had made, the swelling of her face, which was down a little, and the perkiness of her turquoise nightgown, Jack stood and said, "Talk to Rachel. I'll be back." Ben was no threat, and he had something to do.

From the bank of phones down the hall, he called Jill. At the sound of her voice, he felt a guilty tug. "Hey."

"Hey, yourself," she said with pleasure. "I was wondering when you'd remember I was here."

His guilt increased. "It's been a rough couple of days. The girls are pretty upset. I'm still at the hospital. Rachel hasn't woken up."

"I know."

"Ah. You called my office."

"No." She sighed. "I didn't want Tina to know that you hadn't called me, so I called the hospital."

He felt even worse. "I'm sorry, Jill. I've had a lot on my mind."

"You could have called," she chided. "Didn't you think I'd want to know how Rachel was doing?"

She would. She was that kind of person. And he couldn't say why he hadn't called. That was one of many things that were muddled up in his mind.

But she expected an answer. So he said, "I've been trying to juggle everything here—work, the girls, Rachel. It's a nightmare."

"One phone call, Jack. It would have taken ten seconds."

Ten seconds, max. But damn it, she wasn't as harried as he was. "You could have called me in Big Sur," he countered. "Rachel's number is listed."

There was a silence. Then a sad "I think you forgot."

He pushed a hand through his hair. "I didn't forget."

"I think it didn't matter enough to you to talk with me."

"No," he sighed, "there's just nothing to tell. Not so long ago I was in conference with some of the best medical minds around, and *they* had nothing to say. There's nothing, Jill. We can't do a damn thing but sit here and wait."

"You're missing my point. If I meant anything to you, you'd want to hear my voice. It would be a comfort."

How could her voice be a comfort when it reminded him of the dozens of loose ends he had left hanging in the city? He put his elbow on the top of the phone and his head on his fist. "This isn't a good time, Jill. It just isn't."

"Is that my answer?"

He sighed. "No. It isn't. But I'm grappling with something difficult. I need a little time."

"You always need time."

"You knew that when we met. You knew I had a demanding life."

"I didn't count on the demands coming from your ex-wife," she said, then caught herself. "God, I'm sorry, Jack. That was selfish of me. She's in a coma. She may die."

"She's not dying. My guess is she'll wake up by the first of the week."

He heard a cautious "I won't see you until then? Not even on Saturday night?"

Over the past few months, Jack had spent every Saturday night with Jill that he hadn't either been with the girls or out of town—and he looked forward to those nights. He relaxed with Jill. He could count on her to be stimulating, physically and intellectually. He did love her—until she got that tomorrow look in her eye. Then he felt boxed in, which was what he felt now.

"Can't do it this Saturday," he said, annoyed. What did she think he would do with the girls while he drove three hours north on a Saturday night? Okay, Samantha was fifteen and would probably have plans of her own, but she was too young to drive, they lived in the middle of nowhere, and their mother was critically ill. "I have to be there for the girls. They have lists of things for me to do for them this weekend, and between all that, I'll be taking them to visit their mother. The doctors want them to talk with her. They say the girls will keep her focused, maybe help bring her back. Time'll be tight this weekend."

Jill said, "I see."

But she didn't. He heard hurt between those two little words. "Maybe Monday, when they're at school," he said, because he was going to have to drive up to the office again whether Rachel woke up or not. "Want to plan on lunch?"

She was that easily pleased. The smile returned to her voice. "I'd like that."

"Say, one o'clock, at Stars?"

"Not Stars. Here. I'll make lunch."

Lunch at her house would be a longer affair. It would be harder to eat and run, and he didn't know how much time he would have. But Jill was special. Of the women he had dated since the divorce, she came closest to being right for him. She didn't mind his travels. She was wonderful at business dinners. One on one, she was a charming companion and a devoted lover. During the few times she had seen the girls, they had gotten along well. How not to get along with Jill? She deserved better than days without a call.

So he said, "Sounds good. I'll look forward to it.

Thanks for being understanding, Jill. That's the biggest help to me right now."

He hung up the phone feeling like a total heel.

THE FEELING followed him right back into Rachel's room.

Ben was saying something to her and looked up, red-faced. "We were talking about the show."

Jack couldn't resist. "What was Rachel saying?"

"Not—a whole lot. I was telling her that you've been looking through her work. What do you think? Do we have a shot at going ahead?"

Jack hadn't looked through her work. He hadn't been in her studio other than to check the fax machine, and then he had walked in and out without seeing a thing. It was deliberate. He knew that. The why of it, like the why of not calling Jill at least once a day, wasn't clear.

So he stated the obvious. "We have a shot at having a show if she wakes up. If she doesn't . . ." He waggled his hand.

"How many pieces are done?"

"I'm not sure. I didn't count."

"Maybe I should take a look."

"Nah. There's no need for you to drive all the way down." There was the possessiveness again. The man might be benign enough, but Jack didn't want him in Rachel's house. "I'll do the counting tomorrow, when I'm not worried about getting the girls to school. Will you be at the gallery this weekend?"

"Sunday, from twelve to five."

"I'll stop in." He put out his hand. "Thanks for stopping by. We really appreciate it."

Ben shook his hand. He looked back at Rachel as though wanting to say something, thought twice, and quietly left.

JACK actually dozed off sitting in the chair by Rachel's bed. One minute he put his head down beside her hand, the next he woke up with a jolt.

"I'm sorry. I didn't mean to wake you."

He looked groggily at the woman who had arrived. She wasn't a natural beauty. Her nose was too long, her face too narrow, her silver hair too thin. But she was put together nicely, wearing a silk tunic and slim pants, and there was a gentleness to her. There was also a wonderful smell. It appeared to come from the large, zippered container she held.

She felt familiar, soothing.

He stood. "I've met you, haven't I?"

Her eyes smiled. "I'm Faye Lieberman. I've been by before. Rachel and I are in book group together."

"Ah. Faye of the beautiful blue flowers," he said. "You're one of the golfers."

She blushed. "Well, I'm not very good at it, but my husband wanted to retire here to play, so I figured that if I didn't learn, I'd be bored silly." She set the zippered container on the tray table. "This is dinner. There should be leftovers for the weekend. I figured you could use a little something homemade by now. Heating instructions are inside."

"Bless you," he said. They could indeed use a little something homemade. He was touched. "That's very sweet of you."

"It's nothing. How's Rachel?"

"Lying here listening, but not saying a word."

Faye went to the bed rail and touched Rachel's arm. "I'm here, Rachel. I brought food for your family. Not exactly chicken soup. Jack, here, needs something more solid. At least, that's what my Bill always says. Chicken soup is for children and invalids. We know better, though, don't we?" She glanced at Jack. "Rachel made my chicken soup recipe once a week through much of the winter. Not that it gets very cold here. I kind of miss that, the change of seasons."

"Where are you from?"

"Originally New England. Then D.C. My husband was with the State Department." To Rachel, she said, "He signed up for your investment course."

"Rachel's investment course?"

Faye smiled and moved a hand to erase the misconception. "Rachel took it and liked it. We figured it would give Bill something to do. We'd like to invest a little money for our grandchildren. Right now, college seems a long way off, but it isn't getting cheaper. How are the girls?"

The girls! Jack shot a look at his watch. "Waiting to be picked up at school as we speak." He squeezed Faye's shoulder and eyed the zippered bag. "They'll be thrilled. It's been take-in all week. You're a good soul to remember us."

She waved off his praise. "It's in the genes. This is what Jewish mothers do best. Enjoy."

THEY did that—all five of them. Samantha had invited Lydia and Shelly to stay overnight in Big Sur, a fact that

Jack didn't learn until the two additional girls were jammed into the BMW, at which point it seemed more of an effort to say no and pry them out.

Maybe Katherine was right. A bigger car would help. Still, it seemed premature.

The insulated bag held chicken in a wine-and-tomato sauce, with carrots and potatoes. To a person, they ate well and with good humor. Samantha and her friends alternately tossed their hair behind one shoulder or another and chatted about everyone and everything that came to mind. Hope, with her own hair in a scrunchy at her nape and Guinevere on her lap, listened to them with something like awe, and Jack wasn't much different. Samantha and company moved from topic to topic in stream-of-consciousness style and had an opinion on just about everything. Jack was intrigued by the sheer stamina of their mouths.

It wasn't until the next morning, though, that he understood the deeper implication of the sleepover. "Of *course,* they're coming shopping with me," Samantha said when Jack had the temerity to suggest that he drop the two girls at their homes on the way. "That's the whole point! I can't pick out a dress myself, and you're not a woman. If Mom can't be here, I want my friends."

He wanted to say, *No way! I have my hands full with my own two kids. I don't need two extras. Besides, I can't bring an army to the ICU—not to mention that they can hardly all fit in my car!*

He also wanted to say, *What is that under your eyes? Since when do you wear eyeliner? Does your mother know about that?*

But he didn't want Samantha growing grumpy again, not when they were beginning to get along. So he bit down both thoughts.

They hit Saks. They hit Benetton. By the time they hit the three other specialty stores, he was regretting his decision. Had it been just Samantha and he, she would have found something at the first store, and they would have been long since done. Hope was getting antsy. *He* was getting antsy.

"One more stop," he informed them when they were standing on the street corner, debating which way to go. "The next place is it. So think hard. There was a perfectly good dress back at Saks."

The girls held a prolonged three-way summit. When they finally agreed to return there, Jack exchanged a smug look with Hope. The smugness disappeared when the dress Samantha carried to the cash register wasn't the baby blue one he had meant. This one was short, slim, and black.

"Uh, Sam, isn't that one a little too . . . much?"

"Too much how?"

"Sophisticated?"

"I'm fifteen."

"You look about twenty-two in that dress."

"That's the point," she said with a sudden broad smile.

That smile did something to Jack. It gave him a glimpse of the beautiful young woman she was quickly becoming. He felt a jolt inside, a startling burst of pleasure and pride, followed closely by fear. Fifteen was nearing the age of consent. Was he ready for that? No. Could he prevent it? No.

"Would your mother like this dress?" he asked, suspecting that the Rachel who loved color and flow would have her qualms.

"She would *love* it," Sam said and, with another of those killer smiles, held out a hand for his credit card.

JACK gave serious thought to getting that new car during the ride from Carmel to Monterey. Lydia and Shelly insisted that they wanted to see Rachel, so five of them piled in again, but the dress was the final straw. For an itty-bitty thing, it caused a huge stir. Samantha wanted it hung. When there was no room for that, she decided that it should lie flat, but there was even less room for that. Jack, who knew something about fabrics, finally informed her that she could ball the thing up and it would bounce right back into shape without a wrinkle, especially once she had it on, it was that tight. That set her off. She finally agreed to drape it over the seat, but she wasn't happy with him, which meant that all his efforts to please had gone for naught. He would have given his right arm just then for a Cherokee.

Buying a car was something big, though. It was a major expense—and, yes, Rachel would need something new, but even if she was awake when they got to the hospital, she wouldn't be driving for a while, and then she would want to pick out her own car. He had done it for her once before, and wasn't making the same mistake twice.

They had been married for seven years. Her red VW was far older than that and had died and been revived more than once. It was still chugging along, but it badly needed a new radiator. Thinking to surprise her, now that he was finally making good money, Jack drove it off one morning under the guise of doing repairs and returned home with a Volvo. She had been heartsick. It was one of the first all-out, top-of-the-lungs arguments they'd had—or one of the last? He couldn't recall. Arguing wasn't their style. And she had calmed down. Rachel wasn't one to beat a dead horse. The VW was gone. The Volvo was theirs. The dignity of her surrender had made him feel worse.

He hadn't thought about that argument in years, had always chalked it up to a case of principle and pride on Rachel's part, the feminist in her wanting to make her own decisions. At the time, his star was rising fast. Hers was on hold while she raised the kids. She had a right to be feeling defensive.

Only, she hadn't said that she wanted to make her own decisions. She had said that she wanted them to make decisions together. She had said that that was what couples did, and didn't he *want* her input?

Well, he did. She should have known that. But before long she was starting to make more of *her* own decisions, all without consulting him. She claimed he was out of town. He suspected it was tit for tat on an ongoing scale.

All of which had nothing to do with the present. He asked her about a new car. She didn't answer. So the decision was his. And he wasn't rushing out to buy.

He could lease one, he supposed. But even that was a lengthy commitment. After all, he was only filling in until Rachel woke up.

Better to wait.

JACK lingered with Rachel. He moved her hands around his, lacing their fingers, spooning their fists. He brushed her hair. He studied her face.

The girls knew their way around the hospital well

enough to take themselves to the cafeteria for cold drinks, a while later for lunch, a while after that for frozen yogurt. Lydia's mother came to visit and left with Lydia and Shelly. A refreshingly docile Katherine came and went, as did Charlie with the pink streak in her hair, Jan with the no-nonsense manicure, the mommy's beeper, and a golfer's tan, and a nondescript Nellie and Tom.

When others were in the room, Jack backed off. He didn't know these people. They were part of the life that Rachel had made without him. Oh, they were cordial. They introduced themselves and said kind things about the girls. But the situation was as awkward for them as it was for him. He was the bad guy in a room full of good guys.

Still, he outstayed them all. He helped the weekend nurse bathe Rachel and exercise her limbs. When her lips looked dry, he got Vaseline from the nurses' station. When her head looked uncomfortably angled, he propped it with pillows.

"When are we leaving, Daddy?" Hope asked every hour or so. Her cat was with Duncan. She wanted to get her.

Jack understood that; still, he put it off. He told himself that since the weekend staff didn't know Rachel, he could help out, but there was more to it. He felt better when he was with her, felt that his being there was a good thing in a bad time. He felt *decent* being with her, felt calmer. There wasn't any static here. There were no choices to make. All that was asked of him was to be, to talk, to assist. It was life at its primal best.

But Samantha was due at another friend's for a birthday overnight, and Hope, who kept trying to bury herself in a book, was giving him the most beseeching little looks, so he finally trundled them off.

RACHEL'S studio waited.

After dropping Hope at Duncan's, Jack drove back to the little local market for groceries. He put the leftovers of Faye's chicken into the oven. He put a load of laundry in the washing machine. He sat out under the redwoods, breathing woodsy air. The midday warmth had ebbed. It was a clear, cool, sweetly fragrant late afternoon.

Hope joined him, and they sat together for a while. He ran his hand along Guinevere's back, feeling warmth and weakness. He prayed that Hope was right, that the cat wasn't suffering. He knew Hope was.

Rachel's studio waited.

Jack put dinner on the table and took his time eating. Between bites, he asked Hope about school, about her friends, about the book she was reading. He told her he was proud of the way she was taking care of Guinevere, and when she burst into tears, he leaned over her chair and wrapped his arms around her. She still smelled of little girl, all warm and sweaty. He knew it wouldn't be long before she would be wanting short, skinny black dresses, too. For now, though, she was all innocence.

He wanted to say something about the cat, but he couldn't think of anything to make her feel better. So he just held her. It seemed fine.

When her tears slowed, he said, "Hey. Want to give me a hand?"

"W-with what?" she asked against his arm.

"Mom's paintings. We have to see what's what, so we can tell ole Ben what to do about a show. I've been putting off going in there."

"Why?"

"I don't know. I guess because I've always liked her work."

"So why don't you want to look at it?"

"I do." He realized that didn't jibe with what he had said before. "But her work always gets to me."

"Makes you sad?"

"Not sad."

"Happy?"

"It makes me . . . *feel*."

Hope looked up at him, her eyes wet but wide. "She was doing sea otters on Monday. They are—*so*—*neat*. They're still on the easel. Want to see?"

She was beautiful from the inside out, his youngest daughter. Sweet, sensitive. Too often dominated by her older sister, but not tonight. Tonight she was the little girl who used to crawl into his lap and make him feel like a million bucks.

He smiled. "If you take me."

THEY spent an hour in the studio. Then Hope went to her room to read, and Jack spread the contents of his portfolio on the kitchen table to work. He had barely taken a look at what was there when he turned around and went back to the studio.

Rachel had made things easy. Tacked to her board was a list of the paintings that she had planned to include in the show. The pieces she had been working on just prior to the accident stood closest to the easel. Other pieces stood in clearly marked stacks. He had gone through them with Hope as a buffer. She saw subject matter and felt mood, but was most concerned about telling Jack little stories that went with each. He let her talk, pleased to see her focused on something other than the cat.

Now he went through the pieces, studying each one, moving on, then back. Rachel painted wildlife. In addition to the sea otters so graphically depicted, there were gray whales and Arctic wolves, egrets, quail, and loon. There were deer in snow and deer in high grass. There was a meadow of butterflies, and a rattlesnake so well camouflaged that a casual viewer would miss it. There was a coyote, looking Jack in the eye with such a vivid mix of fear and warning that he nearly backed off.

This was why he had put off seeing Rachel's work. He had always found it strong to the point of being intimidating. Whether she used oils, watercolors, acrylics, or pastels, she caught something so real and direct that he felt it—a look, a mood, a need. There was no mystery to why her following was growing. In a state and age where environmental concerns were rising, she captured the vulnerability of the wild.

Take the rattlesnake. There might well have been a caption below it that said the damned thing wanted nothing more than to fade into the woodwork and that it wouldn't harm a thing unless it feared harm to itself.

Powerful stuff to create with just the stroke of a brush or palette knife. He could never do anything like that, didn't have the vision or the skill. She was far more talented than he.

He suspected that that was why he had pursued architecture. True, he had been on that track before meeting Rachel. But they'd had such fun with each other that for a short time he had toyed with the idea of spending a lifetime painting with her. He hadn't, ostensibly because one of them needed to earn money. Deep down inside, though, he knew that his work would always be inferior to hers.

Still, they *had* had fun.

He went through her pieces again. Eleven paintings were done and ready to frame. Seven, including the otters, were finished except for the background, which held sketchy forms but no more. Field sketches and photographs were affixed to the back of each piece.

His best guess? She would need a week and a half to finish the seven. And the framing? The moldings were stacked in long strips by the baseboard. She had picked a wide wood frame, so simple and natural that it would enhance rather than compete. Pushing it, she could do the framing in several days.

Two weeks of work for a show two weeks away. It would have been a cinch, if the artist weren't in a coma.

HE had planned to tell Ben Wolfe exactly that at the gallery Sunday afternoon, but before he could say a word, Ben led him into an adjoining room. Three paintings, framed much as Rachel planned to frame the rest, hung in an alcove. Ceiling spots hit each canvas in such a way that the subject was perfectly lit and riveting. Ben knew his stuff.

"We had four," he explained, seeming taller and stronger on his own turf. "One of them sold last week. Another of the four isn't for sale at all. Rachel won't let it go. Not that I blame her. I'd hold on to it, too, if it were mine. It's my all-time favorite." He was looking at the one he meant, but Jack had already picked it out. A layman might not have caught the difference between the three. Not only wasn't he a layman, but he was personally involved.

The painting that Ben loved, that Rachel refused to sell, was one that she and Jack had done together. The subject was a pair of bobcat pups on a fallen log, the background a meadow surrounded by trees. They had come on the scene during a busman's weekend hiking through—yes—the same Santa Lucias that Rachel now called home. She had done the pups, he the background.

The pups were more vivid now than he remembered them being. She might have touched them up, but the background was exactly as it had been—all his.

"What do you love about it?" Jack asked Ben. So maybe he, too, needed stroking.

Ben, in his innocence, didn't hesitate to tell him. "The background is complimentary to the rest, but different, very subtly different. It makes the bobcats more striking."

"Have you told Rachel that?"

"Many times."

"What does she say?"

"Just that it was done a long time ago. So where do we stand? How many more paintings are in her studio?"

Eleven, Jack thought, but he was still looking at the picture he and Rachel had done together. She hadn't told Ben about his participation. Dishonest, perhaps, but interesting. The piece wasn't for sale. That was good.

"Do we have a shot at the show?" Ben asked.

"I, uh, I think . . . yeah, actually, I think we do," Jack said, because they definitely had a shot at it. That wasn't the real question. The *real* question was how Rachel would feel if Jack picked up a brush and collaborated with her again.

chapter nine

JACK WAS FEELING stronger. He didn't know why, since Rachel's condition hadn't changed. He figured it had to do with being more rested. Life in Big Sur didn't make evening demands. He had slept more in the last few days than he had in months.

It surprised him. By rights, he should have been lying awake worrying about Rachel and the girls and what might be if Rachel didn't recover. He should have been losing sleep over work and the firm, should have been staring at the ceiling wondering what to do about Jill. And he did think about all those things—but during the day. Rachel's bed was firm, and even if the scent of her on the sheets roused the devil of his id, he had always slept well when he was with her.

He thought about that now, driving south along the coast with the girls in the car. Rachel was a cuddler. For him, that had meant having a breath of warmth against back, front, arm, or hip, depending on how she was burrowed. She snuggled in as though his body were a magnet. During the night, at least, he had always felt competent and strong.

So sleeping better was one possible reason for his current mood.

Another might be the drive itself. He used to find driving relaxing, way back, before they moved to the city. What he felt now reminded him of that. Traffic always thinned after Carmel, allowing him to catch more of the passing scenery—the beach, artichoke fields, the touch of purple where wildflowers were starting to bloom on the low hills swelling beyond. He could feel himself mellowing once he reached this stretch, could feel himself breathing more deeply. Not even the spot where the accident had occurred changed that.

Or maybe it was Rachel's work. He kept thinking about the gallery, about Ben's favorite painting, about the ones in her studio waiting to be finished. He kept thinking that it would be fun to paint again.

It was like there was something new and different in his life. Something exciting. Challenging. *Meaningful* was the word that came to mind, which was odd, since his life was *plenty* meaningful. But there it was.

THE PHONE was ringing when they walked in the door. Samantha ran for it. Jack followed her into the kitchen and waited nervously. If something had happened at the hospital—good *or* bad—he would turn right around and return to Monterey.

Samantha passed him the phone with a look of frustration. "It's David."

Jack felt his own frustration as he took the phone. David had been sending messages all week. He wanted work done, but Jack's mind was elsewhere. "How're you doing, David?"

"Jack? Jack? Is it really you?"

Jack looked out the window. The early evening sun snagging the tops of the redwoods spilled a glow through airy needles and on down densely scaled bark. There was something settling about it. His voice was more forgiving than it might otherwise have been. "It's been a long day, pal."

"No change, then?"

"No change. What's up?"

"I just got a call. Flynn's gone."

"To Buffalo? It's about time."

"To Walker, Jansen, and McCree."

Walker, Jansen, and McCree. The competition. Michael Flynn had defected. He was the third one in six weeks. At least he wouldn't have taken any accounts with him. Clients weren't drawn to Michael. He was a follower, not a leader.

"Will you be long?" an aggrieved Samantha asked.

Jack held up a hand to silence her and said to David, "Okay. We can live with this. It makes sense. WJM's work is more local than ours. Michael has young kids and doesn't want to travel."

"I agree with you there, but what about you? You're the one who'll have to fly to Buffalo in his place."

Habit kicked in. For a split-second, Jack looked ahead to the workweek and debated what he could shift around or cancel to allow for several days in New York. Then he realized that he had already canceled and shifted to the limit to clear the next patch for Rachel.

She had to wake up. It would be a week tomorrow. It was time.

In the meanwhile, there was a solution. There was always a solution. He made a quick mental assessment of the office situation vis-à-vis the Buffalo project. "Brynna Johnson can do it."

David made a disapproving sound. "Brynna's only a draftsperson."

"She's more experienced than the others, and she knows Buffalo. Besides, I think she's great."

"She's pregnant."

Jack hadn't known that. "No kidding? But that's okay. We can still move her up."

"What's the point of doing that if she'll be leaving?"

"Will she?"

"You know how women are these days. What'll happen— trust me, this happens *all* the time—is that she'll say she's taking a standard maternity leave, then at the end of it she'll tell us she's not coming back. Why should we make a woman like that a project manager?"

"Because she's talented," Jack said, thinking of his daughters being in the same boat one day, "and because maybe if we put out for her, she'll put out for us. It's a matter of instilling loyalty."

David snorted. "Loyalty? Good God, I haven't heard that word in a while. Has anyone else?"

Fine. So loyalty wasn't something they had talked much about. But it was time. Instability in the lower echelons of the firm made things harder for the people on top. Jack had to be able to rely on his associates. He hadn't realized how much, until now.

"Maybe if she feels she's moving up with us," he said, "she'll come back after the baby. How far along is she?"

"I don't know. Three months? Four months?"

Jack remembered Rachel at four months. She had barely looked pregnant with Samantha, had looked it a little more with Hope. The early change had been in her breasts and her belly, both gently swollen, creamy, soft.

That was what Jack had seen. The rest of the world had seen that by the fourth month, Rachel had outgrown morning sickness and was feeling good. She hadn't wanted coddling, hadn't wanted extra attention, hadn't wanted anyone telling her not to do what she normally did. All she asked for was the occasional hot fudge sundae with mocha almond ice cream. That was her favorite, her very favorite. The ecstatic look on her face—the way she sucked off each spoonful, scraping the very last of the fudge from the rim of the dish—was a sight to behold.

Rachel in her fourth month of pregnancy had been confident and strong. Brynna Johnson struck Jack as the same type.

"Brynna can go to Buffalo," he decided. "Unless she doesn't want to. In which case we'll send Alex Tobin. But Brynna's my first choice."

"Dad, I need the phone," Samantha whined.

David said, "Why not go yourself? If Rachel is stable—"

"She's in a coma. I can't leave now."

"Okay. Forget traveling. I'll settle for getting you back in the office. Hell, I'll settle for four hours a day. Do it while the girls are in school. If Rachel is unconscious, she won't know you're gone, and if she wakes up, hell, if she wakes up she won't *want* you there. We have work to do, Jack. It'll only wait so long."

Jack and David went back a long way. They had met as draftsmen sharing the bottom rung of the ladder and, commiserating, had started the climb together. Jack was the stronger designer, David the better businessman, but they shared identical dreams of success, recognition, and monetary reward. Early on in those bottom-rung days, when such dreams were a mainstay of survival, they decided to form a firm together someday. It made good business sense. Between their different strengths, their shared goals, and the diversity of their cultural backgrounds, they covered a good many bases.

For two years, the dream remained a dream. They slowly climbed the ladder, becoming junior architects, then project architects. Then, in the blink of an eye, everything changed. On the day when David charmed a large company into hiring them independently of the firm where they worked, they resigned and formed Sung and McGill. In the thirteen years since, they had been of one mind as to what was needed to make the firm a success—and they might still be. Jack just wished his partner was more sensitive.

"I need understanding here, Dave. I need help."

"I gotcha. But for how long? She's your past; we're your present and future."

"Da-ad?" Samantha made two impatient syllables of his name.

He put a finger in his ear and turned his back. "Do you want to call Brynna, or should I? No. Forget that question." David could be abrasive. He feared what the man might say to Brynna. "I'll call her. I'm driving up tomorrow morning. I'll meet with her and make sure she understands what has to be done."

"Have you talked with Boca?"

"Oh, yeah. I've talked with Boca. The problem is with the footprint, which means altering the whole fuckin' design." Why did he fear it wouldn't be for the last time?

His stomach churned just thinking about it. "Listen, David, I have to get off the phone—"

"To do *what?* Jack, I'm the front guy here. I'm the one running around drumming up work. I need to know you're making progress on something. You are working down there, aren't you? The girls are in school all fuckin' day, and there isn't a hell of a lot you can do for Rachel."

For a minute, Jack was angry enough to hold his tongue. When he was in control again, he said, "Actually, there is. I can paint. Hey, my daughter needs the phone. I have to go, Dave. Later." He hung up the phone.

"Paint what?" Samantha asked, tossing her hair back in a gesture that was at the same time negligent and powerful.

"Your mom's stuff," he answered.

She screwed up her face in horror. "You can't do that. Mom's stuff is hers. You can't mess with it."

The phone rang again. He beat her to it. "Yes?"

"It's Victoria. How's my daughter?"

"You *can't*," Samantha insisted.

"She's the same," he told his mother-in-law, returning the finger to his ear. "The doctors think that's good news."

"I don't. There must be something they can do. I've been asking people here, and they all agree. You don't just sit around and wait. I can't tell you the number of horror stories, *horror* stories, I've heard about times when action wasn't taken that should have been taken. If I were you, I wouldn't want to find myself six months from now looking back and regretting that I didn't push. Didn't my man have *any* suggestions?"

"None that were different from the doctors here."

"The doctors there. Huh. The one I talked with the other day sounded too young to know much. I'd like to consult with someone in New York. I'll be back there later tomorrow. My board was sending flowers. Did they arrive?"

"A few minutes ago, but she's in the ICU, Victoria. It'd be best if you asked people not to send things. We'll only have to give them away." It wasn't the whole truth, but he envisioned Victoria spreading the word and an entire flower shop materializing in Rachel's room.

"You told me not to come, Jack. Has that changed? Is there anything I can do there?"

Samantha tugged at his arm. *Wait,* he mouthed, then said to Victoria, "We're marking time."

"Has your mother been down?"

"I haven't talked with her."

"She doesn't know? That's *terrible,* Jack. Give her a call. She should be told. I'll call you again tomorrow. In the meantime, you know how to reach me."

"It isn't right," Samantha said as he hung up the phone.

"Tell me about it," he muttered, thinking about motherly devotion. If Victoria came to see Rachel, she would drive them all up a tree. And his own mother? A phone call would be bad enough. Somehow, some way she would blame him for the accident.

"So you won't?" Samantha asked.

"Won't what?"

"Mess with mom's work?"

He shifted gears. "I wasn't planning to 'mess' with it. I was planning—I was *toying* with the idea of finishing a few of those pieces so that Ben can go ahead with the show."

"She wouldn't want you doing that."

"Oh? Did you ask?"

Samantha made a face. "That was a mean thing to say."

"Well, did you? No, because your mother is in a coma, which means that none of us can ask, so we don't know *what* she wants. She did want this show. Do you doubt that?"

Samantha grunted what he took to be a no.

"And Ben says the show can't be postponed, so what are we supposed to do?"

"Some of her pictures are finished. They can be in the show."

And if your mother doesn't ever wake up or, worse, dies? It may be now or never, toots, he wanted to say, but he held his temper in check. "Know the picture at the gallery of the bobcat pups in the meadow?"

"Of course I know it," she said in disgust. "Anyone who's been in this house knows it. It was in the living room for years. It's Mom's favorite."

"Right," he said, gaining strength. "Do you know that I helped paint it?" Her withering look said that not only didn't she know it, but that she didn't believe it for a minute. "You were six years old. Your mother and I went hiking in the mountains not far from here. When we came back, that was one of the pictures we painted."

"Like, what part did *you* do?" Samantha mocked. "A *tree?*"

There hadn't been many times when one of his children had angered him to the point of losing control, and this wasn't one, but he wasn't taking any chances. Very deliberately, he tucked his hands in his pockets. Had he been his father, he would have used one of them to take the scornful look off Samantha's face. There had to be a better way.

"Have you ever drawn a tree?" he asked.

"Everyone's drawn trees."

"Yeah?" Catching her wrist in a way that was loose but locked, he strode toward the front door.

"Where are you *taking* me?" she cried. "I have things to *do!*"

He didn't talk, didn't look back, didn't stop until they were in the woods and standing face-to-face with the trunk of one of the largest of the redwoods. It wasn't one of the giant sequoias that grew farther north and inland, just a coast redwood, but it would do fine.

Drawing Samantha in front of him, he held her rigid shoulders and said over the crown of that straight blond hair, "What do you see?"

"Bark," she snapped.

"What else?"

"*Bark.*"

"Okay, what color is it?"

"Red," she said, then slowly, pedantically, "This is a redwood."

"Bright red? Brick red? Mahogany? Maroon?"

"I don't know. Whatever."

"If you were to paint it, what color would you make it? Bright red? Brick?"

When she didn't answer, he squeezed a shoulder.

"Darker than that," she muttered.

"Mahogany?"

"Maybe."

"All of it?"

"What do you mean?"

"Would you paint all of it mahogany?"

"Yes," she bit out.

He released one shoulder, reached over it, and touched a piece of the bark. "But what about this part? The way the light hits, it's darker by a shade or two." He moved his finger. "This part's a shade or two darker than that." And again. "This part's almost black. Can you see that?"

"*Yes,* I can see it."

"If you paint the whole thing mahogany, you'll lose the texture." He swept the pads of his fingers over the bark. "Look at the shape of this piece, wider on top, tapering down. And the way this one waves back and forth. And this sickle-shaped piece? You'd lose these shapes if you did the whole thing one color." He looked higher. "And up there? Where the sunset slants in? It makes the bark more orange than red. So you'd miss that, too, if you did the whole thing mahogany." He looked way up. "Now look at the needles."

"You've made your point."

"Look at them anyway," he said, framing her head with his hands and using only enough pressure as was necessary to tip it up. "The needles are feathery. Rich green. No—more blue-green in this light, I think. Warmer, almost lime, where the sun hits." He paused. "Is it the needles that smell so good, or the bark?"

"I don't know. Is it *my* fault that I'm the only one in this family who can't draw?"

Jack was so surprised by the question that he let her go when she twisted away.

"And just because you know about colors," she blurted out, turning from ten feet away, "doesn't mean you painted part of Mom's picture. If you did, why would she have it hanging in the living room? She divorced you. She wanted you out of her life!"

She stomped off, leaving Jack feeling empty again.

❧ ❧ ❧

"MY FATHER is a jerk," Samantha told Lydia. She was breathing hard. "Who does he think he is, barging in here and taking over? He doesn't know what my mother wants. He hasn't lived with her in six years. No, *longer.* He wasn't *there* for at *least* another six years. Probably even *more.*"

"Aw, Sam, he's not that bad."

"You don't have to live with him. You're not the one he's watching all the time. You don't see him trying to take over everything. *You're* not the one who can't borrow your mother's clothes because *he's* in there all the time. He said he used to help my mother paint, and I'm like, 'Why didn't she ever tell *us* that?' and he doesn't have an answer. I'm *sick* of having him around. I can't do *anything* right when he's here. Know what he wants? He wants me to shut up. He wants me to be sweet and silent and obedient like Hope. But I'm not like Hope. I don't *want* to be like Hope."

"I don't think he wants that. Did he ever say it?"

"He wouldn't say it. But I know. I can see the way he looks at her and the way he looks at me. It's different."

"I thought he was pretty nice."

"That was what he wanted you to think. It was an act."

"He seems really worried about your mother."

"Yeah. Because if she doesn't get better, he'll be stuck with us. That'd cramp his style. Why are you sticking up for him? You don't know the half of it. You should meet the woman he dates. Jill. Jack and Jill. Can you believe it? She's nice enough to make you sick."

"Is he gonna marry her?"

"Poor her, if he does. He's fickle. Before long, he's out looking for better."

"Is that what he did to your mom?"

"Why *else* would they get divorced?" Call waiting clicked. "Why *are* you taking his side? You're supposed to be *my* friend, Lydia. Hold on." She pressed the button. It was Brendan. Normally, talking with Brendan wouldn't hold a candle to talking with Lydia, but Samantha was furious with Lydia just then, so she took the call. "Lydia's being a dweeb," she told Brendan straight out.

"So you know about the party?"

"Know what?"

"Didn't she tell you? She was supposed to."

"Tell me *what?*"

There was a pause, then a meek "Maybe you should call her."

"Brendan. *Tell* me."

"Her parents are staying home," he blurted out.

"*What?*"

"Lydia let it slip that the guys were coming back afterward, too, so they changed their plans. They're gonna be there all night."

"*Lydia* let it slip?" Samantha sighed in disgust. "How could she *do* that?"

"Some of the other parents started calling her parents, so they started asking her questions, and it slipped out."

"I should have known." Lydia had been her best friend since third grade, but lately she was too soft. All along she had been nervous about the party. She was scared that someone would throw up, her parents would find out why, and she'd be the one punished. So now everyone would miss out. "She *is* a dweeb. This ruins the whole thing."

"Why?"

"Forget the beer, if her parents are there."

"Yeah, but my mother thought her parents were going

to be there all along, so now I won't get in trouble. Besides, they'll stay in the other room. It won't be so bad."

"Oh, yuk! You're as pathetic as Lydia is." When he had nothing to say about that, she made a guttural sound. "This prom is going to be totally boring. I'm not sure I want to go."

He was silent for a long minute. "What do you mean?"

"I may not go."

He should have protested. If it had been her, she would have. But that was asking too much of Brendan. Instead, after *another* silence, he said, "What about me?"

"I think you should take Jana," she decided.

"You do?"

"Yes." She wasn't going with a wimp.

"You really don't want to go?"

"I really don't. Call Jana."

He couldn't think of a thing to say to that but a weak "Oh. Okay. See you tomorrow."

Samantha hung up the phone and fumed. She had been waiting *forever* for a prom, for limos and all-night parties and beer. She had been to a zillion dances. If she'd thought this was going to be another one, she'd have bought the dorky blue dress her father liked. But this was a *prom*. It was supposed to be different.

Thank you, Lydia. Thank you, Brendan. Neither of them had any guts. Neither of them had a sense of adventure. They were big babies. Was *she* the only one who wasn't?

She knew of another person who wasn't. Picking up the phone, she pressed in his number. She knew it by heart, had called it many times. Before, she hadn't done anything but listen to his voice.

Her pulse raced when it came to her now, a deep, cool, seventeen-year-old " 'Lo?"

"Hi, Teague. It's Samantha. You know, from the school bus?"

The voice turned smooth around a smile. "I think I know Samantha from the school bus, only she hasn't been there all week."

"My mom's been sick, so my dad's been driving me up. How's things?"

"Better now. I was beginning to think you were avoiding me."

She grinned. "I wouldn't do that. I mean, I go to my dad, 'I really want to take the bus,' and he goes, 'But I want to drive your sister, and she won't go without you.' So I'm stuck in the car."

"Hey. Was it *your* mom who had an accident?"

"It was," Samantha said, feeling important. "She was driving up to Carmel when someone hit her. The car went off the road and over the cliff. She was underwater for ages. They got her breathing again, but she's in a coma, and they don't know if she's going to wake up. We've been spending every minute we can in her hospital room."

"Is it gross?"

Samantha straightened her shoulders. "It's actually fine. After a while, you forget about the machines and tubes. They want us to talk with her, so that's what we do. They say she hears us and that if anything can bring her back, it's our voices."

"Cool."

"The thing is that I've been so *obsessed* with my mom and the hospital that I haven't been thinking about anything else, but my dad said that my mom would want me to go to my prom—it's Saturday night—only I haven't asked anyone yet. So. What do you think? Want to go with me?"

"Where is it?"

Her heart fell. Teague was a junior. *His* prom would be held in a hotel. "It's at school," she murmured and raced on, "but the thing is that we don't have to stay there long. I mean, it's going to be a dumb little prom, but if my mom would want me there, I think I should go. I have a gorgeous black dress that my dad says is too sexy for someone my age, which shows how much *he* knows. So, do you want to go?"

"Sure." His voice was smiling again. "I'll go."

She smiled back. "Awesome!"

HOPE sat on her bedroom floor. A book lay open beside her, but she was studying her calendar, the one Rachel had made her, with a different watercolor for each month. Guinevere was on her lap, curled in a limp little ball, making precious few sounds.

Carefully cradling the cat, she rose and went out in her stocking feet to find her father. He wasn't in the living room or the kitchen, wasn't in the den, wasn't in her mother's bedroom. She found him in the studio. He was leaning against a wall, ankles crossed, arms folded. He was deep in concentration, studying canvases that he had lined up on the opposite side of the room.

She stood quietly by the door, telling herself that maybe she should leave and come back later. But she needed to talk with him.

"Hi, sweetie," he said and looked at her feet. "Where are the boots?"

"In my room. What are you doing?" she asked.

"Looking at your mother's stuff. She's good."

"Are you really going to finish her pictures?"

"I don't know. It was just a thought. What do you think? Would your mother be angry with me if I did?"

Hope didn't think so. She hadn't ever heard Rachel say anything bad about Jack. Sam told her she just wasn't listening, but she was. "Daddy?"

"What, sweetie?"

"It'll be a week tomorrow. Do you think Mommy's going to wake up?"

"I do. It's just taking longer than I had hoped it would."

"What do the doctors say?"

"Not much. They're waiting, too. They're pleased that she's not getting worse."

Hope guessed that if Rachel wasn't getting worse, then the bad stuff she was feeling had to do with her cat. She raised her arms so that she could rub her face in Guinevere's fur. It was as soft as ever. But something wasn't right.

"Guinevere's getting worse," she said. "I don't think she hears me anymore. I clap, and she doesn't even turn her head. She's going to die soon, Daddy."

He pushed away from the wall, crossed the room, and rubbed Guinevere between the ears. "Is she in pain?"

"No. She'd meow if she was." She swallowed. Her throat hurt. She had to force the words out. "Daddy, what'll I do when she dies?"

He thought for a minute. "You'll be sad. You'll grieve for her."

That wasn't what Hope meant. "What will I do with *her?* I mean, I can't just . . . throw her out like she was chicken bones."

He looked cross. "You shouldn't be worrying about this now, Hope. It doesn't accomplish anything. This cat doesn't look to me like she's ready to die."

But Hope felt the urgency of it. "She is. I know it, Daddy. I can *feel* it."

"You're just scared."

"No," she insisted. "It's happening. So what am I going to *do?*"

He frowned, not so much cross now as unsure. "What do you want to do?"

"I want to bury her."

He scratched his head and left his hand up there for a minute. She could see that he didn't know what to do. Samantha was right. He didn't think the way they did.

"Okay," he said, surprising her. "You can bury her. There must be a pet cemetery somewhere around here."

But Hope didn't want a pet cemetery. She didn't want to have to go driving to see Guinevere. She wanted the cat nearby, wanted Guinevere to know that *she* was nearby.

"Or we can bury her in the forest," Jack said, glancing out the window. "Somewhere close. Would you feel better if we did that?"

Much, Hope thought, nodding.

"Done," he said and pulled her close.

She didn't say anything for a minute because her throat hurt again. This time it was in relief, because Sam was wrong. He did understand. That meant he cared.

"Daddy?" she whispered so Sam wouldn't hear. "You won't leave us alone, will you?"

"How could I do that?"

She knew that if Sam annoyed him enough, he could and would. "If Mommy doesn't wake up and you have to go back to the city to work, you could hire someone to stay here."

"I won't."

"Do you promise?"

"I promise."

She sighed. Even more softly, with the smallest bit of breath, she said, "I love you."

He didn't answer, but she felt his cheek against the top of her head, and in that instant, the clock turned back and she believed.

WHEN SHE woke up the next morning, Guinevere hadn't moved from the spot where Hope had put her the night before. Frightened, she leaned close, close enough so that the cat would feel her breath. "Guin?" she whispered, rubbing the cat's cheek with a fingertip. When she felt the smallest movement against her finger, she let out a breath.

She draped an arm lightly around the cat and lay close, thinking, *I love you, Guinevere, I love you,* and heard the whisper of an answering purr. Then it stopped. For several minutes, Hope didn't move. "Guin?" she whispered. She stroked the cat's head and waited for a purr, stroked again, waited again. When there was nothing, she buried her head in Guinevere's cooling fur and began to cry.

"Hope?" Jack called, coming to the door. "Are you up?"

Gulping sobs bubbled up from inside. When she tried to stop them, they only grew louder. She pulled Guinevere closer, hoping she was wrong, hoping she was wrong. Only, she knew better. She could *feel* it, a giant emptiness, a big hole, a huge aloneness.

"Sweetie?" He touched her head. "Hope, what is it?" He touched the cat, left his hand there a minute, and just when she was thinking that she didn't know what she was going to do because everything she loved always left her, he slipped his arms around her and Guinevere both, and leaned over close.

He didn't say anything, just sat there sheltering them, and when Samantha came in asking when they were leaving, he said, "Hope's not going today. Guinevere just died."

"I'm sorry, Hope," Samantha said, softly now, close by.

"We're burying her here," Jack told her. "Want to take the bus today?"

Hope didn't hear an answer. She had started crying again, because the words were too real. *Guinevere just died.* Besides, Samantha wasn't the one she wanted just then. The one she wanted was holding her tight.

IF ANYONE had told Jack that while his wife was in a coma and his firm was floundering, he would be splitting firewood into planks to build a tiny coffin for a cat, he would have had them committed. But it seemed like the best thing to do.

Hope sat on the ground nearby. Guinevere was wrapped in the wash-worn baby afghan that Rachel had crocheted and that Hope had slept with for the first eight years of her life. Tatters and all, it was her prized possession. Once she wrapped Guinevere in it, she stopped crying. She held her bundle as though it were gold.

Jack found satisfaction splitting the logs and putting hammer to nail. When the small coffin was finished, he dug a grave, dug deeper than was probably necessary, but he didn't want other animals digging it up. Besides, it felt good to work, felt good to build up a sweat and breathe hard.

The exertion also tired him out enough so that when Hope placed her little bundle in the coffin and he nailed it shut, put it in the hole, and began covering it with dirt, he didn't feel quite so raw.

Hope cried. It was inevitable. Jack held her against his side and let her get it all out. Then they sat, just sat for a bit—and again it was absurd. The last thing Jack had time for was lingering in the forest on a Monday morning. He had to shower and visit Rachel, then drive on into the city to work. But Hope seemed to want him to do this. And he had to admit there was a peace to it.

They sat side by side facing Guinevere's grave. After a time, in a voice that held the remnants of tears, and reverence, Hope said, "Know why I picked right here?"

"No. Why?"

"The view." She pointed. "See through the trees? That drop-off? That's the canyon opening up."

Jack followed the line of her finger and, yes, saw the drop-off. Beyond, given depth and distance by a whisper of mist, was a palette of forest greens. He turned to Hope to remark on its beauty, but she had shifted her head and narrowed her eyes.

"If you look past it," she said, "way past it—what looks like clouds is really ocean."

"How can you tell?"

"If those were clouds, they would be whitish gray or blackish gray. Those are bluish gray. Can you see?"

Actually, he could.

"Mom taught me that. And to listen." She cocked her head. "Do you hear it?"

"The silence? You bet."

"No," she scolded with a small smile. "The *stream.*"

He listened. "That's silence."

She shook her head.

He might have argued. But if Rachel had heard a stream, there was a stream. He knew not to question it. Rachel *felt* the outdoors. That was one of the things that had first intrigued him about her. In Tucson once, she had made him sit with her for hours in the desert with his eyes closed, listening. He had heard the scampering of a pack rat, the slither of a snake. He had heard wind whispering down the fluted trunk of a saguaro.

Remembering that as he sat here in this breathtakingly lovely place, he had a sense of what Rachel might have given up when she had moved to San Francisco with him. She lived and breathed the fresh outdoors. She connected with flora and fauna as many people didn't. She knew her terrain.

So he listened for the sound of a stream. He swallowed to clear his ears and listened again, sorting the outside world from the flow of blood in his head. And he heard it, a faint, distant *shhhhh* far to the left.

"Over there?" He pointed.

Hope grinned and nodded.

"How far a walk?"

"Five minutes. It runs down the mountains into the ocean. I've walked it all the way down with Mom."

"How does it cross the road?"

"It goes under a bridge. I'll show you sometime," she said, but her voice was less sure, and she didn't look at him.

He knew she was thinking that once Rachel woke up, he would be gone. But even if Rachel woke up that very day, she would still need help. Okay, so she might not want him around all the time. But spring was full and summer approaching. There were new shades of green here. The idea of a streamside walk held appeal.

He smiled, feeling the same sense of anticipation that he had felt driving back to Big Sur the night before.

chapter ten

THE DRIVE from Big Sur to the hospital on a Monday midmorning took an easy forty-five minutes. Jack arrived feeling mellow—only to find another patient in Rachel's room. He hurried to the next room, thinking he had made an innocent mistake, but an entire family of grim-faced strangers there told him he had been right the first time. His heart stopped for the fraction of a second it took for him to reason that he would have been called if Rachel had died. Then, surgery? Nearly as bad.

Holding Hope's hand, he strode to the nurses' station. "Where's my wife?" he asked, and spotted Cindy emerging from a room at the far end of the corridor. He headed there with Hope in tow. "Where's Rachel?"

Cindy waved them along and into the room from which she had just come. It was a regular hospital room, with a TV, a bathroom, and several easy chairs. Katherine was in one of those chairs. Rachel was lying on her side facing her, and for a split-second, unable to see her eyes, Jack thought the change meant she had woken up.

Katherine had a fast smile for Hope, but her expression before and after told him that it wasn't so.

"It's been a week," Cindy said in her slow, gentle way. "Rachel's condition has been steady the whole time. The doctors thought she could be moved."

Jack had a bad feeling. Even after separating it from Guinevere's death, it still felt bad. "You needed her space for someone else."

"Yes, but that's not why we moved her. She's stable. Her stats aren't changing."

"But what if they do? The whole point was for you to know the minute something happened."

"We're monitoring her from here," Cindy said and, yes, he saw the same monitors, the same wires.

"But those aren't connected to the central desk."

"We'll be checking her regularly."

Kara Bates's voice came from the door. "This is what we call an observation room," she said, entering. "It's one step down from the ICU. Rachel will have the kind of attention here that most patients get immediately after surgery."

"It's only been a week," Jack argued, frightened. "What about that guy you pointed out who's been in Intensive Care for a month and a half?"

"He has heart and lung problems. He's not stable. Believe me, Rachel is far better off. She's functioning on her own, perfectly steady. She isn't going anywhere."

Jack fought a sinking feeling without quite knowing its cause. The bruise on the side of Rachel's face was healing—scabbing a reddish brown where it had been scraped, turning green where it had been hit—and the stitches had been removed from the cut on her hand. She looked paler than ever, though, and thin. He worried about that. She had never had pounds to spare.

Hope climbed onto the bed, tucked in her cowboy boots, and sat by her mother's hip. She didn't say anything. After a minute, she gingerly lifted Rachel's hand and put it in her lap. Her head was down. She slowly curled into herself. When she started to sniffle, she lifted Rachel's hand to cover her tears.

Jack caught Katherine's look of alarm. *Guinevere,* he mouthed.

She winced and nodded.

He touched Hope's bowed head, lightly stroking her hair as he had the cat's fur. He wanted to say something, but didn't know what. He imagined that letting Hope know he was with her was what she needed most.

But the sinking feeling inside him was starting to take form. He gestured Kara into the hall. "You're giving up on her," he accused. "You're taking her off the front line because you don't think she's waking up for a while."

"That's not it. We're simply saying that since the accident was nearly a week ago and there haven't been any complications, the chances of one occurring now are low. Cindy will still be her nurse. She'll watch the monitors and do side-side-back rotations every two hours. She'll be in here just as often as she was before. Same with Steve and me. This is standard protocol. In a larger hospital, she might have left Intensive Care even sooner. The fact is, she isn't critical."

"The fact is, she isn't *conscious,*" Jack muttered, but more to himself than to Kara. She patted his elbow and set off down the hall. Cindy and Katherine replaced her.

Since he hadn't gotten anywhere with Kara, he turned

on Cindy. "Rachel is losing weight. Isn't that dangerous?"

Cindy pushed up her glasses and looked back into the room. "No," she said slowly, quietly, "she's getting the nutrients she needs through a drip. We're still hoping that she'll wake up soon."

"I'm glad *someone* is," he said, but his sarcasm faded fast. "It'll be a week tonight. How long can she survive on an IV?"

"Ohhh, another few weeks."

"What then?"

"We'll consider a feeding tube. It goes directly into the stomach."

He wished he hadn't asked. A feeding tube was long-range, big-time stuff, right up there with putting Rachel in a regular room, which smacked of settling in for the long haul. He had done his homework. Next they'd be talking about a nursing home.

He pushed his hands through his hair and tried to wade through a rising panic. "This is not working for me. I can't accept that this is going to go on forever. There has to be more we can do."

"I've been talking to people," Katherine said. "There are other things we might try."

That cleared his thoughts some. Jack wasn't sure he liked the idea of Katherine talking to people about *his* wife's coma, but he was desperate enough to listen.

"We could read to her," Katherine said, "play her favorite music, bring in her favorite food. The smell might reach her. We could burn incense."

"Maybe get the maharishi in here, too," he muttered.

Katherine nearly smiled. "I was thinking of incense that smells like the woods near her house. A little of that might snap her out of it."

Jack wanted to argue but couldn't. Even now, miles away, he could smell those woods. There was a power to that smell.

"Would it work?" he asked the nurse.

"It can't hurt," Cindy said as she had so often before. Looking past them, speaking just a hair above a whisper, she added, "There's nothing scientific about it—for or against." She put on a smile. "Here's Dr. Bauer."

"I'll go visit with Hope," Katherine said, but before she could leave, someone called her name. She looked past Steve Bauer, broke into a grin, and set off to greet a young, good-looking guy wearing purple scrubs.

Watching her, Jack couldn't help but think that there was something to be said for living and working in a smaller place than San Francisco. People saw one another around town. Familiar faces were everywhere. It was kind of nice, when life was shaky.

He hadn't always felt that way. Growing up in a small town where everyone knew every last thing he did, he had choked on intimacy. So he went to college in Manhattan, where the anonymity was a welcome relief. He would have done his graduate work there, too, if he had been accepted. But Tuscon was where the grant money was, and then he met Rachel.

Rachel loved Arizona. She loved the air, the sun, the open space. She loved the desert landscape, claimed that there was a romanticism to it, that she could feel the ghost of Geronimo riding through the brush. She loved the heat, loved wearing skimpy tank tops and shorts and piling her hair on top of her head, even loved sweating.

She had blossomed as a painter in Tucson. With instruction and practice, she became technically proficient. As her personal confidence grew, her work gained strength. Wearing a large, broad-brimmed hat, she spent hour upon hour in the desert, nearly immobile at her easel, brush and palette in hand. She had the patience to wait for desert creatures to appear, and the stillness not to scare them off once they did. When the desert was in bloom, she was in heaven, but her pleasure extended far beyond that. She saw beauty where others saw hard sand and drab growth. Give her a glimpse of the sun angled low, and she turned bland into breathless.

Jack and Rachel were together in Tucson for three years, married for the last, and in all that time they hadn't disagreed on a thing. Then Jack was offered a job in San Francisco, and still they didn't disagree. It made sense for an architect to be in the city, and the firm was a good one in terms of projects, opportunity for advancement, and pay. Rachel voiced her qualms; Jack had answers for each. In the end, it boiled down to the fact that she could work anywhere, and he couldn't. So they moved.

He wondered now if he had been shortsighted. He had taken her from her element without realizing the effect it would have. She might have found cause for new inspiration in Big Sur, but there had been a long stretch of barren years before that. Her work had suffered. He should have seen it.

And then there was the twist of fate that had him driving to the hospital to be with her for the seventh day in a row. If they hadn't moved to San Francisco, she wouldn't have ended up in Big Sur, wouldn't have been driving the coast road at the same time as an elderly woman who had no business driving at all, wouldn't be in a coma right now.

Coming up on one week. Scary.

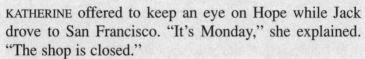

KATHERINE offered to keep an eye on Hope while Jack drove to San Francisco. "It's Monday," she explained. "The shop is closed."

But Jack wanted Hope with him. He saw the sad expression on her face and the tears that remained in a state of perpetual threat. He didn't know whether she was thinking of Guinevere or Rachel, but a drive to the city would be a diversion. He felt closer to her after Guinevere. He imagined they had established a bond, and wanted to keep it going.

He was also feeling low himself, brooding about people giving up on Rachel. Given his druthers, he wouldn't be driving to San Francisco at all, but sitting with her, talking to her, badgering her, challenging her—anything to wake her up. Having Hope with him gave him another purpose.

Besides, she was a shield. She was visible evidence of his responsibilities, proof for all to see of the reasons why he couldn't stay in San Francisco for long.

HE CALLED Jill from the phone down the hall and explained about Guinevere's death, about getting a late start from Big Sur, about Michael Flynn's defection. As gently as he could, he said, "I can't do lunch, Jill. Hope's with me, and we don't have much time. I'm sorry. I'll bet you made something incredible." On top of everything else, Jill was a gourmet cook.

"Not yet. I was going to do risotto primavera right before you came. The ingredients will hold. Will you come tomorrow?"

He closed his eyes and rubbed his brow. "I won't be in the city. Not until later in the week."

There was a pause, then a quiet "Does Rachel know you're there?"

"I don't know. But I can't *not* be there."

After another pause, she asked softly, "Why?"

He felt it coming. The deep stuff. And he didn't want it, didn't want it. So he said, "Because it could make a difference, Jill. The girls' talking to her could help her out of the coma. *My* talking to her could help her out of it. She's the mother of my children. I want her well."

She relented with a sigh. "I know."

"Thursday," he suggested, because he was hurting her and he didn't want that. "How about Thursday. Will the veggies hold until then?"

"It's not about the veggies."

"I know." It was about commitments. "Lunch Thursday. I promise."

THEY stopped at Jack's house before heading for Sung and McGill. While he filled a large sports duffel with clothes, he had Hope pile mail into a shopping bag. They worked quickly. The place felt cold and damp. The sun was out, and still the backyard looked gray.

In the midst of putting everything in the car, Jack had a thought. Returning to his bedroom closet, he pushed sweaters aside on the top shelf and pulled down two framed photographs. One was of Rachel and the girls, one of Rachel alone. Slipping them into a bag, he rejoined Hope.

They stopped at a nearby pastry shop for lunch. The

place was small enough and Jack had been there often enough for someone to show a sign of recognition. His order was filled promptly and efficiently, but no one said a word.

Still, they lingered there. He got Hope a refill of Coke, which she drank, and offered her dessert, which she refused. He ordered a piece of marble cheesecake anyway, handed her a spoon, and made her take a bite. He drank his third cup of coffee.

When he couldn't put it off any longer, they headed for the office, where he spent the bulk of the next three hours arguing with contractors, apologizing to clients, assigning tasks to associates, and avoiding David. He succeeded in everything but the last. David found him wherever he was, asking questions about work, time, and Rachel, adding to the pressure he already felt.

In the sudden silence after one tense bout, Hope asked, "Do you like David?" She had her legs tucked under her on the sofa in his office and was alternately reading a book, doodling, and watching Jack work. David had just stalked out clutching the latest design revision for the Montana resort, which Jack had asked him to present at Tuesday's meeting.

"Sure, I do," Jack said. "David and I go back fifteen years. We've shared some exciting jobs, pretty heady stuff. He does the things I can't, and vice versa. I wouldn't be the architect I am today if it weren't for him. This is our firm. We made it ourselves. We're partners."

Hope thought about that for a minute. "But do you like him?"

Jack used to. He used to admire David's dedication and direction. Lately, he had found the man a little too intense. Still, how to argue when the firm thrived?

"We're a good team. He keeps the fire going under me when I might be tempted to relax."

"Mom doesn't like him," Hope said quietly.

"Really?" It was news to Jack. Rachel had never said a word. "Why not?"

"She says he's hard."

Hard—as in *insensitive, cutthroat,* and *driven?* "Some would say I am, too."

"Mom never said that," Hope said quickly.

"She didn't ever yell and scream and curse me out?" he teased.

A sheepish grin. "Well, maybe. But she always apologized after."

"What did she say?"

"When she apologized?"

"When she was cursing me out."

"Oh, you know"—she lifted a shoulder—"stubborn, selfish. But she said it took two to make a marriage work and two to make it fail, so she was as much at fault as you were."

That was interesting. To hear Samantha talk, Jack had always assumed that his "desertion" was the only thing discussed. He was the bad guy, Rachel the good guy. He couldn't imagine Hope saying something different, if it wasn't so.

He covered his surprise by flipping her doodle pad around. Her pen had recreated Guinevere, capturing vulnerability with a minimum of strokes.

He turned back a page and forward a page. Each one offered a similarly evocative beauty. He had known Hope could draw but had never made much of it—largely, ironically, to protect Samantha, though it appeared that Samantha was well aware of her inability.

But Samantha wasn't there just then. On a note of genuine awe, he told Hope, "You are your mother's daughter."

"What do you mean?"

"You see the same things she does—small, subtle things, feelings—and you can put them on paper. That's more than I can do. It's a real talent."

Hope gave a modest little shrug, but her cheeks were pink. "I loved Guinevere. Drawing her makes me feel like she's still here." Her voice caught. Her eyes fell. "I keep thinking of her back there."

"I know you do."

"I'll miss her."

"You were good to her. I'm proud of you."

Tears gathered on her lower lids. "She's still dead."

"But you made her last days good ones. You were a loyal friend to her." He wanted her happy. "We could get you another cat if you want."

Without a minute's thought, she shook her head. "I want to remember Guinevere for a while. She was always a little scared of new people, and she didn't like playing with toys, but she slept with me from the night we found her, and she always purred when I whispered to her. So if I was loyal, it was because she was loyal. I don't want another cat taking her place so soon."

"BRENDAN says you're not coming with us. Why *not?*" Lydia asked. They were at their lockers at the end of the day. Samantha had avoided Lydia that long.

She scooped her hair off her face. "I'm going with

Teague Runyan. He has a car. It'll be better this way."

"Better for *who?* Teague is trouble. He has a *police* record."

"He was accused of shoplifting. It was a case of mistaken identity. The charges were dropped, so he does *not* have a police record."

"He was suspended from school for cheating."

"For one day. That's how serious it was."

"There's no way my parents will let him into the house."

"If your parents weren't home," Samantha said archly, "they'd never know. Why did you *tell* them there would be guys there?"

"They started asking. I couldn't lie to their faces."

"Well, they're not my parents, so I don't have that worry."

"Does your father know you're going with Teague?"

"Sure. He trusts me."

When Lydia didn't have an answer to that, Samantha felt a small measure of satisfaction. The satisfaction waned, though, when Lydia gathered her books and, shoulders hunching as she hugged them close, walked away alone.

IT WAS LATE afternoon by the time Jack returned to the hospital. Katherine had picked up Samantha at school and returned with a CD player, which was now running softly on the bed stand not twelve inches from Rachel's head.

"Garth," Samantha told him, seeming unperturbed by the change in rooms.

"*She's* a fan, too?" He knew that the girls were and

had assumed that the concert had been for them. His Rachel had been partial to the likes of James Taylor, Van Morrison, and the Eagles.

"A *big* fan," Samantha said.

Hope confirmed it with a nod, which didn't leave much for him to do but to set up the pictures he had brought.

Samantha was immediately drawn to them. "Where'd you get those?"

"I've had them," he said casually. "I want the doctors and nurses who walk in and out to see your mother with her eyes open. I want them to view her as a living, breathing, feeling individual."

"Grandma sure does. Look what she sent."

Three large boxes were stacked by the wall behind the bed. Each one brimmed with hot pink tissue and the kind of frothy white stuff that Rachel hadn't touched since she had cut it up and sewn it into a quilt.

"Nightgowns," Samantha said unnecessarily.

Hope sat on her heels and began looking inside the boxes. "Mom won't wear these. Why did she send them?"

Jack was saved from answering by the arrival of the travel agent, Dinah Monroe. She wore a smart suit and her dark hair in a shiny bob. After fingering the lingerie with genuine admiration, she kissed Rachel's cheek and, in an upbeat tone that warred with the concern in her eyes, told her about the client from hell for whom she had spent most of the day booking an Aegean cruise. More easily, she kidded Samantha about a mutual friend and shared sympathetic memories of Guinevere with Hope. She didn't stay for more than ten minutes and was followed soon after by Eliza, of the dark eyes and dark curls, arriving with warm pecan rolls packed in layers of bags. The minute she opened the innermost one, the sweet scent wafted out. Jack began to salivate. After ten minutes of gentle chatter with Rachel, Katherine, and the girls, she was gone.

The rolls remained in the tray table. Jack was eyeing them and wondering what to do about dinner when a new face appeared. This latest visitor was male but effeminate, Harlan by name, one of Katherine's operators. He hugged the girls and kissed Rachel, chatted with each for a short time, then left. Jack had barely begun to get over the feeling that he was the outsider here when Faye arrived with another zippered bag.

"Brisket," she told him. "Noodles and veggies included. Just heat and serve." She didn't stay much longer than it took to tell Rachel about the abysmal game of golf she had played that day, her surprise enjoyment of the book group's next book, and her three-year-old granddaughter's preschool play. Then she, too, was gone.

Half an hour later, when Charlie Avalon arrived with an earful of beaded hoops and a cedar-scented candle, Jack waved Katherine into the hall. "Tell me the truth," he said when she joined him. "These visitors dovetail too neatly. Someone orchestrated this. Was it you?"

"Definitely. They wanted to come, but it won't do Rachel any good to have them all here at once."

"Did you tell each one what to bring?"

"I didn't have to. They knew what to bring." She frowned. "Do you have a problem with this?"

He did. But he wasn't sure what it was.

Yes, he did. It was the outsider thing. He was feeling usurped.

"The girls have CD players," he said. "I gave them each one last Christmas. They might have wanted to bring Rachel their own."

"If they want to, that's great. They can also bring CDs from home. And books." She studied him. "Are you jealous?"

"Jealous of what?"

"Of my bringing a CD? Of Rachel's friends bringing other things? Of Rachel's friends, period?"

"No. *No*. I'm just surprised. She used to be more of a loner. I had no idea she had so many friends, and *good* friends. They've gone out of their way to help out."

"Don't you have friends who would do the same if the situation was reversed?"

Jack had many, many friends. But *good* friends? Jill would come, for sure. David? He . . . couldn't quite picture it.

"Do Rachel's friends make you feel left out?" Katherine asked.

"Of course not. Why do you say that?"

"It's just how you look, standing over by the window. It's like you're realizing that you don't know who Rachel is now and what she's doing with her life, and even though you're divorced, that bothers you. Is it a control thing?"

He was astounded by her gall. "Are you serious?"

"Uh-huh. From what Rachel says, you had the upper hand in the marriage. Your job, your needs came first. I'd call that controlling. Old habits die hard."

"Thank you, Dr. Freud," he said, then added an annoyed "Is there some reason you're telling me this?"

"Uh-huh. Rachel would do it if she could, but she can't."

"Rachel would *not*." Not *his* Rachel. "She was never one to bicker and carp."

"But she thinks. She feels. She's thought a lot about her marriage since it ended. She's learned to express herself more than she did when she was married."

"She expressed herself plenty then."

Katherine just shrugged.

"Okay, what didn't she say?" Jack asked. When she shrugged again, he said, "I can take it. What didn't she say?"

"Important things. She felt that she let them go by the board. It goes back to control. If Rachel could see you in there with her friends, she'd probably say you were jealous. *And* insecure."

"I'm controlling. I'm jealous. I'm insecure." Jack sputtered out a breath. "You're tough."

As insults went, it was weak. Many women would have taken it as a compliment. Apparently not Katherine. It fired her up.

"I've *had* to be tough, because I've depended on men like you and they've always let me down. That's the first thing Rachel and I had in common."

"Ahhh. Fellow man-haters."

"Not man-haters. We have plenty of male friends."

He couldn't resist. "Like Harlan?"

She stared. "Harlan supports a significant other who has AIDS. He cooks, cleans, buys food, clothes, and medical care. He rushes home to make lunch and has passed up training seminars in New York that might have advanced his career, all to care for his partner. You could take a lesson from Harlan."

Forget Harlan. Forget even that young guy in the purple scrubs. Something else had stuck in his brain. "Rachel has plenty of male friends? Where are they? Is Ben the supposed significant other? Or is she dating lots of guys and playing the field—once-burned, twice-shy kind of thing?"

"You're a fine one to talk," Katherine said. "There you are, holding on to favorite pictures of your ex-wife while you string Jill on for, what, two years now?"

"Hah. Pot calling the kettle black. What's with you and Bauer? He's a good-looking guy, but whenever he shows up, you get all high-voiced and nervous, then turn tail and run." He paused, frowned. "How do you know about Jill?"

"Rachel told me."

"That's interesting. Is *she* jealous?"

"Not on your life. She's been thriving since the divorce. You've seen her work. She couldn't paint in the city. Now she can. Something stifled her back there. I wonder what it was."

Jack knew she was about to tell him—and he had suddenly had enough. He held up a hand. "Your clients may sit in your chair and talk their hearts out, but that's *their* need, not mine. My life is not your business. I don't have to discuss it with you."

"Wasn't that one of the problems with your marriage? Lack of communication?"

Both hands raised now, he stepped back. He was about to return to the room when Katherine said a more gentle "Run if you want, but it won't go away."

"Rachel and I are *divorced*. That's about as far away as it gets."

"Is that why you've been here every day for the past week? Is that why you kept those pictures? You care, Jack."

"Of course, I care. I was with Rachel for two years; we were married for ten. That doesn't mean I need to analyze every little thing that's happened since—including those pictures. She has pictures of me; why the hell shouldn't I have pictures of her? You don't negate twelve good years. You don't just wipe them off the screen like they never happened, and that goes for the feelings involved. Rachel is seriously ill. I'm here for old times' sake, because someone I was intimate with for years could *die. And* because she is the mother of my daughters, who happen to need tending."

"The girls could be staying with me, or with Eliza or Faye. We all know them well, and we have the room. We also live closer to the hospital than the house in Big Sur, but you're driving them back and forth, back and forth, when you really want to be in the city."

"It's what I think is best, and since I'm the next of kin, it's my say."

"Isn't it always?"

"Actually," he let out an exasperated breath, "no. I didn't ask for the divorce. I didn't move out. Rachel did." He pushed a hand through his hair. "Why am I telling you this? My life is none of your business. *Butt out,* will you?"

JACK was still feeling testy when he started the drive back to Big Sur, but the coast did its thing. By the time they passed Big Sur, a mist had risen to buffer him from the world, and he was more pensive than irate.

He spent thirty minutes with his laptop hooked up to Rachel's fax line, and another thirty with Faye's brisket and the girls. There wasn't much talking. Hope was teary eyed. Samantha kept looking at her. All Jack could do was to say the occasional "It'll get better. Things like this take time."

Then the girls went to their rooms, leaving him to his own devices. He told himself to work. Or to paint. Instead, he dumped the bag of mail from his house on the kitchen table, and with barely a glance, threw out all but the bills. That done, he looked around the kitchen. Idly, he opened drawers, thumbed through takeout menus from restaurants in Carmel—Italian, Mexican, Thai. Some had items circled. Others had food stains. All had clearly been used, which was a change. In San Francisco, Rachel had always cooked. She had said it was easy enough, since she worked at home. She still worked at home. Had *he* been the one who kept them in? He had always preferred home cooking after being away, so Rachel had cooked. He supposed that could be called controlling.

He flipped through Rachel's mail, tossing junk in the basket, putting bills next to his. Samantha had already taken a handful of catalogues. And the ones that were left, the ones addressed to Rachel? Most were for outdoor clothing. Several were for artists' goods. The rest were for garden supplies. No surprise there. Nor in the CD collection in the living room. Oh, yes, she had a supply of James Taylor, Van Morrison, and the Eagles, but she had half again as many country discs. He supposed it went with outdoor clothing and garden supplies. He supposed it went with a country life. But he hadn't even thought of Rachel as a romantic. Sweet, sentimental, and sensitive—but romantic?

Actually, now that he thought of it, she was. He recalled returning from a business trip once to something *very* romantic. Rachel had picked him up at the airport, typically breathless but on time. It was dark out. The girls were in the backseat, in their pajamas, giggling behind their hands. Looking back, he guessed they had been six and four, or seven and five, which put the time at two to three years before the divorce. There had been tension at home surrounding this trip. Rachel had been quiet driving him *to* the airport. He was missing a school play in which both of the girls had parts.

"If it was just me, I wouldn't mind," she had said the night before he left; but it was an important trip for him, and it had been productive.

The girls giggled most of the way home from the airport. "What are you guys up to?" he asked more than once, to which they had only giggled more.

What they were up to was a rerun of the play in the living room, with scenery taken right from the school— easily done, since Rachel was the chief set designer— and Rachel playing every part except the girls' parts. Jack applauded roundly, then read good-night stories to each girl in turn. He had thought that the ongoing grins and giggles were simply because he was home.

Then he reached his and Rachel's room and found the place ablaze with daffodils in candlelight. Rachel had unpacked his bag and filled the bathtub with hot water and bubbles. There were daffodils and candles there, too. And fresh raspberries. And wine. Without eating a thing, he felt totally full.

All the more empty by contrast now and needing more of Rachel, he went to her studio. His laptop was still plugged in, resting on a mound of Boca paperwork. The canvases he had placed against the wall the day before hadn't moved. He sat down on the floor and studied them.

After a bit, he began rummaging through her supplies. She had oils and acrylics in tubes, neatly arranged on a work desk. Watercolors were in tin boxes. Brushes of varying widths lay on a cloth with several palette knives. There were more tubes and tins in the storage closet, plus her traveling gear—a heavy-duty manual camera and film, a portable easel, a large canvas bag, a folding seat—plus a supply of sketch pads, pencils, and pens.

There was also a metal file cabinet. He opened it to find her professional records—sales receipts, lists of what painting was at what gallery, expense receipts, tax forms, memos from her accountant. He closed it just shy of seeing how much money she made. He didn't want to know that, didn't want to know that.

Instead, snooping idly, he pulled out a portfolio that was stashed between the file cabinet and the wall. It wasn't a large portfolio, either in size or thickness. Squatting down, he set it against the front of the file cabinet, opened it, and found a sheaf of rag paper bound with a thin piece of blue yarn. He pulled it out, untied the yarn, and sat back, resting the sheaf against his thighs.

The first page was blank, a title page without a title. He turned to the next page and saw something that looked like a baby in the very first stages of development. An embryo. He turned to the next and the next, watching the embryo develop into a fetus with features that grew more distinct and increasingly human. Then, in a moment of silent violence, the sac holding the fetus burst. Jack was shaken. He looked at it for the longest time, unable to turn forward or back. When the shock passed, he went on, and then it was as if the explosion hadn't occurred. The fetus grew page by page into a baby, confined in its sac but in different positions.

It was a little boy. As fingers and toes were delineated, so was a tiny penis.

Again, Jack was shaken. He studied the infant, feeling the utter reality of the child, though it was drawn with nothing more than a blue pen. A blue pen, on high-quality, heavy ivory rag.

Only three pages remained. On the first, the baby was simply larger and more detailed, tiny eyelashes, perfectly shaped ears, thumb in mouth. On the second, his little body was turned in preparation for birth, with only elbows and heels, head and bottom making bumps in the smooth egg shape. On the last, the child had his eyes open and was looking directly at Jack.

So real. Jack felt a chill on the back of his neck. So real. So *familiar.*

Turning back to the first page, he went through the sheaf again. He felt the familiarity begin soon after that silent violence. By the time he turned the last page, he had an eerie thought. He pushed it aside, gathered the pages together, retied the yarn, and returned the sheaf to the portfolio. Closing it tightly, he stashed it back between the file cabinet and the wall.

Still, he saw that last picture. It haunted him through the night and woke him at dawn. He phoned Brynna in Buffalo and his client in Boca, but as soon as he hung up, that baby was back.

Watching the girls in the car, he wondered if they knew anything about a baby, but he couldn't ask. Whether he was wrong or right, mentioning it would open a can of worms.

Rachel knew. But Rachel wasn't saying. That left Katherine.

chapter eleven

NATURALLY, KATHERINE wasn't at the hospital when he arrived, but that was fine. Jack had taken her phone number from Rachel's address book—both numbers, work and home. Standing just outside Rachel's room, he called the work number on his cell phone.

"Color and Cut," came a bubbly young voice.

"Katherine Evans, please."

"I'm sorry. She's with a client. Would you like to make an appointment?"

"Not for my hair," Jack remarked.

"Oh. Uh. Then, can she return your call?"

He gave the sweet young thing his number, pushed the phone in his pocket, and returned to Rachel. Drawing up a chair, he put his elbows on the bed rail.

"So," he said, feeling resentful. "She's your unofficial spokeswoman. Make that *spokesperson*. Might as well be politically correct, here. It looks like I have to go through her to get to you." He half expected a gloating smile. Of course, there was none, which, irrationally, annoyed him more. He rubbed his thumb over those immobile lips, found them dry, applied Vaseline. What excess there was, he rubbed into the back of his hand.

"Remember when we used to ski?" They had done Aspen and Vail. They had done Snowmass and Telluride. The trips were gifts from Victoria, the only gifts from her that they had truly enjoyed. While the girls took lessons, Rachel and Jack skied together. One Chap Stick was all they ever brought, and they shared. "That was fun. This isn't. Rachel? Are you there? Can you hear me? It's been a week, Rachel, a whole week. You may be having a ball in there, but it's getting harder on us out here. Hope needs you to help her with Guinevere's death. She disappeared this morning—didn't show up for breakfast and wasn't in the house at all. I ran to Guinevere's grave. No Hope. I was getting ready to panic when she came down from Duncan's. That's starting to make me nervous. I mean, he's a big guy living alone. Could be he's a pervert." Rachel didn't look upset. Neither had Hope when she returned from Duncan's. Jack had watched her closely for signs of distress, but there were none. "She says she needs his faith. If that's the extent of it, I still feel inadequate. We never talked about religion, you and me. Maybe we should have. Maybe the kids need a faith of their own for times like these."

He stood, bringing her arm up with him, and began to gently put it through its paces. "And Sam. She's a trip. I have no idea what's going on in her head. She vacillates between being an angel and a shrew. I'm never quite sure whether she's listening to what I say or whether she's only nodding while her mind is off somewhere else. Do *you* get through to her?"

The ring of the phone was muffled by his jeans. Gently, he set her arm down. Less gently, he flipped the phone open as he walked to the door. "Yeah?"

"It's Katherine," said a frightened voice. "What's up?"

"I need to talk with you."

There was a silent beat, then, "Rachel's the same?"

"Yeah. Sorry. She's the same."

Katherine swore softly. "Can I ask a favor? Next time you call, please tell them it isn't an emergency."

"But it is," he said, looking back at his wife. "I found a pack of drawings in Rachel's studio. Of a baby. A baby boy."

The silence this time was for more than one beat.

"I need to know what those drawings meant, Katherine. That baby had my eyes."

There was more silence. Finally, she murmured something to someone on her end, then said, "I'll be over in forty-five minutes."

BY THE TIME she arrived, Jack had exercised every appropriate part of Rachel's body. He had talked to Kara Bates. He had talked to Cindy Winston. He had rearranged the framed pictures of Rachel to accommodate several more that the girls had produced, showing Rachel running, painting, laughing, further evidence of the vibrant woman inside the shell on the bed. He had listened to Garth Brooks from start to finish, and had asked himself a dozen questions about the baby whose existence Rachel's best friend hadn't denied.

Katherine entered the room looking wary. Pocketing her keys, she kissed Rachel's cheek. "Mmm. You smell good. So he's been rubbing in cream? Isn't that typical. They'll do anything to get their hands on our bodies."

"Sex was never a problem for us," Jack said, out of

the gate at the crack of the gun. "It was good from start to finish. So, were those drawings wishful thinking on Rachel's part? Or was she really pregnant?"

Katherine looked torn.

"Come on, Katherine," he warned. "You've told me other things about Rachel. Besides, you're not denying it, which means she was. Unless I misinterpreted those drawings, she lost the baby." When Katherine's eyes fell to Rachel, he said a gentler "Look. We don't know what's going to happen here. It's been a whole week. I'm sleeping in her bed, using her shower, digging coffee beans out of a canister shaped like a cuke. I'm using her towels. I'm eating her frozen zucchini bread. I'm putting my shorts in her underwear drawer because I'm getting fuckin' tired of living out of a suitcase, I'm—"

"Yes, she was pregnant."

Suddenly real, it took his breath. He looked at Rachel, trying to imagine it. The pain he felt was gnawing. "How could she pick up and leave me, if she was pregnant?"

Katherine's eyes rounded. "Oh no. She wasn't pregnant when she left. It was *before.*"

"Before." That made even less sense. "No. I would have known."

"From what she told me, she barely knew it herself. Things weren't going well between you. There was less talk, more silence. When she missed a period, she figured it was because of the strain. She didn't have an inkling until she missed a second one, and even then she let it go. Like I said, things weren't good at home. She didn't know what to do."

He shook his head. "I knew her body. Even two months along—"

"She was three months along."

"I'd have seen it."

"Not if she was thinner to start with. The bloat of early pregnancy would have brought her up to normal."

Jack forced himself to think back. Yes, Rachel had lost weight before the split. And despite what he had said, there hadn't been much intimacy at the end. Either he was traveling or one of them was tired. There was a chance he hadn't seen her undressed in anything but the darkest of night.

"But she would have *told* me," he argued. That was what hurt most. A baby affected him directly. A baby was part *his*.

Katherine sighed. "She tried. You were on a trip when she started feeling sick. She called and asked you to come home. You wouldn't."

Swallowing, he focused on Rachel's still face and struggled again to think back. There had been a trip to Toronto two weeks before the split. Yes, she had called, not feeling well, wanting him home. But the trip had been an important one. A large contract had hung in the balance. Turning to Rachel, he said, "I kept asking you what was wrong. You said, nothing terrible. That was what you said, *nothing terrible*. You had stomach pains. Maybe the flu, you said." He looked at Katherine. "She was *miscarrying?*"

Katherine nodded.

He made himself remember more. "She was pale as death when I came home, but she said she was getting better. I was home for four days. Not *once* did she mention a baby." He felt shaky inside, even close to tears. "Then there was a bunch of trips in close sequence." And an ultimatum before the last one. He recalled being annoyed that she seemed to be in . . . in *pain*. Good Lord. She had cause. "When I came back from the last, she was gone," he murmured, before anger killed the tears. "Why didn't she *tell* me?"

"She couldn't."

"She lost a baby I didn't know about, then left because *I* hadn't somehow figured it *out?*"

When Katherine looked reluctant to speak, he wiggled his fingers. "Come on, Katherine. Talk to me. Tell me what she said."

"She said it wasn't just the miscarriage. It was everything about your relationship. The miscarriage was only the clincher. She saw it as a sign that the marriage wouldn't work."

"Christ," he said and pushed his hands through his hair. "Why didn't she tell me *after?*"

"When, after? When you called, it was to arrange to see the girls, not to ask about her. Nothing that happened *after* suggested she was wrong. She was convinced you'd lost your interest in her."

"Well, I hadn't." He felt an overwhelming sadness. "Ahhh, Rachel," he breathed, lifting her hand to his chest, "you should have told me."

"Would it have made a difference?" Katherine asked.

He felt too hollow to be annoyed. "I don't know," he murmured. "Maybe." He would have liked a son. Hell, he would have liked another daughter. They had talked about having more children, but their finances were stretched with two, and then, once Hope was out of diapers, they enjoyed the freedom.

If he had known she was pregnant, they might have talked. She wasn't the only one who thought her partner didn't care anymore. If he had known she was pregnant, he would have come home from that trip.

At least, right now, that sounded like the right thing to

do. Back then, he was in a different place. He was riding high on success, so involved with it and with his work.

"For what it's worth," Katherine said, "she would have lost the baby whether you were there or not. She didn't blame you for the miscarriage, only for not being with her to lend comfort and support when it happened."

"Yeah." He sighed. "Well, I can see that she did." So now he knew what had actually caused that final break. Not that it helped. He still felt abandoned. Rejected. Alone. Baby or no baby, she had gone off and begun a new life.

Thinking about that new life made him think about her friendship with Katherine. "You said you met her at the gynecologist's office. In Carmel?"

"Yes."

"Did she have more trouble after she left the city?"

"No. She was just having a follow-up exam, getting to know a local doctor. We got to talking. There was instant rapport. One thing led to another. We went for coffee, then lunch, then coffee. She was very supportive."

He would have thought it was the other way around. "*She* was supportive?"

Katherine paled. She gave a quick little tip of her head, a dismissal that dismissed nothing.

"Why were you seeing the doctor?" he asked.

He could see her mind working as she stared at him. Then she glanced back at the door. No one was there. She looked down at Rachel. After another minute, she returned to Jack. "I had just been diagnosed with breast cancer."

His eyes widened. It was all he could do not to look at her chest. "Bad?"

She sputtered out a laugh. "That's like being a little pregnant versus a lot pregnant."

"You know what I mean."

"I do. And no, it wasn't bad in that way. Nothing had spread. The lymph nodes were clear. What they found in me was microscopic, tiny *in situ* ductal carcinomas. I'm living proof of the miracle of early detection. If I hadn't had a mammogram, I'd either be dealing with a lump right now or dead." She took a tiny breath. "That was the good news. The bad news was that I had tiny little grains of it in *both* breasts." She made a gesture that would have suggested beheading had it been eight inches higher.

Jack did look this time, because not once—and he had seen Katherine numerous times in the last week, wearing different outfits, *including* sweaters that clung—not *once* had he thought her body was anything but that of an attractive, shapely forty-something female.

She chuckled. "Your mouth is open."

"I know—it's just—I don't see—"

"Reconstruction."

"Ah." He was embarrassed. "Good as new."

"From the outside," she said, and with those three words, her defensiveness was back. Jack hadn't realized it was gone until then. But yes, she had been softer, very human.

"In what ways was Rachel supportive of you?" he asked.

Katherine studied Rachel for a minute before nodding slowly. "She was there for me, the proverbial phone call away. She talked me through many a rough spot."

"Like?"

"Like deciding between lumpectomy and mastectomy. Like choosing a surgeon and a plastic surgeon, and trying to decide which method of reconstruction was best. Like dealing with the knowledge that until the surgery was done and the lymph nodes were tested in the path lab, I didn't *know* whether the cancer had spread. Like wondering if I would survive the *surgery,* much less the disease." The corner of her mouth twitched. "Aren't you glad you asked?"

He was. Otherwise, he wouldn't have had a clue.

"Rachel was there the entire time—before, during, and after," she said.

"You have no family nearby?"

She folded her arms over those perfectly natural-looking breasts. "Have? No. Had? Yes. I was married at the time. My husband had a squeamish stomach."

Ahhhh. She'd had a husband. The missing piece—and apparently a huge one. "He wasn't there *at all?*"

"Well, he was. In a way." Her tone was wry, bitter. "Roy was a golf pro. We moved here from Miami when he got a job offer he couldn't refuse. He ran tournaments at a club in Pebble Beach. That's big stuff. He didn't have the time to sit in doctors' offices holding his wife's hand." She tipped her head, still wry, still bitter. "I could've lived with that. I mean, it *was* boring . . . tense . . . time-consuming. You'd sit in a cold cubicle in a thin paper gown waiting ninety minutes for one of the team of doctors to appear, and for what, a five-minute meeting? And the whole time you're thinking that this is the beginning of the end and you don't want to die. I'm a pretty composed person, but there were times, waiting, when I broke into a sweat and started shaking and thought that if I didn't get out of that damned cubicle in the next minute I'd go stark raving mad!"

Jack would have guessed that Katherine Evans had come out of the *womb* composed. She was composed even then—but only on the outside. He saw that now. Her eyes and her voice conveyed anxiety aplenty.

She drew herself up. "So Roy couldn't take it, and I didn't push. It would have been worse for me having to deal with his nerves on top of my own. I did everything with only a minimal involvement on his part—the doctors, the preop tests, the surgery, the drains, the follow-up appointments. Rachel drove me to some. Other friends drove me to others. I was fine until they dropped me off at my house."

"And then?"

"Then Roy treated me like I was a leper."

Jack swallowed.

"He was giving me space, he said. He didn't want to risk rolling over and hitting me in bed, so he slept in the spare room. He wouldn't sit too close or stand too close lest he inadvertently bump me. We had a huge bathroom—two sinks, separate Jacuzzi and shower, dressing table, and room to spare—but I had it all to myself. He said he didn't want me feeling self-conscious. He was giving me time to get used to the new me." Her tone was straightforward, her mockery all the more powerful for understatement.

"I recovered from the surgery. It was slower than I had expected—they don't tell you the half. But I gradually gained strength and felt better. I told myself I'd been given a gift of life. I went back to work even before I regained full use of my arms."

He didn't follow. "What was wrong with your arms?"

"The lymph nodes come from the armpit, so there's cutting and internal scarring. That was one of the hardest parts of the recovery, another thing no one warned me about. But I was working for someone else at the time, my clients were loyal, and I was tired of being disabled, so I pushed myself. It was the best thing I could have done. Those first few weeks I faded by noon and wound up at home with a heating pad on my back and cold packs on my arms where the muscles ached from fighting the scarring, but before long, I had full range of motion."

She stopped. Looking at Jack, she was wryness personified.

Treating her with care now, he said a cautious "What then?"

"Roy couldn't get it up."

"Excuse me?"

"Sex. He couldn't handle it. He couldn't look at my breasts. I bought sexy black camisoles so that he wouldn't have to see them. It didn't matter."

"Did you kick him out?" He assumed it was a given.

She surprised him by saying, "Not at first. I figured he needed time to adjust. I did, too. The truth was that I wasn't gung ho about sex then, either. Breasts are important sexual conduits. Suddenly I had none." When he glanced at her shapely chest, she said, "Not the same. Even aside from the emotional element—which is major—the physical response just isn't there. The raw matter is gone. I was grappling with that. So Roy was off the hook for a time."

"Until?"

"Until I learned he was screwing a little redhead from Santa Cruz." She rubbed Rachel's shoulder with her fingernails. "So we had that in common, too."

"Hey, I never cheated on Rachel."

"No, but you left her alone."

"I sure as hell didn't when I was home. So maybe I underestimated what she was feeling when I was gone."

"That's putting it mildly."

Jack was feeling too raw to be criticized. He was still trying to deal with the fact of that baby. "You're taking your anger toward Roy out on me. That's unfair. I'm not Roy."

"Would you be attracted to a woman with no breasts?"

"I'm attracted to a woman in a coma," he said before he could censor the thought. Quickly he added, "Forget Roy. There are other men in the world."

She gave a dramatic sigh. "Yes, well, I told myself that, too, and along came Byron. I met him at a hair show in New York. By then I had my own shop, thanks to my divorce settlement. When you have your own shop, you have to be up on the latest styles and techniques. So I met Byron in New York. What a charmer. Flowers, cards, little gifts. When he flew out here to see me, I put him in the guest room. I said I wasn't ready to sleep with him, and I really wasn't. But he was gorgeous, and there was a definite spark, and he was persistent."

"Didn't he—didn't you—"

"We kissed. I touched him."

"But didn't he—" *Touch your breasts?* Jack couldn't imagine not touching Rachel's. He loved their softness and sway, loved the way they changed when he tasted and touched.

Those were the very things that Katherine missed and would never have again. He began to understand her loss.

"Men can forget everything but their own needs if you push the right buttons," she said, "but it was okay. He was good in other respects. We were taking our time getting to know each other. I thought of him as a friend, as well as a possible lover. Then I told him." Jack waited.

She remained composed. Only her eyes showed the pain. "Oh, it was gradual, his withdrawal. The phone calls came fewer and further between. He had a show in

Paris, so he couldn't fly out for Christmas. When I had to be in New York, he had a show in Milan. After a while, it was me making the calls. When I stopped, that was it. After three months of silence, he called to see how I was. I hung up on him." She took a shuddering breath. "Rachel helped me through that, too. So maybe we did feed into each other's anger and hurt." She gave an evil grin. "But boy, did it feel good."

Jack smiled back. How to be offended, when the woman had just opened herself that way? He doubted many people knew that she'd been sick. She was a survivor on many levels.

He had a sudden thought. "That young guy the other day in the purple scrubs?"

"My anesthesiologist. He had a crush on me. Stopped in at my room every day to see how I was. And the woman in the hall, Darlene? My plastic surgeon's nurse. She's back to working the floor."

"And Steve Bauer?"

Too casually, she said, "What about him?"

"Did you know him before?"

"Nope."

"Was I imagining your reaction to him?"

He could see her start to nod. Then her chin came up in defiance. "No."

"There's a spark."

"Uh-huh. But it isn't going anywhere. In the first place, he's a doctor, and I've had enough of those to last a lifetime. In the second place, he's a man. I'll be very happy to keep those at arm's length for a while."

"You don't miss it?"

"Miss what?" she asked, staring at him, daring him to say it.

"Okay." He couldn't imagine it, attractive woman that she was, but, hey, different strokes for different folks. "So you don't miss it."

"I didn't say I didn't," she relented. "I used to love sex. There are times when I miss it a whole lot. Right now, as Rachel would say, it just isn't high on my list."

"What is?"

"Making a go of the shop. Spending time with my friends. Being there for people who were there for me."

Jack knew she meant Rachel. He also knew that her priorities were noble. That made him feel all the worse—not to mention that by virtue of being male, he felt guilty by association with Roy.

"We're not all bad," he said. "I'm here, aren't I?"

She thought about that for a minute, seemingly without rancor. "Have you thought about the possibility that Rachel may only partially recover? What if she wakes up diminished? What if she can't talk right, or walk right? What if she can't paint? What will you do then?"

He hadn't thought that far. He didn't want to do it now. "Let's get her woken up first. Then we'll worry about the rest. It's been a week."

Katherine nodded and glanced at her watch. "I have to get back to work."

"Thank you," Jack said.

"For what?"

He had to think for a minute. The thanks had startled him, too. "For coming today. For telling me what you did. About Rachel, and about you."

"I haven't told many people. I'd appreciate it if you wouldn't—"

"I won't." He hitched his head toward the door and began walking that way. When she joined him, he said,

"Thank you for being there for Rachel. She's lucky to have a friend like you who can receive *and* give."

"That's a nice thing to say."

"I have my moments." On impulse, he gave her a quick hug.

"What was that for?" she asked when he held her back.

"I don't know. It just seemed right."

"I think you just wanted to feel my boobs."

"With my wife watching?" He looked back at Rachel, wondering if she understood the hug. He went still. "Whoa." He strode back to the bed.

Katherine was right beside him. "What?"

"Rachel?" He leaned over her, his heart pounding. "I saw that, Rachel."

"What did she do?"

"Blinked. Flinched. Something." He took her hand. "Rachel? If you hear me, give a squeeze." He waited, felt nothing. "Come on, angel." He held his breath. But there was nothing. "Try a blink." Again he waited. "I saw something. I know you can do it."

"Rachel?" Katherine tried. "Fight it, Rachel. Push your way up. We want to know you're here. Give us a sign. Anything."

They stood side by side, leaning in over Rachel.

"Maybe I was wrong," Jack said. "Jesus. I could have *sworn* . . ."

"Rachel? Talk to us, Rachel. Move for us."

From behind them came Cindy's voice. "What's happening?" When Jack told her, she leaned in on the opposite side and chafed Rachel's jaw. "Rachel! Rachel!"

Jack was watching Rachel closely enough to pick up the slightest movement, but he didn't see a thing. They waited and watched. Cindy called her name again. With a defeated sigh, he straightened. "I don't know. Maybe it was a twitch in my own eye. I wasn't looking for it and suddenly it happened."

"It might have been involuntary," Cindy said. That the words came faster than usual said something about her excitement.

Jack recalled a term Bauer had used. "Posturing?"

"Posturing is larger—odd arm or leg movements. I was thinking more along the lines of what we call 'lightening.' It's a gradual waking that starts with the fingers or toes."

"This wasn't finger or toes," he said, but his hopes were up again. If Rachel wasn't going to just open her eyes and smile in one fell swoop, he could live with a gradual waking. "It was her face. Could that still be the start of something?"

The eyes behind Cindy's thick glasses said maybe or maybe not. And his letdown returned.

"What do we do now?" he asked. "Anything different?"

The nurse squeezed Rachel's arm from elbow to shoulder. She was back to being calm and slow. "We keep talking. When you saw this movement, were you saying anything she might have reacted to?"

Jack looked at Katherine. "We had been talking about personal stuff, but we were done. We walked to the door. I hugged you." He arched a brow. "Maybe she was jealous."

From Cindy came a quiet "Lesser emotions than that have pulled people from comas."

Still to Katherine, Jack said, "She and I are divorced. She wouldn't be jealous."

It was Katherine's turn to arch a brow. But she didn't elaborate and he didn't ask. She had appointments waiting, and he needed time to think.

chapter twelve

FOR A LONG WHILE after Katherine left, Jack sat on Rachel's bed. He traced each of her fingers, and traced the new scar. He put their hands palm to palm, then fitted her palm to his jaw. He thought about the miscarriage, about the little boy they might have had, and what might have been. He thought about country music and about jealousy. And he thought about what he had never imagined Katherine had lived through.

"We think we know so much," he told Rachel, and realized that Katherine had said the same thing, in different words, more than once. So there was a lesson to be learned. He might be slow on the uptake, but he wasn't hopeless.

FAYE LIEBERMAN came at noon. Her smile was as warm as her silver hair. Her pantsuit was silk and soothing. This time she brought a huge tin of home-baked *rugelach,* plus a bag containing two sandwiches. "You haven't eaten yet, have you?" she asked, stopping with her arms suspended halfway through unloading the bag.

"Not yet."

She held out two sandwiches wrapped in opaque white paper. "They're from Eliza's shop. One is turkey with Swiss cheese, lettuce and tomato, and mustard. The other is roast beef with *boursin*. Choose."

"Which do you want?"

She smiled, pressed her lips together, shook her head. "I'm the least liberated of Rachel's friends. If I were you, I'd pick my favorite. You may not be given a choice again."

He had felt comfortable with Faye from the start, and felt even more so now. Smiling, he reached for the one with *R/B* on the wrapper. "Thanks. This is a treat."

Faye produced two Diet Cokes and handed him one. "See? No choice." Eyes smiling, she said to Rachel, "As ex-husbands go, he isn't so bad." The smiled faded. She touched Rachel's cheek.

"She'll be fine," Jack said. "As soon as the bruise inside is healed enough, she'll wake up. It'll be a straight shot home after that."

Faye nodded. For a minute she didn't say anything. Then she pressed a hand to her chest, swallowed, and took a deep breath. After a second one, she said, "Do you know that last Monday night was the first book-group meeting that Rachel ever missed? In five years. That's something."

"It meant that much to her?"

"To her, to all of us."

He gave her the chair nearest Rachel and pulled up a second one. He was done retreating to the window when her friends came by. They were as much a source of information as Katherine was.

He bit into his sandwich, chewed thoughtfully, and swallowed. "Why?"

"Why does it mean so much?" Faye considered it for a minute. "Because we're good friends. We're all different. We have our own lives and don't always see each other between meetings, but we've grown close. Something happens when you're discussing a book and you touch on personal issues. You open up. I probably know these women better than some I see every day. I think it's the fact that our lives are so separate that gives us the freedom to speak."

"Instant-rapport kind of thing?"

"Not instant. It took a while for some of us to feel comfortable with the confessions that others made in the course of discussions. It took that long to . . . bond." She smiled. "Trite word, I know, but that's what we did. We learned to trust. We're not unique. There are a dozen other book groups in town."

"All because of Oprah?"

Faye chuckled. "Ours started *years* before hers. Some of those dozen other book groups have been going twice as long as ours. I've heard of groups that are into their second generation. And ours aren't fan clubs. We aren't afraid to discuss the downside of books." She frowned. "There's a need."

"For downside discussions?"

"For support." Reflective, she took a bite of her sandwich. When she finished chewing, she set it back in its wrapper. "Sixty-somethings like me know what it means to live in a community. When I was a child, I had grandparents in the apartment upstairs, two aunts and their families across the street, a second set of grandparents down the block. My mother had a built-in support group.

Then one by one our parents bought houses and moved to the suburbs, and we went to college and married and lived wherever our husbands took us, and suddenly the support network was gone. So we pushed the kids' carriages through the neighborhood and made friends with other mothers doing the same, and we were fine. Then the kids grew up and we went back to work, and there was no one. Now most young women work. Who's their support group?"

Jack pictured Rachel back in San Francisco. "Their husbands and kids?"

Faye smiled sadly. "Not good enough. Men don't know what women feel, and kids are kids. Women need other women." Smiling more brightly, she touched Rachel's arm and asked her if she remembered *Plain and Simple*. "It's a little book by a woman who leaves the city to spend time with the Amish," she told Jack. "There she finds groups of women who live, work, and play in close proximity to each other. They talk all day, help each other with chores, back each other up. It's the kind of support system the rest of us used to have, but lost."

Jack had designed a language center for a college in Lancaster. Since that was in the heart of Amish country, he knew something about the sect. "Would *you* want to live like an Amish woman does?"

"Not on your life," Faye declared. "I like my luxuries. But there are times when I'm lonely, when my husband is playing golf and I wish there were a clothesline in my backyard and other women in neighboring backyards wanting to talk while we hang out the wash. We all have driers now."

"But backyards are for gossip. Book groups are for intellectual discussion."

"They can't be for both?" she asked, eyes smiling. "Intellectual discussion can be personal. There are times when we discuss the book, and times when we discuss ourselves. Some books have so much meat in them that we don't get to ourselves at all. Others are only good as facilitators."

Jack smiled. *Facilitators.* He had never heard the term used quite that way before, but he supposed it fit.

"The thing is," Faye went on, "that we never know until we get there which way it'll be. The promise of the intellectual is what some of us need. Take me. I'm programmed to be home with my husband at night. I'd never have the courage to leave him alone if it was just to gab with girls. Same with Jan. She has four very young children. Granted they have a nanny—Jan teaches golf at one of the clubs—but the nanny's gone by six. Jan's husband wouldn't dream of baby-sitting the kids without Jan if she didn't have a good reason to be gone."

"What if one of the kids is sick?"

"One of the kids is always sick." She smiled. "Obviously, there are emergencies." She touched Rachel again. "We won't kick Rachel out of the group because she missed last Monday night." She was suddenly sober, suddenly dismayed.

Jack knew what she felt. At times he could take part in normal conversation as though nothing was wrong. Then he looked at Rachel and his insides bottomed out. With the bruise on her face healing, there was more paleness to her. Her freckles stood out, waiting for the rest of her to return to life.

He couldn't conceive of it not happening. But it had been a week. So maybe she had blinked earlier that morning. Since then, *nada.*

"Book group is a commitment," Faye went on, sounding determined to distract them both. "That was a ground rule. We only have seven members. If half of them don't show up, it's not the same."

"It's still strange to me," he said. "Rachel was always such a nonjoiner."

"In the city. It's different in the city. There are people everywhere. There's noise everywhere. There's *action* everywhere. Not so in Big Sur. The canyon is a great isolator. The same thing that Rachel loves about the place is its worst drawback. An artist needs to be alone, but not all the time. I'd guess that Rachel feels more of a need to join a group now than she did in the city."

"Who picks the books?"

"Whoever hosts the meeting."

"Has Rachel hosted?"

"Everyone has. That's another given."

"Isn't it out of the way for you all to drive to Big Sur?"

"No more than it's out of the way for her to drive to us." She let out a breath, suddenly sober again, and Jack knew where her mind went.

"The accident could have happened anywhere," he reasoned, recalling what the state trooper had said at the scene. "She could have been heading to Carmel for a completely different reason, and it could have been a lot worse. Once she wakes up, she'll be fine." When Faye remained grim, he said, "Tell me what books Rachel chose."

As he had hoped, she brightened. He liked it when she smiled. It made reality easier to take.

She was looking at Rachel, mischievously now. "This woman is a romantic at heart. One year, she had us do *A Farewell to Arms*. Another year, she had us do *Tess of the D'Urbervilles*. Both made her cry."

Jack tried to remember if he had ever seen Rachel cry over a book. "Once the girls were born, she didn't read as much. Magazines, yes. But the girls were little then, and active. If she wasn't doing things with them, she was painting. Five minutes of reading in bed at night, and she was out like a light."

"The city exhausted her," Charlie Avalon said from the door. She wore another tank top, a short skirt, and high platform shoes. Today, instead of feathers or beads, a shimmer of silver fell from her left ear. The streak in her hair was as pink as before, but she seemed subdued. Her eyes were on Rachel. Standing there at the door, she looked nearly as young and vulnerable as Hope.

Jack rose. When Charlie didn't enter, Faye went to her. For a minute, they hugged—an unlikely couple on the surface, not so unlikely what with all Faye had said. When Faye returned to the bed, Charlie was with her. She refused the offer of a chair, though, refused the offer of a sandwich, just stood with her hands on the bed rail and her eyes on Rachel.

"I used to live in San Francisco," she said. "We talk about it sometimes."

"Did you hate it as much as she did?" Jack asked.

"More. She was the one defending the place. Restaurants. Funky clothing boutiques. I knew San Francisco was where her marriage went wrong, but she never said much that was negative. Not until *Now You See Her*. It's about a woman who turns forty and suddenly starts to disappear."

"Disappear?"

"Really. Rachel said she felt like that in San Francisco. There were too many artists, too many people, too many noises, too many things going every which way at once, so that she couldn't clear her head and paint. She didn't have an anchor. Vital parts of herself were just floating every which way, up and away."

"Charlie. That's a little dramatic," Faye scolded, and told Jack, "The book is about a woman whose identity comes only through other people—you know, Jack's wife, Samantha's mother, Charlie's friend."

"But Rachel had her own identity," Jack argued. "She was an artist."

"Struggling," Charlie insisted. "She couldn't be self-supporting. Not in San Francisco. She had to rely on you for her basic needs."

"I was her husband. That was my job. What was the problem?"

Charlie looked at Faye, who patted the air with a warning hand. But Charlie Avalon wasn't being warned. Defiant, she said, "She hated the way her mother thought money was the be-all and end-all of life. She feared you were getting to be the same way."

Jack drew back. "When did I throw money around?"

"You bought her a rock."

It was a minute before he realized what she meant. Then he hung his head and rubbed the back of his neck. When he looked up again, he said, "It wasn't a rock. It was a three-carat diamond ring."

"That's a rock."

He blew out a breath. His stomach was starting to knot. "I had a buddy of hers—a totally artsy guy—set it in a shield of platinum and gold. It was unusual. I thought she'd love it."

"She said it was a consolation prize to make up for the traveling you did."

Jack was hurt. "I was trying to tell her that I thought

she was worth the cost of the damned ring and more. I was trying to tell her that since I hadn't had the money for a diamond ring when we got engaged, she deserved a *special* one. I was *trying* to tell her I *loved* her."

There was silence. Pushing the remnants of his sandwich aside, Jack left his chair and braced his elbows on the rail by Rachel's head. She hadn't said she hated the ring. She just hadn't worn it the way he had hoped she would. She should have told him. He could have said what he felt.

He studied her face, looking for answers, looking for *movement*. He took her chin, rubbed it lightly with the pad of his thumb, ran the backs of his fingers along her jaw. Finally he straightened.

"Apparently," Faye said in soft apology, "a ring wasn't what she needed."

"What was?" he asked.

She thought for a minute. With a sad smile, she hitched her chin toward where he stood so close to Rachel. "Maybe this?"

SAMANTHA loaded her backpack with books to bring home, then checked herself out in the mirror inside her locker door. She ran a comb through her hair. She wiped a finger under her eye to get rid of runaway liner and studied something on her forehead. If it grew into a zit just in time for the prom, she would *die*. When she had looked enough and prayed enough, she straightened and tossed her hair back. She mashed her lips together to make them red. Finally, when Lydia didn't show up, she took her baseball jacket from its hook. She was closing her locker when Pam Ardley turned the corner.

"Hey, Samantha!" she called, breaking into a trot. "Wait up!" She was all smiley white teeth and sleek black hair. Cocaptain of the cheerleading squad, she was probably the most popular girl in the class. Samantha wasn't going anywhere, not when Pam Ardley called.

Pam slowed to a walk, then stopped and leaned a shoulder against the locker's edge. "Teague says you asked him to the prom. I think that's awesome. He's hot. We're having a party at Jake Drumble's. Maybe you two want to come?"

Samantha couldn't *believe* it. Jake Drumble played football, basketball, and baseball. If Pam was the most popular girl, he was the most popular boy. And gorgeous? Drop dead.

"I'd like that," she said without raising her voice. She didn't want to seem overeager. Cool was better. Suave was best.

"What can you bring?" Pam asked.

Samantha scooped her hair to the side. "What do you need?" Something told her that salsa and chips weren't on the wish list. Not for a party at Jake's. This was big stuff. Unbelievable.

"Whatever you have at home—vodka, gin. You don't have an ID, do you?"

An ID. No, she didn't have an ID.

Pam waved a hand. "Not to worry. Bring whatever."

"I may have a problem," Samantha warned, but boldly. If she sounded weak, she would give herself away. "My mom's been in a coma for a week, so my dad's with us. It's a nightmare. He drives us here and back. He watches us like a hawk. If he gets even the slightest idea that I'm smuggling out vodka—" Like there was a drop of vodka in the house. There was *nothing* in the house.

Pam waved a hand. "Don't do it. We'll manage without." She stood back and grinned. "I'm glad you're coming, Samantha. I never understood what you were doing with Lydia and the others. They're very young."

"Tell me about it."

Pam started bouncing from one toe to the other of crisp white platform sneakers. "No need. You know. Saturday night at six for something before the prom. See you then." She jogged off.

HOPE had turned the corner unaware and stopped short, watching from the other end of the hall. She didn't move again until Pam was gone. "Sam?"

Samantha whirled around. She put a hand to her chest. "You scared me."

"What did she want?"

She was suddenly nonchalant. "Not much." She closed her locker and slung the backpack on a shoulder. "She's a friend." She started down the hall.

Hope fell into step beside her. "Since when?"

"What do you mean, 'since when?' We've been in the same class for *years*."

"Does Lydia like her?"

"Lydia," Samantha spoke clearly, "is not in this equation."

"Why? Did you guys have a fight?"

"We didn't have to. Lydia and I have been heading in different directions all year. Those guys are young." She swung through the door and started down the stairs.

Hope hurried to keep up. "They're your age."

"In years. That's all. They have no idea how to have fun."

"But you're going with them to the prom, aren't you?"

"I haven't decided," Samantha said as she pushed open the outside door and hit the steps.

Hope followed her, squinting against the sun. "Mallory Jones said you were going with Teague Runyan. I don't think Mom would like that."

Samantha stopped short, came up close, and said with lethal quiet, "Mom's in a coma, and if you say one word to Dad, you're dead." Scooping her hair back, she set off again.

Hope watched her go. Lydia, Brendan, and Shelly were watching, too, but from an even greater distance than Hope.

Halfway to the curb, Samantha turned and yelled, "Are you *coming?*"

Hope ran forward, because Jack was there and she didn't want him waiting, but during the entire drive to the hospital, she tried to decide what to do. Samantha would never forgive her if she told Jack—and it seemed like his mind was somewhere else anyway. If Rachel was still in a coma, the only one left was Katherine. But Katherine wasn't at the hospital when they got there, and when she finally came, it was late, and then Jack said he needed to talk with her and took her out in the hall.

So, while Samantha stared at her forehead in the bathroom mirror, Hope tacked a drawing she had made of her mother up on the bulletin board, then sat beside Rachel and told her that Angela Downing's mother was running Friday's picnic, but Jack was bringing drinks. Whispering, she read Rachel a poem she had written about Guinevere's death. She pulled a jar from her backpack and opened it under Rachel's nose.

"What's *that?*" Samantha asked.

"Paste. Remember all the signs we used to make? Thanksgiving, Christmas, end of the school year, start of the school year." Construction paper cutouts pasted on poster board. "She likes the smell."

Samantha snorted and turned away, but Hope didn't care. She couldn't do much if Sam decided to make a mess of her life with Teague Runyan. But if that happened, she wanted Rachel awake to help clean things up.

JACK stood in the hall with his back to the wall and his hands in his pockets. He didn't know whether to be embarrassed, angry, or hurt. "I was so proud of myself, asking questions and learning little things about Rachel, and then Charlie hits me with the business about trying to buy her off with a ring. Do you know about that?"

Katherine was unruffled. "I didn't know Charlie had said it. But I have seen the ring."

"What did Rachel do? Present it as display number eighteen, proof of Jack's materialism? Did the two of you sit back and laugh? If she thought it was so gaudy, why didn't she sell it and give the money to the International Save the Walrus Foundation or something?"

Katherine looked amused. "For the record, I thought the ring was beautiful. For the record, so did Rachel."

"Charlie said—"

"Charlie is young. Charlie is poor. Charlie is the product of every possible kind of abuse. She is wonderfully loyal to the women in the group and lends a different insight to conversations, but what she told you may have been tinged by her own feelings, not the least of which is envy. Charlie would give her right arm to be married to someone who could support her while she worked. She gave you her own take on the ring. It may not have been a fair representation of what Rachel said."

"What *did* Rachel say?" When Katherine shot him a beseeching look, he said, "I gave her that ring because I loved her. I can't believe she took it any other way."

"You gave it to her at a time when she wanted you, not a ring. She worries, Jack. She sees you buying lavish gifts for the girls."

"On birthdays. For Christmas. And what *should* I do? If they want CD players—or Patagonia jackets—or leather backpacks, and I have the money, why *not?* It's not like I see them all the time. It's not like there's much *else* I can do for them."

"Do you really believe that? What about more time with them? That was what Rachel wanted most. That was what she missed. She didn't want the money. She had it once. It didn't help."

"Ah." Jack pushed a hand through his hair. "We've been down *this* road before, Rachel and I. She had it and spurned it. Me, I grew up poor. Dirt poor. Money means something, after that."

"But it's not *about* money," Katherine said, suddenly impassioned. "You could have made *billions,* and Rachel wouldn't have cared, if you had been there emotionally. But you were so obsessed with work, you lost sight of what mattered. Your days were exhausting. Come night-time, you had less and less left over for Rachel and the girls. I see it, too. You walk in every day with briefcase, laptop, and phone. Hey"—she held up a hand—"I'm not complaining. I think it's great that you're here. I think that if you'd been half as portable with work when you were married, you'd still be married. But are you enjoying it? Doesn't look to me like you are. You look hassled. So some of that's worry about Rachel, but I see you on the phone. I hear you. You're not having fun. How much is enough?"

Jack stared at her silently for a time, then dropped his eyes. "I don't know," he finally said.

But he thought about it when he returned to the room, and thought about it back at the house. He thought about it when he woke up in the middle of the night and found Hope with tear streaks on her cheeks, wrapped in her quilt on the far side of Rachel's bed, sound asleep. He thought about it when he woke up and Hope was gone.

Sitting on the edge of the bed rubbing a stiff shoulder, he still didn't know. He opened the window. The morning chill felt good on his skin. He stretched, flexed that stiff shoulder a time or two, put his hands on the windowsill and his face to the air, and wondered about a place that didn't need screens.

It was a good place. It was a different place. There was no cover price here, no charge for admission. All he had to do was walk, breathe, listen, and look, and the beauty was there.

Just then, *that* was enough.

He pulled his head in and closed the window. Picking up the phone, he called his would-be client in Boca and said that Sung and McGill was withdrawing from the project. Life was too short to be held ransom by a bunch of two-bit politicians, he said. No, he didn't want to take one last crack at it; he had already compromised too much. Yes, he knew he wouldn't be paid if he quit. But he wouldn't be paid, anyway, when perfectly good designs ran into last-minute code interpretations. So he was cutting his losses. Thanks a lot. Bye-bye.

When he hung up the phone, his shoulder felt better, and no wonder. The load had been lightened a little. David would be upset. But that was a passing thought. The one that lingered was that he couldn't wait to tell Rachel.

chapter thirteen

COLOR AND CUT normally opened at nine, but Katherine believed that loyalty stemmed from accommodating the client; hence she was often at the shop far earlier. She had a seven-thirty this Wednesday morning, a young woman who worked a ten-hour stint as concierge at a resort in the valley. Even if Katherine hadn't been fond of her—which she was—she knew that Tracey LaMarr was a showcase for her work. Besides, Tracey was fun to do. She gave Katherine the freedom to try new things and had the kind of thick chestnut hair and pretty features to wear it all well.

Today they had agreed on a partial face frame. Katherine was carefully layering Tracey's hair, using foil and three shades ranging from light brown to ash to create a subtle glow around Tracey's face. There wasn't much talk. Early morning appointments rarely jabbered, and Tracey didn't need therapy. She was refreshingly content with her young marriage and her work. So this was a gentle wake-up time for them both. The sounds of a New Age harp drifted through the shop, along with the scent of freshly brewed coffee. Tracey, a tea drinker like Katherine, was nursing a fragrant lemongrass herb tea when, almost dreamily, she said, "Mmm. There's a nice one."

Katherine followed her line of sight out the front window. The shop was on a street that was a block off Carmel's main drag. This early in the day there was little by way of either vehicular or pedestrian traffic, which meant what Tracey saw stood right out. It was a runner, a man. He was gone before Katherine could do more than admire his shorts and his stride.

"I'm envious," she said, resuming her work. She slipped the tail of her comb under another layer, deftly catching alternate strands. "Certain people have the build to do that." She took a square of foil. "It's a physiological thing. Have you ever run?" She knew that Tracey was into aerobics; they often compared classes and instructors. But running was something else.

"Not me," Tracey said. "If I have to exercise, I'd rather enjoy what I'm doing. Running is torture."

Katherine used a brush to slather the separated hair onto foil with one of the three colors in nearby bowls. "Not so torturous, if your body is made for it. Watch a marathon, and you'll see it. Those runners are *lean*. They're not even heavily muscled, though you know they're in perfect condition." She set the brush aside and folded the foil in half.

"Which comes first," Tracey asked, "the chicken, or the egg? Are they lean because they run? Or do they run because they're lean?"

Katherine started again with the tail of the comb. "Both. I think there's a genetic factor. I tried running two years ago. I was about to turn forty and decided that running a ten k would be a great birthday gift for myself.

That's only six-something miles. Piece of cake." She reached for the foil.

"No?"

"No." A second brush, second color. "After two miles, wicked shin splints. I rested and tried again. Same thing. I backed up to a half mile and slowly added. No go. I had every test in the book done. The only thing they could find was that I was pronating. I changed sneakers. I got orthotics. I did special stretches and longer warm-ups." She folded the foil. "It bought me a mile. So I could do *three* before the pain."

"What did you do for your birthday?"

"A friend threw a party. It was a ball. A little caviar and champagne, a little cake with sugary icing. My shins felt great." She took up the comb. "So that's my running story."

"There he is again."

Katherine's first thought was that it couldn't be the same man, but the stride had the same length and litheness, and those running shorts were the same—navy and of normal length. She noticed things like that. She hated running shorts that showed groin. She also hated ones that were so long and loose that they could hide diapers underneath.

"Sharp guy," she remarked.

"He's looking here," Tracey said.

Katherine noticed that, at the same time that she noticed his hair. It was a brown-gray shade, sweaty and spiked. She had seen that hair before.

She returned to the rhythm of her work—separate hair, insert foil, brush on color, fold foil; separate hair, insert foil, brush on color, fold foil. She had wanted to do this to Rachel's hair, to add a subtle variation in color.

Rachel had been on the verge of giving in when the accident happened.

She missed Rachel. Rachel thought the way she did. Katherine didn't know what she would do if Rachel didn't wake up.

Enya was chanting something soulfully Celtic. Katherine let it take her to another time, another place, and it worked for a bit. Then two things happened. First, she finished with foil and color and turned on a three-headed ultraviolet lamp to speed the processing. Second, she looked out the window again.

"That's his third time around," Tracey said. "Do you know him?"

Katherine sighed. "I do." With a reassuring hand on her client's shoulder, she leaned around the lamps. "You'll need fifteen minutes here. Can I get you anything—more tea, *biscotti?*"

"I'm fine," Tracey said, opening the latest *Vogue.* "Go."

Katherine stripped off her thin rubber gloves—surgical gloves, irony of ironies—and pushed the color cart aside. She checked the appointment book, giving Steve Bauer a chance to leave. But he remained across the street, feet firmly planted in front of the curb, hands on his hips, sweat on his T-shirt, which was navy as well. Though it galled her to admit it, he looked gloriously male.

She went outside.

"I thought it was you," he said, breathing faster than normal.

Katherine worked too many early mornings to know that he didn't normally run down this street. She made no effort to hide her cynicism. "Were you just . . . trying out a new street today?"

Bless him, he didn't even blush. Rather, he took a steadier breath, drew himself up, and smiled. "Actually, the Internet had two numbers, work and home. I called work and got the name of the shop, decided to run by and take a look. I wouldn't have expected you here so early."

"I wouldn't have expected you here so *late*. Don't you have rounds or something to do?"

His eyes sparkled. In broad daylight, they were a striking blue. "Yesterday was my long day," he said, "rounds at dawn, teaching in the city, private patients between surgeries." A trickle of sweat began to roll down his cheek. "I was in the OR until nine last night. I figured I'd sleep in today." He wiped the sweat from his cheek with a shoulder. "So. That's your shop?"

"Uh-huh."

"Looks chic."

"It has to be, in a town like this, or I'd be out of business in no time flat."

"Have you had it long?"

"Five years."

"Ah. Steady clientele?"

She thought about that and conceded, "Steady enough with locals. Tourists fill in the gaps."

"How do tourists know you're here? Do you advertise?"

"I give referral discounts to the hotels."

He smiled. "Clever." He gestured toward an Italian restaurant halfway down the block. "Ever eaten there?"

Katherine was grateful when he looked that way. Always a sucker for blue eyes, she was relieved to be released. "I have. It's great."

Too soon his eyes caught hers again. "I've never tried it. Want to go with me?"

"Mmm, I don't think so."

"Any special reason? Husband, fiancé, significant other?"

She thought about lying, but that wasn't her style. "No. I'm just . . . not interested right now."

Those blue eyes clouded. "Is it me?"

Oh, it was. She liked the way he looked, liked the way he dressed, liked the way he ran. He didn't evade questions. When she thought he was handing her a line, it turned out to be a legitimate one, and even aside from that, there was something intangible going on. She didn't understand what it was. She didn't *know* why a woman fell hard for a particular man. Chemistry, more than *logic?*

Oh, yes, it was him. But she wasn't ready to take another chance. Not yet. Not when she was finally starting to feel good about herself.

It had taken a long time—*another* thing they hadn't warned her about. She was forty-two and finally believing that she wasn't soon going to die. The shop helped. It spoke of a future. The way people looked at her helped, too. They saw not only the healthy woman she was but the attractive woman she wanted to be.

Still, she wasn't ready to take her blouse off for anyone yet, much less a man—which was no doubt jumping the gun. Steve Bauer had asked her out to dinner. He hadn't asked her to bed.

But it was coming. She saw it in those blue eyes. Worse, she felt it in the tiny place in her belly that hadn't been revved up since her surgery. Oh, it was revved up now. She could do it with this man. The question was whether things would go dead if he had a problem with her breasts.

Those eyes were still clouded. He seemed concerned, on the verge of hurt, and Katherine wasn't one to hurt. "No," she said. "It's not you. It's me."

"Why you?"

"Bad experiences." With a regretful smile, she started walking backward toward the shop. "Maybe someday we'll have dinner. Not yet."

His eyes dropped to her mouth, and for a split second, she felt caressed. "I'd settle for lunch," he said with such endearing directness that her smile grew coy.

"Tell you what. Get my friend out of her coma and I might go for that."

"I'm not God."

She shrugged. Turning, she walked with deliberate reserve the rest of the way back to her shop.

JACK reached the hospital before nine. Cindy was bathing Rachel. The only change that had occurred was the arrival of a new, larger-than-ever flower arrangement from Victoria.

"Hi, Rachel," he said, but she showed no sign of hearing. "No more movement?" he asked Cindy.

She shook her head.

From his briefcase, he took a handful of CDs that the girls had pulled from Rachel's collection. Flipping through them, he said, "We have another Garth, we have Clint Black, we have Collin Raye, Shania Twain, and Wynonna. Okay, angel, what'll it be?" When Rachel didn't answer, he said, "Hope said I'd like Collin, so let's do it." He put the CD on low.

While Cindy finished up with Rachel, he disposed of

the flower arrangements that were dead and went to the shop downstairs for replacements. In response to his request for something vivid, the florist pulled out an orange hibiscus and a deep pink kalanchoe. "They'll bloom for months," the man said, and just that quickly, Jack decided on roses and tulips. The roses were yellow, the tulips pink. They would last a week, no more. He wanted Rachel to be home by then.

Cindy had dressed Rachel in a nightshirt that was bright pink with orange and blue splashes—sent by the owner of a Big Sur crafts shop, along with a card that was tacked on the bulletin board beside Hope's drawings and other cards—and was trying to tuck stray strands of Rachel's hair into the loose topknot that Samantha had created with Hope's scrunchy the afternoon before.

"Leave it," he said to the nurse. "It's pretty, curling against her cheek."

Moments later, alone with Rachel, he touched that curl. It was soft, silky. There was life there yet.

Taking one of the roses, he moved it under her nose. "Bright yellow," he said and, studying the rose, pushed himself to see it as Rachel would. "Sunshine. Barely open but wanting to, just the tips starting to curl outward, like delicate paper." He tipped the rose to his own nose. "And fragrant. Smells like sunshine, too. Makes me think beach roses in Nantucket. Remember those? Good vacation." He returned the rose to Rachel's nose, then exchanged it for a tulip. "This one is soft pink. Baby pink. Smooth. Tall and graceful. A dancer. An elegant spring dancer."

He teased the tip of her nose with the tulip. Then he told her about going out to the car that morning and seeing deer in the woods. A doe and two fawns—*blacktails,* he could have sworn he heard her say, though his own memory may have dredged it up. And he told her about Boca.

"See, it isn't just the money," he said, because if it was he would never have blown off a job. Then he leaned closer, so that no one else would hear, and confessed, "Maybe it was, for a while. But it wasn't conscious materialism. It was wanting to be a success. If I got lost in it, I'm sorry. But success has always been a thing for me, more than for you. Back home, I was shit growing up. I still feel that way sometimes. You, you've always been a success. Hell, just growing the girls for nine months and giving birth was a coup."

Oh, he had been proud, and not only of his daughters. Rachel had been the most beautiful, most serene mom during her brief-as-brief-could-be stays in the maternity ward. He remembered lying just this close when she was back home and nursing, watching her doze off with a baby at her breast. She hadn't changed—same gracefully arched brows, same short nose, same freckles. He felt the same familiarity, the same closeness, that had made their best years so good. Even at the end, some things had worked. Like the girls tumbling with him in the yard, while Rachel captured it all on film. Even at the end there were smiles.

But okay, he hadn't been there emotionally for her. She hadn't pointed it out. He had felt her increasing silence. She had felt his increasing distance.

"It's like you get started in one direction and pick up speed, and you may forget where you're going and why, but the momentum takes you there anyway. Only, you find out when you arrive that it isn't where you want to be." He wasn't sure if he was talking about work or about the divorce. Since the divorce was a done deed, he focused on work.

"The problem," he said, pulling shop drawings from his briefcase, "is that I can cancel on a project like Boca because nothing's been signed yet, but there are too many others where the commitment's been made." He unfolded the drawings. They were the designs for Napa—heat and air ductwork, lighting, kitchen fixtures—submitted by the various subcontractors and overnighted to him in Big Sur. They needed study and approval. It was the least he could do after postponing another set of meetings.

He told Rachel about the project, then talked his way through the shop drawings, wondering if what he said meant anything to her. She used to look over his shoulder sometimes when he was working with drawings like these. He had talked her through the plans then.

At least, he thought he had. Maybe he hadn't. Maybe she had been running in and out, busy with the girls. She would have been bored with these. Hell, *he* was bored with these. They had more to do with supervision than design, and design was his love.

He had barely refolded the drawings and put them away when Ben Wolfe arrived. He carried an arrangement of yellow roses, saw the ones Jack had bought, and said a surprisingly gracious, "Great minds think alike." He set his vase on the nightstand. "Today's my birthday. We were going to celebrate."

"Happy birthday," Jack said, but he didn't leave this time. He stood right there with Rachel while Ben made awkward conversation with her. He seemed like a very nice, very decent, very attentive and accommodating man. Jack had the wildest impulse to introduce him to Jill.

When Ben broached the subject of Rachel's show, Jack said that he would be framing her pictures himself. After all, she had all the materials at the house, and he had framed pictures before, or so he reasoned. But he wasn't thinking about framing when Ben left. He was thinking about painting. He had put it off, put it off, thinking that Rachel would wake up and tell him not to do it, but the show was ten days off and she was still asleep, and he didn't *know* whether this six-years-older Rachel would resent his touching her work. Samantha thought she would. Katherine might have an opinion.

Katherine would *definitely* have an opinion. But he had told her to butt out.

He could apologize. That felt like the right thing to do. He wanted to think that she was his friend now, too. He would do it.

UNFORTUNATELY when Katherine came to visit, she wasn't alone. Dinah and Jan were with her. Dinah looked as successful as ever with her smart red suit, gold brooch, and beeper. Jan was no-nonsense and functional, a woman with muscled calves, sun-dried skin, and sheer polish on her nails. Katherine's own nails were burgundy today.

The three looked worried approaching the bed. With forced lightness, they talked to Rachel in turns. One held her hand, another brushed her hair, the third asked Jack what the doctors were saying.

Thinking to learn more about Rachel from them, as he had from Charlie and Faye, he asked about book group. It was a mistake. Suddenly, though he was standing right there, he faded. Their voices grew quiet, more intimate.

They became four close friends—Dinah, Katherine, Jan, and Rachel—four close *female* friends, reminiscing about things they had shared.

"Why did I join?" Dinah asked in response to Jack's question, but oblivious to him now. "Because I love to read. I always have."

"You were the most avid of us," Katherine said. "We rarely chose a book where you hadn't read another by the same author."

"I was so intimidated," Jan confessed. "I felt like the dummy because my life was either hitting golf balls or changing diapers. I came so close to calling and canceling out of that first meeting. Changed clothes three times beforehand."

"You didn't."

"I did. But I needed to talk about that book. Remember it?"

"*Beloved.*"

"I was sure I'd missed most of the meaning."

"Haunting book."

"Strong."

"Scary." It was Jan, again, speaking softly. "But not as scary as *The Fifth Child.*"

"You were pregnant again."

"Waiting for amnio results."

"I read the book and began imagining that this new child would arrive and mess up the family I already had."

"That was your confession book." This from Katherine with a nod.

Dinah chuckled. "Boy, did you let go."

"I was embarrassed."

"But it gave the rest of us permission to do the same," Katherine said. "I did it with *A Prayer for Owen Meany,* which I adored, but which had nothing to do with me directly." She frowned. "So why that book?"

"It was the timing," Dinah suggested. "Byron had just let you down. You needed to vent."

"I vented all right." She touched Rachel's hair. "What did it for Rachel?"

"*Moon Tiger.*"

"*Woman on the Edge of Time.*"

But Katherine was shaking her head. "*Exit the Rainmaker.*"

"Oh my God." Jan laughed. "About the college president who just disappeared one day. I haven't thought of that one in *ages.*"

"What a great discussion."

Katherine nodded. "We asked each other where *we* would go if we were to walk out of our lives and disappear like he did. Remember what Rachel said?" Jack listened as Katherine's voice grew softer, lyrical. "She described a little town in Maine, not much more than a handful of stores backed up to the shore of a lake. There were huge pine forests, long dirt roads leading to cabins in the woods, and skies so clear you could see the northern lights. She said she would live in one of those cabins and know everyone in town. She thought it would be the simplest, most beautiful life."

Dinah snorted. "Not *my* cup of tea. Remember what *I* said? *I'd* get lost in *Gstaad.*"

She may have said more, but Jack didn't hear. He had gone to the window and was looking blindly out over a cluster of Monterey cypress, realizing that the birds he had found on one of those canvases waiting to be finished in Rachel's studio were loons. He hadn't identified them immediately because his mind was on the West

Coast, not the East. Mention of the northern lights had shifted his sights, because he had seen those lights, that sky. The loons were from Maine. They had been floating on the glassy surface of the lake at dusk on every one of the seven nights he and Rachel had spent in the small cabin in the pines that had been their honeymoon suite.

HE BEGAN painting at eight. He worked until three in the morning, layering Rachel's canvas with that lake and its small center island, its border of trees, and an early evening sky shot with a whisper of green and pink. Where the mirror of the lake called for reflections, he made them lighter than real life would have them, and it worked. When he finally set down his palette and brushes, straightened cramped legs one at a time, and stepped back from the easel, his eye was drawn more strongly than ever to Rachel's loons.

It was another hour before he capped the oils and half again as much before he crawled into Rachel's bed. He woke up after three hours of sleep, opened the window, and inhaled the lifting fog. He was tired, but pleasantly so. He had worked hard and done well. He hadn't felt as satisfied in a long, long while.

He showered, shaved, and dressed. When he arrived in the kitchen, Samantha was standing at the counter drinking coffee. She looked like something from a magazine, all tight top and jeans, silky straight hair, and eyes lined in blue.

"You look so grown-up it scares me," he said, meaning every word. The defiance he saw kept him from telling her to get rid of the eyeliner. "Is that all you're having for breakfast?" he asked instead.

"Breakfast is my least favorite meal."

"Since when?"

A look of annoyance came and went. Even her defiance was down. "Daddy? Can we talk about the prom?"

"Is your sister up?"

"Up and gone."

"Gone where?" he asked, fearing.

Samantha didn't have to do more than look in the direction of Duncan's, and suddenly Jack made for the door. He knew that Hope would show up in time to leave, but she had gone to Duncan's one time too many. A niggling in the back of his mind said that he wanted to see more of where she went.

He had lost one child, perhaps because of his own inertia. He couldn't let it happen again. If he didn't go after Hope, and she was ever hurt in any way, Rachel would never forgive him. More, he would never forgive himself.

chapter fourteen

JACK WAS A MAN with a mission as he strode up the hill. He felt little of the early morning chill, saw little of the sun that was just rising high enough to crest the hills in the east, and if the fragrance of the air had any power at all, it served only to keep him from outright panic. During the precious minutes it took him to reach Duncan Bligh's cabin, his imagination worked double-time. He conjured all kinds of ugly images, all kinds of perverse abuse. Quickening his step, he swore at himself repeatedly for not acting sooner.

The cabin was a log box that might have fit neatly into a corner of the adjacent pen. The barn behind it was larger and newer. Sheep clustered between pen and barn, staring at him as he neared.

He crossed the porch and pounded on the door. Hands on his hips, he clenched his jaw and waited. When Duncan opened up, he said angrily, "I don't know what in hell's been going on here, but I want my daughter, and I want her now."

Looking unperturbed—which bothered Jack all the

more—Duncan *ssh-sh*ed him with a finger and glanced into the interior of the cabin. Wondering what all he *hadn't* imagined, Jack barged past him. He hadn't taken more than a handful of steps when he stopped short.

The first thing he saw was a large hearth with a healthy fire radiating warmth. The second was Hope's blond hair, but it was down low, resting against something. That something was the third thing he saw. It was a minute before he identified a small figure in a wheelchair.

"About time you met Faith," Duncan muttered, walking past Jack. He bent low over the figure in the chair and murmured something Jack couldn't hear. Impatiently, he waved Jack forward. "Say hello to my wife."

The woman in the wheelchair looked back at Jack. Her hair was white, her face creased, her spectacles round and small. Her smile was as warm as the fire.

"Hello," she said, more mouthing than sound. Her hand lay on Hope's head, which lay against the crocheted afghan covering her legs. "She's sleeping," she whispered, but she needn't have reassured Jack. One look at the woman and her sweet smile, and his fears were gone. *Duncan's faith.* He couldn't count the number of times he had heard that phrase uttered in the same breath as *solace* and *peace*. The woman and her smile said it all. *Duncan's Faith.*

Jack took a deep, wry breath. *Duncan's Faith.* He was right for swearing at himself. He should have acted sooner. What an imbecile he was.

Releasing the breath with a self-deprecating shake of the head, he extended a hand. "Jack McGill," he said. Her hand was frail in his, but there was a dignity to it. "I'm pleased to meet you."

Faith nodded. "Hope didn't tell you she was coming?"

"No." He glanced at Duncan, who was regarding his wife with such tenderness that Jack was all the more humbled. *Duncan's Faith.* Why hadn't he known?

He hadn't known because he was thickheaded, because he was driven by jealousy where his family was concerned, because he jumped to conclusions at the drop of a hat. And maybe because the girls had hoodwinked him. So there was that.

Duncan walked off. Jack hunkered down in front of the fire so that Faith wouldn't have to look up.

"It's been hard on her," she said, her voice so soft and lyrical that it wouldn't waken Hope. "I don't think she's sleeping nights very well. How is Rachel?"

Jack hadn't called the hospital that morning. He knew that he would have been notified if anything had changed during the night. "She's the same. Do you know, I had no idea you existed? The girls talked about 'Faith' like it was a religion. I'm afraid I've been rude not coming to thank you before this."

"Thank me for what?"

The words came easily. Faith Bligh radiated goodness. Jack felt no threat here, no risk in baring his feelings. "For being kind to the girls. For taking care of Guinevere." He sputtered out a laugh in self-reproach. "I couldn't quite understand why the cat would be better off up here if Duncan was out in the fields all day." At that moment, Duncan was washing dishes in the kitchen that lined the far living room wall. "Now it makes sense."

"He comes back to check on me every few hours." She smiled again. "Not that I'm going anywhere."

"Do you go outside?"

"Oh, yes. I can wheel myself out to the porch. There's

a beautiful view of the valley. But I need Duncan for much beyond that."

Jack was remembering something—something Hope had said on the very first morning after Rachel's accident. He had been trying to assure her that broken legs healed. She had been convinced that it wasn't always the case.

He was frowning, trying to decide whether he could ask and, if so, how to do it, when Faith said, "Some people think I'm crazy living up here, but I've always loved these hills. If I have to be confined, this is a beautiful place to be. Duncan and I used to vacation here before the accident."

"How long ago was that?"

"The accident? Twelve years. A ski lift collapsed. My legs were broken in so many places that walking would have been an ordeal even if my spine hadn't been injured, which it was."

"I'm sorry."

"Don't be. Three died that day. I could have been one of those, and then I would have missed out on the life we've found here." Her eyes sparkled. "My Duncan used to drive a truck. I never saw him. Now I do."

Hope moved her head. She rubbed her eyes against the afghan, turned them toward the fire, opened them slowly, and saw Jack. "Daddy," she breathed, and quickly sat up.

"I was worried," he said, but gently. There was no other way to speak in this home.

"Mom always knows I'm here."

"Well," he said, pushing himself up, "maybe I'll know now, too." He held out a hand. "You have school. Samantha's waiting."

"She had breakfast with us," Faith said with a fond look at Hope.

"I'm sorry for that. We've imposed enough."

"Imposed? Oh, no. Hope is no imposition. She's a joy. This is the least I can do, after all Rachel has done." She reached for Hope's free hand. "Give your mother a kiss for me, will you?"

"OKAY," HE told the girls as he hustled them to the car. "The joke's up. Tell me about your mom and the Blighs."

"They're good friends," Samantha said. "Can we talk about my prom?"

"Not yet," Jack answered, because he was feeling a little foolish knowing so little. "How did they get to be good friends?" he asked, backing out of the drive.

Hope said, "Mom was exploring right after we moved here. She stumbled across their cabin and Faith was on the porch."

"About my prom—"

"Not yet," Jack said, shifting to drive down the hill. "You owe me. Both of you. No one told me Faith was a person."

"No one told you she wasn't."

"You guys let me think your mother was *dating* Duncan."

"We *never* said that."

Hope said, "The thing about Duncan and Faith is that it never seems right talking about them. Mom helps them out, doing marketing and stuff. She always said that Faith was like a favorite aunt. She has coffee up there a lot. They sit and talk. With Faith you don't even *have* to talk and it feels good."

One meeting with the woman, and Jack knew what

Hope meant. Faith radiated understanding, acceptance, calm.

Samantha's voice was a jarring intrusion. "Dad. We need to talk about my prom. There's been a change in plans."

He would have liked to hear more about Faith, because even picturing her brought calm, but Samantha had an agenda of her own, and he was learning that car time was good time. Oh yes, he was a captive audience here, but so was she. She couldn't stomp off when she didn't like what he said.

He turned north onto Highway 1. "What's the change?"

"First of all, I'm not going with Brendan. I'm going with Teague."

Jack felt something by his arm closest to the door. Hope was crowded against the window there. "Teague?" he asked Samantha.

"Teague Runyan. He's a great guy."

"Why the switch?"

"Brendan and I aren't getting along. It doesn't make any sense for us to be stuck with each other when he wanted to be with Jana and I wanted to be with Teague. I mean, everyone's with everyone anyway, so it's no big thing except for going and coming."

Jack followed that—in a way. "Are you still leaving from Lydia's house?"

"No. That's the second change. Teague's picking me up here."

Hope shifted. Jack felt the movement against his arm, decided that he really did need a bigger car, and shot Samantha a look. "How old is this Teague?"

"Seventeen. He's a good driver, and he has a truck. It's, like, indestructible."

In Jack's day, guys wouldn't be caught dead picking up their girls in a truck, if they had another option. So maybe this Teague didn't. Or maybe it was just that times had changed. Trucks were in. And Jack did like the sound of *indestructible*. What he didn't like was the sound of *seventeen*. Seventeen was a dangerous age. "Okay. So I'll meet him when he comes?"

"Uh-huh," Samantha said a little too brightly.

"What else?"

"Else?"

"Is that it for changed plans? You're still doing the limo thing from Lydia's house and back?"

"The party's at Jake Drumble's."

"I've never heard that name either," Jack said a little less easily. Katherine had warned him that things weren't always as they seemed. Just now with Hope, they had proved to be better. He had a feeling it wouldn't be that way with Samantha. "Who is Jake Drumble, where does he live, and what happened to Lydia's party?"

"Oh God, here we go," Samantha cried, "I knew you'd have trouble with this. You are the most . . . *anal* person I know."

"I just *asked.*"

"Like it's the Inquisition," she said with indignation. "It's no—big—thing. As far as you're concerned, the only difference is that Teague will pick me up Saturday and drop me back Sunday."

"Yeah, well, that leaves a whole lot of hours unaccounted for," he said. He felt Hope again. Deliberate? "So. The party's at Jake's. Before and after?"

"I think so. It's not definite about after."

"But you're going back to Lydia's to sleep."

"*No*," She was suddenly impatient. "I'm not *going* with Lydia."

"Not at all?"

"That's the *point*. Like, this is a whole different group. Lydia'll be with Brendan and Jana and Adam and Shelly, and I'll be with Teague and Pam and Jake and Heather."

He was beginning to see the picture. "So Lydia's party is still on, only you're not going. But she's your best friend."

"So?"

He slid her a glance. "So, that doesn't sound right."

Samantha blew out a breath. She folded her arms and stared out the windshield, and Jack was tempted to let it go. The silence was welcome, with his mind so full of other things. But one of those things was Katherine's concern about teenaged girls and proms; another was a little something that was starting to feel like a finger poking his arm where Samantha couldn't see.

"Talk to me, Sam," he said lightly.

"What do you want me to say? Lydia just isn't . . ."

"Isn't . . . sophisticated?"

"No, she isn't, and if I'm with her, I can't be with other kids who are."

"Because those others won't like you if you're with Lydia?"

"They *won't*."

Jack thought about that as he drove. Hope wasn't poking him anymore. She didn't need to. He knew on his own that more than a little something wasn't right. "What about loyalty?" he finally asked. "Lydia's been your best friend for six years. It shouldn't just end in a day."

There was a pause, then a sharp "Your marriage did."

Jack was blindsided for the space of a breath. He

rebounded with a firm "No, it didn't. It was months leading up to the end, and it was painful. It wasn't something
either of us wanted."

"Then why did it happen?"

"Because we'd reached an impasse, but it was
between your mother and me and no one else. There
weren't any third parties. We weren't choosing between
one group or another."

"Just one *lifestyle* or another," Samantha said.

"Okay. I can buy that. But it's a far cry from being
best friends with Lydia one day and deciding she isn't
good enough for you the next. So she isn't sophisticated.
What does that mean? She doesn't use eye makeup? Her
T-shirts aren't tight enough? You seemed happy enough
with her last weekend. Was that an act?"

"No." She made a disgruntled sound. "You don't
understand."

"I'm trying to. But it doesn't feel right."

"This is a *prom,*" she said, enunciating each word.
"It's one night."

"Sounds to me like it's more than that. Sounds to me
like a *lifestyle* decision," he said, using her word.
"You're choosing between groups of friends. That has
long-range implications. So Lydia isn't as sophisticated
as—what's her name?"

"Pam. And it's *all* those kids who aren't as cool."

"But they're nice kids. They come from nice families.
I haven't seen Pam at the hospital visiting your mother. I
haven't seen Teague there, or any of the others you mentioned."

"That's because they're new friends. They don't know
Mom yet. And why do you assume they're not nice? Just
because they're different doesn't mean they aren't as

265

good or even better." Her voice turned pleading. "You don't understand. I am *so* excited about going to the prom with these kids. It'll be awesome," she said with feeling, and because Jack did want her to be happy, he settled into the silence of the drive.

But he had a bad taste in his mouth. After meeting Lydia's mom, he had grown complacent about the prom. What did he know about Pam whoever, *or* about Teague Runyan? Hell, he didn't even like the kid's name, which was sick. But he was Samantha's father. And he was a man. He knew what men did. He knew what *young* men did. Seventeen-year-olds were loose cannons.

They were approaching the tree-lined stretch of Carmel Highlands when he said, "I worry about safety. Are Jake's parents chaperoning this party?"

"As far as I know." She took a quick breath. "Don't you dare call. You'll *humiliate* me."

Well, he didn't want to do that. He wanted to treat Samantha like a mature young woman. "Still," he said because the whole thing with Lydia was sitting wrong in his gut, "there's something to be said for loyalty."

"Oh?" Samantha asked. "Is that why you're racing back to the city to have lunch with Jill today? You dumped Mom because she wasn't sophisticated enough."

"Excuse me?"

Samantha barreled on, clearly driven by that agenda of hers. "She didn't want to party all the time, so you dumped her for Jill. Is that any different from what I'm doing?"

"*Totally.* First of all, I didn't *dump* your mother. If anything, she dumped me. Second, I didn't start dating Jill until a long time after your mother and I split."

"You've been dating her two years. Is it serious? Have you given her a ring or anything?"

"No. We're just friends."

"Don't you think *she*'s thinking about loyalty?"

"Samantha," he said with a sigh, "this isn't your business."

"It *is*. I want to know why loyalty has to matter to me, but not to you."

"Loyalty matters to me. Why do you think I'm here? Why do you think I've spent the better part of the past week and a half at your mother's bedside?"

"Why have you?" Samantha asked. "Has it occurred to you that she might not want you there?"

"Yes. It has. But that doesn't change the way I feel. Sitting with your mother feels like the right thing to do. So I ask *you* what feels right—going to the prom with friends you know and trust, or blowing them off to be with a whole other group?"

"This is hopeless," she grumbled and said for what had to have been the third time, "You *don't* understand." This time she turned her head away.

"No," he sighed, feeling defeated. "I guess I don't."

JILL lived in a modest house in Seacliff, which was in northwest San Francisco, overlooking the Pacific. When Jack arrived, at one, he felt a sense of dread. Jill was perfect. Her blond hair was adorably layered, her makeup pleasantly light, her skirt and blouse artsy, her scent spicy—though the scent might well have come from the kitchen. She had decided against the risotto that she would have cooked Monday and, instead, had made a warm Oriental salad with fresh tuna, spaghetti-thin wonton crisps, a dressing that was light and contained herbs Jack had never heard of, and warm, home-baked olive bread.

The granite kitchen island was set with rattan mats, linen napkins, and fresh flowers. One look, one smell, and Jack sensed the effort she had made to make things special. The kiss she gave him tasted of relief, which made him feel worse.

They sat side by side on tall stools, thighs touching, arms occasionally entwined. Jill asked first about Rachel and listened in concern while he tried to verbalize the jolt he still felt each morning walking into that hospital room and seeing her lying inert. He told of helping the nurse bathe her and work her limbs to keep them pliant. He told of talking to Rachel about the girls and the past in the hope of eliciting a response.

Then Jill asked him about work. Fresh from two hours at the office, he talked about that for a while. David had been upset over Boca, but they had worked it through. More worrisome to Jack was his partner's lukewarm response to his latest Montana design, which he described to Jill to her nodding approval. He told her about sending Brynna to Buffalo, elevating Alex to a project manager for Napa and San Jose, and alerting the others that he needed backup for Austin. He told her that he had just learned about a new project that might be interesting.

He asked Jill about the final take from the benefit the week before, and listened while she outlined plans for the next year's benefit, proposed several days before. He asked about her tennis lessons and asked how her diabetic mother was doing.

When they stopped talking, Jill slipped her arms around his waist. She rested her head on his shoulder, then raised her face. They kissed once, and again. She slipped off her stool, came between his legs, and wrapped her arms around his neck. Her breasts settled against his chest. As she kissed him again, she undulated ever so slowly.

Jack tried to get into it. He told himself that it might work after all, that Jill was an incredible woman, that he would be a fool to let her go. He tried to feel, but nothing came, so he tried to fantasize. But Rachel's was the only face he could see, and his body wasn't falling for the switch. It knew the difference between the women. He had spent more than a few hours of late painfully aroused in Rachel's bed. The only pain he felt now was the knowledge that he couldn't keep doing this and, because of that, he was about to hurt Jill.

Her mouth was doing its very best against his throat when he took her arms and gently disengaged. He put his forehead to hers. "This isn't working," he said quietly. "I . . . can't."

She drew back frightened, studied his face. "Is it Rachel?"

"It's everything."

"But is it her?"

He wasn't sure. Early on, Katherine had asked him why he was still at her bedside. Samantha had asked him the same thing that morning.

"Do you love her?" Jill asked.

"I don't know. I don't know. My life just seems to be turning on end."

"You need space. That's okay. I'll wait. You can take your time. I'm not going anywhere."

He felt a stab of annoyance. It was a minute before he realized that the annoyance wasn't *at* her, but *for* her. She was too good. He could take advantage of her offer in no time.

Clasping her hands together in his, he said, "I can't do this anymore, Jill. It isn't fair to you."

Her voice went high, urgent. "Am I complaining?"

"No. That's the problem. You don't complain. You don't demand. You don't give me ultimatums."

"I don't have to. You know what I want."

"I do, and you've been patient, waiting, wanting it to happen, but it isn't going to."

"How do you *know?* Your life is turning on end; you just said so. Why not wait? Why call it off now?"

"Because," he said with greater feeling, "it's not going to happen. It's not, Jill."

"But—"

"Shh." He pressed a finger to her lips, stroked the blond hair that was so much like Rachel's but not. He spoke in a half whisper, urgent now himself. "Listen to me. Please. I love you, Jill, I do, but as a person, a friend. It won't ever end in marriage, which is what you want, what you *should* have."

Her eyes were large, teary. "Why . . . won't it? What's . . . missing?"

"Nothing. Nothing in you. It's me. I'm just . . . I'm just . . ."

"Still in love with Rachel?"

He released a breath. "Maybe. I honestly don't know. But I don't feel free now. My marriage is still there. Unfinished business."

"Rachel ended it. She left you. You always told me that."

"It helped keep me angry, but there are reasons why she left, things I didn't know about until now. I have to talk with her, Jill. I won't know where I'm going until I do."

Bewildered, Jill asked, "Was it *that* good with her?"

That good and better, he would have said if he hadn't cared so much, but he was hurting Jill enough without. "It was different. Unique in its way. Rachel and I have a history, Jill. We go way back."

"What if she doesn't wake up?"

"Then I'll have the girls. And regrets." He sighed, running his hands up and down her arms. "Don't add to the regrets, Jill. I could keep this going between us and just take what I want. But I'm trying to do the right thing. Help me? Please?"

"IT'S DONE," he told Rachel barely two hours later. Jill had cried at the end. They had agreed to talk from time to time. He was feeling empty, alone. But he had done the right thing. "She was a perfectly lovely woman, but Christ, you have a hold on me. You always did. I was dating someone when we met. Remember? I broke up with her, too."

Only, then, Jack had been madly in love with Rachel. Now, they weren't married anymore. But he remembered clear as day the tingling he had felt deep inside whenever she talked, touched him, even *looked* at him. He remembered the anticipation of seeing her and the pleasure when he did. It had been that way through the birth of the kids. Even after they'd started to want different kinds of everyday lives, there were times when a word, a look, or a touch could start the tingling.

"Were things so bad at the end?" he asked, studying her face. It was healing by the day. Her color was improving. He wanted to think that was propitious.

He curled and uncurled the fingers of her right hand,

271

then did the same with the left. "Maybe we jumped the gun. Gave up too soon. Let it happen without enough of a fight. We had good stuff going." He concentrated on her ring finger, so slim and bare. "Didn't we?" He searched her face for a blink or a twitch.

"I keep thinking about that baby. Feeling that loss. Thinking maybe that would've done it, made us yell and scream and get it all out. Six years. What we could have had and done in six years." He felt a wave of weariness. "Talk to me," he whispered plaintively. "*Tell* me."

Katherine turned into the room. He took a tired breath, sighed, straightened. "How goes it?"

"Not bad. And here?"

Jack shrugged. He followed her gaze to the tray table that was covered with papers.

"Are you getting much done?" she asked without spite.

"Nah. I spread stuff out and pretend, but it's hard to concentrate. What I'm working on feels stale. I was in the office this morning and got a call about a new project. If I hadn't been right there, I wouldn't ever have known. My partner would have said thanks, but no thanks."

"Why?"

"The job is to build a private home. Granted, there are four acres to work with and the client wants more an estate than a home, but it's smaller than most of our recent jobs. David thinks it's a step back for us."

"What do you think?"

"I think," he said, flexing his spine side to side, "that it'd be a fun job to do. It's in Hillsborough. Local. The zoning's all done. The client knows my work. He wants me to use what I've done in the past as a springboard. I.e., he wants something new and imaginative."

Katherine nodded her approval. Jack wanted to think Rachel approved, too.

He sat back and smiled. "So, how's the good doctor?"

For a minute he saw the old, defensive Katherine. Then his smile registered, and she softened. "Sent me flowers yesterday afternoon," she said.

"That's impressive."

She gave a one-shouldered shrug. "Byron sent me flowers, too. The good doctor is as much in the dark about you-know-what as Byron was then."

"You don't think Bauer is used to medical quirks?"

"Quirks? That's rich. And I'm sure he is. But that's a problem in itself. If he deals with medical . . . quirks all day long, why ever would he want to face them at night?"

"The flip side of that argument is that he's become so inured to them, he wouldn't notice."

"He'd notice."

"Are they that bad?" Jack asked, frankly curious. From the outside, nothing was wrong. Absolutely nothing.

"Well, they aren't," Katherine conceded. "They just . . . take a little getting used to. There are scars."

"Few people make it to forty without those."

"It's the idea of the whole thing."

"That may be more in your mind than anyone else's."

"Possibly." She paused. "Why are you pushing this?"

"Pushing what?"

"The good doctor and me. Why do I need a man?"

Jack sat back. "There's an interesting question. From what I've gathered, you and Rachel are two peas in a pod, very much alike, yes? Strong, independent women?"

Katherine considered that. "I'd say so."

"Okay. Early on, I said that Rachel never really needed

me. You said I was wrong. If you tell me how she needed me, there might be a message for you." When she didn't immediately respond, he said, "I assume you two talked about it."

"Not in as many words. Strong, independent women like us don't use the word *need*. We use the word *want,* like we have the power to choose." But she grew reflective as she focused on Rachel. "She sometimes talks about things she misses."

"Like?"

"Help with the girls. Raising kids is hard. The bigger they get, the bigger the issues. Rachel misses having you there to talk things through with."

"She always had answers."

"Maybe when the girls were little. She had to. You weren't around, and little kids need immediate response. Big kids, big problems require more thought. That's the discussion she misses."

You weren't around. Well, he was, but not enough. He had missed some important times for the girls. And for Rachel? Okay. He should have been there more. He certainly should have known about that baby. He should have cut that trip short and come home. If he was haunted by the loss of that child now, he could imagine what Rachel had felt at the time.

She should have told him. He should have been there.

But if he had been there for her all along, she *might* have told him.

Accepting his share of the blame, he sighed. "What else did she miss?"

"I don't know," Katherine said, seeming embarrassed. She pushed her fingers through her hair from underneath, then shook her head. "I know what *I* miss. I miss someone to be with after work. Someone to share wine with. Someone to share silence. Sharing. I guess that's it. I'd venture to say that Rachel misses that."

"Sounds to me she found some of it with Faith Bligh. Sharing the silence over coffee."

"Not the same. There's something about lying in bed late at night or very, very early in the morning, talking, silent, whatever."

Memory had Jack right back there, lying with Rachel. They were special times, which had started coming fewer and farther between. Then they had ended. "When you work and have kids, you're exhausted."

But it was a stock excuse. Katherine's arched brow said as much.

You make time for what you want, Rachel had said once. And she had tried. He recalled a time when he was due back from a trip in the evening. She hired a baby-sitter and made reservations at Postrio weeks in advance, then picked him up at the airport and drove him there. He proceeded to tell her that he had eaten at the place six times in the last month and couldn't bear to do it again.

He had missed the point, which wasn't form but substance. He realized that now, with no pride at all.

"I miss taking vacations with Rachel," he offered.

He was rewarded when Katherine said, "She misses being pampered once in a while."

"Strong, independent women need pampering?"

"We're human, too."

"Any man can suffice for that."

She shook her head. "Only certain ones. It's an . . . intangible something. A man can be in a room with fifty women and fall for only one. A woman can be in a room with fifty men and fall for only one. Why? I don't know the answer. Do you?"

Jack didn't. But he hadn't fallen in love with Jill the way logic said he should. "Does Rachel have that . . . whatever with Ben?"

Katherine laughed. "Not quite."

He was immensely pleased. "Really?"

"What do *you* think?"

"Well, the guy doesn't turn *me* on," he said, then asked a cautious "She hasn't found it with anyone else?"

Katherine slowly shook her head. Softly she said, "It's a very special quality. When it works, it works. Rachel had it with you. She still thinks about that. She thinks about it a lot."

SO DID JACK, most notably Katherine's use of the present tense. He might have taken it more lightly if it had come from anyone else. But Katherine said what she meant.

He could ask her for specifics, could prod and dig. But did he want to risk her saying that Rachel was simply analyzing and understanding the past, rather than feeling it in the present?

No.

Because the fact was that he *did* feel things now. He felt things every time he touched her, whether applying skin cream or exercising her limbs. He felt things looking at her mouth, or at those freckles that promised such spirit. He felt things walking down the hospital corridor and turning in at her room. Anticipation. Purpose. Rightness.

Fine to say that he was here out of guilt, or for the girls, or for old times' sake, but the truth was that he still felt a connection with Rachel. Unfinished business, he had told Jill. He wondered if it was more than that. One of the things he had loved most about Rachel when they first met was believing that she brought out the best in him. He wondered if she still could.

SO HE SAT with her following his talk with Katherine, and though he didn't deliberately think about work, his mind wandered there on its own. Looking at Rachel, holding her hand, he began to talk out the Montana project, and suddenly he saw a design possibility. No, it wasn't the one he had originally wanted, or any one of his subsequent revisions, but yes, it would work.

Fearful that he might lose it once he left Rachel, he pulled up a pad and quickly sketched out his thoughts, then booted up his laptop and drew it there. He saved what he drew and took longer studying it, but way deep down in his fast-beating heart he knew it was finally, finally right.

His agonizing was over. The client would be pleased. The resort would be built in this design. Done deal.

RIDING THE TIDE of that sense of accomplishment, he painted in Rachel's studio again that night. He was up until four in the morning this time, but the satisfaction was worth it. He woke up to have breakfast with the girls and drive them down the road to the bus stop, to call the hospital for an update on Rachel, and to fax the new design from his laptop to the office. Ignoring E-mail from

David, he went back to bed and slept until ten. Even then, he took the time to drink a leisurely cup of coffee, sitting on the fallen log in Rachel's woods, watching the foraging of half a dozen wild turkeys, big brown things the likes of which he couldn't imagine cooking and carving.

He didn't bother to shave. Rachel never minded stubble. He stopped at the market for a dozen two-liter bottles of assorted sodas and, feeling another bit of accomplishment, dropped them at school just in time for Hope's class picnic. Then he went on to Monterey.

He had known that Rachel was still comatose. What he hadn't known was that she had new guests.

chapter fifteen

JACK WAS ALWAYS amazed when he saw Victoria Keats. She looked younger each time—and it wasn't generosity toward his ex-mother-in-law that made him think that. It was fact. She was six years older now than when he had seen her last, but she didn't look a minute of it. Her eyes were bright and wide, her skin smooth. He figured she was on her third face-lift. She was always on the run, hence well toned, and not only had impeccable taste in clothes but refused to believe that trendiness had either age or business limits. She wore a chic wrap dress in a jersey print, produced by a designer whose styles were making a dramatic comeback. The print was heavy in brown, black, and beige. She wore sheer brown stockings and stylish brown heels. Her hair was a tasteful platinum, drawn back into a knot at the nape of her neck. Her face had a moisturized glow; her lipstick was a flattering coral.

She was extraordinary looking, particularly in comparison to the plain woman standing at the foot of Rachel's bed.

"Mom!" Jack said to the plain woman, feeling the

same tug at his heart that he felt each time he saw her. "I didn't expect you here!"

"Of course, you didn't," scolded Victoria Keats. "You didn't call her, because you wanted to spare her the worry, but Rachel is, after all, her daughter-in-law and the mother of her grandchildren. Eunice was so upset when I told her about the accident that she insisted on meeting me here."

Jack was about to ask how his mother, who rarely left Oregon, had managed to get to Monterey on her own, when Victoria said, "Well, Rachel doesn't look as bad as I thought she would. That's a nasty scrape on her face, but it looks to be healing well, and the doctor tells me her leg will be just fine. It looks like she's sleeping." She patted Rachel's arm. "Well, you go right ahead and sleep, darling, that's the best thing for you. The doctor assures me it's only a matter of days before you'll be awake and then you'll have to face this man." The look she turned on Jack might have been a scowl if her face had worked properly. The smooth stretch of her skin watered down dismay into puzzlement. "You look like something the cat dragged in. You know, they did tell me that comas can be psychological."

They had told Jack that, too. Everything about Rachel suggested that she was healing well. Since they didn't know why she wasn't waking up, they were looking for excuses. Personally, he couldn't believe she wanted this.

"She may be terrified of facing you," Victoria said. "Is that how successful architects dress these days? It must be a West Coast thing, because they would never walk around New York looking like that. In New York they're a dapper group, which they *have* to be; it's part of the statement they make, knowing about fashion and style, *and* good grooming. But then, in New York, *everyone* has higher standards. When was the last time you shaved?"

"Yesterday morning."

"Your father shaved every day," Eunice reminded him.

"It looks like longer than that," Victoria decided, giving him a slow head-to-toe, "but we won't put you on the spot. After all, you do have a lot on your hands. Rachel, they tell me he's been here every day. Now isn't that something? He's living with the girls in Big Sur, and after all that hullaballoo about preferring to live in the city, aside from the stubble he doesn't look bad. Well, he could use a pair of tailored slacks; those jeans have seen better days, as have the loafers—are those Cole-Haans? No, they wouldn't be. You need Cole-Haans—the leather is exquisite—but that would be for the city, and if you're living in the country now, I suppose what you have on is all right. Oh my"— she lifted Rachel's hand—"look at your nails. Someone did a *beautiful* French manicure. It makes your nails look longer and more elegant. *How* many years did I tell you that you ought to let them grow?"

"She paints," Jack said. He had rounded the bed, greeting his mother with a shoulder touch along the way—a grand show of affection, by his family's standards. Taking root opposite Victoria, he put a protective hand against Rachel's neck. "Long nails get in the way."

"I don't see why they should," Victoria argued, "not if she uses a brush. Of course, that manicure calls for something classic and white, certainly something more elegant than flannel," she said in distaste. "And lime green? Oh my. Lime green is not terribly classy. Subtle is the way to go, subtle and rich. But where is the lingerie I *sent?*"

"In Big Sur . . ."

"I sent it *here*."

"I know, but—"

"Ah! Didn't I read once that silk and electronic devices like monitors don't work well together?" She hit her beautifully smooth forehead—but gently. "I should have remembered! I could as easily have sent cotton. We could have shopped in the city," she told Eunice, then told Jack, "I rented a car at the airport, fetched Eunice at the train, and here we are, but I should have thought to stop. Honestly, I assumed that she had everything she needed."

"She does."

"Do you know how *rude* drivers are around here? I have never been honked at so much. And *trucks?* All *over* the place, getting larger and longer by the day. You take your hands in your life trying to pass one of *those* on the highway. I thought about hiring a driver, but I wanted this to be a break from business. You know"—she was pensive, looking at Eunice—"we *should* have stopped in the city. There's a marvelous restaurant at the Huntington, although we probably aren't dressed right—"

Victoria was, Jack thought. Eunice was not. She wore a plain white blouse, a just-below-the-knee skirt, and serviceable tie shoes. What with her home-cut gray hair and a tightness in her face that had nothing to do with plastic surgery, she looked every one of her seventy-something years. His heart ached for her. She would have stood out at the Huntington like a donkey at Ascot.

"—and we did want to get down here as soon as possible," Victoria was saying. "Maybe another time. I hear Diane loves the place."

"Diane?" Jack asked.

"Your *senator*," Victoria said.

Eunice confirmed his ignorance with a dismayed "Jack."

Victoria waved it aside. "Naturally, the city was *covered* with fog, so it was probably just as well we didn't stop. We'll have another chance. I have to say, Jack, I kept expecting you to move Rachel to the city. I was *not* terribly impressed with the way I was treated when I called here on the phone. Fine to say that the important thing is the quality of the medical care, but the term *bedside manner* is a broad one, and it comes right down from management, at least, that's what I say to *my* management team. So I was expecting the worst, and then I met Kara in person, but what a lovely young woman!" She confided, "And what *gorgeous* pearl earrings. *There's* a woman who knows how to make a statement. As it happens, I know her parents. They're a side branch of the Philadelphia Bateses, who have a summer place in Newport. A *fine* family."

"Aren't Kara's parents younger than you?" Jack said.

"Jack!" cried Eunice, but Victoria was undaunted.

"Not by much," she assured him. "She's the youngest of four, she told me. A lovely girl. And where are yours? I'd like to see my granddaughters. I don't come this way often, and I can't stay long. It's quite pathetic, with my own daughter in a coma, but the board of directors is holding its quarterly meeting in New York on Monday. I have to fly back tomorrow. I know you said not to come at all, Jack, but I had to, even for this little time. Where *are* those girls?"

"School," Jack said. Single words had less of a chance of being cut off.

"Well, how do they get here from there? They are coming, aren't they? I would think that the *very* best

283

thing for Rachel is to have her daughters here. Of course, they're probably the ones responsible for that music." She winced. "What awful stuff. I turned it right off. There has to be something more appropriate."

"Appropriate?"

"If she's listening to music, it might as well be something worthwhile. Rachel used to love symphonies. Did you know that she wanted to be a concert pianist?"

A concert pianist? Jack thought not. Victoria had wanted it. Not Rachel. Victoria had given them a piano as a wedding gift, and they had toted it from Tucson to San Francisco because one didn't sell a Steinway, especially if it was a gift from a parent—not until you were divorced, which Rachel had promptly done. Before then, in her inimitably irreverent way, she had used it as a table for photographs, the girls' projects, and wine and hors d'oeuvres. The bench was perpetually open and filled with green plants.

Concert pianist? To Jack's recollection, Rachel had never actually sat down and played the damned thing.

No. That was wrong. She had played it one night, near the end of their marriage. He had come home from work and had more work to do. The girls were asleep. Startled by the bits of sound coming from the living room, he had gone down and found her there. The plants were on the floor, the piano bench an actual seat for once. Her left elbow was on top of the piano, left palm on her forehead, right hand on the keys. She was picking out a slow, soft, sad tune that might indeed have been an echo of Beethoven.

He had leaned against the archway, struck by the pensive picture she made. For the longest time, she didn't know he was there, and he watched, just watched, wishing he had the time and skill to paint her that way. Then she looked up and brightened. "Done with work?"

"No. But I heard you playing. You're very good."

"I am not. That was the extent of my expertise. Three painful years of lessons, and I can't coordinate the right hand with the left, so one-handed single notes are the best you get."

"It's strange, seeing you there. What made you play?"

She studied the keys, pensive again, sad. "I don't know. I don't feel like doing anything else. I feel . . . aimless." Her eyes found his.

"I'll give you some of *my* aim," he said, slapping the woodwork as he straightened. "I wish I had less. There's at least two more hours of work up there." As he started off, he called back, thinking about an important meeting he had the next morning, "Is my pin-striped suit back from the cleaners?"

He had cut her off. Only now, looking back, did Jack realize that. He had cut her off for the sake of his own agenda, had done just what her mother always did.

And Victoria was rattling on. ". . . never seemed to be time for lessons and practice, and then she was too old. I had the most *delightful* lunch *à la Rive Gauche"*—pronounced the French way—"with a flautist. What was her name? . . . *Geneviève,* I believe. She was talking about what it took to play at that level and the touring that was involved . . ."

Jack moved his hand against Rachel's jaw. He hadn't given the piano playing incident a second thought. He wondered how many similar memories were hidden— wondered if they would be as condemning. He had cut Rachel off because he couldn't deal with her problem. Selfish of him. Blind of him. *Just* like Victoria, who was managing the conversation even here. And Eunice? Eunice was her usual, caustic self. She didn't say much but had a consistently negative way of saying it. Jack had visited briefly at Christmas, *briefly* being the operative word. An hour or two in the same house with his mother, his sister and brothers, and their families, and he was desperate to leave. The whole lot of them were negative. Their major delight in life was in finding fault and placing blame. He knew it was a cover-up for insecurity, but it got old fast.

Still, he kept trying, hoping it would be different, angry when it wasn't. Visiting there had been easier when Rachel was with him. Her physical presence reminded him that his life was different.

"Positively *grueling,*" Victoria was saying, "and that was even *before* the recording dates. That's such a large part of it now, you know; it's become as commercial as anything *we* do, but you can almost understand it, what with the cost of sending an entire symphony orchestra on the road."

"It's greed," scoffed Eunice. "The food chain."

"Well, it's a shame. This young woman had taken two days off and looked as though she needed another two *weeks*. Are you hungry, Eunice? I haven't had a *thing* since breakfast, which was in Los Angeles ages ago."

"Los Angeles?" Jack asked.

"Well, I flew Nice to Paris to London. Would you believe that Los Angeles was the closest I could get to here from London on such short notice, unless I wanted to go through Miami, which I did not, thank you; I don't speak Spanish. So I spent the night at the Beverly Hills Hilton. I always like staying there. It isn't the Pierre, but it's close. I went down for an early breakfast, and who should be sitting two tables over but Paul. Now *there* is a stunning man. And decent? I remember what he said once when he was asked whether it was difficult being faithful to Joanne. 'Why go out for hamburger when I can have steak at home?' he said, or words to that effect." She pressed her chest. "Isn't that heartwarming? Not that I need steak for lunch, but is there anywhere nearby where Eunice and I can get a decent lunch—salad, quiche, whatever? Hospital cafeterias are pathetic. I don't mind driving, either. There must be something worthwhile in the center of town."

Jack gave her a name and directions, and the two of them left. The silence was heavenly.

Putting his elbows on the bed rail, he let his eyes roam Rachel's face, touching on all the old familiar spots, divining the same solace he always had in the past with her when visiting family. He could take Victoria. After a while, he just tuned her out. He didn't have to talk; she did it all. She didn't want to hear, wouldn't listen to anyone but herself.

Eunice was harder for him. She was his mother. For a time in his life, she had bathed him, clothed him, fed him. He remembered precious few times when she had smiled, or hugged him, or praised him. He was the only one of his siblings who had broken out and made good. Eunice had never been interested in hearing the details of his career, and he hadn't offered them. He continued to send her money, which she chose not to spend. The only way he had known that she was pleased with his marriage was the satisfaction with which she agreed to the festivities, and the fact that she blamed him for the divorce.

In Eunice, he saw a woman he had often wished wasn't his mother—and though he kept expecting God to strike him dead for thinking it, the thought still came.

It might have been nice to have felt loved, might have been nice to have a mother who showed feelings and shared her thoughts.

Rachel did those things. He had fallen in love with her, in part, because when they were together, they were the antithesis of their parents.

At least, he had always thought it. Suddenly he wondered.

IN A STROKE of luck, Katherine arrived soon after the mothers returned. Jack immediately enlisted her to stay while he went for the girls.

"I can't leave her alone with those two," he whispered at the door. "Let her know you're there. She needs someone sane at her side."

Having met Victoria before, Katherine stayed.

DRIVING from the hospital to the school, he savored the silence. The return trip was louder. Between Hope telling him that the drinks were *the* best part of the picnic after the ooey-gooey peanut butter brownies that one of the mothers had made, and Samantha telling him that she had aced a biology test, gotten an A-minus on an English paper, and had the *neatest* lunch with Pam and Heather, there wasn't time to tell them about the grandmothers until they were at the hospital.

They grew quiet then. They flanked Jack in the elevator, watching the lights above the door, and walked beside him down the hall. They offered their cheeks to their grandmothers for the kind of mutant kisses that came, in Victoria's case, from not wanting her skin disturbed, and in Eunice's, from being awkward with physical gestures. They weathered Victoria's seamless chatter and Eunice's evaluative scrutiny from positions close to Jack and were visibly relieved when, with profuse apologies and another round of those barely-there kisses, the two women left.

Jack felt so many things in the aftermath of their visit that he couldn't begin to sort them out, except for one. Just because his mother would choke on a compliment didn't mean he had to. Looking from one daughter to the other, he said, "Y'know, I'm really proud of you guys."

"Why?" Samantha asked.

"For being kind. And respectful. They aren't easy women, either of them, but they are your grandmothers."

"I hope I look the way Gram Victoria looks when I'm her age."

Hope, who was using the electric controls to raise Rachel's head, asked, "Why does she talk so much?"

Nervousness? Jack thought. *Selfishness? Control?* "It's just her way."

"Thank God Mom doesn't do that," Samantha said. "I'd lose my mind."

Hope adjusted the pillows to support Rachel's head. "If Mom was like that, I wouldn't ever talk. I'd just get tired of trying."

"That's pretty much what your mom did," Jack said, watching Hope pull a fistful of something from her pocket. "She was a quiet lady when I met her. What have you got there?"

"Unshelled peanuts." She put several in Rachel's hand and very carefully folded her fingers around them. "There was a whole bag of them at the picnic. Mom loves peanuts." She started cracking one.

Samantha screwed up her face. "You'll get crumbs all over the sheets." To Jack, she said, "So if Mom was quiet because her mother wouldn't shut up, did you talk a lot because yours didn't?"

Jack thought back. "No. No one talked much in my house."

"Why not?"

"My parents didn't want it. They didn't think we had anything to offer."

"They told you that?"

"Not as politely. But that was the gist of it."

"Wow. Amazing that you and Mom talked at all!"

IT *WAS* AMAZING, Jack realized. Driving back on the coast road that night, he thought about what he had felt meeting Rachel in that laundromat in Tucson, nearly eighteen years before. She had opened him up with a combination of quiet, sweetness, curiosity, and chemistry, and she had opened up herself. They told each other things they hadn't told anyone else, and because that felt so good, it became self-perpetuating. They shared feelings and fears. It was quality communication, interspersed with silences that were made special by that exchange of honest thought.

At some point they had stopped talking. He tried to look back and figure out when—it was surely before the piano incident—but then he reached the River Inn, where he had promised to take the girls to dinner, and by the time they got home, he wanted to paint, and then he was lost.

THE NIGHT'S subject was quail. Rachel had painted a covey roosting low in a sycamore tree. Her work was detailed and exact—the male with his larger, curved plume and blue-gray feathers, the female with her reduced features and scaled belly. Using acrylics and a palette knife, she had re-created the exact texture of the feathers. Even before Jack studied the photographs affixed to the back of the canvas, he knew that the background had to be the duller tans and browns of winter, against which the birds would be simultaneously camouflaged and crisp. He hadn't been in the Santa Lucias during that cool, rainy season, and wondered if he could do it justice. Then he realized that the justice had been done in Rachel's rendition of the quails. He was like a male dancer in the ballet, boosting the prima ballerina into the air, supporting her in her landing.

Several years ago, that might have bothered him. But he had a name in his own right. Supporting Rachel this way, being background, felt good.

He worked with care, but it flowed. He used brushes exclusively, wanting nothing as crisp as the palette knife would carve, but there were wide brushes and narrow brushes. He used umbers, ochers, siennas, and grays, mixing and matching until he had the right feel for a background that would highlight the quails.

By the time he was done, the adrenaline was flowing fast and hard. Tired as he was, it was a while before he fell asleep.

HOPE was the first one awake on Saturday morning. She stood for a time watching her sister sleep, then stood for a time watching Jack sleep. Slipping a fleece jacket over her nightshirt and her boots on her feet, she let herself out of the house, picked a handful of newly blue lupine from the roadside, and ran through the forest to Guinevere's grave. She brushed the dirt with her hand until it looked artful, and carefully arranged the flowers in a way she hoped Guinevere would like. Then, sitting on her heels, she wrapped her arms around her knees and rocked slowly, back and forth, back and forth, until worrisome images of her grandmothers faded and worrisome images of Samantha faded. Closing her eyes, she focused on Rachel and Jack and the safety she had felt when she was little.

She wanted that again.

SAMANTHA had planned to sleep her usual Saturday-morning late, but she woke up when Hope left her room and couldn't fall back to sleep. Her head was a battlefield of emotions. The prom came first; she was totally excited. But she was angry at Jack for making her feel guilty about Lydia, and *furious* at the grandmothers for giving her an empty kind of feeling. That empty feeling made her worry more about Rachel.

She missed her. They disagreed on lots of things, but at least Rachel cared. Samantha wasn't sure Jack did, and she knew the grandmothers didn't. There was always Katherine. But Katherine wasn't family.

Samantha wished she were twenty-one. If she were, she wouldn't be worrying about a prom. She wouldn't be worrying about whether or not to wear a bra, whether or not to wear nylons, whether or not to wear the three-inch heels Heather had lent her. If she were twenty-one, she wouldn't be worrying about a zit on her forehead. Or about what to drink. Or about what to do when Teague kissed her.

Rachel would have told her what to do. But Rachel wasn't there, only Jack, and that annoyed her.

JACK set off early with Hope. Samantha had pleaded exhaustion and stayed home, and a part of him wished he could, too. That part was tired of the drive to Monterey, tired of sterile corridors, hushed silences, smells of sickness. That part felt the monotony of visiting a comatose Rachel.

But not visiting her would be worse. Besides, the day's visit would be short. He had promised Samantha to be back by noon with food.

They stopped at Eliza's for hot coffee and brought it along, moving the cup under Rachel's nose in the hope that the smell would reach her. They put on a T-shirt that Eliza had sent; it had Rachel's name spelled in large, hand-painted letters. While Hope used a tiny scissors to cut exquisitely detailed snowflakes from white paper she had brought, they talked about the weather, about the grandmothers, about Samantha's prom.

Then Hope hung the snowflakes from the IV pole and whispered, "Tell her about the quails."

Jack hesitated. He hadn't told Rachel about doing *any*

painting. Hope loved what he had done, but Samantha refused even to look. If he viewed his daughters as the two sides of his wife—Hope the commonsense Rachel, Samantha the emotional one—he feared that on this issue, Rachel might side with Samantha.

Suddenly it struck him that that might be good. If there were psychological reasons for her continuing coma, angering her might shock her out of it. If she didn't want him finishing her paintings—didn't want it bad enough— she would wake up and tell him.

So he told her about the loons he had done Wednesday night, the deer he had done Thursday night, and the quails he had done Friday night. He gained momentum talking about the colors he had used and the effects he had sought, got caught up in excitement and satisfaction. His face was no more than a foot from Rachel's the whole time, but he saw no movement.

They left when Faye arrived, and stopped again at Eliza's, this time for a big bag of sandwiches, and yes, Jack was impatient standing in line. He took a deep breath, told himself that he wasn't in a rush to get anywhere, smiled at Hope, and wasn't as frayed as he thought he would be when they reached the front of the line. He was actually in the middle of paying when he had a thought. "Pecan rolls for Duncan and Faith?"

Hope's surprised smile was all the answer he needed. He bought a dozen.

JACK had initially thought he might do schematic drawings for the Hillsborough job, and there was more of Rachel's work to do, but he barely lasted in the studio for twenty minutes. For one thing, there was another fax from David, the follow-up to a phone message, neither of which he wanted to answer. For another, it didn't seem right closeting himself there and leaving the girls alone.

Samantha had gone back to her room after lunch, so it was just Hope, curling beside him on the living room sofa with a book. Her presence was a lulling warmth. He sprawled lower, put his head back, and slept for an hour. When he woke up, he stretched, then had a distinct urge to move.

"Is Samantha still in her room?" he asked, sitting up.

"Yes."

"On the phone?"

"No. She's making herself beautiful."

It was said with enough sarcasm that he chided, "You'll be doing it, too, before long. Want to go for a walk?"

She nodded and closed her book.

Jack knocked on Samantha's closed door. "Sam? Come for a walk with us?"

"I just washed my hair," she called out.

"You could still come."

"Take Hope. I'll stay here."

Jack stood at her door for another minute. As difficult as she was at times, he really did want her along. There was something about the three of them being together that seemed more important after the grandmothers' visit. He wanted family, damn it, he did. He *liked* being with his daughters. They filled up the emptiness of childhood memories, made his life more *full*.

There was also something about Samantha's prom being that night. It was a milestone. He wanted to do something to mark it, wanted to somehow make up for Rachel missing it.

"Are you sure?" he called a final time.

"*Positive,*" she yelled.

Fearing he would make things worse if he pushed, he let it go.

HE HAD BROUGHT his hiking boots from the city the Thursday before. He hadn't worn them since the divorce, but they felt good on his feet. He put water and snacks in a backpack, slipped it on, and left with Hope.

She had temporarily traded her lucky boots for hiking boots of her own, and a good thing it was. The winding trek she led him on, between spreading redwood trunks, aspens, and fir, was arduous. At times they climbed, at others they walked straight. Where the sun broke through the overhead boughs, it touched them, but the air remained cool, particularly as they approached the stream. Jack felt the anticipation of it, heard the crescendoing rush of water. When it came into sight, he discovered it was as much waterfall as stream, spewing over a rocky bed in tiered cascades.

They stopped and knelt by its side, saying nothing, just watching the bubbling play and listening to the flow.

When they stood, Hope said, "It's loudest this time of year. By fall, it's only a trickle." She led him across a rough-planked bridge and on through a fragrant eucalyptus grove to open meadow, and the temperature jumped. "See Duncan's sheep?" she asked.

They grazed in random clusters in the sun. It was a bucolic bouquet of color, with the deep green of live oaks in the distance blanching to the newer green of the spring grass, interspersed with patches of red poppy and yellow iris and the sheep, with their gray-white coats and their brown eyes and muzzles, paying them scant heed as they crossed the top of the meadow.

They continued on through oak and madrone on no path Jack could see, but Hope seemed to know where to go, and she went at a clip. By the time the land tipped and chaparral took over, a path emerged. It was even warmer here. As they walked, Jack pulled off his sweat-shirt and tied it around his waist. They moved higher, into a stand of pines, and beyond those, the world sud-denly gaped open.

They came on it so quickly that he wasn't prepared. "Wow!"

Hope slanted him a knowing smile. "Isn't it neat?"

"I'll say." They were higher than he had thought, looking into the belly of the canyon over the tops of pines and firs. Just as spectacular was the succession of ridges beyond. Those more distant, near the ocean, were dusted with fog.

Jack had taken his daughters to Muir Woods more than once, and those woods were beautiful. But this was something else. Rachel knew what breathtaking meant.

They sat on the ground looking out, legs crossed, drinking bottled water and munching granola. "Do you come here often with your mom?" he asked.

She chomped on a nut. "Uh-huh. We both love it. You look out and the world just keeps going."

Jack looked out, and the world *did* just keep going. The ocean did that. But there was also the sense of end-less fingers of granite, patchy with pine, cedar, or fir, stretching for miles down the coast.

Muir Woods didn't have that. You could close your eyes and pretend, but it wasn't the same. The city was too close. Here, it was easier to breathe, in every sense of the word.

He glanced at Hope, about to say that, then stopped. She, too, was looking out, but her brows were drawn. "What's wrong?"

Her eyes flew to his, then returned to the view. It was a minute before, quietly, she said, "Do you think Mom will ever come here again?"

His insides shifted. It wasn't the knotting he used to feel; that was better. This was something higher, something more closely tied to his heart. "I want to think so."

"But you don't know."

"None of us do."

"What if she dies?"

"She's not about to do that."

"What if she stays in a coma for years?"

Ten days before, he would have denied the possibility. *Five* days before, he would have denied it. But the doctors had taken Rachel out of Intensive Care and settled her into a regular room. She was nearing the end of her second comatose week. Everything else seemed to be healing but her head. Her GCS score hadn't budged.

Still, in a coma for *years?* They were just words. He couldn't grasp their meaning.

Hope picked raisins from the granola and put them one by one into her mouth. She took a drink of water and gazed out over the trees, frowning again. "Daddy?"

"Hmm?"

"Remember the other morning when you were telling Sam about loyalty?"

"Um-hmm."

"I feel bad for Lydia. But I can't say anything to Sam."

"Why not?"

"Because she's my sister. I owe the same loyalty to her that she owes to Lydia. So I have to support what she's doing. Don't I?"

"Not if you think what she's doing is wrong."

Hope swiveled on her bottom and faced him. Her eyes were large and expectant. "I do."

He wasn't sure what she wanted. "Maybe you should tell her."

"She'll kill me. You're going to meet her date tonight, aren't you?"

"That's the plan."

"What if you don't like him? Will you tell her not to go?"

He heard an urgency. "Do you *not* like the guy?"

"Would you make her stay home?"

"From her prom? I don't know, Hope. That might be going too far."

Her eyes teared up. "I have a bad feeling, like I did before Guinevere died."

Jack picked a strand of blond hair from her sweaty cheek. "Oh, sweetie."

"Don't *you?*"

The truth was that he hadn't thought much about Samantha's date, largely because there wasn't a hell of a lot he could do about it. He had made his best argument on Lydia's behalf, but he couldn't force Samantha to be with people she didn't want to be with. He knew. He had been there. His parents had said one thing; that was incentive enough to do the other.

Yes, it scared him where Samantha was concerned. And yes, he had *lots* of bad feelings, but they were more worry than omen, and had to do as much with Rachel and with Sung and McGill as with Samantha.

He caught Hope's hand. It was small, not yet womanly, but with promise. "At some point," he said, thinking it out as he spoke, "a parent has to trust that upbringing will guide a child when he isn't around. You've both been close to your mother. She raised you well. She may not be here to send Samantha off to the prom, but I want to think that Samantha will know what her mother expects."

Hope stared at him. "She knows. That doesn't mean she'll do."

Which was exactly what Jack thought seconds earlier. "Do you know something I don't?"

She said a quick "no."

"What's she planning?"

Both shoulders came up. "I don't know."

"Are you sure?"

She nodded vigorously.

He didn't believe her, but he couldn't force the issue. There was that thing about loyalty, *thank you, Jack*. If he wanted to know what Samantha was planning, he was going to have to ask Samantha.

chapter sixteen

THE SMARTEST THING Samantha did was to start getting ready very early. She ended up taking two showers when her hair didn't blow right the first time. Her deodorant took forever to dry; she botched her eyeliner and had to start all over with that; and though she had decided that sheer black stockings looked more sophisticated than none, she still hadn't made up her mind on the bra issue when it was time to put on the dress.

She owned two black bras. Each had straps. If she reached a certain way, which she was bound to do when she danced with Teague, who was at *least* six-two, the straps showed.

She rummaged through Rachel's drawers for a strapless bra. The only things of interest she found were her father's boxer shorts and some framed photographs. She didn't know why her mother kept them. Rachel *hated* Jack. He might talk a blue streak about loyalty, but talk was all it was. They were divorced. That said it all.

She shoved the drawers closed and turned to leave.

"Everything all right?" Jack asked from the door. He

looked sweaty and relaxed, like he'd had a good time in the woods with his favorite daughter.

Everything is not all right, she wanted to cry. *My mother is in a coma, my father is a jerk, and I don't have a strapless bra.* "Just fine," she ground out and brushed past him.

"Doesn't sound it," he said, following her down the hall.

She whirled on him. "I'm nervous. All right? This is a big night. Just leave me alone."

He held up a hand and backed off—and even *that* angered her. She wanted to argue. She wanted to scream and shout and let off the steam that was building inside. A part of her even wanted to cry, but she'd be damned if she would do that in front of him. Hope cried. Samantha didn't.

Beside, she didn't have time to do her eyes *again.*

BY SIX, Jack was freshly showered and in the kitchen, spooning chip dip into a bowl. Having spent most of the hike back through the woods thinking that Rachel's coma couldn't possibly be psychological since she wouldn't have missed Samantha's prom for the world, and wondering what she would have done for a send-off, he had mixed up her favorite dip recipe, while Hope arranged crackers on a dish around the bowl. They had barely put it in the living room when the doorbell rang.

"Oh God," Samantha wailed from her room. *"Talk to him. I'm not ready."*

Jack opened the door to a young man who was just his height, but dark-haired, dark-eyed, dark-jawed. He was wearing a tux . . . barely. Where a pleated shirt should have been was a white T-shirt; where a cummerbund should have been was a wide leather belt; and the scuffed black shoes sticking out from his pants looked to Jack to be boots.

O-kay, Jack thought. *Times have changed. Go with the flow.* He extended a hand. "I'm Samantha's dad."

The returning handshake was firm, perhaps cocky, even defiant. "Teague Runyan."

Jack drew him into the house with the kind of firm hand that said he had no choice in the matter. "Samantha says you live here in Big Sur?"

"Up the street a little," he said, tossing his head in a direction that could have been north or south. "How's Samantha's mom?"

"She's the same. Thank you for asking. Does she know your folks?"

"She may. They run the gas station right outside the center."

Jack nodded. He knew of two gas stations there. Both gouged.

Hope approached with the dip and crackers, staring smilelessly at Teague.

"Hey, Hope," Teague said. "Did you make this?" He topped a cracker with dip and popped it whole into his mouth. "Mm. Good."

Jack waited until he had swallowed. "So, what's the plan?"

"Plan?" Teague asked, brushing cracker salt off his hands.

"For tonight."

"I don't know. It's Samantha's prom. She made the arrangements."

"When can I expect her back?"

Teague looked mystified.

"When do your folks expect you back?"

"Sometime tomorrow."

"Tomorrow, as in the wee hours of the morning?"

He thought about that. "Nah."

"Later tomorrow morning?"

"Maybe. Maybe afternoon. It depends how late we sleep."

That wasn't what Jack wanted to hear. "Where will this sleeping be?"

Teague shrugged. "It's Samantha's prom."

"Hi, Teague," Samantha said. She stood at the edge of the living room, looking gorgeous enough to take Jack's breath. He was suddenly terrified.

"Hey," said Teague by way of greeting. "Ready to go?"

There was no *You look great,* no *Here's a corsage,* no *Have some of this dip, it's great; thanks, Hope.* Jack didn't like those boots, or that wide leather belt. There was something on the T-shirt that was too faded to make out. No matter. He didn't like the T-shirt, either.

He crossed to Samantha, pointing her back into the hall, and kept going until he was in her bedroom, glancing behind only to make sure she followed.

Oh, she did that, but she wasn't happy. "I have to go," she hissed.

"You look beautiful," he said, taking her off guard. He could have sworn he saw a look of disbelief on her face, before she grew cautious.

"I do?"

"I wish your mother could see." He had an idea. "Wait. I'll get a camera . . ."

She grabbed his arm. "No, Daddy, *please*. He's *waiting.*"

He should have had the camera ready, should have thought ahead. "You really do look spectacular," he said and felt another kick of terror. She was growing up too fast. "Can we talk about curfews?"

She looked at him like he had horns. *"Curfews?* This is an all-nighter. You *knew* that."

"I knew you were sleeping at Lydia's, but that's changed. So tell me the plans. I want to know where you'll be."

"The prom is at school."

"That's not the part that worries me." He rummaged through the refuse on her desk for a pen and tore a scrap of paper from the nearest notebook. "There are parties before and after. I need phone numbers."

"You do *not,*" she cried. "You *can't* check up on me. If you call, I'll *die.*"

"What if your mother wakes up?"

That got her. She stood with her eyes wide and her mouth half open.

He compromised. "Give me names, then. Just names." He could always call directory assistance. "The party before is at Jake's—is it Jake Drummer?"

"Drumble."

"Where's the party after?"

"Pam's, I think, but I'm not sure. It depends on who leaves the prom when, whether we want something to eat, and what we feel like after that, so I don't know."

Jack wouldn't run *his* business that way. "Would your mother be satisfied with that answer?"

"Yes. She trusts me."

"So do I. It's the other kids I don't trust." He had another idea. "Take my cell phone."

Again, that where-are-*you*-from look. "Why?"

"So we can be in touch."

She looked horrified. "Kids don't take cell phones to proms. Besides, where would I *put* it? This dress does *not* have pockets."

"A purse?"

She held up a thin thing on even thinner straps.

He sighed. "Okay. No phone. What's Pam's last name?"

She gave it grudgingly. He had barely begun scribbling it down when she started out of the room. "Wait," he said, because he was uneasy still.

She turned back with an impatient *"What?"*

"Call me if there's a problem."

"Are you expecting one?"

"No." He approached her. "I just wanted to say it. I won't tell you when to be home. I'll trust you know what you're doing. But I'd like a call by ten tomorrow morning, please."

"Ten? *Dad.*"

"Samantha, you're only fifteen. All I'm asking for is a phone call."

"Fine," she said and disappeared into the hall.

He followed her back to the living room, arriving just as she swept Teague to the door.

"Bye," she said with a wave to no one in particular, and before Jack could say that they needed something solid in their stomachs and why didn't they have crackers and dip, before he could open his mouth to warn Teague that if anything went wrong there would be hell to pay, they were gone.

JAKE DRUMBLE'S house was a zoo. Samantha had never seen so many kids in such a small place in her life, and they weren't all from her school. She would have recognized faces. The boys were huge, with the kinds of big necks and wide shoulders that went with playing football. The girls were perky and bright and talking in tight little clumps.

"Do you know these people?" Teague asked, snapping up two beers from the bar and putting one in her hand.

"I think they're football buddies of Jake's," she said and, for a split second, feeling alone and lost, would have given anything for the sight of Lydia or Shelly.

"Talk about slabs," Teague said under his breath.

She forced a laugh. "Hey. There's Pam. Pam!" She led Teague through the crowd, stopping now and again when she felt resistance against her hand to look back and find him talking to one girl or another. She couldn't blame those girls. He was the coolest guy in the place. She hooked an elbow through his when they reached Pam, so that no one would doubt that he was Sam's for the night.

They talked and laughed with Pam and Jake, then moved on to talk and laugh with Heather and Drew. They munched on nachos and drank beer, ate popcorn and drank beer. Teague was the perfect date, always knowing when she needed a refill, always knowing where to find it.

"How're you doing?" he said with a grin as he backed her into a corner.

She was feeling light-headed and free. "I'm doing fine. This is a great party."

Putting his hands on either side of the wall, he gave

her the weight of his body. His mouth was inches from hers. "I could do with fewer people. You're sweet." He erased those inches with a kiss that was so soft and gentle that all of her earlier worries seemed absurd. His mouth moved, showing hers what to do, and was gone before she wanted it to be.

"Nice?" he asked.

She grinned. "Mmmm."

"More?"

"Um-hm."

It was a deeper kiss this time, more mobile and open. Samantha had read about breathlessness. She had read about feeling a fire inside, but she hadn't experienced either in response to a kiss until then.

Rachel would not be pleased. She believed in restraint, in saving it for someone special, but who was to say Teague wasn't? There was such a thing as instant attraction, not to mention love at first sight. And was Rachel a virgin when she married Jack? Samantha thought not. So who were *either* of them to criticize her? Besides, if Rachel was so worried, she would have woken up from the damn coma. She would have *been* there to give orders and warnings, instead of leaving it to Jack. She would have demanded a detailed itinerary as a condition for leaving the house, would have phoned some of the other parents, and Samantha would have been docked for sure. If her mother were well, she wouldn't be here right now.

That thought made her head buzz in a grating way. To still it, she poured herself into Teague's kiss, not a very hard thing to do, for at that minute he took her hands, put them behind him, and pressed his hips to hers, and oh, what she felt! When she caught her breath, his tongue

entered her mouth. Startled then, she would have pulled
back if there had been anywhere to go, but the wall was
behind her, his hands were framing her face, and he was
saying into her mouth, "Don't stop. It's cool. Take my
tongue." And he was right, it was cool, unbelievably
grown-up and sexy, the feel of that tongue sliding in and
out against hers, and his body, anchoring hers when it
started to tremble. "Ride the feeling," he whispered, and
she did. Her mouth fell open a little, then a little more,
then even more, and suddenly her tongue caught the
wave.

Breathing hard, he made a guttural sound and put his
forehead to hers. "Whooh. We gotta go somewhere."

Samantha was barely beginning to understand what
he meant when the room began to empty. "The prom,"
she managed to say.

"No. Somewhere alone."

"The prom," she insisted. She wasn't missing her first
prom for the world. She wanted people to see her with
Teague Runyan. They were a great-looking couple.
Lydia would *die* when she saw how cool they looked, not
to mention the fact that super kissers had to be super
dancers. Samantha wasn't doing anything else until she
danced with Teague.

She did, actually. She shared another beer with him in
the truck, driving between Jake's house and school. They
finished it parked in a dark corner of the lot, away from
the others. This time when he gave her an open-mouthed
kiss, right at the start, she knew just what to do. She was
feeling smart and strong. The only thing she was thinking about was having a good time. Life was too short to
be uptight about drinking. Look at her mother, a good little do-bee who followed every rule in the book and was

now lying in a coma because someone she didn't know had hit her car.

Teague came over her in the cab of the truck, holding her head while he kissed her, then dropping a hand to her breast. Samantha had ended up wearing no bra, so she felt every inch of his fingers. Startled, she cried out into his mouth, but he soothed her with words she barely heard, and his kneading felt good, so good.

"Fuck the prom," he whispered.

"No, no," she said and pulled away. He was moving too fast, scaring her a little. She wanted to know what she was doing, wanted to be in control. "I want to go." She took his hand and dragged him from the truck. Seconds later, he had her pinned against its side.

"You're a tease, Samantha."

"No. I *want* to go to the prom."

"Can we do this after?" he asked, pushing both breasts up, lowering his head to kiss the swell he had created above her dress.

It felt a little rougher now, not as good. She wanted to tell him that, but the words didn't come, and all she could think to do was to slither out from under him and say, "This is my *prom.*" If she was relieved that he came along without a fight, she forgot it the next minute. This *was* her prom. She was with the coolest guy in the world, and she turned him on. It didn't get much better than that.

But it did. The school gym was transformed by dark red lights into something pretty neat, and with everyone she knew in the world watching, Teague was an *awesome* dancer. He didn't move much, just kind of throbbed in time to the music with his eyes on her the whole time. She felt the same tingling inside as when he kissed her, so that when the slow dancing came, body to body, it was a relief.

She put her head on his shoulder and moved with him, feeling tired now, more mellow. When he said he needed air, she didn't argue. They walked outside, back to the truck. He popped open a couple of beers and chugged his fast, helped her with hers, and opened a third. He kissed her, touched her. She pulled him back into the school.

JACK and Hope stood in Rachel's studio, surrounded by wood moldings that would soon be frames.

"Are you sure you know how to do this?" Hope asked.

"You bet," Jack said. "I've done it before." But not in years, and never for a show. "Those lengths of wood"— he pointed their way—"have to be cut to size with that"—his finger shifted—"miter saw. Then you predrill nail holes, apply wood glue, hammer in nails, clamp in that"—he pointed toward a heavy metal contraption— "miter vise. Piece of cake."

"But . . . but what about putting the picture in it?"

"Not tonight. The frame has to dry in the vise. Then it fits on the canvas, and we pack it in with nails."

Hope grinned. "Piece of cake."

"You bet." If it didn't come out well, he could dump the framing on Ben. "I was thinking you'd help. It isn't hard. Want to?"

Hope's eyes told it all, even before she said an excited "Yes."

"Which picture first?" he asked.

After giving careful consideration to the canvases that were lined up and ready, Hope pointed to the loons. "That's my favorite."

Jack didn't know if she had chosen it to please him, but

he wasn't about to argue. The loons were his favorite, too. When he projected himself into the scene, he felt closer to Rachel, which was something he very much wanted to feel on this night. He had thought that taking a break from the hospital would be good, but he missed being there. He had called. Rachel was the same. Still, he felt unnerved.

No doubt some of that had to do with Samantha. He didn't think he had handled her well, but hell, he was groping blind. Maybe Rachel would have known what to do and say. Then again, maybe not. In any case, he would have liked her input. They used to discuss things— Rachel had rightly told that to Katherine. Now Jack was feeling the loss firsthand. Deciding whether to punish the temper tantrum of a four-year-old with a spank or time alone in the bedroom was a far cry from deciding whether to insist on a curfew, forbid drinking, or lay down the law about sex—and Teague Runyan was into sex. Jack didn't doubt it for a minute. The guy was too good looking, too physically developed, too cocksure of himself not to be experienced.

Jack should have insisted Samantha take the phone.

Whether she would have used it was another matter entirely.

His stomach was knotting for the first time in days. Taking a deep breath to relax it, he scooped up a bunch of the moldings and the miter saw. "Okay," he told Hope as he carried them to the worktable, "let's see what we can do."

SAMANTHA and Teague left the prom shortly after ten and followed Pam and Jake to Ian McWain's house. The music was canned here, but there was pizza, beer, and a punch that was incredibly sweet and good. Samantha was starting to recognize more faces, so she didn't feel so alone when Teague wandered off. But he wasn't gone long. He was never gone long. He always returned, eyes bright at the sight of her, arms catching her up and swinging her around.

She was relieved. He seemed to be having a good time, which must have said something for his feelings for her. If he didn't like her, he would be bored. He would be aching to leave. He would be standing against a wall with a scowl on his face.

But he was treating her like she was gold, grinning nonstop, bringing her drinks, dancing body to body regardless of how fast the beat, and he wasn't the only one warming to the night. Minute by minute, the kids grew looser and louder, the music faster, the dancing wilder than it had been at school. When the dining room table was cleared of pizza boxes, bottles, and cans, and became a dance floor, there was hysterical laughter all around. Laughter turned to applause when one couple jumped up and began necking. The applause was joined by raucous calls when a girl removed the top of her dress as she boogeyed.

Teague was holding Samantha from behind now, doing that same throbbing thing to the beat of the music with his body flush to hers. He had his arms wrapped around her and was alternately nibbling on her ear and moving his hands along the undersides of her breasts, teasing, teasing, she knew, and it felt good.

"Look at her," he whispered, leaving his mouth open, and Samantha couldn't seem to focus anywhere else. The girl on the table was laughing and singing with her arms over her head now, her bare breasts bobbing to the beat of the dance. Samantha might have been embarrassed, if that part of her hadn't been muted. She was high, feeling part of the crowd, part of the fun, part of Teague Runyan even, so that when he maneuvered her back, swiped a pair of fresh long-necks with one hand, and led her outside, she wasn't alarmed. She could hear the beat even from here. Teague felt it, too. They danced in the dark, body to body in a way she would never have thought to do, never have *dared* to do before, but it was nice, drinking beer as they danced, so nice, exciting, even dangerous. She was dizzy with laughter and dance. She felt sexy and adult. When Teague took her hand and, laughing, ran toward his truck, she went right along.

Pulling her close on the bench, with an arm around her and his beer dangling between her breasts, he started driving.

"Where to?" she asked, wondering how he could see, since her world was still spinning, but he was older, larger, protective.

"Somewhere quiet," he said. "You're too special to share."

There was nothing she could say to that, so she smiled, closed her eyes, and buried her face in the rough spot under his jaw where his beard was a darkening shadow, and even that was erotic. None of the other boys she knew had to shave more than once or twice a week. Teague's stubble was a manly thing.

They hadn't driven far when he pulled the truck off the road. Killing engine and lights, he took a long drink, put the bottle on the floor of the cab, and turned to her. He didn't say anything, just caught her face and held it while he kissed her. She tasted beer first, then his tongue, and it was firmer now, but welcome. Her body was a mass of tingles, confusing almost, so that the only thing it knew was that it needed something more.

He held her face until she was into the kiss, then he lowered both hands to her breasts. He kneaded them and found her nipples, tugging until she felt it all the way to her belly. She arched her back, wildly dizzy but feeling good, especially when something changed. It was a full minute of bliss before she realized that her breasts were bare, scooped right out of that stretchy dress. She looked down at them in amazement, until his head blocked the view, and then while his thumb rolled one nipple, his lips caught the other, and suddenly the sensation was too great. She made a sound of protest, feeling dizzy and high and confused.

"Ride with it," he whispered and, shifting, lowered her to the seat.

"Teague, I don't—this isn't—"

"Sure it is," he said in that grown-up, sexy way he had. He was moving against her now, making a place between her thighs and slipping a hand there. She tried to close her legs, but he rubbed her, and it felt so good that for a minute she let him, let him, even moved against him until the dizziness prevailed.

"We—have to—stop," she whispered, trying to think straight when a part of her wanted him to keep on, but more of her was frightened. His teeth were rougher on her nipple now, and she didn't know how, but his hand was suddenly inside her nylons, touching things he shouldn't be touching.

"No," she said, trying to slip out from under him the way she had at the truck earlier, but she was on her back with her legs wide, and his weight pinned her this time.

His hips were moving rhythmically, allowing only enough room for his hand, which rubbed and opened.

"I'll do it with my finger first," he said, breathing hard, and she started to squirm. It wasn't fun anymore. She pushed at his shoulders for leverage, but his finger followed. He was hurting her.

She tried to scramble back. "Let me *go!*"

"I'll get you ready—"

"I feel sick," she cried, and it was true. Through the nausea and the dizziness, she found his hair and pulled.

"What the—"

Kick him in the groin, her mother had always said, and Samantha did it. It didn't matter that she couldn't do it very hard, but it moved him enough for her to wriggle free, tug at the truck door, and fall out.

"What the hell'd you do *that* for?" Teague yelled through the open door.

But she'd had enough of music and dancing and beer, and more than enough of Teague Runyan. Tugging her clothing back into place, she ran. She stumbled when her heels caught in the grass, caught herself, and barreled on. She ran through a small wooded stretch, ran until she couldn't breathe, then stopped and was violently ill in someone's pitch black backyard. Holding her stomach, she backed up to the dark house, slid down to the ground, turned sideways against the wood, and drew her knees close. When more threatened to erupt from her stomach, she swallowed it down. She took shallow breaths, listening hard in between. She couldn't hear Teague, couldn't see Teague, but there was a noise in her head and her eyes wouldn't stay in one place long enough for her mind to figure out what she saw.

She lost the battle with her stomach and threw up

again. As soon as she was done, she pushed up and away
from the house. When she searched the street from
behind a tree and saw no sign of the truck, she ran in
what she hoped was the opposite direction. She turned a
corner and sat on the edge of the road to regain strength
in her legs, then forced herself up and ran until she
rounded another corner. She retched again and sank to
the ground, praying that no one would see her. She was
in a residential area. She had no idea which one. Her
head was starting to hurt. If she'd been able to dig a hole,
she would have climbed in and pulled the dirt in over her.
She felt sick and embarrassed and scared.

She started off again, clutching her shoes to her chest
and walking in her stocking feet, trying to recognize the
names on street signs and failing. She turned one corner
just as a pickup approached, and ducked behind a shrub,
but it wasn't Teague's truck. She walked on, feeling sick
in deeper ways now. She turned another corner and
another pickup passed. She didn't duck away this time,
just kept walking as though she knew exactly where she
was headed, all the time wondering where she *was* headed and what she was going to do. When the same truck
passed a third time, more slowly, she was uneasy.

"Hey, baby," said a voice that sounded older and more
dangerous than Teague's, and suddenly she'd had
enough of being alone. Terrified, she turned in at the
nearest walk and fumbled in her purse as though for the
house keys. When the truck drove off, she stole away.

She ran the length of several blocks through people's
backyards, and emerged desperate to find a phone. She
felt sick enough to vomit again, and wanted to lie down,
just lie down and sleep while her mother kept watch,
only her mother was in the hospital in a coma, and she

couldn't call Lydia, after what she'd done, and *she didn't have a phone!*

She listened, trying to separate out traffic sounds from the other ones in her head. She walked another block and listened again, then headed in the direction she thought would be right. Her head hurt, her breasts hurt, her stomach hurt, her feet hurt. Looking behind her when she thought she heard another truck, she missed a break in the sidewalk and fell on her wrist, and that hurt, too.

She imagined what might happen if those men found her, or if Teague did. She imagined wandering around all night, freezing in the night air, making it to morning and not knowing what to do then.

More frightened by the minute, wanting only to be home, she began to cry softly. She was nearly frantic by the time she reached the end of another block and recognized the name on the street sign. *Thank God thank God thank God,* she murmured and started running again. It wasn't more than five minutes before she found her phone. She lifted the receiver, dialed the number, and waited for her father to answer.

chapter seventeen

JACK WAS PAINTING when the phone rang, and felt an instant jolt. He didn't have to look at the clock to know that something was wrong. He had sent Hope to bed at midnight, more than an hour before. Either Rachel was in trouble or Sam was.

Dropping palette and brush, he grabbed up the phone. "Hello?"

There was a pause, then a broken "Daddy? Come pick me up."

He swallowed hard. Not Rachel. Relief. Fear. "Where are you? What happened?"

"I don't feel good."

"Too much to drink?" It was the least of the evils.

"I feel *sick*. Can you come?"

He was already wiping his hands. "Right now. Tell me where you are." When she gave him a set of cross streets, he asked for the house address.

"It's a pay phone," she cried. "Can you come *soon?*"

He could do the drive in thirty-five minutes if he

pushed it, but a pay phone? "Are you alone?" Where in the hell was her date? And *what had he done?*

"Hurry, Daddy."

"Samantha, do I need to call an ambulance? Or the police? Is there trouble—"

"*I just want to come home!*"

"Okay, sweetheart, okay—I'm on my way—just stay there—don't *move*—and if anyone stops, call the cops, okay?"

She said a shaky "Okay."

He had a thought. "Give me five minutes, then call me in the car." He wasn't sure what all had happened, but he didn't want to hang up and imagine her alone and sick for the length of his drive. Better to talk her through the time. That way, if she passed out or ran into another kind of trouble, he could call an ambulance himself.

"I don't know the number," she wailed.

He told her and made her repeat it. "Five minutes, okay?"

"Okay."

He hung up the phone to find a wide-awake Hope inches behind him. "Can I come?"

He didn't answer, just took her hand and, snatching up his wallet in the kitchen, ran with her out to the car.

FIVE MINUTES passed, then ten, and the car phone didn't ring. He gripped the wheel and pushed the car as fast as he could through a shifting fog, praying she would still be there when he arrived.

"Okay," he said to Hope. "What do you know that I don't?"

"Nothing."

"Loyalty changes sometimes, you know. Showing loyalty to your sister right now means helping get her home safe and sound."

"She knew I didn't like what she was doing, so she didn't tell me. You were the one who was supposed to ask where she was going."

"I did and it didn't get me very far." So he was trying to blame Hope, but that wasn't fair. Hope was right. It was his job, and he had bungled it.

At least Samantha had had the sense to call.

IT WAS AFTER two in the morning when he reached Carmel. The streets were deserted. He found the intersection Samantha had named, spotted the phone booth, pulled up fast, and saw nothing. He left the car, looking in every direction, thinking she might have been standing, waiting, somewhere else, when he heard her call.

"Daddy?" For all her maturity and bravado, she was a wisp of a girl, huddled on the floor of the phone booth, her tear-streaked face looking green in the night light. "I messed up the number," she cried; "couldn't remember. It wouldn't go through. I tried *everything.*"

He knelt, lifted her up and into his arms. Hope ran beside him and helped him fit her into the front seat and strap her in, then ran around the car and snaked behind the driver's seat into the back. He slipped off his jacket and covered Samantha up, because she was trembling, bare armed and bare shouldered in the nippy night air. Then he put a hand on the top of her head.

"Do we need a hospital?" he asked softly. He hadn't

seen bruises or blood, but he wasn't looking at the places that scared him most.

She shook her head. "I just drank too much."

"Where's your date?"

She began to cry. "He wanted—to do things—I didn't."

Jack's heart ached. "Good girl," he said, softly still. Leaning over, he pressed a kiss to the crown of her head, then turned the car for home.

HE DROVE to Big Sur slowly and sensibly, despite the hour. The car seemed a safe place between wherever it was that Samantha had been and whatever Jack was going to have to face when they got home. For most of the drive, Samantha huddled under his jacket and slept, and it seemed a natural thing to do with the fog rolling in. He touched her head every few minutes. He told her to tell him if she felt sick and wanted to stop. But her eyes remained closed and her breathing even. She didn't look drunk. She wasn't convulsing, and the way she stirred every so often suggested sleep, not unconsciousness. He could tell that she had thrown up, and assumed she had lost whatever hadn't already made it into her bloodstream. He guessed that whatever manner of sick she was had to do with heart as well as body.

He wanted to do things I didn't, she had said, and it haunted Jack, ate at his stomach, what those things might be. But he didn't ask. He remembered being grilled by his father when he was Samantha's age—worse, remembered his *sister* being grilled by his father, guilty until proven innocent. Jack wouldn't do that to Samantha.

So, was the alternative silence? Jack had been taught

silence by a father who needed to place blame and a mother who loathed dissension. Rachel had been taught it by a mother who knew everything about everything. When Jack met Rachel, they had been like souls freed from confinement, talking at length and with substance. Then time passed and old habits returned. Yes, that was what had happened. He saw. He understood. But silence wasn't the answer in dealing with Samantha. They couldn't sweep what had happened under the rug. There had to be talk.

WHEN THEY got home, he carried her to her room. While she showered, he stared out at the forest through the living room glass, wondering whether she was washing evidence away. She claimed she didn't need a hospital. If he insisted, he would be saying he didn't believe her, didn't trust her. It was a no-win situation.

The water went off. He gave her enough time to get into bed, then went to her room to make sure she was all right. He didn't turn on the light. After a minute, he adjusted to the dark and made his way to her bed. The window was hand-high open. The smell of moist earth, leaves, and bark drifted in. It was a cool, familiar comfort.

Samantha had the quilt up to her chin. If she had been sleeping he would have left, but her eyes were open and wet. He hunkered down by her face.

"What I need to know most," he said gently, "is whether he . . . touched you in ways he shouldn't have." He wasn't sure how else to ask. The truth was that he didn't know for sure whether Samantha had been a virgin to begin with.

She didn't answer at first. So he said, "If it was rape—"

"No."

"Date rape."

"*No.*"

He waited for her to say more. When she didn't, he said, "Talk to me, Sam. I'm worried. I'm scared. You're upset. I want to help." After another minute, he said, "If your mother was here, she'd be doing what I am. She'd be sitting right here talking to you. It's not prying. It's not accusing or finding fault. It's trying to make sure that you don't need medical care, or that we don't need legal help. But I have to tell you," he added with a small laugh, "I'll strangle the guy if he raped you."

"He didn't," she whispered.

"But you ended up alone in a phone booth in the middle of town." He tried to tease her into talking. "Want to tell me what happened—I mean, as much as you think my sensitive ears can take?"

She closed her eyes. One tear, then another slid out of the downward corners. He felt the pain of each. When she covered her face with a hand and broke into long, deep sobs, he felt that, too—felt it in helplessness, inadequacy, and fear.

He wished Rachel was there. *He* didn't know how to talk to a fifteen-year-old girl. This was *woman* stuff.

But Rachel wasn't there and might not be for a while. He didn't like that thought, but it was a reality he had to face. Besides, Samantha wasn't telling him to leave. That seemed significant.

Sitting back on his heels, he continued to stroke her head until her crying slowed. Then he blew out a breath. "I wouldn't want to be your age for all the tea in China."

She sniffled. "Why not?"

"It's in between nowhere." How well he remembered.

"You aren't a child anymore, so you can't just play and be cute and play dumb when things go wrong. Your body is doing weird things. You feel grown-up, but you're not that either. You can't drive a car, or make the kind of money you want to spend, and you can't do what you want when you want it, even though that's just what you want to do. You're expected to do a lot of grown-up stuff because you need the experience, only you don't *have* the experience, so half the time you don't know what in the hell you're doing. No. I'd like to be twenty-seven again. But fifteen? Not on your life."

"What was so great about twenty-seven?"

He thought about that. "Your mom."

Samantha started to cry again.

He moved his hand on her head.

"I *need* her."

"I know. But she isn't here, so we're going to try to work this through together the way she would. Want to tell me about tonight? Or do you want to sleep?" He kept expecting to be tired himself, but he was all keyed up.

She grunted. "I slept in the car. I'm not sleepy now."

He thought about putting a light on. But there was something about the foggy dark, something so dense as to be a buffer. "Tell me, then. I want to hear."

"That's because you love knowing"—her voice caught—"what a *loser* I am."

Fiercely, he said, "You aren't a loser. If you were, you'd still be at some party with kids making fools of themselves, drinking and laughing at nothing and dancing on tables and taking off their clothes—"

Her eyes went wide. "How did *you* know?"

"I've been there, sweetie. Your music may be different from what mine was, and God knows there are more beer labels to choose from these days, but human nature hasn't changed much."

"Did you know Teague would have beer in his car?"

"No. I didn't want to know that. It doesn't surprise me, though."

"You didn't like him."

"How *could* I? He didn't even tell you how pretty you looked. And you looked pretty, Sam—prettier, I'd bet, than most everyone at that prom. So. Did he just leave you at the phone booth, or what?"

"I ran there. He was somewhere . . . blocks away. He probably went back to the party."

"Nice guy," Jack muttered, but couldn't leave it at that. "If he was cool, he'd have followed you and driven you home. If he was *really* cool, he'd have kept his hands to himself in the first place. You're a minor. We're talking statutory rape."

"It didn't *get* that far. Besides, it wasn't all his fault. I let him, a little."

Jack had figured that. He took Samantha's hand and kissed it. It smelled of soap, good and clean and healthy. Quietly, he said, "Letting him, a little, is okay as long as you trust the guy and there isn't booze involved. I'm guessing there was more than beer."

"Punch."

"Spiked with vodka." When she didn't deny it, he said, "That was what made you sick. The rule of thumb is that if you have vodka first, the beer's okay. Beer first, and vodka will make you sick. Mind you, I'm not saying drinking's all right. It isn't. Drinking makes people do dumb things. It makes them do *tragic* things." His voice rose. "I didn't smell anything on Teague when he got here. When did he start drinking? Was he drinking in the truck? At the end there, was he *drunk?*"

In that split second, Jack heard his father's voice. In the next second, he regained control of himself. "Don't answer," he said softly. "It's over and done. And maybe I shouldn't be telling you how to drink and how not to drink. Maybe that's giving the wrong message. Only, kids *do* drink sometimes, and if I want you safe, you need to know. Knowledge is the key. It's right up there with experience." He paused. "See, the downside of being a grown-up is that you're held accountable for your actions. Okay, so you weren't raped. You could have been killed if Teague crashed the truck. You could have died of alcohol poisoning, or an overdose of something that someone slipped into that punch. Someone *else* could have died. That's the kind of thing you carry with you all your life. I don't want that for you, Samantha. I really don't. A big part of growing up is learning when to be cautious. It's realizing that there are consequences to everything you do."

She was quiet for so long that he wondered if she had fallen asleep, and part of him felt that was fine. He liked the note he had ended on. For a father muddling his way through, he wasn't doing so bad.

He should have known better.

In the same quiet, very grown-up voice he had used, Samantha asked, "How does all that fit in with the divorce? Are you accountable for your actions in a marriage, too?"

It was a minute before he said, "Yes."

"Then you accept the blame for that?"

"No. It takes two to make a marriage, and two to break it." Which was what Hope said Rachel had said, and quite an admission on his part. Two weeks before, he would have blamed the breakup of the marriage on Rachel. She was the one who had walked out.

Only, her leaving San Francisco was a symptom, not a cause. He could concede that now. The cause of the breakup went deeper. Rachel may have been abandoned in the broadest sense. He may have put his work first.

"But how could you guys just let it go?" Samantha asked, and there were tears in her voice again.

"We didn't."

"You *did*," she cried with a vehemence that reminded him of something. Katherine had said that she was obsessed with the divorce. Katherine might be right. "You didn't argue about it, you just split," she charged. "What was *your* side of the story?"

He wasn't sure he should say, not without Rachel there. But Samantha sounded like she needed an answer. "I felt," he began, considering it, "that your mother didn't want me. That we had grown apart, maybe needed different things. I was tied to the city because of work, and that was the last place your mother wanted to be."

"Then it was about *place?*"

Two weeks ago he might have said that, might have boiled down the cause of the break to a word or two. But it was more complex. He saw that now. "Place was only a symptom of other things."

"But you loved her."

"Yes."

"Do you still?"

He thought about the hand-around-the-heart feeling he experienced walking into that hospital room every day. "Probably."

"So why didn't you *fight* to keep her? Wasn't it worth it? Weren't *we* worth it?"

The question stunned him. "Yes. *Yes*."

"I kept thinking about that when I was waiting for you to come get me. I kept thinking you were right. We weren't worth it. Me, especially me."

"Are you *crazy?*"

"See?" she cried. "You'd *never* say that to Hope."

"No, I'd say other things to Hope, because Hope and you are different people. Different. Not better or worse."

"She's *lovable* and I'm not."

"But I do love you."

"I'm *not* lovable. I say too much."

"That's one of the things that *makes* you lovable. I always know where I stand. That's a real plus in a relationship. Honesty. Trust. Ease. Well, sometimes we don't have ease, you and me, but that's because you're your age and I'm mine, and you let me *know* when I'm being . . . being . . ."

"Old."

He sighed. "I guess. So, see, we can talk about that, too."

She turned onto her back and stared at the ceiling. "I couldn't talk to Teague. Not the way I wanted to. I was afraid he'd think I was a *kid*."

"Teague's crud," Jack said. "You can do better, Sam."

"I thought he *was* better. Shows how much *I* know."

"You knew enough to get the hell away from the guy when things started to get out of control. Didn't you?" When she didn't instantly answer, he felt another moment's doubt. "The truth, Sam. Didn't you? Or," he pushed himself to say, "do we need to talk about the facts of life?"

She shot him a glance. "Mom already has, but I didn't do it with Teague. He wanted to. That was when I left."

"See? You learned. That's what growing up is about. What went wrong with Brendan and Lydia?"

Unexpectedly, Samantha started crying again. When she tried to turn onto her side away from him, he rolled her right back.

"Talk it out, sweetheart."

Between sobs, she said, "I blew them off, so now I don't have them—and I won't have Pam and Heather, because Teague must have gone back there and told them what happened. I'm not going to be able to show my face in school again, not *ever*. I am such a *fuckup*."

"No. No, you're not."

But she wouldn't be assuaged. "I messed up, just like I messed up with Mom. If it hadn't been for me, she wouldn't have had the accident."

"How do you figure that?"

"We had a fight that afternoon."

"What happened in the afternoon has nothing to do—"

"It does, because she was thinking about the fight and brought her book to the studio, and if she hadn't had to get it there later, she would have left the house earlier."

"Don't do that, Sam," he warned. "If you do, I have to."

"Have to what?"

"Blame me. Do you think it hasn't occurred to me that if I'd been around more for your mother in San Francisco, she wouldn't have moved down here in the first place? If she hadn't moved down here, she wouldn't be in that hospital. But it doesn't do any good to think that way. It's done. Over. Not your fault or my fault, but the fault of the woman who was driving the other car."

"She's dead, isn't she?"

He figured that if Samantha was old enough to drink

beer and vodka and do God knew what with a boy she'd never dated before, she was old enough to know the truth. "Yes. She's dead. So we have to let it go, Sam. We can't blame her, and we can't blame us. We have to do what we can to help your mother wake up. And we have to carry on and move forward here. I think you should call Lydia later."

"I *can't*. She's not going to want to talk to me! I was *horrible* to her!"

"You could apologize."

"That wouldn't work."

"Why not?"

"Because."

"That's not a real answer, Samantha. Try again."

"She won't want me back."

"Do you want her back?"

"*Yes*. She's my *friend.*"

"More so than Pam?"

Samantha thought about that. "Yes. I feel safer with Lydia."

"Tell her that." When she didn't speak, he said, "That's your strength, expressing yourself. It's a precious thing, Sam. Not everyone has what it takes inside to do it. I know it's hard, but the important things in life are. You have to put yourself out there and risk the possibility that she's feeling so hurt that she won't want any *part* of you, but I don't think that'll happen. Lydia strikes me as a forgiving person."

Samantha started to cry again.

"What's wrong now?" he asked, because he thought they had it all worked out.

"I miss Mom."

Feeling a wrenching inside, he smoothed the hair

back from her face. "Me, too," he said and realized that he did, very much.

HE CONTINUED to stroke her hair until she quieted. Then he heard something new and went to the window. It sounded like rain. Only it wasn't raining.

Samantha came up beside him, wrapped in her quilt. "It's fog feet."

Fog feet. That had to be a Rachel expression.

"It's like," she said, "when the fog is so thick that it makes noise moving through the forest."

He looked at her. "Want to go outside? Nah. You feel lousy."

"I'll go," she said.

So they went outside, Jack in his paint-spattered sweat suit, Samantha in her nightgown and quilt. They were both barefooted—crazy, Jack knew, but somehow feeling the earth beneath their feet was important. They didn't go far, just to a level spot where the tree trunks rose and narrowed and stretched toward branches that spawned needles, and the sky.

They didn't move, didn't speak. They felt the moisture on their faces, a gentle curative, and listened to the steady, soothing sound of fog feet, and it occurred to Jack that this was a gift, standing here with his daughter, after the night that had been. He tried to think of when he had last felt as content, and realized it had been in these same woods. Then he had been with Hope. Now Samantha.

"I used to stand like this with Mom," she whispered so softly that he might have missed it if he hadn't been so close. She didn't say anything else. She didn't have to, because Rachel was suddenly with them, so strong a presence that Jack actually looked behind him, half expecting her to take form from the fog.

Did he still love her? There was no *probably* about it. And saying that he missed her told only half the story. The truth—realized, admitted only now, with the fog so thick that only the largest things in life were visible— was that he had been missing her for months.

HE WOKE UP Sunday morning, feeling her in bed with him, memory was so strong. Her hand moved on his chest, side to side through a matting of hair, and down his belly. The soft, sexy voice in his ear said that she loved it when he was this hard, so hard that he shook. He smelled the warm woman of her, kissed the wet woman in her, and came in a climax so cruel that for long minutes after, he lay with an arm over his eyes, breathing hard, swearing again and again.

His heartbeat had barely begun to steady when the peal of the phone sent it through the roof. Sunday morning at eight, with Samantha and Hope safe in bed?

"Jack? It's Kara. Rachel's thrown a clot."

chapter eighteen

" 'THROWN A CLOT.' What does that mean?" Samantha asked. They were in the car, speeding back to Monterey. She looked pale, almost green. Jack suspected that had as much to do with it being the morning after as with Rachel's condition. He had given her aspirin before they left. She was holding her head still against the headrest.

Hope had her lucky boots back on and was leaning forward between their seats, waiting for his answer.

He tried to repeat the gist of what Kara had told him. "On rare occasions, a broken bone—in Mom's case, her leg—creates a clot, a wad that enters the bloodstream and moves through the veins. Sometimes it gets stuck in the head or the heart. Sometimes it gets stuck in the lungs. That's where your mom's got stuck."

"How do they know?"

"They did a scan."

"Before that, how did they know something was wrong?"

"The monitors she's been connected to showed changes in the oxygen level in her blood. The problem was discovered as soon as it happened." He had asked that right off. If there had been a delay because she had been moved from Intensive Care to a regular room, he would have screamed.

"But what *is* the problem?" Samantha persisted. "Like, could she die from this?"

Bite your tongue. Words from his past. And wrong, here, because Samantha was only asking what Hope was surely wondering. Not addressing it would frighten them more.

"She could, Sam," he said, "but she won't, because we've got Bauer and Bates with her right now. The problem is that a clot can cut the flow of blood. In your mother's case, that's the last thing they want. Her brain is healing. It needs all the oxygen it can get, and since blood carries oxygen, they don't want anything slowing the flow." There was also a little problem with pneumonia, if a lung infection developed. That could kill her. But he wasn't mentioning it now.

"So do they operate and cut it out?"

According to Kara, operating posed more of a risk to Rachel's system than they cared to take. "They're treating it medically, with something they call a clot buster. It's heavy-duty stuff that will break up the clot."

"Right away?"

Hadn't he asked it himself, with the very same fear? "They hope so."

"What if it doesn't?"

"Don't look for trouble, Sam."

"But—"

"Sam." He took her hand. "Let's work together here. It doesn't do any good to think the worst. I don't know much more than you do. But we're due for a break, aren't we?" When she didn't answer, he gave her hand a jiggle. "Aren't we?"

"Yes," she whispered and closed her eyes.

He held her hand for a while. It comforted him, as did the weight of Hope's cheek on his shoulder.

KARA had forgotten to tell Jack three small things.

First, Rachel was back in ICU. They discovered that when they arrived at her room, found it empty, and in a panic ran down the hall.

Second, her lips and the area surrounding them were blue, which would have been frightening enough without the third thing. That was the gasping sound she made.

"What's happened," Kara explained as Jack and the girls watched Rachel in horror, "is that because there's a block, the blood can't participate in ventilation. Blood carrying oxygen can't get to her lungs to exchange with blood carrying carbon dioxide. The gasping you hear is her attempt to get more oxygen to her lungs. She sounds a lot worse than she is."

That was putting it mildly. To Jack's ears, Rachel sounded on the verge of death. He was appalled. "How long until the medicine starts working?"

"We're hoping to see results within a few hours."

THE FIRST HOUR crept. Rachel's gasping breaths counted the seconds.

Jack didn't know what to do. He was frightened and unsure, as terrified by the grating sounds Rachel made as he was by the tinge of her skin. For a time, he simply stood with an arm around each of the girls, but they were all tired. Eventually, they sat down on the bed, the girls on one side, Jack on the other. He tried to think of things to say, but it seemed important, so important, to listen to those gasping sounds, to hear the slightest change, to imagine that there were words in there somewhere.

"She sounds *awful*," Samantha whispered at one point.

Jack nodded. He held Rachel's hand, occasionally touched her face or her neck, and thought it ironic that when the scrapes on the side of her face were nearly healed, she should be turning blue. His stomach was tight, his insides chilled. Prayers came to him from a long-ago childhood of enforced practice. His memory fragmented them and they emerged watered down, but he thought them anyway. *Dear God, help her . . . give her strength . . . let her heal . . . serve you again . . .*

THE SECOND HOUR began, and the gasping went on undiminished.

"Hang in there," Jack murmured. "You can lick this, Rachel. Breathe long and slow, long and slow." He made a dry sound.

"What?" Samantha asked.

"We've done this before, your mom and me. When you were born. I coached her. 'Hang in there, Rachel. You can do it. Breathe long and slow.' Then out you came."

"Yelling and screaming?"

"No." He paused, smiled. "Actually, yes. You were vocal from birth. Very vocal. You let us know when you wanted something, all right."

"What about me?" Hope asked.

"Less vocal." His smile was for Rachel now. The memories were sweet. "In some ways, that was harder. You didn't tell us as much, so we had to guess. You guys were different even then. Your mom claimed you were different in the womb."

"How could she tell?" Hope asked.

"The way you moved. Sam was more active even then."

"But I slid out easier."

"Second deliveries are like that. She had to work harder with Sam." He heard that breathing again, as loud as ever. His smile faded. "Long and slow. Hang in there, angel. You're doing good, you're doing good."

KATHERINE arrived looking pale, upset, and totally different from any other way Jack had seen her. Her face was washed clean, curls a dozen shades of beige caught up in a ponytail. She wore a lightweight warm-up suit and sneakers. Only her fingernails were done, but even then, lighter. They were pink.

Jack took comfort in her presence. Even pale and upset, she conveyed competence. She knew what to say, what to ask. If there was something he wasn't doing for Rachel that should be done, she would tell him. She was his friend now, too. They were allies in the same war.

When he sent the girls to the cafeteria for drinks, she said, "Thanks for calling. I was working out. I got your message as soon as I got back." She made a general gesture toward her hair and face, apologetic, Jack thought. "Just took time to shower."

"You look great," he said. When she gave him a skeptical look, he added, "I'm serious. All natural. Very Rachel. Thanks for coming." He touched Rachel's lips. They were parted, air grating in and out. "I didn't expect this. The girls are pretty shaken. *I'm* pretty shaken."

"The medicine will work," Katherine said firmly.

"I've been praying. It's the first time in years. I don't want to lose her, Katherine. Do you think she wants to hear that?"

Katherine looked at him and sighed. "You're not a bad-looking guy. Need a haircut. Need a shave. But you clean up good. So, yeah. She'd want to hear it. What woman wouldn't?"

"I think you're missing my point," Jack said, but the girls returned then, and when Katherine took her tea with thanks and suggested that Jack take the girls back to the cafeteria for breakfast, he figured he'd leave well enough alone.

"HI THERE."

Katherine was leaning over the bed rail, letting Rachel know she was rooting for her, when Steve Bauer walked in. She had known he would appear, had felt it in her gut well before she decided to forgo makeup and mousse. She figured it was time to give him a preview of the less glamorous side of the woman she was.

"What's happening here?" she asked, straightening.

"Clot. Drip. Wait."

"Ahh. Thanks."

He approached the bed, studied Rachel, then the monitor. He adjusted the solution dripping from the IV bag, then leaned in and said in a voice loud and authoritative enough to be heard over her breathing, "Rachel? I'm speeding up the drip. You won't feel the change, but it should help."

Katherine sensed his worry. "Should she have already responded?"

He checked the wall clock. "No. But she can use more."

"How does something like this affect the coma? Can it snap her out of it?"

"It can. It may not." He turned his blue eyes on her, along with a small smile. "How are you?"

"Nervous."

"I'm flattered."

"Nervous about *Rachel,*" she said, focusing again on her friend. There was no pretending she was asleep, not with the noise she made with every breath.

"I'm envious. How far back do you two go?"

"Six years." But she had never had a friend like Rachel. "I feel like I've known her forever, we're that much alike."

"You look more alike now than usual."

"Ashen skin? Blue lips?"

"Unadorned. You look pretty."

Jack had said the same thing, but it felt different coming from Steve. She squeezed Rachel's hand. "He's hitting on me again."

"No. Just saying I'm in for the long haul." Before she could begin to analyze *that,* he said, "So you and Rachel are alike. Tell me how."

Katherine could do that. "She's an only child. So am I. She grew up in the city. So did I. She hated it. So did I."

"Why?"

"In Rachel's case, she felt pressured to conform to a way of life she didn't like."

"In yours?"

"I felt lost. I like bumping into people I know."

"Like Rick Meltzer?"

Rick was the anesthesiologist who had called out her name. She should have known Steve would notice. "Like Rick," she admitted, since denying it would only make him curious. "I also like privacy. Drive half an hour from here, and you're in the middle of nowhere. For someone like Rachel, that's important. She's artistic. We have that in common, too."

"Then it isn't just—" He made a speedy snipping motion.

"No. It isn't just." She held his gaze. "There's an art to coloring and styling hair. Even in that, Rachel and I are alike."

"How?"

"We're both adherents of realism. We spend our professional lives trying to bring out the best and most beautiful of what nature has to offer." She looked at Rachel again, suddenly resentful of what she saw. "I don't think she'd like these blue lips."

"We don't either, but they're telling us what's going on inside."

"Can she do herself harm, gasping like this?"

"No. She needs the air."

"When will the medication kick in?"

"Hard to tell. Another two or three hours. Maybe more." He was holding Rachel's shoulder. "I've seen her work. I stopped in at P. Emmet's."

Katherine was surprised. She had thought detachment was a medical school basic. "Aren't you risking emotional involvement doing that?"

"Yes. The more you know, the harder it is when

patients fail, or when you have to recommend one of two lousy alternatives. The flip side is that when patients respond and recover, there's greater satisfaction. The brute fact is that medicine is becoming a service profession. The customer wants his doctor to be involved. Isn't that why Jack brought in these pictures? Or why Rachel is wearing a T-shirt with her name in big bright letters? It's why I'm asking you these questions."

"And here I thought you had an ulterior motive," Katherine said, knowing that he did. He wanted to learn about her, so he was asking about Rachel.

Those blue eyes said she was right. "Does she like to travel?" he asked.

Katherine sighed. He was incorrigible. Something about his persistence was nice, though. If he wanted her bad enough . . . "Yes. She travels for work. She'd like to travel more for fun, but money's tight. Paying for three. You know."

"I do. Does she like movies?"

"Good ones." She arched a brow. "There aren't any around, so don't even suggest it."

"I wasn't about to. You'd feel guilty going to a movie with Rachel struggling in here, but you have to eat, and I can't go far from the hospital. I was thinking something quick and easy, like smoked salmon on the Wharf."

Katherine couldn't help but grin. "With the tourists?"

"It's quick. It's easy. It's public. Tell you what. I'll be in and out of here for another few hours. If you're hungry at two, meet me out front. My car is the dark green CJ-7." He briefly turned away to check the speed of the drip, looked back at the monitor for another minute, then, with an endearingly vulnerable glance at Katherine, left the room.

WHEN JACK returned with the girls, he was discouraged to find that nothing had changed. Rachel's coloring was as poor as before, her breathing as labored.

"Bauer was just here," Katherine said. "He didn't seem overly concerned."

But Jack was. He kissed Rachel's hand and pressed his mouth to the scar there. It was a fine line, growing finer by the day, but her hand was thinner. All of her was thinner. She was fading away right before his eyes. It struck him that this was his punishment. He had let Rachel walk out of his life. Had let her. Samantha was right. He hadn't fought.

He had been preoccupied and too proud. He had let the silence win.

"*Goddammit,*" he muttered, cursing both that silence and the gut-wrenching noise Rachel was making, and suddenly his eyes filled with tears. He squeezed them shut, swallowed, and pressed Rachel's hand to his brow.

"Hey, guys," Katherine said to Samantha and Hope, "let's take a walk. Your parents need some private time."

Jack didn't look, but he knew when they were gone. He felt the special connection with Rachel that used to reduce the rest of the world to fringe. Memory, or reality? He wasn't sure. But it was strong, and a good sign maybe, if she was still putting out vibes.

Taking a steadying breath, he lowered her hand from his eyes. "I don't know if you can hear me, Rachel, but there are things I need to say. There are things *we* need to say. If you wanted to get my attention, you couldn't have done it better. It's been an . . . enlightening few weeks."

He whispered his thumb over her eyelids, feeling tissue-thin, soft skin that was surprisingly warm. "I want to talk about what happened. We never did that. We just kind of split up and went separate ways. Stopped talking over the piano." He was haunted by his memory of her picking out sad tunes that night, when she had given him an opening and he had walked away. "We fell back into who we were before we met, but that wasn't us. It was me. It was you. It wasn't us. Together we were something different, something better than we'd been. When did we lose that?"

Through the ruckus of gasps, he imagined her voice, thoughtful and warm as it was in the best of times, but there were no words, no answers, no insight.

Suddenly angry, he whispered, "Don't you leave me in the lurch, Rachel Keats. Keats—God, I hate that. With all due respect to fuckin' women's rights, I hate it. You should be Rachel McGill. Or I'll be Jack Keats. But we should be the same." He took a shuddering breath and said, fiercely, "We had a pretty damn nice marriage, Rachel. I want it back. Don't you die on me now."

He watched her face closely, hoping for a reaction. "Did you hear what I said?" he fairly yelled. "I want it back!"

She didn't move, didn't blink, just took one gasping breath after another.

Frightened, he pulled up a chair and sat back.

chapter nineteen

JACK WAS IN the same chair an hour later. Samantha had squeezed in beside him and was sleeping under his arm. Hope was dozing, curled on her side against Rachel's hip. Noon had come and gone. Rachel was still blue, still gasping.

Samantha stirred. She looked at him groggily, then less groggily at Rachel. "No better?" she asked.

"Not yet. How's your head?"

"Okay." She settled back against him in a way that spoke of how far they had come. If the chair was crowded, he didn't care. He wouldn't have moved for the world.

"I keep thinking about Lydia," she said softly. "I should tell her about Mom."

With only a minor stretch, he pulled the cell phone from his pocket, turned it on, and held it out.

It was a minute before she took it. "What if she hangs up when she hears my voice?"

"She won't hang up." If she did, he would never forgive her. Samantha was headed in the right direction. He didn't want her derailed. "She's not that kind of person. Isn't that the lesson here?"

Samantha fingered the phone for a long time. "Maybe I should wait." He thought of the things he wanted to say to Rachel, things he should have said before, things he might never, ever have a chance to say. "Do it now, Sam. That's a lesson we *all* have to learn. If you know something's right, don't let it go."

SAMANTHA wanted privacy. Calling Lydia to grovel was hard enough. Doing it in public would be worse. So she walked to the end of the corridor and wedged herself in a lonely corner, and even then she hesitated. If Lydia refused to talk, she didn't know what she'd do. But Rachel had given her a perfect excuse. The blood clot was something to tell Lydia. Lydia adored Rachel. *All* of Samantha's friends adored Rachel. They thought she was the nicest, most interesting, most *fun* of the moms. Of course, they didn't have to live with her.

Feeling guilty to have thought that, she pressed in Lydia's number. When Lydia's mother answered, Samantha's throat closed. In that instant, she would have given *anything* to hear her own mother's voice.

She cleared her throat. "Hi, Mrs. Russell. Is Lydia up?"

"Samantha! We missed you last night. I thought for sure you'd stop over. Did you have fun?"

Samantha's eyes teared up. She debated lying, but she was too tired, too nervous, too needy. "No. It wasn't . . . what I thought. Is everyone still there?"

"Shelly just left. I think Lydia's in the shower. Hold on. I'll check."

Samantha turned in against the wall and waited.

"Yes, she's in the shower," Mrs. Russell said a little too brightly. "Is there a message?"

No *Hold on, she's getting out,* no *She'll call you right back*—either of which Lydia would have done the week before. "Um, it's kind of important. My mom is worse."

There was a gasp, then the kind of worried "Oh dear" that Samantha would never have heard from Pam, Heather, or Teague, let alone any of their mothers. "Hold on, Samantha." She was an ally now. "Let me get her out."

Samantha pressed her head to the wall. It seemed forever until Lydia's voice came through. It, too, was worried, but there was a distance to it. "What happened to your mom?"

Acting as though nothing had ever come between them, Samantha told her about the clot and ended with, "She's making an awful sound. It's very scary."

There was a silence on the other end, then a wary "Do you want me to come?"

Groveling sucked. If Samantha was willing to forgive and forget, she didn't know why Lydia couldn't. "Not if you don't want to."

"I want to if you want me to be there. Do you?"

"Yes."

"Okay."

The line went dead before Samantha could say another word. The coward in her was relieved to be let off the hook. But the hook was still there, so she felt dread. She also felt humbled. Lydia hadn't sounded young or stupid. She had taken the phone when she had every right not to. It remained to be seen how she would be in person, but maybe Jack was right. Maybe there was a lesson here.

She jumped when the phone in her hand rang. Thinking that Lydia wanted to say more, even reconcile there and then, she pressed *send* and was about to speak when a loud male voice beat her to it.

"It's about time you turned on the fuckin' phone, Jack. I've been leaving messages at every number you have, and you don't call me back? We're partners in this business, pal. You gotta carry some of the weight. I know Rachel's sick and you have a lot on the brain, but so do I. The natives are getting restless in Montana. They hired an architect, they want some plans, and I don't think they're gonna like those new ones you faxed. What's going on with you? Are we talking midlife crisis here? I'm getting the distinct impression you don't care about work anymore. Tell me this is a temporary thing." He paused, waited. "Jack?"

"This is Samantha," she said, standing taller. "If you want to speak with my father, you'll have to hold on." Dropping the phone to her side, she walked with deliberate leisure back to Rachel's room.

JACK saw her coming. He took heart from her composure, until she handed him the phone and said, "It's David. He is . . . *fuckin'* mad."

He stared at her for the time it took to rake his upper lip with his teeth. Then he took the phone and stepped into the hall. "How're you doin', Dave?"

"I'd be doing better if I thought you just weren't *getting* my messages. Why haven't you called?"

"Rachel's in the middle of a crisis."

"What kind of crisis?"

"She's having trouble breathing. She can't get enough oxygen."

"Where are the fuckin' doctors?"

"Right here, but they're doing all they can. We're waiting. That's all we can do."

"Jesus." He gave a long, loud sigh. "How long this time, Jack? When are you coming back on board?"

"I don't know."

"Not good enough. I'm trying to run a business. We need you here, Jack."

"I can't *be* there. Not now."

"When?"

"I'll let you know," Jack ground out and turned off the phone.

When Samantha raised a fist and said, "Yesssss," he smiled. It was a single fine moment in the middle of a mess.

KATHERINE had no intention of going to the Wharf for lunch. It felt wrong, with Rachel so sick. She wanted to be at the hospital, rooting, supporting, fighting for her right by her side.

But Jack and the girls were doing that, Jack surprisingly well. And they were family. Besides, she was hungry. She'd had nothing but tea all day.

There was still the matter of how she looked. The sweat suit was fine, but the hair? The skin? She prided herself on being a walking ad for her shop. She wouldn't win many customers looking like this.

But this was Fisherman's Wharf, the major tourist attraction in Monterey. She wouldn't look any different from the average visitor. She might not gain customers, but she sure wouldn't lose them. And she *was* hungry. By promising to be back in an hour with lunch for Jack and the girls, she made it a practical mission and easier to justify.

She went down to the front door, assuming that a CJ-7 was a snappy sports car. The dark green car that waited, though, was an old-fashioned Jeep, with a roll bar on top, neither roof nor windows, and what looked like tin for doors.

"Wow," she said, fastening her seat belt first thing— second thing being grateful that her hair wasn't loose. "Quite a car."

He grinned. "Thanks." He worked the stick shift, stepped on the gas, and the car headed out. "It's an eighty-six. I had to look for two years. Then I found it in La Jolla. *CJ* means *civilian Jeep*. Know any Jeep history?"

"Uh, no. Beauty school doesn't go that far."

He laughed. "Neither does med school. Jeeps go back to World War Two—1941—when the army needed a reconnaissance vehicle that would go anywhere. Lore has it that the name *Jeep* is a derivation of *GP*—general purpose. The first CJs hit the road as early as forty-six. So there's your trivia for the day."

She had to admit there was a classic feel to the thing. The dashboard was metal—dark green to match the outside of the car—with chrome circling the dials. He touched that chrome once or twice. She couldn't begrudge him the affection.

He took his time driving—enjoying the fresh air, she imagined, because she surely was. The May sun was relaxingly warm, the ocean air a far cry from the hospital's sterility.

Despite his promise to make it quick, he parked a distance away. Katherine didn't fault him on it, nor did she rush the pace as they walked to the Wharf. She figured she owed herself the leisure after two weeks of shuttling between work and the hospital. She figured Steve deserved it, too. Without the lab coat, he looked totally casual—sport shirt rolled up his forearms, old jeans, sneakers. She could have sworn he was taking the same reinvigorating breaths she was.

Tourists were milling in groups at the head of the Wharf. They joined one group that circled a tiny monkey who was stuffing his pockets with the quarters children offered, but Katherine could only watch so long. "I always feel bad for that poor little thing," she murmured when they broke away and set off.

They passed storefront after storefront as they ambled down the pier. Had she been there alone, Katherine would have simply picked out a grill, ordered food, eaten, and left. But the ambling was pleasant, and the Wharf wasn't long. They reached its end just as a bench opened up. Steve parked her there and left, returning several minutes later with cups of clam chowder, grilled-salmon sandwiches, and iced tea.

Katherine rather liked being waited on. She had spent so much of her adult life doing for herself that it was a treat. She ate every last bit of her portion, not in the least embarrassed, since Steve ate every last bit of his, and with the very same grinning gusto. Passing the bench on to another pair of eaters, they stood a bit longer watching a seal in the water. When they spotted a group of kayakers on the bay, he told her that he was a canoeist. She told him she had never learned to swim. He told her it was easy. She said that was nice. He told her she didn't know what she was missing. She said she'd take his word for it. They smiled at each other, no offense taken either way.

Walking back up the pier, she bought sandwiches and chowder for the McGills. Steve guided her to the car.

He didn't immediately start it, but turned to her and sat back. "Thanks. I needed that."

Feeling safe enough, she smiled back. "So did I. Thank you."

He looked out the windshield, pensive. Then he looked at her. "There. That didn't hurt, did it?"

She laughed. "No, Doctor."

"I'm serious." She could see that he was. There was no humor in his eyes, just concern and that same vulnerability. "I know it's hard to do things like play tourist on the Wharf when people you know are in Intensive Care," he said, "but I *live* with people I know being in Intensive Care. Part of me wants to be back at that hospital watching Rachel. That part would be at the hospital twenty hours a day. So I make a concerted effort to leave. That thing about emotional involvement? I have to balance it somehow. Walking the Wharf helps. Canoeing helps. Gardening helps."

"Gardening? Oh dear. I have a brown thumb."

"I said that once, too. Funny, how resilient nature is. I do my best, and it may not be everything a plant needs, but it's more than the thing would get without." He stretched his fingers, palms to the steering wheel. "I kind of look at medicine the same way. Take Rachel. Thirty years ago, without drugs like mannitol and streptokinase, she would have died. Yes, I want her awake. I want her awake *now*. I do the best I can. It may not be everything she needs, but she'd be worse off without." His eyes found hers and held for a silent minute. Then, quietly, he said, "I'm a good guy, Katherine. You can trust me."

She knew he was talking beyond Rachel, and the air grew charged. She tore her eyes away, focused on her lap, then on a brick building adjacent to the parking lot.

"I've been divorced for ten years," he said. "I've had it with dating."

She chewed on her cheek.

"So if I come on faster than you want," he continued, "it's because I don't see the point in beating around the bush when someone appeals to me. Few women have. You do."

She put her elbow on the door and pressed her knuckles to her forehead.

"Say the word, and I'll get lost," he said.

She wanted to say the word, wanted to say *any* word, but none came.

"Either tell me to get lost," he said without a bit of smugness, "or give me a kiss."

"That's not a fair choice."

"Ask Rachel about fair. Look, I know the timing of this stinks, but I'm fifty-three. I'm too old to play games. Do you want me to get lost?"

She thought about that. There was something about him, something beyond those blue eyes and that fit body, that appealed to her, too. "No."

"Then kiss me."

She eyed him from under her fist. "Why?"

"I want to see if it works."

"What a male thing to say."

"And because I said it, you're totally turned off."

"I should be." But she wasn't, because it went two ways. If his kiss left her cold, she wouldn't have to worry about the rest. They could be friends without the threat of anything more.

"Okay," she said and looked at her watch. "One minute. Then we have to leave." She leaned over and put her lips to his, moved them a little, backed off. "Am I doing a solo here?"

Smiling, he shook his head. He slid one hand around her neck and moved gentle fingers into her hair, slid the other around her shoulder in a gentle message that rose to her jaw before she could begin to fear it would head south. His hands framed her face. His eyes touched her lips. He took his time, moved closer, tipped his head, took more time. His mouth was an inch from hers when, with a less than steady breath, he drew back, faced front, cleared his throat, and turned the key in the ignition.

Katherine stared in disbelief. "What are you doing?"

"Minute's up."

She knew that, but her insides were humming. She would have been flexible on the time. "I thought you didn't play games."

Shifting in his seat, he headed out of the parking lot. "I don't. It works. Wasn't that the point of the exercise?"

"Works for *who?*" she cried. "Is that *your* idea of a kiss?"

"Oh, no." His laugh was quintessentially male. "But it works, Katherine. Tell me you didn't feel it."

She jabbed a finger at her lips. "I didn't feel a damn *thing.*"

He shot her one look, then, when she didn't relent, shot her another. Seconds after that, he pulled over to the curb, took her into his arms, and without once giving her cause to tense up by going anywhere near her breasts, gave her a kiss that spelled trouble.

SAMANTHA stood beside Rachel's bed watching the door. Her head was throbbing again, her stomach was twisting. Her wrist ached and her feet hurt. Going to school in the morning was unthinkable. She didn't care if finals were coming up. She would make them up in the summer, when no one else was around. By fall, people would forget.

It was thirty minutes since she had called Lydia. Jack had his elbows on the bed rail. He was staring at Rachel. Hope was looking around the room, sitting cross-legged with her butt against Rachel's cast. Barely five minutes passed without either Kara or a nurse stopping in. Samantha wished Cindy was there, but she wasn't on duty until tomorrow morning.

Hope straightened her legs and slid off the bed. Her boots hit the floor with a thunk. "I'm getting stuff from the other room. This room could be *anyone's.*" She strode into the hall.

"She shouldn't do that," Samantha warned. "The point is getting Mom back there as soon as the medicine works."

Jack had straightened. He was flexing his neck, dipping his head from side to side. "That is the point. But then there's Murphy's Law. It says that as soon as we move everything here, she'll be ready to move back. Hold the fort," he said and left.

Rachel's breathing was louder than ever in the silence that remained.

Samantha went to the door and looked down the hall just as Jack turned into Rachel's regular room. In the other direction, several nurses were clustered, heads together. Lydia was nowhere in sight.

Back at the bed, she curled her fingers over the rail. Just thinking about the fiasco of the prom, she felt lost and sick and scared. The best part, the *best* part, was getting home. She didn't know how many of the other dads would have been as supportive as hers had been. So it was possibly a fluke. So maybe he wouldn't have come for her if he'd been working his head off in the city. So maybe if Rachel woke up he would be gone again.

But, boy, it had been nice listening to fog feet with him. It reminded her of times before the divorce.

The blue tint around Rachel's mouth brought back another memory. "Omigod, Mom, remember Halloween? We always had *the* best costumes. Hershey's Kisses and Crayola boxes and bunches of grapes. And makeup out of food coloring and flour? Blue lips? *Purple* lips?"

"Sam?"

She whirled around. Not knowing what to say, she turned right back to Rachel. When she sensed Lydia beside her, and still there weren't any words, she dared a look. Lydia's eyes were on Rachel, reflecting the same horror Samantha had felt seeing her mother like this for the first time.

"Can't they *do* something?"

Samantha waved at the IV pole. "It's up there. We have to wait for it to work."

"Oh." She wrapped her arms around her middle. "Does she know about last night?"

"You mean, did my telling her cause this?" It wasn't

the vote of confidence Samantha needed. "No, Lydia. I haven't told her. She did this all on her own."

"You don't have to get angry. She'd be upset about last night, and you know it."

Samantha looked at her then. "What do you know about last night?"

"You want me to say? In front of your Mom?"

"Yeah, I want you to say." Rachel would have to know sometime. Better when she couldn't speak.

Lydia kept her eyes on Rachel. "You went to Ian's but left there with Teague and got so sloshed you passed out, so he drove you home. At least, that's what Teague said when he got back to the party. He ended up with Marissa Fowler, who was supposed to be with Mark Cahill. Mark's Amanda's cousin. He picked her up at my house this morning."

"And told *everyone* that story?" Nightmare!

"Told Amanda and Shelly and me. Is it true?"

"No, it is not true. I didn't get sloshed or pass out, and Teague did not drive me home. He came on so strong that I could nail him for rape, hands down—only it never got past the attempted stage. I ran away before it did. Me sloshed? Try Teague. And stoned. My father came and got me."

Lydia's eyes were wide. "You had to *call* him?"

"I wanted to call you, but I didn't think you'd care."

Lydia looked suddenly close to tears, and totally like the sweet person Samantha loved. "You're stupid, you know that?" she cried.

Samantha was about to say she was right, when Hope walked in loaded down with cards, signs, and pictures. Jack followed with vases of flowers, which he set on the windowsill. Hope sank to the floor and opened her arms.

Samantha said to Lydia, "We're counting on Murphy's Law. Want to help?"

JACK was buoyed when sweet, unsophisticated, loyal Lydia stayed. He couldn't help but think that if Samantha could go through life with friends like this one, she would survive and flourish. She certainly had a role model in her mother. Rachel had Faye and Charlie, Dinah, Jan, and Eliza. She had bridge friends, and friends at the girls' school. She had Ben. And she had Katherine—who returned with an incredibly good lunch.

Steve Bauer arrived minutes later. He checked Rachel's chart, the monitor, and the IV drip. He lifted her lids and studied her pupils. He called her name, then leaned closer and called it again. He left the room to order another lung scan. Within minutes, the necessary equipment was wheeled in. Jack sent the three girls out to walk around in the sun. He and Katherine waited in the hall.

He stuck his hands in his pockets and blew out a frustrated breath.

"She'll make it," Katherine insisted. "There are too many people working too hard to make her live."

"The point isn't just to make her live. It's to make her wake up and be well." He thought about Faith Bligh. "She could wake up not whole. You asked me once what I'd do then. I think I'd be destroyed."

"Would you leave?"

"No." It was a sober admission. "No. I couldn't." When Katherine said nothing, he met her gaze. It was open and warm. "What?" he asked, vaguely embarrassed.

"Man has risen to the occasion," she declared. The words were no sooner out of her mouth than her eyes flew toward Rachel's room. "Oh, man," she murmured, folding her arms on her chest.

Jack followed her gaze. All he could see was Steve Bauer, alternately watching the technicians and looking out into the hall at them. And there was Katherine, with windblown air and warm apricot cheeks.

"Did I miss something?" he asked.

She bowed her head and made a strangled sound. "Don't ask. This is *so* not the right time."

He disagreed. If that strangled sound she had made was related to a laugh, the time was right. "I could use a lift. Make me smile."

She was sober when she raised her head. "He's a great kisser. What should I do?"

Jack did smile. He liked the doctor. The smile faded when he realized what she meant. "Ah. The old breast thing."

She settled against the wall and looked into the room again. She kept her arms folded and her voice low. "He didn't try to touch them, but he will. Men always do. It's only a matter of time."

Jack tried to imagine what he would want if he were Bauer. He thought about Rachel. All too well he remembered arriving at the hospital that morning, unprepared for what he would find. "I think you should tell him. If it were dark, would he know?"

"By feel? Yes. Silicone was the best, but it's been banned. Mine are saline. There's a difference."

"Then tell him. You'll be too nervous to enjoy it, if you don't."

She made another of those strangled sounds. "Yeah,

well, I'd have thought that, too, before he kissed me. I didn't have time to think of much, it was that good. I mean, he did *everything* right."

"It's chemistry."

"It was chemistry with Byron. Funny how body mutilation can kill a good thing." She pressed her lips together and met his gaze.

"And you don't want it killed," Jack said, "so there's more at stake this time."

She nodded.

Jack tried to think of all the women he had dated. The ones before Rachel hadn't been anything special. The ones after had been nice enough, but Jill was the first he had viewed as a friend. For a while he had thought she might be it. But she wasn't Rachel. Poor Jill wasn't Katherine, either.

Hard to believe, but he liked Katherine a lot. Totally aside from all that she gave Rachel and the girls, she did things for him, too. Like now. Confiding in him. Telling him things he guessed she would normally tell only another woman. She made him feel like his opinion mattered, which was quite a compliment from a woman as strong as Katherine.

"There's an analogy here," he said, reaching out to tuck in a windblown piece of hair, then leaving it because it looked so nicely undone. "Samantha was sure Lydia wouldn't want any part of her. I told her it was a test. If Lydia didn't, then she wasn't the friend Samantha thought, so the loss wasn't as great. The same goes for you. Any man who loses it because of what you've been through isn't worth your while."

"Easy to say. You're not the one baring all."

He understood that. It had to be hard for Katherine to

open herself to the kind of rejection she had already experienced twice. "But breasts are only a small part of a woman, and pretty fickle things, when you get down to it. They swell, they shrink, they sag. Intelligence is more constant. So is warmth, and humor. So is loyalty. Truthfully? If Steve was younger, I'd warn you off. Breasts mean more to young guys. They're a symbol. I'd be lying if I denied it. But Steve's not a kid. He's been around the block. Look at him in there with Rachel. He doesn't have to be here. It's Sunday. Give a guy like that the choice between a bimbo with natural knockers and an intelligent, warm, funny, loyal, beautiful woman with rebuilt ones— come on, Katherine, no contest. Hell, I'd go after you myself if I weren't still in love with my wife."

JACK'S wife remained unresponsive to the clot buster. The scan showed no noticeable improvement in the passage of air through her lungs, and on the outside, to the eyes and ears of the people who loved her, the symptoms didn't ease. The doctor said it would take longer. He wouldn't say how *much* longer.

Sitting with her that afternoon, Jack thought about love, but he couldn't relate to it in the abstract, only in specifics. Eighteen years ago, love had meant spending every free minute with Rachel. Seventeen years ago, it meant making monthly payments on a small diamond ring. Sixteen years ago, it meant marrying her; fifteen years ago, having a child.

Men like action, Katherine had said during one of their earliest discussions. He had made it into a semantic argument, but the truth was that he did like action. Having admitted that he loved Rachel, he wanted to *do* something. Talking to her, moving her arms, applying Vaseline to her lips or scented lotion to her legs was only part of that.

He wanted to believe she would wake up, and wanted things to be right when she did. He had gotten Hope through her picnic and Samantha through her prom. Okay, so he had canceled doctor and dentist appointments, but they could be done later. Right now, he needed to paint. He needed to frame. He needed to buy a car.

chapter twenty

THE CAR JACK BOUGHT was technically a truck. It was a
large, loaded, four-wheel-drive vehicle with power, luxury, and class, and if Charlie Avalon wanted to accuse
him of flaunting his money, he didn't care. He wanted
the best for Rachel and the girls. He didn't know why in
the hell he had busted his butt to make money or what in
the hell he was saving it for, if not this.

And he could afford it. How well, he discovered in
Rachel's studio that night. He hadn't planned on scruti-
nizing his finances, had hooked his laptop to the modem
for the sole purpose of transferring money from one
account to another for the car. Then he set about framing
more of Rachel's pieces. The girls were helping. Hope
had done it once, and Samantha was a quick study. In no
time, he had Samantha predrilling holes and Hope applying wood glue. He was the one using the miter saw to cut
the molding to size, then hammering the nails in once the
wood was glued, but neither job was taxing. His mind
wandered. Transferring money had put a bug in his ear.
So, when it was time for a break, he went back to the lap-

top and accessed other of his bank records. After another round of leveling and bracketing corners, he accessed his investment accounts.

He hadn't deliberately saved money in the years since his divorce. He simply hadn't spent much. He also discovered, several links later, that San Francisco real estate was at a healthy high, which meant that the value of his house had appreciated considerably.

He was, it seemed, fairly well off. For a guy who had started with nothing—with *less* than nothing when school loans were factored into the equation—he had done well.

That thought gave him the same kind of good feeling that Katherine's confiding in him had.

When Hope put her head down on the worktable, he sent her to bed. Samantha worked a while longer. He knew she had to be exhausted, given what she had been through the night before, but he suspected she was feeling some of what he was. As important as visiting with Rachel was, after a while it was discouraging. Working here, there was progress.

She didn't say anything about the paintings themselves. Given the strength of her initial objections, he guessed that was asking too much. He chose to let her prolonged attentiveness to the framing speak for itself. By the time she finally went off to her room, six paintings were one step away from being done and ready to hang.

Alone, Jack went to work on a wolf. It was a beautiful thing, lying low in a carpet of khaki green summer grass, with the top of its head and body outlined, white fur backlit by the sun. Rachel had gone to the Arctic the summer before, with the girls this time. Studying the photographs she had taken, he wished he had been along. He found prints of wolves in packs, hunting, and at play. There was a primal power to them, foiled by surroundings that looked quiet and serene, in those things much like Big Sur. He felt Rachel's appreciation in these prints, in her field sketches, in the wolf she had brought to life with her brush. Jack's challenge was to render that appreciation in an understated backdrop.

She had used mixed media for this one—india ink for the detail of eye and muzzle, acrylic for the fur, watercolor for experimental patches of distant grass. The choice was just right. She had that vision. He was awed enough to hesitate, wondering if he was foolish to touch the canvas, if he could do it justice or would only ruin it.

Then he pictured Rachel, blue around the lips and gasping for air. Wanting, wanting to do it for her, he dug deep inside and began.

Warming up with a large brush on the distant grasses, he used a light watercolor wash of gray, ocher, umber, and green. He gave it depth with charcoal and sap green, gave it warmth with sepias. Layering acrylic over watercolor edges, he moved inward. He kept the grasses neutral in color, but textured. Though Rachel hadn't put flowers on her canvas, they were on her field sketches. Several photographs depicted them well, cotton flowers, like the wolf, caught from behind by the sun.

Did she want them added?

It was his decision to make, but no decision, really. He saw harmony between animal and plant life in a barren land. The flowers were a must.

He stayed with acrylics to re-create the small cotton buds. When they didn't capture the halo effect he wanted, he switched to a white pencil with a dulled tip, blending the lines with his finger, then a tissue, then a cotton swab. Nearly there, he put a scrap of paper toweling around the end of the swab and polished the buds. Satisfied at last, he stepped back.

IT WAS NEARLY five in the morning when he cleaned up. He slept for two hours and awoke exhausted. Samantha said she was too tired for school. Hope said she wanted to be with Rachel. He called the hospital, praying that Rachel had improved, but she hadn't.

He pushed his hands through his hair. "I'll be running around talking with the doctors. Your mother would want you in school, and it would do my mind good to know you're there. I'll pick you up right after. You can see her then."

Samantha argued as they drove, but he held firm. He needed time alone with the doctors to express fears that he didn't want the girls to hear.

When he pulled up at the school, Samantha didn't budge. Where a mutinous pout would have been days before, now there was sheer apprehension.

He tried to understand what she was feeling. "Lydia had no problem with this."

"There's all the other kids. And Pam and Heather. And *Teague.*"

"Teague," he said, monitoring his language with care, "is not worth your spit. As for Pam and Heather, they're not much better if they side with him. Life is about making choices, Sam. You can go in there and try to salvage something with Pam and Heather. Or you can stick with

Lydia." When she didn't speak, he said, "It's hard. I know."

"It's *mortifying.*"

"Yes." He sighed. "But the sooner it's done, the sooner it's done, if you get my drift." He put his elbows on the steering wheel and watched a line of reluctant teenagers stumble from a bus. He looked back at Samantha. If she wore makeup, it was light and more in keeping with the natural curl that, for a change, she'd left in her hair. "I was wrong the other night."

"You? Wrong?"

"When I told you how gorgeous you looked all dressed up. You did look gorgeous, but you look even better now. More beautiful. More you."

She flipped down the visor and moved her head in the mirror. "I look dorky."

"Beautiful. Anyone says different, they're jealous."

She scooped her hair back. Without the sleek swing, the effect was more feminine.

"Here goes nothing," she mumbled, flipping up the visor. She opened the door and had barely stepped out when Lydia came toward her. The door closed with a solid new-car thud.

One down, Jack thought, and looked back at Hope. She seemed a great distance behind him, belted safely in, but too far away. When he motioned her forward, she unbuckled herself, shimmied into the passenger's seat, and sat.

"What, sweetie?"

So softly that it was nearly a whisper, she said, "I have a funny feeling."

"Funny feeling?"

"I want to be with Mom. Like I was with Guinevere."

Jack's heart buckled. He reached over and pulled her into a hug over the center console. "Your mother isn't dying," he said into her hair. "We won't let her die."

"I said that about Guinevere."

"Guinevere had a tumor."

"Is a tumor any different from a blood clot?"

"God, yes," he said, wondering how long she'd been agonizing over that. "A blood clot isn't poisonous in itself. It just gets in the way until we break it up. A tumor has bad stuff in it. It grows and spreads and does sick things to the places it touches." It was a simplification, possibly inaccurate, but hell, he was doing his best. "They can just give her a megadose of that medicine to bust up the clot, then we'll fight harder than ever to wake her up."

"How?" came her small voice.

"I don't know. I don't know, but we'll think of a way."

THEY couldn't give Rachel a megadose of medicine. They hadn't even continued the drip through the night. "It's a question of weighing the risks against the benefits," Steve explained. They were in the hall—Jack, Steve and Kara, two residents and a nurse who had worked with Rachel, and Cindy. "Anticoagulants thin the blood and break up the clot, but thinning the blood raises the risk of bleeding elsewhere. We don't want Rachel bleeding."

Jack agreed. But he was frantic. "Why isn't she responding?"

Steve shook his head. When none of the others offered an explanation, he said, "We'll start another dose of the same drip, and then just watch her closely."

JACK did that himself. Lowering the bed rail, he sat on the bed and exercised Rachel's hands and arms. He told her that the medicine was working in places they couldn't see, and that it was only a matter of time before her breathing quieted and her coloring improved. He went so far as to say that once those things happened, she would wake up.

"Sounds like a course in the power of positive thinking," David Sung said from the door. He wasn't a tall man, but he wore his suits well. Today's was a light gray plaid. His hair, eyes, and shoes were dark, shiny, and straight.

He entered the room with those dark eyes on Rachel and put the heels of his hands on the bed rail across from Jack. "I thought I'd come see for myself what's happening here, maybe give you a little support." He swore softly. "I can see why you're scared. I hadn't realized it was this bad."

Jack was just edgy enough to lash out. "Did you think I was joking? Made it all up, just looking for an excuse to get out of work for a couple of weeks?"

David held up his hands. "Hey, this isn't my fault."

Wasn't it? If David hadn't pushed, the business wouldn't have grown as fast, Jack wouldn't have been sucked in and blinded, Rachel wouldn't have left him and moved to Big Sur and been hit by a car on the coast road.

But no. Too easy to shift blame. Jack could have stopped the treadmill at any time. He could have stepped off.

David pushed his hands into his pants pockets. It was

a sure sign of deliberate restraint. "Let's start over. Is she showing any improvement?"

Jack blew out a breath. "Nah. Not yet."

"How're the girls doing with this?"

"Hangin' in there."

In the silence that followed, Jack didn't look at his partner. He didn't want to talk business, but business was all they shared. Once, he had thought it might be different. But David had never had a family. He had divorced one wife after another. Even after Jack, too, was divorced, they didn't mesh on a personal level the way they had when they were back on the bottom rung.

David cleared his throat. "Listen, Jack, I don't mean to be the heavy . . . " He tore his eyes from Rachel and glanced back at the hall. "Uh, can we—can we talk out there? It doesn't seem right talking work in here."

"It's okay. It's good for Rachel to hear voices. Say what you want."

It was a minute before David did. His voice was subdued, but the words came fast. "You're right. This is a family emergency. It's tough. I'm sorry I didn't see that sooner"—he took a breath—"but the truth is, I'm worried. Something's going on here that I don't get."

Jack threaded his fingers through Rachel's. They looked bare. He wondered what she had done with her wedding ring.

"We had no business losing Boca," David said. "We can't afford things like that, any more than we can afford to take on the kind of house designing we did ten years ago. The word over lunch at Moose's is that we're passé. So rather than doing client development, I'm doing damage control. This isn't where I want to be at this point in my life."

"Me, neither," Jack said. Odd, given Rachel's condition, but only now was his middle starting to knot.

"So okay, we lost Boca. It was more trouble than it was worth. Okay, we lost associates. We can hire others. But on principle alone we can't do Hillsborough. It's too small, too minor. We need Montana, which is still up in the air but which is ours if you can get up there to argue the last design in person, and"—he grew expectant—"we need Atlantic City."

"What's in Atlantic City?"

"A new hotel," he said with barely banked glee. "Big gloss, big press, big bucks."

Jack didn't share his excitement. He wasn't even curious to know more. He didn't like the feel of that knot in his middle, didn't like the buzz that business talk put in his head.

And David went on, still gleeful, still dense. "I've been courting these guys for weeks. They've seen enough of your work to think that they might get something a little different from what the others would do. They want us out there, both of us. We're talking high-rise, Jack."

High-rise? He was talking a casino. A fuckin' casino.

Jack raised Rachel's arm, angled it slowly across her chest. This movement was personal, even intimate. So was Hope's painting of Guinevere, taped to the wall, and the single small braid that Samantha had made on one side of the mass of Rachel's waves. What David described was so far removed from any of this as to be otherworldly.

"Well?" David said, both hands out now, inviting response. "Come on. Did I do good, or did I do good?" He rubbed his hands together. "This could do it, Jack. It's a biggie, one step beyond Montana. No one'll be laughing at Moose's if we get this nailed down. It'll mean doing some significant hiring, but we can handle it. Would-be draftsmen are picking up their degrees as we speak. They're looking for jobs. The timing couldn't be better. Okay, it'll mean travel for you and me, but, hey, you can't—"

Jack's warning look stopped him short.

David dropped his hands. He stared at Jack over the bed for several long, silent minutes. When Jack made no attempt to either look away or soften, David sighed.

"I think," he said with deliberate care, "that we've come to a crossroads. There's this new deal on the table. It's the moment of truth. I have to know if you're in, or out."

In or out. In or out. In or out. An ultimatum?

David's eyes remained steady. "The harsh reality is this. Ideally, Rachel gets better, and you return to your own life. I want that, Jack. I want it like nothing else. But harsh reality says there's another side. There's the chance that Rachel *won't* get better, and you have to shift things around to accommodate the girls, but sooner or later you'll have to work, Jack." He was suddenly pleading. "We've known each other, what, fifteen years? Thirteen of those we've been partners, working hard for the same thing, and we're right there, right there, pal. We're on the verge of grabbin' that big brass ring we've been running so hard after. Don't blow it now, Jack. Don't lose sight of what matters. We're too close." His words hung in the air. Finally, he let out a breath and straightened.

Jack tore his eyes away and returned them to Rachel. He counted the breaths she hauled in and pushed out, indeed a harsh reality. No, he couldn't blame David for her physical condition. But the man stood for everything that had gone wrong between Rachel and him.

"Are you in?" David asked.

Was he? Did he want that big brass ring? Did he want to design that casino and keep running until the next big gold ring came into sight? Was there satisfaction in it? Or challenge? Or *fun?* Did he want the same thing for this firm now that David did?

The choice wasn't cut-and-dried. Building his own firm had been his goal for as long as he could remember. He had given it his heart and soul for years.

Don't lose sight of what matters, David had said. That was the clincher.

Jack raised his eyes and slowly shook his head. He was tired of evading David, tired of erasing messages, crumbling faxes, deleting E-mail, and feeling guilty about it. He was tired of doing projects he didn't like. He was tired of traveling. He was tired of the kind of tension that knotted his middle. "It's not working for me anymore. I want out."

David looked startled. "Out? Out of the *firm?*"

"Wasn't that what you asked?"

"Yeah, but I didn't expect you'd chuck it. This is your firm as much as it's mine."

"Actually," Jack said with a sigh, "it hasn't been that for a while. Isn't that what's been wrong between you and me? It's more yours than mine. I've been pulling back for a while."

David continued to look stunned. Jack couldn't remember when he had ever seen his partner that way. David's confidence had been a mainstay of the partnership. Jack was sorry to undermine it now, but if David

Sung was nothing else, he was a hustler. He would survive.

"Regardless of what happens with Rachel," Jack said, "I want to downsize. I want to represent people; you want to represent conglomerates. I want Hillsborough. You want Atlantic City. It's time we split."

"Just like *that?*"

Jack rubbed his forehead. His thoughts were fragmented, but they were all headed in one direction. "Not just like *that*. There were good years. And there are details. People to reassure. Tina, some of the others. Assets to split." *Still,* David was stunned. "Why are you surprised? You're here now. You *see.*" Loudly, rhythmically, Rachel breathed in, breathed out, breathed in, breathed out. "This is not a vacation. It's my *life.*"

Perplexed now, David asked, "Was it a choice, then? Me, or your marriage?"

"Christ, no." Jack pushed his hands through his hair. "It's been me all along. Me, biting off more than I wanted to chew. Me, learning the *hard* way that I'd bitten off more than I wanted to chew. I just want out, David. I'm tired."

David looked appalled. "Do you *know* what you're giving up?"

Jack actually laughed. "No. I'm too tired to give it much thought. All I know is I'm out."

"*Fuckin' A.*"

Jack was tired of that, too. It had been funny once. Not anymore.

Suddenly it seemed that David needed to recoup the emotional advantage he had lost. More sharply, he said, "She left you once. So now you're out of work. Does she need that?"

"Hey," Jack warned. "We did well together for too long to become enemies now. Let's just quit while we're ahead."

"Are you gonna open your own fuckin' firm, or what?" Jack's voice rose. "I don't *fuckin'* know."

David stared at him for the longest time, then turned on his heel. The last Jack saw of him he was shaking his head and picking up the pace of those shiny black shoes. Only when he was completely gone from sight did the enormity of what Jack had done hit him, and then he was as stunned as David had been. Stunned, but relieved. Relieved. Incredibly relieved. Though he hadn't planned it this way, another of those weights had been lifted. He was suddenly breathing easier.

Then it struck him that he wasn't the only one who was. He looked at Rachel, swallowed, listened. The noise was easing, it definitely was. Holding his breath that he wasn't imagining it, he rang for the nurse.

SAMANTHA was fine as long as she was with Lydia. Lydia was the charm that instantly put her back in good standing with Shelly and Brendan, which said something for how badly Samantha had underestimated Lydia's strength. Come second period, though, she was on her own, heading for American history with Pam.

She took her seat without looking around and focused on the teacher, which was fine, until the teacher began to drone. Her pen slowed and her mind wandered. She imagined that every other bored person in the room was staring at her back, and kept her eyes on the teacher and a confident mask on her face, all the while remembering how foreign she had felt at that party and how scared she'd been with Teague. She didn't look back, not even when she thought she heard the rustle of note passing behind her.

An eternity later, the bell rang. She closed her note-book, pushed her things together, and slid out from behind the desk. She had no sooner reached the hall than Pam fell into step beside her and said, "I don't care what the others say, I still think you're okay. So you couldn't handle Teague. I had a feeling he'd be a little much for you."

"A little much?" Samantha asked, feeling something but not sure what it was.

"Well, I mean, he's more than you're used to, isn't he? Like, he's totally cool. Is *Bar-rendan* totally cool?"

Annoyance. That was what Samantha felt. She had seen Pam drinking, dancing, laughing her head off over a half-naked dancer. Pam had seen her leave the party with Teague. Had she tried to stop them? "No, Brendan isn't—"

"See?" Pam cut in. "I *knew* you'd agree. So I forgive you. If you want to sit with us at lunch, we'll let you. By the way, is that natural curl? What, did you sleep too late to blow it out?" She was walking at an angle to look, bouncing on the balls of her feet. "I know *the* best stylist in the center. He'll get that straight."

"I don't want it straight," Samantha said. *More beau-tiful. More you.* It was something her mother would have said, too.

Pam made a face. "You like it *curly?*"

Samantha stopped walking. "Actually, I do."

Pam stopped, too. "It's very . . . Lydia."

Life is about making choices. "Thanks," Samantha said

with a pleased smile. "Hey, I have Spanish. I have to run."

Pam tossed her shiny black, stick-straight hair over a shoulder. "So, are you meeting us for lunch, or not?" she asked. "Because if you're not, that's it. I mean, forget it. I'm through sticking my neck out. If you want to be with Lydia, *be* with Lydia."

Samantha took a last good look at the most popular girl in the class. She moved closer, focused in. "Is that eye makeup? No, it's a blackhead, right there on the side of your nose. *Gar-rowsss*. Do you have a skin doctor? Like, I never needed it, but there's one I've heard *great* things about." She glanced at the clock. "Omigod. I'm late. See you around."

HOPE tried to concentrate, but she had that *feeling*. Something was happening; only, when she tried to decide whether it was something good or bad, she couldn't. Her head was too full of things that had to do with her mother and her father—whether her mother would wake up, whether they'd get back together, what would happen if they did, what would happen if they *didn't,* whether Rachel would *die* first—and Hope still missed Guinevere, still woke up mornings aching to hold her.

The class ended. She filed out with the others, but when they turned right, she turned left. She ducked into the bathroom and closed herself in a stall, but stayed only long enough for the bathroom to empty. Then she went out and walked down the hall like she had every reason to be headed for the door. *If you hold your chin up and act like you know what you're doing, people will think that you do,* Rachel always said. She had been talking about going to things like birthday parties, because Hope *knew* that everyone would be staring when she got there, unless she pretended that they were all just waiting for her to arrive because she was the best part of the group. At least, that's what Rachel said.

Hope held her chin up and pretended there was a note filed in the principal's office saying that her mother was waiting outside to take her to the dentist. She fingered her jaw as she went down the steps, frowned toward the curb where the parents usually waited, even looked off down the street. She checked her watch. Apparently her mother was late. She figured she'd walk down a little way to intercept her. That wasn't against the rules. She wasn't in elementary school anymore.

Off she went. She walked with confidence until she reached the corner, then turned it and ran until she came to a spot where she could catch a bus. No one else was waiting, which meant that either the bus had just come or there was no bus at all. It didn't run during the winter. She couldn't remember whether it started up again in April, or May.

For a long time, she stood there with her backpack on her back, thinking that she was wearing her lucky boots and that it was about time they did something. She shifted from one foot to the other. She sat down on the curb. She stood again and hopped from foot to foot like a runner waiting for a traffic light to change. Something was happening. She knew it was.

She shrugged out of the backpack and was scrounging around inside to see if she had enough money for a taxi when her boots delivered and the bus came down the road.

BAUER hurried in. So did Bates, Winston, and everyone else on the floor who had been involved with Rachel's care. The monitor showed improved oxygenation; the gasping was softer; and while her lips weren't the soft pink that Jack loved, they were definitely less blue.

There were high fives all around. Rachel might still be comatose, but everything in medicine was relative.

Long after they were gone, Jack was still grinning, breathing one loud, relieved sigh after another against Rachel's hand. Then, because he needed to hug her and it had been too long, he slid his arms under, carefully drew her up, and fitted her upper body to his. She felt thin and limp; his memory fleshed her out and gave her shape. She smelled hospital white; his own hands supplied threads of paint thinner; his imagination supplied lilies. He closed his eyes on unwanted tears and gave several more immense sighs.

He didn't know how long he held her. There was no rush, no rush at all. When he opened his eyes, Katherine was smiling.

Very gently, he settled Rachel into the pillows. He could have sworn her lips were more pink than they had been when he had picked her up, and guessed that it was from holding her, perhaps from nearness or the change of position. In any case, it was a gratifying sight.

"Steve called and told me the news," Katherine said. "He was nearly as excited as I was." She came to the bed. "This is a good sign. A good sign."

Jack thought so, too. As far as the doctors were concerned, the medicine had finally kicked in. As far as Jack was concerned, Rachel had been listening in on his conversation with David and had reacted with a show of support. He was grinning again, grinning still. He felt so tired, so good, so *shocked*. "Katherine, I just deep-sixed my job."

"You what?"

He told her about David's visit. "We'll be dissolving the firm."

"Wow," she said, then, "Good for you. You'd outgrown it. Besides, you have a name. You can work on your own, whenever, wherever."

"Yeah, well, I want to work out of Big Sur, but that's Rachel's turf. For all I know, she wants no part of me."

"Is that what you think?"

"I don't *know* what to think, since she isn't talking. You're her best friend. You've heard her side. Do you think she'd consider giving it another try?"

Katherine held up her hands. "Not my place to say."

"You know her. Give me a hint."

Cautious, she said, "A try, as in living together? Remarrying?"

"Remarrying," Jack said, since it was a day of shockers. He felt a twisting inside when Katherine looked troubled. "Come on. Say it. I'm a big boy."

"It's not that. It's this. One crisis is over, but the other goes on. You want her back based on memories of how it was during the best of times. But what if it isn't ever like that again? What if she wakes up and can't walk or talk?"

"We've been through this before."

"What if there's permanent brain damage, so that she can't think the way she used to? What if she can't understand what it takes to paint? Or to cook a meal, or drive a car, or bathe?"

"Why are you obsessed with this?"

"Because it's part of what it means to love Rachel."

"But why are you *pessimistic?*"

"I'm *not*," she cried, then composed herself and said a quieter "I'm not, but I could be. I could assume that next month or next year I'll find that they didn't get it all and my cancer has spread. For a year or two after my diagnosis, I panicked every time I felt a pain. Then I decided that hope was a better way to go. I choose to believe that I'll live to grow old. But there are no guarantees. If I become involved with someone, he has to know that."

Ahhh. Jack understood. She was asking him what she would have to ask Steve Bauer. Jack could argue that Rachel's situation was more traumatic. If Katherine woke up one day with a recurrence of cancer, there would be treatment and remission and, still, the possibility of some good time. If Rachel woke up mentally diminished, there would be nothing.

No. That was wrong. There would be something. But it would be different.

He guessed that was what Duncan had experienced with Faith. Life after the accident was different. Duncan changed jobs. He learned to do things around the house. He gave up much of what was social in their lives, all because he loved Faith.

If that old, leathery clod of a mountain man could do it, Jack certainly could.

One thing was for sure. If Rachel woke up disabled, he didn't trust that anyone else could take care of her the way he would.

He said a quiet "You didn't answer my question. Do I have a chance? Is the feeling there? Or gone?"

Katherine looked past him at something and brightened, then frowned almost as quickly.

Jack turned to find Hope at the door. Her hair was a mess of blond waves. She was breathless and sweaty. Wide eyes were on Rachel.

He started toward her, but she ran past to the bed. "I *knew* it!" she cried, breaking into an excited smile. "I *knew* something was happening, only I didn't know which way it would go." She hugged Jack, jumping up and down, then gave Rachel a big, smiling, smacking kiss on the cheek. When she straightened, she breathed out a satisfied sigh and looked triumphantly from Jack to Katherine and back.

Jack felt as though he ought to scold her, but he couldn't figure out what for. It was Katherine who finally cleared her throat and said, "Uh, Jack, maybe you should call the school before they call the cops, and tell them she's with you?"

KATHERINE had to return to work, Jack had to call his lawyer, and Hope had to put several more braids in Rachel's hair. By the time she announced she was hungry, Jack was starved. He took her to lunch in downtown Monterey and returned to the hospital in time to open more gifts from Victoria—cotton nightgowns, perfume and powder, and no less than a dozen CDs, all symphonies. They had moved Rachel back to a regular room, where Jack promptly fell asleep with his head on the bed near her hand. When he woke up, it was time to get Samantha. He talked with his lawyer again while the girls were busy with Rachel, then he told Rachel about dissolving the firm. He drove the girls back to Big Sur, cooked dinner, and went to the studio.

Samantha worked with him for a while before heading off to make calls. Jack was relieved enough that she was back to normal to let her go. Hope continued to work by his side until he finally sent her to bed. They had framed another six pictures that night. Twelve were done in all. They couldn't do much more until Jack finished painting.

He chose a canvas depicting a great egret spreading its wings for takeoff. His task was to fill in the murky dusk of the Florida Everglades against which the white bird was poised. He had barely taken up palette and brush when Hope returned. She wore a T-shirt that reached her knees and nothing on her legs and feet.

"Everything okay?" he asked.

She nodded. Her hands were linked behind her. She looked like she just wanted to hang around. So Jack started talking about the canvas. He told her why he mixed certain colors and showed her the effect of different brushes.

She watched what he did, nodded, said the kind of distracted "Uh-huh" that suggested her mind wasn't on it. After a few minutes she began wandering around the studio. He watched her make one leisurely turn, then another. Each time, she stopped at the desk backed against the wall.

"Hope?"

She shot him a smile that was a little too bright, shrugged, and moved on. But she was back in the same spot three minutes later.

He set down his things and went to the desk. His laptop was there, closed. Several shop drawings lay under it, but they wouldn't interest her. They didn't interest *him.* He had only planned to study them later as a concession to his lawyer, who suggested that he complete as much of the firm's work as he could until a dissolution agreement was signed.

"What's going on in that pretty head of yours?" he asked.

She spoke quickly, barely opening her mouth. "There's other stuff here. I'm not supposed to know."

"What stuff?"

"Sketches."

"Where?"

She made an offhand gesture toward the desk. "Behind."

From where Jack stood, he saw nothing. Only when he leaned over to where the desk hit the wall did he see the edge of something wedged behind. Dragging the desk forward, he removed a slim portfolio. He set it down with care, remembering the last time he had opened a surprise portfolio. Then he had learned about a child he had lost.

With some trepidation, he opened this one—and was suddenly back in life drawing class, sitting with Rachel, drawing nudes. She had used charcoal on thick ivory rag. The view was a rear one—hips, torso, shoulders, head. Without a face it might have been anonymous. But that was his shape, his hair, his scar at the back of the elbow, all drawn with such feeling that the sorrow of things lost rushed through him.

He paused. The scar was from a runaway piece of scaffolding. It was six months old. Rachel had seen it and commented on it once when he had come for the girls.

Wishing that she was right there right then, he turned from one sheet to the next to the next. Some had been done with charcoal, others with watercolor. Some had features as distinct as his profile, others were as faceless as the first. But her voice spoke, answering his question in each and every one.

Is the feeling there? Or gone? Katherine hadn't answered because Hope arrived. Hope must have heard.

She had given him a gift, but by the time he turned to thank her, she had gone.

chapter twenty-one

JACK SHOULD HAVE been used to being woken by the phone, but he jumped as high as ever when it rang Tuesday morning at dawn.

He reached it on the first grab. "Yes?"

"Mr. McGill?" The voice was authoritative. "This is Janice Pierce. I'm one of the residents—"

"What happened?" he cut in, sitting up.

"Rachel is starting to move."

He was utterly still for a second. Then he dared breathe, but barely. "She's waking up?"

"Not exactly. She's moving her fingers and toes."

"Moving them how?"

"Wiggling. It's spontaneous. Not in response to commands. We call it 'lightening,' as in limbs that have been dead weight becoming lighter. Typically, it starts from the outside and moves in. It definitely boosts her GCS score."

"Which means?"

"She may be starting to wake up."

"May be," he repeated, wanting to hope, but Rachel

had moved before. He had seen her blink, flinch, whatever.

"It doesn't always lead to full awakening," she said. "This could be as good as it gets. But it's more than we've had so far. We thought you'd want to know."

THE GIRLS had heard the phone and were beside him even before he hung up. He told them what Janice had said. Within five minutes, they were dressed and in the car.

The air outside was moist. Fog floated in pale gray bands through the woods and over the narrow road. Sitting higher in the new car than he had in the old, Jack should have been able to see more, but anything too distant was a blur.

As he turned onto the highway and picked up speed, he struggled not to get carried away. He had read enough to know that comatose responses were unreliable. The movement might end before they reached the hospital, having been nothing more than the last little spasms in limbs that would never move again. Or this kind of movement could go on forever, never spreading beyond fingers and toes.

Still, his hopes edged up along with the sun behind the fog.

WHEN THEY arrived, Rachel was propped on her left side. There was no sign of movement. Pillows held her in place. She lay as still as ever.

Fearful, Jack eased lank blond hair back from a face

that was growing thinner by the day. "Hi, Rachel. Hi, angel. They told us you're moving. Can we see?"

"Hi, Mommy." Hope crowded in beside him. "It's me. We didn't even have breakfast; we just came here first."

"*Move,* Mom," ordered Samantha.

"She won't move if you tell her like that."

"Come on, Rachel," Jack coaxed. "Sun's coming up. It's gonna be a nice one. *That's* poetic, don't you think?"

"*There,*" Samantha cried, pointing at the sheet. "Her foot."

Jack moved the sheet away. When there was nothing, he tickled her sole.

Hope said a worried "That *always* makes her laugh."

"How can she not feel it?" Samantha asked.

"She's still comatose," Kara said as she joined them. "The movement isn't conscious. It usually comes in waves, brief periods of activity alternating with periods of rest."

"Ah!" Jack cried, victorious. "Her ankle jerked!"

"I saw it!"

"Me, too!"

Energized, he straightened. "What do we do now?" he asked the power-pearl lady. "How do we get her to do more?"

"Keep doing what you've been doing. Something's working."

KATHERINE was coming out of the shower when the phone rang. The mirror was covered with steam, but she wrapped herself in a bath sheet before she passed.

"She's starting to move," Jack said without preamble

and went on to describe what he'd seen. "It could be nothing or the proverbial last gasp, but I don't want to let anything go that might help. I thought I'd call her friends and get them in here. Bombard her with stimulation. Can you give me numbers?"

Katherine's first instinct was to make the calls herself. Then she took a slow, understanding breath and went for her address book.

Five minutes later, she returned to the bathroom. The mirror was clearing from the bottom up. She loosened her towel, figuring that this would be easy as pie with her face obscured. She could be more objective that way, less emotional. Rachel was moving right along. She should, too.

But . . . not yet. Opening the medicine chest wide so that the mirror faced the wall, she quickly slathered her body with cream and put on a bra and a blouse. Covered up, she relaxed. She reached for panty hose and let excitement about Rachel erase every negative thought.

JACK called the numbers Katherine gave him, plus others he found in the phone book. He called Faith Bligh. He called Victoria, then remembered a message that she had left for him. She was in either Chicago or Detroit, he couldn't remember which. He settled for leaving a message on her machine in New York.

When Cindy came to bathe Rachel, he drove the girls to school. Then he turned around and drove back to Big Sur. Having lined up successive visits by Dinah, Charlie, and the bridge player, Bev, he knew that Rachel would have stimulation until he returned. Between now and then, he had something urgent to do.

The sun was making short shrift of the fog, unveiling a day as full of color as any Jack had seen. The farmland flanking the road just south of Carmel was green with lettuce and artichoke; the hills beyond were wild mustard yellow. Granite outcroppings on the shore side of the road were a richer gray, almost slate under an emerging blue sky. Beyond rock, the ocean was kelp-green, then aqua descending into a deep, dark charcoal blue. The sky was endless and new.

Turning off the highway at Rachel's road, he felt the glow of familiarity. Oak, sycamore, redwood, even scrub chaparral—all substantial, all thriving. He climbed from the car that was really a truck and stretched, smiled, filled his lungs with air so clear that his body tingled. Inside, the phone began to ring. Hopeful, terrified, he rushed to get it. "Mr. McGill?"

"Yes." He didn't recognize the voice, but the hospital had dozens of doctors.

"My name is Myron Elliott. I'm a developer. I want to talk business."

Jack felt an instant letdown. "What business?"

"I heard about your break with David Sung. I wanted to approach you before others do. My company specializes in building resorts. We like the designs you did in Montana. If you're wondering how we saw those, the answer is a spy, but I won't dwell on that, because I understand that your time is short. We talked with David a month ago, but the price he quoted was, well, ridiculous. I was hoping you'd be more flexible."

Totally aside from the fact that Jack didn't want to be thinking business, he was mildly put off. "Why would I be?"

"You may be joining another firm or going solo, but

in either case, you need to establish your name quickly. We're not as big as the group doing Montana, but we're getting there. We won't overpay, but we'll pay. We'll also offer you more than one project. That would take a load off your mind, wouldn't it?"

It certainly would, if assuring a steady income was his major concern. It was definitely a concern. But major? "Uh, look, I'm not sure I can think about this right now. I'm in the middle of a family emergency. If you give me your number, I'll get back to you." He wrote down the number on the flap of an envelope on the counter.

"We'd like to move ahead on this immediately," the man said. "When will I hear from you?"

Jack pressed thumb and forefinger to his brow. "Today's Tuesday. Give me a week?"

"Can you make it sooner? I need to know if we're in the ballpark. If we are, we'll hold off on seeking other bids until we see something from you."

Jack felt a gnawing in his stomach. The man was right. He needed work. A group that promised more than one job would give him instant security. But a resort? "Friday. I'll call you Friday."

"Good. Great. Talk with you then."

Jack hung up feeling uncomfortable. He didn't want to be thinking about this now. But at some point he had to. According to his lawyer, David was claiming, as his, every prospective client that hadn't yet been signed. Jack could take him to court. Those clients had been developed on Sung and McGill time. They should be split half-and-half.

Did Jack have the stomach for a court case? No. Did Jack *want* those clients? No. He wanted a smaller, more humane practice. That was all.

Tearing off the phone number, he stuffed it in his pocket and went to work. He moved in and out of the house like a man possessed, carrying framed canvas after framed canvas to the car that was, *thankfully,* a truck. When twelve were carefully stacked around foam buffers, he closed the hatch and drove right back to Carmel and P. Emmet's.

Ben was waiting. They quickly carried the pieces inside and stood them against a wall not far from the three paintings already there. Ben's excitement was obvious. He hadn't expected there would be so many new ones. What kept Jack waiting nervously were the man's thoughts about what he saw.

Ben moved in, hunkered down before one, moved on to the next, moved back.

When Jack couldn't bear the suspense, he said, "Well? What do you think?"

"I think she's brilliant," Ben said. "She captured everything I wanted her to. These have the same feeling as the bobcat pups. She listened, she heard, she did." He darted Jack a glance. "Nice job with the frames."

Feeling validated and exuberant, Jack grinned. "Thanks."

WHEN KATHERINE got a midmorning cancellation, she had her receptionist move the two appointments following it to the afternoon, and headed for the hospital.

Cindy was with Rachel, slow-talking as she exercised her limbs. Katherine stood silently, watching in vain for movement. But Cindy was smiling. "Watch." She took a pen from her pocket and pressed it against Rachel's thumbnail. She pressed harder. Rachel pulled her thumb away.

Katherine's heart raced. "Do it again," she said. The movement had been so small, she wanted to make sure it was real.

Cindy pressed with the pen, and there it was, a tiny recoil.

Katherine clapped her hands together, put them to her mouth, and beamed. She was enough of a realist to know they had a long way to go. Reponse to pain was bottom-line basic, but it was a step beyond the random move-ment begun earlier that morning, far and away the best thing they had seen in two whole weeks.

JACK was at the hospital by noon, staking out a bedside spot. By two he regretted making so many calls. Rachel had a steady stream of visitors, but he wanted to be alone with her. When he imagined her opening her eyes, he wanted to be the first thing she saw. Wanted to be the *only* thing she saw. Wanted her to know that he had been there more than anyone else.

It was juvenile. But he was getting nervous. Charcoal sketches might suggest she still loved him; same with framed pictures stashed in a drawer. But the fact remained that she had chosen to leave him. He under-stood now why she had. It was his job to show her that things had changed.

So he sat beside her and talked with the friends who came. He kept track of her movements, looking for the little more that suggested she was coming further out of the coma. She continued to do small things with fingers and toes, occasionally twitching an ankle, elbow, or knee, but there wasn't anything new until that evening. He was helping the night nurse turn her when she moaned. When they repeated the motion, she repeated the moan. Then she settled into silence.

They were small sounds, but his heart soared. He called the girls, who were back in Big Sur after dinner with Katherine. He called Katherine, who had returned to Carmel. He kissed Rachel's pale cheek and told her that she was wonderful, that she was strong, that she could do it, and he waited.

The expectancy was so strong and his adrenaline flowing so fast that he didn't think he would feel tired. But nights on end of moonlighting in Rachel's studio and catching precious few hours of sleep took its toll. He was dead asleep in his chair by the bed when the night nurse came to turn Rachel again.

There was no moan this time. Nor was there motion. Jack would have been discouraged if the nurse hadn't been able to evoke the thumbnail response. It was still there, that recoil.

"Go home," she urged. "We'll call if there's any change. Once she wakes up, she'll need you even more. You should be rested for that."

Jack wasn't so sure about the needing-him-even-more part, but he liked the way it sounded, and the girls were alone. He drove home.

HE FELL into bed at eleven and slept straight until Hope shook his shoulder. His eyelids were heavy. With an effort, he raised one.

"We're taking the bus," she whispered.

He came awake fast then, startled to see that it was light, and late. "No, I'll get ready," he said, pushing himself up, but his head was nearly as heavy as his eyes.

"Sleep longer," Samantha said from the door. "I called the hospital. She's doing the same stuff, but she isn't awake. They promised they'd call when she is."

Jack wanted to get up anyway, but he made the mistake of putting his head down for one last minute after the girls left. He was asleep in seconds.

He slept for another three hours. When he woke up, he called the hospital. Rachel hadn't come any further, but she hadn't regressed. They were pleased.

Jack tried to be pleased, too, but he kept thinking about the possibility that she would be stuck at that point for the rest of her life. He meant what he'd told Katherine. He would take care of her. He would set her up in the canyon she loved and care for her much as Duncan cared for Faith, but, Lord, he didn't want it to come to that. He wanted Rachel with him, in every sense of the word.

Sipping hot coffee, he stood in his boxers at the wall of windows overlooking the forest. It was another beautiful day. The fog had burned off, leaving the earth beneath the redwoods a rich mahogany broken by patches of deep sorrel green. Higher up, where the boughs hung, the needles were a lighter green. Pretty. Peaceful.

He turned around. Same with the house. Pretty. Peaceful. The floors were of natural wood, the sofa was red-and-maroon plaid. The church bench was green, with lilac flowers on fat cushions. The planters that flanked the bench were a deep purple with orange splashes, and brimming with chaotically leggy plants.

Pretty? Peaceful? But the house *was*. It was fun and

full of life, very much the irreverent Rachel he had met so long ago. If the customary brush to use on a subject was a number five filbert bristle, she would use a number five bristle round just to see what she could do. In some cases she ended up with the filbert after all; in others she ended up with something wonderfully unique. That was the Rachel he felt in this house. It was the Rachel he had married.

With that thought, he set off for the bedroom. He searched the dresser and the night table, searched the closet and the bathroom. He searched the kitchen cabinets that he didn't regularly use. He searched the storage pantry. He stood in the living room with his hands on his hips and wondered where she would have put it.

If she had kept it.

She might not have.

He went to the studio and stood, again, with his hands on his hips. He had been working here. He knew what was where. He had explored. But she had hidden pictures of a baby that had died. She had hidden charcoal sketches. Granted, Hope knew about this latter.

On a hunch, he strode back through the house to Hope's room. Everything here was sweet. What better spot for a ceramic angel—and there it was on the dresser, a fat little postmodern cherub with wings, keeping watch over a crystal cut box filled with trinkets, a tiny ceramic cat that may or may not have resembled Guinevere, a comb and brush, a smattering of scrunchies, and a pile of acorns.

If Rachel had wanted something cherished, she couldn't have chosen a better guardian than Hope.

He picked up the angel, turned it over, and slipped two small latches hidden under the wings. He lifted off a back panel, pulled out a velvet bag, and emptied its contents in his hand. There were the pearl earrings Rachel had worn at their wedding, given to her the night before by her father, who had died two months later. There was a National Honor Society key. There was a watch with Minnie Mouse on the face. And the ring.

It wasn't the big flashy ring. He suspected that was in a safety deposit box along with numerous lavish pieces of jewelry given her by Victoria over the years. The ring in his hand was simple and gold. It was the only one that mattered.

JACK was heading for the car, bent on getting that ring on Rachel's finger, when Duncan Bligh came striding down the hill, bellowing, "Saw your truck on my way up from the lower pasture, figured you hadn't left." He stomped to a halt. "My wife wants to see Rachel. I thought I'd drive her up after work. Any problem with that?"

"Uh, no. None." When Jack got his bearings, he was touched. He knew that Faith didn't get out often. "Rachel would really like it. I mean, she's not awake yet, but it could help."

With a single nod, the older man turned to leave.

"Wait," Jack said on impulse and waved an arm back. "I'm heading there now. Since I have the truck, I could put the chair in the back. Show me what to do, and I'll get her in and out."

Duncan's expression was unfathomable. "She doesn't go far without me."

"It means she'd be able to spend longer with Rachel."
Duncan looked up toward his cabin. "I suppose."

After another minute, he started climbing. "Get the truck."

JACK had selfish reasons for wanting Faith in his car. He envisioned forty-five minutes of conversation that would naturally turn on Rachel. There were gaps in his knowledge of her early years in Big Sur. If anyone could fill them in, it was Faith.

And the conversation was easy. Faith was chatty, sitting in her long flowered dress that hid pencil-thin, useless legs. What she chatted about, though, was Big Sur. She talked about the early cattle ranchers and those who traded sea otter pelts. She told of lime smelting and smuggling, of arduously long trips from Monterey by stagecoach. She gave a blow-by-blow of the building of the highway and had something to say about each bridge they passed.

"Tourism has been a mainstay in these parts since the turn of the century," she said, "but tourists rarely understand what living here means. It's an isolated life, and we like it that way. We keep our private roads unpaved and our lives simple. There's little privately owned land, and even less chance for development. Electricity is a recent thing in some canyons. We all lose it regularly during storms. We have no fast-food chains, no banks, no supermarkets." Daylight flashed off her spectacles. "It's a quiet life. We socialize among ourselves from time to time, but people who decide to live here are usually self-sufficient sorts. Artists, yes. Writers. Ranchers, like us. Retirees. People who work at the resorts. Free spirits. Have you walked the beach?" she asked and went on to tell of solstice celebrations, whale sightings, and riptides.

Jack listened to every word, hooked not only by what she said but by the lyrical way she said it. It wasn't until they reached the hospital that he realized he had been warned.

JACK and Rachel were divorced. The hospital personnel knew it. Rachel's friends knew it. Faith Bligh knew it.

So Jack felt a little awkward about the wedding ring. Technically, he had no right putting it on her hand. But he wanted it there. He wanted to think it might help. He wanted her to see it when she woke up.

He thought he did it brilliantly. After parking Faith on Rachel's right side, he went immediately to her left side. He took her hand while he kissed her cheek, then straightened. Holding her hand close to his chest, he worked her fingers through a round of exercises. Slipping the ring on was part of the motion. No matter that it was looser than it had ever been. It was on.

Faith saw it instantly. The eyes behind those small, round glasses flew there—stricken eyes, because she was grappling with seeing Rachel this way. Seconds later, still stricken, she looked back at Rachel's face.

Jack sighed. "Well, hell, I'm trying everything. There's part of me that says if she doesn't want the ring there, she'll open her eyes and tell me so."

"She used to wear it sometimes," Faith said. Her eyes searched Rachel's face. He imagined she was looking for permission to speak.

"At the beginning?" he asked.

"Every year. On the Fourth of July."

Independence Day. Their wedding anniversary. *"Why?"*

"She said there were good things to remember, but it wasn't easy. She always breathed a sigh of relief when that day was done. I kept telling her to put it behind her. If I spent my days thinking about all I could do if my legs worked, I'd be a sour woman. Rachel, bless her, never turned sour. She learned to live with those memories."

"Did you know about the baby?"

Faith tugged a shawl close on her shoulders. "She told me."

"She should have told *me*."

Faith thought about that. Her creased face was gentle with its little white cap. There was no accusation when she spoke, only resignation. "She said she was also pregnant on your wedding day, and that she wouldn't use that hook again to make you feel guilty or get you back."

He was startled. "We didn't marry because she was pregnant." He pushed his hands into his hair and laughed. "God, that's funny. Victoria had that monstrosity of a wedding planned long before we knew about Sam. I was locked into the marriage by *that*, not by any baby. Victoria didn't care that Rachel was pregnant. It didn't show. No one knew. But if I'd decided I'd had it with that pomp and circumstance, Victoria would have had the shotgun out fast. No, I wanted that baby. Rachel and I both did. Why in the devil would she think I was forced?"

Faith's brow furrowed. "Have you ever had a disagreement with someone? Hung up the phone and walked away and started thinking about the disagreement? Made assumptions and generalizations about the person, and built them up, built them up until they took on the reality of your anger or hurt? Then you saw the person again, and it was suddenly forgotten, just a petty disagreement that carried none of the weight you gave it?" She smiled that warm, sad smile. "Emotions can be potent. They shade things in ways that may have nothing to do with reality. Rachel was feeling the loss of that child. She was upset. She was hurt that you hadn't wanted to come home from your trip even without knowing she was pregnant. It confirmed what she had been fearing for months, that you didn't care. She thought using the pregnancy to manipulate you was the oldest, lowest trick in the book."

That did sound like Rachel. She was principled. Sad here, but true. She should have told him. But he should have come home even without knowing. He should have let her know how much she meant to him, but he had stopped doing that. He had shut down. The trip to Toronto was only the last in a growing case for emotional neglect. He was guilty, and now six years had been lost.

He ran the pad of his thumb over the scrapes that were nearly healed. Her freckles were ready and waiting, as were her lips, her ears, her hair. Her broken leg still needed time in its cast, but her hands could paint.

Where are you, Rachel?

As though in answer to the question, she moved her eyes.

chapter twenty-two

JACK LEANED CLOSER. "Rachel?" Her eyeballs were moving behind their lids. "Rachel?" She could have been dreaming. "Rachel, wake up! Come on, honey. I know you hear me. Open those eyes. *Open* those eyes."

The movement continued for a minute, then stopped. He waited. Nothing.

He grabbed her shoulders, finding them so thin and frail that he held gently, but he held. "Don't go back to sleep, Rachel. *Please* don't. It's time to *wake up!*" But she was doing it again, using the round bristle brush because someone told her to use the bristle filbert. "Okay." He removed his hands and straightened. "You want to sleep, sleep. It's your choice. Me, I'd like to talk with the people who've been so kind as to come here. I'd also like to wake up in time for a showing at P. Emmet's. I wouldn't want to work so long and hard to build a career to the point of being invited by a gallery like that, only to *sleep* through the whole damn thing!"

He crossed his arms and stood back, frustrated enough to be angry. "She's doing this deliberately," he told Faith. "It's a control thing. She's getting back at me for years when she thought I was controlling her, but it's *her* fault for not speaking up. She never talked about control. What did she say? *I don't like San Francisco. I don't want to live in San Francisco. I don't want to be alone in San Francisco.* So what did she do? She left *me* alone there. Gave me a taste of my own medicine. Well, I learned. Isn't that enough?"

Faith simply smiled her sweet, sad smile.

RACHEL didn't move her eyes again, but by the time Jack brought the girls, her lids were ajar. Not much. Just enough to see a tiny rim of white. Just enough to spark the fear that she might open her eyes and spend the rest of her life staring at nothingness. The doctors couldn't get a pupil dilation, but they called this progress. Jack called it torment. He was frantic with impatience.

"That looks totally gross, Mom," Samantha said. "You always tell me to do things well or not at all. Eyelids like that aren't doing it well."

Hope was ducking down, trying to look under those lids and see something that might see her. She had barely straightened when she saw the wedding band. Her eyes flew to Jack. He was wondering whether she thought he had searched her room and would be angry, when she said, "Where did you find this? Did she send it to you? I always wondered where it was."

"She kept it," Jack said. Unsure, he looked from Hope to Samantha and back. "I thought it might help. Anyone have a problem with this?"

❧ ❧ ❧

NO ONE did. The girls were as restless as he was as the hours passed, and as reluctant to leave Rachel. Ben stopped by. Jan stopped by. Steve and Kara came in and prodded and tested and talked. Nellie stopped by. Charlie stopped by. Cindy turned Rachel, who moaned, then settled back into place with those same barely open eyes. Duncan picked up Faith. Steve came again. Katherine brought in McDonald's for dinner. They waved fries under Rachel's nose.

By nine, Jack and the girls were the only ones left. Hope was pale and yawning, Samantha's mood was sour, Jack was beat.

Still, they waited. They took turns talking to Rachel, saying the same things over and over again, badgering her, begging her, half expecting her to open her eyes if for no other reason than to shut them up.

By ten, they were ready to leave. They drove home in silence. Halfway there, it started to rain. Jack turned off the highway at the bank of mailboxes, downshifted, and felt an odd power climbing into the canyon. He pulled in at the house. They climbed out and stood in the rain.

"I'm taking a walk," he said, suddenly needing action. Walking in the rain at night was something Rachel would do. "Anyone coming?"

"Me."

"Me."

The only thing they did before leaving was to check the answering machine. There were messages for Samantha from Lydia, Shelly, and Brendan. There were messages for Jack from his lawyer and the potential Hillsborough client. Victoria had called from Detroit, ecstatic to hear the news and promising another call. There was no message from the hospital.

Taking raincoats, Jack's cell phone, and the large flashlights that Rachel kept on hand for the outages that Faith had said were frequent in winter, they pulled up their hoods and set off. In open meadow, the rain would have been harder, but the trees gentled the drops. Their pit-pat was a steady whisper. The air was cool and smelled of damp earth and wood.

Hope led the way to the spot where Guinevere was buried. After several minutes there, they moved on with Samantha in the lead, but she turned back and halted the others before they had gone far.

"I'll take you to my place, but it is mine. You can't come here again. Wait. Close your eyes. I'll lead you."

"Nuh-uh," Jack said. "I'm not walking with my eyes closed. If you want to share, you share. Come on, Sam. It's too dark to see a hell of a lot. I wouldn't recognize anything in daylight."

"Hope would."

"No, I won't," Hope promised. "I *swear.*"

Short of shining a light in her face, Jack couldn't see Samantha's expression. But she turned and began walking again. Less than five minutes later, over a course so circuitous that Jack was as lost as he was sure Samantha intended, they arrived at her place. It was another red-wood grove, this one with wide trunks that spread and hollowed and straddled uneven ground.

Samantha escaped from the rain into one. Hope slipped into another close by. Jack took shelter in the largest, to the right of the others, in easy view. He skimmed his light at each, saw small bits of color from their slickers, and turned off his light.

The night was thick and black. There was no moon, no fog, just a dense forest under a high, dense cover of clouds. The steady pit-pat of rain was the only real sound. The laughter beside him was pure fantasy, as was Rachel snuggling close. He heard, he felt, he craved.

He settled back, praying that nothing live was behind him, then nearly died when, after a quick scurrying sound, something hit his side.

He twisted away. "Jesus Christ!"

"It's *me*," Hope whispered. "Shhh. I don't want her to know I'm here. She'll think I'm a wimp. But yours is *better* than mine."

Jack laughed. "Damn it, Hope, you just took ten years off my life." But he had an arm around her and was holding her close. When another scurrying sound came, they both yelled.

"What is *wrong* with you people?" Samantha cried, crowding in. "I mean, like, who do you think is out here? *Jason?* Pu-leeze."

Jack was laughing again. He pictured the three of them filling a single redwood trunk, a jumble of arms, legs, and bodies not very different from the jumble on the hill in the photograph that lay facedown in Rachel's drawer, and he was suddenly light-headed. Oh yeah, exhaustion did that, but there was more to it. Crammed in a pitch black hole with his daughters, with more than a few clods of mud and the smell of wet wood and raincoats, he had recaptured something he had thought forever lost.

It was one heartrending thought. Another was that Rachel knew the three of them were there.

She couldn't, of course, unless she was dead and watching from above, but he refused, absolutely refused, to buy into that. No. She was still in a coma, and even if the phone in his pocket rang to say she had woken up, she couldn't possibly know where they were. He was fantasizing again. But boy, was the feeling real.

IT STAYED real. Rachel was with them when they traipsed back through the woods to the house and shook themselves off. She took a shower with Jack, put on a robe that matched his, helped him make hot chocolate for the girls. She took her turn kissing them good night and followed him into the bedroom.

He shook off the fantasy when he climbed into bed, but it returned in a flash. He sat up and stared into the dark. He thought about how tired he was. He looked at his watch.

It was twelve-thirty. He had a sudden urge to drive back to the hospital.

He called there instead and was told that Rachel hadn't woken.

He lay down again and slept for two hours. He called the hospital, lay down again, slept for three hours this time. He called the hospital. He lay down. He got up and opened the window. The rain continued, peaceful and clean, restorative. And he felt it, felt Rachel.

When he turned away from the window, Hope was at the door. She didn't say anything, just hung on the knob and looked at him.

"Are you sensing things?" he asked.

She nodded.

"Me, too." He ran his hands through his hair. So maybe they were both going mad, wanting something so much that it became real in their minds. The only thing he knew for sure was that he wouldn't be able to fall back to sleep. "Wanna take a drive?"

HOPE was belted sideways into the backseat. Samantha was in front, with an elbow against the door and a fist to her chin. Her eyes were closed. Jack kept both hands on the wheel and an even foot on the gas.

The rain had slowed to a drizzle. It was nearly thirty minutes past sunrise on a gray day. Traffic was light. No one spoke.

Jack pulled into what they had come to think of as their normal place in the parking lot, then backed out and picked another spot. The old one hadn't worked. This one might. He looked at the girls, daring them to ask. Neither did.

As they left the car and entered the hospital, he tried to stay calm, but he didn't have the patience to wait for the elevator. He found the stairs and took them two at a time, while the girls trotted close behind. They swung onto Rachel's floor, strode quickly down the hall, and turned into her room—and so help him, despite all cautionary thoughts, he expected to see Rachel propped higher, with her eyes open and alert, and a smile in the works.

He stopped just inside the room. Samantha was on his left, Hope on his right. Rachel was on her back, her eyes that same little bit open that they had been the night before.

"Mom?" Hope called.

Samantha wailed a soft "No change!"

Jack swallowed. His body drained of energy and felt like rubber. Disappointment lay thick in his throat.

He approached the bed. Sitting by Rachel's hip, he put an arm on either side of her and gave her the lightest, softest kiss on the mouth.

"What *happened,* Daddy?" Hope asked.

"I don't know, honey. I guess we got ourselves wound up with wanting."

"This is getting old," Samantha complained.

He let out a breath, then spoke with angry force. "You're toying with us, Rachel. That is not fair. It is not *nice.*" He pushed off from the bed and went to the window, but seconds later he was back at the bed, arms straddling Rachel again.

This time he stared. He looked at her long and hard, willing her to open those barely open eyes. Her lips were pink, her freckles mauve, her hair gold. The rest of her was paler than pale, and thin.

He continued to stare. Something was going on in there. Her eyes were darting around. He saw a pinch between her brows at the very same spot where the worry line was on his own face. It happened a second time, a tiny frown.

He poured himself into it this time, digging deep, cursing her for punishing them with this unbearable waiting game, willing her finally, finally, finally awake. He heard one of the girls call, but he didn't respond. Everything he had was focused on Rachel.

Another frown came. Her eyes began moving more slowly. He caught his breath when she did. Again one of the girls spoke. Again he ignored it.

Come on, Rachel, come on, come on, Rachel.

Her lids fluttered. They shut, then pressed together. Slowly they rose.

Jack was afraid to breathe. After initial gasps from

behind him, there was no sound at all. Rachel's eyes stayed on his face, stayed there so long that he half feared she was still comatose. Then her eyes broke from his and moved past to Hope.

"Mommy?" Hope cried.

Her eyes shifted to Samantha, who said a breathless "Omigod."

When those eyes returned to him, they were confused. Slowly she moved her fingers into a loose fist with the thumb inside. Puzzled eyes went to Hope, to Samantha, and back to him. Jack was beginning to think she might have amnesia when she looked at the girls again and smiled. In a voice that was weak but very Rachel, she asked, "What's doing?"

He gave a shout of relief, and suddenly the girls were crowding in, hugging Rachel, talking and laughing at the same time, and though Jack felt the same exuberance they did and wanted to hug her, too, he gave them room. This was the most important thing, after all, Rachel and her girls. She was awake. She was back. With another shout of relief, he left to tell the doctors the news.

KATHERINE was in bed when Jack called. She bolted upright, ecstatic. "Wide awake?" she asked.

"Wide awake!"

"Speaking? Remembering?"

"She's confused about what happened and what day it is, and she's weak, but awake!"

"Oh, Jack, that is *the* best news! Has Steve been by?"

"He's on his way."

"So am I," she said and hurried into the shower. It was

only when she was under the spray and surrounded by steam that she remembered Jack's dilemma. She was rooting for him. She planned to tell Rachel that.

She turned off the shower and stepped out, letting the steam fill the room. With her back to the mirror, she rubbed skin cream all over her body. By then, the mirror was fully fogged. She worked on her hair by feel, using the humidity to enhance the curls.

Wrapping a towel around her, she returned to the bedroom. The clothes she had chosen weren't right. There would be celebrating today, even, perhaps, if she could work appointments around it, a special lunch. In any event, she would see him. So she picked an outfit she loved, soft pants and a two-tiered top, and returned to the bathroom.

Hooking the clothes hanger over the door, she reached for her bra, thought twice, and exchanged it for panty hose. She pulled them up carefully, flexed her ankles, slipped a hand inside along her hip to even the stretch. Then she reached for the bra again.

She held it, turned it. It was black, one of Victoria's Secret's sleekest numbers. She looked wonderful with it on. She looked sexy with it on. Steve would like it.

And with it off? Her plastic surgeon said her breasts looked good. So did Rachel, who was the only other person in the world she had trusted enough to show. She trusted Steve. At least, she thought she did. He knew what he faced. He had surely seen worse. She didn't think he would run from her, screaming and limp.

It was time she showed the same courage.

The mirror was to her right, and clear now. Drawing herself tall with a deep, deep breath, she stepped before it, and for the first time in months and months, took a good long look.

EXCITEMENT spread down the hall. Doctors came and did their tests. Nurses came and helped. Families of other patients, framed in envy, stood outside looking in.

Jack didn't know what to do. He watched it all from beside the bed, from a spot just behind Rachel's head. He was there, but he wasn't. He felt relief and worry, happiness and fear. He was the ex-husband, relegated to silence again.

chapter twenty-three

RACHEL EMERGED from her coma thinking it was just another day of waking up with Jack on her mind, until she found him there in the flesh, inches from her face, looking worried and involved. Her first thought was that something had happened to one of the girls, but she saw them in her periphery, as alive and intense as Jack. So she went on to thinking that she had imagined Big Sur and six years of life without him. When she looked directly at the girls, though, she saw that they were too old, too tall. Jack's hair was less pecan and more beige, his jaw was rougher, his brow more creased. Oh yes, those six years had passed. With Jack? In San Francisco, with Big Sur wishful thinking?

No. Big Sur was too clear in her mind and heart. She couldn't have dreamed the woods, the cabin, the coast any more than she could have dreamed the aloneness. She was definitely divorced. But there was a wedding band on her finger. It was bigger than it had been last time she had put it on, which was as odd as the way her body felt—tired, heavy, weak.

She was clearly in a hospital. How else to explain coarse white sheets and a medicinal smell? So now she was frightened as well as confused. But the people she loved were all there and alive. Jack must have been the one who brought the girls. He wouldn't stay. He never stayed.

Thinking that mothers had to be strong, she mustered a smile for Samantha and Hope. "What's doing?"

Suddenly, like a paused video starting to play, the two of them came to life. Displacing Jack, they began hugging her, laughing, chattering about an accident she didn't remember, a coma she didn't remember, a broken leg, a blood clot, twitching, moaning, gross half-opened eyes.

She didn't remember any of it. She couldn't grasp the fact that she had been lying there for sixteen days—though the doctors and nurses who came in to look and prod confirmed it. It did explain her weakness and the thinness of her fingers. She had lost weight. Sixteen days without solid food would do that. Other than soreness from intravenous needles, though, she felt no pain. Apparently she had slept through that.

The girls jabbered on about Jack staying at Big Sur, Jack driving them to school, Jack being at the hospital every single day. Jack didn't say anything. He had backed off to the side somewhere. She closed her eyes. Too much too soon. He had come through as a father. She was grateful for that.

She rested a bit. Life was hazy. Sixteen days were a long time to have missed. There were things she was supposed to have done. One by one, those thoughts began to congeal.

When she opened her eyes to ask, Samantha and Hope were sitting on the bed on either side of her, looking at her with wide, frightened eyes. She guessed a sixteen-day coma would do that, too. "I'm here," she said, smiling, when their features abruptly relaxed. But she was still feeling confused. She asked what day of the week it was and what time. She asked why the girls weren't in school.

"We've waited too long for this," Samantha told her. "Dad said we could skip."

Rachel wondered what else he had said they could do. Sunday fathers had a way of indulging. Jack usually did it with money. He would have other means, if he was seeing the girls every day. It sounded like he had scored points. The two of them were pushing his virtues awfully hard, which was especially not like Samantha.

A sweet nurse—*Cindy,* the girls informed her; *she's been helping Dad take care of you; she's wonderful*—cranked up her head a little, then a little more. She was dizzy, but it passed, and the girls began again. Samantha listed off all of the people who had come to visit. Hope told her about the flowers and the cards, the lingerie and the perfume. Samantha told her about Faye's brisket and Eliza's pecan rolls. Hope told her about Katherine's crush on the doctor.

When Samantha told her about the prom, Rachel was heartsick. When Hope told her about Guinevere, Rachel cried.

Jack went off somewhere, which was fine. This was the life she was used to now, just the girls and her. But as soon as he disappeared, the girls started talking about him again.

"He drove down in the middle of the night right after the accident."

"He loves the woods. He takes *us* for walks."

415

"He dug around for the recipe and made your favorite dip for my louse of a prom date, Teague."

"He even made a *coffin* for Guinevere."

"He bought you a new car, Mom. You'll *love* it."

"He framed your pictures, so the show's going on."

"He hasn't worked in two weeks. I think he's changed."

Rachel smiled and nodded, then dozed off, which was a wonderful way of escaping what she didn't want to hear. When she woke up, the girls were staring at her again, frozen, scared.

"Come *on,* you guys," she said, with a laugh this time. "You can't panic every time I fall asleep."

"But you don't know how *awful* it was," Samantha cried, and the two of them proceeded to tell her again, until she couldn't help but get their drift.

"Tell me about the show," she said. "You said that your father framed my pictures?"

"Framed them and delivered them," Hope said.

Samantha added, "Ben's setting things up. We haven't seen much of him lately. Dad's the one who's been here most."

Before Rachel could ask about the less-than-subtle lobbying, Katherine arrived—dear Katherine, who would have kept an eye on the girls even if Jack hadn't shown up—suave Katherine, who actually blushed when the doctor who had earlier introduced himself as Steve returned to the room. The crush Hope had mentioned? *Katherine?* Rachel was overwhelmed. But that wasn't the first thing she asked when she and Katherine finally got a minute alone.

She wiggled her ring finger. "What's with this?"

"Did you ask him?"

"No. Katherine, did *you* call him after the accident?"

"I did," she said, looking defiant. "I figured you'd want him here."

"*Want* him here? He shut down on me. You *know* it still hurts."

"You still love him. That's why it hurts. That's why I called."

"It hurts to *see* him."

"You don't think he feels that, too? You think he's been here for sixteen days for his health?"

"He's here for the girls."

"And you."

"He feels obligated."

"He cares."

"Caring isn't love, and even if it was, you can love someone and still shut them out." Worn out, Rachel closed her eyes and said a muddled "We've been through this, Katherine. You know how I feel."

"So take the ring off," Katherine said.

Rachel didn't, because she was too tired, and a fresh round of medical people were there when she woke up, which would have meant making a public thing of it. Besides, she figured the ring might be a charm. She had been wearing it when she had come out of the coma. She figured she would wear it until she got home.

LEAVING RACHEL'S room, Katherine saw Steve from a distance and, stopping where she was, watched him talk with a nurse, lean down to study a computer, straighten, turn, and smile when a colleague approached. She found such pleasure in watching.

Why him? Because he was skilled, smart, kind, and sensitive? Because he was the right age for her? Because he was the right height, the right weight, the right everything, physically?

When he looked down the hall and saw her, he grinned, said something to his colleague, and started toward her with that lean-limbed walk. He was grinning broadly when he arrived.

"You owe me lunch," he said.

She grinned back. How not to? His pleasure was infectious. She felt its warmth at the same time that she felt a contradictory chill, deep inside, in a spot she couldn't place. "I know."

He gave her a once-over that raised both the warmth and the chill. "You look great." He glanced at his watch, then said in a coaxing way, "I can buy a couple of free hours this afternoon. Can you?"

Katherine made a show of looking at her own watch. That chilly spot inside was growing worse. She grimaced. "I don't know. Thursdays are packed."

"Forget *hours,* plural. Try one hour. Any chance?"

She winced. "I'm already starting off late, being here now. How about Monday?"

His face went through changes—disappointment to doubt to caution—which was another thing about him that worked for her. She could see what he felt. He was definitely suspicious when he said, "Isn't that restaurant closed on Mondays?"

"Only off-season. It's open now."

"Then it's a date?"

"Uh-huh," she said, grateful for the reprieve. "The shop's closed Mondays. I'm free."

"I'll make reservations, say at one o'clock?"

She nodded vigorously.

He smiled again. His lids lowered a hair, gaze dropped to her lips. He mouthed the kind of tiny kiss that no one could see but her, and set off back down the hall leaving her hotter than ever—but only from her knees up. As she headed for the elevator, she located the chill. It was lower.

She had cold feet.

BY THURSDAY afternoon, word had spread that Rachel was awake. By evening, friends were coming by to see for themselves.

Jack had felt awkward enough when just the girls and Katherine were talking with Rachel. It was worse now. He had come to respect her friends and they him, but hearing them sing his praises felt like . . . charity. Rachel didn't do more than glance at him every once in a while, and then, without giving a clue as to what she felt.

So he idled in the hall on the phone, calling his lawyer at home, calling Tina Cianni at home. He intercepted a man delivering a huge bouquet of balloons from Victoria—*incredible! appropriate!*—and with Hope's gleeful help, tied them to Rachel's IV pole. Superfluous once again, he ambled to the door, then leaned against the wall just beyond it. When Steve returned for a last evening look, he caught him before he entered the room.

"What happens now? Is she out of the coma free and clear?" He shared the same fear the girls did every time Rachel closed her eyes. "I read a newspaper story once about a guy who came out of a coma and was talking with his family, as lucid as Rachel. He lapsed back into a coma the next day and later died."

Steve said, "As I recall, that fellow had been comatose for several years. Rachel's case is more logical. Her head was injured. It took sixteen days for it to heal enough for her to regain consciousness. We'll do scans in the morning, but I don't expect to see anything wrong. She'll be on meds for a while to minimize chance of the swelling returning, maybe a lightweight anticoagulant for six months to make sure there isn't another clotting problem, but that's it."

"When can she go home?" It would be a moment of truth. He had been sleeping in Rachel's bed.

"The IV will come out later," Steve explained. "We'll start her on a liquid diet and move on to soft solids when she's up to it. We'll monitor her oxygenation level for another day, get her out of bed in the morning. We want her eating and walking. Once that's done and she's regained full bladder tone, she's yours."

Jack wished it was as easy as that. "Best guess, how many days till she's out?"

"Three. She should be home by Sunday."

THE GIRLS slept soundly that night. Jack knew, because he looked in on them every few hours. Their ordeal was ending. They were excited enough about Rachel's awakening not to be worried about Jack's future role in their lives, but he sure was. He was worried sick. Sleep came only in short stretches, broken by restlessness and fear. He called the hospital several times during the night. Rachel remained out of her coma. Between hours of healthy sleep, she was drinking juice and eating pudding.

Friday morning, he went to the hospital alone. Her IV pole was gone. Her hair was damp and waving gently, her face was shiny clean. The tray table held a plate with dried egg streaks and toast crumbs, and an empty cup of coffee. She was reading the newspaper, looking as thin and small as Hope in a huge magenta T-shirt. The wedding band was still on her finger, but she looked startled to see him.

"How are you feeling?" he asked, standing just inside the door. Despite all that had been, coming closer seemed an intrusion on her turf. If she wanted him there, she had to let him know.

"Better," she said. "Where are the girls?"

"School. They've missed too much of it. They'll be here this afternoon."

She nodded.

"So," he said, "they got you up for a shower?"

She smiled and nodded. "Uh-huh. They wrapped the cast in plastic. It was a little bulky, plaster and crutches. They're giving me a waterproof one later."

"That's good." He slipped his hands in the pockets of his jeans and looked around. "Do you need anything? Candy? Magazines?"

"No, thanks. I'm fine. When are you going back to the city?"

"I don't know. Not for a while. You'll need some help."

"The girls can help. School will be out in a few weeks."

"Well, between now and then. Unless you'd rather have someone else. If you'd rather have a nurse, I'll hire one."

"That might be best if you have to get back to the city."

A deep dark hole was eating his insides. He had just *said* that he didn't have to go, hadn't he? Hadn't anything the girls said registered with her?

"Perfect timing," said Steve Bauer as he slipped past Jack and went to the bed. "I want you taking another walk down the hall. Jack can take you."

"I'm still tired from the last one."

"You ate. Good. We'll get more in here in a little while. Fatten you up a little. The more you walk, the stronger you'll be and the faster the plumbing will start up again. As soon as that happens, you can go home." He held out a hand.

She sighed, took it, and pushed herself to a seated position. When she was steady there, he handed her a furry red slipper. She fitted it to her foot—bending stiffly, Jack thought. Steve gave her a single crutch, helped her up, then gave her the other. When both crutches were in place, she stood for a minute with her head down.

"Okay?" Steve asked quietly. Jack envied him the intimacy.

She nodded and took several uneven steps.

"Hand hurt?" Steve asked.

"A little, but it's okay," she said. Her voice was as shaky as the rest of her looked.

"Is she up for this?" Jack asked. He imagined her falling and hurting herself more.

But Steve kept an arm around her back, preventing that. "She can't go home until she is." When they reached Jack, he said, "Your turn."

THEY walked slowly and haltingly down the corridor.

"Okay?" Jack asked; then after several more steps, "Hanging in there?" When they reached the end, he said, "You're doing great," and when they were halfway back, "Nearly there."

She gave him single-word answers, clearly concentrating on keeping her balance. By the time they were back in the room, she had broken into a sweat. He helped her into bed and asked if she needed anything. She shook her head and closed her eyes.

Jack was devastated.

"HOW'S MOM?" Hope asked as soon as she climbed into the car. She was still wearing her cowboy boots, which told Jack she wasn't yet completely relaxed.

"She's great," he said and pushed open the door for Samantha, who promptly repeated the question. "She's been up and hobbling around. Had a sandwich for lunch."

"Did you get it for her?" Hope asked.

"Eliza dropped it off before I could." With a glance in the rearview mirror, he pulled away from the curb.

"But you've been with her all day," Samantha said.

"Yup."

"So did you guys talk?"

He shot her a curious glance. "About?"

"Stuff, Daddy," Hope said, leaning in between the seats. "You know. Your living with us and all."

He had figured they were getting at that. It followed, after all of the good things they had told Rachel the day before. "Is your seat belt fastened, Hope?"

"Well, did you?" Samantha asked.

Jack darted glances in the rearview mirror until he heard the click that said Hope was belted in.

"*Dad.*"

"No, Samantha. We didn't talk about that. Your mother's just been through an ordeal." He had been telling himself that all day. "She's concentrating on getting up and eating. Her first priority is getting home."

"What happens then?"

"What do you mean?"

"Are you staying?"

"That depends."

"On what?"

He drove silently, until she repeated the question. He caught Hope's eyes in the rearview mirror. She was waiting for his answer, too.

"On things that your mother and I decide to do," he finally said. "But there's a whole lot of other *stuff* we need to think about before we think about that, so I'd appreciate it if the two of you backed off. Okay?"

"SO DAD'S been here all day?" Samantha asked.

They hadn't been there five minutes. Jack was at the window looking out, listening to the girls tell Rachel about school. He hung his head when he heard the question, pursed his lips, waited.

"He has," Rachel said. "It's tricky getting used to crutches. He walked me up and down a few times. He brought me a hot fudge sundae."

"With mocha almond ice cream?" Hope asked in obvious delight.

"Uh-huh. It was good. I'm still sleeping a lot. Funny,

you'd think after sixteen days I wouldn't be tired."

"I think Dad should stay with us," Samantha said. "You know, like, after you get home?"

Jack put a hand to the back of his neck.

"We'll talk about that later," Rachel said.

"When later? You may be home in two days. He's really a good guy, Mom."

"I never said he wasn't."

"Maybe you need to hear his side of the story."

"Samantha," Jack warned, turning to face them.

Hope said, "He did *everything* while you were sick. I mean, he came right down from the city that first day and shopped and cooked and drove us around. He even drove Faith to see you. Did you know he did that?"

"No," Rachel said without looking at Jack. "I'm grateful to him."

"He left the *firm* for you!" Samantha cried.

Jack said, "No, I didn't, Sam."

Blond hair flying, she looked at him fast. "You *did!*"

"I left it for me. For me, Sam. It wasn't working for me anymore, so I gave it up. Don't lay that on your mother, too. It's not like I'm out of work. My phone's been ringing. I can get clients now that I couldn't get before. New doors are open now." He stopped. He didn't know why he had said all that. It wasn't what he wanted to tell Rachel.

"Fine," Samantha said, staring at him with his very own defiant eyes. "But if you go back to San Francisco, I'm going, too."

"Samantha!" Rachel cried, sounding totally displeased, even hurt.

"I can live both places, can't I? And, anyway, it's summer. I can get a job there."

Jack said, "You're not doing that."

"I will!"

"No, you won't, because your mother's going to need your help, and besides, I won't be in San Francisco. I'm moving here. I like it here. I'll buy my own place if I have to." The timing was all wrong to say that. The idea was half-baked. It would never work if Rachel was against it. He resented his daughter forcing the issue. This wasn't Samantha's business. It wasn't Hope's business. It was between Rachel and him. That was all. Rachel and him.

The fact that Katherine was suddenly standing in the door didn't help. Annoyed, he stalked past her, right out of the room, then realized it was another wrong thing to do. He should have told Katherine to take his daughters away. They had given Rachel a rundown on what the last few weeks had been like for them. He needed to tell her what it had been like for him.

But he couldn't turn around and go back. Forget talking. Rachel was barely looking at him. He might have started seeing things differently in the last few weeks, but she sure hadn't.

Disgusted, he went down the hall to the bank of telephones. It was Friday. He had told Myron Elliott that he would call. There was no point in delaying. Regardless of where he lived, Jack didn't want the job.

"WHY DIDN'T you *say* something?" Samantha asked.

"He *loves* you, Mommy," Hope said.

Katherine had approached the bed. "Can I talk to your mom, guys?"

"Someone better," Samantha remarked and, with a

look of disgust at Rachel, grabbed Hope's arm and hauled her out of the room.

Rachel watched them go. "That was a quick honey-moon."

"Why *didn't* you?" Katherine asked.

Rachel's eyes flew to her face. She didn't understand the edge in Katherine's voice. "Why didn't I what?"

"Say something to Jack."

"About what?"

"His leaving the firm. His moving here."

Rachel tried to replay the conversation without opening herself to hurt. "Did he ask my opinion?"

"Do you need a formal invitation? Come on, Rachel. The guy hasn't left your side. Help him out a little here."

"Help him with *what?*" Rachel cried. "Maybe I don't want him moving here. Fine, the girls are attached to him, but maybe I don't want to have to see him all the time. Big Sur is mine. Why does he think he can just barge right in?"

"He loves you, Rachel."

Rachel closed her eyes and turned away.

"Tell him you love him back," Katherine said.

Rachel's heart was aching. It was a veteran at that, where Jack McGill was concerned. "I don't know if I can," she said. She had precious little energy when her heart ached. It had been aching so long.

"What are you afraid of?"

"Depending on him and being abandoned again."

"You'd rather live the rest of your life without?"

Rachel opened her eyes and looked at Katherine hard. She could understand that her daughters would have con-flicting loyalties, but her best friend should be on *her* side. "He hasn't said he loves me either, y'know, and don't say he's shown it, because it's not the same. If he loves me, let him say it. Let him go out on a limb and take a risk that I'll say no. Wouldn't *you* do that, if you wanted something bad enough?"

Katherine looked at her a minute longer, then headed for the door. Rachel wanted to ask where she was going, but didn't have the strength.

KATHERINE kept her head down and scowled as she walked. She was angry at Rachel for being stubborn, angry at Steve for being persistent, angry at herself for being afraid to take the kind of risk she just told her best friend to take. She was angry at Jack. And then, there he was at the bank of phones.

JACK had made his call and didn't know what to do next. His life was in a limbo—professionally, personally. The phone booth seemed as good a way station as any.

"What are you doing?" Katherine asked, looking and sounding again like the woman who had thought him lower than low several weeks before.

He was feeling raw. He didn't need prodding from her. Pushing away from the booth, he held up a hand and set off for the elevator. "Not now, Katherine."

"If not now, when?" she asked, keeping up with his stride easily. "You told me you loved her and wanted back into the marriage. Why don't you tell *her?*"

He put a hand over his ear. "Not now, Katherine?"

"Then *when?* What's with you and silence? What's this whole thing been about? Haven't you lost enough time? Jesus, Jack, haven't you learned *any*thing?"

He stopped short and put his face in hers. "Have you?"

That got her fast. She swallowed, blinked, pulled back. She frowned in the direction of the nurses' station, then lowered her eyes.

"Yeah," she said, suddenly humble, "I want to think I have. I took a good look at myself, and you were right. What I have isn't so bad." Flattening a hand on her chest, she seemed to be speaking more to herself than to him. "Am I pleased with these? No. But I can live with them. I can live with them."

She dropped her hand, straightened her spine, raised her eyes to his, and said with determination, "I'm gonna give it a shot, risk that ole rejection, because maybe there's something that's worth it." She smiled, becoming the friend he wanted, needed. "So what's with you? Can't you just do it, too?"

She made it sound easy. He started walking again. "You're talking apples and oranges."

"I'm talking trust," she said, beside him still.

"Christ, Katherine, where's *hers?* She knows I'm done with the firm. She knows I'm done with San Francisco. She *knows* I've been here taking care of her." He stopped at the elevator and faced her. "She hasn't said a goddamned word about *any* of it."

Katherine stared at him, stared deep. He felt genuine caring—from her, from him—when she put a hand on his arm. "Three weeks ago, I'd have said you were a guy through and through. Guys don't think, they don't analyze, they don't understand. They just *do*—whatever, whenever, however. But you can be more than a guy,

429

Jack." She squeezed his arm. "Why isn't she talking?" She tapped her head. "Think."

She looked at him a minute longer, took a deep breath that he could have sworn reverberated with courage, did an about-face, and started back down the hall.

BY THE TIME she reached the nurses' station, Katherine was starting to tremble. She consciously laced her fingers and kept them low when she asked if Steve was around. There was some confusion and consulting of one another behind the desk. Katherine was starting to wonder if her bravado would hold over for another day when he emerged from a door far down the hall. He spotted her. His blue eyes smiled and closed in fast. The shaking inside her went deeper.

He was still smiling when he reached her. His hands were in his pockets, pushing back the lapels of his lab coat. He raised his brows. "Can you take a break?" Katherine whispered.

He spoke briefly with the nurse at the desk, walked Katherine to the elevator, pushed the buttons both outside and inside. The ride was short, and they were alone. He leaned against one wall, she leaned against the other. She spent the entire time running through all the things she had seen and learned that suggested he was worthy of trust, but it was thinking about Jack and Rachel that kept her on track. If she expected them to risk something of themselves, she had to be willing to do it herself.

The elevator took them to the lowest level. Steve stuck a finger toward outside, then a thumb toward a long corridor. "Is this about Rachel?" he asked. When she shook her head, he followed the thumb. Holding her hand, he led her down the corridor, around a corner, and into a room that was small and dark. He leaned against the door to shut it, at the same time pushing his fingers deep into her hair. "This is so gorgeous," he whispered, using the leverage to bring her in for a kiss. His mouth was as willful as it had been on Sunday, but no stick shift stood between them now. They were in full body contact. A deep breath caused an undulation. Katherine didn't know whose breath it was, but the shaking in her belly grew worse.

It was a while before he dragged his mouth away. When he wrapped his arms around her, her head had nowhere to go but his shoulder. She smelled the starch of his lab coat, and something male beneath it.

Her chest was flush to his. She wondered if he felt anything strange.

"Where are we?" she asked. Beyond the sound of their own heavy breathing, she heard the hum of a machine in the wall.

"Broom closet," he murmured into her hair. "I've always wanted to do it in a broom closet. If a doctor is worth his salt, he's done it in a broom closet, right?"

"On TV," she chided, but the darkness helped. "We have to talk, Steve. *I* have to talk. You need to know certain things about me before this relationship goes any further."

He made a humming sound, leaned down a little, and lifted her closer. He felt like a man in ecstasy.

"The thing is," she began, wanting to give in and melt, but fearing disaster, "there are never guarantees in any relationship, because no one knows what the future holds. I mean, look at Rachel, perfectly healthy one day and comatose another through no single fault of her own. We think we'll be here next week, but we don't know for sure. I mean, *you* could be running down the street and be hit by a car, and *zap,* you're gone, just like that—God forbid, I *don't* want that to happen . . . Steve, I have breast cancer."

There should have been an abrupt silence with her announcement. But life hadn't stopped. There were heartbeats, ongoing breaths, and the hum of that machine in the wall.

He drew her closer. His voice was deep and sure. "Wrong tense. You *had* breast cancer. It's gone."

She caught her breath. "Excuse me?"

"Past tense. You're cured."

She drew her head back, unable to see him but needing the distance. "You *know?*"

"You looked familiar when I saw you after Rachel's accident, and you kept bumping into hospital personnel who knew you, too. I put two and two together and checked our database."

"So much for my privacy!" she cried and would have pushed him away if he hadn't had his hands locked at the small of her back. "That's a breach of ethics, Steve."

"Probably, but I was desperate. You were special, and you didn't want any part of me. I had to know why."

She had *agonized* over this. "Why didn't you *tell* me you knew?"

"I couldn't. It had to be this way. I had to know you cared enough about me to share it."

"Well, I do," she complained. She swallowed, feeling close to tears. "It's been a long time since I cared enough." Her breasts were flush as ever against his chest. "Last time I did, he dumped me as soon as he learned."

"Does it feel like I will?"

Not only was he still holding her, but he was hard. She wanted to believe, oh, she did. "Maybe it's a perversion," she muttered.

"No. It's just not as big a thing as you think, Katherine. We all have something."

"What do *you* have?"

"Me, personally, now? Nothing. But my dad died at forty-two of prostate cancer, and his dad died at forty-eight of lung cancer, so there's part of me that feels like I'm living on borrowed time, which is maybe why I want that time to be good. I bought the CJ-7 when I turned fifty. I always wanted a car like that. I figured that if I wasn't already dead, a topless car wouldn't kill me, and—want to know something?—I love that car. It's probably the cheapest one I've ever owned, but I've never enjoyed driving another as much. It's just plain fun. You fit in it well."

"I had reconstruction," she blurted out, because he seemed too cheery to have gotten the whole picture. "Have you ever made love to a woman with reconstructed breasts?"

"No, but they don't feel so bad right now. There's more to you than your breasts," he said, just as Jack had. "I can appreciate that. I've seen enough in my line of work to know about putting the emphasis on the right syl-*la*-ble."

Priorities. Rachel was going to love him. "My husband couldn't hack it. He couldn't look, couldn't touch. He couldn't get an erection."

"I don't have that problem."

No. He didn't. At least, not right then. "Talking's different from doing."

He cupped her face in the dark. "Want to try now? I'll do it now."

She had to laugh. She half-believed that he would.

"I have a feeling your breasts bother you more than they'll bother me," he said with such gentleness that her hackles couldn't rise.

It struck her that he might be right.

"We can work with it," he said. "If my touching them turns you off, I'll wait. I could kiss you all night and get pleasure enough from that." He cleared a thick throat and said through a smile, "Well, almost. There's"—he swallowed—"a kind of pressure down low, but I can wait, I can wait." He took a deep, shaky breath. "There's pleasure to be had from an erection alone. Enjoyment of the process." He ducked his head and caught her lips in a kiss that started innocently enough but quickly escalated.

Katherine didn't know how he managed to do it. He had her as into the thing as he was, using her tongue and teeth with an enthusiasm she shouldn't have been able to feel, given the circumstances, but he did taste divine.

Her breasts would have loved him. She was dreadfully sorry they weren't there.

But *she* was there. She was alive and well, and she had found a caring man who claimed to be willing to live with saline. Granted, the proof of the pudding was in the eating. But she had never gotten this far before. Maybe, just maybe, things were looking up.

chapter twenty-four

JACK WAS MORE than a guy. He thought, he analyzed, he understood. He was waiting for Rachel to talk. Rachel was waiting for him to talk. Whoever talked first took the greater risk.

The thing was that if he didn't take any risk, he was sure as hell going to end up with the kind of life he had just had. That life was gray, foggy, muzzy, damp. It was flat.

Rachel's life had depth. It had color and warmth. She could afford to wait for him to speak. She had less to lose if they never did.

So it was up to him.

That was what his brain said. His heart said that he couldn't bare all with the girls there, and when the girls weren't there, Katherine was, or Charlie, or Faye, and then the girls were back.

Evening came. He drove them home. The coast road was bathed in the amber of a setting sun that gilded wild-flowers, granite boulders, layer after layer of greening hills. There was a poignance to its beauty, a soft whisper from the surf. *Tell her, ask her, beg her,* it said, repeating its message with the rush of the waves.

At the bank of mailboxes, he turned off the highway and started up the hill. If the message hadn't already been ingrained in him, the canyon would have done it. There wasn't a sound from the woods when he climbed from the car, just that nagging whisper all around. *Tell her, ask her, beg her.*

"Uh . . ." He stopped on the front porch. Samantha and Hope were already inside. "Hey . . . uh."

Hope came back to the door. "What's wrong?"

He pushed his hands into his hair, feeling a sudden dire need. "Where'd Sam go? *Sam?*"

Samantha came up behind Hope.

"Listen, can you two look out for yourselves for a while?"

"We're not babies," Samantha said, but kindly. "Where are you going?"

He was already heading back to the car. "I, uh, need to talk with your mom."

The drive back to Carmel wasn't as easy. The sun set. The road grew darker. He turned on his headlights, but they didn't show him what he needed to do. It wasn't until he passed the Highlands and saw the lights of Carmel across the bay that he had a clue.

RACHEL hovered on the brink of tears. With each hour that passed, the reality of the accident, the coma, and the blood clot sank in deeper. She had never been one to dwell on her own mortality, but it was hard not to now. She was vulnerable. She was human. She thought about Katherine and about Faith. Just picturing them gave her strength.

So there was that, and the girls, and her work, and Jack. And Jack. And more Jack. She was trying to process all she had been told about him, trying to figure out what was what and where it went. She liked putting things in piles. She didn't care if there was a mess within a pile, as long as there was a semblance of order, pile to pile.

Since the divorce, she had kept Jack in a pile of his own. It wasn't a neat pile. Dozens of thoughts and emotions were stacked randomly and high. For the most part, she managed to keep them separate from the rest of her life. The occasional spillover was quickly contained. That was how she survived.

Now, though, Jack was scattered everywhere. He touched the girls. He touched Katherine. He touched friends in Carmel, touched the house in Big Sur, touched Duncan and Faith. He touched her work.

She wanted to sort and separate, but her heart kept messing things up. She couldn't unwind Jack from those other people and things.

Then he appeared at the door to her room and her heart moved right up to her throat. She swallowed, but it didn't budge.

"Hi," he said. After several seconds on the threshold, he came inside. "I dropped the girls back home." He put his hands on his hips and looked around the room. Then his eyes returned to hers.

Say something, she told herself, but her throat was closed and her eyes moist. *Say something,* she cried, directing the plea to him.

"I thought maybe—" he began and cleared his throat. "I know it's late—well, there's—" He took a breath and asked straight out, "Do you want to take a ride?"

She hadn't expected that. The tears hung on her lids. Something more than her throat squeezed her heart. Standing there, all six two of him—with his sport shirt rolled to the elbow, faded jeans, his weathering hair, and unsureness—he looked so *dear.*

"You haven't been out of this place in two and a half weeks," he went on. "I have the new car downstairs. I won't keep you out long—unless you're nervous being in a car, after the accident."

"I don't remember the accident."

"If you're too tired—"

"I'm not," she said. She pushed herself up, carefully easing her casted leg over the side. Her nightgown fell to her ankles. She reached for her crutches.

"If I carry you, you won't wear yourself out," he said with such gentleness that the tears returned. She brushed them away with the heels of her hands and nodded. It wouldn't be the first time that he had carried her, but it would be the first time since well before the divorce. It would be the first time in six long years that their bodies had been so close.

"I've been doing this for seventeen days," he corrected as he slipped his arms under her. He lifted her with the same exquisite gentleness that had been in his voice.

She held herself stiffly at first.

"Not comfortable?" he asked as he headed for the door.

"Awkward." She wanted to wrap her arms around his neck, bury her face against his throat, and hang on, but she was frightened. Giving in to a want could mean trouble if the want was taken away again. "Is this allowed?"

He strode to the nurses' station and said to two nurses and a resident, "I'm taking my wife for a ride. We'll be gone an hour. Is there any reason we shouldn't?"

The nurses looked at each other, then at the resident, who was nonplussed. "It isn't normally done."

"That's not a good reason," Jack said. "Medically, any problem?"

He reached for the phone. "I'll check with Dr. Bauer."

Jack took that as permission and set off down the hall.

I'm not your wife, Rachel thought, but didn't say it. She didn't want to argue over words, not when being carried felt so nice. She settled in a little and thought about seeing the car. She thought about smelling fresh air, rather than hospital sterility. She thought about feeling alive.

The night was warm and clear. It no sooner enveloped her when her eyes filled with tears again. She took a deep breath, then gasped when she saw where Jack was headed. A tall halogen light lit the car well. "It's red!" she cried. "The girls didn't tell me it was red! I haven't had a red car since–"

"Since the VW. I thought it was time." He freed a hand enough to open the door and carefully settled her inside. He adjusted the seat to make more room for her cast and fastened the seat belt before she could do it herself.

"Why?" Rachel asked when he slid behind the wheel.

He started the car. "Why what?"

"Why did you think it was time?"

He left the parking lot and drove several blocks before he said, "Because you loved that car. I shouldn't have sold it the way I did."

Rachel was startled by the admission so long after the fact, but there was too much to see and do to dwell on it. She rolled down her window and put her face to the warm breeze that blew in as he drove. Her lungs came alive, hungry for more. "Where are we going?"

"P. Emmet's."

The show! Exciting! Her paintings were like her children, now all dressed up in their new frames and on display. She had seen Samantha and Hope. She wanted to see her work. But, "At *this* hour?"

"It's Friday night. They're open late."

"It's nearly ten."

"No, it's not," Jack said. But it was. He looked at the clock and swore. "Well, we're going anyway. I want you to see the paintings."

"We won't be able to get in."

"We'll get in."

She didn't argue, didn't have the strength. Jack was determined. It was all in his hands.

Laying her head against the headrest, she said, "I haven't thanked you for doing the framing. I'm grateful."

"You had everything there. The girls helped."

She rolled her head to look at him. Six years hadn't changed his profile. His hair remained thick and too long in the back. His nose was straight, his mouth strong, his chin and neck firm. She had always thought him beautiful. That hadn't changed.

"Thank you for staying with them," she said.

He nodded, but didn't speak.

When tears pricked her lids, she looked forward again. They used to talk, used to go on and on about whatever they wanted, or keep utterly still, but there was an ease. She felt no ease now, only a dull ache inside. It hurt to be with Jack like this, locked out as surely as she had been at the end. It hurt. She had warned Katherine.

"There's no point in this," she said, feeling tired and

weak. Her paintings could wait. What she wanted most in that instant was to bury her head in a pillow and cry.

"We're almost there."

"Jack, they're *closed.*"

He didn't answer, simply drove on through the back streets of Carmel and pulled up in front of the gallery. The place looked dark and deserted. Swearing, he left the car and peered in the front window. Using his hands as blinders, he tried to see more. He knocked on the glass, went to the door and knocked harder.

"Custodian," he called to Rachel. He knocked again, studied the door, jabbed his thumb on the bell. He cupped his hands on the glass and peered inside again. He hit the bell several more times.

Rachel was picturing a person wearing headphones to blunt the noise of a vacuum when Jack turned to her and raised a victorious fist. Seconds later, a man was on the inside of the door, waving a hand no, shaking his head.

Jack spoke loudly. "My wife is the artist whose show is about to open. She's been in the hospital in a coma. I stole her out to show her this. Two minutes. That's all we'll need."

The man opened his hands in a helpless gesture.

Jack held up a finger, telling him to wait. In two long steps, he was at the car, lifting Rachel out, carrying her to the door.

"See her cast?" he yelled through the glass. "This is legitimate, bud."

"Show him ID," Rachel tried, because, having come this far, being this close, she wanted in.

Her arms were around his neck. He looked at her, so close, so tender. "My name, not yours," he said with regret. She watched the little line come and go between his eyes. Gently lowering her to her good foot, he anchored her to his side while he removed his watch and held it up. "It's a Tag. Want it? It's yours."

"Jack!"

"I don't need it," Jack said as the man opened the door.

Rachel saw that he was an older man. His head had a constant shake. "I don't want your watch," he mumbled, barely opening his mouth. "I want my job. Place is closed. No one's s'posed to be here but me."

"This is the artist."

"Could be a thief."

"Does she look like a thief? Her name's Rachel Keats. Look." He thumbed the window. "See this notice. Rachel Keats." To Rachel, he said, "Was Ben putting your picture on a flyer?" Before she could say she didn't think so, he told the man, "Go inside and look for a flyer. Check out the picture. It's her face."

The man scratched his nose. His head continued to wag. "I don't know."

Jack lifted Rachel again, shouldered the door open, and entered the gallery. Rachel felt a little naughty, but excited, very excited.

"Mr. Wolfe won't like this," came a complaint from behind, but Jack went right on through to the room where shows were hung, the room where Rachel had previously only dreamed of seeing her things.

It was dark, almost eerily silent. She held her breath there in his arms, catching it when he suddenly turned and went back to the wall. She held on tighter when he angled himself to snag the lights with an elbow. When they came on, he carried her to the center of the room and carefully lowered her. Standing behind, he slipped

his arms around her waist and put his chin on her head.
The familiarity of the pose alone would have made her
cry, except that she was distracted—and not by the voice
from behind that said, again, "Mr. Wolfe won't like this."
She barely breathed. Her eye ran around the room, not
knowing where to settle, wanting to see everything at
once. She felt surrounded, overwhelmed. These were her
babies, but more in content, more in style, more in *numbers*. When tears blurred her vision, she pushed both
hands against her eyes to stem them. Leaving her hands
over her mouth, she began with the bobcats. That canvas
was her favorite. She had already seen it framed and
hung, likewise the two that flanked it, but then came the
butterflies . . . and the rattlesnake. And the gray whale.
And the sheep. And her Arctic wolf, her lone Arctic wolf,
with the sun making a full-length halo of its white fur.

She gasped. She hadn't finished the Arctic wolf.
"Omigod." She hadn't finished the quail . . . or the deer .
. . or the great egret, either. "*Omigod.*" The loons. The
loons, sitting on that mirrored surface of a lake at dusk,
with the island in the center and the sky lit by the aurora
borealis. Jack had done this. No one else could have. He
had done it for her so beautifully, *so beautifully.* He might
as well have put her on a pedestal and draped that plain
stone pillar with variations of the softest, richest, most
exquisite velvet.

There was no stopping her tears this time. They came
hard and fast along with huge, wrenching sobs. She was
touched and lonely and needy and wanting and afraid, so
afraid that those paintings were as good as it got.

When Jack turned her into his chest, she coiled her
arms around his neck and clung. "Don't cry, angel," he
begged, "please don't cry. I only want you to be happy."

She wanted to say that what he had done was so beautiful that she was more happy than she would ever, ever be again. She wanted to say that she missed the days when they painted together and that she wanted to do it again. She wanted to say she loved him, only she couldn't stop crying.

She had never cried like this. She had never cared like this.

She felt his arms around her, felt movement, and the next thing she knew they were sitting on the floor. He cradled her close, absorbing the spasms of her weeping with a soft rocking.

Then he began to speak. His head was bowed over hers, his arms protective, his voice beseeching but loud enough to carry over her sobs. "It wouldn't have occurred to me if I hadn't come in here and seen the bobcats. Ben was raving about them, saying that the canvas was his all-time favorite, and I remembered how we'd done it together. He didn't know that, so he wouldn't know if I did it again, and I was torn, Rachel, totally torn. You got this show all on your own, not because of the bobcats but because of the whole body of your work. That was you, your skill, your talent, your perseverance. I wouldn't have done a thing if you'd shown signs of waking up, but you didn't. The longer it went on, the more we realized how long it *could* go on, and then I started thinking that if you didn't wake up, there wouldn't be another show. I wanted you to have at least one, Rachel. I figured you'd worked too hard and too long not to."

He held her head to his chest. Her sobs had slowed to hiccuping murmurs. She was hanging on every word.

"I was feeling helpless there in the hospital," he said. "I talked to you and helped move you, but you weren't waking up. I'd get back to Big Sur at night wanting to do something useful. I couldn't stand the sight of my own work, and the materials were all in your studio, waiting, so I decided to try one, just one." She felt the swell of his chest when he drew in air and a warm reverence when he blew it out against her hair. "It was incredible. I haven't painted like that in years. I haven't been lost in anything like that in years. I felt more alive, more talented, more purposeful.

"So I've been dreaming," he said. "Know what of?"

She shook her head under his hand, against his chest, all too aware of her own dreams and wanting, wanting so badly.

"Of us doing more of this. I don't want a name role in it. You keep the name. I'll still design, but smaller things again, houses for people who can smile at me and love what I've done. I had that in the beginning, but it's been gone for so long that I barely remember it. What you barely remember, you don't miss until something happens to jog your memory. That's what sitting at your bedside did, Rachel, jogged my memory. I remembered things about my work and things about us, things that maybe I didn't want to remember because they were so good, and they were gone."

Rachel knew what he meant. She *knew* what he meant.

"I don't regret going into architecture. I grew up needing money, and architecture gave me that, but I have enough of it now. I've had enough of it for years. Never saw *that,* boy. You always talked about priorities and mine were messed up, but sitting at your bedside fixed that, too. So I want to design houses and paint your backgrounds. I want to live in Big Sur and be with the girls, and I want us to talk, Rachel. We let old habits take over, but if we broke them once, we can do it again. I want us to talk. I want us to be married."

Rachel started crying again, but it was a gentler weeping this time, from the heart, not the gut. Twisting, she drew herself up against him. Her tears wet his neck, but she held on tightly, held on until she needed a kiss.

His mouth moved on hers, reinforcing everything he had said, taking her to places she hadn't been in too many long years. She felt his hunger and tasted his need, weak with it all, when he finally broke the kiss and framed her face with his hands. "I never stopped loving you," he whispered. "Never did."

She could see it in his eyes. But the light had been there once before and died. "You shut me out," she accused in a nasal voice.

"I was stupid. I was proud. I didn't know what mattered." He threw back an accusation. "You walked away."

"I was hurting. I had to distance myself from the source of the pain."

"I didn't know you were pregnant when you called me that time. I should have come. I'm sorry you lost the baby. It would have been something."

"Yes." She had mourned that child. It would have been . . . something. "Did you really leave the firm?"

"I did. What do you think?"

"I think it's good. David brought out the worst in you."

"He may have. Do you mind that I finished your pictures?"

"I love that you finished my pictures. What's with Jill?"

"Over. I knew there was no future. What's with Ben?"

"Nothing. Nothing. Nothing."

"I like your friends."

"They like you. What'll you do with your house?"

"Sell it. We could buy something bigger, but I like the place you have."

"Really? Are you sure? You're not just saying that?"

"Really. I'm sure. I'm not just saying that."

"Will you like it in five years?" she asked, knowing he knew what she meant. It was there in his eyes, with his love.

"I've been alone. Five years, ten years, twenty years living with you in that house is so much more than what I was facing before . . ." His voice broke. His eyes were moist.

Rachel touched his lips. *I love you,* she mouthed and said it again in a kiss. When it was done, he gave a huge sigh of the relief she felt and hugged her with arms that shook.

From somewhere off to the side came an edgy "Mr. Wolfe won't like this."

No, Rachel figured, he wouldn't. She also figured he had known all along that something was missing in her life. She suspected that in his own kind way he would be pleased to know she had found it again.

THREE WISHES

Well-Wishes

A Personal
Note from the Author

I've always been a wish maker. I wish at the sight of evening's first star, on pulling the long end of the turkey wishbone, in secret notes written on birch bark and tossed onto a campfire, and, of course, over birthday candles. Some of my wishes are general and constant, most notably for good health and happiness. Others are more specific.

On the occasion of the publication of this book, I offer three of the latter. First, anniversary wishes to Steve; I vote for another thirty years. Second, graduation wishes to Andrew and Jeremy; may you each find deep satisfaction in whatever field you choose to enter. Third, wedding wishes to Jodi and Eric, with the sweetest dreams of good health, happiness, and—I can't resist—true love always.

I've made other wishes this year. Thanks to my agent, Amy Berkower, and my editor, Laurie Bernstein, many have already come true. You both know what's left. We'll wish together.

Chapter

~ 1 ~

*I*t wasn't the first snow of the season. Panama, Vermont, lay far enough north to have already seen several snow-dusted dawns. But this wasn't dawn, and these flakes didn't dust. From early afternoon right on into evening, they fell heavy and fat and wet.

Truckers stopping at the diner complained of the roads growing slick, but the warning carried little weight with locals. They knew that the sun would be back, even an Indian summer before winter set in. Snowfall now was simply frosting on the cake of another wildfire fall, thick flakes silencing the riot of colorful leaves, draping a plump white shawl on the town green's oak benches, on marigolds that lingeringly lined front walks, on a bicycle propped against an open front gate.

The scene was so peaceful that no one imagined the accident to come, least of all Bree Miller. Winter was her favorite season. There was something about snow that softened the world, made it make-believe for the briefest time, and while she wasn't a woman prone to fancy—would have immediately denied it if accused—she had her private moments.

She didn't bother with a jacket. The memory of summer's heat was all too fresh. Besides, with locals wanting to eat before the weather worsened and with truckers bulking up, the diner had been hopping, so she was plenty warm without.

She slipped out the door, closing it tight on the hum of conversation, the hiss and sizzle of the grill, the sultry twang of Shania Twain. In the sudden hush, she ran lightly down the steps, across the parking lot, then the street. On the far side, she flattened her spine to the crusty trunk of a large maple whose amber leaves hung heavy with snow, and looked back.

The diner was a vision of stainless steel and neon, rich purples and greens bouncing off silver, new and more gallant through a steady fall of snow. Gone were little items on her fix-it list—the scrape Morgan Willis's truck had put on a corner panel, a dent in the front railing, bird droppings off the edge of the roof. What remained was sparkling clean, warm, and inviting, starting with the diner's roadside logo, concentric rings of neon forming a large frying pan with the elegant eruption of FLASH AN' THE PAN from its core. Behind that were golden lamps at each of ten broad windows running the diner's length and, in booths behind those lamps, looking snug and content, the customers.

The diner wasn't Bree's. She just worked there. But she liked looking at it.

Same with Panama. Up the hill, at the spot where East Main leveled into an oval around the town green, snow capped the steel roofs of the row of tall Federals and beyond, white on white, the church steeple. Down the hill, at the spot where the road dipped past the old train depot, snow hid the stains that years of diesel abuse had left and put a hearty head on the large wood beer stein that marked the Sleepy Creek Brewery.

Panama was ten minutes off the highway on the truck route running from Concord to Montreal. Being neither here nor there was one of its greatest strengths. There were no cookie-cutter subdivisions, no planned developments with architect-designed wraparound porches. Porches had been wrapping around houses in Panama since the days of the Revolution, not for the sake of style but for community. Those porches were as genuine as the people who used them. Add the lack of crime and the low cost of land, and the town's survival was ensured. Bright minds sought haven here and found inspiration. The brewery was but one example. There was also a bread company, workshops producing hand-carved furniture and wooden toys, and a gourmet ice cream factory. Native Panamanians lent stability. Newcomers brought cash.

Bree drew in a snow-chilled breath, held it deep in her lungs, let it slowly out. The occasional snowflake breached the leaves overhead to land in an airy puff on her arm, looking soft, feeling rich, in those few seconds before melting away. On impulse, she slid around the tree trunk to face the woods. Here, the snow picked up the diner's lights in a mystical way. Drifting leaves whirled about, forest fairies at play, Bree fancied. From nowhere came childhood images of carousels, clowns, and Christmas, all more dream than memory. She listened hard, half expecting to hear elf sounds mixed in with those of nocturnal creatures. But, of course, there were none.

Foolish Bree. High on snow. Time to go inside.

Still she stood there, riveted by something that made her eyes mist and her throat ache. If it was wanting, she didn't know what for. She had a good life. She was content.

Still she stood there.

Behind her came a fragment of conversation when the diner door opened, and the subsequent growls, muted by billowing flakes, of one big rig, then a second. By the time the semis had rumbled out of the parking lot, cruised down the hill, and turned toward the highway, the only sound left was the cat's-paw whisper of snow upon snow.

The diner door opened again, this time to a louder "Bree! I need you!"

Brushing tears from her eyes, she pushed off from the bark. Seconds later, she was running back across the road, turning her head against the densest of the flakes, suddenly so desperate to be back inside, where everything made sense, that she grew careless. She slipped, fought for balance with a flailing of arms, landed in the snow all the same. Scrambling up, she brushed at the seat of her black jeans and, with barely a pause to shake her hands free of snow, rushed inside, to be met by applause, several wolf whistles, and a "Way to go, Bree!"

The last was from a trucker, one of the regulars. Another round of applause broke out when she wrapped her icy hands around his bull neck and gave an affectionate squeeze on her way to the kitchen.

Flash, the diner's owner and executive chef, met her at the swinging door. A near-full gallon of milk hung from his fingers. "It's bad again," he said, releasing the door once she was inside. "What're we gonna do? Look of the roads, no delivery's coming anytime soon."

"We have extra," Bree assured him, opening the refrigerator to verify it.

Flash ducked his head and took a look. "That'll be enough?"

"Plenty."

"Seventeen's up, Bree," the grillman called.

The diner sat fifty-two, in ten booths and twelve counter stools. At its busiest times, there were lines out the door, but bad weather slowed things down. Barely thirty-five remained now. LeeAnn Conti was serving half. The rest were Bree's.

Balancing four plates holding a total of twelve eggs, twelve rashers of bacon, six sausages, six slabs each of

4

maple nut and raisin toast, and enough hash browns to crowd everything in, she delivered supper to the men in seventeen, the booth to the right of the door. She had known the four all her life. They, too, had gone to the local schools and stayed to work in the area, Sam and Dave at the lumber mill three towns over, Andy at his family's tackle store, Jack at the farm his father had left his brother and him. They were large men with insatiable appetites for early-evening breakfast.

The Littles, two booths down, were another story. Ben and Liz had fled a New York ad agency to run their own by way of computer, fax, and phone from Vermont. Along with seven-year-old Benji, five-year-old Samantha, and two-year-old Joey, they hit the diner several times a week to take advantage of Flash's huge portions, easily splitting three orders of turkey, mashed potatoes, and peas, or biscuit-topped shepherd's pie, or American chop suey. They were currently sharing a serving of warm apple crisp and a large chocolate chip cookie.

At Bree's appearance, the two-year-old put down his hunk of cookie, scrambled to his feet on the bench, and opened his arms. She scooped him up. "Was everything good?"

He gave her a chocolaty grin that melted her heart.

"Anything else here?" she asked his parents.

"Just the check," said Ben. "That snow keeps coming. Driving won't be great."

When Joey squirmed, Bree kissed the mop of his hair and returned him to the bench. At the side counter, she tallied the check, then put it on their table and set to cleaning the adjacent booth, where the drivers of the newly departed big rigs had been. She cleared the dirty dishes, pocketed her tip, wiped down the black Formica, straightened shakers, condiment bottles, and the small black vase that held a spray of goldenrod. She set out new place mats, oval replicas of the frying pan from the logo, with the regular menu printed in its center. Specials—"The Daily Flash"—were handwritten on each of two elliptical chalkboards high behind either end of the counter.

She moved several booths down to Panama's power elite —postmaster Earl Yarum, police chief Eliot Bonner, town meeting moderator Emma McGreevy. Before them were dishes that had earlier held a beef stew, a pork chop special, and a grilled chicken salad. All three plates, plus a basket of sourdough rolls, were empty, which was good news. When sated, Earl, Eliot, and Emma were innocuous.

Bree grinned. "Ready for dessert?"

"Whaddya got?" Earl asked.

"Whaddya want?"

"Pie."

"O-kay. We have apple, peach, and blueberry. We have pumpkin. We have strawberry rhubarb, banana cream, maple cream, maple pecan, pumpkin pecan, lemon meringue—"

"Anything chocolate?" Earl asked.

"Chocolate pecan, chocolate mousse, chocolate rum cream—"

"How about a brownie?"

She might have guessed they were headed there. Earl was predictable.

"One brownie," she said, and raised questioning brows at Emma. "Tea?"

"Please." Emma never had anything but tea.

Eliot played his usual game, letting Bree list as many ice cream flavors as she could—Flash owned part of Panama Rich and stocked every one of its twenty-three flavors— before ordering a dish of plain old strawberry.

Working around LeeAnn, the grillman, the cook, the dishwasher, and Flash, Bree warmed the brownie and added whipped cream, hot fudge, and nuts, the way Earl liked it, and scooped up Eliot's ice cream. She served a chicken stir-fry to Panama's only lawyer, Martin Sprague, in the six spot at the counter, and pork chops and chili to Ned and

Frank Wright, local plumbers, two stools over. With carafes in either hand, she topped off coffees down the row of booths, then worked her way along the counter.

At the far end sat Dotty Hale and her daughter, Jane. Both were tall and lean, but while Dotty's face was tight, Jane's was softer in ways that had little to do with age. Not that Bree was impartial. Jane was one of her closest friends.

LeeAnn had her elbows on the counter before them. In contrast to the Hales, she was small and spirited, with short, spiked blond hair and eyes that filled her face. Those eyes were wider than ever. "Abby Nolan spent the night *where?* But she just *divorced* John."

"Final last week," Dotty confirmed, with the nod of a bony chin. "Court papers came in the mail. Earl saw them."

"So why's she sleeping with him?"

"She isn't," Jane said.

Dotty turned on her. "This isn't coming from *me*. Eliot was the one who saw her car in John's drive." She returned to LeeAnn. "Why? Because she's pregnant."

LeeAnn looked beside herself with curiosity. "With *John's* child? *How?*"

Bree smiled dryly as she joined them. "The normal way, I'd think. Only the baby isn't John's. It's Davey Hillard's."

Dotty looked wounded. "Who told you that?"

"Abby," Bree said. She, Abby, and Jane had been friends since grade school.

"Then why'd she spend the night with John?" LeeAnn asked.

"She didn't," Jane said.

"Were you there?" Dotty asked archly.

"Abby just went to talk," Bree said to divert Dotty's attention from Jane. "She and John are still friends. She wanted to break the news to him herself."

"That's not what Emma says," Dotty argued. Emma was her sister and her major source of gossip. "Know what else she says? Julia Dean got a postcard."

"Mother," Jane pleaded.

"Well, it's *fact*," Dotty argued. "Earl saw the postcard and told Eliot, since he's the one has to keep peace here and family being upset can cause trouble. Julia's family is *not* thrilled that she's here. The postcard was from her daughter in Des Moines, who said that it was a *shame* that Julia was isolating herself, and that she understood how upset she had been by *Daddy's* death, that they *all* were, but three years of mourning should be enough, so when was she coming home?"

"All that on a postcard?" Bree asked. She didn't know much more about Julia than that she had opened a small flower store three years before and twice weekly arranged sprigs in the diner's vases. She came by for an occasional meal but kept to herself. She struck Bree as shy but sweet, certainly not the type to deserve being the butt of gossip.

"Julia's family doesn't know about Earl," Jane muttered.

"Really." Bree glanced toward the window when a bright light swelled there, another eighteen-wheeler pulling into the parking lot.

"And then," Dotty said, with a glance of her own at that light, "there's Verity. She claims she saw another UFO. Eliot says the lights were from a truck, but she insists there's a mark on the back of her car where that mother ship tailed her."

LeeAnn leaned closer. "Did she see the baby ships again, the squiggly little pods?"

"I didn't ask." Dotty shuddered. "That woman's odd."

Bree had always found Verity more amusing than odd and would have said as much now if Flash hadn't called. "Twenty-two's up, LeeAnn."

Bree stayed LeeAnn with a touch. "I'll get it."

She topped off Dotty's coffee and returned the carafes to their heaters. Scooping up the chicken piccata with angel hair that was ready and waiting, she headed down the counter toward the booths. Twenty-two was the last in the row, tucked in the corner by the jukebox. A lone man sat there, just as he had from time to time in the last seven months. He never said much, never invited much to be said. Most often, like now, he was reading a book.

His name was Tom Gates. He had bought the Hubbard place, a shingle-sided bungalow on West Elm that hadn't seen a stitch of improvement in all the years that the Hubbards' health had been in decline. Since Tom Gates had taken possession, missing shingles had been replaced, shutters had been straightened, the porch had been painted, the lawn cut. What had happened inside was more murky. Skipper Boone had rewired the place, and the Wrights had installed a new furnace, but beyond that, no one knew. And Bree had asked. She had always loved the Hubbard place. Though smaller than her Victorian, it had ten times the charm. She might have bought it herself if she'd had the nerve, but she had inherited her own house from her father, who had inherited it from his. Millers had lived on South Forest for too many years to count and too many to move. So she contented herself with catching what bits of gossip she could about restoration of the bungalow on West Elm.

None of those bits came from Tom Gates. He wasn't sociable. Good-looking. Very good-looking. Too good-looking to be alone. But not sociable.

"Here you go," Bree said. When he moved his book aside, she slid the plate in. She wiped her palms on the back of her jeans and pushed her hands in the pockets there. "Reading anything good?"

His eyes shifted from his dinner back to the book. "It's okay."

She tipped her head to see the title, but the whole front looked to be typed. "Weird cover."

"It hasn't been published yet."

"Really? How'd you get it?"

"I know someone."

"The author?" When he shook his head, the diner's light

shimmered in hair that was shiny, light brown, and a mite too long. "Are you a reviewer?" she asked.

He shifted. "Not quite."

"Just an avid reader, then," she decided. Not that he looked scholarly. He was too tanned, too tall, too broad in the shoulders. Coming and going, he strode. Flash bet that he was a politician who had lost a dirty election and fled. Dotty bet he was a burned-out businessman, because Earl told of mail from New York. LeeAnn bet he was an adventurer recouping after a tiring trek.

Bree could see him as an adventurer. He had that rugged look. His buying a house in town didn't mean much. Even adventurers needed to rest sometimes, but they didn't stay put for long. Panama bored men who loved risk. This one would be gone before long.

It was a shame, because Tom Gates had great hands. He had long, lean, blunt-tipped fingers and moved them in a way that suggested they could do most anything they tried. Bree had never once seen dirt under his nails, which set him apart from most of the men who ate here, and while he didn't have the calluses those men did, his hands looked well used. He had cut himself several months back and had needed stitches. The scar was nearly two inches long and starting to fade.

"I just finished the new Dean Koontz," she said. "Have you read it yet?"

He was studying his fork. "No."

"It's pretty good. Worth a shot. Can I get you anything else? Another beer?" She hitched her chin toward the long-neck on the far side of his plate. "You know that's local, don't you? Sleepy Creek Pale. It's brewed down the street."

His eyes met hers. They were wonderfully gray. "Yes," he said. "I do know."

She might have been lured by those eyes to say something else, had not the front door opened just then to a flurry of flakes and the stamping boots of four truckers. Shaking

10

snow from heads and jackets, they called out greetings, slapped the palms of the men in seventeen, and slid into sixteen, which meant they were Bree's.

"Nothing else?" she asked Tom Gates again. When he shook his head, she smiled. "Enjoy your meal." Still smiling, she walked on down the line. "Hey, guys, how're you doin'?"

"Cold."

"Tired."

"Hungry."

"A regular round for starters?" she asked. When the nods came fast, she went to the icebox on the wall behind the counter, pulled open the shiny steel door, and extracted two Sleepy Creek Pales, one Sleepy Creek Amber, and a Heineken. Back at the booth, she fished a bottle opener from the short black apron skimming her hips and did the honors.

"Ahhhhh," said John Hagan after a healthy swallow. "Good stuff on a night like this."

Bree glanced out the window. "How many inches would you say?"

"Four," John answered.

"Nah, there's at least eight," argued Kip Tucker.

"Headed to twenty," warned Gene Mackey for the benefit of a passing, predictably gullible LeeAnn.

"Twenty?"

Bree nudged Gene's shoulder. "He's putting you on, Lee. Come on, guys. Behave."

"What fun is that?" Gene asked, hooking her waist and pulling her close.

She unhooked his arm. "All the fun you're getting," she said, with a haughty look. "I'll be back to take your order *once* I'm done scraping down plates."

"I'll have my usual," T. J. Kearns said fast, before she could leave.

"Me, too," said Gene.

John pointed at himself and nodded, indicating beef pot

11

pie topped with mashed potatoes and gravy, served with hunks of bread for dunking and whatever vegetables Flash had that day, buttered.

Kip was eyeing the specials board. "What's he got up there that I want?"

Bree knew Kip. "Brook trout," she said in a cultured way, "sautéed in butter and served on a bed of basmati rice, with sun-dried tomatoes, Portobello mushrooms, and broccoli."

Kip sighed his pleasure. "One up, right here. Thanks, doll."

Panama lay in hill country. Come the first of November, sand barrels sat on most every corner, trucks carried chains, and folks without four-wheel drive put on snow tires. But this wasn't the first of November. It was the ninth of October, and the snow was coming heavy and fast. By eight, only a handful of stragglers remained.

Armed with a laptop computer and her own serving of trout, Bree slid in across from Flash. He was reading the newspaper, alternately sipping coffee and pulling at one of two sticky buns on his plate, no doubt his dinner. She never failed to be amazed that a man who was endlessly artful when it came to creating meals for others had such abominable eating habits himself.

"You're missing good trout," she said.

"I hate bones."

"There aren't any bones. Not in your trout."

"That's what we tell the customers," he said, without looking up, "but I never know for sure if I get them all out, and the fear of it would ruin my meal. Besides"—he looked up then—"there aren't usually any sticky buns left after five. Why are there today?"

Bree opened the laptop. "Because Angus, Oliver, and Jack didn't make it in"—and wisely so, since the three were in their eighties and better at home in a storm.

"Flash?" asked LeeAnn. She shot a look at the last man at the counter. "Gav says he'll drive me home, since I don't have boots or anything, but he can't hang around till we close." Her brows rose.

Flash shot a look at Bree. "Ask her. She's the one who'll have to cover for you."

Bree shooed her off. "No one else is coming in. Not tonight. Go."

LeeAnn went.

"She skips out early too often," Flash said. "You have a soft heart."

"Yours is softer than mine, which is why you didn't say no first. Besides, she has kids at home. I don't."

"Why not?" he asked.

Bree pulled up the supply list. "I think we've been through this before."

"Tell me again. I especially like the part about needing a man to have kids, like you couldn't have any guy who walked in here. Know what turns them on? Your disinterest."

"It isn't disinterest. It's caution."

Caution sounded kinder. Disinterest was probably more to the point. The men who passed through the diner were just fine for conversation and laughs. They gave appreciative looks to her hair, which was thick, dark, and forever escaping whatever she tied it with, and her body, which was of average height and better toned than most. What they liked most, though, was the fact that she served them without argument and, more, that she knew what they wanted before they said it. Her father had liked that, too. She had been his cook, his maid, his tailor, his barber, his social secretary . . . the list went on and on. In the days following his death, she'd had her very first taste of me time. Now, three years later, it was still both novelty and prized possession.

"Caution. Ahh. Well, that is you, Bree. Cautious to a

fault. Have you hired someone to get you a decent heating system, or are you still getting estimates?"

"I'm still getting estimates."

He glanced at the snow. "Time just ran out."

"Give it a day. Sun'll be back."

"You're only postponing the inevitable. Last winter you were racing over here half frozen. Why wait? You have money."

"I have money for a new car. That's first on my list. Heating is second."

"That's crazy."

"Why? I have a woodstove in the kitchen and quilts in every room. I can stay warm whether the furnace works or not. But I can't go anywhere without a car." She tapped the laptop's screen. "We have to talk about getting a new milk supplier."

"No."

She softened her tone. "Stafford's local. We both want to support him, but his deliveries are late more often than not, and lately a full quarter of what he brings is bad. Think back two hours. You were in a panic."

"I was tired, is all. Stafford's working the kinks out."

"He's been working the kinks out for two years, but they aren't going away."

"Give him a little longer," Flash said. He flipped up his paper and resumed reading.

Bree didn't know whether to laugh or cry. Oh, yes, Flash was softhearted, a sucker if the truth were told, though that was a good half of the diner's charm. He was an artist. Try as he might to look like a trucker in the black jeans, purple T-shirt, and bill cap that were the diner's uniform, he couldn't pull it off. Even without the long mane spilling from the hole in the back of his cap, he had too gentle a look, and that was even before he waved off the difference when one of the town's poorest came up short on cash at the end of a meal.

Not that Bree was complaining. Had her boss been anyone else, she would still be waitressing, period. But Flash wasn't hung up on formalities. She was good with numbers, so he had her balance the books. She was good with deadlines, so he had her pay the bills. She worked with the people who printed their place mats, the people who serviced the drink machines, the people who trucked in fresh eggs, vegetables, and fish.

Hungry, she dug into her trout and broccoli. Focusing on the computer screen, she plugged in the week's expected deliveries, noted shortages that had arisen, set up orders to be placed as soon as she hooked the computer to the modem in the back office. Flash was a softie there, too. That modem had been installed within twenty-four hours of her saying it might be nice.

The sound of spinning wheels drew her eye to the window, where a truck was heading out of the lot. After a minute, the tires gained traction, the sound evened out, and taillights disappeared in the thickening snow.

By eight-fifty, the last of the diners had left, fifty-two places had been wiped down and set for breakfast, dishes had been washed, food put away, the grill scraped. Minutes after Flash officially called it a night, the staff was gone.

Bree was pulling on her jacket when he said, "I'll drive you home."

She shook her head. "Driving is slow. It'll be faster if I walk." Tugging up the leg of her jeans, she showed him her boots. "Besides, you live downhill, I live uphill. No need backtracking in weather like this."

But Flash was insistent. Taking her arm, he guided her out the door.

The world had changed dramatically since Bree's earlier foray into the storm. With the exception of bare pavement where others of the staff had parked and just left, everything was pure white, and colder, far colder than before.

15

"It's too early for this," Flash grumbled as they approached his Explorer. While he dug behind his seat for a scraper, Bree started on the windows with the sleeve of her jacket. When he took over with the brush, she climbed inside. Leaning over the gearshift, she started the engine and, once the windshield was clear, turned on the wipers.

Since the parking lot had last been plowed, another several inches of snow had fallen. Between those inches and what had been left around cars that were parked, the lot was ragged. Flash gunned his engine to back the Explorer over the pile of snow at its own rear, then shifted into drive. The Explorer jolted its way to the street.

Bree stared hard out the windshield. As far as she could tell, the only thing marking the road was the slightly lower level of snow there. The headlights of the Explorer swung a bright arc onto East Main. Flash accelerated. His tires spun, found purchase, started slowly up the hill. They hadn't gone far when the spinning resumed. The Explorer slid sideways. He braked, downshifted, and tried again.

"Bad tires?" she asked.

"Bad roads," he muttered.

"Not if you're going downhill. Let me walk. Please?"

He resisted through several more tries, shifting from drive to reverse and back in an attempt to gain traction, and he always did, but never for long. The Explorer had barely reached the first of five houses that climbed the hill to the town green when, sliding sideways and back this time, he gave in.

Bree pulled up her hood and slid out. "Thanks for trying. See you tomorrow." Shutting the door, she burrowed into her jacket and started up the hill.

At first, with the Explorer coasting backward, its headlights lit her way. When Flash turned at the diner's driveway and came out headfirst, the lights disappeared. Moments later, even the sound of his engine was gone.

In the silence, Bree trekked upward. The snow on the

road wasn't deep, rising only to the top of her boots, but she had the same problem the Explorer had. With the drop in temperature, the thin layer of packed snow left by the plow had frozen under the new-fallen stuff. She kept slipping on the steepening incline.

Tightening her hood, she tucked her hands in her pockets and plodded on. When she slipped again, her arms flew out for balance, hands bare and cold. She wished she had gloves, wished it even more in the next instant, when she lost her footing and landed wrist deep in the snow. Straightening, she shook herself off and went on. One more slip, though, and she trudged to the side of the road. The snow was deeper there, well past her calves, which made the walking harder but safer.

Head bowed against the steady fall of snow, she leaned into the climb. She had walked the same route for years, barely had to lift her eyes to know where she was. One foot rose high after the other to clear the drifts. By the time she passed the last of the houses, her thighs were feeling the strain. She felt instant relief when the road leveled off at the top.

Turning left, she started around the town green under the gaslights' amber glow. There were no cars about, just snow-shrouded shapes in driveways. Wood smoke rose from high chimneys to scent the air. Snow slid, with a rush and a thud, down tall steel panels from roof to ground.

The curve of the road took her past the Federal that housed the bank, with smaller offices above for the town's lawyer, realtor, and chiropractor. The one beside it housed the Chalifoux family, the one beside that the Nolans, the one beside that the library. Farther on, in a more modest house, lived the minister and his family. At the end of the oval, spire high, large green shutters and doors finely edged in snow, was the church.

The wood fence circling the churchyard had disappeared under the snow, as had the split-rail one around the town green. But the green wasn't to be missed. A true common area, it had recently been host to sunbathers, picnickers, and stargazers. Now the limbs of maples, birches, and firs hung low to the ground under the weight of the snow, transforming stately trees into weepers.

The sound of an engine broke the silence. At the opposite end of the green, a pickup coasted down from Pine Street and cruised slowly around the oval. When it reached Bree, it stopped.

Curtis Lamb rolled down his window. "Just comin' from work?"

Bree raised an arm to shield her eyes from the snow. "Yeah."

"Want a lift?"

But Curtis lived downhill, not far from Flash. She smiled, shook her head, gestured toward Birch Hill, just beyond the church. "I'm almost there. You go on."

Curtis rolled up his window. The pickup went slowly forward, turned right at the bank, and started down East Main.

Bree resumed the hike. She was making good time now, was actually enjoying the snow. It was cleansing, coming so soon after summer's sweat.

Another engine broke the stillness, with a growing sputter. Bree guessed the vehicle was climbing Birch Hill. Its headlights had just appeared when a second pickup swooped down Pine, far off to her right. It was going fast, too fast. She watched it skid onto the oval, regain traction, and barrel toward her end.

Eager to be out of its way, she quickened her step. At the corner, she turned onto Birch Hill. The car climbing it—a bare-bones Jeep—was twenty feet off but approaching steadily, so she hopped from the street into the deeper snow at the side.

The pickup kept coming. Alarmed by its speed, fascinated in a horrified way, Bree stopped walking. The pickup looked to be dull blue and old. She figured that whoever was driving was either drunk, inexperienced, or just plain dumb.

"Slow down," she warned. At the rate it was going, it would surely skid when it turned. And it was going to have to turn, either right onto Birch Hill or left around the oval. If it went straight, it would hit her head-on.

Suddenly frightened, she moved. Running as quickly as she could through the deep snow, she started down Birch Hill, but it was an ill-timed move. Seconds after she passed the Jeep, she heard the crunch of metal on metal. Then the Jeep was skidding back, sliding faster than she could run and in the god-awful same direction.

Its impact with her was quieter. She felt a searing pain and a moment's weightlessness, then nothing at all.

Chapter

2

The first hit sent the Jeep skidding sideways and back. When the pickup tried to swerve away, it skidded into a broadside hit that crushed the Jeep against a stone wall. On the rebound, the pickup ricocheted back to the center of the road and sailed off down the hill.

Tom Gates didn't see that. He had only one thought in mind. Heart pounding, he rammed his shoulder once against the Jeep's door, realized that it was too damaged to open, and scrambled over the gearshift to the passenger's door. When it wouldn't budge, he raised his feet, kicked out the glass, and tumbled through. He grazed the edge of the stone wall on his way to the snow but was on his feet in an instant, racing back over the wall and around the Jeep.

He searched the road and saw nothing. He fell to his knees beside the Jeep, searched underneath, ran to where it met the wall, and, putting everything he had into the effort, moved the Jeep enough to see that no one was trapped there, not even down by the tires.

Frantic, he looked around. He was sure that someone had

turned the corner seconds before the pickup hit him. He had hit whoever it was. He was sure of that, too.

He had just spotted a dark lump in the snow when a light came on in the house deep in the yard. "Anyone hurt?" Carl Breen hollered.

"Yeah," Tom hollered back. "Call an ambulance."

He stumbled to his knees by the inert shape, reached out to touch it, paused. What to do without causing greater injury? The legs looked normal, no grotesque angles there, but an oversize jacket hid everything above. Crouching over the head, he saw a face, which meant that whoever it was wasn't suffocating in the snow, assuming that whoever it was hadn't died on impact. At least he saw no blood in the snow.

"Hey," he said urgently, "hey. Can you hear me?"

A hood covered half of the face. When he loosened its strings and eased it back, recognition was instant. No matter that her normal coloring had gone ashen. If the fineness of her features hadn't given her away, stray wisps of dark hair would have.

Tom closed his eyes and rocked back on his heels. It was Bree, sweet Bree from the diner.

"Christ," he whispered, coming forward. He touched her cold cheek and pulled the hood up again to protect her face from the falling snow. He felt her neck for a pulse, though his own was pounding so hard he didn't know whose he perceived. Her skin under her clothing was warm, though. Taking hope from that, he pulled off his jacket and spread it over her.

That was when he saw her hand, little more than a small band of knuckles at the end of her sleeve. It was cold and limp. Taking it gently, he rubbed it to warm it up.

"Bree?"

She didn't move, didn't moan, didn't blink.

He slipped a hand inside the hood and put it to her cheek. "Can you hear me, Bree?"

A beam of light swung past him, then returned. Squinting into it, he saw Carl Breen trudging through the snow. His wool topcoat flapped over wash-worn pajamas. He had a southwester on his head and unlaced galoshes on his feet.

The beam of the flashlight shifted to Bree. "Is she dead?" Carl asked.

"Not yet. Did you call?"

"Ambulance is on its way."

"How long will it take?"

"Good weather? Ten minutes. This weather? Twenty."

"*Twenty?*" Tom cried. "Christ, we need something sooner than that."

Carl was bending over, lifting the edge of her hood. "What was she, coming from work?"

"Twenty minutes is too long. She can't lie here that long."

"Won't have to. Chief's on the way. Travis, too. He's a paramedic. Need a blanket?"

"Yes." While Carl plodded back to the house, Tom kept one hand around Bree's and the other on her cheek, so she would know that someone was there.

"Christ, I'm sorry," he murmured. "Ten feet up or back, and I'd have missed you." He leaned close, looking for movement. "Are you with me, Bree?" He didn't know what he would do if she died, couldn't conceive of living with that. Being a self-centered bastard was one thing. Causing someone's death was something else entirely.

"Hang on, baby," he murmured, looking at the road, rocking impatiently. "Come on, come on. What's taking so fucking long?"

Carl returned, unzipping a high-tech sleeping bag. "My grandson's," he explained, and shook it out over Bree. Squatting, he said, "Quite some noise, that crash. What happened?"

Tom shot another glance at the street. "Where are they?"

"Chief was down Creek Road when I called. He'll be

coming up East Main." He shone his flashlight on Tom's face. "You're bleeding." Tom pushed the light away, still Carl saw fit to inform him, "Your face got cut."

Tom felt nothing but fear. Again he searched Bree's throat for a pulse, sure he felt one this time, though it was weak. Slipping his hand inside the hood, he cupped her head. "They're almost here, Bree. Help's almost here."

Miraculously, then, it was. In what seemed the best thing to have happened to Tom in months, the headlights of the Chevy Blazer that served as a cruiser for Eliot Bonner, Panama's police department, preceded it by seconds around the corner. Travis Fitch followed close in his own car. Both vehicles pulled in at either end of the Jeep, doors opening in tandem, drivers running through the snow in the crisscross of headlights.

Travis, in his early thirties and beanpole long, wore dark pants and a dark hooded jacket. Eliot was a bit older, a bit shorter, a bit heavier. In his plaid jacket and orange wool cap, he looked more like a hunter than a police chief, which, given Panama's minimal law enforcement needs, wasn't far off the mark.

Though Tom shifted to allow Travis access, he kept the back of his fingers against Bree's cheek. "She hasn't moved," he said, giving in to traces of panic, "hasn't opened her eyes or said anything."

Travis was feeling around under the coverings.

The police chief hunkered down beside Tom. In a gravelly voice to match his beer belly, he said, "Jeep's a mess. What happened?"

Tom was watching Travis, wondering if he knew what he was doing. "A truck hit me. I hit her."

"Must've done it real hard, to throw her so far. Where's the truck?"

Tom twisted to look down the road. It was nowhere in sight. Swearing softly, he twisted back to Bree. "What do you feel?" he asked Travis.

"Neck's okay. Spine's okay. I think the problem's inside."

"What do you mean, inside?"

"Stomach, or thereabouts. Somethin's hard."

"She's bleeding internally?"

"Looks that way."

"Who was driving the truck?" the chief asked.

But Tom couldn't think about the truck yet. "Can she bleed to death?" he asked, as Travis worked his way down Bree's legs.

"She could," Travis said. "Nothing's broken down here, leastways nothing I can feel."

"How do you stop the bleeding?"

"I don't. Surgeons do." He re-covered Bree and pushed to his feet. "I'm calling ahead. They'd better get in someone good." He loped back through the snow to his car.

"Where will they take her?" Tom asked Bonner. He didn't want Bree to die, did not want Bree to die. For the first time in seven months, he wished he were back in New York. There, she would have had top doctors, no questions asked. Here, he wasn't so sure.

"There's a medical center in Ashmont," Bonner answered.

There certainly was. Tom had been there. It had been just fine for stitching up his hand, but Bree hadn't been cut by a saw. "She needs a *hospital*."

"She needs fast care," the chief replied. "No chopper's taking off in this snow, so she's going to Ashmont. They'll get a surgeon up from Saint Johnsbury. If he sets off now, he'll reach Ashmont by the time she's ready."

"Does Ashmont have operating rooms?"

Bonner screwed up his face. "Hell, man, we're not hicks. Our operating rooms may not be as state-of-the-art as yours, but they get the job done. We don't like dying any more'n you do, y'know."

Tom straightened. He wasn't the helpless type. Yet what

he felt now ranked right up there with what he had felt all those months before, standing alone at his mother's graveside with nothing to do but grieve. "Someone has to call her family."

"Well, there isn't any of that to speak of," Bonner advised, "not for Bree. Her mother left her when she was a baby. Her father raised her, but he's been dead three years now. There weren't any sisters or brothers. No husband. No kids."

That surprised Tom. He had watched Bree work. She had always seemed so self-possessed, so grounded, that he had assumed she had the solid backing of family. He pictured her with a husband and a child or two, maybe a mother or sister to help with the kids while she worked. He had envied her that, had envied her for belonging.

Bonner rose. "Flash is as close to family as she has. I'll give him a call."

He set off just as Travis returned. "The ambulance is three minutes away. No sense my moving her. They'll have a long board."

Tom sat on his knees in the snow. He touched Bree's neck, her forehead, her cheek, wanting to do something and feeling hamstrung. He brushed snow from her hood, for what good that did. She had been at the wrong place at the wrong time. So had he.

Desperate for someone to blame, he looked skyward. The clouds were a dense night gray, still heavy with snow. "It's October, for Christ's sake. When's this supposed to stop?"

Carl, who continued to hold his flashlight on Bree, said, "Weatherman says morning."

"Yeah, like he said this was gonna be rain."

"Difference of a few degrees, is all."

Tom might have said what he thought of that if the ambulance hadn't circled the town green just then. Its engine was all business, giving it away even before it pulled around the corner, red and white lights flashing, and ground to a halt.

Leaning over Bree, Tom felt a fast relief, a sharp fear, and something almost proprietary. He talked softly, telling her that help had come, that she was going to be all right, that she shouldn't worry about anything. He wasn't pleased when the ambulance crew hustled him aside, or when one of them threw a blanket around him and poked at his face. He was most bothered when they wouldn't let him ride with Bree.

"I'm all she has right now," he argued, acutely aware of the "right now." Bree might not have family, but she had friends. He had seen the way she had with people. Flash would be only the start. Once word spread that she was hurt, friends would rush to her bedside, and he would be the outsider, the villain of the piece.

The grasp Eliot Bonner took of his arm said it was happening already. "We need to talk, you and me. We'll follow in the cruiser. Unless," he added dryly, "you were a doctor back in the city." The ambulance doors closed. "You never did say what you were."

Soon after Tom had come to town, the police chief had stopped by. "Offering a welcome," he had said, with a too wide smile, and a welcome might have been part of it. Tom wasn't so untrusting as to deny that. But the bottom line had been curiosity about Panama's newest resident.

In the ten minutes that they had spent talking on the front walk, Tom had been vague. More than anything, he had wanted anonymity, and he still wanted it. But having been involved in an accident in which one of Panama's own was badly hurt, he was in a precarious position. He might have a history of lying to friends and family—worse, of lying to himself—but he knew better than to lie to the law.

"I'm a writer," he said.

Bonner sighed. "Ah, jeez. Another writer. Searching for inspiration, am I right?"

"Not really." There was so much else for him to seek before he sought that.

"Then what?"

Tom didn't answer. He had come to Panama to distance himself from the arrogant, self-absorbed man he'd become. He had wanted time alone to think, to soul-search, to look inside and see what bits of decency were left—all of which was self-indulgent, none of it remotely relevant to what had happened that night.

For the first time, watching the ambulance pull away, he felt cold. There was some comfort in the thought that Bree had his jacket—though he wondered if they had tossed it aside to work on her. He pictured her in a neck brace, strapped flat, being hooked up to monitors and IVs. He prayed she was holding her own.

The chief ushered him toward the Blazer. "You're shaking. Not goin' into shock on me, are you? Better get in."

The offer was for the passenger's side, rather than the backseat, which was the good news. The bad news was that shaking was the least of it. Climbing in was a challenge. Tom's body was starting to hurt.

Bonner eyed him from behind the wheel. "You okay?"

"I'm okay." The paramedic had given him gauze for his cheek. Pressing it there, Tom waved Bonner on after the ambulance. It was already out of sight, gone too fast with Bree.

The Blazer took up a slow, safe, frustrating pace through the snow. "So. What happened?"

The shaking increased, radiating outward from his belly.

"Gates?"

Tom forced himself to think back, but things were fuzzy. "I was coming up the hill toward the green."

"Slippin' around, were you?"

He didn't remember slipping around. "Not particularly. The Jeep holds the road."

"Why were you out?"

There hadn't been any special reason. He had been restless, even lonely. He had been thinking how different his life was, at that moment, from what had gone before. There had surely been regret, surely self-pity. "I just felt like being out."

"Were you drinking?"

Tom slid the man a long look. "You leaned in close when you reached the scene. Did you smell booze on my breath?"

Bonner smirked. "Nope. Just coffee."

"You saw me at the diner. I had one beer with my chicken. Bree asked if I wanted another. I didn't. LeeAnn poured the coffee. I had two cups." The wipers pushed snowflakes from side to side. Peering out between them, Tom envisioned himself in a tunnel of light formed by the Blazer's headlights. The eeriness of it gave him a chill. "Where's the ambulance?"

"Up a ways. So. You had your coffee, then you left. What time was that?"

"Eight, give or take." His left side ached. He changed position to ease it, still he felt the Blazer's every shift. "I went home, stayed half an hour, then left."

"To go joyriding in the snow."

"Not joyriding." He hadn't felt any joy, hadn't felt any joy in too long to remember. "Just riding."

"Where?"

"Around town. Out toward Lowell. Into Montgomery. Like I said, the Jeep holds the road."

"So you wanted to see how good it was in the snow?"

"If you're asking whether I was pushing to see how fast I could go before spinning out, I wasn't. Come on, Bonner. You looked at tire tracks back there. Did it look like I was weaving coming up the hill?"

"Nope."

"As soon as the truck hit, I was gone. It was like being at the wrong end of a bulldozer, pushed sideways into the wall."

"When did you first see the truck?"

Tom took a deep breath and swallowed it fast when he

felt pain. Bruised ribs, he guessed, plus cuts on his hands
from fleeing the Jeep, plus God only knew what up and
down his left side, where the truck had hit him hard. But all
that was nothing compared to what had happened to Bree.

"Gates?"

Squeezing his eyes shut, he struggled to re-create those
lost seconds. Finally, he sighed and looked up. "All I remember is the headlights closing in."

"What kind of truck was it?"

"I don't know."

"Color?"

Again he tried to recall. "It wasn't a big truck. More
likely a pickup. Color? Black, maybe? Hell, I couldn't see
much in the glare of the lights. Take a look at my Jeep,
though. It'll have paint in the scrapes."

"I looked. The truck was maroon."

"What about the tires?"

"Consistent with a pickup, but bald. When did you first
see Bree?"

"I didn't see her. Not directly. I was aware of passing a
dark shape just before the truck came around the corner, but
it didn't register as anything more than a shadow, maybe a
lamppost. I didn't know it was a person until I heard the
thud. *Felt* the thud." He felt it again, and again, and again.
He doubted he would live long enough to forget it. It raised
the hair on the back of his neck. "How much longer till
we're there?"

"Not long. So you don't have any idea who was driving
the truck?"

Tom expelled a frustrated breath. "If I knew, don't you
think I'd say?"

"Beats me. I don't know you much."

"Trust me. I'd say."

"Yeah? Funny that you would. Most guys would be clam-
ming up around now."

"Only if they have something to hide. I don't. That guy

hit me. You studied the scene. You know that. There wasn't a hell of a lot I could have done differently.''

"Still, you're city. I'd have thought you'd be yelling and screaming for a lawyer."

"I *am* a lawyer." He hadn't intended to say it, but there it was.

Bonner sent him a guarded look. "I thought you said you were a writer."

"I am. I write about law."

"Ah, *jeez.*" His head went back with the oath. "Another one lookin' to be the next Grisham."

"Actually," Tom said, because he figured Bonner would run a check on him and find out anyway, and then, of course, there was his damnable pride, which survived despite months of trying to kill it, "I was writing before Grisham ever did."

"That's what they all say."

"I was published before Grisham ever was."

The chief paused. "That so?" Cautious interest. "Have I read anything of yours?"

"While the Jury Was Out." One look at the chief and he had his answer. "Lucky I have a common name, huh? I've been here seven months, and no one's figured it out. Christ, they will now," he muttered, refocusing on the road. "How much longer?"

"Not much. Why the secret?"

"It's been a rough few years. I needed downtime. I needed to be someplace where people didn't know who I was."

"Why's that?"

Taking aim at that damnable pride, he said, "I ran into trouble."

"Legal trouble?"

"Ego trouble."

He stared out the window at the outskirts of Ashmont. Small frame houses came closer together now, lights on here and there. The Blazer fell in behind a plow that was spewing sand and slowed to give it space.

Tom felt a surge of impatience. "Pass him."

"Not me. I'd rather be safe than sorry. I'd think you would, too. You don't need two accidents in one night. So. You got famous and bought into the hype."

Tom lifted the gauze from his cheek, glanced at it, put it back. "Something like that."

"Weren't there movies, too?"

"Yeah."

"Are you loaded?"

"Not now."

"Poor?"

"No." Tom looked at Bonner. "If she doesn't have insurance, I'll cover her bills."

"That's nice and generous, thank you, but Bree won't have any part of it. She's an independent sort. Besides, don't feel guilty. If you hadn't been where you were, that truck would've hit her directly, and it was bigger than you."

"So if she dies, she'll be less dead?" Tom asked. "Besides, it isn't guilt."

"Then what?"

Redemption was the word that came to mind, and it didn't sound right. But he did know, for all he was worth, that this time he couldn't turn his back.

The Ashmont Medical Center was small and relatively new, a two-story brick building at the end of a long drive curving back behind the old stone town hall. Tom remembered the parking lot as being neatly landscaped, but the peaceful feeling he remembered, from things green and flowered, was gone. Halogen lights on the snow turned the scene a garish yellow.

There was a small emergency entrance at the side of the building. The ambulance stood there, empty. Within seconds of the Blazer's pulling up behind it, Tom was out. He pushed through the door and approached the nurse at the desk.

"Bree Miller?" he asked, though he knew at a glance that she wasn't there. The emergency area was negligible. Each of three cubicles was open and quiet. That meant she was either upstairs or in the morgue.

He was tied in knots envisioning the latter scenario, when the nurse rounded the desk. She was a competent-looking sort, less laid-back than the typical local. "You must be the other injured party. I was told to watch for you."

"His name's Tom Gates," Bonner said. "He needs stitching. Check his ribs. And his hands."

Tom wasn't being touched until he had some news. "How is Bree?"

"She's upstairs."

"Is she alive?"

"Yes."

He released a small breath. "Is the surgeon here yet?"

"No, but he's close."

Ignoring protests by both the nurse and his body, he strode toward the elevator, spotted the stairs on the near side, and slipped through the door. Minutes later, he approached the second-floor nurses' station. "I'm looking for Bree Miller," he said. He saw a slew of patients' rooms, what looked to be a kitchen, a supply area, an open lounge, and a lot of closed doors.

This nurse was younger and gentler, but focused. Rising to meet him, she reached for the gauze he still held to his cheek. "Were you in the accident, too?"

"Yes, but I'm fine."

She was studying the gash on his cheek. "This has to be stitched. How'd you get past Margo?"

"I just went. Tell me more about Bree, and I'll go back. Where is she?"

"If I tell you, you might head that way, and if you do, you'll contaminate everything they're trying to keep sterile."

Tom backed off. "Okay. Just give me an update. Has she regained consciousness?"

"Not that I know of."

"The paramedic at the scene said she was bleeding internally. Did the EMTs find anything else?"

"Bruises, but bleeding's the first worry."

"My blood type is A. Will that help?"

"No. She's B. We have some here, and a list of donors. We've already called in a few."

Things were bad, then. Tom felt weak. "How many doctors are here?"

"Normally, one. We called in another of our own. The surgeon coming from St. Johnsbury makes three."

"Have your two ever done anything like this?" He knew he sounded snobbish, but refused to take back the question even when the nurse looked vaguely annoyed.

"Yes," she said. "Doctors here know everything and do everything. They're better rounded than city doctors. They have to be." She took his arm. "I think you should go back downstairs."

He held his ground. "Where can I wait afterward? I want to know how she is the minute they're done. I want to talk to the surgeon."

"You're shaking."

He had been trying to ignore that, but he kept hearing that *thud* again and was feeling sick. "Wouldn't you be shaking if it was your car that hit someone?"

"Yes, but there's nothing you can do for her right now," she said, pleading now. "The doctors are working on her, and you can't be there. So let Margo patch you up. Please?"

What with cleaning, stitching, and X-raying, Tom was downstairs for an hour. During that time, the doctor from St. Johnsbury arrived and Bree's surgery began.

When Tom finally made it back upstairs, Flash O'Neil was in the waiting room. The police chief must have filled him in on the details of the accident, because other than a quiet "You okay?" he didn't ask questions.

It was nearly midnight. Tom lowered himself onto a vinyl sofa and sat, first, with his head low against dizziness, then, as time passed, with his eyes closed and his legs sprawled stiffly. Any movement in the region of the operating room brought him up straight, but news was scarce. He sat forward again, then back, shifted gingerly, stretched out. Had he been a religious man, he might have prayed, but it had been years since he'd done that. After his mother died, he hadn't felt worthy, and before, well, he hadn't felt the need. He had been his own greatest source of strength, his own inspiration, his own most blind, devoted, and bullheaded fan.

So here he was.

Somewhere around one, Flash began to talk. He had his elbows on his knees and his hands hanging between, and was studying the floor, looking lost. "Bree was the first person I ever met in Panama. I heard the diner was for sale and came to see it. She waited on me and my wife, sold us on the town with that friendly way she has. After we bought the place, we had to close down a month for renovations. Bree was the only one who said she'd wait out the month and work for us when we reopened. She did more than wait. She was right there with us, making suggestions during the renovations—you know, things that people around here would like that we didn't know, not being from here. She and Francie—my wife—they got along fine."

Tom had never seen a wife. "What happened to Francie?"

"She left. Proved to be a *real* flash in the pan," he muttered. "Not Bree, though. She's worked for me for fourteen years now. I oughta make her a partner."

A nurse ran down the hall from the operating room. Tom came to his feet.

She held up a hand, shook her head as she passed, and disappeared. A minute later, she returned carrying an armload of supplies, but she had no more time for him then. It was the young nurse from the station who came to report, "It's going slow. She lost a lot of blood."

Again Tom felt the frustration of not being in New York, and while part of him knew that the going might have been just as slow there, it was small solace.

"I started to drive her home," Flash said, with more emotion now, "but the hill was so bad I gave up. If I'd stuck with it, this wouldn't have happened."

Tom made a disparaging sound. "It wasn't your fault."

"So whose fault was it?"

"Whoever drove that truck."

"So who drove it?"

"How the hell would I know?"

"You were there. It was your car that hit Bree. What were you, asleep at the wheel?" The words were barely out before Flash held up a hand. "Sorry. I'm scared."

Tom knew how *that* was. "Are you and Bree together?"

Flash made a sputtering sound. "Nah. She won't have me. She likes going home alone. Says she needs it after a day at work. But, man"—he gave a slow head shake—"she's my right hand at the diner. If anything happens . . ."

"It won't," Tom said.

"How do you know?"

"I just know."

"How?"

He opened his mouth to answer, and closed it again. One part of him feared Bree's dying as much as Flash feared it, but there was another part, a part that said the accident had happened for a reason and that her dying right now wasn't it.

True, that kind of thinking wasn't logical, and he was a logical guy—cold, calculating, and shrewd, his father had accused him of being, before turning his back on him for good. Maybe his father was right. With regard to family and friends, Tom had been cold, calculating, and shrewd.

Not so professionally. He had been creative and caring in

his defense of clients, creative and caring in the construction of a plot. And he definitely had an imaginative streak. *Something* had to explain the eeriness he had felt when passing through the tunnel of light that the Blazer had carved in the snow. He felt that eeriness still, felt it deep in his tired bones.

While Tom waited for news with his eyes closed, his legs braced, and his arms cradling his bruised ribs, down the hall in the operating room, Bree watched with fascination as five skilled professionals tried to restart her heart.

Chapter

~ 3 ~

"*W*ake up, Bree. Time to wake up."

Bree struggled to open her eyes. It was a minute of starts and stops, and what seemed a great expenditure of energy, before she succeeded.

"That's it. You can hear me, can't you?"

She nodded, more a thought than an act, and tried to look around. The woman who had spoken was pale green. Beyond was a room that was dimly lit, cool, and sterile, totally different from where she had been seconds before. That place had been bright and warm. The memory of it brought a wisp of calm.

"She's awake?" asked another voice, this one male, and for a minute she thought it was *his*. But this face had features. The other had been too bright to see.

So how had she known it was male? And how had it smiled? Or had she only imagined a smile?

"Hi there, Bree," came this new one again. "Welcome back." The voice was familiar, but nothing else.

"Do I know you?" she asked in a whispery croak.

37

"I'm Paul Sealy, one of the ones who've been working on you for the last five hours."

She tried to moisten her tongue, but her whole mouth was dry. "Where am I?"

"In the recovery room. How do you feel?"

She felt confused. Sad, like she'd been someplace nicer and didn't want to be back. But happy to be here, too.

"Any pain?"

Maybe, in her midsection, but it was more dull than excruciating. The thoughts that came and went were harder to handle. She kept picturing herself on the operating table, kept *seeing* herself there, as if she had left her body behind and was rising to a gentler place. If she didn't know better, she would have thought she had died and gone to heaven. But this clearly wasn't heaven. So she'd been sent back down to earth. Which was a *really* weird idea.

Far easier to stop thinking and just drift off to sleep.

That first day passed in groggy spurts. She dozed and woke, dozed and woke. There were questions about comfort and pain, much poking and prodding, an overall jostling when she was wheeled down the hall to her room. Doctors and nurses hovered. More than once, she fought through a private fog to tell them that she would be fine, because she knew that she would be. She wasn't sure how she knew, but she did.

That was the only certainty she had. Between the lingering anesthesia and the drugs they gave her for pain, she was confused about where she was and why she hurt. She was confused about who was with her, seeing familiar faces one minute and new faces another, and each time she remembered what had happened in the operating room, she was confused about what was real and what was dream.

Sleep continued to be a lovely escape.

By the second morning, the effects of the anesthesia had worn off and she was awake enough to respond to the nurses attending her. Yes, her stomach hurt. No, she wasn't dizzy. No, she wasn't nauseated. Yes, she was thirsty.

None mentioned the surgery. She guessed that they were leaving that to Paul Sealy. By the time he showed up, it was late morning, snow was dripping past her window from the roof under a repentant October sun, her mind was clearing, and she needed feedback.

Standing by her bedside, with his hand in the pocket of his lab coat, he told of the tearing in her abdomen. "There was extensive bleeding. We had to find its source and stop it, then piece you back together again. It was touch-and-go for a while."

In a scratchy voice, she asked, " 'Touch-and-go'?"

He softened the words with a smile. "We lost your pulse for a bit."

"I died?"

"Not exactly. We kept you going until your heart started back up on its own."

"You used electric shock." It wasn't a question, but the doctor didn't realize that.

"Actually, we did. It's the most effective thing in situations like yours."

"How long was my heart not beating?"

He waved a hand. "Not long enough to cause any damage."

But Bree wanted to know. It had seemed an eternity that she had watched them work on her, and then there was the upward floating, and the bright light, and the sense of total and utter well-being. "Seconds? Minutes?"

"Your brain was never without oxygen," he said, which didn't answer the question, so she tried a different angle.

"How many of you were working on me?" She had seen five.

"There were seven—three doctors and four nurses."

"At the time when my heart stopped?"

He thought back. "No. There were five in the room then

—Jack Warren and I, two nurses, and Simon Meade, up from St. Johnsbury."

Simon Meade. The tall one in the dark-blue scrubs. The one who had applied the paddles that shocked her back to life. It had taken more than one application.

"I felt those shocks," she murmured. It had been at the very end. She had been at peace with herself and the world, totally happy, then, *whap!*

The doctor smiled. "Patients often say that, but it's actually only the thought of the procedure that hurts. You were completely anesthetized."

"I felt them," Bree insisted, but softly, because there was a chance he was right. What she thought she had seen didn't make sense. Maybe it was her imagination. She was heavily medicated. Maybe she was pulling images from the past. After all, she had watched *ER*. She knew what went on in operating rooms.

She also knew about near-death experiences—hard for an avid reader not to, what with so many books and magazine articles on the subject. So maybe what she had thought was real was nothing more than the power of suggestion. Maybe she had dreamed it up, after all.

But the dream wouldn't be dispelled. It penetrated her discomfort in bits and snatches, in ever greater detail as the day progressed. Friends stopped by to say hello, only to be hurried along by the nurses. Flash was one of the few who were allowed to stay.

He arrived late in the afternoon, with a platter of goodies from the diner. Bree was awake, but a long way from eating anything solid. Her stomach hurt. Her whole body hurt— cheek, arm, hip, legs. The last thing she felt was hungry. Thirsty, yes. Hungry, no.

"Not even one little cookie?" Flash pleaded. "I brought the shortbreads just for you. You love them."

"*You* love them," she said, in a raspy voice, and grimaced

against the pain of movement when she reached toward the cup on the bed table. "I'm so dry. Help me, Flash. I can't reach that cup." When he moved it closer, she fished out several ice chips and put them in her mouth.

"What have we here?" Flash asked on his way to the window. A bubble bowl on the sill was filled with flowers, exquisitely arranged. "Pink geraniums, purple somethings, white crocuses. And lots of local ornamental grass. From Julia Dean. That's so nice." He returned to the bed. "I talked with the doctors. Another five days here, they said, and you'll be home. A couple of weeks at home, and you'll be back at the diner. Jillie's filling in while you're gone, and if you don't feel like waitressing after that, she'll stay on. You can just sit in the office and manage the place. I'm paying you either way. You don't have to worry about a thing."

Bree wasn't worried. She hadn't thought about what would come after, was still trying to figure out what had come before. "I died on the operating table."

"No, you didn't. Your heart stopped for a few beats before they started it up again. That's not dying."

But she wasn't being put off. Flash was one of her best friends. She needed to tell him what had happened. "I knew when it stopped. I felt things."

He looked skeptical. "What kinds of things?"

"Lightness. Out-of-my-body kinds of things. I went through the ceiling."

"So did I when Eliot told me about the accident. I knew I should have driven you all the way home. If I had, you wouldn't be lying here now. Whoever was driving that truck is in deep shit."

He wasn't listening. Frustrated, Bree closed her eyes. But a greater need forced them open again. "What do you know about near-death experiences?"

"As much as I want," he said, with a snort that said he didn't think they were real. "When we die, we die. I don't believe in heaven or hell."

He didn't believe in God, either. He had told her that more than once, and while she didn't agree with him, she respected his feelings. She also respected the fact that he had a graduate degree in art history from Columbia. He wasn't dumb.

"What if I said I'd had a look at heaven?" she asked.

"I'd say it's the medication talking. They have you on morphine. That's strong stuff."

She gave a tiny head shake. "It's not the medication."

"No? Listen to you. Your words are slurred. It's the medication."

Possibly. Still, she saw that scene and felt that light, felt the *benevolence* of it. "I don't usually believe in things like this."

"Damn right you don't," Flash scolded. "Verity does. Do you want people laughing at you the way they laugh at her?"

"But I see this so *clearly,*" she pleaded.

"I'm telling you, it's the morphine and, if not that, the anesthesia. It'll pass." With more fear than humor, he added, "It better. I need you with your feet on the ground. You're the sane one, Bree. Don't flip out on me, huh?"

Bree wasn't flipping out. He was right. She *was* the sane one.

But each time she closed her eyes, she was back in the operating room, hovering over the table, then rising, rising, and then there was that light. As confused as she was about what was real and what wasn't, she couldn't deny the calm that flowed through her each time she thought of that light.

And there was more to the experience. She hadn't told Flash the half of it. More returned with each wakeful stretch, much of it sketchy still, but exciting, baffling, even scary, if what she thought she had heard was true.

Dusk fell. Bree dreamed about the operating room again, dreamed of hovering above it and looking down. This time she saw a mole on the nape of the neck of one of the nurses.

She awoke convinced that it wasn't a dream at all. She *had* seen a mole in the operating room that night. But how, if she had been unconscious? There was only one way.

Shaken, she forced her eyes open. The only light in the room was the dim glow of a corner lamp. It was a gentle light, less harsh than the overheads, but reassuring. She wouldn't have wanted to wake up to total darkness and wonder which world she was in.

She lay without moving for a while, trying to separate pain from other needs, deciding whether she wanted to act on any and, if so, how. First priority, easiest to meet, was water. Her mouth was still abominably dry.

She had barely reached for the overhead bar, in an attempt to sit up, when the chair in the corner came alive. Her eyes widened on the man who approached. Uncommon height, tapering body, light-brown hair long grown out of a stylist's cut—no mistaking his identity.

He poured fresh water into the cup from the pitcher beside it, flexed the straw so that she could drink more easily, and slipped an arm behind her. "Don't use your stomach muscles. Let me do the work."

She stared at him, wondering why he was there but too dry to ask. And he was right. She felt less pain when she let him take her weight. With her upper body raised just enough, she drank, paused, drank again, then whispered, "Why am I so dry?"

"It's from the anesthesia. The IV pumps in fluids, but it doesn't seem to make a difference."

"Actually, it does," she remarked, because the bathroom was second on her list.

"Ah." He set the water back on the table. "I think, for that, maybe a nurse."

"No. They had me up before. If you can just help me across the room." She moved the covers aside and got her legs over the edge of the bed, though not without the kind of pain that had her taking quick, shallow breaths.

43

"Can I carry you?"

"No," she gasped. "I need to walk. Not only for the stomach. The rest of me is stiffening up not doing anything."

He eyed her swollen cheek. "The rest of you is bruised, too. The only thing that'll cure it is time and rest." He looked away, looked right back. "I'm sorry, Bree. If there'd been any way I could have avoided hitting you, I would have."

She had known that, from the moment Eliot had told her about the accident. Tom had always struck her as a decent sort. He was respectful at the diner, and he left great tips. Besides, she remembered how the accident had happened and knew that he had been in the Jeep, not the pickup. From the look of his own face—a cruel line of stitches beneath a dilly of a shiner—he hadn't escaped unscathed. Yet here he was. *The* Thomas Gates.

Hard to take in, that little twist. Had she felt better, she might have been awed, but tackling celebrity status wasn't high on her list just then. Nor was talking books. Prioritywise, her body was calling the shots.

Holding the mass of bandages that covered her stomach, she inched to the edge of the bed and, with his help, shifted her weight to her feet. It was a long minute of unsteady breaths before she could straighten enough to walk.

He supported her with one arm, guided the IV pole with the other while she shuffled forward. By the time she was finished in the bathroom, she couldn't get back to bed fast enough.

Tom helped her in, got the IV business straight, covered her up. "There's Jell-O in the kitchen," he said. "Will you tell me when you want some?"

She nodded, eyes already closed, and sought memory of the light to ease her pain.

She must have dozed, because when she opened her eyes again, the wall clock's small hand had moved from nine to ten. A nurse was checking her bandages, taking her vital signs, adjusting the IV drip, administering pain medication. Bree tried to look for a mole, but the light was too dim, the angle wrong. The woman had barely vanished into the night hush of the hall, when Bree remembered Tom.

Her eyes flew to the chair in the corner, and there he was. Slouched low, with his head against the back of the chair and his fingers laced over his middle, he looked decidedly unfamous. The book in his lap suggested he planned to stay awhile.

At first she thought he was sleeping. His eyes were hooded, his body was perfectly still. Then his mouth moved in the touch of a smile.

She hadn't seen him smile before. He was usually serious and withdrawn. But his smile was something, even just that touch. It reminded her of those great hands of his, which she now pictured poking at a word processor. That made her think of the kind of life he must have led before coming to Panama, which made her think of the kind of people he must have known, which made her think that she was *nothing* by comparison, which made her wonder why he was glued to the chair in her room.

Since she didn't want to think it was guilt, she didn't ask. "How'd you get the nurses to let you stay?" she asked instead.

He stretched. "I convinced them that if I can be a help to you here, there's less work for them."

"Do they know you write books?"

There was a brief, thick silence, then a wary "I hope not. Who told you? Eliot?"

"Yes."

"I'd rather you forget it. I didn't much like the man who wrote those books. I was trying to put distance between him and me."

"Was it working?"

"I don't know. My life is different here, that's for sure. Not being known helped."

45

"I won't tell."

"You're not the problem. Eliot is. One word to Emma, and Dotty will know, and once Dotty knows, the world knows." He sniffed in a long, loud breath. "But that's fine." Setting the book aside, he pushed himself out of the chair. "It had to happen sooner or later. How do you feel?"

She hurt. But she was also thinking that her mouth felt like sand and that something smooth, cool, and moist would feel good. "Did you mention Jell-O?"

"I did. Name your wish—strawberry, cherry, or lime." Name your wish. Weird. "Cherry."

"Bathroom first?"

"Please."

He helped her there, then helped her back. He fluffed the pillow and turned it, held the water for her, settled her in. She was grateful to rest while he went for the Jell-O, but drew the line when he offered to feed her. So he cranked up the head of the bed and retreated to the chair while she ate.

It was slow going. Her hand was shaky, her whole arm ached. She felt weak, despicably weak, and reminding herself of what she'd been through didn't help. What did help was thinking about the light. It gave her strength.

She wanted to tell Tom about it, wanted him to say that she hadn't imagined anything, that near-death experiences did happen, that the light and all the rest was real. But she would be mortified if he was skeptical, too, especially now that she knew who he was.

So she finished her Jell-O, let him crank down the head of the bed, closed her eyes, and drifted off.

She awoke slowly, didn't open her eyes, didn't move, just thought—about the light first, because she had been dreaming of that, then about the silence of the night, then about her stomach. During one of the doctor's checks, she'd had a glimpse of what was under the bandages. The incision was huge, actually two crisscrossing cuts. Granted they were a small price to pay for life, but they weren't pretty.

She had seen those incisions when they were wide open. They hadn't been pretty then, either. Hard to believe that that body had been hers.

So maybe it hadn't been. Maybe she had conjured the scene from a movie.

Only those had been strands of *her* hair escaping the cap on her head, and she had heard the people around her chanting, "Come on, Bree, hang on . . . you can do it, Bree."

It had been *so real*. She *wanted* it to be real. She had never been in the presence of anyone as cheerful and loving and good as that being in the light. The high of being with him was like nothing she had ever felt smoking Curtis Lamb's homegrown pot, and Curtis Lamb's pot was good.

With a sigh, she opened her eyes. They went first to the clock, which read two, then to the man who sat in the chair, reading. Still there. Amazing.

Tell him, Bree. He'll laugh. *So what?* So he's Thomas Gates!

At the silent sound of his name, Tom looked up and saw that she was awake, propped his cheek on a fist, and smiled, and suddenly it didn't seem fair that he was who he was and that she should care whether he laughed at her or not. It didn't seem fair that, even banged up, he looked good. It didn't seem fair that she was out of his league.

"Aren't you tired?" she grumbled, more accusation than question.

"No. I slept most of the day."

"You don't have to stay here. The accident wasn't your fault."

"That's not why I'm here."

"Then why?"

It was a minute before he said, "Because this beats sitting in the snow waiting for an ambulance, or sitting outside an operating room waiting for the doctors to come out."

She forgot her pique. "You were here then?"

He nodded.

Cautious now, she asked, "How much did they tell you about the surgery?"

"Enough," he said, in a way that said it all, and it was like an invitation, only she couldn't get herself to accept.

But why not? she asked herself. *Forget who he is. One Panamanian winter, and he'll be gone. What does it matter if he thinks you're nuts?*

She closed her eyes and listened for the turning of pages to suggest he had gone back to his book, but there was none. Finally, without opening her eyes, she asked, "Did they tell you my heart stopped?"

"Oh, yeah."

"Scary, huh?"

"Oh, yeah," he said, with feeling.

Then, because in order to write the way he did he had to be worldly, and because something about dying and being reborn told her to take the risk, she opened her eyes and said, "Do you believe in near-death experiences?"

He was silent for a time, sitting with the book in his lap and his ankle on his knee. "I don't know."

"Do you know anyone who's had one?"

"No. But that doesn't mean anything." Setting the book aside, he pushed up from the chair—gingerly, she thought, but she promptly forgot it when he approached the bed and asked, "Did you have one?"

She looked for mockery, saw none. "Maybe. I don't usually believe in things like that."

"Neither do I. But that doesn't mean anything, either. Sometimes seeing is believing."

"Oh, I saw," Bree drawled, emboldened by his encouragement. She felt suddenly heady, but her tongue was dry again.

Tom slid her up, held the straw to her lips. After turning her pillow, he lowered her to its fresh, cooler side. Then he sat down on the spare patch of bed by her hip. "Tell me what you saw." He seemed genuinely curious.

Buoyed by that, she said, "First, I heard. I heard them say they'd lost a pulse, and I heard their fear. Then it was like something sucked me out of my body and up, and I was looking down on what was happening. They did CPR. There were two of them working on that, and one monitoring my signs, and another shooting me with adrenaline, only my blood pressure kept falling, and I wouldn't breathe on my own. They were getting really scared; I could hear it in them. Only *I* wasn't scared"—and she felt a wave of calm now—"because I was with this . . . thing, and it was *so nice.*" She didn't know where she found the strength to talk, but the words kept coming. "It didn't have arms I could see, but its arms were open in welcome. It was strong but gentle. And powerful. It could do whatever it wanted—miracles, I swear. Maybe what happened to me *was* a miracle. I don't know. I only know that I was with this very bright being. It was visually bright and smart bright, and pure and kind and sweet, and it *loved* me."

She closed her mouth on the rush of words, afraid that she had gone too far.

But Tom looked intrigued. "What happened then?"

"Do you think I'm losing it?"

"No."

"This is pretty bizarre."

"Tell me what happened next."

"They applied electric shocks. They had to do it twice. Each time, it jolted my whole body. It really *is* like you see on TV, only it's not so much fun when it's your own body down there. It was awful to watch, awful to *feel.*"

"You *felt* it?" he asked.

"Only the last time. Before that, I was with this person, this being, and I was happy and peaceful and *relieved.*"

"Relieved. Why?"

She wasn't sure. The word had just popped out. "Relieved to be there, I guess. Maybe relieved to know that *there* existed. Was it heaven?"

49

"I don't know. Did you see anything beyond this being?"

Shaking her head, she reached for water.

He held the cup and put the straw to her mouth. "What did it look like?"

After several sips, she let the straw fall away. "Light. It was nothing but light. It didn't have a face, but it smiled and was beautiful, and it spoke." She frowned. "There wasn't any voice. I just . . . felt its thoughts."

"What was it thinking?"

"I'm not sure I can find the words," she said, holding back for the first time. This was the newest part of her recollection, potentially the silliest. Self-consciousness kept her from risking sounding like a fool to this virtual stranger, who was a handsome one at that. She may have nearly died, but she had a little pride, after all.

He returned the cup to the bed tray.

Whispering, she asked, "Are you leaving now?"

He shook his head. "I'll stay awhile."

"You don't have to. I'll be going back to sleep. I won't need anything until morning."

"Then I'll just read." He left the bed and crossed to the chair. Easing into it, he stretched out and crossed his ankles.

He was wearing running shoes. That was the last thing she noticed about him before she closed her eyes, but it wasn't the last thing she thought. The last thing she thought was that she didn't care if he *was* driven by guilt: no one had ever spent the night sitting by her bedside before.

It was the pain that did it. After sleeping for nearly two hours, she woke up feeling awful. Tom was beside her in an instant, ringing for the nurse, then running to get her when she didn't come fast enough.

The morphine brought instant relief. It also enveloped Bree in a dull haze that lowered her inhibitions. Alone with Tom again, with him sitting on the side of the bed like he was her very best friend, she said in a molasses-thick voice, "There's more to the story of the being of light."

"More?"

"More bizarre. I keep hearing something he said. Thought. Whatever."

"What was it?"

"Three wishes. I have three wishes." Her voice was slurred, but the words came anyway. "I died. Only it wasn't my time. So I was sent back with a gift. Three wishes before I die again. Like a reward."

"To make up for the accident?"

The being of light hadn't said. "Maybe." She waded through the haze in search of other possibilities. "Or to make up for my mother. Or my father. But my life's good. So maybe it's just *because*." She closed her eyes. With an effort, she opened them again. "This part's harder to believe than the rest."

"Why?"

It took a minute of pushing her thoughts past the morphine before she recalled. "Wishes lie ahead. The rest, the bright light and all, is past."

"So there's no way to prove whether the bright light was real, but there is a way to prove whether the wishes are or not."

"Ex*actly*."

"Do you want them to be?"

She frowned. "I guess." She wasn't sure. But she didn't know why.

"Only guess? Aren't there things you'd wish for?"

"Yes." Something nagged at the back of her mind.

"So?"

Then she remembered. "Three wishes before I die again." Was that the message she had received, or were the drugs confusing her? She looked at Tom. "I guess I'm a little worried about what happens after the third wish." She watched his face for understanding. When nothing came, she continued. "It's like this. It seems like I've come back to use the wishes, but if that's true, does it also mean that once I've used the third one, my time will be up? Will I have to go back?"

His eyes widened and his chin came up. "Ah. I see what you mean."

That chin was slightly square, slightly stubbled. She stared at it until Tom waved a hand before her eyes. Then she blinked, took a sleepy breath. "It's okay." Her voice was distant. "They're probably not real anyway." Seeing something after the fact, she frowned and lifted the hand he had waved. His palm was covered with barely scabbed cuts.

When she looked questioningly at him, he said, "Getting out of the Jeep."

She looked at his cheek. "That'll leave a scar."

"It'll add character. I can use that."

Her eyelids were growing heavy. "Maybe I'll wish for no scar for you."

"Don't you dare."

"Then no scars for me."

"You wouldn't waste a wish on that, would you?"

"Maybe not." Her lids drifted shut. Whether it was the thinking of the being of light, or being with Tom, or floating on a morphine high, she felt peaceful. "Maybe I can use only two. Save the third up. Know what I mean?"

"That's a thought."

Smiling, she gave herself over to whatever it was that felt so good.

Bree was sleeping when Tom left. The morning nurses had just arrived, the sun was newly up, and he was desperate to ease his own aches with a long, hot bath and a long, firm bed. First, though, he needed information.

He drove home in the car he had rented the day before. Snow still lay on the roadside, but two days of melt under sun and mild air had thinned it considerably. Limbs that had fallen under the weight of the snow had been moved aside. Fall foliage had reemerged. The roads themselves were wet but clear, the spatter under the tires a steady *shushhhh* through his open window.

West Elm was off Pine Street, two miles up from the town green. The houses here were farther apart than the ones in the center of town, and hidden from each other behind evergreen shields. That was the first thing Tom had liked about the bungalow. The second was the modesty of it, the third its difference from his earlier homes.

He turned into the driveway along ruts widened by melt and climbed out in time to hail the newsboy, who was pedaling his mountain bike through the slush on the road. The paper he carried wasn't a local. Panama wasn't big enough for that. This one was out of Burlington and had local news at the back.

Tom fished a dollar from his pocket.

The boy stopped, straddling the bike. "They told me you're s'posed to subscribe."

"I swore off newspapers when I left New York."

"So why do you keep flagging me down?"

"I just need a fix now and then." Specifically, he wanted to see if there was mention of the accident and, if so, his identity. He tucked the dollar in the boy's pocket. "The Johnsons are on vacation. This is for theirs."

Folding the paper under his arm, he slogged back to the car and drove on to the carport. Entering the kitchen, he kicked off his sneakers, dropped the paper on the table in passing, and took the stairs two at a time. There were three bedrooms on the second floor of the house. The only room whose door was open was the one with his king-size bed. He opened the door at the end of the hall and went in.

This was the room he had designated as his office when he had moved to Panama seven months before. He could count on both hands the number of times he had been in it since then, and it showed. Unopened cartons stood exactly where the movers had placed them. Walls and windows were bare. The only color to speak of came from a pair of overstuffed briefcases that lay on the handsome mahogany desk behind which he had once practiced law.

He unzipped one of the briefcases, removed a laptop computer, plugged it in, and booted it up. While it hummed on its own through obligatory openers, he rubbed his aching side. He bent over the desk, realized that his body wouldn't take that for long, dragged over the chair, and adjusted the angle of the laptop. The first thing he saw was that he had mail.

No surprise there. Weekly messages came from his agent like clockwork.

He debated passing it by; but there was always the chance that someone else wondered how he was.

Clicking into his mailbox, he found one, two, three messages from Nathan Gunn, sent in, yes, each of the last three weeks. He didn't have to read them to know that Nathan wanted another book. The plea was always the same.

At least Nathan cared enough to keep contact. No one else did, for which Tom had no one to blame but himself. Friends who had once E-mailed him regularly had deleted his name from their address books months before.

That bothered him, but the self-pity that usually followed the thought didn't come. Closing the file, he logged on to the Internet, typed in NEAR-DEATH EXPERIENCES at the blank, and clicked on Search.

Chapter

4

$\mathcal{T}$om read dozens of personal recountings of near-death experiences. He read excerpts from books, comments from researchers, transcripts of interviews. He read until he was bleary-eyed and too tired even for the hot bath his bruised body craved. Leaving his clothes in a heap, he crawled into bed and fell into a dead sleep until noon, and the only thing that brought him awake then was the pain of inadvertently turning onto his left side.

He took the bath and a painkiller, fell back into bed, and slept until early evening. Then it was hunger that woke him. He hadn't eaten since he had woken at roughly the same hour the day before, scarfed down several slices of leftover pizza, and driven to the hospital.

Leftover pizza wouldn't do it this time. After a hot shower, he headed for the diner.

The roads were clear and dry. The only evidence of the storm that had hit three days before was the lingering sogginess of the earth and the occasional patch of unmelted snow. The air was warm, the foliage vivid even in twilight. It was the kind of sweet October night Tom had dreamed of when he moved north, the kind of night when he might have walked through his yard to the brook and followed it upstream, sat on a moonlit bench, and done the kind of connecting with himself that he needed to do. It was the kind of quiet night when he would have been able to hear his innermost thoughts, had he not been preoccupied with Bree.

The diner was doing a brisk Sunday business. Every booth was taken, with two parties of four waiting and only one empty place at the counter. Tom preferred the privacy of a booth, but he was too hungry to wait, too anxious to be on his way to the hospital. He eased through the eight standing just inside the door and was halfway to the empty stool when the hum of conversation dimmed. In its place, loud without it, were the slap of burgers on the grill, the clink of dishes in the kitchen, and Vince Gill sounding lonely and sad.

Tom wasn't a novice at being in the spotlight. He had been a star quarterback in high school and college, the stroke of his crew boat in law school, an articulate champion of the poor working out of the public defender's office, an equally articulate, often flamboyant savior of the rich as a private practitioner of increasingly national prominence. As a writer, he had been followed by the spotlight from his very first sale, which had made *Time, Newsweek,* and *People* magazines, to the very last, when an argument that had taken place at Lutèce between him and his publisher, coincidentally his lady of the moment, was reported in some detail on *Inside Edition.*

At the time, believing that even bad publicity was good, he hadn't been bothered. But this was different. This spotlight invaded the space that he was trying to put between himself and the past.

He didn't know these people well. They were the kind of small towners for whom he had carelessly signed books at malls, the kind who wrote him letters care of his publisher and received form letters from his publisher in return. The old Tom would have seen them as nothing more than a vehicle for his own adulation. That Tom would have looked around the diner with a grin, hitched his chin in recognition of the attention, held up a falsely modest hand, and said, *My thanks, folks, but please, go ahead and eat.*

The new Tom, the one who didn't know whether the sudden silence reflected his past fame or the fact that his car had been the one to hit a woman these people loved, kept his eyes straight and walked forward. He was nowhere near as confident as he looked when he slipped onto the stool. With brief, unreturned glances at Frank Wright on his left and Martin Sprague on his right, he studied the menu on his mat, then looked up at the chalkboard's specials.

Flash entered his line of vision. He was wiping his hands on a towel, but his eyes quickly went past Tom to the booths behind. His voice followed, loud with meaning. "You folks waiting for something?"

There were several grunts and an inarticulate word or two. Anything more was lost when the surrounding conversation resumed.

Flash gave Tom a dry look. "Walk in here with a shiner like that, and that's what you get. How're you feeling?"

"Arthritic," Tom said. Then, because Flash seemed Bree's closest friend, and because she was Tom's major concern, he asked, "Have you seen Bree today?"

"A little while ago. She's hangin' in there. She said you spent the night. Said you were a help. That was good of you."

"It was the least I could do."

"How did she seem to you?"

"She was uncomfortable."

"I mean mentally," Flash said, more hesitant now. "Did she seem confused?"

"Not terribly."

"Did she say anything much?"

Tom knew what he was getting at. What he didn't know was whether anyone other than Flash knew Bree's thoughts. With Frank at his left elbow and Martin at his right, both ignoring his presence and surely listening to his every word, he chose those words with care. "She mentioned what she had been through. I thought she was coherent."

"You did?"

Tom nodded and, when Flash looked relieved, asked, "How's the veal?"

"Tender and light."

"I'll try it. With a tall ice water."

Flash seemed to want to say more. After a look down the counter, though, he wiped his hands again and disappeared into the kitchen.

The grillman called out an order for LeeAnn, who passed Tom without a glance. Frank finished his blueberry crisp, dug money out of his pocket, and studied the check. Martin forked up American chop suey to a steady beat.

Tom studied the diner's reflection in the stainless steel over the grill. He picked out faces he knew—Curtis Lamb and John Dillard, a boothful of local truckers, Sandy and Jack Swartz with little Tyler, the trio of Earl, Eliot, and Emma. People were looking at him, no doubt about that. He guessed they were talking about him, too. Once, he had craved the attention, so he deserved the discomfort it brought now. Be careful what you wish for, his mother had always said. She was right about that, too.

Frank put a handful of money on the counter and left. Jillie delivered a pizza to the man two stools over and breezed back past Tom to the kitchen. LeeAnn strode by with an armload of dirty plates and not a word.

Tom was feeling like a pariah by the time Flash set down a glass of water and said, "I hear your Jeep was totaled."

"The axle's gone."

"Are you getting another?"

"Jeep? No. I want something heavier."

"Self-protection?"

For sure, Tom thought, and said as much with a look.

Flash moved on. In the stainless steel, Tom watched the occupants of one of the booths slide out and head for the door. LeeAnn had barely reset the table when a new foursome slid in.

Martin Sprague ran a napkin across his mouth. "Hear you're a lawyer," he said, without looking at Tom.

Tom would have denied it, had there been any point. "I was."

"Not much need for lawyers in Panama."

"I didn't come here to practice."

"That's good. I do what has to be done."

Tom imagined that he did. Panama was hardly infested with crime. Since he had come, the only offense he had heard about was the case of a four-year-old child stealing a handful of artificial flies from the tackle shop. Martin Sprague might be getting along in years, but Tom guessed that the legal needs in a town like this were tame enough for him to handle. "Are you the only lawyer here?"

"Not enough work for any others."

"What type of things do you do?"

"Nothing you'd be interested in," Martin said, and raised a sharp voice. "LeeAnn, where's my check?"

Tom took a drink of water, set down the glass, ran his fingers up and down its sides. The cuts on his palms were beginning to scab. The cool felt good.

Martin moved away the instant LeeAnn gave him his check, and waited for his change by the cash register at the end of the counter.

Eliot Bonner slid onto the stool on Tom's left.

Tom shot him a look. "You're brave. Everyone else hurried off when I came. Is it the writing that did it, or the accident?"

"Both, I'd guess. No one thought twice about you when you didn't make noise. Now you stand out. Panama's like a boat. You up and rocked it."

"Yeah, well, I didn't do it on my own. I have a totaled Jeep and a battered body to prove it." And then there was Bree. "Any luck tracing that truck?"

"Nope. I talked with local departments. Talked with the state police. I was hoping one or the other would have caught someone driving stupid that night. There were a couple of other accidents and an arrest or two, but nothing involving a pickup. Hard to believe, what with so many trucks around here. Lucky, maybe." He smirked. "Bree says it was blue, you say black, your Jeep says maroon."

"Trust the Jeep," Tom advised and might have made a remark about physical evidence holding up in court, if his veal hadn't come just then. He began to salivate instantly. It looked and smelled as good as anything he had had in New York. Of course, he might have salivated over stale meat loaf, he was so hungry.

"There are a dozen people in town with maroon pickups," Bonner said. "Every one of them's got alibis. None's got dents consistent with what happened."

Tom decided that Flash hadn't been bragging without cause. The veal was tender and light, the Madeira sauce pleasantly mild. He chased a second mouthful with helpings of new potatoes and grilled asparagus.

"What about maroon pickups in neighboring towns?" he asked as he ate.

"We're working on it. Bree said not to bother. Said she's alive and that's all that matters."

Tom put his fork down. "It is, assuming whoever was driving that pickup got enough of a scare to change his ways, but that's a big assumption. He probably didn't even know I hit Bree, probably thought he'd just hit another car. He's probably out there telling himself, No sweat, car's insured, no one's the worse for the wear." Tom realized how angry he was. "Who's to say the next time he careens around in the snow he won't hit a bunch of kids and kill one or more outright?"

"Told her that myself."

"He must have been stoned or drunk. How else could a human being do what he did and then just drive away? Hell, she nearly died."

Bonner squinted up at the stainless steel. "I heard she did. Heard she died on the table. Heard she made it to heaven, before someone sent her back. She tell you about it?"

Tom wanted to say that what Bree told him was privileged information, only they weren't lawyer and client. He wasn't quite sure what they were—friends, maybe—but whatever, he wasn't betraying her. "Heaven?" he echoed. "Did she tell you that?"

"Nah. My cousin works with Paul Sealy. Bree told Paul."

Bree had told Paul, who told his coworker, who told Eliot, who would tell Earl and Emma. Emma would tell Dotty, who would tell anyone else in town who cared to listen.

Tom was angry on Bree's behalf. "Did Bree tell Paul in confidence?"

"Who knows. Look, it's no big thing. She won't sue Paul, any more'n she'll press charges against whoever was driving that truck. If you ask me, it's a lot of hokum, this near-death business, but I don't blame Bree. She had a scare. She earned the right to hallucinate. I just don't want someone having a *real*-death experience because I didn't catch the bastard the first time around." He pushed himself off the stool, straightened the belt under his belly, cleared his throat. "So. I hear you've been on Larry King."

Tom stared at him, then beyond. Conversation was abruptly down again. Half the diner was looking their way.

With a thanks-for-nothing look at the chief, he returned to his veal.

"More than once," Bonner went on. "He musta liked you."

"He liked what I did," Tom muttered, jabbing at his food with his fork. "I wrote about incendiary cases. It made for an easy show."

"What about Barbara Walters?"

Tom snorted. "You've done your homework."

"It's my job. I'm all Panama's got. So. How'd she treat you? Did she put you on the spot? She can be a tough one sometimes. Course, that's what people like about her. Boy, she's been at it for a long time now. How'd she look in person?"

Tom raised a piece of veal, pondered it, returned it to his plate. Whoever in the diner hadn't known who he was before this would know now, and it wouldn't stop there. It was only a matter of time before the whole town knew.

So let them know something else, he decided. With a resigned sigh and a meaningful look at the faces turned his way, he said loudly and to the point, "I bought a house in Panama because it seemed like the kind of place where people respected each other, the kind of place where I could go about my business without being questioned about the past. I chose Panama because I wanted privacy, and because it was far away from New York." Though his gaze settled on Bonner, his voice was a warning for the rest. "If I wanted to tell the world I was here, I'd have taken out an ad in the *Times*. If the media track me here, I'm gone. Am I getting through?"

Miraculously, he finished his dinner. No doubt stubbornness was part of it, since his hunger had left with the mention of Larry King. It wasn't that he had a gripe with the man, or with Barbara Walters or any of the others who had interviewed him. The majority of those interviewers had simply asked the questions Tom's publicist had fed them. They were questions Tom had helped formulate, each designed to show yet another flattering side, and he hadn't felt a bit of guilt doing it. That was how the game was played. He had left those interviews walking on air, totally enamored with himself, sold on the flattery.

Thinking back on it made him sick to his stomach. But he needed food if he planned to stay at the hospital again, and he most definitely did plan to stay. He felt good when he was there, felt decent and different and right. So he finished the veal, drank two cups of coffee, ordered desserts to go, and left.

When Tom started high school, he was five feet eight, which would have been a fine height for a fifteen-year-old if he hadn't wanted to play football. He had come off a summer of painting houses during the day and playing ball at night, so he was tanned and fit, but he lacked the bulk that the older players had.

"You're scrappy," his mother pointed out when she caught him moping around on the eve of tryouts.

"That doesn't matter. I won't make it. I'm too small."

"Smallness is a state of mind," she said, as she puffed up every cushion in the living room except those on which he was slouched. "Walk onto that field with your head high, and you'll look a foot taller. Look the coach in the eye, and he'll think you're more solid. Carry yourself like a quarterback, and people will see you as one."

It worked. He played backup to a senior quarterback that freshman year, then starting quarterback for his remaining three years. By the time he graduated, he was six four and strong. Though he no longer needed pretense, the lesson in projecting confidence was ingrained.

It stood him in good stead now. For the third night in a row, well after visiting hours ended, he walked into the medical center past the nurse at the desk, swung into the stairwell, climbed the stairs, and strode down the second-floor corridor to Bree's room as though he had every right in the world to be there. No matter that the nurses on duty were new and that his battered face made him look like a thug. Then again, perhaps they knew exactly who he was and didn't dare stop him. Whatever, no one looked twice.

He was the one to blink when Bree was nowhere in sight.

* * *

Bree sat in the dark of the deserted lounge at the far end of the hall. The music drifting from wall speakers was classical, soft and soothing, exactly what she needed. Her room had grown oppressive. Even now, well after the last of her friends had left, she could still hear them telling her that they missed her, that they wished her a speedy recovery, that any out-of-body visions would end once her mind cleared.

The thing was that her mind was perfectly clear. She had slept most of the morning, had cut back on pain pills, and if anything, her memory of that time in the operating room had sharpened. She didn't tell her friends that. They weren't inclined to listen, and she didn't have the strength to make her case. Sitting here, with the mild night air whispering in through half-open windows, she found it hard to believe that a major snowstorm had hit three days before, much less that she had died, gone to heaven, and returned.

It was all at the same time crystal clear and totally unreal. Unreal that it had snowed so hard so early in the season. Unreal that she had been at just that spot on Birch Hill at just that moment. Unreal that she had watched the goings-on in the operating room. Unreal that she felt the calming force of that bright light still. Unreal that silent Tom from the diner was Thomas Gates of national renown.

Thomas Gates. Unreal.

Shifting gingerly in the wingback chair, she started to raise her legs to tuck her cold feet beneath her. When the soreness in her abdomen wouldn't allow for the movement, she settled for layering one foot over the other and burying her hands in the folds of her robe.

She knew about Thomas Gates. Being a fan of his books, she had read articles on him. Many hadn't been flattering. He wasn't supposed to be very nice.

Odd, but the Tom Gates she knew seemed perfectly nice.

Releasing a breath, she put her head against the back of the chair and closed her eyes. She remembered those articles in detail. Thomas Gates was reputed to be callous and conceited, but she hadn't seen either trait in him, and as for being the womanizer the articles implied, he hadn't womanized in Panama. He hadn't come on to her as had other men in the diner, hadn't leered or teased or touched her in inappropriate ways.

Footsteps came from the hall, and suddenly he was there. Thinking she might have imagined him, she blinked, but he remained.

She hadn't wished him there. She was being careful not to make wishes accidentally. But she was inordinately pleased that he'd come.

"Hi," he said. Backlit as he was, she couldn't see his face, but his voice was gentle, smiling.

Her heart beat a little faster. She smiled back. "Hi."

"Walk all the way down here yourself?"

"Uh-huh." Dryly, she added, "It took everything I had."

He made a show of looking around. "No more IV. That's progress."

"Uh-huh. I had solid food for dinner. Chicken."

"Bet it wasn't as good as Flash's."

"No. But that's okay. I was full after two bites." She felt revived now that he had come. "Want to turn on a light?"

"Not if you prefer the dark."

"I don't."

He slipped a hand under the shade of a nearby lamp. The soft light that filled the room made him real, in an unreal sort of way. He was gorgeous, with his tousled hair and his athlete's build, and he was *there*.

"I didn't think you were coming," she said.

"I promised I would. You just slept through the promise."

No. She had heard. Then she had wondered if she had simply dreamed it up because she wanted it so much. "I thought you might go home and think about it and decide I was loony."

"If you are, then so are a hell of a lot of other people."

He lowered a leather knapsack from his shoulder at the same time that he lowered himself to a chair. The knapsack settled on the floor between his knees. He unstrapped the top and pulled out a folder that was a solid inch thick. "Printouts from my computer. They're personal accounts of other people who have experienced what you did."

Bree's heart beat even faster than before. She looked from the folder to Tom and back. She didn't know whether to be more pleased that there were others like her or that Tom had made the effort of seeking them out.

The first took precedence. Taking the folder from him, she put it on her lap and covered it with a proprietary hand. Cautiously, she asked, "Did you read them?"

"Every one."

"What do they say?"

"Much of what you do," he answered gently. He had his elbows on his thighs. His hands dangled between. "An accident or a medical crisis occurs. The victim is conscious of leaving his body, rising up above it, and looking back down. Sometimes it happens at the scene of the accident, sometimes in an operating room. He sees people working on him, hears their voices. Then there's the light. It's always very bright. It's always benevolent. It conveys a sense of well-being. It speaks without actually talking."

"It *did*," Bree breathed, delighted. She hadn't realized how alone she had felt until she suddenly felt less so. "What else?" She put her fingertips together in front of her mouth and tried to contain her excitement.

"There's a lot of the same uncertainty that you feel. The person knows he's had an out-of-body experience, but he's still not sure."

"Ex*actly.*"

"He knows people don't believe him, but he can't forget what happened. He's afraid to talk about it. Some people hold it in for years—twenty-five, by one account."

"Oh, my. But I know the fear that person felt." She

reversed her feet, putting the bottom one on top. "Did anyone else mention being promised three wishes?"

Tom gave a quick head shake. "That doesn't mean anything. No two accounts I read were exactly alike. One person said that the air around the being of light was purple.
Another passed through a tree during his experience and
woke up covered with sap. Another left his body and floated
around the city for a while before waking up in the hospital.
Another tried to open a door while he was out of his body,
but couldn't. Some remember feeling a sense of belonging
when they're with this being."

Bree had, now that she thought of it.

Tom went on. "Lots of people report being sucked out of
their bodies and up through a dark tunnel. The bright light
is at the end of that tunnel. Some of them report hearing a
buzzing or jangling noise. Some say they fought it, fought
the noise and the light, fought being sucked up."

Bree shook her head. She hadn't experienced anything
like that. There had been nothing to fight. She had simply
been in her body one minute and out of it the next. Once
she was with the being of light, she wouldn't have fought
anyway. That being had been compelling. If anything, she
had been sad to leave it.

"Some people say they were given a choice and made a
conscious decision to return to life. Others believe they were
returned to life for a reason. Being granted three wishes is a
reason."

"But no one else mentioned getting wishes?" she asked,
knowing that the concept would be more credible if it had
happened before.

The small lines that furrowed his brow did nothing negative. Black eye and all, he looked great.

"No one else mentioned getting wishes," he said. "One
person mentioned coming back to take care of a sick parent,
another coming back to be with a lover, but neither mentioned it as a response to a wish. There were reports from

people who said that they had done things wrong and were being given a second chance, and reports from people who said that the being of light showed them what hell looked like, so they were reformed. Some specifically said they'd been to heaven. They wrote about seeing dead relatives and friends."

"I didn't," Bree said, and was grateful for it. She might have liked to see her father, but if the dead congregated, he would have been with his parents, and they were dour people. Their presence in a room put a damper on everyone and everything. It would have surely dulled the luster of the being of light. She was glad that had remained unspoiled.

Of course, it was still possible that the being didn't exist. "What do you think?" she asked Tom. "Was it real, what happened to me?"

Again those small creases touched his forehead. He frowned at his palms, let them fall to his thighs, and met her gaze. "I don't know. Your claim is certainly more plausible than some of the others. Take young children having near-death experiences. Kids of three or four, even seven or eight, are imaginative. They're wide open to the power of suggestion. And I have a hard time believing near-death experiences reported by people who acknowledge that they were either stoned or drunk at the time. I also have a hard time believing the stories written by people whose lives were unstable to begin with. They may be prone to hallucinating. Same with a person who suffers a severe head injury.

"Then there are those people who report a cataclysmic awakening. They're walking down the street and—wham— they suddenly see something or know something or feel something that may or may not have to do with God. I wouldn't call that a near-death experience. An epiphany, maybe. Same thing with people who recover from a serious illness and report having seen Saint Peter and the pearly gates. Serious illnesses naturally spawn thoughts of mortality, which naturally spawn thoughts of religion."

Bree shook her head. "Not in me. My dad was a Congregationalist, but I'm not much of anything."

Tom smiled and sat straighter. "So then there are people like you. They're well-adjusted adults. They're intelligent. They may or may not be religious, but they're good people. They aren't hopped up or soused, they're in accidents not of their own making, and somewhere along the line their hearts stop. Medical personnel verify it and reverse it. These momentarily dead return to the world of the living with stories that are so much alike that it gives you chills. These people come from all walks of life. They don't know each other. They may or may not have ever read an account of a near-death experience, still the experiences they report have eerie similarities." He blew out a breath. "Hard not to believe people like that."

Bree felt suddenly lighthearted. "You're very convincing."

"When you sum it up, it *is* convincing. The only theory I found at all plausible made the argument that the end of life is like the very beginning, that things come full circle, that there are parallels between the birth process and near-death accounts. The dark tunnel that some people claim they're sucked into at the moment of death is like the birth canal. The bright light is what the delivery room must seem like to the newborn after the dark of the womb. Same with the noise. The implication is that at the moment of death, or just prior to death, the human mind reverts in time to the moment of birth."

"Then what I saw were memories?" She shook her head again. "Babies aren't given three wishes. Besides, I saw a mole."

"A mole."

"On the neck of one of the nurses who was in the operating room that night. She was bending over me, and it was on the back of her neck. How could I have seen it there if I wasn't above her?" Bree held up a hand. "Okay. I know.

Maybe she was in the recovery room when I woke up, and I saw it when she turned away from me, and I'm just confusing the two locations. But there was only one nurse in the recovery room—I asked—and she wasn't in the operating room during the time my heart stopped, and besides, she doesn't have a mole. I checked."

"Have you checked the OR nurses?"

"One. She didn't have a mole. The other has long hair. She only puts it up when she's in the operating room." Bree tucked her hands inside each other on the folder. "I should just come out and ask her about it, but I feel silly." At times, she felt silly, period. "Word's already going around town. What if the whole near-death thing is bogus?" She reversed her feet again, rubbing them together to generate heat. Flash had brought her robe, which was fleece, large and warm, but he hadn't thought to bring slippers. The hospital provided foam ones that were barely better than nothing.

Tom slid to the floor, shifted her feet to his lap, and began to chafe them. The warmth of it went all the way to her cheeks.

"You don't have to do that," she said.

"I want to."

"You must have better things to do with your time."

He shook his head, looking pleased.

"You're feeling guilty," she insisted, "but I told you, the accident wasn't your fault." And he was a celebrity and movie-star handsome. But did she move her feet out of his grasp? No. "This is embarrassing."

"Why? You have nice feet. Nice icy feet."

"They're always that way."

"My mom used to say that it's a female thing, that women's warmth is concentrated in the region of their hearts, so their extremities suffer."

Bree laughed, then hugged her middle when the movement hurt.

Tom's hands stopped. Troubled eyes went to her stomach. "I'm sorry."

"Don't be. It's fine now. But what a nice thought. You say things like that in your books, little gems of wisdom. Is that where you get them, from your mom?"

His reply was snide. "I never thought so. I thought it was all me."

"Is she still alive?"

Quietly, he said, "She died last year."

"I'm sorry."

"Me, too."

When he resumed his rubbing, it seemed more a massage, a gentle kneading that involved both of his hands and both of her feet, from the tips of her toes to her ankles.

Closing her eyes, she gave herself up to the feeling. It occurred to her that she could easily spend a wish on a permanent foot masseur, if the business of wishes was real.

She wondered if it was. No one else had ever reported being granted three wishes.

So maybe it was just her. Or maybe someone had used all three wishes and died before writing about it.

She wouldn't use the third wish, wouldn't take the risk. Then again, maybe *none* of it was real.

The massage stopped. Tom reached into his bag, pulled out a sweater, and was about to wrap it around her feet, when she said, "I'm getting tired. I'd better go back to bed."

He returned the sweater to the knapsack, pushed to his feet, and hitched the knapsack to his shoulder. Holding the folder in one hand, he helped her up with the other. He kept one arm around her as they walked.

She had made it to the lounge on her own. Aside from the bend in her middle, she was remarkably steady. Even tired, she could have made it back to her room on her own. But she let Tom help her into bed, let him straighten the covers and pull them up. She watched him put the folder on the table where she could reach it when she was ready, watched him pull a book from the knapsack.

"That thing's full of goodies," she mused.

His face brightened, rendering him devilishly handsome. She could see why he was called a lady-killer. "As a matter of fact." He reached in again and produced two take-out containers. "Pudding. One for you, one for me."

She was touched. He had brought a sweater and a book, which meant that he was staying. And now pudding.

Thinking that he might stay longer if he had *both* puddings, she touched her stomach and said, "That was so sweet of you. But the chicken filled me up. Honestly."

He set one container on the bedstand and opened the second. "Don't like tapioca?"

He put it down and was reaching for the other, when she said, "I love tapioca, but I'm stuffed. Really. You eat it."

"This one's Indian pudding."

She took a quick breath. "Indian pudding?" Indian pudding was her favorite.

He upped the ante. "There's a microwave in the kitchen. I could heat it for you."

She was sorely tempted.

"Then, once it's hot, I could raid the freezer and add a little vanilla ice cream."

That did it. "Just a very, very, *very* little."

He gave her a smile that warmed her all over. Watching him head for the kitchen, she decided that she didn't need three wishes as long as Tom Gates was around.

On Monday night, he pulled a pair of wool socks from his knapsack. They were soft, clean, and large, and clearly his, which made them more special than if he had spent a fortune on fancy slippers. They warmed her feet perfectly.

On Tuesday night, just when she was starting to feel hungry, he showed up with a meal from the diner and said, "Flash recommended the Yankee special, but the risotto sounded lighter and too good to pass up. Interested?" Was she ever, and *not* for the Yankee special. The Yankee special was a pot roast reminiscent of the kind her grandmother had made every Thursday without fail, and while Flash's pot roast was light-years better, memory had her avoiding the dish. Risotto, on the other hand, she loved.

On Wednesday night, he brought her a book. It was one of the advance reading copies his agent had sent, a legal thriller that tackled the issue of privacy and had made him think, he said, as many of the others hadn't. He thought she might enjoy it and was interested in her opinion. Would she read it? he asked. Like she would ever say no.

On Thursday night, when the walls of her room were starting to close in, he helped her steal past the nurses' station for a quick trip to the rooftop deck. Her pace was slow, but the freshness of the night justified the effort. She felt that she had never in her life seen so many stars. They seemed to fill the sky in ways that suggested a million worlds beyond.

Friday morning, a full week after the accident and an hour before her discharge, she formally met Dr. Simon Meade from St. Johnsbury. He examined her and removed her stitches. Then he drew up a chair and in a kindly voice broke the news that she would never be able to have a child. "When we reconstruct people's insides like we did yours, their bodies develop scar tissue," he explained. "It gets in the way of conception."

Bree was startled. "No children? Ever?"

"I can't say the chances are zero, but they're pretty slim. You haven't had any yet, have you?"

She shook her head.

"And you're how old?"

"Thirty-three."

"You're less fertile now than you were ten years ago. Put that together with scarring, and you have a problem."

Bree hadn't been thinking about having a child. She hadn't been feeling desperate about it, hadn't heard any biological clock ticking. So she was surprised when her eyes filled with tears.

"I'm sorry," the doctor said. "This is the worst part of my job. The good news is that you're alive. If you'd been left lying in the snow, you'd have bled to death."

She knew that. And she was grateful. And she really *hadn't* had her heart set on having children.

Still, there was an awful emptiness, a sudden sense of loss.

"In every other respect, you're healing well," the doctor went on. "I agree with Dr. Sealy. No reason why you can't go home. Take it easy for the next few weeks. Add activity a little at a time. Listen to your body. It'll tell you what you can do."

She continued to stare at him through tear-filled eyes.

He rose from the bed, gave her hand a pat, and smiled. "I have to get back to St. Johnsbury. This is a long way to come to make rounds."

She swallowed the lump in her throat.

"Well, then," he said, "good luck to you." He turned toward the door.

"Dr. Meade?" When he looked back, she said, "What if I lie perfectly still?"

He seemed confused.

"If I lie perfectly still, will less scar tissue grow?"

"No. Scarring is a natural part of healing."

"There's no way to prevent it?"

"No."

She swallowed again, took a breath, thought of the benevolent being of light, and felt less alone. It was all right, she reasoned. So she wasn't destined to be a mother. She supposed it made sense. She hadn't grown up in a house full of kids. She didn't have a maternal role model, or even a husband. She wouldn't know what to do with a child of her own. Besides, she didn't want to be tied down, after being finally free after so long.

So fate had simply formalized what her instincts had always known.

She rubbed her eyes with the heels of her hands, took another breath, and smiled at the doctor, who lifted a hand in farewell and turned again toward the door.

That was when she saw the mole on the back of his neck.

Once the breakfast rush at the diner was over, Flash came to the hospital and drove Bree home. She didn't tell him what the doctor had said, didn't see the point, since she didn't know how she felt about it herself. All her rationalization notwithstanding, there was still an unexpected emptiness. So she pushed it from her mind.

The weather helped. The sun was bright and the air warm; the roads were dry. It was the type of autumn day she loved, the type when the smallest pile of raked leaves, heated by the sun, perfumed the air for miles. If the jostling of the Explorer as it barreled along caused her discomfort, it was soothed by the rush of the breeze past her face.

The roads grew progressively familiar. Not a thing had changed while she had been gone, it seemed. The Crowells' rusted Chevy still sat in the tall grasses of the field beside their house, the Dillards' front lawn was still filled with pumpkins for sale, the Krumps' three-year-old triplets still clustered on the big old tire that swung from the sprawling oak at the side of their house.

Everything was just as it had been prior to the snow a week before—just the same, yet different. The trees looked larger, the sun brighter, the colors richer. The smiles of the people they passed were broader, their waves higher. Even Bree's old Victorian seemed less prim as it welcomed her home.

She went up the front walk hugging the bubble bowl that Julia Dean had sent. The few flowers left in it were so feeble that Flash had wanted to leave it behind, but Bree wouldn't hear of it. Julia's arrangement had been the first splash of color she had seen, waking up in her hospital room. Then, it had seemed a link between the world she had glimpsed beyond and the earthly one to which she'd returned. Her need for that link was greater now than ever.

Chapter

5

$\mathcal{T}$om was unsure of his place, with Bree suddenly home. Each time he drove past her house that first day, a different car was parked there. Talk at the diner revolved around who was sitting with her when, who was cooking for her when, who was cleaning for her when. Directly or indirectly, most everyone in town had a role.

For the first time in years, he thought about his own hometown, small and so like this one. He hadn't appreciated it then, but he did now. Having lived in the city, having been one of those who were too busy—or self-important—to care about a neighbor's woes, having felt the brunt of isolation during his last few months there, he found it heartwarming to see Panama rally around Bree. A schedule was drawn up to ensure that during those first few days, at least, she was never alone.

No one asked him to take a turn. So he approached the group that surrounded Flash, making final arrangements. Jane Hale had known Bree since childhood, LeeAnn Conti had worked with her for years. Dotty Hale and Emma

McGreevy, both a generation above, spoke for the town. Liz Little was simply a friend.

"I'd like to do my part," he said. "I feel responsible for her needing the help."

All six regarded him with eyes that ranged from cautious to cold—a sobering experience for a man who had once had the power to charm by virtue of simply walking into a room.

"Thank you," said Emma, with a curt smile, "but we take care of our own."

He absorbed the rebuff as his due. But it didn't stop him. "I'd like to be considered one of your own."

Emma looked at his fading shiner and the livid line beneath it. "After half a year? I think not. Besides, we don't need help with Bree. We have it all arranged."

"All but the nights," he said, when she would have closed the circle and shut him out. He had overheard enough to know where they stood. "You're still working that out. I can help."

Emma fingered the short strand of pearls that circled her neck. "You wouldn't know what to do."

"Bree says he does," Jane said in a quiet voice.

Dotty scowled at her. "What's there to do in a hospital? This is at home."

"I can help there, too," Tom said.

"Can you cook?" asked Liz.

Emma waved a hand. "No need for him to cook. We have plenty of food."

"It'd be nice if he could heat up what's there."

Emma tried shaking her head. "No matter. He can't stay with her."

Jane dared a soft "Why not?"

"Good *God,* Jane," Dotty flared, "how can you even *ask* that? He said it himself. He's responsible for putting her there."

"It wasn't his fault," offered Flash. "She doesn't blame him."

"Still," Dotty insisted, "looking at him will only remind her of bad things."

"He's famous," said LeeAnn, with a curious glance Tom's way.

Emma grunted. "More like *in*famous. Goodness, LeeAnn, Dotty's been waving those articles in front of your nose for a week now."

"Do you really want Bree to spend the night with a womanizer?" Dotty asked.

"*Alleged* womanizer," Tom corrected. "Just because the tabloids loved writing about me doesn't mean everything they said was true."

Dotty brushed his comment aside. "You can't stay with her. It isn't proper."

"Why not?" Jane asked again.

"Because . . . he's . . . male."

"So's Flash," Liz said, "and he's spending the night."

"Bree's like my sister," Flash reasoned. "I've known her for years."

"So have you," Dotty told her daughter. "You're a selfish one, wanting him there to spare you the work."

"That's not it at all. I *do* want to help. In fact, I can sleep better at her house than at ours. You wake up all the time."

"Do I tell you to get up with me? I do not. It's not *my* fault you sleep so lightly every little noise spooks you. Good *God,* Jane. I'm your mother. You complain about me, you complain about Bree . . ."

Tom saw Julia Dean watching them from a booth. She looked torn, as though she wanted to join the group but didn't dare. What with the way they weren't welcoming him, Tom didn't blame her. What with the way Dotty was going after Jane, he *really* didn't blame her.

"The thing is," he said to end the last, "you all have other things to do during the day. I don't. I can sleep all day if I want. Look at you, Liz. You can't sleep all day. You have three young kids."

"But I love Bree," Liz said. "She house-sits with our cats whenever we go away, and she never lets me pay her for it. I owe her this."

"Me, too," Tom said, but Emma was moving on, paper and pencil in hand.

"All right. It's Liz tonight, LeeAnn tomorrow night, Flash Sunday, Jane Monday. Abby wants Tuesday night, and then we'll regroup." Throwing a smug look Tom's way, she drew a line across the bottom of the list, and that was that.

But Tom couldn't stay away. He left the diner at eight, saw two cars in Bree's drive, drove past and down the turnpike to the mall, where he rented a movie. Reversing the trip, he arrived back at Bree's shortly after nine. The two cars had been replaced by Liz Little's Suburban. Satisfied that Bree was in capable hands, he went home and put the movie in the VCR. He watched it for half an hour, before turning it off and snatching up the keys to his car.

Bree's Victorian was a behemoth of a house. It was tall and lean, made all the more so by its setting on a rise. *Staid* was one word Tom might have used to describe it, *stark* another. In the absence of a moon, not even the dim lamplight seeping from the lower-floor windows added cheer. The house felt cold. He never would have matched it with Bree.

Climbing the front steps, he crossed the porch to knock softly on the old wood door. After a minute's wait, he gave another knock. He was about to go around to the back, when the door opened.

Having fully expected to see Liz, he was startled to find Bree. She looked so waiflike in the meager porch light, with dark eyes in a pale face, framed by long, dark, damp hair, and the rest of her lost in her huge fleece robe, that something tripped inside him.

"Hey," he half whispered. "I didn't mean to get you up. Where's Liz?"

Bree's voice wasn't much louder than his, though he suspected she had sheer physical weakness to blame. "On the phone. One of the kids is sick. She's talking with Ben." She reached for his arm and drew him in, then closed the door and leaned against it.

He stayed close. "How do you feel?"

"Tired. Friends keep coming. And I'm grateful. But it's hard to say no when they want to talk."

"Go on to bed. I'll talk with Liz."

For an instant, looking up at him, she seemed on the verge of tears, and for the life of him he didn't know what to do. What he wanted to do was hold her, but that didn't seem right. So instead he simply asked, "Are you okay?"

She swallowed, nodded, and eased away from the door. He followed her as far as the bottom of the winding staircase, and then it took everything he had just to watch, instead of walking beside her or even carrying her up. But they weren't at the hospital anymore. This was personal stuff.

When she had reached the top and disappeared down the hall, he looked around. The foyer in which he stood was large and opened to an even larger living room. Furnished in dark woods with frayed fabrics, both areas looked tired. Like the outside of the house, they didn't fit Bree.

Liz Little's voice came from the back of the house. Following the sound, he found himself in a kitchen that was old but functional and clean. Liz had the telephone cord wrapped around her hand and was saying, with what sounded like dwindling patience, "On his forehead. Hold it flat on his forehead until the strip changes color." She paused. "I *know* he won't lie still, but believe me, it's easier doing it this way than the other way." She paused again. "Well, *hold* him there. Come on, Ben," she pleaded, "you're a whole lot stronger than he is. You can immobilize him for two minutes." She listened, pushed a hand through her hair, spotted Tom. She held his gaze while she said,

"Yes, I'm *thrilled* that he wants me, but the fact is that I'm not there."

"Go," Tom mouthed. "I'll stay."

Liz declined his offer with the wave of her hand. "No, Ben, he doesn't specifically need me. He needs one of us, and you're there. It's good for him to know that you can take care of him as well as I can." She paused. "Of course you can. You're a great parent. Besides, wasn't that a major reason why we gave up our old jobs and came here, so you could be with the kids more?" Another pause, then a frown and a cry. "I *do* love my kids. I'd be home in a minute if I thought Joey was very sick. He was fine when I left."

When she paused this time, Tom actually heard Ben yelp.

Liz's eyes went wide. "Oh, yuck," she finally said. "All over you?" She made a face. "Okay, sweetheart, sit him in a tepid tub. I'll be there in ten minutes."

She hung up the phone and looked apologetically at Tom. "You don't mind?"

"Not if you don't." He was counting on Liz being more accepting of him than the others. She had been an outsider herself not so long ago. "Bree's gone to bed. I'll just sit around down here."

Liz rummaged in her bag. "There's enough food to feed an army," she said, with a glance at foil-wrapped bundles on the counter. "I'll settle things at home and come back."

"No need. I'm here until the next person shows up."

"That won't be until ten tomorrow morning."

"Ten is fine."

Liz came up with her keys. "The others will kill me."

"Tell you what," Tom said. "Come back at nine, and they'll never know."

She stared at him for a minute. "That's sly."

He didn't say anything.

For another minute she stared, then she opened the back door. "You really wrote those books?"

He nodded.

"How many in all?"

"Six."

"I can't imagine writing one, let alone six."

"Then we're even. I can't imagine cleaning up after a sick kid."

She gave him a grudging smile. "I'll be back tomorrow morning at nine. Thanks."

Tom stood at the base of the front stairs, his hand on the mahogany newel post, his eye on the landing above. He was as unsettled remembering Bree with tears in her eyes as he had been at the time. Wanting to make sure she was all right, he started the climb.

At the top, all was dark. Only when his eyes adjusted did he make out three open doorways. That a fourth was closed was underscored by a pale line of light at its base.

His knock was little more than the brush of knuckles on wood, too soft to disturb sleep if that was where she was. He listened for sound, heard none. Slowly, carefully, he turned the knob and opened the door.

The light came from a small lamp that stood by the side of the bed. Both the lamp and the bed frame were made of wrought iron. Everything else was either white—bedding, draperies, ceilings, walls, and wood—or yellow—throw pillows, lamp shades, and carpet.

The bedroom was smaller than he guessed the others in the house to be, with space for little more than a double bed, a chest of drawers, and a big old upholstered chair. But framed pictures stood on the chest, and books were stacked by the chair, and though the wind chimes hanging at the window were still, they added charm. There were no ruffles or bows, nothing showy or overly feminine. Even the flower arrangement on the dresser, a fresh one with Julia Dean's unmistakable stamp on it, was bright and honest, like Bree.

The quilt was bunched at the bottom of the bed. She lay above it, curled up with her back to the door. Her robe was dark against the sheets, her hair dark against the pillow.

Quietly, he rounded the bed, to find that her eyes were open and sad. They climbed to his and held.

When he sat by her hip and touched her cheek, she closed her eyes. Within seconds her lashes were wet.

He felt the same tripping sensation he had earlier, even stronger now, and suddenly it didn't matter that he wasn't a Panamanian, didn't matter that her needs now weren't for impersonal things like Jell-O, wool socks, or Internet printouts. It didn't matter that he might be crossing a line. He had no choice but to gather her up and let her cry.

Cry Bree did. Tom's chest was the best thing that had happened to her all day. It gave her permission to be weak for a change, made her feel that if she broke down, the world wouldn't end. Crying eased the tension that had been building in her since morning, eased the sorrow she hadn't expected to feel. It eased the confusion of coming home to a house that was the same as before, in a body that wasn't. It eased her fear of a world where anything at all could happen and leave her wondering what was real and what wasn't.

But tears were real. And Tom's chest was real.

She ran out of the first before the second left, but by then she was sleeping too soundly to notice.

LeeAnn drove to Bree's straight from work on Saturday night. By the time Tom arrived an hour later, her boyfriend was brooding on the front steps in the dark. Though Tom had seen the man numerous times at the diner, they had met formally only the week before. Gavin was the mechanic who had declared Tom's Jeep a total loss.

"What's up?" Tom asked.

Gavin grunted. "Nothin' at all."

Guessing that that was the man's gripe in a nutshell, Tom went past him up the steps and across the porch. He had barely knocked on the door when LeeAnn pulled it open, looking ready to do battle. She closed her mouth when she saw Tom instead of Gavin, and glanced uneasily past him to the porch steps.

Tom slipped into the house. "Crossed signals?"

LeeAnn was clearly peeved. "No. He knew I promised to spend the night here. He just isn't happy about it, what with my having a baby-sitter for the night. It won't help that you're here. I told *him* he couldn't come in."

"Why can't he?"

Her cheeks reddened while she searched for an answer. Tom guessed it had to do with sex.

She tipped up her chin. "If you're here to see Bree, she's eating dinner."

"I'm sorry. I didn't mean to interrupt."

"You're not interrupting me. I ate before. I'm just keeping her company." She scowled at Gavin. "He was supposed to tend bar at his uncle's place in Ashmont, but he got the night off at the last minute. I mean, what am I supposed to do? I'm already committed."

"Bree will probably be going to bed soon."

"But I have to be here in case she wakes up and feels sick."

"Do you think she will?"

LeeAnn thought about that. "No. She told me she slept well last night." The look she shot at Gavin this time was softer. "I mean, it's not like she really needs me. I didn't even have to bring food from the diner, there's so much here already." She darted a quick look at Tom. "How long did you want to stay?"

Tom shrugged. "Ten minutes, ten hours. You tell me."

She thought for another minute, then shook her head. "I shouldn't." But she looked tempted. "My ex's mother has the kids. She's probably already put them to bed. She may be asleep herself. It'd be silly to wake her." She drew her teeth over her lips. "I have to work tomorrow." She tacked on, "I could use a good night's sleep."

Tom understood perfectly.

LeeAnn alternated hesitant glances between him and Gavin. "Maybe I could go out for a little while. I mean, if you're going to be here anyway."

"Sure," Tom said, with an innocent shrug.

"I mean, what would be *really* good is if I could get some sleep and come back later."

"What time would that be?"

She dipped her head to the side in a timid shrug of her own. "I don't know. One, two. I mean, three would be really great."

"I slept most of the day, so I'll probably still be up then. I have a movie. You could watch it with me."

"Well, if you're only watching a movie, I could sleep longer," she said, confidentially now. "Like until four or five. *Six* would be *really* awesome. I mean, I could be back here by seven, no questions asked. Bree would *never* be up before seven. She isn't a morning person. She doesn't get to the diner before noon. She likes taking her time waking up."

"Then it'd be pretty safe for you to come back at seven."

"For sure." She paused, looking at him askance. "Did you really break Courteney Cox's heart, like the *Star* said you did?"

"I've never met Courteney Cox."

"That's good. Because if you broke her heart, I couldn't trust you with Bree. Bree is too nice to be hurt." A sound came from the porch. Her eyes flew there, then shot back to Tom. In a voice that held a hint of conspiracy, she whispered, "So if I tell Bree I'm going out for a couple of hours, you'll cover for me till I get back?"

Tom was glad to do it.

He had a head start Sunday night. Right about the time he was finishing off the pasta special at the diner, in short order Jillie went home sick and the grillman burned his hand. Flash, who had wanted to leave early to stay with Bree, slid in across from Tom.

"You were going over there anyway, weren't you?" he asked, in a voice low enough not to carry beyond the booth.

Tom nodded.

"Think you could stay till I get there? It shouldn't be later than ten."

It was actually fifteen minutes before ten. By ten, Flash was stretched out on the floor in front of the television in Bree's den, snoring softly.

"So much for the movie I thought was riveting," Tom remarked, though he wasn't hurting any. He took satisfaction in seeing that Bree was wide awake, looking rested and riveted indeed. Each day, her face was regaining more of its natural color, and while she still moved with care, she was greatly improved.

The den had been a welcome discovery, the only room other than Bree's bedroom with her personal stamp. Filled with a large, cushiony sofa and chairs, a low coffee table that she claimed she ate dinner on more often than not, and shelves of books, it was a room after his own heart.

Bree looked away from the movie long enough to say, "Let's give him a few minutes and see if he wakes up."

The snoring grew louder.

She leaned down from the sofa, jiggled his shoulder, and gave a gentle "Shhh."

Flash turned his head, and the snoring stopped. It resumed with a vengeance moments later.

Bree sent Tom a beseechful look, so sweet it made him laugh. "Don't look at *me*," he said. *"I"*'m not the one making the noise."

"Why do men do this? Snoring in bed is one thing, but doing it in a room full of people? My father used to turn on the radio in the living room and snore to the music. It ruined it for me." She leaned sideways. "Flash!" She gave his shoulder a sharp jab. "Wake up!"

Tom felt a moment's sympathy for Flash when he bolted up, looking dazed. "What?"

"Go home," she said, with affection. "Sleep in your own bed."

He ran a hand over his face. "No. I'm okay. I'll just go in the other room and stretch out on the sofa. A few minutes is all I need."

"This is ridiculous, Flash. There's no need for you to spend the night here. There's no need for *anyone* to spend the night." She rubbed his shoulder where she had jabbed it. "The thought is sweet. But I'm so much better."

"You're still in pain."

"Much less now."

"What if it gets worse? What if you get up in the middle of the night and pass out?"

"I won't. Please, Flash? I love you for wanting to help, but what'll make me feel best is if you go home and sleep so I can finish watching this movie in peace. Besides, Tom's here."

Tom sat a little straighter, felt a little better.

Flash wasn't so happy. "That's why I have to be. Dotty would have a fit if she heard I left you two alone."

"Like he's taking advantage of me. Come on, Flash."

"I'll never hear the end of it."

"Are *you* going to tell her?" Bree asked.

"Me? Christ, no."

"Well, I'm not, and Tom won't. So please, go home to bed."

"You're kicking me out?"

"Yes!" She softened the rebuff with a gentle smile. "I'm tired of people being here all the time. I like having my house to myself."

"Tom's staying."

"Tom's different."

"How?"

Bree seemed at a momentary loss. Tom held his breath

while she searched for an answer. Finally, she tipped up her chin and quite logically said, "Tom's recovering, too. He rests when I rest, so his sitting with me kills two birds with one stone. Besides, he'll leave if I ask, and he won't be hurt. Easy. No hassle."

"I'm easy, too," Flash said.

She smiled. "I know. Know what you can *really* do to help?"

"What?"

"Get them to cancel the night shift. Please?"

Bree was relieved when the stream of visitors slowed. She wasn't used to being coddled. Once, she would have wished for it with all her might. Now she found it stifling.

She liked stretching out on the sofa without making excuses for not going to bed, liked getting up without apologizing for not sleeping longer. She liked walking in the backyard without someone telling her that it was too cool or, worse, going out there with her and tainting the fresh air with human speech.

Tom understood. He was as pleased as she to sit out back on the trunk of a fallen maple and listen to the rap of a woodpecker, the hoot of an owl, the rustle of squirrels in the dry autumn leaves. When he spoke, it was in the same hushed voice she used, and he was just as good when they were inside. As he had in the hospital, he sensed what she needed without having to ask. He talked when she was in the mood for talking, opened a book and read when she grew tired, made tea when she was thirsty, made himself scarce when she needed time alone. He didn't rush to make her bed the minute she left it, didn't balk when the movie she wanted to watch began at eleven at night, and he made her a breakfast of sweet apple pie with a wedge of sharp cheddar—melted—a totally indulgent, thoroughly enjoyable treat that none of her other caretakers would have allowed.

As relationships went, it was the most unusual one she had ever had. They didn't talk about his books. They didn't talk about her tears. Many a time they sat silently, each of them reading, sharing the occasional look and smile. She knew little about him, save what she had read. She had no idea what he wanted from her or where he was headed. Still, she felt closer to him for the silence, and for all the other nonverbal things that he did. He calmed her, like the being of light she still saw in her dreams. He made her feel cared for, even loved.

Talk around town, passed on to her like little get-well gifts, with varying degrees of delight, was that he was dangerous, but she had never felt that. To the contrary. He was so perfect for her that he seemed unreal. And that was okay. Something had happened that night on the operating table, something that said life was too short to analyze things too much, something that relaxed her and made her see and do and feel things that weren't entirely sensible.

So what if Tom had a whole other life waiting for him in New York? So what if his feelings started and stopped at guilt? So *what?*

Falling for Tom wasn't sensible. But it sure felt good.

Chapter

6

$\mathcal{T}$om made a point of eating at the diner every night before going to Bree's. He wanted to be seen as a regular there, wanted to be accepted, wanted to feel he was part of the town.

Funny. Belonging hadn't been something he had thought much about when he chose Panama. He had sought a place to hide in while he figured out what to do with the rest of his life. Panama had fit the bill, first and foremost, because it wasn't New York. If someone had suggested that he was actively seeking small-town flavor, he would have denied it. He had grown up in a small town and left at the first opportunity, thinking bigger was better.

He had to rethink that now. Panamanians seemed perfectly happy, perfectly content, perfectly intelligent and enterprising, even sophisticated in a modern, media-driven way. The town wasn't poverty-stricken. Anyone who wanted to get out could get out. That so few did said something.

He thought about it as he sat in his booth day after day,

while the townsfolk mingled comfortably among themselves.

He also thought about the surprising relief he felt now
that his identity was known. It was nice not to have to avert
his eyes or hide behind a three-day stubble, nice not to have
to fear discovery. Not that anyone here seemed impressed
by who he was. Glances his way were few and far between.

He thought his ego would mind, even just a little. That it
didn't was a sign of how far he had come. But then, being
ignored in as close-knit a town as Panama was deliberate. It
told him that people were fully aware of what he was doing,
and were watching and waiting.

By the time he was into his second week of spending
nights at Bree's, the waiting ended. He began having visitors
to his booth.

It started simply enough, with Sam, Dave, Andy, and
Jack—all local boys, Bree's contemporaries and friends—
shuffling over on their way out the door. They loomed over
him, four solid men made more solid by layers of November
clothing and more imposing by the earnestness of their expressions.

"We hear you've been at Bree's a lot," said Andy, whose
experience in sales at his family's tackle store apparently
made him the designated speaker. "She's a friend of ours.
We'll be checking up on her to make sure she's all right. We
thought you oughta know that."

Before Tom could react, they shuffled off.

Eliot Bonner stayed longer. The following day, after
eating with Emma and Earl, he slid in with his coffee cup,
facing Tom. "Saw your car at Bree's again last night," he
said. "Is somethin' going on that I should know about?"

No beating around the bush, Tom thought, and he said,
"That depends. We played backgammon and watched TV.
Are there town ordinances against either of those?"

"No. Can't say there are. So are you gonna keep going over there?"

Tom waited only long enough to make a show of giving his answer some thought. "For a while. She doesn't seem to mind."

"Maybe she's star struck."

He smiled at that. "I doubt it." Bree never mentioned his work.

"Are you planning to stay in town?"

He had given himself a year. Now he sensed he might need longer. "I have a house here. I'm registered to vote here."

"Doesn't mean a thing," Eliot said. "What keeps you going to Bree's? Is it guilt?"

"No." It might have been at first, but that was gone.

"Then what?"

He thought about the comfort he felt when he was with her. It was honest, pure, even uplifting, if he wanted to be lyrical about it. It was also addictive. He was coming to depend on seeing Bree each day.

To Eliot, he simply said, "I like Bree."

"So where's it headed?"

He was beginning to ask himself the same question. "Nowhere for now. She's a long way from being recovered."

"Nah. Knowing Bree, she'll be back here in two weeks, tops. So I'm warning you. Be careful."

"Careful?"

"What you do with Bree. She's a nice girl. Know what I mean? I don't want anything happening to her now that things are finally looking up. Boy." He shook his head. "Her father was a long time dying." He sniffed in a breath, leaned forward, confided, "He was a tough one, Haywood Miller was. Not abusive. Nothing physical. But one cold son of a bitch. The one who could have made all the difference to Bree was the mother, but she didn't want any part of either of them. If I'd had *my* way, I'd have gone after her for abandonment. Course, I wasn't the chief then. I was still working at the lumber mill, right there alongside Haywood, except for the year he was gone. It was a month after he came back before any of us knew he'd brought a baby with him. He hadn't been much of a talker before he left, but after, he was even worse. We only learned about the baby because he had to take it to the hospital when it got sick."

"Why the secret?"

"Go ask him. He was a strange bird. The miracle of it is that Bree's so normal. She's got a strength in her most people don't." He raised a warning finger. "So don't mess with it, you hear?" He sat back. As an afterthought, he took a drink of his coffee.

"How did her father die?" Tom asked.

Still holding his coffee cup, Eliot slid out of the booth. "Terminal ill humor," he said and stalked off.

Tom was finishing his own coffee when Martin Sprague took Eliot's place. The tired look that Martin always wore was even more so than usual. With his face drawn and his eyebrows lowered, he was all business.

"I think you should know that I handle Bree's legal affairs," he said, without prelude.

Tom was taken aback. Not sure how to respond, he settled for a polite "Yes?"

"So if you're broke because you spent it all," Martin warned, "don't go looking for money from her. She doesn't have any."

"I'm not broke."

"You wouldn't be the first to think she's loaded, coming from that family, but I handled Haywood's legal affairs and his father's before him, so I know. There's no money left. None."

"Was there once?"

"Once. Osgood Miller owned some of the best hardwood forest for miles around. He was good with the trees, but he didn't have an ounce of business sense. When he should've been building his own lumberyard so that he could make the most of what he cut, he was putting his money into foolish things. Most of it was gone before Bree was born. The rest went after. Haywood wasn't any better with money than Ozzie. Between them, they lost the land, the trucks, the name. The house was all Bree got, and it's a sad old pile of wood."

Tom had stopped seeing the frayed parts. Bree divided her time between the bedroom and the den, so he did, too. Both of those rooms were brighter.

"It looks okay to me," he said.

"Look closer," Martin advised, pushing himself out of the booth. "Walls are rotting, furnace is dying. She's going to have to put big money into the place before long." With a final look, he said, "So you'd best stay where you are."

If that meant staying at the bungalow and away from Bree, Tom couldn't comply. The time he spent with her was more rewarding than anything he had done in years. When she smiled, or laughed, or looked up at him with a face full of warmth, he felt like a million bucks, so much so that he started staying longer. Rather than leaving after breakfast, he lingered into the morning. Rather than waiting until nine at night to return, he began going straight from the diner. He took her for drives when she was feeling shut in, took her for walks through the backyard leaves when she wanted exercise, took her to the general store for soft-serve Oreo fudge frozen yogurt when she had a sudden sharp craving. Eliot was right. She was recovering fast.

At the end of her second week at home, he took her to the diner. Visiting royalty couldn't have received a more rousing welcome. She was escorted from booth to booth, from one seat of honor to the next. Superfluous, Tom fell into the background.

Emma found him there. "Could I have a minute, please?"

she asked, and gestured toward the empty booth at the far end of the row. As soon as they were seated, she faced him straight out and said, "I'm worried about Bree."

"She's healing well."

"That's not what worries me. People are starting to talk."

"About . . . ?"

"Bree. And you."

Surprise, surprise. "Ah."

"You spend too much time with her. Her friends are feeling left out. I can't tell you how many come up to me to ask if I know what's going on."

Tom was curious. "What do you say?"

"What *can* I say? *I* don't know what's going on. What *is* going on?"

He was trying to figure it out himself. All he felt safe saying was, "Nothing sinister."

"Maybe not, but your presence is putting a wedge between Bree and her friends, and that's an awful thing to happen. One day you'll be gone, and then where will Bree be? She needs her friends. They're her family, now that poor Haywood is gone." Her eyes grew distant. She fingered her pearls in dismay. "Poor Haywood. All those years, and he never recovered." She refocused on Tom. "She was a free spirit, Bree's mother was, and he fell for her hard. When he came back without her, he was the shadow of a man."

"I was under the impression he was the shadow of a man before."

Emma frowned. "Who told you that? That's not true at all. Haywood might have been quiet, but he stood on his own two feet. He was always proper and polite. He never missed a town meeting. He went to church every Sunday."

Some of the worst scoundrels did, Tom mused.

"Poor Haywood," Emma went on, lost in it now. "He didn't have an easy time, with a mother like that. Hannah Miller was a rigid woman. She gave new meaning to the words *proper* and *polite*. Long after the rest of the women eased up, she was still wearing dresses that buttoned up to her chin. Everything around her was neat as a pin. Everything was regimented. She was the kind of woman who made the rest of us grateful for our own mothers."

"Did she help raise Bree?"

"She had to. Poor Haywood couldn't have done it on his own, what with needing to work to earn money for food. There wasn't any day care center in the basement of the church in those days. Ozzie was dead, or just as good as dead, so the burden of it all was on poor Haywood." She shook her head. "What that woman did to him . . ."

Tom was about to ask whether she was talking about Hannah Miller or Bree's mother, when Dotty materialized at the booth. As sisters went, there was little physical resemblance between the two women. Though the younger of the two, Dotty was taller, thinner, and grayer than Emma, who never failed to look the part of town leader with her stylish suit, her light makeup, her hair that was a tad too auburn.

Their differences were exaggerated now by Dotty's scowl. "What are you telling him, Emma?"

"I'm just giving him a history lesson," Emma said, sliding out of the booth. "Don't get all ruffled up, sister."

"You're the one always telling me *I* talk too much."

"You do," Emma declared, and walked off.

Dotty glared after her, then, still glaring, turned back to Tom. "Don't ask me why we voted *her* town meeting moderator. She's been insufferable ever since."

"How long's it been?" Tom asked. He had arrived in town shortly before the last town meeting but hadn't bothered to go. He wondered if Emma's election was one of the things he had missed.

Apparently it wasn't.

"Eight years," Dotty replied, "and each one of those it gets worse. She thinks she can stick her nose into everyone else's business, sitting there with Earl and Eliot each and every day. John must be turning over in his *grave*. He wanted his wife in his home. He'd never have let her do what she does if he'd been alive. If he knew the *half* of it, he'd lock her up." She slid into the booth. Her manner sweetened. "What was she telling you?"

"She was talking about poor Haywood," Tom said.

Dotty rolled her eyes. "Poor Haywood, my foot. She always had her eye on him was her problem, but he couldn't talk his way out of a paper bag, much less court a woman, so she married John, and even *then* she kept an eye on Haywood. Did she tell you he was handsome?"

"No."

"That's a surprise. Usually it's the first thing she says. Well, he *was* handsome, I have to admit. Handsome and dull. And drab. And sour. Even *he* knew there was something wrong with his life. That's why he left that year. He went down to Boston to see about getting work there. Then he met that woman."

"Bree's mother?"

"What other? He never used her name, once he was back here. She couldn't have been more than twenty. Haywood, he was nearing forty. He happened to run into her in a sandwich shop one day, and that was all it took." She threw up a hand. "He was gone. Crazy in love. But a love like that never lasts, not between a woman so young and spirited and a man with his feet rooted so deep in New England soil. He needed to come back here to live, and she couldn't do that, so he came back alone, he and Bree." Her voice went higher. "Can you imagine turning your back on a baby that way?"

Tom, who knew well how to play devil's advocate, imagined that there might be situations in which walking away from a baby was the most compassionate thing to do, particularly when the baby had a father and a home. He didn't know enough about Bree's mother's situation to judge one way or the other.

"So what happened?" Dotty asked, sounding affronted.

"People talked. They talked when he came back to town without a word as to where he'd been and what he'd done, and they talked when they learned there was a baby and no wife. They talked about that child from the time she was old enough to walk down the street by herself, and they *still* talk, when you get them going. So"—she looked him dead in the eye—"that's why what you're doing to her is wrong."

He drew his head back. "What am *I* doing to her?"

"It doesn't matter. That's my point. They'll talk if you give them the slightest cause, and she deserves better."

Tom couldn't help himself. "Maybe you could tell them not to talk. Maybe you could set an example. You know, live and let live?"

Dotty straightened. "Are you saying that *I* talk? I'm no worse than anyone else in this town. My goodness, if *I* don't talk, the others will anyway, and then all the *wrong* things will be heard." She scooted across the bench and out of the booth. "You have no call to attack me. I was only giving you friendly advice." With a righteous look, she was gone.

Jane Hale caught up with him in the parking lot when he went out to bring the car around for Bree. She glanced back to make sure they were alone, pulled her coat tighter around her with fingers whose nails were bitten short, and said in a quiet voice, "I'm sorry about my mother. She tells herself she's doing the right thing. Don't let her put you off."

Tom smiled. What Jane lacked in looks she more than made up for in gentleness. It was hard not to like her. "I won't. She only did what other people have been doing all week."

"They're worried, is all. They like Bree. So do I. She's my oldest friend. I mean, she isn't old, but we've been friends a long time."

He indicated his understanding with a nod.

She glanced back again, drew her collar up higher against

the brisk air. "We became friends in first grade. She was lonely because her grandmother kept her apart, and I was lonely because, well, my mother was always right *there*, so it was better sometimes not to have friends at the house." She looked down, then behind her, then straight at him again. "I'm not complaining. My mother loves me. I wish Bree had that."

"Didn't her father love her?"

"I suppose. But he was unhappy. Maybe he wanted to be a good parent but didn't know how. Bree's mother must have been the colorful one. Bree had to get her spirit from someone, and it wasn't from him." She was instantly contrite. "I shouldn't say that, his being dead and all." She paused, then blurted, "But I remember him, and he was grim. Bree's mother was probably the most exciting thing that ever happened to him. It's like he spent the rest of his life mourning her."

"Is that what Bree thinks?"

Jane nodded. "We used to talk about it. She always wondered about her mother. She used to imagine all kinds of things, mostly pretty things, flattering things."

"Didn't her father tell her anything?"

"Her grandmother wouldn't let them talk about her, and after Hannah died, well, I guess the course was set. Haywood got quieter and quieter and more and more dark. Bree was keeping house for him and pretty much raising herself. She started working part-time at the diner when she was fifteen, just to get away. She wanted to be with people who talked and smiled and laughed. The diner was more of a home to her than the house on South Forest." She dug her hands into her pockets. "Here I am, jabbering on like my mother."

"There's a difference," Tom said, which was as close as he would come to criticizing Dotty in front of Jane. "Did Bree's mother ever try to reach her?"

"No."

"Did Bree ever try to hunt her down?"

"No. By the time Haywood died, she'd lost interest."

Tom thought about the Bree he was coming to know. "She's remarkable to have overcome all that."

"Yes." Jane seemed suddenly less concerned about who might see her in the parking lot than about what she wanted Tom to know. "That's why people are protective of her."

"I understand."

"They're worried she'll come to depend on you and then you'll leave."

"She's getting more independent by the day."

"She may be more vulnerable because of the accident."

"Because of her near-death experience, you mean?"

Jane nodded.

"I'll keep that in mind," he said.

"Jane!" The voice was distant but definitely Dotty's.

Jane gasped. With a last, pleading look that made him envious of the loyalty she felt for Bree, she slipped off between the cars so that she wouldn't be anywhere near Tom when her mother tracked her down.

Flash had his say when he stopped by to visit Bree several days later. Tom had been reading in the den, while Bree napped on the sofa there. She opened unfocused eyes at the sound of the back door opening and closing. He tossed another log on the fire and motioned her to stay where she was.

"Just as well," Flash said, when Tom explained. "I have to talk to you alone." He set a foil-wrapped bundle on the counter. "Lasagna, with sausage and extra cheese. She needs fattening up."

Tom's hand went to his stomach. Several day before, it had been an extra-rich fettuccine Alfredo, a few days before that, a thick-gravied beef stew. When Bree refused to eat either, he was the one who ended up stuffed.

"It's still warm," Flash went on. "If you use it for dinner, all it'll need is ten minutes in a hot oven. Put what's left over in the fridge. It'll be even better tomorrow." Bracing himself against the counter, he looked at Tom. "I'm not here because of me. I want you to know that. I don't think you're so bad, and besides, Bree's been taking care of herself for a long time with regard to everything else, so I'm sure she can take care of herself with regard to this, too. The problem is, being so close to Bree and all, I don't hear the end of it. Half the town's on my back to learn what I can."

Tom leaned against the enamel sink and folded his arms. "I'm not sure what's left that the others haven't asked, but you're welcome to give it a shot."

"You want to make fun of us, go ahead, but you ought to know that what's happening here is highly unusual."

"My helping Bree? Isn't that what this town is about? If I weren't here right now, someone else from town would be."

"No. Bree wouldn't have had that. Remember when she told me to cancel the nighttime detail? That was the Bree this town knows, the independent-to-a-fault Bree. Her letting you hang around is not normal, and don't tell me she needs you to fetch and carry, because she's perfectly capable of doing that for herself. More*over*," he said, with gusto, "this is the first time since I've known her that she's had a man in this house."

Tom was startled but pleased. "No kidding?"

"Don't get me wrong. She isn't some shrinking violet. She's had relationships with men. But none of those has ever stayed here one night, let alone however many you have."

"Sixteen," Tom put in.

"Christ. Are you paying *rent?*"

"No, and for what it's worth, I sleep on the sofa while she's up in her bed."

"No matter," Flash said. "Bree likes her space." He frowned. "Maybe it's different since she isn't coming to work. She has a lot of people there. Here she doesn't. So she's lonely. You know?"

Tom didn't point out that she continued to choose his company over that of others who offered to come. "Tell me. Who has she dated in town?"

"No one," was Flash's automatic response. Then, as though the temptation to be the one to tell was too much to resist, he said, "At least not since I've been here. I heard she and Curtis Lamb were a number in high school, but there hasn't been anyone local since then."

Tom waited, then asked, "That's it? Just Curtis Lamb?"

"From Panama."

Again Tom waited.

And again it was as if Flash couldn't resist. "Men are always coming to the diner from one place or another. They pass through once a week, once a month. She had a thing for a while with a trucker, and for a while after that with a computer salesman, but she never brought them back here. It was kind of a rule she had. They were both good-looking guys, too, both love-'em-and-leave-'em types. She wanted to be the one doing the loving and leaving."

"You make her sound hardhearted."

"No. She just knows how to protect herself."

"If she knows how to protect herself, why are you all so worried about me?" Tom asked.

"Because she lowered the bridge and let you in. So now people are wondering why you're still here and how long you're planning to stay."

"Ah," Tom said.

"What does that mean?"

It meant that Tom didn't know the answers. He had never felt as innocent an attraction to a woman as he felt toward Bree. Hell, he hadn't even kissed her. "Just . . . 'ah.' "

"What does *that* mean?"

"Hi, Flash," Bree said from the door. She crossed to him, slipped an arm around his waist, and kissed his cheek. "How's my favorite boss today?"

Flash glowered. "Lousy. I tried to do the payroll and screwed up the figures. I need you, Bree. When are you coming back?"

Julia Dean phoned Tom at home. She identified herself, apologized for disturbing him, then said, "I missed Bree's visit to the diner the other day. Listening to people talk about it was a little confusing. One said she looked good, another said she was pale. One said she moved like she hurt, another said no way would anyone know what had happened. You see her all the time. You'd know, more than they would. How is she?"

Tom heard genuine concern. "She's much better."

"Really?"

"Really."

She breathed a sigh of what sounded like genuine relief. "That's good. I was worried."

"She loves the flowers you send." New arrangements were delivered each week. "They have a special place on her bureau, so she can see them when she wakes up. You ought to stop over sometime. She'd like that."

Tom heard genuine pleasure in Julia's reply. "Well, she'll be back in the diner before long. I'll see her there. Will you give her my best until then?"

Tom did it again, anticipated Bree's wishes and made them come true. Just when she was itching to see the inside of the place where he lived when he wasn't with her, he invited her over.

"The house isn't much to see," he warned, pulling in under the carport, but she disagreed. Just as she had known, the bungalow had charm. The kitchen opened to a breakfast room, dining room, and screened porch, all overlooking a stone terrace. There was a large family room and a larger living room and, up one flight, three bedrooms and two baths. The ceilings were lower than hers, the wooden floor planks wider and pegged, the hearth of fieldstone and raised.

The fact that nearly every room held cartons Tom hadn't unpacked, and that he hadn't done any decorating, and that there wasn't a single family picture in sight, told her he was unsettled, neither here nor there, unsure of who he was and where he was headed. From the looks of it, he could fill a U-Haul in an hour and be gone from town ten minutes later.

That thought made her uneasy. It sent a different message from the one she usually received, one of a man who was staying right where he was. When he was with her at her house, he was committed. She had been with enough men to know.

Tom was hooked, for now at least, and so, God help her, was she.

When he took her by the hand and led her from room to room, the physical connection lessened the forlorn feeling of the house. It disappeared completely when he led her outside.

"This is what I really wanted you to see," he said, and instantly she understood. Just beyond the terrace rose the sound of the brook. It lured them across a lawn covered with dry, snapping leaves, down a slope roughened by tree roots, and over a border of pebbles. The brook itself was an undulating swath that varied in width from three feet to six, and in depth from two inches to several dozen. Fall rain, added to their one major storm and a handful of night snows, kept the current moving. Clear water sped over rocky clusters whose colors ran from ivories to mossy greens, blues, and grays. Though clouds covered the sun, the sway of dappling evergreens gave the water sparkle.

Bree put her palms together. "A magical place."

"Maybe."

"Definitely," she said, lowering herself to a large rock.

"Tired?"

"No. I just want to look."

"There's even better looking upstream a little way. Want to try it?"

She answered by pushing herself right back to her feet and leading the way. It wasn't far. The instant she turned a bend, she saw the falls. They were minifalls, really, tumbling little more than four feet, but all the sweeter for their size. Bundles of mud, sticks, and stones at either end suggested beavers at work. On the shore, perfectly set for viewing, was a bench.

"I found it the day I came to look at the house," Tom said. "Look at the worn spots on the seat. The Hubbards must have spent hours here, maybe even whoever owned the place before them. It looks ancient."

Bree ran a hand over the weathered wood in awe, then turned and fit her backside to the indentation on the left. Stretching an arm over the bench arm nearest her, she took a deep breath and grinned up at Tom.

He sat down on her right, stretched an arm over the bench arm on his side, took a deep breath, and grinned right back.

Bree took a second deep breath, then a third. She looked up at the fir fronds above them, then across the brook into the forest. The hardwoods were largely bare. What few leaves still clung to their limbs were curled there, faded and dry. Evergreens swelled around them as though freed for the first time since spring.

In that instant, she felt invincible. In that instant, she chose to believe. She was healthy, Tom was devoted, life held the promise of love and three wishes.

"I used to hate fall," she said. "I hated it when the trees lost their leaves. I always thought it was a time of death."

"You see death differently now."

"Uh-huh," she said, and unexpectedly, her throat went tight. She didn't know of another man who would let her talk, much less hear her, the way Tom did. He was special. Very, very special.

"Do you think about it much?" he asked.

Her near-death experience. "Uh-huh." She thought about it more and more as she began doing those things she had done before the accident, like driving a car, paying Flash's bills, taking walks in the woods. Everything was the same, yet nothing was.

"I would, too," he said. "I do, actually. I think about what I'd be feeling if I were in your shoes."

She spent a minute loosening the knot in her throat, then asked, "What would you be feeling?"

He took a breath that expanded his chest. "Regrets. For missed opportunities."

She didn't want to think of his other life, the one with "unsettled" written all over it. But that life was part of Tom, and she was feeling strong, feeling *invincible*. So she said, "*You* missed opportunities?"

"For the things that counted." He took a quicker, lighter breath. "I'd also be feeling hope. Like I'm just beginning the rest of my life and can do things differently this time."

The look he gave her brought the lump back to her throat. It stayed there when he threw an arm around her shoulders and drew her close.

"I'm not leaving, Bree," he said.

Wanting to believe, wanting to believe so badly, she closed her eyes. He smelled the way he looked, clean and male and outdoorsy, a Vermont man now with his wool jacket open over flannel, over thermal, over just a glimpse of warm, hairy skin. He wore his jeans low and slim, like the best of the Panamanians. Only his running shoes set him apart.

I'm not leaving, Bree.

Nestling against him, she felt something bright touch her eyelids. Cracking them open, she squinted up at the spot where a single brilliant ray of sun breached clouds and trees. It was only an instant before it was gone, but that was enough.

She was invincible. She was in love.

Chapter

7

"If you had three wishes, what would they be?" Bree asked, looking from one to another of her boothmates, Liz to LeeAnn to Jane. Her laptop was closed, several hours of catch-up bookkeeping done.

"Three wishes?" Jane asked unsurely.

"Dream stuff?" Liz asked hopefully.

"I know what I'd ask for," LeeAnn announced. "First, I'd wish for money—oh, maybe a million dollars. Then I'd wish for a yacht, I mean, like a big one with beautiful bedrooms and a crew to serve *me* food. Then I'd wish for a prince."

Jane grimaced. "A prince?"

"A real one. Doesn't have to be a major one. But real. I want a tiara."

"A tiara." Liz sighed. "That's sweet. But I wouldn't wish for that."

"What would you wish for?" Bree asked, just as Liz's Joey scampered up. He gave his mother a huge grin, squealed, turned, and raced back to the other end of the diner.

"A nanny," Liz said. "But not just any nanny. Mary Poppins, so I wouldn't feel so awful when Ben and I close the office door and go to work."

"That's only one wish," LeeAnn said. "What else?"

Liz thought for a minute. "A time-share in the Caribbean. With airline tickets there for the next fifteen years. And a beach for the kids. That's all one wish."

"What's the third?"

Liz grinned. "Thick curly hair. I've always wanted that."

Bree wouldn't have made curly hair one of her own wishes. She turned to Jane, whose thick straight hair was her single greatest asset.

"I like my hair," Jane said.

Bree laughed at the echo of her thoughts. "What would you wish for?"

"A trip to Disneyland."

LeeAnn shot up a hand. "Me, too. Make that one of mine. Disneyland with my kids."

"Not me," Liz drawled, as Joey returned. He was either skipping or galloping, hard to tell what, with his legs so small and his diaper so big. When Liz made a grab for him, he shrieked unintelligibly, whirled around, and ran off. "But I'd pay Mary Poppins to take my kids there for me."

Bree watched Joey for a fascinated minute before returning to Jane. "Why Disneyland?"

"Because I think it'd be fun. I always wanted to go." She didn't have to say that life with Dotty wasn't fun, or that Dotty left Panama only when she absolutely, positively had to. Those were givens.

"Okay," Bree said. "Disneyland. What else?"

With surprisingly little pause, Jane said, "I'd wish for a scholarship to art school."

Liz gave her a curious smile. "No kidding?"

Bree should have guessed it. Even without formal training, Jane was an artist. She designed all the church flyers and calligraphed all the town notices. Her work was such a staple in Panama that it was largely taken for granted.

"What's the third?" LeeAnn asked.

Jane swallowed. "Courage. I'd wish for courage."

No one spoke. Bree, who knew that for Jane, courage meant freedom, gave her friend's hand a squeeze. "You can wish for that," she whispered.

"Like the lion in *The Wizard of Oz*," LeeAnn crowed, then turned to Bree. "What about you?"

"Me?"

"What would your three wishes be?" Liz asked, narrowing her eyes. "Wait a minute. I recall your refusing to make a wish when you blew out the candles on your birthday cake last year. What was it you said, that wishes couldn't compete with elbow grease? So why the sudden interest in them?"

Bree shrugged and said lightly, "I don't know. An idle mind. You know. It's kind of fun to think about. No big thing, really."

"So what would yours be?" Jane asked.

"First," LeeAnn teased, "you'd wish to be back at work."

Bree glanced at the computer. "I already am." She had been in for a few hours every afternoon that week.

"You haven't waitressed yet. You'd wish for that, because you miss it so much."

"I do. I miss seeing everyone."

Flash appeared from nowhere. "Your wish is granted. I'm putting you on the schedule for light hours next week. Can you handle it?"

She was handling long walks, driving a car, doing the books. Waitressing was the next step, and a good thing it was. She feared she was becoming too dependent on Tom. "I can."

"Thank you." He stared at LeeAnn. "I need *someone* who'll work, instead of sitting around talking all day."

"I'm coming," LeeAnn said, but the minute he left, she turned expectantly to Bree.

So did Liz. "I bet you'd wish for a new car, one that would take you for miles without fading out like your old one does. If you had a new car, you could drive to California. You told me you wanted to do that."

She had wanted it once. Her father had mentioned that her mother had come from there, and Bree had imagined looking her up. But she didn't know if her mother was anywhere near California now, much less how to find out. Besides, right now there was plenty to keep her in Panama.

"What about Tom?" asked Jane, with intuitive precision. "Would you wish for him?"

"I would, if I were you," LeeAnn said.

"LeeAnn!" Flash hollered.

She shot him a look, grumbled something about wishing for longer breaks, and slid out of the booth. Joey wormed into her place and tucked his head against Liz, who cradled him close and asked, "So would you wish for Tom?"

Bree made a noncommittal face.

"You like him," Jane said.

"What's not to like?" Bree asked.

Liz was suddenly sober. "Plenty, says the grapevine. He goes through money like water. He has a wicked temper. He breaks contracts."

"The grapevine knows all that firsthand?" Bree asked. No answer was necessary. "Firsthand, I know that he's always kept his word to me. If he says he's coming over, he comes over. He's never lost his temper, never even come close. And he doesn't waste his money. I was with him when he bought his new truck. He'd done research and knew what the dealer's cost was. He was patient but firm with the salesman, so he got a great deal. Besides, I don't know what I'd have done without him these past few weeks."

"How long do you think he'll stay in Panama?" Jane asked.

Bree didn't know.

"More to the point," Liz said, "do you want him to stay? That's what a wish is about."

"I think he cares about you," Jane said.

Liz arched a brow. "He spends enough time at your house. It really is remarkable, considering who he is. Think about it. You have a world-famous author, who just happens to be gorgeous, sleeping over every night." Her brow went higher in speculation. Then she caught herself, pressed her fingertips to her mouth in self-chiding, and held them off to the side. "Not my business."

Bree looked at Joey, who was all warm and cozy, with his thumb in his mouth and his eyes half closed, and felt an unexpected pang of envy. She raised her eyes to Liz. "It's innocent between Tom and me."

"Then you haven't . . . is it . . . *can* you yet?"

"I can." The doctor had checked her out earlier that week and had rattled off all the things she could do. Sex was on the list. "But we haven't."

"Why not?" Jane asked quietly.

Liz's eyes went wide. "No chemistry?"

"There is. I think." There was. She knew. She had felt it, looking at his hands, at his long, long legs, at the sprinkling of hair she saw when he rolled back the cuffs of his shirt.

Jane gave her a look.

"Okay," Bree conceded, because Jane knew she was no nun. "That sounds odd coming from me, but what I'm trying to say is that with my being sick and all, chemistry has been low on my list."

Liz grinned. "So now you're not sick. I repeat. If you had three wishes, would you wish for Tom?"

Bree didn't know. Tom was either the best thing that had ever happened to her or the worst. He was strong but sensitive, self-sufficient but attentive, everything she wanted in a man and had never had. He was also a man whose past might easily rise up to claim him again, in which case he would be gone.

Liz and Jane weren't the only ones to warn her. Most everyone she ran into had some little confidence to share about Tom. Eliot said he was slick, Emma said he was cocky, Dotty said he was rude. Flash bet he'd be going back to New York. LeeAnn bet he'd be going back to Hollywood. Martin Sprague went so far as to say that Bree's father would die a second time if he knew she was seeing a man like that.

"A man like what?" Bree had asked.

"Shrewd. He's too smart to be sitting here doing nothing. Mark my words, he's out for something. Know what I think? I think he's writing. Wouldn't surprise me at all to see Panama as his next book, and you'd be right in the center of it, Bree Miller. Could be he's using you. Could be he's using all of us."

Bree didn't think so. She had seen Tom's house. His office had cobwebs. Okay, so there weren't any cobwebs on his computer. But he wasn't writing. At least she didn't think he was.

The thing was that the more she was warned off Tom, the more strongly she was drawn. Defending someone who had no one else was only part of it. She was good for him in other ways, ways that had nothing to do with making his bed or cooking his food, neither of which he had ever asked her to do. He was at peace when he was with her. She could see it in the comfortable slant of his shoulders, the restful ease of those wonderful hands of his, the pleasure that lit his face and made it younger and warmer—all of that a far cry from the man who used to sit with downcast eyes in his lonely diner booth.

So was it real or an act? Was he a godsend or a nightmare?

"What's wrong?" Tom asked from the bedroom door. His voice held the gentle huskiness of recent sleep.

It was three in the morning. She had woken half an hour

earlier, used the bathroom, and had been shifting in bed ever since. Her movements must have wakened him.

"Just restless," she said.

"Nervous about waitressing tomorrow?"

"No. Just restless."

"Want some warm milk?"

She didn't think warm milk would do it this time, and said as much with the shake of her head. Sighing, she switched on the lamp. Then she pushed herself up, piled the pillows against the wrought-iron swirls, and sat against them.

He grinned knowingly. "Want to talk?"

"Yes."

His shirt was open, the top snap of his jeans undone, his feet bare. He looked warm from sleep, raw and appealing, as he settled cross-legged on the bed, facing her. Was she attracted to him? Was she ever!

"Why so restless?" he asked.

"Three wishes."

"Aha. That'll do it. Are you thinking that they're real?"

"No. But they're interesting to think about. I keep asking myself what I'd wish for."

"What would you?"

"I don't know. I always come up with dumb things, like a trip somewhere or a new watch or a big-screen TV."

"Those aren't dumb things."

"They're material things. I don't want to waste a wish on something material." She had decided that much after talking with her friends. Not that she faulted them. To them, talk of three wishes was make-believe, and make-believe was just for fun. "What about you?" she asked Tom. "If you had three wishes, what would they be?"

He thought about it for a while. His frown deepened. Finally, looking resigned, he said, "I'd wish to turn back the clock and redo certain things."

"What things?" she asked, but less surely. She sensed that if he answered, they would be treading new ground.

He studied the quilt for a minute. Then he raised his eyes to hers. "I've always been competitive. I was that way as a little kid. I was that way in college and law school. I was that way as a lawyer, right from the start, driven to do better and be better. I went for the best cases, even when that meant taking them from lawyers who may have been just as good but weren't as forceful. I strode my way to the top, and when I had to climb on other people to get there, I reasoned that my clients were the winners and that was all that mattered.

"When I wrote my first book, it was the same. I'd established my name as a lawyer, so I had access to the most powerful literary agent, no questions asked. We had a publicist working even before my manuscript was sent to editors. That book could have been a dud and it would have been published, we were so successful at creating hype. Some editors called in bids even before they finished reading the thing."

"That book *was* good," Bree said.

He smiled sadly. "Lots of books are good. Lots of books are *better.* So why did mine hit it big? Because I was clever. Once that book hit the top of the best-seller lists, anything I wrote that was marginally good was guaranteed to make it, too, because the hype continued to build. Success fueled success. There were reviews and interviews. There were profiles in magazines. There were publishing parties in New York and screening parties in L.A. I was," he said with something of a sneer, "rich and arrogant and famous."

Bree sat forward and took one of his hands. He studied the mesh of their fingers.

"I wasn't a nice man. Did you know I was married?"

"No."

"Not many people did. Her name was Emily. We were college sweethearts. She worked to support us while I was in law school. So how did I thank her? Once I graduated, I buried myself in the law and ignored her. Two years of that,

114

and she asked for a divorce, and would you believe I was startled? I had no idea she was unhappy, no idea at all. That's how attentive I was."

Bree didn't know what to say.

"She remarried soon after, and no wonder. She was a great girl. She has four kids now. From what I hear, she's really happy. I'd turn back the clock with her, too."

"You still love her?" Bree didn't see how that could be. She hadn't died, gone to heaven, and returned, only to fall in love with a man who still loved his ex-wife. Then again, what did she know?

"No. It's not about love. It's about the bastard I was even after the divorce. She came to a book signing of mine once. The line was around the block when I got to the store. I saw her standing there and should have pulled her out of line and brought her inside with me. But I was all caught up in myself. I waved and walked on, like it was my due and not hers." He looked to the side. "I did things like that a lot— saw someone I knew and rather than acknowledging the relationship, treated the person like just another one of my fans. It happened in restaurants, in airports, at parties. I have a knack for condescension. I have a history of dropping people."

"Had," Bree whispered.

His eyes returned to their hands. "After Emily, I had two long-term relationships with women. The first was with a female associate who worked at my firm. We were together for three years. I dropped her when my first movie came out, because I didn't see her fitting in with a Hollywood crowd. The second was a production assistant on the second movie. She was Hollywood through and through—long legs, blond hair, blue-jeans glamour. I was with her for two years, when she started making noises about marriage." He snapped his fingers. "That was it. I was outta there. But not before I told her that if she thought she had anything that a thousand other women didn't have, too, she was nuts." He let out a disgusted burst of breath. "I was not nice at all. And *then* there's my family." The eyes that met Bree's were filled with self-reproach. "I haven't talked much about them, have I? They are my one, single greatest source of shame."

She might have denied it, might have tried to lighten his burden with empty words. But she wanted their relationship to be an honest one. This was Tom's moment of confession.

"I come from a small town in Ohio," he said. "There were six of us kids, five boys and Alice. She was the youngest. I was right above her. My father worked for the highway department, and not in administration. He plowed snow and patched roads and pitched roadkill into the back of the truck. We were working class all the way. I was the first to make it out. I got a football scholarship. Boy, were they proud of me. They treated me like a king when I came to visit. It wasn't more than once or twice a year, and then only for a few days at the most. There was always something to keep me away—spring training, a trip with my friends, catch-up studying—and they accepted that. It didn't occur to them that I didn't want to be small-town anymore, that I was separating myself from everything they stood for. My two oldest brothers got on my case once, and I let them have it, told them how hard it was trying to make it in a cutthroat world and the fact that they didn't understand just went to show how little *they* knew." He raked his teeth over his upper lip. "Only I didn't say it like that. The words I used were more crude."

He stared at her, inviting her disdain.

She said nothing.

Still staring, still daring, he said, "After I hit it big, I sent money, mostly around holiday time, usually to make up for not going out there myself. At one point, I didn't see them for two years. In the middle of that time, I actually did a media thing in Cleveland. They could've driven up in two hours, or I could've driven down. But I didn't even tell them

I was coming. They found out after the fact. My mother took it hard."

Memory broke his stare, visibly taking him back. "She was a plucky lady—petite, like my sister Alice, but strong-willed. I used to think my dad wore the pants in the family. He came home from work, planted himself in that big old armchair of his, and let us wait on him. Only she was the one telling us what to bring him. She kept the house and paid the bills and made us do our homework. Long after he'd fallen asleep in that chair, she was folding laundry or mopping the floor or cutting hair." He smiled. "It wasn't until I was eighteen that I ever went to a barber." He grew quiet.

Still Bree said nothing. She would have given anything to have a mother who did those kinds of things. She would have given anything to have someone care that way.

Tom's quiet lingered, then yielded to sorrow. "I never could think of her as being sick. Being sick just wasn't part of who she was. Maybe that's why I didn't go back."

"What was wrong with her?"

"Cancer. Maybe she couldn't think of herself as being sick, either, because she let it go for so long that by the time she finally went to the doctor, it had spread to her bones. I remember when they called to tell me. There were three messages on my answering machine before I finally called back, and then, even though I'd been totally independent and separate from them for nearly twenty years, it was like I'd been hit in the stomach." He broke off. Self-loathing returned. "I recovered. She didn't. I kept myself busy. She got weaker." He swallowed. "Oh, I said all the right things about getting a second opinion, a specialist from New York, an experimental protocol from Houston. I might have wanted those things if I'd been in her shoes. But she didn't. She wanted to stay where she was with the doctor she knew. So I went back to my own arrogant life, thinking that I'd done all I could. Only I never visited."

"Never?" Bree asked in disbelief and, yes, disappointment. She couldn't conceive of having a mother—let alone a good one—and not treating her well.

"I did visit, just not enough. I went once in the beginning, another time about halfway through. It was painful. Easier to stay away." He looked Bree in the eye, challenging again. "That's the kind of person I was. I did what suited me. They used to leave messages saying that she was weakening, or that the cancer had spread more, and I'd send a card or leave a phone message, because it was easier that way. I always had an excuse. Either I was working on a book or off doing publicity. The pathetic thing is that I wasn't writing. I didn't have time to write. I was too busy being a star."

The line between his brows deepened. "I was vacationing with a group of equally famous and sybaritic friends when she died. We were on a boat on the Adriatic. My family had no idea where I was. They left message after message on my answering machine. When I didn't answer any of them, they had no choice but to go ahead with the funeral." His voice broke. "I showed up a week later."

"Oh, Tom."

He held up a hand. "Don't feel sorry for *me*. I got off easy. Hell, I missed out on the pain of having to go through the whole drawn-out ordeal of a funeral." His Adam's apple moved. "The thing is, there's a purpose to the ordeal. Funerals are outlets for grief. I was trying to deny the pain and my guilt, and I didn't have that outlet. And suddenly the pain and the guilt and the grief cleared all the other nonsense from my head, and I had a clear vision of what my life had become. That answering machine I mentioned? While I was sailing merrily through the Adriatic, while my mother was being embalmed and my family was trying to reach me, no one else was. Once I erased their messages, there was nothing. I was in pain, and no one came around. And it was my fault. Absolutely my own fault. I was a lousy friend, a lousy person."

Without a second thought, Bree came forward and curved her hands around his neck. His pain was real as real could be. She was desperate to ease it.

He raced on, the dam broken. "I tried calling my father, but he wouldn't talk with me. Neither would my brothers. My sister did. We'd always had a special relationship, being the last of the six. But it was awkward with her, too. So I got on a plane and flew out there. I went straight to the cemetery." He took a shaky breath. Tears brimmed on his lower lids. "Looking at that grave with the dirt that hadn't had time to grow grass . . . looking at that stone that had just barely been carved . . . I thought . . . I thought that was the most awful moment in my life, but I was wrong. I hadn't been there more than ten minutes when my father arrived. He came up the hill with his head down and his shoulders huddled, like he was ninety years old. He couldn't have been more than twenty feet away when he looked up and stopped dead in his tracks. He straightened his spine, took a cold breath, and told me what he thought of me. Then he turned right around and walked back down the hill."

Bree held her breath. "Did you go after him?"

"I called, but he didn't stop, and it was weird, after all those years, but I just couldn't leave my mother, couldn't leave her alone in that place, so I stayed awhile. Then I went to the house. He was there. I saw him through the window. He was there, but he refused to open the door when I knocked, and he's right. Looking at me—knowing the opportunities I had that the others didn't have—knowing everything I didn't do when I could have—knowing all that I squandered—knowing how I let *my own mother* down at a time when there was literally no tomorrow . . . all that must be hell for him."

Present tense. "Still? You haven't talked with him since then?"

"I try. I call every few weeks. He won't talk." He looked down. "That was ten months ago. I went back to New York after that, but I hated it. Nothing fit me the way it had before. I didn't call people, they didn't call me. I sat alone in the loft that I had thought was so chic, and I hated the chrome and the leather and the gloss, and in the middle of that . . . starkness, all I could do was think about the people I wanted to be with, who I couldn't be with because, one by one over the years, I had picked them off and tossed them away like they were pieces of lint messing up my Armani tux."

He stopped talking. Slowly, he raised his eyes. They were bleak, challenging her to say what a worm he was.

But Bree couldn't. She didn't know the Tom who had done those things. The one she knew had been attentive to a fault. He had given up nights of sleep to see to her, had put his own needs second to hers. "You haven't tossed me away," she said, going at the tension in his jaw with small strokes of her thumbs.

She felt a faint easing in him. "Things are different here. The change has been good."

"Things here are basic. And you're basically good."

"I don't know as I'd go *that* far," he said, but she could see that he was pleased, pleased and so very close to her that when the first glints of warmth reached his eyes, she felt them.

Her thumbs slid up and back under his jaw. "What about writing?" It was time she asked about that.

In a reprise of disdain, he grunted. "I haven't written anything worth reading in four years."

"That's not true."

"Tell me honestly. Which of my books did you think were stronger, the first or the last?"

She thought back. "It's hard to compare. The last one was shorter—"

"And more shallow and less well plotted. I went through the motions of writing, but I wasn't involved. That last book was awful."

Bree wouldn't have used the word *awful*. But he was right about depth and plotting. "Still, lots of people read it."

"They sure did. It sat right at the top of the best-seller lists, so I told myself it was great. Now I can say that it wasn't. That'd be my second wish. To rewrite that book and the one before it."

"And the third wish?"

His eyes softened. A small smile touched his mouth. "A kiss."

Pleased, she smiled back, pointed to her lips, raised her brows.

"Yes, you," he said.

Something about the reality of what was about to happen caught a tiny train of her thought, and for an instant, just an instant, she wondered if she was buying trouble, playing with fire, with a man like Tom. Then the instant passed. It didn't have a chance against all he had come to mean to her.

"Consider this your lucky day," she said, and didn't have far to go, not with Tom meeting her halfway, but it wasn't his mouth she thought of first. It was his hands, one cupping the back of her head, the other threading through her hair in gentle possession, then both moving to shift her head, hold it, caress it with exquisite intimacy. She had guessed that his hands could do anything they tried, and she was right. His hands knew how to kiss.

Not that his mouth did a bad job. It was gentle but firm, soothing, challenging. It opened hers and ate from it, staying one step ahead in anticipation of her needs, and when those needs escalated to the point where her insides were humming and breath was scarce, it knew to withdraw.

Too fast. She clutched his shoulders and tried to steady herself. *Too hot, too fast*. He put his forehead to hers. There was heat there, too.

He dragged in a long, deep, shuddering breath and let it out with a tortured moan that said he wanted more but had no intention of taking it then.

Different. So different from other men. And sweet.

What if he loved me? Bree thought, then chased the thought away and simply enjoyed the moment for its closeness, which was so much more than she'd ever had that it was beautiful even if there wasn't love.

After several minutes' cooling, Tom pulled the pillows down from the wrought iron at the head of the bed and set them where they belonged. He switched off the light, helped Bree slide under the quilt, and stretched out on top of it. He lay on his side, facing her. Incredibly, given the pleasure of it, they weren't even touching when they fell asleep.

As November nights went, this one was cold. Had Bree's furnace gone on, Tom would have been fine. But the room was chilly when he woke up, and Bree seemed plenty warm, all bundled up. So he slipped under the side of the quilt where she wasn't, pulled it up to his neck, and went back to sleep.

Bree opened her eyes at dawn. Her head lay on Tom's arm, her cheek on his shirt just above his elbow. He lay on his side with his eyes closed, dark lashes resting not far from the yellowing remnants of a bruise and a fading suture line. She reached up to touch it but stopped just shy and drew her hand back. Holding it tucked to her throat, she looked more.

His hair fell onto his forehead from a mussed, off-center part. His ear was neatly formed and small-lobed, his sideburns neither short nor long. A day's growth of beard added even greater texture to his face than that already left by the sun. His tan was just starting to fade.

That tan had been the cause for much speculation. LeeAnn had bet it was from the jungle, Flash from a tanning parlor, Dotty—with a disapproving sniff—from a beach "for *naked* people." Bree had always figured that a man didn't have to be nude to get tanned on his face, throat, and arms, which was as much as any of them had ever seen of Tom, until now.

Now, with his shirt unbuttoned, Bree saw that the tan covered his chest—no surprise, since she knew that he had spent much of the summer in the yard behind his house, preparing the ground and laying stone for the terrace she so admired. She imagined that his chest muscles had grown while he was doing that work, though she assumed they hadn't been small to start with. But they were certainly impressive, tight and well formed, his skin dusted with tawny hair that spread wide before tapering. His entire torso tapered along with it, right down to a lean waist and hips that were angled slightly forward.

She let her hand go this time. The backs of her fingers brushed the hair at the center of his chest and found it surprisingly soft, but the warmth coming from the skin beneath it was no surprise. Even more than the quilt, he had kept her warm while the rest of the room got colder and colder.

The furnace needed another kick. One of these days, even that wouldn't work.

Then again, if she had Tom in her bed, the furnace could die for good and she wouldn't care. His warmth was a wonder. She could feel it stealing into her, stealing ever so slowly, deeper and deeper.

Fingers spread, her palm whispered its way down his chest to the tauntingly low point where the snap of his jeans lay open. She withstood the taunting for only a minute before, less steadily, folding her hand over the snap and holding on tight. The heat there was intense, his hardness unmistakable.

"Having fun?" came a thick voice from above.

Bree tried to find a reason why she shouldn't do this. Nothing came to her, except that life was too short for one to pass some things up. She had died and come back. Next time she could as easily die for good. So maybe Tom had a dark side, and maybe, just maybe, he would break her heart. But right here, right now, he had the power to make her feel loved. And right here, right now, that was all she wanted.

Was she having fun? "I *am*," she said, with a grin.

"Can I join in?"

She raised her mouth in answer, and in that very instant knew she had made the right choice. His kiss was everything she had dreamed a morning kiss would be. It held the sweetness of rest, the warmth of intimacy, the fire of awakening. Slipping fully into his arms was the most natural, most exciting thing in the world. It was where they had been headed since she had woken up in the hospital little more than a month before and found him there.

He fit her. Hands, chest, hips, legs—everything wound and pressed in its proper place as though it had been there dozens of times before. Only the arousal was new. It simmered through kisses, grew more heated through touches. It positively sparked when clothing came off, and when the freedom of that allowed for even greater intimacy, it burst into flame.

Bree had expected to feel twinges of pain when she stretched hard against him, but there were none. Nor were there any when his kisses moved down her body, because in this, too, he knew where she had been. His gentleness was a turn-on, as was the catch in his breath when he first saw her scars and the feel of his mouth there moments later.

If this was love, Bree had never even come close to receiving it before. If this was love, she never wanted to feel anything but.

He knew what she wanted and gave it, always in charge, ever careful. In a voice that was low but made rough by desire, he let her know that. *Can I? Does this hurt? Let me kiss you there*. He never gave her the brunt of his weight, not even when he made a place for himself between her thighs, and then, though the drive in him had his arms shaking as he held himself above her, he asked if he needed a condom.

Bree shook her head, a frantic no. Her men always wore condoms, but there was no need, no need at all with Tom. She urged him lower. For the care he took when he entered her, she might have been a virgin.

Emotionally, she was. For the very first time, her heart was involved, and the beauty of that was stunning. It enhanced everything she felt, made everything hotter and richer, drove her higher than she would have thought possible several weeks before. It made her feel that anything, *anything* was possible if she only dared take the chance. For a split second, at the very first moment of orgasm, her world was so blindingly bright that she thought she had died again. The realization that she hadn't only heightened the pleasure.

Tom felt pretty damn good. He had his favorite corner booth, a good book, a super turkey club with a double dose of Flash's curly fries, his favorite Sleepy Creek Pale, and Bree. She was moving from table to table, from the counter to the grill to the kitchen. Every time he caught her eye, she blushed.

Finally, she slid into his booth with her back to the rest of the diner and, trying to be stern, whispered, "Stop *looking* at me that way. I can't do my job. My hands start shaking. I forget what I'm supposed to be doing. It's embarrassing."

"You're doing just fine."

"You know what I mean."

"How do you feel?"

"Surprisingly good."

"Doesn't surprise *me*," he said. The second time around, she had made love to him in ways she couldn't have if she hadn't been healed. She was more woman than he had ever held in his arms.

Now she looked him in the eye, touched her tongue to the bow of her lips and left it there for a reminiscent moment, before pulling it back in, giving him a smart look, and sliding out of the booth. He imagined that her hips swayed as she sauntered away.

Moaning softly, he shifted on the bench. He was staring after Bree, thinking that redemption felt sinfully good, when a blond mess of hair surfaced on the other side of the table. It was a minute before Joey Little's face appeared.

"Hello," said Tom.

Joey stared.

"Well, hello back," Tom said.

Joey looked away for only as long as it took to settle himself on the bench.

"Have you had lunch?" Tom asked.

Joey nodded.

"What did you eat?" Tom asked. When Joey didn't answer, he said, "You have a macaroni-and-cheese mustache."

Joey sucked in his lips.

"Macaroni and cheese?" Tom asked.

Joey nodded.

Tom reached for the cap he had twisted off his beer bottle. He set it in front of him, took aim, and gently flicked it toward Joey. When it barely moved past the center of the table, he brought it back and tried again. This time it landed within inches of the table's edge.

Joey looked at the bottle cap, then at Tom.

Tom nodded, gestured that he should try.

A small hand came up and gave the cap a nudge. When the cap barely moved, the hand gave it a shove. There was progress this time, but not enough. Coming up on his knees, Joey gave the cap a wallop. Tom caught it on its way to the floor and held it in his lap.

Joey waited. When the cap didn't reappear, he stood on the bench seat, put his hands on the table, and looked down at Tom's side of the bench. Then, as quickly as he'd pushed himself up, he collapsed and disappeared. Seconds later, under the table, tiny fingers were prying Tom's hand open and retrieving the prize. Seconds after that, Joey was up on the bench again, setting the cap on the table, taking aim.

* * *

Tom figured it was a sign. It didn't matter that the child was two. Kids were wise. Instinctively, they knew friend from foe. Joey Little had decided that he was a friend. It was a start.

Once he was convinced that Bree was holding up well waitressing for the first time, that Flash was watching her closely, and that, in any case, she was having too much fun seeing all the regulars to leave, he settled his bill. Then he drove to the bungalow on West Elm, took a single-edge razor from the tool kit under the kitchen counter, and slit open the first of the cartons of books that hadn't seen the light of day since he left New York.

He was back at the diner at five to pick her up, drove her home to the Victorian on South Forest, and gave her a full-body massage that put the foot warming he had given her at the hospital to shame. Later, in the claw-footed bathtub that barely, just barely, held two and was ideal for that reason, he told her that he loved her.

Chapter

8

*L*ife was good.

No, Bree decided. Life was *great*. She was madly in love with a guy who loved her back, a guy whose main purpose in life seemed to be to please her. There were times when she was sure she was either dreaming or hallucinating, but when she pinched herself, Tom stayed right there, smiling at her like she was the answer to his prayers.

A few months back, she wouldn't have believed that she could have found a man who was as kind, as intelligent, as *famous,* as loving. That, though, was before she had seen the being of light. The peace she had felt with that being was the same peace she felt with Tom. Same goodness. Same love. There were times when she wondered if Tom wasn't the incarnation of that being, times when she wondered if she had died and been sent back to earth for the sole purpose of being with him, times when she wondered if she *wasn't* the answer to his prayers. She was good for him. He needed laid-back, and she was laid-back. He needed open and sincere, and she was open and sincere. Though she was small-town, she read the books he read and could hold her own in any discussion he started. She gave his life a focus, something he hadn't had in too long a time. And she pleased him sexually. Oh, yes, she did. She could hear it in the sounds that came from his throat when she ran a hand down the center of his chest to his belly, could feel it in the tremors that shook him when her tongue found the smooth skin at his groin; and when he threw back his head and bared his teeth in the course of a long and powerful climax, then slowly sank down beside her with a look of pure love on his face, she knew it was true.

She hadn't told him that she couldn't have kids.

But if he loved her, that wouldn't matter.

If he would be gone by spring, it *really* wouldn't matter.

In any case, she had time.

Besides, she couldn't dwell on the future. The being of light had taught her that, though, like the three wishes, it was a lesson she had absorbed without hearing the words. More important, living for the moment was something she could *do*. It was something she could act on immediately.

She wasn't ready to act on the three wishes. Not yet.

Thanksgiving in Panama had been a communal affair since the days of the town's founding fathers. In those early days, the leading families, whose houses all circled the green, prepared grand turkey dinners and opened their doors to the town. As those families died or moved on and the town's population grew, things changed. The houses around the green still opened their doors, but now everyone chipped in with the work.

Bree had been assigned to the Nolans' house. She brought two huge salads and Tom. After eating the main part of their dinner there, they strolled from house to house for dessert, as tradition decreed.

"Not great when it's raining," Bree remarked, remembering the mess of many another Thanksgiving Day. There was no rain on this one, though. From the start, the clouds were thick and white. By strolling time, it had begun to flurry. The town green became an enchanted place then, filled with townsfolk wearing brightly colored hats, jackets, and scarves, their faces flushed by good food and drink, and light white stuff falling innocuously around.

Bree couldn't have wished for a nicer day. From early morning to late night, she glowed. Tom rarely left her side, and then only to fill her dinner plate, refill her glass, or fetch her coat. He wasn't possessive. He simply doted on her in the nicest, most subtle of ways.

The significance of his presence beside her wasn't lost on the town. She hadn't come partnered to a town event since she had gone to her high school prom with Curtis Lamb. Nor, though, was Tom's presence beside her a surprise. It was common knowledge that he dropped her at the diner every noon, picked her up when her shift was done, and spent most nights at her house.

But something happened that Thanksgiving Day. A bit of the goodwill that the town afforded one of its own, and in even larger measure one as well liked as Bree, spilled over onto Tom. They didn't exactly open their arms. A wariness remained. But they included him in the talk.

More to the point, they questioned him. Curiosity took over where distrust had left off.

He was asked about being a lawyer. He was asked about being a writer. He was asked about his family. He was asked the same questions over and over again, first at the Nolans', later at other houses, and he answered with unending patience. Only Bree knew how hard the family ones were for him.

In a private moment's reminiscence, as they leaned against the warm brick of the Nolans' fireplace, he said, "Our house was always busy on Thanksgiving. My brothers played football, too, so there was always a game. Afterward everyone poured back to the house—friends, family, coaches, teachers. It was a little like this, actually."

He didn't have to say that he wondered what his family was doing this Thanksgiving Day. Bree had seen him lift the phone that morning and hold it to his chest for a long moment when he thought he was alone, before quietly putting it back. She could see the sadness in his eyes now when he looked at one family after another of parents, grandparents, aunts, uncles, in-laws, and kids.

If she had three wishes, she might wish for Tom to make that call. But it wasn't her place to suggest it. The best she could do was to help field his sorrow.

She was prepared to do that. What she wasn't prepared for was fielding a sorrow of her own, unexpected pangs at times when she saw those families that were larger by one child than they had been the year before. She looked at the runny noses and the hands greasy from turkey skin, and reminded herself that she hadn't wanted to have kids.

Still, the pangs came.

In the days following Thanksgiving, Joey Little became a regular at Tom's booth. At first he stayed on his side of the table, shoving the bottle cap toward Tom, slipping underneath to retrieve it from Tom's hand, and scrambling back to his own side. In time, he took to stealing under the table and coming up to sit beside Tom. Gradually, his silences gave way to giggles and shrieks.

One particularly high shriek brought Liz on the run. She found Joey scrunched under Tom's arm, making faces at his upside-down reflection in the soup spoon Tom held.

"Oh, dear," she said. "Is he bothering you?"

Tom gave the little boy a squeeze. "No way. We're best buddies, Joey and me."

"He can be a handful."

"I've got big hands," he said without a second thought. He had played this way with his nieces and nephews on the rare occasions when he'd visited. Children fascinated him. Their motives were clear, their instincts straight from the gut.

He was pleased when Liz slipped in across from him. "What did you think of Thanksgiving?" she asked. "Kind of different, huh?"

He had done Thanksgiving at the Ritz in Laguna Niguel, at a posh estate north of Manhattan, and on the slopes in Aspen. "Different from anything I've done in recent years," he told Liz now, then added, "Nicer. I liked it."

"So did Bree. I've never seen her look so happy. I wasn't the only one to think so. Lots of people said it. I guess we have you to thank."

The old Tom would have taken all the credit. The new Tom wasn't falling into that trap. "Bree's had an interesting fall. She sees things differently. She's happy to be alive."

"It's more than that," Liz said and sat back. "So are you going to break her heart and leave, or are you staying?"

"I won't break her heart." He couldn't do that without breaking his own, and he had never been a masochist.

"That's only half an answer."

Tom sensed that Liz was a friend. He liked her husband, felt an affinity for them both. They, too, came from the city. They, too, had professional lives independent of Panama. They, too, adored Bree.

So he confided, "I don't know the other half. I haven't decided that yet."

"Martin Sprague is convinced you're writing a book set in Panama."

"I'm not. I'm not writing, period."

"Martin wants to think you are, because the alternative is that you might just hang out a shingle and practice law on his turf."

Tom cleared his throat. "I sensed he was worried about that. But I won't."

Liz studied the table. She scrubbed at Joey's smudgy fingerprints with the arm of her sweater. "You could. There's a need."

"Martin handles it."

"Barely," she said, and raised her eyes to his. "Don't mistake me. He's a wonderful man. He's handled Panama's needs for years. The problem is that some of us who are new to Panama have needs that are new, too." She took a breath. "Ben and I design ad campaigns for small businesses. Last summer we made a presentation to one of our clients. The president didn't like it and hired a cut-rate firm instead. Suddenly now the company is running print ads that are identical to the ones we proposed. That's theft."

"Doesn't Martin agree?"

"He doesn't call it theft. He calls it an unfair business practice, and he says it'll cost us more to go after them than we'd have made in the first place. I'm not sure he's comfortable doing the going after."

"He isn't a litigator."

"No." She paused, looking him in the eye. "You are."

He had set himself up and been caught. Clever Liz. "I'm not practicing law."

"You could."

He shook his head.

"Why not?" she asked.

"First, I haven't practiced law in eight years. Second, I'm not a member of the local bar. Third, you said it: this is Martin's turf."

"Do you agree with him that this isn't worth going after?"

"I couldn't say that without knowing more. Intellectual law wasn't my specialty. Don't you have lawyers in New York?"

"We thought we did until we called. Apparently there isn't enough money at stake for their tastes, and they're right, in a way. With us, it's the principle of the thing. We don't have copyright protection. It never got that far."

"Then you may not have a case."

"We have the ads we designed. We have a copy of the ads being run. We know that the same things the president of the company said he objected to in our ads are right there in the ads being run."

"Can you prove it?"

"We have a tape of our meeting with him."

"Stating his objections?"

"Yes."

Tom was tempted. But there were still the three points he had ticked off.

"Don't say anything now," Liz said, clever in that, too. "Just think about it. Okay?" She looked around. "Where's Joey?"

Tom pointed down to his left. Curled up, pleasantly warm against him, was Joey Little, fast asleep.

Bree found new surprises each time she went to Tom's house. One day it was the family room with endless shelves filled with books and not a carton in sight. Another day it was cartons gone from the kitchen, their contents now in the cabinets. Another day it was oil paintings hung on the living room walls.

Most touching were the framed photographs that began appearing. Most were small, many were faded. Each had a story.

"There's my oldest brother, Carl," Tom told her. "And, in descending order, Max, Peter, Dan, and me. This is my sister, Alice, all dressed up for a sixth-grade dance. Notice that her date is nowhere in sight. He was scared of us."

"He wasn't."

"Well, only for a little while, and then he came back. He decided that he was more scared of what we'd do to him if he didn't. He lived right down the road. We'd known him all his life. He was a nice kid. Alice ran circles around him, though."

Bree picked up another picture. After checking back to the first and making allowances for the passage of time, she said, "This is Max?"

"And his wife, Sandra, taken on their wedding day. They'd been childhood sweethearts, but Sandra went off to school and married someone else. When the marriage fell apart, she came back home. Max had been waiting. No way could he have married anyone else. The kids are from her first marriage. They've had two of their own since this picture was taken."

"They look like a peaceful family."

"They are," Tom said.

"How many grandchildren are there in all?"

"A dozen at last count."

Bree heard pride. Looking up, she also saw longing. Touched, she set the picture down and lifted a third.

"That's my dad," Tom said, pointing to a large man who stood, shoulders back, with a proprietary hand on the hood of what must have been at the time a brand-new Chevrolet. Scattered over, in front of, and beside the car were Tom, his five siblings, two dogs, and one cat. "He saved for years for that car. It was the first new one he ever bought. We used to crowd around his chair and look at the dealer's brochure. He'd go back each year for a new brochure, he was that long saving up. He wouldn't buy it on time, had to have the whole amount saved. He finally bought the car in sixty-five. Carl and Max had their licenses, but it was months before he let either of them drive it. Max had an accident the very first time he took it out."

Bree caught her breath. "What did your dad do?"

"He yelled and screamed until my mother told him to keep still. Max drained his savings to pay for the repairs. Years later, he learned that Dad had paid for the repairs himself and banked Max's money for him. It paid for his honeymoon with Sandra."

That said something about the man, Bree decided. It said that regardless of how hard he looked, he had a soft spot inside. She wondered if any of it was left.

Studying the picture, she decided that Tom's brothers took

after his father far more than he did. He and Alice were the different ones, resembling each other in coloring and smile. "You and Alice must take after your mom. Why isn't she in any of these pictures?"

"She's taking them."

"Do you have one of her?"

"Upstairs."

It was on the dresser that had previously been bare, a simply framed snapshot of a twenty-something Tom with a woman who was an older version of his sister, Alice. Bree looked at the picture for a long time. When she looked up at Tom, his eyes were still on it.

"My law school graduation," was all he said.

"She must have been proud."

He nodded and set the picture back on the dresser.

"Call them, Tom," Bree whispered.

Tucking his hands in the pockets of his jeans, he looked off toward the window. "I want to."

"Then *do* it."

He looked back at her with something akin to panic. "What if he hangs up?"

"Call Alice, then. You were closest to her."

"What if *she* hangs up?"

"What if she doesn't?"

Contacting his family was Tom's decision to make. But Bree knew she had given him something to think about when, after staring at her in amazement, he shook his head, chuckled, and hooked an elbow around her neck. "You're tough," he said, dragging her close.

"Maybe I'll wish for it, you know?"

"Don't you dare," he scolded. "Those wishes are yours."

So he had something of his father, after all, Bree mused. Hard voice, soft heart.

"What would I wish for?" she asked, filled to overflowing with the moment's joy. "I'm too happy to want a thing. There's absolutely nothing I need."

"You need a new furnace," he said. "Wish for that."

She screwed up her face. "I'm not wasting a wish on a furnace."

"Yours is on its last leg. Maybe I'll get you a new one."

"Don't you *dare*." She tossed his words right back. She wouldn't *allow* him to do it. After all, if things went the way she hoped they would, she wouldn't be living in the house on South Forest for long.

That was something to wish for, if she was into wishing.

Serious snow arrived the first week in December, with the cold air and ice that went along with the season. To say that life in Panama slowed down implied that it couldn't handle the snow, which wasn't the case at all. The town handled the snow just fine now that sand barrels were in place and plows were hooked up. What slowed life down was tradition, specifically the East Main Slide.

"Come again?" Tom asked, when Bree took a break from waitressing and slid into his booth, close beside him, to explain what the diner's buzz was about.

"The East Main Slide. It's a race. It starts at the town green and ends at the bottom of the hill. School lunch trays, cardboard boxes, trash can lids, chairs—anything unconventional can be used. There are prizes for the fastest, the slowest, the most original, the oldest, and the youngest. Actually, anyone who finishes gets a prize."

"Everyone wins?" Tom asked. "What fun is that?"

Bree smiled. Tom Gates might be a world traveler, but he had a lot to learn about Panama, Vermont. Pleased to be his teacher, she said, "You only win if you finish, and you only finish if you go from top to bottom without stopping. You can take a running start off the green at the top of the hill, but then you have to stay on for a single continuous ride. If you tip over, you're out. If you go off course, you're out. If anyone gives you a push or any other kind of help, you're out."

She could see Tom's mind starting to work. He suddenly looked very young.

"When?" he asked.

"If the snow stops? Tomorrow at noon. There are heats, six sleds per heat."

"One person per sled?"

"Any number per sled, as long as it stays the same from start to finish."

"Can anyone enter?"

"Uh-huh."

"Do you?"

"I did once, when I was in high school. Three friends and I took the legs off an old porch bench and waxed the bottom slats. We thought we could steer by shifting our weight around." She slowly shook her head.

"Went off the road?"

"Real quick."

"Did that turn you off trying again?"

"No. But my father kept saying I was crazy to risk getting hurt, and then once I started working for Flash, I was needed here. The diner is halfway down the hill. It's the only pit stop for spectators. We dole out hot chocolate all afternoon." At least that was what she had done for the past God-only-knew-how-many years, but it sounded boring as hell to her now. "I wouldn't be against entering. People don't usually get hurt." Certainly not as she had been hurt during an innocent walk home from work.

Tom was clearly interested. "Are you up for it?" he asked. "Physically?"

Bree straightened. Physically, she felt great. Emotionally, she felt great. She wasn't afraid of getting hurt this year. If she'd been meant to die, she would be dead already. And damn it, she *wasn't* pouring hot chocolate all afternoon.

"I'm up for it. Got any ideas?"

His idea, to which they devoted all that evening and most of the next day, involved cutting a four-foot piece from a wide tree trunk that had fallen in his woods, slicing it in half, hollowing out its insides, sticking a rudimentary rudder through a hole in its rear, waxing its bottom, and canoeing down East Main. They weren't the fastest or the slowest, weren't the oldest or the youngest or the most original, but they did finish.

Bree had never had so much fun in her life.

The next week, Tom had a glimpse of what winters in Panama were like. A second storm hit, dumping a foot of snow on top of the fourteen inches already fallen and frozen. The roads were quickly cleared and sanded, so he was able to drive Bree to work, but there was something confining about having that much snow on the ground. He was bored.

Just for the heck of it, he climbed up to the room he called his office. It was the only room in the house that wasn't unpacked, and he didn't unpack it now. He simply turned on his computer, plugged it into the phone jack, called up Lexis, and did some legal research.

Then, just for the heck of it, because Bree had another few hours of work and he had nothing better to do, he typed up some thoughts on the Littles' case as Liz had outlined it, suggested possible strategies, and, taking those, composed a prototype of the kind of letter that Martin Sprague might want to think of writing to the company president who had rejected the Littles' plan. He put everything in a five-by-seven envelope and slid it into the book he was reading.

Then, just for the heck of it, because he knew that Martin ate at the diner every Monday, Wednesday, and Friday, and this was Wednesday, and because he'd planned to go there anyway and eat with Bree when she finished work, he drove over. If Martin hadn't been there, he would have left the envelope in his book and disposed of it later. If Martin had had people sitting on either side of him at the counter, he would have done the same thing. But the stool on Martin's left was wide open.

"How're you doin'?" Tom asked, pulling himself onto that wide-open stool. He winked at Bree, who winked right back but instinctively knew to steer clear.

"Not bad," Martin said.

"I have a favor to ask."

Martin grew wary. "What's that?"

"I was talking with Liz Little about her work, and she mentioned the unfair-competition problem she has. That's not my field, mind you, but it interested me, so I did some research. I think there might be an easy solution to the problem, especially since Liz and Ben have that tape." He waved a hand no when LeeAnn arrived with the coffee carafe, and kept his voice low. "The right threats in the right kind of letter might be enough to get that company president to negotiate a settlement with the Littles."

"What kind of threats?" Martin asked.

Tom shrugged. "Threat of a suit under the Vermont labor laws. Threat of an audit. Threat of an injunction. Any one of those will cost a small business more money than it wants to spend. At least it seems that way to me. But I could be all wrong. Like I said, intellectual property isn't my field, and anyway, I'm not a member of the local bar. You'd be the person to handle this." He slid the envelope out of his book and across the counter until it was anchored under Martin's plate. "Want to take a look? Give me your opinion on whether you think the case has merit? As far as Liz is concerned, I forgot about it right after she mentioned it, so she doesn't expect anything. But she and Ben are good people. It doesn't seem fair that they shouldn't be paid for ideas that are theirs. If a session at a negotiating table can get them some cash, that's good." He slapped the counter and pushed off from his stool. "They're your clients. It's your call."

By the third week in December, the diner was decked out for Christmas. Place mats had been printed with a Santa hat topping the frying pan. Snowflakes hung from the ceiling tiles. A decorated tree stood by the jukebox, which was restocked with holiday songs that Flash kept playing at his own expense. The small black vases on each of the tables held bouquets of red dogwood stems, sprigs of holly berries, and mistletoe. Even The Daily Flash reflected the season. One day it offered "Santa sushi"; the next, "Christmas carbonara"; the next, "Niçoise Noël."

"Too tacky?" a cautious Bree asked Tom, knowing that he had seen grander and more sophisticated holiday touches.

"Definitely tacky. But *great,*" he said, gilding a season that Bree was seeing through new eyes and loving as never before.

Christmases with her grandparents had been sober affairs. They had viewed the holiday as a day for prayers of gratitude for the Savior's birth and hadn't seen any connection between celebrating his birth and giving gifts to each other or to Bree. Her father had given her small toys when she was a child, justifying it to his parents by saying that he didn't want her to think that Santa didn't love her, too, but the practice stopped the very first year she had outgrown her belief in Santa.

Bree hadn't missed the presents. She had desperately missed the cheer.

There was that and more this year. The diner's festiveness was only the start. There was the annual clothing drive at the church, which was as much a Christmas cookie exchange as anything else. There was the annual dance celebrating the winter solstice, at which she learned the joy of slow dancing with Tom. And there was the approach of Christmas itself.

Tom surprised her on the twenty-third by decorating her house while she was at work, turning the sour-faced Victorian old maid into something surprisingly gay.

"But I wanted to help," was her only complaint, half-hearted at best, she was so touched by what he'd done, and even *then* she got her wish. After Tom dropped her at work the next morning, Flash ushered her right back outside.

"What are you doing?" she cried, when he wouldn't let go of her arm.

"You're taking the day off," he said, "and don't tell me there's work to do, because we both know you don't care as much as you used to. You don't give me lists of things to do anymore. Hell, you've even stopped crapping about Stafford, though his milk still goes bad. I don't want you at work today. I want you out here."

She was about to ask *Out where?* when she faced front and saw a grinning Tom. His truck was idling and warm. He was clearly in on the joke.

Bree went along without a fight, hiding her delight until there was just too much to contain. Tom took her into his snowy woods to cut a tree for his house, popped popcorn to string, opened packages of tinsel, little hanging doodads, and red velvet bows. When everything was in its place, he hoisted her up to place the glittery star on the top of the tree.

That night, they joined the rest of the town for midnight services, and there was something extra special in that, too. Though never before terribly religious, Bree felt blessed. Sitting in church beside Tom, with all the people she knew seated nearby, she experienced the same sense of belonging she had felt with the being of light.

In other respects, too, she was aware of the being of light. She didn't know if that being was God, Jesus, Saint Peter, or another figure entirely, but sitting in that church, she felt its warmth, felt its love.

In the oddest way, Bree felt like a newborn, which was probably why she indulged herself when, returning to Tom's house after church, she found a pile of gifts for her beneath his tree. With a child's excitement, she opened every last one.

"Don't you want to save a few for morning?" he teased, laughing.

She merely shook her head and slipped off another ribbon. She had gifts for him at her house. If she had been able to wait, they might have opened their gifts together. But it was out of the question.

She opened fun gifts—a hand-carved backgammon set, books that were on her list to read, a new Garth Brooks CD. She opened practical gifts—a cashmere sweater set that she would never have splurged on herself, a scarf and mitten set, a waffle maker.

Tom saved the best for last, and then, like the star at the top of the tree, the present he handed her glittered. It was a pair of earrings that looked suspiciously like diamond studs.

She swallowed, looked up at him, swallowed again, and even then only managed an awed whisper. "These aren't . . . they look like . . . are they?"

He nodded, grinned. "Real."

It took a long minute of trying to steady her hands before she fitted the posts into the holes in her ears, a long minute of ogling in the mirror, a long, *long* minute of hugging Tom in thanks when her throat was too knotted for speech, and a long, long, *long* time after that before they fell asleep.

Bree didn't need any three wishes. She decided that again on Christmas Day, and nothing in the days that followed convinced her otherwise. Tom made the week an unending celebration. He cooked a goose one night, took her to dinner at an inn outside Burlington another. On the weekend between the holidays, he drove her to Boston, where they saw *The Nutcracker,* slept at the Four Seasons, ate brunch at the Ritz, and browsed through Newbury Street shops.

Bree had been to Boston before, but never as lavishly, and never in the company of her dream man. During the drive home, she sat back, turned her head to Tom, and grinned. "I've died and gone to heaven. That's all there is to it."

"Again?"

"Still."

It did seem that way. Then came New Year's Eve and, after the champagne, a tiny pop in her bubble.

Chapter

9

"Do you believe in making New Year's resolutions?" Bree asked Tom. They were on their way home from a party thrown by the Littles. He held her hand but was quieter than usual.

"I don't know," he said. "I used to make them when I was a kid. I'd resolve not to fight with my brothers, or to clean my room without being asked. By the time I got to high school, I was resolving to get better grades. By the time I got to college, better grades weren't enough. I was resolving to get A's."

Disdain had crept into his voice. Bree hadn't heard that in a while. "What happened after that?" she asked.

"I got the A's. I got most everything I wanted without making resolutions, so I stopped." He shot her a look. "I was arrogant as hell."

"Was," she echoed, satisfied to hear the past tense at last. She raised his hand and ran her mouth over the scar that had healed to a thin ridge. "So do you believe in them?"

He thought about it. "I do. They imply a willingness to grow."

"So what are yours?"

He shot her another look. "You first."

"I asked you."

"I'm driving. I can't concentrate. You can. What are your New Year's resolutions?"

"Just one," she said. "To live life to the fullest."

She watched for his reaction. It was a small, pensive smile. "I like that."

"And yours?"

He turned onto West Elm and cruised over the snow-crusted road to the shingle-sided bungalow. Ice crunched under the truck's tires on the drive. He pulled up under the carport.

"Tom?"

"I'm thinking."

Bree felt a touch of unease. It was not that she didn't want him to think, just that something that was taking so long had to be heavy. She didn't have to be a genius to know that it was related to the future. New Year's resolutions always were.

Tom reached for the door handle. Bree reached for his arm.

He stared at the steering wheel, his lower teeth clenching his upper lip, then sighed. "My New Year's resolution is to figure out my life."

She caught her breath. He caught her hand.

"That came out wrong," he said. "I don't need to figure out you and me. It's the rest that's murky. I need to decide what's fitting in where."

It had been only a matter of time, Bree knew. Living in the here and now couldn't last forever. But it had been nice. She had been able to accept diamond earrings from Tom as a simple gift of love, had been able to live day to day without any expectation beyond seeing him after work. She had been perfectly content, *more* than content, living for the moment. Doing that, she had been free of disappointment.

Now, suddenly, she was afraid. For the first time in weeks, she wondered if Tom would leave town.

He opened the truck's door, drew her across the seat and out after him, and threw an arm around her shoulders as they walked into the house. They dropped their jackets in the kitchen.

Bree followed him into the family room and watched while he started a fire. When the kindling caught and the flames spread, she turned to the bookshelves lining the walls. Her gaze went straight to the books Tom had written. They were six in a row in an unobtrusive spot, off to the side and higher than eye level, and should have been lost among hundreds of other books. But they weren't. From the day he had put them there, she had been acutely aware of their presence.

"Do you want to write?" she asked.

He was hunkered down, stoking the flames with his back to her. "I don't know. I've been rereading what I've already written. The early ones aren't bad."

She folded her arms around her middle. "Do you have new ideas?"

"At first I didn't. But that's changed. Right now, ideas are the easy part. If I pick up a newspaper, I get ideas."

"What's the hard part? The writing?"

"No. Writing was never a problem for me."

"So what's the hard part?"

"What comes after."

Ahh. His nemesis. "Fame."

He dusted his palms on his jeans and pushed himself to his feet. Shoving his hands in his pockets, he looked at her. "I'm not sure I can trust myself to handle it well."

"Kind of like an alcoholic in a room with a bottle?"

"Kind of like that, and anyway, I don't know if I want to write. I know I can. I just don't know if I want to."

"How do you decide?"

He scratched his head. "Beats me." He left his hand on

his head. "You want to live life to the fullest. Well, so do I. There are times when I feel like I'm already doing that. I'd say nine-tenths of my life is that way, that happy. Then there's the one-tenth that says my father was right. I have skills that I'm wasting." He crossed to where she stood and hung his arms over her shoulders. "The thing is, I can't sit around here each day while you go to work. It isn't right."

"I don't mind," Bree insisted, afraid, so afraid. "I like working at the diner. Besides, I don't need fancy things. You could have given me beach stones instead of diamonds, and I'd have loved them just as well. If it's a matter of money—"

"It isn't. It's the principle of the thing."

A man of principle was one to admire, she reasoned, though it did little to ease her fear. What eased her fear was thinking of the being of light, which loved her and wouldn't let anything bad happen. And then there were her three wishes. If they were real, she would use one of those in a heartbeat to keep Tom.

Two weeks into January, Tom went to New York. He had made a lunch date with his agent and a dinner date with the lawyers with whom he had once practiced. Bree saw the sense in it. She knew that he needed to mend fences before he could decide if he liked what was inside. That didn't mean she wasn't jittery from the moment she learned he was going.

Tom insisted that she drive the truck while he was gone. "I don't trust your old car," he said, which annoyed her no end.

"Then let me buy a new one. You keep talking me out of it."

"You don't need a new one. You have the truck."

"It's *your* truck," she said. "I want *my* truck." She hated thinking that way. But wasn't he going to *his* New York, while she stayed behind in *her* Vermont? Weren't they from different worlds, after all? And hadn't she done just fine for herself before he came along? She resented the idea that she had become suddenly dependent, resented the idea that she had given so much of herself to a man who might, just might, throw it back in her face. "I can negotiate a deal on a car. I've done it before."

"Wait," he begged. "We'll go together when I get back."

Thinking of his return began to make her feel better.

Seeing him dressed in a suit, ready to leave, didn't. She stared at him for so long that he looked down at himself. He touched his tie, brushed his lapels, checked his fly.

Then he looked back at her and read her thoughts. "Weird, huh? I'm a stranger to me, too."

From the neck up he was fine. His hair was neatly combed, though longer, she wagered, than it had ever been when he had worn this suit. Add that to the slim line of the scar on his cheekbone, and he was the man she knew and loved. From the collar down was the problem.

"You look stuffy," she said, when what she was really thinking was that between that longer-than-lawyerly hair, the prominent scar, the suit and the stunning body beneath it and *everything* about his face, from his eyes to his straight nose to his squared chin, he would stop traffic, which meant that God only knew what possibilities lay open to him in New York, but in any case he would *never* come back.

"Two days, Bree. That's all."

She wanted to believe it, but there were so many possible glitches. "What if something's too good to resist?"

"Nothing will be. I just need to talk through some things. I need to see what's there and what isn't."

"There'll be women."

"I won't be looking at women."

"They'll be looking at you."

Suit and all, he gave her a bear hug. "I love you. I'm immune."

She grunted against his designer lapel. "That's what they all say. I'm going to wish for you to return."

"Bree." He held her back. "Don't. That'd be a total waste. I'll be back day after tomorrow. My tickets say it. I say it."

Bree took a deep breath and pictured the being of light. It was real. The mole on the back of Simon Meade's neck proved it. The being of light wouldn't let her lose Tom. Would it?

Worst case, there were still those wishes.

Afterward she would blame it on loneliness, frustration, and simply thinking about the wishes once too often. At the time, all she knew was that she had woken in her own ancient house without Tom, and she was cold.

Scrambling out from under the quilt, she pushed icy feet into slippers and trembling arms into her robe. Pulling the belt tight, she glanced at the clock on her way to the door. It was six in the morning. She hadn't slept well. She missed Tom, missed his bed, missed his warmth.

The house was dark, but her feet knew it well. They plodded with due speed and much annoyance down the stairs to the first floor, then through the kitchen and down a narrower flight to the basement, which was framed in stubbly cement and colder than cold. The furnace was at the far end. She pulled the light chain there, shivered, and scowled.

She jiggled one knob, then another. She made sure the pilot light was on. She checked to see that the dampers were open. She turned a dial and gave the furnace a shove. When nothing happened, she shoved it again. Her breath came out white when she swore.

Tom had warned her. Flash had warned her. She hadn't listened. She didn't want to listen even now, because the *last* thing she wanted to do was to pour money into this house. She didn't want to *be* here. She wanted to be with Tom. But Tom was living it up in New York, having all kinds of fun with his friends, maybe even making plans to return there and wondering how to break the news to her.

She needed a miracle, was what she needed. Right here. Right now.

Feeling desperate and cross enough to be brash, she squeezed her eyes shut, laced her fingers together with her knuckles by her chin, and dared the being of light to put up or shut up. "I . . . wish . . . for . . . heat." Picturing that being, she said it again, louder this time, to make sure it heard. "I . . . wish . . . for . . . *heat.*"

Opening her eyes, she tucked her hands under her arms, glared at the furnace, and waited for it to turn on.

It didn't.

She rocked back on her heels, tucked her hands in tighter, and waited longer.

Nothing.

Turning on her cold-enough-to-be-nearly-numb heel, she stomped back upstairs and lit the woodstove in the kitchen. By the time it was radiating warmth, she was wrapped in a quilt in a chair inches away, brooding over a mug of hot tea, telling herself that maybe, just maybe, wishes took time.

She arrived at the diner at ten, two hours before she was due to start work. If three layers of sweaters and two of socks hadn't given her away, her scowl would have.

"Aha," Flash gloated. "What did I tell you? If you'd listened to me, you'd still be lying in bed, nice and warm. How cold is the house?"

"Cold," Bree grumbled, though she suspected disappointment was as much behind her mood as the chill in her bones. She had waited at the house for nearly four hours, *four hours,* and her wish hadn't come true. Okay, she had money to fix the furnace. A new car could wait. But the thought of having three wishes had been kind of nice.

Flash wrapped her hands around an apricot bran muffin that was fresh from the oven and warm. "Sit and eat. The Wrights will handle the heating, and they won't charge you an arm and a leg. They'll be in for lunch. We'll give them the news then."

* * *

When the Wrights came in at noon, they were the ones with the news. "Can't eat now," Ned said. "Just got word on the scanner." As he spoke, the whine of the town's fire alarm began to sound from the top of the hill to alert the volunteer force. "There's a fire over on South Forest."

Bree had the worst thought. "South Forest?"

"Don't know whose house."

She saw Eliot turn into the diner's lot with his lights flashing and ran to the door. When he climbed from the cruiser looking straight at her, she knew. Grabbing her jacket, she joined him. Horror was shaking her so badly that she didn't trust herself to drive.

Within minutes, they were at the scene. There wasn't much she could do but stand and watch. There were no flames shooting through the roof, only thick black smoke, but the flames were on their way. The second floor was fully engulfed, the first floor long gone. She imagined that the basement was nothing but a charred concrete shell.

Feeling helpless, discouraged, and quite personally at fault, she watched while the men she knew—plumbers, carpenters, and electricians transformed into firefighters—directed thick streams of water through the upper windows. Glass shattered. Water was re-aimed. The air was filled with the acrid scent of a burning past.

She didn't want to think about the damage, about the loss of a history, about memories that would never be the same, but she thought about all those things. She was the last of the Millers. This house was all she had.

"This wasn't what I meant by heat!" she wailed to no one in particular. "It wasn't what I meant *at all!*" Her voice held both upset and accusation. She wanted to blame someone else, some*thing* else. But her cry was lost to the awful sound of fire and the thunder of water from yards and yards of canvas hose.

As word spread through Panama, friends arrived to stand with her, but they were small solace for the ravage she

151

witnessed. By the time the flames were out, nearly half the town was there, and she was feeling completely alone.

"You'll rebuild, Bree."

"The house will be better than ever."

"You can stay with us. Our attic room is perfect."

"Take the room over our garage. It's yours."

Her eyes remained on the ruin of her house. She couldn't seem to drag them away, not even when they filled with tears.

Jane slipped an arm around her. Quietly, she said, "You'll stay with Tom?"

Bree nodded. She was practically living at his house anyway. That's where she would have been last night, if he hadn't been in New York. She wouldn't have slept at her own house, wouldn't have woken up lonely and cranky and cold, wouldn't have dared the being of light to make good on its promise, wouldn't have forfeited a wish out of spite.

There was plenty of heat at Tom's house.

So had her wish come true in some perverted sense?

Many hours later, warm as toast under the down comforter on Tom's bed, she was no closer to an answer. Her stomach turned each time she pictured the blackened remains of her house. It had taken two showers before the stench of the smoke left her hair, and a bath filled with scented oils before her skin let her forget.

By that time, she was worried again. Tom hadn't called. He had said that he would, had *promised* it—his word, not hers. If he hadn't been able to get through at her house, he would have tried here, unless he was so wrapped up in being back in New York that he forgot. She was scared, so scared.

Sitting up, she hugged her knees to still the shaking inside. Fine. If he gave her up and went back to his life in New York, she would take the insurance money from the house on South Forest and buy this house from him. She had always wanted it. She could live here without him and go back to her own life, which had been just fine before him. Just fine. Yes, it had been. Just fine before Tom.

The digital clock turned. It was midnight. He should have *long since* called.

Grabbing for the phone at the side of the bed, she called information, got the number of his hotel, and, on the second try, pressed all the right buttons. A hotel operator answered. Bree asked for Tom. After a pause came word that he had checked out that afternoon.

She didn't know what to think or do. In a bid for calm, she tried to recapture the comfort of the being of light. For the first time, she couldn't. She could picture a great ball of light, but the picture was an intellectual one. She couldn't feel it. Emotionally, she was detached. And suddenly she was back in the world she had known before that October night, only it didn't seem as wonderful to her now as it had seemed then. Now it seemed programmed and parochial. It seemed lonely. It seemed boring. Ironic, but it even seemed *barren.*

Unable to sit still with those thoughts, wanting to recapture the present, she left the bed and began walking from room to room. That was how she found herself upstairs, looking out over the front yard from the spare bedroom, when a pair of headlights lit the street. Her pulse skittered when she saw that the headlights belonged to a taxi, which pulled up in front of the bungalow.

It was Tom, back home a day early. Because New York had been so good that his mind was made up?

Heart pounding, she watched him turn away from the cab and lope up the walk. She ran down the stairs, opened the door just as he reached it, and held back in fear for only as long as it took him to drop his bag. When he reached for her, she was there, holding tight to his neck, clinging in a way she would never have done in her other life but which was the only thing that made sense in this one. It was a long minute before she realized that the shaking wasn't all coming from her. He was holding her that tightly.

"I went by the house," he said, in a voice so raw she barely recognized it. "What happened?"

"Fire," was all she had a chance to say, because anything else would have been lost in his kiss. It was a kiss that tasted of fear and a desperate need for reassurance, as much of it his as hers.

When it ended, he took her face in his hands. "When?" His thumbs brushed at her tears.

"Lunchtime today." She wormed her arms inside his and touched his face right back, needing to know more, feel more, to prove he was there. "I called your hotel. They said you checked out."

"I had to get back here. Were you at work when it happened?"

She nodded and burst into tears. "Why didn't you *call?*"

"I tried, but your phone just rang." He pulled her close. "When I tried the diner, the line was busy, and then I was sitting in the airplane on the goddamned runway for three hours while the fuckin' air traffic control computers were down. Aw, honey, don't cry. Please don't cry."

She tried to stop—told herself that there was a message in his wearing jeans and a sweater under his coat and not his despicable suit—but it didn't work. "I was scared!"

"So was I," he said against her hair. "Scared in New York, scared back here. I love you, Bree."

She locked her hands at the center of his back and cried harder. She didn't want him to leave, didn't want him to leave *ever again!*

He held her for another minute, running his hands over her back, telling her he loved her, begging her not to cry. When he urged her inside and shut the door behind him, he leaned against it and pulled her tight to his side. "I bought you something."

She ran the back of her hand past her eyes. "I don't want anything. Just you."

"You heard me say that."

154

"Huh?"

"The exact same words. I was saying them the whole time I was in New York. I didn't like the traffic. I didn't like the crowds. I didn't like Nathan saying that he could get me good money for a three-book deal but *great* money for a four-book deal. I didn't like my law partners trying to measure in dollars and cents the kind of clients I could bring in from the entertainment industry. The hotel was pretentious, the restaurants overpriced, and the air polluted. I kept asking myself what in the hell I was doing there, when the only thing I wanted was you."

Bree raised her head. "It was?"

"Is." In the near dark, his eyes were fierce, his voice was compelling. "I was supposed to see Nathan again today, but I canceled. I walked up and down the streets and thought about the people I'd planned to stop in and see, and I didn't stop in and see a one. The only thing I wanted to do was shop." He reached into his pocket and drew out a box. It was small, square, and blue, and had a neat white bow tied around it.

Bree looked from the box to his face and back.

"Open it," he coaxed.

She released her hold of him and took the box from his hand, untied the ribbon, and lifted the top. Inside was another box. She looked at Tom again.

"Go on," he said, and took the outer box from her when she removed the inner one.

Afraid to hope, she held it in her hand. Then she lifted the lid. There, on a dark field, lay a pear-shaped diamond set in platinum, and slowly but surely the light returned to her life, radiating outward from the diamond, speaking of belonging and love, filling her with warmth. "This is . . . ?"

"It is."

She looked up. "Are you asking . . . ?"

"I am."

"Oh my *God,*" she breathed, and she threw her arms

around his neck. Seconds later, she was back looking at the ring. She had never owned anything like it, had never *dreamed* of owning anything like it. "You bought this in New York?"

"It's the only important thing I did the whole time I was there."

Bree was short of breath. Holding the ring box in her hand, she hugged Tom again. "Thank you," she whispered against his cheek, seconds before drawing back to look inside the box once more. The ring was still there.

"Put it on."

She was about to. Then she had a thought that wiped the smile from her face. Without hesitancy, because she knew it had to be said, she blurted, "I can't have kids, Tom. I can't. There's scar tissue."

He went still. "From the accident?"

She nodded. "You want kids. I know you do. I've heard you talk about your nieces and nephews. I've seen you with Joey Little."

He was shaking his head. "We'll adopt."

"It isn't the same."

"It *is*." He removed the ring from its box and slipped it on her finger. Then he raised it to his mouth, kissed it, and looked her in the eye. "I wasn't thinking about kids while I was walking around New York. I was thinking about you."

"But you want family. That's what you've missed."

"Right, and the root of family is a man and a woman. If the root stinks, the whole thing fails." He gave her a crooked grin. "There's no other woman I want to root with."

She could feel the sincerity in him. Tears welled again.

"Marry me, Bree?"

No matter that she had his diamond on her finger: hearing the words in the air stole her breath. She must have looked dumbfounded, because he laughed. The sound was full and rich, as she imagined life with him would be. "I thought for sure you'd decide it was New York that you loved," she cried. "I was lying here thinking it was all over, like a dream that ends in one second of waking up." The ring sparkled as she turned her hand. Its light brought a special kind of calm.

"I wished for heat," she told him, at three in the morning. They had made love, made pizza, and made more love. Now they lay in the sweet redolence of passion and sweat, Bree with her cheek over the strong beat of Tom's heart. Her hand lay nearby on his chest, fingers splayed. She flexed the third one to see the diamond sparkle. The excitement of it nullified fatigue.

Tom must have felt the same way, because there was nothing sleepy about his voice. "Wished for it?"

"Closed my eyes, pictured the being of light, and wished. Nothing happened. I waited and waited, then finally went to the diner. By noontime, the house was on fire."

He chuckled. "So here you are in a house with plenty of heat, and here you'll stay. You got your wish."

She raised her head. "Did I? I wished for heat, and there was a fire. Was it my wish or something more logical, like an erratic old furnace? I've thought about this, Tom. In the figurative sense, I did get my wish. But what about the literal sense? Did I actually cause that fire by wishing for heat?"

"If you're feeling guilty, don't."

"I can't help it. That was a *home*."

"It was a thing. It can be replaced." He stroked her cheek, suddenly serious. "I'm sorry about the business about kids, Bree. I'm sorry you had to hear that from the doctor and keep it all to yourself. If you'd told me, I could have shared the pain."

"You did. You came to my house that night and held me when I cried."

"You should have told me why you were crying."

"You'd only have felt more guilty about the accident. I don't want you feeling that. I don't want to think you gave me this ring because of guilt."

"Selfishness is more like it. You're the best thing that's happened to my life. Giving you a ring is the first step in tying you down. So. What do you think? We could get married next week, or next month. A Valentine's Day wedding might be nice."

Bree put her head down, smiled against his chest, and savored the moment. "We'll decide."

"When?"

"Soon. I've never been engaged before. I want to enjoy it for a while."

That night, she dreamed she had a baby. It was a little boy, a miniature version of Tom as he'd been in the family pictures she had seen. He was perfectly formed and alert, focusing startlingly clear eyes on them as though, right from that moment of birth, he knew exactly who they were. Paternal pride swelled Tom so that he grew a whole twelve inches, there and then. As for Bree, she was filled with so much love that she just . . . burst.

She awoke with a start, feeling that love still. And the sadness of knowing that the dream was only a dream? It was forgotten, first in Tom's arms, then in the excitement that filled the diner when her friends saw the ring.

Chapter

10

"Who'd have thought it," Jane said, after oohing and ahhing over the ring. Her excitement was genuine. Since she would have given anything to be married herself, that was doubly meaningful. "I am so-o-o"—she hugged Bree —"happy for you. It's a dream come true."

Bree glanced at the put-up shelf, saw that no orders were ready yet, and took Jane's arm. "I have to talk with you." She led her through the diner's kitchen to the small office at the rear and shut the door. "I need your opinion."

Jane held up her hands. "I know *nothing* about weddings."

"Not about that." Bree hadn't begun to think about that. A wedding would be a while in the coming. Other things were more immediate. "You know me as well as anyone. You know that I'm sensible. You know that I'm levelheaded. Aren't I?"

Jane nodded vigorously.

"Do you believe me when I say I had an out-of-body experience?"

Jane opened her mouth, then closed it. After a minute, she said, "You wouldn't have said you had one if you didn't believe you had."

"But do you believe they're possible?"

"I might not if anyone else was saying it, but you don't dream things up."

Bree pressed her lips together. She debated for a final minute. Then, taking a deep breath, she told Jane about the three wishes. Jane's eyes grew larger and larger.

"You mean you can make things happen just by wishing them?"

"I don't know. I don't know if I did. That's the problem."

"How's it a problem? You got heat. You got an even better place to stay. You always hated your house."

"But the house is my inheritance. I didn't mean to burn it down when I made that wish."

"Did you go over there this morning?"

"No. I'm a coward. Tom went." It was gruesome, he said, and he urged her to wait until the shock wore off. One part of her wanted to know what remained and what didn't. The rest of her—the part that didn't want anything touching her happiness—was content to stay away. "He said that the fire inspector came in from St. Johnsbury. What if he says it was *arson?* Will they accuse me of it?"

"Arson means using matches and gasoline. You didn't do anything like that."

"No. I just wished."

Jane considered that for a minute, scrunched up her nose, shook her head. "That probably had nothing to do with it."

"Then the wishes aren't real?"

Jane looked doubtful, but Bree couldn't give it up. Simon Meade had a mole on the back of his neck. She could only have seen it from outside herself, which meant that her out-of-body experience had been real. If that was so, she didn't see why the being of light and his three wishes couldn't be real, too. "Maybe I should ask Verity."

"Don't ask Verity. Verity is crazy."

"Not crazy. Just eccentric."

"She thinks thunder is the sound of God bowling."

"So did I, when I was younger."

"Then you grew up."

And Verity hadn't grown up? Not so long ago, Bree might have agreed with Jane. That was before things had happened to her that she would have sworn were impossible. "Maybe I'm crazy, too. I swear I was told I had three wishes to make. I swear I was sent back to earth just to make them."

"Then try another," Jane suggested. "Something specific, so you'll know if it worked. Heat is too vague. It can be taken lots of ways. This time, wish for a *thing*."

"I don't want a *thing*."

"It may be the only way you'll know if the wishes are real."

"But if they are, that will be my second wish. And then what?"

"You'll make a third."

"And *then* what?" Three strikes and you're out, was what she was thinking.

Jane simply grinned. "Happiness forever after?" Her grin faded in the next breath when the office door flew open.

"Jane." Dotty gave a long-suffering sigh and a withering look. "I have been waiting outside for twenty minutes. You're supposed to drop me home if you want the car, and you need the car if you're going to Ashmont. They're expecting you at the community center in thirty minutes."

"It doesn't take long to get there," Jane said, though she quickly gave Bree a hug and moved toward the door.

Bree knew Dotty hadn't been waiting any twenty minutes. Jane had been checking the front lot until Bree dragged her back to the office, and that had been no more than five minutes before. But arguing with the woman would only make things worse for Jane.

"Don't I get to see the ring?" Dotty asked Bree.

Bree would have liked to hide it. But that would have made things worse for Jane, too. And besides, mere mention of the ring made Bree grin. She held out her hand.

Dotty turned her ring finger one way, then the other. "It looks like a decent diamond."

"Mother."

Dotty frowned at Jane. "What?"

"It's a *perfect* diamond."

"You're a jeweler now? For all you know, this diamond is cracked or chipped or inferior or *fake*. 'It's a perfect diamond.' That shows how much *you* know. It would be *another* thing if you'd ever had a diamond of your own."

Bree took back her finger. "Jane's no fool. If the choice was between a lousy guy and no diamond, I'd pick no diamond, too."

"Ward Hawkins is a disgusting man," Jane said under her breath.

Bree agreed. He lived two towns over and had been married four times. He proposed to Jane on a regular basis.

Dotty snorted. "At least he offered." With an arch look at her watch, she left the office.

"Go," Bree urged Jane. "We'll talk later."

"I'm really happy about your ring."

"I know. Now go." She gave a gentle push. Jane was barely gone when Flash appeared. He was looking back at the pair.

"Why does Jane take it?" he asked. "Why doesn't she just leave?"

Bree had asked Jane that many a time. She answered Flash the same way Jane always answered her. "Where would she go?"

"*Anywhere* would be better than living with Dotty."

"On what? What's she got for money?"

"Same thing you have. The difference is that you work."

"So does Jane, only she doesn't get paid for it."

"She should charge for her artwork."

"She can't. The town won't pay."

"Neither will I, if you don't get back up front."

Bree left the office. "Food's up?"

"Not yet. But everyone wants to see your ring. Now that you're engaged to marry a celebrity, you're a celebrity yourself. It's kind of a fairy tale, y'know?"

Tom's celebrity status was reinforced, now that he was engaged to marry the town's own celebrity. Bree's popularity in Panama had people acknowledging him with a warmth that had previously been withheld. He was congratulated at the post office when he went for his mail, at the bank when he went to deposit royalty checks he had picked up in New York, and at the hardware store when he went to buy paint for the spare bedroom's wall. He was given thumbs-up by walkers as he drove around the green, and once he reached Bree's house, he was even congratulated by local men who were helping the fire inspector sift through the ruins.

"Just how fast does the grapevine work?" he asked Eliot Bonner after he returned to the diner to wait out the last of Bree's shift. They sat on adjacent stools, nursing beers.

Eliot chuckled. "When there's a diamond involved? Lightning fast. It's a nice ring."

Tom caught it glinting on Bree's finger as she worked around the diner. It wasn't the biggest diamond he had seen in Tiffany's that day, but bigger wasn't better. He had learned that the hard way and wasn't making the same mistake twice. He had spent hours picking just the right ring for Bree. This one had her brilliance, her simplicity, her grace. It was as beautiful on her hand as he had imagined it would be, and she looked beautiful with it there. Glowing from within. Radiant. They were clichés, but they fit.

"So now that you're marrying into the town," Eliot broke in, "I guess you're staying?"

Tom smiled. "I guess I am." It hadn't been a conscious decision. But the only pleasure he had found in New York had been in shopping for Bree, and once that was done, he couldn't leave fast enough. Heading back to Panama, he was heading home. He loved Bree and he liked her friends. He liked the fresh air and the slower life. He even liked the physical exertion of shoveling snow twice a week. Okay, so gossip was a staple and he'd had enough of gossip to last a lifetime. But that was a small minus against lots of pluses. The town was like a large extended family, which wasn't a bad thing to have if one was estranged from one's own. Tom thought he couldn't find a better place to raise kids.

"What'll you do here?" Eliot asked.

"Finish unpacking. Paint a few rooms. Maybe build a garage." It wasn't productive in the way his father meant, but it satisfied him for now.

"Make it nice for Bree," Eliot ordered. "She deserves nice things." He shook his head. "Too bad about the house. It was old, but it wasn't bad. What'll you do? Rebuild and sell?"

Tom tipped the Sleepy Creek Pale to his mouth. He even liked the *beer* here. "That's up to Bree. It's hers."

"She'll get insurance money. She could keep that and just bulldoze what's left of the house and sell the land." He swiveled toward Tom, looking puzzled. "It's the damnedest thing. The fire inspector couldn't figure out what caused the fire. Couldn't find a thing. We all know she had a bad furnace, but she said the pilot light wasn't doing a thing when she left for work. So what happened? There could have been a spark. Only there wasn't much around the furnace but concrete. So what was it that caught so bad? The inspector couldn't find one thing burned more than another. It was all pretty even. He figures there was some kind of flukey explosion, you know"—he used his hands—"*pffff,* with flames hitting the ceiling rafters. That would have done it."

"I suppose," Tom said. He could picture an explosion, a sudden wild burst of light not unlike the luminous being

Bree swore she had seen. He wasn't saying that he believed her wish had caused the fire, but he wasn't ruling it out. Bizarre things happened sometimes. Take his life. Five years ago, ten years ago—hell, twenty years ago—he would never have imagined finding happiness in a small town with a local girl. Even when he had been at the height of his fame he had never felt as good, as *full,* as he did now—even with the knowledge of what the accident had done to Bree. He would spend his life making that up to her, and what a nice, rich life it would be.

"Hi, guys," said Bree, but her eyes were all for Tom, which made him feel even fuller than before, which should have been impossible but apparently wasn't.

The weirdest thing was that he hadn't even noticed her the first time he had come to the diner. He had been too deeply mired in his own pain to be admiring a butt and legs. But Bree had nice ones. He had come to realize that in the months after his arrival, when the rawness of his situation began to ease and he started looking around him, but even then he wasn't consciously aware of being drawn to her. He just knew he liked her. He liked her hair, which was dark and thick and slightly disobedient, and her eyes, which were hazel and warm. He liked the way a smile lit her face, as though her pleasure was thorough. And yeah, he liked her butt and her legs.

Come late summer, he had begun looking forward to seeing her at the diner, but it wasn't until after the accident, when he watched her for hours on end, when he touched her and let her lean on him, that he felt the force of physical attraction. By then, the emotional attraction was established and strong. He supposed that was what had made the physical one so powerful.

And powerful it was, but not in the typical way. He didn't need to look at her mouth or her breasts or her belly to feel it. All he had to do was look into her eyes.

Eliot loudly cleared his throat. "Ah, kids, excuse me."

Tom jumped. He hadn't realized Eliot was still there.

Bree blushed. Sending Eliot an embarrassed grin and Tom a last look, she headed for the booths.

Tom took a steadying breath.

"You're hit bad," Eliot remarked.

Slowly, Tom raised his head. His eyes found the stainless-steel wall panel and, in the reflection of the diner, found Bree. The image was vaguely distorted and pretty even then. He took another breath. "Tell me about it."

"Nah-uh. Got something else to tell you. Martin says you helped him on a case."

Tom looked at him in surprise.

"Some business with the Littles," Eliot went on. "They'll be coming into some money that they didn't think they'd get."

"Hey, Tom," said LeeAnn in passing, "what an *awesome* ring."

Tom smiled his thanks but was glad she didn't linger. "Martin told you I helped?" he asked Eliot.

"Yup. Surprised me, too. I don't know if Martin took your suggestions because he thought they were good, or if he was afraid that if he didn't you'd do the work yourself, but the important thing is that the Littles are getting what's due them." He frowned at his coffee cup, tapped the rim with his thumbs. "Can I ask you something?"

Tom steeled himself for a warning about butting in on Martin's business.

"I got a phone call the other day," Eliot said, in a voice that was low and private. "Don't quite know what to do about it."

Tom didn't, either, if it was what he thought. "Media?" he asked, wondering if his praise of the discretion of the townsfolk of Panama had been premature.

"No. It was a call from the family of one of the people who recently moved to this town." Eliot ran his tongue over his lower lip, shot Tom a warning look. "Can I trust you won't talk?"

Tom was so relieved that he would have promised most anything. Confidentiality was a cinch. "Yes."

Eliot's back curved around his secret. His voice went even lower. "It was from Julia Dean's son. He said he thought she was in trouble. Thought someone was holding her hostage."

"Holding her hostage? I doubt that. I see her coming and going."

"I told him the same thing. He said he meant mentally. He thinks the woman's been brainwashed or is somehow else being controlled by another person. He asked me to investigate. So I made a point of dropping by the flower shop to talk with Julia, and she seemed perfectly fine to me. When I called the son back and told him, I thought he'd be pleased." Eliot shook his head no. "He wants me to charge her with theft."

"Theft of what?"

Eliot's eyes flew past Tom. Even before Tom could turn, his shoulder was clasped. "Hey, Chief, is this the guy?"

Four large men stood there. Tom recognized them as truckers who had been at the diner before.

"Sure is," Eliot said. "Tom Gates, meet John Hagan, Kip Tucker, Gene Mackey, T. J. Kearns."

Four beefy hands shook Tom's in turn, each one accompanied by a comment.

"You got a great girl. Bree's the best."

"One look at her face and we could see something was up."

"I'd'a gone after her myself, if I wasn't already married."

"Take care of her, man."

Tom watched them trail off. As he swiveled forward again, he felt the same fullness he had earlier. Celebrity status had never been so good.

"Money," Eliot said by his ear. "From the trust left by her husband. Seems she was supposed to use the interest only, but she went ahead and helped herself to more. When

167

I told him she had the flower shop and a small house, he was surprised. He thought she was just working for a florist and renting a place. I thought it'd calm him to know where the money went. Just the opposite. He got more angry."

"How could he not know what she was doing?" Tom asked, but the minute the question was out, he realized its absurdity. *His* family didn't know much more about his current life than his address and phone number, which was all he had shared with them, and that by letter. He had hoped they might write back and ask. When they hadn't done so he blamed them for not wanting to know, which was probably a cop-out on his part.

Probably? Definitely.

For the second time in as many minutes, Eliot dragged him back to the subject at hand. "The son and a daughter live in Des Moines. Julia visits them twice a year, but she doesn't talk about them much around here, so I'd guess she doesn't talk about us much when she's there. It's like she's got two separate lives."

"There's no crime in that."

"That's what I told him. He said it'd be okay if it weren't for the money."

Tom didn't know much more about wills and estates than he knew about intellectual property law, but certain things were basic law school fare. "If there's a trust, there's a trustee."

"She's it."

"Then her husband must have trusted her."

"That's what I told the son. He said she changed after he died. The thing is," Eliot said, shifting awkwardly on his stool, "I could tell Julia about the calls, but I don't much care to. She's a nice lady, y'know?"

Tom did. She was quiet and pleasant, she worked hard, and she was talented. She had sent Bree four flower arrangements in all, one at the hospital, three others during her recuperation at home. He often saw her arranging fresh flowers in the small table vases here at the diner. Flash had told him that her prices were dirt cheap.

So she wasn't a businesswoman. So she needed to take money from the trust fund to survive. That wasn't a crime, either.

"Does the son have a case?" Eliot asked.

"You can't know that without reading the trust instrument. Many trust instruments allow for emergency disbursement of money. If this one does, it may be a question of the son differing with his mother's definition of emergency. In any event, there's nothing you can do. If charges are brought, they have to be brought in Des Moines, if that's where the trust was drawn up and executed. The son has to go to authorities there."

Eliot nodded. "I pretty much told him that. I just wasn't sure if I should be doing anything more on this end. I wouldn't want to be accused of shirking my responsibility."

"Will you look at her?" Flash interrupted to ask. Bree was serving an early-evening breakfast to the local boys Sam, Dave, Andy, and Jack. "She's on cloud nine. Didn't make a peep when another gallon of milk turned up bad." He moved on.

Tom watched Bree until she winked at him on her way back to the kitchen. Strengthened, he told Eliot, "I wouldn't worry about shirking your responsibility. There isn't much you can do in a case like this without violating Julia's civil rights." That was a field of law about which he did know a lot. Some of his most celebrated cases involved civil rights issues.

Eliot took a deep breath that uncurled his spine. "Good. I like the woman." He snorted. "If you ask me, I'd rather have Julia in my town than her greedy son, any day."

What stuck with Tom about the discussion wasn't Julia or her son; it was the fact that their lack of communication was so common a problem. Things happened in families.

Angry words were spoken, hurt was inflicted. Oh, those things happened among friends, too, but that was different. People were more vulnerable where family was concerned. The angry words were hotter, the hurt was more painful. Silences grew to become as obtrusive as the most bothersome of family members.

Breaking the silence was the problem. It took strength, and in his instance it meant dealing with pride and with fear. He had been grappling with both for months. What made the difference now were his feelings for Bree.

She was sleeping soundly when he left the bedroom and picked up the phone in his office. It was eleven at night. With any luck, his father would be asleep.

He punched out the number and waited nervously, holding his finger over the disconnect button, wavering right up until the moment he heard Alice's voice rather than his father's.

"Hi, Lissa. It's Tom."

There was a stunned pause, then a soft "I know who it is. No one else calls me that anymore. No one else has your voice."

Compliment or complaint, he wasn't sure. "It's been a while."

"A long one," she said. She had never been one to beat around the bush. Spunky, was what she was called.

"How are you?" he asked.

"Okay. And you?"

"Not bad. Actually, I'm pretty good."

"Are you back in New York?"

"No. I'll be staying here in Vermont."

There was another pause, then a skeptical "Staying, as in permanently?"

"Funny, isn't it? I was in such a rush to see the world. Now here I am in another small town."

"They're good for some things." She sounded expectant, as if she was waiting for the second shoe to fall.

He let it. "I've met a woman here. Her name's Bree. We're engaged."

"Engaged to be *married?*"

He smiled at her astonishment. "Yes."

"Are you sure?"

He knew she was remembering the pride he had taken in being named one of the twenty-five most eligible bachelors by *People.* He had strutted around for days after the issue had come out.

"I'm sure. Bree's a remarkable woman. I've been wanting to tell you about her for a while. You'll like her a lot, Lissa. I'd love you to meet her."

Her voice hardened a touch. "Will you bring her here to visit?"

He wanted to. But if he went there now, it would be a nightmare of a visit. More quietly, he said, "I need to do some patching up there first."

"That's wise."

"They're still angry?"

"Shouldn't they be?" she asked. "They won't ever forget what you did, Tom, and it wasn't only when Mom died."

"I know."

"Dad doesn't want your money."

Tom knew that, too. Every check he sent was returned uncashed. More quietly, he asked, "How is he?"

"Old and mean and crotchety."

"More so than usual?"

"You could say that." There was a change in her voice then, a crack in the spunk. "He isn't pleased with me. I did the unthinkable."

Tom could think of only one thing that was unthinkable for a daughter of Harris Gates.

"That's right," she singsonged. "I'm pregnant."

His first response was excitement, his second was to think.

"Right again," she said in his silence. "Pregnant and unmarried."

171

"That's still great . . . I think. Who's the guy?"

"Someone I work with."

"Are you marrying him?"

"No."

"Why not?"

"I don't love him."

"Did he ask?"

"Yes. I said no."

"Do you want the baby?"

"I'm not on the witness stand," she protested, in a way that said Tom's grilling was the latest of many.

"I'm sorry," he said gently. "I just want to know if you're happy."

"I am. Yes, I want the baby. I love babies, and I'm not getting any younger."

"You're only thirty-eight."

"Thirty-nine next month."

And still living in her father's house, much as Bree had done until her father had died. In theory, that showed either great strength or great weakness. Tom knew it was the former in both women. They were a lot alike. "When's the baby due?"

"April."

Three months off. So she was six months pregnant. And he hadn't known.

He tried to picture his little sister with a round belly and couldn't quite. He imagined that wasn't the case to his father's disapproving eye. "Come live with us, Lissa," he said on impulse. "Have the baby here."

There was sadness in Alice's voice when she said, "And give up my life here? I can't do that, Tom. You left when you were eighteen and didn't look back. I've been here all along. I can't leave now. I won't do that to myself, and I won't do it to the people I love."

"But if Dad is making your life miserable—"

"He'll come around. If not before, then after. He may

have gripes with his kids, but he loves his grandkids. If you'd spent any time around here, you'd know that."

Tom did know it. There had been grandkids aplenty before the estrangement. He had seen his father with them. At the time, he had attributed the softness to age. Now he realized that that was only part of it.

"Then will you just come to visit?" he asked. Even beyond introducing Bree to Alice, he wanted Alice to see Panama. He knew she would like it.

"That might be hard."

"Because of work?" Alice wrote for the local newspaper.

"Because of Dad. And Carl and Max and Peter and Dan."

The opposition was formidable. Tom took it step by step. "Would you come for my wedding?"

"When is it?"

"Soon, I hope."

"I can't promise anything, Tom."

But she hadn't hung up at the sound of his voice, which was something. "I'm happy about the baby, Lissa. If anyone will be a great mom, it's you. Do you need anything?"

"You mean like money?" she asked, with an edge.

Yes, that was what he had meant. It had been an automatic thing. Less automatically, more thoughtfully, he said, "Support of any kind."

"I have what I need."

"Will you let me know if you don't?"

She didn't answer.

"Can I call you again?" he asked, and this time he waited.

After what seemed an eternity, she whispered a soft, "As long as he doesn't know," and quietly hung up the phone.

Bree woke up when Tom came back to bed. She assumed he had just gone to the bathroom and was surprised to find his hands and feet cold. When he drew her into the curve of his body, she shivered. "Where've you been?" she murmured against the pillow.

"On the phone," Tom breathed against her hair. "I called my sister."

Bree opened her eyes. "You did?" She turned in his arms to see him, though it was too dark to see much. "How was it?"

"Nice."

"She didn't hang up?"

He chuckled. It was a sweet sound, which said he was feeling pleased. "Only at the end. I told her about you. I invited her to the wedding. I said I'd get back to her with a date. So. What do you think?"

Bree slipped her arms around his neck. "I think it's great. I'm proud of you. You took the first step."

He gave her a squeeze. "About the wedding. What do you think?"

"I think I can't set a date until I get used to being engaged. Tell me about Alice. Was she friendly?"

"Mostly."

"Mostly?"

"She's between a rock and a hard place."

"Between your dad and you?"

"And my brothers and me. It won't be easy, reconciling."

"But you want it. I know you do."

"I do."

She beamed. "I'm *so glad* you called her."

He drew back his head. "You didn't wish for it, did you?"

"Me? No." When he continued to look at her, she said, "I swear I didn't. But I might have. That would have been something worthwhile to spend a wish on."

He sighed, relaxed, and drew her in tight. "I used to think family wasn't important."

"It is."

"I'm sorry I never knew yours."

"Don't be," Bree said. Her grandparents would have been scandalized by Tom's reputation. Her father would have positively faded into the woodwork beside him. "It's better this way."

"What about your mother?"

"What about her?"

"Do you ever think about her?"

Bree did. More often in the last few months. "Sometimes."

"Do you ever think about tracking her down?"

"I used to think about doing it. Then time passed and I let it go. Maybe I should wish for her," she said on a whim. "Y'know, make that one of my three wishes. It'd be a good one, don't you think?"

"It would. Hypothetically."

"I know, I know. You're afraid I'll set my heart on seeing her, and then if the wish doesn't work, I'll be upset."

"I don't want you upset."

"But it'd be a good wish," she reasoned, warming to the idea. "It isn't greedy, like for something material. And it isn't vague. If I wish for my mother, she either shows up or she doesn't. Then I'll know, one way or another."

"About the wishes."

"About the wishes." She snuggled closer, warm and suddenly sleepy again. "I'm happy for you, Tom," she whispered.

"Me, too," he whispered back.

The idea of wishing for her mother might have come on a whim, but Bree couldn't believe how perfect it was. Getting engaged was something to share with a parent, and this woman was the only parent Bree had left. If ever there was a time to try to reach her, it was now.

So while Tom was putting coffee on to brew one morning the following week, she came close to him at the counter and said, "I'm doing it, Tom. I'm wishing for my mother."

He stopped mid-scoop. "A real wish?"

"If that's what they are."

He finished measuring coffee into the filter. By the time he was done, she saw telltale lines between his brows and by his mouth.

"What?" she asked.

He turned to her. "I don't want you hurt."

"By what? The wishes not being real? Or her not being what I want her to be?"

"Either."

Bree had given both possibilities plenty of thought. "It's okay if the wishes aren't real. But I have to know one way or another, and I won't unless I try something else. The fire may have been caused by the furnace. It may have been a coincidence at the time that I made my wish. This is different. What would be the chance of the woman materializing after all these years at exactly the same time that I'm wishing her to appear?"

"Slim."

"Very. Her name was Matty Ryan. My father met her in Boston and followed her to Chicago. I was born there. He never brought her back here. So maybe she doesn't know where I am. This would help both of us."

Tom looked pained.

"Okay," Bree conceded. "Maybe she could have found me if she wanted to. But what if she was afraid I wouldn't want to see her after all this time?"

"Do you know for sure that she's still alive?"

"No. But she was twenty when I was born, so she'd only be fifty-three now. That's not very old. Think about it," she said, when he remained doubtful. "What do I have to lose? Worst-case scenario, no one shows up, so I can forget the business about the dreams."

"Worst-case scenario," he corrected, "she shows up and isn't what you want her to be." He took her face in coffee-scented hands. "As long as you recognize that that's a possibility, it's okay."

She wrapped her fingers around his wrists, wanting him to know how sure she was that making this wish was right. "My grandparents said she didn't want me, and my father never disagreed. So that's what I've believed all my life.

Isn't *that* the worst-case scenario? That she doesn't want me?" Her eyes softened. She allowed herself to feel the excitement she had been trying to stem. "But what if she does? I've read stories about women who gave babies up for adoption and were reunited with them years later. What if I could have a reunion like that with my mother? What if there were *reasons* why she gave me up? My father loved her. I used to see a look in his eyes that I never understood until I met you. I feel it in me when I look at you, the same wanting I saw in his eyes. He never stopped loving her. But what if she didn't love him? What if his love frightened her? What if she felt *suffocated* by it? What if she had no money at all and thought I'd be better off with my father? What if she just assumed he would pour some of that love into me?"

A silence fell between them.

"He didn't," Tom said sadly.

"No. I wasn't her. She must have been special."

He folded her in his arms. "So are you."

She could feel his conviction in the way he held her. It gave her strength. "I want to do this, Tom."

He took her face again and kissed her this time. She imagined she tasted vulnerability, even desperation, in him.

"It'll be okay," she soothed. "Don't you see? I could have gone looking for her years ago, but I didn't feel strong enough then. I couldn't take the risk. I didn't have enough to hold me up if she turned her back and walked away. Now I do." She rose on tiptoe, stretched her arms way up past his neck, and held on tight. The sense of fullness was back, richer than ever. She breathed it in and smiled.

"And if it's the second wish?" he whispered. "What then?"

"No more wishes."

It must have been the right answer, because after another minute, he held her back and she knew she had won. The worry lines had left his face. Anticipation was in their place.

"So how do you do it?" he asked. "Is there a ritual?"

She felt a burst of excitement. "There were never any specific instructions. I guess I'll just do what I did last time." She laced her fingers and shut her eyes. In the next instant, they popped open again. "You won't laugh, will you?"

"Of course not."

"This must look pretty silly to someone who doesn't believe."

"Bree."

"Okay." She closed her eyes tighter this time, brought her laced hands to her chin, and said, "I . . . wish . . . to see . . . my mother." She conjured up an image of the being of light, waited until she felt the warmth of it and its calm, and said the words again.

Then she opened her eyes. They met Tom's expectant ones. Only their breathing broke the silence. Slowly, she unlaced her fingers, let her hands fall to her sides, and relaxed.

For the longest time, they simply looked at each other. Finally, Tom whispered, "What now?"

"Now we wait."

Chapter

~ 11 ~

$\mathcal{B}$ree sat on pins and needles through breakfast and a morning of stripping gray paint from the pine moldings in Tom's living room. Working side by side, she and Tom exchanged the occasional expectant glance. The slightest sound from outside brought their heads around, but the doorbell didn't ring.

Bree refused to be discouraged. "It could take a while. The fire didn't happen until six hours after the wish. Maybe I have to be at work. You know, thinking about other things."

She was grateful, though, when, rather than dropping her off at the diner, Tom parked and came in. He read in his corner booth while she worked, then switched to the counter when the lunch business picked up. His presence reassured her, as did the ring on her hand. They made her feel less alone than she might otherwise have felt.

Regulars came and went. Of the new faces that appeared, not a one was female.

Lunchtime passed. Bree grew more edgy. "What do you think?" she asked Tom, back in his booth now.

"She could be coming a distance. Let's give it more time."

His voice held no mockery. He was as into the wish as she was. She would have loved him for that alone, if she hadn't loved him already.

"What if it takes days?" she asked, impatient now.

He slid her an encouraging smile. "You've waited this long."

Yes. She had. Waiting now, she remembered those years. Bits and snatches of the old curiosity—questions about her mother's appearance, taste, and personality—had been distracting her all day, so that she had forgotten things like Carl Breen taking his scrambled eggs dry and Travis Fitch wanting his chili with cheese. But Tom was right. She had waited this long. A little longer wouldn't hurt.

She returned to work. After another hour of only locals walking through the door, though, she had another thought. "A watched pot never boils," she told Tom. "I think you should leave."

Tom shook his head. "I'm staying with you."

"What if she's waiting at the house?"

That gave him pause. "Do you think she might be?"

"I don't know," Bree said, feeling bewildered. "I don't know *anything*." Pushing loose strands of hair back from her cheek, she eyed the door. "This is frustrating."

He closed his book. "What would make you feel best?"

She weighed the comfort of his being there against the fear that her mother might be looking for her elsewhere. "If she goes to the house on South Forest and sees that it's burned out, she might stop somewhere in town and ask. Most people would direct her here. Some might direct her to your place. Or she might just know to go there," she added more softly, because there wouldn't be any rational explanation for that. But then, there was no rational explanation for the idea of three wishes, yet here she was, having made a second one.

"I think," she said, "that we should cover our bases. Just to be sure."

He nodded. "I'll go back there and check. I'll check South Forest, too." He slid out of the booth. "Will you be okay here?"

She looked up at him and swallowed, pressed her face to his shoulder, breathed in the clean, male scent that was his alone. In that instant, she knew that she would never, *never* have been able to do this without his support. He was her safety net if the wish went all wrong.

"I'll be fine," she said. "I have ordering to do. I can set the computer up right here and watch the door. No one much is coming. Suppertime's still a ways off."

Promising to be back before then, Tom left. Bree opened the laptop at his booth, from where she could see both the diner and the parking lot entrance. Her eye kept wandering to the latter.

At half past three, daylight was waning, but it wasn't that as much as the late-January cold that reduced Panama to grays and whites. The ground was snow-crusted, the roads were dirty. The evergreens looked drab and withdrawn. Frost lined most everything in sight, from windows to truck bumpers to tree limbs to breath.

With the disposal of Christmas decorations, the job of providing color fell to the human population of the town. As Bree watched, a group of neon-jacketed students from the regional high school piled out of a souped-up red Chevy and came in for snacks. A truckload of telephone company workers, wearing orange reflecting vests and ruddy cheeks, ordered hot coffee and sandwiches. Angus, Oliver, and Jack shuffled in for sticky buns, wearing their plaid jackets and bright wool caps. Julia Dean pulled up in her yellow van, with a load of fresh flowers.

Bree always admired Julia's work, but never more so than in the dreary winter months. Julia saw color where others didn't. She could walk into the woods and return with armloads of shrubbery stems, fir fronds, and berry sprigs. Alone, they were beautiful. With the addition of a single hothouse flower, they were striking. Of all the bills Bree paid for Flash in a month, the one she did with the most pleasure was the one submitted quietly, almost apologetically, by Julia.

A car turned off East Main. Bree's eye was back on the window in time to see it pull up beside the front steps in the space reserved for the handicapped. Though the marking was hidden under the snow, regulars to the diner knew not to park there. That was the first thing to alert Bree. The second was the car itself, a sporty little Mercedes that should have had the same winter muck on its flanks as all the other cars in the lot, but didn't. The third thing was the driver. She rose from the car to an average height and ran a hand through hair that was shorter than Bree's, though just as dark. When the wind caught that hair seconds later, she turned and quickly locked up the car. Holding the lapels of a stunning navy suit closed against the cold, she trotted up the steps.

Bree's heart began to pound. She watched the woman enter the diner, straighten her collar, and look around, more curious than searching. Her gaze touched Bree and moved on. Bree was trying to decide if it had lingered a second longer on her than on others, when the woman strode toward her.

Bree didn't breathe.

The woman slid in two booths away, set a briefcase-type purse on the table, loosened the silk scarf around her neck, and studied the menu.

Her coloring was right, Bree decided. So were her features. Her skin looked young, and her hair had no gray, though Bree knew that both qualities could be artificially achieved. But the neck never lied. Nor did the hands. Judging from the two, this woman could easily be fifty-three.

LeeAnn rounded the counter, and in a flash Bree was up, waving her off. "I'll take this one," she said, fumbling nervously for her order pad. She was at the table before she managed to fish a pen from her apron.

"Hi," she said, with a breathless smile. "Welcome." She tucked a strand of hair behind her ear, wishing she had done something more with it, fearing she looked a mess. The wind might have caught this woman's hair when she had stepped from her car, but every strand had fallen back into place. She looked professional and sophisticated and smelled expensive, all of which was consistent with the car, the suit, and the large emerald ring on her hand.

She glanced at Bree and back down without a smile.

Bree wasn't discouraged. She figured that if the woman had any character at all, she had to be scared out of her wits, seeing her daughter for the first time in thirty-three years. She had taken pains to look nice. That much was clear. The diner hadn't seen anyone dressed as well in years. Nor had the town, for that matter.

Bree searched for an opener that was less threatening than just coming right out and confronting the woman. "Is this your first time in Panama?" she finally asked.

"Definitely."

"Are you just passing through?"

"God willing." She waved a negligent hand at the menu, put that same hand to her throat, and raised direct eyes to Bree. "I am parched. Could you bring me some Perrier, please? And I'd like to eat something hot but light. What do you recommend?"

The CEO of a large corporation, Bree decided. Being a take-charge type was necessary and commendable for someone in that kind of position. No doubt she had hundreds, even thousands, of employees on her payroll. No doubt she had more than one office and more than one home. No doubt she had frequent-flier mileage piling up right and left. She had been to exotic places and met exotic people. She had ambition.

Bree wondered if that ambition was what had made her decide to give up her child. And if she had decided the other way, what might Bree's life have been like? One thing was for sure. This woman—a onetime free spirit, if the story was right—had left Haywood Miller in the dust.

"Excuse me," the woman said. "You are here to take my order, aren't you?"

Bree dropped her pen. She bent to pick it up. "Yes. I'm sorry. You wanted Perrier. And something hot and light. Did you see the specials board?"

"No. Is there anything on it that's hot and light?"

Bree started to point to the board, then caught the woman's expression. Its impatience said that she didn't want to look herself but wanted a recommendation. Wondering if this was a test, Bree suggested, "Homemade vegetable soup. Flash purées the vegetables, so the soup is healthy and hearty without feeling heavy. He serves it with toasted Parmesan bread sticks."

"That sounds fine," the woman said, and turned to her purse. She drew out a pair of glasses, a pad of paper, and a thick fountain pen that looked luxurious to hold. She uncapped it, then looked up at Bree. "Is there a problem?"

Bree hurried off for the water, all the while telling herself that if the woman was short-tempered, it was nerves. Even the most skilled CEO would feel awkward in a situation like this. Running a business was one thing. Dealing with a sensitive family matter was something else. Bree couldn't imagine anything more sensitive—and intimate—than mother and daughter meeting this way.

"Here you go," she said, and set down a tall glass. Normally, she would have set the bottle of Perrier beside it. This time she did the pouring herself. When the glass was full, she carefully set the bottle behind it. "The soup will be right up."

The woman frowned. "I wanted a twist of lime."

Bree left. She sliced a fresh lime and returned. After setting the plate down by the glass, she smoothed the narrow band of her apron. It was an unconscious gesture, meant to ease the nest of knots in her stomach, but in the doing, Bree saw a side benefit. No thinking, breathing woman could miss her ring. It was just as stunning as this woman's emerald. Surely, it was an opener.

The woman didn't take it.

Casually, Bree asked, "Where are you from?"

The woman darted her a glance over the top of her glasses. "New York." Setting the pen aside, she took several lime slices, squeezed them over the water, dropped them in, and took a drink.

"Are you on your way there now?"

She shook her head. "Montreal." She picked up the pen and began writing.

"On business?"

A nod this time.

Bree would probably have been just as tight-mouthed, had she been in this woman's shoes. Nobody in her right mind would tip her hand too soon or put herself in a position of vulnerability unless she knew she would be well received.

"My dad had a friend once. Actually, more than a friend. He was madly in love with her. The way he described her, she could have been you." It wasn't quite true. Bree's father hadn't done much describing, despite Bree's pleas. But the fib was for a good cause.

"Hm," the woman said in acknowledgment but little else. She sounded unimpressed, even uninterested. Bree wondered if that, too, was a cover.

"Were you ever in Boston?"

Sighing, the woman set down her pen. "I grew up in Boston."

"You did? Not California?"

"No. Not California."

"Did you ever live in California?"

"No." She glanced toward the kitchen, then looked back at Bree. "Is my soup ready yet? I have to get some work done here."

"I'll check."

Bree dashed straight through the kitchen to the employees' bathroom. She brushed her hair, pinched her cheeks hard, reglossed her lips. Cursing softly, she brushed lint from her black jeans. Then she washed her hands, buffed her ring on her thigh, and went for the soup.

By the time she returned to the table, the woman was talking on a cellular phone. In the process of sliding the soup bowl onto the place mat, Bree caught phrases like "grand jury" and "show cause" and excitedly revised her theory. She left to give the woman privacy, but the minute the phone was set aside, she returned.

"I'm sorry, I couldn't help overhearing some of what you were saying. Are you a lawyer?" She was about to say that her fiancé was, too, which would give them a small bit of common ground, when the woman shot her a quelling look.

"No, I'm not a lawyer. Look, I've come a long way today, and I'm tired and hungry." She picked up her spoon and arched a brow.

Bree forced an apologetic little laugh. "Sorry," she said, and withdrew, discouraged for the first time. Tom had warned her that the mother she found might not be the one she wanted, and that was okay. She hadn't expected that they would fall into each other's arms and be inseparable. She didn't want it, didn't need it. She had her own life. She'd done just fine without a mother up to now and could do just fine again.

If this woman *was* her mother.

Feeling shaky and unsure, she returned to her own booth and closed the laptop. Flash was napping in the office, sprawled in the chair with his feet on the desk. She stole in, set down the computer, and stole out, then called Tom from the kitchen phone and whispered a frantic "She's here—at least I think it's her, but I don't know for sure. She's beautiful and rich, and so different from anyone who usually comes that I don't know what to say to her or how to get her to say whether she is who I think she is."

"What's she doing now?"

"Eating soup. But she isn't admitting anything, she isn't very friendly at all, and I don't know what to *say.*"

"Hang in there, honey. I'm on my way."

Bree hung up, ran to the door, and peeked through the window. The woman was still there, looking elegant and out of place. It would have been worse if the diner had been full, but the predinner lull was in effect. LeeAnn was at the counter, talking to Gavin, Julia was arranging the last of her stems, the grillman and the cook were smoking out back.

Taking a damp cloth and a deep breath, Bree went out front and began to wipe down unoccupied bench seats in anticipation of the evening crowd. It was a job that justified her looking from booth to booth.

The woman alternately jotted down notes and spooned up her soup. Her hand was steady, her movements were smooth. At one point, she made another phone call. She looked thoughtful, distant. From time to time, she glanced up. Each time, Bree averted her eyes and poured herself into her work, but the more she thought about what was happening, the more frightened she grew. Time was passing. Before long, the woman would finish her soup, pay her bill, and be gone. If this was Bree's wish fulfillment—this one brief meeting with her mother—she wanted to know.

She pictured the being of light and let the peace of it calm her, but there were no answers to be had in that calm. *Tell me she's it,* she begged. *Give me a sign. Just so I'll know I've seen her once, so I'll know my wish came true.*

Nothing.

Then Tom, she pleaded, peering through frosty windows to search East Main for a sign of his truck. *Bring him quickly. He'll know what to do. He can carry this off better than me.*

But Tom wasn't there. She was on her own, just as she had been for most of her life, and why? Because some woman—perhaps this one—had decided she didn't want to be a mother, well after the deed had been done.

Desperate to know the why of that, she tucked the damp cloth behind the counter and went to the booth where the woman sat. "I have to ask you something," she said, in a voice that surely betrayed her fear but was the best she could do.

The woman took a wallet from her large leather purse. "How much do I owe you?"

"Does the name Haywood Miller mean anything to you?"

A ten came out of the wallet. "I'm afraid not. Do you have my check?"

Bree took the pad from her pocket. "Thirty-five years ago, Haywood Miller was working in Boston when he met a woman named Matty Ryan. I was thinking you might be her."

"Me?" The woman shuddered. She gestured toward Bree's pad. "I have to be going. I owe you what—five, six dollars?"

"They fell in love, but something happened, and they had to separate. He never forgot her. He loved her until the day he died."

The woman set down the ten and reached for her purse. "This should cover it."

"Wait. I need to know. This may be my only chance."

But the woman was tucking the purse under her arm and starting for the door.

Bree caught her arm. "This sounds bizarre, but you may be my mother."

Cold eyes pinned her in place. "Your *mother?* Oh, please. Look, I don't know any Haywood Miller, and my name isn't Matty Ryan, and I pray that no daughter of mine would accost a stranger in a diner. Now"—she glanced at Bree's hand on the sleeve of her suit—"if you don't release my arm, I'll charge you with assault."

Bree let go. She watched the woman leave the diner, climb into her car, and speed off down East Main toward the highway. By then, her eyes were flooded with tears.

"It's all right," came a soft voice behind her. A tentative hand touched her shoulder. "She isn't your mother." Julia Dean was there, looking heartsick. "I couldn't help but overhear."

Bree looked at Julia, then beyond. Most everyone in the diner was watching her. She made an embarrassed sound, shook her head, and went to the end of the row of booths. Julia came right along.

Elbows on the jukebox, Bree pressed her fingers under her eyes to stem the tears. "It's okay. Really. I don't know what I expected." She grew angry. "A woman would have to be pretty cold to abandon her newborn baby. She'd have to be pretty selfish to go through life without ever calling on the phone or sending a card. She'd have to be *heartless* to just vanish." She blew out a shaky breath. "I used to wait on my birthday. I figured she couldn't forget that date. But she did. Every year. I thought she might come when my father died, but I guess that didn't mean anything to her, either." She turned pleading eyes to Julia. "What kind of a person *does* that?"

Julia didn't answer. Looking as pained as Bree felt, she moved her hand in small, light circles on Bree's shoulder. Finally, gently, she said, "There may be a reason. She may not have done all those things out of choice. She may have thought about you a lot."

Bree wanted to believe it. She almost could, hearing it in Julia's sure voice. Still, there was the lingering scent of the woman who had just come and gone. "That woman didn't look like she was even curious."

"She isn't your mother."

"How can I know that? How can I be sure?"

"Your mother wouldn't talk to you like that. She wouldn't sit here and order you around. She wouldn't come all this way just to hurt you."

"How do you *know?*"

"Because you're not like that," Julia said, with a small

squeeze and more of that quiet confidence. "And everyone in town says you take after your mother."

Bree sighed. "No one here has ever met her."

"It makes sense, though, doesn't it?"

"I suppose." She sure didn't take after her father.

A winded Tom rushed to her side, with a dismayed "I missed her."

Bree leaned into him. "You did. Boy. She was something."

"Not your mother," Julia repeated, and left her with Tom.

"No?" Tom asked Bree.

"She denied it."

"What else is new?"

"She was really beautiful. That was always one of my dreams. But she wasn't very nice. Maybe I came on too strong. Maybe I scared her away."

"Maybe Julia's right and she isn't the one."

"Maybe. But how will I know, Tom? How will I know for sure?"

As miraculous as Tom's presence in her life was, he didn't have an answer. Back home that night, when he questioned her about the woman who had come to the diner, Bree told him everything she remembered, right down to the pale pink of the woman's nail polish. But Bree didn't have the number of her license plate, and Tom agreed that a sporty red Mercedes wasn't any more unique in New York than a woman who wore a smart navy suit and carried a briefcase-type purse with a cellular phone inside.

So the woman was gone. Left behind, ongoing, was the matter of the three wishes.

Tom disagreed with the ongoing part. "It's over, Bree. That's it. Two wishes, no more."

"But what if they weren't wishes?"

"What if they were? I won't take that chance."

"*I*'m the one taking the chance."

"No, no, honey," he said, with a firm head shake and as determined a look as she had ever seen. "It's my chance, too. I'm the one who loves you. I'm the one who needs you. I'm the one who wants to live with you for the rest of my life. It may have been your chance three months ago, but now it's *our* chance. I say forget about the wishes. You've made two, and we can't prove they didn't come true. I don't want you trying a third. Not after what you said to me in the hospital about your fear of your time being up once you spend that last wish."

Bree might have argued more if she had felt he was being controlling for the sake of having control, but all she saw beneath his vehemence was love.

"Let's set a date," he said.

She searched his eyes. They were a strong sterling gray in a season of grays, but warmer and more uplifting than any other gray in town. She wondered if they would stay that way even when the reality of her not being able to have a child set in. "You need to think about it more."

"What's to think about?"

"Kids."

"I've already thought about that. It's settled. Like the matter of three wishes. Over and done. A no-brainer. We'll adopt."

"Think about it, Tom."

"What do you think I do all the time you're at work?"

"Paint walls. Strip woodwork. Sand floors."

"And think about you." He paused, frowned. "Is there something else, something I don't know about, that's holding you back?"

"God, no. I love you."

"But you don't trust me."

"Of course I do."

"It's my track record, isn't it?"

"No! I've never trusted anyone the way I trust you."

"Then why don't you believe that I mean what I say?

The issue of kids is okay. Before I met you, I'd given up the idea of having kids, period."

"You come from a big family. You want one of your own, I know you do."

"Small family, big family, we can have what we want, and *don't*"—he held up a warning hand—"don't say adopting isn't the same, because I disagree." He took a step back. "Adopting is a nonissue. I can say that a dozen times, but you don't seem to want to be convinced. So there has to be something else on your mind. Maybe when you figure out what it is, you'll let me know."

His face was a mess of anger and hurt that she didn't know how to address, and then it was too late. For the very first time in their relationship, he backed off.

It was a while before Bree found the something else that was giving her pause, and then it came only after she stepped away from the relationship and looked at the whole. Childbearing was an issue, but more for her than for him. She was the one who still had to come to terms with her body's failings. In the excitement of being with Tom, falling in love, and getting his ring, she hadn't done that. She had been happy to be swept up in a world as fantastic as anything she had ever seen in her private little dreams.

The deeper issue had to do with the whole of that fantastic world. Until last October, she had been a realist. Then the accident happened, and her life had changed. But threads of the realist remained. They were reminding her of where Tom had come from, what he had been, and the sheer improbability of his landing in Panama, let alone as her lover. They were tweaking the far reaches of her mind into wondering now whether all that was real. They were trying to reconcile the life she had thought was perfectly fine before with this new one, which seemed too good to be true.

Bree could think of only one person in town who could help her decide if it was.

Chapter

~ *12* ~

*N*o one in Panama knew exactly when Verity Greene had come to town. It might have been twenty years before. It might have been twenty-two, or eighteen. People simply started seeing her walking across the green or browsing in the library or the general store. If she attended town events, it was at a distance. Likewise, she came to the diner at odd times and only when the counter stool at the far end was free. She minded her own business and spoke only when spoken to, and then with a southern accent that charmed Bree but made others all the more wary.

What she said didn't help if endearing herself to the town was her goal. She was forever contradicting popular sentiment. Though she did it with a smile—and often quite sensibly, Bree thought—she was considered odd. No one understood how her mind worked. No one had cause to find out.

Her house was as much a mystery as she was. It was a small cottage that stood about as far out of town as it could stand and still be in Panama. To get to it meant driving deep into the woods on a rutted path. No one seemed to have known the path existed, much less the cottage, before Verity had taken root there.

From the first, she was considered bohemian. She wore long skirts, vivid crocheted vests, and voluminous blouses. Her hair was long, dark, and wavy, and was held back by a bandanna that covered her forehead. She was always impeccably clean, though as far as anyone in town knew, she had neither hot water nor indoor plumbing. As far as anyone in town knew, she had no electricity, either. She grew her own herbs and vegetables, stripped the best blueberry patches before anyone else could find them, and was thought to eat small animals as they died in the woods. She had no apparent source of income. As for her name, few believed it was real.

Theories had abounded over the years. One theory held that she was an outcast from a commune that had thrived in the seventies in southern Vermont. Another held that she was the daft daughter of a southern billionaire. A third held that she was a witch.

Bree had never believed the last. She had talked with Verity, and while the woman had unusual views and no qualms about sharing them when asked, she seemed harmless. More, she seemed lonely, though when Bree suggested that to others, few agreed. The general consensus was that Verity chose to live as she did. Whether out of fear or respect, the town let her be.

Eliot was one of the few to have ever been to the cottage in the woods. He had described how to get there to Emma, who had told Dotty, who told Jane, who told Bree, who set off in Tom's truck first thing in the morning under the guise of shopping for clothes. She rarely shopped for clothes, *hated* shopping for clothes, and Tom knew it, but he didn't question her. He hadn't said much at all since their talk about setting a wedding date. He had held her, showered with her, made oh-so-sweet love to her. He had fixed her breakfast and eyed her longingly through the eating, but he hadn't said much. Nor had she. She just didn't know what to say.

After stopping at the diner to smuggle food from the back room reserves, she drove to the town line. Once there, she made a U-turn and drove very slowly back until she spotted the twin-trunked birch that was visible only from that direction. Beside it were the faint ruts that marked Verity's road.

The woods were surprisingly dark given the sun above and the snow below. Bree turned on her headlights and jolted along for what seemed an age. The jolting echoed the thud of her heart, which said she had no idea what she was in for. But she didn't stop and turn around. Verity was her last, best, whimsical hope.

When the road finally ended, it was Verity's old orange VW Bug that marked her arrival. The cottage itself was nearly hidden under a cluster of pines.

Uneasy, Bree knocked on the door. She waited several minutes and knocked again. She shifted the bags in her arms and was about to knock a third time, when she saw Verity's startled face at the window. Seconds later, the door opened.

The startled look remained, making Bree wonder when Verity's last visitor had come. Though she was dressed, she wasn't wearing her normal bandanna. Bree hoped she hadn't come at an awkward time.

She held out the bags. "For you."

Verity looked puzzled.

"It's not much, just soup and stew and some other wintry things. I'd have brought your usual," she added, with a tentative smile, "only it wouldn't travel well." Verity's usual was one hot dog, an order of fries, and a Coke. Bree had always thought it a sedate order for someone who was supposedly bizarre, though a perfectly sensible one for someone who normally lived on homegrown goods.

Verity's expression softened. Quietly, she accepted the bags and carried them into the cottage. Bree took a breath for courage and followed, though only enough to close the door. From there, she looked cautiously around. The whole of the place was a single large room, with a kitchen at its far end and a sleeping loft above. The walls were made of exposed logs, the heat was from a wood-burning stove. Baskets of brightly colored yarns were strewed around, a cozy touch. The fragrance that filled the room came from a window garden, where herbs were warmed by a string of sunbeams piercing the pines.

Bree wasn't sure what she had expected—incense smoke, the bodies of little creatures hung to dry, a world of dark corners and eerie sounds—but the cottage held none of that. It was simply furnished, commendably neat, startlingly conventional.

Verity returned to her. In the absence of the bandanna, wisps of gray hair glittered through darker strands. A long shawl covered her blouse and the top of her skirt. She wore thick socks but no shoes.

Bree tucked her hands in her pockets. "I like your place. I didn't know you had lights." She also saw a refrigerator and a television. "You must have your own generator."

"And a satellite dish," Verity said, in her light southern way.

"Ah. Shows how much *we* know." Bree smiled.

Verity looked around the cottage but said nothing.

Bree cleared her throat. "You're probably wondering why I'm here."

"You brought food."

"It's a bribe. I need your advice."

Verity's brows went up. When they came down, she smiled. "I don't think I'm one to be giving advice."

But Bree stood her ground. It was Verity or nothing.

Verity must have sensed her resolve. With a glance toward the back of the cottage, she asked, "Would you like some tea?"

Bree's hands were cold, perhaps from the outdoors, more

likely from nerves. She rubbed them together. "That would be nice."

She followed Verity to the kitchen and sat at a scarred wooden table while Verity heated water, warmed a pot, and opened a tin of loose tea leaves. Bree smelled their scent as soon as they hit the air, even more when Verity spooned some into the pot and poured in boiling water. The smell that rose as the tea steeped was raw, rich, and sweet.

Settling in across the table, Verity folded her hands. "What advice do you think I can give?"

Bree had thought long and hard about what words to use. Convinced that her own clumsiness had turned off the woman in the diner and not wanting to do the same here, she had practiced scripts that gently and gradually related the problem. Sitting here, though, with a woman whose home held no pretense, she realized those scripts were misconceived. So, bluntly, she said, "Strange things have happened to me. You're the expert on strange things."

Verity's mouth twitched at that. "UFOs, CE5s, NDEs, OBEs, ESP. I'm not really an expert. Just an observer."

"And a believer."

"Sometimes."

"Do you believe in near-death and out-of-body experiences?"

"Like the ones you had? Yes." The word had two syllables.

"Why?"

Politely, Verity asked, "Why not?"

"Because there's no way to prove that they're real. They happen to people in the middle of traumas, and then they're over and done. Most of my friends think I imagined what happened to me."

Verity rose, took cups and saucers from the cupboard, and set them on the table. They were of fine china, white with delicate green leaves inside a bright gold rim, perfectly matched and unchipped. The stream of tea that filled one, then the other, was a deep shade of bronze. It smelled even richer than before.

Verity settled into her seat. She looked from one cup to the other, seeming to take in the whole picture. Then, sprightly, she raised her head and smiled. In the next instant, her eyes widened. Leaving the table again, she took a package from the bread bin, unwrapped it, cut several slices of whatever it was, and set them on a plate.

"A tea party isn't complete without sweets," she said, as she set down the plate and returned to her chair. "It's apple cake. The apples are from my own trees."

Bree wasn't hungry, but she took a piece of cake. Verity's pride was a tangible thing. Bree couldn't bear the thought of hurting her. Not that she needed to lie about the cake. It was moist, sweet, delicious. She told Verity so and took pleasure in her smile, then set to wondering how to return to the subject at hand.

Verity did it for her. After taking a sip of her tea, she said in a voice that was tea-party conversational, "Your friends think you imagined what happened, because they aren't open to the idea of a different dimension."

Bree blinked. A different dimension. "Am *I?*"

"Not the you who was raised by your father and grandparents. But the you who likes to stand in the woods and dream."

"How . . . ?"

"I've seen you. I'm a woods walker, too. I've seen the look on your face."

There was no point in denying it, not here, not to Verity, not when Bree's curiosity was whetted. "What kind of different dimension?"

"It's an energy channel. One step above man's everyday level of functioning. It consists of pure thought and feeling."

"Does it take a near death to reach it?"

"No. Psychics do it without. And many people who have

near deaths don't reach it. Only the ones with open minds. The ones willing to believe. The others are weighted down by the physical world. They never rise."

"But I've always been a realist," Bree argued.

Teacup in hand, Verity sat back with a smug smile.

Okay, Bree reasoned. So she dreamed. But did that make her different from others?

"You believe in positives," Verity said. "You're an optimist. That's how you survived living with your father all those years. You made a life for yourself at the diner. You looked outward. You saw the glass as half full." She paused. "Those forest fairies stirred up by the wind?"

Bree's eyes went wide.

Verity smiled and shook a gently chiding finger. "Your face doesn't hide much. I've watched you watch them. Some people see drifting leaves. You and I, we see life."

You and I. Bree had a startling thought.

But Verity was speaking on, slowly and softly, with only the faintest of drawls. "You believe in a world of possibility. Not everyone does. Your friends don't, which is why they have trouble believing what you experienced. That, and they're jealous."

Of Tom? Of her diamond ring? "Of what?"

"Of the inner peace you found."

"What inner peace?" Bree cried. "I am totally confused. My life used to be sensible and predictable. Then the accident happened, and nothing's been the same since."

"Are things worse?"

"No." She hadn't meant to complain. Or maybe she had. "Better?"

"So much so that sometimes I think it's too good to be true."

Verity studied her for a minute, then nodded. "Thomas Gates."

Bree sighed. "Oh, yes. Thomas Gates. Most of the time I forget that half the world knows who he is. Then I remember, and I can't believe he loves me."

"He seems happy."

"Well, he thinks he is now, but what if he should change his mind?"

"Are you going to throw away what you have on the chance that he will?"

Bree started to speak, then stopped. Put that way, the answer was obvious. It told only half the story, though. "If he had happened to me before all this, I could probably believe it faster. But first there was the accident, then the out-of-body experience, now the wishes. Put Tom in the middle of it, and I don't know what's real and what isn't."

Verity was frowning. "Wishes?"

Bree hesitated. Then she reminded herself that this was a woman who not only saw forest fairies but had argued more than once in favor of UFOs, psychics, and, yes, a bowling alley in heaven. So she told her about the three wishes, from her first awareness of them, to the fire, to the woman at the diner. She argued both sides, coincidence versus wish. "Do you see why I'm confused? And then there's the part of me that thinks the only reason I'm back here is for the wishes, and that after the third one, the being of light will reclaim me."

"Oh my," Verity said. "What makes you think that?"

"I don't know. Maybe it was the drugs I was on right after the accident. Maybe it's nothing but a human kind of fear." Most people feared death, didn't they? It was the most natural thing in the world, wasn't it? "Do you think the wishes are real?"

Verity considered the question. "They could be."

"Was that my mother who came to the diner?" When Verity shrugged, Bree again had that startling thought. Again she set it aside. "After the third wish, do I die?"

Verity raised both shoulders and kept them up this time.

"Can I risk it?"

The shoulders dropped. "That depends on what the wish is and how much it matters to you." She thought for a minute. "I probably would."

"Even if it means death?"

"What if it means life?"

"You mean a happier life?"

"Happier. Safer. Freer. Most people live like this." She drew a level line with her hand. "Some people live like this." She drew a higher line. "Having an open mind makes part of the difference. Risk makes the rest."

In a moment's frustration, Bree scanned the room. It held most every creature comfort. "This doesn't look too risky."

"Now it isn't. It was when I first came here. I had never lived alone. I had never taken care of myself. I didn't have a generator then, just the clothes on my back."

Regretful of her outburst, Bree brought the tea to her mouth. She let the nearness of the scent tease her taste buds for a minute, took a sip, and, in the smooth, rich heat, found a temporary balm. More calmly, she asked, "Why did you come?"

Verity smiled. "Not for the UFOs, though I do think this is where they land."

"What did you leave?"

The smile faded. "A man who swore to kill me if I left."

Bree gasped.

Verity waved a hand. "It's an old story. Not an uncommon one. It's nowhere near as exotic as the stories people tell about me in town."

"How many of them are real?"

"Not many. It may be possible to commune with the dead, but I've never done it. I have been followed by strange lights and do believe in UFOs, but I've never come face-to-face with an alien. I have come face-to-face with a bear. I was so frightened that I froze. The bear got bored and walked away. So people say I can control wild beasts with a single look. I let them believe it."

"Why?"

"Because it frees me to be and do whatever I want. For years I couldn't."

It sounded so sensible and unbizarre that Bree took the opening it offered. No hopes up, she told herself. Just curious. "Where did you live before you came here?"

"Atlanta."

"Have you ever lived in California?"

"No."

It was possible that Bree's father might have been either wrong or misled. "Have you ever been to Chicago?"

"Once. Fifty years ago. I was ten. We were visiting relatives there."

That would make her sixty, not the fifty-three that Bree's mother would be. In that, too, Haywood Miller might have been wrong or misled. "Do you have any children?"

"No. My husband wouldn't share me that much."

What if she had run away, had an affair with Haywood, and conceived Bree? What if that was the only way in the world she could have had a child? What if, years later, she had come to Panama to watch Bree grow? That didn't explain why she had never revealed herself to Bree. But what if Haywood had forbidden her to? What if that had been part of the deal? What if she had changed her looks so that Haywood himself hadn't recognized her?

Trying to stay calm, she asked, "What brought you to Panama?"

"I closed my eyes and pointed."

"Pointed?"

"I needed to leave the South. So I opened a map of the North, closed my eyes, and pointed."

"Did you know anyone here before you came?"

Verity shook her head. Then she tipped it and gave a small, knowing smile. "I thought you thought the woman in the diner was your mother."

Bree felt a stab of embarrassment. Throwing it off, she raised her chin. "I don't know that for sure. When I wished for heat, I got a fire. So I moved to Tom's, where I have heat. I got my wish, but in a roundabout way. My seeing the woman at the diner led to my confrontation with Tom, which led to my coming here.''

Gently, Verity said, "I'm not your mother."

"Would you tell me if you were?"

"Yes. I believe in telling the truth."

"Verity."

"Yes?"

"Your real name?"

Her eyes twinkled. Her accent thickened. "It is. Right on my birth certificate."

Bree couldn't argue with a birth certificate. "Do you really think that God is bowling when it thunders?"

"Do you know otherwise?"

"When hot air hits cold air, there's lightning. The sound comes from that."

"Does air make noise? Do clouds?"

"Scientists say so."

"Does it make sense?"

Bree saw her point.

"Think back," Verity went on. "Did I ever say for sure that God bowled? Or did I say it was *possible?*"

Bree was caught. "Possible."

"Is it?"

"I guess."

Verity's smile was wide. "See? You do have an open mind, just like me, though not because we're blood kin. Both of us experienced a life threat. That freed us up."

Freedom was one thing, lunacy another, was what Bree was thinking.

Verity said, "Freedom is relative. So is happiness and reality and risk. Sometimes, in order to be free, we have to take risks. Sometimes, in order to be *happy,* we have to take risks. As for what's real and what isn't, it's like beauty, in the eye of the beholder. Reality is one thing for one person, and another for another. We make our reality. It can be what we want, or what we need."

"What if my reality is different from Tom's? What if he really is that other person, the famous one who lives in the fast lane?"

"And if he is? What would you lose?"

"The most wonderful thing in my life."

"Well, there you have it."

"Have what?"

"Your answer. The thing that brought you here, what's real and what isn't. If Thomas Gates is the most wonderful thing in your life, why question it? You're an optimist. Deep down inside, past that old inbred cautiousness, you believe in possibility. It doesn't matter if a *thing* is real. If the *possibility* is, that's what counts."

Bree's spirits rose higher with each jolt of the truck during the return trip on Verity's rutted path. At its end, the forest's darkness gave way to a near-blinding light that Bree took as her special being's approval of the visit. Waiting only long enough for her eyes to adjust, she turned onto the main road and, ebullient, headed for Tom.

The house was so quiet when she reached it that for an instant she feared she had waited too long. After searching the rooms on the first floor, she ran up the stairs. *"Tom?"*

"In here," came his voice from the end of the hall.

She went to the door of his office. He had yet to unpack the cartons there, but they were pushed aside, which was an improvement, and there was a lamp on the desk. He sat in its light with his computer open, gestured that she should wait, tapped at the keyboard. After reading from the screen, he jotted something on a long yellow pad, tossed down his pen, and pushed himself back.

There was an instant's hesitancy when he looked at her, an instant's reminder of their confrontation. Then came a slow grin and the sexiest "Hey" she'd ever heard, but he didn't leave the chair.

So she went to him. "Hey yourself." Stopping between

his legs, she looped her arms around his neck and kissed him once with her lips, a second time with her teeth, a third time with her tongue.

He circled her waist. "Must have been one hell of a shopping trip."

She smiled down into his smiling face. "It was. Whatcha been doing?"

"Exploring the feasibility of obtaining a waiver of the ban on federal subsidizing of nonregulated growth material for the Allsworthys' farm down the road."

The only thing she could understand of his answer was the bottom line. "Another case?"

He shrugged, but his smile remained. Every few days something new popped up, some legal problem that Martin Sprague didn't know how to handle. Tom refused to take credit for the work, but the whole town knew what was what.

"I love you," she said.

He drew in a deep breath. It came out ragged. "I was hoping you'd say that."

"Let's get married."

He rolled his eyes.

She was more specific. "This weekend."

Slowly, he straightened. "Do you mean it?"

"Uh-huh."

"This weekend is three days off," he warned, but she felt his excitement.

"We don't need printed invitations."

"Are you sure?"

"About printed invitations?"

"About the date."

"Positive." She was making her own reality, tying Tom down, then giving him a last chance to escape. "Unless you'd rather wait."

The eloquent look he gave her was followed by another kiss. This one was longer and deeper than the three that had come before and tasted of commitment. Odd, but it made Bree feel free.

She smoothed his hair back and studied him, trying to see the brash and successful man whose face was on the books on the shelf. But there were no traces of that man here. This one was more handsome, more honest, more decent. His hair was longer and his coloring more healthy. He had a scar on his cheek that lent character, and wonder in his eyes. This one was the man who loved her enough to believe in her fantasies and wait through her doubts.

"You are the most wonderful thing in my life," he said, in a voice that was hoarse with emotion. They were the very same words she had used not so long before at Verity's house, and would have erased the last of her qualms if those hadn't already been gone.

All that remained was a world of possibility, one so large and bounteous that Bree couldn't have explored it all in an hour, a day, a year. But she tried. She touched Tom's face and his neck with her hands, then her mouth. She unbuttoned his shirt and touched his chest, unbuckled his belt and unzipped his jeans. She touched everything inside, stroked until she had created a new reality that was larger, harder, and so much more exciting than the old that she slipped to her knees.

Tom jerked at the touch of her lips. "Christ, Bree."

She didn't stop. The idea that anything in the world was possible gave her a certain freedom, which gave her a certain power. That power meant taking the thickness of him into her mouth while she held his thighs apart with her hands. It meant milking him to the point of release, then rising up, pushing aside her blouse and bra, and offering him her breasts. It meant watching his wonderful long-fingered hands knead them, then lifting her nipples to his tongue, and if there was brazenness in that, she had no regrets. The power was hers, the freedom, the possibility. All these were her reality with Tom.

With a sudden tousling of hands, clothes, and breath came the desperate drive toward consummation. There was Tom's hoarse "That's it, baby . . . lift . . ."

And her own breathless "Wait . . . there . . . oh, my . . ."

"Higher . . . wrap your legs . . . yessss . . ."

"Touch me . . . *there!*"

"You're so hot . . ."

"I can't . . . hold back . . . Tom!"

Her last conscious thought before her climax consumed conscious thought was that this was a reality she could live with.

The next morning, riding high on Bree's love and knowing that he would never feel bolder, Tom called his father. The older man's gruff "Hello" had him gripping the phone more tightly.

"Dad? It's Tom."

Silence.

"Dad?" His heart was beating up a storm, but nothing at all came from the other end of the line.

So he tried "How are you?"

When that didn't evoke a response, he jumped in with, "Something's happened here, something really exciting. I've been wanting to tell you about it for a long time—" He thought he heard a click. "Dad?" he tested, fearful. "Dad?"

When a dial tone came on, he let out a disappointed breath and quietly hung up the phone.

If Bree hadn't believed that anything was possible, she would never have believed the kind of wedding that occurred three days later. When she set the date with Tom, she had envisioned something small, a simple church ceremony with a brief reception at either the diner, an inn in a neighboring town, or even Tom's house. That was before the townsfolk got wind of her plans.

Flash, who was the first to know, insisted that he was catering whatever, wherever. Jane, who agreed to be Bree's maid of honor, insisted that the whole of the town should be invited, since the whole of the town loved Bree. Jane called Dotty, who called Emma, who called Eliot and Earl, and before lunchtime of that very first day, the entire town was involved.

The pastor, who was thrilled with the idea of having a large and captive audience, promised to set up folding chairs in every available space in the church and perform the most beautiful ceremony Bree had ever seen. The organist secured a list of Bree's favorite songs and, insisting that the organ alone wouldn't do, called for a choir rehearsal that night. Emma, being as close to a mayor as the town had, insisted that the reception be held in the town hall, which had been newly painted in anticipation of the March town meeting anyway and was, after all, "the only suitable place for a town-wide event."

Volunteers began calling Flash to offer help in preparing the food. The owners of the Sleepy Creek Brewery pledged kegs of their best sellers. The owner of the local bread company announced plans for a huge four-tiered wedding cake.

By the time Bree dropped by the shop to talk flowers with Julia Dean, Julia had already gathered buckets of imported blooms. "I have people out collecting greens enough to decorate the church and the town hall," she said, with satisfaction. "All you have to do is tell me what flowers you want to carry, and I'll make up a bouquet. What are you wearing?"

Bree was feeling slightly breathless. "I don't know yet. I'm going shopping later. I don't think I can get a gown so late, but I should be able to find a pretty suit or a dress."

Julia set the stems she was clipping in a pail of water. Coming out from behind the counter, she stood back and studied Bree, up and down, for a quiet minute. Then, even more quietly, she said, "I have a gown you could wear."

Bree's heart tripped. "A wedding gown?"

"Can I show it to you?"

Too touched to refuse, Bree followed her out the back door and across the drive to the small house where Julia lived. Once inside, they climbed two flights of stairs to the attic. There, hanging in a small cedar closet, covered with wrapping that Julia carefully removed, was the wedding dress of Bree's dreams. It was ivory in color and Victorian in style, with a high neck, long sleeves, and a hem layered with ruffles and lace. Delicate beads dotted the bodice, right down to the fitted torso.

Bree swallowed. "It looks so slim."

"You're slim. Do you like it?"

"I *love* it."

"Try it on."

Bree tore her eyes from the gown. "Really?"

Julia nodded, looking pleased.

"Right now?"

"It'll save you a trip to the mall."

Bree knew that she could look for weeks and weeks and not find anything half as beautiful as this gown. Without another word—and only a brief thought to the scars Julia might see—she slipped off her jeans and shirt. By that time, Julia had tiny buttons unbuttoned and the back zipper down. Bree stepped carefully into the dress. Just as carefully, she drew it on. Julia helped her straighten the fabric and secured the zipper.

It fit. Perfectly. Amazed by that, and awed by the dress, Bree smoothed her hands over her stomach while Julia did up the tiny buttons, adjusted the shoulders, gently pulled at the sleeves. When Julia came around to the front and stepped back to look, Bree held her breath.

Julia's eyes teared. "At the time I wore this," she whispered, "I was sure it had been made for me and no one else. I was wrong."

"It looks okay?"

Julia's "Oh, my" said it looked a far sight better than that, and Bree could feel it. Everything was right—the style, the fit, the length.

"When I sold my house in Des Moines and came here," Julia said, in a distant voice, "I thought about giving it away, but I couldn't. My wedding day was glorious. When my daughter got married, she wanted something new. So this has been wrapped up all that time. Something must have been telling me to take it along." Julia raised her eyes. Though they remained moist, her voice was clear. "I would be honored if you would wear it, Bree. It would mean the world to me."

"To *you*," Bree breathed, through her own film of tears. "It would mean the world to *me*." She imagined walking down the aisle of the church in this dress, imagined putting her hand in Tom's, imagined walking back up the aisle as his wife, and her throat swelled. Then she imagined dancing through a boisterous reception at the town hall, and had a thought that caught her breath up short. "What if I spill something on it?"

Julia laughed and brushed at her tears. "It'll clean."

"I'd feel *terrible*."

"I won't," Julia said, but she had turned away. Pulling a box from the closet shelf, she removed its lid and reached inside. It seemed that the magic wasn't over. She drew out a veil to match the dress and lifted it above Bree's head.

"My hair's a mess!"

"Just a quick look," Julia insisted. She set the band of the veil in place and, as though she were touching gold, arranged Bree's hair around it. Then she stood back and smiled.

"Yes?" Bree whispered.

"Yes," Julia said, and held up a finger. She went to the far end of the attic, bent her knees, moved this way and that. Then she motioned for Bree to come.

Bree walked on tiptoe so that the hem of the gown

wouldn't touch the floor. The fabric made an elegant swishing sound as she moved. Once Julia had Bree positioned, she saw her reflection on the window. There were four pieces to it, where the mullions divided the glass, and while the image was remarkably clear, it was a total dream.

Bree could only stare.

"Quite something, isn't it?" Julia asked.

"Oh, yes."

"You look stunning."

"Tom will *die.*"

"I certainly hope not."

"I look like a bride."

"You *are* a bride, or will be. Day after tomorrow. Oh, my."

"Too soon?" Bree asked, turning to her. "This is happening so fast I feel like I'm out of breath. Am I rushing it?"

"Not if you love Tom."

"I do."

"Then why wait?"

Good old commonsense Bree couldn't think of an answer.

"I was engaged for a week," Julia told her. "My husband was going into the army. We decided to get married before, rather than wait."

"Did you ever regret it?"

"Regret marrying Teddy?" Julia's smile was wistful. "No. I adored him. We had a wonderful life together. He's been gone three years. I still miss him."

"Is that why you left Des Moines?"

"It's one of the reasons. Everything there reminded me of him. And then there were the children. Not children any longer. Adults. A son and a daughter, both married, with kids. I was too close to them. Our relationship wasn't healthy. We needed distance between us."

"You must miss them."

"Not as much as I thought I would." She laughed. "That sounds terrible, but the truth is that I'm busier here than I was there, and then, each time I start thinking that it's family time, something happens here to make me feel as if the people here are family, too. Like this wedding. It's going to be special."

"It isn't the first wedding the town has put on."

"But it'll be the best. You're respected here, Bree. Loved."

Bree saw tears refill Julia's eyes. Her own throat grew tight. Laughing brokenly, she said, "Let's not start this again."

Julia nodded, wiped the corners of her eyes, straightened, and smiled. "So. Since flowers this time of year will have to come a distance, we can choose whatever we want." Thoughtful, she studied the dress. "What do you think? Would you like white tulips with baby's breath? Lily of the valley? Something with sweet alyssum or roses?"

Tom had been warned to wear a tuxedo, but he wasn't prepared for the sight of Bree when she appeared at the back of the church and began her walk down the aisle. She was a vision in ivory and lace, primly covered from neck to foot but provocative where the dress clung, and beautiful, so beautiful that she stole his breath.

She carried a bouquet of small white flowers and greens, and wore a veil that shaded her face, but he saw her eyes through it, saw her eyes and felt her love. When she reached him and he draped the veil back over her hair, the feeling intensified.

Incredibly, it just kept growing. If, a mere year before, someone had told him that he would be marrying a small-town girl in a wedding put on by her town, he would have laughed himself silly. But there was nothing silly about the wedding Panama gave them. It was the most touching wedding he had ever attended. From the church that was packed to the gills, to the town hall that wasn't much different, to Flash's food, to live music from a jazz band, a string trio, and a barbershop quartet, to the strobe lights of no less than four self-appointed photographers and two videographers, to smiles and wishes and handshakes that never stopped coming—he had never in his life been the recipient of so much sheer goodwill, and all because of the woman at his side.

He only wished that his family were there. He wished they could see Bree, wished they could feel the decency and caring in this room. He wanted them to be part of his new life, but his father had refused to talk to him, and when he finally reached his sister, she had declined his invitation to come. He offered to pay her way, to pay the way of any or all who would come, but she held firm. She had told his brothers that he had called, she said. She had argued in his defense, but the anger was still there. She begged for time. When he argued that a wedding was a onetime event, she argued that a mother's funeral was, too, and he had been silenced. His mother would have loved Bree, he knew, would have loved her spirit and her strength. At the drop of a hat, she would have become the mother Bree had never had.

On her wedding day, though, Bree didn't look to be missing a mother. She had dozens of mothers, dozens of sisters and brothers. Her face was wreathed in smiles from the minute he slipped a wedding band on her finger, through laughter and dance and food, to the minute she fell asleep against him in the wee hours of Sunday morning at the inn where they spent the night. Come morning, when they drove to Boston to catch a plane to the Caribbean, she was smiling still.

Tom had chartered a boat with a captain and a cook. It was the perfect way to island-hop without hassle. Their stateroom was luxurious, the food gourmet, and the schedule theirs for the making each morning when they arose.

He had done the Caribbean before, but this time was

different. This time, he did it through Bree. Through her eyes he saw the brilliance of aqua water and the novelty of sun and warm sand in the middle of winter. Through her ears he heard the flap of sail against mast, the rustle of the palms, the laughter of native children on the docks. Through her hands he felt the beat of a steel band on Nevis, through her nose smelled goodies at a patisserie on St. Bart's.

Between the joy she took in each new thing she saw and the joy he took in her, Bree made his week. They returned to Panama tanned, happy, and rested. He was more in love with her than ever.

Chapter

13

*M*ud season in Panama wasn't attractive. With the last major melt of winter's snow, the ground grew sodden. Hillsides seeped onto hardtop and slithered down lawns. The half of Panama's roads that were unpaved became all but impassable for anything that didn't have chains, while the rest of the roads were just messy. Cars grew mud-spattered, shoes and boots caked. Those patches of snow that lingered in shady spots were edged with dirt. The town green became something to avoid.

The onset of mud season occurred anywhere from the fifteenth to the thirtieth of March. It lasted from two to three weeks. During any other time of the year, there were things to do outside. During these few weeks, there was nothing. Cabin fever raged. Tempers were short. The coming of spring seemed improbable.

The general assumption was that the founding fathers of Panama had held the town meeting at the end of March because, lacking snowplows, they couldn't mobilize themselves sooner. Modern-day Panama wasn't as concerned with snow as with creating a diversion in this bleakest, dirtiest, most boring of times. To that end, the town meeting was drawn out over three nights and sandwiched between parties before and after.

Bree was looking forward to the week, not because she was feeling bleak, dirty, or bored, but because she was happy. She was back working at the diner, which she loved. She had blissful memories of her wedding and honeymoon, and, still, healthy traces of a Caribbean tan, which she loved. And she was married to Tom, which she really, *really* loved. The fear that he would come to have second thoughts hadn't materialized. Nothing had changed with their marriage to dampen his ardor. He was as attentive, as protective, as interested and loving, as he had been before. She was deliriously happy.

So her reaction to the partying took her by surprise. Seeing families, seeing families with *children,* caused the same pangs she had felt in November. She thought she had come to terms with not being able to have a child. After the holidays and Tom's repeated assurances that it didn't matter to him, she thought she was comfortable with the idea. Then she saw Tom at the dinners and dances and fairs that brought the town together, only now he wasn't just looking at warm family groupings from afar. He was in the middle of them.

It started with Joey Little. But Joey had friends. When those friends discovered that Tom had infinite patience and kid-friendly shoulders, they were all clamoring to climb up. Tom loved it. He was large and physical. He could toss giggling children around with such care that anyone watching laughed, too. He removed little noses and held them between his fingers, could pull quarters out of ears or throw shadows of wolves, witches, and turkeys onto the wall. He was a kid when he was with kids. He was meant to be a father.

Bree needed to talk about that, but she couldn't talk with Tom. She knew how he felt. He had expressed it often enough. She needed to figure out what *she* wanted to do. So, as casually as she could, she raised the subject with friends.

Flash was the first. "Do you miss having children?" she asked one afternoon in the diner's kitchen. He was experimenting with dessert presentations and had spread raspberry sauce on a plate.

"How could I have kids?" he asked, preoccupied as he dropped a glob of white cream in the center. He took a knife and drew it from white to red, one way, then another. "I'm a kid myself."

"I'm serious."

"Me, too. How could I take care of a kid? I can barely take care of myself."

"That's not true," she scolded, though, thinking about it later, she wasn't so sure.

So she drove out to see Verity. Verity was a perfect example of someone who could take care of herself. Bree brought a piece of wedding cake from those sliced and frozen, and scolded Verity for having left the reception too early to get one fresh.

"It was better that I left," Verity said. She was crocheting, working so nimbly that Bree had trouble following the in-and-out of the hook. "You don't need people making a connection between us. Besides, I don't do well in crowds."

"Because of the children?"

Verity's hands stilled, though her eyes remained on her work. "Why do you ask that?"

"Children make noise. They don't allow for peace and quiet. Or for privacy."

"I never wanted the privacy. The peace and quiet is part of me. It has been so all my life. That was the only way I survived my marriage as long as I did. I used to withdraw into myself." Her fingers returned to activity. "I wouldn't have been able to do that if I'd had children."

"Are you sorry?"

"That I didn't have children?" She didn't break the rhythm of her work. "Given the circumstances, no. I didn't want to have his children. With another man, maybe. In another life, maybe. But it's too late in this one. No herbal potion or alien encounter will bring it about. I'm well past my childbearing years. And yes," she added, "I've come to like the privacy."

The only other woman Bree knew who prized privacy as much as Verity was Julia. Indeed, she sensed that Julia told her as much about herself as she told anyone, and that wasn't much. But the wedding dress had created a bond between them. Bree enjoyed being with her. She had taken to stopping in at the flower shop to talk whenever she passed.

As fate had it, on this day Julia was tying a huge pink bow around the neck of a vase filled with pink and white tulips, a gift for the barber's son's wife, who had just given birth to a daughter. Bree watched for a minute, then asked, "When you do up arrangements like these, do you think back to when your own children were born?"

"Sometimes," Julia said. She gave the ribbon a twist. "It was a special time."

"Was it hard?"

"Childbirth?" She smiled. "No. The cause was good."

"Labor can go on forever."

Julia gave a negligent nose-scrunch. "The worst comes only at the end, and then there are drugs to help. Drugs hurt the baby, you say? Well, our kids didn't seem damaged any. In my day, mothers weren't as quick to martyr themselves. After the children were born, yes. Child rearing was our major occupation. We often put it before our own best interests. At the time of birth? No. Ignorance was bliss."

"Kind of like a reward for surviving pregnancy?"

"Oh, I liked being pregnant. I liked it very much." She held back the vase, looked at it, then turned it to Bree.

But Bree was trying to convince herself that she didn't want to be pregnant. "I've heard awful stories."

"You're talking to the wrong people," Julia said. She paused, raised hopeful brows, lowered her voice. "Are you pregnant?"

"Good Lord, no. I just got married. It's too soon to be having a baby. So much has happened to me so quickly that I need time to adjust. I like working, and I like being alone with Tom and anyway, he's still trying to decide what to do about *his* work, so it wouldn't be fair to impose kids on him yet."

"I don't think children would be an imposition with that one," Julia said.

Bree knew she was right, which didn't help things much. She trusted Julia's judgment. But she needed an ally. So she raised the subject with Jane, leaning in close across the counter after the lunchtime crowd had thinned. "Do you worry about getting older? Does that thing about the biological clock ever get you to wondering?"

Jane sighed. "All the time. But what can I do? I don't draw men like you do."

"The right man just hasn't seen you. Someday he will." Bree believed it. Jane was too good a person to go through life alone.

"Someday," Jane said, and sighed. "I may be too old for kids by then."

"You could adopt. Single mothers do. Michelle Pfeiffer did. So did Rosie O'Donnell. The way some men are, a woman's better doing it alone anyway."

"Doing what alone?" Dotty asked, taking the stool beside Jane.

Jane gave Bree a look that said You should have warned me she was there, but Bree hadn't noticed it herself.

"Having kids," LeeAnn put in, having caught the conversation in passing. "Look at me. I've done it alone, haven't I?" She left again before anyone could answer.

"Look at her," Dotty muttered under her breath. *"Don't* look at her. She's no example of motherhood, doing that thing to her hair. Besides, it's just fine for a pretty little Hollywood face to adopt a child. Those women don't have to worry about paying the bills."

"Neither do I," Jane said quietly. She was looking at Bree. "I have a home. The oil is paid for. So's the electricity and the phone."

Dotty drew back and stared at her. It was only when Bree looked at Dotty that Jane did, too. "Don't worry, Mother. I'm not having a child."

"Having? I *hope* not. Good God, Bree. Are you putting bugs in her ear now that you're married? Well, she isn't, for one thing, and for another, you shouldn't be having a child yourself. You just got married. You don't know if the marriage will last."

"It will last," Jane said.

"The voice of experience. She's an expert on marriage *and* on babies."

"Adoption was the subject," Jane corrected.

"Don't you dare do that, either. I'm not up for raising another child."

"If it was my child, I'd be doing the raising."

"Like you do the cooking?" Dotty asked.

Bree tried to defuse the situation. "Verity was saying—"

"Verity?" Dotty turned to her. "That woman has nothing worthwhile to say. You talk with her too much, Bree. You encourage her."

"To do what?"

"To come into town. Fine. We can't keep her out of town meeting. But she doesn't have to be lurking around at the crafts fair. People won't buy what she crochets. She makes us all nervous. And showing up at your wedding?" Dotty reared back. "I wouldn't have liked that one bit, if it had been me."

"Verity is harmless," Jane said before Bree could stop her.

Dotty picked right up where she had left off. "That shows

how much you know. You've been here when she's been talking nonsense. Don't you *know* it's nonsense?"

"She says things to shock us."

"Oh, she does? Who told you that?"

"I did," Bree said.

Dotty sighed. "Bree. Why do you tell Jane things like that? She believes them."

Looking straight ahead, Jane said, "Verity makes sense when you talk with her alone."

"Is that what you've been doing? Is *that* where the talk about adopting a child came from?" She pushed out a breath. "God save us from idiots." She left the stool with an impatient "Are you coming?"

As she walked off, Bree touched Jane's arm.

In a shaky whisper, Jane said, "One day she'll push me so far that courage won't matter. I hate her." She put a fingernail to her mouth.

Bree pulled it down. "You don't. She's your mother."

Jane wrapped a remorseful arm around Bree's neck. "I'm sorry. I know you never had a mother. I am selfish, like she says."

"If you were selfish, you'd have moved out long ago." Bree set her back. "Apply to art school."

"Art school?" Jane looked suddenly panicked. "It's a dream, that's all."

"Make it come true. Apply. You'll get in."

"You've never said this before."

"I should have. It's *so possible.*"

"I'm thirty-five. I'd be the oldest in the class."

"I bet you wouldn't be. But even if you are, so what? Apply, Jane. You *will* get in."

"And then what? How will I pay for it? How will I live?"

"*Jane!*" Dotty called from the door of the diner.

Bree held Jane's arm when she would have fled. "Scholarship. Dorm. Job. You can get all of them. Then you'll be free."

Jane looked torn.

"Think about it."

Jane nodded quickly and ran after Dotty, only to stop halfway there and run back. Anger tightened her face. "Don't listen to what she said about having children. Have them now, Bree. You'll make the best mother in the whole wide world."

So Flash didn't want children because he was part child himself. That didn't apply to Bree, who had never really been a child at all.

Verity hadn't had children because the circumstances were wrong. That didn't apply to Bree, either. She was married at the right time to the right man in the right place, with the right amount of love and desire and money.

Julia, bless her soul, had not only loved being pregnant but loved giving birth, which shot a great big hole through the complaints Bree had heard. And Julia was right about Tom. Being a father wouldn't be an imposition on him. He wanted family more than anything. He would thrive.

So would she, Bree knew. Jane was right. She would make a great mother. It didn't matter that she had never had one of her own to learn from. She loved children. She loved Tom. She would love his child. It made sense.

What didn't make sense was how to do it, because if the doctor was right and she couldn't conceive, the only way to achieve it was through a wish. But she still didn't know if the wishes were real. The fire was listed as accidental. The woman in the diner was long gone. Two wishes spent? Or none?

So, okay. She could wish, and nothing might happen. She would know for sure that the wishes weren't real, they could adopt a baby, and that would be that.

But if the wishes were real and this was her third, what then? She could live happily ever after with Tom and his child, and thank God every day that she'd had the courage to take the risk. Or she could die.

A bizarre thought, that one. And totally unfounded. She had no proof that she would die. She didn't even know where she'd gotten the idea.

But given the possibility of it, no matter how remote, was wishing for a child an irresponsible thing to do? A child without a mother—she knew how *that* was. Tom would have the burden of raising it alone.

But Panama was filled with people who loved them. Her wedding had shown her that. And Tom wasn't Haywood. He was strong and outgoing and able. If he was left to raise their child alone, he would have plenty of help.

She didn't want to die. She wanted to be with Tom. She wanted to be with their child. But if she didn't risk a wish, there might be no child at all.

What do I do? she asked the being of light, but it didn't answer. *Are the wishes real? Do I dare?*

In the end it came down to greed. Having Tom's baby was the one thing that could make her life more complete than it was. She tried to talk herself out of it: told herself that what she had with Tom was so much more than most women ever had that she should be satisfied, told herself that they could adopt a baby, told herself that making a third wish wasn't worth the risk.

Then she saw Tom at town meeting, standing to discuss the pros and cons of keeping town positions under the civil service system, and all the while he was talking, his hands were behind his back, doing funny little things to entertain two restless children in the row behind, and she knew. She knew she could debate forever, but the truth was that her heart had already made up her mind. She'd had enough of being sensible and cautious. Expecting the worst was no way to live. These days, she was banking on optimism and hope. These days, she was squeezing the best out of life.

More than anything else, she wanted to give Tom a child. She didn't have to close her eyes to imagine that child. She could see it clear as day, just as she could feel her own joy. That joy justified the risk.

So she did it. That night, after town meeting adjourned, when she was in the bathroom before joining Tom in bed, she laced her fingers together by her chin, closed her eyes tight, and whispered, "I . . . wish . . . to have Tom's child." She pictured the being of light and repeated the words. "I . . . wish . . . to have Tom's child."

For long minutes she stood there, with her heart pounding at the gravity of what she'd done. But the wish was sent. She couldn't take it back. Trembling, she imagined it rising on a starbeam and finding the being of light. As she homed in on that being, its luminescence was as strong as ever before, and soothing. Gradually, the pounding of her heart eased, and her trembling gave way to an overall calm. She drew in a slow, deep, satisfied breath and let it out. Smiling, she combed through her hair, smoothed the silk of her negligee, and went to join Tom.

It happened that night. She was convinced by the sense of fulfillment she experienced as she lay against him afterward. They were both bare and damp. From a microscopic near-nothing deep inside, her body glowed.

She didn't tell him, neither then nor the following week, when a home test confirmed what the tiny dot of heat that glowed more strongly inside her each day told her was true. Nor did she worry. She was committed. There was no turning back.

Between repairing winter's damage to the grounds, preparing the malleable ground for the garage he planned to build, and playing newlywed with Bree, a busy month passed before Tom asked about her period. She had figured he would ask in time. He was always attuned to those days when she was feeling bloated and crampy. "How did I miss it?"

"You didn't." She kept her voice low, her excitement in check, but barely. "It's late."

He was instantly on the alert. "How late?"

"Two weeks." Bits of excitement escaped. "What do you think?"

"I think you should do a test."

"I did. It says I am. But I'm not supposed to be."

Tom made no effort to control his excitement, which was precisely what Bree wanted to hear. "Doctors can be wrong," he said. "It won't be the first time. Did you call him?"

She nodded.

"Why didn't you *tell* me? What did he say?"

"I have an appointment two weeks from now. By then, he can decide it with a physical exam, and I didn't tell you because I don't want us getting our hopes up. He said it'd be a real fluke." She had clung to that thought. A fluke was something that was improbable, that happened rarely but happened nonetheless. It was something that defied the odds but might indeed have happened on its own, without any wish at all.

Tom took her arms. His eyes were wide and bright. "The test said you are. That's incredible."

She nodded again, grinning widely now.

He put a hand on her stomach and said in a hushed voice, "Do you feel it?"

The look on his face was precious, not to mention the awe in his voice. He looked as though he had been given the most precious gift possible, and in that instant, third wish or not, she was so, *so* glad she had done what she had.

She covered his hand. "It's too small to feel yet, but I swear I do. It's a little warm spot in the middle of everything else down there. I've been feeling it since it happened."

"You *have?* And you *didn't tell me?*"

"I thought it was just happiness. Love."

He made a sound deep in his throat, ever so gently took her face in his hands, and, moving his thumbs against her cheeks, said, "You've turned my life around, Bree. Whether you're pregnant or not, you've saved me from a whole other fate. How do I thank you for that?"

By way of answering his own question, he spent those two weeks making Bree the center of his life. He brought her breakfast in bed every morning, gave her flowers, spent his free time at the diner, told her many times a day just how beautiful she looked. When they were in bed, he was hungry, if solicitous, but she had no cause for caution on that score. Her baby had taken root and wasn't being dislodged, and she wanted Tom. There wasn't a time when he turned to her that she wasn't ready. Even when she emerged from a deep sleep to find him hard against her, she was quickly aroused. Her body was extrasensitive, her breasts fuller, her insides moist. She climaxed often and well.

He was spoiling her. She loved every second of it.

Mud season ended with April's lengthening daylight and a gradual hardening of the ground. Tom and Bree spent hours on the bench by the brook, listening to the rush of the water, smelling the promise of spring in the damp ground, watching the return of migrating birds.

Bree had been happy before, but those two weeks gave new meaning to the word. She shared a joy with Tom that was innocent and complete. If, indeed, God had put man on earth for the purpose of procreation, He was smiling on them now. Their life together was rich in satisfaction and love. Bree was back to pinching herself, wondering if it all was real.

Tom didn't question the pregnancy for a minute. Everything that had happened since that October night had been unexpected. This was just one more thing.

But what a wondrous thing it was! He thought he had been the happiest man in the world when Bree set a date for their wedding, but that happiness had been topped on their wedding day, when she appeared at the church looking like a dream, walked down the aisle only to him, and smiled up through tears when he slipped his ring on her finger. They had been married for barely two months, had known each other for barely six, but she was as much a part of his life as his heart.

And now this. A child. Bree's child. Bree's and his.

Paul Sealy was stunned. Returning to his desk after Bree's examination, he looked from one of them to the other, shook his head, blew out a breath. "How to explain it? I've specialized in gynecology for twenty years. Infertility is an increasing problem, often for very new reasons, but this wasn't a situation like that. It was an age-old case of an injury causing scar tissue that would interfere with conception. I've seen dozens of cases like it. In some, surgery solved the problem. Simon and I discussed it. We didn't think that would help here, or we'd have suggested it." He focused on Bree. "We never would have put you through the agony of thinking you couldn't have children if we hadn't thought the chance of it was better than ninety-nine percent." He frowned, puzzled. "I'm usually pretty good at prognoses."

"Is that what it was?" Bree asked. "Ninety-nine percent?"

"I'd have said ninety-nine point five, odds against."

"So I'm the one in two hundred people who got pregnant in spite of the scarring?"

"Looks that way."

"And you're sure she's pregnant?" Tom asked. He knew *she* was sure, could see the conviction in her eyes and her smile, could feel it in her hand, which he held so tight that her fingers would have choked had they been her neck. But he wanted to hear it again.

"Oh, I'm sure," the doctor said, still amazed. "The signs are all there. She's six weeks along. Whew. I'm sorry for the heartache we caused. We messed up."

Damn straight! Tom thought. Bree had come close to not marrying him, because her doctors had messed up. He could strangle them for that, either strangle them or sue them, though he doubted Bree would allow either. Sitting beside him, she was benevolence incarnate.

"No heartache now that a baby's coming," she said in a serene voice.

Tom would share that serenity once he knew a little more. "Is there no scar tissue, then?" he asked the doctor.

"Apparently not as much as I expected."

"Will it affect the pregnancy in any way?"

"It shouldn't. But I think we can plan on taking the baby by cesarean section."

"Why?"

"Her uterus has been cut and repaired. It hasn't had much time to recover. I wouldn't want to risk a rupture during hard labor. A cesarean is no problem, though. We won't even use general anesthesia. A spinal block will do it. Many a woman who delivers vaginally has that." He frowned, tapped a fist in the air, murmured, "I was so sure." With a final head shake, he brought himself back. "I don't foresee any complications with the pregnancy itself. You're perfectly healthy, Bree. You've had an amazing recovery from the accident."

She shot Tom a look that said he was partly responsible. His chest swelled.

Sealy reached for a prescription pad and a pen. "You'll take vitamins daily. Eat a balanced diet. I'll see you monthly until the seventh month and more often after that." He glanced at her record and pulled up a calendar. "As I figure it, you're due . . ." The tip of his pen counted out the weeks. "Too much," he said, with a chuckle, and raised his eyes. "As I figure it, you're due on or about Christmas. I'd say there's magic in that."

I'd say there's magic in that.
Tom heard those words over and over during the ride

back from Ashmont, and with growing concern. If Bree shared that concern, she didn't let on. She was exuberant the whole way. The only thing to upset her was when he refused to let her sit close and belted her in on the passenger side, but she held his hand in both of hers, as though she would float away if she didn't, and she didn't stop beaming.

It was almost enough to make him forget. When she turned her smile on him, he felt the force of it deep inside. He lived to make her happy.

But he kept hearing those words. *I'd say there's magic in that.* And he had to know.

"Bree?"

"What if it's a boy?" she asked in a dreamy voice.

Helplessly, he smiled. "What if it is?"

"He'll look like you."

"He could look like you."

"No-o," she wailed, shaking his hand. "I want a little Tom."

A little Tom. The thought of it made him so proud that he thought he would burst. But there was still the other. "Bree?"

"We'd name him Tom, wouldn't we? Tom, junior?"

"Maybe he should have a name all his own. My mother's family name was Wyatt."

"Wyatt," Bree repeated. "That's a *great* name. If it's a girl, she can be Chloe."

"Chloe. Where did that come from?"

"Nowhere. I just like it. Chloe Gates. It flows. I used to dream of changing my name to Chloe, but I couldn't let go of Bree. It's one of the few things I have of my mother."

Tom knew that she thought about her mother a lot, more so since the incident at the diner. He had actually talked with the private investigator who had helped him on many a case in the past, but they had precious little to work with to decide whether the second wish had come true or not. "Her name wasn't Bree."

"No, but she chose it for me. My grandparents always hated it. Keeping it was one of the few things my father ever did against their wishes. That and going to Boston in the first place. I've always thought Bree was short for something. Brianna, or Brittany. Or Bridget. Can you imagine me as a Bridget?"

He couldn't. Shifting gears, he pulled the truck onto the shoulder of the road.

She twisted to look out the rear window. "What's wrong?"

He parked and faced her. "I need to know something, Bree. Did you wish for the baby?"

She started to blink, caught herself. "Of course I did. I wished ten times over. It's what I want more than anything else in the world."

"But did you *wish?* You know, do the ritual? Did you use your last wish for this?"

"You heard Dr. Sealy. He said my conceiving wasn't an impossibility."

"Bree."

She didn't say anything. She didn't have to. The look on her face said it all.

"Oh, baby," he breathed, feeling a deep, tingling fear. He hooked his arm around her neck, brought her face to his shoulder, and closed his eyes. "Why, Bree? *Why?*"

She clasped a fistful of his flannel shirt. Her voice came from his collar, words spilling fast in argument, as though she was trying to convince herself, too. "Because you'll be the very best father, and because I want your baby, and because if I was given three wishes, I was meant to use them. I don't know where I got the notion that the world would end once I used the last wish. We don't know that at all, and anyway, the more I think about it, the more I say that we're crazy to believe in three wishes. Life doesn't happen like that. When you pull a quarter out of Joey Little's ear, it's sleight of hand. That's all magic is, an illusion, but there's a rational explanation for it. So yes, I made a wish, but that's not why I'm pregnant. I'm pregnant because I love you, and because we wanted it so much, and because we'll be good parents, and because you turn me on so much that my body is entirely open when we make love. Scar tissue didn't have a chance against that."

Tom couldn't help it. He laughed. "Christ, what's medical school in the face of logic like that?"

"I'm serious."

"So am I." His laughter ended. Fear was suddenly a living, breathing thing inside him. "What if you're wrong? What if the wishes *are* real? What if the thing about the third wish is true? What if that really *does* mean . . ." He couldn't finish.

In a quiet voice, she said, "I'm not going to die."

Hearing the word loosed his fear. Wrapping both arms around her, he buried his face in her hair. "If something happened, I'd never forgive myself. I don't want to live without you. I *can't*. You're everything good that's come into my life, everything good that I've become." She was shaking her head no against him, but he believed what he said. "You are. You're my heart and soul. You're my conscience. When I'm with you, I feel more at peace than at any other time in my life. I don't feel driven. I don't feel competitive. I'm a decent person when I'm with you. A *caring* person. A *happy* person. I fell in love with *you,* not with the idea of having a baby. I don't need a baby. If we could go on living just the way we have for the last few months, I'd be happy. The baby's no good without you."

She pushed at him so suddenly that he couldn't hold her. The next thing he knew, her eyes were flashing. "Don't say that. Don't *think* it. That's pretty much what my father thought. I don't *ever* want a child of mine raised that way." She softened, grew pleading, touched his face. "Don't you see? This is what our love is about. It's what lives after *both* of us are gone. We all die, Tom. Sooner or later we do."

He saw her tears and was lost. It was like that every time. When she cried, her emotion became his. "Oh, Bree," he whispered.

"We do."

"But I want it to be later."

"It will be."

"I wish you'd talked with me first." He might have talked her out of it. He might have suggested they try to get pregnant without wishing for it. Of course, they had made love many dozens of times since November. He hadn't once worn a condom. Her body had been entirely open then, too. And she hadn't conceived.

That realization made him all the more fearful.

"You'd have said no," she said.

"Probably."

"So we'd have argued. I thought this all out, Tom. Really I did. I went over every argument, and the ones about *wanting* to have our baby were the best, but then there were the ones about not trying. About not trying and always wondering. About letting ten years go by and still wondering, and regretting, and then finding it was too late to try." She tipped up her chin in defiance. "Besides, it's my body."

Tom cursed liberated women then, but he felt the same little catch inside that he always felt when the bottom line was clear. He wanted to be angry with her, but he loved her too much for that. So he sighed. "Well, it's done. You are pregnant."

Her eyes lit. "I am so happy. Be happy, too."

"How not to be?" he asked. "As long as I don't think."

If he was nothing else, though, Tom was a thinking creature. More, he was a *deliberating* creature. It was the single trait most responsible for his success as a lawyer. He could look at a case from every angle, could analyze every argument and devise a strategy that, nine times out of ten, worked.

So he began deliberating. On trial was the validity of Bree's three wishes. The plaintiff was his own peace of mind. His goal was to prove, beyond the shadow of a doubt, that one of those three wishes had not been granted.

As he interpreted the testimony of the fire inspector, the cause of the fire could never be proved one way or another.

Likewise, given the doctor's suspension of disbelief, the pregnancy.

The one piece of evidence that hadn't been established as clearly, and therefore held the most promise, was the positive identification of Bree's mother.

Chapter

~ 14 ~

Tom had the best of intentions. He called his investigator friend and put him on the case. A few phone calls later, the investigator reported that the little bit of information on Bree's mother that was filed in records at the hospital in Chicago where Bree was born led nowhere, which meant that either the woman had given false information or the address she gave the hospital had been so tentative that no trail remained. Tom put him back to work checking out New York women who drove small red Mercedeses, women who were possibly involved in litigation and who traveled to Montreal on business.

Then life distracted him.

First, there was the weather. Mid-May brought clear skies and warm sun, fragrant apple blossoms, budding trees, and greening grass. Even beyond framing a two-car garage on the far side of the carport, there were chores to do, like replacing storm windows with screens, cutting back trees that were growing too near the house, cleaning the yard, and doing the season's first mowing. The year before, when he was alone and raw, these chores had been therapeutic. This year, they were a pleasure.

Second, there was Bree. How could he dwell on dark fears when she was so happy? She smiled through morning sickness, smiled through afternoon fatigue. She cut back her work hours to four a day and was right there puttering around the house with him, smiling all the while. If she ever thought about a less than happy ending to their story, she didn't let on. She was exhilarated and beautiful. His love for her grew with each day that passed.

Third, there was the phone. It rang more and more often with calls from people wanting legal advice. Those calls came from a growing circle of towns, from families and small-time entrepreneurs with problems that were novel enough to stump their local lawyers. In some instances, Tom shared thoughts off the top of his head. Others required research. He found the thinking a challenge, an easy return to law after a time away, but he never billed a client. That would have made the challenge a job rather than an intellectual exercise. If a case required follow-up, he referred it to Martin Sprague.

Martin proved to be a pleasant surprise. He was a plodding workhorse of a lawyer, making up in follow-through what he lacked in creativity. Tom was pleased to direct work his way, not only because of that, or because the man needed the work, but because Tom was a Panamanian now, and Panamanians supported each other.

Fourth, there was his family. He wanted to tell them about Bree and the baby, but he didn't think he could have borne it if his father hung up again, not when what he had to say was so close to his heart. So he bought a point-and-shoot camera and began writing letters. The first few were short and direct. They included pictures of Bree and him, and while he hoped for a reply, he didn't expect one. Each week, he sent a new letter. By the beginning of June, he was sending pictures of the house with its freshly painted porch and of Bree at the brook. He also dropped notes to his brothers, lighthearted, undemanding little things that said he was thinking of them.

He talked with his sister every few weeks. She had given birth to a boy and was doing well, and, yes, Harris Gates had come around. She thanked Tom for the large package of baby clothes he and Bree had sent. But she didn't invite him to the christening.

Tom didn't blame her. His presence would have detracted from the occasion. But he wasn't holding that against Alice. If anything, he grew more determined to check regularly on the baby and her.

By late June, the investigator had reached a dead end. He had amassed a file of information on New York business-women of the right age who owned sporty red Mercedeses, but Bree couldn't make a positive identification from the photos he offered.

"Not surprising," he said. "The car may be owned by the woman's husband or her boss. It may be leased. I've checked hotels and motels in Montreal, but I can't find the record of a car like that registered at any of the cheap ones on the day in question, and the expensive ones keep their records under lock and key. Times have changed, Tom. Thanks to guys like you suing the pants off them, places like that are locked up tight. And as for the litigation angle, *nada*. It could be she was talking about a friend that day."

Tom wasn't as disappointed as he thought he would be. He was coming around to Bree's thinking that the pregnancy had resulted from natural causes, which meant that the woman at the diner had been no one in particular and that the fire on South Forest had been pure coincidence. The natural-cause approach was the one that made sense, the one any levelheaded man would take.

Being a levelheaded man, though, Tom was cautious. He got second and third opinions from doctors in New York,

who studied Bree's records and agreed with Sealy and
Meade that while the chances of Bree's conceiving were
slim, they had existed. The New York doctors also agreed,
after seeing results of the tests Paul had run on Bree in May,
that she was healthier than many an expectant mother. They
assured Tom that her heart was steady and strong, and saw
no reason whatsoever why Tom should drag Bree to New
York for the birth.

So he pushed away the three-wish theory and espoused
that of natural causes. Natural causes were easier to swallow
than wishes. Natural causes were what he *wanted* to believe,
because his life with Bree was rich. They were rarely apart,
and then only for brief stretches. Many a day, he stayed at
the diner while she worked, and he was seldom the only one
in his booth. He had friends now, friends of hers, friends of
his own. People looking for him knew to find him there. If
the subject was law, he jotted notes on a paper napkin. If
the subject was social, he sat back and relaxed. In both
cases, he was more content than he had ever been, not to
mention within easy reach of Bree.

She was his soul mate. He didn't know another word to
describe it. She thought the way he did, felt the way he did.
They were both small-town people at heart. She had known
it all along. He had simply been longer in the learning.

Her quickness was only one of the things he loved about
her. He had never been in a relationship that was so well
balanced. When he felt like reading, she wanted to read.
When she was hungry, he wanted to eat. When he wanted
to walk in the woods, she was one step ahead. When she
wanted to lie in the sun, he had chairs drawn up before she
had changed her clothes. They went barefoot in the grass
and deep-kissed under the lilacs. They talked and laughed
and read each other's minds, and they rarely argued. She
was his best friend. He would never have imagined a wife
would be that, and it kept getting better.

July brought warmer sun and richer greens. Fireworks lit
Panama's sky on Independence Day, marking the first of an

endless string of summer celebrations. There were concerts on the green, warm evenings spent on nubby blankets, listening to the regional high school's marching band or singing along with Panama's barbershop quartet. There were cookouts in the lot behind the town hall, softball games in the schoolyard, a make-your-own-sundae orgy to introduce Panama Rich's twenty-fourth flavor, Oooey Gooey, which was a concoction of vanilla and mocha ice creams, caramel, fudge, marshmallow, and nuts. Even on evenings when nothing formal was planned, people gathered on the town green.

Tom bought a more sophisticated camera. It became a regular at his side, in his hand, at his eye. He photographed Bree in profile in the morning sun, with one hand on the new swell of the baby and a dreamy look in her eye. She had started wearing maternity clothes—early, she said, but her other clothes were too tight in the bust and belly, and besides, she admitted proudly, she felt pregnant and wanted to *look* it. He photographed her in every imaginable pose at home, photographed her in a huddle with Flash and LeeAnn at the diner and laughing with Jane and Julia on a bench on the green. He photographed the barber through the front window of his shop, the bread truck loading up for a day's deliveries, the bottlers at Sleepy Creek Ale taking a cool beer break in the parking lot of the brewery at day's end.

In its summer mode, the diner offered fresh lemonade and lime rickeys, soft-serve frozen yogurt, and iced cappuccinos. The Daily Flash listed two cold salads for every hot special and promoted Oooey Gooey. Picnic tables covered the grass in front of the diner. Sandwiches to go were the rage.

The sounds of Panama were of lawn mowers, sprinklers, and fun, the scents were of warm grass, hazy sunshine, and grilled chicken. For Tom, though, the essence of the season was captured by the Panama Rich ice cream truck with its jingle-jangle bell, its pied piper following, and the old-fashioned ice cream sandwiches it sold, meant to be eaten from the outer edges in.

The dog days of August had set in when Martin Sprague called and invited Tom to his office for a meeting. Ostensibly, the topic of discussion was a case Tom had referred. But he had never been asked to the office before.

On the second floor of the Federal that housed the bank, it consisted of two rooms overlooking the town green. One room was for a secretary, who wasn't there when Tom arrived. The other room was for Martin. It had the smell of old papers and the look of a man who was busier than he had expected to be. Folders lay in odd spots beside books that bulged where random objects had been inserted to mark a place. A standing fan, slowed by the heat, swiveled sluggishly from side to side. Only the computer that sat on a small side cabinet looked fresh, as much a guest there as Tom.

"It's not much," Martin said, with an awkward look around. "But it serves my needs."

He gestured Tom into one of two straight-back chairs and went to sit behind the desk. After pulling out a handkerchief and mopping his forehead, he jumped back up and opened the cabinet under the computer. It proved to be a small refrigerator. "Cold drink?"

"Sure."

Even with the fan, the office was warm. Four windows were open, two on either side of the wall behind the desk, but there was no breeze coming in off the green. Tom wore the T-shirt and denim cut-offs that were the summer uniform in Panama. Martin was the only man in town who wore a suit at any time of year. This day, mercifully, his shirt sleeves were short.

"You can have root beer or root beer," he said. Straightening, he handed one of two bottles to Tom. Then he returned to the desk and opened the nearest folder.

"The Ulrich business. I got your notes. You're right. It's a standard age-discrimination case, but the thing is that what you're suggesting involves going to court, and I don't do that. So I've been sitting here thinking that I could call Don Herrick over in Montgomery and he could take it to court, but then I said that that didn't make sense, not with you living right here in town and looking like you're going to stay. Are you?"

Tom could see that Martin was uneasy, but it seemed a different uneasiness from the one that, months earlier, had had the man warning him off. There was more curiosity than resistance this time.

"I'm staying."

Martin pushed the Ulrich folder out of the way and ferreted another from the pile. He opened it and fished through the papers there. Gruffly, without looking at Tom, he said, "I did some calling. You practiced for more than five years in New York, so you don't have to take any test to get admitted to the bar here. You have to file an application and do a clerkship. That's three months working under a local lawyer, someone like me. You're pretty much already doing that." He raised his root beer but set it back down without drinking. Both hands grasped the corners of the papers before him. "So," he said, looking anywhere but at Tom, "what do you think?"

Tom was stunned.

"And don't say you don't know local law," Martin grumbled, "because you do by now. You've done as much work for me in a handful of months as a kid out of law school does in a year. Local law? Hell, it's *national* law, more and more. And *don't* say most of this stuff isn't your field, because you did well enough with it in spite of that. You were the one who hooked the paper company up with investors and helped them avoid a takeover. So that's not your field. There's other stuff that is. Well?"

Tom held the cold drink can to the fast-beating pulse at

his wrist. "I wasn't planning on practicing law when I came here."

"That's what you said."

"It wasn't just words. I meant it. I'm not looking to take away from your practice."

Martin waved a resigned hand. "They're going to you for different things. Things I can't do. Things I don't want to do. They'll keep coming to me for their wills and estates, and their mortgage problems, and their lease agreements, but if I don't get help on the rest"—his bewildered gaze encompassed the papers on the desktop—"they'll go to someone else. It occurs to me"—he shot Tom a skittish glance—"you could do your thing and I could do my thing and we'd have a corner on the market. Know what I mean?" He sniffed.

"I think so."

"Hell, if we don't do the work, someone else will, and I'd rather the money be in our pockets. Course, the money's not like New York money. Nor's the practice. You already know the kinds of cases we get up here. Pretty tame, by comparison. Could be you'd be bored."

Tom doubted it. "I have a life besides law here. I don't want to work the way I did in New York." He felt no competitiveness, no driving hunger. Practicing law in Panama would be more fun than work.

"All these cases, and you never asked for a referral fee," Martin said.

"I'm not in it for the money."

"It isn't right. I say we make an agreement. You fill out an application to join the Vermont Bar and do your clerkship with me. You keep whatever money you bring in, after expenses." He sat back with a there-it-is, take-it-or-leave-it look on his face.

Tom found himself smiling. As agreements went, it was refreshingly simple.

Martin mopped his forehead. "I can put you in the next room and put Celia in a room down the hall."

"I have an office at home. I can work there." He glanced at the computer. "Is that functional?"

"It is. I'm not. And I won't promise to be. I don't trust those things. Look, this isn't the fiftieth floor of some skyscraper. It's the second floor of a building that's got no air-conditioning in a town that's got nothing but volunteers in its fire department. The clients don't come in wearing fancy clothes, and if you want to take them to lunch, it's Flash's or nothing. We're not fancy here, but we have legal needs, too."

"It's a deal," Tom said, feeling pleased.

Martin looked surprised. "You don't want to think about it?"

"Nah. It's good."

Martin scowled. "Don't think you can do your clerkship and then open up a separate office down the street from me, because I'm putting a noncompetition clause into our agreement. And *don't* think you can move in here and take everything over yourself in two years when I croak, because I'm only sixty-six. I'm not croaking so fast."

"I hope not. The last thing I want to do is wills and estates and mortgages and leases. I'll handle the other stuff."

"You're satisfied with that?"

"Yes."

Martin rose from his seat only enough to stick out his hand. Tom shook it, and it was done.

Incredibly, Martin smiled. It was an odd smile, tight but pleased. Closing the Ulrich folder, he passed it over and sat back. "There's something else I need you to do." He took a swig of his root beer, set the bottle down, ran a hand back over thin hair. "It's a touchy situation. There's a woman in Des Moines wants to hire me. Her mother's living here. Julia Dean?"

At mention of Des Moines, Tom had immediately pictured Julia. "Yes?"

"Eliot knows about this. The son called him not long ago. He said he told you."

Tom nodded. "I told him that the son had to work through authorities in Des Moines if he wanted to claim mishandling of a trust fund."

"He's decided not to do that until he has evidence against his mother." He paused, made a face. "Evidence against his *mother?*" He grunted his disapproval. "The daughter's angle is to hire someone local to observe Julia and report on her instability."

"Instability?" Tom would have laughed if Martin weren't so serious. "Bree and Julia have become close. From what I've seen, Julia's entirely stable."

"I always thought so myself, but I figured if I didn't look into it, the daughter would hire someone else, and I'd rather give Julia an edge with me. Or with you."

"We're not psychiatrists."

"The daughter didn't ask for one. She said anyone with two eyes would do. She told me to hire whoever. I'm hiring you. So to speak."

Tom had defended many guilty people in his day. It had been his job to force the prosecution to prove his client guilty beyond the shadow of a doubt. Along the way, he had made mincemeat of witnesses who testified against him, had discredited the creditable, besmirched the innocent. In some instances, those witnesses suffered afterward. He knew of several who had lost jobs as the result of doubts he had cast on their testimony, others whose marriages were hurt—and those were only the ones he *knew*. During the first months of his self-imposed exile, he had given thought to those he *didn't* know and felt more than a little guilt.

Determined not to repeat his sins, he didn't skulk around watching Julia Dean. That wouldn't do in as small a town as Panama, where people saw things and talked. The mail Julia received created gossip enough. He didn't want to give fodder for more.

Julia was well liked. Flash wasn't the only one to rave about her work, though he did so on a regular basis—and she was regular herself, arriving like clockwork every Tuesday and Friday to arrange fresh flowers in the diner's vases. Tom had never heard a derogatory word spoken about her, had never seen anything to suggest mental upset, much less instability. He didn't want her hurt by even the hint of suspicion.

So he began by calling her daughter in the hope that a talking-to would appease the woman, but Nancy Anderson was upset. She proceeded to repeat much of what the son had told Eliot the first time around. "She hasn't been herself since my father died. When I ask her what's wrong, she denies anything is, but I know my mother, Mr. Gates. She spent a lifetime hating to travel. She always liked staying home. Then my father died, and she packed up and moved halfway across the country to a town where she knows no one."

"She knows people here now. She knows everyone in town. Maybe she just needed to make a change."

"She always hated change."

"Your father's death forced a change," Tom pointed out. He wasn't playing therapist, was simply expressing pure common sense. "It's possible that she couldn't bear to stay there doing the same things as always but without him."

"No. It's something else. She was so determined when she moved. It's like one day she just snapped. And then there's the trust fund."

"Do you or your brother need money? Is that the problem?"

"No, but what if we do someday? My father left that for us. There was enough so that she could live off the interest, only she isn't. But that's not the main reason we're doing this," she insisted. "We're worried."

Tom didn't doubt it. Judging from Nancy Anderson's voice, she was legitimately bewildered and more than a little hurt. "There's no cause for worry. She has a very nice life here."

"A *flower* shop?"

"Is that out of character, too?"

"No. She used to grow flowers in the yard. She used to *dance* out there. Flowers do something to her. They make her wild. You can understand why I'm worried."

Tom had seen Bree dance through wildflowers by the brook. He still held the image, clear as day and sweet.

"Does she have a man there?" Julia's daughter asked. "Because if a man is behind her taking that money, it *really* worries me."

"There's no man that I know of. The grapevine would have said if there were. Have you asked her about the money?"

"I can't. She'll think that's all I'm worried about, and it isn't. Really it isn't."

"What, exactly, do you want us to do on this end?"

"Watch her. The police chief wouldn't do anything. So I'm prepared to pay to have the job done. I want someone to look at her closely and see how she is."

"Why don't you? Why don't you fly out for a visit?"

"I wanted to when she first moved there, but she told me not to. Each time I mention it, she waves a hand and says it's easier for her to visit us here. I think she's hiding something."

"There may not be anything illegal in that."

"Or there may be. We want to know why she's doing what she is."

Tom suspected that a good mother-daughter heart-to-heart would solve the problem, but he was a fine one to talk. His father had hung up on him once, and he hadn't called again. Parent-child relationships involved great emotional risk, regardless of the ages of the parties involved.

"I have to tell you, Mrs. Anderson," he warned, "Julia has many friends in this town. She's known for being kind, talented, and reliable. I don't think you'll find anyone here willing to say she isn't stable." Mindful that the daughter might go elsewhere if she didn't get what she wanted from him, he bought time by adding, "I'll find out what I can. In the meantime, I want you to consider the possibility that your mother just needed to try something new. All right?"

Tom drove to the flower shop after he dropped Bree at work. A sign on the door said that Julia was weeding in the garden out back, and sure enough, there she was, sitting in the flower beds looking perfectly content, with a misshapen straw hat on her head and the occasional bee humming about.

She was an attractive woman, slim and of average height. Her brown hair was streaked with silver, but it remained thick. When she pulled it up into a clip, as she often did when delivering flowers to the diner, she looked a decade younger than the fifty-something she was. The peaceful look she wore helped.

Tom smiled. He liked Julia. More, he identified with her. She, too, had come to Panama knowing no one and had made a life for herself here. Unstable? Hell, from the look of her, she was rock solid and thriving.

When she spotted him, he glanced at the low ceiling of clouds. "You're taking your chances."

"Chances of what?" she answered, with a smile. "Getting wet? I won't melt. This time of year, it's cooler working under clouds than sun. How's Bree?"

"Fine. She's at the diner."

"She told me the morning sickness ended."

"Finally."

"It was worse on you than on her, I imagine. Men suffer during pregnancies."

"Thank you," he said appreciatively.

She tipped her head back to see him better from under the hat. "Are you here for flowers?"

"I'm here for you." He swatted at a hovering bee. "Can we talk while you work?"

"Of course," she said, but she set her weeding fork aside and tugged off her gloves. Her serenity wavered. "Is something wrong?"

He settled on a nearby patch of grass. "Martin Sprague got a call from your daughter. She's worried about you."

With a single definitive nod, Julia sighed. "Why doesn't that surprise me?"

"She doesn't understand why you're doing what you are."

"What did she want Martin to do?"

"Give an unbiased opinion of your mental state."

"For what purpose?" Julia asked, then said, "Don't answer. I don't want to hear." She pushed the hat back with her wrist. "I spent the better part of thirty years doting on Nancy and Scott. They can't understand why I'm not doing it still."

"Why aren't you?"

"Because they're adults. Nancy is thirty, Scott is twenty-eight. They're both married, both parents themselves. They don't need me. At least they shouldn't."

"Your daughter says she saw a change when your husband died."

"No doubt. Teddy died a slow, painful death. He was only fifty-two. I had been in love with him since I was ten. Then he was gone, and I needed to be someplace where I didn't see his face all the time."

"Why Panama?"

"There was no flower shop."

"Did you look at other towns?"

"I didn't have to, once I found Panama." A bee flew near. She gracefully waved it off. "My children think this was a sudden decision on my part. They might not understand the truth, which is that during the last months of Teddy's life, he was so sick and sitting by his bedside was so painful for me that the only way I could survive was by daydreaming. I studied maps and did my research and made my plans. I loved him with all my heart, and I buried a part of me with him, but the rest of me needed to move. Does that sound callous?"

It didn't to Tom. Nor did it sound like the voice of an unstable woman.

Reaching sideways, Julia bare-handedly tore a clump of weeds from the ground. She tossed the clump into a half-filled bag. Brushing off her hands, she asked, "Did she tell you about the trust fund?"

Tom nodded.

"That *really* has them hot and bothered. Oh, they don't come out and say it. They say things like, 'Isn't setting up a business risky at your age?' Like I have one foot in the grave," she drawled. "It's my fault, I suppose. When we knew Teddy was dying and were trying to get used to the idea, I kept telling them about the trust fund because I wanted them to know that Teddy had provided for them. Here, too, they may not understand the truth."

"Which is?"

"That Teddy meant for me to use as much or as little of that money as I wanted. He put it in writing. I have a copy of that paper. So does our lawyer. The children won't go to him, because he was a close friend of Teddy's and mine, and they're sure he'll side with me. But we both do have copies of that paper." She ran her palm over a pool of orangy-pink impatiens. "I bought the house here with what I got from my house in Des Moines, but I dipped into the trust fund to set up the shop. There's plenty left for my children." She turned beseeching eyes on Tom. "For years I gave them everything I could, even when there were things I wanted that I couldn't have. For years I put them first. Now it's my turn."

"Have you told Nancy that?"

"In gentler terms. But she doesn't hear, and her brother goads her on."

"Would you like me to talk to her? Explain a little of that?"

Julia grew hopeful. "Would you?"

"Should I mention the paper your husband left?"

"If you have to." She smiled a silent thanks. "You're a good man, Tom. Bree is lucky to have you. Unless people are right and her father became so withdrawn that he couldn't see beyond himself, he would have liked you, too."

"He was a tough man."

"Unsatisfied. From what I hear."

"Lovesick. From what *I* hear. He never got over Bree's mother."

A distant roll of thunder drew Julia's head around. "Maybe if he'd been a stronger man," she said when she looked back at Tom.

"Or if she'd been a stronger woman," he countered. "What would possess a woman to walk away and never look back?"

"She may have had good reason."

"*Good* reason?"

Julia arched a brow at his sarcasm. "Things aren't always as they seem, Tom. Take your reasons for coming here now. My children say that because I left them and moved away, something's wrong with my mind. But the reasons I gave you make sense, don't they? So maybe Bree's mother had reasons, too."

He scratched his head. "Yeah, well, it's hard for me to come up with a scenario that makes her a saint."

"None of us are saints. The truth usually lies somewhere in the middle."

He leaned back on the heels of his hands. "What's the middle ground here? What could possibly justify a woman's leaving her baby with its father and dropping off the face of the earth?"

Julia looked bemused. "Well, I don't know."

"Guess."

She frowned, shook her head, shrugged. "Maybe she had other ties, other responsibilities?"

"No tie could be as strong as the one between mother and child. Unless she already had a family. But if she did, she had no business carrying on with Haywood Miller in the first place."

Julia responded sadly. "You do sound like my kids. If I didn't know better, I'd think I was talking to one of them right now."

"Okay. So I'm being judgmental. I'm angry on Bree's behalf. If the woman wasn't free, she shouldn't have been with Haywood. If she was already married, she was cheating on her husband."

"So it would seem. But we don't know the particulars."

Tom's face hardened. "I've been trying to learn the particulars. I've tried to locate her, but I can't. She's done one hell of a job covering her tracks."

"After how many years?"

He conceded the point. Thirty-three years was a long time. With most of those years predating the age of computers, a track wouldn't need much covering. It would easily fade on its own.

Another roll of thunder came, still distant, but louder than the last. Julia raised her voice. "So focus on what you *do* know. See if any sense comes from that."

"All we know for sure is that the woman came from California, that she met Haywood in Boston, and that she gave birth to Bree in Chicago."

"Were they together the whole time she was pregnant?"

"The grapevine says they were."

"So where was her husband?"

Tom sighed in frustration. "You tell me."

Julia took him literally. "Somewhere else entirely, I'd guess. Maybe he was a traveling salesman. Or in the service." She frowned. "This would have been in the sixties?"

"Early sixties."

A furrow of pain crossed her face. "The first of our men were already lost in Vietnam by 1962."

Tom was drawn to her expression. "I thought it was later."

"No. It started then." She smiled sadly. "No great mystery how I know, Tom. My husband was among the first to be sent there. You can't imagine what it's like, the not knowing, the worrying. I knew women whose husbands were missing in action. That's a devastating thing. It leaves a woman feeling lost and alone."

"And vulnerable? Is that what you're suggesting? Vulnerable enough to fall into another man's arms?"

"It's possible. Don't you think?"

"But even so," Tom persisted, coming forward, folding his legs, elbows on knees. "Even allowing for the possibility of a war widow finding comfort with another man, why would she leave him once she had his baby?"

"Honestly, Tom, how would *I* know? All I'm suggesting is that you're doing just what my kids are doing. You're assuming the worst. Like the story between me and my kids, maybe there's more to this one that would make you see her choice differently." She waved a hand. "I mean, for the sake of the argument, what if a woman was told that her husband had died at war, and then it turned out that the report was wrong, that he wasn't dead and was coming home, just like in the movies. It happens, you know, and stranger things than that. Would you still be so angry?"

Tom softened, but only a tad. "Even so, even if there was something as far-fetched as that to explain it—thirty-three years without a word? We're back to square one. Even if she had reason to leave, how could she abandon the child without a trace?"

Julia nodded sympathetically. "You're right. We're back to square one. There are endless possibilities—we could speculate for days. Without more details, we can't ever know for sure why she left her child." She paused, seeming again to want to stick up for the woman, as she had done for herself minutes before. "Have you considered the possibility that this wasn't solely the woman's choice? Maybe the baby's father had a say. Maybe he made her leave."

"Why would he do that?"

"Hurt. Anger. You're a man. You tell me. Maybe refusing her contact with the child was his way of punishing her."

"But Haywood died three years ago," Tom argued. "If that were it, wouldn't she have shown up now that he's dead?"

"Maybe she's dead, too. Or maybe she *has* shown up."

"Ah. The woman in the diner. But you were there. You overheard what she said. You were convinced she wasn't Bree's mother."

"Maybe *she* wasn't. Strangers are in and out of the diner all the time. Bree's mother could have been one of them. For all we know, she's passed through here every summer since Haywood died just to look at Bree and see how she's doing. For all we know, she passed through here summers for years *before* that, too."

"Without identifying herself?"

"Sure. It'd be risky to come forward after all that time, don't you think?"

"Because of Bree? Bree is the kindest, most gentle woman in the world."

Julia replied slowly. "You didn't see her with that woman, Tom. She was very angry. I've never seen her like that before."

"Do you blame her?"

"Not at all. She missed having a mother. She has a right to that anger."

"I'll say," Tom avowed. With the first large, spattering drop of rain, he unfolded his legs.

Rising beside him, Julia brushed at the seat of her pants. "I don't envy the woman. It's a sad situation. Truly." She bent to retrieve her weeding fork.

Tom grabbed the bag full of weeds, and they set off for the shop. When the raindrops came faster, they quickened their steps, running at the end. They were laughing by the time they were inside.

"Look at it *pour*," Julia said, giving her hat a good shake as she peered through the rain. "But this is good. My flowers need it. I'm doing a wedding in Montgomery next week. I want the lilies to look their best."

"Business is good?"

"Business is fine."

"Do you enjoy it?"

"Yes. I've always been a flower person. Put me in a room with fresh roses, and I get a little high."

Free association took Tom from picturing Julia high on roses, to seeing her dancing through flower beds, to recalling the original reason for his visit. "I'll give Nancy a call and tell her we've talked. I can probably convince her to ease off a little. It would be even better if you two sat down together. If it's her brother who's getting her wound up, she needs someone giving her the other side. When will you be seeing her again?"

"Thanksgiving."

"Don't want to do it sooner?"

Julia shook her head. "I'll warn you now. She's upset because I told her I wouldn't come for Christmas, too. I have every other year. But this year I want to be here. I wouldn't miss the birth of your baby for the world."

Thinking of Christmas, Tom felt alternately exhilarated and terrified. "Bree's delivering by cesarean section. I thought the doctor might set a date, but he wants her to go into labor on her own. She could be late. Maybe you should rethink that."

"No. I want to be here."

Tom didn't argue this time. Something in her eye said she wasn't budging.

* * *

As soon as he returned to the house, Tom called Nancy Anderson. He described his visit with Julia and did his best to paint a picture of the contentment he had seen. When Nancy mentioned the trust fund once, then a second and third time, he told about the paper her father had signed. She seemed almost relieved. Tom imagined she was grateful to have an argument to give her brother.

A good lawyer never became personally involved with his client. It was a basic rule. But Nancy wasn't actually his client, since no money had exchanged hands, and he cared deeply for Julia. So he offered to meet her at the airport, if Nancy chose to come for a visit.

Chapter

~ 15 ~

*D*ear Dad, Tom wrote in early September.

Hard to believe that Labor Day has come and gone. I took the enclosed pictures at the town's celebration—a huge barbecue held in a pumpkin field. The pumpkins weren't quite ready for harvest, but that was the point. The whole town showed up to cheer them on. That's Bree in the first picture, with our friends the Littles and their kids. That's Bree in the second picture with the troika who run the town—left to right, the police chief, the postmaster, and the town meeting moderator. In the third picture, Bree is with her friends Angus, Oliver, and Jack, and her boss, Flash. Flash is a good soul. You'd like him. He isn't thrilled with Bree right now, since she's cut back to working only a few hours a day, but I don't like her on her feet all day when there's no need for her to work at all.

She didn't want me sending the next picture. She says she looks fat. I say she looks pregnant and beautiful. She's just starting her sixth month. She's gained ten pounds and is feeling great. We love listening to the baby's heartbeat.

The doctor is afraid we'll start making extra appointments just to use his stethoscope, and I don't rule it out. That heartbeat is something else. So's the baby's movement. We can actually see it now, a definite ripple. I guess after six kids you got pretty used to that, but this is my first.

You'll be pleased to know that I'm getting back to practicing law. A local lawyer and I are working together. It's an apprenticeship for me, since I'm not a member of the Vermont Bar. I've applied for that, though, and hope to be sworn in in another few months.

Practicing here is different from practicing in New York. The cases aren't blockbuster ones, but they deal with real people and real problems. In that sense, they're more rewarding. Also, practicing here allows for a gentler lifestyle. I'm working out of an office at home, which is a five-minute drive from my mentor's office in town. And I'm really only working part time, so that I can spend the rest of the time with Bree. I want to be involved in raising the baby. It'll work this way.

When I finally unpacked the cartons that were piled in my office, I found the family photographs that I framed when I first started to practice. Among them was one of all of us taken at my high school graduation. Do you remember it? We were on the front porch getting ready to leave, and Minna came from next door to take the picture so Mom could be in it, too. It's one of the few of all of us. I have it on my desk.

I hope you're well. I'll write again soon.

Love, Tom

Dear Alice, Bree wrote in mid-September.

Thank you so, so, so much for sending the picture of little Jimmy. He is precious. I see you in him, and even a little of Tom. Tom stood looking at the picture for the longest time. He still keeps picking it up. So you know how much it means to him that you sent it.

THREE WISHES

Only three and a half months of waiting left for us. I go back and forth between being so impatient I can't sit still and being terrified. I don't tell Tom about the terrified part. It's silly, isn't it? I mean, doctors have childbirth down pat. What could go wrong? We had amniocentesis done, so we know that the baby's healthy, but we didn't ask for the sex. We want that to be a surprise. It's kind of neat that our kids will be less than a year apart, don't you think?

We've been working to get the baby's room ready. Tom sanded and lacquered the floor. He painted the ceiling white and the walls yellow. I made a clown border with stencils using navy blue, white, and red, so it'll be good for a boy or a girl. Believe it or not, Tom stood at the bottom of the ladder the whole time I was painting it. He was afraid I'd fall.

We've also started buying a few things. Thank you for the recommendation on the carriage. We bought it, and a crib. The crib is white. I start crying every time I look at it.

I know Tom has asked you himself, but I would love it, too, if you would come visit. I was an only child. The idea of having a sister-in-law is wonderful. We have a sleep sofa in the third bedroom, and a crib for Jimmy. I know that your father wouldn't like the idea of your coming, but if there's any way you can get around that, please consider it. It would mean a lot to me to meet you before our baby is born. It would mean a lot to Tom, too. Say the word, and he'll send tickets. You could fly into Burlington or Boston. We'll meet you in either place. Just let us know.

The trees are starting to turn. It's just beautiful up here. Please come.

Love, Bree

P.S. My stretched stomach itches something fierce. Any suggestions?

Dear Nathan, Tom wrote in early October.

I enjoy getting your little notes. Being out of the main-stream, I didn't know that my favorite publisher was fired, much less that the publishing house was bought. I didn't know that Ben Harps's book hit the lists, either. I'm pleased for him and pleased for you. Maybe someone like Ben can get you to stop E-mailing me. He's young and hot. If you haven't sold him to Hollywood yet, you will. His stuff is good.

I know I told you I'd think about writing again, and I have. But it isn't going to happen, Nathan, not now, maybe not ever. Drop all the hints you want, but you won't make me jealous of Ben or anyone else.

I've gone back to practicing law. Yes, up here. Don't be so startled. It's like going back to my roots. Very satisfying. Bree is expecting a baby in December, so there's plenty to keep me busy. I'm happier than I've ever been. Be happy for me.

Yours, Tom

Dear Dad, Tom wrote in mid-October.

Bree and I spent last weekend in Nantucket. These pictures are from there. The one of the two of us was taken by the owner of the bed-and-breakfast where we stayed. It was a charming place, small and quiet on a private way that led to the beach. We spent hours walk-ing there and browsing through the shops in town. Bree had never been there. Her excitement made it like the first time for me, too.

A funny thing happened. When we stopped in at a lit-tle sandwich place, I was recognized by a woman who interviewed me several years back for Vanity Fair. *She came right up and started asking questions. Two years ago, I would have answered. This time, I refused. I may have offended her, but I don't care. I'm done with that life. All I could think was that she was intruding on my time with my wife.*

258

Bree is wonderful. She's starting to look very preg-
nant and has trouble keeping going endlessly the way
she used to, but she doesn't complain. She's a trouper
—the warmest, most interesting and loving woman I've
ever met. Based on past performance, I don't deserve
her. I'm trying to change that.

We had cause to celebrate in Nantucket. It was the
first anniversary of the accident that brought us to-
gether. It scares me to think how close I came to losing
her. Had she died that night, I never would have known
this kind of love. Okay, if I hadn't known it, I wouldn't
have missed it, but boy, it makes me think.

If you felt for Mom what I feel for Bree, I can under-
stand why you were so hurt by what I did. If a child of
mine ever did that to Bree, I would be angry, too. All I
can say is that I didn't know, and that I'm sorry.

Enclosed is a small painting done by one of the
local artists on the island. The view of the dunes is one
that we saw each day. I hope you can get a feel for it
through the oils.

Love, Tom

P.S. We're out of double digits. Only nine weeks until the
baby is due.

With eight weeks to go, Bree was sitting in the breakfast
room, feeling lazy and replete in the morning sun, when the
phone rang. Setting the newspaper aside, she rose to get it.

"Hello?"

"Bree?" The voice was tentative, new. "This is Alice."

Bree caught her breath. "Alice." There was only one
person with that name. "Alice," she breathed, half relieved,
half awed. "How *are* you?"

"Feeling like a traitor, but otherwise fine. I got my editor
to send me to a seminar in Boston. I just landed."

"In *Boston?*" Bree's voice went higher. "Tom will be *so excited!* Can we see you? Will you come here? Where can we pick you up? How long do you have?"

"Three days. I have the baby with me."

"Oh my God! Tom'll *die* when he finds out. He just left to meet with his law partner in town. I'll call him there. We can be on our way in less than an hour. You should have called before you left. We'd have been there to meet you."

"I didn't know if I'd have the courage to call. I'm not sure I should be doing this."

"Of course you should."

"My father wouldn't be pleased."

"You're not making *him* come."

"This is pretty last-minute."

"Are you kidding? Tom's been dreaming of this for *months.*" So had Bree, more so of late. "Will you come back here with us?"

"If it's no trouble."

"None. Where should we meet you?"

They arranged to meet at the downtown hotel where the seminar was being held. While Tom and Bree were en route, Alice attended two lectures. When they arrived, she was sitting in the lobby, as petite as Bree had pictured her, with Tom's shiny brown hair and gray eyes. The baby was a sleeping wad strapped to her front.

Bree was entranced by the look on Tom's face when he first saw her. It combined longing and love with intense relief. He stopped just inside the revolving door. Alice rose. She didn't come toward them, but her unsureness ended his. He crossed the space in seconds, wrapped her in his arms, baby and all, and held them both for a long, silent time.

The forty-eight hours that they had together couldn't have been more perfect. As Boston fell behind mile by mile, so did the hard feelings that had kept them apart. By the time they reached Panama, all awkwardness was gone. The town was a pocket that the past couldn't touch.

Tom wanted to show Alice the town green, the church where he and Bree had been married, the office above the bank. Bree wanted to show her the town hall, where their wedding reception had been held, the general store, and the diner. Alice wanted to see the bungalow, the bench by the brook, the pumpkin field where the Labor Day barbecue had taken place.

They saw it all. The weather was perfect, the foliage vivid even a week past its peak. Townsfolk waved as they drove by and approached when they stopped. Alice's enthusiasm matched Tom's pride. Both matched Bree's happiness. She couldn't even be envious of Tom's intimate ease with his sister, because Alice was just as easy with her. In no time at all, she felt she had known Alice forever.

They spent time at the bungalow and time at the diner. Tom baby-sat Jimmy while Bree took Alice to meet Julia, and when they should have returned, they traded grins instead and went to Verity's cottage in the woods.

Alice was spirited and fun. Bree adored her.

And the baby? What could Bree say? He was smiley and sweet, wanting nothing more than dry diapers, mother's milk, and the occasional bit of attention. Tom gave him far more than that, uncle and nephew a sight to behold. If Bree had even the tiniest lingering doubt about having risked a third wish on their own child, it was dispelled by the sight of Tom stretched out on the floor, watching in fascination while the baby played inches away.

All too quickly, Alice's time in Panama ended. With Boston's approach, mile by mile, came threads of sadness.

"Will you tell Dad you saw us?" Tom asked.

"Not yet. But he isn't indifferent. He reads your letters, reads them more than once. And he studies the pictures."

"Will he talk if I call?"

"I don't know. He visits the cemetery twice a week.

That's when he comes home all stoic and hard. I'll work on him, Tom. I can't promise anything more than that." She hugged him, then opened her arms to Bree with a what-can-I-say expression.

Bree held her tight. "Thank you," she whispered. "You've made him so happy by coming. Him *and* me." Alice would be a wonderful aunt to her child. Bree felt a profound sense of relief knowing that Tom and the baby would have family, should anything happen to her.

By the end of October, Bree stopped waitressing. She went to the diner every day, but what work she did was either by computer or by phone. Before and after, she sat talking with friends.

"Only two months left," Jane said. They sat side by side at the counter, having late-morning muffins and tea. "Can you stand it?"

"Barely."

"You look good."

"I feel good." She truly did—strong, energetic, and happy, so happy sometimes that she burst into tears. Waking up beside Tom each day was a dream, all the more so waking up *pregnant* beside him each day. Julia had been right about the joy of pregnancy, though Bree figured the father-to-be made the difference. Tom loved everything about her pregnant body. Rarely did a night pass when he didn't remove her nightgown to run his hands, ever so slowly, over the mound of her belly. He loved the fullness of her breasts, loved the bump of her navel and the vertical line beneath it. He loved putting his ear to the baby and listening, and she loved pushing her hands into his hair or rubbing his bare shoulders and watching them, father and child.

If only there weren't that fear. It came and went, a scary little shred. She was seeing the doctor twice a month now. He swore all was just as it should be. The baby was bigger and more active. But December neared.

"I want everything to go well," she told Jane.

"What's not to go well?"

She fiddled with the crumbs on her plate. "Remember I told you about the three wishes?"

Jane nodded.

"I think this was one."

"The *baby?*"

"After the accident, the doctor told me I couldn't have kids."

"Oh, Bree. You didn't tell me that."

"I didn't tell anyone. I didn't want to think about it. I told Tom before we got married. He was furious when I told him I wished for a baby."

"Why? What better thing to wish for?"

"It might have been the third wish." When the look on Jane's face said she still didn't get it, Bree added, "There's a part of me that thinks I was put back on earth for Tom and the wishes, and that once the third one is granted, I'll die."

"That's *crazy,*" Jane scolded. She lowered her voice, but the fire remained. "Don't say it, don't think it, don't *breathe* it."

"I can't *help* it," Bree cried. Most of the time she believed that the pregnancy had happened on its own, but there was no way she could be absolutely, positively sure that the wishes hadn't been involved. She wrapped her fingers around Jane's arm. "Promise me you'll be there for Tom and the baby if anything happens."

"Don't even *mention* the possibility—"

"Promise me, Jane. You're my best friend. I want you to say it."

"I'll be there, but it won't be necessary. Nothing's going to happen. You'll fly through the delivery. Afterward you and I will sit here and *laugh* that you thought for even *one minute* what you just thought." She shivered. "God, Bree, that's *awful.*"

But Bree felt better with Jane's promise secured. Dark

images faded. Only bright ones remained. She smiled at those. "I'm okay now."

Jane eagerly changed the subject. "The shower's going to be at Abby's house. She insisted, and since the Nolans have the nicest house on the green, and since Abby's babysitter can watch the other kids, too, it seems right. Next Friday at five. Okay?"

"You guys don't have to do this."

"Yes, we do. Besides, it's already done. Everyone knows. We're not canceling." Jane's gaze shifted.

Bree looked around and smiled more broadly when she found Verity leaning against the edge of the next stool. "Hi. Sit and have a muffin with us?" She raised a hand to LeeAnn, but Verity drew it back down.

"I can't stay," she said softly. "I just wondered if you knew the sex of the baby. I'm crocheting something."

"Oh, Verity." Bree was touched.

"I want to make the color right."

"That's *so sweet* of you. But I don't know what the sex is."

Verity nodded. "Then I'll make it generic." She left the stool and was gone without another word.

Bree understood the rush when Dotty took her place, looking back at the door. "Good thing you didn't tell her. The last thing you need is something Verity makes."

"I would have told her, if I'd known the sex. I'd love to have something Verity makes. She's very talented."

"She's weird."

"She's my friend." Bree turned to Jane. "She's coming to the shower, isn't she?"

"I invited her."

"You did?" Dotty asked. "You said you wouldn't."

"You told me not to. I didn't answer."

Dotty made a guttural sound. "You're impossible." With a look of disgust, she left.

Jane kept her eyes on her tea. "I'm no more impossible than she is."

"You're not impossible. There's no comparison."

"I applied."

It was a minute before Bree understood what she meant. "To art school? That's *great*."

"I don't know if I'll get in."

"You will."

"I don't know if I'll get a scholarship."

"You *will*."

Jane let out a weary breath. "I hope so. I can't take much more, Bree."

"You won't have to. Oh, I'm *so pleased* you did it. When will you hear?"

"After the fifteenth of December."

That pleased Bree even more. It meant she would know before the baby came, which meant that she would be able to lobby for Jane if Dotty gave her trouble, which she was sure to do. Dotty was a difficult woman.

Bree leaned close and, tongue in cheek, said, "Maybe your mom will have other plans next Friday at five?"

Dotty was at the shower. Verity was not. Bree kept thinking about that afterward. Worried, she drove to the cottage the next day.

Verity seemed unsure from the moment she opened the door. She invited Bree in and set about making tea, but she didn't quite look Bree in the eye.

So Bree said, "I missed you yesterday. Why weren't you there?"

Still without making eye contact, Verity said a breezy, "Oh, I hadn't finished making what I wanted to make," as though that were all there was to it, but Bree doubted it was.

"You could have come anyway. You didn't have to bring a gift."

Verity poured the tea.

"Dotty said something to you, didn't she?" Bree asked.

A plate of sliced pumpkin bread joined the tea.

"Why do you listen to her, Verity? She's one of those people you talked about who have a closed mind."

Verity slipped a slice of the bread onto Bree's dish. When Bree made no move to touch it, she sat back in her own seat, with her shoulders slumped. "She said you didn't want me to come. She said that you would never say anything to me, that you're too polite." She looked up. "You are polite, I know that."

"I wanted you there. I *told* Dotty that. I told her you and I are friends. I'm sorry, Verity. She's a witch."

Verity laughed at that.

It was a minute before Bree realized what she had said. Then she laughed, too. "She is. Not you. Her." She sobered. "I really did want you there. I want people to know we're friends."

Verity's smile turned sad. "No, you don't. You don't want that kind of stigma."

"There's no stigma. Not for me. I don't care what people think about our friendship."

"Your husband might."

"Tom? Oh, no. When I told him what I suspected Dotty did to you, he said . . . I won't repeat it—it was crude." And Verity was a southern lady, sitting there with her fine china and linen napkins. She still looked bohemian. But she was refined and sensitive.

"Dotty isn't alone. There are others who share her feelings. You have a baby to think about now. Maybe she's right. Maybe the baby would be better off sleeping under someone else's afghan."

Bree slid her arms across the table to touch Verity's hands. "I would be *honored* if my baby had an afghan made by you. It would bring luck."

Verity looked like she wanted to believe that.

"The baby may need luck," Bree said quietly, straightening. "If this is the third wish, I don't know what's going to happen." She wished Verity could read the tea leaves in her cup.

"You did the right thing," Verity said. "I've seen your husband's face when he's looking at you. That expression is as close to holy as we have here on earth."

"What if I die?" Bree asked. She couldn't ask anyone else quite as directly.

"You died once," Verity said. "Think back to how that was."

"I keep trying to, but I can't."

"Earthly images have come in the way."

Yes. She supposed they had. Swept up in the joy of life, she had distanced herself from the being of light. She had wanted to feel normal.

But she wasn't normal. She would never be normal.

"Take a deep breath," Verity said. "Close your eyes. Clear your mind."

Bree took a deep breath. She closed her eyes. She cleared her mind.

After a minute, Verity spoke again, but softly. "Now remember what happened that night."

That night. Bree recalled walking through the snow. She saw Tom's Jeep coming up the hill and, looking toward the far end of the green, saw the pickup barreling toward them. She relived the fear she had felt at the last minute, felt the pain of being hit, saw herself on the operating table, seconds from death.

Something took over her thought process then. Without a conscious effort to re-create it, she felt herself leaving her body and rising, rising past the room's ceiling. Her mind's eye looked up, drawn there by a light that grew brighter and brighter until it filled everything in its path. Love was there. Peace was. And happiness.

Bree grew stronger. Fear vanished, done in by the sheer beauty of the place where she was. Here, anything was possible. Every outcome was positive. Whatever happened was meant to be.

Calmer now, she drew in a deep, slow breath. Drowsy but

renewed, she opened her eyes. They fell on Verity. "Thank you," she said softly, and smiled.

Dear Dad, Tom wrote on Thanksgiving night.

I'm sitting in the family room with the fireplace lit and Bree curled up beside me, sleeping. We had a great day. Thanksgivings in Panama involve the whole town, so those of us without extended family don't feel so alone. That doesn't mean we don't think about what might have been.

I'm sorry we couldn't have been there with all of you. I'm sorry you wouldn't let us come. I respect the fact that you aren't ready to see me. Still, it's hard. Bree is at the end of her eighth month. The doctor doesn't want her flying after this, and once the baby's born, we'll have to stay put for a while. I wished she could have met you—and you her—before the baby's birth. She has no family at all besides me. She's hungry for it.

I know you're angry at Alice for coming to visit, but I want you to know that in all the time we talked, she never once criticized you. She never once said she thought you were wrong to be angry. Don't think that by her coming here, I got my way. If anything, her visit reminded me that I don't have all of you.

Bree loved having her here and wants her to come back. I wish you'd encourage her to.

I wish you'd come yourself, if not now, then once the baby is born. My offer of tickets is still open, for as many of you as will come. My house is small. Not everyone would fit here, but we have friends in town who will gladly house the overflow.

I was wrong, Dad. The way I behaved even before Mom got sick was wrong, and afterward, what I did was inexcusable. Mom's gone now. I can never apologize to her. I can never move past this with her. But I'd like to with you. I'm not asking you to forget. I'm not even asking you to forgive. What I'm asking is if we can bury the hatchet and maybe recapture some of the good times. You're the only grandfather my child will ever have.

Love, Tom

Two weeks later, Bree was at peace. The doctor pronounced her in fine health, if still a ways from delivering, and she wasn't thinking about what-ifs. She had decided that nothing would get her down, and nothing did. Even eighteen pounds fatter, she was enjoying being a woman of leisure for the first and last time.

The season was perfect for that. She had the diner's best seat for watching the East Main Slide and got first crack at the cookie exchange during the annual clothing drive at the church. She spent hours reading before a blazing fire, and hours more at Verity's with yarn and crochet hook in hand.

Her joy was in spending time with those she cared most about. Tom topped the list, of course. Behind him came Jane, Liz, and Abby. Verity's spot was more private, Julia's more special.

She was with Julia on this day, watching her arrange greens in the diner's little black vases, when the front door opened. With the lunch rush over and the dinner rush yet to start, new arrivals stuck out.

Bree didn't turn. She was too bulky to do it with ease and, after the first seconds, too busy watching Julia's face. Her eyes had widened. Her skin had blanched. Her hands were suspended around the greens.

Slowly, she lowered them. "Oh, my," she said. "Oh, *my.*" She shot Bree a moment's frightened glance and slid out of the booth.

Only then did Bree turn. The newcomer was a woman, close to her own age, with thick dark hair spilling from a pretty wool hat, flushed cheeks, and a homespun look. Julia gave her a hug, then took her hand and stood for what seemed an unsure minute, before leading her back to the booth.

Looking as nervous as Bree had ever seen her, she said, "Bree, this is my daughter, Nancy. Nancy Anderson, Bree Miller."

Tom spent the afternoon in Montpelier, negotiating with federal prosecutors in an attempt to forestall a client's indictment for mail fraud. He carried a cellular phone, as Bree did. They had agreed she would call at the slightest hint of labor, but the phone didn't ring.

When he arrived home, Bree was setting the table. The instant she saw him, she dropped what she was doing and grabbed his shoulders. "You'll never guess what. Julia's daughter showed up, right out of the blue. It's the first time she's ever been here. Julia got so pale I thought she'd seen a ghost."

Tom hadn't heard from Nancy since he had suggested she come. "Julia's daughter? Nice. I take it Julia recovered?"

"It took a while. They've had some differences. Julia was cautious at first." She gave him a wide grin. "Hi, handsome. How was your day?"

He laughed. It was a joy, the way she did that each time he came home from wherever he was. He caught her mouth in a kiss and moved his hand on her belly. "Hard as a rock. Muscles contracting?"

"A lot. But I feel good."

"No pains?"

"None. Tom, they're coming for dinner."

"Who?" It took him a minute. "Here?" He counted the place settings. "Bree, you're not making dinner."

"That's what Julia said. But it's all made. Flash did it, three courses' worth. We just have to heat and serve."

"You won't. I will."

"I knew you'd say that." She unknotted his tie.

He unbuttoned his collar. "So what's the daughter like?"

"Very nice."

"You sound surprised."

"I was. Am." She frowned, then grew sheepish. "I think I was jealous. I've had Julia all to myself, then suddenly this stranger waltzes right in. Nancy looked even more nervous than Julia, though. I felt bad for her. We talked for a while at the diner, then Julia left to show her around town. They're coming at seven."

Something about the evening made an impression on Tom, but he couldn't put his finger on it. Neither he nor Nancy mentioned their earlier talk. She was entirely pleasant, apparently reassured after seeing Julia's life for herself. Julia seemed happy, even relieved, that her daughter had come. Bree was delighted to be doing something special for Julia, who had come to mean so much to her.

Three women, all smiling, talking comfortably, enjoying the night.

Naturally, Tom pulled out his camera. Nancy wasn't staying in Panama for long. Pictures of her visit would be special.

It wasn't until a full week later that he finished up the roll of film by shooting Bree at her heaviest and most lovely. He dropped off the film to be developed, but by the time he picked it up, he was so preoccupied between Christmas preparations and wondering when Bree's labor would begin, how they would get to the hospital in case of snow, and whether Bree would be all right, that he set the pictures aside without a glance.

Chapter

~ *16* ~

$\mathcal{S}$now came on the twenty-first of December. The flakes were large and nearly as thick as they had been on that fateful day fourteen months before. This time, though, the town was prepared. Roads were plowed and sanded throughout the day, particularly the ones near West Elm. Everyone knew Bree was about to deliver. No one wanted her stuck when her time finally came.

Tom wasn't looking forward to driving in the snow, but Bree had her last scheduled appointment with Paul Sealy that afternoon, and he wasn't having her miss it. Well before they reached the medical center, he decided that if Paul said Bree was anywhere near delivery, they were staying.

Paul said she hadn't begun to dilate.

That made Tom nervous. He had read an Internet piece about women dying from obstructed labor and figured that a failure to dilate could cause that. Granted, those women lived in third world countries. Still.

"Is it a problem?" he asked Paul, calmly so that he wouldn't worry Bree, though she looked far calmer than he felt.

"No problem at all," Paul said. "Sometimes we know the exact date when a woman conceived and still miss the delivery date. Every woman is different. Every pregnancy is different. She may not deliver for another ten days."

It occurred to Tom that Paul could do the cesarean now and avoid the uncertainty of weather. But he didn't ask, because of that other uncertainty. It sat like lead in the back of his mind. He wasn't ready for the baby to be born. He wanted more time alone with Bree.

Slowly, carefully, he drove her home through the snow. They passed the town hall, where, despite the weather, the Winter Solstice Dance was about to begin, but neither of them wanted to party, not with others at least. Tom built a fire in the family room, stir-fried a healthy dinner, popped popcorn, played music. They swayed more than danced, rubbed against each other, laughed. Then they lay in each other's arms on the sofa, watching the flames.

"We have diapers," Bree said, running through the list for the *third* last time. "We have a baby bathtub and towels. We have baby powder and baby lotion. We have baby books. We have baby clothes and a baby seat. We have a snowsuit. We have formula just in case—"

Tom didn't like those words. "Shhh," he whispered, and held her more tightly.

"In case I don't have enough milk," she specified.

"You will." How could she not? She was woman personified, with her warm smell and the richness of a body ripe with child. Her breasts had grown full, her stomach round and firm. During the last few weeks, when intercourse would have been awkward, they had pleasured each other in different ways. Tom's orgasms had been intense. From the sounds Bree made, hers had, too. She was the sweetest thing he had ever tasted, the sexiest thing he had ever held.

His camera couldn't capture her spirit, though Lord knew, he had tried. But two-dimensional images were finite. They couldn't convey the heart of her, and her soul. She brought depth to his life, brought optimism and innocence and goodness.

Yet again he wondered if he should have insisted that she deliver in New York. But she was happy here. She had faith in Paul. Having come to know him well, so did Tom.

"I love you," she whispered against his mouth.

He hugged her but didn't speak. His throat was too thick to allow it.

On the twenty-second, Bree helped Tom decorate— "helped" being a relative term, since he wouldn't let her do much. She would have argued, had there been even a remote chance of her winning. But Tom had assured her there wasn't, so she settled for directing the goings-on.

Bree didn't miss out on the fun in the woods. She was all bundled up with Tom and Ben Little, picking the tree she wanted, cheering while they chopped it down, guiding them back to the house, and, once inside, steering them around corners until the tree was in place in the family room. She decorated the lower limbs, Tom the upper ones, with more tinsel, bigger bows, brighter decorations, than the year before. Come time for the star, he sat her right up on his shoulder and held her tight while she did the honors. It was a charmed time. Mistletoe hung in every doorway, big fat candles scented every room, and through it all, carols played, soft, sweet, and poignant.

Friends dropped by for eggnog and hot cider, starting the holiday early, a dream come true for Bree. She loved the sights, sounds, and smells of Christmas—all real now, as they hadn't been that October night fourteen months before when she had stood in the snow across from the diner and dreamed. Her life was rich and brimming. There was nothing she wanted that she didn't have. She felt blessed—and that was even before she saw Tom's gift to her. It arrived shortly before dusk, with a giant red bow on its shiny red roof—her very own brand-new luxury four-wheel-drive vehicle.

"With baby seat," Tom said, and there it was, belted into the back.

Bree was speechless. They never had gotten around to shopping together for her car. It simply hadn't been high priority, what with Tom's truck being right there and their going most everywhere together anyway. She hadn't dreamed he would do this on his own. For the longest time, she just stood there, looking at her gift, stunned.

"Do you like it?"

"I *love* it." She threw her arms around his neck and hugged him as tightly as she could, given the baby between them. Seconds later, she pulled back to lumber in behind the wheel, opening a palm. "Give me the keys. I'm going for a ride."

Tom shook his head.

"Tom," she protested. "Come on, Tom."

"After the baby's born."

"I won't hurt the baby. I'll go slow."

"You can't even reach the wheel."

"I can," she said, demonstrating. Her elbows were nearly straight, but no matter. "Just to the end of the driveway and back."

She finally wore him down. He actually allowed her to drive to the end of the street and back. She was in heaven.

On the morning of the twenty-third, Tom woke up in a cold sweat. He had dreamed that Bree's side of the bed was icy, and he put a fast hand there. She was warm and awake. He pulled her close.

"You're shaking," she whispered.

She's here, he told himself. *She'll always be here,* he told himself. "How long have you been up?"

"A while. I was watching you sleep."

He curved a hand to her belly. "How's baby?"

"All snug and settled in."

"Smart kid knows a good thing."

"What did you dream?"

"Nothing much." It hadn't taken much to cause the sweat. One thought. Just one. He could avoid it most of the time by obsessing over Christmas preparations, but he had less control over night thoughts.

Bree touched his face. "Things will be fine."

"I know."

Her eyes lit. "This time next week we'll be parents."

He brought her hand to his mouth, kissed it, held it there.

"We've done everything right," she reasoned. "For baby *and* me. We had all their tests—heart, lungs, blood—and they couldn't come up with a thing, not the *tiniest thing* that's wrong. We'll make it through this delivery just fine, all of us. I know it. I know it right here." She touched her heart.

What could Tom say to that? He couldn't tell her about the ominous feeling he had. It was the exact opposite of his utter conviction, in the waiting room with Flash on the night of the accident, that she would be fine. Okay, so he had more at stake now. But why such a strong premonition? And what could he say to Bree?

Not a damn thing, except "Wyatt for a boy, Chloe for a girl?"

She grinned and nodded. "I want a big christening, with everyone there and Julia as godmother."

"Not Jane?"

"Jane's going to art school. Dotty doesn't know it yet, but she is. She'll be a great visiting aunt, but Julia's *here*. She has the time and the love. It would mean a lot to her. . . . And I've been thinking: the land on South Forest? Let's sell it."

"Are you sure? We can wait longer. It's not going anywhere."

"I'm positive. You're good with money. Invest it for the baby. And call Alice as soon as the baby's born. She'll tell your father. He'll call us, I know he will."

"You sent them nice gifts."

She smiled. "It was easy."

"All with personal notes."

"What else did I have to do with my time? You won't let me do anything." She moved her lips over his, teasing, smiling. "I love the truck, Tom. Thank you. I can't wait till you see your gift."

"What is it?"

"I'm not telling. It's coming tomorrow morning."

"Give me a hint."

"If I do that, you'll guess."

"I won't. I promise."

She laughed. Her thumb found his chin, moved up his cheek to the scar on the bone, then over his temple, across his brow, and into his hair. She did that often—looked at him like he was the best thing to ever come down the road —and it never failed to both humble him and fill him with pride. If there had been a life before Vermont, he couldn't remember it. He had never felt so content, so satisfied, so fulfilled, so loved.

It was the morning of the twenty-fourth when his gift arrived, the large riding mower that he had sworn to buy in the fall, then forgotten in the excitement of everything else.

"I have this image," Bree said, "of you mowing the grass with the baby on your lap. Promise you'll do it?"

Tom promised. He had no choice. He shared the image and loved the gift. What he didn't like was the feeling he had—in this, in talk of godparents and christenings, in stocking the house with supplies enough to keep them for months—that she was making provisions for when she was gone.

"Don't do this," he whispered, pushing his hands into her hair and holding her face to his.

She didn't pretend not to know what he meant but clung to his wrists, her eyes bright with tears. "I just love you so much."

Words, tears, touch—all went straight to his heart. Fiercely, determinedly, he said, "That's why we'll be fine. You said it yourself. We've taken every precaution. The baby will be fine. *You*'ll be fine." He pressed her face to his chest.

"I'm tired of waiting," she said, in a moment's rare complaint. "I want it over, Tom."

"Soon, angel, soon."

The day alternately sped and dragged. Bree was calm one minute and shaky the next. She unpacked and repacked the baby's little bag, and unpacked and repacked her own. She washed the few clothes that she and Tom had worn since she had done the wash the day before, dusted tables that hadn't had time to gather dust, ran the dishwasher, made the bed. She checked the freezer for the tenth time to make sure it was packed with food. She called Flash. She called Julia. She called Jane. She called Alice.

Everything was done. It was barely noon.

She was in the family room, wondering what to do with herself, when Tom said, "Open your gifts." They were gaily wrapped and stacked under the tree—gifts for her, gifts for him, even gifts for the baby.

She considered it but shook her head. "Nah. I'll wait till morning."

"You didn't last year. Remember that?"

Grinning, she slid her arms around his waist. "Last year was my first Christmas. This year I'm more mature. But you can open yours, if you're impatient."

"I already got mine, even besides this one." He patted her belly. "Want to go to the diner for lunch?"

That was good for two hours. A movie at the mall was good for another two. It was dusk by the time they returned to town, blustery and gray, but Christmas Eve. Trees on the green were strung with bright lights. Every window in sight had a candle. The church at the head of the oval was bathed in white. The air was rife with wood smoke and pine.

Bree felt an odd unreality as they rounded the green, felt almost distanced from the holiday, though in its midst. She felt distracted. She felt *removed*.

Back at the house, Tom built up the fire. She napped against him and woke up feeling like a ten-ton load. She wasn't hungry for dinner. She felt stuffed even before she began. So she nibbled while Tom ate, and peppered the meal with frequent reassurances, lest he worry.

The plan was to attend midnight services with the rest of the town. She had showered and was standing before the closet in her robe, doubting that even her maternity clothes would fit over her pitifully swollen stomach, when her water broke. For a minute she just stood there looking down, knowing what had happened but paralyzed. Then she came alive with a long, broken breath.

"Tom? *Tom!*"

Tom was alerted by the alarm in her voice, well before he saw the puddle on the floor or the panic on her face. It was the latter that kept him calm.

"What do you feel?" he asked.

"Wet," she said, in a high voice.

"Any contractions?"

"Not yet."

"Okay," he said. He knew what to do, had been holding mental rehearsals for days. After guiding her to the bathroom and helping her dry off, he sat her on the toilet seat, with instructions not to move, and called Paul Sealy.

She was still on the toilet seat when he returned, which said something about her fear.

He took her face in his hands. "Paul's on his way." He kissed her eyes and her nose. "Let's get you dressed."

She nodded and did what she could to help, but she was shaking so badly her contribution was negligible.

Tom didn't mind. He had enough energy for both of them. "Left leg ... I've got it; now the right ... that's my girl," he soothed, and when the bottom half was done, he did the same for the top. "There . . . second arm, there you go. Now over the head. Good." He combed her hair with his fingers. "Okay?"

She nodded convulsively. "Okay."

By the time she was belted into his truck, she was feeling mild contractions. "What if it comes fast?" she asked. "What if we don't get there in time?"

"We'll get there in time."

"Drive fast."

Holding her hand the whole way, kissing it from time to time, he drove as fast as he dared. He wouldn't have minded being stopped by a cop and getting an escort, but it was Christmas Eve. He doubted cops were on patrol, in this neck of the woods at least. Houses were lit, people inside. The roads were quiet.

The last time Tom had made this trip at night, he had been terrified that Bree would die. A tiny part of him had the same fear now.

"I love you, Tom," she said in a tremulous voice.

"You'll be fine, Bree. This is our baby being born. It's the best Christmas gift in the world."

"Christmas. Oh, Lord." She took a shaky breath and smiled at Tom. "Last chance to bet. What do you think? Wyatt or Chloe?"

"I'll love either one."

"Bet, Tom. Just for fun. Loser does middle-of-the-night diapers for a week."

"I say Wyatt."

"So do I. What happens now?"

"We do diapers together." Tom liked the thought of that, but it left his mind seconds later. Pulling up at the medical center's emergency entrance, assailed by the fear he had tried to assuage, he wondered—again—why he hadn't taken Bree back to New York, where the best doctors in the world would have assured that she'd live. The answer came with the appearance of Paul Sealy and the nurses they both knew and trusted, running out to help Bree into a wheelchair.

Tom wouldn't be separated from her. He held her hand when they wheeled her inside and took her upstairs, letting go only to pull scrubs on. Then he was leaning over her, talking her softly through lengthening contractions, trying to calm her, trying to calm himself—all the while fearing that he was on a runaway train on a downhill track with no hope of stopping, no chance of regaining control. Too quickly, she was changed, prepped, and wheeled into the operating room. Too quickly, she was given a spinal, the anesthesiologist was monitoring her vital signs, and a drape was put up at the spot where her belly began.

"I love you," Tom whispered against her knuckles, taking heart in the strength of her fingers. Their eyes clung. When hers filled with tears, he kissed them away. Then he smiled. "You're beautiful. And so strong."

"What's he doing?" she whispered.

"Getting the baby out." He smoothed dark strands of hair back from her cheeks, which were pale but wonderfully warm.

"I can't feel it."

"Remember he said you wouldn't? That's the spinal."

"I love you," she mouthed.

He mouthed the words back, brushing more tears away with his hand.

Then, from the other side of the sheet, came a pleased, "Well, well. It looks like we have a healthy, perfectly formed little . . . *boy* . . . who is . . . getting . . . ready . . . to cry."

The cry came, lusty and long. Bree broke into a smile, but it swam through the tears in Tom's eyes. He touched her face, kissed her, touched her neck, kissed her, so relieved, *so relieved* that she was alive and happy and his. "A boy," he breathed.

"I'm *so glad,*" Bree cried, laughing.

Her laughter died on a fast, indrawn breath when the nurse appeared on their side of the drape with the loosely wrapped baby. He was red and wrinkly, clearly in need of something more than the cursory wiping they'd done, but he was the most beautiful thing Tom had ever seen. It struck him then, as it hadn't quite done during the months when process had overshadowed product, that this was his flesh and blood. This little thing was a human being. It was the little boy he and Bree had made.

His hand shook when he took the baby from the nurse, and his touch was awkward. But nothing would have kept him from it. Holding his minutes-old child had been a fantasy of his, but only half. He satisfied the other half by carefully placing the tiny bundle in Bree's waiting arms.

She was crying again, smiling as widely as he. He felt light-headed, and no wonder. A huge weight had been lifted from his shoulders. Bree was alive. *Alive.* And they had a son.

At right about the time when midnight services were in progress, Bree was wheeled to a room not unlike that in which she had stayed the year before. This time, though, the air was festive, and she was wide awake and full of energy. The fact that once the spinal wore off she would feel the pain of the surgery didn't matter. She loved Tom. She loved the baby. And she was alive.

From where she lay, she had a front-row view of Tom's face as he stood by the baby's crib, at the foot of her bed. She loved his awe, loved his love, loved his excitement and pleasure and gratitude. She loved life, even loved the *after*-life that had enhanced her appreciation of all this. She felt bold and strong, felt so very happy that if she died right then, she would have died luckier than most.

It was a heartrending admission, but not one that she had time to dwell on. Julia and Jane arrived shortly thereafter.

They had been tipped off when she and Tom hadn't shown up at church, and when a call to the house went unanswered, they'd headed here. Since it was the holiday, and since they swore they were next closest to Bree after Tom, the nurses let them in.

"He's beautiful, he's beautiful," Jane said.

Julia didn't speak, but the look on her face, in her eyes, said the same thing, and when she went to Bree, took her hand, and held it tight, Bree heard even more. Julia was happy. She was pleased for Bree and pleased for Tom. She was proud of the baby—though not even yet aware Bree wanted her to be godmother to Wyatt. That request was in the note accompanying the gift Bree had left at Julia's house for Christmas day.

Minutes later, Flash arrived. He was followed by Liz and Abby. No one cared about the hour. It was the holiday, and a nicer thing couldn't have happened. Bree lay in bliss, feeling no pain at all, with her husband sitting close by her side and their son asleep at the foot of the bed.

By two in the morning, the nurses shooed away everyone but Tom. By three, Bree shooed off him, too.

"You need sleep," she said.

"No, I don't." He had one arm over her head, the other holding her hand. Clearly, he didn't want to move.

"Well, then, I do."

"I'll stay and watch you sleep."

"I won't sleep if I know you're here, but if neither of us do, who'll take care of the baby tomorrow? I won't be able to do much, and I'll feel awful if I know you got no sleep at all. Besides, the baby won't be doing anything more for a while." She had already put him to her breast, though her milk wasn't in yet. Tom had changed his first diaper. They had oohed and ahhed over every inch of baby body, from tiny fingers and toes to Bree's mouth, Tom's eyes, and a thatch of auburn hair that came from God knew where.

"Sleep for a few hours. Then call Alice and your dad. Load up the camera, and come back at eight. Maybe by then they'll let me up. You can help me to the bathroom, kind of like old times, y'know?"

He didn't budge.

She gave his hand a teasing shake. "I'll be here."

He breathed a sigh of relief. "You will, won't you." He kissed her, then went to the crib and kissed the baby. When he returned to kiss Bree again, there was a catch in his voice. "You are the most wonderful woman in the world." He sandwiched her hands between his and brought them to his mouth. "Know what I'm imagining now?"

She shook her head.

"Growing old with you," he said. "Watching the baby grow and have babies of his own. Walking down a lane, slowly when we can't go faster. Sitting on the porch in the sun when our creaky old bones need the heat. Aren't those incredible pictures?"

They were. They lingered with Bree long after Tom finally left, and they had her smiling into the night. Up until then, she hadn't dared think so far ahead. Now she could, and the thoughts brought a certain serenity. It swelled within her, as light, bright, and buoyant as the being of light that had started all this.

Were the wishes real? She believed that they were. She had conceived a child because she wished it, which meant she wouldn't have any more children, but that was fine, so fine. She had Tom and Tom's child, and a happiness that knew no bounds at all. The being of light had been good to her. She owed it deep, deep thanks.

Closing her eyes, she conjured it up. There was no waiting this time. It was right there, had probably been there all along through such a momentous night. She felt its love and approval, and the warmth of its smile. She smiled back when it opened its arms in welcome. Feeling radiant and ethereal, maternal and loved, she released a long, slow, satisfied breath and went up for a hug.

Chapter

~ 17 ~

$\mathcal{T}$om couldn't sleep. He tried to only because Bree had asked, but kept jumping up to check the clock, striding from room to room, bursting with pride and relief. He wanted to go right back to the hospital, but he knew Bree needed sleep. So he busied himself readying his camera for the first photographs of his son.

He was returning the camera to its case when he remembered the last roll that had been developed. The envelope lay unopened on top of cookbooks on the kitchen counter. He pulled the pictures out and went straight for the ones of a beatific Bree at the height of her pregnancy. Helplessly, he smiled. She was something else.

Smiling now at the thought of photographing mother and child, he absently flipped through the rest of the pictures, taken during Nancy Anderson's visit. He was at the bottom of the pile when his smile faltered. Flipping back a few, he looked more closely at one picture, then another, and another. All were of Nancy, Julia, and Bree together. In each, the three women wore look-alike smiles—and suddenly,

suddenly, it made total sense: Julia knowing that the woman in the diner wasn't Bree's mother . . . Julia offering Bree her own wedding gown . . . Julia in her garden, defending Bree's mother to Tom . . . Julia offering encouragement and support as Bree's pregnancy progressed.

He might have felt a twinge of anger, if all hadn't been so right with the world. But it was a time of forgiveness. And he wanted Bree to know.

He picked up the phone to call, changed his mind, and raced upstairs for a shower. He had just finishing dressing, intent on driving to the hospital, creeping into Bree's room, and doing his best to contain his excitement until she woke on her own, when the phone rang.

It was five in the morning. He reached for it with a grin, thinking it was his incredible wife on his brainwave again, but it wasn't.

"Mr. Gates, this is Dr. Lieber at the medical center." His voice was tense, the tone urgent. "I think you should come."

Tom went cold. "What's wrong?"

"We really need you here."

His heart started to pound. "What's wrong?"

"I'm afraid we have a problem."

"What kind of problem?"

"With Bree. She's had an attack."

For a minute, he couldn't breathe. "Attack?"

"Heart attack."

Oh, God. His voice rose. "Is she alive?"

"I think you should come."

"Is she *alive?*" he yelled.

There was a pause, then a quiet "No. We did everything we could, but she had been gone too long when we found her. I'm sorry."

The cold spread through him, ice in his veins.

"Will you come?" the doctor asked.

Tom swallowed. "Yes. Fifteen minutes." He hung up

the phone and stared at it, pushed a hand through his hair, blinked.

Three wishes. One for heat, one for a mother, one for a child. And after the last?

It couldn't be, he argued with himself. There had to be a mistake. She had made it through the delivery, had been *fine* just two hours before. Besides, she couldn't have had a heart attack. She was too healthy for that. She was too *young* for that.

He swallowed again, feeling sick to his stomach. So was the call a joke? Not possible. No one, *no one,* would joke that way, especially not on Christmas morning.

If it wasn't a joke, though, it might be a mistake. Telling himself that was it, he lifted his keys from the kitchen table as he ran past. He was already in the truck when he thought to call Julia. Leaving the door ajar, he raced back inside and was nearly at the phone, when he changed his mind. He couldn't call her. Bree wasn't dead. There had been a mistake, that was all.

He drove through the predawn dark at the kind of speed he hadn't dared attempt the night before, but Bree wasn't in the car now, and time was of the essence. He had to get to the medical center to straighten things out.

Leaving the truck at the front entrance, he ran inside and up the stairs. One look at the somber faces gathered at the nurses' station, stark against a backdrop of tinsel and cheer, and the cold in him became dread.

Paul Sealy separated himself from the group. Looking devastated, he clutched Tom's arm. "The nurse checked at three-fifty. Bree and the baby were both sleeping. When she made rounds less than an hour later, Bree was gone."

Tom didn't understand.

Paul didn't seem to, either. "Her heart just stopped. There was no warning. No violence. The resident used defibrillators, but it was too late. She must have died right after that three-fifty check."

Tom frowned. He ran a hand through his hair.

"I don't know what happened," Paul said. "We tested her. Her heart was sound."

"Where is she?" Tom asked in a raw voice.

"In her room. We moved the baby to the nursery. He's doing fine."

Tom barely heard the last. He was already on his way down the hall to the room where he had left Bree alive such a short time before. He paused briefly at the door. She was sleeping. That was all. Sleeping. Three steps, and he was beside the bed, but the instant he touched her cheek, he knew.

It was cold as ice. He felt her neck, her arm, her hand. All cold, too cold.

He chafed her hand to warm it up and called her name in that same raw voice. Her face was pale and waxy, her lashes as dark on her cheeks as her hair was on the pillow. Her nose was delicate, her chin gently rounded. Her lips were curved in a soft, sweet smile.

She looked serene, even happy and beautiful, too beautiful to be dead.

"Oh, baby," he whispered, bringing her hand to his mouth. It smelled of the lilac bath oil she had used the night before, and of antiseptic, where the anesthesiologist had swabbed it for a drip.

As he stood there, the smell of the antiseptic faded, leaving only a lilac softness. Against it, he made a long, low, keening sound.

No joke. No mistake. Bree—his Bree—was gone.

Time ceased to count. He sat beside her on the bed, holding her hand, stroking her arm, kissing her cheek. He told her he loved her and breathed warmth into her cold fingers. Pressing them to his throat, he studied her face, tracing every feature, memorizing texture and shape. He struggled to accept that she wouldn't—wouldn't ever again—come awake and break into the smile that he loved.

At some point, Paul joined him. Quietly, he asked, "Is there anything I can do?"

Hit by a sudden insane fury, Tom turned on him fast. *What happened?* he wanted to scream. *She was in your care, so why weren't you here? Why didn't someone check her sooner? You knew she died once, man. You knew it! How could you have done all those tests and not known her heart was weak?*

His fury deflated with the realization that her heart hadn't been weak. The most he could manage was a stricken "Bring her back."

Paul ran a hand around his neck. "What I'd give to be able to. The few patients I've lost died because of accident, catastrophic illness, or old age. I've never lost someone like Bree before."

Neither had Tom. He touched her cheek. The chill of her skin went right through him, bottling things up somewhere deep in his gut.

"Is there anyone I can call?" Paul asked.

Julia. Tom had to call Julia. But he wasn't ready to share Bree yet. So he shook his head no.

Dawn broke after seven. Tom hadn't moved, other than to touch another part of Bree—her hair, her hip, her leg. Her feet were cold. Her feet were always cold, she had told him once. He remembered telling her what his mother had said about a woman's warmth being centered around her heart.

So was a man's, he thought now. His heart was broken. What warmth it had held had just seeped right out through the crack. He was nearly as cold as Bree.

"Tom?" came a frightened voice from behind. Julia was at the door, ghostly pale and visibly shaking. Her eyes were on Bree. "I woke up an hour ago with such an odd feeling. I couldn't shake it. So I drove over. They stopped me at the desk." She approached, still looking at Bree. She carried a small gift. It fell to the floor, unnoticed, when she put out a hand to touch Bree's face.

Then she covered her mouth. Her gaze flew to Tom.

"It was her heart," he said.

"No. She's just sleeping. Smiling at sweet dreams."

Tom shook his head.

"But she was fine," Julia protested. "Healthy. *Strong*. Women don't die having babies. Not here. Not anymore." She whirled toward the door, as if to summon a doctor to treat what ailed Bree.

Tom stopped her with a hoarse "It's too late. She's gone."

"No."

"She is. I've been with her since a little after five. She isn't here anymore."

Julia shook her head in denial still, but when she looked back at Bree, she started to cry.

Tom held her, for his sake as much as hers. They shared something, Julia and he. They both loved Bree deeply. Julia's tears expressed his own grief in ways that the ice inside him wouldn't allow.

After a time, she drew back and pressed a tissue to her eyes. Her voice was ragged and low. "I was going to tell her today. I wrote it all out in a little book for her to read, everything that happened back then, my reasons and what I felt." She shot him a teary look. "You guessed the truth. After that day in the garden?"

"No. Not until a few hours ago. I was looking through pictures of you and Nancy and Bree. There's a family resemblance." He thought to correct the tense, but couldn't, couldn't.

Julia touched Bree's shoulder. She smoothed out the material of the hospital gown and ever so gently kneaded the skin beneath. Her smile was so sad that if Tom's heart had still been whole, it would have shattered right then.

"Beautiful Bree," she whispered. "Beautiful from the start." Her words began to flow, seeming appropriate, even soothing. "I was so frightened when I learned I was pregnant. But she was life, after months focused on death. I loved her the whole time I carried her, and Haywood loved me. He made me forget about Vietnam. We built a make-believe life together. I was so happy when Bree was born. Somehow, I thought, somehow it would all work out."

She fell silent. Tom brought Bree's hand to his mouth and kissed it. Looking up, he wondered if she knew he was there. He wondered if she knew Julia was, too, and if she was listening to Julia's tale. He wanted that more than anything.

"Did your family know about Bree?" he asked.

Julia's sigh was rough. "God, no. We were Catholics. I had committed adultery. They wouldn't have understood. I had gone east to be with the wife of one of Teddy's war buddies, and they didn't even understand that. Teddy was an MIA. They thought I should be waiting at home by the phone. But, *Lord,* was it oppressive. I called home once a week to see if there was word. I couldn't bear calling more often than that. Bree was two weeks old when I learned that Teddy was found. They had brought him to a hospital in Germany. He had lost a leg and was going to need care. I didn't know what to do."

"Did you love Haywood?" Tom asked, as Bree would have.

"Like I loved Teddy?" Julia gave another sad smile before looking back at Bree. "Haywood was something to think about when I couldn't bear thinking about Teddy." Her voice shrank. "But I loved Bree. I did." Fresh tears slid down her cheeks. With near reverence, she drew a circle from Bree's cheek, over her forehead, past her other cheek, to her chin. "Bree," she whispered. "Oh, Bree. Maybe if I'd been older, or more sure of myself. I was convinced that Teddy was dead. When I found out he wasn't, I felt so guilty. I had betrayed my wedding vows while my husband was living a nightmare. The pain of leaving you seemed just punishment for that."

"Did you ever have second thoughts?"

"All the time. But Teddy was sick at first, and then Nancy was born, and Scott, and time passed, and it would have been even harder to tell them about Bree. Besides, Haywood had forbidden me to contact her. He threatened to expose me if I did. I had to wait until he died. Teddy died the month before." She shivered. "An eerie coincidence."

Nothing surprised Tom. Nothing at all.

"All this time," Julia said with regret, "all this time I've been here, and I didn't speak up. I was afraid she wouldn't want me. It was enough to just see her. So I didn't say a word until the day she thought that other woman was her mother, and even then I didn't tell the whole truth."

Tom was struck by the precision with which Bree's wish had come true. On the very day when she had wished to see her mother, Julia had come forward. The woman in the Mercedes had been a red herring.

"You were born in California?" he asked.

"Near Sacramento."

"Who was Matty Ryan?"

"Me. Ryan is my maiden name. Martina was my middle name. When I was little, everyone called me Matty. Everyone but Teddy. I was always Julia to him."

"Where did the name Bree come from?"

"My father. Bryce." She touched Bree's hair. "Haywood let you keep that at least. I wasn't sure he would. It meant so much to me when I found out. My father was a powerful man, with a shock of thick auburn hair." Her chin trembled. "Oh, Bree," she whispered, "I should have told you sooner." Softly, she wept.

Tom lifted the forgotten gift from the floor. It was small and compact, as a journal would be. He tucked it against Bree. "I think she knew. She told me how much you meant to her. She wanted you to be the baby's godmother."

Julia's sobs deepened. Her words came, broken and wrenched, from behind the tissue she pressed to her nose.

"I was so happy—early this morning—couldn't sleep—so I opened Bree's gift—an album for baby pictures—along with this." She pulled a folded paper from her pocket and passed it to Tom.

Dear Julia, he read. *This gift is really from my baby, so you'll have a place to put pictures of him (I just know it's a boy). He's going to love you. He'll know that he can go to you when he has a problem. He'll know that you love him. Since I know all that, too, I'd be honored if you'd be his godmother. I'd be honored if you'd think of Tom and the baby and me as your family in Panama.*

You've come to be special to me. I can't explain what happens, but something does when we're together. You always make me feel better, even when I didn't feel bad to start with. I especially needed you these past months. Being pregnant has been a little scary for me. You helped me get through it. I'm lucky you're here. Thank you for being my friend. Love, Bree

Tom stared at the note for a bit, then carefully folded it and returned it to Julia. He held her shoulder, but it was a while before he could speak. "I didn't know she wrote that. I'm glad she did." But the poignancy of it left him feeling more hollowed out than ever.

When Julia quieted, sniffling, she glanced at the foot of the bed. "Where is the baby now?"

"In the nursery."

"Have you been there?"

"No."

"I'll help, Tom. Will you let me?"

What choice did he have? He couldn't begin to think about the baby. He couldn't think about the future, period. More than once he had been in the courtroom when a defendant was sentenced to life in prison without parole. He had truly tried to imagine what it would be like to face endless years of a cold and barren life. For the very first time now, he understood how it felt.

* * *

The thing about small-town life was that the choices were limited. Panama had a single undertaker and a single grave-yard. Tom made the necessary arrangements from the hospital and stayed with Bree until the hearse arrived. Only when they took her could he leave.

Knowing she would have wanted it, he brought the baby home. The nurses dressed him in the tiny clothes that were in his little bag and wrapped him in blankets against the cold. Julia held him close, while Tom drove. Together they settled him in the crib Bree had picked out, and for the longest time, Tom just stood, looking around.

Bree was there—in the bunny lamp on the bureau, the framed clown prints, the turtle mobile over the crib. She had tested a dozen rocking chairs for comfort before buying one that was white, with a cushion of navy and yellow. She had placed it by the window with love.

Where are you, Bree? the panic in him cried. *I need you here. I can't do this. Not alone.*

Baffled, he wandered from room to room on legs that were wooden, muscles that were tight. Bree was everywhere —on the bedroom dresser, in the bathroom medicine chest, on his office walls, the family room bookshelves, and the kitchen counters. The scent of her led him, the echo of her voice followed. He kept turning to her and finding her not there. Aloneness closed in on him, barren and stark.

Then the doorbell rang. It was Flash, looking as lost as Tom felt. On his heels came a sobbing Jane, needing to be held. She was followed minutes later by her mother and Emma. In short order, as word spread, others arrived—Liz, Abby, Martin, and LeeAnn, Eliot and Earl and their wives, the minister who had married Tom and Bree not a year before. None seemed aware that it was Christmas morning. Their grief was heavy, their compassion heartfelt.

By midday, the house had filled with townsfolk wanting to pay their respects. Bree's childhood friends came, her father's childhood friends came, newer friends came, diner regulars came. They opened the door for each other. They answered Tom's phone. They brought food, though he couldn't eat a thing. They expressed condolences, shed tears, spoke about Bree in hushed tones. When they left, others arrived. Tom was hugged by friends and acquaintances alike. One and all, they were grief-stricken.

The baby was the only bright spot. Visitors who crept upstairs to the nursery returned smiling. "He's a handsome boy," one told Tom, and another, "Tall and strapping, like his daddy."

As for Tom, he didn't know how he felt about the baby. He was tired enough, numb enough, to confess it to Jane when she caught him in the kitchen alone. He had been rearranging foil-wrapped packages on the counter, needless busywork what with all the women taking charge of the food, but he didn't know what else to do with himself. He couldn't laugh, couldn't cry. Once a master of small talk, he couldn't handle it now.

Jane began with a confession of her own. "I know about the wishes, Tom. Bree told me. She was worried this might happen."

He thrust a hand through his hair. "She knew more than I did. I should have listened."

"She didn't *know*, not for sure. She just worried. But she was so excited about the baby. She wanted to give him to you. She wouldn't want you having regrets."

"How not to? She gave me back my life, so what did I do? I took hers."

"You didn't."

"She died because she had my baby."

"She *chose* to have your baby."

"Yeah, well." He rolled tension from his shoulders. "I wish she hadn't. I wish she'd asked me. I'd have chosen her over a baby."

"He's innocent, Tom. Whatever you do, don't blame him."

Tom kept telling himself the very same thing. It would be so easy to say that if it hadn't been for the baby, Bree would be there. So easy, so cruel, so morally wrong.

He sighed. "I don't know if I can do this."

"Do what?"

"Live without Bree."

"You lived without her before."

"And made a mess of things."

"You have the baby now. He'll keep you on track."

Tom stared out at the terrace that Bree had loved, toward the woods Bree had loved and the brook Bree had loved. "I wanted Bree. I wanted to be a parent with her. It won't be the same."

"Don't you love him?" Jane asked.

"I do." He drew in a breath. It burst from him seconds later. "But how do you swallow something like this? Who do you get angry at? Who do you blame? What do you do?"

A soft knock came at the back door. Tom saw Verity through the glass and, feeling an odd need to connect with her, opened the door. She was hugging a gift-wrapped bundle. When she hesitated, looking carefully past him to see who else would know she was there, he drew her inside.

She didn't say anything at first, didn't look capable of it. Her eyes were filled with a grief so intense that Tom understood why he wanted her there.

"It isn't often that people like Bree come along," she finally said. Her soft southern drawl was slowed by sorrow.

"She died too soon."

"I keep asking myself if I could have stopped this from happening."

"That's two of us."

"She died doing what she wanted."

Tom was moved to argue but couldn't. He recalled Bree's face in death. That smile, that serenity, would be with him forever.

"She wanted you to be happy," Verity said.

"Without her?"

"She didn't know that for sure, so she took the risk. She didn't regret it."

"But now I'm alone with her baby."

"It's your baby."

"He needs Bree."

"He can't have her. So who's going to love him and raise him the way she would have?"

Tom knew who. He just didn't know how.

Verity shot a nervous look at Jane, then beyond when Dotty and Emma suddenly appeared. "I have to leave," she whispered, and turned.

But Tom caught her arm. He gestured toward the bundle she clutched. "What did you bring?"

Still whispering, she said, "It can wait."

Jane was suddenly beside him. "You made something, didn't you?"

Verity looked uncomfortable. "It's not much. I wanted it to be ready for the shower."

"I'm sorry about the shower. Bree wanted you there. I wanted you there. Whatever my mother said was mean and dead wrong."

There was an indignant murmur from behind. Jane ignored it.

So did Tom. Bree had admired Verity. She would have wanted this gift.

With a brief spurt of feeling—defiance, as much as anything, at a time when he felt powerless—he said, "We'd like what you made, the baby and I."

Verity held the bundle for another awkward minute before finally unfolding her arms. There were actually two packages. The smaller of them, on top, had been hidden. As soon as they were in Tom's hands, she was out the door and gone.

From behind came Dotty's arch "At least she had the good sense to use the back door."

Tom looked at Jane, who was looking right back at him. In silent agreement, he lowered the bundles to the table.

"Why don't I just put those away for you," Emma offered.

But he was already opening the largest, the one with bright baby wrapping. He imagined Bree tearing at the paper in excitement and felt a vicarious thread of it himself. There was tissue inside the wrapping. Peeling it back, he lifted out an afghan. It was crib-size, navy, yellow, and white to match the baby's room, and more beautiful than anything he and Bree had seen in the stores.

"It's wonderful," Jane breathed, moving a hand over the fine crocheted wool.

Dotty sputtered. "Did she think the baby wouldn't already have a crib blanket?"

Tom said, "The one he has now wasn't handmade. I'd rather use this one. Bree would have."

"Bree would be *alive* if it weren't for that woman."

He looked at Dotty. "How do you figure that?"

"Verity Greene egged her on. Bree was too old to have children."

"Mother! That's crazy. Besides, *you* told her to *wait*."

"Oh, hush."

"No, *you* hush," Jane said, drawing herself even taller than Dotty. "Bree did what she wanted. No one made her do anything. If she took chances, it was because she didn't want to live with the alternative. It's taken me a while, but I understand what she felt."

Dotty nodded. "So you're going to art school. If you aren't careful, you'll end up like Bree."

"Better that than living with the alternative."

Dotty gasped.

Emma led her from the room, saying, "She's upset. She'll come around."

Jane stared after them with her jaw set, then turned on Tom. "I *have* come around, and about time! Yes, I'm going to art school. Especially now. I'll do it for Bree as much as for me." Her eyes filled with tears. She pressed bitten fingernails to her mouth. Brokenly, she said, "I'm going to miss her so much."

Tom couldn't speak. The void in his life was gaping again, the emptiness of Bree's absence. He wished he could cry. The emotion backing up in him was painful.

Then Jane handed him the smaller package. It had Christmas wrapping and a card with his name on it in Bree's handwriting. His first instinct was to put it with the others under the tree. He couldn't deal with them yet. They were the last gifts he would ever get from Bree. Once opened, they would be gone.

But something had him taking this package from Jane and opening the card. *Dear Tom,* he read. *I had Verity teach me to crochet. I'm not very good at it, but this is the result. I was working on it all those afternoons I spent at her house these past few weeks. It's a scarf, in case you couldn't tell. Don't look too closely. It's got lots of mistakes. More love than mistakes, though. I adore you. Bree.*

Tom spent the night in the nursery, with the burgundy scarf wrapped around his neck. Pure exhaustion kept him asleep on the carpet while the baby slept. He awoke when the baby did, and changed him and fed him, as Julia had taught him to do. Then he sat in the pretty white rocker and rocked him back to sleep, as Bree would have done, and all the while her voice didn't call and her smile didn't show.

It hit him then that speculative talk about beings of light and three wishes was all well and good, but death was real. It was a hard, final, scientific fact.

He rocked harder now, seeking solace and finding none. With each passing minute, the pain of missing her grew.

Pain of missing her.

Fear of the future.

Dread. Sheer dread. They were burying her the following afternoon. He didn't know how he could stand there, cold all the way to his marrow and alone as never before, and watch.

*   *   *

But he wasn't alone. Crowds of people were already gathered at the graveyard by the church when he arrived, and then, while he waited at its entrance, the hearse inched its way through roads clogged with even more who had come. The whole town was in attendance, it seemed. As often as people reached out to touch the coffin as it was carried from the hearse down the narrow cemetery path, they reached out to touch Tom, who followed.

That kept him from being as cold as he might have been. It was a dreary day. Snow a foot deep lay over the graveyard. Though he wore a dark suit and a topcoat and Bree's burgundy scarf, his head and his hands were bare.

At the grave site, people closed in around him. He was barely aware of who was where, knew only that they were near and that they cared. The minister spoke simply. The choir soloist sang beautifully. Tom's eyes clung to the casket, to Bree. She was wearing the dress she had worn at their wedding. Julia had insisted on it. Tom would always remember her as she had been that day, his bride, his first and last, only truly innocent love.

When they would have lowered her into the ground, he felt a moment's jarring panic. Reaching out, he grabbed the wood and held it as though to keep her from the finality of death. But the wood was cold. What Bree was—her hope, her vitality, her love—wasn't there.

The reality of it pressed on his shoulders. Bereft, he stepped back. The coffin was lowered slowly into the ground. Watching it settle, he felt an ache so intense he began to shake.

Then, suddenly, a single ray of sun broke through the clouds and touched the wood, giving it a soft chestnut color and the warmth he sought. He closed his eyes, opened them again, and the warmth remained. His body steadied. His heart lifted. As surely as any dream he had ever had, he felt her presence. It began in the warmth of that improbable ray of sun and moved into the scarf around his neck, but it didn't stop there. He felt it in the people who wrapped their arms around him and held him, one after another, before leaving the graveyard. He saw it in the white-spired church where they had been married, on the town green where they had laughed, down the streets where they had walked. He even knew it would be in the bungalow on West Elm, where their son lay sleeping under his grandmother's watchful eye.

Bree was his soul mate. Her death couldn't change that. She was the ray of sun in a dark day, had been that for him from the first, and she was with him still, cheating death in her own imaginative way. Indeed, he felt her presence so strongly that when the crowd finally cleared, he half expected that she would be there.

Instead, standing a short distance across the newly tamped snow was his father.

Something inside Tom cracked. He was vaguely aware that Alice was there and that three of his brothers were, too, but it was his father who held his gaze, his father who drew his aging body up to Tom's height and started toward him, his father who didn't stop until he was close, then stood for a silent sad minute.

Tom wasn't sure what he saw then, because his eyes were filled with tears. But he felt things he had been too frozen to feel, felt love and grief and need. He felt regret and apology, felt acceptance, and suddenly he was ten years old, coming home to a place of unconditional love.

One open arm was all the invitation he needed. Wrapping both of his around his father, he buried his face in the collar of a coat where the scent of home was familiar and warm even after so many years away, and he cried as he hadn't been able to do before. He cried for Bree, cried for his mother, cried for things that had been lost in the morass of success. It all came out in low gulps that might have embarrassed him had his father made any move to set him back. But even when Tom was finished and held on still, his father held him right back.

In time, the others joined them. He embraced his brothers, holding each in silent thanks, and shared more tears with Alice, who had known Bree and felt her loss. He led them to the graveside, knowing Bree would appreciate that, and knew from the warmth inside him that she did. Then, finding warmth in this, too, he invited them home.

He felt a new urgency now. As short as the drive was, he grew impatient. Once there, he left his family with those closest friends who had gathered again at the house and ran up the stairs to the baby's room. Julia was leaning against the crib rail, rubbing the baby's back. Tom could see that she had been crying. He knew the exact instant when she saw that he had been, too.

"I just fed him," she said. "He's nearly asleep." She searched his face in relief and understanding, squeezed his arm, and left the room.

The baby lay under the afghan Verity had made. Tom drew it back and lifted him, one hand under his head and back, the other under his bottom. The baby didn't object. He didn't make faces or squirm. Little arms and legs barely left the fetal position. Eyes that had been nearly closed slowly opened.

Tom felt their warmth, and in that instant, Bree was with him again. The baby had her mouth, her neat ears, the shape of her face, her peaceful disposition. She had bequeathed him these things. He would wear them well. But he had other things, too, even aside from Tom's eyes. He had his own nose and chin, his own sweet voice, and a brain that made his tiny fingers move in gentle ways that were determined by no one but him.

Settling him in the crook of his elbow, Tom slipped a finger into those tiny ones. They promptly curled around it and held on. He lowered himself to the rocker and started it swinging slowly, soothingly, back and forth.

Bree approved. He could feel the force of her ear-to-ear smile. And if that didn't make sense? Tough. He felt it anyway. When she smiled that way, he felt strong. He felt that he could be a good father, that he could be a good *person,* that he could survive after all and make her proud. When she smiled that way, he *believed.*

"He's a fine-looking boy," came a gruff voice from the door.

Tom looked up. "His name's Wyatt."

Harris Gates came in for a closer look. "Definitely a mix of the two of you. Oh, I know. I never met her. But I saw those pictures. She looked like a good person."

"The best," Tom said. He drew in a deep breath, deeper than any he had taken since Bree had died. The pain was still there, but bearable now. "It's amazing. Two years ago, I didn't know she existed. We really only knew each other for fourteen months. Sometimes I think those fourteen months were preordained. Maybe they were all we were meant to have." He stroked the baby's silky auburn hair and swallowed. His eyes brimmed with new tears. Unembarrassed, he let them stay. "I used to think that she had come back to life solely for me to redeem myself."

"Haven't you?"

Had he? He had given Bree a home she loved, jewelry, a wedding, a honeymoon, a truck. He had been her cook, her waiter, her chauffeur. He had listened when she talked. He had been with her morning and night, taking pleasure from her pleasure. He had made her the center of his universe and had loved her with all his heart.

Could redemption have felt so *good?* Anything was possible.

"She wrote me a note," his father said. "It was with the gift she sent. She said you'd made her happier than she thought a person could be. Was she wrong?"

Tom studied the baby. His tiny cheek was against the scarf his mother had made. His eyes were closed, his little mouth pursing in sleep. Tom remembered Bree's mouth doing something like that, then spreading into a smile of delight when he woke her with a kiss. "No. She wasn't wrong."

"Did you do it only because of the accident? Because you felt you owed her?"

"No. It was because of her. Because I loved her. Because I wanted to make her happy. Because making her happy made *me* happy." Which sounded selfish again. "So am I still the bottom line?"

His father shook his head no.

Tom studied his craggy face. Age had thinned it and added creases and marks, but it remained a solid face, one people admired. His mother certainly had. Tom had seen her searching for it out the parlor window at the close of the day, even that last time he had seen her, when he had refused to admit to himself how ill she was. "I made some awful mistakes."

"Yes," his father said. "You did." There was silence, then a rough flurry. "So did I. I should have accepted your apology sooner, should have met your Bree. I missed my chance. Now it's too late."

Thinking about that, watching the baby sleep in his arms, Tom remembered the words on the card that had come with his scarf. *Don't look too closely,* Bree had written. *It's got lots of mistakes. More love than mistakes, though.*

More love than mistakes. He supposed that was what life was about. She had been a wise woman, his Bree.

Gently, he touched the soft spot on the baby's head. The pulse beating there was little more than a whisper, but a sweet one. He tipped his head back to the ceiling. It was the crisp white that he'd painted it, made more brilliant by the beam of the lamp Bree had bought. In the shower of that light, he felt her nearness and smiled.

~ *Epilogue* ~

*P*hotographs are wonderful things. They capture moments that would otherwise be lost and save them for all time. Some say photographs are flat, lifeless things. I say not. When the camera is in skilled hands, a photograph comes alive to capture a world of emotions.

Tom Gates's house is filled with photographs like that. I'm always amazed when I baby-sit Wyatt and find more on display. There are usually new ones of Wyatt, of course. Tom never tires of photographing him. But there are others that aren't newly taken, are only newly printed and framed. Those are of Bree.

You see, it's a two-way street. Tom documents Wyatt's life with him for Bree to see and Bree's life with him for Wyatt to see.

Oh, I know. You're thinking that Bree can't really *see* those pictures. Well, maybe she can't. Then again, maybe she can. I've seen Tom agitated over something one minute and, in the next, suddenly take a breath, draw himself up, and grow calm. He doesn't say it, but I know he's thinking of Bree. So is she present in his house?

I can't say she isn't.

She was actually the one to start the thing with photographs, and I don't mean the album she gave me. Among the gifts she left wrapped under the Christmas tree was a special one for Wyatt. It contained a double-hinged frame holding three pictures of her that Tom had taken during their all-too-brief marriage. No one looking at them can help but smile. They capture everything that was Bree—her warmth, her spirit, her love of the life that she found.

It took Tom months to open those last Christmas gifts. Long after the tree had been taken down, he kept them in a pile. He claimed that he had the only gifts he wanted, his son and the burgundy scarf Bree had crocheted. Only when spring arrived, and the daffodil bulbs that, against my better horticultural judgment, he had planted on her grave one bleak January day burst into glorious yellow bloom, did he feel strong enough to open the rest. There were books he had wanted, a legal print for his office, and driving gloves. There was a fine leather briefcase with his initials embossed. There was a small glass heart with multicolored swirls inside, good for nothing more than the thought it carried. Even now, five years later, Tom tucks it in his pocket every day.

Those first few months after Bree died were the hardest for him. Often I would find him in the rocking chair, with the baby asleep on his chest, tears in his eyes, and a stricken look on his face. As though she were an amputated limb, he kept feeling Bree there and mourned all over again when he found that she wasn't. In time, he adjusted to the idea that what remained of her was pure spirit.

That didn't mean he stopped missing her. He stayed home a lot that first year, bonding with Wyatt, yes, but unable to go out and just have fun. I had been the same after Teddy died. Feelings of emptiness, of guilt at being the one to survive, of fear of a future without, were overwhelming. Holidays in particular—the first this, the first that, without the person you loved more than life—were brutal. Occasionally, Tom strapped Wyatt to his chest and went through the motions, but anyone who looked could see his heart wasn't in it.

Two things changed that. No, three things. No, *four* things.

First, there was the town. If Panamanians were nothing else, they were persistent. They kept a close eye on Tom, bringing him food long after the funeral was over, calling often to see how he was, popping by to dote on the baby. They included him in their plans even when he resisted, protected him when the press finally found him, treated him as though he had lived in town for years. They let him know in dozens of wordless ways that he wasn't alone.

Second, there was Tom's family. His sister and brothers left two days after the funeral, but his father stayed on for a time. The end of their estrangement meant the world to Tom, all the more so as Wyatt grew bigger. Every few months, one Gates or another came to town. Whenever Tom felt too much time had elapsed, he packed Wyatt up, and the two of them flew home. Family had been Tom's backbone as a child. It was again now.

Third, there was work. Martin was the best partner Tom could have had. He might have felt threatened when Tom's identity first came out, but that feeling had disappeared entirely by the time Bree died. In fact, their roles reversed. Martin became more assistant than mentor. Under Tom's tutelage, he did the legwork that Tom couldn't do during those first dark days. By the time Tom felt up to returning to work, a thriving practice was waiting, so much so that he and Martin hired an associate. Even when he began to function well, Tom refused to work full time. He wanted to raise his son, Wyatt.

Yes, Wyatt. Wyatt was the fourth and probably the single most influential factor in getting Tom's heart working again. How *not* to smile and laugh with a child like that? I had worried that Tom's grieving would make Wyatt a serious child, but the reverse happened. Wyatt was an early smiler, an early tease, an early talker who loved being with people. Oh, he knew where his bread was buttered. He loved his daddy first and foremost, no doubt about that. But when his daddy took him to the diner, which he so often did, he was in his half-pint glory. By the age of three he had a killer smile and an uncanny sensitivity to people's moods. He had Tom's capacity to charm and Bree's outgoing nature, and was fearless, energetic, and imaginative. More than anyone or anything else, he led Tom back to the world of the living.

Tom has dozens of pictures of him scattered around the house and dozens more in albums—bulging, like mine—that are as popular bedtime fare as any story. *Remember this one, Daddy? Grammy, look at this one, it's you and me. Tell me again, Daddy, I want to hear about the time you took this one.* Some of the pictures are in color, some in black and white. Some show Wyatt alone, others show him playing with friends, at the diner helping Flash fix Earl his brownie sundae, picking blueberries with Verity, celebrating graduation from art school with Jane.

Jane has done well. She is working as court artist for a media group in greater Boston and is dating the detective who testified in one of her cases. Dotty says he's a thug who's only after her money, but since there isn't much of that, and since the detective in question comes from a family with *three* times as much, I doubt it's so. Besides, Tom's detective friend knows him and vouches for his character.

Tom is protective of Jane.

He is protective of Verity.

He is protective of me, too. Even back in those first days after Bree's death, he never betrayed me. My relationship to her was a secret we shared. He felt it was my job to tell people, my *right* to do it. He gave me time. And there was no rush. My presence in Wyatt's life aroused no suspicion. People knew that Bree and I had grown close. As the baby's godmother, it was only natural for me to help out with his care.

A quick word here, before I go on. I *helped*. That's all. There was never any question about who Wyatt's primary caretaker was. From the start, Tom did all the things that men of my generation rarely did. He diapered and fed, bathed and played, taught and disciplined. He never walked away from a chore, no matter how dirty it was. He was more attentive than ever when the child was fussy or sick.

Wyatt knows that I'm his grandmother. He's known since he was old enough to understand, because the whole town knew by then. Did the grapevine have a field day with that one! Word spread like lightning, not all of it kind. For a short time I was an outsider again, the woman who had cheated Haywood and Bree, the one who had come to town with a "hidden agenda" and been less than honest for four years. I was honest then, though. I bared my soul and invited their censure as part of my penance. When understanding and forgiveness came instead, I knew that Panama was truly my home.

All that, though, came after another trial. Before I told the town, I had to tell Nancy and Scott. It was hard. I had kept secrets from them far longer than from Panama. Nancy was the quicker to come around, understandably so, since she had met Bree and liked her. Whereas she could identify with the despair I had felt thinking Teddy was dead, Scott identified with his father and had more trouble accepting my infidelity. Of course, Scott was nothing if not competitive. When Nancy began visiting me in Panama, he wasn't about to let her get a foot up on him, so he visited, too. By then the trust fund was reflecting a healthy stock market and beginning to grow. Scott was appeased.

I have a good life here in Panama. My work as a florist is only as demanding as I want it to be, which means that I can meet my little kindergartner at the school bus any day when Tom is in court. Naturally, Tom apologizes. He respects the fact that I have a business to run, and if I didn't love him for other things, I would love him for that. But it is a joy for me to be able to do for Wyatt in ways that I didn't do for Bree. I've been given a second chance. There's closure in that.

I see closure coming on another front, too. Tom needs a woman. Wyatt may be only five now, but soon enough, he'll be older and wanting to spend much of his time with his friends.

Tom knows that. He has taught Wyatt enough about Bree so that mention of her is a regular part of the child's existence. That will always be so, for *both* of them. But they need to move on.

Those times when I grow angry at the thought that Bree died too young, I think of the accident that snowy October night. She died then. Had she not been revived, she would never have known Tom or me. She would never have experienced the joy she had. She would never have left a piece of herself behind in Wyatt. So I see those fourteen months as a gift.

Finally, Tom does, too. He knows now that he can survive without Bree. He can be a good parent and a fine lawyer and live the kind of life that would have made Bree proud. She is an irrevocable part of who he is. But just as she willingly gave her life to give him a child, he knows that she wouldn't want him growing old alone.

A new woman has just moved to town, a widow with a teenage daughter and a successful statistical analysis business that she plans to run from her house. That house is a charming Cape newly built on the site of the old Miller house on South Forest. Yes, it took Tom this long to do anything with the lot. He held it for two years after Bree died, finally razed the burned-out old house and left the land empty for another two years before building the Cape, and *then* he was fussy about who bought it. He personally helped this woman secure a mortgage. Her name is Diana, shortened to Dee.

Too much of a coincidence, you say?

I might have said it once, too. That was before Bree's three wishes.

But were the wishes real? you ask.

It's a fair question. A fluke spark from a faulty furnace could have caused the house fire. Bree had seen me around town for three years before she wished to see her mother. And more than one doctor told Tom of the feasibility that intense emotion of the type she had felt at the baby's birth could have caused her healthy heart to stop.

So *were* the wishes real? I'll never know for sure. All I know is that Bree believed they were. In those last fourteen months of her life, she came to believe that anything was possible.

I like to think it is.

Two great books— one great price!

Each book features two classics by your favorite authors together in one collectible volume!

Coast Road • Three Wishes
Barbara Delinsky

The Taming • The Conquest
Jude Deveraux

Twin of Ice • Twin of Fire
Jude Deveraux

Velvet Song • Velvet Angel
Jude Deveraux

Angel Creek • A Lady of the West
Linda Howard

Shades of Twilight • Son of the Morning
Linda Howard

Guardian Angel • The Gift
Julie Garwood

Castles • The Lion's Lady
Julie Garwood

Honey Moon • Hot Shot
Susan Elizabeth Phillips

Scandalous • Irresistible
Karen Robards

Homeplace • Far Harbor
JoAnn Ross

The Callahan Brothers Trilogy
JoAnn Ross

POCKET BOOKS
A Division of Simon & Schuster
A VIACOM COMPANY

Visit **www.simonsays.com**

charabanc noun SEE **bus**.

character noun 1 *This brand of tea has a character all of its own.* SEE **characteristic** noun, distinctiveness, flavour, idiosyncrasy, individuality, integrity, peculiarity, quality, stamp, taste, uniqueness.
2 *She has a forceful character.* attitude, constitution, disposition, individuality, make-up, manner, nature, personality, reputation, temper, temperament.
3 *She's a well-known character.* figure, human being, individual, person, personality, [*informal*] type.
4 *She made us laugh—she's such a character!* [*informal*] case, comedian, comic, eccentric, [*informal*] nut-case, oddity, [*uncomplimentary slang*] weirdo.
5 *a character in a play.* part, persona, portrayal, role.
6 *the characters of the alphabet.* cipher, figure, [*plural*] hieroglyphics (*Egyptian hieroglyphics*), ideogram, letter, mark, rune, sign, symbol, type.

characteristic adjective *I recognized his characteristic walk.* distinctive, distinguishing, essential, idiosyncratic, individual, particular, peculiar, recognizable, singular, special, specific, symptomatic, unique.

characteristic noun *He has some odd characteristics.* attribute, distinguishing feature, feature, hallmark, idiosyncrasy, peculiarity, symptom, trait.

characterize verb 1 *The play characterizes Richard III as a villain.* describe, delineate, depict, draw, portray, present.
2 *The cuckoo is characterized by its familiar call.* brand, differentiate, distinguish, identify, individualize, mark, recognize, typify.

charade noun *He wasn't really upset—his behaviour was just a charade.* acting, deceit, deception, fabrication, make-believe, masquerade, mockery, [*informal*] play-acting, pose, pretence, [*informal*] put-up job, sham.

charge noun 1 *an increase in charges.* cost, expenditure, expense, fare, fee, payment, postage, price, rate, terms, toll, value.
2 *They left the dog in my charge.* care, command, control, custody, keeping, protection, responsibility, safe-keeping, trust.
3 *a criminal charge.* accusation, allegation, imputation, indictment.
4 *Some of the horses fell in the charge.* assault, attack, incursion, invasion, offensive, onslaught, raid, rush, sortie, strike.

charge verb 1 *What do they charge for a coffee?* ask for, exact, levy, make you pay, require.
FOR VERBS WITH THE BUYER AS SUBJECT, SEE **pay** verb.
2 *They charged me with the duty of cleaning the hall.* burden, command, commit, empower, entrust, give, impose on.
3 *What crime did they charge him with?* accuse, blame, [*formal*] impeach, [*formal*] indict, prosecute, tax.
4 *The cavalry charged the enemy line.* assail, assault, attack, [*informal*] fall on, rush, set on, storm, [*informal*] wade into.

charger noun SEE **horse**.

chariot noun OTHER VEHICLES: SEE **vehicle**.

charisma noun SEE **charm** noun.

charitable adjective SEE **generous, kind**.

charity noun 1 *He helped us out of charity, not self-interest.* affection, altruism, benevolence, bounty, caring, compassion, consideration, generosity, goodness, helpfulness, humanity, kindness, love, mercy, philanthropy, sympathy, tender-heartedness, unselfishness, warm-heartedness.
OPPOSITES: SEE **selfishness**.
2 *The animals' hospital depends on our charity.* [*old-fashioned*] alms or almsgiving, bounty, donations, financial support, gifts, [*informal*] hand-outs, largesse, offerings, patronage, self-sacrifice.
3 *We collected for charity.* a good cause, the needy, the poor.

charlatan noun SEE **cheat** noun.

charm noun 1 *Everyone falls for his charm!* allure, appeal, attractiveness, charisma, fascination, hypnotic power, lovable nature, lure, magic, magnetism, power, pull, seductiveness, sex appeal.
2 *magic charms.* curse, enchantment, incantation, SEE **magic**, mumbo-jumbo, sorcery, spell, witchcraft, wizardry.
3 *a charm on a silver chain.* amulet, lucky charm, mascot, ornament, talisman, trinket.

charm verb *He charmed us with his singing.* allure, attract, beguile, bewitch, cajole, captivate, cast a spell on, decoy, delight, enchant, enrapture, entrance, fascinate, hold spellbound, intrigue, lure, mesmerize, please, seduce, soothe.

charming adjective *charming manners.* alluring, SEE **attractive**, disarming, endearing, lovable, seductive, winning, winsome.

chart noun 1 *a weather chart.* map, sketch-map.

2 *an information chart.* diagram, graph, plan, table.

charter noun SEE **document** noun.

charter verb *to charter an aircraft.* employ, engage, hire, lease, rent.

charwoman noun SEE **servant**.

chary adjective SEE **cautious**.

chase verb **1** *The dog chased a rabbit.* drive, follow, hound, hunt, pursue, track, trail.
2 [*informal*] *I chased round trying to finish my jobs.* SEE **hurry**.

chasm noun *a deep chasm.* abyss, canyon, cleft, crater, crevasse, drop, fissure, gap, gulf, hole, hollow, opening, pit, ravine, rift, split, void.

chaste adjective **1** *People in some religious orders remain chaste.* celibate, continent, [*formal*] immaculate, inexperienced, innocent, moral, pure, sinless, uncorrupted, undefiled, unmarried, virgin, virginal, virtuous.
OPPOSITES: SEE **immoral**.
2 *a chaste dress.* austere, becoming, decent, decorous, maidenly, modest, plain, restrained, simple, tasteful.
OPPOSITES: SEE **ornate, sexy, vulgar**.

chasten verb **1** *They chastened me for my slowness.* SEE **punish**.
2 *She was chastened by her failure to reach the finals.* SEE **humble** verb.

chastise verb SEE **punish**.

chastity noun *sexual chastity.* abstinence, celibacy, continence, innocence, maidenhood, purity, sinlessness, virginity, virtue.

chat noun, verb SEE **talk** noun, verb.

château noun SEE **castle**.

chattels noun SEE **possessions**.

chatter noun, verb SEE **talk** noun, verb.

chatterbox noun SEE **talkative (talkative person)**.

chatty adjective SEE **talkative**.

chauffeur noun driver.

chauvinism noun [*Chauvinism* means *exaggerated patriotism,* but is now also used to mean *sexism.*] SEE **patriotism**, sexism, SEE **prejudice** noun.

chauvinist, chauvinistic adjectives SEE **patriotic**, sexist, SEE **prejudiced**.

chauvinist noun SEE **prejudiced (prejudiced person)**.

cheap adjective **1** *a cheap buy. a cheap price.* bargain, budget, cut-price, [*informal*] dirt-cheap, discount, economical, economy, fair, inexpensive, [*informal*] knock-down, low-priced, reasonable, reduced, [*informal*] rock-bottom, sale, under-priced.
OPPOSITES: SEE **expensive**.
2 *cheap quality.* inferior, poor, second-rate, shoddy, tatty, tawdry, tinny, worthless.
OPPOSITES: SEE **superior**.
3 *cheap humour. cheap insults.* contemptible, crude, despicable, facile, glib, ill-bred, ill-mannered, mean, silly, tasteless, unworthy, vulgar.
OPPOSITES: SEE **worthy**.

cheapen verb *The actors' silly giggling cheapened the performance.* belittle, debase, degrade, demean, devalue, discredit, downgrade, lower the tone (of), popularize, prostitute, vulgarize.

cheat noun **1** *Don't trust him—he's a cheat.* charlatan, cheater, [*informal*] conman, counterfeiter, crafty person, deceiver, double-crosser, extortioner, forger, fraud, hoaxer, impersonator, impostor, [*informal*] phoney, [*informal*] quack, racketeer, rogue, [*informal*] shark, swindler, trickster, [*informal*] twister.
2 *The whole thing was a cheat.* artifice, bluff, chicanery, [*informal*] con, confidence trick, deceit, deception, [*slang*] fiddle, fraud, hoax, imposture, lie, misrepresentation, pretence, [*informal*] put-up job, [*informal*] racket, [*informal*] rip-off, ruse, sham, swindle, [*informal*] swizz, treachery, trick.

cheat verb **1** *He cheated me by selling me an unroadworthy car.* bamboozle, beguile, bilk, [*informal*] con, deceive, defraud, [*slang*] diddle, [*informal*] do, double-cross, dupe, [*slang*] fiddle, [*informal*] fleece, fool, hoax, hoodwink, outwit, [*informal*] rip off, rob, [*informal*] short-change, swindle, take in, trick.
2 *to cheat in an examination.* copy, crib, plagiarize.

check adjective *a check pattern.* SEE **chequered**.

check noun **1** *We reached our destination without any check.* SEE **interruption**.
2 *I took the car to the garage for a check.* check-up, examination, [*informal*] going-over, inspection, investigation, [*informal*] once-over, scrutiny, test.
3 [*American*] *a check for 10 dollars.* SEE **cheque**.
to keep in check SEE **check** verb.

check verb **1** *to check someone's progress. to check a horse.* arrest, bar, block, bridle, control, curb, delay, foil, govern, halt, hamper, hinder, hold back, impede, inhibit, keep in check, obstruct, regulate, rein, repress, restrain, retard, slow, slow down, stem (*to stem the tide*), stop, stunt (*to stunt growth*), thwart. **2** *We checked our answers. They checked the locks on the doors.* [*American*] check out, compare, cross-check, examine, inspect, investigate, monitor, research, scrutinize, test, verify.

check-up noun SEE **check** noun.

cheek noun [*informal*] *She's got a cheek!* arrogance, audacity, boldness, brazenness, effrontery, impertinence, impudence, insolence, [*informal*] lip, [*informal*] nerve, pertness, presumptuousness, rudeness, [*informal*] sauce, shamelessness, temerity.

cheeky adjective *a cheeky manner. a cheeky remark.* arrogant, audacious, bold, brazen, cool, discourteous, disrespectful, flippant, forward, impertinent, impolite, impudent, insolent, insulting, irreverent, mocking, pert, presumptuous, rude, [*informal*] saucy, shameless, [*informal*] tongue-in-cheek.
OPPOSITES: SEE **respectful**.

cheer noun **1** *Give the winners a hearty cheer!* acclamation, applause, cry of approval, encouragement, hurrah, ovation, shout of approval. **2** [*old-fashioned*] *Be of good cheer!* SEE **happiness**.

cheer verb **1** *We cheered the winners.* acclaim, applaud, clap, shout.
OPPOSITES: SEE **jeer**.
2 *The good news cheered us.* comfort, console, delight, divert, encourage, entertain, exhilarate, gladden, make cheerful, please, solace, uplift.
OPPOSITES: SEE **sadden**.
to cheer up *The weather cheered up. Cheer up—we're nearly home!* become more cheerful, brighten, [*informal*] buck up, make more cheerful, [*informal*] perk up, [*slang*] snap out of it, take heart.

cheerful adjective *a cheerful mood.* animated, bright, buoyant, cheery, [*informal*] chirpy, contented, convivial, delighted, elated, festive, gay, genial, glad, gleeful, good-humoured, SEE **happy**, hearty, jaunty, jocund, jolly, jovial, joyful, joyous, jubilant, laughing, light (*a light heart*), light-hearted, lively, merry, optimistic, [*informal*] perky, pleased, rapturous, sparkling, spirited, sprightly, sunny, warm-hearted.
OPPOSITES: SEE **sad**.

cheerfulness noun animation, brightness, cheeriness, elation, festivity, gaiety, good-humour, SEE **happiness**, jollity, laughter, merriment, optimism, sprightliness.
OPPOSITES: SEE **depression**.

cheerio interjection SEE **goodbye**.

cheerless adjective *a cheerless rainy day.* bleak, comfortless, dark, depressing, desolate, dingy, disconsolate, dismal, drab, dreary, dull, forbidding, forlorn, frowning, funereal, gloomy, grim, joyless, lack-lustre, melancholy, miserable, mournful, sad, sober, sombre, sullen, sunless, uncongenial, unhappy, uninviting, unpleasant, unpromising, woeful, wretched.
OPPOSITES: SEE **cheerful**.

cheery adjective *a cheery manner.* airy, blithe, carefree, SEE **cheerful**, good-humoured, pleasant.

chef noun cook.

chemical noun compound, element, substance.

SOME CHEMICALS: acid, alcohol, alkali, ammonia, arsenic, chlorine, fluoride, litmus.

CHEMICAL ELEMENTS AND THEIR SYMBOLS: actinium *Ac*, aluminium *Al*, americium *Am*, antimony *Sb*, argon *Ar*, arsenic *As*, astatine *At*, barium *Ba*, berkelium *Bk*, beryllium *Be*, bismuth *Bi*, boron *B*, bromine *Br*, cadmium *Cd*, caesium *Cs*, calcium *Ca*, californium *Cf*, carbon *C*, cerium *Ce*, chlorine *Cl*, chromium *Cr*, cobalt *Co*, copper *Cu*, curium *Cm*, dysprosium *Dy*, einsteinium *Es*, erbium *Er*, europium *Eu*.

fermium *Fm*, fluorine *F*, francium *Fr*, gadolinium *Gd*, gallium *Ga*, germanium *Ge*, gold *Au*, hafnium *Hf*, helium *He*, holmium *Ho*, hydrogen *H*, indium *In*, iodine *I*, iridium *Ir*, iron *Fe*, krypton *Kr*, lanthanum *La*, lawrencium *Lr*, lead *Pb*, lithium *Li*, lutetium *Lu*, magnesium *Mg*, manganese *Mn*, mendelevium *Md*, mercury *Hg*, molybdenum *Mo*.

neodymium *Nd*, neon, *Ne*, neptunium *Np*, nickel *Ni*, niobium *Nb*, nitrogen *N*, nobelium *No*, osmium *Os*, oxygen *O*, palladium *Pd*, phosphorus *P*, platinum *Pt*, plutonium *Pu*, polonium *Po*, potassium *K*, praseodymium *Pr*, promethium *Pm*, protactinium *Pa*, radium *Ra*, radon *Rn*, rhenium *Re*, rhodium *Rh*, rubidium *Rb*, ruthenium *Ru*.

samarium *Sm*, scandium *Sc*, selenium *Se*, silicon *Si*, silver *Ag*, sodium *Na*, strontium *Sr*, sulphur *S*, tantalum *Ta*, technetium *Tc*, tellurium *Te*, terbium *Tb*, thallium *Tl*, thorium *Th*, thulium, *Tm*, tin *Sn*, titanium *Ti*, tungsten *W*, uranium *U*, vanadium *V*, xenon *Xe*, ytterbium *Yb*, yttrium *Y*, zinc *Zn*, zirconium *Zr*.

chemist noun 1 OTHER SCIENTISTS: SEE **scientist**.
2 *I went on to the chemist's for some medicine.* [*old-fashioned*] apothecary, [*American*] drug-store, pharmacist.

chemistry noun OTHER SCIENCES: SEE **science**.

cheque, cheque-card nouns [*American*] check, SEE **money**.

chequered adjective 1 *a chequered pattern.* check, criss-cross, in squares, like a chessboard, patchwork, tartan, tessellated.
2 *a chequered career.* SEE **changeable**.

cherish verb *I cherish the present you gave me.* be fond of, care for, foster, keep safe, look after, love, nourish, nurse, prize, protect, treasure, value.

cherry adjective SEE **red**.

cherub noun SEE **angel**.

cherubic adjective SEE **angelic**.

chess noun CHESSMEN: bishop, castle or rook, knight, king, queen, pawn.
TERMS USED IN CHESS: castle, check, checkmate, mate, move, stalemate, take.

chest noun 1 *a tool chest.* box, case, casket, coffer, crate, strongbox, trunk.
2 *a person's chest.* breast, rib-cage.
RELATED ADJECTIVE: pectoral.

chestnut adjective SEE **brown** adjective.

chevron noun SEE **badge**.

chew verb *to chew food.* bite, champ, crunch, SEE **eat**, gnaw, masticate, munch, nibble.

chewy adjective 1 *chewy toffee.* elastic, flexible, [*formal*] malleable, pliant, springy, sticky, stiff.
OPPOSITES: SEE **brittle**.
2 *chewy meat.* gristly, leathery, rubbery, tough.
OPPOSITES: SEE **tender**.

chic adjective SEE **elegant, fashionable**.

chicanery noun SEE **trickery**.

chick noun SEE **bird**.

chicken noun bantam, broiler, chick, cockerel, fowl, hen, pullet, rooster.

chicken verb **to chicken out** SEE **withdraw**.

chicken-feed noun SEE **small** (**small amount**).

chicken-hearted adjective SEE **cowardly**.

chide verb SEE **scold**.

chief adjective 1 *the chief guest.* first, greatest, highest, major, most honoured, most important, principal.

OPPOSITES: SEE **unimportant**.
2 *the chief cook.* arch (*the arch enemy*), head, in charge, leading, most experienced, oldest, senior, supreme, top, unequalled, unrivalled.
OPPOSITES: SEE **junior**.
3 *the chief facts.* basic, cardinal, central, dominant, especial, essential, foremost, fundamental, high-priority, indispensable, key, main, necessary, outstanding, overriding, paramount, predominant, primary, prime, salient, significant, substantial, uppermost, vital, weighty.
OPPOSITES: SEE **unimportant**.

chief noun *Who's the chief around here?* administrator, authority-figure, [*informal*] bigwig, [*informal*] boss, captain, chairperson, chieftain, commander, commanding officer, commissioner, controller, director, employer, executive, foreman, [*informal*] gaffer, [*American*] godfather [= *chief criminal*], governor, head, leader, manager, master, mistress, officer, organizer, overseer, owner, president, principal, proprietor, responsible person, [*uncomplimentary*] ring-leader, ruler, superintendent, supervisor, [*informal*] supremo.
OPPOSITES: SEE **employee**.

chiefly adverb especially, essentially, generally, mainly, mostly, predominantly, primarily, principally, usually.

chieftain noun SEE **chief** noun.

child noun 1 *a growing child.* [*informal*] babe, baby, [*Scottish*] bairn, [*informal, from Italian*] bambino, boy, [*uncomplimentary*] brat, girl, [*uncomplimentary*] guttersnipe, infant, [*formal*] juvenile, [*informal*] kid, [*formal*] minor, [*informal*] nipper, offspring, toddler, [*informal*] tot, [*uncomplimentary*] urchin, youngster, youth.
2 *a child of wealthy parents.* daughter, descendant, heir, issue, offspring, progeny, son.
expert in children's illnesses paediatrician.

childbirth noun SEE **birth**.

childhood noun adolescence, babyhood, boyhood, girlhood, infancy, minority, schooldays, [*informal*] your teens, youth.

childish adjective [*Childish* is a word used by adults to describe behaviour or qualities they disapprove of, whereas *childlike* is used to describe qualities people generally approve of.] *It's childish to make rude noises.* babyish, foolish, immature, infantile, juvenile, puerile, silly.
OPPOSITES: SEE **mature**.

childlike adjective [See note under *child- ish.*] *a childlike trust in people's goodness.* artless, frank, guileless, ingenuous, innocent, naïve, natural, simple, trust- ful, unaffected, unsophisticated.
OPPOSITES: SEE **artful**.

chill adjective SEE **chilly**.

chill noun *The chill penetrated to our bones.* SEE **cold** noun.

chill verb 1 *The wind chilled us to the bone.* cool, freeze, make cold.
OPPOSITES: SEE **warm** verb.
2 *to chill food.* keep cold, refrigerate.

chilly adjective 1 *a chilly evening.* cold, cool, crisp, fresh, frosty, icy, [*informal*] nippy, [*informal*] parky, raw, sharp, wintry.
OPPOSITES: SEE **warm** adjective.
2 *a chilly greeting.* aloof, cool, dispassion- ate, frigid, hostile, ill-disposed, remote, reserved, [*informal*] standoffish, un- forthcoming, unfriendly, unresponsive, unsympathetic, unwelcoming.
OPPOSITES: SEE **friendly**.

chime noun, verb SEE **bell**.

chimney noun flue, funnel, smoke- stack.

chimpanzee noun SEE **monkey**.

china noun crockery, earthenware, por- celain, SEE **pottery**.

chink noun 1 *a chink in the wall.* cleft, crack, crevice, cut, fissure, gap, open- ing, rift, slit, slot, space, split.
2 *the chink of glasses.* VARIOUS SOUNDS: SEE **sound** noun.

chip noun 1 *I knocked a chip off the cup.* bit, flake, fleck, fragment, piece, scrap, shaving, shiver, slice, sliver, splinter, wedge.
2 *I noticed a chip in the cup.* crack, damage, flaw, gash, nick, notch, scratch, snick.

chip verb *I chipped the cup.* break, crack, damage, gash, nick, notch, scratch, splinter.

chipboard noun OTHER KINDS OF WOODEN MATERIAL: SEE **wood**.

Several English words, including *chiro- podist* and *chiropractor*, are related to Greek *kheir = hand.*

---

chiropodist noun pedicurist.

chiropractor noun manipulator, [*male*] masseur, [*female*] masseuse, osteopath, physiotherapist.

chirp noun, verb VARIOUS SOUNDS: SEE **sound** noun.

chirpy adjective SEE **cheerful**.

chirrup noun, verb VARIOUS SOUNDS: SEE **sound** noun.

chisel verb SEE **cut** verb.

chit noun SEE **note** noun.

chit-chat noun SEE **talk** noun.

chivalrous adjective *a chivalrous knight.* bold, brave, chivalric, courageous, courteous, courtly, gallant, gener- ous, gentlemanly, heroic, honourable, knightly, noble, polite, respectable, true, trustworthy, valiant, valorous, worthy.
OPPOSITES: SEE **cowardly**, **dishonour- able**, **rude**.

chivvy verb SEE **urge** verb.

chlorinate verb SEE **disinfect**.

chloroform noun SEE **anaesthetic**.

chock noun *a chock of wood.* block, chunk, lump, piece, slab, wedge, [*infor- mal*] wodge.

chocolate adjective SEE **brown** adjective.

chocolate noun OTHER SWEETS: SEE **sweet** noun (**sweets**).

choice adjective SEE **excellent**.

choice noun 1 *The choice was between two good candidates.* alternative, choosing, dilemma, need to choose, option.
2 *The older candidate was our choice.* decision, election, liking, nomination, pick, preference, say, vote.
3 *The greengrocer has a good choice of vegetables.* array, assortment, diversity, miscellany, mixture, range, selection, variety.

choir noun choral society, chorus, vocal ensemble.
OTHER MUSICAL GROUPS: SEE **music**.

choke verb 1 *This collar is choking me.* asphyxiate, smother, stifle, strangle, suffocate, throttle.
2 *The firemen choked in the smoke.* gag, gasp, retch, suffocate.
3 *The roads were choked with traffic.* block, [*informal*] bung up, clog, close, congest, fill, jam, obstruct, smother, stop up.

choleric adjective SEE **angry**.

choose verb 1 *They chose a new leader. I chose a green anorak.* adopt, appoint, decide on, distinguish, draw lots for, elect, fix on, identify, isolate, name, nominate, opt for, pick out, [*informal*] plump for, select, settle on, show a preference for, single out, vote for.
2 *I chose to do it myself.* decide, deter- mine, prefer, resolve.

choosy adjective SEE **fussy**.

chop verb *to chop wood.* cleave, SEE **cut** verb, hack, hew, slash, split.
to chop down cut down, fell.

to chop off amputate, detach, dock, lop, lop off, sever.

to chop up cut up, dice, divide, mince, share out, subdivide.

to chop and change SEE **change** verb.

chopper noun **1** axe, cleaver.
OTHER TOOLS: SEE **tool**.
2 helicopter.

choppy adjective *a choppy sea.* rippled, roughish, ruffled, turbulent, uneven, wavy.
OPPOSITES: SEE **smooth**.

chore noun *chores around the house.* boring work (SEE **boring**), burden, drudgery, duty, errand, job, task, work.

choreography noun SEE **dance** noun.

chorister noun SEE **singer**.

chortle verb SEE **laugh**.

chorus noun **1** choir, choral society, vocal ensemble.
OTHER MUSICAL GROUPS: SEE **music**.
2 *We all sang the chorus.* refrain, response.

in chorus SEE **together**.

christen verb *Tony was christened Antony.* baptize, dub, name.

Christmas noun the festive season, Noel, [*informal*] Xmas, Yule, Yuletide.

Several English words, including *chromatic* and *monochrome,* are related to Greek *khroma = colour.*

---

chromatic adjective **1** SEE **colourful**.
OPPOSITE: monochrome.
2 *the chromatic scale.* semitone.
OPPOSITE: diatonic.

chrome noun chromium.
chrome yellow SEE **yellow**.

Several English words, including *chronic, chronological, chronometer,* etc., are related to Greek *khronos = time.*

---

chronic adjective **1** *a chronic illness.* ceaseless, constant, continual, continuous, deep-rooted, everlasting, habitual, incessant, incurable, ineradicable, ingrained, lifelong, lingering, permanent, persistent, unending.
OPPOSITES: SEE **acute, temporary**.
2 [*informal*] *His driving is chronic!* SEE **bad**.

chronicle noun *a chronicle of events.* account, annals, diary, history, journal, narrative, record, saga, story.

chronological adjective *chronological order.* consecutive, sequential.

chronology noun calendar, dating, diary, order, schedule, sequence, timetable, timing.

chronometer noun clock, timepiece, watch.

chrysalis noun STAGES OF INSECT LIFE: SEE **insect**.

chubby adjective *a chubby figure.* buxom, dumpy, SEE **fat** adjective, plump, podgy, portly, rotund, round, stout, tubby.

chuck verb [*informal*] *Stop chucking rubbish in the water.* cast, ditch, dump, fling, heave, hurl, jettison, lob, pitch, shy, sling, throw, toss.

to chuck away, to chuck out discard, dispose of, reject, scrap, throw away.

chuckle verb SEE **laugh** verb.

chuffed adjective SEE **pleased**.

chug verb VARIOUS SOUNDS: SEE **sound** noun.

chum noun SEE **friend**.

chummy adjective SEE **friendly**.

chump noun SEE **idiot**.

chunk noun *a chunk of cheese. a chunk of wood.* bar, block, brick, chuck, [*informal*] dollop, hunk, lump, mass, piece, portion, slab, wad, wedge, [*informal*] wodge.

church noun

CHURCH BUILDINGS: abbey, basilica, cathedral, chapel, convent, monastery, nunnery, parish church, priory.

PARTS OF A CHURCH: aisle, belfry, buttress, chancel, chapel, cloister, crypt, dome, gargoyle, nave, porch, precinct, sacristy, sanctuary, spire, steeple, tower, transept, vestry.

THINGS YOU FIND IN A CHURCH: altar, Bible, candle, communion-table, crucifix, font, hymn-book, lectern, memorial tablet, pew, prayer-book, pulpit.

WORDS TO DO WITH CHURCH: Advent, angel, Ascension Day, Ash Wednesday, baptism, benediction, christening, Christmas, communion, confirmation, Easter, Good Friday, gospel, hymn, incense, Lent, martyr, mass, Nativity, New Testament, Old Testament, Palm Sunday, patron saint, Pentecost, prayer, preaching, psalm, requiem, Resurrection, sabbath, sacrament, saint, scripture, sermon, service, Whitsun, worship.

PEOPLE CONNECTED WITH CHURCH: archbishop, bishop, cardinal, chaplain, choirboy, choirgirl, churchwarden, clergyman, cleric, congregation, curate, deacon, deaconess, elder, evangelist, friar, layman, minister, missionary, monk, non-conformist, nun, padre, parson, pastor, Pope, preacher, prelate, priest, rector, sexton, sidesman, verger, vicar.

churchyard noun burial-ground, cemetery, graveyard.

churlish adjective SEE **rude**.

churn verb SEE **agitate**.

chute noun *a water-chute*. incline, ramp, slide, slope.

chutney noun pickle, relish.

ciao interjection SEE **goodbye**.

cinder noun *a cinder from a fire*. ash, clinker, ember.

cinder-track noun SEE **racecourse**.

cine-camera noun SEE **camera**.

cinema noun films, [*informal*] the movies, the pictures.

cipher noun SEE **character, code**.

circle noun 1 *a perfect circle*. ring.
2 *a large circle of friends*. association, band, body, clique, club, company, fellowship, fraternity, gang, SEE **group** noun, party, set, society.

LINES AND SHAPES IN RELATION TO A CIRCLE: arc, chord, diameter, radius, sector, segment, tangent.

VARIOUS CIRCULAR SHAPES OR MOVEMENTS: band, belt, circlet, circuit, circulation, circumference, circumnavigation, coil, cordon, curl, curve, cycle, disc, ellipse, girdle, globe, gyration, hoop, lap, loop, orb, orbit, oval, revolution, rotation, round, sphere, spiral, tour, turn, wheel, whirl, whorl.

circle verb 1 VARIOUS WAYS TO MAKE A CIRCLE OR TO MOVE IN A CIRCLE: circulate, circumnavigate, circumscribe, coil, compass, corkscrew, curl, curve, encircle, girdle, gyrate, hem in, loop, orbit, pirouette, pivot, reel, revolve, ring, rotate, spin, spiral, surround, swirl, swivel, tour, wheel, whirl, wind.
2 *The plane circled before landing*. go round, turn, wheel.
3 *Trees circled the lawn*. encircle, enclose, encompass, girdle, hem in, ring, skirt, surround.

circuit noun 1 SEE **circle** noun.
2 *a racing circuit*. SEE **racecourse**.
3 *I completed one circuit in record time*. lap, orbit, revolution.
4 *We made a circuit of the antique shops*. journey round, tour of.

circuitous adjective *a circuitous route*. curving, devious, indirect, labyrinthine, meandering, oblique, rambling, roundabout, serpentine, tortuous, twisting, winding, zigzag.
OPPOSITES: SEE **direct** adjective.

circular adjective 1 *a circular shape*. elliptical, oval, round.
2 *a circular argument*. cyclic, repeating, repetitive.

circular noun *an advertising circular*. advertisement, leaflet, letter, notice, pamphlet.

circulate verb 1 *I circulated round the room to speak to my friends*. SEE **circle** verb, go round, move about.
2 *We circulated a notice about our sale*. [*formal*] disseminate, distribute, issue, [*formal*] promulgate, publicize, publish, send round, spread about.

circulation noun 1 *the circulation of the blood*. flow, movement, pumping, recycling.
2 *the circulation of information*. broadcasting, dissemination, distribution, spread, transmission.
3 *the circulation of a newspaper*. distribution, sales-figures.

circumference noun *It's a mile round the circumference of the field*. border, boundary, circuit, edge, exterior, fringe, limit, margin, outline, outside, perimeter, periphery, rim, verge.

circumlocution noun SEE **verbiage**.

circumnavigate verb SEE **travel** verb.

circumscribe verb SEE **restrict**.

circumspect adjective SEE **cautious**.

circumstances noun [*usually plural*] *Don't jump to conclusions before you know the circumstances*. background, causes, conditions, considerations, context, contingencies, details, facts, factors, influences, particulars, position, situation, surroundings.

circumstantial adjective *circumstantial evidence*. conjectural, unprovable.
OPPOSITES: SEE **provable**.

circumvent verb SEE **evade**.

circus noun big top.

WORDS TO DO WITH A CIRCUS: acrobat, clown, contortionist, juggler, lion-tamer, ring, ringmaster, tightrope, trainer, trapeze, trapeze-artist.

cirrus noun SEE **cloud** noun.

cistern noun *a water cistern*. reservoir, tank.
OTHER CONTAINERS: SEE **container**.

citadel noun acropolis, bastion, castle, fort, fortification, fortress, garrison, stronghold, tower.

cite verb *She cited several authorities to support her case.* adduce, advance, [*informal*] bring up, enumerate, mention, name, quote, [*informal*] reel off, refer to, specify.

citizen noun *the citizens of a town or country.* [*old-fashioned*] burgess, commoner, denizen, householder, inhabitant, national, native, passport-holder, ratepayer, resident, subject, taxpayer, voter.

citrus fruit noun VARIOUS CITRUS FRUITS: clementine, grapefruit, lemon, lime, mandarin, orange, satsuma, tangerine.

city noun *London is a large city.* conurbation, metropolis, town.
RELATED ADJECTIVE: urban.

civil adjective 1 *I know you're angry, but try to be civil.* affable, civilized, considerate, courteous, obliging, SEE **polite**, respectful, well-bred, well-mannered.
OPPOSITES: SEE **impolite**.
2 *civil defence. civil liberties.* communal, national, public, social, state.
civil engineering SEE **engineering**.
civil rights freedom, human rights, legal rights, liberty, political rights.
civil servant administrator, bureaucrat, mandarin.

civilian adjective, noun
OPPOSITE: military.

civility noun SEE **politeness**.

civilization noun *the civilization of the ancient Egyptians.* achievements, attainments, culture, organization, refinement, sophistication, urbanity, urbanization.

civilize verb *Could we civilize monkeys?* cultivate, educate, enlighten, humanize, improve, make better, organize, refine, socialize, urbanize.

civilized adjective *a civilized nation. civilized behaviour.* cultivated, cultured, democratic, developed, educated, enlightened, orderly, polite, sophisticated, urbane, well-behaved, well-run.
OPPOSITES: SEE **uncivilized**.

clad adjective SEE **clothed**.

cladding noun SEE **covering**.

claim verb 1 *I claimed my reward.* ask for, collect, demand, exact, insist on, request, require, take.
2 *He claims that he's an expert.* affirm, allege, argue, assert, attest, contend, declare, insist, maintain, pretend, profess, state.

clairvoyant adjective *I could foretell the future if I had clairvoyant powers.* extrasensory, oracular, prophetic, psychic, telepathic.

clairvoyant noun fortune-teller, oracle, prophet, seer, sibyl, soothsayer.

clamber verb *We clambered over the rocks.* climb, crawl, move awkwardly, scramble.

clammy adjective *a clammy atmosphere. clammy hands.* damp, dank, humid, moist, muggy, slimy, sticky, sweaty.

clamour noun *The starlings made a clamour.* babel, commotion, din, hubbub, hullabaloo, noise, outcry, racket, row, screeching, shouting, storm (*a storm of protest*), uproar.

clamour verb *They clamoured for attention.* call out, cry out, exclaim, shout, yell.

clamp verb SEE **fasten**.

clan noun *a Scottish clan.* family, house, tribe.

clandestine adjective SEE **secret** adjective.

clang noun, verb, **clangour** noun
VARIOUS SOUNDS: SEE **sound** noun.

clank noun, verb VARIOUS SOUNDS: SEE **sound** noun.

clannish adjective *a clannish family.* cliquish, close, close-knit, insular, isolated, narrow, united.

clap noun 1 *a clap of thunder.* SEE **sound** noun.
2 *a clap on the shoulder.* SEE **hit** noun.

clap verb 1 *We clapped her performance.* applaud.
2 *He clapped me on the shoulder.* SEE **hit** verb, pat, slap, smack.

claptrap noun SEE **nonsense**.

clarify verb 1 *Clarify what you want us to do.* define, elucidate, explain, gloss, illuminate, make clear, throw light on.
OPPOSITES: SEE **confuse**.
2 *I passed the wine through a filter to clarify it.* cleanse, clear, filter, purify, refine.

clarion adjective SEE **clear** adjective, **loud**.

clash noun 1 *the clash of cymbals.* SEE **sound** noun.
2 *a clash between enemies.* SEE **conflict** noun.

clash verb 1 *The cymbals clashed.* VARIOUS SOUNDS: SEE **sound** noun.
2 *The rival gangs clashed. The colours clash.* SEE **conflict** verb.

3 *My interview clashes with my dentist's appointment.* SEE **coincide**.

clasp noun 1 *a gold clasp.* brooch, buckle, catch, clip, fastener, fastening, hasp, hook, pin.
2 *a loving clasp.* cuddle, embrace, grasp, grip, hold, hug.

clasp verb 1 *to clasp things together.* SEE **fasten**.
2 *to clasp someone in your arms.* cling to, clutch, embrace, enfold, grasp, grip, hold, hug, squeeze.
3 *to clasp your hands.* hold together, wring.

clasp-knife noun SEE **knife** noun.

class noun 1 *in a class of its own.* category, classification, division, genre, genus, grade, group, kind, league, order, quality, rank, set, sort, species, sphere, type.
2 *social class.* caste, degree, grouping, standing, station, status.

TERMS SOMETIMES USED TO LABEL SOCIAL CLASSES: aristocracy, bourgeoisie, commoners, the commons, gentry, lower class, middle class, nobility, proletariat, ruling class, serfs, upper class, upper-middle class, the workers, working class.

---

3 *a class in a school.* band, form, group, set, stream.

class verb SEE **classify**.

classic adjective [It is useful to distinguish between *classic = excellent or typical of its kind,* and *classical = of the ancient Greeks and Romans,* or *classical = having an elegant style like that associated with classical times.*]
1 *a classic goal.* admirable, consummate, copybook, excellent, exceptional, exemplary, fine, first-class, first-rate, flawless, SEE **good**, ideal, [*informal*] immaculate, masterly, memorable, model, perfect, superlative, supreme, [*informal*] vintage.
OPPOSITES: SEE **commonplace**.
2 *classic works of literature.* abiding, ageless, deathless, enduring, established, immortal, lasting, time-honoured, undying.
OPPOSITES: SEE **ephemeral**.
3 *a classic case of chicken-pox.* archetypal, characteristic, regular, standard, typical, usual.
OPPOSITES: SEE **unusual**.

classic noun *This book is a classic!* masterpiece, model.

classical adjective [See note under *classic.*]

1 *classical civilizations.* ancient, Attic, Greek, Hellenic, Latin, Roman.
OPPOSITES: SEE **modern**.
2 *a classical style of architecture.* austere, dignified, elegant, pure, restrained, simple, symmetrical, well-proportioned.
OPPOSITES: SEE **exuberant**.
3 *classical music.* established, harmonious, highbrow.
OPPOSITES: SEE **modern, popular**.

classification noun *the classification of knowledge.* categorization, SEE **class** noun, codification, ordering, organization, systematization, tabulation, taxonomy.

classified adjective *classified information.* confidential, [*informal*] hush-hush, private, restricted, secret, sensitive, top secret.

classify verb *We classified the plants according to the shape of their leaves.* arrange, catalogue, categorize, class, grade, group, order, organize, [*informal*] pigeon-hole, put into sets, sort, systematize, tabulate.

classy adjective SEE **stylish**.

clatter noun, verb VARIOUS SOUNDS: SEE **sound** noun.

clause noun 1 *a clause in a legal document.* article, condition, item, paragraph, part, passage, provision, proviso, section, subsection.
2 *a clause in a sentence.* LINGUISTIC TERMS: SEE **language**.

claw noun *a bird's claws.* nail, talon.

claw verb *The animal clawed at its attacker.* graze, injure, lacerate, maul, rip, scrape, scratch, tear.

clean adjective 1 *a clean floor. clean clothes.* dirt-free, hygienic, immaculate, laundered, perfect, polished, sanitary, scrubbed, spotless, tidy, unsoiled, unstained, washed, wholesome.
OPPOSITES: SEE **dirty** adjective.
2 *clean water.* clarified, clear, decontaminated, distilled, fresh, pure, purified, sterilized, unadulterated, unpolluted.
OPPOSITES: SEE **impure**.
3 *clean paper.* blank, new, plain, uncreased, unmarked, untouched, unused.
OPPOSITES: SEE **used**.
4 *a clean edge. a clean incision.* neat, regular, smooth, straight, tidy.
OPPOSITES: SEE **jagged, ragged**.
5 *a clean fight.* chivalrous, fair, honest, honourable, sporting, sportsmanlike.
OPPOSITES: SEE **dishonourable**.
6 [*informal*] *a clean joke. clean thoughts.* chaste, decent, good, innocent, moral, respectable, upright, virtuous.
OPPOSITES: SEE **indecent**.
to make a clean breast (of) SEE **confess**.

clean verb VARIOUS WAYS TO CLEAN THINGS: bath, bathe, brush, buff, cleanse, decontaminate, deodorize, disinfect, dry-clean, dust, filter, flush, groom, hoover, launder, mop, polish, purge, purify, rinse, sand-blast, sanitize, scour, scrape, scrub, shampoo, shower, soap, sponge, spring-clean, spruce up, sterilize, swab, sweep, swill, vacuum, wash, wipe, wring out.
OPPOSITES: SEE **contaminate, dirty** verb.

cleanse verb SEE **clean** verb.

clean-shaven adjective beardless, shaved, shaven, shorn, smooth.
OPPOSITES: SEE **shaggy**.

clear adjective 1 *clear water.* clean, colourless, crystalline, glassy, limpid, pellucid, pure, transparent.
OPPOSITES: SEE **opaque**.
2 *a clear sky.* bright, cloudless, sunny, starlit, unclouded.
OPPOSITES: SEE **cloudy**.
3 *a clear conscience.* blameless, easy, guiltless, innocent, quiet, satisfied, sinless, undisturbed, untarnished, untroubled, unworried.
OPPOSITES: SEE **troubled**.
4 *a clear outline. a clear signal. clear handwriting.* bold, clean, definite, distinct, explicit, focused, legible, obvious, plain, positive, recognizable, sharp, simple, unambiguous, unmistakable, visible, well-defined.
OPPOSITES: SEE **indistinct**.
5 *a clear sound.* audible, clarion (*a clarion call*), distinct, penetrating, sharp.
OPPOSITES: SEE **muffled**.
6 *a clear explanation.* clear-cut, coherent, comprehensible, intelligible, lucid, perspicuous, unambiguous, understandable, unequivocal, well-presented.
OPPOSITES: SEE **confused**.
7 *a clear case of cheating.* apparent, blatant, conspicuous, evident, glaring, indisputable, manifest, noticeable, obvious, palpable, perceptible, plain, pronounced, straightforward, unconcealed, undisguised.
OPPOSITES: SEE **disputable**.
8 *a clear road. a clear space.* empty, free, open, passable, uncluttered, uncrowded, unhampered, unhindered, unimpeded, unobstructed.
OPPOSITES: SEE **congested**.

clear verb 1 *The fog cleared.* disappear, evaporate, fade, melt away, vanish.
2 *Wait for the water to clear. The weather cleared.* become clear, brighten, clarify, lighten, uncloud.
3 *I cleared the misty windows.* clean, make clean, make transparent, polish, wipe.

4 *I cleared the weeds from my garden.* disentangle, eliminate, get rid of, remove, strip.
5 *She cleared the blocked drainpipe.* clean out, free, loosen, open up, unblock, unclog.
6 *The court cleared him of all blame.* absolve, acquit, [*formal*] exculpate, excuse, exonerate, free, [*informal*] let off, liberate, release, vindicate.
7 *If the alarm goes, clear the building.* empty, evacuate.
8 *The horse cleared the fence.* bound over, jump, leap over, pass over, spring over, vault.
to clear away SEE **remove**.
to clear off SEE **depart**.
to clear up 1 *Clear up the mess.* clean, remove, put right, put straight, tidy.
2 *I asked her to clear up a difficulty.* answer, clarify, elucidate, explain, make clear, resolve, solve.

clear-cut adjective *Her proposal was clear-cut.* clear, coherent, definite, distinct, explicit, intelligible, lucid, plain, positive, precise, specific, straightforward, unambiguous, understandable, unequivocal, well-defined, well-presented.

clearing noun *a clearing in the forest.* gap, glade, opening, space.

clearway noun SEE **road**.

cleavage noun SEE **split** noun.

cleave verb SEE **cut** verb.

cleaver noun axe, chopper, knife.

cleft noun SEE **split** noun.

clemency noun SEE **mercy**.

clement adjective *clement weather.* balmy, calm, favourable, gentle, mild, peaceful, pleasant, temperate, warm.

clench verb 1 *to clench your teeth. to clench your fist.* clamp up, close tightly, double up, grit (your teeth), squeeze tightly.
2 *to clench something in your hand.* clasp, grasp, grip, hold.

clergyman noun VARIOUS CLERGYMEN: archbishop, bishop, canon, cardinal, chaplain, cleric, curate, deacon, deaconess, dean, evangelist, minister, ordained person, padre, parson, pastor, preacher, prelate, priest, rector, vicar.
OPPOSITES: SEE **layman**.

cleric noun SEE **clergyman**.

clerical adjective 1 *clerical work.* office, secretarial.
2 [= *of clerics, of clergymen*] *clerical duties.* ecclesiastical, pastoral, priestly, spiritual.

clerk noun VARIOUS PEOPLE DOING CLERI-CAL WORK: assistant, bookkeeper, computer operator, copyist, filing clerk, office boy, office girl, office worker, [informal] pen-pusher, receptionist, recorder, scribe, secretary, shorthand-typist, stenographer, typist, word-processor operator.

clever adjective *a clever child. a clever idea.* able, academic, accomplished, acute, adroit, apt, artful, artistic, astute, brainy, bright, brilliant, canny, capable, [uncomplimentary] cunning, [uncomplimentary] crafty, [uncomplimentary] cunning, [informal] cute, [informal] deep (*She's a deep one!*), deft, dextrous, discerning, expert, gifted, [informal] handy, imaginative, ingenious, intellectual, intelligent, inventive, judicious, keen, knowing, knowledgeable, precocious, quick, quick-witted, rational, resourceful, sagacious, sensible, sharp, shrewd, skilful, skilled, [uncomplimentary] slick, smart, subtle, talented, [uncomplimentary] wily, wise, witty.
OPPOSITES: SEE **stupid, unskilful**.
a clever person [informal] egghead, expert, genius, [uncomplimentary] know-all, [sexist] mastermind, prodigy, sage, virtuoso [=*a brilliant performer*], wizard.

cleverness noun ability, acuteness, astuteness, brilliance, [uncomplimentary] cunning, expertise, ingenuity, intellect, intelligence, mastery, quickness, sagacity, sharpness, shrewdness, skill, subtlety, talent, wisdom, wit.
OPPOSITES: SEE **stupidity**.

cliché noun *He talks uninterestingly in boring clichés.* banality, commonplace, familiar phrase, hackneyed expression, platitude, well-worn phrase.

client noun *a client of the bank.* [plural] clientele [=*clients*], consumer, customer, patron, user.

clientele plural noun SEE **client**.

cliff noun bluff, crag, escarpment, precipice, rock-face, sheer drop.

climate noun 1 SEE **weather** noun.
2 *a climate of opinion.* ambience, atmosphere, disposition, environment, feeling, mood, spirit, temper, trend.

climax noun 1 *The music built up to a climax.* crisis, culmination, head, highlight, high point, peak, summit.
OPPOSITES: SEE **bathos**.
2 *a sexual climax.* orgasm.

climb noun *a steep climb.* ascent, gradient, hill, incline, rise, slope.

climb verb 1 *She climbed the rope.* ascend, clamber up, go up, mount, move up, scale, swarm up.

2 *The plane climbed steeply.* defy gravity, levitate, lift off, soar, take off.
3 *The road climbs steeply.* incline, rise, slope up.
4 *They climbed the mountain.* conquer, reach the top of.
to climb down SEE **descend, retreat** verb.

climber noun 1 mountaineer, rock-climber.
2 CLIMBING PLANTS INCLUDE: clematis, creeper, honeysuckle, hops, ivy, runner bean, vine.

clinch verb *to clinch a deal.* agree, close, conclude, confirm, decide, make certain of, ratify, settle, shake hands on, sign, verify.

cling verb 1 *Ivy clings to the wall.* adhere, fasten on, stick.
2 *The baby clung to its mother.* clasp, clutch, embrace, grasp, hug.

clinic noun health centre, infirmary, medical centre, sick-bay, surgery.

clinical adjective SEE **unemotional**.

clinker noun *clinker from a furnace.* ash, burnt remains, cinders, embers.

clip noun 1 *a paper clip.* VARIOUS FASTENERS: SEE **fastener**.
2 *a clip from a film.* excerpt, extract, fragment, passage, quotation, section, trailer.
3 [informal] *a clip on the ear.* SEE **hit** noun.

clip verb 1 *to clip papers together.* SEE **fasten**, pin, staple.
2 *to clip a hedge.* crop, SEE **cut** verb, dock, prune, shear, snip, trim.
3 *to clip someone on the ear.* SEE **hit** verb.

clique noun SEE **group** noun.

cloak noun 1 *She wrapped a cloak around her.* cape, coat, cope, mantle, wrap.
2 *The thief operated under the cloak of darkness.* SEE **cover** noun.

clobber verb SEE **defeat** verb, **hit** verb.

clock noun 1 INSTRUMENTS USED TO MEASURE TIME: alarm-clock, chronometer, digital clock, grandfather clock, hour-glass, pendulum clock, sundial, watch.
2 *The car had only 1000 miles on the clock.* SEE **dial**.

clod noun SEE **lump** noun.

clog noun SEE **shoe**.

clog verb *The drain was clogged with leaves.* block, [informal] bung up, choke, close, congest, dam, fill, jam, obstruct, plug, stop up.

cloistered adjective SEE **secluded**.

clone noun SEE **copy** noun, **twin** noun.

close adjective 1 *a close position.* adjacent, adjoining, at hand, handy (for), near,

neighbouring, point-blank (*point-blank range*).
OPPOSITES: SEE **distant**.
2 *a close relationship*. affectionate, attached, dear, devoted, familiar, fond, friendly, intimate, loving, [*informal*] thick.
OPPOSITES: SEE **unfriendly**.
3 *a close comparison*. alike, analogous, comparable, compatible, corresponding, related, resembling, similar.
OPPOSITES: SEE **dissimilar**.
4 *a close crowd*. compact, congested, cramped, crowded, dense, [*informal*] jam-packed, packed, thick.
OPPOSITES: SEE **thin** adjective.
5 *a close examination*. attentive, careful, concentrated, detailed, minute, painstaking, precise, rigorous, searching, thorough.
OPPOSITES: SEE **cursory**.
6 *close about her private life*. confidential, private, reserved, reticent, secretive, taciturn.
OPPOSITES: SEE **open** adjective.
7 *close with money*. illiberal, mean, [*informal*] mingy, miserly, niggardly, parsimonious, penurious, stingy, tight, tight-fisted, ungenerous.
OPPOSITES: SEE **generous**.
8 *a close atmosphere*. airless, fuggy, humid, muggy, oppressive, stifling, stuffy, suffocating, sweltering, unventilated, warm.
OPPOSITES: SEE **airy**.

close noun **1** *By the close of business, the shop had taken £1000*. cessation, completion, conclusion, culmination, end, finish, stop, termination.
2 *the close of a piece of music*. cadence, coda, finale.
3 *the close of a play*. curtain, denouement, ending.

close verb **1** *Close the door*. bolt, fasten, lock, seal, secure, shut.
2 *The road was closed*. bar, barricade, block, obstruct, stop up.
3 *We closed the party with "Auld lang syne"*. complete, conclude, culminate, discontinue, end, finish, stop, terminate, [*informal*] wind up.
4 *Close the gap*. fill, join up, make smaller, reduce, shorten.

closet noun SEE **cupboard**.

clot noun **1** *a clot of blood*. [*formal*] embolism [= *obstruction of an artery or vein*], lump, mass, thrombosis [= *clot of blood within the body*].
2 [*informal*] *He's a silly clot!* SEE **idiot**.

clot verb *When you cut yourself, blood clots and forms a scab*. coagulate, coalesce, congeal, curdle, make lumps, set, soli-

dify, stiffen, thicken.

cloth noun *cloth to make clothes and curtains*. fabric, material, stuff, textile.

SOME KINDS OF CLOTH: astrakhan, bouclé, brocade, broderie anglaise, buckram, calico, cambric, candlewick, canvas, cashmere, cheesecloth, chenille, chiffon, chintz, corduroy, cotton, crepe, cretonne, damask, denim, dimity, drill, drugget.

elastic, felt, flannel, flannelette, gaberdine, gauze, georgette, gingham, hessian, holland, lace, lamé, lawn, linen, lint, mohair, moiré, moquette, muslin, nankeen, nylon, oilcloth, oilskin, organdie, organza, patchwork, piqué, plaid, plissé, plush, polycotton, polyester, poplin.

rayon, sackcloth, sacking, sailcloth, sarsenet, sateen, satin, satinette, seersucker, serge, silk, stockinet, taffeta, tapestry, tartan, terry, ticking, tulle, tussore, tweed, velour, velvet, velveteen, viscose, voile, winceyette, wool, worsted.

---

clothe verb *She always clothes her children nicely*. array, attire, cover, deck, drape, dress, garb, outfit, robe, swathe, wrap up.
OPPOSITES: SEE **strip** verb.
to clothe yourself don, dress in, put on, wear.

clothed adjective *warmly clothed*. [*old-fashioned*] apparelled, attired, clad, dressed, fitted out, [*informal*] turned out (*well turned out*), wrapped up.

clothes noun apparel, attire, [*informal*] clobber, clothing, costume, dress, finery [= *best clothes*], garb, garments, [*informal*] gear, [*informal*] get-up, outfit, [*old-fashioned*] raiment, [*informal*] rig-out, trousseau [= *a bride's clothes*], underclothes, uniform, vestments [= *priest's clothes*], wardrobe, wear (*leisure wear*), weeds (*widow's weeds*).
RELATED ADJECTIVE: sartorial.

VARIOUS GARMENTS: anorak, apron, belt, bib, blazer, blouse, bodice, breeches, caftan, cagoule, cape, cardigan, cassock, chemise, chuddar, cloak, coat, cravat, crinoline, culottes, cummerbund, décolletage, doublet, dress, dressing-gown, duffel coat, dungarees, frock.

gaiters, garter, gauntlet, glove, gown, greatcoat, gym-slip, habit (*a monk's habit*), SEE **hat**, housecoat, jacket, jeans, jerkin, jersey, jodhpurs, jumper, kilt, knickers, leg-warmers, leotard, livery, loincloth, lounge suit.

mackintosh, mantle, miniskirt, mitten, muffler, necktie, négligé, night-clothes, night-dress, oilskins, overalls, overcoat, pants, parka, pinafore, poncho, pullover, pyjamas, raincoat, robe, rompers.

sari, sarong, scarf, shawl, shirt, SEE **shoe**, shorts, singlet, skirt, slacks, smock, sock, sou'wester, spats, stocking, stole, suit, surplice, sweater, sweatshirt, tail-coat, tie, tights, trousers, trunks, t-shirt, tunic, tutu, SEE **underclothes**, uniform, waistcoat, wet-suit, wind-cheater, wrap, yashmak.

PARTS OF A GARMENT: bodice, buttonhole, collar, cuff, hem, lapel, pocket, sleeve.

clothing noun SEE **clothes**.

cloud noun 1 KINDS OF CLOUD: altocumulus, altostratus, cirrocumulus, cirrostratus, cirrus, cumulonimbus, cumulus, mackerel sky, nimbostratus, rain cloud, storm cloud, stratocumulus, stratus.
2 *a cloud of steam.* billow, haze, mass, mist, puff.

cloud verb *Mist clouded our view.* blur, conceal, cover, darken, dull, eclipse, enshroud, hide, mantle, mist up, obfuscate, obscure, screen, shroud, veil.

cloudburst noun SEE **rain**.

cloudless adjective *a cloudless sky.* bright, clear, starlit, sunny, unclouded.
OPPOSITES: SEE **cloudy**.

cloudy adjective 1 *a cloudy sky.* dark, dismal, dull, gloomy, grey, leaden, lowering, overcast, sullen, sunless.
OPPOSITES: SEE **cloudless**.
2 *cloudy windows.* blurred, blurry, dim, misty, opaque, steamy, unclear.
3 *cloudy liquid.* hazy, milky, muddy, murky.
OPPOSITES: SEE **transparent**.

clout noun, verb SEE **hit** noun, verb.

clown noun buffoon, comedian, comic, fool, jester, joker.

cloying adjective sweet, syrupy.
OPPOSITES: SEE **refreshing**.

club noun 1 *a club to hit someone with.* bat, baton, bludgeon, cosh, cudgel, stick, truncheon.
2 *a football club. a book club.* association, circle, company, group, league, order, organization, party, set, society, union.

club verb *to club someone to death.* SEE **hit** verb.
to club together SEE **combine**.

clubbable adjective SEE **sociable**.

clue noun *I don't know the answer—give me a clue.* hint, idea, indication, inkling, key, lead, pointer, sign, suggestion, tip.

clump noun *a clump of daffodils. a clump of trees.* bunch, bundle, cluster, collection, SEE **group** noun, mass, shock (*a shock of hair*), thicket, tuft.

clumsy adjective 1 *clumsy movements. a clumsy person.* awkward, blundering, bumbling, bungling, fumbling, gangling, gawky, graceless, [*informal*] ham-fisted, heavy-handed, hulking, inelegant, lumbering, maladroit, shambling, uncoordinated, ungainly, ungraceful, unskilful.
OPPOSITES: SEE **dainty, skilful**.
2 *a clumsy raft.* amateurish, badly made, bulky, cumbersome, heavy, inconvenient, inelegant, large, ponderous, rough, shapeless, unmanageable, unwieldy.
OPPOSITES: SEE **neat**.
3 *He made a clumsy remark about her illness.* boorish, gauche, ill-judged, inappropriate, indelicate, indiscreet, inept, insensitive, tactless, uncouth, undiplomatic, unsubtle, unsuitable.
OPPOSITES: SEE **tactful**.
a clumsy person botcher, bungler, [*informal*] butterfingers, fumbler.

cluster noun *a cluster of trees. a cluster of people.* assembly, batch, bunch, clump, collection, crowd, gathering, SEE **group** noun, knot.

clutch noun 1 [*usually plural*] *He had us in his clutches.* clasp, control, evil embrace, grasp, grip, hold, possession, power.
2 *a clutch of eggs.* SEE **group** noun.

clutch verb *He clutched the rope.* catch, clasp, cling to, grab, grasp, grip, hang on to, hold on to, seize, snatch.

clutter noun *We'll have to clear up all this clutter.* confusion, disorder, jumble, junk, litter, lumber, mess, mix-up, muddle, odds and ends, rubbish, untidiness.

clutter verb *Her belongings clutter up my bedroom.* be scattered about, fill, lie about, litter, make untidy, [*informal*] mess up, muddle, strew.

coach noun 1 *a motor coach.* bus, [*old-fashioned*] charabanc.
OTHER VEHICLES: SEE **vehicle**.
2 *a football coach.* instructor, teacher, trainer.

coach verb *to coach a football team.* instruct, prepare, teach, train, tutor.

coagulate verb clot, congeal, curdle, [*informal*] jell, solidify, stiffen, thicken.

coal noun anthracite, coke.
OTHER FUELS: SEE **fuel** noun.

coalesce verb SEE **combine**.

coalition noun SEE **combination**.

coarse adjective 1 *coarse cloth. coarse sand.* bristly, gritty, hairy, harsh, lumpy, rough, scratchy, sharp, stony.
OPPOSITES: SEE **soft**.
2 *coarse language.* bawdy, blasphemous, boorish, common, crude, earthy, foul, immodest, impolite, improper, impure, indecent, indelicate, offensive, ribald, rude, smutty, uncouth, unrefined, vulgar.
OPPOSITES: SEE **polite**.

coast noun beach, coastline, seaboard, sea-shore, seaside, shore.

coast verb *to coast down a hill on a bike.* cruise, drift, free-wheel, glide, sail.

coastal adjective *a coastal town.* maritime, nautical, naval, seaside.

coastline noun SEE **coast** noun.

coat noun 1 KINDS OF COAT YOU CAN WEAR: anorak, blazer, cagoule, cardigan, dinner-jacket, doublet, duffel coat, greatcoat, jacket, jerkin, mackintosh, overcoat, raincoat, tail-coat, tunic, tuxedo, waistcoat, wind-cheater.
OTHER GARMENTS: SEE **clothes**.
2 *an animal's coat.* fleece, fur, hair, hide, pelt, skin.
3 *a coat of paint.* coating, cover, covering, film, finish, glaze, layer, membrane, patina, sheet, veneer, wash.
coat of arms badge, crest, emblem, heraldic device, insignia.

coat verb SEE **cover** verb.

coax verb *We coaxed the animal back into its cage.* allure, beguile, cajole, decoy, entice, induce, inveigle, persuade, tempt, wheedle.

cobble noun pebble, stone.

cobble verb *to cobble something together.* botch, knock up, make, mend, patch up, put together.

cobbled adjective *a cobbled street.* OTHER SURFACES: SEE **road**.

cobbler noun shoemaker, shoe-mender, shoe-repairer.

cock noun SEE **bird**.

cockerel noun SEE **chicken** noun.

cocksure adjective SEE **confident**.

cocktail noun OTHER DRINKS: SEE **drink** noun.

cocky adjective SEE **bumptious**.

cocoon noun SEE **wrapping**.

coda noun SEE **end** noun.

coddle verb *to coddle a baby.* SEE **pamper**.

code noun 1 *The Highway Code. a code of conduct.* etiquette, laws, manners, regulations, rule-book, rules, system.
2 *a message in code.* cipher, Morse code, secret language, semaphore, sign-system, signals.

codger noun SEE **man** noun.

codicil noun SEE **appendix**.

codify verb SEE **systematize**.

coeducational adjective *a coeducational school.* mixed.

coerce verb *I was coerced into joining the gang.* bludgeon, browbeat, bully, compel, constrain, dragoon, force, frighten, intimidate, press-gang, pressurize, terrorize.

coercion noun *We prefer you to work voluntarily rather than by coercion.* browbeating, brute force, bullying, compulsion, conscription [*into the armed services*], constraint, duress, force, intimidation, physical force, pressure, [*informal*] strong-arm tactics, threats.

coffee noun KINDS OF COFFEE: black coffee, café au lait, espresso, Irish coffee, white coffee.

coffer noun *coffers full of money.* box, cabinet, case, casket, chest, crate, trunk.

coffin noun sarcophagus.

cog noun tooth.

cogent adjective *a cogent argument.* compelling, conclusive, convincing, effective, forceful, forcible, indisputable, irresistible, persuasive, potent, powerful, rational, strong, unanswerable, weighty, well-argued.

cogitate verb SEE **think**.

Cognac noun brandy.

cognate adjective SEE **related**.

cognition noun SEE **understanding**.

cognizant adjective SEE **aware**.

cog-wheel noun gearwheel, toothed wheel.

cohabit verb live together.

cohere verb *When you squeeze a handful of snow, the flakes cohere to make a snowball.* bind, cake, cling together, coalesce, combine, consolidate, fuse, hang together, hold together, join, stick together, unite.

coherent adjective *a coherent argument. coherent speech.* articulate, clear, cohering, cohesive, connected, consistent, convincing, intelligible, logical, lucid,

orderly, organized, rational, reasonable, reasoned, sound, structured, systematic, understandable, well-structured.
OPPOSITES: SEE incoherent.

cohesive adjective SEE **coherent**.

cohort noun SEE **armed services**.

coiffure noun SEE **hair-style**.

coil noun VARIOUS COILED SHAPES OR MOVEMENTS: circle, convolution, corkscrew, curl, helix, kink, loop, ring, roll, screw, spiral, twirl, twist, vortex, whirl, whorl.
the coil SEE **contraception**.

coil verb *The sailor coiled the rope. The snake coiled round a branch.* bend, curl, entwine, loop, roll, snake, spiral, turn, twine, twirl, twist, wind, writhe.

coin noun *a fifty pence coin.* bit, piece.
coins *I haven't any coins, only notes.* change, coppers, loose change, silver, small change.
SEE ALSO **money**.
collector of coins numismatist.

coin verb 1 *It's a serious offence to coin money.* forge, make, mint, mould, stamp.
2 *We coined a new name for our group.* conceive, concoct, create, devise, dream up, fabricate, hatch, introduce, invent, make up, originate, produce, think up.

coincide verb 1 *My birthday coincides with a bank holiday.* clash, coexist, fall together, happen together, synchronize.
2 *Our answers coincided.* accord, agree, be identical, be in unison, be the same, concur, correspond, harmonize, match, square, tally.

coincidence noun *We met by coincidence.* accident, chance, fluke, luck.

coincidental adjective SEE **chance** adjective.

coitus noun SEE **sex**.

cold adjective 1 *cold weather. a cold wind. a cold place.* arctic, biting, bitter, bleak, chill, chilly, cool, crisp, cutting, draughty, freezing, fresh, frosty, glacial, icy, inclement, keen, [*informal*] nippy, numbing, [*informal*] parky, penetrating, perishing, piercing, polar, raw, shivery, Siberian, snowy, unheated, wintry.
OPPOSITES: SEE **hot**.
2 *cold hands.* blue with cold, chilled, dead, frostbitten, frozen, numbed, shivering, shivery.
OPPOSITES: SEE **warm** adjective.
3 *a cold attitude. a cold heart.* aloof, callous, cold-blooded, cool, cruel, distant, frigid, hard, hard-hearted, heartless,

indifferent, inhospitable, inhuman, insensitive, passionless, phlegmatic, reserved, standoffish, stony, uncaring, unconcerned, undemonstrative, unemotional, unenthusiastic, unfeeling, unfriendly, unkind, unresponsive, unsympathetic.
OPPOSITES: SEE **kind** adjective, **passionate**.

cold noun 1 *Our cat doesn't like the cold.* chill, coldness, coolness, freshness, iciness, low temperature, wintriness.
OPPOSITES: SEE **heat** noun.
to feel the cold freeze, quiver, shake, shiver, shudder, suffer from hypothermia, tremble.
2 *She's got a nasty cold.* chill, cough.
SYMPTOMS OF A COLD: catarrh, coughing, runny nose, sneezing, sniffing, snuffling.

cold-blooded adjective [*Cold-blooded* properly refers to animals whose body temperature varies with the temperature of their surroundings, but it is often used to describe *inhuman* aspects of human behaviour or character.] *a cold-blooded killing.* barbaric, brutal, callous, cold, cold-hearted, SEE **cruel**, dispassionate, hard-hearted, heartless, impassive, inhuman, insensitive, merciless, pitiless, ruthless, savage, unemotional, unfeeling.
OPPOSITES: SEE **humane**.

cold-hearted adjective SEE **cold-blooded**.

cold-shoulder verb SEE **ostracize**.

colic noun stomach ache, [*informal*] tummy ache.

collaborate verb 1 *The work gets done more quickly when we collaborate.* band together, [*uncomplimentary*] collude, [*uncomplimentary*] connive, co-operate, join forces, [*informal*] pull together, team up, work together.
2 *to collaborate with an enemy.* be a collaborator, join the opposition, [*informal*] rat, turn traitor.

collaboration noun *collaboration between partners.* association, [*uncomplimentary*] collusion, [*uncomplimentary*] connivance, concerted effort, co-operation, partnership, tandem, team-work.

collaborator noun 1 *I need a collaborator to help me.* accomplice (*in wrongdoing*), ally, assistant, associate, co-author, colleague, confederate, fellow worker, helper, helpmate, partner, [*joking*] partner-in-crime.
2 *a collaborator with the enemy.* blackleg, [*informal*] Judas, quisling, [*informal*] scab, traitor, turncoat.

collage noun SEE **picture**.

collapse noun *An earthquake caused the collapse of the hotel.* break-up, cave-in, destruction, downfall, end, fall, ruin, ruination, subsidence, wreck.

collapse verb 1 *Many buildings collapsed in the earthquake.* buckle, cave in, crumble, crumple, disintegrate, fall apart, fall in, fold up, give in, [*informal*] go west, sink, subside, tumble down.
2 *People collapsed in the heat.* be ill, [*informal*] bite the dust, faint, fall down, founder, [*informal*] go under.
3 *Ice-cream sales collapsed in the cold weather.* become less, crash, deteriorate, drop, fail, slump, worsen.

collapsible adjective *a tripod with collapsible legs.* adjustable, folding, retractable, telescopic.

collar verb SEE **capture**.

collate verb SEE **arrange**.

colleague noun SEE **collaborator**, **fellow**.

collect verb 1 *Squirrels collect nuts.* accumulate, agglomerate, aggregate, amass, bring together, garner, gather, harvest, heap, hoard, lay up, pile up, put by, reserve, save, scrape together, stockpile, store.
2 *A crowd collected to watch the fire.* assemble, cluster, come together, congregate, convene, converge, crowd, forgather, group, muster, rally round.
OPPOSITES: SEE **disperse**.
3 *We collected a large sum for charity.* be given, raise, secure, take.
4 *I collected the bread from the baker's.* acquire, bring, fetch, get, obtain.

collected adjective SEE **calm** adjective.

collection noun 1 accumulation, array, assortment, cluster, conglomeration, heap, hoard, mass, pile, set, stack.

VARIOUS COLLECTIONS OF PEOPLE AND THINGS: anthology (*of poems, etc.*), arsenal (*of weapons*), assembly (*of people*), batch (*of cakes, etc.*), company, congregation (*of worshippers*), crowd, gathering, SEE **group** noun, library (*of books*), stockpile (*of weapons*).

---

2 *a collection for charity.* [*old-fashioned*] alms-giving, flag-day, free-will offering, offertory, voluntary contributions, [*informal*] whip-round.

collective adjective *a collective decision.* combined, common, composite, co-operative, corporate, democratic, group, joint, shared, unified, united.
OPPOSITES: SEE **individual** adjective.

college noun academy, conservatory, institute, polytechnic, school (*art school, etc.*), university.

collide verb **to collide with** *The car collided with the gate-post.* bump into, cannon into, crash into, SEE **hit** verb, knock, meet, run into, slam into, smash into, strike, touch.

collier noun coal-miner, miner.

colliery noun coal-mine, mine.

collision noun *a collision on the motorway.* accident, bump, clash, crash, head-on collision, impact, knock, pile-up, scrape, smash.

colloquial adjective *colloquial language.* chatty, conversational, everyday, informal, slangy, [*formal*] vernacular.
OPPOSITES: SEE **formal**.

colloquy noun SEE **conversation**.

collude verb SEE **connive**.

collusion noun SEE **conspiracy**.

collywobbles noun 1 [*slang*] *I had collywobbles after eating too much fruit.* [*informal*] belly-ache, stomach-ache, [*informal*] tummy-ache.
2 [*slang*] *I had collywobbles before my interview.* SEE **nervous** (**to be nervous**).

colonist noun *Some of the early colonists were cruel to the native population.* colonizer, explorer, pioneer, settler.
OPPOSITES: SEE **native** noun.

colonize verb *to colonize a territory.* found a colony in, move into, occupy, people, populate, settle in, subjugate.

colony noun 1 *At one time Britain had colonies all over the world.* dependency, dominion, possession, protectorate, province, settlement, territory.
2 *a colony of ants.* SEE **group** noun.

coloration noun SEE **colour** noun.

colossal adjective *A colossal statue towered above us.* SEE **big**, elephantine, enormous, gargantuan, giant, gigantic, huge, immense, mammoth, massive, mighty, monstrous, monumental, prodigious, titanic, towering, vast.
OPPOSITES: SEE **small**.

colour noun 1 coloration, colouring, hue, shade, tincture, tinge, tint, tone.

SUBSTANCES WHICH GIVE COLOUR: cochineal, colourant, colouring, cosmetics, dye, make-up, SEE **paint** noun, pigment, pigmentation, stain, tincture, woad.

VARIOUS COLOURS: amber, azure, beige, black, blue, brindled, bronze, brown, buff, carroty, cherry, chestnut, chocolate, cobalt, cream, crimson, dun, fawn, gilt, gold, golden, green, grey, indigo, ivory, jet-black, khaki, lavender, maroon, mauve, navy blue, ochre, olive, orange, pink, puce, purple, red, rosy, russet, sandy, scarlet, silver, tan, tawny, turquoise, vermilion, violet, white, yellow.

---

2 *colour in your cheeks.* bloom, blush, flush, glow, rosiness, ruddiness.
colours *the colours of a regiment.* banner, ensign, flag, standard.
colour verb **1** *to colour a picture.* colour-wash, dye, paint, shade, stain, tinge, tint.
2 *His fair skin colours easily.* blush, bronze, brown, burn, flush, redden, tan.
OPPOSITES: SEE **fade**.
3 *An umpire shouldn't let her prejudices colour her decisions.* affect, bias, distort, impinge on, influence, pervert, prejudice, slant, sway.
colourful adjective **1** *colourful flowers. a colourful scene.* bright, brilliant, chromatic, gaudy, iridescent, multicoloured, psychedelic, showy, vibrant.
OPPOSITES: SEE **colourless, pale** adjective.
2 *a colourful description.* exciting, florid, graphic, picturesque, rich, stimulating, striking, telling, vivid.
OPPOSITES: SEE **dull** adjective, **plain** adjective.
3 *a colourful personality.* dashing, distinctive, dynamic, SEE **eccentric**, energetic, flamboyant, flashy, glamorous, interesting, lively, publicity-seeking, unusual, vigorous.
OPPOSITES: SEE **restrained**.
colouring noun SEE **colour** noun.
colourless adjective **1** *a colourless substance.* albino, black, faded, grey, monochrome, neutral, SEE **pale** adjective, [*informal*] washed-out, white.
2 *a colourless personality. a colourless scene.* boring, characterless, dingy, dismal, dowdy, drab, dreary, dull, insipid, lacklustre, shabby, tame, uninteresting, vacuous, vapid.
OPPOSITES: SEE **colourful**.
colt noun SEE **horse**.
column noun **1** *columns supporting a roof.* pilaster, pile, pillar, pole, post, prop, shaft, support, upright.
2 *I write a column in a local newspaper.* article, feature, leader, leading article, piece.
3 *a column of figures. a column of writing.* vertical division, vertical section.
4 *a column of soldiers.* cavalcade, file, line, procession, queue, rank, row, string, train.
columnist noun SEE **journalist**.

coma noun SEE **unconsciousness**.
comatose adjective SEE **unconscious**.
comb verb **1** *to comb your hair.* arrange, groom, neaten, smarten up, spruce up, tidy, untangle.
2 *I combed the house in search of my pen.* hunt through, ransack, rummage through, scour, search thoroughly.
combat noun *a fierce combat.* action, battle, bout, clash, conflict, contest, duel, encounter, engagement, fight, SEE **martial (martial arts)**, skirmish, struggle, war, warfare.
combat verb *to combat crime.* battle against, contend against, contest, counter, defy, face up to, fight, grapple with, oppose, resist, stand up to, strive against, struggle against, tackle, withstand.
combatant noun SEE **fighter**.
combination noun *a combination of things. a combination of people.* aggregate, alliance, alloy, amalgam, amalgamation, association, blend, coalition, compound, concoction, concurrence, confederacy, confederation, conjunction, consortium, conspiracy, federation, fusion, link-up, marriage, merger, mix, mixture, partnership, syndicate, synthesis, unification, union.
combine verb **1** *to combine resources.* add together, amalgamate, bind, blend, bring together, compound, fuse, integrate, intertwine, interweave, join, link, [*informal*] lump together, marry, merge, mingle, mix, pool, put together, synthesize, unify, unite.
2 *to combine as a team.* associate, band together, club together, coalesce, connect, co-operate, gang together, join forces, team up.
combustible adjective *Don't smoke near combustible materials.* flammable, inflammable.
OPPOSITE: incombustible.
combustion noun SEE **fire** noun.
come verb **1** *Visitors are coming tomorrow.* appear, arrive, visit.
2 *Spring came suddenly this year.* advance, draw near, materialize, occur.
3 *Tell me when we come to my station.* approach, arrive at, get to, near, reach.
to come about SEE **happen**.
to come across SEE **find**.
to come clean SEE **confess**.
to come out with SEE **say**.
to come round SEE **recover**.
to come up SEE **arise**.
to come upon SEE **find**.
come-back noun SEE **retort** noun.

comedian noun buffoon, clown, comic, SEE **entertainer**, fool, humorist, jester, joker, wag.

come-down noun SEE **anticlimax**.

comedy noun buffoonery, clowning, facetiousness, farce, hilarity, humour, jesting, joking, satire, slapstick, wit. SEE ALSO **entertainment**.

comestibles noun SEE **food**.

comet noun ASTRONOMICAL TERMS: SEE **astronomy**.

comfort noun 1 *to live in comfort.* affluence, contentment, cosiness, ease, luxury, opulence, relaxation, well-being.
2 *We tried to give the injured woman some comfort.* aid, cheer, consolation, encouragement, help, moral support, reassurance, relief, solace, succour, sympathy. OPPOSITES: SEE **discomfort**.

comfort verb *He was upset, so we tried to comfort him.* assuage, calm, cheer up, console, ease, encourage, gladden, hearten, help, reassure, relieve, solace, soothe, succour, sympathize with.

comfortable adjective 1 *a comfortable chair. a comfortable place to rest.* [informal] comfy, convenient, cosy, easy, padded, reassuring, relaxing, roomy, snug, soft, upholstered, warm.
2 *comfortable clothes.* informal, loose-fitting, well-fitting, well-made.
3 *a comfortable life-style.* affluent, agreeable, contented, happy, homely, luxurious, pleasant, prosperous, relaxed, restful, serene, well-off. OPPOSITES: SEE **uncomfortable**.

comfy adjective SEE **comfortable**.

comic adjective *a comic situation. comic remarks.* absurd, amusing, comical, diverting, droll, facetious, farcical, funny, hilarious, humorous, hysterical, jocular, joking, laughable, ludicrous, [informal] priceless, [informal] rich (*That's rich!*), ridiculous, SEE **sarcastic**, sardonic, satirical, side-splitting, silly, uproarious, waggish, witty.

comic noun 1 *A comic sang songs and made us laugh.* SEE **comedian**.
2 *She bought a comic to read on the train.* SEE **magazine**.

command noun 1 *Do you always obey commands?* behest, bidding, commandment (*the Ten Commandments*), decree, directive, edict, injunction, instruction, order, requirement, ultimatum, writ.
2 *She has command of the whole expedition.* authority (over), charge, control, direction, government, management, power (over), rule (over), supervision, sway (over).

command verb 1 *He commanded us to stop.* adjure, bid, charge, compel, decree, demand, direct, enjoin, instruct, ordain, order, require.
2 *A captain commands his ship.* administer, be in charge of, control, direct, govern, head, lead, manage, reign over, rule, supervise.

commandant noun SEE **officer**.

commandeer verb *The police commandeered a passing car to help in the emergency.* appropriate, confiscate, hijack, impound, requisition, seize, sequester, take over.

commander noun captain, SEE **chief** noun, commanding-officer, general, head, leader, officer-in-charge.

commandment noun SEE **command** noun.

commando noun SEE **armed services**.

commemorate verb *a ceremony to commemorate those who died in war.* be a memorial to, be a reminder of, celebrate, honour, keep alive the memory of, pay your respects to, pay tribute to, remember, salute, solemnize.

commence verb SEE **begin**.

commend verb *The boss commended our effort.* acclaim, applaud, approve of, compliment, congratulate, eulogize, extol, praise, recommend. OPPOSITES: SEE **criticize**.

commendable adjective SEE **praiseworthy**.

commensurate adjective SEE **comparable**, **proportionate**.

comment verb 1 *I heard several comments about the way we played.* animadversion [= *hostile comment*], criticism, mention, observation, opinion, reference, remark, statement.
2 *Teachers write comments on pupils' work.* annotation, footnote, gloss, note.

comment verb *I commented that the weather had been bad.* explain, interject, interpose, mention, note, observe, remark, say.

commentary noun 1 *a commentary on a football match.* account, broadcast, description, report.
2 *We wrote a commentary on the novel we were studying.* analysis, criticism, critique, discourse, elucidation, explanation, interpretation, notes, review, treatise.

commentator noun *a radio commentator.* announcer, broadcaster, journalist, reporter.

commerce noun *A healthy economy depends on commerce.* business, buying and selling, dealings, financial trans-actions, marketing, merchandising, trade, trading, traffic.

commercial adjective 1 *commercial deal-ings*. business, economic, financial, mercantile.
2 *a commercial success*. financially suc-cessful, monetary, money-making, pecuniary, profitable, profit-making.

commercial noun *a TV commercial*. [*in-formal*] ad, [*informal*] advert, advertise-ment, [*informal*] break (*commercial break*), [*informal*] plug.

commercialize verb [*Commercialize* can mean *to make commercial or profit-able*, but it can also mean *to debase or spoil something by making it commercial*: e.g. *Christmas has become commercia-lized*.] SEE **debase**.

commiserate verb *We commiserated with the losers*. comfort, condole, con-sole, express sympathy for, feel for, SEE **sympathize**.
OPPOSITES: SEE **congratulate**.

commission noun 1 *a commission in the armed services*. appointment, pro-motion, warrant.
VARIOUS RANKS: SEE **rank** noun.
2 *a commission to paint a portrait*. book-ing, order, request.
3 *a commission to investigate a complaint*. SEE **committee**.
4 *a salesperson's commission on a sale*. allowance, [*informal*] cut, fee, percent-age, [*informal*] rake-off, reward.

commissioner noun SEE **official** noun.

commit verb 1 *to commit a crime*. be guilty of, carry out, do, enact, execute, perform, perpetrate.
2 *to commit valuables to someone's safe-keeping*. consign, deliver, deposit, entrust, give, hand over.
to commit yourself *I committed myself to help with the jumble sale*. contract, covenant, guarantee, pledge, promise, undertake, vow.

commitment noun 1 *The builder had a commitment to finish the work on time*. assurance, duty, guarantee, liability, pledge, promise, undertaking, vow, word.
2 *The Green party has a commitment to conservation*. adherence, dedication, de-termination, involvement, loyalty.
3 *I checked my diary to see if I had any commitments*. appointment, arrange-ment, engagement.

committed adjective *a committed mem-ber of a political party*. active, ardent, [*informal*] card-carrying, dedicated, devoted, earnest, enthusiastic, fervent,

firm, keen, passionate, resolute, single-minded, staunch, unwavering, whole-hearted, zealous.
OPPOSITES: SEE **apathetic**.

committee noun GROUPS WHICH MAKE DECISIONS, ETC.: advisory group, as-sembly, board, cabinet, caucus, com-mission, convention, council, discus-sion group, junta, jury, panel, parliament, quango, synod, think-tank, working party.
SEE ALSO **meeting**.

commodious adjective SEE **roomy**.

commodity noun SEE **product**.

common adjective 1 *common knowledge*. accepted, collective, communal, general, joint, mutual, open, popular, public, shared, universal.
OPPOSITES: SEE **individual** adjective.
2 *a common happening*. average, [*infor-mal*] common or garden, SEE **common-place**, conventional, customary, daily, everyday, familiar, frequent, habitual, normal, ordinary, popular, prevalent, regular, routine, [*informal*] run-of-the-mill, standard, traditional, typical, unsurprising, usual, well-known, wide-spread.
OPPOSITES: SEE **uncommon**.
3 [*informal*] *common behaviour*. boorish, churlish, coarse, crude, disreputable, ill-bred, loutish, low, plebeian, rude, uncouth, unrefined, vulgar, [*informal*] yobbish.
OPPOSITES: SEE **refined**.
4 *of common birth*. lowly.
OPPOSITES: SEE **aristocratic**.

common noun *We play football on the common*. heath, park.

commoners noun SEE **class** noun.

commonplace adjective *a commonplace event. a commonplace remark*. banal, bor-ing, SEE **common** adjective, familiar, for-gettable, hackneyed, humdrum, me-diocre, obvious, ordinary, pedestrian, plain, platitudinous, predictable, rou-tine, standard, trite, undistinguished, unexceptional, unexciting, unremark-able, unsurprising.
OPPOSITES: SEE **distinguished, memor-able**.
a commonplace remark banality, cliché, platitude, truism.

commons noun SEE **class** noun.

commonsense adjective SEE **sensible**.

commonwealth noun SEE **country**.

commotion noun *a commotion in the street*. [*informal*] ado, agitation, [*infor-mal*] bedlam, [*informal*] brouhaha, bother, brawl, [*informal*] bust-up, chaos, clamour, confusion, contretemps, din, disorder, disturbance, excitement, ferment, flurry, fracas, fray, furore, fuss, hubbub, hullabaloo, hurly-burly, incident, [*informal*] kerfuffle, noise, [*informal*] palaver, pandemonium, [*informal*] punch-up, quarrel, racket, riot, row, rumpus, [*informal*] shemozzle, sensation, [*informal*] stir, [*informal*] to-do, tumult, turbulence, turmoil, unrest, upheaval, uproar, upset.

communal adjective *communal washing facilities.* collective, common, general, joint, mutual, open, public, shared.
OPPOSITES: SEE **private**.

commune noun SEE **community**.

commune verb SEE **communicate**.

communicate verb 1 *to communicate information.* advise, announce, broadcast, convey, declare, disclose, disseminate, divulge, express, impart, indicate, inform, intimate, make known, mention, [*in computing*] network, notify, pass on, proclaim, promulgate, publish, put across, relay, report, reveal, say, show, speak, spread, state, write.
2 *to communicate with other people.* commune, confer, contact [= *communicate with*], converse, correspond, discuss, get in touch, interrelate, make contact, speak, talk, write (to).
3 *to communicate a disease.* give, infect someone with, pass on, spread, transfer, transmit.
4 *This passage communicates with the kitchen.* be connected, lead (to).

communication noun *Animals have various methods of communication.* communicating, communion, contact, [*old-fashioned*] intercourse, understanding one another.

METHODS OF HUMAN COMMUNICATION: announcement, bulletin, cable, SEE card, communiqué, computer, conversation, correspondence, dialogue, directive, dispatch, document, FAX, gossip, [*informal*] grapevine, information, intelligence, intercom, intimation, SEE **letter**, the media [SEE BELOW], [*informal*] memo, memorandum, message, news, note, notice, proclamation, radar, report, rumour, satellite, signal, speaking, statement, talk, telegram, telegraph, telephone, teleprinter, transmission, walkie-talkie, wire, word, writing.

THE MASS MEDIA: advertising, broadcasting, cable television, newspapers, the press, radio, telecommunications, television.

---

communicative adjective *a communicative person.* frank, informative, open, out-going, sociable, SEE **talkative**.
OPPOSITES: SEE **secretive**.

communion noun SEE **communication**, **fellowship**.

communiqué noun SEE **communication**.

communism, communist nouns POLITICAL TERMS: SEE **politics**.

community noun *Most people like to live in a community.* colony, commonwealth, commune, country, SEE **group** noun, kibbutz, nation, society, state.

commute verb 1 *to commute a prison sentence.* adjust, alter, curtail, decrease, lessen, lighten, mitigate, reduce, shorten.
2 *to commute into the city every day.* SEE **travel** verb.

compact adjective 1 *compact soil.* close-packed, compacted, compressed, dense, firm, heavy, solid, tight-packed.
OPPOSITES: SEE **loose**.
2 *a compact encyclopaedia.* abbreviated, abridged, brief, compendious, compressed, concentrated, condensed, short, small, succinct, terse.
OPPOSITES: SEE **diffuse** adjective.
3 *a compact tool-box.* handy, neat, portable, small.
OPPOSITES: SEE **large, spacious**.
compact disc OTHER RECORDS: SEE **record**.

compact noun SEE **agreement**.

companion noun *He took a companion with him.* accomplice, assistant, associate, colleague, comrade, confederate, confidant, consort, [*informal*] crony, escort, fellow, follower, SEE **friend**, SEE **helper**, [*informal*] henchman, mate, partner, stalwart.

companionable adjective SEE **friendly**.

company noun 1 *We enjoy other people's company.* companionship, fellowship, friendship, society.
2 [*informal*] *We've got company coming on Sunday.* callers, guests, visitors.
3 *a company of friends.* assemblage, band, body, circle, community, coterie, crew, crowd, entourage, gang, gathering, throng, troop.
4 *a theatrical company.* association, club, ensemble, group, society, troupe.
5 *a trading company.* business, cartel, concern, conglomerate, consortium, corporation, establishment, firm, house, line, organization, partnership, [*informal*] set-up, syndicate, union.

6 *a company of soldiers.* SEE **armed services.**

comparable adjective *I got better quality at a comparable price. The work she does is not comparable to yours.* analogous, cognate, commensurate, compatible, corresponding, equal, equivalent, parallel, proportionate, related, similar.
OPPOSITES: SEE **dissimilar.** [Usually *incomparable* is NOT the opposite of *comparable.*]

comparative adjective *Once she was poor, but now she lives in comparative luxury.* relative.

compare verb **1** *Compare these sets of figures.* check, contrast, correlate, draw parallels between, juxtapose, make connections between, match, parallel, relate, set side by side, weigh.
2 *You can't compare the two teams.* equate, liken.
3 *Their team cannot compare with ours.* compete with, emulate, equal, match, rival, vie with.

comparison noun analogy, contrast, correlation, difference, distinction, juxtaposition, likeness, parallel, resemblance, similarity.

compartment noun *a compartment to keep belongings in. a compartment to sleep in.* alcove, area, bay, berth, booth, cell, chamber, [*informal*] cubby-hole, cubicle, division, kiosk, locker, niche, nook, pigeon-hole, section, space, subdivision.

compassion noun SEE **mercy, sympathy.**

compatible adjective **1** *People who live together must be compatible.* SEE **friendly,** harmonious, like-minded.
2 *The work he did was not compatible with his terms of employment.* accordant, congruent, consistent, consonant, matching, reconcilable.
OPPOSITES: SEE **incompatible.**
to be compatible with SEE **match** verb.

compatriot noun fellow citizen.

compel verb *You can't compel me to join in.* bind, SEE **bully** verb, coerce, constrain, dragoon, drive, exact, force, impel, make, necessitate, oblige, order, press, press-gang, pressurize, require, [*informal*] shanghai, urge.
to be compelled *They'll be compelled to use the motorway if they want to get here for tea.* be bound, be certain, be obliged, have, must, be sure.

compelling adjective SEE **irresistible.**

compendium noun *a compendium of information.* condensation, digest, handbook, summary.

compensate verb *to compensate someone for damage.* atone, [*informal*] cough up, [*formal*] indemnify, make amends, make reparation, make up, offset, pay back, pay compensation [SEE **compensation**], recompense, redress, reimburse, repay.

compensation noun *How much compensation did they get?* amends, damages, [*formal*] indemnity, recompense, refund, reimbursement, reparation, repayment, restitution.

compère noun *the compere of a TV programme.* anchor-man, announcer, disc jockey, host, hostess, linkman, Master of Ceremonies, MC, presenter.

compete verb *to compete in a sport.* be a contestant, enter, participate, perform, take part, take up the challenge. [Also use verbs appropriate to the particular sport: *jump, race, swim, throw,* etc.]
to compete against be in competition with [SEE **competition**], challenge, conflict with, contend against, emulate, SEE **fight** verb, oppose, rival, strive against, struggle with, undercut, vie with.

competent adjective *a competent builder. a competent performance.* able, acceptable, accomplished, adept, adequate, capable, clever, effective, effectual, efficient, experienced, expert, fit, [*informal*] handy, practical, proficient, qualified, satisfactory, skilful, skilled, trained, workmanlike.
OPPOSITES: SEE **incompetent.**

competition noun **1** *The competition between contestants was fierce.* competitiveness, conflict, contention, emulation, rivalry, struggle.
2 *a football competition. a prize competition.* challenge, championship, contest, event, game, heat, match, quiz, race, rally, series, tournament, trial.

competitive adjective **1** *competitive games.* aggressive, antagonistic, combative, contentious, cut-throat, hard-fought, keen, lively, sporting, well-fought.
OPPOSITES: SEE **co-operative.**
2 *competitive prices.* average, comparable with others, fair, moderate, reasonable, similar to others.
OPPOSITES: SEE **exorbitant.**

competitor noun *the competitors in a quiz.* adversary, antagonist, candidate, challenger, contender, contestant, entrant, finalist, opponent, participant, rival.

compile verb *to compile a magazine.* arrange, assemble, collect together, compose, edit, gather together, marshal, organize, put together.

complacent adjective [Do not confuse with *complaisant.*] *You can't be complacent when the job is only half-finished.* confident, contented, pleased with yourself, self-congratulatory, self-righteous, self-satisfied, smug, unconcerned, untroubled.
OPPOSITES: SEE **anxious.**

complain verb *We complained about the awful service.* [*informal*] beef, [*slang*] bind, carp, cavil, find fault (with), fuss, [*informal*] gripe, [*informal*] grouch, grouse, grumble, lament, moan, object, protest, whine, [*informal*] whinge.
OPPOSITES: SEE **approve (approve of).**
to complain about cast aspersions on, censure, condemn, criticize, decry, disparage, [*informal*] knock, [*informal*] slate.
OPPOSITES: SEE **praise** verb.

complaint noun 1 *We had complaints about the noise.* accusation, [*informal*] beef, charge, condemnation, criticism, grievance, [*informal*] gripe, grouse, grumble, moan, objection, protest, stricture, whine, whinge.
2 *Flu is a common complaint in winter.* affliction, ailment, disease, disorder, SEE **illness**, indisposition, infection, malady, malaise, sickness, upset.

complaisant adjective [Do not confuse with *complacent.*] *She's always helpful and complaisant.* accommodating, acquiescent, amenable, biddable, compliant, co-operative, deferential, docile, obedient, obliging, pliant, polite, submissive, tractable, willing.
OPPOSITES: SEE **obstinate.**

complement noun [Do not confuse with *compliment.*] *The ship carried its full complement of passengers.* aggregate, capacity, quota, sum, total.

complement verb [Do not confuse with *compliment.*] *Her guitar-playing complemented his singing perfectly.* complete, make complete, make perfect, make whole, top up.

complete adjective 1 *the complete story.* comprehensive, entire, exhaustive, full, intact, total, unabbreviated, unabridged, unedited, unexpurgated, whole.
2 *a complete job of work.* accomplished, achieved, completed, concluded, ended, faultless, finished, perfect.
OPPOSITES: SEE **incomplete.**
3 *complete disaster. complete rubbish.* absolute, arrant, downright, extreme, [*informal*] out-and-out, outright, pure, rank, sheer, thorough, thoroughgoing, total, unmitigated, unmixed, unqualified, utter, [*informal*] wholesale.

OPPOSITES: SEE **qualified.**

complete verb 1 *to complete a job of work.* accomplish, achieve, carry out, clinch, close, conclude, do, end, finalize, finish, fulfil, perfect, perform, round off, terminate, [*informal*] wind up.
2 *to complete a questionnaire.* answer, fill in.

complex adjective *a complex substance. a complex task.* complicated, composite, compound, convoluted, elaborate, [*informal*] fiddly, heterogeneous, intricate, involved, manifold, mixed, multifarious, multiple, multiplex, sophisticated.
OPPOSITES: SEE **simple.**

complexion noun *a healthy complexion.* appearance, colour, colouring, look, pigmentation, skin, texture.
WORDS TO DESCRIBE COMPLEXIONS: black, brown, clear, dark, fair, freckled, pasty, ruddy, sickly, spotty, swarthy, tanned, white.

compliant adjective SEE **obedient.**

complicate verb *Don't complicate things by asking for food that's not on the menu.* compound, confuse, elaborate, make complicated (SEE **complicated**), mix up, muddle, tangle.
OPPOSITES: SEE **simplify.**

complicated adjective *a complicated task. a complicated plan.* complex, convoluted, difficult, elaborate, entangled, hard, intricate, involved, knotty (*a knotty problem*), perplexing, problematical, sophisticated, tangled, tortuous, [*informal*] tricky, twisted, twisting.
OPPOSITES: SEE **straightforward.**

complication noun *I thought the job was easy, but then I found a complication.* complexity, confusion, difficulty, [*informal*] mix-up, problem, ramification, setback, snag, tangle.

complicity noun SEE **involvement.**

compliment noun [Do not confuse with *complement.*] [*often plural*] *Give our compliments to the chef.* accolade, admiration, appreciation, approval, commendation, congratulations, [*formal*] encomium, [*formal*] eulogy, [*formal or joking*] felicitations, flattery, honour, [*formal*] panegyric, plaudits, praise, testimonial, tribute.
OPPOSITES: SEE **insult** noun.

compliment verb [Do not confuse with *complement.*] *to compliment someone on their performance.* applaud, commend, congratulate, [*informal*] crack up, eulogize, extol, [*formal*] felicitate, give credit, [*formal*] laud, praise, salute, speak highly of.
OPPOSITES: SEE **criticize, insult** verb.

complimentary adjective 1 *complimentary remarks.* admiring, appreciative, approving, commendatory, congratulatory, eulogistic, favourable, flattering, fulsome, generous, laudatory, rapturous, supportive.
OPPOSITES: SEE **critical, insulting.**
2 *complimentary tickets.* free, [*informal*] give-away, gratis.

comply verb **to comply with** *I complied with the rules.* accede to, acquiesce in, agree to, assent to, conform to, consent to, defer to, fall in with, follow, fulfil, obey, observe, perform, satisfy, submit to, yield to.
OPPOSITES: SEE **defy.**

component noun *components of a car.* bit, constituent part, element, essential part, ingredient, item, part, piece, [*informal*] spare, spare part, unit.

compose verb 1 *The village was composed of small huts.* build, compile, constitute, construct, fashion, form, frame, make, put together.
2 *Mozart composed a lot of music.* arrange, create, devise, imagine, make up, produce, write.
3 *Have a cup of tea and compose yourself.* calm, control, pacify, quieten, soothe, tranquillize.
to be composed of *A hockey team is composed of 11 players.* comprehend, consist of, comprise, contain, embody, embrace, include, incorporate, involve.

composed adjective SEE **calm** adjective.

composer noun OTHER WRITERS: SEE **writer.**

composite adjective SEE **complex.**

composition noun 1 *the composition of a team. the composition of a chemical.* constitution, content, establishment, formation, formulation, [*informal*] make-up, structure.
2 *a musical composition.* [*formal*] opus, piece, work.
VARIOUS COMPOSITIONS: SEE **music.**

compos mentis SEE **sane.**

composure noun SEE **tranquillity.**

compound noun 1 *a chemical compound.* alloy, amalgam, blend, combination, composite, composition, fusion, synthesis.
SEE ALSO **mixture**: but note that in chemical terms *compound* and *mixture* are not the same.
2 *a compound for animals.* [*American*] corral, enclosure, pen, run.

compound verb 1 *to compound substances.* SEE **combine.**
2 *The bad weather compounded our difficulties.* SEE **aggravate, complicate.**

comprehend verb *Can you comprehend what I'm saying?* appreciate, conceive, discern, fathom, follow, grasp, know, perceive, realize, see, [*informal*] twig, understand.

comprehensible adjective *a comprehensible explanation.* clear, easy, intelligible, lucid, meaningful, plain, self-explanatory, simple, straightforward, understandable.
OPPOSITES: SEE **incomprehensible.**

comprehension noun SEE **understanding.**

comprehensive adjective *a comprehensive account of a subject.* all-embracing, broad, catholic, compendious, complete, detailed, encyclopaedic, exhaustive, extensive, full, inclusive, thorough, total, universal, wide-ranging.
OPPOSITES: SEE **selective.**

comprehensive school OTHER SCHOOLS: SEE **school.**

compress verb *to compress ideas into a few words. to compress things into a small space.* abbreviate, abridge, compact, concentrate, condense, constrict, contract, cram, crush, flatten, [*informal*] jam, précis, press, shorten, squash, squeeze, stuff, summarize, telescope, truncate.
OPPOSITES: SEE **expand.**

compressed adjective *a compressed account of my life.* abbreviated, abridged, compact, compendious, concise, condensed, shortened, summarized, telescoped, truncated.

comprise verb *This album comprises the best hits of the year.* be composed of, consist of, contain, cover, embody, embrace, include, incorporate, involve.

compromise noun *The two sides reached a compromise.* bargain, concession, [*informal*] give-and-take, [*informal*] halfway house, middle course, middle way, settlement.

compromise verb 1 *The two sides compromised.* concede a point, go to arbitration, make concessions, meet halfway, negotiate a settlement, reach a formula, settle, [*informal*] split the difference, strike a balance.
2 *He compromised his reputation by getting involved in a scandal.* discredit, dishonour, imperil, jeopardize, prejudice, risk, undermine, weaken.

compromising adjective *a compromising situation.* damaging, discreditable, disgraceful, dishonourable, embarrassing, ignoble, improper, questionable, scandalous, unworthy.

compulsion noun 1 *Slaves work by compulsion, not by choice.* being compelled, coercion, duress (*under duress*), force, necessity, restriction, restraint.

2 *an irresistible compulsion to eat.* addiction, drive, habit, impulse, pressure, urge.

OPPOSITES: SEE **option**.

compulsive adjective **1** *a compulsive urge.* besetting, compelling, driving, instinctive, involuntary, irresistible, overpowering, overwhelming, powerful, uncontrollable, urgent.

2 *a compulsive eater.* addicted, habitual, incorrigible, incurable, obsessive, persistent.

compulsory adjective *The wearing of seat-belts is compulsory.* binding, de rigueur, imperative, imposed, incumbent, inescapable, mandatory, obligatory, official, required, stipulated, unavoidable.

OPPOSITES: SEE **optional**.

compunction noun SEE **conscience**.

compute verb *to compute figures.* add up, assess, calculate, count, estimate, evaluate, measure, reckon, total, work out.

computer noun mainframe, [*informal*] micro, microcomputer, mini-computer, personal computer, PC, word-processor.

SOME TERMS USED IN COMPUTING: bit, byte, chip, cursor, data, database, data-processing, desk-top publishing, [*adjective*] digital, disc, disc-drive, firmware, floppy-disc, hard copy, hard disc, hardware, input, interface, joystick, keyboard, machine-code, [*adjective*] machine-readable, memory, menu, micro, microchip, micro-processor, monitor, mouse, network, output, printer, printout, processor, program, retrieval, robotics, silicon chip, software, spreadsheet, terminal, VDU, window, word-processing.

---

comrade noun SEE **companion**.

con noun, verb SEE **cheat** noun, verb.

concatenation noun SEE **sequence**.

concave adjective SEE **curved**, dished.
OPPOSITE: convex.

conceal verb blot out, bury, camouflage, cloak, cover up, disguise, envelop, hide, hush up, keep dark, keep quiet, keep secret, mask, obscure, screen, suppress, veil.

OPPOSITES: SEE **reveal**.

concealed adjective camouflaged, cloaked, disguised, furtive, hidden, SEE **invisible**, secret, unobtrusive.

OPPOSITES: SEE **obvious**, **visible**.

concede verb **1** *I conceded that I was wrong.* acknowledge, admit, agree, allow, confess, grant, make a concession, own, profess, recognize.

2 *After a long fight he conceded.* capitulate, [*informal*] cave in, cede, [*informal*] give in, resign, submit, surrender, yield.

conceit noun SEE **pride**.

conceited adjective arrogant, [*informal*] bigheaded, boastful, bumptious, [*informal*] cocky, egocentric, egotistic, egotistical, haughty, [*informal*] high and mighty, immodest, overweening, pleased with yourself, proud, self-satisfied, [*informal*] snooty, [*informal*] stuck-up, [*informal*] swollen-headed, supercilious, vain, vainglorious.

OPPOSITES: SEE **modest**.

conceited person SEE **show-off**.

conceivable adjective SEE **credible**.

conceive verb **1** *to conceive a baby.* become pregnant.

2 *to conceive an idea.* [*informal*] bring up, conjure up, create, design, devise, [*informal*] dream up, envisage, form, formulate, germinate, hatch, imagine, invent, make-up, originate, plan, produce, realize, suggest, think up, visualize, work out.

concentrate noun *fruit-juice concentrate.* distillation, essence, extract.

concentrate verb **1** *Please concentrate on your work.* apply yourself (to), attend (to), be absorbed (in), be attentive (to), engross yourself (in), focus (on), think (about), work hard (at).

OPPOSITE: be inattentive (SEE **inattentive**).

2 *The crowds concentrated in the middle of town.* accumulate, centre, cluster, collect, congregate, converge, crowd, gather, mass.

OPPOSITES: SEE **disperse**.

3 *to concentrate a liquid.* condense, reduce, thicken.

OPPOSITES: SEE **dilute** verb.

concentrated adjective **1** *concentrated fruit-juice.* condensed, evaporated, strong, undiluted.

OPPOSITES: SEE **dilute** adjective.

2 *concentrated effort.* all-out, committed, hard, intense, intensive, thorough.

OPPOSITES: SEE **half-hearted**.

concept noun SEE **idea**.

conception noun **1** *She has no conception of how difficult it is.* SEE **idea**.

2 *the conception of a baby.* begetting, beginning, conceiving, fathering, fertilization, impregnation.

concern noun **1** *concern for others.* attention, care, consideration, heed, interest, involvement, responsibility, solicitude.

2 *It's no concern of theirs.* affair, business, matter.
3 *a matter of great concern to us all.* anxiety, burden, cause of distress [SEE **distress**], fear, worry.
4 *a business concern.* company, corporation, enterprise, establishment, firm, organization.

concern verb *Road safety concerns us all.* affect, be important to, be relevant to, interest, involve, matter to, [*formal*] pertain to, refer to, relate to.

concerned adjective [The meaning of *concerned* varies according to whether the word comes before or after the noun it describes: compare the examples given here.] **1** *The concerned parents asked for news of their children.* SEE anxious, bothered, caring, distressed, disturbed, fearful, solicitous, touched, troubled, unhappy, upset, worried.
OPPOSITES: SEE **callous**.
2 *If you want the truth, talk to the people concerned.* connected, implicated, interested, involved, relevant, referred to.
OPPOSITES: SEE uninvolved, SEE **detached**.

concerning preposition *information concerning our holiday.* about, apropos of, germane to, involving, re, regarding, relating to, relevant to, with reference to, with regard to.

concert noun VARIOUS ENTERTAINMENTS: SEE **entertainment**.

concerted adjective *a concerted effort.* collaborative, collective, combined, co-operative, joint, mutual, shared, united.

concession noun *If you're under 16 you get a concession.* adjustment, allowance, reduction.
to make a concession SEE **concede**.

conciliate verb SEE **pacify, reconcile**.

conciliation noun SEE **negotiation, reconciliation**.

conciliator noun SEE **peacemaker**.

concise adjective *a concise dictionary. a concise account.* abbreviated, abridged, brief, compact, compendious, compressed, concentrated, condensed, laconic, pithy, short, small, succinct, terse.
OPPOSITES: SEE **diffuse** adjective.

conclave noun SEE **meeting**.

conclude verb **1** *The concert concluded with an encore.* cease, close, complete, culminate, end, finish, round off, stop, terminate.
2 *When you didn't arrive, we concluded that the car had broken down.* assume, decide, deduce, gather, infer, judge, reckon, suppose, surmise, SEE **think**.

conclusion noun **1** *the conclusion of a journey. the conclusion of a concert.* close, completion, culmination, end, finale, finish, peroration, rounding-off, termination.
2 *Now that you've heard the evidence, what's your conclusion?* answer, assumption, belief, decision, deduction, inference, interpretation, judgement, opinion, outcome, resolution, result, solution, upshot, verdict.

conclusive adjective *conclusive evidence.* convincing, decisive, definite, persuasive, unambiguous, unanswerable, unequivocal.
OPPOSITES: SEE **inconclusive**.

concoct verb *to concoct excuses. to concoct something to eat.* SEE **cook** verb, cook up, contrive, counterfeit, devise, fabricate, feign, formulate, hatch, invent, make up, plan, prepare, put together, think up.

concomitant adjective SEE **accompanying**.

concord noun SEE **harmony**.

concordat noun SEE **agreement**.

concrete adjective *concrete evidence.* actual, definite, existing, factual, firm, material, objective, palpable, physical, real, solid, substantial, tactile, tangible, touchable, visible.
OPPOSITES: SEE **abstract** adjective.

concretion noun SEE **mass** noun.

concubine noun SEE **lover**.

concur verb **1** *The doctor concurs with my diagnosis.* accede, accord, agree, assent.
2 *Our opinions often concur.* coincide, come together, harmonize, meet, unite.

concurrent adjective *You can't attend two concurrent events!* coexisting, coinciding, concomitant, contemporaneous, contemporary, overlapping, parallel, simultaneous, synchronous.

condemn verb **1** *We condemn violence. We condemn criminals.* blame, castigate, censure, criticize, damn, decry, denounce, deplore, disapprove of, disparage, rebuke, reprehend, reprove, revile, [*informal*] slam, [*informal*] slate, upbraid.
OPPOSITES: SEE **commend**.
2 *They were condemned by the evidence. The judge condemned them.* convict, find guilty, judge, pass judgement, prove guilty, punish, sentence.
OPPOSITES: SEE **acquit**.

condense verb **1** *to condense a book.* abbreviate, abridge, compress, contract, curtail, précis, reduce, shorten, summarize, synopsize.

OPPOSITES: SEE **expand**.

2 *to condense a liquid.* concentrate, distil, reduce, solidify, thicken.
OPPOSITES: SEE **dilute** verb.

3 *Steam condenses on a cold window.* become liquid, form condensation [SEE **condensation**].
OPPOSITES: SEE **evaporate**.

condensation noun *condensation on the windows.* haze, mist, [*formal*] precipitation, [*informal*] steam, water-drops.

condescend verb [*often joking*] *Would you condescend to accompany me?* deign, lower yourself, stoop.

condescending adjective *a condescending attitude.* disdainful, haughty, imperious, lofty, patronizing, [*informal*] snooty, supercilious, superior.

condiment noun *condiments to flavour food.* garnish, relish, seasoning.
CONDIMENTS INCLUDE: chutney, mustard, pepper, pickle, salt, spices.

condition noun **1** *in good condition, in bad condition.* case, circumstance, fettle (*in fine fettle*), fitness, health, [*informal*] nick, order, shape, situation, state, [*informal*] trim.
2 *a medical condition.* SEE **illness**.
3 *conditions of membership.* limitation, obligation, proviso, qualification, requirement, restriction, stipulation, terms.

conditional adjective *a conditional agreement. conditional surrender.* dependent, limited, provisional, qualified, restricted, safeguarded, [*informal*] with strings attached.
OPPOSITES: SEE **unconditional**.

condolences noun SEE **sympathy**.

condom noun SEE **contraception**.

condone verb *Do you condone his sin?* allow, connive at, disregard, endorse, excuse, forgive, ignore, let someone off, overlook, pardon, tolerate.
OPPOSITE: be unforgiving.

conducive adjective *Warm, wet weather is conducive to the growth of weeds.* advantageous, beneficial, encouraging, favourable, helpful, supportive.
to be conducive to SEE **encourage**.

conduct noun **1** *good conduct.* actions, attitude, bearing, behaviour, demeanour, manner, ways.
2 *the conduct of the nation's affairs.* administration, control, direction, discharge, handling, leading, management, organization, running, supervision.

conduct verb **1** *The curator conducted us round the museum.* accompany, convey, escort, guide, lead, pilot, steer, take, usher.
2 *The chairman conducted the meeting well.* administer, be in charge of, chair, command, control, direct, govern, handle, head, lead, look after, manage, organize, oversee, preside over, regulate, rule, run, superintend, supervise.
to conduct yourself *Didn't we conduct ourselves well!* act, behave, carry on.

conduit noun SEE **channel** noun.

cone noun VARIOUS SHAPES: SEE **shape** noun.

confectioners noun sweet-shop.

confectionery noun SEE **sweet** noun (**sweets**).

confederate noun SEE **ally**.

confederation noun SEE **alliance**.

confer verb **1** *to confer an honour on someone.* accord, award, bestow, give, grant, honour with, impart, invest, present.
2 *You may not confer with each other during the exam!* compare notes, consult, converse, debate, deliberate, discourse, discuss, exchange ideas, [*informal*] put your heads together, seek advice, talk, talk things over.

conference noun consultation, convention, council, deliberation, discussion, SEE **meeting**, symposium.

confess verb *to confess guilt.* acknowledge, admit (to), be truthful (about), [*informal*] come clean (about), concede, [*informal*] make a clean breast (of), own up (to), SEE **reveal**, unbosom yourself, unburden yourself.

confession noun *a confession of guilt* acknowledgement, admission, declaration, disclosure, profession, revelation.

confidant, confidante nouns SEE **friend**.

confide verb **to confide in** consult, have confidence in, open your heart to, speak confidentially to, [*informal*] spill the beans to, [*informal*] tell all to, tell secrets to, trust, unbosom yourself to.

confidence noun **1** *to face the future with confidence.* certainty, credence, faith, hope, optimism, positiveness, reliance, trust.
OPPOSITES: SEE **doubt** noun.
2 *I wish I had her confidence.* aplomb, assurance, boldness, composure, conviction, firmness, nerve, panache, self-assurance, self-confidence, self-possession, self-reliance, spirit, verve.
OPPOSITES: SEE **diffidence**.
confidence trick SEE **deception**.
to have confidence in SEE **trust** verb.

confident adjective 1 *confident of success.* certain, convinced, hopeful, optimistic, positive, sanguine, sure, trusting.
OPPOSITES: SEE **doubtful**.
2 *a confident person.* assertive, assured, bold, [*uncomplimentary*] cocksure, composed, definite, fearless, secure, self-assured, self-confident, self-possessed, self-reliant, unafraid.
OPPOSITES: SEE **diffident**.

confidential adjective 1 *confidential information.* classified, [*informal*] hush-hush, intimate, [*informal*] off the record, personal, private, restricted, secret, suppressed, top secret.
OPPOSITES: unclassified, SEE **public** adjective.
2 *a confidential secretary.* personal, private, trusted.

configuration noun SEE **shape** noun.

confine verb *The police confined the home supporters at one end of the ground.* bind, cage, circumscribe, constrain, [*informal*] coop up, cordon off, cramp, curb, detain, enclose, gaol, hem in, [*informal*] hold down, immure, imprison, incarcerate, intern, isolate, keep, limit, localize, restrain, restrict, rope off, shut in, shut up, surround, wall up.
OPPOSITES: SEE **free** verb.

confinement noun 1 *confinement in prison.* SEE **imprisonment**.
2 = *childbirth.* SEE **birth**.

confines plural noun SEE **boundary**.

confirm verb 1 *The strange events confirmed his belief in the supernatural.* authenticate, back up, bear out, corroborate, demonstrate, endorse, establish, fortify, give credence to, justify, lend force to, prove, reinforce, settle, show, strengthen, substantiate, support, underline, vindicate, witness to.
OPPOSITES: SEE **disprove**.
2 *We shook hands to confirm the deal.* [*informal*] clinch, formalize, guarantee, make legal, make official, ratify, validate, verify.
OPPOSITES: SEE **cancel**.

confiscate verb *The police confiscated his air gun.* appropriate, impound, remove, seize, sequester, take away, take possession of.

conflagration noun SEE **fire** noun.

conflict noun 1 *conflict between rivals.* antagonism, antipathy, contention, difference, disagreement, discord, dissention, friction, hostility, opposition, strife, unrest, variance (*to be at variance*).
2 *conflict on the battlefield.* action, battle, brawl, brush, clash, combat, confrontation, contest, encounter, engagement, feud, fight, quarrel, [*informal*] set-to, skirmish, struggle, war, warfare.

conflict verb 1 *Her account of events conflicts with mine.* [*informal*] be at odds, be at variance, be incompatible, clash, compete, contend, contradict, contrast, differ, disagree, oppose each other.
2 SEE **fight** verb, **quarrel** verb.

conflicting adjective *conflicting views.* SEE **incompatible**.

conform verb *The club has strict rules and will throw you out if you don't conform.* acquiesce, be good, behave conventionally, comply, [*informal*] do what you are told, fit in, [*informal*] keep in step, obey, [*informal*] see eye to eye, [*informal*] toe the line.
to conform to *to conform to the rules.* abide by, accord with, agree with, be in accordance with, coincide with, comply with, concur with, correspond to, fit in with, follow, harmonize with, keep to, match, obey, square with, submit to, suit.
OPPOSITES: SEE **differ**, **disobey**.

conformist noun conventional person [SEE **conventional**], traditionalist, yesman.
OPPOSITES: SEE **rebel** noun.

conformity noun *Military discipline requires conformity from all soldiers.* complaisance, compliance, conventionality, obedience, orthodoxy, submission, uniformity.

confound verb SEE **amaze**.

confront verb 1 *to confront your enemies.* accost, argue with, attack, brave, challenge, defy, face up to, oppose, resist, stand up to, take on, withstand.
OPPOSITES: SEE **avoid**.
2 *to confront someone unexpectedly.* encounter, face, meet.

confuse verb 1 *Don't confuse the system.* disarrange, disorder, jumble, mingle, mix up, muddle, tangle.
2 *The complicated rules confused us.* agitate, baffle, bemuse, bewilder, confound, disconcert, disorientate, distract, [*informal*] flummox, fluster, mislead, mystify, perplex, puzzle, [*informal*] rattle.
3 *I confuse the twins.* fail to distinguish, muddle.

confused adjective 1 *a confused argument.* aimless, chaotic, disconnected, disjointed, disordered, disorderly, disorganized, garbled, [*informal*] higgledy-piggledy, incoherent, irrational, jumbled, misleading, mixed up, muddled, muddle-headed, obscure, rambling, [*informal*] topsy-turvy, unclear, unsound, woolly.

2 *a confused state of mind.* addled, addle-headed, baffled, bewildered, dazed, disorientated, distracted, flustered, fuddled, [*informal*] in a tizzy, inebriated, muddle-headed, [*informal*] muzzy, nonplussed, perplexed, puzzled.
OPPOSITES: SEE **sane**.

confusion noun **1** [*informal*] ado, anarchy, bedlam, bother, chaos, clutter, commotion, confusion, din, disorder, disorganization, disturbance, fuss, hubbub, hullabaloo, jumble, maelstrom, [*informal*] mayhem, mêlée, mess, [*informal*] mix-up, muddle, pandemonium, racket, riot, rumpus, shambles, tumult, turbulence, turmoil, upheaval, uproar, welter, whirl.
2 *I saw the confusion on their faces.* bemusement, bewilderment, disorientation, distraction, mystification, perplexity, puzzlement.

confute verb SEE **disprove**.

congeal verb *Blood congeals to form a clot. Water congeals to ice.* clot, coagulate, coalesce, condense, curdle, freeze, harden, [*informal*] jell, set, solidify, stiffen, thicken.

congenial adjective *congenial company. congenial surroundings.* acceptable, agreeable, amicable, companionable, compatible, SEE **friendly**, genial, kindly, SEE **pleasant**, suitable, sympathetic, understanding, well-suited.
OPPOSITES: SEE **uncongenial**.

congenital adjective *congenital deafness.* hereditary, inborn, inbred, inherent, inherited, innate, natural.

congested adjective *a congested road. a congested space.* blocked, clogged, crowded, full, jammed, obstructed, overcrowded, stuffed.
OPPOSITES: SEE **clear** adjective.

conglomeration noun SEE **mass** noun.

congratulate verb *We congratulated the winners.* applaud, SEE **compliment** verb, felicitate, praise.
OPPOSITES: SEE **commiserate, reprimand** verb.

congratulations noun SEE **compliment** noun.

congregate verb *On summer evenings, we congregate in the park.* accumulate, assemble, cluster, collect, come together, convene, converge (on), crowd, forgather, gather, get together, group, mass, meet, muster, rally, rendezvous, swarm, throng.

congregation noun SEE **group** noun.

congress noun SEE **assembly**.

congruent adjective SEE **identical**.

conical adjective cone-shaped, pointed.

conifer noun VARIOUS TREES: SEE **tree**.
RELATED ADJECTIVE: coniferous.

conjectural adjective SEE **hypothetical**.

conjecture noun, verb SEE **guess** noun, verb.

conjugal adjective SEE **marital**.

conjunction noun *a conjunction of events.* SEE **combination**.

conjure verb *The wizard conjured stones to move.* bewitch, charm, compel, enchant, invoke, raise, rouse, summon.
SEE ALSO **magic** noun (**to do magic**).
to conjure up SEE **produce** verb.

conjuring noun *The entertainer didn't fool us with his conjuring.* illusions, legerdemain, SEE **magic** noun, sleight of hand, tricks, wizardry.

conjuror noun SEE **entertainer**, illusionist, magician.

connect verb **1** *to connect things together.* attach, combine, couple, engage, fasten, fix, interlock, join, link, tie.
OPPOSITES: SEE **disconnect**.
2 *to connect ideas in your mind.* associate, bracket together, compare, make a connection between, put together, relate, tie up.
OPPOSITES: SEE **dissociate**.

connection noun *I don't see the connection.* affinity, association, bond, coherence, contact, correlation, correspondence, interrelationship, join, link, relationship, [*informal*] tie-up, unity.
OPPOSITES: SEE **separation**.

connive verb **to connive at** SEE **condone**.

connoisseur noun SEE **expert** noun.

connotation noun *What are the connotations of the word "food"?* association, implication, insinuation, reverberation, suggested meaning, undertone.
COMPARE: denotation.

connote verb *The word "food" may connote "greed".* have connotations of [SEE **connotation**], imply, suggest.
COMPARE: denote.

connubial adjective SEE **marital**.

conquer verb **1** *to conquer a territory.* annex, capture, occupy, overrun, possess, quell, seize, subject, subjugate, take, win.
2 *to conquer an opponent.* beat, best, checkmate, crush, defeat, get the better of, humble, [*informal*] lick, master, outdo, overcome, overpower, overthrow, overwhelm, rout, silence, subdue, succeed against, [*informal*] thrash, triumph over, vanquish, worst.

3 *to conquer a mountain.* climb, reach the top of.

conqueror noun SEE **winner**.

conquest noun *the conquest of a territory.* annexation, appropriation, capture, defeat, invasion, occupation, overthrow, subjection, subjugation, [*informal*] takeover, triumph (over), victory (over), win (against).

consanguinity noun SEE **relationship**.

conscience noun *Vegetarians have a conscience about eating animals.* compunction, ethics, misgivings, morals, principles, qualms, reservations, scruples, standards.

conscience-stricken adjective SEE **ashamed**.

conscientious adjective *a conscientious worker.* accurate, attentive, careful, diligent, dutiful, exact, hard-working, honest, meticulous, painstaking, particular (*She's particular about details*), punctilious, responsible, scrupulous, serious, thorough.
OPPOSITES: SEE **careless**.

conscious adjective **1** *In spite of the knock on his head, he remained conscious.* alert, awake, aware, compos mentis, sensible.
OPPOSITES: SEE **unconscious**.
2 *a conscious act. a conscious foul.* calculated, deliberate, intended, intentional, knowing, planned, premeditated, self-conscious, studied, voluntary, waking, wilful.
OPPOSITES: SEE **accidental**.

conscript noun SEE **soldier**.

conscript verb SEE **enlist**.

consecrate verb **1** *They consecrated a temple to their god.* dedicate, devote, hallow, make sacred, sanctify.
OPPOSITES: SEE **desecrate**.
2 *to consecrate a king.* SEE **enthrone**.

consecrated adjective *The churchyard is consecrated ground.* blessed, hallowed, holy, religious, revered, sacred, sanctified.
OPPOSITES: SEE **accursed**.

consecutive adjective *She was away for three consecutive days.* continuous, following, one after the other, running (*three days running*), sequential, succeeding, successive.

consensus, consent nouns SEE **agreement**.

consent verb *They consented to come with us.* agree, undertake.
OPPOSITES: SEE **refuse** verb.
to consent to *She consented to my request.* allow, approve of, authorize, comply with, concede, grant, permit.

consequence noun **1** *The flood was a consequence of all that snow.* aftermath, by-product, corollary, effect, end, [*informal*] follow-up, issue, outcome, repercussion, result, sequel, side-effect, upshot.
2 *The loss of one penny is of no consequence.* account, concern, importance, moment, note, significance, value, weight.

consequent adjective *consequent effects.* consequential, ensuing, following, resultant, resulting, subsequent.

conservation noun *the conservation of the environment.* careful management, economy, maintenance, preservation, protection, safeguarding, saving, upkeep.
OPPOSITES: SEE **destruction**.

conservationist noun ecologist, environmentalist, [*informal*] green, preservationist.

conservative adjective **1** *conservative ideas.* conventional, die-hard, hidebound, moderate, narrow-minded, old-fashioned, reactionary, sober, traditional, unadventurous.
OPPOSITES: SEE **progressive**.
2 *a conservative estimate.* cautious, moderate, reasonable, understated, unexaggerated.
OPPOSITES: SEE **extreme** adjective.
3 *conservative politics.* right-of-centre, right-wing, Tory.
POLITICAL TERMS: SEE **politics**.

conservative noun conformist, die-hard, reactionary, [*political*] right-winger, [*political*] Tory, traditionalist.
POLITICAL TERMS: SEE **politics**.

conservatory noun glass-house, greenhouse, hothouse.

conserve noun *apricot conserve.* SEE **jam** noun.

conserve verb *to conserve energy.* be economical with, hold in reserve, keep, look after, maintain, preserve, protect, safeguard, save, store up, use sparingly.
OPPOSITES: SEE **waste** verb.

consider verb **1** *to consider a problem.* cogitate, contemplate, deliberate, discuss, examine, meditate on, mull over, muse, ponder, reflect on, ruminate, study, think about, [*informal*] turn over, weigh up.
2 *I consider that he was right.* believe, deem, judge, reckon.

considerable adjective *a considerable amount of rain. a considerable margin.* appreciable, big, biggish, comfortable, fairly important, fairly large, noteworthy, noticeable, perceptible, reasonable, respectable, significant, sizeable,

substantial, [*informal*] tidy (*a tidy amount*), tolerable, worthwhile.
OPPOSITES: SEE **negligible**.

considerate adjective *It was considerate to lend your umbrella*. altruistic, attentive, caring, charitable, friendly, gracious, helpful, kind, kind-hearted, obliging, polite, sensitive, solicitous, sympathetic, tactful, thoughtful, unselfish.
OPPOSITES: SEE **selfish**.

consign verb *to consign something to its proper place*. commit, convey, deliver, devote, entrust, give, hand over, pass on, relegate, send, ship, transfer.

consignment noun *a consignment of goods*. batch, cargo, delivery, load, lorry-load, shipment, van-load.

consist verb **to consist of** *What does this fruit salad consist of? What does the job consist of?* add up to, amount to, be composed of, be made of, comprise, contain, embody, include, incorporate, involve.

consistent adjective **1** *a consistent player. a consistent temperature*. constant, dependable, faithful, predictable, regular, reliable, stable, steady, unchanging, unfailing, uniform, unvarying.
2 *His story is consistent with hers*. accordant, compatible, congruous, consonant, in accordance, in agreement, in harmony, of a piece.
OPPOSITES: SEE **inconsistent**.

consolation noun *Music can give you consolation when you're depressed*. cheer, comfort, ease, encouragement, help, relief, solace, succour, support.
consolation prize prize for runner-up, second prize.

console verb *to console someone who is unhappy*. calm, cheer, comfort, ease, encourage, hearten, relieve, solace, soothe, sympathize with.

consolidate verb *This season she consolidated her reputation as our best athlete*. make secure, make strong, reinforce, stabilize, strengthen.
OPPOSITES: SEE **weaken**.

consonant adjective SEE **consistent**.

consort noun OTHER ROYAL FIGURES: SEE **royal**.

consort verb **to consort with** *to consort with criminals*. accompany, associate with, befriend, be friends with, be seen with, fraternize with, [*informal*] gang up with, keep company with, mix with.

consortium noun SEE **group** noun.

conspicuous adjective *a conspicuous landmark. a conspicuous mistake*. apparent, blatant, clear, discernible, dominant, evident, flagrant, glaring, impressive, manifest, notable, noticeable, obvious, patent, perceptible, prominent, pronounced, self-evident, showy, striking, unconcealed, unmistakable, visible.
OPPOSITES: SEE **inconspicuous**.

conspiracy noun *a conspiracy to defraud*. cabal, collusion, [*informal*] frame-up, insider dealing, intrigue, [*often joking*] machinations, plot, [*informal*] racket, scheme, treason.

conspirator noun plotter, schemer, traitor, [*informal*] wheeler-dealer.

conspire verb *Several men conspired to defraud the company*. be in league, collude, combine, co-operate, hatch a plot, have designs, intrigue, plot, scheme.

constable noun SEE **policeman**.

constant adjective **1** *a constant cough. a constant rhythm*. ceaseless, chronic, consistent, continual, continuous, endless, eternal, everlasting, fixed, incessant, invariable, never-ending, non-stop, permanent, perpetual, persistent, predictable, regular, relentless, repeated, stable, steady, sustained, unbroken, unchanging, unending, unflagging, uniform, uninterrupted, unremitting, unvarying, unwavering.
OPPOSITES: SEE **changeable, irregular**.
2 *a constant friend*. dedicated, dependable, determined, devoted, faithful, firm, loyal, reliable, staunch, steadfast, true, trustworthy, trusty.
OPPOSITES: SEE **fickle, unreliable**.

constellation noun ASTRONOMICAL TERMS: SEE **astronomy**.

consternation noun SEE **dismay** noun.

constituent noun SEE **part** noun.

constitute verb **1** *In soccer, eleven players constitute a team*. compose, comprise, form, make up.
2 *We constituted a committee to organize a jumble sale*. appoint, bring together, create, establish, found, inaugurate, make, set up.

constitution noun **1** *the constitution of a committee*. SEE **composition**.
2 *the country's constitution*. SEE **government**.

constrain verb SEE **compel**.

constraint noun SEE **compulsion**.

constrict verb SEE **tighten**.

constriction noun *a constriction in the throat*. SEE **blockage**, narrowing, pressure, [*formal*] stricture, tightness.

construct verb *to construct a shelter.* assemble, build, create, engineer, erect, [*formal*] fabricate, fashion, fit together, form, [*informal*] knock together, make, manufacture, pitch (*a tent*), produce, put together, put up, set up.
OPPOSITES: SEE **demolish**.

construction noun 1 *The construction of a shelter took an hour.* assembly, building, creation, erecting, erection, manufacture, production, putting-up, setting-up.
2 *The shelter was a flimsy construction.* building, edifice, erection, structure.

constructive adjective *a constructive suggestion.* advantageous, beneficial, co-operative, creative, helpful, positive, practical, useful, valuable, worthwhile.
OPPOSITES: SEE **destructive**.

construe verb SEE **interpret**.

consul noun SEE **official** noun.

consult verb *Please consult me before you do anything.* ask, confer (with), debate (with), discuss (with), exchange views (with), [*informal*] put your heads together (with), question, refer (to), seek advice (from), speak (to).

consume verb 1 *to consume food.* devour, digest, eat, [*informal*] gobble up, [*informal*] guzzle, swallow.
2 *to consume your energy. to consume your savings.* absorb, deplete, drain, eat into, employ, exhaust, expend, swallow up, use up, utilize.

consumer noun *Shops try to give consumers what they want.* buyer, customer, purchaser, shopper.

consuming adjective *a consuming passion.* SEE **irresistible, powerful**.

consummate adjective *a consummate artist.* SEE **skilful**.

consummate verb **to consummate marriage** SEE **sex**.

contact noun 1 *an electrical contact.* connection, join, touch, union.
2 *contact between people.* SEE **communication, meeting**.

contact verb *I'll contact you when I have some news.* approach, call, call on, communicate with, correspond with, [*informal*] drop a line to, get hold of, get in touch with, notify, phone, ring, speak to, talk to.

contagion noun SEE **illness**.

contagious adjective *a contagious disease.* catching, communicable, infectious, spreading, transmittable.
OPPOSITE: non-infectious.

contain verb 1 *This box contains odds and ends. This book contains helpful information.* be composed of, comprise, consist of, embody, embrace, hold, include, incorporate, involve.
2 *Please contain your enthusiasm!* check, control, curb, hold back, keep back, limit, repress, restrain, stifle.

container noun holder, receptacle, repository, vessel.

SOME CONTAINERS: bag, barrel, basin, basket, bath, beaker, billy-can, bin, SEE **bottle**, bowl, box, briefcase, bucket, butt, caddy, can, canister, carton, cartridge, case, cask, casket, casserole, cauldron, chest, churn, cistern, coffer, coffin, crate, creel, cup.

decanter, dish, drum, dustbin, envelope, flask, glass, goblet, hamper, handbag, haversack, hod, hogshead, holdall, holster, jar, jerry-can, jug, keg, kettle, knapsack, luggage, money-box, mould, mug, pail, pan, pannier, pitcher, pocket, portmanteau, pot, pouch, punnet, purse.

rucksack, sachet, sack, satchel, saucepan, scuttle, skip, suitcase, tank, tankard, tea-chest, teapot, test tube, thermos, tin, trough, trunk, tub, tumbler, urn, vacuum flask, vase, vat, wallet, water-butt, watering-can, wine-glass.

---

contaminate verb *Chemicals contaminated the water.* adulterate, defile, foul, infect, poison, pollute, soil, taint.
OPPOSITES: SEE **purify**.

contemplate verb 1 *We contemplated the view.* eye, gaze at, look at, observe, regard, stare at, survey, view, watch.
2 *We contemplated what to do next.* cogitate, consider, deliberate, examine, mull over, plan, reflect on, study, think about, work out.
3 *I contemplate taking a holiday soon.* envisage, expect, intend, propose.
4 *She sat quietly and contemplated.* [*informal*] day-dream, meditate, muse, ponder, reflect, ruminate, think.

contemplative adjective *a contemplative mood.* SEE **thoughtful**.

contemporaneous adjective SEE **contemporary**.

contemporary adjective 1 [= *belonging to the same time as other things you are referring to*] *contemporary events.* coinciding, concurrent, contemporaneous, simultaneous, synchronous, topical.
COMPARE: earlier, later.
2 [= *belonging to the present time*] *contemporary music.* current, fashionable, the

latest, modern, newest, present-day, [*informal*] trendy, up-to-date, [*informal*] with-it.
OPPOSITES: SEE **old**.

contempt noun *Our contempt for their bad behaviour was obvious.* derision, detestation, disdain, disgust, dislike, disparagement, disrespect, SEE **hatred**, loathing, ridicule, scorn.
OPPOSITES: SEE **admiration**.
to feel contempt for SEE **despise**.

contemptible adjective *a contemptible crime.* base, beneath contempt, despicable, detestable, discreditable, disgraceful, dishonourable, disreputable, hateful, ignominious, inferior, loathsome, [*informal*] low-down, mean, odious, pitiful, [*informal*] shabby, shameful, worthless, wretched.
OPPOSITES: SEE **admirable**.

contemptuous adjective *a contemptuous sneer.* arrogant, condescending, derisive, disdainful, dismissive, disrespectful, haughty, [*informal*] holier-than-thou, insolent, insulting, jeering, patronizing, sarcastic, scathing, scornful, sneering, [*informal*] snooty, supercilious, withering.
OPPOSITES: SEE **admiring**.
to be contemptuous (of) SEE **denigrate**, **sneer**.

contend verb 1 *We had to contend with strong opposition.* compete, contest, dispute, SEE **fight** verb, grapple, oppose, SEE **quarrel** verb, rival, strive, struggle, vie.
2 *I contended that I was right.* affirm, allege, argue, assert, claim, declare, maintain.
to contend with *We had a lot to contend with.* cope with, deal with, manage, organize, put up with, sort out.

content adjective SEE **contented**.

content noun 1 *Butter has a high fat content.* constituent, element, ingredient, part.
2 *She smiled with content.* SEE **contentment**.

content verb SEE **satisfy**.

contented adjective *a contented expression.* cheerful, comfortable, complacent, content, fulfilled, gratified, SEE **happy**, peaceful, pleased, relaxed, satisfied, serene, smiling, smug, uncomplaining, untroubled, well-fed.
OPPOSITES: SEE **dissatisfied**.

contention noun SEE **argument**.

contentious adjective 1 *a contentious crowd of objectors.* SEE **quarrelsome**.
2 *a contentious problem.* SEE **controversial**.

contentment noun *a smile of contentment.* comfort, content, contentedness, ease, fulfilment, SEE **happiness**, relaxation, satisfaction, serenity, smugness, tranquillity, well-being.
OPPOSITES: SEE **dissatisfaction**.

contest noun *a sporting contest.* bout, challenge, championship, [*informal*] clash, combat, competition, conflict, confrontation, duel, encounter, SEE **fight** noun, game, match, [*informal*] set-to, struggle, tournament, trial.

contest verb 1 *to contest a title.* compete for, contend for, fight for [SEE **fight** verb], [*informal*] make a bid for, strive for, struggle for, take up the challenge of, vie for.
2 *to contest a decision.* argue against, challenge, debate, dispute, doubt, oppose, query, question, refute, resist.

contestant noun *a contestant in a competition.* candidate, competitor, contender, entrant, participant, player.

context noun *Words only have meaning if you put them in a context.* background, frame of reference, framework, milieu, position, situation, surroundings.

contiguous adjective SEE **adjoining**.

continental quilt noun duvet, eiderdown.

contingency noun *Be prepared for all contingencies.* SEE **accident**.

contingent noun SEE **group** noun.

continual adjective *a continual process of change. continual bickering.* constant, continuing, SEE **continuous**, endless, eternal, everlasting, frequent, interminable, lasting, limitless, ongoing, perennial, permanent, perpetual, persistent, recurrent, regular, relentless, repeated, unending, unremitting.
OPPOSITES: SEE **occasional**, **temporary**.

continuance noun SEE **continuation**.

continuation noun 1 *the continuation of a journey.* carrying on, continuance, continuing, extension, maintenance, prolongation, protraction, resumption.
2 *a continuation of a book.* addition, appendix, postscript, sequel, supplement.

continue verb 1 *We continued the search while it was light.* carry on, keep going, keep up, persevere with, proceed with, prolong, pursue, [*informal*] stick at, sustain.
2 *We'll continue work after lunch.* recommence, restart, resume.
3 *This rain can't continue for long.* carry on, endure, go on, keep on, last, linger, live on, persist, remain, stay, survive.

4 *Continue the line to the edge of the paper.* extend, lengthen.

continuous adjective *continuous bad weather. exhausted by continuous effort.* ceaseless, chronic (*chronic illness*), SEE **continual**, incessant, never-ending, non-stop, [*informal*] round-the-clock, [*informal*] solid (*I worked for 3 solid hours*), sustained, unbroken, unceasing, uninterrupted.

contort verb SEE **twist** verb.

contour noun *the contours of the countryside.* curve, form, outline, relief, shape.

contraband noun *smugglers' contraband.* booty, illegal imports, loot.

contraception noun birth-control, family planning.
VARIOUS METHODS OF BIRTH-CONTROL: cap, coil, condom, contraceptive pill, [*informal*] the pill, rhythm method, spermicide, sterilization, vasectomy.

contract noun *a business contract.* agreement, bargain, bond, commitment, compact, concordat, covenant, deal, indenture, lease, pact, settlement, treaty, understanding, undertaking.

contract verb **1** *Most substances contract as they cool.* become denser, become smaller, close up, condense, decrease, diminish, draw together, dwindle, fall away, lessen, narrow, reduce, shrink, shrivel, slim down, thin out, wither.
OPPOSITES: SEE **expand**.
2 *A local firm contracted to build our extension.* agree, arrange, close a deal, covenant, negotiate a deal, promise, sign an agreement, undertake.
3 *She contracted a mysterious illness.* become infected by, catch, develop, get.

contraction noun **1** *Contraction of the timbers left gaps in the fence.* diminution, narrowing, shortening, shrinkage, shrivelling.
2 *"Jim" is a contraction of "James".* abbreviation, diminutive, shortened form.

contractual adjective *a contractual obligation.* agreed, binding, formal, formalized, legally enforceable, signed and sealed, unbreakable.

contradict verb *It's considered rude to contradict other people's views.* challenge, confute, controvert, disagree with, dispute, gainsay, impugn, oppose, speak against.
OPPOSITES: SEE **confirm**.

contradictory adjective *contradictory opinions.* antithetical, conflicting, contrary, discrepant, different, incompatible, inconsistent, irreconcilable, opposed, opposite.

OPPOSITES: SEE **consistent**.

contraption noun apparatus, contrivance, device, gadget, invention, machine, mechanism.

contrary adjective **1** [pronounced *con*trary] *She spoke for the motion, and I put the contrary view.* contradictory, conflicting, converse, different, opposed, opposite, other, reverse.
OPPOSITES: SEE **similar**.
2 [pronounced *con*trary] *contrary winds.* adverse, hostile, inimical, opposing, unfavourable, unhelpful.
OPPOSITES: SEE **favourable**.
3 [pronounced con*trary*] *a contrary child.* awkward, cantankerous, defiant, difficult, disobedient, disobliging, intractable, obstinate, perverse, rebellious, [*informal*] stroppy, stubborn, uncooperative, wayward, wilful.
OPPOSITES: SEE **co-operative**.

contrast noun *a contrast between two things.* antithesis, comparison, difference, differentiation, disparity, dissimilarity, distinction, divergence, foil (*act as a foil to*), opposition.
OPPOSITES: SEE **similarity**.

contrast verb **1** *The teacher contrasted the work of the two students.* compare, differentiate between, discriminate between, distinguish between, emphasize differences between, make a distinction between, set one against the other.
2 *His style contrasts with mine.* be set off (by), clash (with), deviate (from), differ (from).

contrasting adjective *contrasting colours. contrasting opinions.* antithetical, clashing, conflicting, different, dissimilar, incompatible, opposite.
OPPOSITES: SEE **similar**.

contretemps noun SEE **mishap**.

contribute verb *to contribute money to charity.* bestow, donate, [*informal*] fork out, give, provide, put up, sponsor (*to sponsor an event or a person*), subscribe, supply.
to contribute to *Good weather contributed to our enjoyment.* add to, encourage, SEE **help** verb, reinforce, support.

contribution noun **1** *a contribution to charity.* donation, fee, gift, grant, [*informal*] handout, offering, payment, sponsorship, subscription.
2 *The weather made an important contribution to our enjoyment.* addition, encouragement, SEE **help** noun, input, support.

contributor noun **1** *a contributor to charity.* backer, benefactor, donor, giver, helper, patron, sponsor, subscriber, supporter.

2 *a contributor to a magazine.* columnist, correspondent, free-lance, journalist, reporter, writer.

contrite adjective SEE **penitent**.

contrivance noun SEE **device**.

contrive verb **1** *We contrived to get there in spite of a bus strike.* SEE **manage**.
2 *He contrived a way to do it.* SEE **plan** verb.

control noun *Who is in control? A teacher needs good control in the classroom.* administration, authority, charge, command, direction, discipline, government, guidance, influence, jurisdiction, management, mastery, orderliness, organization, oversight, power, regulation, restraint, rule, strictness, supervision, supremacy.
to gain control of annex, seize, steal, take over, usurp, win.
to have control of SEE **control** verb.

control verb **1** *The government controls the country's affairs. Managers control the workforce.* administer, [*informal*] be at the helm of, be in charge of, [*informal*] boss, command, conduct, cope with, deal with, direct, dominate, engineer, govern, guide, handle, have control of, lead, look after, manage, manipulate, order about, oversee, regiment, regulate, rule, run, superintend, supervise.
2 *They built a dam to control the floods.* check, confine, contain, curb, hold back, keep in check, master, repress, restrain, subdue, suppress.

controversial adjective *a controversial decision.* arguable, contentious, controvertible, debatable, disputable, doubtful, [*formal*] polemical, problematical, questionable.
OPPOSITES: SEE **straightforward**.

controversy noun *controversy about the building of a motorway.* altercation, argument, contention, debate, disagreement, dispute, dissension, issue, [*formal*] polemic, quarrel, war of words, wrangle.

controvert verb SEE **contradict**.

contumely noun SEE **insult** noun.

contusion noun SEE **bruise** noun.

conundrum noun SEE **riddle** noun.

conurbation noun SEE **town**.

convalesce verb *to convalesce after an illness.* get better, improve, make progress, mend, recover, recuperate, regain strength.

convalescent adjective *convalescent after an operation.* getting better, improving, making progress, [*informal*] on the mend, recovering, recuperating.
convalescent home SEE **hospital**.

convector noun SEE **fire** noun.

convene verb **1** *The chairman convened a meeting.* bring together, call, [*formal*] convoke, summon.
2 *The meeting convened at two o'clock.* SEE **assemble**.

convenient adjective *a convenient shop. a convenient tool. a convenient moment.* accessible, appropriate, at hand, available, handy, helpful, labour-saving, nearby, neat, opportune, suitable, timely, usable, useful.
OPPOSITES: SEE **inconvenient**.

convention noun **1** *a convention of business people.* SEE **assembly**.
2 *a human rights convention.* SEE **agreement**.
3 *It's a convention to give presents at Christmas.* custom, etiquette, formality, matter of form, practice, rule, tradition.

conventional adjective **1** *conventional behaviour. conventional ideas.* accepted, accustomed, common, commonplace, correct, customary, decorous, everyday, expected, habitual, mainstream, normal, ordinary, orthodox, prevalent, regular, routine, [*informal*] run-of-the-mill, standard, straight, traditional, unsurprising, usual.
OPPOSITES: SEE **unconventional**.
2 [*uncomplimentary*] *Don't be so conventional!* bourgeois, conservative, formal, hackneyed, hidebound, pedestrian, rigid, stereotyped, [*informal*] stuffy, unadventurous, unimaginative, unoriginal.
OPPOSITES: SEE **independent**.

converge verb *Motorways converge in one mile.* coincide, combine, come together, join, meet, merge.
OPPOSITES: SEE **disperse, diverge**.

conversant adjective SEE **knowledgeable**.

conversation noun [*informal*] chat, [*informal*] chin-wag, [*formal*] colloquy, communication, [*formal*] conference, dialogue, discourse, discussion, exchange of views, gossip, [*informal*] heart-to-heart, [*formal*] intercourse, [*informal*] natter, phone-call, [*informal*] powwow, SEE **talk** noun, tête-à-tête.

converse adjective SEE **opposite** adjective.

converse verb [= *have a conversation*] SEE **talk** verb.

convert verb **1** *We converted the attic to a games-room.* SEE **adapt**.
2 *She converted me to a new way of thinking.* change, change someone's mind, convince, persuade, re-educate, reform, regenerate, rehabilitate, save (= *convert to Christianity*), win over.

convertible noun SEE **car**.

convex adjective bulging, SEE **curved**, domed.
OPPOSITE: concave.

convey verb 1 *to convey goods*. bear, bring, carry, conduct, deliver, export, ferry, fetch, forward, import, move, send, shift, ship, take, transfer, transport.
2 *What does his message convey to you?* communicate, disclose, impart, imply, indicate, mean, reveal, signify, tell.

conveyance noun SEE **vehicle**.

convict noun *Convicts were transported to Australia*. condemned person, criminal, culprit, felon, malefactor, prisoner, wrongdoer.

convict verb *to convict someone of a crime*. condemn, declare guilty, prove guilty, sentence.
OPPOSITES: SEE **acquit**.

conviction noun 1 *He spoke with conviction*. assurance, certainty, confidence, firmness.
2 *She has strong religious convictions*. belief, creed, faith, opinion, persuasion, principle, tenet, view.

convince verb *He convinced the jury. He convinced them that he was innocent*. assure, [*informal*] bring round, convert, persuade, prove to, reassure, satisfy, sway, win over.

convincing adjective *convincing evidence*. conclusive, decisive, definite, persuasive, unambiguous, unarguable, unequivocal.
OPPOSITES: SEE **inconclusive**.

convivial adjective SEE **sociable**.

convocation noun SEE **assembly**.

convoke verb SEE **summon**.

convoluted adjective SEE **complicated**.

convolution noun SEE **coil** noun.

convoy noun *a convoy of ships*. armada, fleet, SEE **group** noun.

convulsion noun 1 *The doctor treated him for convulsions*. attack, fit, involuntary movement, paroxysm, seizure, spasm.
2 *a volcanic convulsion*. disturbance, eruption, outburst, tremor, turbulence, upheaval.

convulsive adjective *convulsive movements*. jerky, shaking, spasmodic, [*informal*] twitchy, uncontrolled, uncoordinated, violent, wrenching.

cook noun chef.

cook verb *to cook a meal*. concoct, heat up, make, prepare, warm up.

RELATED ADJECTIVES: culinary, gastronomic, SEE **taste** verb.
to cook something up SEE **plot** verb.

WAYS TO COOK FOOD: bake, barbecue, boil, braise, brew, broil, casserole, coddle (*eggs*), fry, grill, pickle, poach, roast, sauté, scramble (*eggs*), simmer, steam, stew, toast.
OTHER THINGS TO DO IN COOKING: baste, blend, chop, grate, freeze, infuse, knead, mix, peel, sieve, sift, stir, whisk.
SOME COOKING UTENSILS: baking-tin, basin, billy-can, blender, bowl, breadboard, breadknife, carving knife, casserole, cauldron, chafing dish, chip-pan, coffee grinder, colander, corkscrew, SEE **crockery**, SEE **cutlery**, deep-fat-fryer, dish, food-processor, frying-pan, jug, kettle, ladle, liquidizer, microwave, mincer, mixer, pan, pepper-mill, percolator, plate, pot, pressure-cooker, rolling-pin, rôtisserie, salt-cellar, saucepan, scales, skewer, spatula, spit, strainer, timer, tin-opener, toaster, whisk, wok, wooden spoon.
OTHER KITCHEN EQUIPMENT: SEE **kitchen**.

cooker noun SEE **stove**.

cooking noun baking, catering, cookery, cuisine.

cool adjective 1 *cool weather*. chilly, SEE **cold** adjective, coldish.
2 *a cool drink*. chilled, iced, refreshing.
OPPOSITES: SEE **hot**.
3 *a cool reaction to danger*. SEE **brave**, calm, collected, composed, dignified, elegant, [*informal*] laid-back, level-headed, quiet, relaxed, self-possessed, sensible, serene, unflustered, unruffled, urbane.
OPPOSITES: SEE **frantic**.
4 *cool feelings*. aloof, apathetic, dispassionate, distant, frigid, half-hearted, indifferent, lukewarm, negative, offhand, reserved, [*informal*] stand-offish, unconcerned, unemotional, unenthusiastic, unfriendly, unresponsive, unwelcoming.
OPPOSITES: SEE **passionate**.
5 *a cool request for £1000*. bold, cheeky, impertinent, impudent, shameless, tactless.

cool verb 1 *to cool food*. allow to get cold, chill, freeze, ice, lower the temperature of, refrigerate.
OPPOSITES: SEE **heat** verb.
2 *to cool someone's enthusiasm*. abate, allay, assuage, calm, dampen, lessen, moderate, [*informal*] pour cold water on, quiet, temper.
OPPOSITES: SEE **inflame**.

coolie noun SEE **worker**.

coomb noun SEE **valley**.

coop noun *a chicken coop*. SEE **enclosure**.

coop verb **to coop up** SEE **confine**.

co-operate verb *We need two people to co-operate on this job*. aid each other, assist each other, collaborate, combine, conspire (=*co-operate in wrongdoing*), help each other, [*informal*] join forces, [*informal*] pitch in, [*informal*] play ball, [*informal*] pull together, support each other, work as a team, work together.
OPPOSITES: SEE **compete**.

co-operation noun aid, assistance, collaboration, co-operative effort [SEE **co-operative**], co-ordination, help, joint action, team-work.
OPPOSITES: SEE **competition**.

co-operative adjective **1** *As everyone was co-operative, we finished early*. accommodating, comradely, constructive, hard-working, helpful to each other, keen, obliging, supportive, united, willing, working as a team.
OPPOSITES: SEE **competitive**, **unco-operative**.
2 *a co-operative effort*, collective, combined, communal, concerted, co-ordinated, corporate, joint, shared.
OPPOSITES: SEE **individual** adjective.

co-opt verb SEE **appoint**.

co-ordinate verb SEE **organize**.

cop noun SEE **policeman**.

cope verb *Shall I help you, or can you cope?* carry on, get by, make do, manage, survive, win through.
to cope with *She coped with her illness cheerfully*. contend with, deal with, endure, handle, look after, suffer, tolerate.

copier noun SEE **reprographics**.

copious adjective *copious supplies of food*. abundant, ample, bountiful, extravagant, generous, great, huge, inexhaustible, large, lavish, liberal, luxuriant, overflowing, plentiful, profuse, unsparing, unstinting.
OPPOSITES: SEE **scarce**.

copperplate noun SEE **handwriting**.

coppice, copse nouns *a coppice of birch trees*. SEE **wood**.

copulate verb SEE **mate** verb.

copy noun **1** *a copy of a letter. a copy of a work of art*. carbon-copy, clone, counterfeit, double, duplicate, facsimile, fake, forgery, imitation, likeness, model, pattern, photocopy, print, replica, representation, reproduction, tracing, transcript, twin, Xerox.

2 *a copy of a book*. edition, volume.
SEE ALSO **book** noun.

copy verb **1** *to copy a work of art. to copy someone's ideas*. borrow, counterfeit, crib, duplicate, emulate, follow, forge, imitate, photocopy, plagiarize, print, repeat, reproduce, simulate, transcribe, xerox.
2 *to copy someone's voice or mannerisms*. ape, imitate, impersonate, mimic, parrot.

coquette noun (=*a flirtatious person*). SEE **flirtatious**.

coquettish adjective SEE **flirtatious**.

coral reef SEE **island**.

cord noun *a length of cord*. cable, catgut, lace, line, rope, strand, string, twine, wire.

cordial adjective SEE **friendly**.

cordial noun SEE **drink** noun.

cordon noun *a cordon of policemen*. barrier, chain, fence, line, ring, row.

cordon verb **to cordon off** SEE **isolate**.

corduroy noun KINDS OF CLOTH: SEE **cloth**.
corduroys SEE **trousers**.

core noun **1** *the core of an apple. the core of the earth*. centre, heart, inside, middle, nucleus.
2 *the core of a problem*. central issue, crux, essence, kernel, [*slang*] nitty-gritty, nub.

cork noun *a cork in a bottle*. bung, plug, stopper.

corkscrew noun SEE **spiral** noun.

corn noun *a field of corn*. SEE **cereal**.

corner noun **1** *a corner where lines or surfaces meet*. angle, crook (*the crook of your arm*), joint.
2 *a quiet corner*. hideaway, hiding-place, hole, niche, nook, recess, retreat.
3 *the corner of the road*. bend, crossroads, intersection, junction, turn, turning.

corner verb *After a chase, they cornered him*. capture, catch, trap.

corner-stone noun SEE **foundation**.

cornucopia noun SEE **plenty**.

corny adjective SEE **hackneyed**.

corollary noun SEE **consequence**.

coronation noun enthronement, crowning.

coroner noun SEE **official** noun.

coronet noun crown, diadem, tiara.

corporal adjective SEE **physical**.
corporal punishment SEE **punishment**.

corporate adjective SEE **collective**.

corporation noun 1 *a business corporation.* company, concern, enterprise, firm, organization.
2 *the city corporation.* council, local government.

corps noun SEE **armed services**.

corpse noun body, cadaver, carcass, remains, skeleton.

corpulent adjective SEE **fat** adjective.

corral noun SEE **enclosure**.

correct adjective 1 *the correct time. correct information.* accurate, authentic, exact, factual, faithful, faultless, flawless, genuine, precise, reliable, right, strict, true.
OPPOSITES: SEE **inaccurate, wrong**.
2 *the correct thing to do.* acceptable, appropriate, fitting, just, normal, proper, regular, standard, suitable, tactful, unexceptionable, well-mannered.
OPPOSITES: SEE **inappropriate, wrong**.

correct verb 1 *to correct a fault.* adjust, alter, cure, [*informal*] debug (*to debug a computer system*), put right, rectify, redress, remedy, repair.
2 *to correct pupils' homework.* assess, mark.
3 *to correct a wrongdoer.* SEE **rebuke**.

correlate verb SEE **compare**.

correlative adjective SEE **corresponding**.

correspond verb 1 *Her story corresponds with mine.* accord, agree, be consistent, coincide, concur, conform, correlate, fit, harmonize, match, parallel, square, tally.
2 *I corresponded with a girl in Paris.* communicate with, send letters to, write to.

correspondence noun *A secretary deals with his boss's correspondence.* letters, memoranda, [*informal*] memos, messages, notes, writings.

correspondent noun SEE **writer**.

corresponding adjective *When I got a more responsible job I expected a corresponding rise in pay.* analogous, appropriate, commensurate, complementary, correlative, equivalent, matching, parallel, reciprocal, related, similar.

corridor noun hall, passage, passageway.

corroborate verb SEE **support** verb.

corrode verb 1 *Acid may corrode metal.* consume, eat away, erode, oxidize, rot, rust, tarnish.
2 *Many metals corrode.* crumble, deteriorate, disintegrate, tarnish.

corrugated adjective *a corrugated surface.* creased, [*informal*] crinkly, [*formal*] fluted, furrowed, lined, puckered, ribbed, ridged, wrinkled.

corrupt adjective 1 *a corrupt judge. corrupt practices.* [*informal*] bent, bribable, criminal, crooked, dishonest, dishonourable, false, fraudulent, unethical, unprincipled, unscrupulous, unsound, untrustworthy.
2 *corrupt behaviour. a corrupt individual.* debauched, decadent, degenerate, depraved, [*informal*] dirty, dissolute, evil, immoral, iniquitous, low, perverted, profligate, rotten, sinful, venal, vicious, wicked.
OPPOSITES: SEE **honest**.

corrupt verb 1 *to corrupt an official. to corrupt the course of justice.* bribe, divert, [*informal*] fix, influence, pervert, suborn, subvert.
2 *to corrupt the innocent.* debauch, deprave, lead astray, make corrupt [SEE **corrupt** adjective], tempt, seduce.

corsage noun SEE **bouquet**.

cortège noun cavalcade, SEE **funeral**, parade, procession.

cosh verb SEE **hit** verb.

cosmetics noun make-up, toiletries.

VARIOUS COSMETICS: cream, deodorant, eye-shadow, lipstick, lotion, mascara, nail varnish, perfume, powder, scent, talc, talcum powder.

Several English words, including *cosmic*, *cosmopolitan*, and *cosmos*, are related to Greek *kosmos* = *world*.

cosmic adjective *cosmic space.* boundless, endless, infinite, limitless, universal.

cosmonaut noun astronaut, space-traveller.

cosmopolitan adjective *Big cities usually have a cosmopolitan atmosphere.* international, multicultural, sophisticated, urbane.
OPPOSITES: SEE **provincial**.

cosmos noun galaxy, universe.

cosset verb SEE **pamper**.

cost noun *the cost of a ticket.* amount, charge, expenditure, expense, fare, figure, outlay, payment, price, rate, value.

cost verb *This watch costs £10.* be valued at, be worth, fetch, go for, realize, sell for, [*informal*] set you back.

costermonger noun [old-fashioned]
barrow-boy, market-trader, SEE **seller**,
street-trader.

costly adjective SEE **expensive**.

costume noun *actors' costumes.* [formal]
apparel, attire, SEE **clothes**, clothing,
dress, fancy-dress, garb, garments, [in-
formal] get-up, livery, outfit, period
dress, [old-fashioned] raiment, robes,
uniform, vestments.

cosy adjective *a cosy room. a cosy atmosphere.* comfortable, [informal] comfy,
homely, intimate, reassuring, relaxing,
restful, secure, snug, soft, warm.
OPPOSITES: SEE **uncomfortable**.

cot noun SEE **bed**.

coterie noun SEE **group** noun.

cottage noun SEE **house** noun.

cotton noun 1 KINDS OF CLOTH: SEE **cloth**.
2 *cotton to sew on a button.* thread.

couch noun SEE **seat** noun.

couchette noun SEE **bed**.

council noun 1 *a council of war.* SEE
assembly.
2 *the town council.* corporation.
council house SEE **house** noun.

councillor noun [Do not confuse with
counsellor.] member of the council, official.

counsel noun [Do not confuse with *council*.] 1 *counsel for the defence.* SEE **lawyer**.
2 *She gave me good counsel.* SEE **advice**.

counsel verb *The careers officer coun-
selled me about a possible career.* advise,
give help, guide, have a discussion with,
listen to your views.

counsellor noun [Do not confuse with
councillor.] adviser.

count verb 1 *Count your money.* add up,
calculate, check, compute, enumerate,
estimate, figure out, keep account of,
[informal] notch up, number, reckon,
score, take stock of, tell, total, [informal]
tot up, work out.
2 *It's taking part that counts, not winning.*
be important, have significance, matter,
signify.
to count on *You can count on my support.*
bank on, believe in, depend on, expect,
have faith in, rely on, swear by, trust.

countenance noun *a sad countenance.*
air, appearance, aspect, demeanour,
expression, face, features, look, visage.

countenance verb *They would not countenance our suggestion.* SEE **approve**.

counter noun 1 *a counter in a shop or café.*
bar, sales-point, service-point.
2 *You play ludo with counters.* disc, token.

counteract verb *a treatment to counteract
poison.* act against, be an antidote to,
cancel out, SEE **counterbalance**, fight
against, foil, invalidate, militate
against, negate, neutralize, offset, oppose, resist, thwart, withstand, work
against.

counter-attack noun, verb SEE **attack**
noun, verb.

counterbalance verb *Their strength in
defence counterbalances our strength in
attack.* balance, compensate for, SEE
counteract, counterpoise, counter-
weight, equalize.

counterblast noun SEE **response**.

counter-espionage noun SEE **spying**.

counterfeit adjective *counterfeit money.
a counterfeit work of art.* artificial, bogus,
copied, ersatz, fake, false, feigned,
forged, fraudulent, imitation, pastiche,
phoney, [childish] pretend, sham, simulated, spurious.
OPPOSITES: SEE **genuine**.

counterfeit verb 1 *to counterfeit money.*
copy, fake, forge.
2 *to counterfeit an illness.* feign, imitate,
pretend, sham, simulate.

countermand verb SEE **cancel**.

counterpart noun *The sales manager
phoned his counterpart in the rival firm.*
corresponding person or thing, equivalent, match, opposite number, parallel
person or thing.

counter-productive adjective *Our attempt to help her was counter-productive.*
negative, worse than useless.

countless adjective *countless stars. a
countless number.* endless, immeasurable, incalculable, infinite, innumerable, many, measureless, myriad,
numberless, numerous, unnumbered,
untold.
OPPOSITES: SEE **finite**.

country noun 1 *the countries of the world.*
canton, commonwealth, domain, em-
pire, kingdom, land, nation, people,
principality, realm, state, territory.
POLITICAL SYSTEMS FOUND IN VARIOUS
COUNTRIES: democracy, dictatorship,
monarchy, republic.
2 *There's some attractive country near
here.* countryside, green belt, landscape,
scenery.
RELATED ADJECTIVES: SEE **rural**.

countryside noun SEE **country**.

county noun [old-fashioned] shire.

coup, coup d'état nouns SEE **revolution**.

coupé noun SEE **car**.

couple noun SEE **pair** noun.

couple verb 1 *to couple two things together.* combine, connect, fasten, hitch, join, link, match, pair, unite, yoke.
2 *to couple sexually.* SEE **mate** verb.

coupon noun *Save ten coupons and get a free mug.* tear-off slip, ticket, token, voucher.

courage noun audacity, boldness, [*informal*] bottle, bravery, daring, dauntlessness, determination, fearlessness, fibre (*moral fibre*), firmness, fortitude, gallantry, [*informal*] grit, [*informal*] guts, heroism, indomitability, intrepidity, mettle, [*informal*] nerve, [*informal*] pluck, prowess, resolution, spirit, [*slang*] spunk, [*formal*] stoicism, valour. OPPOSITES: SEE **cowardice**.

courageous adjective audacious, bold, brave, cool, daring, dauntless, determined, fearless, gallant, game, heroic, indomitable, intrepid, lion-hearted, noble, plucky, resolute, spirited, stalwart, stoical, tough, unafraid, uncomplaining, undaunted, unshrinking, valiant, valorous. OPPOSITES: SEE **cowardly**.

courier noun 1 *A courier delivers packages.* carrier, messenger, runner.
2 *A courier helps tourists.* guide, representative.

course noun 1 *a normal course of events.* advance, continuation, development, movement, passage, passing, progress, progression, succession.
2 *a ship's course.* bearings, direction, path, route, way.
3 *a course of treatment at hospital.* programme, schedule, sequence, series.
4 *a course in college.* curriculum, syllabus.
5 *a golf course.* links.
6 *a racecourse.* SEE **racecourse**.
7 *a course of a meal.* SEE **meal**.
of course SEE **undoubtedly**.

course verb SEE **flow** verb, **hunt** verb.

court noun 1 SEE **courtyard**.
2 *a monarch's court.* entourage, followers, palace, retinue.
3 *a court of law.* [*old-fashioned*] assizes, bench, court martial, high court, lawcourt, magistrates' court.
LEGAL TERMS: SEE **law**.

court verb 1 *to court attention.* [*informal*] ask for (*She's just asking for attention*), attract, invite, provoke, seek, solicit.
2 [*old-fashioned*] *to court a boyfriend or girlfriend.* date, [*informal*] go out with, make advances to, make love to [SEE **love** noun], try to win, woo.

courteous adjective SEE **polite**.

courtesan noun SEE **prostitute** noun.

courtesy noun SEE **politeness**.

courtier noun [*old-fashioned*] *a king's courtiers.* attendant, follower, lady, lord, noble, page, steward.

courtyard noun court, enclosure, forecourt, patio, [*informal*] quad, quadrangle, yard.

cousin noun MEMBERS OF A FAMILY: SEE **family**.

couturier noun SEE **designer**.

cove noun SEE **bay**.

coven noun SEE **group** noun.

covenant noun SEE **agreement**.

covenant verb SEE **agree**.

cover noun 1 *a cover to keep the rain off.* canopy, cloak, clothes, clothing, coat, SEE **covering**, roof, screen, shield, tarpaulin.
2 *a jam-pot cover.* cap, lid, top.
3 *a cover for papers or a book.* binding, case, dust-jacket, envelope, file, folder, portfolio, wrapper.
4 *cover from a storm.* hiding-place, refuge, sanctuary, shelter.
5 *A helicopter gave them cover from the air.* defence, guard, protection, support.
6 *the cover of an assumed identity.* camouflage, concealment, cover-up, deception, disguise, façade, front, mask, pretence, veneer.

cover verb 1 *A cloth covered the table. Cloud covers the hills. Fresh paint will cover the graffiti.* blot out, bury, camouflage, cap, carpet, cloak, clothe, cloud, coat, conceal, curtain, disguise, drape, dress, encase, enclose, enshroud, envelop, face, hide, hood, mantle, mask, obscure, overlay, overspread, plaster, protect, screen, shade, sheathe, shield, shroud, spread over, surface, tile, veil, veneer, wrap up.
2 *Will £10 cover your expenses?* be enough for, match, meet, pay for, suffice for.
3 *An encyclopedia covers many subjects.* comprise, contain, deal with, embrace, encompass, include, incorporate, involve, treat.

covering noun *a light covering of snow.* blanket, cap, carpet, casing, cladding, cloak, coating, cocoon, cover, facing, film, layer, mantle, pall, sheath, sheet, shroud, skin, surface, tarpaulin, veil, veneer, wrapping.

coverlet noun SEE **bedclothes**.

covert adjective SEE **secret** adjective.

cover-up noun SEE **deception**.

covet verb SEE **desire** verb.

covetous adjective SEE **greedy**.

covey noun SEE **group** noun.

cow noun SEE **cattle**.

cow verb SEE **frighten**.

coward noun [*informal*] chicken, deserter, runaway.
OPPOSITES: SEE **hero**.

cowardice noun cowardliness, desertion, evasion, faint-heartedness, SEE **fear** noun, [*informal*] funk, shirking, spinelessness, timidity.
OPPOSITES: SEE **heroism**.

cowardly adjective *a cowardly person. a cowardly action.* abject, afraid, base, chicken-hearted, cowering, craven, dastardly, faint-hearted, fearful, [*informal*] gutless, [*old-fashioned*] lily-livered, pusillanimous, spineless, submissive, timid, timorous, unheroic, [*informal*] yellow.
OPPOSITES: SEE **brave**.
to be cowardly [*informal*] chicken out, cower, desert, [*informal*] funk it, run away.

cowed adjective SEE **afraid**.

cower verb *The naughty dog cowered in a corner.* cringe, crouch, flinch, grovel, hide, quail, shiver, shrink, skulk, tremble.

cox, coxswain nouns SEE **sailor**.

coy adjective *Don't be coy: come and be introduced.* bashful, coquettish, demure, diffident, embarrassed, modest, reserved, retiring, self-conscious, sheepish, shy, timid.
OPPOSITES: SEE **forward** adjective.

crabbed adjective SEE **bad-tempered**.

crack noun 1 *the crack of a whip.* VARIOUS SOUNDS: SEE **sound** noun.
2 *a crack on the head.* SEE **hit** noun.
3 [*informal*] *a witty crack.* SEE **joke** noun.
4 *a crack in a cup. a crack in a rock.* break, chink, chip, cleavage, cleft, cranny, craze, crevice, fissure, flaw, fracture, gap, opening, rift, split.

crack verb 1 *The whip cracked.* VARIOUS SOUNDS: SEE **sound** noun.
2 *to crack a cup. to crack a nut.* break, chip, fracture, snap, splinter, split.
3 *to crack a code. to crack a problem.* SEE **solve**.
to crack up [*informal*] SEE **disintegrate**, **praise** verb.

crackle noun, verb VARIOUS SOUNDS: SEE **sound** noun.

crackpot noun SEE **madman**.

cradle noun *a baby's cradle.* SEE **bed**.

cradle verb *to cradle someone in your arms.* SEE **hold** verb.

craft noun 1 *the craft of thatching.* art, handicraft, job, skilled work, technique, trade.
VARIOUS CRAFTS: SEE **art**.
2 *I admired the thatcher's craft.* SEE **craftsmanship**.
3 *He wins by craft rather than by honest effort.* SEE **deceit**.
4 *All sorts of craft were in the harbour.* SEE **vessel**.

craftsman noun SEE **artist**.

craftsmanship noun artistry, cleverness, craft, dexterity, expertise, handiwork, knack, [*informal*] know-how, SEE **skill**, workmanship.

crafty adjective *a crafty deception.* artful, astute, calculating, canny, clever, cunning, deceitful, designing, devious, [*informal*] dodgy, [*informal*] foxy, SEE **furtive**, guileful, ingenious, knowing, machiavellian, scheming, shrewd, sly, [*informal*] sneaky, tricky, wily.
OPPOSITES: SEE **innocent**, **straightforward**.
a crafty person SEE **cheat** noun.

crag noun *a steep crag.* bluff, cliff, precipice, rock.

craggy adjective *a craggy pinnacle.* jagged, rocky, rough, rugged, steep, uneven.

cram verb 1 *to cram into a confined space.* compress, crowd, crush, fill, force, jam, overcrowd, overfill, pack, press, squeeze, stuff.
2 *to cram for an examination.* SEE **study** verb.

cramp verb *Your presence cramps my style.* SEE **restrict**.

cramped adjective *cramped accommodation.* crowded, narrow, restricted, tight, uncomfortable.
OPPOSITES: SEE **roomy**.

crane noun *a crane for loading freight.* davit, derrick, hoist.

crane verb *to crane your neck.* SEE **stretch** verb.

cranium noun skull.

crank noun SEE **eccentric** noun.

cranky adjective SEE **eccentric** adjective.

cranny noun *a cranny in a rock.* SEE **crack** noun.

crash noun 1 *a loud crash.* VARIOUS SOUNDS: SEE **sound** noun.
2 *a rail crash. a crash on the motorway.* accident, bump, collision, derailment, SEE **disaster**, impact, knock, pile-up, smash, wreck.
3 *a crash on the stockmarket.* collapse, depression, fall.

crash verb 1 *to crash into someone.* bump, collide, SEE **hit** verb, knock, lurch, pitch, smash.
2 *to crash to the ground.* collapse, fall, plunge, topple.

crash-dive noun, verb SEE **dive** noun, verb.

crash-helmet noun KINDS OF HEAD-GEAR: SEE **hat**.

crass adjective SEE **stupid**.

crate noun *We packed our belongings in crates.* box, carton, case, packing-case, tea-chest.

crater noun *The explosion left a crater.* abyss, cavity, chasm, hole, hollow, opening, pit.

cravat noun necktie.

crave verb SEE **desire** verb.

craven adjective SEE **cowardly**.

craving noun SEE **desire** noun.

crawl verb 1 *I crawled along a narrow ledge.* clamber, creep, edge, inch, slither, wriggle.
2 [*informal*] *She got high marks because she crawled to the teacher.* SEE **obsequious** (to be obsequious).

craze noun *the latest craze.* diversion, enthusiasm, fad, fashion, infatuation, mania, novelty, obsession, passion, pastime, rage, trend, vogue.

crazed adjective SEE **crazy**.

crazy adjective 1 *The dog went crazy when it was stung by a wasp.* berserk, crazed, delirious, demented, deranged, frantic, frenzied, hysterical, insane, lunatic, SEE **mad**, [*informal*] potty, [*informal*] scatty, unbalanced, unhinged, wild.
OPPOSITES: SEE **sane**.
2 *a crazy comedy.* absurd, confused, daft, eccentric, farcical, foolish, idiot, illogical, irrational, ludicrous, nonsensical, preposterous, ridiculous, senseless, silly, stupid, unreasonable, weird, zany.
OPPOSITES: SEE **sensible**, **straight**.
3 [*informal*] *crazy about snooker.* SEE **enthusiastic**.

creak noun, verb VARIOUS SOUNDS: SEE **sound** noun.

creamy adjective *a creamy liquid.* milky, oily, rich, smooth, thick, velvety.

crease noun *a crease in a piece of cloth.* corrugation, crinkle, fold, furrow, groove, line, pleat, pucker, ridge, ruck, tuck, wrinkle.

crease verb *to crease a piece of paper.* crimp, crinkle, crumple, crush, fold, furrow, pleat, pucker, ridge, ruck, rumple, wrinkle.

create verb *to create something new. to create trouble.* [*old-fashioned*] beget, SEE

begin, be the creator of [SEE **creator**], breed, bring about, bring into existence, build, cause, conceive, concoct, constitute, construct, design, devise, engender, establish, form, found, generate, give rise to, hatch, institute, invent, make, make up, manufacture, occasion, originate, produce, set up, shape, think up.
OPPOSITES: SEE **destroy**.
to create a work of art compose, draw, embroider, engrave, model, paint, print, sculpt, sketch, throw (*pottery*), weave, write.
OTHER WORDS TO DO WITH ART: SEE **art**.

creation noun 1 *the creation of the world.* beginning, birth, building, conception, constitution, construction, establishing, formation, foundation, generation, genesis, inception, institution, making, origin, procreation, production, shaping.
OPPOSITES: SEE **destruction**.
2 *The dress is her own creation.* achievement, brainchild, concept, effort, handiwork, invention, product, work of art.

creative adjective *a creative imagination.* artistic, clever, fecund, fertile, imaginative, inspired, inventive, original, positive, productive, resourceful, talented.
OPPOSITES: SEE **destructive**.

creator noun 1 *the creator of an empire. the creator of a TV programme.* architect, begetter, builder, designer, deviser, discoverer, initiator, inventor, maker, manufacturer, originator, parent, producer.
2 *the creator of a work of art.* artist, author, composer, craftsman, painter, photographer, potter, sculptor, smith, weaver, writer.
3 *the Creator.* SEE **god**.

creature noun animal, beast, being, brute, mortal being.
VARIOUS SPECIES: SEE **animal** noun, **bird**, **fish**, **insect**, **reptile**, **snake**.

crèche noun SEE **nursery**.

Several English words, including *credentials, credible, credulous,* etc., are related to Latin *credere = to believe.*

---

credentials noun *You must show your credentials before they'll let you in.* authorization, documents, identity card, licence, passport, permit, proof of identity, warrant.

credible adjective [Do not confuse with *creditable.*] *The report about Martian visitors is not credible.* believable, conceivable, convincing, imaginable, likely,

persuasive, plausible, possible, reasonable, tenable, thinkable, trustworthy.
OPPOSITES: SEE incredible.

credit noun 1 *Her success brought credit to the school.* approval, commendation, distinction, esteem, fame, glory, honour, [*informal*] kudos, merit, praise, prestige, recognition, reputation, status.
OPPOSITES: SEE dishonour.
2 *a credit balance at the bank.* plus, positive.
OPPOSITE: debit [SEE debt].
3 *to buy on credit.* SEE loan noun.
credit card SEE money.
in credit [*informal*] in the black, solvent.

credit verb 1 *You won't credit her farfetched story.* accept, believe, [*informal*] buy, count on, depend on, endorse, have faith in, reckon on, rely on, subscribe to, [*informal*] swallow, swear by, trust.
OPPOSITES: SEE disbelieve.
2 *I credited you with more sense.* attribute to, ascribe to, assign to, attach to.
3 *The bank credited £10 to my account.* add, enter.
OPPOSITES: SEE debit.

creditable adjective [Do not confuse with *credible*.] *a creditable performance.* admirable, commendable, estimable, excellent, good, honourable, laudable, meritorious, praiseworthy, respectable, well thought of, worthy.
OPPOSITES: SEE unworthy.

credulous adjective *You must be credulous if she fooled you with that story.* easily taken in, [*informal*] green, gullible, innocent, naïve, [*informal*] soft, trusting, unsuspecting.
OPPOSITES: SEE sceptical.

creed noun *a religious creed.* beliefs, convictions, doctrine, dogma, faith, principles, tenets.

creek noun SEE bay, estuary, inlet.

creep verb 1 *to creep along the ground.* crawl, edge, inch, move slowly, slink, slither, worm, wriggle, writhe.
2 *to creep quietly past.* move quietly, slip, sneak, steal, tiptoe.

creeper noun *Creepers had grown over the ruin.* SEE climber.

creepy adjective *creepy noises in the dark.* disturbing, eerie, frightening, ghostly, hair-raising, macabre, ominous, scary, sinister, spine-chilling, [*informal*] spooky, supernatural, threatening, uncanny, unearthly, weird.
OPPOSITES: SEE natural, reassuring.

cremate verb SEE burn verb.

cremation noun SEE funeral.

crenellated adjective SEE indented.

creosote noun wood-preservative.

crescent adjective *a crescent moon.* bow-shaped, curved.

crest noun 1 *a crest on a bird's head.* comb, plume, tuft.
2 *the crest of a hill.* apex, brow, crown, head, peak, ridge, summit, top.
3 *the school crest.* badge, emblem, insignia, seal, sign, symbol.

crestfallen adjective SEE downcast.

cretin noun SEE idiot.

crevasse noun [Do not confuse with *crevice*.] *a crevasse in a glacier.* SEE chasm.

crevice noun [Do not confuse with *crevasse*.] *a crevice in a wall.* SEE crack noun.

crew noun *a ship's crew.* SEE group noun.

crib noun *a baby's crib.* SEE bed, cot, cradle.

crib verb *to crib in a test.* cheat, copy, plagiarize.

crick noun *a crick in the neck.* SEE pain noun.

cricket noun CRICKETING TERMS: bail, batsman, bowler, boundary, cricketer, fielder, fieldsman, innings, lbw, maiden over, over, pad, run, slip, stump, test match, umpire, wicket, wicket-keeper.

crime noun *The law punishes crime.* delinquency, dishonesty, [*old-fashioned*] felony, illegality, law-breaking, misconduct, misdeed, misdemeanour, offence, racket, sin, transgression of the law, wrongdoing.

VARIOUS CRIMES: abduction, arson, blackmail, burglary, extortion, hijacking, hold-up, hooliganism, kidnapping, manslaughter, misappropriation, mugging, murder, pilfering, poaching, rape, robbery, shop-lifting, smuggling, stealing, theft, vandalism.

criminal adjective *a criminal act.* [*informal*] bent, corrupt, [*informal*] crooked, [*formal*] culpable, dishonest, felonious, illegal, illicit, indictable, nefarious, [*informal*] shady, unlawful, SEE wrong adjective.
OPPOSITES: SEE lawful.

criminal noun *The law punishes criminals.* convict, [*informal*] crook, culprit, delinquent, felon, hooligan, law-breaker, [*formal*] malefactor, offender, outlaw, recidivist, [*old-fashioned*] transgressor, villain, wrongdoer.

VARIOUS CRIMINALS: assassin, bandit, blackmailer, brigand, buccaneer, burglar, desperado, gangster, gunman, highwayman, hijacker, kidnapper, mugger, murderer, outlaw, pickpocket, pirate, poacher, racketeer, rapist, receiver, robber, shop-lifter, smuggler, swindler, terrorist, thief, thug, vandal.

crimson adjective SEE **red**.

cringe verb *to cringe in fear*. blench, cower, crouch, dodge, duck, flinch, grovel, quail, quiver, recoil, shrink back, shy away, tremble, wince.

crinkle noun, verb SEE **crease** noun, verb.

cripple noun SEE **disabled (disabled person)**.

cripple verb 1 *to cripple a person*. disable, dislocate (*a joint*), fracture (*a bone*), hamper, hamstring, incapacitate, lame, maim, mutilate, paralyse, weaken.
2 *to cripple a machine*. damage, make useless, put out of action, sabotage, spoil.

crippled adjective 1 *a crippled person*. deformed, SEE **disabled**, handicapped, hurt, incapacitated, injured, invalid, lame, maimed, mutilated, paralysed.
2 *a crippled vehicle*. damaged, immobilized, out of action, sabotaged, useless.

crisis noun 1 *the crisis of a story*. climax.
2 *We had a crisis when we found a gas leak*. danger, difficulty, emergency, predicament, problem.

crisp adjective 1 *crisp biscuits*. brittle, crackly, crispy, crunchy, fragile, hard and dry.
OPPOSITES: SEE **soft**.
2 *a crisp winter morning*. SEE **cold** adjective.
3 *a crisp manner*. SEE **brisk**.

criss-cross adjective SEE **chequered**.

criterion noun SEE **measure** noun, touchstone.

critic noun 1 *a music critic*. analyst, authority, commentator, judge, pundit, reviewer.
2 *a critic of the government*. attacker, detractor.

critical adjective 1 *Critical* can mean either (a) *unfavourable* (*a critical review of the dreadful new LP*) or (b) *showing careful judgement* (*a critical analysis of Shakespeare's plays*). (a) = *unfavourable*. captious, censorious, criticizing [SEE **criticize**], deprecatory, derogatory, fault-finding, hypercritical, [*informal*] nit-picking, scathing, slighting, uncomplimentary, unfavourable.

OPPOSITES: SEE **complimentary**.
(b) = *showing careful judgement*. analytical, discerning, discriminating, intelligent, judicious, perceptive.
OPPOSITES: SEE **imperceptive**.
2 *a critical decision*. crucial, SEE **dangerous**, decisive, important, key, momentous, vital.
OPPOSITES: SEE **unimportant**.

criticism noun 1 *unfair criticism of our behaviour*. censure, diatribe, disapproval, disparagement, judgement, reprimand, reproach, stricture, tirade, verbal attack.
2 *literary criticism*. analysis, appraisal, appreciation, assessment, commentary, critique, elucidation, evaluation, notice (*a favourable notice in the papers*), [*informal*] puff [= *a flattering notice*], review.

criticize verb 1 *She criticized us for being noisy. She criticized our efforts*. belittle, berate, blame, carp, [*informal*] cast aspersions on, castigate, censure, [*old-fashioned*] chide, condemn, decry, disapprove of, disparage, fault, find fault with, [*informal*] flay, impugn, [*informal*] knock, [*informal*] lash, [*informal*] pan, [*informal*] pick holes in, [*informal*] pitch into, [*informal*] rap, rate, rebuke, reprimand, satirize, scold, [*informal*] slam, [*informal*] slate, snipe at.
OPPOSITES: SEE **praise** verb.
2 *to criticize an author's work*. analyse, appraise, assess, evaluate, judge, review.

critique noun SEE **criticism**.

croak noun, verb VARIOUS SOUNDS: SEE **sound** noun.

crock, crocks nouns SEE **crockery**.

crockery noun ceramics, china, crocks, dishes, earthenware, porcelain, pottery, tableware.

VARIOUS ITEMS OF CROCKERY: basin, bowl, coffee-cup, coffee-pot, cup, dinner plate, dish, jug, milk-jug, mug, plate, [*American*] platter, pot, sauceboat, saucer, serving dish, side plate, soup bowl, sugar-bowl, teacup, teapot, [*old-fashioned*] trencher, tureen.
VARIOUS COOKING UTENSILS: SEE **cook**.

crocodile noun alligator.

croft noun SEE **farm** noun.

croissant noun SEE **bread**.

crony noun SEE **friend**.

crook noun 1 *the crook of your arm*. angle, bend, corner, hook.

2 [*informal*] *The cops got the crooks.* SEE **criminal** noun.

crooked adjective **1** *The picture hangs crooked.* angled, askew, awry, lopsided, offcentre.
2 *a crooked road. a crooked tree.* bent, bowed, curved, curving, deformed, misshapen, tortuous, twisted, twisty, winding, zigzag.
3 *a crooked salesman.* SEE **criminal** adjective.

croon verb SEE **sing**.

crop noun *a crop of fruit.* gathering, harvest, produce, sowing, vintage, yield.

crop verb **1** *Animals crop grass.* bite off, browse, eat, graze, nibble.
2 *A barber crops hair.* clip, SEE **cut** verb, shear, snip, trim.
to crop up *A difficulty cropped up.* appear, arise, come up, emerge, happen, occur, spring up, turn up.

cropper noun **to come a cropper** SEE **fall** verb.

crosier noun SEE **staff** noun.

cross adjective *She's always cross when she comes in from work.* SEE **angry**, annoyed, bad-tempered, cantankerous, crotchety, [*informal*] grumpy, ill-tempered, irascible, irate, irritable, peevish, short-tempered, testy, tetchy, upset, vexed.
OPPOSITES: SEE **even-tempered**.

cross noun **1** *marked with a cross.* intersecting lines, X.
RELATED ADJECTIVE [= *cross-shaped*]: cruciform.
2 *a cross I have to bear.* affliction, burden, difficulty, grief, misfortune, problem, sorrow, trial, tribulation, trouble, worry.
3 *a cross between two breeds. a cross between soup and stew.* amalgam, blend, combination, cross-breed, half-way house, hybrid, mixture, mongrel [= *a cross between two breeds of dog*].

cross verb **1** *lines which cross.* criss-cross, intersect, intertwine, meet, zigzag.
2 *to cross a river.* bridge, ford, go across, pass over, span, traverse.
3 *The trains crossed at high speed.* pass.
4 *Don't cross him when he's in a temper.* annoy, block, frustrate, hinder, impede, interfere with, oppose, stand in the way of, thwart.
to cross out SEE **cancel**.
to cross swords SEE **quarrel** verb.

cross-breed noun hybrid, mongrel.

cross-check verb SEE **check** verb.

cross-examine verb *to cross-examine a witness.* SEE **question** verb.

cross-eyed adjective [*informal*] boss-eyed, squinting.

crossing noun *a sea crossing.* SEE **journey** noun.

CROSSINGS OVER A RIVER, ROAD, RAILWAY, ETC.: bridge, causeway, flyover, ford, level-crossing, overpass, pedestrian crossing, pelican crossing, subway, stepping-stones, underpass, zebra crossing.

---

crosspatch noun SEE **angry** (angry person).

cross-question verb SEE **question** verb.

cross-reference noun SEE **note** noun.

crossroads noun interchange, intersection, junction.

crotchety adjective SEE **cross** adjective.

crouch verb *They crouched in the bushes.* bend, bow, cower, cringe, duck, kneel, squat, stoop.

crow verb **1** *The cock crows every morning.* VARIOUS SOUNDS: SEE **sound** noun.
2 *to crow about an achievement.* SEE **boast** verb.

crowd noun **1** *a crowd of people.* army, assembly, bunch, circle, cluster, collection, company, crush, flock, gathering, SEE **group** noun, horde, host, mass, mob, multitude, pack, rabble, swarm, throng.
2 *a football crowd.* audience, gate, spectators.

crowd verb *We crowded together. They crowded us into a small room.* assemble, bundle, compress, congregate, cram, crush, flock, gather, herd, huddle, jostle, mass, muster, overcrowd, pack, [*informal*] pile, press, push, squeeze, swarm, throng.

crowded adjective *a crowded room.* congested, cramped, full, jammed, jostling, overcrowded, overflowing, packed, swarming, teeming, thronging.
OPPOSITES: SEE **empty** adjective.

crown noun **1** *a monarch's crown.* coronet, diadem, tiara.
2 *the crown of a hill.* apex, brow, crown, head, peak, ridge, summit, top.

crown verb **1** *to crown a monarch.* anoint, appoint, enthrone, install.
2 *to crown your efforts with success.* cap, complete, conclude, consummate, finish off, perfect, round off, top.

crowning adjective *her crowning achievement.* culminating, deserved, final, highest, hoped for, perfect, successful, supreme, top, ultimate.

crowning noun *the crowning of a monarch.* coronation, enthronement.

crucial adjective *a crucial decision. a crucial part of an argument.* central, critical, decisive, important, major, momentous, pivotal, serious.
OPPOSITES: SEE **peripheral.**

crucifix noun cross, [*old-fashioned*] rood.

crude adjective 1 *crude oil.* natural, raw, unprocessed, unrefined.
OPPOSITES: SEE **refined.**
2 *crude workmanship.* amateurish, awkward, bungling, clumsy, inartistic, incompetent, inelegant, inept, makeshift, primitive, rough, rudimentary, unpolished, unrefined, unskilful, unworkmanlike.
OPPOSITES: SEE **dainty, skilful.**
3 *crude language.* SEE **indecent.**

cruel adjective 1 *a cruel action. a cruel person.* atrocious, barbaric, barbarous, beastly, blood-thirsty, bloody, brutal, callous, cold-blooded, diabolical, ferocious, fierce, flinty, grim, hard, hard-hearted, harsh, heartless, hellish, implacable, inexorable, inhuman, inhumane, malevolent, merciless, murderous, pitiless, relentless, remorseless, ruthless, sadistic, savage, spiteful, stern, stony-hearted, tyrannical, unfeeling, unjust, unkind, unmerciful, unrelenting, vengeful, vicious, violent.
OPPOSITES: SEE **kind** adjective.
2 *cruel disappointment.* SEE **severe.**

cruise noun *a sea cruise.* SEE **journey** noun.

cruise verb SEE **travel** verb.

crumb noun *a crumb of bread.* bit, fragment, grain, morsel, particle, scrap, shred, speck.

crumble verb 1 *Rotten wood crumbles.* break up, decay, decompose, deteriorate, disintegrate, fall apart, [*of rubber*] perish.
2 *He crumbled the cake onto his plate.* break into pieces, crush, fragment, grind, pound, powder, pulverize.

crumbly adjective *crumbly soil.* friable, granular, powdery.
OPPOSITES: SEE **solid, sticky.**

crumple verb *Don't crumple your clothes!* crease, crush, dent, fold, pucker, rumple, wrinkle.

crunch verb 1 *The dog crunched up a bone.* break, champ, chew, crush, grind, masticate, munch, scrunch, smash, squash.
2 *Footsteps crunched on the gravel.* VARIOUS SOUNDS: SEE **sound** noun.

crusade noun *a crusade against drugs.* campaign, drive, movement, struggle, war.

crush noun *I couldn't fight my way through the crush.* congestion, SEE **crowd** noun, jam.

crush verb 1 *to crush a finger in the door.* break, bruise, crumple, crunch, grind, SEE **injure,** mangle, mash, pound, press, pulp, pulverize, smash, squash, squeeze.
2 *to crush your opponents.* conquer, defeat, humiliate, mortify, overcome, overpower, overthrow, overwhelm, quash, quell, rout, subdue, thrash, vanquish.

crust noun *the crust of a loaf. the crust of the earth.* coat, coating, covering, incrustation, outer layer, outside, rind, scab, shell, skin, surface.

crustacean noun CRUSTACEANS INCLUDE: crab, lobster, shrimp.

crusty adjective 1 *a crusty loaf.* crisp.
2 *a crusty manner.* SEE **gruff.**

crutch noun *a crutch for a lame person.* prop, support.

crux noun *the crux of a problem.* centre, core, crucial issue, essence, heart, nub.

cry noun *a bird's cry. a cry of pain.* battle-cry, bellow, call, caterwaul, [*formal*] ejaculation, exclamation, hoot, howl, outcry, roar, scream, screech, shout, shriek, yell, yelp.

cry verb 1 *It was so sad it made me cry.* blubber, grizzle, shed tears, snivel, sob, wail, weep, whimper, whinge.
2 *Who cried out?* bawl, bellow, call, caterwaul, clamour, exclaim, roar, scream, screech, shout, shriek, yell, yelp.
to cry off SEE **withdraw.**

crypt noun *a church crypt.* basement, cellar, undercroft, vault.

cryptic adjective *a cryptic message.* coded, concealed, enigmatic, hidden, mysterious, obscure, occult, perplexing, puzzling, secret, unclear, unintelligible, veiled.
OPPOSITES: SEE **intelligible, plain** adjective.

crystal noun glass, mineral.
RELATED ADJECTIVE: crystalline.

crystalline adjective SEE **transparent.**

cub noun YOUNG ANIMALS: SEE **young** adjective.

cubby-hole noun SEE **compartment.**

cube noun cuboid, hexahedron.
RELATED ADJECTIVES: cubical, cuboidal.
OTHER SHAPES: SEE **shape** noun.

cubicle noun *changing cubicles at the swimming baths.* SEE **compartment.**

cuddle verb *to cuddle a baby.* caress, clasp lovingly, dandle, embrace, fondle, hold closely, huddle against, hug, kiss, nestle against, nurse, pet, snuggle against.

cudgel noun *armed with cudgels.* baton, bludgeon, cane, club, cosh, stick, truncheon.

cudgel verb *The attackers cudgelled him unconscious.* batter, beat, bludgeon, cane, [*informal*] clobber, cosh, SEE **hit** verb, pound, pummel, thrash, thump, [*informal*] thwack.

cue noun *Don't miss your cue to speak.* hint, prompt, reminder, sign, signal.

cuff noun PARTS OF A GARMENT: SEE **clothes**.
off-the-cuff SEE **impromptu**.

cuff verb SEE **hit** verb.

cuisine noun SEE **cooking**.

cul-de-sac noun SEE **road**.

culinary adjective *culinary skill.* to do with cooking.

cull verb 1 *to cull flowers.* SEE **pick** verb.
2 *to cull animals.* SEE **kill**.

culminate verb *The gala culminated in a firework display.* build up to, climax, close, conclude, end, finish, reach a finale, rise to a peak, terminate.

culottes noun SEE **trousers**.

culpable adjective *culpable negligence.* blameworthy, criminal, SEE **deliberate** adjective, guilty, knowing, liable, punishable, reprehensible, wrong.
OPPOSITES: SEE **innocent**.

culprit noun *They punished the culprit.* SEE **criminal** noun, delinquent, felon, malefactor, miscreant, offender, trouble-maker, wrongdoer.

cult noun 1 *a religious cult.* SEE **denomination**.
2 *The new pop-idol inspired a cult.* craze, enthusiasts [SEE **enthusiast**], fan-club, fashion, following, party, school, trend, vogue.

cultivate verb 1 *to cultivate land.* dig, farm, fertilize, hoe, manure, mulch, plough, prepare, rake, till, turn, work.
2 *to cultivate crops.* grow, plant, produce, raise, sow, take cuttings, tend.
3 *to cultivate good relations with your neighbours.* court, develop, encourage, foster, further, improve, promote, pursue, try to achieve.

cultivated adjective 1 *a cultivated way of speaking.* SEE **cultured**.
2 *cultivated land.* agricultural, farmed, farming, planted, prepared, tilled.

cultivation noun *the cultivation of the land.* agriculture, agronomy, culture, farming, gardening, horticulture, husbandry.

cultural adjective *The festival included sporting and cultural events.* aesthetic, artistic, civilized, civilizing, educational, elevating, enlightening, highbrow, improving, intellectual.
OPPOSITES: SEE **lowbrow**.

culture noun 1 *a nation's culture.* art, background, civilization, customs, education, learning, traditions.
2 *the culture of rare plants.* breeding, SEE **cultivation**, growing, nurturing.

cultured adjective *a cultured person.* artistic, civilized, cultivated, educated, erudite, highbrow, knowledgeable, scholarly, well-bred, well-educated, well-read.
OPPOSITES: SEE **ignorant**.

culvert noun SEE **drain** noun.

cumbersome adjective SEE **clumsy**.

cummerbund noun SEE **belt** noun.

cumulative adjective *the cumulative effect of something.* accumulating, building up, developing.

cunning adjective 1 *a cunning deception.* artful, SEE **crafty**, devious, dodgy, guileful, insidious, knowing, machiavellian, sly, subtle, tricky, wily.
2 *a cunning way to do something.* adroit, astute, SEE **clever**, ingenious, skilful.

cunning noun 1 [*uncomplimentary*] *Foxes have a reputation for cunning.* artfulness, chicanery, craftiness, deceit, deception, deviousness, duplicity, guile, slyness, trickery.
2 *The inventor showed great cunning in solving the problem.* cleverness, expertise, ingenuity.

cup noun 1 THINGS TO DRINK FROM: beaker, bowl, chalice, glass, goblet, mug, tankard, teacup, tumbler, wineglass.
2 *a cup presented on sports day.* award, prize, trophy.

cupboard noun VARIOUS KINDS OF CUPBOARD: cabinet, chiffonier, closet, dresser, filing-cabinet, food-cupboard, larder, locker, sideboard, wardrobe.
OTHER FURNITURE: SEE **furniture**.

cupidity noun SEE **greed**.

cur noun SEE **dog** noun.

curable adjective *a curable disease.* operable, remediable, treatable.
OPPOSITES: SEE **incurable**.

curate noun SEE **clergyman**.

curator noun *the curator of a museum.* archivist, SEE **custodian**.

curb verb *to curb someone's enthusiasm.* bridle, check, contain, control, deter, hamper, hinder, hold back, impede,

inhibit, limit, moderate, repress, restrain, restrict, subdue, suppress.
OPPOSITES: SEE **encourage**, **urge** verb.

curdle verb *Milk curdles.* clot, coagulate, congeal, go lumpy, go sour, thicken.
to curdle your blood SEE **frighten**.

cure noun 1 *a cure for a cold.* antidote, corrective, medicine, nostrum, palliative, panacea [= *a cure for everything*], prescription, remedy, restorative, solution, therapy, treatment.
2 *Her unexpected cure amazed the doctors.* SEE **recovery**.

cure verb 1 *The pill cured my headache.* alleviate, counteract, ease, heal, help, palliate, relieve, remedy, treat.
OPPOSITES: SEE **aggravate**.
2 *I cured the fault in the car.* correct, [*informal*] fix, mend, put right, rectify, repair, solve.

curfew noun SEE **restriction**.

curio noun SEE **antique** noun.

curiosity noun *I couldn't restrain my curiosity.* inquisitiveness, interest, meddling, nosiness, prying.

curious adjective 1 *curious questions.* inquiring, inquisitive, interested, [*informal*] nosy, prying, puzzled.
OPPOSITES: incurious, SEE **indifferent**.
to be curious SEE **pry**.
2 *a curious smell.* abnormal, bizarre, extraordinary, funny, mysterious, odd, peculiar, puzzling, queer, rare, strange, surprising, unconventional, unexpected, unusual.
OPPOSITES: SEE **normal**.

curl noun VARIOUS CURLED SHAPES: bend, SEE **circle** noun, coil, curve, kink, loop, ringlet, scroll, spiral, swirl, turn, twist, wave, whorl.

curl verb 1 *The snake curled round a branch.* bend, SEE **circle** verb. coil, corkscrew, curve, entwine, loop, spiral, turn, twine, twist, wind, wreathe, writhe.
2 *to curl your hair.* crimp, frizz, perm.

curly adjective *curly hair.* crimped, curled, curling, frizzy, fuzzy, kinky, permed, wavy.
OPPOSITES: SEE **straight**.

currency noun SEE **money**.

current adjective 1 *current fashions.* contemporary, fashionable, modern, prevailing, prevalent, [*informal*] trendy, up-to-date.
OPPOSITES: SEE **old-fashioned**.
2 *a current passport.* usable, valid.
OPPOSITES: SEE **out-of-date**.
3 *the current government.* existing, extant, present, reigning.

current noun *a current of air or water.* course, draught, drift, flow, jet, river, stream, tide.

curriculum noun *the school curriculum.* course, programme of study, syllabus.

curry verb **to curry favour** SEE **flatter**.

curse noun 1 *I let out a curse.* blasphemy, exclamation, expletive, imprecation, malediction, oath, obscenity, profanity, swearword.
OPPOSITES: SEE **blessing**.
2 *Pollution is a curse in modern society.* SEE **evil** noun.

curse verb *I cursed when I hit my finger.* blaspheme, damn, fulminate, swear, utter curses [SEE **curse** noun].
OPPOSITES: SEE **bless**.

cursed adjective SEE **hateful**.

cursory adjective *a cursory inspection.* brief, careless, casual, desultory, fleeting, hasty, hurried, perfunctory, quick, slapdash, superficial.
OPPOSITES: SEE **thorough**.

curt adjective *a curt answer.* abrupt, brief, brusque, gruff, laconic, monosyllabic, offhand, rude, sharp, short, succinct, tart, terse, uncommunicative, ungracious.
OPPOSITES: SEE **expansive**.

curtail verb *to curtail a debate.* abbreviate, abridge, break off, contract, cut short, decrease, [*informal*] dock, guillotine, halt, lessen, lop, prune, reduce, restrict, shorten, stop, terminate, trim, truncate.
OPPOSITES: SEE **extend**.

curtain noun *Close the curtains.* blind, drape, drapery, hanging, screen.

curtain verb *to curtain the windows.* drape, SEE **hide** verb, mask, screen, shroud, veil.

curtsy verb bend the knee, bow, genuflect (*before an altar*), salaam.

curve noun arc, arch, bend, bow, bulge, camber, SEE **circle** noun, convolution, corkscrew, crescent, curl, curvature, cycloid, loop, meander, spiral, swirl, trajectory, turn, twist, undulation, whorl.

curve verb arc, arch, bend, bow, bulge, SEE **circle** verb, coil, corkscrew, curl, loop, meander, spiral, swerve, swirl, turn, twist, wind.

curved adjective arched, bent, bowed, bulging, cambered, coiled, concave, convex, convoluted, crescent, crooked, curled, [*formal*] curvilinear, curving, curvy, looped, meandering, rounded, serpentine, shaped, sinuous, snaking, spiral, sweeping, swelling, tortuous, turned, twisted, undulating, whorled, winding.

cushion noun bean-bag, bolster, hassock, headrest, pad, pillow.

cushion verb *to cushion the impact of a collision.* absorb, bolster, deaden, lessen, mitigate, muffle, protect from, reduce the effect of, soften, support.

cushy adjective SEE **easy**.

custodian noun *the custodian of a museum.* caretaker, curator, guardian, keeper, overseer, superintendent, warden, warder, [*informal*] watch-dog, watchman.

custody noun 1 *The animals were left in my custody.* care, charge, guardianship, keeping, observation, possession, preservation, protection, safe-keeping.
2 *He was kept in police custody.* captivity, confinement, detention, imprisonment, incarceration, remand [*on remand = in custody*].

custom noun 1 *It's our custom to give presents at Christmas.* convention, etiquette, fashion, form, formality, habit, institution, manner, observance, policy, practice, procedure, routine, tradition, way.
2 *The shop offers discounts to attract custom.* business, buyers, customers, patronage, support, trade.

customary adjective *It was customary to give a tip to the waiter.* accepted, accustomed, common, conventional, established, expected, fashionable, general, habitual, normal, ordinary, popular, prevailing, regular, routine, traditional, typical, usual, wonted.
OPPOSITES: SEE **unusual**.

customer noun *a shop's customers.* buyer, client, consumer, patron, purchaser, shopper.
OPPOSITES: SEE **seller**.

customs noun *You may have to pay customs on imports.* SEE **tax** noun.
customs officer SEE **official** noun.

cut noun 1 *a cut on the finger. a cut in a piece of wood.* gash, graze, groove, [*formal*] incision, SEE **injury**, [*formal*] laceration, nick, notch, rent, rip, slash, slice, slit, snick, snip, split, stab, tear, wound.
2 *a cut in prices.* cut-back, decrease, fall, lowering, reduction, saving.

cut verb 1 VARIOUS WAYS TO CUT THINGS: amputate (*a limb*), axe, carve, chip, chisel, chop, cleave, clip, crop, dissect, dock, engrave (*an inscription on something*), fell (*a tree*), gash, gouge, grate (*into small pieces*), graze, guillotine, hack, hew, incise, lacerate, lop, mince, mow (*grass*), nick, notch, pare (*skin off fruit*), pierce, poll, pollard (*a tree*), prune (*a growing plant*), reap (*corn*), saw, scalp, score, sever, shave, shear, shred, slash, slice, slit, snick, snip, split, stab, trim, whittle (*wood with a knife*), wound.
TOOLS FOR CUTTING: SEE **cutter**.
2 *to cut a long story.* abbreviate, abridge, bowdlerize, censor, condense, curtail, digest, edit, précis, shorten, summarize, truncate.
3 *to cut expenditure.* SEE **reduce**.
cut and dried SEE **definite**.
to cut in, to cut someone off *to cut in when someone is talking. to cut someone off on the phone.* SEE **interrupt**.
to cut short *to cut your holiday short.* SEE **curtail**.

cute adjective SEE **attractive, clever**.

cutlass noun SEE **sword**.

cutlery noun [*informal*] eating irons.

ITEMS OF CUTLERY: breadknife, butter knife, carving knife, cheese knife, dessert-spoon, fish knife, fish fork, fork, knife, ladle, salad servers, spoon, steak knife, tablespoon, teaspoon.

cut-price adjective SEE **cheap**.

cutter noun 1 VARIOUS SHIPS: SEE **vessel**.
2 VARIOUS TOOLS FOR CUTTING: axe, billhook, chisel, chopper, clippers, guillotine, SEE **knife** noun, lawnmower, SEE **saw**, scalpel, scissors, scythe, secateurs, shears, sickle.

cutthroat adjective *cutthroat competition.* SEE **merciless**.
cutthroat razor SEE **razor**.

cutthroat noun *a murderous cutthroat.* SEE **killer**.

cutting adjective *cutting remarks.* acute, biting, caustic, SEE **hurtful**, incisive, keen, mordant, sarcastic, satirical, sharp, trenchant.

cutting noun *a newspaper cutting.* SEE **extract** noun.

cycle noun 1 *a cycle of events.* circle, repetition, revolution, rotation, round, sequence, series.
2 *A cycle is a cheap form of transport.* KINDS OF CYCLE: bicycle, [*informal*] bike, moped, [*informal*] motor bike, motor cycle, penny-farthing, scooter, tandem, tricycle.

cycle verb SEE **travel** verb.

cyclic adjective *a cyclic process.* circular, recurring, repeating, repetitive, rotating.

cyclone noun SEE **storm** noun.

cyclostyle verb SEE **reprographics**.

cylinder noun OTHER SHAPES: SEE **shape** noun.

cynical adjective *a cynical outlook.* doubting, [*informal*] hard, misanthropic, negative, pessimistic, questioning, sceptical, sneering.
OPPOSITES: SEE **optimistic**.

cynicism noun SEE **doubt** noun.

cyst noun SEE **growth**.

D

dab verb SEE **touch** verb.

dabble verb 1 *to dabble in water.* dip, paddle, splash, wet.
2 *to dabble in a hobby.* potter about, work casually.

dabbler noun *a dabbler in astrology.* amateur, dilettante, potterer.
OPPOSITES: SEE **expert** noun.

daddy-long-legs noun crane-fly.

daffodil noun narcissus.

daft adjective SEE **silly**.

dagger noun [*old-fashioned*] dirk, SEE **knife** noun, stiletto.

daily adjective *a daily occurrence.* diurnal, everyday, SEE **regular**.

dainty adjective 1 *dainty embroidery.* charming, delicate, exquisite, fine, meticulous, neat, nice, pretty, skilful.
OPPOSITES: SEE **clumsy**, **crude**.
2 *a dainty eater.* choosy, discriminating, fastidious, finicky, fussy, well-mannered.
OPPOSITES: SEE **gross**.

dais noun SEE **platform**.

dale noun SEE **valley**.

dally verb *Don't dally: we must move on.* dawdle, delay, [*informal*] dilly-dally, hang about, idle, linger, loaf, loiter, play about, procrastinate, saunter, [*old-fashioned*] tarry, waste time.

dam noun *a dam across a river.* bank, barrage, barrier, dike, embankment, wall, weir.

dam verb *to dam the flow of a river.* block, check, hold back, obstruct, restrict, stanch, stem, stop.

damage noun *Did the accident cause any damage?* destruction, devastation, harm, havoc, hurt, SEE **injury**, loss, mutilation, sabotage.

damage verb 1 *A gale damaged the tree. Frost can damage water-pipes.* break,

buckle, burst, [*informal*] bust, crack, SEE **destroy**, [*informal*] do a mischief to, fracture, harm, hurt, impair, injure, mutilate, [*informal*] play havoc with, ruin, rupture, strain, warp, weaken, wound, wreck.
2 *Someone damaged the paintwork.* blemish, chip, deface, disfigure, flaw, mar, mark, sabotage, scar, scratch, spoil, vandalize.
3 *Corrosion damaged the engine.* cripple, disable, immobilize, incapacitate, make inoperative, make useless.

damaged adjective *damaged goods.* broken, faulty, flawed, hurt, injured, misused, shop-soiled, unsound.
OPPOSITES: SEE **undamaged**.

damages noun *to pay damages to someone.* SEE **compensation**.

damaging adjective *the damaging effects of war.* calamitous, deleterious, destructive, detrimental, disadvantageous, evil, harmful, injurious, negative, pernicious, prejudicial, ruinous, unfavourable.
OPPOSITES: SEE **helpful**.

dame noun *a pantomime dame.* SEE **woman**.

damn verb SEE **condemn**, **curse** verb.

damnable adjective SEE **hateful**.

damnation noun doom, everlasting fire, hell, perdition, ruin.
OPPOSITES: SEE **salvation**.

damp adjective 1 *damp clothes. a damp room.* clammy, dank, dripping, moist, perspiring, soggy, sticky, sweaty, unaired, unventilated, wet.
2 *damp weather.* dewy, drizzly, foggy, humid, misty, muggy, raining, wet.
OPPOSITES: SEE **dry** adjective.

damp, dampen verbs 1 *to damp a cloth.* SEE **moisten**.
2 *to damp someone's enthusiasm.* SEE **discourage**.

damsel noun SEE **girl**.

dance noun 1 choreography, dancing.
RELATED ADJECTIVE: choreographic.
2 *We went to a dance.* ball, barn-dance, [*Scottish & Irish*] ceilidh, [*informal*] disco, discothèque, [*informal*] hop, [*informal*] knees-up, party, SEE **social** noun, square dance.

KINDS OF DANCING: aerobics, ballet, ballroom dancing, break-dancing, country dancing, disco dancing, flamenco dancing, folk dancing, Latin American dancing, limbo dancing, morris dancing, old-time dancing, tap-dancing.

VARIOUS DANCES: bolero, cancan, conga, fandango, fling, foxtrot, gavotte, hornpipe, jig, mazurka, minuet, polka, polonaise, quadrille, quickstep, reel, rumba, square dance, tango, waltz.

dance verb *We danced all night. I danced for joy.* caper, cavort, frisk, frolic, gambol, hop about, jig about, jive, jump about, leap, prance, rock, skip, [*joking*] trip the light fantastic, whirl.

dancer noun ballerina.

dandle verb SEE **nurse** verb.

danger noun 1 *a danger of frost.* chance, liability, possibility, risk, threat.
2 *He faced the danger bravely.* crisis, distress, hazard, insecurity, jeopardy, menace, peril, pitfall, trouble, uncertainty.
OPPOSITES: SEE **safety**.

dangerous adjective 1 *dangerous driving. a dangerous situation.* alarming, breakneck (*speed*), [*informal*] chancy, critical, explosive (*an explosive situation*), grave, [*slang*] hairy, hazardous, insecure, menacing, [*informal*] nasty, perilous, precarious, reckless (*driving*), risky, uncertain, unsafe.
OPPOSITES: SEE **safe**.
2 *dangerous lions. dangerous criminals.* desperate, SEE **ruthless**, treacherous, unmanageable, unpredictable, violent, volatile, wild.
OPPOSITES: SEE **tame** adjective.
3 *dangerous chemicals.* destructive, harmful, noxious, toxic.
OPPOSITES: SEE **harmless**.

dangle verb *A rope dangled above my head.* be suspended, droop, flap, hang, sway, swing, trail, wave about.

dank adjective *a dank atmosphere.* chilly, clammy, damp, moist, unaired.

dapper adjective SEE **smart** adjective.

dappled adjective *dappled with patches of light.* blotchy, brindled, dotted, flecked, freckled, marbled, motley, mottled, particoloured, patchy, pied, speckled, spotted, stippled, streaked, varicoloured, variegated.

dare verb 1 *Would you dare to make a parachute jump?* gamble, have the courage, risk, take a chance, venture.
2 *He dared me to jump.* challenge, defy, provoke, taunt.

daredevil noun SEE **daring** (daring person).

daring adjective *a daring explorer. a daring feat.* adventurous, audacious, bold, SEE **brave**, brazen, [*informal*] cool, dauntless, fearless, hardy, intrepid,

plucky, reckless, unafraid, valiant, venturesome.
OPPOSITES: SEE **timid**.
a daring person adventurer, [*informal*] daredevil, hero, stunt man.

dark adjective 1 *a dark room. a dark sky.* black, blackish, cheerless, clouded, coal-black, dim, dingy, dismal, drab, dull, dusky, funereal, gloomy, glowering, glum, grim, inky, moonless, murky, overcast, pitch-black, pitch-dark, [*poetic*] sable, shadowy, shady, sombre, starless, sullen, sunless, unilluminated, unlit.
OPPOSITES: SEE **bright**.
2 *dark colours.* dense, heavy, strong.
OPPOSITES: SEE **pale** adjective.
3 *a dark complexion.* black, brown, brunette [=*dark-haired*], dark-skinned, dusky, swarthy, tanned.
OPPOSITES: SEE **blond, pale** adjective.
4 *a dark secret.* SEE **hidden**.

darken verb 1 *The sky darkened.* become overcast, cloud over.
2 *Clouds darkened the sky.* blacken, dim, eclipse, obscure, overshadow, shade.
OPPOSITES: SEE **brighten**.

darling adjective SEE **dear**.

darling noun beloved, dear, dearest, love, loved one, sweetheart.

darn verb *to darn socks.* SEE **mend**, sew up, stitch up.

dart noun arrow, bolt, missile, shaft.

dart verb *to dart about.* bound, SEE **dash** verb, fling, flit, fly, hurtle, leap, move suddenly, shoot, spring, [*informal*] whiz, [*informal*] zip.

dash noun 1 *a dash to the finishing-post.* chase, race, run, rush, sprint, spurt.
2 [=*punctuation mark*] hyphen.

dash verb 1 *to dash home.* bolt, chase, dart, fly, hasten, hurry, move quickly, race, run, rush, speed, sprint, tear, [*informal*] zoom.
2 *to dash your foot against a rock.* SEE **hit** verb, knock, smash, strike.

dashboard noun facia, instrument panel.

dashing adjective *a dashing figure.* SEE **lively, smart** adjective.

dastardly adjective SEE **cowardly**.

data noun [*Data* is a plural word. We don't say *Have you a data?* but *Have you any data?* It is, however, often used with a singular verb: *The data is in a computer file* rather than *The data are ...*] details, evidence, facts, figures, information, statistics.

date noun 1 *the date of my birthday.* SEE **time**.

2 *a date with a friend.* appointment, assignation, engagement, fixture, meeting, rendezvous.

dated adjective *a dated style.* SEE **old-fashioned.**

daub verb *to daub paint.* SEE **smear.**

daughter noun FAMILY RELATIONSHIPS: SEE **family.**

daunt verb *I was daunted by the size of the task.* alarm, depress, deter, discourage, dishearten, dismay, SEE **frighten,** intimidate, overawe, put off, unnerve.
OPPOSITES: SEE **encourage.**

daunting adjective *a daunting task.* SEE **arduous.**

dauntless adjective SEE **brave.**

davit noun SEE **crane** noun.

dawdle verb *Don't dawdle: we haven't got all day.* be slow, dally, delay, [*informal*] dilly-dally, hang about, idle, lag behind, linger, loaf about, loiter, move slowly, straggle, [*informal*] take your time, trail behind.
OPPOSITES: SEE **hurry** verb.

dawn noun **1** daybreak, first light, [*informal*] peep of day, sunrise.
OPPOSITES: SEE **dusk.**
2 *the dawn of a new age.* SEE **beginning.**

day noun **1** *There are seven days in a week.* twenty-four hours.
RELATED ADJECTIVES: SEE **daily.**
VARIOUS TIMES OF THE DAY: afternoon, dawn, daybreak, dusk, evening, [*poetic*] eventide, gloaming, midday, midnight, morning, night, nightfall, noon, sunrise, sunset, twilight.
2 *Most people are awake during the day.* daylight, daytime, light.
OPPOSITE: night.
3 *Things were different in grandad's day.* age, epoch, era, period, time.

daybreak noun SEE **dawn.**

day-dream noun *a day-dream about being rich and famous.* dream, fantasy, hope, illusion, meditation, pipe-dream, reverie, vision, wool-gathering.

day-dream verb dream, fantasize, imagine, meditate.

daylight noun SEE **day, light** noun.

daze verb *The blow dazed him.* SEE **stun.**

dazzle verb SEE **light** noun [**to give light**].

deacon, deaconess nouns SEE **clergyman.**

dead adjective **1** *a dead animal. a dead body.* cold, dead and buried, deceased, departed, inanimate, inert, killed, late *(the late king)*, lifeless, perished, rigid, stiff.
OPPOSITES: SEE **alive, living.**

2 *a dead language. a dead species.* died out, extinct, obsolete.
OPPOSITES: SEE **existing.**
3 *dead with cold.* deadened, insensitive, numb, paralysed, without feeling.
OPPOSITES: SEE **sensitive.**
4 *a dead battery. a dead engine.* burnt out, defunct, flat, inoperative, not going, not working, no use, out of order, unresponsive, used up, useless, worn out.
OPPOSITES: SEE **operational.**
5 *The party was dead until Frank arrived.* boring, dull, moribund, slow, uninteresting.
OPPOSITES: SEE **lively.**
6 *the dead centre.* SEE **exact** adjective.
a dead person body, cadaver, carcass, corpse, [*informal*] goner, mortal remains, [*slang*] stiff.

deaden verb **1** *to deaden a sound. to deaden a blow.* check, cushion, damp, hush, lessen, muffle, mute, quieten, reduce, smother, soften, stifle, suppress, weaken.
OPPOSITES: SEE **amplify, sharpen.**
2 *to deaden a pain. to deaden feeling.* alleviate, anaesthetize, blunt, desensitize, dull, numb, paralyse.
OPPOSITES: SEE **aggravate, intensify.**

deadline noun *the deadline for competition entries.* latest time, time-limit.

deadlock noun *Negotiations reached deadlock.* halt, impasse, stalemate, standstill, stop.
OPPOSITES: SEE **progress** noun.

deadly adjective *a deadly illness. deadly poison.* dangerous, destructive, fatal, SEE **harmful,** lethal, mortal, noxious, terminal.
OPPOSITES: SEE **harmless.**

deadpan adjective SEE **expressionless.**

deaf adjective hard of hearing.
OTHER HANDICAPS: SEE **handicap.**

deafen verb *The noise deafened us.* make deaf, overwhelm.

deafening adjective *a deafening roar.* SEE **loud.**

deal noun **1** *a business deal.* agreement, arrangement, bargain, contract, pact, settlement, transaction, understanding.
2 *a great deal of trouble.* amount, quantity, volume.

deal verb **1** *to deal cards.* allot, apportion, assign, dispense, distribute, divide, [*informal*] dole out, give out, share out.
2 *to deal someone a blow on the head.* administer, apply, deliver, give, inflict, mete out.
3 *to deal in stocks and shares.* buy and sell, do business, trade, traffic.

to deal with 1 *I'll deal with this problem.* attend to, come to grips with, control, cope with, get over, grapple with, handle, look after, manage, overcome, see to, SEE **solve**, sort out, surmount, tackle, take action on.
2 *I want a book that deals with insects.* be concerned with, cover, explain, treat.

dealer noun *a car dealer. a dealer in antiques.* merchant, retailer, shopkeeper, stockist, supplier, trader, tradesman, wholesaler.

dean noun SEE **clergyman**.

dear adjective **1** *dear friends.* beloved, close, darling, intimate, SEE **lovable**, loved, valued.
OPPOSITES: SEE **hateful**.
2 *dear goods.* costly, exorbitant, expensive, over-priced, [*informal*] pricey.
OPPOSITES: SEE **cheap**.

dear noun *He's a dear!* SEE **darling**.

dearth noun *a sad dearth of talent.* SEE **scarcity**.

death noun **1** *We mourn the death of a friend.* [*formal*] decease, demise, dying [SEE **die** verb], end, loss, passing.
2 *The accident resulted in several deaths.* casualty, fatality.
to put to death SEE **execute**.

deathless adjective SEE **immortal**.

débâcle noun SEE **disaster**.

debar verb *debarred from driving.* SEE **ban** verb.

debase verb *They debased that lovely music by using it in an advert.* commercialize, degrade, demean, depreciate, devalue, lower the tone of, pollute, reduce the value of, ruin, soil, spoil, sully, vulgarize.

debatable adjective *a debatable question.* arguable, contentious, controversial, controvertible, disputable, doubtful, dubious, moot (*a moot point*), open to question, problematical, questionable, uncertain.
OPPOSITES: SEE **certain, straightforward**.

debate noun *a debate about animal rights.* SEE **argument**, conference, consultation, controversy, deliberation, [*formal*] dialectic, discussion, [*formal*] disputation, dispute, [*formal*] polemic.

debate verb *We debated the pros and cons of the matter.* argue, consider, deliberate, discuss, dispute, [*informal*] mull over, question, reflect on, weigh up.

debauch verb SEE **seduce**.

debauched adjective SEE **immoral**.

debilitate verb SEE **weaken**.

debility noun SEE **weakness**.

debit verb *The bank debited £10 from my account.* cancel, remove, subtract, take away.
OPPOSITES: SEE **credit** verb.

debonair adjective SEE **carefree**.

debrief verb SEE **question** verb.

debris noun *debris from a crashed aircraft.* bits, detritus, flotsam [=*floating debris*], fragments, litter, pieces, remains, rubbish, rubble, ruins, waste, wreckage.

debt noun **1** *Can you pay off your debt?* account, arrears, bill, debit, dues, score (*I have a score to settle*), what you owe.
2 *I owe you a great debt for your kindness.* duty, indebtedness, obligation.
in debt bankrupt, insolvent, SEE **poor**.

debtor noun bankrupt, defaulter.

début noun SEE **performance**.

débutante noun SEE **girl**.

decade noun PERIODS OF TIME: SEE **time** noun.

decadent adjective *a decadent society.* SEE **corrupt** adjective, declining, degenerate, immoral.
OPPOSITES: SEE **moral** adjective.

decamp verb SEE **depart**.

decant verb SEE **pour**.

decanter noun OTHER CONTAINERS: SEE **container**.

decapitate verb behead, SEE **kill**.

decay verb **1** *Dead plants and animals decay.* break down, decompose, degenerate, fester, go bad, moulder, putrefy, rot, shrivel, waste away, wither.
OPPOSITES: SEE **grow**.
2 *Most substances decay in time.* corrode, crumble, deteriorate, disintegrate, dissolve, fall apart, oxidize, perish, spoil.

deceased adjective SEE **dead**.

deceit noun *We saw through his deceit.* artifice, bluff, cheating, chicanery, [*informal*] con, craftiness, cunning, deceitfulness, deception, dishonesty, dissimulation, double-dealing, duplicity, feint, [*informal*] fiddle, fraud, guile, hoax, imposture, insincerity, lie, lying, misrepresentation, pretence, ruse, sham, stratagem, subterfuge, swindle, treachery, trick, trickery, underhandedness, untruthfulness, wile.
OPPOSITES: SEE **honesty**.

deceitful adjective *a deceitful person. a deceitful trick.* cheating, crafty, cunning, deceiving, deceptive, designing, dishonest, double-dealing, false, fraudulent, furtive, hypocritical, insincere, lying, secretive, shifty, sneaky, treacherous, [*informal*] tricky, [*informal*] two-faced,

underhand, unfaithful, untrustworthy, wily.
OPPOSITES: SEE **honest**.

deceive verb *I had no intention to deceive. His disguise deceived me.* [*informal*] bamboozle, be an impostor, beguile, betray, blind, bluff, cheat, [*informal*] con, defraud, delude, [*informal*] diddle, doublecross, dupe, fool, [*informal*] fox, [*informal*] have on, hoax, hoodwink [*informal*] kid, [*informal*] lead on, lie, mislead, mystify, [*informal*] outsmart, outwit, pretend, swindle, [*informal*] take for a ride, [*informal*] take in, trick.

decelerate verb brake, decrease speed, go slower, lose speed, slow down.
OPPOSITES: SEE **accelerate**.

decent adjective 1 *decent behaviour. decent language.* acceptable, appropriate, becoming, befitting, chaste, courteous, decorous, delicate, fitting, honourable, modest, polite, presentable, proper, pure, respectable, seemly, sensitive, suitable.
OPPOSITES: SEE **indecent**.
2 [*informal*] *a decent meal.* agreeable, SEE **good**, nice, pleasant, satisfactory.
OPPOSITES: SEE **bad**.

decentralize verb SEE **disperse**.

deception noun *I was taken in by the deception.* bluff, cheat, cheating, chicanery, [*informal*] con, confidence trick, cover-up, craftiness, cunning, deceit, deceitfulness, dishonesty, dissimulation, double-dealing, duplicity, fake, feint, [*informal*] fiddle, fraud, hoax, imposture, lie, lying, misrepresentation, pretence, ruse, sham, stratagem, subterfuge, swindle, treachery, trick, trickery, underhandedness, untruthfulness, wile.

deceptive adjective *a deceptive argument. deceptive appearances.* delusive, fallacious, false, fraudulent, illusory, insincere, misleading, specious, spurious, treacherous, unreliable.
OPPOSITES: SEE **genuine**.

decide verb *Please decide what to do.* adjudicate, choose, conclude, determine, elect, fix on, judge, make up your mind, opt for, pick, resolve, select, settle.

decided adjective SEE **definite**.

Several English words, including *decathlon, decimal, decimate,* etc., are related to Latin *decem = ten.*

---

decimal adjective metric.

decimate verb [Originally *decimate* meant *to kill one in ten.* Now it usually means *to kill a large number.*] SEE **destroy**.

decipher verb SEE **decode**.

decision noun *The judge announced his decision.* conclusion, findings, judgement, outcome, result, ruling, verdict.

decisive adjective 1 *decisive evidence.* conclusive, convincing, crucial, final, influential, positive, significant.
OPPOSITES: SEE **inconclusive**.
2 *a decisive person. decisive action.* decided, SEE **definite**, determined, firm, forceful, forthright, incisive, resolute, strong-minded, unhesitating.
OPPOSITES: SEE **hesitant**.

deck noun *the deck of a ship.* floor, level.

deck verb SEE **decorate**.

declaim verb SEE **speak**.

declamation noun SEE **speech**.

declaration noun *a formal declaration of intentions.* affirmation, announcement, assertion, avowal, confirmation, deposition, disclosure, edict, manifesto, proclamation, profession, pronouncement, protestation, revelation, statement, testimony.

declare verb *He declared that he would never steal again.* affirm, announce, assert, attest, avow, certify, claim, confirm, contend, disclose, emphasize, insist, maintain, make known, proclaim, profess, pronounce, protest, report, reveal, SEE **say**, show, state, swear, testify, witness.

decline noun *a decline in productivity. a decline in population.* decrease, degeneration, deterioration, downturn, drop, fall, falling off, loss, recession, reduction, slump, worsening.

decline verb 1 *to decline an invitation.* forgo, refuse, reject, turn down.
OPPOSITES: SEE **accept**.
2 *His health declined.* decrease, degenerate, deteriorate, die away, diminish, drop away, dwindle, ebb, fail, fall off, flag, lessen, sink, wane, weaken, wilt, worsen.
OPPOSITES: SEE **improve**.

declivity noun SEE **slope** noun.

decoction noun SEE **extract** noun.

decode verb *to decode a cryptic message.* [*informal*] crack, decipher, explain, figure out, interpret, make out, read, solve, understand, unscramble.
OPPOSITES: SEE **encode**.

decompose verb SEE **decay**.

decontaminate verb SEE **purify**.

décor noun *Do you like the new décor in our lounge?* colour scheme, decorations, design, furnishings, interior design, style.

decorate verb **1** *to decorate a room with flowers.* adorn, array, beautify, [*old-fashioned*] bedeck, deck, embellish, festoon, garnish, make beautiful, ornament, [*uncomplimentary*] prettify, [*uncomplimentary*] tart up.
2 *to decorate a room with a new colour-scheme.* colour, [*informal*] do up, paint, paper, refurbish, renovate, wallpaper.
3 *to decorate someone for bravery.* give a medal to, honour, reward.

decoration 1 *beautiful decorations.* accessory, adornment, arabesque, elaboration, embellishment, embroidery, filigree, finery, flourish, frill, ornament, ornamentation, tracery, [*plural*] trappings, trimming.
2 *a decoration for bravery.* award, badge, medal, ribbon, star.

decorative adjective *decorative details.* elaborate, fancy, non-functional, ornamental, ornate.
OPPOSITES: SEE **functional**.

decorator noun painter.

decorous adjective *decorous behaviour.* appropriate, becoming, befitting, correct, SEE **decent**, dignified, fitting, presentable, proper, refined, respectable, sedate, staid, suitable, well-behaved.
OPPOSITES: SEE **unbecoming**.

decorum noun *He behaved with great decorum.* decency, dignity, etiquette, good manners, gravity, modesty, politeness, propriety, respectability, seemliness.

decoy noun bait, enticement, lure, red herring, stool-pigeon.

decoy verb attract, bait, draw, entice, inveigle, lead, lure, seduce, tempt.

decrease noun *a decrease in wages.* contraction, cut, cut-back, decline, diminuendo [= *decrease in loudness*], downturn, drop, fall, falling off, reduction.
OPPOSITES: SEE **increase** noun.

decrease verb **1** *We decreased speed.* abate, curtail, cut, lessen, lower, reduce, slacken.
2 *Our speed decreased.* contract, decline, die away, diminish, dwindle, fall off, lessen, peter out, shrink, slim down, subside, [*informal*] tail off, taper off, wane.
OPPOSITES: SEE **increase** verb.

decree noun *an official decree.* act, command, declaration, edict, fiat, law, order, ordinance, proclamation, regulation, ruling, statute.

decree verb *The government decrees what we must pay in taxes.* command, decide, declare, determine, dictate, direct, ordain, order, prescribe, proclaim, pronounce, rule.

decrepit adjective *a decrepit old car.* battered, broken down, derelict, dilapidated, feeble, frail, infirm, SEE **old**, ramshackle, tumbledown, weak, worn out.

decry verb SEE **criticize**.

dedicate verb **1** *The church is dedicated to St Paul.* consecrate, hallow, sanctify, set apart.
2 *I dedicate my poem to my father's memory.* address, inscribe.
3 *He dedicates himself to his work.* commit, devote, give (yourself) completely, pledge.

dedicated adjective *dedicated fans.* committed, devoted, enthusiastic, faithful, keen, loyal, single-minded, zealous.

dedication noun **1** *I admire her dedication to the job.* adherence, allegiance, commitment, devotion, faithfulness, loyalty, single-mindedness.
2 *the dedication in a book.* inscription.

deduce verb *The policeman deduced that I was involved.* conclude, draw the conclusion, extrapolate, gather, infer, [*informal*] put two and two together, reason, work out.

deduct verb *to deduct tax from your pay.* [*informal*] knock off, subtract, take away.
OPPOSITES: SEE **add**.

deduction noun **1** [In this sense, *deduction* is related to the verb *deduct*.] *a deduction off your bill.* allowance, decrease, discount, reduction, subtraction.
2 [In this sense, *deduction* is related to the verb *deduce*.] *My deduction was correct.* conclusion, inference, reasoning.

deed noun **1** *a heroic deed.* achievement, act, action, adventure, effort, endeavour, enterprise, exploit, feat, performance, stunt, undertaking.
2 *the deeds of a house.* contract, documents, [*formal*] indenture, papers, records, [*formal*] title.

deem verb SEE **judge** verb.

deep adjective **1** *a deep pit.* bottomless, fathomless, unfathomable, unplumbed.
2 *deep feelings.* earnest, extreme, genuine, heartfelt, intense, serious, sincere.
OPPOSITES: SEE **shallow**.
3 *deep in thought.* absorbed, concentrating, engrossed, immersed, lost, preoccupied, rapt, thoughtful.

4 *a deep subject.* abstruse, arcane, SEE
difficult, esoteric, intellectual, learned,
obscure, profound, recondite.
OPPOSITES: SEE **easy**.
5 *deep sleep.* heavy, sound.
OPPOSITES: SEE **light** adjective.
6 *a deep colour.* dark, rich, strong, vivid.
OPPOSITES: SEE **pale** adjective.
7 *a deep voice.* bass, booming, growling,
low, low-pitched, resonant, reverberating, sonorous.
OPPOSITES: SEE **high**.

deepen verb SEE **intensify**.

deer noun DEER AND SIMILAR ANIMALS:
antelope, [*male*] buck, caribou, chamois,
[*female*] doe, elk, fallow deer, gazelle,
gnu, [*male*] hart, [*female*] hind, impala,
moose, reindeer, roe, [*male*] roebuck,
[*male*] stag, wildebeest.
OTHER ANIMALS: SEE **animal** noun.

deface verb *Vandals defaced the statue.*
damage, disfigure, injure, mar, mutilate, spoil, vandalize.

defamation noun SEE **slander** noun.

defamatory adjective SEE **slanderous**.

defame verb SEE **slander** verb.

default verb SEE **wrong (to do wrong)**.

defeat noun *a humiliating defeat.* beating, conquest, downfall, [*informal*]
drubbing, failure, humiliation, [*informal*] licking, overthrow, [*informal*]
put-down, rebuff, repulse, reverse, rout,
setback, subjugation, thrashing,
trouncing.
OPPOSITES: SEE **victory**.

defeat verb *to defeat an opponent.* beat,
best, checkmate, [*informal*] clobber,
confound, conquer, crush, [*informal*]
flatten, foil, frustrate, get the better of,
[*informal*] lay low, [*informal*] lick, master, outdo, outvote, outwit, overcome,
overpower, overthrow, overwhelm, put
down, quell, repulse, rout, ruin, [*informal*] smash, subdue, subjugate, suppress, [*informal*] thrash, thwart, triumph over, trounce, vanquish, win a
victory over.
to be defeated SEE **lose**.

defeated adjective *the defeated team.* beaten, bottom, last, losing, unsuccessful,
vanquished.
OPPOSITES: SEE **winning**.

defecate verb SEE **excrete**.

defect noun *a defect in a piece of work.*
blemish, bug (*in a computer program*),
deficiency, error, failing, fault, flaw,
imperfection, inadequacy, lack, mark,
mistake, shortcoming, spot, stain, want,
weakness.

defect verb *The traitor defected to the
enemy.* desert, go over.

defective adjective SEE **faulty**.

defence noun **1** *What was the accused
woman's defence?* alibi, apology, case,
excuse, explanation, justification, plea,
testimony, vindication.
2 *a defence against attack.* SEE **barricade**,
cover, deterrence, fortification, guard,
protection, rampart, safeguard, security, shelter, shield.

defenceless adjective SEE **helpless**.

defend verb **1** *to defend yourself against
attackers.* cover, fortify, guard, keep
safe, preserve, protect, safeguard,
screen, secure, shelter, shield, [*informal*] stick up for.
OPPOSITES: SEE **attack** verb.
2 *He defended himself in court.* champion,
justify, plead for, speak up for, stand up
for, support, uphold, vindicate.
OPPOSITES: SEE **accuse**.

defendant noun accused, appellant,
offender, prisoner.

defensible adjective *a defensible argument.* SEE **justifiable**.

defensive adjective **1** *a defensive style of
play.* cautious, defending, protective,
wary, watchful.
OPPOSITES: SEE **aggressive**.
2 *defensive remarks.* apologetic, faint-
hearted, self-justifying.
OPPOSITES: SEE **assertive**.

defer verb **1** *We deferred the remaining
business until next week.* adjourn, delay,
hold over, postpone, prorogue (*parliament*), put off, [*informal*] shelve, suspend.
2 *I deferred to her superior experience.* SEE
yield.

deference noun SEE **respect** noun.

deferential adjective SEE **respectful**.

defiant adjective *a defiant attitude.* aggressive, challenging, disobedient, insolent, insubordinate, mutinous, obstinate, rebellious, recalcitrant,
refractory, stubborn, truculent, uncooperative, unyielding.
OPPOSITES: SEE **co-operative**.

deficient adjective *Their diet is deficient
in vitamins.* defective, imperfect, inadequate, incomplete, insufficient, lacking,
meagre, scanty, scarce, short, unsatisfactory, wanting, weak.
OPPOSITES: SEE **adequate, excessive**.

deficit noun *The company had a deficit in
their accounts.* loss, shortfall.
OPPOSITES: SEE **excess**.

defile noun *a mountain defile.* SEE **pass**
noun.

defile verb *I felt defiled by the filth.* contaminate, corrupt, degrade, desecrate, dirty, dishonour, infect, make dirty [SEE **dirty** adjective], poison, pollute, soil, stain, sully, taint, tarnish.

define verb 1 *A thesaurus simply lists words, whereas a dictionary defines them.* clarify, explain, formulate, give the meaning of, interpret.
2 *The fence defines the extent of our land.* bound, be the boundary of, circumscribe, demarcate, determine, limit, mark out, outline.

definite adjective 1 *definite opinions. a definite manner.* assured, categorical, certain, clear-cut, confident, cut-and-dried, decided, determined, emphatic, exact, explicit, fixed, incisive, particular, precise, settled, specific, sure, unambiguous, unequivocal.
OPPOSITES: SEE **indefinite**.
2 *definite signs of improvement.* apparent, clear, discernible, distinct, marked, noticeable, obvious, perceptible, plain, positive, pronounced, unmistakable.
OPPOSITES: SEE **imperceptible**.

definitely adverb *I'll definitely come tomorrow.* beyond doubt, certainly, doubtless, for certain, indubitably, positively, surely, unquestionably, without doubt, without fail.

definition noun 1 *a dictionary definition.* elucidation, explanation, interpretation.
2 *the definition of a photograph.* clarity, clearness, focus, precision, sharpness.

definitive adjective [Do not confuse with *definite.*] *the definitive account of someone's life.* agreed, authoritative, conclusive, correct, final, last (*He's written the last word on the subject*), official, permanent, reliable, settled, standard.
OPPOSITES: SEE **provisional**.

deflate verb 1 *to deflate a tyre.* let down.
OPPOSITE: inflate.
2 *to deflate your pride.* SEE **humble** verb.

deflect verb *to deflect a blow.* avert, divert, fend off, head off, intercept, parry, prevent, turn aside, ward off.

defoliate verb SEE **strip** verb.

deform verb SEE **distort**.

deformed adjective *a deformed tree.* bent, buckled, contorted, SEE **crippled**, crooked, defaced, disfigured, distorted, gnarled, grotesque, malformed, mangled, misshapen, mutilated, twisted, ugly, warped.

deformity noun malformation.

defraud verb SEE **cheat** verb, [*informal*] diddle, embezzle, [*informal*] fleece, rob, swindle.

defray verb *I've enough money to defray expenses.* cover, foot (*foot the bill*), meet, pay, refund, repay, settle.

defrost verb de-ice, warm, unfreeze.

deft adjective *deft movements.* adept, adroit, agile, clever, dextrous, expert, handy, neat [*informal*] nifty, nimble, proficient, quick, skilful.
OPPOSITES: SEE **clumsy**.

defunct adjective SEE **dead**.

defuse verb SEE **safe** (to make safe).

defy verb 1 *to defy someone in authority.* confront, disobey, face up to, flout, refuse to obey, resist, stand up to, withstand.
OPPOSITES: SEE **obey**.
2 *I defy you to produce evidence.* challenge, dare.
3 *The jammed door defied my attempts to open it.* baffle, beat, defeat, elude, foil, frustrate, repel, resist, thwart, withstand.

degenerate adjective *degenerate behaviour.* SEE **immoral**.

degenerate verb *His behaviour degenerated.* become worse, decline, deteriorate, regress, retrogress, sink, slip, weaken, worsen.
OPPOSITES: SEE **improve**.

degrade verb *Bad living conditions degrade people.* brutalize, cheapen, corrupt, debase, dehumanize, demean, deprave, desensitize, harden, humiliate, lower, make uncivilized.

degrading adjective *a degrading experience.* brutalize, cheapening, corrupting, dehumanizing, demeaning, depraving, dishonourable, humiliating, ignoble, lowering, shameful, undignified, unworthy.
OPPOSITES: SEE **uplifting**.

degree noun 1 *a high degree of skill.* calibre, extent, grade, intensity, level, measure, order, standard.
2 *of high degree. of low degree.* class, position, rank, standing, station, status.
3 *a polytechnic degree.* SEE **qualification**.

dehumanize verb SEE **degrade**.

dehydrate verb *Take care not to dehydrate in the heat.* desiccate, dry out, dry up.

de-ice verb *to de-ice the windscreen.* clear, defrost, unfreeze.

deify verb idolize, treat as a god, venerate, worship.

deign verb *He doesn't deign to talk to unimportant people like me.* condescend, demean yourself, lower yourself, stoop.

deity noun *pagan deities.* divinity, god, goddess, godhead, idol, immortal, power, spirit.

dejected adjective *a dejected mood.* SEE **depressed**.

delay noun *a delay in proceedings.* check, filibuster, hitch, hold-up, moratorium, pause, postponement, set-back, wait.

delay verb 1 *The fog delayed the traffic.* bog down, cause a delay, check, detain, halt, hinder, hold up, impede, keep back, keep waiting, make late, obstruct, retard, set back, slow down, stop.
2 *to delay a meeting.* defer, hold over, postpone, put back, put off, suspend.
3 *You'll lose your chance if you delay.* be late, [*informal*] bide your time, dawdle, [*informal*] dilly-dally, hang back, hesitate, lag, linger, loiter, pause, [*informal*] play for time, procrastinate, stall, [*old-fashioned*] tarry, temporize, wait.

delectable adjective SEE **delicious**.

delegate noun *a delegate at a conference.* agent, ambassador, envoy, legate, messenger, representative, spokesperson.

delegate verb *They delegated me to speak on their behalf.* appoint, assign, authorize, charge, commission, depute, empower, entrust, mandate, nominate.

delegation noun *a delegation to pass on our complaints.* commission, deputation, mission, representative group.

delete verb *to delete someone from a list.* blot out, cancel, cross out, edit out, efface, erase, expunge, obliterate, remove, rub out, strike out, wipe out.

deleterious adjective SEE **damaging**.

deliberate adjective 1 *deliberate insults.* calculated, conscious, contrived, culpable, intended, intentional, knowing, organized, planned, pre-arranged, premeditated, prepared, studied, wilful.
OPPOSITES: SEE **unplanned**.
2 *deliberate movements.* careful, cautious, circumspect, considered, methodical, painstaking, slow, thoughtful, unhurried.
OPPOSITES: SEE **hasty**.

deliberate verb SEE **discuss**, **think**.

deliberation noun SEE **discussion**, **thought**.

delicacy noun 1 *We admired the delicacy of the craftsmanship.* accuracy, care, cleverness, daintiness, exquisiteness, fineness, fragility, intricacy, precision.
2 *She described the unpleasant details with great delicacy.* discrimination, finesse, sensitivity, subtlety, tact.
3 *The table was loaded with delicacies.* rarity, speciality, treat.

delicate adjective 1 *delicate material. delicate plants.* dainty, diaphanous, easily damaged, fine, flimsy, fragile, frail, gauzy, slender, tender.
OPPOSITES: SEE **strong**.
2 *a delicate touch.* gentle, feathery, light, soft.
OPPOSITES: SEE **clumsy**.
3 *delicate workmanship.* accurate, careful, clever, deft, exquisite, intricate, precise, skilled.
OPPOSITES: SEE **crude**.
4 *a delicate flavour. delicate colours.* faint, gentle, mild, muted, pale, slight, subtle.
OPPOSITES: SEE **harsh**.
5 *delicate machinery.* complex, easily broken, fragile, intricate, sensitive.
OPPOSITES: SEE **robust**.
6 *a delicate constitution.* feeble, puny, sickly, unhealthy, weak.
OPPOSITES: SEE **healthy**.
7 *a delicate problem.* awkward, confidential, embarrassing, private, problematical, prudish, ticklish, touchy.
OPPOSITES: SEE **straightforward**.
8 *a delicate treatment of a problem.* considerate, diplomatic, discreet, judicious, prudent, sensitive, tactful.
OPPOSITES: SEE **tactless**.

delicious adjective *delicious food.* appetizing, choice, delectable, enjoyable, luscious, [*informal*] mouth-watering, palatable, savoury, [*informal*] scrumptious, succulent, tasty.
OPPOSITES: SEE **unpleasant**.

delight noun *A hot bath is a great delight.* bliss, ecstasy, enchantment, enjoyment, [*formal*] felicity, gratification, happiness, joy, paradise, pleasure, rapture.

delight verb *The music delighted us.* amuse, bewitch, captivate, charm, cheer, divert, enchant, enrapture, entertain, enthral, entrance, fascinate, gladden, please, ravish, thrill, transport.
OPPOSITES: SEE **dismay** verb.

delighted verb SEE **pleased**.

delightful adjective SEE **pleasant**.

delineate verb SEE **describe**.

delineation noun SEE **description**.

delinquency noun SEE **crime**.

delinquent noun *a juvenile delinquent.* criminal, culprit, defaulter, hooligan, law-breaker, miscreant, offender, [*informal*] tear-away, vandal, wrongdoer, young offender.

deliquesce verb SEE **dissolve**, **melt**.

delirious adjective *delirious with joy.* [*informal*] beside yourself, crazy, demented, deranged, SEE **drunk**, ecstatic,

excited, feverish, frantic, frenzied, hysterical, irrational, light-headed, SEE mad, wild.
OPPOSITES: SEE sane, sober.

delirium noun ecstasy, SEE excitement, fever, hysteria, SEE madness.

deliver verb 1 *to deliver letters or goods to an address.* bear, bring, convey, distribute, give out, hand over, make over, present, supply, take round, transfer, transport, turn over.
2 *to deliver a lecture.* give, make, read, SEE speak.
3 *to deliver a blow.* aim, deal, SEE hit verb, launch, strike, throw (*a punch*).
4 *to deliver someone from slavery.* SEE rescue verb.

deliverance noun SEE rescue noun.

delivery noun 1 *a delivery of vegetables.* batch, consignment, distribution, shipment.
2 *the delivery of a message.* conveyance, dispatch, transmission.

dell noun SEE valley.

delude verb SEE deceive.

deluge noun *We got soaked in the deluge.* downpour, flood, inundation, rainfall, rainstorm, rush, spate.

deluge verb *They deluged me with questions.* drown, engulf, flood, inundate, overwhelm, submerge, swamp.

delusion noun *a misleading delusion.* deception, dream, fantasy, hallucination, illusion, mirage, misconception, mistake.

delusive adjective SEE deceptive.

delve verb *to delve into the past.* burrow, dig, explore, investigate, probe, research, search.

demagogue noun SEE agitator, leader.

demand noun *The manager agreed to the workers' demands.* claim, command, desire, expectation, importunity, insistence, need, order, request, requirement, requisition, want.

demand verb 1 *I demanded a refund.* call for, claim, command, exact, expect, insist on, order, request, require, requisition, want.
2 *"What do you want?" she demanded.* SEE ask.

demanding adjective 1 *a demanding child.* SEE importunate.
2 *a demanding task.* SEE difficult.

demarcation noun SEE boundary.

demean verb *She demeans herself by doing his dirty work.* abase, cheapen, debase, degrade, disgrace, humble, humiliate, lower, make (yourself)

cheap, [*informal*] put (yourself) down, sacrifice (your) pride, undervalue.

demeanour noun SEE attitude, behaviour.

demented noun SEE crazy.

demerit noun SEE fault noun.

demesne noun SEE territory.

demise noun SEE death, end noun.

demo noun SEE demonstration.

demobilize verb *After the war the soldiers were demobilized.* disband, dismiss, release, return to civilian life.

democracy noun POLITICAL TERMS: SEE politics.

democratic adjective *democratic government.* chosen, elected, elective, popular, representative.
OPPOSITES: SEE undemocratic.

demolish verb *to demolish old buildings.* break down, bulldoze, SEE destroy, dismantle, flatten, knock down, level, pull down, raze, tear down, undo, wreck.
OPPOSITES: SEE build.

demon noun devil, fiend, goblin, imp, spirit.

demonstrable adjective *a demonstrable fact.* certain, clear, evident, incontrovertible, irrefutable, palpable, positive, provable, undeniable, verifiable.

demonstrate verb 1 *to demonstrate how to do something.* describe, display, embody, establish, exemplify, exhibit, explain, expound, illustrate, indicate, manifest, prove, represent, show, substantiate, teach, typify.
2 *to demonstrate in the streets.* lobby, march, parade, picket, protest.

demonstration noun 1 *a demonstration of how to do something.* confirmation, description, display, evidence, exhibition, experiment, expression, illustration, indication, manifestation, presentation, proof, representation, show, test, trial.
2 *a political demonstration.* [*informal*] demo, march, parade, picket, protest, rally, sit-in, vigil.

demonstrative adjective *a demonstrative person.* affectionate, effusive, emotional, fulsome, loving, open, uninhibited, unreserved, unrestrained.
OPPOSITES: SEE reserved.

demoralize verb SEE discourage.

demote verb *The boss demoted her to a less responsible position.* downgrade, put down, reduce, relegate.
OPPOSITES: SEE promote.

demur verb SEE object verb.

demure adjective *a demure expression.* bashful, coy, diffident, modest, prim, quiet, reserved, reticent, retiring, sedate, shy, sober, staid.
OPPOSITES: SEE **bumptious**.

den noun *a den in the garden.* hide-away, hide-out, hiding-place, hole, lair, private place, retreat, sanctuary, secret place, shelter.

denial noun *The jury didn't believe his denial of guilt.* abnegation, disclaimer, negation, rejection, renunciation, repudiation.
OPPOSITES: SEE **admission**.

denigrate verb *It was unkind to denigrate her achievement.* be contemptuous of, belittle, blacken the reputation of, criticize, decry, disparage, impugn, malign, [*informal*] run down, sneer at, speak slightingly of, traduce, vilify.
OPPOSITES: SEE **praise** verb.

denizen noun SEE **inhabitant**.

denomination noun 1 *a Christian denomination.* church, communion, creed, cult, persuasion, sect.

VARIOUS CHRISTIAN DENOMINATIONS: Anglican, Baptist, Congregational, Episcopalian, Lutheran, Methodist, Moravian, Orthodox, Presbyterian, Protestant, Revivalist, Roman Catholic, United Reformed.
COMPARE: ecumenical.

---

2 *I need coins of the right denomination for the slot machine.* category, class, designation, size, type, value.

denote verb *What does this word denote?* be the sign for, express, indicate, SEE **mean** verb, signify, stand for.
COMPARE: connote.

denouement noun [Literally, *denouement* means *untying a knot.*] *the denouement of the plot of a play.* climax, SEE **end** noun, [*informal*] pay-off, resolution, solution, [*informal*] sorting out, [*informal*] tidying up, unravelling.

denounce verb *to denounce a traitor. to denounce wickedness.* accuse, attack verbally, blame, brand, censure, complain about, condemn, declaim against, decry, fulminate against, [*informal*] hold forth against, inform against, inveigh against, report, reveal, stigmatize, [*informal*] tell of.
OPPOSITES: SEE **praise** verb.

dense adjective 1 *dense fog. a dense liquid.* concentrated, heavy, opaque, thick, viscous.
OPPOSITES: SEE **thin** adjective.

2 *a dense crowd. dense undergrowth.* compact, close, impenetrable, [*informal*] jam-packed, lush, massed, packed, solid.
OPPOSITES: SEE **sparse**.

3 *a dense pupil.* crass, dim, dull, foolish, obtuse, slow, stupid, [*informal*] thick, unintelligent.
OPPOSITES: SEE **clever**.

dent noun *a dent in a flat surface.* concavity, depression, dimple, dint, dip, hollow, indentation, pit.

dent verb *I dented the car.* bend, buckle, crumple, knock in, push in.

Several English words, including *dental, dentist, denture, indented,* etc., are related to Latin *dens, dentis = tooth.*

---

dental adjective to do with teeth.

dentist noun OTHERS WHO LOOK AFTER OUR HEALTH: SEE **medicine**.

denture noun false teeth, plate, SEE **tooth**.

denude verb *to denude a hillside of vegetation.* bare, defoliate, deforest, expose, make naked, remove, strip, unclothe, uncover.
OPPOSITES: SEE **clothe**.

denunciation noun *We were amazed to hear the witness's denunciation of the accused.* accusation, censure, condemnation, denouncing, incrimination, invective, stigmatization, verbal attack.
OPPOSITES: SEE **praise** noun.

deny verb 1 *to deny an accusation.* contradict, disagree with, disclaim, disown, dispute, oppose, rebuff, refute, reject, repudiate.
OPPOSITES: SEE **acknowledge**.

2 *Her indulgent parents don't deny her anything.* begrudge, deprive of, refuse.
OPPOSITES: SEE **give**.

to deny yourself SEE **abstain**, **fast** verb.

deodorant noun anti-perspirant.
OTHER TOILETRIES: SEE **cosmetics**.

deodorize verb air, freshen up, purify, refresh, sweeten, ventilate.

depart verb 1 *to depart on a journey.* begin a journey, [*informal*] clear off, decamp, disappear, embark, emigrate, escape, exit, go away, leave, make off, [*informal*] make tracks, migrate, [*informal*] push off, quit, retire, retreat, [*slang*] scram, set off, set out, start, take your leave, vanish, withdraw.
OPPOSITES: SEE **arrive**.

2 *to depart from your script.* deviate, digress, diverge, stray from.
OPPOSITE: stick to.

departed adjective SEE **dead**.

department noun **1** *a government depart-ment. a department in a large shop.* branch, division, office, part, section, sector, subdivision, unit.
2 [*informal*] *Ask someone else—it's not my department.* area, domain, field, function, job, line, province, responsibility, specialism, sphere.

departure noun disappearance, embarkation, escape, exit, exodus, going, retirement, retreat, withdrawal.
OPPOSITES: SEE **arrival**.

depend verb **to depend on 1** *My success will depend on good luck.* be dependent on [SEE **dependent**], hinge on, rest on.
2 *I depend on you to be good.* bank on, count on, need, rely on, trust.

dependable adjective *a dependable worker.* conscientious, consistent, faithful, honest, regular, reliable, safe, sound, steady, true, trustworthy, unfailing.
OPPOSITES: SEE **unreliable**.

dependence noun **1** *dependence on others.* confidence (in), need (for), reliance (upon), trust (in).
2 *dependence on drugs.* SEE **addiction**.

dependent adjective [Do not confuse with noun *dependant = a person who depends on your support*.] **dependent on 1** *Everything is dependent on the weather.* conditional on, connected with, controlled by, determined by, liable to, relative to, subject to, vulnerable to.
OPPOSITES: SEE **independent (of)**.
2 *dependent on drugs.* addicted to, enslaved by, [*informal*] hooked on, reliant on.

depict verb *to depict a scene.* delineate, describe, draw, illustrate, narrate, outline, paint, picture, portray, represent, reproduce, show, sketch.

deplete verb *The holiday has depleted our savings.* consume, cut, decrease, drain, lessen, reduce, use up.
OPPOSITES: SEE **increase** verb.

deplorable adjective *deplorable be-haviour.* SEE **bad**, blameworthy, discreditable, disgraceful, disreputable, lamentable, regrettable, reprehensible, scandalous, shameful, shocking, unfortunate, unworthy.
OPPOSITES: SEE **praiseworthy**.

deplore verb **1** *We deplore suffering.* grieve for, lament, mourn, regret.
2 *We deplore vandalism.* SEE **condemn**, deprecate, disapprove of.

deploy verb *The boss deployed the workers effectively.* arrange, bring into action, distribute, manage, position, use systematically, utilize.

deport verb *They used to deport people for minor crimes.* banish, exile, expatriate, expel, remove, send abroad.

deportment noun SEE **bearing**.

depose verb *to depose a monarch.* demote, dethrone, dismiss, displace, get rid of, oust, remove, [*informal*] topple.
OPPOSITES: SEE **enthrone**.

deposit noun **1** *a deposit on a car.* down-payment, initial payment, part-payment, payment, retainer, security, stake.
2 *a deposit in the bottom of a container.* accumulation, dregs, layer, lees, precipitate, sediment, silt, sludge.

deposit verb **1** *Deposit the dirty plates by the hatch.* [*informal*] dump, lay down, leave, [*informal*] park, place, put down, set down.
2 *I deposited my money in the bank.* bank, pay in, save.
3 *The flood deposited a layer of mud.* precipitate.

depository noun SEE **depot**.

depot noun **1** *a stores depot.* arsenal [= *arms depot*], base, cache, depository, dump, hoard, store, storehouse.
2 *a bus depot.* garage, headquarters, station, terminus.

deprave verb *Do sadistic films deprave the viewers?* brutalize, corrupt, debase, degrade, influence, pervert.

depraved adjective *a depraved person. depraved behaviour.* SEE **bad**, corrupt, degenerate, dissolute, evil, immoral, lewd, perverted, profligate, reprobate, sinful, vicious, vile, wicked.
OPPOSITES: SEE **moral** adjective.

deprecate verb SEE **deplore**.

deprecatory adjective SEE **critical**.

depreciate verb [Do not confuse with deprecate.] *The value of antiques is not likely to depreciate.* become less, decrease, deflate, drop, fall, go down, lessen, lower, reduce, slump, weaken.
OPPOSITES: SEE **appreciate**.

depredation noun SEE **pillage** noun.

depress verb **1** *The weather depressed us.* discourage, dishearten, dispirit, enervate, grieve, lower the spirits of, make sad [SEE **sad**], sadden, tire, upset, weary.
OPPOSITES: SEE **cheer** verb.
2 *Bad news depresses the stock market.* bring down, deflate, make less active, push down, undermine, weaken.
OPPOSITES: SEE **boost** verb.

depressed adjective broken-hearted, crestfallen, dejected, desolate, despairing, despondent, disappointed, disconsolate, discouraged, disheartened, dismal, dismayed, dispirited, doleful, [*informal*] down, downcast, downhearted, friendless, gloomy, glum, hopeless, [*informal*] in the doldrums, [*informal*] in the dumps, languishing, [*informal*] low, melancholy, miserable, morose, pessimistic, sad, suicidal, unhappy, weary, woebegone, wretched. OPPOSITES: SEE **cheerful**.
depressed person depressive.

depressing adjective SEE **sad**.

depression noun 1 *a mood of depression.* [*informal*] blues, dejection, desolation, despair, despondency, doldrums (*in the doldrums*), gloom, glumness, heaviness, hopelessness, low spirits, melancholy, misery, pessimism, sadness, unhappiness, weariness. OPPOSITES: SEE **cheerfulness**.
2 *an economic depression.* decline, hard times, recession, slump. OPPOSITES: SEE **boom** noun.
3 *a meteorological depression.* area of low pressure, cyclone, low. OPPOSITE: anticyclone.
4 *a depression in the ground.* cavity, concavity, dent, dimple, dip, excavation, hole, hollow, indentation, pit, rut, sunken area. OPPOSITES: SEE **bump** noun.

deprive verb **to deprive of** deny, dispossess of, prevent from using, refuse, rob of, starve of, strip of, take away.

deprived adjective *deprived families.* disadvantaged, needy, SEE **poor**.

deputation noun SEE **delegation**.

depute verb SEE **appoint**.

deputize verb **to deputize for** *I deputized for the manager when she was ill.* act as deputy for [SEE **deputy**], cover for, do the job of, replace, represent, stand in for, substitute for, take over from, understudy [= *deputize for an actor*].

deputy noun *The mayor was ill, so his deputy conducted the ceremony.* agent, assistant, delegate, [*informal*] fill-in, locum, proxy, relief, representative, reserve, replacement, second-in-command, [*informal*] stand-in, substitute, supply, surrogate, understudy, [*informal*] vice [and words with prefix *vice-*, e.g. *vice-captain*, etc.].

derailment noun SEE **accident**.

deranged adjective SEE **mad**.

derelict adjective *derelict buildings.* abandoned, broken down, decrepit, deserted, desolate, dilapidated, forlorn, forsaken, neglected, ruined, tumbledown.

dereliction noun SEE **neglect** noun.

deride verb SEE **mock** verb.

de rigueur SEE **customary**.

derision noun SEE **scorn** noun.

derisive adjective *derisive laughter.* SEE **scornful**.

derisory adjective *I rejected her derisory offer without hesitation.* SEE **laughable**.

derivation noun SEE **origin**.

derivative adjective *Their music seemed very derivative.* SEE **imitative**.

derive verb 1 *I derive pleasure from my garden.* acquire, gain, get, obtain, receive.
2 *He derived his ideas from a text book.* borrow, collect, crib, draw, glean, [*informal*] lift, pick up, procure, take.
to be derived *This word is derived from Latin.* arise, come, descend, develop, originate, proceed, spring, stem.

derogatory adjective SEE **uncomplimentary**.

derrick noun SEE **crane** noun.

descant verb SEE **sing**.

descend verb 1 *to descend a hill. to descend by parachute.* come down, climb down, drop down, fall down [SEE **fall** verb], go down, move down, sink down.
2 *The hill descends gradually.* dip, drop, fall, incline, slant, slope. OPPOSITES: SEE **ascend**.
to be descended *She's descended from a French family.* come, originate, proceed, spring, stem.
to descend from *to descend from a bus.* alight from, disembark from, dismount from, get off.
to descend on *Bandits descended on the camp. Our friends descended on us at Christmas.* SEE **attack** verb, **visit** verb.

descendant noun *a descendant of a Victorian scientist.* heir, successor.
descendants children, family, issue, line, lineage, offspring, posterity, progeny, [*formal*] scion. OPPOSITES: SEE **ancestor**.

descent noun 1 *a steep descent.* declivity, dip, drop, fall, incline, slant, slope, way down. OPPOSITES: SEE **ascent**.
2 *aristocratic descent.* ancestry, background, blood, derivation, extraction, family, pedigree, genealogy, heredity, lineage, origin, parentage, stock, strain.

describe verb 1 *An eyewitness described what happened.* delineate, depict, detail, explain, express, narrate, outline,

recount, relate, report, sketch, tell about.
2 *The novelist describes her as a tyrant.* characterize, portray, present, represent, speak of.
3 *to describe a circle.* draw, mark out, trace.

description noun 1 *a vivid description.* account, characterization, commentary, delineation, depiction, explanation, narration, outline, portrait, portrayal, report, representation, sketch, story, word-picture.
2 *I haven't seen anything of that description.* SEE **kind** noun.

descriptive adjective *descriptive writing.* colourful, detailed, explanatory, expressive, graphic, illustrative, pictorial, vivid.

desecrate verb *to desecrate a holy place.* abuse, contaminate, debase, defile, pollute, profane, treat blasphemously or disrespectfully or irreverently, vandalize, violate.
OPPOSITES: SEE **bless, revere.**

desert adjective 1 *desert conditions.* arid, barren, dry, infertile, sterile, uncultivated, waterless, wild.
OPPOSITES: SEE **fertile.**
2 *a desert island.* desolate, isolated, lonely, solitary, unfrequented, uninhabited.
OPPOSITES: SEE **inhabited.**

desert noun wasteland, wilderness.

desert verb 1 *to desert your friends.* abandon, betray, forsake, give up, jilt, [*informal*] leave in the lurch, maroon (*maroon someone on an island*), [*informal*] rat on, renounce, strand, [*informal*] walk out on, [*informal*] wash your hands of.
2 *to desert a sinking ship.* abandon, leave, quit, vacate.
3 *The soldiers deserted.* abscond, decamp, defect, go absent, run away.

deserter noun *a deserter from the army. a deserter from a cause.* absentee, apostate, backslider, betrayer, defector, disloyal person [SEE **disloyal**], fugitive, outlaw, renegade, runaway, traitor, truant (*from school*), turncoat.

deserve verb *to deserve a reward.* be good enough for, be worthy of, earn, justify, merit, rate, warrant.

deserving adjective *a deserving winner. a deserving cause.* admirable, commendable, creditable, good, laudable, meritorious, praiseworthy, worth supporting, worthy.
OPPOSITES: SEE **unworthy.**

desiccate verb SEE **dry** verb.

design noun 1 *a design for a new car.* blueprint, drawing, model, pattern, plan, prototype, sketch.
2 *an old design.* model, style, type, version.
3 *a jazzy design of dots and lines.* arrangement, composition, configuration, pattern.
4 *I wandered about without any design.* aim, end, goal, intention, object, objective, purpose, scheme.
to have designs SEE **plot** verb.

design verb *Architects design buildings. We designed this book to help you find words.* conceive, construct, contrive, create, devise, draft, draw, draw up, fashion, intend, invent, make, plan, plot, project, propose, scheme, sketch.

designer noun author, contriver, creator, deviser, inventor, originator.

DESIGNERS OF VARIOUS PRODUCTS: architect, artist, couturier, fashion designer, graphic designer, hair stylist, interior designer, stage designer.

---

designate verb SEE **appoint.**

designation noun SEE **title** noun.

designing adjective SEE **crafty.**

desirable adjective SEE **attractive, sexy.**

desire noun 1 *a desire to do good.* ache, ambition, craving, fancy, hankering, [*informal*] itch, longing, urge, want, wish, yearning, [*informal*] yen.
2 *desire for food or drink.* appetite, gluttony, hunger, thirst.
3 *desire for money.* avarice, covetousness, cupidity, greed, miserliness, rapacity.
4 *sexual desire.* ardour, lasciviousness, libido, love, lust, passion.
5 [*formal*] *It is the king's desire that you attend.* entreaty, petition, request, wish.

desire verb *What do you most desire?* ache for, covet, crave, fancy, hanker after, [*informal*] have a yen for, hunger for, [*informal*] itch for, like, long for, lust after, need, pine for, prefer, [*informal*] set your heart on, thirst for, want, wish for, yearn for.
2 [*formal or old-fashioned*] *He desired me to step inside.* SEE **ask**, beg, entreat, importune, petition, request.

desist verb SEE **cease.**

desk noun bureau, lectern, writing-table.
OTHER FURNITURE: SEE **furniture.**

desolate adjective 1 *a desolate place.* abandoned, bare, barren, benighted,

bleak, cheerless, depressing, deserted, dismal, dreary, empty, forsaken, gloomy, [*informal*] god-forsaken, inhospitable, isolated, lonely, remote, unfrequented, uninhabited, wild, windswept.
OPPOSITES: SEE **idyllic**.
2 *He was desolate when his dog died.* bereft, companionless, dejected, SEE **depressed**, disconsolate, distressed, forlorn, forsaken, inconsolable, lonely, melancholy, neglected, sad, solitary, wretched.
OPPOSITES: SEE **cheerful**.

despair noun *a state of despair.* anguish, dejection, depression, desperation, despondency, gloom, hopelessness, melancholy, SEE **misery**, pessimism, wretchedness.
OPPOSITES: SEE **hope** noun.

despair verb give up, [*informal*] lose heart, lose hope.
OPPOSITES: SEE **hope** verb.

desperado noun bandit, brigand, SEE **criminal** noun, cutthroat, gangster, gunman, outlaw, ruffian, thug.

desperate adjective **1** *The starving refugees were desperate.* beyond hope, despairing, hopeless, inconsolable.
2 *a desperate situation.* acute, bad, critical, drastic, grave, irretrievable, serious, severe, urgent.
3 *desperate criminals.* dangerous, impetuous, reckless, violent, wild.

despicable adjective SEE **contemptible**.

despise verb be contemptuous of, condemn, deride, disapprove of, disdain, feel contempt for, SEE **hate** verb, have a low opinion of, look down on, [*informal*] put down, scorn, sneer at, spurn, undervalue.
OPPOSITES: SEE **admire**.

despondent adjective SEE **depressed**.

despot noun SEE **dictator**.

despotic adjective SEE **dictatorial**.

dessert noun [*informal*] afters, fruit, pudding, sweet.
OTHER COURSES: SEE **meal**.

dessert-spoon noun SEE **cutlery**.

destination noun *the destination of a journey.* goal, objective, purpose, target, terminus.

destined adjective **1** *My plans were destined to fail.* bound, certain, doomed, fated.
2 *I foresaw the destined outcome.* inescapable, inevitable, intended, ordained, predestined, predetermined, preordained, unavoidable.

destiny noun chance, doom, fate, fortune, karma, kismet, lot (*Accept your lot*), luck, providence.

destitute adjective *destitute beggars.* bankrupt, deprived, down-and-out, homeless, impecunious, impoverished, indigent, insolvent, needy, penniless, SEE **poor**, poverty-stricken, [*informal*] skint.
OPPOSITES: SEE **wealthy**.
destitute people beggars, down-and-outs, [*informal*] the have-nots, paupers, the poor, tramps, vagrants.

destroy verb abolish, annihilate, blast, break down, crush, decimate [see note under *decimate*], SEE **defeat** verb, demolish, devastate, devour, dismantle, eliminate, SEE **end** verb, eradicate, erase, exterminate, extinguish, extirpate, finish off, flatten, get rid of, SEE **kill**, knock down, lay waste (to), level, liquidate, make useless, pull down, put out of existence, raze, ruin, sabotage, scuttle, shatter, smash, stamp out, undo, uproot, vaporize, wipe out, wreck.
OPPOSITES: SEE **create**.

destruction noun *We deplore the destruction of wildlife.* annihilation, damage, decimation [see note under *decimate*], demolition, depredation, devastation, elimination, end, eradication, erasure, extermination, extinction, extirpation, havoc, holocaust, SEE **killing**, liquidation, overthrow, pulling down, ruin, shattering, smashing, undoing, uprooting, wiping out, wrecking.
OPPOSITES: SEE **conservation, creation**.

destructive adjective *a destructive storm. destructive criticism.* adverse, antagonistic, baleful, baneful, calamitous, catastrophic, damaging, dangerous, deadly, deleterious, detrimental, devastating, disastrous, fatal, harmful, injurious, internecine, lethal, malignant, negative, pernicious, pestilential, ruinous, violent.
OPPOSITES: SEE **constructive**.

desultory adjective SEE **disjointed**.

detach verb *to detach one thing from another.* cut loose, cut off, disconnect, disengage, disentangle, divide, free, isolate, part, release, remove, segregate, separate, sever, take off, tear off, uncouple, undo, unfasten, unfix, unhitch.
OPPOSITES: SEE **attach**.

detachable adjective *a detachable hood.* loose, removable, separable, separate.
OPPOSITES: SEE **integral**.

detached adjective **1** *a detached house.* free-standing, separate, unconnected.
COMPARE: semi-detached, terraced.

2 *a detached point of view.* aloof, cool, disinterested, dispassionate, impartial, impassive, independent, neutral, non-partisan, non-party, objective, unbiased, uncommitted, unconcerned, unemotional, uninvolved, unprejudiced.
OPPOSITES: SEE **committed**.

detail noun *Her account was accurate in every detail.* aspect, circumstance, complexity, complication, fact, factor, feature, ingredient, intricacy, item, [*plural*] minutiae, nicety, particular, point, refinement, respect, specific.

detail verb 1 *She detailed the relevant facts.* SEE **describe**.
2 *I was detailed to do the job.* SEE **assign**.

detailed adjective *a detailed description.* complete, complex, [*uncomplimentary*] fussy, giving all details, [*uncomplimentary*] hair-splitting, intricate, minute, specific.
OPPOSITES: SEE **general**.

detain verb 1 *The police detained the suspect.* arrest, capture, confine, gaol, hold, hold in custody, imprison, intern, restrain.
OPPOSITES: SEE **release** verb.
2 *What detained you? Who detained you?* buttonhole, delay, hinder, hold up, impede, keep, keep waiting, prevent, retard, slow, stop, waylay.

detainee noun SEE **prisoner**.

detect verb *to detect a fault.* become aware of, diagnose, discern, discover, expose, feel, [*informal*] ferret out, find, hear, identify, note, notice, observe, perceive, recognize, reveal, scent, see, sense, sight, smell, sniff out, spot, spy, taste, track down, uncover, unearth, unmask.

detective noun investigator, SEE **policeman**, [*informal*] private eye, sleuth.

détente noun SEE **reconciliation**.

detention noun SEE **imprisonment**.

deter verb *How can we deter the wretched starlings?* check, daunt, discourage, dismay, dissuade, frighten off, hinder, impede, intimidate, obstruct, prevent, put off, repel, send away, stop, [*informal*] turn off, warn off.
OPPOSITES: SEE **encourage**.

detergent noun cleaner, soap, washing-powder, washing-up liquid.

deteriorate verb *His work deteriorated. The buildings deteriorated.* crumble, decay, decline, degenerate, depreciate, disintegrate, fall off, get worse, [*informal*] go downhill, lapse, relapse, slip, weaken, worsen.

OPPOSITES: SEE **improve**.

determinate adjective SEE **limited**.

determination noun *Marathon runners show great determination.* [*informal*] backbone, commitment, courage, dedication, doggedness, drive, firmness, fortitude, [*informal*] grit, [*informal*] guts, perseverance, persistence, pertinacity, resolution, resolve, single-mindedness, spirit, steadfastness, [*uncomplimentary*] stubbornness, tenacity, will-power.

determine verb 1 *to determine a number.* SEE **calculate**.
2 *to determine the cause of an accident.* SEE **decide**.

determined adjective 1 *He's determined he will succeed.* adamant, bent (*on succeeding*), certain, convinced, decided, definite, firm, insistent, intent (*on succeeding*), resolved, sure.
OPPOSITES: SEE **doubtful**.
2 *a determined woman.* assertive, decisive, dogged, [*uncomplimentary*] obstinate, persistent, pertinacious, purposeful, resolute, single-minded, steadfast, strong-minded, strong-willed, [*uncomplimentary*] stubborn, sworn (*sworn enemies*), tenacious, tough, unwavering.
OPPOSITES: SEE **irresolute**.

deterrent noun *I put a net over my strawberries as a deterrent to the birds.* barrier, caution, check, curb, difficulty, discouragement, disincentive, dissuasion, hindrance, impediment, obstacle, restraint, threat, [*informal*] turn-off, warning.
OPPOSITES: SEE **encouragement**.

detest verb SEE **hate** verb.

detestable adjective SEE **hateful**.

dethrone verb SEE **depose**.

detonate verb *to detonate a bomb.* SEE **explode**.

detour noun *I wasted time making a detour.* deviation, diversion, indirect route, roundabout route.
to make a detour SEE **deviate**.

detract verb **to detract from** *Damage detracts from the value of an antique.* SEE **reduce**.

detractor noun SEE **critic**.

detriment noun SEE **harm** noun.

detrimental adjective SEE **harmful**.

detritus noun SEE **debris**.

devalue verb SEE **reduce**.

devastate verb 1 *A hurricane devastated the town.* damage severely, demolish, destroy, flatten, lay waste, level, overwhelm, ravage, raze, ruin, wreck.

2 [*informal*] *We were devastated by the bad news.* SEE **dismay** verb.

develop verb **1** *People develop. Plans develop.* advance, age, evolve, get better, grow, flourish, improve, mature, move on, progress, ripen.
OPPOSITES: SEE **regress**.
2 *A storm developed.* arise, [*informal*] blow up, come into existence, [*informal*] get up, work up.
3 *She developed a cold. He developed a posh accent.* acquire, contract, cultivate, evolve, foster, get, pick up.
4 *Develop your ideas.* amplify, augment, elaborate, enlarge on.
5 *Our business will develop next year.* branch out, build up, diversify, enlarge, expand, extend, increase, swell.

development noun **1** *the development of science. the development of trade.* advance, betterment, enlargement, evolution, expansion, extension, [*informal*] forward march, furtherance, growth, improvement, increase, progress, promotion, regeneration, reinforcement, spread.
2 [*informal*] *We'll let you know of any developments.* change, gain, happening, incident, occurrence, outcome, result, upshot.
3 *The land is earmarked for industrial development.* building, conversion, exploitation, use.

deviant adjective *deviant behaviour.* SEE **abnormal**.

deviate verb *to deviate from the usual path.* depart, digress, diverge, err, go astray, go round, make a detour, stray, swerve, turn aside, vary, veer, wander.

deviation noun SEE **abnormality, detour**.

device noun **1** *a clever device for opening wine-bottles.* apparatus, appliance, contraption, contrivance, gadget, implement, instrument, invention, machine, tool, utensil.
2 *a device to distract our attention.* dodge, expedient, gambit, gimmick, manœuvre, plan, ploy, ruse, scheme, stratagem, stunt, tactic, trick, wile.
3 *a heraldic device.* badge, crest, design, figure, logo, motif, shield, sign, symbol, token.

devil noun the Adversary, demon, the Evil One, fiend, imp, Lucifer, Satan, spirit.

devilish adjective demoniac, demoniacal, diabolic, diabolical, SEE **evil** adjective, fiendish, hellish, infernal, satanic, wicked.
OPPOSITES: SEE **angelic**.

devilment, devilry nouns SEE **mischief**.

devious adjective **1** *a devious route.* circuitous, crooked, deviating, indirect, periphrastic, rambling, roundabout, tortuous, wandering, winding.
OPPOSITES: SEE **direct** adjective.
2 *a devious person. a devious explanation.* calculating, cunning, deceitful, SEE **dishonest**, evasive, insincere, misleading, scheming, [*informal*] slippery (*a slippery customer*), sly, sneaky, treacherous, underhand, wily.
OPPOSITES: SEE **straightforward**.

devise verb *to devise a plan.* conceive, concoct, contrive, design, engineer, form, formulate, imagine, invent, make up, plan, plot, prepare, project, scheme, think out, think up.

devoted adjective SEE **loyal**.

devotee noun SEE **enthusiast**.

devotion noun SEE **love** noun, **piety**.

devotional adjective SEE **religious**.

devour verb **1** *to devour food.* SEE **eat**.
2 *Fire devoured the forest.* SEE **destroy**.

devout adjective SEE **pious**.

dew noun SEE **moisture**.

dexterity noun SEE **skill**.

dextrous adjective SEE **skilful**.

Diabolical and *diabolism* are related to Latin *diabolus* = *devil*. Compare French *diable*.

diabolical adjective **1** *diabolical cruelty.* SEE **devilish**.
2 [*informal*] *a diabolical standard of driving.* SEE **bad**.

diadem noun coronet, crown, tiara.
OTHER FORMS OF HEAD-DRESS: SEE **hat**.

diagnose verb *to diagnose an illness.* detect, determine, distinguish, find, identify, isolate, name, pinpoint, recognize.

diagnosis noun *What's the doctor's diagnosis?* analysis, conclusion, explanation, identification, interpretation, opinion, pronouncement, verdict.

diagram noun *an explanatory diagram.* chart, drawing, figure, flow-chart, graph, illustration, outline, picture, plan, representation, sketch, table.

dial noun *the dials on a dashboard.* clock, digital display, face, instrument, pointer, speedometer.

dial verb *to dial a number.* call, phone, ring, telephone.

dialect noun *a London dialect. a local dialect.* accent, brogue, idiom, jargon, language, patois, pronunciation, register, speech, tongue, vernacular.

dialectic noun SEE **reasoning**.

dialogue noun *a dialogue between two people.* [*informal*] chat, [*informal*] chinwag, [*formal*] colloquy, conversation, debate, discourse, discussion, duologue, exchange, interchange, [*old-fashioned*] intercourse, [*formal*] oral communication, talk.

diameter noun SEE **circle** noun.
RELATED ADJECTIVE: diametrical.

diamond noun OTHER PRECIOUS STONES: SEE **jewel**.
a diamond shape lozenge, rhombus.

diaper noun *a baby's diaper.* nappy.

diaphanous adjective *diaphanous fabric.* airy, SEE **delicate**, filmy, fine, gauzy, light, see-through, sheer, thin, translucent.
OPPOSITES: SEE **opaque, thick**.
diaphanous fabric gauze, net, veil.

diarrhoea noun dysentery, [*informal*] gippy tummy, [*informal*] holiday tummy, looseness of the bowels, [*informal*] the runs, [*informal*] the trots.
OTHER COMPLAINTS: SEE **illness**.

diary noun *a daily diary of events.* appointment book, chronicle, engagement book, journal, log, record.

diatonic adjective *a diatonic melody.*
COMPARE: atonal, chromatic.
OTHER MUSICAL TERMS: SEE **music**.

diatribe noun SEE **censure** noun.

dice verb *to dice with death.* SEE **gamble** verb.

dicey adjective SEE **risky**.

dichotomy noun *an odd dichotomy in his attitude.* ambivalence, divergence, division, doubleness, duality, split.

dictate verb 1 *I dictated while he wrote it down.* read aloud, speak slowly.
2 *Should parents dictate what their children do?* command, decree, direct, enforce, give orders, impose, [*informal*] lay down the law, make the rules, ordain, order, prescribe, state categorically.

dictator noun autocrat, [*informal*] Big Brother, despot, SEE **ruler**, tyrant.

dictatorial adjective *a dictatorial ruler.* absolute, authoritarian, autocratic, [*informal*] bossy, despotic, dogmatic, dominant, domineering, illiberal, imperious, intolerant, oppressive, overbearing, repressive, totalitarian, tyrannical, undemocratic.
OPPOSITES: SEE **democratic**.

dictatorship noun POLITICAL TERMS: SEE **politics**.

diction noun 1 *a poet's diction.* SEE **vocabulary**.
2 *unclear diction.* SEE **pronunciation**.

dictionary noun VARIOUS WORD-LISTS: concordance, glossary, lexicon, thesaurus, vocabulary, wordbook.

dictum noun SEE **saying**.

didactic adjective 1 *a didactic story.* SEE **instructive**.
2 *a didactic manner.* lecturing, pedagogic, pedantic.

diddle verb SEE **cheat** verb.

die verb 1 *All mortal creatures die.* [*informal*] bite the dust, [*informal*] breathe your last, cease to exist, come to the end, [*formal*] decease, depart, [*formal*] expire, fall (*to fall in war*), [*informal*] give up the ghost, pass away, [*slang*] kick the bucket, pass away, [*informal*] peg out, perish, [*slang*] snuff it, starve [= *die of hunger*].
2 *The flowers died.* droop, fade, wilt, wither.
3 *The flames died.* become less, decline, decrease, disappear, dwindle, ebb, end, fail, fizzle out, go out, languish, lessen, peter out, stop, subside, vanish, wane, weaken.
4 [*informal*] *I'm dying to meet you.* SEE **long** verb.

die-hard noun SEE **conservative** noun.

diet noun 1 *a healthy diet.* fare, SEE **food**, nourishment, nutriment, nutrition.
2 *a slimmer's diet.* abstinence, fast, rations, self-denial.
SPECIAL DIETS: vegan, vegetarian.

differ verb 1 *My feelings differ from yours.* be different, contrast (with), deviate, diverge, vary.
OPPOSITES: SEE **conform**.
2 *We differed about where to go.* argue, be at odds with each other, clash, conflict, contradict each other, disagree, dispute, dissent, fall out, oppose each other, quarrel, take issue with each other.
OPPOSITES: SEE **agree**.

difference noun 1 *a difference in price. a difference in meaning.* comparison, contrast, differential, differentiation, discrepancy, disparity, dissimilarity, distinction, diversity, incompatibility, incongruity, inconsistency, nuance, unlikeness, variety.
OPPOSITES: SEE **similarity**.
2 *a difference in our plans.* alteration, change, development, deviation, modification, variation.

3 *a difference of opinion.* argument, clash, conflict, controversy, debate, disagreement, disharmony, dispute, dissent, quarrel, strife, tiff, wrangle.
OPPOSITES: SEE **agreement**.

different adjective **1** *different colours. different opinions.* assorted, clashing, conflicting, contradictory, contrasting, deviating, discordant, discrepant, disparate, dissimilar, distinguishable, divergent, diverse, heterogeneous, ill-matched, incompatible, inconsistent, miscellaneous, mixed, multifarious, numerous, opposed, opposite, [*informal*] poles apart, several, sundry, unlike, varied, various.
OPPOSITES: SEE **identical, similar**.
2 *I'm always getting different ideas.* altered, changed, changing, fresh, new, original, revolutionary.
OPPOSITES: SEE **unchanging**.
3 *It's different to have jam with fried potatoes.* abnormal, anomalous, atypical, bizarre, eccentric, extraordinary, irregular, strange, uncommon, unconventional, unorthodox, unusual.
OPPOSITES: SEE **conventional**.
4 *Everyone's handwriting is different.* distinct, distinctive, individual, particular, peculiar, personal, separate, singular, special, specific, unique.
OPPOSITES: SEE **indistinguishable**.

differentiate verb SEE **distinguish**.

difficult adjective **1** *a difficult problem.* abstruse, advanced, baffling, complex, complicated, deep, [*informal*] dodgy, enigmatic, hard, intractable, intricate, involved, [*informal*] knotty, [*informal*] nasty, obscure, perplexing, problematical, thorny, ticklish, tricky,
OPPOSITES: SEE **easy, straightforward**.
2 *a difficult climb. a difficult task.* arduous, awkward, burdensome, challenging, demanding, exacting, exhausting, formidable, gruelling, heavy, herculean, [*informal*] killing, laborious, onerous, punishing, rigorous, severe, strenuous, taxing, tough, uphill.
OPPOSITES: SEE **easy, light** adjective.
3 *difficult neighbours. a difficult child.* annoying, disruptive, fussy, headstrong, intractable, obstinate, obstreperous, refractory, stubborn, tiresome, troublesome, trying, uncooperative, unfriendly, unhelpful, unresponsive, unruly.
OPPOSITES: SEE **tractable**.

difficulty noun *a difficulty to overcome.* adversity, challenge, complication, dilemma, embarrassment, enigma, [*informal*] fix (*I'm in a bit of a fix*), [*informal*] hang-up, hardship, [*informal*] hiccup, hindrance, hurdle, impediment, jam,

obstacle, perplexity, plight, predicament, problem, puzzle, quandary, snag, [*informal*] spot (*I'm in a bit of spot*), [*informal*] stumbling-block, tribulation, trouble, [*informal*] vexed question.

diffident adjective *a diffident manner.* backward, bashful, coy, distrustful, doubtful, fearful, hesitant, hesitating, inhibited, insecure, introvert, meek, modest, nervous, private, reluctant, reserved, retiring, self-effacing, sheepish, shrinking, shy, tentative, timid, timorous, unadventurous, unassuming, underconfident, unsure, withdrawn.
OPPOSITES: SEE **confident**.

diffuse adjective *a diffuse piece of writing.* digressive, discursive, long-winded, loose, meandering, prolix, rambling, vague, verbose, [*informal*] waffly, wandering, wordy.
OPPOSITES: SEE **concise**.

diffuse verb SEE **spread** verb.

dig verb **1** *to dig a hole.* burrow, delve, excavate, gouge out, hollow out, mine, quarry, scoop, tunnel.
2 *to dig the garden.* cultivate, fork over, [*informal*] grub up, till, trench, turn over.
3 *to dig out information.* find, probe, research, search.
4 *to dig someone in the back.* jab, nudge, poke, prod, punch, shove, thrust.
to dig up disinter, exhume.

digest noun *a digest of the latest research.* SEE **summary** noun.

digest verb **1** *to digest food.* absorb, assimilate, dissolve, SEE **eat**, [*formal*] ingest, process, utilize.
2 *to digest information.* consider, ponder, study, take in, understand.

digit noun **1** *Add up the digits.* figure, integer, number, numeral.
2 *We have five digits on each hand and foot.* finger, toe.

dignified adjective *dignified behaviour. a dignified ceremony.* becoming, calm, decorous, elegant, formal, grave, imposing, impressive, majestic, noble, proper, refined, sedate, serious, sober, solemn, stately, tasteful, upright.
OPPOSITES: SEE **undignified**.

dignify verb SEE **honour** verb.

dignitary noun *The dignitaries entered in procession.* important person, [*informal*] VIP, worthy.

dignity noun *They behaved with dignity.* calmness, decorum, eminence, formality, glory, grandeur, gravity, greatness, honour, importance, majesty, nobility, pride, propriety, respectability, seriousness, solemnity, stateliness.

digress verb *to digress from your subject.* depart, deviate, diverge, go off at a tangent, ramble, stray, veer, wander.

digs noun SEE **lodgings**.

dike noun [Note that the two senses of *dike* are almost opposite in meaning.]
1 *a dike to drain the marsh.* channel, conduit, ditch, watercourse, waterway.
2 *a dike to prevent flooding.* dam, earthworks, embankment, wall.

dilapidated adjective *a dilapidated building.* broken down, crumbling, decayed, decrepit, derelict, falling down, in disrepair, in ruins, neglected, ramshackle, rickety, ruined, [*informal*] run-down, tottering, tumbledown, uncared for.
OPPOSITE: well-maintained.

dilate verb SEE **enlarge**.

dilatory adjective SEE **slow** adjective.

dilemma noun *caught in a dilemma.* [*informal*] catch-22, difficulty, doubt, embarrassment, [*informal*] fix, [*informal*] jam, [*informal*] mess, [*informal*] pickle, plight, predicament, problem, quandary, [*informal*] spot (*I'm in a bit of a spot*).

dilettante noun amateur, dabbler.

diligent adjective *a diligent worker.* assiduous, busy, careful, conscientious, devoted, earnest, energetic, hardworking, indefatigable, industrious, painstaking, persevering, persistent, pertinacious, scrupulous, sedulous, studious, thorough, tireless.
OPPOSITES: SEE **lazy**.

dilly-dally verb SEE **dawdle**.

dilute adjective *dilute acid.* adulterated, diluted, thin, watered down, weak.
OPPOSITES: SEE **concentrated**.

dilute verb *You dilute orange squash with water.* adulterate, make less concentrated, reduce the strength of, thin, water down, weaken.
OPPOSITES: SEE **concentrate**.

dim adjective 1 *a dim outline in the mist.* bleary, blurred, cloudy, dark, dingy, dull, faint, foggy, fuzzy, gloomy, grey, hazy, indistinct, misty, murky, obscure, pale, shadowy, unclear, vague.
OPPOSITES: SEE **bright, clear** adjective.
2 [*informal*] *You are dim if you can't understand that!* SEE **stupid**.
to take a dim view SEE **disapprove**.

dim verb 1 *Cloud dimmed the sky.* blacken, cloud, darken, dull, make dim, mask, obscure.
2 *The lights dimmed.* become dim, fade, go out, lose brightness, lower.
OPPOSITES: SEE **brighten**.

dimension noun SEE **measurement**.

dimensions *a room of large dimensions.* capacity, extent, magnitude, proportions, scale, scope, size.

diminish verb 1 *Our enthusiasm diminished as time went on.* become less, contract, decline, decrease, depreciate, dwindle, lessen, peter out, reduce, shrink, shrivel, subside, wane.
OPPOSITES: SEE **increase**.
2 *Don't diminish the importance of his contribution.* belittle, demean, devalue, minimize, undervalue.
OPPOSITES: SEE **exaggerate**.

diminutive adjective SEE **small**.

dimple noun SEE **hollow** noun.

din noun *a deafening din.* clamour, clatter, commotion, crash, hubbub, hullabaloo, noise, outcry, pandemonium, racket, row, rumpus, shouting, tumult, uproar.

dine verb SEE **eat**.

dinghy noun OTHER BOATS: SEE **vessel**.

dingo noun SEE **dog** noun.

dingy adjective *dingy colours. a dingy room.* colourless, dark, depressing, dim, dirty, discoloured, dismal, drab, dreary, dull, faded, gloomy, grimy, murky, old, seedy, shabby, soiled, worn.
OPPOSITES: SEE **bright, fresh**.

dining-room noun cafeteria, carvery, refectory, restaurant.
OTHER ROOMS IN A HOUSE: SEE **room**.

dinky adjective SEE **small**.

dinner noun banquet, feast, SEE **meal**.

dint noun SEE **dent** noun.

dip noun 1 *a dip in the sea.* bathe, dive, immersion, plunge, soaking, swim.
to take a dip SEE **bathe** verb.
2 *a dip in the ground.* concavity, declivity, dent, depression, fall, hole, hollow, incline, slope.

dip verb 1 *to dip something in liquid.* douse, drop, duck, dunk, immerse, lower, plunge, submerge.
2 *to dip down.* descend, dive, go down, slope down, slump, subside.

diploma noun *a life-saving diploma.* award, certificate, SEE **qualification**.

diplomacy noun *She showed great diplomacy in ending the dispute.* delicacy, discretion, finesse, skill, tact, tactfulness.

diplomat noun 1 ambassador, consul, government representative, negotiator, politician.
2 [used loosely] *Being a diplomat, she smoothed over their differences.* diplomatic person [SEE **diplomatic**], peacemaker, tactician.

diplomatic adjective *a diplomatic reply.* careful, considerate, delicate, discreet, judicious, polite, politic, prudent, sensitive, subtle, tactful, thoughtful, understanding.
OPPOSITES: SEE **tactless.**

dipsomaniac noun alcoholic, drinker, drunkard, toper.

dire adjective 1 *a dire calamity,* SEE **dreadful.**
2 *a dire warning.* SEE **ominous.**
3 *dire need.* SEE **urgent.**

direct adjective 1 *a direct route.* nonstop, shortest, straight, undeviating, unswerving.
OPPOSITES: SEE **indirect.**
2 *a direct answer.* blunt, candid, explicit, frank, honest, outspoken, plain, pointblank, sincere, straightforward, unambiguous, uncomplicated, unequivocal.
OPPOSITES: SEE **evasive.**
3 *direct opposites. a direct contradiction.* absolute, categorical, complete, decided, diametrical, exact, head-on, [*informal*] out-and-out, utter.

direct verb 1 *to direct someone to the station.* guide, indicate the way, point, route, show the way, tell the way.
2 *to direct a letter.* address.
3 *to direct an attack on someone.* aim, point, target, train (on), turn (on).
4 *to direct a project.* administer, be in charge of, command, conduct (*an orchestra*), control, govern, handle, lead, manage, mastermind, oversee, produce (*a play*), regulate, rule, run, stage-manage, superintend, supervise, take charge of.
5 *He directed us to begin.* advise, bid, charge, command, enjoin, instruct, order, tell.

direction noun 1 *Which direction did he take?* aim, approach, bearing (*compass-bearing*), course, orientation, path, point of the compass, road, route, tack, track, way.
PRINCIPAL COMPASS-BEARINGS: east, north, north-east, north-west, south, south-east, south-west, west.
2 [*usually plural*] *The kit comes with directions for assembly.* guidance, guidelines, instructions, orders, plans.

directive noun SEE **command** noun.

director noun SEE **chief** noun.

directorate noun SEE **board** noun.

directory noun *a telephone directory.* catalogue, index, list, register.
OTHER KINDS OF BOOK: SEE **book** noun.

dirge noun lament, mournful song [SEE **mournful**].
OTHER SONGS: SEE **song.**

dirk noun SEE **dagger.**

dirt noun 1 *Clean up the dirt.* dust, filth, garbage, grime, impurity, mess, mire, muck, pollution, refuse, rubbish, slime, sludge, smut, stain, tarnish.
2 *Chickens scratched about in the dirt.* clay, earth, loam, mud, soil.

dirty adjective 1 *a dirty room. dirty clothes.* black, dingy, dusty, filthy, foul, grimy, grubby, marked, messy, mucky, muddy, nasty, scruffy, shabby, smeary, soiled, sooty, sordid, squalid, stained, sullied, tarnished, travel-stained, uncared for, unclean, unwashed.
OPPOSITES: SEE **clean** adjective.
2 *dirty water.* cloudy, impure, muddy, murky, polluted, untreated.
OPPOSITES: SEE **pure.**
3 *dirty tactics.* SEE **corrupt** adjective. dishonest, illegal, [*informal*] low-down, mean, rough, treacherous, unfair, ungentlemanly, unsporting.
OPPOSITES: SEE **honest, sporting.**
4 *dirty language.* coarse, crude, improper, indecent, SEE **obscene,** offensive, rude, smutty, vulgar.
OPPOSITES: SEE **decent.**

dirty verb *Try not to dirty your clothes.* SEE **defile,** foul, make dirty [SEE **dirty** adjective], mark, [*informal*] mess up, smear, smudge, soil, spatter, spot, stain, streak, sully, tarnish.
OPPOSITES: SEE **clean** verb.

disability noun *a physical disability.* affliction, complaint, disablement, handicap, impairment, incapacity, infirmity, weakness.

disable verb 1 *The accident temporarily disabled her.* cripple, debilitate, enfeeble, [*informal*] hamstring, handicap, immobilize, impair, incapacitate, injure, lame, maim, paralyse, weaken.
2 *The storm disabled the generators.* damage, make useless, put out of action, stop working.

disabled adjective *a disabled person.* bedridden, crippled, deformed, handicapped, having a disability, immobilized, incapacitated, infirm, lame, limbless, maimed, mutilated, paralysed, paraplegic, weak, weakened.
disabled person amputee, cripple, invalid, paraplegic.

disabuse verb SEE **disillusion.**

disadvantage noun *It's a disadvantage to be small if you play basketball.* drawback, handicap, hardship, hindrance, impediment, inconvenience, liability, [*informal*] minus, nuisance, privation, snag, trouble, weakness.

disadvantaged adjective SEE **handicapped.**

disaffected adjective SEE **dissatisfied**.

disagree verb argue, bicker, clash, conflict, differ, dissent, fall out, quarrel, squabble, wrangle.
OPPOSITES: SEE **agree**.
to disagree with 1 *He disagrees with everything I say.* argue with, be at variance with, contradict, counter, deviate from, dissent from, object to, oppose, take issue with.
2 *Onions disagree with me.* SEE **upset**.

disagreeable adjective SEE **unpleasant**.

disagreement noun *There was a disagreement between them.* altercation, argument, clash, conflict, controversy, debate, difference of opinion, disharmony, dispute, dissension, dissent, divergence, inconsistency, lack of sympathy, misunderstanding, opposition, quarrel, squabble, [*informal*] tiff, variance, wrangle.
OPPOSITES: SEE **agreement**.

disallow verb *to disallow a goal.* cancel, dismiss, refuse, reject, veto.
OPPOSITES: SEE **allow**.

disappear verb **1** *The fog disappeared.* become invisible [SEE **invisible**], cease to exist, clear, disperse, dissolve, dwindle, ebb, evaporate, fade, melt away, recede, vanish, wane.
2 *He disappeared round the corner.* depart, escape, flee, fly, go, pass, run away, walk away, withdraw.
OPPOSITES: SEE **appear**.

disappoint verb *The weather disappointed us.* be worse than expected, chagrin, [*informal*] dash (a person's) hopes, disillusion, dismay, displease, fail to satisfy, frustrate, [*informal*] let down, upset, thwart, vex.
OPPOSITES: SEE **delight** verb, **satisfy**.

disappointed adjective *a disappointed man.* crestfallen, dejected, discontented, disenchanted, disgruntled, disillusioned, dissatisfied, downcast, downhearted, frustrated, let down, SEE **sad**, unhappy.
OPPOSITES: SEE **contented**.

disapprobation noun SEE **disapproval**.

disapproval noun *Her frown showed her disapproval.* anger, censure, condemnation, criticism, disapprobation, disfavour, dislike, displeasure, dissatisfaction, hostility, reprimand, reproach.
OPPOSITES: SEE **approval**.

disapprove verb **to disapprove of** *They all disapprove of smoking.* be displeased by, blame, censure, condemn, criticize, denounce, deplore, deprecate, dislike, disparage, frown on, jeer at [SEE **jeer**],

look askance at, make unwelcome, object to, regret, reject, take exception to, [*informal*] take a dim view of.
OPPOSITES: SEE **approve**.

disapproving adjective *a disapproving look.* [*informal*] black (*I gave him a black look*), censorious, critical, deprecatory, disparaging, reproachful, slighting, unfavourable, unfriendly.
OPPOSITES: SEE **favourable**.

disarm verb **1** *to disarm your opponent.* make powerless, take weapons away from.
2 *to disarm after a war.* demobilize, disband your troops.

disarming adjective SEE **charming**.

disarray noun SEE **disorder**.

disaster noun **1** *a sudden disaster.* accident, blow, calamity, cataclysm, catastrophe, crash, misadventure, mischance, misfortune, mishap, reverse, tragedy.

VARIOUS DISASTERS: air-crash, avalanche, derailment, earthquake, epidemic, fire, flood, hurricane, landslide, plague, road accident, shipwreck, tidal wave, tornado, volcanic eruption.

---

2 [*informal*] *Our play was a disaster.* débâcle, failure, fiasco, [*informal*] flop, [*informal*] mess-up, [*informal*] wash-out.
OPPOSITES: SEE **success**.

disastrous adjective *a disastrous fire. a disastrous failure.* SEE **bad**, calamitous, cataclysmic, catastrophic, crippling, destructive, devastating, dire, dreadful, fatal, ruinous, terrible, tragic.
OPPOSITES: SEE **successful**.

disband verb SEE **disperse**.

disbelief noun distrust, doubt, incredulity, mistrust, scepticism, suspicion.
OPPOSITES: SEE **belief**.

disbelieve verb *Don't think I disbelieve your story.* be sceptical of, discount, discredit, doubt, have no faith in, mistrust, reject, suspect.
OPPOSITES: SEE **believe**.

disbelieving adjective SEE **incredulous**.

disc noun **1** circle, counter, plate, token.
2 *a recorded disc.* album, compact disc, digital recording, LP, SEE **record** noun, single.
3 *a computer disc.* diskette, floppy disc, hard disc.
disc jockey OTHER BROADCASTERS: SEE **broadcaster**.

discard verb *I discarded some old clothes.* cast off, [*informal*] chuck away, dispense with, dispose of, [*informal*] ditch, dump, eliminate, get rid of, jettison, reject, scrap, shed, throw away.

discern verb *We discerned a change in the weather.* become aware of, be sensitive to, detect, discover, discriminate, distinguish, make out, mark, notice, observe, perceive, recognize, see, spy.

discernible adjective *a discernible change in the weather.* SEE **noticeable.**

discerning adjective *a discerning judge.* SEE **perceptive.**

discharge noun *discharge from a wound.* emission, pus, secretion, suppuration.

discharge verb 1 *The chimney discharged thick smoke.* belch, eject, emit, expel, exude, give off, give out, pour out, produce, release, secrete, send out.
2 *to discharge a gun.* detonate, explode, fire, let off, shoot.
3 *to discharge an employee from a job.* dismiss, fire, make redundant, remove, sack, throw out.
4 *to discharge a prisoner.* absolve, acquit, allow to leave, clear, dismiss, excuse, exonerate, free, let off, liberate, pardon, release.

disciple noun *The great teacher had many disciples.* acolyte, admirer, apostle, devotee, follower, pupil, student, supporter.

disciplinarian noun *a strict disciplinarian.* authoritarian, autocrat, despot, [*informal*] hard-liner, [*informal*] hard taskmaster, martinet, [*informal*] slavedriver, [*informal*] stickler (*a stickler for good manners*), tyrant.
OPPOSITE: libertarian.

discipline noun *firm discipline.* control, management, obedience, order, orderliness, self-control, strictness, system, training.

discipline verb 1 *You must discipline a young dog.* break in, control, drill, educate, instruct, restrain, train.
2 *We disciplined those who disobeyed.* chasten, chastise, correct, penalize, punish, reprimand, reprove, scold.

disciplined adjective *a disciplined army.* SEE **obedient,** orderly, well-behaved, well-trained.
OPPOSITES: SEE **undisciplined.**

disclaim verb *to disclaim responsibility.* deny, disown, forswear, reject, renounce, repudiate.
OPPOSITES: SEE **acknowledge.**

disclose verb SEE **reveal.**

disco noun SEE **dance** noun.

discolour verb *Spilt acid discoloured the floor.* bleach, SEE **dirty** verb, fade, mark, spoil the colour of, stain, tarnish, tinge.

discomfit verb SEE **disconcert.**

discomfort noun *the discomfort of a hard chair.* ache, distress, hardship, irritation, pain, soreness, uncomfortableness, uneasiness.
OPPOSITES: SEE **comfort** noun.

discompose verb SEE **disturb.**

disconcert verb *Bright light disconcerted her.* agitate, bewilder, confuse, discomfit, disturb, fluster, nonplus, perplex, [*informal*] put off (*It puts me off*), [*informal*] rattle, ruffle, throw off balance, trouble, unsettle, upset, worry.
OPPOSITES: SEE **reassure.**

disconcerting adjective *The play was spoiled by a lot of disconcerting noise.* distracting, disturbing, offputting, unsettling, upsetting, worrying.
OPPOSITES: SEE **reassuring.**

disconnect verb *to disconnect a telephone.* break off, cut off, detach, disengage, sever, take away, uncouple, unhitch, unplug.

disconnected adjective *a disconnected argument.* SEE **disjointed.**

disconsolate adjective SEE **sad.**

discontented adjective SEE **dissatisfied.**

discontinue verb SEE **end** verb.

discord noun 1 *discord between friends.* argument, clash, conflict, contention, difference of opinion, disagreement, disharmony, dispute, friction, SEE **quarrel** noun.
OPPOSITES: SEE **agreement.**
2 *discords in music.* cacophony, discordant sound [SEE **discordant**], jangle, SEE **noise.**
OPPOSITES: SEE **harmony.**

discordant adjective 1 *discordant sounds.* atonal, cacophanous, clashing, dissonant, grating, grinding, harsh, jangling, jarring, shrill, strident, tuneless, unmusical.
OPPOSITES: SEE **harmonious.**
2 *discordant opinions. a discordant voice.* conflicting, contrary, differing, disagreeing, incompatible, inconsistent, opposite, SEE **quarrelsome.**
OPPOSITE: assenting [SEE **assent** verb].

discount noun *a discount on the full price.* abatement, allowance, concession, cut, deduction, [*informal*] mark-down, rebate, reduction.

discount verb *We discounted his unlikely story.* disbelieve, disregard, ignore, overlook, reject.

discourage verb 1 *The threat of violence discouraged us.* cow, damp (*It damped our*

enthusiasm), dampen, daunt, demoralize, depress, disenchant, dishearten, dismay, dispirit, frighten, hinder, inhibit, intimidate, [*informal*] put down, [*informal*] put off, scare, [*informal*] throw cold water on, unman, unnerve.
2 *How can we discourage vandals?* check, deflect, deter, dissuade, prevent, put an end to, repress, restrain, stop.
OPPOSITES: SEE **encourage**.

discouragement noun *The loud music was a discouragement to conversation.* constraint, [*informal*] damper, deterrent, disincentive, hindrance, impediment, obstacle, restraint, setback.
OPPOSITES: SEE **encouragement**.

discouraging adjective *discouraging advice.* daunting, demoralizing, depressing, dispiriting.

discourse noun KINDS OF DISCOURSE: SEE **conversation**, disquisition, dissertation, essay, literature, monograph, paper, speech, thesis, treatise.
VARIOUS KINDS OF WRITING: SEE **writing**.

discourse verb *He discoursed on his pet topic.* SEE **speak**.

discourteous adjective SEE **rude**.

discover verb *We discovered a secret spot. I discovered some new facts.* ascertain, come across, detect, [*informal*] dig up, [*informal*] dredge up, explore, find, hit on, identify, learn, light upon, locate, notice, observe, perceive, recognize, reveal, search out, see, spot, [*slang*] sus out, track down, uncover, unearth.
OPPOSITES: SEE **hide** verb.

discoverer noun *the discoverer of penicillin. discoverers of new lands.* creator, explorer, finder, initiator, inventor, originator, pioneer, traveller.

discovery noun *a new discovery.* breakthrough, disclosure, exploration, [*informal*] find, innovation, invention, revelation.

discredit verb **1** *to discredit someone.* attack, defame, disgrace, dishonour, ruin the reputation of, slander, slur, smear, vilify.
2 *to discredit someone's story.* challenge, disbelieve, dispute, [*informal*] explode, prove false, refuse to believe, show up.

discreditable adjective SEE **shameful**.

discreet adjective [Do not confuse with *discrete*.] *I asked a few discreet questions.* careful, cautious, circumspect, considerate, delicate, diplomatic, guarded, judicious, polite, politic, prudent, sensitive, tactful, thoughtful, wary.
OPPOSITES: SEE **indiscreet**.

discrepancy noun *a discrepancy between two versions of a story.* conflict, SEE **difference**, disparity, dissimilarity, divergence, incompatibility, incongruity, inconsistency.
OPPOSITES: SEE **similarity**.

discrete adjective [Do not confuse with *discreet*.] SEE **distinct**.

discretion noun *Handle confidential matters with discretion.* SEE **diplomacy**, good sense, judgement, maturity, prudence, responsibility, sensitivity, tact, wisdom.
OPPOSITES: SEE **tactlessness**.

discriminate verb **1** *Can you discriminate between butter and margarine?* differentiate, distinguish, make a distinction, tell apart.
2 *It's wrong to discriminate against people because of their religion, colour, or sex.* be biased, be intolerant, be prejudiced, show discrimination [SEE **discrimination**].

discriminating adjective *a discriminating judge of wine.* choosy, critical, discerning, fastidious, [*uncomplimentary*] fussy, particular, perceptive, selective.
OPPOSITES: SEE **undiscriminating**.

discrimination noun **1** *She shows discrimination in her choice of music.* discernment, good taste, insight, judgement, perceptiveness, refinement, selectivity, subtlety, taste.
2 *racial discrimination. positive discrimination.* bias, bigotry, chauvinism, favouritism, intolerance, male chauvinism, prejudice, racialism, racism, sexism, unfairness.
OPPOSITES: SEE **impartiality**.

discursive adjective *a discursive essay.* SEE **rambling**.

discuss verb *to discuss a problem.* argue about, confer about, consider, consult about, debate, deliberate, examine, [*informal*] put heads together about, talk about, [*informal*] weigh up the pros and cons of, write about.

discussion noun *a lively discussion.* argument, SEE **conference**, consideration, consultation, conversation, debate, deliberation, dialogue, discourse, examination, exchange of views, symposium, talk.

disdain noun, verb SEE **scorn** noun, verb.

disdainful adjective SEE **scornful**.

disease noun *suffering from a disease.* SEE **illness**.

diseased adjective SEE **ill**.

disembark verb *to disembark from a ship.* alight, go ashore, land.
OPPOSITES: SEE **embark**.

disembodied adjective *a disembodied voice.* bodiless, SEE **ghostly**, immaterial, incorporeal, insubstantial, intangible, unreal.

disembowel verb SEE **kill**.

disenchant verb SEE **disillusion**.

disengage verb SEE **detach**.

disentangle verb 1 *to disentangle a knot.* sort out, straighten, undo, unknot, unravel, untangle, untie, untwist.
OPPOSITES: SEE **entangle**.
2 *The fish disentangled itself from the net.* disengage, extricate, free, liberate, release, rescue, separate.
OPPOSITES: SEE **enmesh**.

disfavour noun SEE **disapproval**.

disfigure verb *He was disfigured in a fire.* damage, deface, deform, make ugly [SEE **ugly**], mar, mutilate, scar, spoil.
OPPOSITES: SEE **beautify**.

disgorge verb SEE **pour**.

disgrace noun 1 *He never got over the disgrace of his court-case.* blot on your name, [*formal*] contumely, degradation, discredit, dishonour, embarrassment, humiliation, ignominy, opprobrium, scandal, shame, slur, stain, stigma.
2 [*informal*] *The way he treats his dog is a disgrace!* SEE **outrage**.

disgraceful adjective *disgraceful behaviour.* SEE **bad**.

disgruntled adjective SEE **dissatisfied**.

disguise noun *I didn't recognize him in that disguise.* camouflage, cloak, costume, cover, fancy dress, front, [*informal*] get-up, impersonation, make-up, mask, pretence, smoke-screen.

disguise verb 1 *to disguise your looks.* blend into the background, camouflage, dress up, make inconspicuous, mask, screen, shroud, veil.
2 *to disguise your feelings.* conceal, cover up, falsify, gloss over, hide, misrepresent.
to disguise yourself as counterfeit, dress up as, imitate, impersonate, mimic, pretend to be, [*informal*] take off.

disgust noun *I couldn't hide my disgust at the rotten food.* abhorrence, antipathy, aversion, contempt, detestation, dislike, distaste, hatred, loathing, nausea, repugnance, repulsion, revulsion.
OPPOSITES: SEE **liking**.

disgust verb *The rotten food disgusted me.* appal, be distasteful to, displease, horrify, nauseate, offend, outrage, put off, repel, revolt, shock, sicken, [*informal*] turn your stomach.
OPPOSITES: SEE **please**.

disgusting adjective *disgusting food, disgusting cruelty.* loathsome, nauseating, offensive, repugnant, repulsive, revolting, sickening, SEE **unpleasant**.

dish noun 1 *an earthenware dish.* basin, bowl, casserole, SEE **container**, plate, [*old-fashioned*] platter, tureen.
2 *Stew is a nutritious dish.* concoction, food, item on the menu, recipe.

dish verb [*informal*] *to dish someone's chances.* SEE **spoil**.
to dish out SEE **distribute**.
to dish up SEE **serve**.

disharmony noun SEE **discord**.

dishearten verb *The feeble applause disheartened us.* depress, deter, SEE **discourage**, dismay, put off, sadden.
OPPOSITES: SEE **encourage**.

disheartened adjective SEE **depressed**.

dishevelled adjective *dishevelled hair.* bedraggled, disarranged, disordered, messy, ruffled, rumpled, [*informal*] scruffy, slovenly, tangled, tousled, uncombed, unkempt, untidy.
OPPOSITES: SEE **neat**.

dishonest adjective *a dishonest deal. a dishonest salesman.* [*informal*] bent, cheating, corrupt, criminal, crooked, deceitful, deceiving, devious, disreputable, fair, false, fraudulent, immoral, insincere, lying, mendacious, misleading, [*formal*] perfidious, [*informal*] shady, [*informal*] slippery, specious, swindling, thieving, [*informal*] underhand, unethical, unprincipled, unscrupulous, untrustworthy, untruthful.
OPPOSITES: SEE **honest**.

dishonesty noun corruption, crookedness, deceit, deviousness, falsity, immorality, insincerity, mendacity, perfidy, speciousness.
OPPOSITES: SEE **honesty**.

dishonour noun *There's no dishonour in losing.* blot on your reputation, degradation, discredit, disgrace, humiliation, ignominy, indignity, [*formal*] opprobrium, reproach, scandal, shame, slur, stain, stigma.
OPPOSITES: SEE **honour** noun.

dishonourable adjective *dishonourable behaviour.* base, blameworthy, compromising, SEE **corrupt** adjective, despicable, discreditable, disgraceful, disgusting, dishonest, disreputable, ignoble, ignominious, improper, infamous, mean, outrageous, reprehensible, scandalous, shabby, shameful, shameless, treacherous, unchivalrous, unethical, unprincipled, unscrupulous, untrustworthy, unworthy, wicked.
OPPOSITES: SEE **honourable**.

dishy adjective SEE **sexy**.

disillusion verb *They became disillusioned about the glory of war.* disabuse, disappoint, disenchant, SEE **enlighten**, reveal the truth to, undeceive.
OPPOSITES: SEE **deceive**.

disincentive noun SEE **discouragement**.

disinclined adjective SEE **unwilling**.

disinfect verb *to disinfect a wound.* cauterize, chlorinate (*water*), clean, cleanse, decontaminate, fumigate (*a room*), purify, sanitize, sterilize.
OPPOSITES: SEE **infect**.

disinfectant noun antiseptic, carbolic, cleaner, germicide.

disingenuous adjective SEE **insincere**.

disinherit verb *to disinherit an heir.* cut off, cut you out of a will, deprive you of your inheritance or birthright.

disintegrate verb *The wreck disintegrated. The team disintegrated when the captain quitted.* become disunited, break into pieces, break up, crack up, crumble, decay, decompose, degenerate, deteriorate, fall apart, lose coherence, rot, shatter, smash up, splinter.

disinter verb *to disinter a body.* dig up, exhume, unbury, unearth.
OPPOSITES: SEE **bury**.

disinterested adjective SEE **unbiased**. [Don't use *disinterested* as a synonym for *uninterested*. A disinterested referee is not *an uninterested referee*.]

disjoin verb SEE **separate** verb.

disjointed adjective *a disjointed story.* aimless, broken up, confused, desultory, disconnected, dislocated, disordered, disunited, incoherent, jumbled, loose, mixed up, muddled, rambling, unconnected, uncoordinated, wandering.
OPPOSITES: SEE **coherent**.

dislike noun *I tried to hide my dislike of the food.* antagonism (to), antipathy (to), aversion (to), contempt (for), detestation, disapproval, disgust (for), distaste (for), SEE **hatred**, loathing, revulsion (from).
OPPOSITES: SEE **liking**.

dislike verb *I dislike shopping.* avoid, despise, detest, disapprove of, feel dislike [SEE **dislike** noun], SEE **hate** verb, loathe, scorn, [*informal*] take against.
OPPOSITES: SEE **like**.

dislocate verb *to dislocate your shoulder.* disengage, disjoint, displace, misplace, [*informal*] put out, put out of joint.

dislodge verb SEE **displace**.

disloyal adjective *a disloyal ally.* faithless, false, insincere, perfidious, seditious, subversive, treacherous, treasonable, [*informal*] two-faced, unfaithful, unreliable, untrustworthy.
OPPOSITES: SEE **loyal**.
disloyal person SEE **deserter**.

disloyalty noun *We couldn't forgive his disloyalty.* betrayal, double-dealing, duplicity, faithlessness, falseness, inconstancy, infidelity, perfidy, treachery, treason, unfaithfulness.
OPPOSITES: SEE **loyalty**.

dismal adjective 1 *dismal surroundings.* SEE **gloomy**.
2 [*informal*] *a dismal performance.* SEE **feeble**.

dismantle verb *to dismantle a building or machine.* demolish, knock down, strike, strip down, take apart, take down.
OPPOSITES: SEE **assemble**.

dismay noun *We listened with dismay to the bad news.* agitation, alarm, anxiety, apprehension, astonishment, consternation, depression, disappointment, discouragement, distress, dread, SEE **fear** noun, gloom, horror, pessimism, surprise.

dismay verb *The bad news dismayed us.* alarm, appal, daunt, depress, devastate, disappoint, discourage, disgust, dishearten, dispirit, distress, SEE **frighten**, horrify, scare, shock, unnerve.
OPPOSITES: SEE **encourage**.

dismember verb *to dismember a body.* amputate (*limbs*), cut up, disjoint, divide, remove the limbs of.

dismiss verb 1 *to dismiss a class.* free, let go, release, send away.
2 *to dismiss employees.* [*informal*] axe, banish, [*formal*] cashier, disband, discharge, [*informal*] fire, give notice to, [*informal*] give them their cards, [*informal*] give the push to, lay off, make redundant, sack, [*informal*] send packing.
3 *to dismiss an idea.* discard, discount, disregard, drop, get rid of, give up, [*informal*] pooh-pooh, reject, repudiate, set aside, shelve, wave aside.

dismount verb *to dismount from a horse.* alight, descend, get off.

disobedient adjective *a disobedient dog. a disobedient class.* badly behaved, contrary, defiant, disorderly, disruptive, fractious, headstrong, insubordinate, intractable, mutinous, SEE **naughty**, obstinate, obstreperous, perverse, rebellious, recalcitrant, refractory, riotous, self-willed, stubborn, uncontrollable,

undisciplined, ungovernable, unmanageable, unruly, wayward, wild, wilful.
OPPOSITES: SEE **obedient**.

disobey verb 1 *to disobey the rules.* break, contravene, defy, disregard, flout, ignore, infringe, rebel against, resist, transgress, violate.
2 *Soldiers must never disobey.* be disobedient, mutiny, protest, rebel, revolt, rise up, strike.
OPPOSITES: SEE **obey**.

disorder noun 1 *disorder in the streets.* anarchy, brawl, clamour, commotion, disorderliness, disturbance, fighting, fracas, fuss, hubbub, lawlessness, quarrelling, rioting, rumpus, tumult, uproar.
OPPOSITES: SEE **peace**.
2 *the disorder on my desk.* chaos, confusion, disarray, disorganization, jumble, mess, muddle, shambles, untidiness.
OPPOSITES: SEE **tidiness**.

disorderly adjective 1 *a disorderly class.* SEE **disobedient**.
2 *disorderly work.* SEE **disorganized**.

disorganized adjective *disorganized work.* careless, chaotic, confused, disorderly, haphazard, illogical, jumbled, messy, muddled, scatter-brained, [*informal*] slapdash, [*informal*] slipshod, [*informal*] sloppy, slovenly, unmethodical, unplanned, unstructured, unsystematic, untidy.
OPPOSITES: SEE **neat, systematic**.

disorientate verb SEE **confuse**.

disown verb *I'll disown you if you misbehave.* cast off, disclaim knowledge of, renounce, repudiate.

disparage verb SEE **criticize**.

disparaging adjective SEE **uncomplimentary**.

disparate adjective SEE **different**.

disparity noun SEE **difference**.

dispassionate adjective *a dispassionate look at a problem.* calm, cool, SEE **impartial**, level-headed, unemotional.
OPPOSITES: SEE **emotional**.

dispatch noun *A messenger brought dispatches.* bulletin, communiqué, letter, message, report.

dispatch verb 1 *to dispatch a parcel.* consign, convey, forward, post, send, transmit.
2 *to dispatch a wounded animal.* dispose of, finish off, SEE **kill**, put an end to.

dispel verb SEE **disperse**.

dispensable adjective SEE **inessential**.

dispensary noun pharmacy.

dispense verb 1 *to dispense charity.* allocate, allot, apportion, deal out, distribute, dole out, give out, mete out, provide, share.
2 *to dispense medicine.* make up, prepare, supply.
to dispense with *We dispensed with the formalities.* abolish, cancel, dispose of, do without, get rid of, jettison, make unnecessary, relinquish, remove.

dispenser noun chemist, pharmacist.

disperse verb 1 *to disperse a crowd.* break up, disband, dismiss, dispel, dissipate, divide up, drive away, send away, send in different directions, separate.
2 *The crowd dispersed.* disappear, dissolve, melt away, scatter, spread out, vanish.
OPPOSITES: SEE **collect**.
3 *The company dispersed its workforce throughout the country.* decentralize, devolve, distribute, spread.
OPPOSITES: SEE **centralize**.

dispirited adjective SEE **depressed**.

displace verb 1 *Vibration displaced part of the mechanism.* disarrange, dislocate, dislodge, disturb, misplace, move, put out of place, shift.
2 *Newcomers displace older players.* crowd out, depose, dispossess, oust, replace, succeed, supersede, supplant.

display noun *a gymnastics display.* demonstration, exhibition, pageant, parade, presentation, show, spectacle.

display verb *to display your knowledge.* air, demonstrate, disclose, exhibit, flaunt, flourish, give evidence of, parade, present, produce, put on show, reveal, show, show off, vaunt.
OPPOSITES: SEE **hide** verb.

displease verb SEE **annoy**.

displeasure noun SEE **annoyance**.

disport verb **to disport yourself** SEE **play** verb.

disposable adjective 1 *disposable income.* at your disposal, available, usable.
2 *a disposable razor.* expendable, replaceable, [*informal*] throwaway.

dispose verb *A general disposes his troops for battle.* arrange, array, group, place, position, set out
to dispose of *to dispose of rubbish.* deal with, destroy, discard, dump, get rid of, give away, jettison, scrap, sell, throw away.
to be disposed to *Are you disposed to lend me £100?* be inclined to, be liable to, be likely to, be ready to, be willing to.

disposition noun 1 *the disposition of troops.* SEE **arrangement**.

2 *a friendly disposition.* SEE **character**.

dispossess verb SEE **deprive**.

disproportionate adjective *Little jobs can use up a disproportionate amount of time.* excessive, inordinate, unbalanced, uneven, unreasonable.
OPPOSITES: SEE **proportionate**.

disprove verb *to disprove an allegation.* confute, controvert, discredit, [*informal*] explode, invalidate, negate, rebut, refute, show to be wrong.
OPPOSITES: SEE **prove**.

disputable adjective SEE **debatable**.

dispute noun *a dispute between rivals.* SEE **debate** noun, **quarrel** noun.

dispute verb **1** *We disputed the rights and wrongs of the affair.* SEE **debate** verb.
2 *No one disputed the referee's decision.* argue against, challenge, contest, contradict, controvert, deny, doubt, impugn, oppose, quarrel with, question.
OPPOSITES: SEE **accept**.

disqualify verb *to disqualify someone from driving.* debar, declare ineligible [SEE **ineligible**], preclude, prohibit.

disquiet noun SEE **anxiety**.

disquisition noun SEE **discourse** noun.

disregard verb **1** *to disregard advice.* brush aside, despise, discount, dismiss, disobey, disparage, [*informal*] fly in the face of, forget, ignore, [*informal*] make light of, neglect, overlook, pay no attention to, [*informal*] pooh-pooh, reject, shrug off, slight, snub, turn a blind eye to.
OPPOSITES: SEE **heed**.
2 *I disregarded the boring parts of the book.* exclude, leave out, miss out, omit, pass over, skip.

disrepair noun *buildings in a sad state of disrepair.* bad condition, collapse, decay, dilapidation, neglect, ruin, shabbiness.
OPPOSITES: SEE **renovation**.

disreputable adjective **1** *a disreputable firm.* dishonest, dishonourable, [*informal*] dodgy, dubious, infamous, questionable, [*informal*] shady, suspect, suspicious, unreliable, unsound, untrustworthy.
OPPOSITES: SEE **reputable**.
2 *a disreputable appearance.* raffish, unconventional.
OPPOSITES: SEE **respectable**.

disrespectful adjective SEE **rude**.

disrobe verb SEE **undress**.

disrupt verb *A fire-practice disrupted work.* break the routine of, break up, confuse, dislocate, disturb, interfere with, interrupt, intrude on, spoil, throw into disorder, unsettle, upset.

disruptive adjective *disruptive pupils.* SEE **unruly**.

dissatisfaction noun *I expressed dissatisfaction at the poor service.* annoyance, chagrin, disappointment, discontentment, dismay, displeasure, disquiet, exasperation, frustration, irritation, mortification, regret, unhappiness.
OPPOSITES: SEE **satisfaction**.

dissatisfied adjective *dissatisfied customers.* disaffected, disappointed, discontented, disgruntled, displeased, [*informal*] fed up, frustrated, unfulfilled, SEE **unhappy**, unsatisfied.
OPPOSITES: SEE **satisfied**.

dissect verb SEE **analyse, cut** verb.

dissemble verb SEE **pretend**.

disseminate verb SEE **spread** verb.

dissension, dissent nouns SEE **disagreement**.

dissent verb SEE **disagree**.

dissertation noun SEE **discourse** noun.

disservice noun SEE **harm** noun.

dissident noun [*uncomplimentary*] agitator, dissenter, independent thinker, non-conformer, protester, [*uncomplimentary*] rebel, [*informal*] refusenik.
OPPPOSITE: conformist.

dissimilar adjective *dissimilar clothes. dissimilar personalities.* contrasting, different, disparate, distinct, distinguishable, divergent, diverse, heterogeneous, incompatible, opposite, unlike, unrelated, various.
OPPOSITES: SEE **similar**.

dissimulation noun SEE **pretence**.

dissipate verb **1** *to dissipate your energy.* SEE **disperse**.
2 *to dissipate your wealth.* SEE **squander**.

dissipated adjective SEE **immoral**.

dissociate verb *The editor dissociated herself from the views in the article.* back away, cut off, detach, distance, divorce, isolate, SEE **separate** verb.
OPPOSITES: SEE **associate**.

dissolute adjective SEE **immoral**.

dissolve verb **1** [It's useful to note a distinction between *dissolve = disperse in a liquid* (*Sugar dissolves in tea*) and *melt = become liquid by heating* (*Ice melts*).] become liquid, deliquesce, diffuse, disappear, disintegrate, disperse, liquefy.
2 *to dissolve a partnership.* break up, bring to an end, cancel, dismiss, divorce, end, sever, split up, suspend, terminate, [*informal*] wind up.

dissonant adjective SEE **discordant**.

dissuade verb **to dissuade from** advise against, argue (someone) out of, deter from, discourage from, persuade (someone) not to, put off, remonstrate (with someone) against, warn against.
OPPOSITES: SEE **persuade**.

distance noun 1 *the distance between two points.* breadth, extent, gap, [*informal*] haul (*a long haul*), interval, journey, length, measurement, mileage, range, reach, separation, space, span, stretch, width.
2 *He keeps his distance.* aloofness, coolness, isolation, remoteness, separation, [*informal*] standoffishness, unfriendliness.
OPPOSITE: closeness.

distance verb *to distance yourself from someone.* be unfriendly (with), keep away, keep your distance, remove, separate, set yourself apart, stay away.
OPPOSITES: SEE **involve**.

distant adjective 1 *distant places.* far, faraway, far-flung, [*informal*] god-forsaken, inaccessible, outlying, out-of-the-way, remote.
OPPOSITES: SEE **close** adjective.
2 *a distant manner.* aloof, cool, formal, haughty, reserved, reticent, unenthusiastic, unfriendly, withdrawn.
OPPOSITES: SEE **friendly**.

distasteful adjective SEE **unpleasant**.

distend verb SEE **swell**.

distended adjective SEE **swollen**.

distil verb *to distil water. to distil spirit from wine.* extract, purify, refine, vaporize and condense.

distilled adjective *distilled water.* pure, purified, refined, vaporized and condensed.

distinct adjective 1 [See note under *distinctive.*] *distinct footprints in the mud. a distinct sound.* apparent, clear, clearcut, definite, evident, noticeable, obvious, patent, plain, recognizable, sharp, unambiguous, unmistakable, visible, well-defined.
OPPOSITES: SEE **indistinct**.
2 *Organize your ideas into distinct sections.* contrasting, detached, different, discrete, dissimilar, distinguishable, individual, separate, special, unconnected.

distinction noun 1 *I can't see any distinction between the twins.* contrast, difference, differentiation, discrimination, dissimilarity, distinctiveness, individuality, particularity, peculiarity.
OPPOSITES: SEE **similarity**.

2 *I had the distinction of being first home.* celebrity, credit, eminence, excellence, fame, glory, greatness, honour, importance, merit, prestige, renown, reputation, superiority.

distinctive adjective [Do not confuse with *distinct*. *Distinct* means *clear writing*; *distinctive handwriting* is *writing you don't confuse with someone else's.*] characteristic, different, distinguishing, idiosyncratic, individual, inimitable, original, peculiar, personal, singular, special, striking, typical, uncommon, unique.

distinguish verb 1 *Can you distinguish between butter and margarine?* SEE **choose**, decide, differentiate, discriminate, judge, make a distinction, separate, tell apart.
2 *In the dark we couldn't distinguish who she was.* ascertain, determine, discern, know, make out, perceive, pick out, recognize, see, single out, tell.

distinguished adjective 1 *distinguished work.* acclaimed, conspicuously good, SEE **excellent**, exceptional, first-rate, outstanding.
OPPOSITES: undistinguished, SEE **ordinary**.
2 *a distinguished actor.* celebrated, eminent, famed, famous, foremost, great, illustrious, important, leading, notable, noted, prominent, renowned, wellknown.
OPPOSITES: SEE **unknown**.

distort verb 1 *to distort a shape.* bend, buckle, contort, deform, twist, warp, wrench.
2 *to distort the truth.* exaggerate, falsify, garble, misrepresent, pervert, slant, twist.

distorted adjective *a distorted account of what happened.* biased, coloured, false, one-sided, perverted, prejudiced, slanted, twisted.

distract verb *Don't distract the driver.* bewilder, confuse, disconcert, divert, harass, perplex, puzzle, sidetrack, trouble, worry.

distracted adjective *distracted with grief.* SEE **sad**.

distraction noun 1 *The TV is a distraction when I'm working.* bewilderment, cause of confusion, SEE **distress** noun, interference, interruption, upset.
2 *He's always looking for some new distraction.* amusement, diversion, enjoyment, entertainment, fun, interest, pastime, pleasure, recreation.
3 *The ants tormented me to distraction.* delirium, frenzy, insanity, madness.

distraught adjective SEE **agitated, sad.**

distress noun *It was painful to see her distress.* adversity, affliction, anguish, anxiety, danger, desolation, difficulty, discomfort, dismay, fright, grief, heartache, misery, pain, poverty, privation, sadness, sorrow, suffering, torment, tribulation, trouble, worry, wretchedness.

distress verb *The bad news distressed us.* afflict, alarm, bother, [*informal*] cut up, dismay, disturb, frighten, grieve, harrow, hurt, make miserable, pain, perplex, perturb, sadden, scare, shake, shock, terrify, torment, torture, trouble, upset, worry, wound.
OPPOSITES: SEE **comfort** verb.

distribute verb 1 *They distributed free samples.* allocate, allot, assign, circulate, deal out, deliver, [*informal*] dish out, dispense, dispose of, divide out, [*informal*] dole out, give out, hand round, issue, mete out, share out, take round.
2 *Distribute the seeds evenly.* arrange, disperse, disseminate, scatter, spread, strew.

district noun *a rural district. an urban district.* area, community, locality, neighbourhood, parish, part, province, quarter (*of a town*), region, sector, vicinity, ward, zone.

distrust verb *I distrust dogs that bark.* be sceptical about, be wary of, disbelieve, doubt, have misgivings about, have qualms about, mistrust, question, suspect.
OPPOSITES: SEE **trust** verb.

distrustful adjective SEE **suspicious.**

disturb verb 1 *Don't disturb her if she's asleep.* agitate, alarm, annoy, bother, discompose, disrupt, distract, distress, excite, fluster, frighten, perturb, pester, ruffle, scare, shake, startle, stir up, trouble, unsettle, upset, worry.
2 *Don't disturb the papers on my desk.* confuse, disorder, [*informal*] mess about with, move, muddle, rearrange, reorganize.

disturbance noun *a disturbance in the street.* SEE **commotion.**

disunited adjective *The committee was disunited on the main issue.* divided, polarized, split.
OPPOSITES: SEE **united.**

disunity noun difference of opinion, disagreement, division, polarization.
OPPOSITES: SEE **solidarity.**

disused adjective *a disused railway line.* abandoned, closed, dead, discarded, discontinued, idle, neglected, obsolete, superannuated, unused, withdrawn.

OPPOSITES: SEE **operational.**

ditch noun *a drainage ditch.* aqueduct, channel, dike, drain, gully, gutter, moat, trench, watercourse.

ditch verb [*informal*] *We ditched the idea.* SEE **abandon.**

dither verb SEE **hesitate.**

ditty noun SEE **song.**

diurnal adjective daily.

divan noun SEE **bed.**

dive verb *to dive into water. to dive down.* crash-dive, descend, dip, drop, fall, go diving [SEE **diving**], go under, jump, leap, nosedive, pitch, plummet, plunge, sink, submerge, subside, swoop.

diver noun frogman, scuba-diver.

diverge noun 1 *to diverge from the path.* branch, deviate, divide, fork, go off at a tangent, part, radiate, separate, split.
2 *Our views diverge.* SEE **differ.**

diverse adjective SEE **various.**

diversify verb *The shop has diversified into a wider range of goods.* branch out, expand, spread out.

diversion noun 1 *a traffic diversion.* detour, deviation.
2 *We organized diversions for the guests.* amusement, distraction, entertainment, game, hobby, pastime, play, recreation, relaxation, sport.

diversity noun SEE **variety.**

divert verb 1 *They diverted the plane to another airport.* change direction, redirect, re-route, shunt (*a train*), switch.
2 *She diverted us with funny stories.* amuse, cheer up, delight, distract, entertain, keep happy, recreate, regale.

diverting adjective SEE **funny.**

divest verb SEE **strip** verb.

divide verb 1 *The path divides. We divided into two groups.* branch, break up, diverge, fork, move apart, part, polarize, split.
OPPOSITES: SEE **converge.**
2 *We divided the food between us.* allocate, allot, apportion, deal out, dispense, distribute, give out, halve, parcel out, pass round, share out.
OPPOSITES: SEE **gather.**
3 *I divided the potatoes according to size.* arrange, categorize, classify, grade, group, sort out, separate, subdivide.
OPPOSITES: SEE **mix.**

dividend noun interest, SEE **money.**

dividers noun compasses.

divine adjective *divine beings.* angelic, celestial, god-like, heavenly, holy, immortal, mystical, religious, sacred, spiritual, superhuman, supernatural, transcendental.

divine verb SEE **guess** verb.

diving noun deep-sea diving, scuba diving, snorkelling, subaqua swimming.

divinity noun 1 SEE **god**.
2 *the study of divinity.* religion, religious studies, theology.

division noun 1 *the division of land into building plots.* allocation, apportionment, cutting up, dividing, partition, splitting.
2 *a division of opinion.* disagreement, discord, disunity, feud, SEE **quarrel** noun, rupture, schism (*in the church*), split.
3 *a box with divisions for various tools.* compartment, part, section, segment.
4 *a division between two rooms or territories.* boundary, demarcation, divider, dividing wall, fence, partition, screen.
5 *a division of an organization.* branch, department, section, subdivision, unit.

divorce noun *Their marriage ended in divorce.* annulment, [*informal*] break-up, [*formal*] decree nisi, separation, [*informal*] split-up.

divorce verb SEE **separate** verb.
to be divorced annul a marriage, dissolve a marriage, part, separate, [*informal*] split up.

divulge verb SEE **reveal**.

dizziness noun faintness, giddiness, vertigo.

dizzy adjective *I feel dizzy when I look from a height.* bewildered, confused, dazed, faint, giddy, light-headed, muddled, reeling, shaky, swimming, unsteady.

do verb [The verb *do* can mean many things. The words given here are only a few of the synonyms you could use.] 1 *to do a job.* accomplish, achieve, carry out, commit, complete, execute, finish, fulfil, organize, perform, undertake.
2 *to do the garden.* arrange, attend to, cope with, deal with, handle, look after, manage, work at.
3 *to do sums.* answer, give your mind to, puzzle out, solve, think out, work out.
4 *to do good.* bring about, cause, effect, implement, initiate, instigate, produce, result in.
5 *Will £10 do?* be acceptable, be enough, be satisfactory, be sufficient, be suitable, satisfy, serve, suffice.
6 *Do as you like.* act, behave, conduct yourself, perform.
7 [*informal*] *The rotten cheat did me!* SEE **swindle** verb.
to do away with SEE **abolish**.
to do up SEE **decorate**, **fasten**.

docile adjective *a docile animal.* SEE **obedient**.

dock noun PLACES WHERE SHIPS UNLOAD, ETC.: berth, boat-yard, dockyard, dry-dock, harbour, haven, jetty, landing-stage, marina, pier, port, quay, slipway, wharf.

dock verb 1 *We can't land until the ship docks.* anchor, berth, drop anchor, moor, tie up.
2 *to dock a dog's tail.* SEE **cut** verb.
3 *to dock someone's wages.* SEE **reduce**.

docker noun stevedore.

docket noun SEE **label** noun.

doctor noun general practitioner, [*informal*] GP, medical officer or MO, medical practitioner, physician, [*uncomplimentary*] quack, surgeon.
OTHERS WHO LOOK AFTER OUR HEALTH: SEE **medicine**.

doctrinaire adjective SEE **dogmatic**.

doctrine noun *religious doctrines.* axiom, belief, conviction, creed, dogma, maxim, orthodoxy, precept, principle, teaching, tenet.

document noun VARIOUS DOCUMENTS: certificate, charter, deed, diploma, form, instrument, legal document, licence, manuscript or MS, passport, policy (*insurance policy*), print-out, record, typescript, visa, warrant, will.

documentary adjective 1 *documentary evidence.* authenticated, recorded, written.
2 *a documentary film.* factual, non-fiction.

doddery adjective SEE **old**.

dodge noun *a clever dodge.* device, knack, manœuvre, ploy, ruse, scheme, stratagem, trick, [*informal*] wheeze.

dodge verb 1 *to dodge a snowball.* avoid, duck, elude, evade, fend off, move out of the way of, swerve away from, turn away from, veer away from.
2 *to dodge work.* shirk, [*informal*] skive, [*informal*] wriggle out of.
3 *to dodge a question.* equivocate, fudge, hedge, side-step.

dodgems noun bumper cars.

dodgy adjective 1 [*informal*] *a dodgy customer.* SEE **cunning**.
2 [*informal*] *a dodgy problem.* SEE **difficult**.

dog noun bitch, [*childish*] bow-wow, [*uncomplimentary*] cur, dingo, hound, mongrel, pedigree, pup, puppy, whelp.
RELATED ADJECTIVES: canine, doglike.

SOME BREEDS OF DOG: Alsatian, basset, beagle, bloodhound, borzoi, boxer, bulldog, bull-terrier, cairn terrier, chihuahua, chow, cocker spaniel, collie, corgi, dachshund, Dalmatian, foxhound, foxterrier, Great Dane, greyhound, husky, Labrador, mastiff, Pekingese or Pekinese, Pomeranian, poodle, pug, retriever, Rottweiler, setter, sheepdog, spaniel, terrier, whippet.

dog verb SEE **follow**.

dogfight noun SEE **battle** noun.

dogged adjective SEE **determined**.

doggerel noun SEE **poem**.

dogma noun *religious dogma.* article of faith, belief, conviction, creed, doctrine, orthodoxy, precept, principle, teaching, tenet, truth.

dogmatic adjective *You won't argue him out of his dogmatic position.* assertive, authoritarian, authoritative, categorical, certain, dictatorial, doctrinaire, [*informal*] hard-line, hidebound, imperious, SEE **inflexible**, intolerant, legalistic, narrow-minded, obdurate, obstinate, opinionated, pontifical, positive.

OPPOSITES: SEE **open-minded**.

dogsbody noun SEE **servant**.

doldrums noun in the doldrums SEE **depressed**.

dole noun [*informal*] *living on the dole.* benefit, income support, social security, unemployment benefit.
on the dole SEE **unemployed**.

dole verb to dole out SEE **distribute**.

doleful adjective SEE **sad**.

doll noun cuddly toy, [*childish*] dolly, figure, [*racist*] golliwog, marionette, puppet, rag doll.

dollop noun SEE **mass** noun.

dolorous adjective SEE **sad**.

dolt noun SEE **idiot**.

domain noun 1 [*old-fashioned*] *the king's domain.* SEE **country**.
2 *the domain of science.* area, concern, field, speciality, sphere.

dome noun convex roof, cupola.

domed adjective SEE **convex**.

Several English words, including *domestic, domesticity,* and *domicile,* are related to Latin *domus* = home.

domestic adjective 1 *domestic arrangements.* family, household, in the home [SEE **home**], private.
OPPOSITES: SEE **public** adjective.
2 *domestic air services.* inland, internal, national.
OPPOSITES: SEE **foreign**.
3 *domestic animals.* SEE **domesticated**.
domestic science home economics.

domesticated adjective *domesticated animals.* house-trained, tame, tamed, trained.
OPPOSITES: SEE **wild**.

domesticity noun *a simple life of domesticity.* family life, home-making, housekeeping, staying at home.

domicile noun SEE **residence**.

dominant adjective 1 *a dominant influence. the dominant issues.* chief, commanding, dominating, influential, leading, main, major, powerful, predominant, presiding, prevailing, primary, principal, ruling, supreme, uppermost.
2 *a dominant feature in the landscape.* biggest, SEE **conspicuous**, eye-catching, highest, imposing, largest, obvious, outstanding, tallest, widespread.

dominate verb 1 *The captain dominated the game.* be the dominant person in [SEE **dominant**], control, direct, govern, influence, lead, manage, master, monopolize, rule, take control of, tyrannize.
2 *A castle dominates our town.* be the dominant thing in [SEE **dominant**], dwarf, look down on, overshadow, tower over.

domineering adjective *a domineering person.* SEE **tyrannical**.

dominion noun SEE **territory**.

don noun *an Oxford don.* SEE **lecturer**.

don verb *to don a disguise.* clothe yourself in, dress in, put on, wear.

donate verb SEE **give**.

donation noun SEE **gift**.

donkey noun jackass, [*informal*] jenny.

donkey-work noun SEE **work** noun.

donor noun *a donor to a charity.* benefactor, contributor, giver, philanthropist, provider, sponsor.
OPPOSITES: SEE **recipient**.

doodle verb SEE **draw** verb, scribble.

doom noun 1 *It is his doom to suffer.* SEE **fate**.
2 *She faced her doom bravely.* SEE **end** noun.

doomed adjective 1 *All mortals are doomed to die.* condemned, fated, intended.

2 *The voyage was doomed from the start.* accursed, bedevilled, hopeless, ill-fated, ill-starred, luckless.

doomsday noun apocalypse, end of the world, judgement day.

door noun barrier, doorway, [*informal*] SEE **entrance** noun, SEE **exit**, French window, gate, gateway, opening, portal, postern, revolving door, swing door.

dope noun **1** [*informal*] *addicted to dope.* SEE **drug** noun.
2 [*informal*] *You silly dope!* SEE **idiot**.

dope verb *to dope a horse.* SEE **drug** verb.

dopey adjective SEE **silly, sleepy**.

Several English words, including *dormant* and *dormitory,* are related to Latin *dormire* = to sleep.

---

dormant adjective **1** *Many living things are dormant in winter.* asleep, comatose, hibernating, resting, sleeping.
OPPOSITES: SEE **awake**.
2 *a dormant illness. a dormant volcano.* inactive, inert, latent, passive, quiescent, quiet.
OPPOSITES: SEE **active**.

dormitory noun bedroom, sleeping-quarters.
OTHER ROOMS: SEE **room**.

dose noun *a dose of medicine.* dosage, measure, portion, prescribed amount, quantity.

dose verb SEE **drug** verb.

doss verb SEE **sleep** verb.

dossier noun *a secret dossier.* file, folder, records, set of documents.

dot noun *Join up the dots.* full stop, mark, point, speck, spot.

dot verb *Sheep dot the hillside.* fleck, mark with dots, punctuate, scatter with dots, speckle, spot.

dotage noun SEE **old (old age)**.

dote verb SEE **love** verb.

dotty adjective SEE **silly**.

double adjective *a double railway-track.* doubled, dual, [*in music*] duple, duplicated, paired, twin, twofold.
double Dutch SEE **nonsense**.
double glazing SEE **window**.

double noun *I saw your double in town.* clone, copy, duplicate, [*informal*] look-alike, [*informal*] spitting image, twin.

double verb *We must double our efforts.* duplicate, increase, multiply by two, reduplicate, repeat.

to double back backtrack, do a U-turn, retrace your steps, return, turn back.
to double up *She doubled up with pain.* bend over, collapse, crumple up, fold over, fold up.

double-cross verb SEE **betray**.

double-decker noun SEE **bus**.

doublet noun SEE **coat** noun.

doubt noun **1** *I had my doubts.* agnosticism [= *religious doubts*], anxiety, cynicism, disbelief, distrust, fear, hesitation, incredulity, indecision, misgiving, mistrust, qualm, reservation, scepticism, suspicion, worry.
OPPOSITE: SEE **confidence**.
2 *There's some doubt about the arrangements.* ambiguity, confusion, difficulty, dilemma, perplexity, problem, query, question, uncertainty.
OPPOSITES: SEE **certainty**.

doubt verb **1** *I doubt whether he can afford it.* be dubious about, feel uncertain about [SEE **uncertain**], hesitate, lack confidence.
OPPOSITE: be confident [SEE **confident**].
2 *I doubt her honesty.* be sceptical about, disbelieve, distrust, fear, mistrust, query, question, suspect.
OPPOSITES: SEE **trust** verb.

doubtful adjective **1** *I'm doubtful about her honesty.* agnostic, cynical, disbelieving, distrustful, dubious, hesitant, incredulous, sceptical, suspicious, uncertain, unclear, unconvinced, undecided, unsure.
OPPOSITES: SEE **certain**.
2 *a doubtful decision.* ambiguous, debatable, dubious, equivocal, [*informal*] iffy, inconclusive, problematical, questionable, suspect, vague, worrying.
OPPOSITES: SEE **clear** adjective, **indisputable**.
3 *a doubtful ally.* irresolute, uncommitted, unreliable, untrustworthy, vacillating, wavering.
OPPOSITES: SEE **dependable**.

douche noun shower.

dour adjective SEE **stern** adjective.

douse verb **1** *to douse with water.* SEE **drench**.
2 *to douse a light.* SEE **extinguish**.

dovetail verb SEE **fit** verb.

dowager noun SEE **woman**.

dowdy adjective *dowdy clothes.* colourless, dingy, drab, dull, [*informal*] frumpish, old-fashioned, shabby, [*informal*] sloppy, slovenly, [*informal*] tatty, unattractive, unstylish.
OPPOSITES: SEE **smart** adjective, **stylish**.

down adjective *You seem down today.* SEE **depressed**.

down noun *pillows filled with down.* feathers, fluff, fluffy material.

downcast adjective SEE **depressed**.

downfall noun SEE **ruin** noun.

downgrade verb SEE **demote**.

downhearted adjective SEE **depressed**.

downhill adjective SEE **downward**.

downpour noun SEE **rain** noun.

downright adjective *a downright lie.* SEE **categorical**.

downs noun SEE **hill**.

downstairs adjective *a downstairs room.* ground-floor, lower.

down-trodden adjective SEE **oppressed**.

downturn noun SEE **decline** noun.

downward adjective *a downward path.* descending, downhill, easy, falling, going down, slanting, sloping. OPPOSITES: SEE **upward**.

downy adjective *downy material.* feathery, fleecy, fluffy, furry, fuzzy, soft, velvety, woolly.

dowry noun SEE **money**.

doze verb SEE **sleep** verb.

drab adjective *drab colours.* cheerless, colourless, dingy, dismal, dowdy, dreary, dull, flat, gloomy, grey, grimy, lacklustre, shabby, sombre, unattractive, uninteresting. OPPOSITES: SEE **bright**.

Draconian adjective SEE **harsh**.

draft noun [Don't confuse with *draught.*] 1 *a draft of an essay.* first version, notes, outline, plan, rough version, sketch. 2 *a bank draft.* cheque, order, postal order.

draft verb 1 *to draft an essay.* outline, plan, prepare, sketch out, work out, write a draft of. 2 *to draft someone into the army.* SEE **conscript** verb.

drag verb 1 *The tractor dragged a load of logs.* draw, haul, lug, pull, tow, trail, tug. OPPOSITES: SEE **push**. 2 *Time drags if you're bored.* be boring, crawl, creep, go slowly, linger, loiter, lose momentum, move slowly, pass slowly. OPPOSITE: pass quickly.

dragon noun OTHER LEGENDARY CREATURES: SEE **legend**.

dragoon verb SEE **compel**.

drain noun *a drain to take away water.* channel, conduit, culvert, dike, ditch, SEE **drainage**, drainpipe, duct, gutter, outlet, pipe, sewer, trench, watercourse.

drain verb 1 *to drain marshland.* dry, dry out, remove water from. 2 *to drain oil from an engine.* bleed, clear, draw off, empty, remove, take off, tap. 3 *The water drained through the sieve.* leak out, ooze, seep, strain, trickle. 4 *The exercise drained my energy.* consume, deplete, SEE **exhaust** verb, sap, spend, use up.

drainage noun *mains drainage.* sanitation, sewage system, sewers, waste disposal.

drake noun SEE **duck** noun.

drama noun 1 *theatrical drama.* acting, dramatics, histrionics, improvisation, SEE **literature**, melodrama, play, show, stagecraft, SEE **theatre**, theatricals. 2 *a real-life drama.* action, crisis, SEE **excitement**, suspense, turmoil.

dramatic adjective 1 *a dramatic performance.* SEE **theatrical**. 2 *a dramatic rescue.* SEE **exciting**.

dramatist noun playwright. OTHER WRITERS: SEE **writer**.

dramatization noun *dramatization of a novel.* screenplay, script, stage or TV version.

dramatize verb 1 *to dramatize a novel for TV.* adapt, make into a play, rewrite, write a dramatization [SEE **dramatization**]. 2 *Don't dramatize a quite ordinary event.* exaggerate, make too much of, overdo, overstate.

drape verb SEE **cover** verb.

drastic adjective *a drastic remedy.* desperate, dire, extreme, harsh, severe.

draught noun [Don't confuse with *draft.*] 1 *a draught of air.* breeze, current, movement, puff, wind. 2 *a draught of ale.* drink, pull, swallow.

draughtsman, draughtswoman nouns OTHER ARTISTS AND CRAFTSMEN: SEE **artist**.

draughty adjective SEE **cold** adjective, windy.

draw noun *a prize draw.* competition, lottery, raffle.

draw verb 1 *The horse drew the cart.* drag, haul, lug, pull, tow, tug. 2 *to draw a big crowd.* allure, attract, bring in, coax, entice, invite, lure, persuade, pull in, win over. 3 *to draw a tooth. to draw money from a bank. to draw a sword.* extract, remove, take out, unsheathe (*a sword*), withdraw. 4 *to draw names from a hat.* choose, pick, select.

5 *to draw a diagram.* depict, doodle, map out, mark out, outline, paint, pen, pencil, portray, represent, sketch, trace.
6 *to draw a conclusion.* arrive at, come to, deduce, formulate, infer, work out.
7 *The two teams drew 1–1.* be equal, finish equal, tie.
to draw out *to draw out chewing-gum. to draw out a conversation.* elongate, extend, lengthen, make longer, prolong, stretch.
to draw up 1 *The bus drew up.* brake, halt, pull up, stop.
2 *The lawyer drew up a contract.* compose, make, prepare, write out.
3 *I drew myself up.* make yourself tall, stand erect, stand straight, stand upright, straighten up.

drawback noun SEE **disadvantage**.

drawers noun [*old-fashioned*] bloomers, briefs, knickers, panties, pants, underpants.

drawing noun cartoon, design, graphics, illustration, outline, SEE **picture** noun, sketch.

drawing-room noun living-room, lounge, sitting-room.
OTHER ROOMS: SEE **room**.

drawl verb SEE **speak**.

drawn adjective *She looked drawn.* SEE **strained**.

dray noun SEE **cart**.

dread noun, verb SEE **fear** noun, verb.

dreadful adjective **1** *a dreadful accident.* alarming, appalling, awful, dire, distressing, fearful, frightening, frightful, ghastly, grisly, gruesome, harrowing, horrible, horrifying, indescribable, monstrous, shocking, terrible, tragic, unspeakable, upsetting.
2 [*informal*] *dreadful weather.* SEE **bad**.

dream noun **1** *Odd things happen in dreams.* delusion, fantasy, hallucination, illusion, nightmare, reverie, trance, vision.
2 *a dream of fame and riches.* ambition, aspiration, day-dream, ideal, pipe-dream, wish.

dream verb *I dreamed I could fly.* day-dream, fancy, fantasize, hallucinate, have a vision, imagine, think.
to dream up SEE **invent**.

dreary adjective SEE **boring, gloomy**.

dredge verb **to dredge up** SEE **discover**.

dregs noun *dregs at the bottom of a cup.* deposit, grounds (*of coffee*), lees (*of wine*), remains, sediment.

drench verb *The rain drenched us.* douse, drown, flood, inundate, saturate, soak, souse, steep, wet thoroughly.

dress noun **1** *formal dress.* apparel, attire, SEE **clothes**, clothing, costume, garb, garments, [*informal*] gear, outfit, [*old-fashioned*] raiment.
2 *a woman's dress.* frock, gown, robe, shift.

dress verb **1** *Dad dressed the children.* attire, clothe, cover, provide clothes for, put clothes on.
OPPOSITES: SEE **undress**.
2 *A nurse dressed my wound.* attend to, bandage, bind up, care for, put a dressing on, tend, treat.

dresser noun SEE **cupboard**.

dressing **1** *a dressing on a wound.* bandage, compress, plaster, poultice.
2 *salad dressing.* French dressing, mayonnaise.

dressing-gown noun housecoat, négligé.

dressmaker noun couturier, seamstress.

dribble verb **1** *He dribbled over his food.* drool, slaver, slobber.
2 *Rain dribbled down the window.* drip, flow, leak, ooze, run, seep, trickle.

drier noun airer, spin-drier, tumble-drier, wringer.

drift noun **1** *a drift of snow.* accumulation, bank, heap, mound, pile, ridge.
2 *the drift of a speech.* SEE **gist**.

drift verb **1** *The boat drifted downstream.* be carried, coast, float, move slowly.
2 *We had nowhere to go, so we drifted about.* meander, move casually, ramble, stray, walk aimlessly, wander.
3 *The snow drifted.* accumulate, gather, make drifts, pile up.

drill noun **1** *military drill.* discipline, exercise, instruction, practice, [*slang*] square-bashing, training.
2 [*informal*] *You know the drill.* SEE **routine**.
3 *Sow the seeds in a drill.* SEE **furrow**.

drill verb **1** *to drill through something.* bore, penetrate, perforate, pierce.
2 *to drill soldiers.* discipline, exercise, instruct, rehearse, train.

drink noun alcohol, beverage, [*informal*] bevvy, [*informal*] booze, [*joking*] grog, [*informal*] gulp, liquor, [*informal*] nightcap, [*informal*] nip, [*often plural*] refreshment. sip, swallow, swig, [*joking*] tipple (*What's your tipple?*).

SOME NON-ALCOHOLIC DRINKS: barley-water, cocoa, coffee, cordial, juice, lemonade, lime-juice, milk, mineral water, nectar, orangeade, pop, sherbet, soda-water, squash, tea, water.

SOME ALCOHOLIC DRINKS: ale, beer, bourbon, brandy, champagne, chartreuse, cider, cocktail, Cognac, crème de menthe, gin, Kirsch, lager, mead, perry, [*informal*] plonk, port, punch, rum, schnapps, shandy, sherry, vermouth, vodka, whisky, wine.

CONTAINERS YOU DRINK FROM: beaker, cup, glass, goblet, mug, tankard, tumbler, wine-glass.

drink verb [*informal*] booze, gulp, guzzle, [*formal*] imbibe, [*informal*] knock back, lap, partake of, [*old-fashioned*] quaff, sip, suck, swallow, swig, [*informal*] swill.

drip noun *a drip of oil.* bead, dribble, drop, leak, splash, spot, sprinkling, trickle.

drip verb *Water dripped into the basin.* dribble, drizzle, drop, fall in drips, leak, plop, splash, sprinkle, trickle, weep.

dripping noun SEE **fat** noun.

drive noun 1 *a drive in the country.* excursion, jaunt, journey, outing, ride, run, trip.
2 *the drive to succeed.* ambition, determination, energy, enterprise, enthusiasm, initiative, keenness, motivation, persistence, [*informal*] push, zeal.
3 *a publicity drive.* campaign, crusade, effort.

drive verb 1 *to drive a spade into the ground.* bang, dig, hammer, hit, impel, knock, plunge, prod, push, ram, sink, stab, strike, thrust.
2 *to drive someone to take action.* coerce, compel, constrain, force, oblige, press, urge.
3 *to drive a car. to drive sheep.* control, direct, guide, handle, herd, manage, pilot, propel, send, steer.

to drive out SEE **expel**.

drivel noun SEE **nonsense**.

driver noun chauffeur, motorist.

drizzle noun SEE **rain** noun.

droll adjective SEE **funny**.

dromedary noun camel.

drone noun VARIOUS SOUNDS: SEE **sound** noun.

droop verb *The flag drooped.* be limp, bend, dangle, fall, flop, hang, sag, slump, wilt, wither.

drop noun 1 *a drop of liquid.* bead, blob, bubble, dab, drip, droplet, globule, pearl, spot, tear.
2 *a drop of whisky.* dash, [*informal*] nip, small quantity, [*informal*] tot.
3 *a drop of 2 metres.* descent, dive, fall, plunge, SEE **precipice**.

4 *a drop in prices.* cut, decrease, reduction, slump.

OPPOSITES: SEE **rise** noun.

drop verb 1 *to drop to the ground.* collapse, descend, dip, dive, fall, go down, jump down, lower, nosedive, plummet, [*informal*] plump, plunge, sink, slump, subside, swoop, tumble.
2 *to drop someone from a team.* eliminate, exclude, leave out, omit.
3 *to drop a friend.* abandon, desert, [*informal*] dump, forsake, give up, jilt, leave, reject.
4 *to drop a plan.* discard, scrap, shed.

to drop behind SEE **lag**.

to drop in on SEE **visit** verb.

to drop off SEE **sleep** verb.

droppings noun SEE **excreta**.

dross noun SEE **rubbish**.

drown verb 1 *The flood drowned everything in the area.* SEE **flood** verb, **kill**.
2 *The music drowned our conversation.* be louder than, overpower, overwhelm, silence.

drowse verb SEE **sleep** verb.

drowsy adjective SEE **sleepy**.

drubbing noun SEE **defeat** noun.

drudge noun SEE **servant**.

drudgery noun SEE **work** noun.

drug noun 1 *a medicinal drug.* cure, medicament, medication, medicine, painkiller, [*old-fashioned*] physic, remedy, sedative, stimulant, tonic, tranquillizer, treatment.
2 *an addictive drug.* [*informal*] dope, narcotic, opiate.

VARIOUS DRUGS: barbiturate, caffeine, cannabis, cocaine, digitalis, hashish, heroin, insulin, laudanum, marijuana, morphia, nicotine, opium, phenobarbitone, quinine.

drug verb anaesthetize, [*informal*] dope, dose, give a drug to, [*informal*] knock out, medicate, poison, stupefy, treat.

Druid noun SEE **priest**.

drum noun 1 VARIOUS DRUMS: bass-drum, bongo-drums, kettledrum, side-drum, snare-drum, tambour, tenor-drum, [*plural*] timpani, tom-tom.
OTHER PERCUSSION INSTRUMENTS: SEE **percussion**.
2 *a drum of oil.* SEE **barrel**.

drunk adjective *The revellers got drunk.* delirious, fuddled, inebriated, intoxicated, over-excited, riotous, uncontrollable, unruly.

SOME OF THE MANY SLANG SYNONYMS ARE: blotto, boozed-up, canned, legless, merry, paralytic, pickled, plastered, sozzled, tiddly, tight, tipsy.
OPPOSITES: SEE **sober**.

drunkard noun alcoholic, [*informal*] boozer, dipsomaniac, drunk, [*informal*] tippler, toper, [*slang*] wino.
OPPOSITES: SEE **teetotaller**.

drunken adjective *drunken revellers*. [*informal*] boozy, SEE **drunk**, inebriate, inebriated, intoxicated.
OPPOSITES: SEE **sober, teetotal**.

dry adjective 1 *dry desert*. arid, barren, dehydrated, desiccated, moistureless, parched, thirsty, waterless.
OPPOSITES: SEE **wet** adjective.
2 *dry wine*. OPPOSITE: sweet.
3 *a dry book*. boring, dreary, dull, tedious, tiresome, uninteresting.
OPPOSITES: SEE **interesting**.
4 *a dry sense of humour*. [*informal*] deadpan, droll, expressionless, laconic, lugubrious, unsmiling.
OPPOSITES: SEE **lively**.

dry verb [Also **to dry out, to dry up**] become dry, dehumidify, dehydrate, desiccate, go hard, make dry, parch, shrivel, towel (*to towel yourself dry*), wilt, wither.
OPPOSITES: SEE **wet** verb.

dryness noun *the dryness of the desert*. aridity, barrenness, drought, thirst.

Several English words, including *dual, duel, duet, duologue, duplicate*, etc., are related to Latin *duo = two*.

---

dual adjective *dual controls*. binary, coupled, double, duplicate, linked, paired, twin.
dual carriageway SEE **road**.

dub verb 1 SEE **name** verb.
2 *to dub a sound track*. add, re-record, superimpose.

dubious adjective 1 *I was dubious about her honesty*. SEE **doubtful**.
2 *a dubious character*. [*informal*] fishy, [*informal*] shady, suspect, suspicious, unreliable, untrustworthy.

duck noun drake, duckling.

duck verb 1 *I ducked when he threw a stone*. avoid, bend, bob down, crouch, dip down, dodge, evade, sidestep, stoop, swerve, take evasive action.
2 *They ducked me in the pool*. immerse, plunge, push under, submerge.

duct noun SEE **channel** noun.

ductile adjective *ductile substances*. flexible, malleable, plastic, pliable, pliant, tractable, yielding.
OPPOSITES: SEE **brittle**.

dud adjective SEE **useless**.

dudgeon noun **in high dudgeon** SEE **indignant**.

due adjective 1 *Subscriptions are now due*. in arrears, outstanding, owed, owing, payable, unpaid.
2 *I gave the matter due consideration*. adequate, appropriate, decent, deserved, fitting, just, mature, merited, proper, requisite, right, rightful, sufficient, suitable, well-earned.
3 *Is the bus due?* expected, scheduled.

due noun *Give him his due*. deserts, entitlement, merits, reward, rights.
dues SEE **fee**.

duel noun, verb SEE **fight** noun, verb.

duet noun duo.

duffer noun SEE **idiot**.

dug-out noun canoe.

dulcet adjective SEE **sweet** adjective.

dull adjective 1 *dull colours*. dim, dingy, dowdy, drab, dreary, faded, flat, gloomy, lacklustre, lifeless, matt (*matt paint*), plain, shabby, sombre, subdued.
OPPOSITES: SEE **bright**.
2 *a dull sky*. cloudy, dismal, grey, heavy, leaden, murky, overcast, sullen, sunless.
OPPOSITES: SEE **clear** adjective.
3 *a dull sound*. deadened, indistinct, muffled, muted.
OPPOSITES: SEE **distinct**.
4 *a dull pupil*. dense, dim, dim-witted, obtuse, slow, SEE **stupid**, [*informal*] thick, unimaginative, unintelligent, unresponsive.
OPPOSITES: SEE **clever**.
5 *a dull edge to a knife*. blunt, blunted, unsharpened.
OPPOSITES: SEE **sharp**.
6 *a dull conversation*. boring, commonplace, dry, monotonous, prosaic, stodgy, tame, tedious, unexciting, uninteresting.
OPPOSITES: SEE **interesting**.

dull verb 1 *to dull a sound*. SEE **muffle**.
2 *to dull a pain*. SEE **relieve**.

dumb adjective 1 *dumb with amazement*. inarticulate, [*informal*] mum, mute, silent, speechless, tongue-tied, unable to speak.
2 [*informal*] *He's too dumb to understand*. SEE **stupid**.

dumbfounded adjective SEE **amazed**.

dummy noun 1 *The revolver was a dummy.* copy, counterfeit, duplicate, imitation, model, sham, substitute, toy.
2 *a ventriloquist's dummy.* doll, figure, manikin, puppet.
3 *a baby's dummy.* teat.
dummy run SEE **practice**.

dump noun 1 *a rubbish dump.* junk yard, rubbish-heap, tip.
2 *an ammunition dump.* cache, depot, hoard, store.

dump verb 1 *to dump rubbish.* discard, dispose of, [*informal*] ditch, get rid of, jettison, reject, scrap, throw away.
2 [*informal*] *Dump your things on the table.* deposit, drop, empty out, let fall, offload, [*informal*] park, place, put down, throw down, tip, unload.

dumps noun **in the dumps** SEE **depressed**.

dumpy adjective SEE **fat** adjective.

dun adjective SEE **brown** adjective.

dunce noun SEE **fool** noun.

dune noun *dunes behind the beach.* drift, hillock, hummock, mound, sand-dune.

dung noun SEE **excreta**, manure, muck.

dungeon noun [*old-fashioned*] gaol, lock-up, pit, prison, underground chamber, vault.

dunk verb SEE **dip** verb.

duo noun SEE **pair** noun.

duologue noun SEE **dialogue**.

dupe verb SEE **trick** verb.

duple adjective SEE **double** adjective.

duplicate adjective *a duplicate key.* alternative, copied, corresponding, identical, matching, second, twin.

duplicate noun *a duplicate of an original document.* carbon copy, clone, copy, double, facsimile, imitation, likeness, photocopy, photostat, replica, reproduction, twin, Xerox.

duplicate verb 1 *to duplicate documents.* copy, photocopy, print, reproduce, Xerox.
2 *If you both do it, you duplicate the work.* do again, double, repeat.

duplicator noun SEE **reprographics**.

duplicity noun SEE **deceit**.

durable adjective SEE **lasting**.

duration noun SEE **time** noun.

duress noun SEE **force** noun.

dusk noun evening, gloaming, gloom, sundown, sunset, twilight.
OPPOSITES: SEE **dawn**.

dusky adjective SEE **dark**.

dust noun *chalk dust.* dirt, grime, grit, particles, powder.

dust verb SEE **clean** verb.

dust-jacket noun SEE **cover** noun.

dusty adjective 1 *a dusty substance. dusty soil.* chalky, crumbly, dry, fine, friable, gritty, powdery, sandy, sooty.
OPPOSITES: SEE **solid, wet** adjective.
2 *a dusty room.* dirty, filthy, grimy, grubby, mucky, uncleaned, unswept.
OPPOSITE: SEE **clean** adjective.

dutiful adjective *a dutiful worker.* careful, compliant, conscientious, devoted, diligent, faithful, hard-working, loyal, obedient, punctilious, reliable, responsible, scrupulous, thorough, trustworthy.
OPPOSITES: SEE **irresponsible**.

duty noun 1 *a sense of duty towards your employer.* allegiance, faithfulness, loyalty, obedience, obligation, responsibility, service.
2 *household duties.* assignment, business, [*informal*] chore, function, job, office, role, task, work.
3 *customs duty.* charge, customs, dues, levy, tariff, tax, toll.

duvet noun SEE **bedclothes**.

dwarf adjective SEE **small**.

dwarf noun midget, pigmy.

dwarf verb *The elephant dwarfed the tortoise.* dominate, look bigger than, overshadow, tower over.

dwell verb **to dwell in** SEE **inhabit**.

dwelling noun SEE **house** noun.

dwindle verb SEE **decrease** verb.

dye noun, verb SEE **colour** noun, verb.

dying adjective declining, fading, moribund.
OPPOSITES: SEE **thriving**.

Several English words, including *dynamic, dynamite,* and *dynamo,* are related to Greek *dunamis = power.*

---

dynamic adjective *a dynamic leader.* active, committed, driving, energetic, enterprising, enthusiastic, forceful, [*informal*] go-ahead, [*uncomplimentary*] go-getting, highly motivated, lively, powerful, pushful, [*uncomplimentary*] pushy, spirited, vigorous.
OPPOSITES: SEE **apathetic**.

dynamite noun SEE **explosive** noun.

dynamo noun generator.

dynasty noun SEE **family**.

dyspepsia noun indigestion.

dyspeptic adjective SEE **irritable**.

E

eager adjective *an eager pupil. eager to hear the news.* agog, anxious (*anxious to please*), ardent, avid, bursting, committed, [*formal*] desirous, earnest, enthusiastic, excited, fervent, impatient, intent, interested, keen, [*informal*] keyed up, motivated, passionate, [*informal*] raring (*raring to go*), voracious, zealous.
OPPOSITES: SEE **apathetic.**

eagerness noun *I began the work with great eagerness.* alacrity, ardour, commitment, desire, earnestness, enthusiasm, excitement, fervour, impatience, intentness, interest, keenness, longing, motivation, passion, thirst (*thirst for knowledge*), zeal.

ear noun ear-drum, lobe.
RELATED ADJECTIVE [= *of hearing*]: aural.

early adjective **1** *early flowers.* advanced, first, forward.
OPPOSITES: SEE **late.**
COMPARE: punctual.
2 *an early baby.* premature.
OPPOSITES: SEE **overdue.**
3 *early civilizations. an early computer.* ancient, antiquated, SEE **old,** primitive.
OPPOSITES: SEE **advanced, recent.**

earliest adjective SEE **first.**

earmark verb SEE **reserve** verb.

earn verb **1** *to earn money.* [*informal*] bring in, [*informal*] clear (*He clears £300 a week*), fetch in, get, [*informal*] gross, make, net, obtain, realize, receive, [*informal*] take home, work for.
2 *to earn success.* attain, deserve, gain, merit, warrant, win.

earnest adjective **1** *an earnest request.* grave, heartfelt, impassioned, serious, sincere, solemn, thoughtful, well-meant.
OPPOSITES: SEE **casual, flippant.**
2 *an earnest worker.* committed, conscientious, determined, devoted, diligent, eager, hard-working, industrious, involved, purposeful.
OPPOSITES: SEE **casual, half-hearted.**

earnings noun SEE **pay** noun.

earth noun **1** *the planet Earth.* SEE **planet.**
2 *fertile earth.* clay, dirt, ground, humus, land, loam, soil, topsoil.

earthenware noun [*formal*] ceramics, china, crockery, [*informal*] crocks, porcelain, pots, pottery.

earthly adjective [Do not confuse with *earthy.*] *earthly pleasures.* human, materialistic, mundane, SEE **physical,** secular, temporal.
OPPOSITES: SEE **spiritual.**

earthquake noun quake, shock, tremor, upheaval.
RELATED ADJECTIVE: seismic.

earthy adjective [Do not confuse with *earthly.*] *an earthy sense of humour.* SEE **bawdy.**

ease noun **1** *The plumber did the job with ease.* dexterity, easiness, effortlessness, facility, nonchalance, simplicity, skill, speed, straightforwardness.
OPPOSITES: SEE **difficulty.**
2 *Now she's retired and leads a life of ease.* aplomb, calmness, comfort, composure, contentment, enjoyment, happiness, leisure, luxury, peace, quiet, relaxation, repose, rest, serenity, tranquillity.
OPPOSITES: SEE **stress** noun.

ease verb **1** *to ease pain.* allay, alleviate, assuage, calm, comfort, lessen, lighten, mitigate, moderate, pacify, quell, quieten, relieve, soothe, tranquillize.
OPPOSITES: SEE **aggravate.**
2 *to ease pressure or tension.* decrease, reduce, relax, slacken, take off.
OPPOSITES: SEE **increase** verb.
3 *to ease something into position.* edge, guide, inch, manœuvre, move gradually, slide, slip.
to ease off *The rain eased off.* SEE **lessen.**

easy adjective **1** *easy work.* [*informal*] cushy, effortless, light, painless, pleasant, undemanding.
OPPOSITES: SEE **difficult, heavy.**
2 *an easy machine to use. easy instructions to follow.* clear, elementary, facile, foolproof, [*informal*] idiot-proof, manageable, plain, simple, straightforward, uncomplicated, understandable, user-friendly.
OPPOSITES: SEE **complicated, difficult.**
3 *an easy person to get on with.* accommodating, affable, amenable, docile, SEE **easy-going,** friendly, informal, natural, open, tolerant, unexacting.
OPPOSITES: SEE **difficult, intolerant.**
4 *an easy life. easy conditions.* carefree, comfortable, contented, cosy, leisurely, peaceful, relaxed, relaxing, restful, serene, soft, tranquil, unhurried, untroubled.
OPPOSITES: SEE **stressful.**
free and easy SEE **easygoing.**

easygoing adjective *an easygoing attitude.* calm, carefree, SEE **casual,** cheerful, even-tempered, [*informal*] free and easy, genial, [*informal*] happy-go-lucky, indulgent, informal, [*informal*] laid-back, lax, lenient, liberal, nonchalant, patient, permissive, placid, relaxed, tolerant, unexcitable, unruffled.
OPPOSITES: SEE **strict, tense** adjective.

eat verb *to eat food.* consume, devour, digest, feed on, [*formal*] ingest, live on, [*old-fashioned*] partake of, swallow, take.

VARIOUS WAYS TO EAT: bite, bolt, champ, chew, crunch, gnaw, gobble, gorge yourself, gormandize, graze, gulp, guzzle, [*informal*] make a pig of yourself, [*formal*] masticate, munch, nibble, overeat, peck, [*informal*] scoff, [*informal*] slurp, [*informal*] stuff yourself, taste, [*informal*] tuck in, [*informal*] wolf it down.

TO EAT AT A PARTICULAR MEAL: banquet, breakfast, dine, feast, lunch, [*old-fashioned*] sup.

THINGS TO EAT: SEE **food**.

---

to eat away. *The river ate the bank away.* crumble, erode, wear away.
to eat into *Acid can eat into metal.* cause to decay, corrode, oxidize, rot, rust.

eatable adjective *Is the food eatable?* digestible, edible, fit to eat, good, palatable, safe to eat, wholesome.
OPPOSITES: SEE **inedible**.

eaves noun *the eaves of a roof.* edge, overhang.

eavesdrop verb SEE **listen**.

ebb verb 1 *The tide ebbed.* fall, flow back, go down, recede, retreat.
2 *Her strength ebbed.* SEE **weaken**.

ebullient adjective SEE **exuberant**.

eccentric adjective 1 *eccentric behaviour.* aberrant, abnormal, absurd, bizarre, cranky, curious, freakish, [*informal*] funny, grotesque, idiosyncratic, ludicrous, SEE **mad**, odd, outlandish, out of the ordinary, peculiar, preposterous, queer, quirky, ridiculous, singular, strange, unconventional, unusual, [*informal*] way-out, [*informal*] weird, [*informal*] zany.
OPPOSITES: SEE **conventional**.
2 *eccentric circles.* irregular, off-centre.
COMPARE: concentric.

eccentric noun [All these synonyms are used *informally*] character (*She's a bit of a character*), crackpot, crank, freak, oddity, weirdie, weirdo.

echo verb 1 *The sound echoed across the valley.* resound, reverberate, ring, sound again.
2 *The parrot echoed what I said.* ape, copy, imitate, mimic, reiterate, repeat, reproduce, say again.

eclectic adjective *eclectic tastes.* SEE **catholic**.

eclipse verb 1 *to eclipse a light.* block out, blot out, cloud, cover, darken, extinguish, obscure, veil.
2 *to eclipse someone else's achievement.* dim, excel, outdo, outshine, overshadow, put into the shade, surpass.

economic adjective [= *to do with economics.* Don't confuse with *economical.*] *economic affairs.* budgetary, business, financial, fiscal, monetary, money-making, trading.

economical adjective [= *to do with saving money.* Don't confuse with *economic.*]
1 *Cycling is more economical than going by bus.* careful, cost-effective, [*uncomplimentary*] SEE **miserly**, parsimonious, prudent, sparing, thrifty.
OPPOSITES: SEE **wasteful**.
2 *Beans make an economical meal.* cheap, [*informal*] cheese-paring, frugal, inexpensive, low-priced, reasonable.
OPPOSITES: SEE **expensive**.

economize verb *If you're poor you have to economize.* be economical [SEE **economical**], cut back, save, [*informal*] scrimp, skimp, spend less, [*informal*] tighten your belt.
OPPOSITES: SEE **squander**.

economy noun 1 *economy in the use of your money.* frugality, [*uncomplimentary*] meanness, [*uncomplimentary*] miserliness, parsimony, providence, prudence, thrift.
OPPOSITE: wastefulness.
2 *I cancelled the holiday as an economy.* cut (*a cut in expenditure*), saving.
3 *the national economy.* budget, economic affairs [SEE **economic**], wealth.

ecstasy noun *an ecstasy of pleasure.* bliss, SEE **delight** noun, delirium, elation, enthusiasm, euphoria, exaltation, fervour, frenzy, trance, [*old-fashioned*] transport.

ecstatic adjective *an ecstatic welcome.* blissful, delighted, delirious, elated, enraptured, enthusiastic, euphoric, exultant, fervent, frenzied, gleeful, SEE **happy**, joyful, overjoyed, [*informal*] over the moon, rapturous.

eddy noun *an eddy in the water.* circular movement, swirl, vortex, whirl, whirlpool.

eddy verb *The water eddied between the rocks.* move in circles, swirl, whirl.

edge noun 1 *the edge of a knife.* acuteness, keenness, sharpness.
2 *the edge of a cup.* brim, brink, lip, rim.
3 *the edge of an area.* border, boundary, circumference, frame, kerb (*of a street*), limit, margin, outline, outlying parts,

outskirts (*of a town*), perimeter, periphery, side, suburbs (*of a town*), verge.
4 *the edge of a dress.* edging, fringe, hem, selvage.

edge verb **1** *I edged the dress with lace.* bind, border, fringe, hem, make an edge for, trim.
2 *We edged away.* creep, inch, move stealthily, sidle, slink, steal.

edgy adjective SEE **nervous**.

edible adjective *I don't think conkers are edible.* digestible, eatable, fit to eat, good to eat, palatable, safe to eat, wholesome.
OPPOSITES: SEE **inedible**.

edict noun SEE **order** noun.

edifice noun SEE **building**.

edify verb SEE **educate**.

edit verb *to edit a film, book, etc.* adapt, alter, assemble, compile, get ready, modify, organize, prepare, put together, supervise the production of.

VARIOUS WAYS TO EDIT A PIECE OF WRITING, ETC.: abridge, amend, annotate, bowdlerize, censor, condense, correct, cut, dub (*sound*), emend, format, polish, proof-read, rearrange, rephrase, revise, rewrite, select, shorten, splice (*film*).

---

edition noun **1** *a Christmas edition of a magazine.* copy, issue, number.
2 *a first edition of a book.* impression, printing, publication, version.

educate verb *to educate people about hygiene. to educate students.* bring up, civilize, coach, counsel, discipline, drill, edify, guide, improve, indoctrinate, inform, instruct, lecture, rear, school, teach, train, tutor.

educated adjective *an educated person.* civilized, cultivated, cultured, enlightened, erudite, informed, knowledgeable, learned, literate, numerate, sophisticated, well-bred, well-read.

education noun coaching, curriculum, enlightenment, guidance, indoctrination, instruction, schooling, syllabus, teaching, training, tuition.

PLACES WHERE YOU ARE EDUCATED: academy, college, conservatory, kindergarten, play-group, polytechnic, SEE **school**, sixth-form college, tertiary college, university.

PEOPLE WHO EDUCATE: coach, counsellor, demonstrator, don, governess, guru, headteacher, instructor, lecturer, pedagogue, professor, SEE **teacher**, trainer, tutor.

---

eel noun elver [= *young eel*].

eerie adjective *eerie sounds in the night.* creepy, SEE **frightening**, ghostly, mysterious, [*informal*] scary, [*informal*] spooky, strange, uncanny, unearthly, unnatural, weird.

efface verb SEE **obliterate**.

effect noun **1** *One effect of overeating may be obesity.* aftermath, consequence, impact, influence, issue, outcome, repercussion, result, sequel, upshot.
2 *The rosy lighting gave an effect of warmth.* feeling, illusion, impression, sense.
to put into effect SEE **effect** verb.

effect verb [Do not confuse with *affect*.] *to effect changes.* achieve, bring about, bring in, carry out, cause, create, [*formal*] effectuate, enforce, execute, implement, initiate, make, put into effect.

effective adjective **1** *an effective cure for colds.* effectual, [*formal*] efficacious, efficient, potent, powerful, real, strong, worthwhile.
2 *an effective goalkeeper.* able, capable, competent, impressive, productive, proficient, successful, useful.
3 *an effective argument.* cogent, compelling, convincing, meaningful, persuasive, striking, telling.
OPPOSITES: SEE **ineffective**.

effectual adjective SEE **effective**.

effectuate verb SEE **effect** verb.

effeminate adjective [*Effeminate* and its synonyms have sexist overtones, and are usually uncomplimentary. Compare *feminine*.] *effeminate behaviour.* camp, effete, girlish, [*informal*] pansy, [*informal*] sissy, unmanly, weak, womanish.
OPPOSITES: SEE **manly**.

effervesce verb boil, bubble, ferment, fizz, foam, froth, sparkle.

effervescent adjective *effervescent drinks.* bubbling, bubbly, carbonated, fizzy, foaming, sparkling.

effete adjective SEE **effeminate**, **feeble**.

efficacious adjective SEE **efficient**.

efficient adjective *an efficient worker. an efficient use of resources.* able, capable, competent, cost-effective, economic, effective, effectual, efficacious, impressive, productive, proficient, successful, thrifty, useful.
OPPOSITES: SEE **inefficient**.

effigy noun SEE **sculpture** noun.

effluent noun SEE **sewage**.

effort noun 1 *strenuous effort.* diligence, endeavour, exertion, industry, labour, pains, strain, stress, striving, struggle, toil, [*old-fashioned*] travail, trouble, work.
2 *a real effort to win.* attempt, endeavour, go, try.
3 *She congratulated us on a good effort.* accomplishment, achievement, feat, job, outcome, product, production, result.

effortless adjective SEE **easy**.

effrontery noun SEE **insolence**.

effusion noun SEE **flow** noun.

effusive adjective SEE **demonstrative**.

egalitarian adjective *egalitarian views.* democratic, populist.
OPPOSITES: SEE **élitist**.

egg verb **to egg on** SEE **encourage**.

egghead noun SEE **intellectual** noun.

egocentric adjective SEE **selfish**.

egoism noun egocentricity, self-centredness, self-importance, selfishness, self-love, self-regard.

egotism noun SEE **pride**.

egotistical adjective SEE **conceited**.

egregious adjective SEE **bad**.

egress noun SEE **exit** noun.

eiderdown noun duvet, quilt.
OTHER BEDCLOTHES: SEE **bedclothes**.

ejaculate verb 1 SEE **speak**.
2 SEE **eject**.

eject verb 1 *to eject someone from a building or country.* banish, [*informal*] boot out, deport, discharge, dismiss, drive out, evict, exile, expel, get rid of, [*informal*] kick out, oust, remove, sack, send out, throw out, turn out.
2 *to eject smoke or liquid.* belch, discharge, disgorge, ejaculate [= *eject semen*], emit, spew, spout, vomit.

eke verb **to eke out** *to eke out a food supply.* economize on, ration, spin out, stretch out, supplement.

elaborate adjective 1 *an elaborate plan.* complex, complicated, detailed, intricate, involved, thorough, well worked out.
2 *elaborate carvings.* baroque, decorative, fancy, fantastic, fussy, grotesque, intricate, ornamental, ornate, rococo, showy.
OPPOSITES: SEE **simple**.

elaborate verb *to elaborate a simple story.* add to, amplify, complicate, decorate, develop, embellish, expand, expatiate on, fill out, give details of, improve on, ornament.
OPPOSITES: SEE **simplify**.

elapse verb *Many days elapsed before we met again.* go by, lapse, pass.

elastic adjective *elastic material.* bendy, ductile, flexible, plastic, pliable, pliant, rubbery, [*informal*] springy, [*informal*] stretchy, yielding.
OPPOSITES: SEE **brittle, rigid**.

elated adjective SEE **ecstatic**.

elder noun SEE **official** noun.

elderly adjective SEE **old**.

elect adjective [Note: *elect* goes *after* the noun it describes.] *the president elect.* [also going *after* the noun] designate, to be; [going *before* the noun] chosen, elected [SEE **elect** verb], prospective.

elect verb *to elect a leader.* adopt, appoint, choose, name, nominate, opt for, pick, select, vote for.

election noun *the election of a leader.* ballot, choice, poll, selection, vote.

electioneering noun campaigning.

electorate noun constituents, electors, voters.

electric adjective 1 *an electric motor.* SEE **electrical**.
2 *an electric performance.* SEE **electrifying**.

electrical adjective *electrical equipment.* battery-operated, electric, mains-operated.

SOME ITEMS OF ELECTRICAL EQUIPMENT: accumulator, adaptor, battery, bell, bulb, cable, capacitor, charger, circuit, dynamo, electric heater, electric motor, electrode, electromagnet, electrometer, electrophorus, electroscope, element, flex, fuse, generator, insulation, lead, light, meter, plug, power-point, socket, switch, terminal, torch, transformer, wiring.

electrician noun electrical engineer.

electricity noun *Is the electricity on?* current, power, power supply.

electrifying adjective *an electrifying performance.* amazing, astonishing, astounding, electric, exciting, hair-raising, stimulating, thrilling.

electrocute verb SEE **kill**.

elegant adjective *an elegant building. elegant clothes.* artistic, SEE **beautiful**, chic, courtly, dignified, fashionable, graceful, gracious, handsome, modish, noble, [*informal*] posh, refined, smart, sophisticated, splendid, stately, stylish, tasteful.
OPPOSITES: SEE **inelegant**.

elegy noun dirge, lament, requiem.

element noun 1 *an element of truth in her story.* component, constituent, factor, feature, fragment, hint, ingredient, part, small amount, trace.
2 *Ducks are in their element swimming in a pond.* domain, environment, habitat, sphere.
elements 1 *We battled against the elements.* SEE **weather** noun.
2 *the elements of a subject.* SEE **rudiments**.
3 CHEMICAL ELEMENTS: SEE **chemical**.

elementary adjective *an elementary problem.* basic, early, SEE **easy**, first (*the first stages*), fundamental, initial, primary, principal, rudimentary, simple, straightforward, uncomplicated.
OPPOSITES: SEE **advanced, complex**.

elephantine adjective SEE **large**.

elevate verb SEE **raise**.

elevated adjective SEE **high**.

elevator noun hoist, lift.

elicit verb [Do not confuse with *illicit.*] *to elicit information.* derive, draw out, extort, extract, SEE **obtain**.

eligible adjective *eligible to apply for a job.* acceptable, allowed, appropriate, authorized, competent, equipped, fit, proper, qualified, suitable, worthy.
OPPOSITES: SEE **ineligible**.

eliminate verb 1 *to eliminate mistakes. to eliminate ants from your garden.* abolish, annihilate, delete, destroy, dispense with, do away with, eject, end, eradicate, exterminate, finish off, get rid of, SEE **kill**, put an end to, remove, stamp out.
2 *Our team was eliminated from the competition.* cut out, drop, exclude, knock out, leave out, omit, reject.

élite noun *These experienced workers are the élite of their profession.* aristocracy, the best, first-class people, flower, meritocracy, nobility, top people.

élitist adjective SEE **snobbish**.

elixir noun SEE **essence, remedy** noun.

elocution noun SEE **speech**.

elongate verb SEE **lengthen**.

elope verb SEE **run** verb (**to run away**).

eloquent adjective [See note at *loquacious.*] *an eloquent speaker.* articulate, expressive, fluent, forceful, [*uncomplimentary*] glib, moving, persuasive, plausible, powerful, unfaltering.
OPPOSITES: SEE **inarticulate**.

elucidate verb SEE **clarify, explain**.

elude verb *to elude capture.* avoid, circumvent, dodge, escape, evade, foil, get away from.

elusive adjective 1 *an elusive criminal.* [*informal*] always on the move, evasive, fugitive, hard to find.
2 *The poem's meaning is elusive.* ambiguous, baffling, deceptive, hard to pin down, indefinable, puzzling, shifting.

emaciated adjective *emaciated bodies.* anorectic, bony, cadaverous, gaunt, haggard, skeletal, skinny, starved, SEE **thin** adjective, undernourished, wasted away.

emanate verb SEE **originate**.

emancipate verb *to emancipate slaves.* deliver from slavery, discharge, enfranchise, free, give rights to, liberate, release, set free.
OPPOSITES: SEE **enslave**.

emasculate verb SEE **weaken**.

embalm verb SEE **preserve** verb.

embankment noun bank, causeway, dam, earthwork, mound, rampart.

embargo noun SEE **ban** noun.

embark verb 1 *to embark on a ship.* board, depart, go aboard, leave, set out.
OPPOSITES: SEE **disembark**.
2 *to embark on a project.* begin, commence, start, undertake.

embarrass verb *They embarrassed me by telling everyone my secret.* chagrin, confuse, disconcert, disgrace, distress, fluster, humiliate, make (someone) blush, make (someone) feel embarrassed [SEE **embarrassed**], mortify, [*informal*] put (someone) on the spot, shame, upset.

embarrassed adjective *an embarrassed silence.* abashed, ashamed, awkward, bashful, confused, disconcerted, distressed, flustered, humiliated, mortified, [*informal*] red in the face, self-conscious, shamed, shy, uncomfortable, upset.

embarrassing adjective *an embarrassing mistake.* awkward, disconcerting, distressing, humiliating, shameful, touchy, tricky, uncomfortable, uneasy, upsetting.

embassy noun *a foreign embassy.* consulate, delegation, legation, mission.

embed verb SEE **fix** verb, **insert**.

embellish verb SEE **ornament** verb.

embers noun ashes, cinders, coals.

embezzle verb *to embezzle funds.* appropriate, misappropriate, SEE **steal**, take fraudulently.

embezzlement noun *embezzlement of funds.* appropriation, fraud, misappropriation, stealing, theft.

embittered adjective *embittered by failure.* bitter, disillusioned, envious, resentful, sour.

emblazon verb SEE **ornament** verb.

emblem noun *The olive branch is an emblem of peace.* badge, crest, device, image, insignia, mark, regalia, seal, sign, symbol, token.

embody verb SEE **include.**

embolden verb SEE **encourage.**

embolism noun *a pulmonary embolism.* clot, obstruction, thrombosis.

emboss verb SEE **ornament** verb.

embrace verb 1 *She embraced him lovingly.* clasp, cling to, cuddle, enfold, fondle, grasp, hold, hug, kiss, snuggle up to.
2 *She's quick to embrace new ideas.* accept, espouse, receive, take on, welcome.
3 *The syllabus embraces all aspects of the subject.* bring together, comprise, embody, enclose, gather together, include, incorporate, involve, take in.

embrasure noun SEE **window.**

embrocation noun liniment, lotion, ointment, salve.

embroider verb SEE **ornament** verb.

embroidery noun needlework, sewing, tapestry.

embroil verb *Don't get embroiled in an argument.* SEE **involve.**

embryo noun foetus.

embryonic adjective *an embryonic organism. an embryonic idea.* early, immature, just beginning, rudimentary, underdeveloped, undeveloped, unformed.

emend verb SEE **alter.**

emerge verb *He didn't emerge from his bedroom until noon.* SEE **appear,** arise, come out, [*old-fashioned*] issue forth, [*informal*] pop up, surface.

emergency noun *She always keeps calm in an emergency.* crisis, danger, difficulty, predicament, serious situation.

emigrant noun OPPOSITE: immigrant.

emigrate verb *to emigrate to another country.* leave, quit, set out, SEE **travel** verb.

eminent adjective 1 *an eminent actor.* august, celebrated, distinguished, esteemed, familiar, famous, great, illustrious, important, notable, noteworthy, renowned, well-known.
OPPOSITES: SEE **unknown.**
2 *an eminent landmark.* conspicuous, elevated, high, noticeable, obvious, outstanding, prominent, visible.
OPPOSITES: SEE **inconspicuous.**

emit verb *Chimneys emit smoke. Transmitters emit radio signals.* belch, discharge, eject, exhale, expel, give off, give out, issue, radiate, send out, spew out, transmit.
OPPOSITES: SEE **absorb, receive.**

emollient adjective *an emollient cream.* softening, soothing.

emolument noun SEE **pay** noun.

emotion noun *His voice was full of emotion.* agitation, excitement, feeling, fervour, passion, sentiment, warmth.
SEE ALSO **anger** noun, **love** noun, etc.

emotional adjective *an emotional farewell. an emotional speech.* demonstrative, SEE **emotive,** fervent, fiery, heated, impassioned, intense, moving, passionate, romantic, touching, warm-hearted.
SEE ALSO **angry, loving,** etc.
OPPOSITES: SEE **unemotional.**

emotive adjective *emotive language.* affecting, biased, SEE **emotional,** inflammatory, loaded, moving, pathetic, poignant, prejudiced, provocative, sentimental, stirring, subjective, tear-jerking, touching.
OPPOSITES: SEE **dispassionate, objective** adjective.

empathy noun SEE **understanding.**

emperor noun SEE **ruler.**

emphasis noun *She put special emphasis on certain words.* accent, attention, force, importance, intensity, priority, prominence, strength, stress, urgency, weight.

emphasize verb *She emphasized the important points.* accent, accentuate, dwell on, focus on, foreground, give emphasis to, highlight, impress, insist on, [*informal*] play up, [*informal*] press home, spotlight, stress, underline.

emphatic adjective *an emphatic denial.* SEE **categorical.**

empire noun SEE **country.**

empirical adjective *empirical knowledge.* gained through experience, observed, practical.
OPPOSITES: SEE **theoretical.**

employ verb 1 *to employ workers.* engage, give work to, have on your payroll, hire, pay, take on, use the services of.
2 *to employ modern methods.* apply, use, utilize.

employed adjective active, busy, earning, engaged, hired, involved, occupied, working.
OPPOSITES: SEE **unemployed.**

employee noun [*old-fashioned*] hand, [*informal*] underling, worker.
employees staff, workforce.

employer noun boss, chief, [*informal*] gaffer, head, manager, owner, taskmaster. [An employer can be a business rather than an individual: SEE **company**.]

employment noun *What's her employment?* business, calling, craft, job, line, living, occupation, profession, trade, vocation, work.

emporium noun SEE **shop**.

empower verb SEE **authorize**.

empty adjective 1 *empty space. an empty room. an empty van.* bare, blank, clean, clear, deserted, desolate, forsaken, hollow, unfilled, unfurnished, uninhabited, unladen, unoccupied, unused, vacant, void.
OPPOSITES: SEE **full**.
2 *empty threats. empty compliments.* futile, idle, impotent, ineffective, insincere, meaningless, pointless, purposeless, senseless, silly, unreal, worthless.
OPPOSITES: SEE **effective**.

empty verb *Empty your cup. Empty the building.* clear, drain, evacuate, exhaust, pour out, unload, vacate, void.
OPPOSITES: SEE **fill**.

emulate verb SEE **rival** verb.

enable verb 1 *The extra money enabled us to have a holiday.* aid, assist, equip, help, make it possible, provide the means.
2 *A passport enables you to travel to certain countries.* allow, authorize, empower, entitle, license, permit, qualify, sanction.
OPPOSITES: SEE **prevent**.

enact verb 1 *to enact a law.* SEE **pass** verb.
2 *to enact a play.* SEE **perform**.

enamoured adjective SEE **love** noun (**in love**).

encampment noun *a military encampment.* camp, camping-ground, campsite.

encase verb SEE **enclose**.

enchant verb *The ballet enchanted us.* allure, bewitch, captivate, charm, delight, enrapture, enthral, entrance, fascinate, spellbind.

enchantment noun SEE **delight** noun, **magic** noun.

encircle verb SEE **enclose**.

enclave noun SEE **territory**.

enclose verb 1 *to enclose animals within a fence.* cage, confine, cordon off, encircle, encompass, envelop, fence in, hedge in, hem in, imprison, pen, restrict, ring, shut in, surround, wall in.
2 *to enclose something in an envelope, box, etc.* box, case, cocoon, conceal, contain, cover, encase, enfold, insert, package, parcel up, secure, sheathe, wrap.

enclosed adjective *an enclosed space.* confined, contained, encircled, fenced, limited, restricted, shut in, surrounded, walled.
OPPOSITES: SEE **open** adjective.

enclosure noun 1 *an enclosure for animals.* arena, cage, compound, coop, corral, court, courtyard, farmyard, field, fold, paddock, pen, pound, ring, run, sheepfold, stockade, sty.
2 *an enclosure in an envelope.* contents, inclusion, insertion.

encode verb OPPOSITES: SEE **decode**.

encomium noun SEE **praise** noun.

encompass verb SEE **enclose, include**.

encore noun *She sang an encore.* extra item, repeat performance.

encounter noun 1 *a friendly encounter.* meeting.
2 *a violent encounter.* battle, brush (*a brush with the authorities*), clash, collision, confrontation, dispute, SEE **fight** noun, struggle.

encounter verb *I encountered fierce opposition.* clash with, come upon, confront, contend with, [*informal*] cross swords with, face, grapple with, happen upon, have an encounter with, meet, [*informal*] run into.

encourage verb 1 *We encouraged our team.* abet, animate, applaud, cheer, [*informal*] egg on, embolden, give hope to, hearten, incite, inspire, rally, reassure, rouse, spur on, support.
2 *Advertising encourages sales.* aid, be conducive to, be an incentive to, boost, engender, foster, further, generate, help, increase, induce, promote, stimulate.
3 *Encourage people to stop smoking.* advocate, invite, persuade, prompt, urge.
OPPOSITES: SEE **discourage**.

encouragement noun *We need a little encouragement.* applause, approval, boost, cheer, incentive, inspiration, reassurance, [*informal*] shot in the arm, stimulation, support.

encouraging adjective *encouraging news.* auspicious, cheering, comforting, favourable, heartening, hopeful, optimistic, promising, reassuring.

encroach verb *to encroach on someone's territory.* enter, impinge, SEE **intrude**, invade, trespass, violate.

encrust verb SEE **cake** verb.

encumber verb SEE **hamper** verb.

encyclopaedic adjective *Her encyclopaedic knowledge amazes me.* SEE **comprehensive**.

end noun 1 *the end of the garden.* boundary, edge, limit.
2 *the end of an event.* cessation, close, coda (*of a piece of music*), completion, conclusion, culmination, curtain (*of a play*), denouement (*of a plot*), ending, finale, finish, [*informal*] pay-off, resolution.
3 *the end of a journey.* destination, expiration, home, termination, terminus.
4 *the end of a queue.* back, rear, tail.
5 *the end of a walking-stick.* ferrule, point, tip.
6 *the end of life.* SEE **death**, demise, destiny, destruction, doom, extinction, fate, passing, ruin.
7 *an end in view.* aim, aspiration, consequence, design, effect, intention, objective, outcome, plan, purpose, result, upshot.

end verb 1 *to end your work.* break off, bring to an end, complete, conclude, cut off, discontinue, [*informal*] drop, halt, put an end to, [*informal*] round off.
2 *to end a life.* abolish, destroy, eliminate, exterminate, [*informal*] get rid of, SEE **kill**, [*informal*] put an end to, ruin, scotch (*to scotch a rumour*).
3 *When does term end?* break up, cease, close, come to an end, culminate, expire, finish, reach a climax, stop, terminate.

endanger verb *Bad driving endangers others.* expose to risk, imperil, jeopardize, put at risk, threaten.
OPPOSITES: SEE **protect**.

endearing adjective *endearing ways.* appealing, attractive, charming, disarming, enchanting, engaging, lovable, sweet, winning.
OPPOSITES: SEE **repulsive**.

endeavour verb SEE **try** verb.

endless adjective 1 *endless space.* boundless, everlasting, immeasurable, infinite, limitless, measureless, never-ending, unbounded, unlimited.
2 *an endless afterlife.* eternal, immortal, undying.
3 *an endless supply.* ceaseless, constant, continual, continuous, everlasting, incessant, inexhaustible, interminable, perpetual, persistent, unbroken, unending, unfailing, uninterrupted.

endorse verb 1 *to endorse a cheque.* sign.
2 *to endorse someone's opinion.* agree with, approve of, condone, SEE **confirm**, subscribe to.

endow verb SEE **provide**.

endowment noun SEE **money**.

endurance noun *The big climb was a test of endurance.* ability to endure [SEE **endure**], determination, fortitude, patience, perseverance, persistence, pertinacity, resolution, stamina, staying-power, strength, tenacity.

endure verb 1 *to endure pain. to endure a storm.* bear, cope with, experience, go through, put up with, stand, [*informal*] stick, [*informal*] stomach, submit to, suffer, tolerate, undergo, weather, withstand.
2 *Life on earth will endure for a long time yet.* carry on, continue, exist, last, live on, persevere, persist, prevail, remain, stay, survive.

enduring adjective *an enduring friendship.* SEE **lasting**.

enemy noun adversary, antagonist, assailant, attacker, competitor, foe, opponent, opposition, the other side, rival, [*informal*] them (*us and them*).
OPPOSITES: SEE **ally** noun, **friend**.

energetic adjective *an energetic person. an energetic game.* active, animated, brisk, dynamic, enthusiastic, fast, forceful, hard-working, high-powered, indefatigable, lively, powerful, quick-moving, spirited, strenuous, tireless, unflagging, vigorous.
OPPOSITES: SEE **lethargic**.

energy noun 1 *She has tremendous energy.* animation, drive, dynamism, enthusiasm, fire, force, [*informal*] get-up-and-go, [*informal*] go (*She's got lots of go*), life, liveliness, might, spirit, stamina, strength, verve, vigour, [*informal*] vim, vitality, vivacity, zeal, zest.
OPPOSITES: SEE **lethargy**.
2 *Industry needs a reliable supply of energy.* fuel, power.

enervate verb SEE **tire**.

enfeeble verb SEE **weaken**.

enfold verb SEE **embrace**, **enclose**.

enforce verb *to enforce the rules.* administer, apply, carry out, execute, implement, impose, inflict, insist on, put into effect.
OPPOSITES: SEE **waive**.

enfranchise verb SEE **emancipate**.

engage verb 1 *to engage workers.* SEE **employ**.
2 *to engage to do something.* SEE **promise** verb.
3 *to engage someone in conversation.* SEE **occupy**.
4 *Cog-wheels engage.* bite, fit together, interlock.

engaged adjective 1 *engaged to be married.* [*formal*] affianced, betrothed, [*old-*

fashioned] promised, [*informal*] unavailable.
OPPOSITES: SEE **unattached.**
2 *engaged in your work.* absorbed, active, busy, committed, employed, engrossed, immersed, involved, occupied, preoccupied, tied up.
OPPOSITES: SEE **idle.**
3 *an engaged telephone-line. an engaged lavatory.* being used, busy, occupied, unavailable.
OPPOSITES: SEE **available.**

engagement **1** *The couple announced their engagement.* betrothal, promise to marry, [*old-fashioned*] troth.
2 *a business engagement.* appointment, arrangement, commitment, date, fixture, meeting, obligation.
3 *a military engagement.* SEE **battle** noun.

engaging adjective SEE **attractive.**

engender verb SEE **generate.**

engine noun **1** KINDS OF ENGINE: diesel engine, electric motor, internal-combustion engine, jet engine, outboard-motor, steam-engine, turbine, turbo-jet, turbo-prop.
2 *a railway engine.* locomotive.

engineer verb SEE **construct, devise.**

engineering noun There are many branches of *engineering,* including: aeronautical, chemical, civil, computer, electrical, electronic, manufacturing, marine, mechanical, plant.

engrave verb SEE **cut** verb, etch.

engraving noun SEE **picture** noun.

engross verb SEE **occupy.**

engulf verb SEE **submerge, surround.**

enhance verb SEE **improve.**

enigma noun SEE **puzzle** noun.

enigmatic adjective SEE **puzzling.**

enjoin verb SEE **command** verb.

enjoy verb **1** *We enjoy outings. I enjoyed her paintings.* admire, appreciate, be pleased by, delight in, indulge in, like, love, luxuriate in, rejoice in, relish, revel in, savour, take pleasure from or in.
2 *Visitors can enjoy the college facilities.* benefit from, experience, have, take advantage of, use.
to enjoy yourself celebrate, [*informal*] gad about, [*informal*] have a fling, have a good time.

enjoyable adjective *an enjoyable party. enjoyable food.* agreeable, amusing, SEE **delicious,** delightful, gratifying, likeable, [*informal*] nice, pleasant, pleasurable, rewarding, satisfying.
OPPOSITES: SEE **unpleasant.**

enlarge verb amplify (*sound*), augment, blow up (*a tyre, a photograph*), broaden (*the river broadened*), build up, develop, dilate (*the pupil of an eye*), diversify (*your interests*), elaborate (*a story or argument*), elongate, expand, extend, fill out, get bigger, grow, increase, inflate (*a balloon, a tyre*), lengthen, magnify, make bigger, multiply, stretch, swell, wax (*the moon waxes and wanes*), widen.
OPPOSITES: SEE **decrease** verb, **shrink.**

enlargement noun SEE **photograph** noun.

enlighten verb SEE **illuminate, inform.**

enlist verb **1** *to enlist troops.* conscript, engage, enrol, muster, recruit.
2 *The men enlisted in the army.* enrol, enter, join up, register, sign on, volunteer.
3 *to enlist someone's help.* SEE **obtain.**

enliven verb SEE **animate** verb.

enmesh verb SEE **tangle** verb.

enmity noun SEE **hostility.**

enormity noun **1** *the enormity of the crime.* SEE **wickedness.**
2 *the enormity of the problem.* SEE **seriousness.**

enormous adjective SEE **big,** colossal, elephantine, gargantuan, giant, gigantic, huge, hulking, immense, [*informal*] jumbo, mammoth, massive, mighty, monstrous, mountainous, titanic, towering, tremendous, vast.
OPPOSITES: SEE **small.**

enough adjective *enough food.* adequate, ample, as much as necessary, sufficient.

enquire verb ask, beg, demand, entreat, implore, inquire, query, question, quiz, request.
to enquire about [*informal*] go into, have an investigation into [SEE **investigation**], investigate, probe, research, scrutinize.

enquiry noun SEE **investigation.**

enrage verb SEE **anger** verb.

enrapture verb SEE **delight** verb.

enrich verb SEE **improve.**

enrobe verb SEE **dress** verb.

enrol verb SEE **enlist.**

ensconce verb SEE **establish.**

ensemble noun **1** GROUPS OF MUSICIANS: SEE **music.**
2 *She wore a new ensemble.* SEE **outfit.**

enshroud verb SEE **cover** verb.

ensign noun SEE **flag** noun.

enslave verb disenfranchise, dominate, make slaves of, subject, subjugate, take away the rights of.
OPPOSITES: SEE **emancipate.**

ensnare verb SEE **trap** verb.

ensue verb SEE **follow**.

ensure verb [Do not confuse with *in-sure*.] *Ensure that you lock the door*. confirm, guarantee, make certain, make sure, secure.

entail verb *What does the operation entail?* SEE **involve**.

entangle verb SEE **tangle** verb.

entente noun SEE **agreement**.

enter verb 1 *to enter a room*. arrive at, come in, go in, move into.
OPPOSITES: SEE **leave** verb.
2 *The bullet entered his leg*. cut into, dig into, penetrate, pierce, push into.
3 *to enter a competition*. engage in, enlist in, enrol in, [*informal*] go in for, join, participate in, sign up for, take part in, take up, volunteer for.
OPPOSITES: SEE **resign, withdraw**.
4 *to enter a name on a list*. add, inscribe, insert, note down, put down, record, register, set down, sign, write.
OPPOSITES: SEE **remove**.
to enter into *They entered into negotiations*. SEE **begin**.

enterprise noun 1 *a bold enterprise*. adventure, business, effort, endeavour, operation, project, undertaking, venture.
2 *She shows enterprise*. SEE **initiative**.

enterprising adjective *Some enterprising girls organized a sponsored walk*. adventurous, ambitious, bold, courageous, daring, eager, energetic, enthusiastic, [*informal*] go-ahead, hard-working, imaginative, industrious, intrepid, keen, pushful, [*uncomplimentary*] pushy, resourceful, spirited, venturesome.
OPPOSITES: SEE **unadventurous**.

entertain verb 1 *to entertain someone with stories*. amuse, cheer up, delight, divert, keep amused, make laugh, occupy, please, regale, [*informal*] tickle.
OPPOSITES: SEE **bore** verb.
2 *to entertain friends at Christmas*. accommodate, be the host or hostess to, cater for, give hospitality to, [*informal*] put up, receive, welcome.
3 *She wouldn't entertain the idea*. accept, agree to, approve, consent to, consider, contemplate, take seriously.

entertainer noun performer.

VARIOUS ENTERTAINERS: acrobat, actor, actress, ballerina, broadcaster, busker, clown, comedian, comic, compère, conjuror, contortionist, co-star, dancer, disc jockey, DJ, jester, juggler, liontamer, magician, matador, minstrel, musician, question-master, singer, star, stunt man, superstar, toreador, trapeze artist, trouper, ventriloquist.

entertaining adjective SEE **amusing**.

entertainment noun amusement, distraction, diversion, enjoyment, fun, night-life, pastime, play, pleasure, recreation, sport.

VARIOUS KINDS OF ENTERTAINMENT: aerobatics, air-show, ballet, bullfight, cabaret, casino, ceilidh, cinema, circus, comedy, concert, dance, disco, discothèque, drama, fair, firework display, flower show, gymkhana, motor show, SEE **music**, musical, night-club, opera, pageant, pantomime, play, radio, recital, recitation, revue, rodeo, show, son et lumière, SEE **sport**, tap-dancing, tattoo, television, theatre, variety show, waxworks, zoo.

enthral verb SEE **captivate**.

enthralling adjective SEE **exciting**.

enthrone verb *to enthrone a king or queen*. anoint, consecrate, crown, make a king or queen, place on the throne.
OPPOSITES: SEE **depose**.

enthuse verb SEE **enthusiastic** (be enthusiastic).

enthusiasm noun 1 *To be successful you need enthusiasm*. ambition, ardour, commitment, drive, eagerness, excitement, fervour, keenness, panache, spirit, verve, zeal, zest.
OPPOSITES: SEE **apathy**.
2 *Her current enthusiasm is judo*. craze, [*informal*] fad, diversion, hobby, interest, passion, pastime.

enthusiast noun *a pop music enthusiast*. addict, admirer, aficionado, [*informal*] buff, devotee, fan, fanatic, [*informal*] fiend, [*informal*] freak, lover, supporter.

enthusiastic adjective *an enthusiastic supporter*. ardent, avid, [*informal*] crazy, delight, devoted, eager, earnest, ebullient, energetic, excited, exuberant, fervent, fervid, hearty, impassioned, keen, lively, [*informal*] mad keen, optimistic, passionate, positive, rapturous, raring (*raring to go*), spirited, unstinting, vigorous, wholehearted, zealous.
OPPOSITES: SEE **apathetic**.
to be enthusiastic enthuse, get excited, [*informal*] go into raptures, [*informal*] go overboard, rave.

entice verb SEE **lure** verb.

entire adjective SEE **whole**.

entitle verb 1 *The voucher entitles you to a refund. Her success entitles her to feel proud.* accredit, allow, authorize, empower, enable, justify, license, permit, warrant.
2 *What did you entitle your story?* call, christen, designate, dub, name, style, title.

entitlement noun *an entitlement to an inheritance.* claim, ownership, prerogative, right, title.

entity noun SEE **thing**.

entomb verb SEE **bury**.

entourage noun *the president's entourage.* attendants, SEE **company**, court (*a royal court*), escort, followers, [*informal*] hangers-on, [*old-fashioned*] retainers, retinue, staff.

entrails noun *an animal's entrails.* bowels, guts, [*informal*] innards, inner organs, [*informal*] insides, intestines, [*formal*] viscera.

entrance noun 1 *You pay at the entrance.* access, door, doorway, entry, gate, gateway, [*formal*] ingress, opening, portal, turnstile, way in.
OPPOSITES: SEE **exit** noun.
2 *I looked up at their entrance.* SEE **arrival**.
entrance hall ante-room, foyer, lobby, porch, vestibule.

entrance verb *The music entranced us.* SEE **delight** verb.

entrant noun *an entrant in a competition.* applicant, candidate, competitor, contender, contestant, entry, participant, player, rival.

entreat verb SEE **request** verb.

entreaty noun SEE **request** noun.

entrench verb SEE **establish**.

entrepreneur noun SEE **businessman**.

entrust verb *They entrusted me with the money.* put in charge of, trust.

entry noun 1 *Please don't block the entry.* SEE **entrance** noun.
2 *an entry in a diary.* insertion, item, jotting, note, record.
3 *an entry in a competition.* SEE **entrant**.

entwine verb SEE **interweave, tangle** verb.

enumerate verb SEE **count** verb, **mention**.

enunciate verb SEE **pronounce**.

envelop verb SEE **cover** verb, **wrap** verb.

envelope noun cover, sheath, wrapper, wrapping.

enviable adjective *an enviable salary.* attractive, desirable, favourable.

envious adjective *envious of her success.* begrudging, bitter, covetous, dissatisfied, [*informal*] green with envy, grudging, jaundiced, jealous, resentful.

environment noun *a natural environment.* conditions, context, habitat, location, setting, situation, surroundings, territory.

environs noun SEE **area**.

envisage noun SEE **visualize**.

envoy noun SEE **messenger**.

envy noun *feelings of envy.* bitterness, covetousness, cupidity, dissatisfaction, ill-will, jealousy, resentment.

envy verb *He envies her success.* begrudge, grudge, resent.

ephemeral adjective *Most newspapers are of ephemeral interest.* brief, evanescent, fleeting, impermanent, momentary, passing, short-lived, temporary, transient, transitory.
OPPOSITES: SEE **eternal, lasting**.

epic noun KINDS OF LITERATURE: SEE **literature**.

epicure noun SEE **gourmet**.

epicurean adjective SEE **hedonistic**.

epidemic noun *an epidemic of measles.* outbreak, plague.

epidermis noun SEE **skin** noun.

epigram noun SEE **saying**.

epilogue noun afterword, postscript.
OTHER PARTS OF A BOOK: SEE **book** noun.
OPPOSITES: SEE **prelude**.

episode noun 1 *a happy episode in my life.* SEE **event**.
2 *an episode of a serial.* chapter, instalment, part, passage, scene, section.

epistle noun SEE **letter**.

epitaph noun *an epitaph on a tombstone.* inscription.

epithet noun description, designation, name, [*informal*] tag, title.

epitome noun *She's the epitome of kindness.* embodiment, essence, personification, quintessence, representation, type.

epoch noun SEE **period**.

epoch-making adjective SEE **important**.

Many English words, including *equable, equal, equate, equilateral,* etc., are related to Latin *aequus* = *even.*

Don't confuse these with words such as *equestrian* and *equine* which are related to Latin *equus* = *horse.*

---

equable adjective SEE **calm** adjective.

equal adjective **1** *equal opportunities.*
equal quantities. corresponding, egalitarian, equivalent, even, fair, identical, level, like, matched, matching, proportionate, the same, symmetrical, uniform.
2 *Is she equal to the job?* SEE **capable**.

equality noun *equality of opportunity.*
balance, correspondence, evenhandedness, fairness, parity, similarity, uniformity.

equalize verb *to equalize scores.* balance, even up, level, make equal, match, [*informal*] square.

equanimity noun SEE **calmness**.

equate verb *You can't equate wealth and happiness.* assume to be equal, compare, juxtapose, liken, match, parallel, set side by side.

equerry noun SEE **official** noun.

equilateral adjective equal-sided.

equilibrium noun SEE **balance** noun.

equinox noun OPPOSITE: solstice.

equip verb *to equip workers with tools. to equip a room with furniture.* arm (*troops*), fit out, furnish, [*informal*] kit out, provide, stock, supply.

equipment noun *equipment you need for a job.* accoutrements, apparatus, furnishings, [*informal*] gear, [*informal*] hardware, implements, instruments, kit, machinery, materials, outfit, paraphernalia, plant, [*informal*] rig, [*informal*] stuff, supplies, tackle, [*informal*] things, tools.

equipoise noun SEE **balance** noun.

equitable adjective *an equitable reward.*
SEE **just** adjective.

equities noun investments.

equivalent adjective SEE **equal**.

equivocal adjective SEE **ambiguous**.

equivocate verb SEE **quibble** verb.

era noun SEE **period**.

eradicate, erase verbs SEE **remove**.

erect adjective *an erect posture.* SEE **upright**.

erect verb *to erect a tent. to erect a flag pole.*
build, construct, elevate, lift up, make upright [SEE **upright**], pitch (*a tent*), put up, raise, set up.

erection noun SEE **construction**.

erode verb *Water erodes the topsoil.* corrode, destroy, eat away, grind down, wear away.

erotic adjective SEE **amorous**.

err verb SEE **misbehave, miscalculate**.

errand noun *an errand to the shops.* assignment, job, journey, mission, task, trip.

erratic adjective *an erratic performance.*
capricious, changeable, fickle, fitful, fluctuating, inconsistent, irregular, shifting, spasmodic, sporadic, uneven, unpredictable, unreliable, unstable, unsteady, variable, wandering, wayward.
OPPOSITES: SEE **consistent**.

erroneous adjective SEE **wrong** adjective.

error noun *factual errors. a fatal error on the motorway.* [*informal*] bloomer, blunder, [*informal*] boob, fallacy, falsehood, fault, flaw, [*informal*] howler, inaccuracy, inconsistency, inexactitude, lapse, misapprehension, miscalculation, misconception, mistake, misunderstanding, omission, oversight, sin, [*informal*] slip-up, [*formal*] solecism, transgression, [*old-fashioned*] trespass, wrongdoing.

erudite adjective SEE **learned**.

erupt verb *Smoke erupted from the volcano.*
be discharged, be omitted, belch, break out, burst out, explode, gush, issue, pour out, shoot out, spew, spout, spurt, vomit.

eruption noun *an eruption of laughter. a volcanic eruption.* burst, explosion, outbreak, outburst.

escalate verb *Fighting escalated as more people joined in.* become worse, build up, expand, grow, increase, intensify, multiply, rise, spiral, step up.

escalator noun lift, moving staircase.

escapade noun *a childish escapade.*
adventure, exploit, [*informal*] lark, mischief, practical joke, prank, scrape, stunt.

escape noun **1** *an escape from gaol.* bolt, break-out, flight, flit, get-away, retreat, running away.
2 *an escape of gas.* discharge, emission, leak, leakage, seepage.
3 *an escape from reality.* avoidance, distraction, diversion, escapism, evasion, relaxation, relief.

escape verb **1** *The prisoner escaped.* abscond, bolt, break free, break out, [*informal*] do a bunk, elope, flee, get away, [*informal*] give someone the slip, run away, [*slang*] scarper, slip away, [*informal*] slip the net.
2 *Oil escaped from a crack.* discharge, drain, leak, ooze, pour out, run out, seep.

3 *She always escapes the nasty jobs.* avoid, dodge, duck, evade, get away from, shirk.
4 *His name escapes me.* baffle, be forgotten by, elude.

escapism noun day-dreaming, fantasy, pretence, unreality, wishful thinking.

eschew verb SEE **avoid**.

escort noun **1** *a protective escort.* bodyguard, convoy, guard, guide, pilot.
2 *escorts to the queen.* attendant, entourage, retinue, train.
3 *an escort at a dance.* chaperon, companion, partner.

escort verb *to escort someone to a party. to escort a prisoner.* accompany, chaperon, guard, [*informal*] keep an eye on, [*informal*] keep tabs on, look after, protect, stay with, usher, watch.

escutcheon noun SEE **shield** noun.

esoteric adjective *esoteric knowledge.* SEE **obscure** adjective, **specialized**.

espalier noun VARIOUS TREES: SEE **tree**.

especial adjective SEE **special**.

espionage noun SEE **spying**.

esplanade noun SEE **path**.

espouse verb *to espouse a cause.* SEE **support** verb.

espy verb SEE **see**.

essay noun KINDS OF WRITING: SEE **writing**.

essay verb SEE **try** verb.

essayist noun VARIOUS WRITERS: SEE **writer**.

essence noun **1** *the essence of a problem. the essence of someone's personality.* centre, character, core, crux, essential quality [SEE **essential**], heart, kernel, life, meaning, nature, pith, quintessence, soul, spirit.
2 *peppermint essence.* concentrate, decoction, elixir, extract, fragrance, perfume, scent, tincture.

essential adjective **1** *essential information for travellers.* basic, chief, crucial, elementary, fundamental, important, indispensable, irreplaceable, key, main, necessary, primary, principal, requisite, vital.
OPPOSITES: SEE **inessential**.
2 *essential features.* characteristic, inherent, innate, intrinsic, quintessential.

establish verb **1** *to establish a business.* base, begin, construct, create, found, inaugurate, initiate, institute, introduce, organize, originate, set up, start.

2 *to establish yourself as leader.* confirm, ensconce, entrench, install, secure, settle.
3 *to establish the facts.* agree, authenticate, certify, confirm, corroborate, decide, demonstrate, fix, prove, ratify, show to be true, substantiate, verify.

established adjective *an established business. an established favourite on TV. established habits.* accepted, confirmed, deep-rooted, deep-seated, entrenched, fixed, indelible, ineradicable, ingrained, long-lasting, long-standing, permanent, proved, proven, recognized, reliable, respected, rooted, secure, settled, traditional, well-known, well-tried.
OPPOSITES: SEE **new, untried**.

establishment noun **1** *the establishment of a new club.* composition, constitution, creation, formation, foundation, inauguration, inception, institution, introduction.
2 *a well-run establishment.* business, concern, factory, household, shop.

estate noun **1** *a housing estate.* area, development.
2 *an estate left in a will.* assets, effects, fortune, goods, inheritance, lands, possessions, property, wealth.

estate car noun SEE **car**.

esteem noun *held in high esteem.* admiration, credit, estimation, favour, honour, regard, respect, reverence, veneration.

esteem verb SEE **respect** verb.

estimable adjective SEE **admirable**.

estimate noun **1** *What's your estimate of the situation?* appraisal, assessment, conjecture, estimation, evaluation, guess, judgement, opinion, surmise.
2 *an estimate of what a job will cost.* calculation, [*informal*] guesstimate, price, quotation, reckoning, specification, valuation.

estimate verb *to estimate how much something will cost.* appraise, assess, calculate, compute, conjecture, consider, count up, evaluate, gauge, guess, judge, project, reckon, surmise, think out, weigh up, work out.

estimation noun *I respect her estimation of the situation.* appraisal, appreciation, assessment, calculation, computation, consideration, estimate, evaluation, judgement, opinion, rating, view.

estrange verb SEE **antagonize**.

estuary noun *a river estuary.* arm of the sea, creek, [*Scottish*] firth, fjord, inlet, [*Scottish*] loch, mouth.

etch verb SEE **engrave**.

etching noun SEE **picture** noun.

eternal adjective 1 *eternal life*. deathless, endless, everlasting, heavenly, immeasurable, immortal, infinite, lasting, limitless, measureless, timeless, unchanging, undying, unending, unlimited.
OPPOSITES: SEE **ephemeral, transitory**.
2 [*informal*] *I'm sick of your eternal quarrelling*. ceaseless, constant, continual, frequent, incessant, interminable, never-ending, non-stop, perennial, permanent, perpetual, persistent, recurrent, relentless, repeated, unceasing, unremitting.
OPPOSITES: SEE **occasional, temporary**.

eternity noun *an eternity in heaven*. afterlife, eternal life [SEE **eternal**], immortality, infinity, perpetuity.

ether noun SEE **anaesthetic**.

ethical adjective *an ethical problem*. SEE **moral** adjective.

ethics noun SEE **morality**.

ethnic adjective *ethnic music*. cultural, folk, national, racial, traditional, tribal.

ethos noun SEE **belief, morality**.

etiolate verb SEE **pale** verb.

etiquette noun *It's polite to observe correct etiquette*. ceremony, civility, conventions, courtesy, decency, decorum, formalities, manners, politeness, propriety, protocol, rules of behaviour, standards of behaviour.

Eucharist noun Communion, Holy Communion, Lord's Supper, Mass.

eulogize verb SEE **praise** verb.

eulogy noun SEE **praise** noun.

eunuch noun SEE **man**.

euphemistic adjective *euphemistic language*. SEE **indirect**.

euphony noun SEE **harmony**.

euphoria noun SEE **happiness**.

euthanasia noun SEE **killing** noun.

evacuate verb 1 *to evacuate people from a building or an area*. clear, move out, remove, send away.
2 *to evacuate a building or an area*. abandon, decamp from, desert, empty, forsake, leave, quit, relinquish, vacate, withdraw from.
to evacuate the bowels SEE **excrete**.

evade verb *to evade your responsibilities*. avoid, [*informal*] chicken out of, circumvent, dodge, duck, elude, escape from, fend off, shirk, shun, sidestep, [*informal*] skive, steer clear of, turn your back on.
OPPOSITES: SEE **accept**.

evaluate verb SEE **assess**.

evanescent adjective SEE **fleeting**.

evangelist noun SEE **preacher**.

evangelize verb SEE **preach**.

evaporate verb *Dew evaporates in the morning*. disappear, disperse, dissipate, dissolve, dry up, melt away, vanish, vaporize.
OPPOSITES: SEE **condense**.

evasive adjective *an evasive answer*. ambiguous, deceptive, devious, disingenuous, equivocal, inconclusive, indecisive, indirect, misleading, non-committal, oblique, prevaricating, shifty, uninformative.
OPPOSITES: SEE **straightforward**.

even adjective 1 *an even surface*. flat, flush, horizontal, level, smooth, straight, true, unbroken, unruffled.
OPPOSITES: SEE **rough**.
2 *an even temper*. SEE **even-tempered**.
3 *the even ticking of a clock*. balanced, consistent, equalized, metrical, monotonous, proportional, regular, rhythmical, steady, symmetrical, unvarying.
OPPOSITES: SEE **irregular**.
4 *even scores*. equal, identical, level, the same.
OPPOSITES: SEE **unequal**.
to get even SEE **retaliate**.

even verb **to even out** *I evened out the wrinkled carpet*. flatten, level, smooth, straighten.
to even up *The next goal evened up the scores*. balance, equalize, level, [*informal*] square.

evening noun dusk, [*poetic*] eventide, [*poetic*] gloaming, nightfall, sundown, sunset, twilight.

evensong noun CHURCH SERVICES: SEE **service**.

event noun 1 *an unexpected event*. affair, business, chance, circumstance, contingency, episode, eventuality, experience, happening, incident, occurrence.
2 *a special event*. activity, ceremony, entertainment, function, occasion.
3 *a sporting event*. bout, championship, competition, contest, engagement, fixture, game, match, meeting, tournament.

even-tempered adjective *an even-tempered character*. calm, composed, cool, equable, even, impassive, imperturbable, peaceable, peaceful, placid, reliable, serene, stable, steady, tranquil, unexcitable.
OPPOSITES: SEE **excitable**.

eventual adjective *the eventual result.* concluding, consequent, ensuing, final, last, overall, resulting, ultimate.

eventuate verb SEE **result** verb.

evergreen noun VARIOUS TREES: SEE **tree**.

everlasting adjective SEE **eternal**.

evermore adverb always, eternally, for ever, unceasingly.

everyday adjective *an everyday happening.* SEE **ordinary, usual**.

everywhere adverb RELATED ADJECTIVE: ubiquitous.

evict verb *to evict a tenant.* [*formal*] dispossess, eject, expel, [*slang*] give (someone) the boot, [*informal*] kick out, oust, put out, remove, throw out, [*informal*] turf out, turn out.

evidence noun *legal evidence. scientific evidence.* confirmation, corroboration, data, demonstration, documentation, facts, grounds, information, proof, sign, statistics, substantiation, testimony.
to give evidence SEE **testify**.

evident adjective *It's evident that he doesn't like work.* apparent, certain, clear, discernible, manifest, noticeable, obvious, palpable, patent, perceptible, plain, self-explanatory, unambiguous, undeniable, unmistakable, visible.
OPPOSITES: SEE **unclear**.

evil adjective **1** *an evil deed. an evil person.* amoral, atrocious, SEE **bad**, base, black-hearted, blasphemous, corrupt, criminal, cruel, dark (*dark deeds*), depraved, devilish, diabolical, dishonest, fiendish, foul, harmful, hateful, heinous, hellish, immoral, impious, infamous, iniquitous, irreligious, machiavellian, malevolent, malicious, malignant, nefarious, pernicious, perverted, reprobate, satanic, sinful, sinister, treacherous, ungodly, unprincipled, unrighteous, vicious, vile, villainous, wicked, wrong.
OPPOSITES: SEE **good**.
2 *an evil smell. an evil mood.* foul, nasty, pestilential, poisonous, troublesome, SEE **unpleasant**, unspeakable, vile.
OPPOSITES: SEE **pleasant**.

evil noun **1** *the fight against evil.* amorality, blasphemy, corruption, SEE **crime**, criminality, cruelty, depravity, dishonesty, fiendishness, heinousness, immorality, impiety, iniquity, [*old-fashioned*] knavery, malevolence, malice, mischief, pain, sin, sinfulness, suffering, treachery, turpitude, ungodliness, unrighteousness, vice, viciousness, villainy, wickedness, wrongdoing.
2 *Pollution is one of the evils of our world.* affliction, bane, calamity, catastrophe, curse, disaster, enormity, harm, ill, misfortune, sin, wrong.

evince verb *to evince interest.* SEE **show** verb.

eviscerate verb SEE **kill**.

evocative adjective *an evocative description.* atmospheric, convincing, descriptive, emotive, graphic, imaginative, provoking, realistic, stimulating, suggestive, vivid.

evoke verb *to evoke a response.* arouse, awaken, call up, conjure up, elicit, excite, inspire, kindle, produce, provoke, raise, stimulate, stir up, suggest, summon up.

evolution noun *the evolution of life. the evolution of an idea.* development, emergence, growth, improvement, maturing, progress, unfolding.

evolve verb *Animals evolved from simple forms of life.* derive, descend, develop, emerge, grow, improve, mature, modify gradually, progress.

ewe noun SEE **sheep**.

ewer noun SEE **jug**.

exacerbate verb SEE **worsen**.

exact adjective **1** *exact measurements.* accurate, correct, dead (*the dead centre*), faultless, meticulous, precise, right, specific, [*informal*] spot-on, strict.
2 *an exact account.* detailed, faithful, scrupulous, true, truthful, veracious.
3 *an exact copy.* flawless, identical, indistinguishable, perfect.
OPPOSITES: SEE **approximate** adjective, **wrong** adjective.

exact verb *to exact payment.* claim, demand, extort, extract, get, impose, insist on, obtain, require.

exacting adjective *an exacting task.* SEE **difficult**.

exaggerate verb **1** *to exaggerate a difficulty.* amplify, enlarge, inflate, magnify, make too much of, maximize, overdo, over-emphasize, overestimate, overstate, [*informal*] pile it on, [*informal*] play up.
OPPOSITES: SEE **underestimate**.
2 *to exaggerate someone's mannerisms.* burlesque, caricature, overact, parody, [*informal*] take off.

exaggerated adjective *exaggerated mannerisms.* burlesque, [*informal*] camp, SEE **excessive**, extravagant, hyperbolical, inflated, overdone, [*informal*] over the top.

exalt verb SEE **praise** verb, **raise**.

exalted adjective *an exalted rank.* SEE **high**.

examination noun **1** *an examination of our finances.* analysis, appraisal, audit, [*informal*] post-mortem, review, scrutiny, study, survey.

2 *a school examination.* assessment, catechism [= *questions and answers about religious knowledge*], exam, oral [= *oral examination*], paper, test, viva or [*Latin*] viva voce.

3 *a medical examination.* [*informal*] check-up, inspection, investigation, probe, scan.

4 *an examination by the police.* cross-examination, enquiry, inquiry, inquisition, interrogation, questioning, trial.

examine verb **1** *to examine evidence.* analyse, appraise, audit (*accounts*), check, [*informal*] check out, explore, inquire into, inspect, investigate, probe, scrutinize, sift, sort out, study, [*slang*] sus out, test, vet, weigh up.

2 *to examine a witness.* catechize, cross-examine, cross-question, [*informal*] grill, interrogate, question.

example noun **1** *Give an example of what you mean.* case, illustration, instance, occurrence, sample, specimen.

2 *She's an example to us all.* ideal, lesson, model, paragon, pattern, prototype.

to make an example of SEE **punish**.

exasperate verb SEE **anger** verb, **annoy**.

excavate verb SEE **dig**.

exceed verb *to exceed the speed limit. to exceed a particular number.* beat, better, excel, go over, outdo, outnumber, outstrip, pass, surpass, top.

exceedingly adverb *exceedingly good cake.* amazingly, especially, exceptionally, excessively, extraordinarily, extremely, outstandingly, specially, unusually, very.

excel verb **1** *Their team excelled ours in every event.* beat, better, do better than, eclipse, exceed, outclass, outdo, outshine, surpass, top.

2 *She's a good all-round player, but she excels in tennis.* be excellent [SEE **excellent**], do best, shine, stand out.

excellent adjective *an excellent player. excellent food.* [*informal*] ace, [*informal*] brilliant, [*old-fashioned*] capital, champion, choice, [*slang*] cracking, distinguished, esteemed, estimable, exceptional, extraordinary, [*informal*] fabulous, [*informal*] fantastic, fine, first-class, first-rate, SEE **good**, gorgeous, great, high-class, impressive, magnificent, marvellous, notable, outstanding, remarkable, [*informal*] smashing, splendid, sterling, [*informal*] stunning, [*informal*] super, superb, superlative, supreme, surpassing, [*informal*] tip-top, [*informal*] top-notch, top-ranking, [*informal*] tremendous, unequalled, wonderful.

OPPOSITES: SEE **bad**, **mediocre**.

except verb SEE **exclude**.

exception noun **1** *an exception from a list.* exclusion, omission, rejection.

2 *an exception from what is normal.* abnormality, anomaly, departure, deviation, eccentricity, freak, irregularity, oddity, peculiarity, quirk, rarity.

to take exception SEE **object** verb.

exceptional adjective **1** *exceptional weather. an exceptional stroke of bad luck.* aberrant, abnormal, anomalous, atypical, curious, deviant, eccentric, extraordinary, memorable, notable, odd, peculiar, phenomenal, quirky, rare, remarkable, singular, special, strange, surprising, uncommon, unconventional, unexpected, unheard of, unparalleled, unprecedented, unpredictable, unusual.

OPPOSITES: SEE **normal**.

2 *an exceptional performance.* SEE **excellent**.

excerpt noun *We read excerpts from '1984'.* [*formal*] citation, clip, extract, fragment, highlight, part, passage, quotation, section, selection.

excess noun **1** *an excess of food.* abundance, glut, over-indulgence, superabundance, superfluity, surfeit.

OPPOSITES: SEE **scarcity**.

2 *an excess of income over expenditure.* profit, surplus.

OPPOSITES: SEE **deficit**.

3 *We were shocked by their excesses.* SEE **extravagance**.

excessive adjective **1** *excessive zeal.* disproportionate, exaggerated, extreme, fanatical, SEE **great**, immoderate, inordinate, intemperate, needless, overdone, profuse, undue, unnecessary.

2 *excessive amounts of food.* extravagant, SEE **huge**, prodigal, profligate, superfluous, unneeded, wasteful.

OPPOSITES: SEE **inadequate**, **moderate** adjective.

3 *excessive prices.* SEE **exorbitant**, extortionate, unrealistic, unreasonable.

OPPOSITES: SEE **low** adjective.

exchange noun **1** *an exchange of prisoners.* replacement, substitution, [*informal*] swap, switch.

2 *exchange of goods.* bargain, barter, deal, trade-in, traffic.

an exchange of views SEE **conversation**.

exchange verb *to exchange one thing for another.* barter, change, convert (*convert pounds into dollars*), interchange, reciprocate, replace, substitute, [*informal*] swap or swop, switch, trade, trade in, traffic.

to exchange words SEE **talk** verb.

excise noun SEE **tax** noun.

excise verb SEE **remove**.

excitable adjective *an excitable crowd.* [*informal*] bubbly, chattery, emotional, SEE **excited**, explosive, fiery, highly strung, hot-tempered, irrepressible, lively, SEE **nervous**, passionate, quick-tempered, restive, temperamental, unstable, volatile.
OPPOSITES: SEE **subdued**.

excite verb 1 *The smell of food excited the animals.* agitate, animate, discompose, disturb, electrify, exhilarate, [*informal*] get going, inflame, intoxicate, make excited [SEE **excited**], move, provoke, rouse, stimulate, stir up, thrill, titillate, [*informal*] turn on, upset.
OPPOSITES: SEE **calm** verb.
2 *My idea excited some interest.* activate, arouse, awaken, cause, elicit, encourage, engender, evoke, fire, generate, incite, motivate, produce, set off, whet (*whet the appetite*).

excited adjective *an excited crowd. an excited reaction.* agitated, animated, aroused, boisterous, delirious, disturbed, SEE **eager**, elated, enthusiastic, SEE **excitable**, exuberant, feverish, frantic, frenzied, heated, [*informal*] het up, hysterical, impassioned, lively, moved, nervous, overwrought, restless, roused, spirited, stimulated, stirred, thrilled, vivacious, wild, [*informal*] worked up.
OPPOSITES: SEE **apathetic**.

excitement noun 1 *feelings of excitement.* agitation, animation, delirium, discomposure, eagerness, enthusiasm, heat (*the heat of the moment*), intensity, [*informal*] kicks, passion, stimulation, suspense, tension, thrill.
2 *A crowd watched the excitement.* action, activity, adventure, SEE **commotion**, drama, furore, fuss, unrest.

exciting adjective *an exciting discovery.* amazing, cliff-hanging, dramatic, electrifying, enthralling, eventful, exhilarating, fast-moving, gripping, hair-raising, inspiring, interesting, intoxicating, moving, [*informal*] nail-biting, provocative, rousing, sensational, stimulating, stirring, suspenseful, thrilling, titillating.
OPPOSITES: SEE **boring**.

exclaim verb call, cry out, [*old-fashioned*] ejaculate, SEE **say**, shout, utter an exclamation [SEE **exclamation**], [*formal*] vociferate, [*informal*] yell.

exclamation noun call, cry, [*old-fashioned*] ejaculation, expletive, interjection, oath, shout, swear word.

exclude verb *to exclude someone from a conversation. to exclude illegal imports.* ban, banish, bar, blacklist, debar, disallow, disown, eject, except, excommunicate (*from the church*), expel, forbid, [*formal*] interdict, keep out, leave out, lock out, omit, ostracize, oust, outlaw, prohibit, proscribe, put an embargo on, refuse, reject, SEE **remove**, repudiate, rule out, shut out, veto.
OPPOSITES: SEE **include**.

exclusive adjective 1 *an exclusive contract.* limiting, restrictive, sole, unique, unshared.
2 *an exclusive club.* classy, closed, fashionable, [*informal*] members only, [*slang*] posh, private, select, selective, snobbish, [*informal*] trendy, [*informal*] up-market.

excommunicate verb SEE **exclude**.

excrement noun SEE **excreta**.

excrescence noun SEE **growth**.

excreta noun droppings, dung, excrement, faeces, manure, sewage, waste matter.

excrete verb defecate, eliminate waste matter, evacuate the bowels, go to the lavatory, relieve yourself.

excruciating adjective SEE **painful**.

exculpate verb SEE **excuse** verb.

excursion noun *an excursion to the seaside.* expedition, jaunt, journey, outing, ramble, tour, trip.

excusable adjective SEE **forgivable**.

excuse noun *a feeble excuse.* alibi, defence, explanation, extenuation, justification, mitigation, plea, pretext, reason, vindication.

excuse verb 1 *to excuse bad behaviour.* condone, explain, forgive, ignore, justify, overlook, pardon, sanction, tolerate, vindicate.
2 *The judge excused the prisoner.* absolve, acquit, discharge, [*formal*] exculpate, exonerate, free, let off, liberate, release.

execrable adjective SEE **bad**.

execrate verb SEE **hate** verb.

execute verb 1 *to execute a manœuvre.* accomplish, achieve, carry out, complete, do, effect, enact, finish, implement, perform.
2 *to execute a criminal.* SEE **kill**, SEE **punish**, put to death.
METHODS USED TO EXECUTE PEOPLE: behead, burn, crucify, decapitate, electrocute, garotte, gas, guillotine, hang, lynch, shoot, stone.

executioner noun hangman, SEE **killer**.

executive noun SEE **manager**.

exemplary adjective *exemplary behaviour.* SEE **admirable**, faultless, flawless, ideal, model, perfect, unexceptionable.

exemplify verb SEE **demonstrate**.

exempt adjective *exempt from paying tax.* excepted, excluded, excused, free, immune, let off, released, spared.
OPPOSITES: SEE **liable**.

exercise noun 1 *Exercise helps to keep you fit.* action, activity, aerobics, effort, exertion, games, gymnastics, PE, sport, [*informal*] work-out.
2 *army exercises. exercises on the piano.* discipline, drill, manœuvre, operation, practice, training.
exercise book jotter, notebook, pad.

exercise verb 1 *to exercise self-control. to exercise power.* apply, bring to bear, display, employ, exert, expend, show, use, utilize, wield.
2 *to exercise your body.* discipline, drill, exert, jog, keep fit, practise, train, [*informal*] work out.
3 *A problem exercised me.* SEE **worry** verb.

exert verb *to exert your authority.* SEE **exercise** verb.

exertion noun SEE **effort**.

exhale verb SEE **breathe**.

exhaust noun *exhaust from a car.* discharge, emission, fumes, gases, smoke.

exhaust verb 1 *to exhaust your resources. to exhaust your energy.* consume, deplete, drain, dry up, empty, finish off, sap, spend, use up, void.
2 *to exhaust yourself.* SEE **tire**.

exhausted adjective 1 *an exhausted oil-well.* drained, dry, empty, finished, used up.
2 *exhausted after a hard game.* breathless, [*informal*] done in, fatigued, gasping, [*slang*] knackered, panting, puffed out, [*informal*] shattered, SEE **tired**, weary, [*informal*] whacked, worn out.

exhausting adjective *exhausting work.* arduous, backbreaking, crippling, demanding, difficult, fatiguing, gruelling, hard, laborious, punishing, sapping, severe, strenuous, taxing, tiring, wearying.
OPPOSITES: SEE **refreshing**.

exhaustion noun debility, fatigue, tiredness, weakness, weariness.

exhaustive adjective *an exhaustive search.* all-out, careful, SEE **comprehensive**, intensive, meticulous, thorough.

exhibit verb 1 *to exhibit paintings.* arrange, display, present, put up, set up, show.

2 *to exhibit your knowledge.* air, demonstrate, [*uncomplimentary*] flaunt, indicate, manifest, [*uncomplimentary*] parade, reveal, [*uncomplimentary*] show off.
OPPOSITES: SEE **hide** verb.

exhibition noun *an art exhibition.* demonstration, display, presentation, show.

exhibitionist noun extrovert, [*informal*] show-off.

exhilarating adjective SEE **exciting**.

exhilaration noun SEE **happiness**.

exhort verb SEE **urge** verb.

exhortation noun *an exhortation to do better.* advice, SEE **encouragement**, lecture, [*informal*] pep talk, sermon.

exhume verb dig up, disinter.

exigent adjective SEE **urgent**.

exiguous adjective SEE **small**.

exile noun 1 *Exile can be a harsh punishment.* banishment, deportation, expatriation, expulsion.
2 *an exile from your own country.* exiled person, deportee, émigré, expatriate, outcast, refugee, wanderer.

exile verb *to exile someone.* banish, deport, drive out, eject, expatriate, expel, send away.

exist verb 1 *Do dragons exist?* be, be in existence, occur.
2 *We can't exist without food.* continue, endure, hold out, keep going, last, live, remain alive, subsist, survive.

existence noun 1 *I don't believe in the existence of ghosts.* actuality, being, life, living, reality.
2 *We depend on the environment for our existence.* continuance, survival.
in existence SEE **existing**.

existing adjective *existing species.* actual, alive, continuing, corporeal, current, enduring, existent, extant, factual, in existence, living, material, ongoing, present, real, remaining, surviving.
OPPOSITES: SEE **non-existent**.

Exit is a Latin word = *he or she goes out.* *Exeunt* is the plural = *they go out.*

---

exit noun 1 *Pass through the exit.* barrier, SEE **door**, doorway, egress, gate, gateway, opening, portal, way out.
2 *We made a hurried exit.* SEE **departure**.

exit verb SEE **depart**.

exodus noun SEE **departure**.

exonerate verb SEE **excuse** verb.

exorbitant adjective *exorbitant prices.* excessive, expensive, extortionate, extravagant, high, outrageous, overpriced, prohibitive, [*informal*] sky-high, [*informal*] steep, [*informal*] stiff, [*informal*] swingeing, top, unrealistic, unreasonable.
OPPOSITES: SEE **competitive, low** adjective.

exorcise verb SEE **expel**.

exotic adjective **1** *exotic places.* alien, different, exciting, faraway, foreign, remote, romantic, unfamiliar, wonderful.
OPPOSITES: SEE **familiar**.
2 *exotic food.* colourful, different, extraordinary, foreign-looking, novel, outlandish, peculiar, strange, striking, unfamiliar, unusual.
OPPOSITES: SEE **ordinary**.

expand verb **1** *to expand a business. to expand a story.* amplify, augment, broaden, build up, develop, diversify, elaborate, enlarge, extend, fill out, increase, make bigger, make longer.
OPPOSITES: SEE **reduce**.
2 *Metal expands in the heat.* become bigger, dilate, grow, increase, lengthen, open out, stretch, swell, thicken, widen.
OPPOSITES: SEE **contract** verb.

expanse noun *an expanse of water or land.* area, breadth, extent, range, sheet, stretch, sweep, surface, tract.

expansive adjective *an expansive talker.* affable, communicative, friendly, genial, open, outgoing, sociable, SEE **talkative**, well-disposed.
OPPOSITES: SEE **curt, unfriendly**.

expect verb **1** *We expected 100 guests.* anticipate, await, bank on, bargain for, count on, envisage, forecast, foresee, hope for, imagine, look forward to, predict, prophesy, reckon on, wait for.
2 *We expect good behaviour.* consider necessary, demand, insist on, rely on, require, want.
3 *I expect he missed the bus.* assume, believe, SEE **guess** verb, judge, presume, presuppose, think.

expected adjective *an expected increase in prices.* awaited, forecast, foreseen, planned, predictable, predicted, unsurprising.
OPPOSITES: SEE **unexpected**.

expectant adjective SEE **pregnant**.

expecting adjective SEE **pregnant**.

expectorant noun cough-mixture, linctus.

expedient adjective *It was expedient to retire gracefully.* advantageous, advisable, appropriate, convenient, desirable, helpful, judicious, opportune, politic, practical, pragmatic, profitable, prudent, sensible, suitable, to your advantage, useful, worthwhile.

expedient noun *His tantrum was simply an expedient to get his own way.* contrivance, device, [*informal*] dodge, manœuvre, means, measure, method, [*informal*] ploy, resort, ruse, scheme, stratagem, tactics.

expedite verb SEE **hurry** verb.

expedition noun *an expedition to foreign parts.* crusade, exploration, SEE **journey** noun, mission, pilgrimage, quest, raid, safari, voyage.

expeditious adjective SEE **quick**.

expel verb **1** *to expel a pupil from a school.* ban, banish, cast out, [*informal*] chuck out, dismiss, drive out, eject, evict (*from your home*), exile (*from your country*), exorcise (*evil spirits*), oust, remove, send away, throw out, [*informal*] turf out.
2 *to expel exhaust fumes.* belch, discharge, emit, exhale, give out, send out, spew out.

expend verb SEE **use** verb.

expendable adjective *expendable materials.* disposable, replaceable, [*informal*] throwaway.
OPPOSITE: reusable.

expenditure noun SEE **expense**.
OPPOSITE: income.

expense noun *the expense of running a car.* charges, cost, expenditure, outgoings, outlay, overheads, payment, price, spending.

expensive adjective *expensive presents.* costly, dear, SEE **exorbitant**, extravagant, generous (*a generous gift*), highpriced, [*informal*] pricey, [*informal*] steep, [*informal*] up-market.
OPPOSITES: SEE **cheap**.

experience noun **1** *You learn by experience.* [*informal*] doing it, familiarity, involvement, observation, participation, practice, taking part.
2 *They want someone with experience.* [*informal*] know-how, knowledge, skill, understanding.
3 *a frightening experience.* adventure, event, happening, incident, occurrence, ordeal.

experienced adjective **1** *an experienced worker.* expert, knowledgeable, practised, professional, qualified, skilled, specialized, trained, well-versed.
OPPOSITES: SEE **inexperienced**.
2 *an experienced man of the world.* knowing, sophisticated, wise, worldly-wise.
OPPOSITES: SEE **innocent**.
an experienced person SEE **expert** noun, [*informal*] old hand, veteran.

experiment noun 1 *scientific experiments.* demonstration, investigation, practical, proof, research, test.
2 *The new bus-service is an experiment.* trial, try-out, venture.

experiment verb *to experiment in a laboratory.* do an experiment, investigate, make tests, research, test, try out.

experimental adjective 1 *experimental evidence.* based on experiments, empirical, proved, tested.
2 *an experimental bus-service.* being tested, exploratory, on trial, pilot, provisional, tentative, trial.

expert adjective *an expert craftsman.* able, [*informal*] ace, [*informal*] brilliant, capable, SEE **clever**, competent, [*informal*] crack, experienced, knowledgeable, master (*a master craftsman*), masterly, practised, professional, proficient, qualified, skilful, skilled, specialized, trained, well-versed.
OPPOSITES: SEE **amateurish, unskilful**.

expert noun *an expert in her subject.* [*informal*] ace, authority, connoisseur, [*informal*] dab hand, genius, [*uncomplimentary*] know-all, master, professional, pundit, specialist, virtuoso [= *an expert musician*], [*uncomplimentary*] wiseacre, [*informal*] wizard.
OPPOSITES: SEE **amateur, ignoramus**.

expertise noun SEE **skill**.

expiate verb *to expiate a crime.* SEE **atone**.

expire verb 1 *The animal expired.* SEE **die**.
2 *My licence expired.* become invalid, come to an end, finish, [*informal*] run out.

explain verb 1 *to explain a problem.* clarify, clear up, decipher, decode, demonstrate, disentangle, elucidate, expound, gloss, illustrate, interpret, resolve, simplify, solve, [*informal*] sort out, spell out, teach, translate, unravel.
2 *to explain a mistake.* account for, excuse, give reasons for, justify, make excuses for, rationalize, vindicate.

explanation noun 1 *an explanation of what happened.* account, clarification, definition, demonstration, description, elucidation, [*formal*] exegesis, explication, exposition, illustration, interpretation, meaning, significance.
2 *the explanation for a mistake.* cause, justification, motivation, motive, reason, vindication.
3 *an explanation beneath a diagram.* caption, gloss, key, legend, rubric.

explanatory adjective *explanatory remarks.* descriptive, expository, helpful, illuminating, illustrative, interpretive.

expletive noun SEE **exclamation**.

explicable adjective *an explicable failure.* accountable, explainable, intelligible, justifiable, straightforward, understandable.
OPPOSITES: SEE **inexplicable**.

explicit adjective *explicit criticism.* clear, definite, detailed, direct, exact, express, frank, graphic, open, outspoken, patent, plain, positive, precise, put into words, said, specific, [*informal*] spelt out, spoken, straightforward, unambiguous, unconcealed, unequivocal, unhidden, unreserved.
OPPOSITES: SEE **implicit**.

explode verb 1 *to explode with a bang.* backfire, blast, blow up, burst, detonate, erupt, go off, make an explosion, set off, shatter.
2 *to explode a theory.* destroy, discredit, disprove, put an end to, rebut, refute.

exploit noun *heroic exploits.* SEE **deed**.

exploit verb 1 *to exploit an advantage.* build on, capitalize on, [*informal*] cash in on, develop, make use of, profit by, work on, use, utilize.
2 *to exploit your employees.* [*informal*] bleed, enslave, ill-treat, impose on, keep down, manipulate, [*informal*] milk, misuse, oppress, [*informal*] rip off, [*informal*] squeeze dry, take advantage of, treat unfairly, withhold rights from.

explore verb 1 *to explore unknown lands.* break new ground, probe, prospect, reconnoitre, scout, search, survey, tour, travel through.
2 *to explore a problem.* analyse, examine, inspect, investigate, look into, research, scrutinize.

explosion noun *a loud explosion.* bang, blast, burst, clap (*of thunder*), crack, detonation, discharge (*of a gun*), eruption (*of a volcano, of noise*), outburst (*of laughter*), report.

explosive adjective *explosive substances. an explosive situation.* SEE **dangerous**, highly charged, liable to explode, sensitive, unstable, volatile.
OPPOSITES: SEE **stable**.

explosive noun EXPLOSIVES INCLUDE: cordite, dynamite, gelignite, gunpowder, TNT.

exponent noun 1 *a talented exponent of jazz.* executant, interpreter, performer, player.
2 *an exponent of a new theory.* advocate, champion, defender, expounder, presenter, propagandist, proponent, supporter, upholder.

export verb *to export goods.* SEE **convey**.

exports noun SEE **goods**.

expose verb SEE **reveal, uncover.**

expostulate verb SEE **protest** verb.

expound verb SEE **explain.**

express adjective **1** *It was his express wish.* SEE **explicit.**
2 *an express train.* SEE **fast** adjective.

express verb *to express ideas.* air, SEE **communicate,** give vent to, phrase, put into words, release, vent, ventilate, word.

expression noun **1** *a verbal expression.* cliché, formula, phrase, phraseology, remark, SEE **saying,** statement, term, turn of phrase, wording.
2 *a facial expression.* air, appearance, aspect, countenance, face, look, mien.

VARIOUS FACIAL EXPRESSIONS: beam, frown, glare, glower, grimace, grin, laugh, leer, long face, poker-face, pout, scowl, smile, smirk, sneer, wince, yawn.

---

3 *She reads with expression.* emotion, feeling, intensity, sensibility, sensitivity, sympathy, understanding.

expressionless adjective *an expressionless face.* blank, [*informal*] dead-pan, emotionless, empty, glassy (*a glassy stare*), impassive, inscrutable, poker-faced, straight-faced, uncommunicative, wooden.
2 *an expressionless voice.* boring, dull, flat, monotonous, uninspiring, unmodulated, unvarying.
OPPOSITES: SEE **expressive.**

expressive adjective **1** *an expressive look.* meaningful, mobile, revealing, sensitive, significant, striking, suggestive, telling.
2 *an expressive voice.* articulate, eloquent, lively, modulated, varied.
OPPOSITES: SEE **expressionless.**

expunge verb SEE **delete.**

expurgate verb SEE **censor.**

exquisite adjective SEE **delicate.**

extant adjective SEE **existing.**

extempore adjective SEE **impromptu.**

extemporize verb SEE **improvise.**

extend verb **1** *to extend a meeting.* draw out, keep going, lengthen, make longer, prolong, protract, [*informal*] spin out.
OPPOSITES: SEE **shorten.**
2 *to extend a deadline.* defer, delay, postpone, put back, put off.
3 *to extend your hand.* give, hold out, offer, present, proffer, put out, raise, reach out, stick out, stretch out.

4 *to extend a business.* add to, build up, develop, enlarge, expand, increase, widen the scope of.
5 *The garden extends to the fence.* continue, go, reach, spread, stretch.

extension noun **1** *an extension to a building.* SEE **addition.**
2 *an extension of a deadline.* delay, postponement.

extensive adjective SEE **large.**

extent noun **1** *The map shows the extent of the estate.* area, bounds, breadth, dimensions, distance, expanse, length, limit, measurement, reach, space, spread, width.
2 *After the storm we saw the extent of the damage.* amount, degree, magnitude, measure, proportions, quantity, range, scope, size.

extenuating adjective *extenuating circumstances.* SEE **mitigating.**

exterior adjective SEE **outside** adjective.

exterior noun SEE **outside** noun.

exterminate verb SEE **destroy.**

extermination noun SEE **destruction.**

external adjective SEE **outside** adjective.

extinct adjective **1** *an extinct volcano.* extinguished, inactive.
OPPOSITES: SEE **active.**
2 *extinct species.* dead, defunct, died out, exterminated, vanished.
OPPOSITES: SEE **existing.**

extinguish verb *to extinguish a fire.* damp down, douse, put out, quench, slake, smother, snuff (*a candle*).
OPPOSITES: SEE **light** verb.

extirpate verb SEE **destroy.**

extol verb SEE **praise** verb.

extort verb *to extort money from someone.* bully, exact, extract, force, obtain by force [SEE **obtain**].

extortionate adjective SEE **exorbitant.**

extra adjective *extra supplies.* added, additional, excess, further, more, other, reserve, spare, supplementary, surplus, unneeded, unused, unwanted.
2 *extra staff.* ancillary, auxiliary, supernumerary, temporary.

extract noun **1** *beef extract.* concentrate, decoction, distillation, essence.
2 *an extract from a newspaper.* [*formal*] citation, [*informal*] clip, clipping, cutting, excerpt, passage, quotation, selection.

extract verb **1** *to extract a tooth.* draw out, pull out, remove, take out, withdraw.
2 *to extract information from a book.* derive, gather, SEE **obtain,** quote, select.

extraordinary adjective *an extraordinary story. extraordinary behaviour.* abnormal, amazing, bizarre, curious, exceptional, fantastic, [*informal*] funny, incredible, marvellous, miraculous, mysterious, mystical, notable, noteworthy, odd, outstanding, peculiar, [*informal*] phenomenal, queer, rare, remarkable, singular, special, strange, striking, stupendous, surprising, [*informal*] unbelievable, uncommon, unheard of, unimaginable, unique, unusual, [*informal*] weird, wonderful. OPPOSITES: SEE **ordinary**.

extrapolate verb SEE **deduce**.

extra-terrestrial adjective SEE **alien** adjective.

extravagance noun *I disapproved of their extravagance.* excess, improvidence, lavishness, over-indulgence, prodigality, wastefulness.

extravagant adjective *an extravagant waste of money.* excessive, SEE **expensive**, [*informal*] fancy, grandiose, improvident, lavish, outrageous, pretentious, prodigal, profligate, profuse, reckless, self-indulgent, [*informal*] showy, spendthrift, uneconomical, unreasonable, unthrifty, wasteful. OPPOSITES: SEE **economical**.
an extravagant person SEE **spendthrift**.

extravaganza noun SEE **show** noun.

extreme adjective **1** *extreme cold. extreme care.* acute, drastic, excessive, greatest, intensest, maximum, severest, utmost.
2 *the extreme edge of the field.* farthest, furthest, furthermost, outermost, ultimate.
3 *extreme opinions.* absolute, avant-garde, exaggerated, extravagant, fanatical, [*informal*] hard-line, immoderate, intemperate, intransigent, militant, obsessive, outrageous, uncompromising, [*informal*] way-out, zealous.
4 *an extreme disaster.* SEE **complete** adjective.

extreme noun *from one extreme to the other.* edge, end, extremity, limit, maximum or minimum, opposite, pole, top or bottom, ultimate.

extremist noun SEE **fanatic**.

extremity noun SEE **extreme** noun.

extricate verb SEE **disentangle**.

extrovert noun [*uncomplimentary*] exhibitionist, good mixer, socializer. OPPOSITES: SEE **introvert**.

extroverted adjective active, confident, outgoing, positive, SEE **sociable**. OPPOSITES: SEE **introverted**.

extrude verb SEE **squeeze** (to squeeze out).

exuberant adjective **1** *an exuberant mood.* animated, boisterous, [*informal*] bubbly, buoyant, cheerful, eager, ebullient, effervescent, elated, energetic, enthusiastic, excited, exhilarated, high-spirited, irrepressible, lively, spirited, sprightly, vivacious. OPPOSITES: SEE **apathetic**.
2 *an exuberant style of decoration.* baroque, exaggerated, highly decorated, ornate, overdone, rich, rococo. OPPOSITES: SEE **classical**.
3 *exuberant growth.* abundant, copious, lush, luxuriant, overflowing, profuse, rank, teeming. OPPOSITES: SEE **sparse**.

exude verb SEE **discharge** verb.

exult verb SEE **rejoice**.

exultant adjective SEE **joyful**.

eye noun PARTS OF THE EYE: cornea, eyeball, eyebrow, eyelash, eyelid, iris, pupil, retina, white.
RELATED ADJECTIVES: optical, ophthalmic.
to keep an eye open SEE **look** verb.

eye verb SEE **look** verb (to look at).

eyelet noun SEE **hole**.

eye-opener noun SEE **surprise** noun.

eyepiece noun SEE **lens**.

eyesight noun *good eyesight.* vision.
WORDS TO DESCRIBE EYESIGHT: astigmatic, long-sighted, myopic, short-sighted.

eyesore noun SEE **blemish**.

eye-witness noun *Eye-witnesses described the accident.* bystander, looker-on, observer, onlooker, spectator, watcher, witness.

F

fable noun SEE **story**.

fabled adjective SEE **legendary**.

fabric noun cloth, material, stuff, textile.
VARIOUS FABRICS: SEE **cloth**.

fabricate verb **1** *to fabricate a building.* SEE **construct**.
2 *to fabricate a story.* SEE **invent**.

fabulous adjective **1** *fabulous monsters.* SEE **legendary**.
2 [*informal*] *a fabulous party.* SEE **excellent**.

façade noun SEE **face** noun.

face noun 1 *a person's face*. air, appearance, countenance, SEE **expression**, features, look, [*slang*] mug, [*old-fashioned*] physiognomy, visage.
2 *the face of a building*. aspect (*a house with a southern aspect*), exterior, façade, front, outside.
3 *A cube has six faces*. facet, side, surface.

face verb 1 *to face one another*. be opposite to, front, look towards, overlook.
2 *to face danger*. come to terms with, confront, cope with, defy, encounter, experience, face up to, meet, oppose, square up to, stand up to, tackle.
3 *to face a wall with plaster*. SEE **cover** verb.

face-lift noun SEE **improvement**.

facet noun SEE **face** noun.

facetious adjective SEE **amusing**.

facia noun dashboard, instrument-panel.

Several English words, including *facile, facilitate,* and *facility,* are related to Latin *facilis = easy*. Compare French *facile*.

---

facile adjective 1 [*uncomplimentary*] *a facile solution to a problem*. cheap, easy, effortless, hasty, obvious, quick, simple, superficial, unconsidered.
OPPOSITES: SEE **thorough**.
2 [*uncomplimentary*] *a facile talker*. fluent, glib, insincere, plausible, shallow, slick, [*informal*] smooth.
OPPOSITES: SEE **profound**.

facilitate verb SEE **help** verb.

facility noun 1 *The facility with which he did the job surprised us*. SEE **ease** noun.
2 *The crèche is a useful facility for working parents*. amenity, convenience, help, provision, resource, service.

facing noun SEE **covering**.

facsimile noun SEE **reproduction**.

fact noun *a known fact*. actuality, certainty, fait accompli, reality, truth.
OPPOSITES: SEE **fiction**.
the facts circumstances, data, details, evidence, information, particulars, statistics

faction noun SEE **party**.

factitious adjective SEE **artificial**.

factor noun *The judge took every factor into account*. aspect, cause, circumstance, component, consideration, contingency, detail, determinant, element, fact, influence, item, parameter, particular.

factory noun PLACES WHERE THINGS ARE MANUFACTURED: assembly line, forge, foundry, manufacturing plant, mill, refinery, shop-floor, workshop.

factotum noun SEE **servant**.

factual adjective 1 *factual information*. accurate, circumstantial, SEE **correct** adjective, demonstrable, empirical, objective, provable, true, well-documented.
OPPOSITES: SEE **false**.
2 *a factual film*. biographical, documentary, historical, real-life, true.
OPPOSITES: SEE **fictional**.
3 *a strictly factual account*. matter-of-fact, plain, prosaic, realistic, unadorned, unemotional, unimaginative.
OPPOSITES: SEE **unrealistic**.

faculty noun 1 *the faculty of sight*. capability, capacity, power.
2 *a faculty for learning languages*. SEE **ability**.

fad noun SEE **craze**.

faddy adjective SEE **fussy**.

fade verb 1 *Sunlight fades the curtains*. blanch, bleach, discolour, whiten.
OPPOSITES: SEE **brighten**.
2 *Daylight faded*. decline, decrease, dim, diminish, disappear, dwindle, evanesce, fail, melt away, pale, vanish, wane, weaken.
OPPOSITES: SEE **increase** verb.
3 *The flowers faded*. droop, flag, perish, shrivel, wilt, wither.
OPPOSITES: SEE **bloom** verb.

faeces noun SEE **excreta**.

fagged adjective SEE **tired**.

fail verb 1 *The engine failed*. break down, [*informal*] conk out, cut out, give out, give up, [*informal*] miss out, stop working.
OPPOSITES: SEE **succeed**.
2 *The attempt failed. The business failed*. be unsuccessful, close down, come to an end, [*informal*] come to grief, [*informal*] crash, fall through, [*informal*] flop, fold, fold up, founder, go bankrupt, [*informal*] go bust, go out of business, meet with disaster, miscarry, misfire, peter out, stop trading.
OPPOSITES: SEE **succeed**.
3 *The light failed*. decline, diminish, disappear, dwindle, fade, get worse, melt away, vanish, wane, weaken.
OPPOSITES: SEE **improve**.
4 *Don't fail to phone!* forget, neglect, omit.
OPPOSITES: SEE **remember**.
5 *She's upset: she thinks she failed us*. disappoint, [*informal*] let down.
OPPOSITES: SEE **please**.

failing noun SEE **weakness**.

failure noun 1 *a power failure.* breakdown, collapse, crash, stoppage.
2 *The attempt ended in failure.* defeat, disappointment, downfall, disaster, fiasco, [*informal*] flop, [*informal*] washout.
OPPOSITES: SEE **success.**

faint adjective 1 *a faint picture. faint colours.* blurred, dim, faded, hazy, ill-defined, indistinct, misty, pale, pastel (*pastel colours*), shadowy, unclear, vague.
OPPOSITES: SEE **clear** adjective.
2 *a faint smell.* delicate, slight.
OPPOSITES: SEE **strong.**
3 *a faint sound.* distant, hushed, low, muffled, muted, soft, subdued, thin, weak.
OPPOSITES: SEE **clear** adjective.
4 *to feel faint.* dizzy, exhausted, feeble, giddy, light-headed, unsteady, weak, [*informal*] woozy.

faint verb become unconscious, black out, collapse, [*informal*] flake out, pass out, swoon.

faint-hearted adjective SEE **timid.**

fair adjective 1 *fair hair.* blond, blonde, flaxen, golden, light, yellow.
2 [*old-fashioned*] *a fair maiden.* SEE **beautiful.**
3 *fair weather.* bright, clear, clement, cloudless, dry, favourable, fine, pleasant, sunny.
4 *a fair referee, a fair decision.* disinterested, even-handed, fair-minded, honest, honourable, impartial, just, lawful, legitimate, non-partisan, open-minded, proper, right, unbiased, unprejudiced, upright.
5 *a fair performance.* acceptable, adequate, average, indifferent, mediocre, middling, moderate, ordinary, passable, reasonable, respectable, satisfactory, [*informal*] so-so, tolerable.

fair noun 1 *the fun of the fair.* amusement park, carnival, fun-fair, gala.
2 *a Christmas fair.* bazaar, festival, fête, market, sale.
3 *a craft fair.* exhibition, show.

fairly adverb *fairly good.* moderately, pretty, quite, rather, reasonably, somewhat, tolerably, up to a point.

fairness noun SEE **impartiality.**

fairy noun OTHER LEGENDARY CREATURES: SEE **legend.**

fairy-tale noun SEE **story.**

fait accompli noun SEE **fact.**

faith noun 1 *faith that something will happen.* belief, confidence, trust.
2 *religious faith.* conviction, creed, devotion, SEE **religion.**
OPPOSITES: SEE **disbelief, doubt** noun.

faithful adjective 1 *a faithful companion.* close, consistent, constant, dependable, devoted, dutiful, loyal, reliable, staunch, trusty, trustworthy, unswerving.
2 *a faithful account of what happened.* accurate, exact, precise, SEE **true.**

faithless adjective SEE **disloyal.**

fake adjective *a fake antique.* artificial, bogus, counterfeit, ersatz, false, fictitious, forged, imitation, [*slang*] phoney, sham, simulated, synthetic, unreal.
OPPOSITES: SEE **genuine.**

fake noun 1 *The picture was a fake.* copy, duplicate, forgery, hoax, imitation, replica, reproduction, sham, simulation.
2 *The so-called expert was a fake.* charlatan, cheat, fraud, impostor, [*slang*] phoney, quack [= *fake doctor*].

fake verb *to fake a posh accent.* affect, copy, counterfeit, SEE **falsify.** feign, forge, fudge, imitate, pretend, put on, reproduce, sham, simulate.

fall noun 1 *a fall in prices.* collapse, crash, decline, decrease, descent, dip, dive, drop, lowering, plunge, reduction, slant, slope, tumble.
2 *the fall of a besieged town.* capitulation, defeat, surrender.

fall verb 1 *He fell off the wall.* collapse, [*informal*] come a cropper, crash down, dive, drop down, founder, keel over, overbalance, pitch, plummet, plunge, slump, stumble, topple, tumble.
2 *Silence fell.* come, come about, happen, occur, settle.
3 *The curtains fell in thick folds.* be suspended, cascade, dangle, dip down, hang.
4 *The water-level fell.* become lower, decline, decrease, diminish, dwindle, ebb, go down, lessen, sink, subside.
5 *The road falls to sea-level.* SEE **descend.**
6 *Millions fell in the war.* SEE **die.**
7 *The besieged town fell.* SEE **surrender** verb.
to fall out SEE **quarrel** verb.
to fall through SEE **fail.**

fallacious adjective SEE **false.**

fallacy noun SEE **error.**

fallible adjective *We're fallible, so we make mistakes.* erring, frail, human, imperfect, liable to make mistakes, uncertain, unpredictable, unreliable, weak.
OPPOSITES: SEE **infallible.**

fallow adjective *fallow land.* dormant, resting, uncultivated, unplanted, unsown, unused.

false adjective 1 *a false idea.* deceptive, erroneous, fallacious, inaccurate, incorrect, inexact, invalid, misleading, mistaken, spurious, unsound, untrue, wrong.
OPPOSITES: SEE **correct** adjective.
2 *a false friend.* deceitful, dishonest, disloyal, double-dealing, double-faced, faithless, lying, treacherous, unfaithful, unreliable, untrustworthy.
OPPOSITES: SEE **trustworthy**.
3 *false documents.* artificial, bogus, concocted, counterfeit, fake, fictitious, imitation, invented, made-up, mock, [*slang*] phoney, pretended, sham, simulated, synthetic, trumped-up, unfounded, unreal.
OPPOSITES: SEE **authentic**.
a false name SEE **pseudonym**.
false teeth dentures, plate.

falsehood noun SEE **lie** noun.

falsify verb *to falsify the facts.* alter, [*informal*] cook (*cook the books*), distort, exaggerate, SEE **fake** verb, misrepresent, oversimplify, pervert, slant, tamper with, tell lies about, twist.

falter verb 1 *to falter in the face of danger.* become weaker, flag, flinch, hesitate, hold back, lose confidence, pause, quail, stagger, stumble, totter, vacillate, waver.
OPPOSITES: SEE **persevere**.
2 *to falter in your speech.* stammer, stutter.

faltering adjective SEE **hesitant**.

fame noun *a superstar's fame.* celebrity, credit, distinction, eminence, glory, honour, importance, [*informal*] kudos, name, prestige, prominence, public esteem, renown, reputation, repute, [*informal*] stardom.

famed adjective SEE **famous**.

familiar adjective 1 *a familiar sight.* accustomed, common, conventional, customary, everyday, frequent, mundane, normal, ordinary, regular, routine, stock (*a stock reply*), usual, well-known.
OPPOSITES: SEE **strange**, unfamiliar.
2 *a familiar relationship. familiar language.* [*informal*] chatty, close, confidential, [*informal*] free-and-easy, SEE friendly, informal, intimate, near, relaxed, unceremonious.
OPPOSITES: SEE **formal**.
familiar with *Are you familiar with this music?* acquainted with, [*informal*] at home with, aware of, conscious of, expert in, informed about, knowledgeable about, trained in, versed in.

familiarize verb *Familiarize the new employee with our routine.* introduce (to), make familiar (with), teach.

family noun 1 [= *children of the same parents*] brood, [*informal*] flesh and blood (*our own flesh and blood*), generation, litter (*a litter of puppies*).
2 [= *the wider set of relations*] clan, kindred, [*old-fashioned*] kith and kin, relations, relatives, tribe.
3 [= *the line from which a person is descended*] *the royal family.* ancestry, blood, clan, dynasty, extraction, forebears, genealogy, house (*a royal house*), line, lineage, pedigree, race, strain.
RELATED ADJECTIVE: genealogical.

MEMBERS OF A FAMILY: adopted child, ancestor, aunt, brother, child, cousin, [*informal*] dad or daddy, daughter, descendant, divorcee, father, [*male*] fiancé, [*female*] fiancée, forefather, foster-child, foster-parent, godchild, godparent, grandchild, grandparent, guardian, husband, [*informal or American*] junior, kinsman or kinswoman, [*old-fashioned*] mater, mother, [*informal*] mum or mummy, nephew, next-of-kin, niece, offspring, orphan, parent, [*old-fashioned*] pater, quadruplet, quintuplet, relation, relative, sextuplet, sibling, sister, son, step-child, step-parent, triplet, twin, uncle, ward, widow, widower, wife.

famine noun *The drought caused widespread famine.* dearth, hunger, malnutrition, scarcity, shortage, starvation, want.
OPPOSITES: SEE **plenty**.

famished, famishing adjectives SEE **hungry**.

famous adjective *a famous person.* acclaimed, celebrated, distinguished, eminent, famed, great, historic, honoured, illustrious, important, legendary, lionized, notable, noted, outstanding, prominent, proverbial, renowned, time-honoured, well-known, world-famous.
OPPOSITES: SEE **unknown**.
famous person SEE **celebrity**.

fan noun 1 *an air-conditioning fan.* blower, extractor, propeller, ventilator.
2 *a pop music fan* SEE **fanatic**.

fanatic noun 1 *a pop music fanatic.* addict, admirer, aficionado, devotee, enthusiast, [*informal*] fan, [*informal*] fiend, follower, [*informal*] freak, lover, supporter.
2 *a political fanatic.* activist, adherent, bigot, extremist, fanatical supporter [SEE **fanatical**], militant, zealot.

fanatical adjective *fanatical political views*. bigoted, extreme, fervent, immoderate, irrational, militant, obsessive, over-enthusiastic, passionate, rabid, single-minded, zealous.
OPPOSITES: SEE **moderate** adjective.

fanciful adjective *a fanciful idea*. SEE **unrealistic**.

fancy adjective *fancy patterns*. SEE **decorative**.

fancy noun 1 *a poet's fancy*. SEE **imagination**.
2 *a fancy to do something*. SEE **whim**.

fancy verb 1 *I fancied I saw pink elephants*. SEE **imagine**.
2 *What do you fancy to eat?* SEE **desire** verb.

fanfare noun MUSICAL COMPOSITIONS: SEE **music**.

fang noun SEE **tooth**.

fanlight noun SEE **window**.

fantasize verb SEE **day-dream** verb.

fantastic adjective 1 *fantastic decoration*. absurd, elaborate, exaggerated, extravagant, fanciful, grotesque, ostentatious, quaint, rococo.
OPPOSITES: SEE **plain** adjective.
2 *a fantastic story about dragons*. amazing, extraordinary, fabulous, far-fetched, imaginative, implausible, incredible, odd, remarkable, strange, unbelievable, unlikely, unrealistic, weird.
OPPOSITES: SEE **realistic**.
3 [*informal*] *We had a fantastic time*. SEE **excellent**.

fantasy noun *a fantasy about the future*. day-dream, delusion, dream, fancy, hallucination, illusion, invention, make-believe, reverie, vision.
OPPOSITES: SEE **reality**.

far adjective *far places*. SEE **distant**.

farce noun SEE **comedy**.

farcical adjective SEE **comic** adjective.

fare noun *the train fare to London*. charge, cost, fee, payment, price.

farewell adjective *a farewell speech*. goodbye, last, leaving, parting, valedictory.

farewell noun *a sad farewell*. SEE **goodbye**, [*informal*] send-off, valediction.

far-fetched adjective SEE **unlikely**.

far-reaching adjective *far-reaching effects*. SEE **influential**.

farm noun [*old-fashioned*] grange.

KINDS OF FARM: arable farm, croft, dairy farm, fish farm, fruit farm, livestock farm, organic farm, plantation, poultry farm, ranch, smallholding.

FARM BUILDINGS, ETC.: barn, barn-yard, byre, cowshed, dairy, Dutch barn, farmhouse, farmstead, farmyard, granary, haystack, milking parlour, outhouse, pigsty, rick, shed, silo, stable, sty.

FARMING EQUIPMENT: baler, combine harvester, cultivator, drill, harrow, harvester, hay fork, hoe, irrigation system, manure spreader, mower, planter, plough, scythe, tedder, tractor, trailer.

FARM WORKERS: [*American*] cowboy, [*old-fashioned*] dairymaid, farm manager, farm worker, labourer, [*old-fashioned*] land-girl, shepherd, stock-breeder, [*old-fashioned*] swineherd, [*old-fashioned*] yeoman.

CROPS GROWN ON FARMS: barley, cereals, corn, fodder, SEE **fruit**, maize, oats, potatoes, rape, rye, sugar-beet, sweet corn, SEE **vegetable**, wheat.

FARM ANIMALS: SEE **cattle**, chicken, cow, duck, fatstock, goat, goose, hen, horse, lamb, livestock, pig, SEE **poultry**, sheep, turkey.

farming noun agriculture, [*formal*] agronomy, crofting, husbandry.
RELATED ADJECTIVES: agricultural.

farrago noun SEE **jumble** noun.

farrier noun blacksmith, smith.

farrow verb SEE **birth (to give birth)**.

fascinate verb 1 *He fascinated us with his tales*. attract, beguile, bewitch, captivate, charm, delight, enchant, engross, enthral, entrance, interest, rivet, spellbind.
2 *Some snakes fascinate their prey*. allure, entice, hypnotize, mesmerize.

fascinating adjective SEE **attractive**.

fascism noun POLITICAL TERMS: SEE **politics**.

fashion noun 1 *He behaved in a strange fashion*. manner, method, mode, way.
2 *the latest fashion in clothes*. convention, craze, cut, [*informal*] fad, line, look, pattern, rage (*it's all the rage*), style, taste, trend, vogue.

fashionable adjective *fashionable clothes*. chic, contemporary, current, elegant, [*informal*] in (*the in thing*), the latest, modern, modish, popular, smart, [*informal*] snazzy, sophisticated, stylish, tasteful, [*informal*] trendy, up-to-date, [*informal*] with it.
OPPOSITES: SEE **unfashionable**.

fast adjective 1 *a fast pace.* breakneck, brisk, expeditious, express (*express delivery*), hasty, headlong, high-speed, hurried, lively, [*informal*] nippy, precipitate, quick, rapid, smart, [*informal*] spanking, speedy, supersonic, swift, unhesitating.
OPPOSITES: SEE **slow** adjective.
2 *Make the rope fast.* attached, fastened, firm, immobile, immovable, secure, tight.
OPPOSITES: SEE **loose** adjective.
3 *fast colours.* fixed, indelible, lasting, permanent, stable.
OPPOSITES: SEE **impermanent.**
4 *fast living.* SEE **immoral.**

fast adverb *travelling fast.* at full tilt, briskly, in no time, post-haste, quickly, rapidly, swiftly.

fast verb *to fast on a holy day.* abstain, deny yourself, diet, go hungry, go without food, starve.
OPPOSITE: indulge yourself [SEE **indulge**].

fasten verb affix, anchor, attach, batten, bind, bolt, buckle, button, chain, clamp, clasp, cling, close, connect, couple, do up (*do up a button*), fix, grip, hitch, hook, knot, join, lace, lash, latch on, link, lock, moor (*a boat*), nail, padlock, paste, pin, rivet (*metal plates*), rope, seal, secure, solder, staple, SEE **stick** verb, strap, tack, tape, tether (*an animal*), tie, unite, weld (*metal*).
OPPOSITES: SEE **undo.**

THINGS USED FOR FASTENING: anchor, bolt, buckle, button, catch, chain, clamp, clasp, clip, dowel, dowel-pin, drawing-pin, SEE **glue** noun, hasp, hook, knot, lace, latch, lock, mooring, nail, padlock, painter, peg, pin, rivet, rope, safety-pin, screw, seal, Sellotape, solder, staple, strap, string, tack, tape, tether, tie, toggle, velcro, wedge, zip.

---

fastener, fastening nouns connection, connector, coupling, link, linkage.

fastidious adjective *a fastidious eater.* choosy, dainty, discriminating, finicky, fussy, particular, [*informal*] pernickety, selective, squeamish.

fat adjective 1 *a fat figure.* chubby, corpulent, dumpy, SEE **enormous,** flabby, fleshy, gross, heavy, obese, overweight, paunchy, plump, podgy, portly, pot-bellied, pudgy, rotund, round, solid, squat, stocky, stout, tubby.
OPPOSITES: SEE **thin** adjective.
2 *fat meat.* fatty, greasy, oily.
OPPOSITE: lean.

3 *a fat book.* bulky, thick, weighty.

fat noun KINDS OF FAT: [*formal*] adipose tissue, blubber, butter, dripping, grease, lard, margarine, oil, suet.

fatal adjective 1 *a fatal dose.* deadly, lethal.
2 *a fatal illness.* final, incurable, malignant, mortal, terminal.
3 *a fatal mistake.* calamitous, destructive, disastrous, vital.

fatality noun *The accident resulted in fatalities.* casualty, death, loss.

fate noun 1 *Fate was kind to him.* chance, destiny, doom, fortune, karma, kismet, luck, nemesis, predestination, providence, the stars.
2 *He met a terrible fate.* death, demise, end.

fated adjective *I was fated to miss that train.* certain, destined, doomed, foreordained, intended, predestined, predetermined, preordained, sure.

fateful adjective *a fateful decision.* SEE **momentous.**

fat-head noun SEE **idiot.**

father noun [*informal*] dad or daddy, parent, [*old-fashioned*] pater.

fathom verb *I can't fathom what he's getting at.* SEE **understand.**

fatigue noun *overcome with fatigue.* debility, exhaustion, feebleness, lethargy, tiredness, weakness, weariness.

fatigue verb SEE **tire.**

fatstock noun farm animals, livestock.

fatten verb *to fatten cattle.* build up, feed up, make fat.

fatty adjective *fatty food.* fat, greasy, oily.

fatuous adjective *fatuous jokes.* SEE **silly.**

fault noun 1 *a fault in the engine.* blemish, defect, deficiency, failure, flaw, imperfection, malfunction, snag, weakness.
2 *a fault in your reasoning.* error, fallacy, inaccuracy, miscalculation, mistake.
3 *The mistake was my fault.* blunder, [*informal*] boob, demerit, failing, guilt, indiscretion, lapse, misconduct, misdeed, negligence, offence, omission, oversight, responsibility, shortcoming, sin, slip, [*informal*] transgression, [*old-fashioned*] trespass, wrongdoing.

fault verb *I can't fault his work.* SEE **criticize.**

faultless adjective SEE **perfect** adjective.

faulty adjective *faulty goods, a faulty argument.* broken, damaged, defective, deficient, flawed, illogical, imperfect, inaccurate, incomplete, incorrect,

inoperative, invalid, not working, out of order, unusable, useless.
OPPOSITES: SEE **perfect** adjective.

fauna noun animal-life, wildlife.
VARIOUS ANIMALS: SEE **animal** noun.

faux pas SEE **mistake** noun.

favour noun 1 *She shows favour towards her friends.* acceptance, approval, bias, favouritism, friendliness, goodwill, grace, liking, preference, support.
2 *He did me a favour.* benefit, courtesy, gift, good deed, good turn, indulgence, kindness, service.

favour verb 1 *She favours the original plan.* approve of, be in sympathy with, champion, choose, commend, esteem, [*informal*] fancy, [*informal*] go for, like, opt for, prefer, show favour to [SEE **favour** noun], think well of, value.
OPPOSITES: SEE **dislike** verb.
2 *The wind favoured our team.* abet, back, be advantageous to, befriend, SEE **help** verb, support.
OPPOSITES: SEE **hinder**.

favourable adjective 1 *a favourable wind. favourable comments.* advantageous, approving, auspicious, beneficial, benign, complimentary, encouraging, following (*a following wind*), friendly, generous, helpful, kind, positive, promising, propitious, reassuring, supportive, sympathetic, understanding, well-disposed.
OPPOSITES: SEE **unfavourable**.
2 *a favourable reputation.* agreeable, desirable, enviable, good, pleasing, satisfactory.
OPPOSITES: SEE **undesirable**.

favourite adjective *a favourable toy.* best, chosen, dearest, esteemed, liked, popular, preferred, well-liked.

favourite noun 1 *mother's favourite* [*informal*] apple of (someone's) eye, darling, idol, pet.
2 *the favourite in a race.* likely winner.

favouritism noun SEE **bias** noun.

fawn verb SEE **flatter**.

fealty noun SEE **loyalty**.

fear noun *trembling with fear.* alarm, anxiety, apprehension, awe, concern, consternation, cowardice, dismay, doubt, dread, faint-heartedness, foreboding, fright, [*informal*] funk, horror, misgiving, panic, [*formal*] phobia, qualm, suspicion, terror, timidity, trepidation, uneasiness, worry.
VARIOUS KINDS OF FEAR: SEE **phobia**.
OPPOSITES: SEE **courage**.

fear verb *to fear the worst.* be afraid of [SEE **afraid**], dread, suspect, tremble at, worry about.

fearful adjective 1 *fearful about the future.* SEE **afraid**.
2 *a fearful sight.* SEE **frightening**.

fearless adjective SEE **courageous**.

fearsome adjective SEE **frightening**.

feasible adjective 1 *a feasible plan.* achievable, attainable, possible, practicable, practical, realizable, viable, workable.
OPPOSITES: SEE **impractical**.
2 *a feasible excuse.* acceptable, credible, likely, plausible, reasonable.
OPPOSITES: SEE **implausible**.

feast noun SEE **meal**.

feat noun *a daring feat.* accomplishment, achievement, act, action, attainment, deed, exploit, performance.

feather noun plume, quill.
feathers down, plumage.

feather-brained adjective SEE **silly**.

feathery adjective downy, fluffy, light, wispy.

feature noun 1 *The crime had some unusual features.* aspect, characteristic, circumstance, detail, facet, peculiarity, point, quality, trait.
2 *a feature in a newspaper.* article, column, item, piece, report, story.
features *a person's features.* countenance, expression, face, lineaments, look, [*formal*] physiognomy.

feature verb *The play featured a new actor.* focus on, give prominence to, highlight, present, promote, show up, [*informal*] spotlight, [*informal*] star.

feckless adjective SEE **ineffective**.

fecund adjective SEE **fertile**.

federate verb SEE **unite**.

federation noun SEE **group** noun.

fee noun *a club membership fee. legal fees.* charge, cost, dues, fare, payment, price, remuneration, subscription, sum, terms, toll.

feeble adjective 1 *feeble after illness.* debilitated, delicate, exhausted, faint, frail, helpless, ill, inadequate, ineffective, listless, poorly, powerless, puny, sickly, useless, weak.
OPPOSITES: SEE **strong**.
2 *a feeble character.* effete, feckless, hesitant, incompetent, indecisive, ineffectual, irresolute, [*informal*] namby-pamby, spineless, vacillating, weedy, [*informal*] wishy-washy.
OPPOSITES: SEE **decisive**.
3 *a feeble excuse.* flimsy, lame, paltry, poor, tame, thin, unconvincing, weak.
OPPOSITES: SEE **convincing**.

feed verb 1 *to feed your children.* cater for, give food to, nourish, provide for, provision, strengthen, suckle.
2 *We fed well.* dine, eat, fare.
to feed on SEE eat.

feel verb 1 *to feel the texture of something.* caress, finger, fondle, handle, hold, manipulate, maul, [*informal*] paw, stroke, touch.
2 *to feel your way in the dark.* explore, fumble, grope.
3 *to feel the cold.* be aware of, be conscious of, detect, experience, know, notice, perceive, sense, suffer, undergo.
4 *It feels cold.* appear, give the feeling of [SEE **feeling**], seem.
5 *I feel it's time to go.* believe, consider, deem, have a feeling [SEE **feeling**], judge, think.

feeling noun 1 *a feeling in my leg.* sensation, sense of touch, sensitivity.
2 *feelings of love. feelings of hate.* ardour, emotion, fervour, passion, sentiment, warmth.
3 *a feeling that something is wrong.* attitude, belief, consciousness, guess, hunch, idea, impression, instinct, intuition, notion, opinion, perception, thought, view.
4 *a feeling for music.* fondness, responsiveness, sensibility, sympathy, understanding.
5 [*informal*], *a Christmassy feeling.* aura, atmosphere, mood, tone, [*informal*] vibrations.

feign verb SEE **pretend**.

feint noun SEE **pretence**.

felicitate verb SEE **congratulate**.

felicitous adjective SEE **appropriate** adjective.

felicity noun SEE **happiness**.

feline adjective cat-like.

fell noun SEE **hill**.

fell verb 1 *to fell an opponent.* bring down, flatten, [*informal*] floor, knock down, prostrate.
2 *to fell trees.* chop down, cut down.

fellow noun SEE **man** noun.

fellowship noun SEE **friendship**, **society**.

felon noun SEE **criminal** noun.

felony noun SEE **crime**.

female adjective, noun SEE **feminine**.
RELATED ADJECTIVE: gynaecological.
OPPOSITES: SEE **male**.

FEMALE PEOPLE: aunt, [*old-fashioned*] damsel, daughter, [*old-fashioned*] débutante, fiancée, girl, girlfriend, grandmother, lady, [*informal*] lass, lesbian, [*old-fashioned*] maid, [*old-fashioned*] maiden, [*old-fashioned*] mistress, mother, niece, sister, spinster, [*old-fashioned or insulting*] wench, wife, woman.

FEMALE CREATURES: bitch, cow, doe, ewe, hen, lioness, mare, nanny-goat, sow, tigress, vixen.

feminine adjective *feminine behaviour. feminine clothes.* [*of males*] effeminate, female, [*uncomplimentary*] girlish, ladylike, womanly.
OPPOSITES: SEE **masculine**.

fen noun bog, lowland, marsh, morass, quagmire, slough, swamp.

fence noun *a garden fence.* barricade, barrier, fencing, hedge, hurdle, obstacle, paling, palisade, railing, rampart, stockade, wall, wire.

fence verb 1 *to fence someone in.* circumscribe, confine, coop up, encircle, enclose, hedge in, immure, pen, surround, wall in.
2 *to fence with foils.* SEE **fight** verb.

fend verb to fend for care for, [*informal*] do for, look after.
to fend off SEE **repel**.

ferment noun *a state of ferment.* agitation, SEE **commotion**.

ferment verb *fermenting wine.* bubble, effervesce, [*informal*] fizz, foam, seethe, work.

ferocious adjective SEE **fierce**.

ferret verb to ferret about SEE **search** verb.

ferrous adjective iron.

ferry noun VARIOUS VESSELS: SEE **vessel**.

ferry verb *to ferry passengers.* SEE **convey**, drive, ship, shuttle, take across, taxi, transport.

fertile adjective 1 *a fertile garden.* abundant, fecund, flourishing, fruitful, lush, luxuriant, productive, prolific, rich, teeming, well-manured.
OPPOSITES: SEE **barren**.
2 *a fertile egg.* fertilized [SEE **fertilize**].
OPPOSITES: SEE **sterile**.

fertilize verb 1 *to fertilize flowers or eggs.* impregnate, inseminate, pollinate.
2 *to fertilize the soil.* add fertilizer to, cultivate, dress, enrich, feed, make fertile, manure, mulch, top-dress.

fertilizer noun compost, dressing, dung, manure, mulch.

fervent adjective *a fervent supporter.* ardent, avid, committed, devout, eager, earnest, enthusiastic, excited, fanatical, fervid, fiery, impassioned, keen, passionate, spirited, vehement, vigorous, warm, wholehearted, zealous.

fervour noun *The fervour of her speech showed she felt strongly.* ardour, eagerness, energy, enthusiasm, excitement, fervency, fire, heat, intensity, keenness, passion, sparkle, spirit, vehemence, vigour, warmth, zeal.

fester verb *The wound festered.* become infected, become inflamed, become poisoned, decay, discharge, gather, go bad, go septic, putrefy, suppurate, ulcerate.

festival noun *a bank-holiday festival.* anniversary, carnival, celebration, commemoration, fair, feast, festivity, fête, fiesta, gala, holiday, jamboree, jubilee, merry-making.

festive adjective *a festive occasion.* cheerful, cheery, convivial, gay, gleeful, happy, jolly, jovial, joyful, joyous, light-hearted, merry, uproarious.

festivities noun *Christmas festivities.* celebrations, entertainment, feasting, SEE **festival**, festive occasion [SEE **festive**], [*informal*] jollification, party, revelry, revels.

festoon verb SEE **decorate**.

fetch verb 1 *to fetch things from the shops.* bear, bring, call for, carry, collect, convey, get, import, obtain, pick up, retrieve, transfer, transport.
2 *How much would our car fetch?* be bought for, bring in, earn, go for, make, produce, raise, realize, sell for.

fetching adjective SEE **attractive**.

fête noun SEE **festival**.

fetid, foetid adjective SEE **smelly**.

fetish noun SEE **obsession**.

fetter noun, verb SEE **chain** noun, verb.

fettle noun SEE **condition**.

feud noun *a feud between two families.* animosity, antagonism, conflict, dispute, enmity, hostility, SEE **quarrel** noun, rivalry, strife, vendetta.

feud verb SEE **quarrel** verb.

fever noun delirium, feverishness, high temperature.
RELATED ADJECTIVE: febrile.

feverish adjective 1 *a feverish illness.* burning, febrile, fevered, flushed, hot, inflamed, trembling.
2 *feverish activity.* agitated, excited, frantic, frenetic, frenzied, hectic, hurried, impatient, restless.

few adjective *We have few buses on Sunday.* [*informal*] few and far between, inadequate, infrequent, rare, scarce,

sparse, sporadic, [*informal*] thin on the ground, uncommon.
OPPOSITES: SEE **many**.

fiasco noun SEE **failure**.

fiat noun SEE **decree** noun.

fib noun, verb SEE **lie** noun, verb.

fibre noun 1 *woven fibres.* filament, hair, strand, thread.
2 *moral fibre.* backbone, SEE **courage**, determination, spirit, tenacity, toughness.

fickle adjective *They have no use for fickle supporters.* changeable, changing, disloyal, erratic, faithless, inconsistent, inconstant, mutable, treacherous, unfaithful, unpredictable, unreliable, unstable, [*informal*] up and down, vacillating, variable, volatile.
OPPOSITES: SEE **constant, stable**.

fiction noun 1 *a work of fiction.* VARIOUS KINDS OF WRITING: SEE **writing**.
2 *Her account was a fiction from start to finish.* concoction, deception, fabrication, fantasy, figment of the imagination, flight of fancy, invention, SEE **lie** noun, [*informal*] tall story.
OPPOSITES: SEE **fact**.

fictional adjective *a fictional story.* fabulous, fanciful, imaginary, invented, legendary, made-up, make-believe, mythical.
OPPOSITES: SEE **factual**.

fictitious adjective *a fictitious name.* apocryphal, assumed, SEE **fake** adjective, false, deceitful, fraudulent, imagined, invented, spurious, unreal, untrue.
OPPOSITES: SEE **genuine, true**.

fiddle noun 1 violin.
2 [*slang*] *a financial fiddle.* SEE **cheat** noun.

fiddle verb 1 *to fiddle with the knobs on the TV.* SEE **fidget**.
2 [*informal*] *to fiddle the accounts.* SEE **cheat** verb.

fiddling adjective *fiddling details.* SEE **trivial**.

fiddly adjective [*informal*] *a fiddly job.* SEE **intricate**.

fidelity noun SEE **loyalty**.

fidget verb *It annoys me when you fidget!* be restless, [*informal*] fiddle about, fret, frisk about, jerk about, [*informal*] jiggle, [*informal*] mess about, move restlessly, [*informal*] play about, twitch, worry.

fidgety adjective *fidgety movements.* agitated, frisky, impatient, jittery, jumpy, nervous, on edge, restive, restless, twitchy, uneasy.
OPPOSITES: SEE **calm** adjective.

field noun 1 *a farm field.* enclosure, [*poetic*] glebe, green, [*old-fashioned & poetic*] mead, meadow, paddock, pasture.
2 *a games field.* arena, ground, pitch, playing-field, recreation ground, stadium.
3 *Electronics isn't my field.* area, [*informal*] department, domain, province, sphere, subject, territory.

field-glasses noun binoculars.
OTHER OPTICAL INSTRUMENTS: SEE optical.

fiend noun 1 *a wicked fiend.* demon, devil, evil spirit, goblin, hobgoblin, imp, Satan, spirit.
2 *a cruel fiend.* SEE **savage** noun.

fiendish adjective SEE **evil** adjective, **fierce.**

fierce adjective 1 *a fierce attack. fierce animals.* angry, barbaric, barbarous, blood-thirsty, bloody, brutal, cold-blooded, cruel, dangerous, fearsome, ferocious, fiendish, homicidal, inhuman, merciless, murderous, pitiless, ruthless, sadistic, savage, untamed, vicious, violent, wild.
OPPOSITES: SEE **humane, kind** adjective.
2 *fierce opposition.* active, aggressive, competitive, eager, heated, furious, intense, keen, passionate, relentless, strong, unrelenting.
OPPOSITES: SEE **gentle.**
3 *a fierce fire.* SEE **fiery.**

fiery adjective 1 *a fiery furnace.* ablaze, aflame, blazing, burning, flaming, fierce, glowing, heated, hot, raging, red, red-hot.
2 *a fiery temper.* angry, ardent, choleric, excitable, fervent, furious, hot-headed, intense, irritable, livid, mad, passionate, violent.

fight noun action, affray, attack, battle, bout, brawl, [*informal*] brush, [*informal*] bust-up, clash, combat, competition, conflict, confrontation, contest, counter-attack, dispute, dogfight, duel, [*informal*] dust-up, encounter, engagement, feud, [*old-fashioned*] fisticuffs, fracas, fray, [*informal*] free-for-all, hostilities, joust, SEE **martial (martial arts),** match, mêlée, [*informal*] punch-up, SEE **quarrel** noun, raid, riot, rivalry, row, scramble, scrap, scrimmage, scuffle, [*informal*] set-to, skirmish, squabble, strife, struggle, tussle, war, wrangle.

fight verb 1 *to fight against an enemy.* attack, battle, box, brawl, [*informal*] brush, clash, compete, conflict, contend, do battle, duel, engage, exchange blows, fence, feud, grapple, have a fight [SEE **fight** noun], joust, quarrel, row, scrap, scuffle, skirmish, spar, squabble,

stand up (to), strive, struggle, [*old-fashioned*] tilt, tussle, wage war, wrestle.
2 *to fight a decision.* campaign against, contest, defy, oppose, protest against, resist, take a stand against.

fighter noun aggressor, antagonist, attacker, belligerent, campaigner, combatant, contender, contestant, defender.

VARIOUS FIGHTERS: archer, boxer, [*informal*] brawler, champion, duellist, freedom-fighter, gladiator, guerrilla, gunman, knight, marine, marksman, mercenary, partisan, prize-fighter, pugilist, sniper, SEE **soldier,** swordsman, terrorist, warrior, wrestler.

figment noun *a figment of the imagination.* SEE **invention.**

figurative adjective *figurative language.* allegorical, metaphorical, poetic, symbolic.
OPPOSITES: SEE **literal.**

figure noun 1 *the figures 1 to 10.* amount, digit, integer, number, numeral, value.
figures *She's good at figures.* accounts, mathematics, statistics, sums.
2 *a diagrammatic figure.* diagram, drawing, graph, illustration, outline, representation.
3 *a plump figure.* body, build, form, physique, shape, silhouette.
4 *a bronze figure.* SEE **sculpture** noun.
5 *a well-known figure.* SEE **personality.**
figure of speech conceit, emblem, image, [*informal*] manner of speaking, trope.

COMMON FIGURES OF SPEECH: alliteration, anacoluthon, antithesis, assonance, climax, ellipsis, hendiadys, hyperbole, irony, litotes, meiosis, metaphor, metonymy, onomatopoeia, oxymoron, parenthesis, personification, simile, synecdoche, zeugma.

figure verb *Macbeth figures in a Shakespeare play.* SEE **appear.**
to figure out 1 *to figure out an answer.* add up, calculate, compute, count, reckon, total, [*informal*] tot up, work out.
2 *to figure out what something means.* comprehend, fathom, make out, puzzle out, reason out, see, understand.

figurine noun SEE **sculpture** noun.

filament noun SEE **fibre.**

filch verb SEE **steal.**

file noun 1 *a file for papers.* binder, box-file, cover, document-case, dossier, folder, portfolio, ring-binder.
2 *single file.* column, line, procession, queue, rank, row, stream, string, train.

file verb 1 *to file rough edges off something.* SEE **smooth** verb.
2 *to file documents.* enter, organize, pigeon-hole, put away, store.
3 *to file through a door.* march, parade, proceed in a line, stream, troop.

filibuster verb SEE **delay** verb.

fill verb 1 *to fill a container.* cram, flood (*with liquid*), inflate (*with air*), load, pack, refill, replenish, [*informal*] stuff, [*informal*] top up.
OPPOSITES: SEE **empty** verb.
2 *to fill a gap.* block, [*informal*] bung up, clog, close up, crowd, jam, obstruct, plug, seal, stop up.
OPPOSITES: SEE **clear** verb.
3 *to fill a need.* fulfil, furnish, meet, provide, satisfy, supply.
4 *to fill a post.* hold, occupy, take up.
to fill out *His figure filled out after his illness.* enlarge, expand, get bigger, make bigger, swell.

filling noun *the filling in a cushion.* contents, insides, padding, stuffing.

filling-station noun garage, petrol station.

fillip noun SEE **impetus**.

filly noun SEE **horse**.

film noun 1 *a film of oil.* coat, coating, covering, layer, membrane, sheet, skin, slick, tissue, veil.
2 *a cinema film.* [*old-fashioned*] flick, motion picture, movie, picture, video.

KINDS OF FILM: cartoon, comedy, documentary, epic, feature, horror film, short, western.

---

filter noun gauze, membrane, mesh, screen, sieve, strainer.

filter verb *to filter a liquid.* clarify, filtrate, percolate, purify, screen, sieve, strain.

filth noun *Clean up this filth!* dirt, SEE **excreta**, garbage, grime, SEE **impurity**, muck, mud, pollution, refuse, scum, sewage, slime, sludge.

filthy adjective 1 *filthy shoes. a filthy room.* caked, dirty, disgusting, dusty, foul, grimy, grubby, impure, messy, mucky, muddy, nasty, slimy, smelly, soiled, sooty, sordid, squalid, stinking, uncleaned, unwashed.
OPPOSITES: SEE **clean** adjective.

2 *filthy language.* SEE **obscene**.

final adjective *the final moments of a game.* clinching, closing, concluding, conclusive, decisive, dying, eventual, last, terminal, terminating, ultimate.
OPPOSITES: SEE **introductory**.

finale noun SEE **conclusion**.

finalize verb SEE **complete** verb.

finance noun *He works in finance.* accounting, banking, business, commerce, investment, stocks and shares.
finances *What's the state of your finances?* assets, bank account, budget, funds, income, money, resources, wealth.

finance verb *The bank helped to finance our business.* back, fund, invest in, pay for, provide money for, sponsor, subsidize, support, underwrite.

financial adjective *financial affairs.* economic, fiscal, monetary, pecuniary.

financier noun SEE **businessman**.

find verb 1 *to find something new.* acquire, arrive at, become aware of, chance upon, come across, come upon, dig up, discover, encounter, expose, [*informal*] ferret out, happen on, hit on, learn, light on, locate, meet, note, notice, observe, reach, recognize, spot, stumble on, uncover, unearth.
2 *to find something that was lost.* get back, recover, rediscover, regain, retrieve, trace, track down.
3 *to find a fault.* detect, diagnose, identify.
4 *He found me a job.* give, pass on, procure, provide, supply.

findings noun *The judge announced his findings.* conclusion, decision, judgement, verdict.

fine adjective 1 *a fine performance.* admirable, commendable, excellent, first-class, SEE **good**.
2 *fine weather.* bright, clear, cloudless, fair, pleasant, sunny.
3 *fine thread. fine china.* delicate, flimsy, fragile, narrow, slender, slim, thin.
4 *fine sand.* minute, powdery.
5 *fine embroidery.* beautiful, dainty, delicate, exquisite, skilful.
6 *a fine distinction.* discriminating, fine-drawn, subtle.

fine noun *a parking fine.* charge, penalty.
OTHER PUNISHMENTS: SEE **punishment**.

finesse noun SEE **delicacy**.

finger noun digit, fingertip, index finger, little finger, middle finger, ring finger.

finger verb SEE **touch** verb.

finicky adjective SEE **fastidious**.

finish noun 1 *the finish of a race.* cessation, close, completion, conclusion, culmination, end, ending, finale, resolution, result, termination.

2 *a shiny finish on the metalwork.* appearance, gloss, lustre, polish, shine, smoothness, surface, texture.

3 *Their performance lacked finish.* completeness, perfection, polish.

finish verb 1 *to finish a job.* accomplish, achieve, break off, bring to an end, cease, complete, conclude, discontinue, end, finalize, halt, perfect, reach the end of, round off, sign off, stop, terminate, [*informal*] wind up.

2 *to finish your rations.* consume, drink up, eat up, empty, exhaust, expend, get through, [*informal*] polish off, [*informal*] say goodbye to, use up.

3 [*informal*] *The effort finished me.* exhaust, tire out, wear out.

to finish off annihilate, destroy, dispatch, exterminate, SEE **kill**.

finite adjective *finite resources. a finite number.* calculable, definable, defined, fixed, known, limited, measurable, numbered, restricted.
OPPOSITES: SEE **infinite**.

fire noun 1 blaze, burning, combustion, conflagration, flames, holocaust, inferno, pyre.

2 *a fire in the lounge.* fireplace, grate, hearth.

KINDS OF FIRE OR HEATING APPARATUS: boiler, bonfire, brazier, central heating, convector, electric fire, SEE **fireworks**, forge, furnace, gas fire, immersion-heater, incinerator, kiln, oven, radiator, stove.

fire verb 1 *The vandals fired a barn.* burn, ignite, kindle, light, put a light to, set alight, set fire to.

2 *to fire pottery.* bake, heat.

3 *to fire your imagination.* animate, enliven, excite, incite, inflame, inspire, rouse, stimulate, stir.

4 *to fire a gun or missile.* detonate, discharge, explode, launch, let off, set off, shoot, trigger off.

5 *to fire someone from a job.* dismiss, make redundant, sack, throw out.

to fire at *I fired at the target.* aim at, bombard, [*informal*] let fly at, shell, shoot at.

firearm noun SEE **gun**.

firelight noun SEE **light** noun.

fireman noun fire-fighter.

fireplace noun SEE **fire** noun.

fireproof adjective *fireproof material.* flameproof, incombustible, non-flammable.
OPPOSITES: SEE **inflammable**.

fire-raiser noun arsonist, pyromaniac.

firewood noun kindling.

fireworks noun pyrotechnics.
VARIOUS FIREWORKS: banger, Catherine wheel, cracker, rocket, Roman candle, sparkler, squib.

firing noun SEE **gunfire**.

firm adjective 1 *firm ground.* compact, compressed, congealed, dense, hard, rigid, solid, stable, stiff, unyielding.
OPPOSITES: SEE **soft**.

2 *a firm fit.* anchored, fast, fixed, immovable, secure, steady, tight.

3 *firm convictions.* adamant, decided, determined, dogged, obstinate, persistent, resolute, unshakeable, unwavering.

4 *a firm arrangement.* agreed, settled, unchangeable.

5 *a firm friend.* constant, dependable, devoted, faithful, loyal, reliable.

firm noun *a business firm.* business, company, concern, corporation, establishment, organization.

first adjective 1 *first signs of spring.* earliest, foremost, initial, leading, soonest.

2 *the first thing to consider.* basic, cardinal, chief, fundamental, key, main, paramount, predominant, primary, prime, principal, uppermost.

3 *first steps in arithmetic.* elementary, introductory, preliminary, rudimentary.

4 *the first version of something.* archetypal, eldest, embryonic, oldest, original, primeval.

5 *the first authority on a subject.* dominant, foremost, head, highest, outstanding, prime, top.

first aid SEE **treatment**.

first name Christian name, forename, given name, personal name.

first-class, **first-rate** adjectives SEE **excellent**.

first-hand adjective *first-hand knowledge.* direct, empirical, personal.

fiscal adjective SEE **financial**.

fish noun OTHER CREATURES: SEE **animal** noun.

VARIOUS FISH: brill, brisling, carp, catfish, chub, cod, coelacanth, conger, cuttlefish, dab, dace, eel, flounder, goldfish, grayling, gudgeon, haddock, hake, halibut, herring, jellyfish, lamprey, ling, mackerel, minnow, mullet, perch, pike, pilchard, piranha, plaice, roach, salmon, sardine, sawfish, shark, skate, sole, sprat, squid, starfish, stickleback, sturgeon, swordfish, [*informal*] tiddler, trout, tuna, turbot, whitebait, whiting.

PARTS OF A FISH: dorsal fin, fin, gills, roe, scales, tail.

fish verb angle, go fishing [SEE **fishing**], trawl.

fisher noun angler, fisherman, trawlerman.

fishing noun angling, trawling.
RELATED ADJECTIVE: piscatorial.
fishing tackle gaff, line, net, rod.

fish-tank noun aquarium.

fishy adjective SEE **suspicious**.

fissure noun SEE **split** noun.

fist noun *a clenched fist.* hand, knuckles.

fisticuffs noun SEE **fight** noun.

fit adjective 1 *The house isn't fit to live in.* adapted, adequate, equipped, good enough, satisfactory, sound.
OPPOSITES: SEE **unfit**.
2 *Her rude song isn't fit for your ears!* apposite, appropriate, apt, becoming, befitting, decent, fitting, proper, right, seemly, suitable.
OPPOSITES: SEE **inappropriate**.
3 *Are you fit to play?* able, capable, competent, in good form, healthy, prepared, ready, strong, well enough.
OPPOSITES: SEE **ill**.

fit noun *a fit of coughing.* attack, bout, convulsion, eruption, explosion, outbreak, outburst, paroxysm, seizure, spasm, spell.

fit verb 1 *My jeans don't fit me.* be the right shape and size for.
2 *Fit the pieces together.* arrange, assemble, build, construct, dovetail, install, interlock, join, match, position, put in place, put together.
3 *Wear clothes to fit the occasion.* accord with, become, be fitting for [SEE **fitting**], conform with, correspond with or to, go with, harmonize with, suit.

fitful adjective SEE **spasmodic**.

fitting adjective *a fitting memorial.* apposite, appropriate, apt, becoming, befitting, decent, due, fitting, proper, right, seemly, suitable, timely.
OPPOSITES: SEE **inappropriate**.

fix noun *I got into a fix.* corner, difficulty, dilemma, [*informal*] hole, [*informal*] jam, mess, plight, predicament, problem, quandary.

fix verb 1 *to fix something into place.* attach, bind, connect, embed, SEE

fasten, implant, install, join, link, make firm, plant, position, secure, stabilize, stick.
2 *to fix a price. to fix a time.* agree, appoint, arrange, arrive at, confirm, decide, establish, finalize, name, ordain, settle, sort out, specify.
3 [*informal*] *to fix a broken window.* make good, mend, put right, repair.

fixative noun SEE **glue** noun.

fixture noun *a home fixture.* date, engagement, game, match, meeting.

fizz verb bubble, effervesce, fizzle, foam, froth, hiss, sizzle.

fizzy adjective *fizzy drinks.* bubbly, effervescent, foaming, sparkling.
OPPOSITE: still.

flabbergasted adjective SEE **surprised**.

flabby adjective [*informal*] *flabby muscles.* SEE **fat** adjective, feeble, flaccid, floppy, limp, loose, out of condition, slack, weak.
OPPOSITES: SEE **firm** adjective.

flaccid adjective SEE **flabby**.

flag noun *decorated with flags.* banner, bunting, colours, ensign, pennant, pennon, standard, streamer.

flag verb 1 *Our interest flagged.* SEE **decline** verb.
2 *The police flagged me down.* SEE **signal** verb.

flagellate verb SEE **whip** verb.

flagrant adjective SEE **obvious**.

flail verb SEE **beat** verb.
to flail about SEE **wave** verb.

flair noun SEE **talent**.

flake noun *flakes of old paint. flakes of flint.* bit, chip, leaf, scale, shaving, slice, splinter, wafer.

flamboyant adjective SEE **showy**.

flame noun SEE **fire** noun.

flame verb blaze, SEE **burn** verb, flare.

flammable adjective SEE **inflammable**.

flap verb *The sail flapped in the wind.* beat, flutter, sway, swing, thrash about, wag, wave about.

flare verb blaze, SEE **burn** verb, erupt, flame.
to flare up SEE **angry (to become angry)**.

flash verb 1 *Lights flashed on and off.* flicker, glare, glint, SEE **light** noun (**to give light**), sparkle, twinkle.

flashlight noun SEE **torch**.

flashy adjective SEE **showy**.

flask noun SEE **bottle** noun.

flat adjective 1 *The snooker-table must be flat.* horizontal, level, levelled.

OPPOSITES: SEE **vertical**.
2 *lying flat in bed.* outstretched, prone, prostrate, recumbent, spread-eagled, spread out, supine.
OPPOSITES: SEE **upright**.
3 *a flat sea.* calm, even, smooth, unbroken, unruffled.
OPPOSITES: SEE **uneven**.
4 *a flat voice.* boring, dry, dull, insipid, lacklustre, lifeless, monotonous, spiritless, tedious, unexciting, uninteresting, unmodulated, unvarying.
OPPOSITES: SEE **lively**.
5 *a flat tyre.* blown out, burst, deflated, punctured.
OPPOSITE: inflated.

flat noun *living in a flat.* apartment, bedsitter, flatlet, maisonette, penthouse.

flatten verb *to flatten a rough surface.* even out, iron out, level out, press, roll, smooth.
2 *They flattened the flowers.* compress, crush, demolish, SEE **destroy**, devastate, level, raze, run over, squash, trample.
3 [*informal*] *He flattened his opponent.* SEE **defeat** verb, fell, floor, knock down, prostrate.

flatter verb 1 be flattering to [SEE **flattering**], [*informal*] butter up, compliment, curry favour with, fawn on, humour, [*informal*] play up to, praise, [*slang*] suck up to, [*informal*] toady to.
OPPOSITES: SEE **insult** verb.

flatterer noun [*informal*] crawler, [*informal*] creep, groveller, lackey, sycophant, [*informal*] toady, [*informal*] yesman.

flattering adjective *flattering remarks.* adulatory, complimentary, effusive, fawning, fulsome, ingratiating, insincere, mealy-mouthed, obsequious, servile, sycophantic, unctuous.
OPPOSITES: SEE **insulting, sincere**.

flattery noun adulation, blandishments, [*informal*] blarney, fawning, [*informal*] flannel, insincerity, obsequiousness, servility, [*informal*] soft soap, sycophancy, unctuousness.

flatulence noun SEE **indigestion**.

flaunt verb SEE **display** verb.

flavour noun 1 *the flavour of food.* SEE **taste** noun.
2 *a film with an oriental flavour.* atmosphere, character, characteristic, feel, feeling, property, quality, style.

flavour verb *I flavoured the meat with herbs.* season, spice.

flavouring noun *peppermint flavouring.* additive, essence, extract, seasoning.

flaw noun *a flaw in someone's work. a flaw in a piece of china.* SEE **blemish**, break, chip, crack, error, fallacy, imperfection, inaccuracy, mistake, shortcoming, slip, split, weakness.

flawed adjective SEE **imperfect**.

flawless adjective SEE **perfect** adjective.

flaxen adjective *flaxen hair.* SEE **fair** adjective.

flay verb SEE **strip** verb.

fleck noun SEE **speck**.

flecked adjective SEE **speckled**.

fledgeling noun BIRDS: SEE **bird**.

flee verb *to flee from invaders.* abscond, [*informal*] beat a retreat, bolt, clear off, disappear, escape, fly, hurry off, make off, retreat, run away, [*slang*] scarper, [*informal*] take to your heels, vanish, withdraw.

fleece noun down, SEE **hair**, wool.

fleece verb SEE **defraud**.

fleet adjective SEE **swift** adjective.

fleet noun *a fleet of ships.* armada, convoy, flotilla, navy, squadron, task force.

fleeting adjective *a fleeting moment.* SEE **brief** adjective, ephemeral, evanescent, impermanent, momentary, mutable, passing, short-lived, transitory.
OPPOSITES: SEE **lasting**.

flesh noun *an animal's flesh.* carrion [= *dead flesh*], fat, meat, muscle, tissue.
flesh and blood 1 *The pain was more than flesh and blood could stand.* the body, human nature, physical nature.
2 *Your children are your flesh and blood.* SEE **family**.

flex noun *a flex for an electric iron.* cable, lead, wire.

flex verb SEE **bend** verb.

flexible adjective 1 *flexible wire.* bendable, [*informal*] bendy, floppy, limp, pliable, soft, springy, supple, whippy.
OPPOSITES: SEE **brittle, rigid**.
2 *flexible arrangements.* adjustable, alterable, fluid, mutable, open, provisional, variable.
OPPOSITES: SEE **immutable**.
3 *a flexible person.* accommodating, adaptable, amenable, compliant, openminded, responsive, tractable, willing to please.
OPPOSITES: SEE **inflexible**.

flick verb SEE **hit** verb.

flicker verb *The candles flickered.* blink, flutter, glimmer, SEE **light** noun (**to give light**), quiver, tremble, twinkle, waver.

flight noun 1 *the flight of a missile.* SEE **journey**, trajectory.

2 *a flight from danger.* SEE **escape** noun.

flimsy adjective 1 *the flimsy wings of a butterfly.* brittle, delicate, fine, fragile, frail, insubstantial, light, slight, thin.
OPPOSITES: SEE **substantial**.
2 *a flimsy structure.* decrepit, gimcrack, loose, makeshift, rickety, shaky, tottering, weak, wobbly.
OPPOSITES: SEE **sturdy**.
3 *a flimsy argument.* feeble, implausible, superficial, trivial, unconvincing, unsatisfactory.
OPPOSITES: SEE **convincing**.

flinch verb *to flinch in alarm.* blench, cower, cringe, dodge, draw back, duck, falter, jerk away, jump, quail, quake, recoil, shrink back, shy away, start, swerve, wince.
to flinch from *to flinch from your duty.* avoid, evade, shirk, shrink from.

fling verb SEE **throw** verb.

flinty adjective SEE **hard**.

flip verb SEE **hit** verb.

flippant adjective SEE **frivolous**.

flipper noun SEE **limb**.

flirt noun [*woman*] coquette, [*man*] philanderer, [*informal*] tease.

flirt verb SEE **love** noun (**to make love**).

flirtatious adjective amorous, coquettish, flirty, [*uncomplimentary*] promiscuous, teasing.

flit verb SEE **move** verb.

float verb 1 *to float on water.* bob, drift, sail, swim.
2 *to float in the air.* glide, hang, hover, waft.
3 *to float a ship.* launch.
OPPOSITES: SEE **sink** verb.

flock noun SEE **group** noun.

floe noun ice, iceberg.

flog verb beat, birch, cane, flagellate, flay, SEE **hit** verb, lash, scourge, thrash, [*slang*] wallop, whack, whip.

flood noun 1 *a flood of water.* deluge, downpour, flash-flood, inundation, overflow, rush, spate, tide, torrent.
OPPOSITES: SEE drought, trickle.
2 *a flood of imports.* excess, large quantity, plethora, superfluity.
OPPOSITES: SEE **scarcity**.

flood verb *The river flooded the town.* cover, drown, engulf, fill up, immerse, inundate, overflow, overwhelm, sink, submerge, swamp.

floodlights noun SEE **light** noun.

floor noun 1 deck, floorboards.
FLOOR COVERINGS: carpet, lino, linoleum, mat, matting, parquet, rug, tiles.

2 *first floor. top floor.* deck, level, storey, tier.

flop verb 1 *The seedlings flopped in the heat.* collapse, dangle, droop, drop, fall, flag, hang down, sag, slump, wilt.
2 *The business flopped.* SEE **fail**.

floppy adjective *floppy lettuce leaves.* droopy, flabby, SEE **flexible**, hanging loose, limp, pliable, soft.
OPPOSITES: SEE **crisp, rigid**.

flora noun botany, plant-life, plants, vegetation.

florid adjective 1 *florid decoration.* SEE **ornate**.
2 *a florid complexion.* SEE **ruddy**.

florist noun flower-shop.

flotilla noun SEE **fleet** noun.

flotsam noun SEE **wreckage**.
flotsam and jetsam SEE **junk**.

flounce verb *She flounced out of the room.* SEE **move** verb.

flounder verb 1 *to flounder in mud.* flail, fumble, grope, move clumsily, stagger, struggle, stumble, tumble, wallow.
2 *to flounder through a speech.* falter, get confused, make mistakes, talk aimlessly.

flourish noun SEE **gesture** noun.

flourish verb 1 *The plants flourished after the rain. Trade flourished in the sales.* be fruitful, be successful, bloom, blossom, boom, burgeon, develop, do well, flower, grow, increase, [*informal*] perk up, progress, prosper, strengthen, succeed, thrive.
OPPOSITES: SEE **fail, wilt**.
2 *He flourished his umbrella.* brandish, flaunt, gesture with, shake, swing, twirl, wag, wave.

flout verb *to flout the rules.* SEE **disobey**.

flow noun *a steady flow.* cascade, course, current, drift, ebb (*the ebb and flow of the tide*), effusion, flood, gush, outpouring, spate, spurt, stream, tide, trickle.

flow verb *Liquids flow.* bleed, cascade, course, dribble, drift, drip, ebb, flood, flush, glide, gush, issue, leak, move in a flow [SEE **flow** noun], ooze, overflow, pour, ripple, roll, run, seep, spill, spring, spurt, squirt, stream, trickle, well, well up.

flower noun *flowers in the garden.* bloom, blossom, floret, petal.
a bunch of flowers arrangement, bouquet, garland, posy, spray, wreath.

VARIOUS FLOWERS: begonia, bluebell, buttercup, campanula, campion, candytuft, carnation, catkin, celandine, chrysanthemum, coltsfoot, columbine, cornflower, cowslip, crocus, crowfoot, cyclamen, daffodil, dahlia, daisy, dandelion.

forget-me-not, foxglove, freesia, geranium, gladiolus, gypsophila, harebell, hollyhock, hyacinth, iris, jonquil, kingcup, lilac, lily, lupin, marguerite, marigold, montbretia, nasturtium, orchid.

pansy, pelargonium, peony, periwinkle, petunia, phlox, pink, polyanthus, poppy, primrose, rhododendron, rose, saxifrage, scabious, scarlet pimpernel, snowdrop, speedwell, sunflower, tulip, violet, wallflower, water-lily.

PARTS OF A FLOWER: axil, bract, calyx, carpel, corolla, perianth, pistil, pollen, sepal, stamen, whorl.

---

flower verb *Most plants flower in the summer.* bloom, blossom, [*poetic*] blow, SEE **flourish** verb, have flowers, open out.

flowery adjective *a flowery style of writing.* SEE **ornate**.

fluctuate verb SEE **vary**.

flue noun chimney.

fluent adjective *a fluent speaker.* articulate, effortless, eloquent, [*uncomplimentary*] facile, flowing, [*uncomplimentary*] glib, natural, polished, ready, smooth, voluble, unhesitating.
OPPOSITES: SEE **hesitant**.

fluff noun down, dust, floss, fuzz, thistle-down.

fluff verb *to fluff a pillow.* make fluffy, shake, soften.

fluffy adjective *fluffy toys.* downy, feathery, fibrous, fleecy, furry, fuzzy, hairy, silky, soft, velvety, woolly.

fluid adjective 1 *a fluid substance.* aqueous, flowing, gaseous, liquefied, liquid, melted, molten, running, [*informal*] runny, sloppy, watery.
OPPOSITES: SEE **solid**.
2 *fluid movements.* SEE **graceful**.
3 *a fluid situation.* SEE **flexible**.

fluid noun *bodily fluids.* fluid substance [SEE **fluid** adjective], gas, liquid, plasma.

fluke noun *a lucky fluke.* accident, chance, stroke of good luck.

flummox verb SEE **baffle**.

flunkey noun SEE **servant**.

fluorescent adjective SEE **glowing**.

flurry noun *a flurry of activity.* SEE **commotion**.

flush adjective SEE **level** adjective.
flush with money SEE **wealthy**.

flush verb 1 *to flush with embarrassment.* blush, colour, glow, go red, redden.
2 *to flush a lavatory.* cleanse, [*informal*] pull the plug, rinse out, wash out.
3 *to flush a bird from its hiding-place.* chase out, drive out, expel, send up.

fluster verb SEE **confuse**.

flutter verb bat (*your eyelids*), flap, flicker, flit, move agitatedly, palpitate, quiver, tremble, vibrate.

flux noun SEE **instability**.

fly noun VARIOUS INSECTS: SEE **insect**.

fly verb 1 *Most birds fly.* ascend, flit, glide, hover, rise, soar, stay in the air, swoop, take wing.
2 *to fly an aircraft.* aviate, pilot, take off (in), travel (in).
3 *to fly a flag.* display, flap, flutter, hang up, hoist, raise, show, wave.
to fly at SEE **attack** verb.
to fly in the face of SEE **disregard**.
to fly off the handle SEE **angry** (to become angry).

flying adjective *a flying machine.* aeronautical, airborne, airworthy, gliding, hovering, soaring, winged.

flying noun [*formal*] aeronautics, airtravel, [*old-fashioned*] aviation, flight, [*informal*] jetting.
flying saucer spaceship, UFO.

flyover noun bridge, overpass, viaduct.

foal noun SEE **horse**.

foal verb SEE **birth** (to give birth).

foam noun 1 bubbles, effervescence, froth, head (*on beer*), lather, scum, spume, suds.
2 *a mattress made of foam.* sponge, spongy rubber.

foam verb *What makes the water foam?* boil, bubble, effervesce, fizz, froth, lather, make foam [SEE **foam** noun].

focus noun 1 *Get the camera into focus.* clarity, correct adjustment, sharpness.
2 *The cathedral is the main focus for tourism.* centre, core, focal point, heart, hub, pivot.

focus verb *to focus a camera.* adjust the lens.
to focus on *Focus on the main problem.* aim at, centre on, concentrate on, direct attention to, fix attention on, home in on, look at, spotlight, think about.

fodder noun *cattle fodder.* feed, food, forage, hay, provender, silage.

foe noun SEE **enemy**.

foetus noun embryo.

fog noun *fog on the motorway.* bad visibility, cloud, foggy conditions [SEE **foggy**], haze, mist, smog.

foggy adjective *foggy weather. a foggy picture.* blurry, clouded, dim, hazy, indistinct, misty, murky, obscure.
OPPOSITES: SEE **clear** adjective.

fogy, fogey noun *an old fogy.* SEE **old-fashioned (old-fashioned person)**.

foible noun SEE **peculiarity**.

foil noun 1 *The thin comedian is a foil to his fat partner.* SEE **contrast** noun.
2 *fighting with foils.* SEE **sword**.

foil verb *The security officer foiled the thieves.* baffle, block, check, frustrate, halt, hamper, hinder, obstruct, outwit, prevent, stop, thwart.

foist verb *He foisted a load of bad fruit on us.* get rid of, impose, offload, palm off.

fold noun 1 *a fold in paper or cloth.* bend, corrugation, crease, furrow, hollow, knife-edge, line, pleat, wrinkle.
2 *a fold for sheep.* SEE **enclosure**.

fold verb 1 *to fold in two.* bend, crease, crinkle, double over, jack-knife, overlap, pleat, tuck in, turn over.
2 *to fold in your arms.* clasp, embrace, enclose, enfold, entwine, envelop, hold close, hug, wrap.
3 *to fold an umbrella.* close, collapse, let down, put down.
4 *The business folded.* SEE **fail**.

folder noun *a folder for papers.* SEE **cover** noun, portfolio.

foliage, folio nouns SEE **leaf**.

folk noun SEE **person**.

folklore noun SEE **tradition**.

follow verb 1 *Follow that car! He follows her everywhere.* accompany, chase, dog, escort, go after, hound, hunt, keep pace with, pursue, shadow, stalk, [*informal*] tag along with, tail, track, trail.
OPPOSITES: SEE **abandon**.
2 *James I followed Elizabeth I.* come after, replace, succeed, supersede, supplant, take the place of.
OPPOSITES: SEE **precede**.
3 *Follow the rules.* attend to, comply with, heed, keep to, obey, observe, pay attention to, take notice of.
OPPOSITES: SEE **ignore**.
4 *Try to follow what I say.* comprehend, grasp, keep up with, understand.
5 *Do you follow snooker?* be a fan of, keep abreast of, know about, support, take an interest in.
6 *It's sunny now, but it doesn't follow that it'll be fine tonight.* be inevitable, come about, ensue, happen, have the consequence, mean, result.

follower noun SEE **disciple**.

following adjective *the following day.* coming, consequent, ensuing, future, later, next, resulting, subsequent, succeeding.
OPPOSITES: SEE **foregoing**.

folly noun SEE **stupidity**.

foment verb *to foment trouble.* See **stimulate**.

fond adjective 1 *a fond kiss.* SEE **loving**.
2 *a fond hope.* SEE **silly**.
fond of *She's fond of him* SEE **love** noun (**in love with**).

fondle verb SEE **caress** verb.

food noun [*old-fashioned*] comestibles, cooking, cuisine, delicacies, diet, [*informal*] eatables, [*informal*] eats, fare, feed (*chicken feed*), fodder (*cattle fodder*), foodstuff, forage (*forage for horses*), [*informal*] grub, SEE **meal**, meat (*meat and drink*), nourishment, [*especially = plant food*] nutriments, [*joking*] provender, provisions, rations, recipe, refreshments, sustenance, swill (*pig-swill*), [*old-fashioned*] tuck, [*old-fashioned*] viands, [*old-fashioned*] victuals.
RELATED ADJECTIVES: cordon bleu, culinary, gastronomic, gourmet.

CONSTITUENTS OF FOOD: carbohydrate, cholesterol, fibre, protein, roughage, vitamin.

VARIOUS FOODS: bacon, batter, beans, biryani, SEE **biscuit**, blancmange, bran, bread, broth, SEE **cake** noun, caviare, SEE **cereal**, charlotte, cheese, cheesecake, chilli, chips, chop suey, chupatti, chutney, coleslaw, cornflakes, cornflour, cream, crisps, croquette, crouton, crumpet, curry, custard.

doughnut, dumplings, egg, SEE **fat** noun, SEE **fish** noun, flan, flour, fondue, fricassee, fritter, SEE **fruit**, ghee, gherkin, glucose, goulash, greens, gruel, haggis, hash, health foods, honey, hot-pot, icecream, icing, jam, jelly, junket, kebab, kedgeree, kipper, kosher food.

lasagne, lentils, macaroni, malt, marmalade, SEE **meat**, milk, mincemeat, mince pies, moussaka, mousse, muesli, noodles, SEE **nut**, oatmeal, omelette, paella, pancake, pasta, pastry, pasty, pâté, pie, pikelet, pizza, porridge, pudding, quiche, rice, risotto, rissole, rolypoly, rusk.

sago, SEE **salad**, sandwich, sauerkraut, sausage, sausage-roll, scampi, schnitzel, seafood, semolina, smorgasbord, sorbet, soufflé, soup, soya beans, spaghetti, stew, stock, sundae, syllabub, syrup, tandoori, tapioca, tart, toast, treacle, trifle, truffle, SEE **vegetable**, vegetarian food, waffle, wholemeal flour, yam, yeast, yogurt or yoghurt.

CONDIMENTS, FLAVOURINGS, ETC.: chutney, colouring, dressing, garlic, gravy, herbs, ketchup, marinade, mayonnaise, mustard, pepper, pickle, preservative, relish, salt, sauce, seasoning, spice, stuffing, sugar, vanilla, vinegar.

fool noun 1 *I am a fool!* [All the synonyms given are normally used *informally*.] ass, blockhead, booby, buffoon, dimwit, dope, dunce, dunderhead, dupe, fathead, half-wit, SEE **idiot**, ignoramus, mug, muggins, mutt, ninny, nit, nitwit, silly person [SEE **silly**], simpleton, sucker, twerp, wally.
2 [*old-fashioned*] *a fool in the king's court.* clown, comic, coxcomb, entertainer, jester.

fool verb *to fool someone with a trick.* [*informal*] bamboozle, bluff, cheat, [*informal*] con, deceive, delude, dupe, [*informal*] have on, hoax, hoodwink, [*informal*] kid, mislead, [*informal*] string along, swindle, take in, trick.
to fool about SEE **misbehave, play** verb.

foolhardy adjective SEE **rash** adjective.

foolish adjective SEE **stupid**.

foolishness noun SEE **stupidity**.

foolproof adjective SEE **simple**.

foot noun 1 *an animal's foot.* claw, hoof, paw, trotter.
2 *the foot of a mountain.* SEE **base** noun.
3 *a metrical foot.* SEE **verse**.

football noun American football, Association football, Rugby football, [*informal*] rugger, [*informal*] soccer.

foothill noun SEE **hill**.

footing noun SEE **base** noun, **basis**.

footling adjective SEE **trivial**.

footloose adjective SEE **independent**.

footman noun SEE **servant**.

footnote noun annotation, note.

footpath noun SEE **path**.

footprint noun footmark, spoor (*of an animal*), track.

footslog noun SEE **walk** verb.

footsore adjective SEE **tired**.

footstep noun footfall, tread.

footwear noun boot, [*mountaineering*] crampon, SEE **shoe**, sock, stocking.

forage noun SEE **food**.

foray noun SEE **attack** noun.

forbear verb SEE **refrain** verb.

forbearance noun SEE **patience**.

forbearing adjective SEE **patient** adjective.

forbid verb *to forbid smoking.* ban, bar, deny (*He denied me the chance*), deter, disallow, exclude, make illegal, outlaw, preclude, prevent, prohibit, proscribe, refuse, rule out, say no to, stop, veto.
OPPOSITES: SEE **allow**.

forbidden adjective 1 *Games are forbidden.* against the law, banned, barred, disallowed, SEE **illegal**, outlawed, prohibited, proscribed, taboo, unlawful, wrong.
OPPOSITES: SEE **permissible**.
2 *This is a forbidden area.* closed, out of bounds, restricted, secret.

forbidding adjective *forbidding storm clouds.* gloomy, grim, menacing, ominous, stern, threatening, SEE **unfriendly**, uninviting, unwelcoming.
OPPOSITES: SEE **friendly**.

force noun 1 *We used force to open the door.* drive, effort, energy, might, power, pressure, strength, vehemence, vigour, weight.
2 *the force of an explosion.* effect, impact, intensity, momentum, shock.
3 *a military force.* army, body, SEE **group** noun, troops.
3 *They took over by force.* aggression, brunt (*We bore the brunt of the attack*), coercion, compulsion, constraint, duress, violence.
4 *I could see the force of her argument.* cogency, effectiveness, persuasiveness, rightness, validity.

force verb 1 *You can't force me to do it.* [*informal*] bulldoze, coerce, compel, constrain, drive, impel, impose on, make, oblige, order, press-gang, pressurize.
2 *We had to force the door.* break open, burst open, prise open, smash, use force on, wrench.
3 *They forced the change on us.* impose, inflict.

forceful adjective SEE **powerful**.

forceps noun pincers, tongs, tweezers.

ford noun river-crossing, water-splash.

ford verb *to ford a river.* SEE **cross** verb, drive through, ride through, wade across.

fore adjective SEE **front** adjective.

forebear noun SEE **ancestor**.

forebode verb SEE **foretell**.

foreboding noun *a foreboding that something is wrong.* anxiety, augury, dread, fear, feeling, intuition, misgiving, omen, portent, premonition, presentiment, warning, worry.

forecast noun *a weather forecast.* augury, expectation, outlook, prediction, prognosis, prognostication, projection, prophecy.

forecast verb SEE **foretell**.

forecourt noun SEE **courtyard**.

forefather noun SEE **ancestor**.

forefront noun *in the forefront of fashion.* avant-garde, front, lead, vanguard, the very front.

foregoing adjective *the foregoing remarks.* above, aforementioned, aforesaid, earlier, just mentioned, preceding, previous.
OPPOSITES: SEE **following**.

foregone adjective **foregone conclusion** SEE **certainty**.

foreground noun *the foreground of a picture.* forefront, front, nearest part.
OPPOSITES: SEE **background**.

forehead noun brow.
PARTS OF YOUR HEAD: SEE **head** noun.

foreign adjective 1 *foreign places.* distant, exotic, far-away, outlandish, remote, strange, unfamiliar, unknown.
OPPOSITES: SEE **familiar, native.**
2 *foreign tourists.* alien, external, immigrant, incoming, international, outside, overseas, visiting.
OPPOSITES: SEE **domestic.**
3 *foreign goods.* imported.
OPPOSITE: indigenous.
4 *Cruelty is foreign to her.* uncharacteristic (of), unnatural (to), untypical (of).
OPPOSITES: SEE **natural.**
5 *a foreign body in his eye.* extraneous, unwanted.

foreigner noun alien, immigrant, newcomer, outsider, overseas visitor, stranger.
OPPOSITES: SEE **native** noun.

foreknowledge noun SEE **forewarning**.

foreland noun SEE **promontory**.

foreman, forewoman nouns boss, SEE **chief** noun, controller, [*of a jury*] spokesman, superintendent, supervisor.

foremost adjective SEE **chief** adjective.

forename noun SEE **name** noun.

forerunner noun SEE **predecessor**.

foresee verb *I foresaw what would happen.* anticipate, envisage, expect, forecast, foretell, have a foretaste of, predict, prognosticate, prophesy.

foreshadow verb SEE **foretell**.

foresight noun *She commended my foresight in bringing an umbrella.* anticipation, caution, farsightedness, forethought, looking ahead, perspicacity, planning, preparation, prudence, readiness.

forest noun coppice, copse, jungle, plantation, trees, woodland, woods.
RELATED ADJECTIVES: arboreal, silvan.

forestall verb SEE **prevent**.

foretaste noun *a foretaste of things to come.* example, SEE **forewarning**, preview, sample, specimen, trailer, [*informal*] try-out.

foretell verb *The omens foretold what would happen.* augur, [*old-fashioned*] bode, forebode, forecast, foreshadow, forewarn, give a foretaste of, herald, portend, presage, prognosticate, prophesy, signify.

forethought noun SEE **foresight**.

forewarning noun *I had no forewarning of trouble.* advance warning, augury, foreknowledge, foretaste, indication, omen, premonition, [*informal*] tip-off.

forewoman noun SEE **foreman**.

foreword noun introduction, prologue.
OTHER PARTS OF A BOOK: SEE **book** noun.

forfeit noun *He had to pay a forfeit.* damages, fine, penalty.

forfeit verb *Because he broke the rules, he forfeited his winnings.* abandon, give up, let go, lose, pay up, relinquish, renounce, surrender.

forgather verb SEE **gather**.

forge noun *a blacksmith's forge.* furnace, smithy, workshop.

forge verb 1 *to forge metal.* beat into shape, cast, hammer out, mould, shape, work.
2 *to forge money.* coin, copy, counterfeit, fake, falsify, imitate, make illegally.
to forge ahead SEE **advance** verb.

forgery noun *The painting was a forgery.* copy, counterfeit, [*informal*] dud, fake, fraud, imitation, [*informal*] phoney, replica, reproduction.

forget verb 1 *I forget things.* be forgetful [SEE **forgetful**], be oblivious (of), disregard, fail to remember, ignore, leave out, lose track (of), miss out, neglect, omit, overlook, skip, suffer from amnesia, unlearn.
OPPOSITES: SEE **remember.**
2 *I forgot my money.* abandon, be without, leave behind.
OPPOSITES: SEE **bring.**

forgetful adjective absent-minded, [*formal*] amnesiac, careless, inattentive, neglectful, negligent, oblivious, unconscious, unmindful, unreliable, vague, [*informal*] woolly-minded.

forgetfulness noun absent-mindedness, [*formal*] amnesia, negligence, oblivion, unconsciousness.

forgivable adjective *a forgivable lapse.*
allowable, excusable, justifiable, negligible, pardonable, petty, understandable, venial (*a venial sin*).
OPPOSITES: SEE **unforgivable.**

forgive verb 1 *to forgive a person for doing
wrong.* [*formal*] absolve, [*formal*] exculpate, excuse, exonerate, let off, pardon,
spare.
2 *to forgive a crime.* condone, overlook.

forgiveness noun absolution, exonera-
tion, mercy, pardon.
OPPOSITES: SEE **retribution.**

forgiving adjective *a forgiving nature.*
SEE **kind** adjective, merciful, tolerant,
understanding.
OPPOSITES: SEE **vengeful.**

forgo verb SEE **abandon.**

fork verb 1 *to fork the garden.* SEE **dig.**
2 *The road forks.* SEE **divide.**
to fork out SEE **pay** verb.

forked adjective *a forked stick.* branched,
divided, split, V-shaped.

forlorn adjective SEE **friendless, sad.**

form noun 1 *human form.* anatomy, body,
build, figure, frame, outline, physique,
shape, silhouette.
2 *What form did it take?* appearance,
arrangement, cast, character, configuration, design, format, framework,
genre, guise, kind, manifestation, manner, model, mould, nature, pattern,
plan, semblance, sort, species, structure, style, system, type, variety.
3 *your form in school.* class, group, level,
set, stream, tutor-group.
4 [*informal*] *It's good form to shake hands.*
behaviour, convention, custom, etiquette, fashion, manners, practice.
5 *an application form.* document, paper.
6 *an athlete's form.* condition, fettle (*in
fine fettle*), fitness, health, performance,
spirits.
7 [*old-fashioned*] *a form to sit on.* bench,
seat.

form verb 1 *A sculptor forms her material.*
cast, construct, design, forge, give form
to, model, mould, shape.
2 *We formed a society.* bring into existence, bring together, constitute, create,
establish, found, make, organize, produce.
3 *They form a good team.* act as, compose,
comprise, make up, serve as.
4 *Icicles formed under the bridge.* appear,
come into existence, develop, grow,
materialize, take shape.

formal adjective 1 *a formal occasion.
formal behaviour.* aloof, ceremonial, ceremonious, conventional, cool, correct,
dignified, [*informal*] dressed-up, official,

orthodox. [*informal*] posh, [*uncomplimentary*] pretentious, proper, reserved,
ritualized, solemn, sophisticated,
stately, [*informal*] starchy, stiff, stiff-
necked, unbending, unfriendly.
2 *formal language.* academic, impersonal, legal, official, precise, specialist,
stilted, technical.
3 *a formal design.* calculated, geomet-
rical, orderly, regular, rigid, symmetrical.
OPPOSITES: SEE **informal.**

formality noun SEE **ceremony.**

former adjective earlier, opening, SEE
previous.
OPPOSITES: SEE **latter.**

formidable adjective *a formidable task.*
SEE **difficult.**

formula noun 1 *a verbal formula.* form of
words, ritual, rubric, spell, wording.
2 *a formula for success.* blueprint,
method, prescription, procedure,
recipe, rule, way.

formulate verb *to formulate a plan.*
create, define, devise, evolve, express
clearly, form, invent, plan, set out in
detail, specify, systematize, work out.

fornicate verb SEE **sex (to have sexual
intercourse).**

forsake verb SEE **abandon, renounce.**

forswear verb SEE **renounce.**

fort noun camp, castle, citadel, fortification, fortress, garrison, stronghold,
tower.

forthcoming adjective SEE **future** adjective.

forthright adjective *forthright views.*
blunt, candid, direct, SEE **frank,** outspoken, plain-speaking, straightforward, unequivocal.
OPPOSITES: SEE **cautious.**

fortification noun SEE **fort.**

fortify verb 1 *to fortify a town.* defend,
garrison, protect, reinforce, secure
against attack.
OPPOSITE: demilitarize.
2 *to fortify yourself for difficulties ahead.*
boost, cheer, encourage, hearten, invigorate, lift the morale of, reassure, stiffen the resolve of, strengthen, support,
sustain.
OPPOSITES: SEE **weaken.**

fortitude noun SEE **courage.**

fortress noun SEE **fort.**

fortuitous adjective SEE **accidental.**

fortunate adjective SEE **lucky.**

fortune noun 1 *good fortune. bad fortune.*
accident, chance, destiny, fate, kismet,
luck, providence.

2 *He left his fortune to a charity.* affluence, assets, estate, inheritance, millions, [*informal*] pile (*She made a pile*), possessions, property, prosperity, riches, treasure, wealth.

fortune-teller noun crystal-gazer, palmist, prophet, soothsayer.

forward adjective **1** *a forward movement.* front, frontal, leading, onward, progressive.
OPPOSITES: SEE **backward**.
2 *forward planning.* advance, early, forward-looking, future.
OPPOSITE: retrospective.
3 [*uncomplimentary*] *too forward for his age.* assertive, bold, brazen, cheeky, familiar, [*informal*] fresh, impertinent, impudent, insolent, over-confident, precocious, presumptuous, pushful, [*informal*] pushy, shameless, uninhibited.
OPPOSITES: SEE **diffident**.

forward verb **1** *to forward a letter.* post on, re-address, send on.
2 *to forward goods.* dispatch, expedite, freight, send, ship, transmit, transport.
3 *to forward someone's career.* accelerate, advance, encourage, facilitate, foster, hasten, SEE **help** verb, help along, [*informal*] lend a helping hand to, promote, speed up, support.
OPPOSITES: SEE **hinder**.

fossilize verb ossify, petrify, turn into a fossil.

foster verb **1** *to foster a happy atmosphere.* cultivate, encourage, promote, stimulate.
2 *to foster a child.* adopt, bring up, care for, look after, nourish, nurse, raise, rear, take care of. [The legal meaning of *adopt* and *foster* is not the same.]

foster-child, foster-parent nouns SEE **family**.

foul adjective **1** *a foul mess. foul air.* contaminated, SEE **dirty** adjective, disagreeable, disgusting, filthy, hateful, impure, infected, loathsome, nasty, nauseating, noisome, obnoxious, offensive, polluted, putrid, repulsive, revolting, rotten, smelly, squalid, stinking, unclean, SEE **unpleasant**, vile.
OPPOSITES: SEE **pure**.
2 *a foul crime.* abhorrent, abominable, atrocious, SEE **cruel**, evil, monstrous, villainous, wicked.
3 *foul language.* abusive, blasphemous, coarse, common, crude, improper, indecent, insulting, SEE **obscene**, offensive, rude, uncouth, vulgar.
4 *foul weather.* foggy, rainy, rough, stormy, violent, windy.

5 *a foul tackle.* against the rules, illegal, prohibited, unfair.

foul verb *Chemicals fouled the drains.* SEE **contaminate**.
to foul up SEE **muddle** verb.

found verb **1** *to found a business.* begin, create, endow, establish, fund, [*informal*] get going, inaugurate, initiate, institute, organize, provide money for, raise, set up, start.
2 *a building founded on solid rock.* base, build, construct, erect.

foundation noun **1** *the foundation of a new association.* beginning, establishment, inauguration, initiation, institution, setting up, starting.
2 *the foundation of a building.* base, basis, bottom, cornerstone, foot, footing, substructure, underpinning.
3 [*plural*] *the foundations of science.* basic principles [SEE **principle**], elements, essentials, fundamentals, origins, rudiments.

founder verb SEE **fall** verb, **sink** verb.

foundling noun orphan, stray, waif.

foundry noun SEE **factory**.

fountain noun *a fountain of water.* fount, jet, spout, spray, spring, well.

fowl noun bird, chicken, hen.

fox noun [*female*] vixen.

fox verb SEE **deceive**.

foxy adjective SEE **crafty**.

foyer noun ante-room, entrance, entrance hall, hall, lobby, reception.

fracas noun SEE **commotion**.

Several English words, including *fraction, fracture, fragile, fragment,* etc., are related to Latin *frangere* = to break.

---

fraction noun *I could afford only a fraction of the amount.* division, part, portion, section, subdivision.

fractional adjective *a fractional amount.* SEE **small**.

fractious adjective SEE **irritable**.

fracture noun *a fracture in a bone.* break, breakage, chip, cleft, crack, fissure, gap, opening, rent, rift, split.

fracture verb *to fracture a bone.* break, cause a fracture in, chip, crack, split, suffer a fracture in.

fragile adjective *Egg-shell is fragile.* breakable, brittle, SEE **delicate**, easily damaged, feeble, frail, insubstantial, slight, thin, weak.
OPPOSITES: SEE **strong**.

fragment noun 1 *a fragment of broken pottery.* atom, bit, chip, crumb, part, particle, piece, remnant, scrap, shiver, shred, sliver, snippet, speck.
2 [*plural*] *smashed into fragments.* debris, shivers, [*informal*] smithereens.

fragment verb SEE **break** verb.

fragmentary adjective *fragmentary evidence.* [*informal*] bitty, broken, disintegrated, disjointed, fragmented, in bits, incoherent, incomplete, in fragments [SEE **fragment** noun], partial, scattered, scrappy, uncoordinated.
OPPOSITES: SEE **complete** adjective.

fragrance noun SEE **smell** noun.

fragrant adjective SEE **smelling**.

frail adjective 1 *a frail person.* delicate, feeble, SEE **ill**, infirm, [*uncomplimentary*] puny, slight, unsteady, vulnerable, weak, [*uncomplimentary*] weedy.
2 *a frail structure.* flimsy, SEE **fragile**, insubstantial, rickety, unsound.
OPPOSITES: SEE **strong**.

frame noun 1 *the frame of a building.* bodywork, construction, framework, scaffolding, shell, skeleton, structure.
2 *a frame for a picture.* border, case, casing, edge, edging, mount, mounting.
a frame of mind SEE **attitude**.

frame verb 1 *to frame a picture.* enclose, mount, surround.
2 *to frame a letter.* SEE **compose**.

framework noun bare bones, frame, outline, plan, shell, skeleton, structure, trellis.

franchise noun SEE **right** noun.

frank adjective *a frank reply, a frank discussion.* blunt, candid, direct, downright, explicit, forthright, genuine, [*informal*] heart-to-heart, honest, ingenuous, [*informal*] no-nonsense, open, outright, outspoken, plain, plainspoken, revealing, serious, sincere, straight from the heart, straightforward, to the point, trustworthy, truthful, unconcealed, undisguised, unreserved.
OPPOSITES: SEE **insincere**.

frankfurter noun SEE **sausage**.

frantic adjective *frantic activity. frantic with worry.* berserk, [*informal*] beside yourself, crazy, delirious, demented, deranged, desperate, distraught, excitable, feverish, [*informal*] fraught, frenetic, frenzied, furious, hectic, hysterical, mad, overwrought, rabid, uncontrollable, violent, wild, worked up.
OPPOSITES: SEE **calm** adjective.

fraternal adjective *fraternal love.* brotherly.

fraternity noun SEE **society**.

fraternize verb SEE **associate** verb.

fraud noun 1 *His fraud landed him in gaol.* chicanery, [*informal*] con-trick, deceit, deception, dishonesty, double-dealing, duplicity, forgery, imposture, [*informal*] sharp practice, swindling, trickery.
2 *The "special offer" was a fraud.* cheat, counterfeit, fake, hoax, pretence, [*informal*] put-up job, ruse, sham, swindle, trick.
3 *The salesman was a fraud.* charlatan, cheat, [*informal*] con-man, hoaxer, impostor, [*slang*] phoney, [*informal*] quack, swindler.

fraudulent adjective *a fraudulent business deal.* bogus, cheating, corrupt, counterfeit, criminal, [*informal*] crooked, deceitful, devious, [*informal*] dirty, dishonest, false, illegal, lying, [*slang*] phoney, sham, specious, swindling, underhand, unscrupulous.
OPPOSITES: SEE **honest**.

fraught adjective [*informal*] *You seem a bit fraught.* SEE **anxious**.

fray noun SEE **fight** noun.

frayed *a frayed collar.* rough at the edges, tattered, threadbare, untidy, worn.

freak adjective *freak weather conditions.* aberrant, abnormal, atypical, exceptional, extraordinary, odd, peculiar, queer, unaccountable, unforeseeable, unpredictable, unusual.
OPPOSITES: SEE **normal**.

freak noun 1 *a freak of Nature.* aberration, abnormality, abortion, anomaly, irregularity, monster, monstrosity, mutant, oddity, quirk, sport, variant.
2 [*informal*] *a keep-fit freak.* SEE **fanatic**.

freckle noun SEE **spot** noun.

free adjective 1 *free to come and go.* able, allowed, at leisure, at liberty, disengaged, idle, loose, not working, permitted, uncommitted, unconstrained, unfixed, unrestrained, unrestricted, untrammelled.
OPPOSITE: restricted.
2 *free from slavery.* emancipated, liberated, released.
OPPOSITE: enslaved.
3 *a free country.* democratic, independent, self-governing, sovereign.
OPPOSITES: SEE **occupied, totalitarian**.
4 *a free gift.* complimentary, gratis, without charge.
5 *Is the bathroom free?* available, open, unoccupied, vacant.
OPPOSITES: SEE **engaged**.

6 *free with your money.* bounteous, casual, generous, lavish, liberal, ready, unstinting, willing.
OPPOSITES: SEE **mean** adjective.
free and easy SEE **informal**.
free-lance independent, self-employed.

free verb **1** *to free someone from prison.* deliver, emancipate, liberate, loose, make free, ransom, release, rescue, save, set free, turn loose, unchain, unfetter, unleash, unlock, unloose.
OPPOSITES: SEE **confine**.
2 *to free an accused person.* absolve, acquit, clear, discharge, [*formal*] exculpate, exonerate, let go, let off, pardon, prove innocent, relieve, spare.
OPPOSITES: SEE **condemn**.
3 *to free tangled ropes.* clear, disengage, disentangle, extricate, loose, undo, unknot, untangle, untie.
OPPOSITES: SEE **tangle** verb.

freedom noun *freedom to do as you please.* autonomy, discretion, independence, latitude, leeway, liberty, licence, opportunity, privilege, scope.
OPPOSITES: SEE **repression, restriction**.

free-for-all noun SEE **fight** noun.

free-standing adjective SEE **separate** adjective.

freeway noun SEE **road**.

free-wheel verb *to free-wheel downhill.* coast, drift, glide, ride.

freeze verb **1** *Water freezes at 0°C.* become ice, become solid, congeal, ice over.
2 *The wind froze us to the bone.* chill, cool, make cold, numb.
3 *to freeze food.* chill, deep-freeze, dry-freeze, refrigerate.
4 *to freeze prices.* fix, hold, keep as they are, peg.

freezing adjective SEE **cold** adjective.

freight noun *Some aircraft carry freight.* cargo, consignment, goods, load, merchandise, shipment.

frenetic, frenzied adjectives SEE **frantic**.

frenzy noun *a frenzy of excitement.* delirium, fit, fury, hysteria, insanity, lunacy, madness, mania, outburst, paroxysm, passion.

frequent adjective **1** *frequent trains. frequent headaches.* constant, continual, countless, incessant, many, numerous, recurrent, recurring, regular, repeated.
2 *a frequent visitor.* common, customary, familiar, habitual, ordinary, persistent, regular.
OPPOSITES: SEE **infrequent, rare**.

frequent verb SEE **haunt**.

fresco noun mural, SEE **picture** noun.

fresh adjective **1** *fresh evidence. fresh ideas. fresh bread.* additional, different, extra, just arrived, new, recent, unfamiliar, up-to-date.
OPPOSITES: SEE **stale**.
2 *fresh water.* clear, drinkable, potable, pure, refreshing, sweet, uncontaminated.
OPPOSITES: SEE **salty**.
3 *fresh air. a fresh atmosphere.* airy, bracing, breezy, circulating, clean, cool, draughty, invigorating, unpolluted, ventilated.
OPPOSITES: SEE **stuffy**.
4 *fresh food.* healthy, natural, newly gathered, raw, unprocessed, untreated, wholesome.
OPPOSITES: SEE **preserved**.
5 *fresh sheets on the bed.* clean, crisp, laundered, untouched, unused, washed-and-ironed.
OPPOSITES: SEE **dirty** adjective.
6 *fresh colours. fresh paint.* bright, clean, glowing, just painted, renewed, restored, sparkling, unfaded, vivid.
OPPOSITES: SEE **dingy**.
7 *fresh after a shower.* alert, energetic, healthy, invigorated, lively, [*informal*] perky, rested, revived, sprightly, spry, tingling, vigorous, vital.
OPPOSITES: SEE **weary** adjective.

fret verb SEE **worry** verb.

fretful adjective SEE **anxious**.

friable adjective SEE **crumbly**.

friar noun mendicant, monk.

friction noun **1** *Bike brakes work by friction against the wheel.* abrasion, chafing, resistance, rubbing, scraping.
2 *There was some friction between the two sides.* SEE **conflict** noun.

fried adjective *fried potatoes.* sauté.

friend noun acquaintance, ally, associate, [*informal*] buddy, [*informal*] chum, companion, comrade, [*male*] confidant, [*female*] confidante, [*informal*] crony, SEE **lover**, [*informal*] mate, [*informal*] pal, partner, pen-friend, playfellow, playmate, supporter, well-wisher.
OPPOSITES: SEE **enemy**.
to be friends associate, consort, fraternize, [*informal*] go around, [*informal*] hob-nob, keep company, mix.
to make friends with befriend, [*informal*] chat up, [*informal*] gang up with, get to know, make the acquaintance of, [*informal*] pal up with.

friendless adjective *a friendless person.* abandoned, alienated, alone, deserted, estranged, forlorn, forsaken, isolated, lonely, ostracized, shunned, shut out, solitary, unattached, unloved.

friendliness noun goodwill, hospitality, kindness, sociability, warmth.

friendly adjective *a friendly person. a friendly welcome.* affable, affectionate, agreeable, amiable, amicable, approachable, attached, benevolent, benign, [*informal*] chummy, civil, close, companionable, compatible, comradely, conciliatory, congenial, convivial, cordial, expansive, SEE **familiar**, favourable, genial, good-natured, gracious, helpful, hospitable, intimate, kind, kind-hearted, likeable, SEE **loving**, [*informal*] matey, neighbourly, outgoing, [*informal*] pally, sociable, sympathetic, tender, [*informal*] thick (*They're very thick with each other*), warm, welcoming, well-disposed.
OPPOSITES: SEE **unfriendly**.

friendship noun *She values our friendship.* affection, alliance, amity, association, attachment, camaraderie, closeness, comradeship, familiarity, fellowship, fondness, friendliness, goodwill, harmony, hospitality, SEE **love** noun, rapport, relationship.
OPPOSITES: SEE **hostility**.

frieze noun *a decorative frieze.* border, edging.

fright noun 1 *The explosion gave them a fright.* jolt, scare, shock, surprise.
2 *You could see the fright in their faces.* alarm, consternation, dismay, dread, fear, horror, panic, terror, trepidation.

frighten verb *The hooligans frightened the passers-by.* alarm, appal, browbeat, bully, cow, curdle the blood of, daunt, dismay, horrify, intimidate, make afraid, menace, persecute, [*informal*] put the wind up, scare, shake, shock, startle, terrify, terrorize, threaten, unnerve.
OPPOSITES: SEE **reassure**.

frightened adjective afraid, alarmed, apprehensive, [*informal*] chicken, cowed, dismayed, fearful, horror-struck, intimidated, panicky, panic-stricken, [*informal*] petrified, scared, terrified, terror-stricken, trembling, unnerved, [*informal*] windy.

frightening adjective alarming, appalling, awful, blood-curdling, [*informal*] creepy, dire, dreadful, eerie, fearful, fearsome, formidable, frightful, ghastly, ghostly, grim, hair-raising, horrific, horrifying, intimidating, menacing, scary, sinister, spine-chilling, [*informal*] spooky, terrifying, traumatic, uncanny, unnerving, upsetting, weird, worrying.

frightful adjective 1 *a frightful accident.* SEE **frightening**, grisly, gruesome, harrowing, hideous, horrible, horrid, macabre, shocking, terrible.
2 [*informal*] *frightful weather.* SEE **bad**.

frigid adjective SEE **cold**.

frill noun SEE **fringe**.

fringe noun 1 *a fringe round the edge of a curtain.* border, edging, flounce, frill, gathering, trimming, valance.
2 *the fringe of a town.* borders, edge, limits, margin, outskirts, periphery.

frippery noun SEE **ornament** noun.

frisk verb 1 *to frisk about.* SEE **frolic**.
2 [*informal*] *to frisk a suspect.* SEE **search** verb.

frisky adjective frolicsome, high-spirited, jaunty, lively, perky, playful, skittish, spirited, sprightly.

fritter verb *to fritter your money.* SEE **waste** verb.

frivolity noun *We enjoy a bit of frivolity on holiday.* facetiousness, fun, fun-and-games, gaiety, joking, levity, light-heartedness, nonsense, playing about, silliness, triviality.

frivolous adjective *frivolous questions. frivolous behaviour.* facetious, flighty, flippant, foolish, jocular, joking, petty, pointless, ridiculous, shallow, silly, stupid, superficial, trifling, trivial, unimportant, unserious, vacuous, worthless.
OPPOSITES: SEE **serious**.

frizzy adjective SEE **curly**.

frock noun dress, gown, robe.

frogman noun diver.

frolic verb caper, cavort, dance, frisk about, gambol, have fun, hop about, jump about, lark around, leap about, play about, prance, rollick, romp, skip, sport.

frond noun SEE **leaf**.

front adjective *the front row.* first, foremost, leading, most advanced.
OPPOSITES: SEE **back** adjective.

front noun 1 bow (*of a ship*), façade (*of a house*), face, facing, forefront, foreground (*of a picture*), frontage (*of a building*), head, nose, van, vanguard (*of an army*).
OPPOSITES: SEE **back** noun.
2 *Troops were sent to the front.* battle area, danger zone, front line.
3 *His cheerfulness was only a front.* appearance, blind, [*informal*] cover-up, disguise, mask, pretence, show.

frontal adjective *a frontal attack.* direct, facing, head-on, oncoming, straight.

frontier noun *a national frontier.* border, borderline, boundary, limit.

frosty adjective SEE **cold** adjective.

froth noun bubbles, effervescence, foam, head (*on beer*), lather, scum, spume, suds.

frown noun VARIOUS EXPRESSIONS: SEE **expression.**

frown verb [*informal*] give a dirty look, glare, glower, grimace, knit your brow, look sullen, lour, lower, scowl.
to frown on SEE **disapprove.**

frozen adjective SEE **cold** adjective, **icy.**

frugal adjective SEE **economical.**

fruit noun berry.

VARIOUS FRUITS: apple, apricot, avocado, banana, bilberry, blackberry, cherry, citrus fruit, coconut, crab-apple, cranberry, currant, damson, date, fig, gooseberry, grape, grapefruit, greengage, guava, hip, kiwi fruit, lemon, lime, litchi or lichee, loganberry, mango, medlar, melon, mulberry, nectarine, olive, orange, papaw or pawpaw, peach, pear, pineapple, plum, pomegranate, prune, quince, raisin, raspberry, rhubarb, satsuma, sloe, strawberry, sultana, tangerine, tomato, ugli.

---

fruitful adjective **1** *a fruitful crop. a fruitful garden.* abundant, copious, fertile, flourishing, lush, plenteous, productive, profuse, prolific, rich.
OPPOSITES: SEE **unproductive.**
2 *a fruitful search.* effective, gainful, profitable, rewarding, successful, useful, worthwhile.
OPPOSITES: SEE **fruitless.**

fruitless adjective *a fruitless search.* abortive, disappointing, futile, pointless, profitless, unavailing, unfruitful, unproductive, unprofitable, unrewarding, unsuccessful, useless, vain.
OPPOSITES: SEE **fruitful.**

frumpish adjective SEE **dowdy.**

frustrate verb *The police frustrated an attempted robbery.* baffle, baulk, block, check, defeat, discourage, foil, halt, hinder, inhibit, prevent, [*informal*] scotch, stop, thwart.
OPPOSITES: SEE **fulfil.**

frustrated adjective inhibited, loveless, lovesick, thwarted.

fry verb sauté.
OTHER WAYS TO COOK: SEE **cook** verb.

fuddled adjective *fuddled with alcohol.* confused, SEE **drunk,** flustered, hazy, mixed up, muddled, stupefied.
OPPOSITE: clear-headed.

fudge verb SEE **fake** verb.

fuel noun KINDS OF FUEL: anthracite, butane, Calor Gas, charcoal, coal, coke, derv, diesel, electricity, gas, gasoline, logs, methylated spirit, nuclear fuel, oil, paraffin, peat, petrol, propane.

fuel verb *to fuel a fire. to fuel someone's anger.* encourage, feed, inflame, keep going, nourish, put fuel on, stoke up, supply with fuel.

fuggy adjective [*informal*] *a fuggy room.* SEE **stuffy.**

fugitive noun *a fugitive from justice.* deserter, escapee, escaper, refugee, renegade, runaway.

fulfil verb **1** *to fulfil an ambition.* accomplish, achieve, bring about, carry out, complete, effect, make it come true, perform, realize.
2 *to fulfil certain requirements.* answer, comply with, conform to, execute, implement, meet, respond to, satisfy.
OPPOSITES: SEE **frustrate.**

full adjective **1** *a full cup. a full cinema.* brimming, bursting, [*informal*] chock-a-block, [*informal*] chock-full, congested, crammed, crowded, filled, jammed, [*informal*] jam-packed, overflowing, packed, stuffed, topped-up, well-filled, well-stocked.
OPPOSITES: SEE **empty** adjective.
2 *a full stomach.* gorged, replete, sated, satiated, satisfied, well-fed.
OPPOSITES: SEE **hungry.**
3 *the full story. a full investigation.* complete, comprehensive, detailed, entire, exhaustive, total, unabridged, uncensored, uncut, unedited, unexpurgated, whole.
OPPOSITES: SEE **incomplete.**
4 *full price. full speed.* greatest, highest, maximum, top.
OPPOSITES: SEE **minimum.**
5 *a full figure.* ample, buxom, generous, SEE **fat** adjective, large, plump, rounded.
OPPOSITES: SEE **slight** adjective.
6 *a full skirt.* baggy, broad, voluminous, wide.
OPPOSITE: close-fitting.

full-blooded adjective SEE **vigorous.**

full-grown adjective adult, grown-up, mature, ready, ripe.

fulminate verb SEE **protest** verb.

fulsome adjective SEE **flattering.**

fumble verb *He fumbled the ball.* grope at, handle awkwardly, mishandle.

fume verb 1 *fuming chimneys.* emit fumes, smoke.
2 *He was fuming because he'd missed the bus.* SEE **angry (to be angry)**.

fumes plural noun exhaust, fog, gases, pollution, smog, smoke, vapour.

fumigate verb SEE **disinfect**.

fun noun amusement, diversion, enjoyment, entertainment, SEE **frivolity**, games, horseplay, jokes, joking, [*joking*] jollification, laughter, merriment, merrymaking, pastimes, play, pleasure, recreation, romp, [*informal*] skylarking, sport, teasing, tomfoolery.
to make fun of SEE **mock** verb.

function noun 1 *the function of the police.* SEE **job**.
2 *an official function.* SEE **event**.

function verb *The computer doesn't function.* SEE **work** verb.

functional adjective *The machine doesn't look elegant—it's purely functional.* practical, serviceable, useful, utilitarian.
OPPOSITES: SEE **decorative**.

functionary noun SEE **official** noun.

fund noun 1 *a charitable fund.* [*often plural*] *He invested all his funds.* capital, endowment, SEE **money**, reserves, resources, riches, savings, wealth.
2 *a fund of jokes. a fund of wisdom.* hoard, [*informal*] kitty, mine, pool, reservoir, stock, store, supply, treasure-house.

fundamental adjective *fundamental principles.* axiomatic, basic, SEE **elementary**, essential, important, key, main, necessary, primary, prime, principal, underlying.
OPPOSITES: SEE **advanced, inessential**.

funeral noun burial, cremation, interment, [*informal*] obsequies, Requiem Mass, wake.

WORDS TO DO WITH FUNERALS: bier, catafalque, cemetery, churchyard, cinerary urn, coffin, cortège, cremation, crematorium, grave, graveyard, hearse, memorial, mortuary, mourner, mourning, pall, sarcophagus, tomb, undertaker, wreath.

funereal adjective dark, depressing, dismal, gloomy, grave, mournful, SEE **sad**, sepulchral, solemn, sombre.
OPPOSITES: SEE **cheerful, lively**.

fun-fair noun

ENTERTAINMENTS AT A FUN-FAIR: amusements, big-dipper, big-wheel, dodgems, merry-go-round, ride, rifle-range, roundabout, side-show, shooting-gallery, switchback.

fungus noun mould, mushroom, toadstool.

funk noun SEE **fear** noun.

funnel noun *a funnel on a steam-ship.* chimney, smoke-stack.

funnel verb *to funnel something into an opening.* channel, direct, filter, pour.

funny adjective 1 *a funny joke.* absurd, amusing, comic, comical, diverting, droll, entertaining, facetious, farcical, hilarious, humorous, hysterical, ironic, jocular, [*informal*] killing, laughable, ludicrous, [*informal*] priceless, ridiculous, risible, sarcastic, satirical, [*informal*] side-splitting, silly, uproarious, witty.
OPPOSITES: SEE **serious**.
2 [*informal*] a funny pain. SEE **peculiar**.

funny-bone noun elbow.

fur noun bristles, coat, down, fleece, hair, hide, pelt, skin, wool.

furious adjective 1 *a furious bull. a furious temper.* SEE **angry**, boiling, enraged, fuming, incensed, infuriated, irate, livid, mad, raging, savage, wrathful.
2 *furious activity.* agitated, frantic, frenzied, intense, tempestuous, tumultuous, turbulent, violent, wild.
OPPOSITES: SEE **calm** adjective.

furl verb SEE **roll** verb.

furnace noun SEE **fire** noun.

furnish verb 1 *to furnish a room.* equip, fit out, fit up.
2 *to furnish someone with information.* give, grant, provide, supply.

furnishings noun SEE **furniture**.

furniture noun antiques, effects, equipment, fittings, furnishings, household goods, [*informal*] moveables, possessions.

ITEMS OF FURNITURE: armchair, bed, bench, bookcase, bunk, bureau, cabinet, chair, chest of drawers, chesterfield, chiffonier, commode, cot, couch, cradle, cupboard, cushion, desk, divan, drawer, dresser, dressing-table, easel, fender, filing-cabinet, fireplace, mantelpiece, ottoman, overmantel, pelmet, pew, pouffe, rocking-chair, seat, settee, sideboard, sofa, stool, suite, table, trestle-table, wardrobe, workbench.

furore noun SEE **commotion**.

furrow noun channel, corrugation, crease, ditch, drill (*for seeds*), fluting, groove, hollow, line, rut, trench, wrinkle.

furrowed adjective 1 *a furrowed brow.* creased, frowning, lined, worried, wrinkled.
2 *a furrowed surface.* corrugated, fluted, grooved, ploughed, ribbed, ridged, rutted.
OPPOSITES: SEE **smooth** adjective.

furry adjective *furry animals.* bristly, downy, feathery, fleecy, fuzzy, hairy, woolly.

further adjective *further information.* additional, extra, fresh, more, new, supplementary.

furthermore adverb additionally, also, besides, moreover, too.

furtive adjective *a furtive look.* concealed, conspiratorial, covert, SEE **crafty**, deceitful, disguised, hidden, mysterious, secretive, shifty, sly, [*informal*] sneaky, stealthy, surreptitious, underhand, untrustworthy.
OPPOSITES: SEE **blatant**.

fury noun *the fury of a storm.* SEE **anger** noun, ferocity, fierceness, force, intensity, madness, power, rage, savagery, tempestuousness, turbulence, vehemence, violence, wrath.

fuse verb *to fuse substances together.* amalgamate, blend, combine, compound, join, meld, melt, merge, solder, unite, weld.

fusillade noun *a fusillade of gunfire.* barrage, burst, firing, outburst, salvo, volley.

fuss noun SEE **commotion**.

fuss verb *Please don't fuss!* agitate, bother, complain, [*informal*] create, fidget, [*informal*] flap, [*informal*] get worked up, grumble, make a commotion [SEE **commotion**], worry.

fussy adjective 1 *fussy about food.* carping, choosy, difficult, discriminating, [*informal*] faddy, fastidious, [*informal*] finicky, hard to please, niggling, [*informal*] nit-picking, particular, [*informal*] pernickety, scrupulous, squeamish.
2 *fussy decorations.* complicated, detailed, elaborate, overdone.

fusty adjective 1 *a fusty atmosphere.* SEE **stuffy**.
2 *fusty ideas.* SEE **old-fashioned**.

futile adjective *a futile attempt to achieve the impossible.* abortive, absurd, empty, foolish, forlorn, fruitless, ineffective, ineffectual, pointless, profitless, silly, sterile, unavailing, unproductive, unprofitable, unsuccessful, useless, vain (*a vain attempt*), wasted, worthless.
OPPOSITES: SEE **fruitful**.

futility noun *the futility of unrealistic ambitions.* absurdity, aimlessness, emptiness, hollowness, ineffectiveness, pointlessness, uselessness, vanity, wasted effort.

future adjective *future events.* approaching, awaited, coming, destined, expected, forthcoming, impending, intended, planned, prospective.
OPPOSITES: SEE **past** adjective.

future noun *a bright future.* expectations, outlook, prospects, time to come.

futuristic adjective SEE **advanced**.

fuzz noun down, floss, fluff, hair.

fuzzy adjective 1 *a fuzzy beard.* downy, feathery, fleecy, fluffy, frizzy, woolly.
2 *a fuzzy picture.* bleary, blurred, cloudy, dim, faint, hazy, ill-defined, indistinct, misty, out of focus, shadowy, unclear, unfocused, vague.
OPPOSITES: SEE **clear** adjective.

G

gabble verb babble, chatter, jabber, mutter, prattle, [*informal*] rattle on, SEE **speak**.

gad verb to gad about SEE **enjoy** (to enjoy yourself).

gadget noun *a gadget for opening tins.* appliance, contraption, contrivance, device, implement, instrument, invention, machine, tool, utensil.

gaff noun SEE **fishing** (fishing tackle).

gaffe noun SEE **mistake** noun.

gaffer noun SEE **chief** noun.

gag noun SEE **joke** noun.

gag verb *to gag someone.* keep quiet, muzzle, prevent from speaking, silence, stifle, suppress.

gaggle noun SEE **group** noun.

gaiety noun SEE **cheerfulness**.

gain noun [*often plural*] *We counted our gains.* achievement, acquisition, advantage, asset, attainment, benefit, dividend, earnings, income, increase, proceeds, profit, return, winnings, yield.
OPPOSITES: SEE **loss**.

gain verb 1 *What do you gain by fighting?* achieve, acquire, bring in, capture,

earn, get, make, net, obtain, pick up, procure, profit, realize, receive, win.
OPPOSITES: SEE **lose**.
2 *The explorers gained their objective.* arrive at, attain, get to, reach, secure.

gainful adjective SEE **profitable**.

gainsay verb SEE **contradict**.

gait noun SEE **walk** noun.

gala noun carnival, celebration, fair, festival, festivity, fête, [*informal*] jamboree, party.

galaxy noun 1 Milky Way, solar system, universe.
2 *a galaxy of famous people.* SEE **group** noun.

gale noun SEE **wind** noun.

gall verb SEE **sore** adjective (**to make sore**).

gallant adjective *a gallant knight.* attentive, SEE **brave**, chivalrous, courageous, courteous, dashing, fearless, gentlemanly, heroic, honourable, intrepid, magnanimous, noble, polite, valiant.
OPPOSITES: SEE **cowardly, rude**.

gallery noun *the gallery in a theatre.* balcony, circle, [*informal*] the gods, upstairs.

galley noun *a galley in a ship.* kitchen.

galling adjective SEE **annoying**.

gallivant verb SEE **enjoy** (**to enjoy yourself**), **travel** verb.

gallop verb SEE **run** verb.

gallows noun *sent to the gallows.* gibbet, scaffold.

galvanize verb *to galvanize someone into action.* SEE **stimulate**.

gambit noun SEE **move** noun.

gamble verb bet, game, [*informal*] have a flutter, risk money, speculate, [*informal*] take a chance, take risks, [*informal*] try your luck, venture, wager.

WAYS OF GAMBLING: backing horses, bingo, cards, dice, drawing lots, lottery, pools, raffle, sweepstake, wager.

PEOPLE WHO GAMBLE: better, gambler, punter, speculator.

PEOPLE WHO SUPERVISE GAMBLING: croupier, bookmaker, turf accountant.

---

gambol verb SEE **frolic**.

game adjective 1 *a game fighter.* SEE **brave**.
2 *game for anything.* SEE **willing**.
3 *a game leg.* SEE **lame**.

game noun 1 *It's just a game.* amusement, diversion, entertainment, frolic,

fun, jest, joke, [*informal*] lark, [*informal*] messing about, pastime, play, playing, recreation, romp, sport.
2 *Shall we play a game?* competition, contest, match, tournament.

SOME GAMES OFTEN PLAYED INDOORS: backgammon, bagatelle, billiards, bingo, cards, charades, chess, crossword puzzle, darts, dice, dominoes, draughts, hoopla, jigsaw puzzle, lotto, ludo, mahjong, marbles, ping-pong, pool, skittles, snooker, solitaire, spelling-bee, table-tennis, tiddly-winks, tombola.

SOME CHILDREN'S GAMES PLAYED OUT OF DOORS: ball, conkers, hide-and-seek, hopscotch, leapfrog, roller-skating, seesaw, skate-boarding, skating, sledging, sliding, tag.

OTHER OUTDOOR GAMES: SEE **sport**.

---

3 *hunting for game.* animals, game-birds, prey.
to give the game away SEE **reveal**.

game verb SEE **gamble**.

gammon noun bacon, ham.

gammy adjective SEE **lame**.

gamut noun SEE **range** noun.

gang noun SEE **group** noun.

gang verb **to gang together** SEE **combine**.

gangling adjective SEE **lanky**.

gangster noun bandit, brigand, criminal, crook, desperado, gunman, mugger, robber, ruffian, thug, tough.

gaol noun [The spellings *gaol* and *jail* are both acceptable. *Gaol* is more common in British official documents; *jail* is more common in America.] borstal, cell, custody, dungeon, guardhouse, jail, [*American*] penitentiary, prison.
OTHER PUNISHMENTS: SEE **punishment**.

gaol verb *He was gaoled for fraud.* confine, detain, imprison, incarcerate, intern, [*informal*] send down, send to prison, [*informal*] shut away, shut up.

gaoler noun guard, prison officer, [*slang*] screw, warder.

gap noun 1 *a gap in a wall.* breach, break, chink, cleft, crack, cranny, crevice, hole, SEE **opening**, rift, space, void.
2 *a gap between events.* breathing-space, discontinuity, hiatus, interlude, intermission, interval, lacuna, lapse, lull, pause, recess, respite, rest.
3 *a gap to be measured.* difference, disparity, distance, interval, space.

gape verb 1 *A chasm gaped.* SEE **open** verb.
2 *He gaped in surprise.* SEE **stare**.

garage noun car-port, filling-station, petrol station, service station.

garb noun SEE **clothes**.

garbage noun SEE **rubbish**.

garbled adjective *a garbled message.* SEE **confused**.

garden noun allotment, patch, plot, yard.
gardens grounds, park.

PARTS OF A GARDEN: arbour, bed, border, compost heap, flower bed, greenhouse, hedge, herbaceous border, hothouse, lawn, orchard, patio, pergola, pond, rockery, rock garden, rose garden, shrubbery, terrace, vegetable garden, walled garden, water garden, window-box.

GARDEN TOOLS AND EQUIPMENT: bill-hook, broom, cloche, cultivator, dibber, fork, hedge-trimmer, hoe, hose, lawn aerator, lawnmower, lawn-rake, mattock, pruning-knife, rake, riddle, secateurs, shears, shovel, sickle, sieve, spade, sprayer, sprinkler, trowel, watering-can, wheelbarrow.

SOME GARDENING ACTIVITIES: cultivation, digging, hedge-cutting, hoeing, lawn-mowing, manuring, mulching, planting, pricking-out, pruning, raking, thinning-out, transplanting, watering, weeding.

RELATED ADJECTIVE: horticultural.

---

gardener noun horticulturist.

gardening noun cultivation, horticulture.

gargantuan adjective SEE **large**.

gargle noun mouthwash.

garish adjective SEE **gaudy**.

garment noun SEE **clothes**.

garner verb SEE **gather**.

garnish verb SEE **decorate**.

garret noun attic.

garrison noun 1 *A garrison of troops defended the town.* contingent, detachment, force, unit.
2 *The enemy took the garrison.* barracks, camp, citadel, fort, fortification, fortress, station, stronghold.

garrotte verb WAYS TO KILL: SEE **kill**.

garrulous adjective SEE **talkative**.

gas noun 1 *poisonous gas.* exhaust, fumes, vapour.
2 *cooking by gas.* OTHER FUELS: SEE **fuel**.

SOME GASES: carbon dioxide, carbon monoxide, coal gas, helium, hydrogen, laughing-gas, methane, natural gas, nitrogen, nitrous oxide, oxygen, ozone, sulphur dioxide, tear-gas.

---

gas verb WAYS TO KILL: SEE **kill**.

gasbag noun SEE **talkative** (**talkative person**).

gash noun, verb SEE **cut** noun, verb.

gasoline noun [*informal*] gas, petrol.

gasp verb 1 *The smoke made them gasp.* blow, breathe with difficulty, choke, gulp, pant, puff, wheeze.
2 *He gasped his message.* SEE **speak**.

gasping adjective breathless, exhausted, puffed, tired out.

gate noun barrier, door, entrance, entry, exit, gateway, kissing-gate, [*poetic*] portal, portcullis, turnstile, way in, way out, wicket, wicket-gate.

gateau noun OTHER CAKES: SEE **cake** noun.

gatecrash verb SEE **intrude**.

gateway noun SEE **gate**.

gather verb 1 *to gather in a pile or crowd.* accumulate, amass, assemble, bring together, build up, cluster, collect, come together, concentrate, congregate, convene, crowd, flock together, forgather, get together, group, grow, herd, marshal, mass, meet, mobilize, muster, round up, swarm round, throng.
OPPOSITES: SEE **divide**, **scatter**.
2 *to gather a harvest.* cull, garner, get in, glean, harvest, heap up, hoard, pick, pick up, pile up, pluck, reap, stockpile, store up.
3 *I gather you've been ill.* conclude, deduce, guess, infer, learn, surmise, understand.

gathering noun *a gathering of people.* assembly, function, [*informal*] get-together, SEE **group** noun, meeting, party, social.

gauche adjective SEE **gawky**, **tactless**.

gaudy adjective [*uncomplimentary*] *gaudy colours.* bright, flamboyant, flashy, garish, loud (*loud colours*), lurid, ostentatious, showy, startling, tasteless, tawdry, vivid, vulgar.
OPPOSITES: SEE **tasteful**.

gauge noun *the gauge of a railway.* measurement, size, span, standard, width.

gauge verb SEE **estimate** verb, **measure** verb.

gaunt adjective 1 *gaunt after an illness.* bony, cadaverous, emaciated, haggard,

hollow-eyed, lank, lean, pinched, skeletal, skinny, starving, thin, wasted away.
OPPOSITES: SEE **healthy, plump.**
2 *a gaunt ruin.* bare, bleak, desolate, forbidding, grim.

gauntlet noun SEE **glove.**

gavel noun SEE **hammer** noun.

gawky adjective *gawky movements.* awkward, blundering, clumsy, gangling, gauche, inept, lumbering, maladroit, uncoordinated, ungainly, ungraceful, unskilful.
OPPOSITES: SEE **graceful.**

gay adjective **1** *gay colours. gay laughter.* animated, bright, carefree, cheerful, colourful, festive, fun-loving, SEE **happy,** jolly, jovial, joyful, lighthearted, lively, merry, sparkling, sunny, vivacious.
2 homosexual, lesbian, [*impolite*] queer.

gaze verb SEE **look** verb.

gazebo noun summer-house.

gazette noun SEE **newspaper.**

gear noun *camping gear.* accessories, apparatus, baggage, belongings, SEE **clothes,** equipment, [*informal*] get-up, harness, instruments, kit, luggage, paraphernalia, rig, stuff, tackle, things.

geezer noun SEE **person.**

gel verb SEE **harden.**

geld verb SEE **castrate.**

gelding noun SEE **horse.**

gem noun SEE **jewel.**

gender noun SEE **sex.**

genealogy noun SEE **descent, family tree.**

general adjective **1** *a general problem. our general experience.* accustomed, collective, common, communal, comprehensive, conventional, customary, everyday, familiar, global, habitual, normal, ordinary, popular, prevailing, regular, shared, typical, universal, usual, widespread.
OPPOSITES: SEE **local, special.**
3 *a general idea of where we are going.* approximate, broad, ill-defined, imprecise, indefinite, in outline, loose, unclear, unspecific, vague.
OPPOSITES: SEE **particular, specific.**
general practitioner SEE **doctor.**

generalize verb *to generalize about something.* be vague, draw general conclusions, speak in general terms.

generally adverb as a rule, broadly, chiefly, commonly, in the main, mainly, mostly, normally, on the whole, predominantly, principally, usually.

Several English words, including *generate, genesis, genetics,* and *genital,* are related to Latin *generare = beget,* and Greek *gen- = be produced.*

generate verb *to generate business.* beget, breed, bring about, cause, create, engender, give rise to, make, produce, propagate, [*informal*] whip up.

generation noun age-group, SEE **family.**

generosity noun bounty, largess, liberality, munificence, philanthropy.

generous adjective **1** *a generous sponsor.* bounteous, bountiful, charitable, [*informal*] free (*free with her money*), liberal, munificent, [*informal*] open-handed, philanthropic, unsparing, unstinting.
OPPOSITES: SEE **mean** adjective.
2 *a generous gift.* SEE **expensive,** princely, valuable.
OPPOSITES: SEE **worthless.**
3 *generous portions of food.* abundant, ample, bounteous, copious, SEE **large,** lavish, liberal, plentiful, sizeable, substantial, unstinting.
OPPOSITES: SEE **scanty.**
4 *a generous attitude.* benevolent, bighearted, forgiving, impartial, kind, magnanimous, open, public-spirited, unmercenary, unprejudiced, unselfish.
OPPOSITES: SEE **selfish.**

genesis noun SEE **beginning.**

genial adjective *a genial welcome.* cheerful, easygoing, SEE **friendly,** good-natured, happy, jolly, kindly, pleasant, relaxed, sunny, warm, warm-hearted.
OPPOSITES: SEE **austere, unfriendly.**

genitals noun [*informal*] private parts, pudenda, sexual organs.

genius noun **1** *He has a genius for maths.* aptitude, bent, flair, gift, intellect, knack, talent.
2 *He's a mathematical genius.* academic, [*informal*] egg-head, expert, intellectual, [*uncomplimentary*] know-all, mastermind, thinker.

genre noun SEE **kind** noun.

genteel adjective SEE **polite.**

gentility noun SEE **manners (good manners).**

gentle adjective **1** *a gentle person.* amiable, biddable, compassionate, docile, easygoing, good-tempered, harmless, humane, kind, kindly, lenient, loving, meek, merciful, mild, moderate, obedient, pacific, passive, peace-loving, pleasant, quiet, soft-hearted, sweet-tempered, sympathetic, tame, tender.
OPPOSITES: SEE **violent.**

2 *gentle music. a gentle voice.* low, muted, peaceful, quiet, reassuring, relaxing, soft, soothing.
OPPOSITES: SEE **harsh**.
3 *a gentle wind.* balmy, delicate, faint, light, soft, warm.
OPPOSITES: SEE **strong**.
4 *a gentle hint.* indirect, polite, subtle, tactful.
OPPOSITES: SEE **tactless**.
5 *a gentle hill.* gradual, hardly noticeable, imperceptible, moderate, slight, steady.
OPPOSITES: SEE **steep** adjective.

gentleman noun SEE **man** noun.

gentlemanly adjective SEE **polite**.

gentry noun SEE **class** noun.

genuflect verb *to genuflect before an altar.* bend the knee, bob, bow, kneel.

genuine adjective **1** *a genuine antique.* actual, authentic, authenticated, bona fide, legitimate, original, real, sterling.
OPPOSITES: SEE **fake** adjective.
2 *genuine feelings.* devout, earnest, frank, heartfelt, honest, sincere, true, unaffected, unfeigned.
OPPOSITES: SEE **insincere**.

genus noun SEE **kind** noun.

geography noun

MAJOR GEOGRAPHICAL AREAS: Antarctic, Arctic, the continents (Africa, Antarctica, Asia, Australasia, Europe, North America, South America), the oceans (Antarctic, Arctic, Atlantic, Indian, Pacific), the polar regions (North Pole, South Pole), the tropics.

EVERYDAY GEOGRAPHICAL TERMS: archipelago, bay, canyon, cape, capital, city, climate, continent, contour, conurbation, country, county, creek, dale, delta, downs, east, equator, estate, estuary, fells, fen, fjord, geyser, glacier, glen, gulf, hamlet, heath, hemisphere, highlands, hill.

industry, inlet, island, isthmus, lagoon, lake, land, latitude, longitude, mainland, north, oasis, parish, pass, peninsula, plain, plateau, pole, prairie, province, reef, relief map, river, sea, south, strait, subtropics, suburb, town, tributary, tropics, valley, village, volcano, west, world.

---

geometry noun SEE **mathematics**.

geriatric adjective SEE **old**.

germ noun **1** *the germ of a new organism. the germ of a new idea.* beginning, embryo, genesis, cause, nucleus, origin, seed.

2 *Germs can cause illness.* [*plural*] bacteria, [*informal*] bug, microbe, microorganism, virus.

germane adjective SEE **relevant**.

germinate verb *Seeds germinate in the right conditions.* begin to grow, bud, develop, grow, root, shoot, spring up, sprout, start growing, take root.

gestation noun SEE **pregnancy**.

gesticulate verb SEE **gesture** verb.

gesture noun *an eloquent gesture.* action, flourish, gesticulation, indication, motion, movement, sign, signal.

gesture verb make a gesture, sign, signal.

VARIOUS WAYS TO GESTURE: beckon, bow, gesticulate, motion, nod, point, salute, shake your head, shrug, smile, wave, wink.

---

get verb [*Get* can mean many things. We also use *get* in many phrases, the meanings of which depend on their context. For example, *to get on* could mean: *make progress* (*Get on with your work*); *step on a bus* (*Get on before it goes*); *be friendly* (*They get on with each other*); or *become older* (*Grandad is getting on*). All we can do here is to give a few synonyms for some of the main senses of *get*.]
1 *What can I get for £10?* acquire, be given, buy, come into possession of, gain, get hold of, obtain, procure, purchase, receive.
2 *Try to get him on the phone.* contact, get in touch with, speak to.
3 *Go and get the ball.* bring, fetch, pick up, retrieve.
4 *She got a prize.* earn, take, win.
5 *I got a cold.* catch, contract, develop, suffer from.
6 *They got the thieves.* apprehend, arrest, capture, catch.
7 *Get someone to help.* cause, persuade.
8 *I'll get tea.* make ready, prepare.
9 *I get what you mean.* comprehend, follow, grasp, understand.
10 *When did you get here?* arrive, reach.
11 *How can I get home?* come, go, travel.
12 *It got cold.* become, grow, turn.

getaway noun SEE **escape** noun.

gewgaw noun SEE **ornament** noun.

ghastly adjective *a ghastly mistake.* SEE **frightful**.

ghetto noun SEE **town**.

ghost noun apparition, [*informal*] bogy, ghostly apparition [SEE **ghostly**], hallucination, illusion, phantasm, phantom, poltergeist, shade, shadow, spectre, SEE spirit, [*informal*] spook, vision, visitant, wraith.

to give up the ghost SEE **die**.

ghostly adjective *a ghostly noise*. creepy, disembodied, eerie, frightening, illusory, phantasmal, scary, spectral, [*informal*] spooky, supernatural, uncanny, unearthly, weird.

ghoul noun SEE **spirit**.

ghoulish adjective SEE **gruesome**.

giant adjective *a giant statue*. colossal, elephantine, enormous, gargantuan, gigantic, huge, immense, [*informal*] jumbo, [*informal*] king-size, SEE **large**, mammoth, massive, mighty, monstrous, prodigious, titanic, vast.
OPPOSITES: SEE **small**.

giant noun colossus, Goliath, giant person (SEE **giant** adjective), leviathan, monster, ogre, Titan, [*informal*] whopper.

gibber verb SEE **talk** verb.

gibberish noun SEE **nonsense**.

gibbet noun SEE **gallows**.

gibbon noun SEE **monkey**.

gibe verb SEE **jeer**.

giblets noun *giblets of a chicken*. insides, offal.

giddiness noun dizziness, faintness, unsteadiness, vertigo.

giddy adjective *a giddy feeling*. dizzy, faint, light-headed, reeling, silly, spinning, unbalanced, unsteady.

gift noun 1 *a birthday gift. a gift to charity*. bonus, bounty, contribution, donation, grant, gratuity, offering, present, tip.
2 *a gift for gymnastics*. ability, aptitude, bent, capability, capacity, flair, genius, knack, talent.

gifted adjective SEE **talented**.

gigantic adjective SEE **giant** adjective.

giggle verb SEE **laugh**, snigger, titter.

gild verb SEE **paint** verb.

gilt adjective gilded, gold-coloured, golden.

gimcrack adjective *gimcrack ornaments*. cheap, [*informal*] cheap and nasty, flimsy, rubbishy, shoddy, tawdry, trashy, trumpery, useless, worthless.

gimmick noun *a publicity gimmick*. device, ploy, stratagem, stunt, trick.

gingerly adjective *a gingerly approach*. SEE **cautious**.

girder noun *a framework of girders*. bar, beam, joist, rafter, RSJ.

girdle noun band, belt, corset, waistband.

girdle verb SEE **surround**.

girl noun [*old-fashioned*] damsel, daughter, débutante, hoyden, lass, [*old-fashioned*] maid, [*old-fashioned*] maiden, schoolgirl, tomboy, virgin, [*old-fashioned or sexist*] wench, SEE **woman**.

girth noun circumference, measurement round.

gist noun *the gist of a message*. direction, drift, essence, general sense, main idea, meaning, nub, point, significance.

give verb 1 *to give money. to give praise*. accord, allocate, allot, allow, apportion, assign, award, bestow, confer, contribute, deal out, [*informal*] dish out, distribute, [*informal*] dole out, donate, endow, entrust, [*informal*] fork out, furnish, give away, give out, grant, hand over, lend, let (someone) have, offer, pass over, pay, present, provide, ration out, render, share out, supply.
OPPOSITES: SEE **take**.
2 *to give information*. deliver, display, express, impart, issue, notify, publish, put across, put into words, reveal, set out, show, tell, transmit.
3 *to give a shout*. let out, utter, voice.
4 *to give punishment*. administer, impose, inflict, mete out.
5 *to give medicine*. dispense, dose with, give out, prescribe.
6 *to give a party*. arrange, organize, provide, put on, run, set up.
7 *to give out heat*. cause, create, emit, engender, generate, give off, produce, release, send out, throw out.
8 *to give under pressure*. be flexible, bend, buckle, distort, give way, warp, yield.
to give away *to give away secrets* SEE **betray**.
to give in *to give in after a fight*. SEE **surrender**.
to give up *to give up smoking*. SEE **abandon**.

glacial adjective SEE **icy**.

glacier noun SEE **ice**.

glad adjective SEE **pleased**.

gladden verb SEE **please**.

glade noun *a forest glade*. clearing, space.

glamorize verb idealize, romanticize.

glamorous adjective 1 *a glamorous filmstar*. SEE **beautiful**.
2 *a glamorous life in show-business*. alluring, colourful, dazzling, enviable, exciting, fascinating, glittering, prestigious, smart, spectacular, wealthy.

glamour noun 1 SEE **beauty**.
2 *the glamour of show-business*. allure, appeal, attraction, excitement, fascination, glitter, high-life, lustre, magic.

glance noun, verb SEE **look** noun, verb.

glare noun 1 *an angry glare.* SEE **expression**.
2 *the glare from a fire.* SEE **light** noun.

glaring adjective SEE **bright, obvious**.

glass noun 1 *window glass.* double glazing, glazing, pane, plate-glass.
2 *a glass of water.* beaker, goblet, tumbler, wine-glass.
glasses VARIOUS OPTICAL INSTRUMENTS: bifocals, binoculars, contact-lenses, eye-glass, field-glasses, goggles, lorgnette, magnifying glass, monocle, opera-glasses, pince-nez, reading glasses, spectacles, sun-glasses, telescope.

glasshouse noun conservatory, greenhouse, hothouse, orangery, vinery.

glasspaper sandpaper.

glassy adjective 1 *a glassy stare.* SEE **expressionless**.
2 *a glassy surface.* glazed, shiny, vitreous.

gleam noun, verb SEE **light** noun.

gleaming adjective SEE **bright**.

glean verb SEE **gather**.

glebe noun SEE **field**.

glee noun SEE **joy**.

gleeful adjective SEE **joyful, triumphant**.

glen noun SEE **valley**.

glib adjective *a glib talker.* articulate, facile, fluent, insincere, plausible, quick, ready, slick, smooth, superficial, SEE **talkative**.
OPPOSITES: SEE **inarticulate, sincere**.

glide verb 1 *to glide across ice or snow.* coast, glissade, move smoothly, skate, ski, skid, skim, slide, slip.
2 *to glide through the air.* drift, float, fly, hang, hover, sail, soar.

glider noun SEE **aircraft**.

glimmer noun, verb SEE **light** noun.

glimpse noun *a quick glimpse.* glance, look, peep, sight, [*informal*] squint, view.

glimpse verb *I glimpsed someone moving between the trees.* discern, distinguish, espy, get a glimpse of, make out, notice, observe, see briefly, sight, spot, spy.

glint noun, verb, **glisten** verb, **glitter** noun, verb SEE **light** noun.

glittering adjective *a glittering occasion.* brilliant, colourful, glamorous, resplendent, scintillating, sparkling, SEE **splendid**.

gloaming noun SEE **evening**.

gloat verb *to gloat over a victim.* boast, brag, [*informal*] crow, exult, rejoice, [*informal*] rub it in, show off, triumph.

global adjective SEE **universal**.

globe noun 1 *the shape of a globe.* ball, orb, sphere.
2 *the globe we live on.* earth, planet, world.

globe-trotter noun SEE **traveller**.

globular adjective SEE **spherical**.

globule noun SEE **drop** noun.

gloom noun 1 *We could hardly see in the gloom.* cloudiness, dimness, dullness, dusk, murk, obscurity, semi-darkness, shade, shadow, twilight.
2 *a feeling of gloom.* SEE **depression**.

gloomy adjective 1 *a gloomy house. gloomy weather.* cheerless, cloudy, dark, depressing, dim, dingy, dismal, dreary, dull, glum, SEE **grim**, heavy, joyless, murky, overcast, shadowy, sombre.
OPPOSITES: SEE **bright**.
2 *a gloomy person.* SEE **depressed**, lugubrious, mournful, saturnine.

glorify verb SEE **praise** verb.

glorious adjective 1 *a glorious victory.* bringing glory [SEE **glory**], celebrated, distinguished, famous, heroic, illustrious, noble, noted, renowned, triumphant.
OPPOSITES: SEE **humiliating**.
2 *a glorious sunset.* beautiful, bright, brilliant, dazzling, excellent, fine, gorgeous, grand, impressive, lovely, magnificent, majestic, marvellous, resplendent, spectacular, splendid, [*informal*] super, superb, wonderful.

glory noun 1 *the glory of winning an Olympic medal.* credit, distinction, fame, honour, [*informal*] kudos, praise, prestige, success, triumph.
2 *glory to God.* adoration, homage, praise, thanksgiving, veneration, worship.
3 *the glory of the sunrise.* SEE **beauty**, brightness, brilliance, grandeur, magnificence, majesty, radiance, splendour.

gloss noun *I polished the table to a high gloss.* brightness, brilliance, burnish, lustre, polish, sheen, shine, varnish.

gloss verb *to gloss over* SEE **disguise** verb.

glossary noun dictionary, phrase-book, vocabulary, word-list.

glossy adjective *a glossy surface.* bright, burnished, glassy, glazed, gleaming, lustrous, polished, reflective, shiny, silky, sleek, smooth.
OPPOSITES: SEE **dull** adjective.

glove noun gauntlet, mitt, mitten.

glow noun 1 *the glow of a light bulb.* SEE **light** noun.

2 *the glow of a fire.* burning, fieriness, heat, incandescence, red-heat, redness.
3 *a glow in your cheeks.* blush, flush, rosiness, warmth.
4 *a glow of excitement.* ardour, enthusiasm, fervour, passion.

glow verb SEE **light** noun **(to give light)**.

glower verb frown, glare, lour, lower, scowl, stare angrily.
FACIAL EXPRESSIONS: SEE **expression**.

glowing adjective **1** *a glowing light.* bright, fluorescent, hot, incandescent, luminous, phosphorescent, radiant, red, red-hot, white-hot.
2 *a glowing recommendation.* complimentary, enthusiastic, fervent, passionate, warm.

glue noun [In addition to the words given here, there are many kinds of glue with proprietary names.] adhesive, cement, fixative, gum, paste, sealant, size, wallpaper-paste.

glue verb *to glue things together.* affix, bond, cement, fasten, fix, gum, paste, seal, stick.

gluey adjective SEE **sticky**.

glum adjective SEE **gloomy**.

glut noun *a glut of fruit.* abundance, excess, plenty, superfluity, surfeit, surplus.
OPPOSITES: SEE **scarcity**.

gluttonous adjective SEE **greedy**.

gnarled adjective *a gnarled old tree.* contorted, distorted, knobbly, knotted, lumpy, rough, rugged, twisted.

gnash verb *to gnash your teeth.* SEE **grind**.

gnaw verb *to gnaw a bone.* bite, chew, SEE **eat**.

go verb **1** *Let's go!* advance, begin, be off, commence, decamp, depart, disappear, embark, escape, get away, get going, get moving, get out, get under way, leave, move, [*informal*] nip along, pass along, pass on, proceed, retire, retreat, SEE **run** verb, set off, set out, [*informal*] shove off, start, take your leave, SEE **travel** verb, SEE **walk** verb, [*old-fashioned*] wend, withdraw.
2 *How far does this road go?* extend, lead, reach, stretch.
3 *The car won't go.* act, function, operate, perform, run, work.
4 *The firework went bang.* give off, make, produce, sound.
5 *Time goes quickly.* elapse, lapse, pass.
6 *Milk soon goes sour.* become, grow, turn.
7 *The butter goes in the fridge.* belong, feel at home, have your proper place.
8 *The light goes in the evening.* die, disappear, fade, fail, give way, vanish.

to go away SEE **depart**.
to go down SEE **sink** verb.
to go in for 1 *I go in for foreign food.* SEE **like** verb.
2 *They go in for competitions.* SEE **enter**.
to go into *Don't go into details.* SEE **investigate**.
to go off *A bomb went off.* SEE **explode**.
to go on *How long can you go on?* SEE **continue**.
to go through *She went through a nasty illness.* SEE **suffer**.
to go to *I want to go to America.* SEE **visit** verb.
to go with 1 *Will you go with me?* SEE **accompany**.
2 *What goes with blue?* SEE **match** verb.
to go without *They went without food.* SEE **abstain**.

goad verb *to goad someone to do something.* badger, [*informal*] chivvy, egg on, [*informal*] hassle, needle, prick, prod, prompt, spur, SEE **stimulate**, urge.

go-ahead adjective SEE **ambitious**.

goal noun *a goal in life.* aim, ambition, aspiration, design, end, intention, object, objective, purpose, target.

goat noun billy-goat, kid, nanny-goat.

gob noun SEE **mouth**.

gobble verb *to gobble food.* bolt, devour, SEE **eat**, gulp, guzzle.

gobbledegook noun SEE **nonsense**.

go-between noun agent, broker, envoy, intermediary, mediator, messenger, middleman.
to act as a go-between SEE **mediate**.

goblet noun SEE **cup**.

god, goddess nouns the Almighty, the Creator, deity, divinity, godhead.
the gods the immortals, pantheon, the powers above.
RELIGIOUS TERMS: SEE **religion**.

godless adjective SEE **irreligious**.

godly adjective SEE **religious**.

godsend noun *Her gift of money was a godsend.* blessing, miracle, stroke of good luck, windfall.

go-getting adjective SEE **ambitious**.

goggle verb gape, gawp, SEE **look** verb, stare.

goggles noun SEE **glass (glasses)**.

going-over noun **1** [*informal*] *I gave the car a going-over.* SEE **inspection**.
2 [*informal*] *The boss gave him a right going-over.* SEE **reprimand** noun.

golden adjective gilded, gilt, yellow.

goldsmith noun jeweller.

golliwog noun SEE **doll**.

gondolier noun SEE **boatman**.

good adjective [We apply the word *good* to anything we like or approve of. The number of possible synonyms, therefore, is virtually unlimited. We give here some of the more common words which express approval.]
1 [= *good* in a general sense] acceptable, admirable, agreeable, appropriate, approved of, champion, commendable, delightful, enjoyable, esteemed, SEE **excellent**, [*informal*] fabulous, fair, [*informal*] fantastic, fine, gratifying, happy, [*informal*] incredible, lovely, marvellous, nice, outstanding, perfect, [*informal*] phenomenal, pleasant, pleasing, praiseworthy, proper, remarkable, right, satisfactory, [*informal*] sensational, sound, splendid, [*informal*] super, superb, suitable, useful, valid, valuable, wonderful, worthy.
2 *a good person. a good deed.* angelic, benevolent, caring, charitable, chaste, considerate, decent, dependable, dutiful, ethical, friendly, helpful, holy, honest, honourable, humane, incorruptible, innocent, just, SEE **kind** adjective, law-abiding, loyal, merciful, moral, noble, obedient, personable, pure, reliable, religious, righteous, saintly, sound, [*informal*] straight, thoughtful, true, trustworthy, upright, virtuous, well-behaved, well-mannered, worthy.
3 *a good musician. a good worker.* able, accomplished, capable, SEE **clever**, conscientious, efficient, gifted, proficient, skilful, skilled, talented.
4 *good work.* competent, correct, creditable, efficient, meritorious, neat, orderly, presentable, professional, thorough, well-done.
5 *good food.* delicious, eatable, nourishing, nutritious, tasty, well-cooked, wholesome.
6 *a good book.* classic, exciting, great, interesting, readable, well-written.
a good person [*informal*] angel, [*informal*] jewel, philanthropist, [*informal*] saint, Samaritan, worthy.

goodbye interjection [Several terms we use when saying goodbye are from foreign languages. Generally, they are used informally.] adieu, adios, arrivederci, auf Wiedersehen, au revoir, bon voyage, ciao, cheerio, farewell, so long. OPPOSITES: SEE **greeting**.

good-for-nothing adjective SEE worthless.

good-humoured adjective SEE **good-tempered**.

good-looking adjective SEE **handsome**.

good-natured adjective SEE **good-tempered**.

goods noun SEE **freight**.

good-tempered adjective accommodating, amenable, benevolent, benign, cheerful, considerate, cordial, friendly, good-humoured, good-natured, helpful, in a good mood, SEE **kind** adjective, obliging, patient, pleasant, relaxed, sympathetic, thoughtful, willing.
OPPOSITES: SEE **bad-tempered**.

goodwill noun SEE **friendliness**.

goody-goody adjective SEE **virtuous**.

gooey adjective SEE **sticky**.

goose noun gander, gosling.

gore noun *covered in gore.* blood.

gore verb *gored by a bull.* SEE **wound** verb.

gorge noun SEE **valley**.

gorge verb *to gorge yourself* SEE **eat**.

gorgeous adjective SEE **beautiful**, **magnificent**.

gormandize verb SEE **eat**.

gormless adjective SEE **stupid**.

gory adjective *a gory wound. a gory battle.* bloodstained, bloody, grisly, gruesome, savage.

gospel noun *preaching the gospel.* creed, doctrine, good news, good tidings, message, religion, revelation, teaching, testament.

gossamer noun cobweb, flimsy material, gauze.

gossip noun **1** *Don't listen to gossip.* casual talk, chatter, hearsay, prattle, rumour, scandal, [*informal*] tattle, [*informal*] tittle-tattle.
2 *Don't listen to him—he's a real gossip.* busybody, Nosy Parker, scandalmonger, SEE **talkative (talkative person)**, tell-tale.

gossip verb *They just stood gossiping.* chat, chatter, [*informal*] natter, prattle, spread scandal, SEE **talk** verb, [*informal*] tattle, tell tales, [*informal*] tittle-tattle.

gouge verb *to gouge out a hole.* chisel, SEE **cut** verb, dig, hollow, scoop.

goulash noun hash, stew.

gourmand noun SEE **greedy (greedy person)**.

gourmet noun connoisseur, epicure, gastronome.

govern verb **1** *to govern a country.* administer, be in charge of, command, conduct the affairs of, control, direct, guide, head, lead, look after, manage, oversee, preside over, reign, rule, run, steer, superintend, supervise.
2 *to govern your temper.* bridle, curb, check, control, discipline, keep in

check, keep under control, master, regulate, restrain, tame.

governess noun SEE **teacher.**

government noun *Any country needs strong government.* administration, bureaucracy, conduct of state affairs, constitution, control, direction, management, regime, regulation, rule, sovereignty, supervision, surveillance.

GROUPS INVOLVED IN GOVERNMENT: Cabinet, constituency, electorate, [*informal*] the Establishment, junta, local authority, ministry, parliament, [*informal*] the powers that be, regime, senate, state.

TYPES OF REGIME: commonwealth, democracy, dictatorship, empire, federation, kingdom, monarchy, oligarchy, republic.

PEOPLE INVOLVED IN GOVERNMENT OR PUBLIC ADMINISTRATION: ambassador, chancellor, Chancellor of the Exchequer, civil servant, consul, councillor, diplomat, elected representative, mayor, Member of Parliament, minister, politician, premier, president, prime minister, SEE **royalty,** Secretary of State (*Home Secretary, Foreign Secretary,* etc.), senator, statesman, stateswoman, viceroy.

---

governor noun SEE **chief** noun.

gown noun dress, frock.

grab verb *Grab what you can.* [*informal*] bag, capture, catch, clutch, [*informal*] collar, get hold of, grasp, hold, [*informal*] nab, pluck, seize, snap up, snatch.

grace noun 1 *grace of movement.* attractiveness, beauty, charm, ease, elegance, fluidity, gracefulness, loveliness, poise, refinement, softness, tastefulness.
2 *God's grace.* beneficence, benevolence, compassion, favour, forgiveness, goodness, graciousness, kindness, love, mercy.
3 *grace before dinner.* blessing, giving thanks, prayer.

graceful adjective 1 *graceful movements.* agile, balletic, deft, easy, flowing, fluid, natural, nimble, pliant, smooth, supple.
OPPOSITES: SEE **clumsy.**
2 *a graceful figure.* attractive, beautiful, dignified, elegant, slim, slender, willowy.
OPPOSITES: SEE **bony, fat** adjective.

graceless adjective 1 *graceless movements.* SEE **clumsy.**
2 *graceless manners.* SEE **rude.**

gracious adjective 1 *a gracious lady.* affable, agreeable, charitable, compassionate, courteous, dignified, elegant, friendly, good-natured, SEE **kind** adjective, pleasant, polite, with grace.
2 *a gracious judge.* SEE **merciful.**
3 *gracious living.* SEE **affluent.**

grade noun 1 *top grade meat.* class, condition, quality, standard.
2 *The examiner re-marked the work and put it up a grade.* category, level, mark, notch, point, position, rank, rung, step.

grade verb 1 *They grade eggs according to size.* arrange, categorize, classify, differentiate, group, range, sort.
2 *Teachers grade students' work.* assess, evaluate, mark, rank, rate.

gradient noun *a steep gradient.* ascent, bank, declivity, hill, incline, rise, slope.

gradual adjective *a gradual increase in prices. a gradual slope.* continuous, even, gentle, leisurely, moderate, slow, steady, unhurried, unspectacular.
OPPOSITES: SEE **steep** adjective, **sudden.**

graduate verb 1 *to graduate at a college or university.* become a graduate, be successful, get a degree, pass, qualify.
2 *to graduate a measuring-rod.* calibrate, divide into graded sections, mark off, mark with a scale.

graffiti plural noun SEE **picture** noun.

graft verb *to graft a bud onto a rose-bush.* implant, insert, join, splice.

grain noun 1 *the grain harvest.* SEE **cereal.**
2 *a grain of sand. a tiny grain.* bit, crumb, fragment, granule, iota, jot, mite, morsel, particle, seed, speck.
RELATED ADJECTIVE: granular.

grammar noun syntax.
LINGUISTIC TERMS: SEE **language.**
grammar school OTHER SCHOOLS: SEE **school.**

gramophone noun SEE **audio equipment.**

grand adjective 1 *a grand occasion. a grand house.* SEE **big,** dignified, glorious, great, important, imposing, impressive, lordly, magnificent, majestic, noble, opulent, [*uncomplimentary*] ostentatious, palatial, posh, [*uncomplimentary*] pretentious, regal, royal, splendid, stately, sumptuous, superb.
OPPOSITES: SEE **modest.**
2 [*often uncomplimentary*] *They're too grand for us.* aristocratic, august, eminent, SEE **grandiose,** haughty, [*informal*] high-and-mighty, patronizing, pompous, upper class, [*informal*] upper crust.
OPPOSITES: SEE **ordinary.**
3 *grand ideas.* SEE **unrealistic.**

grandchild noun granddaughter, grandson.
FAMILY RELATIONSHIPS: SEE **family**.

grandee noun SEE **aristocrat**.

grandeur noun SEE **splendour**.

grandiloquent adjective *grandiloquent language*. bombastic, elaborate, flowery, SEE **grandiose**, high-flown, inflated, ornate, poetic, pompous, rhetorical, turgid.
OPPOSITES: SEE **simple**.

grandiose adjective [*uncomplimentary*] *grandiose ideas*. affected, exaggerated, extravagant, flamboyant, SEE **grand**, SEE **grandiloquent**, ostentatious, [*informal*] over the top, pretentious, showy.
OPPOSITES: SEE **unpretentious**.

grandparent noun [*informal*] gran, [*informal*] grandad, grandfather, grandmother, [*informal*] grandpa, [*informal*] granny.
FAMILY RELATIONSHIPS: SEE **family**.

grant noun *a grant of money*. allocation, allowance, annuity, award, benefaction, bursary, donation, expenses, gift, honorarium, investment, loan, scholarship, sponsorship, subsidy.

grant verb 1 *to grant someone a sum of money*. allocate, allow, allot, award, confer, donate, give, pay, provide.
2 *She granted that I was right*. accept, acknowledge, admit, agree, concede, vouchsafe.

granular adjective *a granular substance*. crumbly, grainy, granulated, gritty, in grains, rough, sandy.
OPPOSITES: SEE **solid**.

granule noun SEE **grain**.

graph noun chart, column-graph, diagram, grid, pie chart, table.

graphic adjective *a graphic description*. SEE **vivid**.

graphics noun SEE **art**.

grapnel noun anchor, hook.

grapple verb **to grapple with 1** *to grapple with an intruder*. SEE **fight** verb, lay hold of, struggle with, tackle, wrestle with.
2 *to grapple with a problem*. attend to, come to grips with, contend with, cope with, deal with, engage with, get involved with, handle, [*informal*] have a go at, manage, try to solve.
OPPOSITES: SEE **avoid**.

grasp verb 1 *to grasp something in your hands*. catch, clasp, clutch, get hold of, grab, grapple with, grip, hang on to, hold, seize, snatch.
2 *to grasp an idea*. apprehend, comprehend, [*informal*] cotton on to, follow, learn, master, realize, take in, understand.
able to grasp prehensile.

grasping adjective *a grasping miser*. SEE **greedy**.

grass noun PLANTS RELATED TO GRASS: bamboo, esparto grass, pampas grass, sugar cane.

AREAS OF GRASS: downland, field, grassland, green, lawn, meadow, pasture, playing-field, prairie, recreation ground, savannah, steppe, [*poetic*] sward, turf, veld, village green.

grasshopper noun cicada, cricket.

grassy adjective grass-covered, green, turfed.

grate noun *a fire in the grate*. fireplace, hearth.

grate verb 1 *to grate cheese*. SEE **cut** verb, shred.
2 *a grating noise*. VARIOUS SOUNDS: SEE **sound** noun.
3 *His manner grates on me*. SEE **annoy**.

grateful adjective *grateful for the gift*. appreciative, indebted, obliged, thankful.
OPPOSITES: SEE **ungrateful**.

gratify verb SEE **please**.

grating noun *iron grating over a drain*. bars, grid, grille, lattice-work.

gratis adjective complimentary, free, without charge.

gratitude noun SEE **thanks**.

gratuitous adjective *gratuitous insults*. groundless, inappropriate, needless, unasked for, uncalled for, undeserved, unjustifiable, unmerited, unnecessary, unprovoked, unsolicited, unwarranted.
OPPOSITES: SEE **justifiable**.

gratuity noun *a gratuity at Christmas*. bonus, [*informal*] perk, present, recompense, reward, tip.

Several English words, including *aggravate*, *grave* (adjective), and *gravity*, are related to Latin *gravis* = *heavy*, *serious*.

grave adjective 1 *a grave decision*. crucial, SEE **important**, momentous, pressing, serious, significant, urgent, vital, weighty.
OPPOSITES: SEE **unimportant**.
2 *a grave illness*. acute, critical, dangerous, major, serious, severe, terminal, threatening, worrying.
OPPOSITES: SEE **slight** adjective.

3 *a grave offence.* criminal, indictable, punishable.
OPPOSITES: SEE **minor.**

4 *a grave expression.* dignified, earnest, gloomy, grim, long-faced, pensive, SEE **sad,** sedate, serious, severe, sober, solemn, sombre, subdued, thoughtful, unsmiling.
OPPOSITES: SEE **happy.**

grave noun *graves where people are buried.* barrow, burial-place, SEE **gravestone,** mausoleum, sepulchre, tomb, tumulus, vault.

gravel noun grit, pebbles, shingle, stones.

gravestone noun headstone, memorial, monument, tombstone.

graveyard noun burial-ground, cemetery, churchyard.

gravitate verb *We all gravitated towards the food.* be attracted to, descend on, head for, make for, move towards.

gravity noun **1** *the gravity of an illness.* acuteness, danger, importance, magnitude, momentousness, seriousness, severity.
2 *the gravity of a state occasion.* ceremony, dignity, earnestness, pomp, sedateness, sobriety, solemnity.
3 *the force of gravity.* gravitation, heaviness, ponderousness, pull, weight.

graze noun *a graze on the knee.* abrasion, laceration, raw spot.

graze verb **1** *grazing cattle.* SEE **eat.**
2 *to graze your knee.* [*formal*] abrade, chafe, scrape, scratch, SEE **wound** verb.

grease noun SEE **fat** noun, lubrication, oil.

greasy adjective **1** *greasy fingers.* fatty, oily, slippery, smeary.
2 *a greasy manner.* fawning, flattering, fulsome, grovelling, ingratiating, [*informal*] smarmy, sycophantic, unctuous.

great adjective **1** *a great mountain. a great ocean.* SEE **big,** colossal, enormous, extensive, huge, immense, large, tremendous.
2 *great pain. great difficulties.* acute, excessive, extreme, intense, SEE **severe.**
3 *a great event.* grand, SEE **important,** large-scale, momentous, serious, significant, spectacular.
4 *a great piece of music.* brilliant, classic, SEE **excellent,** [*informal*] fabulous, famous, [*informal*] fantastic, fine, first-rate, outstanding, wonderful.
5 *a great athlete.* able, celebrated, distinguished, eminent, SEE **famous,** gifted, notable, noted, prominent, renowned, talented, well-known.
6 *a great friend.* SEE **chief** adjective, close, devoted, main, valued.

7 *a great reader.* active, assiduous, SEE **enthusiastic,** frequent, keen.
8 [*informal*] *a great day out.* SEE **good.**
OPPOSITES: SEE **insignificant, small.**

greatcoat noun SEE **coat** noun, overcoat.

greed noun **1** *greed for food.* appetite, craving, gluttony, gormandizing, greediness, hunger, intemperance, insatiability, overeating, ravenousness, self-indulgence, voraciousness, voracity.
2 *greed for possessions.* acquisitiveness, avarice, covetousness, cupidity, desire, rapacity, self-interest, selfishness.

greedy adjective **1** *greedy for food.* famished, gluttonous, gormandizing, hungry, insatiable, intemperate, omnivorous, [*informal*] piggish, ravenous, self-indulgent, starving, voracious.
OPPOSITES: SEE **abstemious.**
2 *greedy for possessions.* acquisitive, avaricious, avid, covetous, desirous, eager, grasping, miserly, [*informal*] money-grabbing, rapacious, selfish.
OPPOSITES: SEE **unselfish.**
a greedy person glutton, [*joking*] good trencherman, gormandizer, gourmand, [*informal*] greedy-guts, guzzler, [*informal*] pig.
to be greedy gobble your food, gorge yourself, gormandize, guzzle, indulge yourself, [*informal*] make a pig of yourself, overeat.

green adjective, noun greenish, verdant.
SHADES OF GREEN: emerald, grass-green, jade, khaki, lime, olive, pea-green, turquoise.
OTHER COLOURS: SEE **colour** noun.
green light SEE **permission.**

greenery noun foliage, leaves, plants, vegetation.

greenhorn noun SEE **inexperienced (inexperienced person).**

greenhouse noun SEE **glasshouse.**

greet verb *to greet visitors.* acknowledge, give a greeting to, hail, receive, salute, say (greeting) to [SEE **greeting**], welcome.

greeting noun salutation, welcome.
OPPOSITES: SEE **goodbye.**

VARIOUS WORDS OF GREETING: good day, good morning (afternoon, evening), hallo, hello, hullo, how do you do, welcome.

GREETINGS USED ON SPECIAL OCCASIONS: condolences, congratulations, felicitations, happy anniversary (birthday,

Christmas, etc.), many happy returns, sympathies, well done.

---

gregarious adjective SEE **sociable**.

gremlin noun SEE **mishap**.

grey adjective *grey hair. grey skies.* ashen, blackish, greying, grizzled, grizzly, hoary, leaden, silver, silvery, slate-grey, whitish.

grid noun 1 *an iron grid.* framework, grating, grille, lattice.
2 *Draw the plan on a grid.* graph paper, network of lines, pattern of intersecting lines, squares.

grief noun *the grief of bereavement.* affliction, anguish, desolation, distress, heartache, heartbreak, misery, mourning, pain, regret, remorse, sadness, sorrow, suffering, tragedy, [*informal*] trials and tribulations, unhappiness, woe.
OPPOSITES: SEE **happiness**.
to come to grief SEE **fail**.

grievance noun SEE **complaint**.

grieve verb 1 *The uncalled-for criticism grieved her.* afflict, cause grief to [SEE **grief**], depress, dismay, distress, hurt, pain, sadden, upset, wound.
OPPOSITES: SEE **delight** verb.
2 *He grieved terribly when his dog died.* feel grief [SEE **grief**], [*informal*] eat your heart out, fret, go into mourning, lament, mope, mourn, suffer, wail, weep.
OPPOSITES: SEE **rejoice**.

grievous adjective 1 *a grievous loss.* causing grief [SEE **grief**], SEE **sad**.
2 *a grievous disaster.* SEE **serious**.

grill noun grid, gridiron, toaster.

grill verb 1 *to grill bacon.* SEE **cook** verb.
2 *to grill a suspect.* SEE **question** verb.

grille noun *a grille over a window.* bars, grating, grid, lattice-work.

grim adjective 1 *a grim expression.* bad-tempered, cruel, dour, fearsome, fierce, forbidding, frightful, ghastly, gloomy, grisly, gruesome, harsh, hideous, horrible, [*informal*] horrid, menacing, merciless, ominous, relentless, severe, stark, stern, sullen, surly, terrible, threatening, unattractive, unfriendly, unrelenting.
2 *grim weather.* SEE **gloomy**.
OPPOSITES: SEE **cheerful, pleasant**.

grimace noun FACIAL EXPRESSIONS: SEE **expression**.

grime noun SEE **dirt**.

grimy adjective *grimy windows.* SEE **dirty** adjective.

grin noun FACIAL EXPRESSIONS: SEE **expression**.

grin verb beam, SEE **laugh**, smile.

grind verb 1 *to grind coffee, corn, etc.* crush, granulate, grate, mill, pound, powder, pulverize.
2 *to grind your teeth.* gnash, rub together.
3 *to grind a knife.* polish, sharpen, whet.
4 *to grind away. to grind down.* abrade, eat away, erode, file, sand, sandpaper, scrape, smooth, wear away.
5 *to grind people down.* SEE **oppress**.
6 *to grind away at a job.* labour, slave, sweat, toil, SEE **work** verb.

grindstone noun SEE **sharpener**.
to keep your nose to the grindstone SEE **work** verb.

grip noun *a firm grip.* clasp, clutch, control, grasp, hand-clasp, hold, purchase, stranglehold.
to come to grips with SEE **deal** verb (**to deal with**).

grip verb 1 *to grip someone's hand.* clasp, clutch, get a grip of [SEE **grip** noun], grab, grasp, hold, seize, take hold of.
2 *to grip someone's attention.* absorb, compel, engross, enthral, fascinate, rivet, spellbind.

gripe verb SEE **complain**.

grisly adjective [Don't confuse with *gristly.*] *a grisly accident.* SEE **gruesome**.

gristle noun *gristle in meat.* cartilage, gristly meat [SEE **gristly**].

gristly adjective [Don't confuse with *grisly.*] *gristly meat.* leathery, rubbery, tough, unchewable, uneatable.

grit noun 1 *grit in my eye.* dust, gravel, sand.
2 [*informal*] *grit in facing danger.* SEE **courage**.

grit verb 1 *to grit your teeth.* SEE **clench**.
2 *to grit the road.* salt, sand, treat.

gritty adjective *something gritty in the food.* abrasive, dusty, grainy, granular, gravelly, harsh, rough, sandy.

grizzle verb SEE **cry** verb.

grizzled, grizzly adjectives SEE **grey**.

groan verb *to groan with pain.* cry out, moan, sigh, wail.

groggy adjective SEE **ill**.

groom noun 1 [= *person who looks after horse*] ostler, stable-lad, stable-man.
2 [= *man on his wedding day*] bridegroom, husband.

groom verb 1 *to groom a horse. to groom yourself.* brush, clean, make neat, preen, smarten up, spruce up, tidy, [*informal*] titivate.
2 *to groom someone for a job.* coach, educate, get ready, prepare, train up.

groove noun *a groove in a surface.* channel, cut, fluting, furrow, gutter, indentation, rut, score, scratch, slot, track.

grope verb *to grope in the dark. to grope for an answer.* cast about, feel about, flounder, fumble, search blindly.

gross adjective 1 *a gross figure.* SEE **fat** adjective.
2 *gross manners.* SEE **vulgar**.
3 *gross injustice.* SEE **obvious**.
4 *gross income.* SEE **total** adjective.

grotesque adjective *grotesque carvings.* absurd, bizarre, deformed, distorted, fantastic, ludicrous, macabre, malformed, misshapen. monstrous, preposterous, ridiculous, strange, ugly, unnatural, weird.

grotto noun cave, cavern, underground chamber.

grouch verb SEE **complain**.

ground noun 1 *the ground someone owns.* area, land, property, terrain.
2 *fertile ground.* clay, earth, loam, soil.
3 *the grounds of a building.* campus, estate, gardens, park, playing-fields, surroundings.
4 *a sports ground.* arena, field, pitch, stadium.
5 *If you accuse someone, be sure of your ground.* argument, basis, case, cause, evidence, foundation, proof, reason.

ground verb 1 *to ground a ship.* beach, run ashore, shipwreck, strand, wreck.
OPPOSITES: SEE **float** verb.
2 *to ground an aircraft.* keep on the ground, prevent from flying.
OPPOSITES: SEE **fly** verb.
3 *On what facts do you ground your argument?* SEE **base** verb.

grounding noun *a thorough grounding in maths.* SEE **teaching**.

groundless adjective *a groundless accusation.* baseless, false, gratuitous, imaginary, irrational, needless, uncalled for, unfounded, unjustified, unproven, unreasonable, unsubstantiated, unsupported, unwarranted.
OPPOSITES: SEE **justifiable**.

groundsheet noun SEE **waterproof** noun.

group noun

VARIOUS GROUPS OF PEOPLE: alliance, assembly, association, band, bevy (*of women*), body, brotherhood, [*informal*] bunch, cadre, cartel, caste, caucus, circle (*of friends*), clan, class, [*uncomplimentary*] clique, club, cohort (*of soldiers*), colony, committee, community, company, conclave (*of cardinals*), congregation (*of worshippers*), consortium, contingent, coterie, coven (*of witches*), crew, crowd, delegation, faction (*a break-away faction*), family, federation, force (*of invaders*), fraternity, gang, gathering, guild (*of workers*), horde, host, knot, league, meeting, [*uncomplimentary*] mob, multitude, organization, party, phalanx (*of soldiers*), picket (*of strikers*), platoon, posse (*of law-enforcers*), [*uncomplimentary*] rabble, ring (*of criminals*), sect, [*uncomplimentary*] shower, sisterhood, society, squad, squadron, swarm, team, throng, troop (*of soldiers*), troupe (*of actors*), union.

GROUPS OF ANIMALS, THINGS, ETC.: accumulation, assortment, batch, battery (*of guns*), brood (*of chicks*), bunch, bundle, category, class, clump (*of trees*), cluster, clutch (*of eggs*), collection, combination, conglomeration, constellation (*of stars*), convoy (*of ships*), covey (*of birds*), fleet (*of ships*), flock (*of birds or sheep*), gaggle (*of geese*), galaxy (*of stars*), herd (*of animals*), hoard, host, litter (*of pigs*), mass, pack (*of wolves*), pride (*of lions*), school, set, shoal (*of fish*), species.
groups of musicians: SEE **music**.

---

group verb 1 *to group things together.* arrange, assemble, bring together, categorize, classify, collect, deploy, gather, herd, marshal, order, organize, put into groups [SEE **group** noun], set out, sort.
2 *to group around a leader.* associate, band, cluster, come together, congregate, crowd, flock, gather, get together, herd, make groups [SEE **group** noun], swarm, team up, throng.

grouse verb SEE **complain**.

grove noun *a grove of trees.* SEE **wood**.

grovel verb *Don't grovel—stick up for yourself!* abase yourself, be humble, cower, [*informal*] creep, cringe, demean yourself, [*informal*] kowtow, prostrate yourself, snivel, [*informal*] toady.

grow verb 1 *Plants grow well in springtime.* become bigger, burgeon, come to life, develop, emerge, evolve, fill out, flourish, germinate, get bigger, increase in size, lengthen, live, make progress, mature, multiply, mushroom, proliferate, put on growth, spread, spring up, sprout, survive, swell, thicken up, thrive.
OPPOSITES: SEE **die**.
2 *I grow roses.* cultivate, farm, help along, nurture, produce, propagate, raise.
OPPOSITES: SEE **kill**.

3 *Her business grew. Her confidence grew.* augment, build up, develop, enlarge, expand, extend, improve, increase, progress, prosper.
OPPOSITES: SEE **shrink**.
4 *She grew more confident.* become, turn.
to grow up become adult, mature.

growl verb snarl.

grown-up adjective adult, fully grown, mature, well-developed.

growth noun **1** *the growth of children.* advance, development, education, getting bigger, growing, maturation, maturing, progress.
2 *the growth of wealth.* accretion, augmentation, enlargement, expansion, improvement, increase, prosperity, success.
3 *growth in the garden.* crop, plants, vegetation.
4 *a growth on the body.* cancer, cyst, excrescence, lump, swelling, tumour.

groyne noun breakwater.

grub noun **1** *a grub in an apple.* caterpillar, larva, maggot.
2 [*informal*] *pub grub.* SEE **food**.

grub verb *to grub up the soil.* SEE **dig**.

grubby adjective *grubby clothes.* SEE **dirty** adjective.

grudge noun *a grudge against someone.* SEE **resentment**.

grudge verb SEE **resent**.

grudging adjective *grudging admiration.* cautious, envious, guarded, half-hearted, hesitant, jealous, reluctant, resentful, secret, unenthusiastic, ungracious, unkind, unwilling.
OPPOSITES: SEE **enthusiastic**.

gruel noun porridge.

gruelling adjective *a gruelling climb.* arduous, backbreaking, demanding, difficult, exhausting, fatiguing, hard, laborious, punishing, severe, stiff, strenuous, taxing, tiring, tough, uphill, wearying.
OPPOSITES: SEE **easy**.

gruesome adjective *a gruesome accident.* appalling, awful, bloody, disgusting, dreadful, fearful, frightful, ghastly, ghoulish, gory, grim, grisly, hair-raising, hideous, horrible, [*informal*] horrid, horrifying, macabre, revolting, sickening, terrible.

gruff adjective **1** *a gruff voice.* harsh, hoarse, husky, rough.
2 *a gruff manner.* SEE **bad-tempered**.

grumble verb SEE **complain**.

grumpy adjective SEE **bad-tempered**.

grunt verb VARIOUS SOUNDS: SEE **sound** noun.

guarantee noun assurance, oath, pledge, promise, surety, warranty.

guarantee verb **1** *to guarantee that a thing works.* assure, certify, give a guarantee, pledge, promise, swear, vouch, vow.
2 *This ticket guarantees your seat.* ensure, make sure of, secure.

guard noun *a prison guard.* custodian, escort, lookout, patrol, security-officer, sentinel, sentry, warder, watchman.
on your guard SEE **alert** adjective.
to stand guard over SEE **guard** verb.

guard verb *A mother guards her young. A warder guards prisoners.* be on guard over, care for, defend, keep safe, keep watch on, look after, mind, oversee, patrol, police, preserve, prevent from escaping, protect, safeguard, secure, shelter, shield, stand guard over, supervise, tend, watch, watch over.
OPPOSITES: SEE **abandon**.

guarded adjective *a guarded remark.* SEE **cautious**.

guardian noun **1** *the guardian of a child.* adoptive parent, foster-parent.
2 *a guardian of public morals.* custodian, defender, keeper, minder, preserver, protector, trustee, warden, warder.

guardsman noun SEE **soldier**.

guerrilla noun SEE **fighter**.

guess noun *a guess about the future.* assumption, conjecture, estimate, feeling, [*informal*] guesstimate, guesswork, hunch, hypothesis, intuition, opinion, prediction, [*informal*] shot in the dark, speculation, supposition, surmise, suspicion, theory.

guess verb *I guess it will cost a lot.* assume, conjecture, divine, estimate, expect, feel, have a hunch, have a theory, [*informal*] hazard a guess, hypothesize, imagine, judge, make a guess [SEE **guess** noun], predict, speculate, suppose, surmise, suspect, think likely.

guesstimate, guesswork nouns SEE **guess** noun.

guest noun **1** *guests at home.* caller, company, visitor.
2 *hotel guests.* boarder, customer, lodger, resident, tenant.

guest-house noun SEE **accommodation**.

guffaw verb SEE **laugh**.

guidance noun *He was new to the job and needed guidance.* advice, briefing, counselling, direction, guidelines, guiding, help, instruction, [*informal*] spoon-feeding, [*informal*] taking by the hand, teaching, tips.

guide noun 1 *a guide who shows the way.* courier, escort, leader, pilot.
2 *maps and guides from the bookshop.* atlas, directory, gazetteer, guidebook, handbook.

guide verb 1 *to guide someone on a journey.* conduct, direct, escort, lead, manoeuvre, navigate, pilot, steer, supervise.
2 *to guide someone in her studies.* advise, brief, counsel, direct, educate, give guidance to [SEE **guidance**], help along, influence, [*informal*] take by the hand, teach, train.
OPPOSITES: SEE **mislead**.

guidelines noun SEE **guidance**.

guile noun SEE **cunning** noun.

guileful adjective SEE **cunning** adjective.

guillotine verb 1 *to guillotine a criminal.* behead, decapitate, SEE **execute**.
2 *to guillotine paper.* SEE **cut** verb.
3 *to guillotine a debate.* SEE **curtail**.

guilt noun 1 *The evidence proved his guilt.* blame, blameworthiness, criminality, culpability, fault, guiltiness, liability, responsibility, sinfulness, wickedness.
OPPOSITES: SEE **innocence**.
2 *a look of guilt on her face.* bad conscience, contrition, dishonour, guilty feelings, penitence, regret, remorse, self-accusation, self-reproach, shame.
OPPOSITES: SEE **virtue**.

guiltless adjective *a guiltless conscience.* above suspicion, blameless, clear, faultless, free, honourable, immaculate, innocent, irreproachable, pure, sinless, untarnished, untroubled, virtuous.
OPPOSITES: SEE **guilty**.

guilty adjective 1 *guilty of wrongdoing.* at fault, blamable, blameworthy, culpable, in the wrong, liable, reprehensible, responsible.
OPPOSITES: SEE **innocent**.
2 *a guilty look.* ashamed, conscience-stricken, contrite, penitent, regretful, remorseful, repentant, shamefaced, sheepish, sorry.
OPPOSITES: SEE **guiltless**.

guise noun SEE **pretence**.

gulf noun 1 *the Gulf of Mexico.* bay.
2 *a deep gulf.* SEE **chasm**.

gullet noun throat.

gullible adjective *He's so gullible he'll believe anything.* credulous, easily taken in, [*informal*] green, impressionable, innocent, naïve, suggestible, trusting, unsuspecting.

gully noun SEE **channel** noun.

gulp verb *to gulp food or drink.* SEE **drink** verb, **eat**.

gum noun *a pot of gum.* SEE **glue** noun.

gummed adjective *gummed paper.* adhesive, gluey, sticky.

gummy adjective SEE **sticky**.

gumption noun [*informal*] *Use your gumption.* common sense, initiative, judgement, [*informal*] nous, sense, wisdom.

gun noun [*plural*] artillery, firearm.

VARIOUS GUNS: airgun, automatic, blunderbuss, cannon, machine-gun, mortar, musket, pistol, revolver, rifle, shot-gun, small-arms, sub-machine-gun, tommygun.

PARTS OF A GUN: barrel, bolt, breach, butt, magazine, muzzle, sights, trigger.

---

gun verb *to gun down* SEE **shoot** verb.

gunfire noun cannonade, firing, gunshots, salvo.

gunman noun assassin, bandit, criminal, desperado, SEE **fighter**, gangster, killer, murderer, sniper, terrorist.

gunner noun SEE **soldier**.

gunpowder noun SEE **explosive** noun.

gunship noun SEE **aircraft**.

gunshot noun SEE **gunfire**.

gurgle verb VARIOUS SOUNDS: SEE **sound** noun.

guru noun leader, SEE **teacher**.

gush noun *a gush of liquid.* burst, cascade, eruption, flood, flow, jet, outpouring, overflow, rush, spout, spurt, squirt, stream, tide, torrent.

gush verb *Liquid gushed out.* come in a gush, cascade, flood, flow quickly, overflow, pour, run, rush, spout, spurt, squirt, stream, well up.
OPPOSITES: SEE **trickle**.

gusher noun oil well.

gust noun SEE **wind** noun.

gusto noun *The musicians played with gusto.* enjoyment, SEE **liveliness**, spirit, verve, zest.

gusty adjective SEE **windy**.

gut adjective *a gut feeling.* SEE **instinctive**.

gut noun [*often plural, informal*] *a pain in the guts.* belly, bowels, entrails, [*informal*] innards, insides, intestines, stomach.
guts [*informal*] *She had guts.* SEE **courage**.

gut verb 1 *to gut an animal.* clean, disembowel, draw, remove the guts of.

2 *to gut a building*. clear, empty, ransack, remove the contents of, strip.

gutless adjective SEE **cowardly**.

gutter noun *a gutter to carry away water*. channel, conduit, ditch, drain, duct, guttering, sewer, sluice, trench, trough.

guttural adjective *a guttural voice*. SEE **throaty**.

guy verb SEE **imitate, ridicule** verb.

guzzle verb SEE **drink** verb, **eat**.

gymnasium noun gym, sports-hall.

gymnastics noun VARIOUS SPORTS: SEE **sport**.

gypsy noun nomad, Romany, traveller, wanderer.

gyrate verb circle, pirouette, revolve, rotate, spin, spiral, turn, twirl, wheel, whirl.

H

habit noun **1** *the habit of shaking hands*. convention, custom, practice, routine, rule, [*old-fashioned*] wont.
2 *the habit of scratching your head*. manner, mannerism, propensity, quirk, tendency, way.
3 *the habit of smoking*. addiction, compulsion, confirmed habit, craving, dependence, fixation, obsession, vice.
to have a compulsive habit be addicted, be a slave, [*informal*] be hooked.
to have a habit of be accustomed to, be used to, do habitually [SEE **habitual**], practice.

Several English words, including *habitable, habitat, habitation*, and *inhabit*, are related to Latin *habitare = to inhabit*. Compare French *habiter*.

habitable adjective *a habitable building*. in good repair, inhabitable, usable.
OPPOSITE: uninhabitable.

habitation noun SEE **home**.

habitual adjective **1** *my habitual route to work*. accustomed, common, conventional, customary, expected, familiar, fixed, frequent, natural, normal, ordinary, predictable, regular, routine, standard, traditional, typical, usual, [*old-fashioned*] wonted.
OPPOSITES: SEE **abnormal**.
2 *a habitual weakness*. addictive, besetting, chronic, established, ineradicable,

ingrained, obsessive, persistent, recurrent.
3 *a habitual smoker*. addicted, conditioned, confirmed, dependent, [*informal*] hooked, inveterate, persistent.
OPPOSITES: SEE **occasional**.

habituate verb SEE **accustom**.

habitué noun SEE **regular** noun.

hack noun **1** SEE **horse**.
2 SEE **writer**.

hack verb SEE **cut** verb.

hackneyed adjective *hackneyed language*. banal, clichéd, cliché-ridden, commonplace, conventional, [*informal*] corny, familiar, feeble, obvious, overused, pedestrian, platitudinous, predictable, stale, stereotyped, stock, threadbare, tired, trite, uninspired, unoriginal.
OPPOSITES: SEE **exciting, new**.

Hades noun SEE **hell**.

Several English words, including *haemophilia, haemorrhage*, and *haemorrhoid*, are related to Greek *haima = blood*.

haemorrhage noun bleeding, internal bleeding.

haemorrhoids noun piles.

haft noun SEE **handle** noun.

hag noun SEE **woman**.

haggard adjective *haggard with exhaustion*. [*informal*] all skin and bone, careworn, drawn, emaciated, exhausted, gaunt, hollow-eyed, pinched, shrunken, thin, tired out, ugly, unhealthy, wasted, withered, worn out, [*informal*] worried to death.
OPPOSITES: SEE **healthy**.

haggle verb *to haggle over the price*. argue, bargain, barter, discuss terms, negotiate, SEE **quarrel** verb, wrangle.

hail verb SEE **greet**.

hair noun **1** *hair on an animal's skin*. bristles, fleece, fur, mane.
2 *hair on your head*. curls, hank, locks, [*informal*] mop, shock, tresses.

WORDS TO DESCRIBE THE COLOUR OF HAIR: auburn, [*male*] blond, [*female*] blonde, brunette, [*informal*] carotty, dark, fair, flaxen, ginger, SEE **grey**, grizzled, mousy, platinum blonde, redhead.
VARIOUS HAIR-STYLES: SEE **hair-style**.

hairdresser noun barber, [*male*] coiffeur, [*female*] coiffeuse, hair-stylist.

hairless adjective bald, bare, clean-shaven, naked, shaved, shaven, smooth.
OPPOSITES: SEE **hairy**.

hairpin adjective *a hairpin bend*. acute, sharp, V-shaped.

hair-raising adjective SEE **frightening**.

hair-splitting SEE **fussy**.

hair-style noun coiffure, cut, hair-cut, [*informal*] hair-do, style.

VARIOUS HAIR-STYLES: bob, crew-cut, dreadlocks, fringe, Mohican, [*informal*] perm, permanent wave, pigtail, plaits, pony-tail, quiff, short back and sides, sideboards, sideburns, tonsure, top-knot.

FALSE HAIR: hair-piece, toupee, wig.

---

hairy adjective *hairy skin*. bearded, bristly, downy, feathery, fleecy, furry, fuzzy, hirsute, long-haired, shaggy, stubbly, woolly.
OPPOSITES: SEE **hairless**.

hale adjective SEE **healthy**.

half-baked adjective SEE **silly**.

half-caste noun half-breed, mulatto, person of mixed race.

half-hearted adjective *half-hearted about her work*. apathetic, cool, easily distracted, feeble, indifferent, ineffective, lackadaisical, listless, lukewarm, passive, perfunctory, uncommitted, unenthusiastic, unreliable, wavering, weak, [*informal*] wishy-washy.
OPPOSITES: SEE **committed**.

half-wit noun SEE **idiot**.

hall noun 1 *the village hall*. assembly hall, auditorium, concert-hall, theatre.
2 *Wait in the hall*. corridor, entrance-hall, foyer, hallway, lobby, passage, vestibule.

hallmark noun SEE **characteristic** noun.

hallowed adjective *hallowed ground*. blessed, consecrated, dedicated, holy, honoured, revered, reverenced, sacred, sacrosanct, worshipped.
OPPOSITE: desecrated [SEE **desecrate**].

hallucinate verb day-dream, dream, fantasize, [*informal*] have a trip, have hallucinations, [*informal*] see things, see visions.

hallucination noun apparition, day-dream, delusion, dream, fantasy, figment of the imagination, illusion, mirage, vision.

halo noun SEE **light** noun.

halt noun 1 *a halt in our progress*. break, interruption, pause, standstill, stop, stoppage.
2 *a railway halt*. platform, station.

halt verb 1 *A traffic-jam halted traffic*. arrest, block, check, curb, impede, obstruct, stop.
2 *Traffic halts at a red light*. come to a halt, come to rest, draw up, pull up, stop, wait.
3 *Work halted when the whistle went*. break off, cease, end, terminate.
OPPOSITES: SEE **start** verb.

halter noun SEE **harness** noun.

halting adjective *halting speech. halting progress*. erratic, faltering, hesitant, irregular, stammering, stumbling, stuttering, uncertain, underconfident, unsure.
OPPOSITES: SEE **fluent**.

halve verb *to halve your income*. bisect, cut by half, cut in half, decrease, divide into halves, lessen, reduce by half, share equally, split in two.

halyard noun SEE **rope** noun.

ham noun SEE **meat**.

ham verb [*informal*] *The actor hammed up the part dreadfully*. act exaggeratedly, [*informal*] camp it up, overact, overdo, overdramatize, [*informal*] send it up.

hamlet noun settlement, village.

hammer noun mallet, sledge-hammer.
to put under the hammer SEE **sell**.

hammer verb *to hammer on the door*. bash, batter, beat, SEE **hit** verb, knock, strike.

hammock noun SEE **bed**.

hamper noun *a picnic hamper*. SEE **basket**.

hamper verb 1 *Bad weather hampered the work*. curb, curtail, foil, hold up, interfere with, obstruct, prevent, restrict, thwart.
2 *My wellingtons hampered me when I ran*. encumber, entangle, fetter, frustrate, handicap, hinder, hold back, impede, restrain, shackle, slow down, trammel.
OPPOSITES: SEE **help** verb.

hamstring verb SEE **cripple** verb.

hand noun 1 *a human hand*. fist, palm.
RELATED ADJECTIVE: manual.
2 *hands on a clock*. pointer.
3 [*old-fashioned*] *factory hands*. SEE **worker**.
at hand, on hand, to hand available, close by, present, waiting, within reach.
to give a hand SEE **help** verb.

hand verb *to hand something to someone*. convey, deliver, give, offer, pass, present, submit.

to hand down *to hand down property.* bequeath, leave as a legacy, pass down, pass on, will.

to hand over 1 *to hand over money.* donate, [*informal*] fork out, give up, pay, surrender, tender.

2 *to hand over a prisoner.* deliver up, extradite, release, [*informal*] turn over.

to hand round *to hand round the drinks.* circulate, deal out, distribute, give out, pass round, share.

handbag noun bag, purse.

handbook noun guide, instruction book, manual.

handicap noun **1** *Luggage is a handicap when you run for a train.* difficulty, disadvantage, drawback, encumbrance, hindrance, inconvenience, [*informal*] minus, nuisance, obstacle, problem, restriction, shortcoming, stumbling-block.

OPPOSITES: SEE **advantage**.

2 *Blindness is a handicap.* defect, disability, impairment, impediment, limitation.

handicap verb *A strong wind handicapped the athletes.* be a handicap to [SEE **handicap** noun], burden, create problems for, disadvantage, encumber, hamper, hinder, hold back, impede, limit, restrict, retard.

OPPOSITES: SEE **help** verb.

handicapped adjective *handicapped people.* disabled, disadvantaged.

SOME WAYS IN WHICH YOU CAN BE HANDICAPPED: autistic, crippled, deaf, disabled, dumb, dyslexic, impaired hearing or sight, lame, limbless, maimed, mute, paralysed, paraplegic, retarded, slow.

---

handicraft noun SEE **art**.

handkerchief noun [*informal*] hanky, tissue.

handiwork noun *Is this your handiwork?* achievement, creation, doing, invention, production, responsibility, work.

handle noun *Hold it by the handle.* grip, haft, hand-grip, helve, hilt (*of a sword*), knob, stock (*of a rifle*).

handle verb **1** *Take care how you handle small animals.* feel, finger, fondle, grasp, hold, [*informal*] maul, [*informal*] paw, stroke, touch, treat.

2 *to handle a rowdy class. to handle a situation.* conduct, control, cope with, deal with, guide, look after, manage, manipulate, supervise.

3 *The car handles well.* manœuvre, operate, respond, steer, work.

4 *We don't handle second-hand goods.* deal in, do trade in, sell, stock, touch, traffic in.

handsome adjective **1** *a handsome man.* attractive, comely, good-looking, personable.

2 *handsome furniture.* admirable, beautiful, elegant, tasteful, well-made.

OPPOSITES: SEE **ugly**.

3 *a handsome gift. a handsome gesture.* big, big-hearted, bountiful, generous, gracious, large, liberal, magnanimous, munificent, sizeable, unselfish, valuable.

OPPOSITES: SEE **mean** adjective.

handwriting noun SEE **writing**.

handy adjective **1** *a handy tool.* convenient, easy to use, helpful, manageable, practical, serviceable, useful, well-designed, worth having.

OPPOSITES: SEE **awkward**.

2 *Keep your tools handy.* accessible, available, close at hand, easy to reach, get-at-able, nearby, reachable, ready.

OPPOSITES: SEE **inaccessible**.

3 *She's handy with tools.* adept, capable, clever, competent, practical, proficient, skilful.

OPPOSITES: SEE **incompetent**.

handyman noun maintenance man, odd-job man.

hang verb **1** *A flag hangs from a flagpole.* be hanging [SEE **hanging**], dangle, droop, swing, trail down.

2 *to hang washing on a line. to hang pictures on a wall.* attach, fasten, fix, peg up, pin up, stick up, suspend.

3 *Smoke hung in the air.* drift, float, hover.

4 *to hang criminals.* SEE **execute**.

to hang about *Don't hang about in the cold.* dally, dawdle, linger, loiter.

to hang back *You'll lose your chance if you hang back.* hesitate, pause, wait.

to hang on *Try to hang on until help comes.* carry on, continue, endure, hold on, keep going, persevere, persist, stay with it, stick it out, wait.

to hang on to *Hang on to the rope.* catch, grasp, hold, keep, retain, seize.

hangdog adjective *a hangdog expression.* SEE **shamefaced**.

hang-glider noun SEE **aircraft**.

hanging adjective dangling, drooping, flopping, pendent, pendulous, swinging loose, suspended.

hangings noun *hangings on the wall.* draperies, drapes, tapestries.

hangman noun executioner.

hang-up noun SEE **inhibition**.

hank noun *a hank of wool.* coil, length, loop, piece, skein.

hanker verb **to hanker after** SEE **desire** verb.

haphazard adjective *The organization was haphazard.* accidental, arbitrary, chaotic, confusing, disorderly, SEE **disorganized**, [*informal*] higgledy-piggledy, [*informal*] hit-or-miss, random, unplanned.
OPPOSITES: SEE **orderly**.

hapless adjective SEE **unlucky**.

happen verb *Did anything interesting happen?* arise, befall, [*old-fashioned*] betide, chance, come about, crop up, emerge, follow, materialize, occur, result, take place, [*informal, sometimes regarded as incorrect*] transpire.
to happen on SEE **find** verb.

happening noun *an unexpected happening.* accident, affair, chance, circumstance, event, incident, occasion, occurrence, phenomenon.

happiness noun bliss, cheer, SEE **cheerfulness**, contentment, delight, ecstasy, elation, euphoria, exhilaration, exuberance. felicity, gaiety, gladness, heaven, high spirits, joy, jubilation, lightheartedness, merriment, pleasure, pride, rapture, well-being.
OPPOSITES: SEE **sorrow** noun.

happy adjective 1 *a happy person. a happy event.* beatific, blessed, blissful, [*poetic*] blithe, SEE **cheerful**, contented, delighted, ecstatic, elated, exultant, felicitous, festive, gay, glad, gleeful, good-humoured, halcyon (*halcyon days*), heavenly, idyllic, jolly, joyful, joyous, laughing, light-hearted, lively, merry, overjoyed, [*informal*] over-the-moon, pleased, proud, radiant, rapturous, relaxed, [*informal*] starry-eyed, thrilled.
OPPOSITES: SEE **unhappy**.
2 *a happy accident.* advantageous, convenient, favourable, fortunate, lucky, opportune, propitious, timely, well-timed.
OPPOSITES: SEE **unlucky**.

happy-go-lucky adjective SEE **carefree**.

harangue noun SEE **speech**.

harangue verb SEE **speak**.

harass verb *Dogs mustn't harass the sheep.* annoy, badger, bait, bother, disturb, harry, [*informal*] hassle, hound, make harassed [SEE **harassed**], molest, persecute, pester, [*informal*] plague, torment, trouble, vex, worry.

harassed adjective *a harassed look.* [*informal*] at the end of your tether, careworn, distraught, distressed, exhausted, frayed, [*informal*] hassled, irritated, pressured, strained, stressed, tired, troubled, vexed, weary, worn out, worried.
OPPOSITES: SEE **carefree**.

harbinger noun SEE **herald** noun.

harbour noun *ships tied up in the harbour.* anchorage, dock, haven, jetty, landing-stage, marina, moorings, pier, port, quay, shelter, wharf.

harbour verb 1 *to harbour criminals.* conceal, give asylum to, give refuge to, give sanctuary to, hide, protect, shelter, shield.
2 *to harbour a grudge.* cherish, cling on to, hold on to, keep in mind, maintain, nurture, retain.

hard adjective 1 *hard concrete. hard ground.* compact, dense, firm, flinty, impenetrable, inflexible, rigid, rocky, solid, stony, unyielding.
OPPOSITES: SEE **soft**.
2 *hard work.* arduous, back-breaking, exhausting, fatiguing, formidable, gruelling, harsh, heavy, laborious, rigorous, severe, stiff, strenuous, tiring, tough, uphill, wearying.
OPPOSITES: SEE **easy**.
3 *a hard problem.* baffling, complex, complicated, confusing, difficult, intricate, involved, knotty, perplexing, puzzling, [*informal*] thorny.
OPPOSITES: SEE **simple**.
4 *a hard heart. hard feelings.* acrimonious, SEE **angry**, callous, cruel, harsh, heartless, hostile, inflexible, intolerant, merciless, pitiless, rancorous, resentful, ruthless, severe, stern, strict, unbending, unfeeling, unfriendly, unkind.
OPPOSITES: SEE **kind** adjective.
5 *a hard blow.* forceful, heavy, powerful, strong, violent.
OPPOSITES: SEE **light** adjective.
6 *a hard time.* calamitous, disagreeable, intolerable, painful, unhappy, unpleasant.
OPPOSITES: SEE **pleasant**.
hard of hearing deaf.
hard up SEE **poor**.

hard-boiled adjective SEE **callous**.

harden verb VARIOUS WAYS SUBSTANCES HARDEN: bake, cake, clot, coagulate, congeal, freeze, gel, jell, ossify, petrify, set, solidify, stiffen, toughen.
OPPOSITES: SEE **soften**.

hard-headed adjective SEE **businesslike**.

hard-hearted adjective SEE **cruel**.

hardly adverb *hardly visible.* barely, faintly, only just, scarcely, with difficulty.

hardship noun *financial hardship.* adversity, affliction, austerity, destitution, difficulty, misery, misfortune, need, privation, suffering, [*informal*] trials and tribulations, trouble, unhappiness, want.

hardware noun equipment, implements, instruments, machinery, tools. VARIOUS TOOLS: SEE **tool**.

hard-wearing adjective *hard-wearing clothes.* durable, lasting, stout, strong, sturdy, tough, well-made. OPPOSITES: SEE **flimsy**.

hardy adjective 1 *a hardy constitution. hardy plants.* fit, healthy, hearty, resilient, robust, rugged, strong, sturdy, tough, vigorous. OPPOSITES: SEE **tender**. 2 *hardy exploits.* SEE **daring**.

hare noun [*male*] buck, [*female*] doe, [*young*] leveret.

hare-brained adjective SEE **silly**.

harelip noun SEE **deformity**.

harem noun seraglio.

hark verb SEE **listen**.

harlot noun SEE **prostitute** noun.

harm noun *Did the storm cause any harm?* damage, detriment, disservice, SEE **evil** noun, havoc, hurt, inconvenience, injury, loss, mischief, pain, unhappiness, [*informal*] upset, wrong. OPPOSITES: SEE **benefit** noun.

harm verb *His captors didn't harm him. Chemicals might harm the soil.* be harmful to [SEE **harmful**], damage, hurt, illtreat, impair, injure, maltreat, misuse, ruin, spoil, wound. OPPOSITES: SEE **benefit** verb.

harmful adjective *a harmful habit. harmful chemicals.* bad, damaging, dangerous, deadly, deleterious, destructive, detrimental, evil, hurtful, injurious, malign, noxious, pernicious, poisonous, prejudicial, unhealthy, unpleasant, unwholesome. OPPOSITES: SEE **beneficial, harmless**.

harmless adjective *harmless animals. a harmless habit.* acceptable, innocent, innocuous, inoffensive, mild, non-addictive, non-toxic, safe, unobjectionable. OPPOSITES: SEE **harmful**.

harmonious adjective 1 *a harmonious group of friends.* amicable, compatible, congenial, co-operative, friendly, integrated, like-minded, sympathetic. OPPOSITES: SEE **quarrelsome**. 2 *harmonious music.* concordant, [*informal*] easy on the ear, euphonious, harmonizing, melodious, musical, sweet-sounding, tonal, tuneful. OPPOSITES: SEE **discordant**.

harmonize verb *I'd like the colours to harmonize.* be in harmony [SEE **harmony**], blend, co-ordinate, correspond, go together, match, suit each other, tally, tone in.

harmony noun 1 *living in harmony.* accord, agreement, amity, compatibility, conformity, co-operation, friendliness, goodwill, like-mindedness, peace, rapport, sympathy, understanding. 2 *musical harmony.* assonance, chords, concord, consonance, euphony, tunefulness. OPPOSITES: SEE **discord**.

harness noun *a horse's harness.* equipment, [*informal*] gear, straps, tackle.

PARTS OF A HORSE'S HARNESS: bit, blinker, bridle, collar, crupper, girth, halter, headstall, noseband, pommel, rein, saddle, spurs, stirrups, trace.

harness verb 1 *to harness a horse.* saddle. 2 *to harness the forces of nature.* control, domesticate, exploit, keep under control, make use of, mobilize, tame, use, utilize.

harp verb *to harp on He harps on about his hobby.* be obsessive, dwell (*I won't dwell on that subject*), keep talking, SEE **talk** verb, talk boringly.

harpoon noun spear.

harridan noun SEE **woman**.

harry verb SEE **harass**.

harsh adjective 1 *a harsh voice.* croaking, disagreeable, discordant, dissonant, grating, guttural, irritating, jarring, rasping, raucous, rough, shrill, stertorous, strident, unpleasant. OPPOSITES: SEE **gentle**. 2 *harsh colours. harsh light.* bright, brilliant, dazzling, gaudy, glaring, lurid. OPPOSITES: SEE **subdued**. 3 *a harsh smell. harsh flavours.* acrid, bitter, unpleasant. OPPOSITES: SEE **mellow**. 4 *harsh conditions.* arduous, austere, comfortless, difficult, hard, severe, stressful, tough. OPPOSITES: SEE **easy**. 5 *a harsh texture.* abrasive, bristly, coarse, hairy, rough, scratchy. OPPOSITES: SEE **smooth** adjective.

6 *harsh criticism.* abusive, bitter, sharp, unkind, unsympathetic.
OPPOSITES: SEE **sympathetic**.
7 *a harsh judge. harsh punishment.* brutal, cruel, Draconian, hard-hearted, merciless, pitiless, severe, stern, strict, unforgiving, unrelenting.
OPPOSITES: SEE **lenient**.

hart noun SEE **deer**.

harum-scarum adjective SEE **reckless**.

harvest noun *a corn harvest.* crop, gathering in, produce, reaping, return, yield.

harvest verb *to harvest the corn.* bring in, collect, garner, gather, mow, pick, reap, take in.

hash noun goulash, stew.
to make a hash of SEE **bungle**.

hasp noun SEE **fastener**.

hassle noun [*informal*] *I don't want any hassle.* altercation, argument, bother, confusion, difficulty, disagreement, disturbance, fighting, fuss, harassment, inconvenience, making difficulties, nuisance, persecution, problem, SEE **quarrelling**, struggle, trouble, upset.
OPPOSITE: peace and quiet [SEE **peace**].

hassle verb *Don't hassle me.* SEE **harass**.

haste noun dispatch, hurry, impetuosity, precipitateness, quickness, rush, SEE **speed** noun, urgency.

hasty adjective **1** *a hasty exit. a hasty decision.* abrupt, fast, foolhardy, headlong, hot-headed, hurried, ill-considered, impetuous, impulsive, [*informal*] pell-mell, precipitate, quick, rapid, rash, reckless, speedy, sudden, summary (*summary justice*), swift.
OPPOSITES: SEE **leisurely**.
2 *hasty work.* brief, careless, cursory, hurried, perfunctory, rushed, short, slapdash, superficial, thoughtless.
OPPOSITES: SEE **careful**.

hat noun head-dress.

VARIOUS HEAD-DRESSES: Balaclava, bearskin, beret, biretta, boater, bonnet, bowler, busby, cap, coronet, crash-helmet, crown, deerstalker, diadem, fez, fillet, headband, helmet, hood, mitre, skull-cap, sombrero, sou'wester, stetson, sun-hat, tiara, top hat, toque, trilby, turban, wig, wimple, yarmulka.

---

hatch verb **1** *to hatch eggs.* brood, incubate.
2 *to hatch a plot.* conceive, concoct, contrive, [*informal*] cook up, devise, [*informal*] dream up, invent, plan, plot, scheme, think up.

hate noun *What's your pet hate?* abomination, aversion, bête noire, dislike, SEE **hatred**, loathing.

hate verb *We hate cruelty. He hates spiders.* abhor, abominate, [*informal*] can't bear, [*informal*] can't stand, deplore, despise, detest, dislike, execrate, fear, feel hostility towards, find intolerable, loathe, recoil from, resent, scorn.
OPPOSITES: SEE **like** verb, **love** verb.

hateful adjective *a hateful sin.* abhorrent, abominable, accursed, awful, contemptible, cursed, [*informal*] damnable, despicable, detestable, disgusting, execrable, foul, hated, heinous, horrible, loathsome, obnoxious, odious, offensive, repellent, repugnant, repulsive, revolting, SEE **unpleasant**, vile.
OPPOSITES: SEE **lovable**.

hatred noun *He made his hatred obvious.* animosity, antagonism, antipathy, aversion, contempt, detestation, dislike, enmity, execration, hate, hostility, ill-will, intolerance, loathing, misanthropy, odium, repugnance, revulsion.
OPPOSITES: SEE **love** noun.

haughty adjective *a haughty manner.* arrogant, boastful, bumptious, cavalier, [*informal*] cocky, condescending, disdainful, [*informal*] high-and-mighty, [*informal*] hoity-toity, imperious, lofty, lordly, offhand, pompous, presumptuous, pretentious, proud, self-important, snobbish, [*informal*] snooty, [*informal*] stuck-up, supercilious, superior.
OPPOSITES: SEE **modest**.

haul noun *a long haul.* SEE **distance** noun.

haul verb *to haul a sledge.* convey, drag, draw, heave, [*informal*] lug, move, pull, tow, trail, tug.

haulage noun *road haulage.* SEE **transport** noun.

haunt verb **1** *to haunt a place.* frequent, [*informal*] hang around, keep returning to, loiter about, visit frequently.
2 *to haunt the imagination.* linger in, obsess, prey on.

have verb [*Have* has many meanings. These are only some of the synonyms you can use.] **1** *I have my own radio.* be in possession of, keep, own, possess.
2 *Our house has six rooms.* consist of, contain, embody, hold, include, incorporate, involve.
3 *They had fun. I had a bad time.* endure, enjoy, experience, feel, go through, know, live through, put up with, suffer, tolerate, undergo.
4 *They all had presents.* accept, acquire, be given, gain, get, obtain, procure, receive.

5 *The thieves had everything.* remove, retain, secure, steal, take.

6 *She had the last toffee.* consume, eat.

7 *We had visitors yesterday.* be host to, entertain, put up.

to have on *Don't believe him—he's having you on.* SEE **hoax** verb.

to have to *I'll have to pay for the damage.* be compelled to, be forced to, have an obligation to, must, need to, ought, should.

to have up *The police had her up for speeding.* SEE **arrest**.

haven noun **1** *a haven for ships.* SEE **harbour** noun.
2 *The climbers found haven in a mountain hut.* asylum, refuge, retreat, safety, sanctuary, shelter.

haversack noun bag, knapsack, rucksack.

havoc noun *The explosion caused havoc.* SEE **carnage**, chaos, confusion, damage, destruction, devastation, disorder, disruption, [*informal*] mayhem, ruin, waste, wreckage.

hawk verb SEE **sell**.

hawser noun SEE **rope** noun.

hay noun fodder, forage.

haystack noun rick.

haywire adjective SEE **chaotic**.

hazard noun *a hazard to traffic.* SEE **risk** noun.

hazard verb SEE **risk** verb.

hazardous adjective *a hazardous journey.* chancy, dangerous, [*informal*] dicey, perilous, precarious, risky, uncertain, unpredictable, unsafe.
OPPOSITES: SEE **safe**.

haze noun cloud, film, fog, mist, steam, vapour.

hazy adjective **1** *a hazy view.* SEE **misty**.
2 *a hazy understanding.* SEE **vague**.

head adjective SEE **chief** adjective.

head noun **1** PARTS OF YOUR HEAD: brain, brow, cheek, chin, cranium, crown, dimple, ear, eye, forehead, gums, hair, jaw, jowl, lip, mouth, nose, nostril, scalp, skull, teeth, temple, tongue.
OTHER PARTS OF YOUR BODY: SEE **body**.
2 *a head for mathematics.* ability, brains, capacity, imagination, intellect, intelligence, mind, understanding.
3 *the head of a mountain.* apex, crown, highest point, summit, top, vertex.
4 *the head of an organization.* boss, SEE **chief** noun, director, employer, leader, manager, ruler.
5 *the head of a school.* headmaster, headmistress, headteacher, principal.
6 *the head of a river.* SEE **source**.

off your head SEE **mad**.
to lose your head SEE **panic** verb.
to put heads together SEE **consult**.

head verb **1** *to head an expedition.* be in charge of, command, control, direct, govern, guide, lead, manage, rule, run, superintend, supervise.
2 *to head a ball.* SEE **hit** verb.
3 *to head for home.* aim, go, make, set out, start, steer, turn.
to head off SEE **deflect**.

headache noun **1** migraine, neuralgia.
2 [*informal*] *Parking can be a headache.* SEE **problem**.

head-dress, headgear nouns SEE **hat**.

heading noun *the heading of a leaflet.* caption, headline, rubric, title.

headlamp noun SEE **light** noun.

headland noun SEE **promontory**.

headlight noun SEE **light** noun.

headline noun *a newspaper headline.* caption, heading, title.

headlong adjective SEE **hasty**.

headquarters noun **1** *the headquarters of an expedition.* base, depot, HQ.
2 *the headquarters of a business.* head office, main office.

headstone noun SEE **gravestone**.

headstrong adjective SEE **obstinate**.

headway noun SEE **progress** noun.

heady adjective SEE **intoxicating**.

heal verb **1** *Wounds heal in time.* get better, knit, mend, recover, unite.
2 *to heal the sick.* cure, make better, remedy, restore, treat.

health noun **1** *your state of health.* condition, constitution, fettle (*in fine fettle*), form (*feeling a bit off-form*), shape (*in good shape*).
2 *We value health.* fitness, robustness, strength, vigour, well-being.

VARIOUS MEDICAL TREATMENTS, ETC.: SEE **medicine**.

VARIOUS ILLNESSES, ETC.: SEE **ill, illness**.

---

healthy adjective **1** *a healthy animal.* in *a healthy condition.* active, [*informal*] blooming, fine, fit, flourishing, good, [*informal*] hale-and-hearty, hearty, [*informal*] in fine fettle, in good shape, lively, perky, robust, sound, strong, sturdy, vigorous, well.
OPPOSITES: SEE **ill**.
2 *healthy surroundings.* bracing, health-giving, hygienic, invigorating, salubrious, sanitary, wholesome.
OPPOSITES: SEE **unhealthy**.

heap noun *a heap of rubbish.* SEE **collection**, mass, mound, mountain, pile, stack.
heaps SEE **plenty**.

heap verb *We heaped up the rubbish.* bank, SEE **collect**, mass, pile, stack.

hear verb **1** *to hear a sound.* catch, listen to [SEE **listen**], overhear, pick up.
2 *to hear evidence in a lawcourt.* examine, investigate, judge, try.
3 *to hear news.* be told, discover, find out, gather, learn, receive.
RELATED ADJECTIVES: auditory, aural.

hearing noun *a court hearing.* case, inquest, inquiry, trial.

hearsay noun SEE **rumour** noun.

heart noun **1** OTHER PARTS OF YOUR BODY: SEE **body**.
RELATED ADJECTIVE [= *of the heart*]: cardiac.
2 *the heart of a forest. the heart of a problem.* centre, core, crux, focus, hub, inside, kernel, middle, nub, nucleus.
3 *Have you no heart?* affection, compassion, feeling, humanity, kindness, love, sympathy, tenderness, understanding.
heart attack cardiac arrest, heart failure.
heart specialist cardiologist.
heart to heart SEE **frank**.
to set your heart on SEE **want** verb.

heartache, heartbreak nouns SEE **sorrow** noun.

heartbreaking adjective distressing, grievous, heartrending, pitiful, SEE **sad**, tragic.

heartbroken adjective broken-hearted, dejected, desolate, despairing, dispirited, grieved, inconsolable, miserable, SEE **sad**, [*informal*] shattered.

heartburn noun indigestion.

hearten verb SEE **encourage**.

heartfelt adjective SEE **sincere**.

hearth noun fireplace, grate.

heartless adjective *heartless cruelty.* cold, SEE **cruel**, icy, steely, stony, unemotional.

heart-searching noun self-examination, self-questioning, thought.

hearty adjective **1** *a hearty welcome.* enthusiastic, sincere, warm.
2 *a hearty appetite.* big, healthy, robust, strong, vigorous.

heat noun **1** *the heat of a fire.* [*formal*] calorific value, fieriness, glow, hotness, incandescence, warmth.

2 *the heat of summer.* closeness, heatwave, high temperatures, hot weather [SEE **hot**], sultriness, warmth.
OPPOSITES: SEE **cold** noun.
3 *the heat of the moment.* ardour, SEE **excitement**, fervour, feverishness, violence.
RELATED ADJECTIVE: thermal.

heat verb VERBS SIGNIFYING TO BE HOT, BECOME HOT, OR MAKE HOT: bake, blister, boil, burn, cook, [*informal*] frizzle, fry, grill, SEE **inflame**, make hot [SEE **hot**], melt, reheat, roast, scald, scorch, simmer, sizzle, smoulder, steam, stew, swelter, toast, warm up.
OPPOSITES: SEE **cool** verb.

heated adjective **1** *heated food.* SEE **hot**.
2 *a heated argument.* SEE **angry, excited**.

heath noun common land, moor, moorland, open country, wasteland.

heathen adjective *heathen beliefs.* atheistic, barbaric, godless, idolatrous, infidel, irreligious, pagan, Philistine, savage, unenlightened.

heave verb *to heave sacks onto a lorry.* drag, draw, haul, hoist, lift, lug, pull, raise, SEE **throw**, tow, tug.
to heave into sight SEE **appear**.
to heave up SEE **vomit**.

heaven noun **1** after-life, Elysium, eternal rest, next world, nirvana, paradise.
OPPOSITES: SEE **hell**.
2 [*informal*] *It's heaven to have a hot bath.* bliss, contentment, delight, ecstasy, felicity, happiness, joy, pleasure, rapture.
the heavens SEE **sky**.

heavenly adjective *heavenly music.* angelic, beautiful, blissful, celestial, delightful, divine, exquisite, lovely, [*informal*] out of this world, SEE **pleasant**, wonderful.
OPPOSITES: SEE **devilish, unpleasant**.

heavy adjective **1** *a heavy load.* SEE **big**, bulky, burdensome, hefty, immovable, large, leaden, massive, ponderous, unwieldy, weighty.
2 *heavy work.* arduous, demanding, difficult, hard, exhausting, laborious, onerous, strenuous, tough.
3 *heavy rain.* concentrated, dense, penetrating, pervasive, severe, torrential.
4 *a heavy crop. heavy with fruit.* abundant, copious, laden, loaded, profuse, thick.
5 *a heavy heart.* burdened, depressed, gloomy, miserable, SEE **sad**, sorrowful.
6 [*informal*] *a heavy lecture.* deep, dull, intellectual, intense, serious, tedious, wearisome.
OPPOSITES: SEE **light** adjective.

heavy-hearted adjective SEE **sad**.

heckle verb *to heckle a speaker.* barrack, disrupt, harass, interrupt, shout down.

hectic adjective *hectic activity.* animated, boisterous, brisk, bustling, busy, chaotic, excited, feverish, frantic, frenetic, frenzied, hurried, lively, mad, restless, riotous, rumbustious, [*informal*] rushed off your feet, turbulent, wild.
OPPOSITES: SEE **leisurely**.

hector verb SEE **intimidate**.

hedge noun barrier, fence, hedgerow, screen.

hedge verb *When I asked for an answer, he hedged.* [*informal*] beat about the bush, be evasive, equivocate, [*informal*] hum and haw, quibble, stall, temporize, waffle.
to hedge in circumscribe, confine, encircle, enclose, fence in, hem in, pen, restrict, shield, surround.

hedonist noun epicurean, hedonistic person [SEE **hedonistic**], pleasure-lover, sybarite.
OPPOSITE: SEE **puritan**.

hedonistic adjective epicurean, extravagant, intemperate, luxurious, pleasure-loving, self-indulgent, sensual, sybaritic, voluptuous.
OPPOSITES: SEE **puritanical**.

heed verb *to heed a warning.* attend to, concern yourself about, consider, follow, keep to, listen to, mark, mind, note, notice, obey, observe, pay attention to, regard, take notice of.
OPPOSITES: SEE **disregard**.

heedful adjective *heedful of people's needs.* attentive, careful, concerned, considerate, mindful, observant, sympathetic, taking notice, vigilant, watchful.
OPPOSITES: SEE **heedless**.

heedless adjective *heedless of other people.* careless, inattentive, inconsiderate, neglectful, thoughtless, uncaring, unconcerned, unobservant, unsympathetic.
OPPOSITES: SEE **heedful**.
heedless of danger SEE **reckless**.

heel verb 1 *to heel a ball.* SEE **kick** verb.
2 *to heel to one side.* lean, list, slope, tilt.

hefty adjective *a hefty man.* beefy, big, brawny, bulky, burly, heavy, heavyweight, hulking, husky, large, mighty, muscular, powerful, robust, solid, [*informal*] strapping (*a strapping lad*), strong, tough.
OPPOSITES: SEE **slight** adjective.

height noun 1 *the height of a mountain.* altitude, elevation, tallness, vertical measurement.

2 [*often plural*] *scaling mountainous heights.* SEE **top** noun.

heighten verb 1 *to heighten the level of something.* build up, elevate, lift up, make higher, raise.
OPPOSITES: SEE **lower**.
2 *to heighten your enjoyment.* add to, augment, boost, enhance, improve, increase, intensify, magnify, maximize, sharpen, strengthen.
OPPOSITES: SEE **lessen**.

heinous adjective SEE **wicked**.

heir, heiress nouns beneficiary, inheritor, successor.

helix noun SEE **spiral** noun.

hell noun eternal punishment, Hades, infernal regions, lower regions, nether world, underworld.
OPPOSITES: SEE **heaven**.

hellish adjective SEE **devilish**.

helm noun *the helm of a ship.* tiller, wheel.
to be at the helm SEE **control** verb.

helmet noun FORMS OF HEAD-DRESS: SEE **hat**.

helmsman noun boatman, cox, pilot, steersman.

help noun *Give me some help.* advice, aid, assistance, avail (*It was of no avail*), backing, benefit, boost, collaboration, contribution, co-operation, friendship, guidance, moral support, relief, succour, support.
OPPOSITES: SEE **hindrance**.

help verb 1 *Help each other. Can I help?* advise, aid, aid and abet, assist, back, befriend, be helpful (to) [SEE **helpful**], boost, collaborate, contribute (to), co-operate, facilitate, forward, further the interests of, [*informal*] give a hand (to), profit, promote, [*informal*] rally round, serve, side (with), [*informal*] spoon-feed, stand by, succour, support, take pity on.
OPPOSITES: SEE **hinder**.
2 *Some medicine might help your cough.* alleviate, benefit, cure, ease, improve, lessen, make easier, relieve, remedy.
OPPOSITES: SEE **aggravate**.
3 *I can't help coughing.* SEE **avoid, prevent**.

helper noun abettor, ally, assistant, collaborator, colleague, deputy, helpmate, partner, [*informal*] right-hand man, second, supporter, [*informal*] willing hands.

helpful adjective 1 *a helpful person.* accommodating, benevolent, caring, considerate, constructive, co-operative, favourable, friendly, helping (*a helping hand*), kind, neighbourly, obliging,

practical, supportive, sympathetic, thoughtful.
OPPOSITES: SEE **unhelpful**.
2 *a helpful suggestion*. advantageous, beneficial, informative, instructive, profitable, valuable, useful, worthwhile.
OPPOSITES: SEE **worthless**.
3 *a helpful tool*. SEE **handy**.

helping adjective *a helping hand*. SEE **helpful**.

helping noun *a helping of food*. amount, plateful, portion, ration, serving, share.

helpless adjective **1** *a helpless invalid*. defenceless, dependent, destitute, feeble, SEE **handicapped**, impotent, incapable, infirm, powerless, unprotected, vulnerable, weak, [*uncomplimentary*] weedy.
OPPOSITES: SEE **independent**.
2 *a helpless ship*. aground, crippled, drifting, stranded, without power.

hem noun *the hem of a skirt*. border, edge, fringe, hemline.

hem verb **to hem in** SEE **surround**.

hen noun SEE **chicken**.

henchman noun SEE **supporter**.

henpeck verb SEE **nag** verb.

herald noun **1** [*old-fashioned*] *the king's herald*. announcer, courier, messenger, town crier.
2 *The cuckoo is the herald of spring*. forerunner, harbinger, omen, precursor, sign.

herald verb *The thunder heralded a change in the weather*. advertise, announce, SEE **foretell**, indicate, make known, proclaim, promise, publicize.

heraldic adjective **heraldic device** badge, coat of arms, crest, emblem, escutcheon, insignia, shield.

heraldry noun heraldic devices [SEE **heraldic**].

Several English words, including *herb, herbaceous, herbicide,* and *herbivorous,* are related to Latin *herba = grass*.

---

herb noun culinary herb.

VARIOUS HERBS: angelica, anise, balm, balsam, basil, borage, camomile, caraway, chervil, chicory, chive, coriander, cumin, dill, fennel, fenugreek, hyssop, liquorice, lovage, marjoram, mint, oregano, parsley, peppermint, rosemary, rue, sage, savory, spearmint, tansy, tarragon, thyme, wintergreen.

---

herbicide noun SEE **poison** noun.

herbivorous adjective *herbivorous animals*. grass-eating, plant-eating, vegetarian.
COMPARE: carnivorous, omnivorous.

herculean adjective **1** *herculean strength*. SEE **strong**.
2 *a herculean task*. SEE **difficult**.

herd noun, verb SEE **group** noun, verb.

hereditary adjective **1** *a hereditary title*. bequeathed, family (*the family name*), handed down, inherited, passed on.
2 *a hereditary disease*. hereditary characteristics. congenital, constitutional, inborn, inbred, inherent, innate, native, natural, transmissible, transmittable.
OPPOSITE: **acquired**.

heresy noun *guilty of heresy*. blasphemy, rebellion, [*informal*] stepping out of line, unorthodox thinking.
OPPOSITES: SEE **orthodoxy**.

heretic noun apostate, blasphemer, dissenter, free-thinker, iconoclast, nonconformist, rebel, renegade, unorthodox thinker.
OPPOSITES: SEE **conformist**.

heritage noun *our national heritage*. birthright, culture, history, inheritance, legacy, past, tradition.

hermaphrodite noun SEE **sex**.

hermetic adjective *a hermetic closure*. airtight, sealed, watertight.

hermit noun monk, recluse, solitary person.

hernia noun rupture.

hero, heroine nouns celebrity, champion, conqueror, daredevil, idol, protagonist [= *leading character in a play*], star, superman, [*informal*] superstar, victor, winner.

heroic adjective *heroic efforts, heroic rescuers*. adventurous, bold, brave, chivalrous, courageous, daring, dauntless, doughty, epic, fearless, gallant, herculean, intrepid, lion-hearted, noble, selfless, stout-hearted, superhuman, unafraid, valiant, valorous.
OPPOSITES: SEE **cowardly**.

heroine noun SEE **hero**.

hero-worship verb SEE **admire**.

hesitant adjective *a hesitant speaker*. cautious, diffident, dithering, faltering, half-hearted, halting, hesitating, indecisive, irresolute, nervous, [*informal*] shilly-shallying, shy, tentative, timid, uncertain, uncommitted, undecided,

underconfident, unsure, vacillating, wary, wavering.
OPPOSITES: SEE **decisive, fluent**.

hesitate verb *I hesitated before jumping into the water.* be hesitant [SEE **hesitant**], delay, dither, falter, halt, hang back, [*informal*] hum and haw, pause, put it off, [*informal*] shilly-shally, shrink back, think twice, vacillate, wait, waver.

hesitation noun caution, indecision, irresolution, nervousness, [*informal*] shilly-shallying, uncertainty, vacillation.

heterogeneous adjective SEE **mixed**.

heterosexual adjective SEE **sex**.

hew verb SEE **cut** verb.

hiatus noun SEE **gap**.

hibernate verb SEE **sleep** verb.

hibernating adjective *a hibernating animal.* asleep, dormant, inactive.

hidden adjective 1 *hidden from view.* concealed, covered, enclosed, invisible, out of sight, private, shrouded, [*informal*] under wraps, unseen, veiled.
OPPOSITES: SEE **visible**.
2 *a hidden meaning.* abstruse, coded, covert, cryptic, dark, implicit, mysterious, mystical, obscure, occult, recondite, secret, unclear.
OPPOSITES: SEE **obvious**.

hide noun *an animal's hide.* fur, leather, pelt, skin.

hide verb 1 *to hide something from view. to hide your feelings.* blot out, bury, camouflage, censor, cloak, conceal, cover, curtain, disguise, eclipse, enclose, mask, obscure, put away, put out of sight, screen, secrete, shelter, shroud, suppress, veil, withhold.
OPPOSITES: SEE **display** verb.
2 *to hide from someone.* disguise yourself, go into hiding, [*informal*] go to ground, keep yourself hidden [SEE **hidden**], [*informal*] lie low, lurk, shut yourself away, take cover.

hideaway noun SEE **hiding-place**.

hide-bound adjective SEE **narrow-minded**.

hideous adjective *a hideous wound.* appalling, disgusting, dreadful, frightful, ghastly, grim, grisly, gruesome, macabre, odious, repulsive, revolting, shocking, sickening, terrible, SEE **ugly**.
OPPOSITES: SEE **beautiful**.

hide-out noun SEE **hiding-place**.

hiding noun *to give someone a hiding* SEE **punish**.
to go into hiding SEE **hide** verb.

hiding-place noun den, hide, hideaway, [*informal*] hide-out, [*informal*] hidy-hole, lair, refuge, sanctuary.

hierarchy noun *The Principal comes at the top of the college hierarchy.* grading, ladder, [*informal*] pecking-order, ranking, scale, sequence, series, social order, system.

hieroglyphics noun SEE **writing**.

hi-fi noun SEE **audio equipment**.

higgledy-piggledy adjective SEE **haphazard**.

high adjective 1 *a high building. a high altitude.* elevated, extending upwards, high-rise, lofty, raised, soaring, tall, towering.
OPPOSITES: SEE **deep, low** adjective.
2 *high in rank.* aristocratic, chief, distinguished, eminent, exalted, important, leading, powerful, prominent, royal, top, upper.
3 *high prices.* dear, excessive, exorbitant, expensive, extravagant, unreasonable.
4 *a high wind.* exceptional, extreme, great, intense, stormy, strong.
5 *a high reputation.* favourable, good, noble, respected, virtuous.
6 *a high sound.* high-pitched, piercing, sharp, shrill, soprano, treble.
high and dry SEE **stranded**.
high and mighty SEE **arrogant**.
high living SEE **luxury**.

highbrow adjective 1 *highbrow literature.* classic, cultural, deep, educational, improving, intellectually demanding, serious.
2 *highbrow music.* classical.
3 *a highbrow person.* academic, bookish, brainy, cultured, intellectual, [*uncomplimentary*] pretentious, sophisticated.
OPPOSITES: SEE **lowbrow**.

high-class adjective SEE **excellent**.

high-falutin adjective SEE **pompous**.

high-fidelity SEE **audio equipment**.

high-handed adjective SEE **arrogant**.

highlight noun *the highlight of the evening.* best moment, climax, high spot, peak, top point.

highly-strung adjective SEE **nervous**.

high-minded adjective SEE **moral** adjective.

high-powered adjective SEE **powerful**.

high-priced adjective SEE **expensive**.

high-speed adjective SEE **fast** adjective.

high-spirited adjective SEE **lively**.

highway noun SEE **road**.

highwayman noun bandit, brigand, SEE **criminal**, robber, thief.

hijack noun, verb SEE **crime**.

hijacker noun SEE **criminal** noun.

hike verb *to hike across the moors.* ramble, tramp, trek, SEE **walk** verb.

hilarious adjective 1 *a hilarious party.* SEE **merry**.
2 *a hilarious joke.* SEE **funny**.

hill noun 1 elevation, eminence, foothill, height, hillock, hillside, hummock, knoll, mound, mount, mountain, peak, prominence, ridge, summit.
Words for *hill* used in particular geographical areas: brae, down, fell, [*plural*] Highlands, pike, stack, tor, wold.
2 *a steep hill in the road.* ascent, gradient, incline, rise, slope.

hilt noun SEE **handle** noun.

hind, hinder, hindmost adjectives SEE **back** adjective.

hind noun SEE **deer**.

hinder verb *Snowdrifts hindered our progress.* arrest, bar, be a hindrance to [SEE **hindrance**], check, curb, delay, deter, endanger, frustrate, get in the way of, hamper, handicap, hit, hold back, hold up, impede, keep back, limit, obstruct, oppose, prevent, restrain, restrict, retard, sabotage, slow down, slow up, stand in the way of, stop, thwart.
OPPOSITES: SEE **help** verb.

hindrance noun *Our heavy shoes were more of a hindrance than a help.* bar, burden, check, deterrent, difficulty, disadvantage, [*informal*] drag, drawback, encumbrance, handicap, impediment, inconvenience, limitation, obstacle, obstruction, restraint, restriction, stumbling-block.
OPPOSITES: SEE **help** noun.

hinge noun *the hinge of a door.* articulation, joint, pivot.

hinge verb *Everything hinges on your decision.* depend, hang, rest, revolve, turn.

hint noun *I don't know the answer: give me a hint.* allusion, clue, idea, implication, indication, inkling, innuendo, insinuation, pointer, sign, suggestion, tip, [*informal*] tip-off.

hint verb *She hinted that we'd get a surprise.* give a hint [SEE **hint** noun], imply, indicate, insinuate, suggest, tip (someone) off.

hire verb *to hire a bus. to hire a hall for a party.* book, charter, engage, lease, pay for the use of, rent, take on.

to **hire out** lease out, let, rent out, take payment for the use of.

hirsute adjective SEE **hairy**.

hiss verb 1 VARIOUS SOUNDS: SEE **sound** noun.
2 *to hiss someone's performance.* SEE **jeer**.

hissing adjective *a hissing sound.* sibilant.

historian noun antiquarian, archivist, chronicler.

historic adjective [Note the difference in meaning between *historic* and *historical.*] *a historic battle.* celebrated, eminent, epoch-making, famed, famous, important, momentous, notable, outstanding, remarkable, renowned, significant, well-known.
OPPOSITES: SEE **unimportant**.

historical adjective [See note under *historic.*] *a historical event.* actual, authentic, documented, real, real-life, true, verifiable.
OPPOSITES: SEE **fictitious**.

history noun 1 *Are you interested in history?* bygone days, heritage, historical events [SEE **historical**], the past.
2 *I enjoy reading history.* annals, chronicles, records.

histrionic adjective actorish, dramatic, theatrical.

hit noun 1 *a hit on the head. a hit with a cricket bat.* [Many of these words are normally *informal.*] bang, bash, belt, biff, blow, buffet, bump, clap, clip, clonk, clout, collision, crack, crash, cuff, drive, flick, flip, hammering, impact, jab, kick, knock, nudge, pat, poke, prod, punch, rap, shot, slap, slog, slosh, slug, smack, smash, smite, sock, stab, stroke, swipe, tap, thump, wallop, whack.
2 *The new record was an instant hit.* success, triumph, [*informal*] winner.

hit verb 1 VARIOUS WAYS TO HIT THINGS: [Many of these words are normally *informal.*] bang, bash, baste, batter, beat, belt, biff, birch, buffet, bump, butt, cane, clap, clip, clobber, clock, clonk, clout, club, collide with, cosh, crack, crash into, cudgel, cuff, dash, deliver a blow, drive (*a ball with a golf-club*), elbow, flagellate, flail, flick, flip, flog, hammer, head (*a football*), jab, jar, jog, kick, knee, knock, lam, lambaste or lambast, lash, nudge, pat, poke, pound, prod, pummel, punch, punt, putt (*a golf-ball*), ram, rap, scourge, slam, slap, slog, slosh, slug, smack, smash, smite, sock, spank, stab, strike, stub (*your toe*), swat, swipe, tan, tap, thrash, thump, thwack, wallop, whack, wham, whip.

2 *The drought hit the farmers.* affect, attack, bring disaster to, damage, do harm to, harm, have an effect on, SEE **hinder**, hurt, make suffer, ruin.
to hit back SEE **retaliate**.
to hit on SEE **discover**.

hitch noun SEE **delay** noun.

hitch verb **1** *to hitch a trailer to a car.* SEE **fasten**.
2 SEE **hitch-hike**.

hitch-hike verb beg a lift, hitch, thumb a lift.

hive noun apiary, beehive.

hive verb **to hive off** SEE **separate** verb.

hoard noun *a hoard of treasure.* cache, heap, pile, stockpile, store, supply, treasure-trove.

hoard verb *Squirrels hoard nuts.* accumulate, amass, be miserly with, collect, gather, keep, lay up, mass, pile up, put by, save, stockpile, store, treasure.
OPPOSITES: SEE **squander**, **use** verb.

hoarding noun *a roadside hoarding.* advertisement, board, display, fence, panel.

hoarse adjective *a hoarse voice.* croaking, grating, gravelly, growling, gruff, harsh, husky, rasping, raucous, rough, throaty.

hoary adjective **1** *hoary hair.* SEE **grey**.
2 *a hoary joke.* SEE **old**.

hoax noun *The alarm was a hoax.* cheat, [*informal*] con, deception, fake, fraud, imposture, joke, [*informal*] leg-pull, practical joke, spoof, swindle, trick.

hoax verb *to hoax someone.* bluff, [*informal*] con, deceive, delude, dupe, fool, [*informal*] have on, hoodwink, lead on, mislead, [*informal*] pull someone's leg, swindle, [*informal*] take for a ride, take in, SEE **tease**, trick.

hoaxer noun SEE **cheat** noun, [*informal*] con-man, impostor, joker, practical joker, trickster.

hobble verb limp, totter, SEE **walk** verb.

hobby noun *a spare-time hobby.* amateur interest, diversion, interest, pastime, pursuit, recreation, relaxation.

hobby-horse noun SEE **obsession**.

hob-nob verb SEE **friend** (**to be friends**).

hocus-pocus noun SEE **trickery**.

hog noun SEE **pig**.

hoi polloi noun SEE **people** noun.

hoist noun block-and-tackle, crane, davit, jack, lift, pulley, winch, windlass.

hoist verb *to hoist crates onto a ship.* heave, lift, lift with a hoist, pull up, raise, winch up.

hoity-toity adjective SEE **haughty**.

hold noun **1** *a firm hold on something.* clasp, clutch, grasp, grip, purchase.
2 *The blackmailer had a hold over him.* authority, control, dominance, influence, power, sway.
3 *the hold of a ship.* cargo-space.

hold verb **1** *to hold in your arms or in your hand.* bear, carry, catch, clasp, cling to, clutch, cradle, embrace, enfold, grasp, grip, hang on to, have, hug, keep, possess, retain, seize, support, take.
2 *to hold a suspect.* arrest, confine, detain, imprison, keep in custody.
3 *to hold a position. to hold an opinion.* continue, keep up, maintain, occupy, preserve, retain, stick to.
4 *to hold a party.* celebrate, conduct, convene, have, organize.
5 *The jug holds one litre.* contain, enclose, have a capacity of, include.
6 *Will this fine weather hold?* be unaltered, carry on, last, persist, remain unchanged, stay.
to hold back *to hold back tears.* block, check, control, curb, delay, halt, keep back, repress, restrain, retain, stifle, stop, suppress, withhold.
to hold out 1 *to hold out your hand.* extend, offer, reach out, stick out, stretch out.
2 *to hold out against opposition.* be resolute, carry on, endure, hang on, keep going, last, persevere, persist, resist, stand fast.
to hold up *to hold up traffic.* delay, detain, hinder, impede, obstruct, retard, slow down.

holdall noun SEE **luggage**.

hold-up noun **1** *a hold-up at a bank.* SEE **crime**.
2 *a hold-up on a journey.* SEE **delay** noun.

hole noun **1** *a hole in the ground.* abyss, burrow, cave, cavern, cavity, chamber, chasm, crater, depression, excavation, fault, fissure, hollow, pit, pocket, pot-hole, shaft, tunnel.
2 *a hole in a fence. a hole in a piece of paper.* aperture, breach, break, chink, crack, cut, eyelet, gap, gash, leak, opening, orifice, perforation, puncture, slit, split, tear, vent.

holiday noun *a holiday from school or from work.* bank holiday, break, day off, half-term, leave, rest, sabbatical, time off, vacation.

SOME KINDS OF HOLIDAY: busman's holiday, camping, caravanning, cruise, honeymoon, pony-trekking, safari, seaside holiday, tour, travelling, trip.

HOLIDAY ACCOMMODATION: apartment, boarding-house, camp-site, flat, guest-house, hostel, hotel, inn, motel, self-catering, villa.

holiness noun devotion, divinity, faith, godliness, piety, [*uncomplimentary*] religiosity, sacredness, saintliness, [*uncomplimentary*] sanctimoniousness, sanctity, venerability.

hollow adjective 1 *a hollow space*. cavernous, concave, deep, empty, unfilled, vacant.
OPPOSITES: SEE **solid**.
2 *a hollow victory*. *a hollow laugh*. cynical, false, futile, insincere, insubstantial, SEE **meaningless**, pointless, valueless, worthless.
OPPOSITES: SEE **meaningful**.

hollow noun *a hollow in a surface*. bowl, cavity, concavity, crater, dent, depression, dimple, dip, dint, dish, hole, indentation, SEE **valley**.

hollow verb **to hollow out** burrow, dig, excavate, gouge, scoop.

holocaust noun annihilation, conflagration, SEE **destruction**, inferno, massacre, pogrom.

holy adjective 1 *a holy shrine*. blessed, consecrated, divine, hallowed, heavenly, revered, sacred, sacrosanct, venerable.
2 *holy pilgrims*. dedicated, devoted, devout, faithful, godly, pious, pure, religious, righteous, saintly, [*uncomplimentary*] sanctimonious.
OPPOSITES: SEE **irreligious**.

homage noun **to pay homage to** SEE **honour** verb.

home noun 1 [= *where I live*] [*old-fashioned*] abode, accommodation, [*formal*] domicile, dwelling, dwelling-place, [*formal*] habitation, SEE **house** noun, household, lodging, residence.
2 [= *where I come from*] birthplace, native land.
3 *a home for the sick or elderly*. [*old-fashioned*] almshouse, convalescent home, hospice, institution, nursing-home.
4 *an animal's home*. habitat, territory.
home help SEE **servant**.

homecoming noun SEE **return** noun.

homeless adjective *homeless families*. abandoned, destitute, down-and-out, evicted, forsaken, itinerant, nomadic, outcast, unhoused, wandering.
homeless people beggars, the destitute, the poor, tramps, vagrants.

homely adjective *a homely atmosphere*. comfortable, congenial, cosy, easy-going, familiar, friendly, informal, intimate, natural, relaxed, simple, unaffected, unpretentious, unsophisticated.
OPPOSITES: SEE **formal**, **sophisticated**.

home-made adjective *home-made clothes*. amateur, [*informal*] DIY or do-it-yourself.
OPPOSITES: SEE **manufactured**.

homesick adjective SEE **sad**.

homework noun assignments, [*informal*] prep, preparation, private study, SEE **work** noun.

homicidal adjective SEE **murderous**.

homicide noun SEE **murder** noun.

homily noun SEE **sermon**.

The prefix *homo-* in words like *homogeneous* and *homosexual* comes from Greek *homos* = *same*.

homogeneous adjective *a homogeneous group*. alike, comparable, compatible, consistent, identical, matching, similar, uniform, unvarying.
OPPOSITES: heterogeneous, SEE **mixed**.

homosexual adjective [*informal*] camp, gay, lesbian, [*uncomplimentary*] queer.
OPPOSITE: heterosexual.

hone noun SEE **sharpener**.

hone verb SEE **sharpen**.

honest adjective *an honest worker*. *an honest answer*. above-board, blunt, candid, conscientious, direct, equitable, fair, forthright, frank, genuine, good, honourable, impartial, incorruptible, just, law-abiding, legal, legitimate, moral, [*informal*] on the level, open, outspoken, plain, pure, reliable, respectable, scrupulous, sincere, square (*a square deal*), straight, straightforward, trustworthy, trusty, truthful, unbiased, unequivocal, unprejudiced, upright, veracious, virtuous.
OPPOSITES: SEE **dishonest**.
to be honest [*informal*] come clean, [*informal*] put your cards on the table, tell the truth.

honesty noun 1 *I didn't doubt his honesty*. fairness, goodness, integrity, morality, probity, rectitude, reliability, scrupulousness, sense of justice, trustworthiness, truthfulness, uprightness, veracity, virtue.
2 *I was surprised by the honesty of his comments*. bluntness, candour, directness, frankness, outspokenness, plainness, sincerity, straightforwardness.
OPPOSITES: SEE **dishonesty**.

honeymoon noun SEE **holiday**.

honorarium noun SEE **payment**.

honorary adjective *an honorary title. an honorary post.* nominal, unofficial, unpaid.

honour noun 1 *She brought honour to the family.* acclaim, accolade, compliment, credit, esteem, fame, good name, [*informal*] kudos, regard, renown, reputation, repute, respect, reverence, veneration.
2 *I had the honour of making a speech.* distinction, duty, importance, privilege.
3 *a sense of honour.* decency, dignity, honesty, integrity, loyalty, morality, nobility, principle, rectitude, righteousness, sincerity, uprightness, virtue.

honour verb *On Remembrance Sunday we honour those who died.* acclaim, admire, applaud, celebrate, commemorate, commend, dignify, esteem, give credit to, glorify, pay homage to, pay respects to, pay tribute to, praise, remember, respect, revere, reverence, show respect to, sing the praises of, value, venerate, worship.

honourable adjective *an honourable action. an honourable person.* admirable, chivalrous, creditable, decent, estimable, ethical, fair, good, high-minded, SEE **honest**, irreproachable, just, law-abiding, loyal, moral, noble, principled, proper, reputable, respectable, respected, righteous, sincere, [*informal*] straight, trustworthy, trusty, upright, venerable, virtuous, worthy.
OPPOSITES: SEE **dishonourable**.

hood noun SEE **hat**.

hoodlum noun SEE **hooligan**.

hoodwink verb SEE **deceive**.

hoof noun SEE **foot**.

hook noun barb, crook, SEE **fastener**, peg (*to hang a coat on*).

hook verb 1 *to hook a fish.* capture, catch, take.
2 *to hook a trailer to a car.* SEE **fasten**.

hooligan noun bully, SEE **criminal** noun, delinquent, hoodlum, lout, mugger, rough, ruffian, [*informal*] tearaway, thug, tough, trouble-maker, vandal, [*informal*] yob.

hoop noun band, circle, girdle, loop, ring.

hoot noun, verb VARIOUS SOUNDS: SEE **sound** noun.

hooter noun horn, siren, whistle.

Hoover verb SEE **clean** verb.

hop verb bound, caper, dance, jump, leap, limp, prance, skip, spring.

hope noun 1 *His hope is to become a professional.* ambition, aspiration, desire, dream, wish.
2 *There's hope of better weather tomorrow.* assumption, expectation, likelihood, optimism, prospect.
OPPOSITES: SEE **despair** noun.

hope verb *I hope that I'll win.* [*informal*] anticipate, be hopeful [SEE **hopeful**], believe, desire, expect, have faith, have hope [SEE **hope** noun], trust, wish.
OPPOSITES: SEE **despair** verb.

hopeful adjective 1 *in a hopeful mood.* confident, expectant, optimistic, positive, sanguine.
OPPOSITES: SEE **pessimistic**.
2 *hopeful signs of success.* auspicious, cheering, encouraging, favourable, heartening, promising, propitious, reassuring.
OPPOSITES: SEE **discouraging**.

hopefully adverb 1 *The hungry dog looked hopefully at the food.* confidently, expectantly, optimistically, with hope.
2 [*informal*] *Hopefully, I'll be fit to play.* all being well, most likely, probably. [Many people think that this is a wrong use of *hopefully*.]

hopeless adjective 1 *hopeless refugees.* beyond hope, demoralized, despairing, desperate, disconsolate, pessimistic, wretched.
2 *a hopeless situation.* daunting, depressing, impossible, incurable, irremediable, irreparable, irreversible.
OPPOSITES: SEE **hopeful**.
3 [*informal*] *a hopeless footballer.* SEE **bad**, feeble, inadequate, incompetent, inefficient, poor, useless, weak, worthless.
OPPOSITES: SEE **competent**.

horde noun *hordes of children from other schools.* band, crowd, gang, SEE **group** noun, mob, swarm, throng, tribe.

horizon noun skyline.

horizontal adjective *a horizontal line.* flat, level, lying down.
OPPOSITES: SEE **vertical**.

horn noun *an animal's horns.* antler.

horoscope noun astrological diagram, [*informal*] your stars, zodiac.

horrendous adjective SEE **horrific**.

Horrible and *horrid* often describe things that are not really important (*horrible food; horrid weather*), whereas *horrific* and *horrifying* describe things that really horrify you (*horrific injuries; horrifying cruelty*).

---

horrible adjective [*informal*] *horrible weather. horrible people.* awful, beastly, disagreeable, dreadful, ghastly, hateful, horrid, loathsome, nasty, objectionable, odious, offensive, revolting, terrible, unkind, SEE **unpleasant**.
OPPOSITES: SEE **pleasant**.

horrid adjective SEE **horrible**.

horrific *a horrific accident.* appalling, atrocious, blood-curdling, disgusting, dreadful, frightening, frightful, grisly, gruesome, hair-raising, harrowing, horrendous, horrifying, nauseating, shocking, sickening, spine-chilling, unacceptable, unnerving, unthinkable.

horrified adjective *horrified onlookers.* aghast, appalled, disgusted, frightened, horror-stricken, horror-struck, shocked, sickened, stunned, unnerved.

horrify verb *The accident horrified us.* alarm, appal, disgust, frighten, harrow, nauseate, scare, shock, sicken, terrify, unnerve.

horrifying adjective SEE **horrific**.

horror noun 1 *a feeling of horror. a horror of spiders.* abhorrence, antipathy, aversion, detestation, disgust, dislike, dismay, dread, fear, loathing, panic, repugnance, revulsion, terror.
2 *I saw the full horror of the disaster.* awfulness, frightfulness, ghastliness, gruesomeness, hideousness.

horror-stricken, horror-struck adjectives SEE **horrified**.

hors-d'œuvre noun OTHER COURSES: SEE **meal**.

horse noun bronco, carthorse, [*old-fashioned*] charger, cob, colt, filly, foal, [*childish*] gee-gee, gelding, hack, hunter, [*old-fashioned*] jade, mare, mount, mule, mustang, [*informal*] nag, [*old-fashioned*] palfrey, piebald, pony, race-horse, roan, skewbald, stallion, steed, warhorse.
RELATED ADJECTIVES: equestrian, equine.
OTHER ANIMALS: SEE **animal** noun.
to ride a horse amble, canter, gallop, trot.

horseman, horsewoman nouns cavalryman, equestrian, jockey, rider.

horseplay noun SEE **misbehaviour**.

horticulture noun cultivation, gardening.

hose noun 1 hosiery, panti-hose, socks, stockings, tights.
2 *a water hose.* hose-pipe, pipe, tube.

hosiery noun SEE **hose**.

hospice noun SEE **home, hospital**.

hospitable adjective SEE **sociable**.

hospital noun clinic, convalescent home, hospice, infirmary, nursing home, sanatorium.

hospitality noun 1 *I gave her hospitality for the night.* accommodation, catering, entertainment.
2 *They thanked us for our hospitality.* SEE **friendliness**, sociability, welcome.

host noun 1 *a host of people.* SEE **group** noun.
2 *the host of a TV programme.* SEE **compère**.

hostage noun captive, prisoner.

hostel noun SEE **accommodation**.

hostile adjective 1 *a hostile crowd.* aggressive, SEE **angry**, antagonistic, antipathetic, attacking, averse, bellicose, belligerent, confrontational, ill-disposed, inhospitable, inimical, malevolent, pugnacious, resentful, unfriendly, unwelcoming, warlike.
OPPOSITES: SEE **friendly**.
2 *hostile weather conditions.* adverse, bad, contrary, opposing, unfavourable, unhelpful, unpropitious.
OPPOSITES: SEE **favourable**.

hostility noun *hostility between enemies.* aggression, animosity, antagonism, antipathy, aversion, bad feeling, belligerence, confrontation, detestation, dislike, enmity, estrangement, hate, hatred, ill will, incompatibility, malevolence, malice, opposition, pugnacity, resentment, unfriendliness.
OPPOSITES: SEE **friendship**.

hot adjective 1 *hot weather. a hot iron.* baking, blistering, boiling, burning, fiery, flaming, oppressive, piping hot (*piping hot food*), red-hot, roasting, scalding, scorching, searing, sizzling, steamy, stifling, sultry, summery, sweltering, thermal (*a thermal spring*), torrid, tropical, warm.
OPPOSITES: SEE **cold** adjective.
2 *a hot temper. in hot pursuit.* angry, eager, emotional, excited, feverish, fierce, heated, hotheaded, impatient, impetuous, intense, passionate, violent.
OPPOSITES: SEE **calm** adjective.
3 *a hot taste.* acrid, biting, gingery, peppery, piquant, pungent, spicy, strong.
OPPOSITES: SEE **mild**.

hot under the collar SEE **angry**.

hotchpotch noun SEE **jumble** noun.

hotel noun SEE **accommodation**.

hotheaded adjective SEE **impetuous**.

hothouse noun SEE **glasshouse**.

hot-tempered adjective SEE **bad-tempered**.

hound noun SEE **dog** noun.

hound verb SEE **pursue**.

hour noun OTHER UNITS OF TIME: SEE **time** noun.

house noun *a house to live in.* abode, [*formal*] domicile, dwelling, dwelling-place, [*formal*] habitation, home, household, lodging, place (*Come to my place*), quarters, residence.

KINDS OF HOUSE: SEE **accommodation**, apartment, bungalow, chalet, cottage, council house, croft, detached house, farmhouse, flat, grange, hovel, homestead, hut, igloo, lodge, maisonette, manor, manse, mansion, penthouse, [*informal*] prefab, public house, rectory, semi-detached house, shack, shanty, terraced house, thatched house, vicarage, villa.
ROOMS IN A HOUSE: SEE **room**.

---

house verb *to house someone.* accommodate, billet, board, [*formal*] domicile, keep, lodge, place, [*informal*] put up, quarter, shelter, take in.

housebreaker noun SEE **burglar**.

household noun establishment, family, home, ménage, [*informal*] set-up.

housekeeper, housemaid nouns SEE **servant**.

house-trained adjective *house-trained animals.* clean in the house, domesticated, tame.

housewife noun SEE **woman**.

housework noun SEE **work** noun.

hovel noun cottage, SEE **house** noun, hut, shack, shanty, shed.

hover verb 1 *to hover in the air.* drift, float, flutter, fly, hang.
2 *to hover about.* be indecisive, dally, dither, [*informal*] hang about, hesitate, linger, loiter, pause, wait about, vacillate, waver.

hovercraft noun OTHER VESSELS: SEE **vessel**.

howl verb VARIOUS SOUNDS: SEE **sound** noun.

howler noun *silly howlers in an exam.* SEE **mistake** noun.

hoyden noun SEE **girl**.

hub noun *the hub of a wheel. a hub of activity.* axis, centre, focal point, heart, middle, pivot.

hubbub noun SEE **commotion**.

huddle verb 1 *to huddle in a corner.* cluster, converge, crowd, flock, gather, heap, herd, jumble, pile, press, squeeze, swarm, throng.
OPPOSITES: SEE **scatter**.

2 *to huddle together to keep warm.* cuddle, curl up, nestle, snuggle.

hue noun SEE **colour** noun, complexion, dye, nuance, shade, tincture, tinge, tint, tone.

hue and cry SEE **pursuit**.

huff noun SEE **annoyance**.

huffy adjective SEE **annoyed**.

hug verb *to hug baby.* clasp, cling to, crush, cuddle, embrace, enfold, fold in your arms, hold close, nurse, squeeze, snuggle against.

huge adjective *Elephants are huge animals. The bank handles huge sums of money.* SEE **big**, colossal, enormous, giant, gigantic, great, [*informal*] hulking, immeasurable, immense, imposing, impressive, incalculable, [*informal*] jumbo-sized, large, majestic, mammoth, massive, mighty, [*informal*] monster, monstrous, monumental, mountainous, prodigious, stupendous, titanic, towering, [*informal*] tremendous, vast, weighty, [*informal*] whopping.
OPPOSITES: SEE **small**.

hulk noun 1 *the hulk of an old ship.* body, carcass, frame, hull, shell, wreck.
2 *a clumsy hulk.* clumsy person, lout, lump, oaf.

hulking adjective [*informal*] *a hulking great parcel.* awkward, bulky, clumsy, cumbersome, heavy, SEE **huge**, ungainly, unwieldy.

hull noun *the hull of a ship.* body, framework.

hullabaloo noun SEE **commotion**.

hullo interjection SEE **greeting**.

hum verb buzz, drone, murmur, purr, sing, SEE **sound** noun, vibrate, whirr.
to hum and haw SEE **hesitate**.

human adjective 1 *the human race.* anthropoid, mortal.
2 *human feelings.* altruistic, SEE **humane**, kind, merciful, philanthropic, rational, reasonable, sympathetic.
OPPOSITES: SEE **inhuman**.
human beings folk, humanity, mankind, men and women, mortals, people [SEE **person**].

humane adjective *Is it humane to kill animals for food?* benevolent, charitable, civilized, compassionate, feeling, forgiving, good, human, humanitarian, kind, kind-hearted, loving, magnanimous, merciful, pitying, sympathetic, tender, understanding, unselfish, warmhearted.
OPPOSITES: SEE **inhumane**.

humanism noun RELIGIONS: SEE **religion**.

humanitarian adjective SEE **humane**.

humanity noun **1** SEE **human (human beings)**.
2 SEE **mercy**.

humanize verb *We hoped that education would humanize our brutal instincts.* civilize, domesticate, educate, make more human [SEE **human**], refine, soften, tame.
OPPOSITES: SEE **dehumanize**.

humble adjective **1** *humble behaviour.* deferential, docile, meek, [*uncomplimentary*] obsequious, polite, respectful, self-effacing, [*uncomplimentary*] servile, submissive, unassertive, unassuming, unpretentious.
OPPOSITES: SEE **proud**.
2 *a humble life-style. humble origins.* commonplace, insignificant, low, lowly, mean, modest, obscure, ordinary, plebeian, poor, simple, undistinguished, unimportant, unremarkable.
OPPOSITES: SEE **important**.

humble verb SEE **humiliate**.

humdrum adjective SEE **ordinary**.

humid adjective *humid weather.* clammy, damp, dank, moist, muggy, steamy, sticky, sultry, sweaty.

humiliate verb *They humiliated us by winning 14–0.* abase, abash, break (someone's) spirit, bring down, chagrin, chasten, crush, deflate, degrade, demean, discredit, disgrace, embarrass, humble, make ashamed, make (someone) feel humble [SEE **humble** adjective], mortify, [*informal*] put (someone) in their place, shame, [*informal*] take down a peg.

humiliating adjective *a humiliating defeat.* chastening, crushing, degrading, demeaning, discreditable, dishonourable, embarrassing, humbling, ignominious, inglorious, mortifying, shaming, undignified.
OPPOSITES: SEE **glorious**.

humiliation noun chagrin, degradation, dishonour, embarrassment, ignominy, indignity, mortification, shame.

humility noun deference, humbleness, lowliness, meekness, modesty, self-effacement, unpretentiousness.
OPPOSITES: SEE **pride**.

hummock noun SEE **hill**.

humorist noun SEE **comedian**.

humorous adjective SEE **funny**.

humour noun **1** *Her humour makes me laugh.* badinage, banter, comedy, facetiousness, jesting, jocularity, jokes, joking, quips, raillery, repartee, [*informal*] sense of fun, wit, witticisms, wittiness.
2 *You're in a good humour!* disposition, frame of mind, mood, spirits, state of mind, temper.

hump noun *a hump in the road.* bulge, bump, curve, knob, lump, mound, protuberance, rise, swelling.

hump verb **1** *The cat humped its back.* arch, bend, curl, curve, hunch, raise.
2 *He humped the sack onto his shoulders.* hoist, lift, raise, shoulder.

humpback noun hunchback, round shoulders, stoop.

humus noun compost, soil.

hunch noun *I have a hunch that they won't come.* feeling, guess, idea, impression, inkling, intuition, suspicion.

hunch verb *to hunch your shoulders.* arch, bend, curl, curve, huddle, hump, shrug.

hunchback noun SEE **humpback**.

hunger noun **1** *a hunger for food.* appetite, craving, SEE **desire** noun, greed, ravenousness.
2 *Hunger kills millions of people.* deprivation, famine, lack of food, malnutrition, starvation.

hungry adjective aching, avid, covetous, eager, famished, famishing, greedy, longing, peckish, ravenous, starved, starving, underfed, undernourished, voracious.

hunk noun SEE **lump** noun.

hunt noun *a hunt for prey.* chase, SEE **hunting**, pursuit, quest, search.

hunt verb **1** *to hunt animals.* chase, course, ferret, hound, poach, pursue, stalk, track down, trail.
2 *to hunt for something you've lost.* ferret out, look for, rummage, search for, seek.

hunter noun huntsman, predator, trapper.

hunting noun KINDS OF HUNTING: beagling, deer-stalking, falconry, fox-hunting, hawking, SEE **hunt** noun, whaling.

hurdle noun **1** *The runners cleared the first hurdle.* barricade, barrier, fence, hedge, jump, obstacle, wall.
2 *There are many hurdles to overcome in life.* difficulty, handicap, hindrance, obstruction, problem, snag, stumbling block.

hurl verb *to hurl something into the air.* cast, catapult, chuck, dash, fire, fling, heave, launch, pelt, pitch, project, shy, sling, throw, toss.

hurly-burly noun SEE **activity**.

hurricane noun cyclone, SEE **storm** noun, tornado, typhoon, whirlwind.

hurried adjective *a hurried decision.* SEE **hasty**.

hurry noun SEE **haste**.

hurry verb 1 *to hurry home.* [*informal*] belt, chase, dash, dispatch, [*informal*] fly, [*informal*] get a move on, hasten, hurtle, hustle, move quickly, rush, speed.
OPPOSITE: go slowly.
2 *If you want to finish, you must hurry.* [*informal*] buck up, [*informal*] shift, [*informal*] step on it, work faster.
OPPOSITES: SEE **dawdle**.
3 *to hurry a process.* accelerate, expedite, quicken, speed up.
OPPOSITES: SEE **delay** verb.

hurt verb 1 *Where do you hurt?* ache, be painful [SEE **painful**], smart, sting, suffer pain [SEE **pain** noun], throb, tingle.
2 *Did they hurt you?* abuse, afflict, agonize, bruise, cause pain to [SEE **pain** noun], cripple, cut, damage, disable, harm, injure, maim, misuse, torture, wound.
3 *The insult hurt her.* be hurtful to [SEE **hurtful**], distress, grieve, pain, torment, upset.

hurtful adjective *hurtful remarks,* biting, cruel, cutting, damaging, derogatory, distressing, hard to bear, harmful, injurious, malicious, nasty, painful, sarcastic, scathing, spiteful, uncharitable, unkind, upsetting, vicious, wounding.
OPPOSITES: SEE **kind** adjective.

hurtle verb *to hurtle along. to hurtle earthwards.* charge, chase, dash, fly, plunge, race, rush, shoot, speed, tear.

husband noun spouse.
FAMILY RELATIONSHIPS: SEE **family**.

husbandry noun agriculture, cultivation, farming.

hush interjection be quiet! be silent! [*informal*] hold your tongue! [*informal*] shut up! silence!

hush noun SEE **silence** noun.

hush verb **to hush up** *to hush up the facts.* conceal, cover up, hide, keep quiet, keep secret, stifle, suppress.

hush-hush adjective SEE **secret** adjective.

husk noun *the husk of a seed.* covering, shell.

husky adjective 1 *a husky voice.* SEE **hoarse**.
2 *a big, husky fellow.* SEE **hefty**.

husky noun *a team of huskies.* SEE **dog** noun.

hussy noun SEE **woman**.

hustle verb *to hustle someone along.* bustle, force, hasten, hurry, jostle, push, rush, shove.

hut noun cabin, den, hovel, lean-to, shack, shanty, shed, shelter.

hutch noun SEE **cage**.

hybrid noun *a hybrid of two species.* amalgam, combination, composite, compound, cross, cross-breed, mixture, mongrel.

hydrant noun SEE **pipe** noun.

hydraulic adjective water-powered.

hygiene noun cleanliness, health, sanitariness, sanitation, wholesomeness.

hygienic adjective *hygienic conditions in hospital.* aseptic, clean, disinfected, germ-free, healthy, pure, salubrious, sanitary, sterilized, unpolluted, wholesome.
OPPOSITES: SEE **unhealthy**.

hyperbole noun exaggeration, overstatement.

hypercritical adjective [Do not confuse with *hypocritical*.] SEE **critical**.

hypermarket noun SEE **shop**.

hypersensitive adjective SEE **sensitive**.

hyphen noun dash.

hypnotic adjective *a hypnotic rhythm.* fascinating, irresistible, magnetic, mesmeric, mesmerizing, sleep-inducing, soothing, soporific, spellbinding.

hypnotism noun hypnosis, magnetism, suggestion.

hypnotize verb bewitch, captivate, dominate, entrance, fascinate, gain power over, magnetize, mesmerize, [*informal*] put to sleep, [*informal*] stupefy.

hypochondriac noun valetudinarian, [*informal*] worrier.

hypocrisy noun *the hypocrisy of people who say one thing and do another.* cant, deceit, deception, double-talk, duplicity, falsity, [*informal*] humbug, inconsistency, insincerity.

hypocritical adjective [Do not confuse with *hypercritical*.] *It's hypocritical to say one thing and do another.* deceptive, false, inconsistent, insincere, [*informal*] phoney, [*informal*] two-faced.

hypothesis noun *an unproved hypothesis.* conjecture, guess, premise, proposition, supposition, theory, [*formal*] thesis.

hypothetical adjective *a hypothetical problem.* academic, conjectural, imaginary, putative, speculative, supposed, suppositional, theoretical, unreal.

ysteria noun *uncontrollable hysteria in he crowd.* frenzy, hysterics, madness, mania, panic.

ysterical adjective 1 *hysterical fans.* berserk, crazed, delirious, demented, distraught, frantic, frenzied, mad, raving, uncontrollable, wild.
2 [*informal*] *a hysterical joke.* comic, crazy, SEE **funny**, hilarious, [*informal*] killing, ridiculous, [*informal*] side-splitting, uproarious.

I

ice noun 1 FORMS OF ICE: black ice, floe, frost, glacier, iceberg, ice-rink, icicle, rime.
2 *a vanilla ice.* ice-cream.

icon noun SEE **picture** noun.

iconoclast noun SEE **rebel** noun.

icy adjective 1 *icy weather.* arctic, SEE **cold** adjective, freezing, frosty.
2 *icy roads.* frozen, glacial, glassy, greasy, slippery, [*informal*] slippy.

idea noun 1 *a philosophical idea.* abstraction, attitude, belief, concept, conception, conjecture, conviction, hypothesis, notion, opinion, theory, view.
2 *the main idea of a poem.* intention, meaning, point, thought.
3 *I have an idea!* brainwave, fancy, guess, inspiration, plan, proposal, scheme, suggestion.
4 *The sample gives an idea of what to expect.* clue, guidelines, impression, inkling, intimation, model, pattern, perception, vision.

ideal adjective 1 *ideal conditions.* best, classic, excellent, faultless, model, optimum, perfect, suitable.
2 *an ideal world.* hypothetical, imaginary, unattainable, unreal, Utopian, visionary.

ideal noun 1 *an ideal worth imitating.* SEE **model** noun.
2 *a person of high ideals.* SEE **principle**.

idealistic adjective *I don't think her idealistic plans will ever materialize.* high-minded, over-optimistic, quixotic, romantic, starry-eyed, unrealistic.
OPPOSITES: SEE **realistic**.

idealize verb *People idealize their heroes.* deify, glamorize, glorify, [*informal*] put on a pedestal, romanticize, worship.

identical adjective *identical twins. identical in appearance.* alike, congruent (*congruent triangles*), corresponding,

duplicate, equal, indistinguishable, interchangeable, matching, the same, similar, twin.
OPPOSITES: SEE **different**.

identifiable adjective *an identifiable accent.* detectable, discernible, distinctive, distinguishable, familiar, known, named, noticeable, perceptible, recognizable, unmistakable.
OPPOSITES: SEE **unidentifiable**.

identify verb 1 *to identify a suspect.* name, pick out, recognize, single out.
2 *to identify an illness.* detect, diagnose, discover, distinguish, pinpoint, [*informal*] put a name to, spot.
to identify with *to identify with a character in a story.* emphathize with, feel for, [*informal*] put yourself in the shoes of, relate to.

identikit noun SEE **picture** noun.

identity noun 1 *Can you prove your identity?* [*informal*] ID, name, nature.
2 *Prisoners sometimes lose their sense of identity.* character, individuality, personality, selfhood, uniqueness.

ideology noun *political ideology.* economic theories, ideas, philosophy, political theories, principles, set of beliefs, underlying attitudes.

idiom noun *It's hard to understand the colloquial idioms of a foreign language.* choice of words, expression, manner of speaking, phrase, phraseology, phrasing, turn of phrase, usage.

idiomatic adjective *idiomatic expressions.* colloquial, natural, well-phrased.

idiosyncrasy noun *Most of us have a few funny idiosyncrasies.* characteristic, eccentricity, feature, habit, mannerism, oddity, peculiarity, quirk, trait.

idiosyncratic adjective *idiosyncratic behaviour.* characteristic, distinctive, eccentric, individual, odd, peculiar, personal, quirky, singular, unique.
OPPOSITES: SEE **common** adjective.

idiot noun [These words are used *informally* and are usually insulting.] ass, blockhead, bonehead, booby, chump, clot, cretin, dimwit, dolt, dope, duffer, dumbell, dummy, dunce, dunderhead, fat-head, fool, half-wit, ignoramus, imbecile, moron, nincompoop, ninny, nitwit, simpleton, twerp, twit.

idiotic adjective SEE **stupid**.

idle adjective 1 *The machines lay idle during the strike.* dormant, inactive, inoperative, in retirement, not working, redundant, retired, unemployed, unoccupied, unproductive, unused.
OPPOSITES: SEE **busy**, **working**.

245

2 *He lost his job because he was idle.* apathetic, good-for-nothing, indolent, lackadaisical, lazy, shiftless, slothful, slow, sluggish, torpid, uncommitted, work-shy.
OPPOSITES: SEE **keen.**
3 *idle speculation.* casual, frivolous, futile, pointless, worthless.
OPPOSITES: SEE **serious.**
an idle person [*informal*] good-for-nothing, idler, [*informal*] layabout, [*informal*] lazybones, loafer, malingerer, shirker, [*informal*] skiver, slacker, sluggard, wastrel.

idle verb **to idle about** be lazy [SEE **lazy**], dawdle, do nothing, [*informal*] hang about, [*informal*] kill time, laze, loaf, lounge about, potter, slack, stagnate, take it easy, vegetate.
OPPOSITES: SEE **work** verb.

idol noun **1** *a pagan idol.* deity, god, icon, image, statue.
2 *a pop idol.* favourite, hero, [*informal*] pin-up, star, [*informal*] superstar.

idolatry noun SEE **worship** noun.

idolize verb SEE **worship** verb.

idyllic adjective *an idyllic scene.* charming, delightful, happy, idealized, lovely, pastoral, peaceful, perfect, unspoiled.
OPPOSITES: SEE **desolate.**

ignite verb *The central-heating boiler won't ignite.* burn, catch fire, fire, kindle, light, set alight, set on fire, spark off.

ignoble adjective *ignoble motives.* base, churlish, cowardly, despicable, disgraceful, dishonourable, infamous, low, mean, selfish, shabby, uncharitable, unchivalrous, unworthy.
OPPOSITES: SEE **noble** adjective.

ignominious adjective *ignominious defeat.* SEE **humiliating.**

ignoramus noun SEE **idiot,** ignorant person [SEE **ignorant**].

ignorance noun *ignorance of the facts.* inexperience, innocence, lack of information, unawareness, unconsciousness, unfamiliarity.
OPPOSITES: SEE **knowledge.**

ignorant adjective **1** *ignorant of the facts.* [*informal*] clueless, ill-informed, innocent, lacking knowledge, unacquainted, unaware, unconscious, unfamiliar (with), uninformed.
OPPOSITES: SEE **knowledgeable.**
2 *You'd be ignorant if you didn't go to school.* illiterate, uncultivated, uneducated, unenlightened, unlettered, unscholarly.
OPPOSITES: SEE **educated.**

3 [*informal*] *He's just plain ignorant!* SEE **stupid.**

ignore verb *to ignore a warning. to ignore your friends.* disobey, disregard, leave out, miss out, neglect, omit, overlook, pass over, [*informal*] shut your eyes to, skip, slight, take no notice of, [*informal*] turn a blind eye to.

ill adjective **1** ailing, bedridden, bilious, [*informal*] dicky, diseased, feeble, frail, [*informal*] funny (*feeling a bit funny*), [*informal*] groggy, indisposed, infected, infirm, nauseated, nauseous, [*informal*] off-colour, [*informal*] out of sorts, pasty, poorly, queasy, queer, [*informal*] seedy, sick, sickly, suffering, [*informal*] under the weather, unhealthy, unwell, weak.
OPPOSITES: SEE **healthy.**
2 *ill effects.* SEE **bad,** damaging, detrimental, evil, harmful, injurious, unfavourable, unfortunate, unlucky.
OPPOSITES: SEE **good.**
ill people the infirm, invalids, patients, the sick, sufferers, victims.
ill will SEE **hostility.**
to be ill ail, languish, sicken.

ill-bred adjective SEE **rude.**

illegal adjective *illegal activities. illegal trade.* actionable, against the law, banned, black-market, criminal, forbidden, SEE **illegitimate,** illicit, invalid, irregular, outlawed, prohibited, proscribed, unauthorized, unconstitutional, unlawful, unlicensed, wrong.
OPPOSITES: SEE **legal.**

illegible adjective *illegible writing.* SEE **bad,** indecipherable, indistinct, obscure, unclear, unreadable.
OPPOSITES: SEE **legible.**

illegitimate adjective **1** *an illegitimate course of action.* against the rules, illegal, improper, inadmissible, incorrect, invalid, unauthorized, unjustifiable, unreasonable, unwarranted.
OPPOSITES: SEE **legitimate.**
2 *an illegitimate child.* bastard, [*old-fashioned*] born out of wedlock, natural.

illicit adjective SEE **illegal.**

ill-fated adjective SEE **unlucky.**

ill-favoured adjective SEE **ugly.**

ill-humoured adjective SEE **bad-tempered.**

illiberal adjective *illiberal views.* SEE **prejudiced.**

illiterate adjective *He is illiterate because he never went to school.* ignorant, unable to read, uneducated.
OPPOSITES: SEE **literate.**

ill-judged adjective SEE **mistaken.**

ill-mannered adjective SEE **rude.**

ll-natured adjective SEE **unkind**.

llness noun *suffering from an illness.* abnormality, affliction, ailment, attack, blight. [*informal*] bug, complaint, condition, contagion, disability, disease, disorder, epidemic, health problem, indisposition, infection, infirmity, malady, malaise, pestilence, plague, sickness, [*informal*] trouble, [*informal*] turn (*He had a nasty turn*), [*informal*] upset, weakness, SEE **wound** noun.

ARIOUS ILLNESSES OR COMPLAINTS: abscess, acne, allergy, amnesia, anaemia, appendicitis, arthritis, asthma, bedsore, beriberi, bilious attack, blister, boil, bronchitis, brucellosis, bubonic plague, bunion, cancer, caries, catalepsy, cataract, catarrh, chicken-pox, chilblains, chill, cholera, claustrophobia, cold, colic, coma, concussion, conjunctivitis, constipation, convulsion, corns, coronary thrombosis, cough, cramp, croup, cystitis.

dandruff, delirium, dermatitis, diabetes, diarrhoea, diphtheria, dipsomania, dropsy, dysentery, dyspepsia, dystrophy, ear-ache, eczema, embolism, enteritis, epilepsy, fever, fits, flu, frostbite, gangrene, gastric flu, glandular fever, goitre, gonorrhoea, gout, gumboil, haemophilia, haemorrhage, haemorrhoids, hay fever, headache, hernia, hypothermia.

impetigo, indigestion, inflammation, influenza, insomnia, jaundice, laryngitis, leprosy, leukaemia, lockjaw, lumbago, malaria, measles, melancholia, meningitis, mental illness, migraine, mongolism, multiple sclerosis, mumps, neuralgia, neuritis, neurosis, paralysis, paratyphoid, pellagra, peritonitis, phobia, piles, plague, pleurisy, pneumonia, polio or poliomyelitis, psychosis, quinsy.

rabies, rheumatism, rickets, ringworm, rupture, scabies, scarlet fever, schizophrenia, sciatica, sclerosis, scrofula, scurvy, sea-sickness, seizure, shingles, silicosis, smallpox, spastic, spina bifida, stomach-ache, stroke, sty, sunstroke, syphilis, tetanus, thrombosis, tonsillitis, toothache, tuberculosis, typhoid, typhus, ulcer, verruca, wart, whooping-cough.

---

llogical adjective *an illogical argument.* absurd, fallacious, inconsequential, inconsistent, invalid, irrational, senseless, SEE **silly**, unreasonable, unsound.
OPPOSITES: SEE **logical**.

ill-omened, ill-starred adjectives SEE **unlucky**.

ill-tempered adjective SEE **bad-tempered**.

ill-treat verb SEE **mistreat**.

illuminate verb 1 *to illuminate a place with lights.* brighten, decorate with lights, light up, make brighter.
2 *to illuminate a problem.* clarify, clear up, elucidate, enlighten, explain, throw light on.

ill-use verb SEE **mistreat**.

illusion noun *an optical illusion.* apparition, conjuring trick, day-dream, deception, delusion, dream, fancy, fantasy, figment of the imagination, hallucination, mirage.

illusionist noun conjuror, magician.

illusory adjective *illusory pleasures.* deceptive, deluding, delusive, false, illusive, SEE **imaginary**, misleading, sham, unreal, untrue.
OPPOSITES: SEE **real**.

illustrate verb 1 *to illustrate a book.* adorn, decorate, illuminate.
2 *to illustrate a story.* depict, draw pictures of, picture, portray.
3 *to illustrate how to do something.* demonstrate, elucidate, exemplify, explain, show.

illustration noun 1 *illustrations in a picture-book.* decoration, depiction, diagram, drawing, photograph, picture, sketch.
2 *This thesaurus gives illustrations of how words are used.* case, demonstration, example, instance, specimen.

illustrious adjective SEE **famous**.

image noun 1 *an image in a mirror. an image on a screen.* imitation, likeness, SEE **picture** noun, projection, reflection.
2 *The temple contained the god's image.* carving, effigy, figure, icon, idol, representation, statue.
3 [*informal*] *She's the image of her mother.* counterpart, double, likeness, spitting-image, twin.

imaginable adjective SEE **credible**.

imaginary adjective *The unicorn is an imaginary beast.* fabulous, fanciful, fictional, fictitious, hypothetical, SEE **illusory**, imagined, insubstantial, invented, legendary, made up, mythical, mythological, non-existent, supposed, unreal, visionary.
OPPOSITES: SEE **real**.

imagination noun *Use your imagination.* artistry, cleverness, creativity, fancy, ingenuity, insight, inspiration, inventiveness, originality, resourcefulness, sensitivity, thought, vision.

imaginative adjective *imaginative paintings. an imaginative story.* artistic, attractive, beautiful, clever, creative, fanciful, ingenious, inspired, inventive, original, poetic, resourceful, sensitive, thoughtful, unusual, visionary, vivid.
OPPOSITES: SEE **unimaginative**.

imagine verb 1 *Imagine you're on a desert island. Imagine what it would be like.* conceive, conjure up, create, dream up, envisage, fancy, fantasize, invent, make believe, make up, picture, pretend, see, think up, visualize.
2 *I imagine you'd like a drink.* assume, believe, conjecture, guess, infer, presume, suppose, surmise, [*informal*] take it.

imbalance noun SEE **bias, inequality**.

imbecile noun SEE **idiot**.

imbibe verb SEE **drink** verb.

imitate verb 1 *to imitate someone's mannerisms. to imitate another person.* ape, caricature, disguise yourself as, echo, guy, impersonate, masquerade as, mimic, parody, parrot, pose as, pretend to be, send up, take off, travesty.
2 *to imitate someone else's example.* copy, emulate, follow, match, model yourself on.
3 *to imitate the sound of the sea.* counterfeit, duplicate, reproduce, simulate.

imitation adjective *The actors carried imitation guns.* artificial, copied, counterfeit, dummy, ersatz, mock, model, sham, simulated.
OPPOSITES: SEE **real**.

imitation noun *an imitation of the real thing.* copy, counterfeit, dummy, duplicate, duplication, fake, forgery, impersonation, impression, likeness, [*informal*] mock-up, model, parody, reflection, replica, reproduction, sham, simulation, [*informal*] take-off, toy, travesty.

imitative adjective *imitative behaviour. an imitative style.* conventional, copied, derivative, fake, mock, plagiarized, traditional, unimaginative, unoriginal.
OPPOSITES: SEE **inventive**.

immaculate adjective SEE **perfect** adjective.

immanent adjective [Do not confuse with *imminent*.] SEE **inherent**.

immaterial adjective SEE **unimportant**.

immature adjective *immature behaviour. an immature person.* adolescent, babyish, backward, callow, childish,

[*informal*] green, inexperienced, infantile, juvenile, puerile, undeveloped, [*of fruit*] unripe, young, youthful.
OPPOSITES: SEE **mature**.

immeasurable adjective SEE **infinite**.

immediate adjective 1 *immediate action.* direct, instant, instantaneous, present, pressing, prompt, quick, speedy, swift, top-priority, unhesitating, urgent.
OPPOSITES: delayed, low-priority.
2 *our immediate neighbours.* adjacent, close, closest, near, nearest, neighbouring, next.
OPPOSITES: SEE **remote**.

immediately adverb at once, directly, forthwith, instantly, now, promptly, [*informal*] right away, straight away, unhesitatingly.

immense adjective SEE **huge**.

immerse verb *to immerse something in water.* bathe, dip, drench, drown, duck, dunk, lower, plunge, submerge.

immersed adjective *immersed in your work.* absorbed, busy, engrossed, interested, involved, occupied, preoccupied, wrapped up.

immersion noun *immersion in water.* baptism, dipping, ducking, plunge, submersion.

immersion heater SEE **fire** noun.

immigrant noun incomer, newcomer, settler.

immigrate verb move in, settle.

imminent adjective [Do not confuse with *immanent*.] *imminent disaster.* about to happen, approaching, close, coming, foreseeable, impending, looming, near, threatening.

immobile adjective 1 *immobile in deep mud.* fast, firm, fixed, immobilized, immovable, motionless, paralysed, secure, solid, static, stationary, still, stuck, unmoving.
2 *immobile features.* frozen, inexpressive, inflexible, rigid.
OPPOSITES: SEE **mobile**.

immobilize verb *to immobilize a vehicle.* cripple, damage, disable, make immobile (SEE **immobile**), paralyse, put out of action, stop.

immoderate adjective SEE **excessive**.

immodest adjective SEE **indecent**.

immoral adjective *immoral behaviour.* abandoned, SEE **bad**, base, conscienceless, corrupt, debauched, degenerate, depraved, dishonest, dissipated, dissolute, evil, [*informal*] fast (*fast living*), impure, SEE **indecent**, licentious, loose, low, profligate, promiscuous, sinful, unchaste, unethical, unprincipled

unscrupulous, vicious, villainous, wanton, SEE **wicked**, wrong.
OPPOSITES: SEE **moral** adjective.
COMPARE: amoral.
an immoral person blackguard, cheat, degenerate, liar, libertine, profligate, rake, reprobate, SEE **scoundrel**, sinner, villain, wrongdoer.

mmorality noun dishonesty, misbehaviour, misconduct, unscrupulousness, SEE **wickedness**.
COMPARE: amorality, morality.

mmortal adjective *immortal souls. an immortal work of art.* ageless, deathless, endless, eternal, everlasting, perpetual, timeless, unchanging, undying.
OPPOSITES: SEE **mortal**.

mmortality noun *the immortality of a work of art.* agelessness, endless life, permanence, timelessness.

mmortalize verb *to immortalize someone's memory.* commemorate, deify, enshrine, keep alive, make immortal, make permanent, perpetuate.

mmovable adjective SEE **immobile**.

mmune adjective *immune to disease.* exempt (from), free (from), immunized (against), inoculated (against), invulnerable, protected (from), resistant, safe (from), unaffected (by), vaccinated (against).

mmunize verb inoculate, vaccinate.

mmunization noun inoculation, vaccination.

mmure verb SEE **imprison**.

mmutable adjective *immutable truths.* constant, dependable, enduring, eternal, fixed, invariable, lasting, permanent, perpetual, reliable, settled, stable, unalterable, unchangeable.
OPPOSITES: SEE **changeable**.

mp noun SEE **spirit**.

mpact noun 1 *Was the car damaged in the impact?* bang, blow, bump, collision, concussion, contact, crash, knock, smash.
2 *The tragedy had a strong impact on us.* effect, force, impression, influence, repercussions, shock.

mpair verb SEE **damage** verb.

mpale verb SEE **pierce**.

mpart verb SEE **give**.

mpartial adjective *an impartial referee.* balanced, detached, disinterested, dispassionate, equitable, even-handed, fair, fair-minded, just, neutral, nonpartisan, objective, open-minded, unbiased, uninvolved, unprejudiced.
OPPOSITES: SEE **biased**.

impartiality noun balance, detachment, disinterest, fairness, justice, lack of bias, neutrality, objectivity, open-mindedness.
OPPOSITES: SEE **bias**.

impassable adjective *an impassable road.* blocked, closed, obstructed, unusable.

impasse noun SEE **deadlock**.

impassioned adjective SEE **passionate**.

impassive adjective SEE **unemotional**.

impatient adjective 1 *impatient to start.* anxious, eager, keen, impetuous, precipitate, [*informal*] raring (*raring to go*).
OPPOSITES: SEE **apathetic**.
2 *impatient because of the delay.* agitated, chafing, edgy, fidgety, fretful, irritable, nervous, restless, uneasy.
OPPOSITES: SEE **calm** adjective, **patient** adjective.
3 *an impatient manner.* abrupt, brusque, curt, hasty, intolerant, quick-tempered, snappy, testy.
OPPOSITES: SEE **easygoing, patient** adjective.

impeach verb SEE **accuse**.

impeccable adjective SEE **perfect** adjective.

impecunious adjective SEE **poor**.

impede verb SEE **hinder**.

impediment noun 1 SEE **hindrance**.
2 *a speech impediment.* SEE **handicap** noun.

impel verb SEE **propel, urge** verb.

impending adjective SEE **imminent**.

impenetrable adjective 1 *impenetrable forest.* dense, impassable, solid, thick.
2 *impenetrable by water.* SEE **impermeable**.

impenitent adjective SEE **unrepentant**.

imperative adjective SEE **necessary**.

imperceptible adjective *imperceptible movement. imperceptible sounds.* faint, gradual, inaudible, infinitesimal, insignificant, invisible, microscopic, minute, negligible, slight, small, subtle, tiny, undetectable, unnoticeable.
OPPOSITES: SEE **noticeable**.

imperfect adjective *imperfect goods. an imperfect success.* broken, damaged, defective, deficient, faulty, flawed, incomplete, incorrect, marred, partial, shopsoiled, spoilt, unfinished, with imperfections.
OPPOSITES: SEE **perfect** adjective.

imperfection noun *a performance with obvious imperfections.* blemish, damage,-

defect, deficiency, failing, fault, flaw, inadequacy, shortcoming, weakness.
OPPOSITES: SEE **perfection**.

imperial adjective SEE **majestic**.

imperil verb SEE **endanger**.

imperious adjective SEE **bossy**.

impermanent adjective *an impermanent relationship*. destructible, ephemeral, evanescent, fleeting, momentary, passing, short-lived, temporary, transient, transitory, unstable.
OPPOSITES: SEE **permanent**.

impermeable adjective *impermeable by water*. hermetic, impenetrable, impervious, non-porous, waterproof, water-repellent, watertight.
OPPOSITES: SEE **porous**.

impersonal adjective *an impersonal manner*. aloof, businesslike, cold, cool, correct, detached, distant, formal, hard, inhuman, official, remote, unapproachable, unemotional, unfriendly, unsympathetic, without emotion.
OPPOSITES: SEE **friendly**.

impersonate verb SEE **imitate**.

impertinent adjective *impertinent remarks*. bold, brazen, cheeky, [*informal*] cocky, [*informal*] cool (*He's a cool customer!*), discourteous, disrespectful, forward, fresh (*Don't get fresh with me!*), impolite, impudent, insolent, insubordinate, insulting, irreverent, pert, SEE **rude**, saucy.
OPPOSITES: SEE **respectful**.

imperturbable adjective SEE **calm** adjective.

impervious adjective 1 *impervious to damp*. SEE **impermeable**.
2 *impervious to criticism*. SEE **resistant**.

impetuous adjective *an impetuous dash for freedom*. careless, eager, hasty, headlong, hot-headed, impulsive, incautious, precipitate, quick, rash, reckless, speedy, thoughtless, spontaneous, [*informal*] tearing (*in a tearing hurry*), unplanned, unpremeditated, unthinking, violent.
OPPOSITES: SEE **cautious**.

impetus noun *Hot weather gives an impetus to swimwear sales*. boost, drive, energy, fillip, force, impulse, incentive, momentum, motivation, power, push, spur, stimulus.

impiety noun blasphemy, godlessness, irreverence, profanity, sacrilege, sinfulness, ungodliness, unrighteousness, wickedness.
OPPOSITES: SEE **piety**.

impinge verb SEE **encroach**.

impious adjective blasphemous, godless, sacrilegious, SEE **wicked**.

implacable adjective SEE **relentless**.

implant verb SEE **insert**.

implausible adjective *an implausible excuse*. far-fetched, feeble, improbable, suspect, unconvincing, unlikely, unreasonable, weak.
OPPOSITES: SEE **plausible**.

implement noun *gardening implements*. appliance, device, gadget, instrument, tool, utensil.

implement verb *to implement a plan*. bring about, carry out, effect, enforce, execute, fulfil, perform, put into practice, realize, try out.

implicate verb *The evidence clearly implicated him in the crime*. associate, connect, embroil, entangle, incriminate, inculpate, involve, show involvement in.

implication noun 1 *What was the implication of her comments?* hidden meaning, hint, innuendo, insinuation, overtone, significance.
2 *He was suspected of implication in the crime*. association, connection, entanglement, involvement.

implicit adjective 1 *implicit criticism*. hinted at, implied, indirect, insinuated, tacit, understood, unexpressed, unsaid, unspoken, unstated, unvoiced.
OPPOSITES: SEE **explicit**.
2 *implicit faith in her competence*. SEE **absolute**.

implore verb SEE **ask**.

imply verb *to imply something without saying it directly*. hint, indicate, insinuate, intimate, mean, point to, suggest.

impolite adjective SEE **rude**.

imponderable adjective *imponderable questions*. SEE **profound**.

import verb *to import goods*. bring in, buy in, SEE **convey**, introduce, ship in.
OPPOSITE: export.

important adjective 1 *important facts an important event*. basic, big, cardinal, central, chief, epoch-making, essential, foremost, fundamental, historic, key, main, major, momentous, newsworthy, noteworthy, once in a lifetime, outstanding, pressing, primary, principal, rare, salient, serious, significant, strategic, urgent, valuable, weighty.
2 *an important person*. celebrated, distinguished, eminent, famous, great, high-ranking, influential, known, leading, notable, powerful, pre-eminent, prominent, renowned, well-known.
OPPOSITES: SEE **unimportant**.

to be important be significant, count, have influence, matter, signify, stand out, take first place.

an important person SEE **celebrity**, mogul, [*informal*] somebody, VIP.

mportunate adjective *importunate requests*. demanding, impatient, insistent, persistent, pressing, relentless, urgent, unremitting.

mportune verb *He's for ever importuning me for money*. SEE **ask**, badger, harass, hound, pester, plague, plead with, press, solicit, urge.

mpose verb *to impose a penalty*. charge with, decree, dictate, enforce, exact, fix, inflict, insist on, introduce, lay, levy, prescribe, set.

to impose on *I don't want to impose on you*. burden, encumber, place a burden on, [*informal*] saddle, take advantage of.

mposing adjective *an imposing castle*. big, dignified, distinguished, grand, grandiose, great, important, impressive, magnificent, majestic, splendid, stately, striking.

mpossibility noun hopelessness, impracticability, unlikelihood.
OPPOSITES: SEE **possibility**.

mpossible adjective *an impossible task*. hopeless, impracticable, impractical, inconceivable, insoluble, insurmountable, out of the question, overwhelming, unachievable, unattainable, unimaginable, unobtainable, unviable, unworkable.
OPPOSITES: SEE **possible**.

mpostor, imposture nouns SEE **cheat** noun.

mpotence noun *His impotence to help made him despair*. feebleness, inability, inadequacy, incapacity, ineffectuality, powerlessness, weakness.

mpotent adjective *impotent to help*. feeble, helpless, inadequate, incapable, incompetent, ineffective, ineffectual, powerless, unable, weak.
OPPOSITES: SEE **powerful**.

mpound verb *to impound someone's property*. SEE **confiscate**.

mpoverished adjective SEE **poor**.

mpracticable adjective SEE **impractical**.

mpractical adjective *an impractical suggestion*. academic, idealistic, SEE **impossible**, impracticable, inconvenient, not feasible, romantic, theoretical, unachievable, unrealistic, unworkable.
OPPOSITES: SEE **practical**.

mprecation noun SEE **curse** noun.

imprecise adjective 1 *imprecise measurements*. approximate, estimated, guessed, inaccurate, inexact, unscientific.

2 *imprecise wording*. ambiguous, SEE **careless**, ill-defined, inexplicit, loose, [*informal*] sloppy, undefined, vague, [*informal*] waffling, [*informal*] woolly.
OPPOSITES: SEE **precise**.

impregnable adjective *an impregnable castle*. impenetrable, invincible, invulnerable, safe, secure, strong, unassailable, unconquerable.
OPPOSITES: SEE **vulnerable**.

impregnate verb SEE **fertilize**.

impress verb 1 *Her hard work impressed me*. affect, be memorable to, excite, influence, inspire, leave its mark on, move, [*informal*] stick in the mind of, stir.

2 *She impressed on us the need for caution*. SEE **emphasize**.

impression noun 1 *The film made a big impression on me*. effect, impact, influence, mark.

2 *I had the impression you were bored*. belief, consciousness, conviction, fancy, feeling, hunch, idea, notion, opinion, sense, suspicion, view.

3 *Granny has clear impressions of her childhood*. memory, recollection.

4 *Our feet left impressions in the snow*. dent, hollow, imprint, indentation, mark, print, stamp.

5 *a new impression of a book*. edition, printing, reprint.

impressionable adjective *impressionable young children*. easily influenced, gullible, inexperienced, naïve, receptive, suggestible, susceptible.
OPPOSITES: SEE **knowing**.

impressive adjective *an impressive win. an impressive building*. affecting, SEE **big**, grand, great, important, imposing, magnificent, majestic, memorable, moving, powerful, remarkable, splendid, stately, stirring, striking, touching.
OPPOSITES: SEE **insignificant**.

imprint verb SEE **print** verb.

imprison verb *to imprison a criminal*. cage, commit to prison, confine, detain, gaol, immure, incarcerate, intern, jail, keep in custody, keep under house arrest, [*informal*] keep under lock and key, lock up, [*informal*] put away, [*informal*] send down, shut up.
OPPOSITES: SEE **free** verb.

imprisonment noun confinement, custody, detention, duress (*under duress*), gaol, house arrest, incarceration, internment, restraint.

improbable adjective *an improbable story.* doubtful, far-fetched, implausible, incredible, preposterous, questionable, unbelievable, unconvincing, unexpected, unlikely.
OPPOSITES: SEE **probable**.

impromptu adjective *impromptu remarks.* [*informal*] ad-lib, extempore, extemporized, improvised, offhand, [*informal*] off the cuff, spontaneous, unplanned, unpremeditated, unprepared, unrehearsed, unscripted.
OPPOSITES: SEE **rehearsed**.

improper adjective 1 *an improper course of action.* ill-timed, inappropriate, incorrect, inopportune, out of place, uncalled for, unsuitable, unwarranted, SEE **wrong** adjective.
2 *improper language.* SEE **indecent**.
OPPOSITES: SEE **proper**.

impropriety noun *I was surprised by the impropriety of his remarks.* bad manners, inappropriateness, indecency, indelicacy, insensitivity, obscenity, rudeness, vulgarity, unseemliness.
OPPOSITES: SEE **propriety**.

improve verb 1 *Her work improved.* advance, develop, get better, move on, progress.
2 *Has he improved since his illness?* get better, [*informal*] pick up, rally, recover, recuperate, strengthen, [*informal*] turn the corner.
OPPOSITES: SEE **decline** verb, **deteriorate**.
3 *The new job improved my finances.* ameliorate, better, enhance, enrich, make better.
4 *Improve your manners!* amend, correct, mend, rectify, refine, reform, revise.
OPPOSITES: SEE **worsen**.
5 *We received a grant to improve our house.* bring up to date, extend, modernize, rebuild, renovate, touch up.

improvement noun 1 *an improvement in behaviour.* advance, amelioration, betterment, correction, development, enhancement, gain, progress, rally, recovery, reformation, upturn.
2 *improvements to our house.* alteration, extension, [*informal*] face-lift, modernization, modification, renovation.

improvident adjective SEE **wasteful**.

improvise verb 1 *to improvise music.* [*informal*] ad-lib, extemporize, make up, perform impromptu [SEE **impromptu**], [*informal*] play it by ear, vamp.
2 *to improvise a meal.* concoct, invent, make do, [*informal*] throw together.

imprudent adjective [Don't confuse with *impudent*.] SEE **unwise**.

impudence noun SEE **cheek**.

impudent adjective [Don't confuse with *imprudent*.] SEE **cheeky**.

impugn verb *to impugn someone's integrity.* SEE **question** verb.

impulse noun 1 *What was the impulse behind your decision?* drive, force, impetus, motive, pressure, push, stimulus, thrust.
2 *a sudden impulse to do something.* caprice, desire, instinct, urge, whim.

impulsive adjective *an impulsive action.* automatic, hare-brained, hasty, headlong, hot-headed, impetuous, impromptu, instinctive, intuitive, involuntary, madcap, precipitate, rash, reckless, spontaneous, sudden, thoughtless, unconscious, unplanned, unpremeditated, unthinking, wild.
OPPOSITES: SEE **deliberate** adjective.

impure adjective 1 *impure water.* adulterated, contaminated, defiled, dirty, SEE **filthy**, foul, infected, polluted, tainted, unclean, unwholesome.
2 *impure thoughts.* SEE **indecent**.

impurity noun *impurities in water.* contamination, dirt, SEE **filth**, foreign body, infection, pollution, taint.

impute verb SEE **attribute** verb.

inaccessible adjective *an inaccessible spot.* cut off, godforsaken, hard to find, inconvenient, isolated, lonely, outlying, out of reach, out-of-the-way, remote, solitary, unfrequented, [*informal*] unget-at-able, unreachable.
OPPOSITES: SEE **accessible**.

inaccuracy noun SEE **mistake** noun.

inaccurate adjective *inaccurate maths. an inaccurate statement.* erroneous, false, faulty, imperfect, imprecise, incorrect, inexact, misleading, mistaken, unfaithful, unreliable, unsound, untrue, vague, wrong.
OPPOSITES: SEE **accurate**.

inactive adjective *Hedgehogs are inactive in winter.* asleep, dormant, hibernating, idle, immobile, inanimate, inert, languid, lazy, lethargic, out of action, passive, quiet, sedentary, sleepy, slow, sluggish, somnolent, torpid, unemployed, unoccupied, vegetating.
OPPOSITES: SEE **active**.

inadequate adjective *an inadequate supply. inadequate preparation.* deficient, imperfect, ineffective, insufficient, little, meagre, niggardly, [*informal*] pathetic, scanty, [*informal*] skimpy, sparse, unsatisfactory.
OPPOSITES: SEE **adequate**.

inadmissible adjective *inadmissible evidence.* SEE **unacceptable.**

inadvertent adjective SEE **unintentional.**

inadvisable adjective *an inadvisable course of action.* foolish, ill-advised, imprudent, misguided, silly, unwise.
OPPOSITES: SEE **advisable.**

inalienable adjective *an inalienable right.* SEE **absolute.**

inane adjective SEE **silly.**

inanimate adjective dead, dormant, inactive, insentient, lifeless, unconscious.
OPPOSITES: SEE **animate** adjective.

inapplicable adjective SEE **inappropriate.**

inappropriate adjective *an inappropriate gift. inappropriate comments.* ill-judged, ill-suited, ill-timed, improper, inapplicable, inapposite, incongruous, incorrect, inopportune, irrelevant, out of place, tactless, tasteless, unbecoming, unfit, unseasonable, unseemly, unsuitable, untimely, wrong.
OPPOSITES: SEE **appropriate.**

inarticulate adjective *an inarticulate speaker.* dumb, faltering, halting, hesitant, SEE **incoherent,** mumbling, mute, shy, silent, speechless, stammering, stuttering, tongue-tied, unclear, unintelligible.
OPPOSITES: SEE **articulate** adjective.

inartistic adjective SEE **unimaginative.**

inattentive adjective *an inattentive driver.* absent-minded, careless, daydreaming, dreaming, heedless, lacking concentration, negligent, preoccupied, unobservant, vague, wandering.
OPPOSITES: SEE **alert** adjective.

inaudible adjective *inaudible sounds.* faint, indistinct, low, muffled, mumbled, muted, quiet, silent, unclear, undetectable, unidentifiable, weak.
OPPOSITES: SEE **audible.**

inaugural adjective SEE **opening** adjective.

inaugurate verb SEE **open** verb.

inauspicious adjective SEE **unfavourable.**

inborn, inbred adjectives SEE **hereditary.**

incalculable adjective SEE **infinite.**

incandescent adjective SEE **glowing.**

incantation noun SEE **spell** noun.

incapable adjective 1 *incapable of doing things for himself.* clumsy, helpless, impotent, inadequate, incompetent, ineffective, ineffectual, inept, stupid, unable, useless, weak.
OPPOSITES: SEE **capable.**
2 [*informal*] *incapable after a couple of drinks.* SEE **drunk.**

incapacitate verb SEE **disable.**

incarcerate verb SEE **imprison.**

incarnate verb SEE **personify.**

incarnation noun SEE **personification.**

incautious adjective SEE **careless.**

incendiary noun 1 [= *an incendiary bomb*] OTHER WEAPONS: SEE **weapons.**
2 arsonist, fireraiser, pyromaniac.

incense verb SEE **anger** verb.

incentive noun *an incentive to work.* bait, [*informal*] carrot, encouragement, inducement, motivation, reward, stimulus, [*informal*] sweetener.

inception noun SEE **beginning.**

incessant adjective *an incessant rhythm. incessant demands.* ceaseless, chronic, constant, continual, continuous, endless, eternal, everlasting, interminable, never-ending, non-stop, perennial, permanent, perpetual, persistent, relentless, unbroken, unceasing, unending, unremitting.
OPPOSITES: SEE **occasional, temporary.**

inch verb *to inch forward.* SEE **creep.**

incident noun 1 *an amusing incident.* affair, circumstance, event, happening, occasion, occurrence.
2 *a nasty incident.* accident, SEE **commotion,** confrontation, disturbance, fight, scene.

incidental adjective *Let's discuss the main point, not incidental issues.* attendant, SEE **chance** adjective, inessential, minor, odd, random, secondary, subordinate, subsidiary.
OPPOSITES: SEE **essential.**

incinerate verb SEE **burn** verb.

incinerator noun SEE **fire** noun.

incipient adjective *an incipient disease.* beginning, developing, early, embryonic, growing, new, rudimentary, starting.
OPPOSITES: SEE **established.**

incise verb SEE **cut** verb.

incision noun SEE **cut** noun.

incisive adjective 1 *an incisive way of dealing with things.* SEE **decisive.**
2 *incisive wit.* SEE **cutting** adjective.

incite verb *to incite violence.* SEE **provoke.**

inclement adjective *inclement weather.* WORDS TO DESCRIBE WEATHER: SEE **weather** noun.

inclination noun *an inclination to doze off.* bent, bias, disposition, fondness, habit, instinct, leaning, liking, partiality, penchant, predilection, predisposition, preference, proclivity, propensity, readiness, tendency, trend, willingness.

incline noun SEE **slope** noun.

incline verb *to incline at an angle.* bend, lean, slant, slope, tilt, tip, veer.
to be inclined *I'm inclined to doze off after lunch.* be disposed, be in the habit (of), be liable, have an inclination [SEE **inclination**], like, prefer.

include verb 1 *The programme includes some new songs.* blend in, combine, comprise, consist of, contain, embody, encompass, incorporate, involve, make room for, mix, subsume, take in.
2 *The price includes transport.* add in, allow for, cover, take into account.
OPPOSITES: SEE **exclude**.

incognito adjective or adverb *to travel incognito.* anonymous(ly), disguised, under a pseudonym, unknown, unnamed, unrecognized.

incoherent adjective *incoherent messages. an incoherent speaker.* confused, disconnected, disjointed, disordered, disorganized, garbled, illogical, SEE **inarticulate**, inconsistent, jumbled, mixed up, muddled, rambling, unclear, unconnected, unintelligible, unstructured, unsystematic.
OPPOSITES: SEE **coherent**.

incombustible adjective fireproof, fire-resistant, flameproof, non-flammable.
OPPOSITES: SEE **combustible**.

income noun earnings, interest, SEE **money**, pay, pension, profits, receipts, revenue, salary, takings, wages.
OPPOSITES: SEE **expenditure**.

incoming adjective 1 *an incoming aircraft.* approaching, arriving, coming, landing, next, returning.
2 *the incoming tide.* flowing, rising.
OPPOSITES: SEE **outgoing**.

incommode verb SEE **inconvenience** verb.

incommunicado adjective *a prisoner held incommunicado.* cut off, isolated, silent, solitary, without communication.

incomparable adjective *incomparable beauty.* SEE **unequalled**.

incompatible adjective *The two accounts are incompatible.* at variance, clashing, conflicting, contradictory, contrasting, different, discrepant, incongruous, inconsistent, irreconcilable.
OPPOSITES: SEE **compatible**.

incompetent adjective *incompetent workers.* bungling, feckless, helpless, [*informal*] hopeless, inadequate, incapable, ineffective, ineffectual, inefficient, inexperienced, inexpert, stupid, unacceptable, unfit, unqualified, unsatisfactory, unskilful, untrained, useless.
OPPOSITES: SEE **competent**.

incomplete adjective 1 *an incomplete story.* abbreviated, abridged, [*informal*] bitty, edited, expurgated, partial, selective, shortened.
2 *incomplete work.* deficient, faulty, imperfect, insufficient, unfinished, unpolished, wanting.
OPPOSITES: SEE **complete** adjective.

incomprehensible adjective *an incomprehensible message.* baffling, beyond your comprehension, cryptic, enigmatic, illegible, impenetrable, indecipherable, meaningless, mysterious, obscure, opaque, perplexing, puzzling, strange, too difficult, unclear, unfathomable, unintelligible.
OPPOSITES: SEE **comprehensible**.

inconceivable *The distances in the universe are inconceivable.* implausible, impossible to understand, incredible, [*informal*] mind-boggling, staggering, unbelievable, undreamed of, unimaginable, unthinkable.
OPPOSITES: SEE **credible**.

inconclusive adjective *inconclusive evidence.* ambiguous, equivocal, indecisive, indefinite, open, uncertain, unconvincing.
OPPOSITES: SEE **conclusive**.

incongruous adjective *an absurdly incongruous couple.* clashing, conflicting, contrasting, discordant, ill-matched, ill-suited, inappropriate, incompatible, inconsistent, irreconcilable, odd, out of place, uncoordinated, unsuited.
OPPOSITES: SEE **matching**.

inconsequential adjective 1 *an inconsequential argument.* SEE **illogical**.
2 *an inconsequential event.* SEE **unimportant**.

inconsiderable adjective *an inconsiderable sum of money.* SEE **negligible**.

inconsiderate adjective *an inconsiderate remark. inconsiderate neighbours.* careless, cruel, insensitive, negligent, rude, self-centred, selfish, tactless, thoughtless, uncaring, unconcerned, unfriendly, unhelpful, unkind, unsympathetic, unthinking.
OPPOSITES: SEE **considerate**.

inconsistent adjective 1 *He is inconsistent in his views.* capricious, changeable,

erratic, fickle, inconstant, patchy, unpredictable, unreliable, unstable, [*informal*] up-and-down, variable.
2 *The stories of the two witnesses are inconsistent.* SEE **incompatible**.
OPPOSITES: SEE **consistent**.

inconsolable adjective SEE **heart-broken**.

inconspicuous adjective *an inconspicuous worker. an inconspicuous act of bravery.* camouflaged, hidden, insignificant, invisible, modest, ordinary, out of sight, plain, restrained, retiring, self-effacing, unassuming, unobtrusive.
OPPOSITES: SEE **conspicuous**.

inconstant adjective SEE **changeable**.

incontestable adjective SEE **indisputable**.

incontinent adjective enuretic, unable to control yourself, uncontrolled.

incontrovertible adjective SEE **indisputable**.

inconvenience noun *the inconvenience of having to change buses.* annoyance, bother, disadvantage, disruption, drawback, encumbrance, hindrance, irritation, nuisance, trouble.

inconvenience verb *Does the noise of the TV inconvenience you?* annoy, be an inconvenience [SEE **inconvenience** noun], bother, disturb, incommode, irritate, [*informal*] put you out, trouble.

inconvenient adjective *an inconvenient moment.* annoying, awkward, bothersome, cumbersome, difficult, embarrassing, inopportune, irritating, tiresome, troublesome, unsuitable, untimely, untoward, unwieldy.
OPPOSITES: SEE **convenient**.

incorporate verb SEE **include**.

incorporeal adjective *incorporeal voices.* disembodied, ethereal, ghostly, impalpable, insubstantial, intangible, spectral, unreal.
OPPOSITES: SEE **physical**.

incorrect adjective SEE **wrong** adjective.

incorrigible adjective *an incorrigible thief.* committed, confirmed, hardened, hopeless, impenitent, incurable, inveterate, SEE **irredeemable**, shameless, unreformable, unrepentant.
OPPOSITES: SEE **penitent**.

incorruptible adjective *an incorruptible judge.* SEE **good**, honest, honourable, just, moral, sound, [*informal*] straight, true, trustworthy, unbribable, upright.
OPPOSITES: SEE **corrupt** adjective.

increase noun *an increase in the size, length, intensity, etc., of something.* addition, amplification, augmentation,

boost, build-up, crescendo, development, enlargement, escalation, expansion, extension, gain, growth, increment, inflation, intensification, proliferation, rise, upsurge, upturn.
OPPOSITES: SEE **decrease** noun.

increase verb **1** *to increase the size, length, intensity, etc., of something.* add to, amplify, augment, boost, build up, develop, enlarge, expand, extend, lengthen, magnify, make greater, maximize, multiply, prolong, put up, raise, [*informal*] step up, strengthen, stretch, swell.
2 *My responsibilities have increased.* escalate, gain (*in size, etc.*), get greater, grow, intensify, proliferate, [*informal*] snowball, spread, [*poetic*] wax.
OPPOSITES: SEE **decrease** verb.

incredible adjective *an incredible story.* extraordinary, far-fetched, implausible, improbable, inconceivable, miraculous, surprising, unbelievable, unconvincing, unimaginable, unlikely, untenable, unthinkable.
OPPOSITES: SEE **credible**.

incredulous adjective *She was incredulous when told she'd won.* disbelieving, distrustful, dubious, questioning, sceptical, suspicious, uncertain, unconvinced.
OPPOSITES: SEE **credulous**.

increment noun SEE **increase** noun.

incriminate verb *to incriminate someone in wrongdoing.* accuse, blame, embroil, implicate, inculpate, involve.
OPPOSITES: SEE **excuse** verb.

incrustation noun SEE **crust**.

incubate verb *Birds incubate eggs.* bring on, brood on, develop, hatch.

inculcate verb SEE **teach**.

inculpate verb SEE **incriminate**.

incumbent adjective SEE **compulsory**.

incur verb *to incur a fine.* [*informal*] be on the receiving end of, bring upon yourself, earn, get, provoke, run up, suffer.

incurable adjective **1** *incurable illness.* fatal, hopeless, inoperable, irreparable, terminal, untreatable.
OPPOSITES: SEE **curable**.
2 *an incurable romantic.* SEE **incorrigible**.

incurious adjective SEE **indifferent**.

incursion noun SEE **raid** noun.

indebted adjective *I'm indebted to you.* [*old-fashioned*] beholden, grateful, obliged, thankful, under an obligation.

indecent adjective *indecent behaviour. indecent language.* [*informal*] blue, coarse, crude, dirty, immodest, impolite,

improper, impure, indecorous, indelicate, insensitive, naughty, SEE **obscene**, offensive, risqué, rude, [*informal*] sexy, [*informal*] smutty, suggestive, tasteless, titillating, unbecoming, unprintable, unrepeatable, unseemly, vulgar.
OPPOSITES: SEE **decent**.

indecipherable adjective SEE **illegible**.

indecision noun SEE **hesitation**.

indecisive adjective SEE **hesitant**.

indecorous adjective *indecorous language*. churlish, ill-bred, inappropriate, SEE **indecent**, rough, tasteless, unbecoming, uncouth, undignified, unseemly, vulgar.
OPPOSITES: SEE **decorous**.

indefatigable adjective SEE **tireless**.

indefensible adjective *Her silly behaviour puts her in an indefensible position*. unjustifiable, unpardonable, untenable, vulnerable, weak.

indefinable adjective SEE **indescribable**.

indefinite adjective ambiguous, confused, equivocal, evasive, general, ill-defined, imprecise, inexact, [*informal*] leaving it open, neutral, uncertain, unclear, undefined, unsettled, unspecific, unspecified, unsure, vague.
OPPOSITES: SEE **definite**.

indelible adjective 1 *indelible ink*. fast, fixed, ineradicable, ingrained, lasting, permanent.
2 *indelible memories*. unforgettable.
OPPOSITE: erasable.

indelicate adjective SEE **indecent**.

indemnify verb SEE **insure**.

indentation noun *an indentation in a surface*. cut, dent, depression, dimple, dip, hollow, nick, notch, serration.

indented adjective *the indented line of the battlements*. crenellated, dented, notched, serrated, toothed, zigzag.

indenture noun SEE **contract** noun.

independence noun *We value independence*. autonomy, being independent [SEE **independent**], freedom, individualism, liberty, nonconformity, self-government.
OPPOSITES: SEE **dependence**.

independent adjective 1 *an independent country*. autonomous, liberated, neutral, nonaligned, self-determining, self-governing, sovereign.
2 *an independent individual*. carefree, [*informal*] foot-loose, free, individualistic, private, self-reliant, separate, unconventional, untrammelled, without ties.
OPPOSITES: SEE **dependent**.
3 *an independent opinion*. SEE **unbiased**.

indescribable adjective *indescribable beauty*. beyond words, indefinable, ineffable, inexpressible, leaving you speechless, stunning, unspeakable, unutterable.
OPPOSITES: SEE **ordinary, prosaic**.

indestructible adjective 1 *indestructible materials*. durable, lasting, permanent, solid, strong, tough, toughened, unbreakable.
OPPOSITES: SEE **impermanent**.
2 *the indestructible spirit of humankind*. enduring, eternal, everlasting, immortal, imperishable.
OPPOSITES: SEE **mortal**.

indeterminate adjective SEE **uncertain**.

index noun *a library index*. alphabetical list, catalogue, directory, register.

indiarubber noun eraser, rubber.

indicate verb 1 *Indicate where you are going*. describe, display, give an indication of [SEE **indication**], intimate, make known, manifest, point out, reveal, say, show, specify.
2 *A red light indicates danger*. be an indication of [SEE **indication**], betoken, communicate, convey, denote, express, mean, register, signal, signify, spell, stand for, symbolize.

indication noun *He gave no indication of his feelings*. clue, evidence, hint, inkling, intimation, omen, portent, sign, signal, suggestion, symptom, token, warning.

indicative adjective *A high temperature is indicative of illness*. meaningful, significant, suggestive, symptomatic.

indicator noun *The indicators showed that the machine was working normally*. clock, dial, display, gauge, index, instrument, marker, meter, pointer, screen, sign, signal, trafficator.

indict verb SEE **accuse**.

indictable adjective *an indictable offence*. SEE **criminal** adjective.

indictment noun SEE **accusation**.

indifferent adjective [Note: *indifferent* is NOT the opposite of *different*.]
1 *I was indifferent about the result*. aloof, apathetic, blasé, bored, casual, cold, cool, detached, disinterested, dispassionate, half-hearted, incurious, neutral, nonchalant, not bothered, uncaring, unconcerned, unemotional, unenthusiastic, unexcited, unimpressed, uninterested, uninvolved, unmoved.
OPPOSITES: SEE **concerned, enthusiastic**.
2 *The food was indifferent*. commonplace, fair, mediocre, middling, moderate, [*informal*] nothing to write home about, SEE **ordinary**, unexciting.
OPPOSITES: SEE **excellent**.

indigenous adjective *indigenous plants.* SEE **native** adjective.

indigent adjective SEE **poor**.

indigestion noun dyspepsia, flatulence, heartburn.

indignant adjective *We were indignant about the way they treated us.* [*informal*] aerated, SEE **angry**, annoyed, cross, disgruntled, exasperated, furious, heated, infuriated, [*informal*] in high dudgeon, irate, irritated, livid, mad, [*informal*] peeved, provoked, [*informal*] put out, riled, sore, upset, vexed.

indignation noun SEE **anger** noun.

indignity noun SEE **humiliation**.

indigo noun SEE **blue** adjective.

indirect adjective 1 *an indirect route.* [*informal*] all round the houses, circuitous, devious, long, meandering, rambling, roundabout, tortuous, winding, zigzag. 2 *an indirect insult.* ambiguous, backhanded, circumlocutory, disguised, equivocal, euphemistic, SEE **evasive**, implicit, implied, oblique.
OPPOSITES: SEE **direct** adjective.

indiscreet adjective *indiscreet remarks.* careless, ill-advised, ill-considered, ill-judged, impolite, impolitic, incautious, injudicious, tactless, undiplomatic, unguarded, unthinking, unwise.
OPPOSITES: SEE **discreet**.

indiscriminate adjective *indiscriminate attacks. indiscriminate praise.* aimless, desultory, general, haphazard, [*informal*] hit or miss, imperceptive, miscellaneous, mixed, random, uncritical, undifferentiated, undiscriminating, uninformed, unselective, unsystematic, wholesale.
OPPOSITES: SEE **selective**.

indispensable adjective *indispensable equipment.* basic, central, crucial, essential, imperative, key, necessary, needed, required, requisite, vital.
OPPOSITES: SEE **unnecessary**.

indisposed adjective SEE **ill**.

indisposition noun SEE **illness**.

indisputable adjective *indisputable facts.* accepted, acknowledged, axiomatic, certain, clear, evident, incontestable, incontrovertible, indubitable, irrefutable, positive, proved, proven, self-evident, sure, unanswerable, unarguable, undeniable, undisputed, undoubted, unimpeachable, unquestionable.
OPPOSITES: SEE **debatable**.

indissoluble adjective SEE **lasting**.

indistinct adjective 1 *an indistinct image.* bleary, blurred, confused, dim, faint, fuzzy, hazy, ill-defined, indefinite, misty, obscure, shadowy, unclear, vague.
2 *indistinct sounds.* deadened, dull, indistinguishable, muffled, mumbled, slurred, unintelligible.
OPPOSITES: SEE **distinct**.

indistinguishable adjective *indistinguishable twins.* identical, interchangeable, the same, twin.
OPPOSITES: SEE **different**.

individual adjective *an individual style.* characteristic, different, distinct, distinctive, exclusive, idiosyncratic, particular, peculiar, personal, private, separate, singular, special, specific, unique.
OPPOSITES: SEE **collective**.

individual noun *Who was that odd individual?* SEE **person**.

indoctrinate verb *to indoctrinate someone with political propaganda.* brainwash, instruct, re-educate, SEE **teach**, train.

indolent adjective SEE **lazy**.

indomitable adjective *indomitable courage.* SEE **brave**, invincible, persistent, resolute, staunch, steadfast, [*uncomplimentary*] stubborn, unbreakable, unconquerable, unyielding.

indubitable adjective SEE **indisputable**.

induce verb 1 *We couldn't induce her to come out.* coax, encourage, incite, influence, persuade, prevail on, [*informal*] talk (someone) into, tempt.
OPPOSITES: SEE **dissuade**.
2 *What induced your cold?* bring on, cause, engender, generate, give rise to, lead to, occasion, produce, provoke.

inducement noun SEE **incentive**.

indulge verb *Older people sometimes indulge children.* be indulgent to [SEE **indulgent**], cosset, favour, give in to, gratify the whims of, humour, mollycoddle, pamper, pander to, spoil, [*informal*] spoon-feed, treat.
OPPOSITES: SEE **deprive**.
to indulge in SEE **enjoy**.
to indulge yourself be self-indulgent, drink (eat, etc.) too much, overdo it, overeat, spoil yourself.

indulgent adjective *indulgent grandparents.* compliant, easygoing, fond, forbearing, forgiving, genial, kind, lenient, liberal, overgenerous, patient, permissive, tolerant.
OPPOSITES: SEE **strict**.

industrial adjective *an industrial area.* industrialized, manufacturing.

industrialist noun businessman, magnate, manufacturer, tycoon.

industrious adjective *an industrious worker.* assiduous, busy, conscientious, diligent, earnest, energetic, enterprising, hard-working, involved, keen, laborious, persistent, productive, sedulous, tireless, zealous.
OPPOSITES: SEE **lazy.**

industry noun 1 *There's a lot of industry in this town.* business, commerce, manufacturing, trade.
2 *We admired the industry of the volunteers.* activity, application, commitment, determination, diligence, effort, energy, hard work, industriousness, keenness, labour, perseverance, persistence, tirelessness, toil, zeal.
OPPOSITES: SEE **laziness.**

inebriated adjective SEE **drunk.**

inedible adjective *inedible food.* bad for you, harmful, indigestible, nauseating, [*informal*] off (*This meat is off*), poisonous, rotten, tough, uneatable, unpalatable, unwholesome.
OPPOSITES: SEE **edible.**

ineducable adjective incorrigible, SEE **stupid,** unresponsive, unteachable.
OPPOSITES: SEE **responsive.**

ineffable adjective SEE **indescribable.**

ineffective adjective 1 *ineffective efforts.* fruitless, futile, [*informal*] hopeless, inept, unconvincing, unproductive, unsuccessful, useless, vain, worthless.
2 *an ineffective salesman.* feckless, feeble, idle, impotent, inadequate, incapable, incompetent, ineffectual, inefficient, powerless, shiftless, unenterprising, weak.
OPPOSITES: SEE **effective.**

ineffectual adjective SEE **ineffective.**

inefficient adjective 1 *an inefficient worker.* SEE **ineffective.**
2 *inefficient use of resources.* extravagant, prodigal, uneconomic, wasteful.
OPPOSITES: SEE **efficient.**

inelegant adjective *inelegant movements. inelegant style.* awkward, clumsy, crude, gauche, graceless, inartistic, rough, SEE **ugly,** uncouth, ungainly, unpolished, unskilful, unsophisticated, unstylish.
OPPOSITES: SEE **elegant.**

ineligible adjective *ineligible for a job.* disqualified, inappropriate, [*informal*] out of the running, [*informal*] ruled out, unacceptable, unfit, unsuitable.
OPPOSITES: SEE **eligible.**

inept adjective *an inept attempt to put things right.* bungling, clumsy, SEE **inappropriate,** incompetent, maladroit.

inequality noun *inequalities between rich and poor.* difference, disparity, dissimilarity, imbalance.
OPPOSITES: SEE **equality.**

inequitable adjective SEE **unjust.**

ineradicable adjective SEE **indelible.**

inert adjective SEE **lifeless.**

inertia noun *The cheering crowd roused us from our inertia.* apathy, deadness, idleness, immobility, inactivity, indolence, lassitude, laziness, lethargy, listlessness, numbness, passivity, sluggishness, torpor.
OPPOSITES: SEE **liveliness.**

inescapable adjective SEE **unavoidable.**

inessential adjective *Leave inessential equipment behind.* dispensable, expendable, minor, needless, non-essential, optional, ornamental, secondary, spare, superfluous, unimportant, unnecessary.
OPPOSITES: SEE **essential.**

inestimable adjective SEE **infinite.**

inevitable adjective *inevitable disaster.* SEE **unavoidable.**

inexact adjective SEE **imprecise.**

inexcusable adjective SEE **unforgivable.**

inexhaustible adjective SEE **infinite.**

inexorable adjective SEE **relentless.**

inexpensive adjective SEE **cheap,** cutprice, low-priced, reasonable.
OPPOSITES: SEE **expensive.**

inexperienced adjective *an inexperienced recruit.* callow, [*informal*] green, immature, inexpert, naïve, new, probationary, raw, unaccustomed, unskilled, unsophisticated, untried, [*informal*] wet behind the ears, young.
OPPOSITES: SEE **experienced.**
an inexperienced person apprentice, beginner, [*informal*] greenhorn, learner, novice, starter, tiro, trainee.

inexpert adjective SEE **unskilful.**

inexplicable adjective *an inexplicable mystery.* baffling, enigmatic, incomprehensible, insoluble, mysterious, mystifying, puzzling, strange, unaccountable, unfathomable, unsolvable.
OPPOSITES: SEE **explicable.**

inexpressible adjective SEE **indescribable.**

infallible adjective *an infallible method.* certain, dependable, foolproof, perfect,

predictable, reliable, sound, sure, trustworthy, unbeatable.
OPPOSITES: SEE **fallible**.

infamous adjective [Note: *infamous* is NOT the opposite of *famous*.] *an infamous crime*. SEE **notorious**.

infant noun baby, SEE **child**, [*informal*] toddler.

infantile adjective [*uncomplimentary*] *infantile behaviour*. adolescent, babyish, childish, immature, juvenile, puerile, SEE **silly**.
OPPOSITES: SEE **mature**.

infantry noun SEE **armed services**.

infatuated adjective besotted, [*informal*] head over heels, in love [SEE **love** noun], obsessed, [*informal*] smitten.

infatuation noun [*informal*] crush, SEE **love** noun, obsession, passion.

infect verb 1 *to infect the water supply. to infect a wound*. blight, contaminate, defile, make infected [SEE **infected**], poison, pollute, spoil, taint.
2 *to infect someone with your laughter*. affect, influence, inspire, touch.

infected adjective *an infected wound*. blighted, contaminated, festering, inflamed, poisoned, polluted, putrid, septic, tainted.

infection noun 1 *The infection spread rapidly*. blight, contagion, contamination, epidemic, pestilence, pollution, virus.
2 *He's off work with some sort of infection*. SEE **illness**.

infectious adjective *infectious diseases*. catching, communicable, contagious, spreading, transmissible, transmittable.

infer verb [Note: *infer* and *imply* are NOT synonyms.] *I infer from what you say that you are unhappy?* assume, conclude, deduce, extrapolate, gather, guess, reach the conclusion, understand, work out.

inferior adjective 1 *inferior rank*. junior, lesser, lower, menial, secondary, second-class, servile, subordinate, subsidiary.
2 *inferior quality*. SEE **bad**, cheap, indifferent, mediocre, poor, shoddy, tawdry, [*informal*] tinny.

inferior noun *The boss is too aloof from her inferiors*. SEE **subordinate** noun.

infernal adjective SEE **devilish**.

inferno noun SEE **fire** noun.

infertile adjective SEE **barren**.

infested adjective *infested with mice*. alive, crawling, overrun, plagued,

ravaged, swarming, teeming, verminous.

infidelity noun 1 *infidelity to a leader*. SEE **disloyalty**.
2 *infidelity to a wife or husband*. adultery, unfaithfulness.

infiltrate verb *to infiltrate the enemy's camp*. enter secretly, insinuate, intrude, penetrate.

infiltrator noun SEE **spy** noun.

infinite adjective *infinite numbers. infinite patience*. boundless, countless, endless, everlasting, SEE **huge**, immeasurable, immense, incalculable, inestimable, inexhaustible, interminable, limitless, never-ending, numberless, uncountable, undefined, unending, unfathomable, unlimited, unnumbered, untold.
OPPOSITES: SEE **finite**.

infinitesimal adjective SEE **tiny**.

infinity noun endlessness, eternity, infinite amount (distance, quantity, etc.) [SEE **infinite**], infinitude, perpetuity, space.

infirm adjective *Infirm people may need our help*. bedridden, crippled, elderly, feeble, frail, SEE **ill**, lame, old, poorly, senile, sickly, unwell, weak.
OPPOSITES: SEE **healthy**.

infirmary noun SEE **hospital**.

infirmity noun SEE **illness**.

inflame verb *to inflame violent feelings*. SEE **anger** verb, arouse, encourage, excite, fire, foment, ignite, kindle, madden, provoke, rouse, stimulate.
OPPOSITES: SEE **cool** verb.

inflamed adjective 1 *an inflamed wound*. festering, infected, poisoned, red, septic, swollen.
2 *inflamed passions*. angry, enraged, excited, feverish, fiery, heated, hot, passionate, roused.

inflammable adjective [Note: *inflammable* is NOT the opposite of *flammable*.] *inflammable chemicals*. burnable, combustible, flammable, volatile.
OPPOSITES: SEE **incombustible**.

inflammation noun *an inflammation of the skin*. abscess, boil, infection, redness, sore, soreness.

inflate verb 1 *to inflate a tyre*. blow up, dilate, distend, puff up, pump up, swell.
2 *to inflate the importance of something*. SEE **exaggerate**.

inflection noun *an inflection in someone's voice*. SEE **tone** noun.

inflexible adjective 1 *inflexible materials.* firm, hard, hardened, immovable, rigid, solid, stiff, unbending, unyielding.
2 *an inflexible attitude.* entrenched, immutable, intractable, intransigent, obdurate, obstinate, resolute, strict, stubborn, unaccommodating, unalterable, uncompromising, unhelpful.
OPPOSITES: SEE **flexible**.

inflict verb *to inflict punishment or pain.* administer, apply, deal out, enforce, force, impose, mete out, perpetrate, wreak.

influence noun *Our trainer had a strong influence on the team.* authority, control, direction, dominance, effect, guidance, impact, power, pressure, pull.

influence verb 1 *Our trainer influenced the way we played.* affect, change, control, determine, direct, dominate, exert an influence on [SEE **influence** noun], guide, impinge on, impress, manipulate, modify, motivate, move, persuade, prompt, stir, sway.
2 *Don't try to influence the referee.* bias, bribe, corrupt, lead astray, prejudice, suborn, tempt.

influential adjective 1 *an influential person.* authoritative, dominant, important, leading, powerful.
2 *an influential idea.* compelling, convincing, effective, far-reaching, moving, persuasive, significant, telling.
OPPOSITES: SEE **unimportant**.

influx noun *an influx of imports.* flood, flow, inflow, inundation, invasion, rush, stream.

inform verb *to inform someone of the facts.* advise, apprise, enlighten, [*informal*] fill in, give information to, instruct, leak, notify, [*informal*] put in the picture, teach, tell, tip off.
to **inform against** *to inform against a wanted man.* accuse, betray, complain about, denounce, give information about, [*informal*] grass on, incriminate, inculpate, report, [*informal*] sneak on, [*informal*] split on, [*informal*] tell of, [*informal*] tell tales about.

informal adjective 1 *an informal greeting. informal clothes. an informal party.* approachable, casual, comfortable, cosy, easy, easygoing, everyday, familiar, free and easy, friendly, homely, natural, ordinary, relaxed, simple, unceremonious, unofficial, unpretentious, unsophisticated.
2 *informal language.* chatty, colloquial, personal, slangy.
3 *an informal design.* asymmetrical, flexible, fluid, intuitive, irregular, spontaneous.

OPPOSITES: SEE **formal**.

information noun 1 *information about what is happening.* announcement, briefing, bulletin, communication, enlightenment, facts, instruction, message, news, report, statement, [*old-fashioned*] tidings, [*informal*] tip-off.
2 *information gathered for a purpose.* data, database, dossier, evidence, intelligence, knowledge, statistics.

informative adjective *an informative booklet.* communicative, enlightening, factual, giving information, helpful, illuminating, instructive, revealing, useful.
OPPOSITES: SEE **evasive**.

informed adjective SEE **knowledgeable**.

informer noun informant, spy, tell-tale.

infrequent adjective *an infrequent guest. infrequent buses.* exceptional, intermittent, irregular, occasional, [*informal*] once in a blue moon, rare, spasmodic, uncommon, unusual.
OPPOSITES: SEE **frequent** adjective.

infringe verb *to infringe the law.* SEE **violate**.

infuriate verb SEE **anger** verb.

infuse verb SEE **instil**.

ingenious adjective [Don't confuse with *ingenuous*.] *an ingenious plan.* artful, astute, brilliant, clever, complex, crafty, creative, cunning, imaginative, inspired, intricate, inventive, original, resourceful, shrewd, skilful, subtle.
OPPOSITES: SEE **unimaginative**.

ingenuous adjective [Don't confuse with *ingenious*.] *an ingenuous beginner.* artless, childlike, frank, guileless, honest, innocent, naïve, open, plain, simple, trusting, uncomplicated, unsophisticated.
OPPOSITES: SEE **sophisticated**.

ingest verb SEE **eat**.

inglorious adjective SEE **shameful**.

ingot noun *a gold ingot.* lump, nugget.

ingrained adjective SEE **established**.

ingratiate verb to ingratiate yourself with be obsequious to [SEE **obsequious**], [*informal*] crawl to, curry favour with, fawn on, flatter, get on the right side of, [*informal*] lick the boots of, [*informal*] suck up to, [*informal*] toady to.

ingratitude noun ungratefulness.
OPPOSITES: SEE **thanks**.

ingredient noun component, constituent, element, part.

inhabit verb *to inhabit a place.* [*old-fashioned*] abide in, dwell in, live in, make your home in, occupy, people, populate, possess, reside in, settle in, set up home in.

inhabited adjective *an inhabited island.* colonized, lived-in, occupied, peopled, populated, settled.
OPPOSITES: SEE **uninhabited**.

inhabitant noun citizen, [*old-fashioned*] denizen, dweller, inmate, native, occupant, occupier, [*plural*] population, resident, settler, tenant, [*plural*] townsfolk, [*plural*] townspeople.

inhale verb *to inhale smoke.* breathe in.

inherent adjective *inherent qualities.* congenital, essential, fundamental, hereditary, immanent, inborn, inbred, ingrained, intrinsic, native, natural.
OPPOSITE: acquired.

inherit verb *to inherit property.* be the inheritor of [SEE **inheritor**], be left, [*informal*] come into, receive as an inheritance [SEE **inheritance**], succeed to.

inheritance noun *a small inheritance from uncle's will.* bequest, estate, fortune, heritage, legacy.

inherited adjective *an inherited title.* family, hereditary, passed down.
OPPOSITE: acquired.

inheritor noun *the inheritor of an estate.* beneficiary, heir, heiress, [*formal*] legatee, recipient, successor.

inhibit verb *to inhibit someone from doing something.* SEE **restrain**.

inhibited adjective *too inhibited to join the fun.* bashful, diffident, formal, frustrated, full of inhibitions [SEE **inhibition**], guarded, [*informal*] prim and proper, repressed, reserved, self-conscious, shy, tense, undemonstrative, unemotional, [*informal*] uptight.
OPPOSITES: SEE **uninhibited**.

inhibition noun 1 [*usually plural*] *Try to overcome your inhibitions.* diffidence, [*informal*] hang-ups, repression, reserve, self-consciousness, shyness.
2 *There's no inhibition on your freedom here.* bar, barrier, check, impediment, interference, restraint.

inhospitable adjective 1 *an inhospitable person.* SEE **unfriendly**.
2 *an inhospitable place.* SEE **desolate**.

inhuman adjective *inhuman feelings.* barbaric, barbarous, bestial, blood-thirsty, brutish, cruel, diabolical, fiendish, heartless, SEE **inhumane**, merciless, pitiless, ruthless, savage, unkind, unnatural.
OPPOSITES: SEE **human**.

inhumane adjective *inhumane treatment of animals.* cold-hearted, cruel, hard, heartless, inconsiderate, SEE **inhuman**,

insensitive, uncaring, uncharitable, uncivilized, unfeeling, unkind, unsympathetic.
OPPOSITES: SEE **humane**.

inimical adjective SEE **hostile**.

inimitable adjective *an inimitable style.* SEE **distinctive**.

iniquitous adjective SEE **wicked**.

initial adjective *an initial payment. an initial reaction.* beginning, commencing, earliest, first, inaugural, introductory, opening, original, preliminary, starting.
OPPOSITES: SEE **final**.

initiate verb *to initiate negotiations.* SEE **begin**.

initiative verb *Show some initiative.* ambition, drive, dynamism, enterprise, [*informal*] get-up-and-go, inventiveness, lead, leadership, originality, resourcefulness.
to take the initiative SEE **begin**.

inject verb *to inject into a vein.* insert, introduce, make an injection.

injection noun *The nurse gave me an injection.* [*informal*] fix, inoculation, [*informal*] jab, vaccination.

injudicious adjective SEE **unwise**.

injunction noun SEE **command** noun.

injure verb break, crush, cut, damage, deface, disfigure, harm, hurt, ill-treat, mar, ruin, spoil, vandalize, SEE **wound** verb.

injurious adjective SEE **harmful**.

injury noun damage, harm, hurt, mischief (*did him a mischief*), SEE **wound** noun.

injustice noun *The injustice of the decision angered me.* bias, discrimination, dishonesty, favouritism, illegality, inequality, inequity, oppression, partiality, prejudice, unfairness, unlawfulness, wrongness.
OPPOSITES: SEE **justice**.

inkling noun *I'd no inkling he was coming.* SEE **hint** noun.

inlet noun SEE **bay**.

inmate noun SEE **inhabitant**.

inn noun [*old-fashioned*] hostelry, hotel, [*informal*] local, pub, tavern.

innards noun SEE **entrails**.

innate adjective SEE **hereditary**.

inner adjective *inner walls. inner feelings.* central, concealed, hidden, innermost, inside, interior, internal, intimate, inward, mental, middle, private, secret.
OPPOSITES: SEE **outer**.

innocent adjective **1** *The trial proved he was innocent.* blameless, free from blame, guiltless.
OPPOSITES: SEE **guilty**.
2 *innocent babes.* angelic, chaste, faultless, [*informal*] green, harmless, honest, incorrupt, inexperienced, ingenuous, inoffensive, naïve, pure, righteous, simple-minded, sinless, spotless, untainted, virtuous.
OPPOSITES: SEE **corrupt** adjective, **experienced**.

innocuous adjective SEE **harmless**.

innovation noun *We propose to introduce some innovations next year.* change, departure, new feature, novelty, reform, revolution.

innovator noun discoverer, experimenter, inventor, pioneer, reformer, revolutionary.

innuendo noun SEE **hint** noun.

innumerable adjective *innumerable stars.* countless, SEE **infinite**, many, numberless, uncountable, untold.

inoculate verb SEE **immunize**.

inoculation noun SEE **immunization**.

inoffensive adjective SEE **harmless**.

inoperable adjective SEE **incurable**.

inoperative adjective SEE **idle** adjective.

inopportune adjective SEE **inconvenient**.

inordinate adjective SEE **excessive**.

inorganic adjective *inorganic fertilizers.* artificial, chemical, dead, inanimate, unnatural.
OPPOSITES: SEE **organic**.

input noun SEE **contribution**.

inquest noun **1** *an inquest to determine how someone died.* hearing, inquiry.
2 [*informal*] *an inquest into why we lost the game.* discussion, exploration, investigation, [*informal*] post-mortem, probe, review.

inquire verb SEE **ask**.

inquiring adjective *an inquiring mind.* SEE **inquisitive**.

inquiry, inquisition nouns SEE **investigation**.

inquisitive adjective *I want to know simply because I'm inquisitive!* curious, inquiring, interested, interfering, meddling, nosy, probing, prying, questioning, sceptical, snooping.
to be inquisitive SEE **pry**.
an inquisitive person SEE **busybody**.

inroad noun SEE **invasion**.

insalubrious adjective SEE **unhealthy**.

insane adjective SEE **mad**.

insanitary adjective SEE **unhealthy**.

insanity noun SEE **madness**.

insatiable adjective SEE **greedy**.

inscribe verb SEE **write**.

inscription noun *the inscription on a memorial.* engraving, epigraph, superscription, wording, writing.

inscrutable adjective SEE **baffling**.

insect noun [*informal*] creepy-crawly.

VARIOUS INSECTS: ant, aphid, bee, beetle, black-beetle, blackfly, bluebottle, bumble-bee, butterfly, cicada, cockchafer, cockroach, Colorado beetle, crane-fly, cricket, daddy-long-legs, damsel-fly, dragonfly, earwig, firefly, fly, glow-worm, gnat, grasshopper, hornet, ladybird, locust, mantis, mayfly, midge, mosquito, moth, sawfly, termite, tsetse-fly, wasp, weevil.

OTHER FORMS OF AN INSECT: caterpillar, chrysalis, grub, larva, maggot.

There are many crawling creatures commonly called *insects* which, strictly speaking, are not insects: e.g. arachnid, centipede, earthworm, mite, slug, spider, woodlouse, worm.

---

insecticide noun pesticide, SEE **poison** noun.

insecure adjective **1** *an insecure foothold.* SEE **dangerous**, loose, precarious, rocky, shaky, uncertain, unsafe, unstable, unsteady, unsupported, weak, wobbly.
2 *an insecure feeling.* SEE **anxious**, exposed, underconfident, vulnerable.
OPPOSITES: SEE **secure** adjective.

inseminate verb SEE **fertilize**.

insensible adjective *insensible after a hit on the head.* [*informal*] dead to the world, inert, knocked out, [*informal*] out, senseless, unaware, unconscious.
OPPOSITES: SEE **conscious**.

insensitive adjective **1** *It's insensitive to joke about people's misfortunes.* callous, SEE **cruel**, imperceptive, obtuse, tactless, [*informal*] thick-skinned, thoughtless, uncaring, unfeeling, unsympathetic.
OPPOSITES: SEE **tactful**.
2 *an insensitive spot on your skin.* anaesthetized, dead, numb, unresponsive, without feeling.
OPPOSITES: SEE **sensitive**.

inseparable adjective always together, attached, indissoluble, indivisible, integral.

insert verb *to insert a wedge. to insert papers in a file.* drive in, embed, implant, interleave (*pages in a book*), introduce, [*informal*] pop in, push in, put in, tuck in.

inside adjective *the inside walls of a house.* indoor, inner, innermost, interior, internal.
OPPOSITES: SEE **outside** adjective.

inside noun bowels (*the bowels of the earth*), centre, contents, core, heart, indoors, interior, middle.
OPPOSITES: SEE **outside** noun.
insides *an animal's insides.* SEE **entrails.**

insidious adjective *insidious propaganda.* SEE **cunning,** furtive, pervasive, secretive, stealthy, subtle, surreptitious, underhand.

insight noun SEE **intelligence, understanding.**

insignia noun SEE **symbol.**

insignificant adjective inconsiderable, irrelevant, lightweight, meaningless, negligible, small, trivial, SEE **unimportant,** unimpressive, valueless, worthless.
OPPOSITES: SEE **significant.**

insincere adjective *insincere compliments.* deceitful, deceptive, devious, dishonest, disingenuous, false, feigned, flattering, hollow, hypocritical, lying, [*informal*] mealy-mouthed, mendacious, [*informal*] phoney, pretended, [*informal*] put on, sycophantic, [*informal*] two-faced, untrue.
OPPOSITES: SEE **sincere.**

insinuate verb *He insinuated that I was lying.* SEE **imply.**

insipid adjective SEE **bland.**

insist verb *He insisted he was innocent.* assert, aver, declare, emphasize, maintain, state, stress, swear, take an oath, vow.
to insist on *She insists on obedience.* command, demand, enforce, [*informal*] put your foot down, require, stipulate.

insistent adjective *an insistent rhythm. insistent requests.* assertive, demanding, emphatic, forceful, importunate, peremptory, persistent, relentless, repeated, unrelenting, unremitting, urgent.

insolence noun *Teachers don't like insolence from pupils.* arrogance, boldness, [*informal*] cheek, defiance, disrespect, effrontery, forwardness, impertinence, impudence, incivility, insubordination, [*informal*] lip, presumptuousness, rudeness, [*informal*] sauce.
OPPOSITES: SEE **politeness.**

insolent adjective *an insolent stare.* arrogant, bold, brazen, [*informal*] cheeky, contemptuous, disdainful, disrespectful, forward, impertinent, impolite, impudent, insulting, presumptuous, rude, saucy, shameless, sneering, uncivil.
OPPOSITES: SEE **polite.**

insoluble *an insoluble problem.* baffling, enigmatic, incomprehensible, inexplicable, mysterious, mystifying, puzzling, strange, unaccountable, unanswerable, unfathomable, unsolvable.
OPPOSITES: SEE **soluble.**

insolvent adjective SEE **bankrupt.**

insomnia noun sleeplessness.

inspect verb *to inspect damage. to inspect someone's work.* check, examine, [*informal*] give it the once over, investigate, make an inspection of, scrutinize, study, survey, vet.

inspection noun check, check-up, examination, [*informal*] going-over, investigation, review, scrutiny, survey.

inspector noun 1 *An inspector checked the standard of work.* controller, examiner, investigator, official, scrutineer, superintendent, supervisor, tester.
2 *a police inspector.* SEE **policeman.**

inspiration noun 1 *the inspiration behind a poem.* creativity, enthusiasm, genius, imagination, influence, motivation, muse, spur, stimulus.
2 *I had a sudden inspiration.* brainwave, idea, thought.

inspire verb *The crowd inspired us to play well.* animate, arouse, [*informal*] egg on, encourage, enthuse, galvanize, influence, motivate, prompt, reassure, spur, stimulate, stir, support.

instability noun *emotional instability. instability in prices.* capriciousness, change, changeableness, fickleness, fluctuation, flux, impermanence, inconstancy, insecurity, mutability, precariousness, shakiness, transience, uncertainty, unpredictability, unreliability, unsteadiness, [*informal*] ups-and-downs, vacillation, variability, variations, weakness.
OPPOSITES: SEE **stability.**

install verb 1 *to install central heating.* establish, fix, introduce, put in, set up.
2 *He installed himself in the best chair.* ensconce, place, plant, position, situate, station.
OPPOSITES: SEE **remove.**

instalment noun 1 *We pay for the TV in instalments.* payment, rent, rental.
2 *an instalment of a serial.* chapter, episode, part.

instance noun *Give me an instance of what you mean.* case, example, illustration, occurrence, sample.

instant adjective *an instant reply.* direct, fast, immediate, instantaneous, prompt, quick, rapid, speedy, swift, unhesitating, urgent.

instant noun *The shooting star was gone in an instant.* flash, moment, point of time, second, split second, [*informal*] tick, [*informal*] twinkling.

instantaneous adjective SEE **instant** adjective.

instigate verb *to instigate a riot.* activate, begin, be the instigator of [SEE **instigator**], bring about, cause, encourage, foment, generate, incite, initiate, inspire, kindle, prompt, provoke, set up, start, stimulate, stir up, urge, [*informal*] whip up.

instigator noun *the instigator of a riot.* agitator, fomenter, inciter, initiator, inspirer, leader, mischief-maker, provoker, ringleader, trouble-maker.

instil verb *to instil knowledge into pupils' minds.* [*informal*] din into, implant, inculcate, indoctrinate, infuse, inject, insinuate, introduce.

instinct noun *People do some things by instinct.* feel, feeling, guesswork, hunch, impulse, inclination, instinctive urge [SEE **instinctive**], intuition, presentiment, sixth-sense, tendency, urge.

instinctive adjective *an instinctive reaction.* automatic, [*informal*] gut (*gut feeling*), impulsive, inborn, inherent, innate, intuitive, involuntary, natural, reflex, spontaneous, unconscious, unreasoning, unthinking.
OPPOSITES: SEE **deliberate** adjective.

institute noun SEE **institution**.

institute verb *to institute a new set of rules.* begin, create, establish, fix, found, inaugurate, initiate, introduce, launch, open, originate, set up, start.

institution 1 *the institution of a new set of rules.* creation, establishing, formation, founding, inauguration, inception, initiation, introduction, launching, opening, setting up.
2 *an institution for blind people.* academy, college, establishment, foundation, home, hospital, institute, SEE **organization**, school, [*informal*] set-up.
3 *Sunday dinner is a regular institution in our house.* convention, custom, habit, practice, ritual, routine, tradition.

instruct verb 1 *The teacher instructed us in a new technique.* SEE **teach**.

2 *He instructed us to wait.* SEE **command** verb.

instruction noun 1 *He gave us instruction in the use of the equipment.* SEE **teaching**.
2 *Obey instructions!* SEE **command** noun.

instructive adjective *an instructive book.* didactic, edifying, educational, enlightening, helpful, illuminating, improving, informative, revealing.

instructor noun SEE **teacher**.

instrument noun *surgical instruments. mathematical instruments.* apparatus, appliance, contraption, device, equipment, gadget, implement, machine, mechanism, tool, utensil.
MUSICAL INSTRUMENTS: SEE **music**.

instrumental adjective *I was instrumental in getting things changed.* active, contributory, helpful, influential, useful.

insubordinate adjective *Many teachers dislike insubordinate children.* defiant, disobedient, SEE **impertinent**, insurgent, mutinous, rebellious, riotous, seditious, undisciplined, unruly.
OPPOSITES: SEE **obedient**.

insubstantial adjective SEE **flimsy**.

insufferable adjective SEE **intolerable**.

insufficient adjective *insufficient supplies.* deficient, inadequate, meagre, poor, scanty, scarce, short, sparse, unsatisfactory.
OPPOSITES: SEE **excessive, sufficient**.

Several English words, including *insular, insulate,* and *peninsula,* are related to Latin *insula* = *island*.

---

insular adjective *Having lived in one place all his life, his views are insular.* closed, limited, narrow, narrow-minded, parochial, provincial.
OPPOSITES: SEE **open-minded**.

insulate verb *to insulate water-pipes.* cocoon, cover, enclose, isolate, lag, protect, surround, wrap up.
OPPOSITES: SEE **bare** verb.

insult noun *I was offended by his insults.* abuse, cheek, contumely, impudence, insulting behaviour [SEE **insulting**], rudeness, slander, slight, snub.
OPPOSITES: SEE **compliment** noun.

insult verb abuse, affront, be insulting to [SEE **insulting**], [*informal*] call someone names, [*informal*] cock a snook at, mock, offend, outrage, patronize, revile, slander, slight, sneer at, snub, [*informal*] thumb your nose at, vilify.
OPPOSITES: SEE **compliment** verb.

insulting adjective *insulting remarks.* abusive, condescending, contemptuous, disparaging, insolent, mocking, offensive, patronizing, SEE **rude**, scornful, scurrilous, slanderous, [*informal*] snide.
OPPOSITES: SEE **complimentary**.

insuperable adjective *insuperable difficulties.* SEE **impossible**, insurmountable, overwhelming, unconquerable.

insupportable adjective SEE **intolerable**.

insurance noun *an insurance against loss or accident.* assurance, cover, indemnity, policy, protection, security.

insure verb *to insure yourself against loss or accident.* cover, indemnify, protect, take out insurance.

insurgent adjective SEE **rebellious**.

insurmountable adjective SEE **insuperable**.

insurrection noun SEE **rebellion**.

intact adjective SEE **undamaged**.

intangible adjective. *The scent of flowers is an intangible quality.* abstract, airy, disembodied, elusive, ethereal, impalpable, incorporeal, indefinite, insubstantial, invisible, unreal, vague.
OPPOSITES: SEE **tangible**.

integer noun SEE **number** noun.

integral adjective 1 *The boiler is an integral part of the heating system.* constituent, essential, indispensable, intrinsic, irreplaceable, necessary, requisite.
OPPOSITES: SEE **detachable**.
2 *The equipment is supplied as an integral unit.* complete, full, indivisible, whole.

integrate verb *We tried to integrate the two groups.* amalgamate, blend, bring together, combine, consolidate, desegregate, fuse, harmonize, join, merge, mix, put together, unify, unite, weld.
OPPOSITES: SEE **separate** verb.

integration noun SEE **union**.

integrity noun *You can trust his integrity.* fidelity, goodness, SEE **honesty**, honour, incorruptibility, loyalty, morality, principle, reliability, righteousness, sincerity, uprightness, virtue.
OPPOSITES: SEE **dishonesty**.

intellect noun SEE **intelligence**.

intellectual adjective 1 *an intellectual student.* academic, [*informal*] bookish, cerebral, cultured, highbrow, SEE **intelligent**, scholarly, studious, thoughtful.
2 *an intellectual book.* cultural, deep, difficult, educational, highbrow, improving, thought-provoking.

intellectual noun *The prof is a true intellectual.* [*informal*] egg-head, genius, highbrow, intellectual person [SEE **intellectual** adjective], member of the intelligentsia, thinker.

intelligence noun 1 *Use your intelligence!* ability, acumen, [*informal*] brains, brightness, brilliance, capacity, cleverness, discernment, genius, insight, intellect, judgement, mind, [*informal*] nous, perceptiveness, quickness, reason, sense, understanding, wisdom, wit (*He didn't have the wit to ask*), wits.
2 *They received intelligence of an impending invasion.* data, facts, information, knowledge, news, notification, report, [*informal*] tip-off, warning.
3 *Our intelligence discovered the enemy's position.* espionage, secret service, spies.

intelligent adjective *an intelligent student. intelligent work.* able, acute, alert, astute, brainy, bright, brilliant, clever, discerning, intellectual, knowing, penetrating, perceptive, perspicacious, profound, quick, rational, sagacious, sharp, shrewd, [*informal*] smart, trenchant, wise, [*informal*] with it.
OPPOSITES: SEE **stupid**.

intelligible adjective *an intelligible message.* clear, comprehensible, decipherable, legible, logical, lucid, meaningful, plain, straightforward, unambiguous, understandable.
OPPOSITES: SEE **incomprehensible**.

intemperate adjective *an intemperate drinker.* SEE **excessive**.

intend verb 1 *What do you intend to do?* aim, aspire, contemplate, design, have in mind, mean, plan, plot, propose, purpose, scheme.
2 *The gift was intended to please you.* design, destine, put forward, set up.

intense adjective 1 *intense pain.* acute, agonizing, extreme, fierce, great, keen, severe, sharp, strong, violent.
OPPOSITES: SEE **slight** adjective.
2 *intense emotions.* ardent, burning, deep, eager, earnest, fanatical, impassioned, passionate, powerful, profound, serious, towering, vehement.
OPPOSITES: SEE **cool** adjective.
3 *an intense person.* SEE **emotional**.

intensify verb *The heat intensified. They intensified the pressure.* add to, aggravate, become greater, boost, build up, deepen, emphasize, escalate, fire, fuel, heighten, increase, magnify, make greater, quicken, raise, redouble, reinforce, sharpen, [*informal*] step up, strengthen.
OPPOSITES: SEE **reduce, soften**.

intensive adjective *intensive effort. intensive enquiries.* [*informal*] all-out, concentrated, detailed, exhaustive, high-powered, thorough, unremitting.

intent adjective *intent on what you're doing.* absorbed, attentive (to), committed (to), concentrating, determined, eager, engrossed, keen, occupied, preoccupied, set, steadfast, watchful.

intent noun *The prosecution had to prove intent to kill.* SEE **intention**.

intention noun *What is your intention?* aim, ambition, design, end, goal, intent, object, objective, plan, point, purpose, target.

intentional adjective *an intentional foul.* calculated, conscious, deliberate, designed, intended, planned, prearranged, premeditated, wilful.
OPPOSITES: SEE **unintentional**.

inter verb SEE **bury**.

The prefix *inter-* is related to Latin *inter = among, between.* The verb *inter* and the noun *interment*, however, are related to a different Latin word, *terra = earth.*

---

interaction noun *the interaction of two influences.* effect on each other, exchange, [*informal*] give and take, interplay, reciprocal effect, [*informal*] to and fro.

intercede verb SEE **intervene**.

intercept verb *I intercepted the messenger before he delivered the message.* ambush, block, catch, check, cut off, deflect, head off, interrupt, obstruct, stop, thwart, trap.

interchange noun 1 *a motorway interchange.* crossroads, intersection, junction.
2 *an interchange of ideas.* exchange, [*informal*] swap.

intercom noun SEE **communication**.

intercourse noun *sexual intercourse* SEE **sex**.

interdict verb SEE **prohibit**.

interest noun 1 *Did he show any interest?* attention, attentiveness, care, commitment, concern, curiosity, involvement, notice, regard.
2 *The information was of no interest.* consequence, importance, moment, note, significance, value.
2 *What are your main interests?* activity, diversion, hobby, pastime, preoccupation, pursuit, relaxation.

interest verb *Astronomy interests me.* appeal to, arouse the curiosity of, attract, capture the imagination of, concern, divert, engage, engross, entertain, SEE **excite**, fascinate, intrigue, involve, stimulate, [*informal*] turn on.
OPPOSITES: SEE **bore**.

interested adjective 1 *an interested listener. interested in your work.* absorbed, attentive, curious, engrossed, enthusiastic, excited, fascinated, intent, keen, preoccupied, responsive.
OPPOSITES: SEE **uninterested**.
2 *Don't consult the owner of the damaged car: she's an interested party.* SEE **biased**, concerned, involved, partial.
OPPOSITES: SEE **disinterested**.
to be interested in SEE **like** verb.

interesting adjective [Things and experiences can be *interesting* in many ways. Only some of the possible synonyms are given here.] *an interesting problem. interesting conversation.* absorbing, challenging, curious, engaging, engrossing, entertaining, exciting, fascinating, important, intriguing, piquant, [*often ironic*] riveting, stimulating, unpredictable, unusual, varied.
OPPOSITES: SEE **boring**.

interface noun *the interface between two regions or systems.* SEE **boundary**, meeting-point.

interfere verb *to interfere in someone's affairs.* be a busybody, butt in, interrupt, intervene, intrude, meddle, molest, obtrude, [*informal*] poke your nose in, pry, snoop, tamper.
to interfere with *to interfere with the smooth running of something.* block, get in the way of, hamper, hinder, impede, obstruct.

interfering adjective *an interfering busybody.* curious, meddlesome, nosy, prying, snooping.

interim adjective *The test isn't finished, but we've produced an interim report.* half-time, halfway, provisional, temporary.

interior adjective, noun SEE **inside** adjective, noun.

interject verb SEE **interpose**.

interlink verb SEE **link** verb.

interlock verb SEE **engage**.

interloper noun SEE **intruder**.

interlude noun SEE **interval**.

intermediary noun SEE **go-between**.

intermediate adjective *an intermediate position.* average, [*informal*] betwixt and between, half-way, mean, medial, median, middle, midway, [*informal*] neither one thing nor the other, neutral, [*informal*] sitting on the fence, transitional.

interment noun [Do not confuse with *internment.*] SEE **funeral**.

interminable adjective SEE **ceaseless**.

intermingle verb SEE **mix**.

intermission noun SEE **interval**.

intermittent adjective *an intermittent fault in a machine.* fitful, irregular, occasional, [*informal*] on and off, periodic, recurrent, spasmodic, sporadic.
OPPOSITES: SEE **continual**.

intern verb SEE **imprison**.

internal adjective *the internal parts of something.* inner, inside, interior, intimate, private.
OPPOSITES: SEE **external**.

international adjective *international travel.* global, inter-continental, worldwide.

internecine adjective SEE **destructive**.

internee noun SEE **captive** noun.

internment noun [Do not confuse with *interment.*] SEE **captivity**.

inter-planetary adjective SEE **space** adjective.

interplay noun SEE **interaction**.

interpolate verb SEE **interpose**.

interpose verb *to interpose remarks in a conversation.* add, contribute, insert, interject, interlard, interpolate, introduce, put in, throw in.

interpret verb *Can you interpret this old writing?* clarify, construe, decipher, decode, elucidate, explain, expound, gloss, make clear, paraphrase, render (*into another language*), rephrase, reword, translate, understand.

interpretation noun *What's your interpretation of her behaviour?* definition, explanation, gloss, reading, understanding, version.

interpreter noun linguist, translator.

interrogate verb SEE **question** verb.

interrogative, interrogatory adjectives asking, inquiring, inquisitive, investigatory, questioning.

interrupt verb 1 *Interrupt if you have any questions.* [*informal*] barge in, break in, butt in, cut in, heckle, intervene, punctuate (*He punctuated the lecture with questions*).
2 *A fire alarm interrupted work.* break in on, break off, call a halt to, cause an interruption in [SEE **interruption**], cut (someone) off, cut short, disrupt, disturb, hold up, stop, suspend.

3 *The new houses interrupt our view.* get in the way of, interfere with, intrude upon, obstruct, spoil.

interruption noun *an interruption in service.* break, check, disruption, division, gap, halt, hiatus, pause, stop, suspension.

intersect verb *motorways intersect.* bisect each other, converge, criss-cross, cross, divide, meet, pass across each other.

intersection noun *a motorway intersection.* crossroads, interchange, junction.

intersperse verb SEE **scatter**.

interstellar adjective SEE **space** adjective.

intertwine verb SEE **interweave**.

interval noun 1 *an interval between events, places, etc.* break, [*informal*] breather, breathing-space, delay, distance, gap, hiatus, lapse, lull, opening, pause, respite, rest, space, wait.
2 *an interval in a play or concert.* adjournment, interlude, intermission, recess.

intervene verb 1 *A week intervened before I saw her again.* come between, happen, intrude, occur.
2 *to intervene in a quarrel.* arbitrate, butt in, intercede, interfere, interrupt, mediate, [*informal*] step in.

interview noun *an interview for a job.* audience, formal discussion, meeting, questioning.

interview verb *A reporter interviewed eye-witnesses.* ask questions, examine, interrogate, question.

interweave verb *The lines interweave in a complex pattern.* criss-cross, entwine, interlace, intertwine, knit, tangle, weave together.

intestines noun bowels, entrails, innards, insides.

intimate adjective 1 *an intimate relationship.* affectionate, close, familiar, SEE **friendly**, informal, loving, sexual.
2 *intimate details.* confidential, detailed, exhaustive, personal, private, secret.

intimate verb SEE **indicate**.

intimidate verb *The strong often intimidate the weak.* browbeat, bully, coerce, cow, daunt, frighten, hector, make afraid, menace, persecute, scare, terrify, terrorize, threaten.

intolerable adjective *intolerable pain.* excruciating, impossible, insufferable, insupportable, unbearable, unendurable.
OPPOSITES: SEE **tolerable**.

intolerant adjective *intolerant of other people's views.* bigoted, chauvinistic, dogmatic, illiberal, narrow-minded, opinionated, prejudiced, racialist, racist, sexist.
OPPOSITES: SEE **tolerant.**

intonation noun *an unusual intonation in her voice.* accent, inflection, sound, tone.

intone verb SEE **sing, speak.**

intoxicant noun SEE **alcohol.**

intoxicated adjective SEE **drunk.**

intoxicating adjective 1 *intoxicating drink.* SEE **alcoholic.**
2 *an intoxicating experience.* exciting, heady, stimulating.

intractable, intransigent adjectives SEE **stubborn.**

intrepid adjective SEE **courageous.**

intricate adjective *intricate machinery. intricate negotiations.* complex, complicated, convoluted, delicate, detailed, elaborate, [*informal*] fiddly, involved, sophisticated, tangled, tortuous.
OPPOSITES: SEE **simple.**

intrigue noun *a political intrigue.* SEE **plot** noun.

intrigue verb 1 *to intrigue against the state.* SEE **plot** verb.
2 *Science intrigues me.* SEE **interest** verb.

intrinsic adjective *The brooch has little intrinsic value.* basic, essential, fundamental, inborn, in-built, inherent, native, natural, proper, real.

introduce verb 1 *to introduce someone to a friend.* acquaint, make known, present.
2 *to introduce a radio programme.* announce, give an introduction to, lead into, preface.
3 *to introduce something new.* add, SEE **begin,** bring in, bring out, broach, create, establish, initiate, offer, pioneer, set up, start.

introduction noun 1 *an introduction to a book or song.* foreword, [*informal*] intro, introductory part [SEE **introductory**], [*informal*] lead-in, opening, overture, preamble, preface, prelude, prologue.
2 *the introduction of a new bus service.* SEE **beginning.**

introductory adjective *an introductory offer. introductory chapters of a book.* early, first, inaugural, initial, opening, prefatory, preliminary, preparatory, starting.
OPPOSITES: SEE **final.**

introspective adjective SEE **introverted.**

introverted adjective *an introverted character.* contemplative, introspective, inward-looking, meditative, pensive, quiet, reserved, retiring, self-contained, shy, thoughtful, unsociable, withdrawn.
OPPOSITES: SEE **extroverted.**

intrude verb *to intrude on a private conversation.* break in, butt in, eavesdrop, encroach, gatecrash, interfere, interrupt, intervene, join uninvited.

intruder noun 1 *intruders at a party.* eavesdropper, gatecrasher, infiltrator, interloper, snooper, [*informal*] uninvited guest.
2 *an intruder on your property.* burglar, housebreaker, invader, prowler, raider, robber, thief, trespasser.

intuition noun SEE **instinct.**

intuitive adjective SEE **instinctive.**

inundate verb SEE **flood** verb.

inure verb SEE **accustom.**

invade verb *to invade enemy territory.* SEE **attack** verb, descend on, encroach on, enter, impinge on, infest, infringe, march into, occupy, overrun, penetrate, raid, subdue, violate.

invalid adjective 1 *an invalid passport.* false, null and void, out-of-date, unacceptable, unusable, void, worthless.
2 *an invalid argument.* fallacious, illogical, incorrect, irrational, unconvincing, unfounded, unreasonable, unscientific, unsound, untrue.
OPPOSITES: SEE **valid.**

invalid noun *an invalid who spends most of the time in bed.* patient, sufferer.

invaluable adjective [Note: *invaluable* is NOT the opposite of *valuable.*] *Your help was invaluable.* incalculable, inestimable, precious, priceless, useful, SEE **valuable.**
OPPOSITES: SEE **worthless.**

invariable adjective *an invariable rule.* certain, constant, eternal, even, immutable, inflexible, permanent, predictable, reliable, rigid, solid, stable, steady, unalterable, unchangeable, unchanging, unvarying.
OPPOSITES: SEE **variable.**

invasion noun 1 *an invasion by an enemy.* SEE **attack** noun, encroachment, incursion, inroad, onslaught, raid, violation.
2 *an invasion of ants.* colony, flood, horde, infestation, spate, stream, swarm, throng.

invasive adjective *invasive weeds in the garden.* burgeoning, colonizing, increasing, mushrooming, profuse, proliferating, relentless, unstoppable.

invective noun SEE **abuse** noun.

inveigh verb to inveigh against SEE **abuse** verb.

inveigle verb SEE **lure** verb.

invent verb to invent something new. be the inventor of [SEE **inventor**], coin [= to invent a new word], conceive, concoct, construct, contrive, [informal] cook up, create, design, devise, discover, [informal] dream up, fabricate, imagine, improvise, make up, originate, plan, put together, think up, trump up (to trump up charges against someone).

invention noun 1 The system is my own invention. brainchild, coinage, contrivance, creation, design, discovery, figment (of the imagination).
2 She let us see her new invention. contraption, device, gadget.
3 His work is full of lively invention. creativity, genius, imagination, ingenuity, inspiration, inventiveness, originality.
4 Her story was pure invention. deceit, fabrication, fantasy, fiction, lies.

inventive adjective an inventive mind. inventive work. creative, enterprising, fertile, imaginative, ingenious, innovative, inspired, original, resourceful.
OPPOSITES: SEE **imitative**.

inventor noun the inventor of something new. architect, author, [informal] boffin, creator, designer, discoverer, maker, originator.

inventory noun SEE **catalogue**.

inverse adjective in inverse proportion. opposite, reversed, transposed.

invert verb capsize, overturn, reverse, turn upside down, upset.

invertebrate adjective VARIOUS ANIMALS: SEE **animal** noun.

invest verb to invest money. buy stocks and shares, put to work, save, use profitably.
to invest in I invested in a new washing-machine. SEE **buy**.

investigate verb to investigate a crime or a problem. consider, examine, explore, follow up, gather evidence about, [informal] go into, inquire into, look into, probe, research, scrutinize, study, [informal] sus out.

investigation noun an investigation into a crime or problem. enquiry, examination, inquiry, inquisition, inspection, [informal] post-mortem, [informal] probe, research, scrutiny, study, survey.

investiture noun the investiture of a bishop. installation, robing.

investment noun SEE **money**.

inveterate adjective an inveterate smoker. SEE **habitual**.

invidious adjective invidious comparisons. discriminatory, objectionable, offensive, undesirable, unjust, unwarranted.

invigilate verb SEE **supervise**.

invigorate verb SEE **animate** verb.

invigorating adjective an invigorating cold shower. bracing, enlivening, exhilarating, fresh, health-giving, healthy, refreshing, rejuvenating, revitalizing, stimulating.
OPPOSITES: SEE **soporific**, **wearying**.

invincible adjective an invincible army. indestructible, indomitable, invulnerable, strong, unbeatable, unconquerable.

invisible adjective an invisible repair. concealed, covered, disguised, hidden, imperceptible, inconspicuous, obscured, out of sight, secret, undetectable, unnoticeable, unnoticed, unseen.
OPPOSITES: SEE **visible**.

invite verb 1 We invite you to join in. ask, encourage, request, summon, urge.
2 Shops want to invite our custom. attract, entice, solicit, tempt.

inviting adjective SEE **attractive**.

invocation noun SEE **prayer**.

invoice noun an invoice showing goods supplied. account, bill, list, statement.

invoke verb to invoke someone's help. appeal to, call for, cry out for, entreat, implore, pray for, solicit, supplicate.

involuntary adjective Blinking is an involuntary movement. automatic, conditioned, impulsive, instinctive, reflex, spontaneous, unconscious, unintentional, unthinking.
OPPOSITES: SEE **deliberate** adjective.

involve verb 1 What does your job involve? comprise, contain, embrace, entail, hold, include, incorporate, take in.
2 Conserving resources involves us all. affect, concern, interest, touch.
3 Don't involve me in your dubious activities! embroil, implicate, include, incriminate, inculpate, mix up.

involved adjective 1 an involved problem. complex, complicated, confusing, convoluted, difficult, elaborate, intricate, [informal] knotty, tangled.
OPPOSITES: SEE **straightforward**.
2 involved in your work. active, busy, caught up, committed, concerned, dedicated, employed, keen, occupied.
OPPOSITES: uninvolved, SEE **detached**.

involvement noun **1** *involvement in sport*. activity, interest, participation. **2** *involvement with criminals*. association, complicity, entanglement, partnership.

invulnerable adjective *The dangerous drivers are those who think they're invulnerable*. indestructible, SEE **invincible**, protected, safe, secure, unwoundable.
OPPOSITES: SEE **vulnerable**.

iota noun SEE **particle**.

Several English words, including *irascible*, *irate*, and *ire*, are related to Latin *ira = anger*.

---

irascible adjective SEE **irritable**.

irate adjective SEE **angry**.

ire noun SEE **anger** noun.

iridescent adjective SEE **colourful**.

irk verb SEE **annoy**.

irksome adjective SEE **annoying**.

iron noun cast iron, steel.
RELATED ADJECTIVE: ferrous.
irons *convicts in irons*. chains, fetters, manacles, shackles.

iron verb *to iron the washing*. flatten, press, smooth.

ironic adjective *I was being ironic when I said their dreadful play was brilliant*. derisive, double-edged, ironical, mocking, sarcastic, satirical, wry.

ironmongers noun hardware store.

irony noun *I don't think they saw the irony in my comments*. double meaning, hidden meaning, sarcasm, satire.

irrational adjective *irrational behaviour. irrational argument*. absurd, arbitrary, biased, crazy, emotional, emotive, illogical, insane, mad, nonsensical, prejudiced, senseless, SEE **silly**, subjective, unintelligent, unreasonable, unreasoning, unsound, unthinking, wild.
OPPOSITES: SEE **rational**.

irreconcilable adjective SEE **incompatible**.

irredeemable adjective *an irredeemable sinner*. beyond redemption, impenitent, SEE **incorrigible**, irretrievable, lost, shameless, unsaveable, wicked.
OPPOSITES: SEE **penitent**.

irrefutable adjective SEE **indisputable**.

irregular adjective **1** *irregular intervals. an irregular rhythm*. erratic, fitful, fluctuating, haphazard, intermittent, occasional, random, spasmodic, sporadic, unequal, unpredictable, unpunctual, variable, varying, wavering.

2 *irregular behaviour. an irregular procedure*. abnormal, anomalous, eccentric, exceptional, extraordinary, illegal, improper, odd, peculiar, quirky, unconventional, unofficial, unplanned, unscheduled, unusual.
3 *an irregular surface*. broken, bumpy, jagged, lumpy, patchy, pitted, ragged, rough, uneven, up and down.
OPPOSITES: SEE **regular**.

irrelevant adjective *Omit irrelevant details*. extraneous, immaterial, inapplicable, inappropriate, inessential, pointless, unconnected, unnecessary, unrelated.
OPPOSITES: SEE **relevant**.

irreligious adjective *If you don't go to church, you aren't necessarily irreligious*. agnostic, atheistic, godless, heathen, humanist, impious, irreverent, pagan, uncommitted, ungodly, unrighteous, wicked.
OPPOSITES: SEE **religious**.

irreparable adjective *irreparable damage*. hopeless, incurable, irrecoverable, irremediable, irretrievable, irreversible, lasting, permanent, unalterable.
OPPOSITE: reparable.

irreplaceable adjective *an irreplaceable work of art*. inimitable, priceless, SEE **rare**, unique.
OPPOSITES: SEE **common** adjective.

irrepressible adjective *irrepressible high spirits*. boisterous, bouncy, ebullient, SEE **lively**, resilient, uncontrollable, ungovernable, uninhibited, unstoppable, vigorous.
OPPOSITES: SEE **sluggish**.

irresistible adjective *an irresistible temptation*. compelling, inescapable, inexorable, not to be denied, overpowering, overwhelming, persuasive, SEE **powerful**, seductive, unavoidable.

irresolute adjective *irresolute about what to choose*. doubtful, fickle, flexible, [*informal*] hedging your bets, SEE **hesitant**, indecisive, open to compromise, tentative, undecided, vacillating, wavering, weak, weak-willed.
OPPOSITES: SEE **resolute**.

irresponsible adjective *irresponsible driving*. careless, conscienceless, feckless, immature, immoral, inconsiderate, negligent, rash, reckless, selfish, shiftless, thoughtless, unethical, unreliable, unthinking, untrustworthy.
OPPOSITES: SEE **responsible**.

irreverent adjective *irreverent behaviour in church*. blasphemous, disrespectful,

impious, profane, SEE **rude**, sacrilegious.
OPPOSITES: SEE **reverent**.

irreversible adjective 1 *an irreversible decision.* SEE **irrevocable**.
2 *irreversible damage.* SEE **irreparable**.

irrevocable adjective *an irrevocable decision.* binding, final, fixed, hard and fast, immutable, irreversible, settled, unalterable, unchangeable.
OPPOSITE: reversible.

irrigate verb *to irrigate the desert.* flood, inundate, supply water to, water.

irritable adjective *an irritable mood. an irritable person.* SEE **angry**, bad-tempered, cantankerous, choleric, cross, crotchety, dyspeptic, easily annoyed, edgy, fractious, grumpy, ill-tempered, impatient, irascible, oversensitive, peevish, pettish, petulant, [*informal*] prickly, querulous, [*informal*] ratty, short-tempered, snappy, testy, tetchy, touchy, waspish.
OPPOSITES: SEE **even-tempered**.

irritant noun SEE **annoyance**.

irritate verb 1 *Rudeness irritates me.* SEE **annoy**.
2 *These spots irritate.* cause irritation, itch, tickle, tingle.

irritation noun 1 *Our neighbours' noise is a continual irritation.* SEE **annoyance**.
2 *My rash causes an irritation.* itch, pain, tickling, tingling.

island noun atoll, coral reef, isle, islet.
RELATED ADJECTIVE: insular.
group of islands archipelago.

isolate verb 1 *The police isolated the trouble-makers.* cordon off, cut off, keep apart, segregate, separate, single out.
2 *The hospital isolated the infectious patients.* place apart, quarantine, set apart.

isolated adjective 1 *an isolated farmhouse.* deserted, desolate, [*informal*] godforsaken, inaccessible, lonely, [*informal*] off the beaten track, outlying, out of the way, private, remote, secluded, sequestered, solitary, unfrequented.
OPPOSITES: SEE **accessible**.
2 *an isolated case of cheating.* abnormal, exceptional, single, uncommon, unique, untypical, unusual.
OPPOSITES: SEE **common** adjective.

issue noun 1 *political issues.* affair, argument, controversy, dispute, matter, point, problem, question, subject, topic.
2 *an issue of a magazine.* copy, edition, instalment, number, printing, publication.

3 *We awaited the issue of the election.* consequence, effect, end, impact, outcome, repercussions, result, upshot.
4 *The duke died without issue.* SEE **offspring**.

issue verb 1 *Smoke issued from the chimney.* appear, come out, emerge, erupt, flow out, gush, leak, rise, spring.
2 *He issued a formal statement.* bring out, circulate, distribute, give out, print, produce, promulgate, publicize, publish, put out, release, send out, supply.

itch noun 1 *an itch in my foot.* irritation, need to scratch, tickle, tingling.
2 *an itch to do something.* ache, desire, hankering, impatience, impulse, longing, lust, need, restlessness, urge, wish, yearning, [*informal*] yen.

itch verb 1 *My skin itches.* be irritated, tickle, tingle.
2 [*informal*] *We itched to be off.* SEE **want** verb.

item noun 1 *items in a sale. an item on a list.* article, bit, component, contribution, entry, ingredient, lot (*in an auction*), object, single thing, thing.
2 *an item in a newspaper.* account, article, feature, piece, report.

itemize verb SEE **list** verb.

itinerant adjective SEE **travelling**.

itinerary noun SEE **route**.

J

jab verb *to jab someone in the ribs.* elbow, SEE **hit** verb, nudge, poke, prod, stab, thrust.

jabber verb SEE **talk** verb.

jack verb **to jack up** SEE **lift** verb.

jackass noun SEE **donkey**.

jacket noun 1 OTHER COATS: SEE **coat** noun.
2 *a jacket for a book, an insulating jacket.* casing, coat, cover, covering, envelope, folder, sheath, skin, wrapper, wrapping.

jack-knife noun SEE **knife** noun.

jack-knife verb SEE **fold** verb.

jackpot noun SEE **prize** noun.

jaded adjective *jaded by lack of success.* bored, [*informal*] done in, exhausted, [*informal*] fagged, fatigued, [*informal*] fed up, listless, spent, tired out, weary.
OPPOSITES: SEE **lively**.

jagged adjective *a jagged edge.* angular, barbed, broken, indented, irregular, ragged, rough, serrated, sharp, snagged, spiky, toothed, uneven, zigzag. OPPOSITES: SEE **even** adjective.

jail SEE **gaol**.

jalopy noun SEE **car**.

jam noun 1 *a jam on the motorway*. blockage, bottleneck, crowd, crush, press, squeeze, throng, traffic jam.
2 *Help me out of a jam!* difficulty, dilemma, embarrassment, [*informal*] fix, [*informal*] hole, [*informal*] hot water, plight, predicament, quandary, tight corner, trouble.
3 *bread and jam*. conserve, jelly, marmalade, preserve.

jam verb 1 *They jammed us into a minibus*. cram, crowd, crush, pack, ram, squash, squeeze, stuff.
2 *Cars jammed the street*. block, [*informal*] bung up, congest, fill, obstruct, overcrowd, stop up.
3 *Jam the door open*. prop, stick, wedge.

jamboree noun SEE **celebration**.

jangle verb VARIOUS SOUNDS: SEE **sound** noun.

janitor noun SEE **caretaker**.

jar noun *a glass jar*. carafe, SEE **container**, crock, flagon, glass, jug, mug, pitcher, pot, urn, vessel.

jar verb 1 *The nasty noise jarred on me*. SEE **annoy**, grate, grind, [*informal*] jangle.
2 *The impact of the collision jarred me*. jerk, jolt, [*informal*] rattle, shake, shock, upset.

jargon noun *I can't understand the technical jargon*. cant, dialect, idiom, language, slang.

jarring adjective *a jarring noise*. annoying, disagreeable, discordant, grating, grinding, harsh, [*informal*] jangling, raucous, unpleasant.

jaundiced adjective SEE **jealous**.

jaunt noun *to go on a pleasure jaunt*. excursion, expedition, SEE **journey** noun, outing, tour, trip.

jaunty adjective *a jaunty tune*, alert, breezy, bright, carefree, [*informal*] cheeky, debonair, frisky, lively, perky, sprightly.

jaw noun chin, mouth.

jazz noun KINDS OF MUSIC: SEE **music**.

jazzy adjective 1 *jazzy music*. animated, lively, rhythmic, spirited, swinging, syncopated, vivacious.
2 *jazzy colours*. bold, clashing, contrasting, flashy, gaudy, loud.

jealous adjective 1 *He's jealous because I won*. bitter, covetous, envious, [*informal*] green-eyed, grudging, jaundiced, resentful.

2 *He's jealous of his reputation*. careful, possessive, protective, vigilant, watchful.

jeans noun SEE **trousers**.

jeer verb **to jeer at** *It's unkind to jeer at the losers*. barrack, boo, disapprove of, hiss, gibe at, heckle, [*informal*] knock, laugh at, make fun of, mock, ridicule, scoff at, sneer at, taunt.
OPPOSITES: SEE **cheer** verb.

jell verb SEE **harden**.

jelly noun RELATED ADJECTIVE: gelatinous.

jeopardize verb SEE **endanger**.

jeopardy noun SEE **danger**.

jerk verb *Jerk the rope when you are ready*. jog, jolt, move suddenly, pluck, pull, tug, tweak, twist, twitch, wrench, [*informal*] yank.

jerkin noun VARIOUS COATS: SEE **coat** noun.

jerky adjective *jerky movements*. bouncy, bumpy, convulsive, erratic, fitful, jolting, jumpy, rough, shaky, spasmodic, [*informal*] stopping and starting, twitchy, uncontrolled, uneven.
OPPOSITES: SEE **steady** adjective.

jerry-built adjective SEE **shoddy**.

jest noun, verb SEE **joke** noun, verb.

jester noun *the king's jester*. buffoon, clown, comedian, comic, SEE **entertainer**, fool, joker.

jet adjective SEE **black** adjective.

jet noun 1 *a jet of water*. flow, fountain, gush, rush, spout, spray, spurt, squirt, stream.
2 *Direct the jet at the fire*. nozzle, sprinkler.
3 *to fly by jet*. VARIOUS AIRCRAFT: SEE **aircraft**.

jettison verb SEE **discard**.

jetty noun *A boat tied up at the jetty*. breakwater, groyne, landing-stage, mole, pier, quay, wharf.

Jew noun WORDS TO DO WITH JEWISH RELIGION: bar mitzvah, kosher food, Passover, rabbi, sabbath, scripture, synagogue, Yom Kippur.
OTHER RELIGIOUS TERMS: SEE **religion**.

jewel noun gem, gemstone, precious stone.
VARIOUS JEWELS: SEE **jewellery**.

jeweller noun goldsmith.

jewellery noun gems, jewels, ornaments, [*informal*] sparklers, treasure.

ITEMS OF JEWELLERY: bangle, beads, bracelet, brooch, chain, charm, clasp, cufflinks, ear-ring, locket, necklace, pendant, pin, ring, signet-ring, tie-pin, watch-chain.
JEWELS AND JEWELLERY STONES: amber, cairngorm, carnelian or cornelian, coral, diamond, emerald, garnet, ivory, jade, jasper, jet, lapis lazuli, moonstone, onyx, opal, pearl, rhinestone, ruby, sapphire, topaz, turquoise.
METALS USED TO MAKE JEWELLERY: gold, platinum, silver.

jib verb SEE **refuse** verb.

jiffy noun SEE **moment**.

jig noun VARIOUS DANCES: SEE **dance** noun.

jiggery-pokery noun SEE **trickery**.

jiggle verb SEE **fidget**.

jilt verb SEE **abandon**.

jingle noun SEE **song**.

jingle verb *coins jingling in his pocket.* chink, clink, jangle, ring, tinkle.
VARIOUS SOUNDS: SEE **sound** noun.

jingoism noun SEE **patriotism**.

jinx noun SEE **curse** noun.

jittery adjective SEE **nervous**.

jive verb SEE **dance** verb.

job noun 1 *a well-paid job.* business, calling, career, employment, livelihood, occupation, position, post, profession, sinecure, trade, vocation, work.
2 *jobs in the house.* activity, assignment, chore, duty, errand, function, housework, pursuit, responsibility, role, stint, task, work.

SOME JOBS PEOPLE DO: accountant, actuary, air hostess, architect, SEE **artist**, astronomer, astronomer, banker, barber, barmaid or barman, barrister, beautician, blacksmith, bookmaker, bookseller, brewer, bricklayer, broadcaster, builder, butler, cameraman, caretaker, carpenter, cashier, caterer, chauffeur, chef, chimney-sweep, cleaner, clergyman, clerk, coastguard, cobbler, commentator, composer, compositor, conductor, constable, cook, courier, croupier, curator.
decorator, dentist, designer, detective, dietician, diver, driver, docker, doctor, draughtsman, dressmaker, dustman,

editor, electrician, engineer, SEE **entertainer**, estate agent, executive, farmer, farrier, fireman, fitter, forester, frogman, gamekeeper, gardener, glazier, groom, groundsman, gunsmith, hairdresser, handyman, hotelier, industrialist, interpreter, joiner, journalist.
labourer, lawyer, lecturer, lexicographer, librarian, lifeguard, lighterman, linguist, locksmith, longshoreman, lumberjack, machinist, manicurist, mannequin, manufacturer, mason, [*male*] masseur, [*female*] masseuse, mechanic, metallurgist, midwife, milkman, miller, milliner, miner, model, musician [SEE **music**], naturalist, night-watchman, nurse, nurseryman.
office worker, optician, parson, pathologist, pharmacist, photographer, platelayer, physiotherapist, pilot, plasterer, ploughman, plumber, policeman, politician, porter, postman, postmaster, postmistress, printer, probation officer, professor, programmer, projectionist, psychiatrist, psychologist, publisher, radiographer, radiologist, railwayman, receptionist, reporter.
saddler, sailor, salesperson, SEE **scientist**, secretary, shepherd, shoemaker, SEE **shopkeeper**, signalman, social worker, soldier, solicitor, stableman, steeplejack, stevedore, steward, stewardess, stockbroker, stoker, stonemason, stunt man, surgeon, surveyor, tailor, taxidermist, teacher, technician, telephonist, teller, test-pilot, traffic warden, translator, treasurer, typist, undertaker, [*male*] usher, [*female*] usherette, vet, [*male*] waiter, [*female*] waitress, warehouseman, woodman.

jobless adjective SEE **unemployed**.

jockey noun rider.

jockey verb *to jockey for position.* SEE **manoeuvre** verb.

jocular adjective SEE **merry**.

jocund adjective SEE **joyful**.

jog verb 1 *to jog someone's elbow.* SEE **hit** verb, jar, jerk, jolt, knock, nudge.
2 *to jog someone's memory.* prompt, refresh, remind, set off, stimulate, stir.
3 *to jog round the park.* exercise, run, trot.

joggle verb SEE **shake**.

join noun *I can't see the join.* connection, joint, knot, link, mend, seam.

join verb 1 *to join things together.* add, amalgamate, attach, combine, connect, couple, dock, dovetail, SEE **fasten**, fit, fix, knit, link, marry, merge, put together, splice, tack on, unite, yoke.

2 *Two rivers join here.* come together, converge, meet.
OPPOSITES: SEE **separate** verb.
3 *to join a crowd.* follow, go with, [*informal*] latch on to, tag along with.
4 *to join a youth club.* affiliate with, become a member of, enlist in, enrol in, participate in, register for, sign up for, volunteer for.
OPPOSITES: SEE **leave** verb.

joiner noun carpenter.

joint adjective *a joint effort.* collective, combined, common, communal, concerted, co-operative, general, mutual, shared, united.
OPPOSITES: SEE **individual** adjective.

joint noun JOINTS IN YOUR BODY: ankle, elbow, hip, knee, knuckle, shoulder, vertebra, wrist.

joist noun beam, girder, rafter.

joke noun *an amusing joke.* [*informal*] crack, funny story, [*informal*] gag, [*old-fashioned*] jape, jest, pleasantry, pun, quip, wisecrack, witticism.

joke verb be facetious, clown, jest, have a laugh, make jokes [SEE **joke** noun].

joker noun SEE **jester**.

jollification noun SEE **merrymaking**.

jollity noun SEE **merriment**.

jolly adjective SEE **joyful, merry**.

jolt verb **1** *The car jolted over the rough track.* bounce, bump, jar, jerk, jog, shake, twitch.
2 *The noise jolted us into action.* astonish, disturb, nonplus, shock, startle, surprise.

jostle verb *The crowd jostled us.* crowd in on, hustle, press, push, shove.

jot verb *to jot down some notes.* SEE **write**.

jotter noun exercise book, notebook, pad.

journey noun **1** *a trade journal.* gazette, magazine, monthly, newspaper, paper, periodical, publication, weekly.
2 *the journal of a voyage.* account, chronicle, diary, log, record.

journalist noun *a newspaper journalist.* columnist, contributor, correspondent, reporter, writer.

journey noun itinerary, peregrination, route, travels, trip.

KINDS OF JOURNEY: crossing (*sea crossing*), cruise, drive, excursion, expedition, flight, hike, jaunt, joy-ride, mission, odyssey, outing, passage (*a sea passage*), pilgrimage, ramble, ride, run, safari, sail, tour, trek, voyage, walk, wanderings.
SEE ALSO **travel** noun.

journey verb go on a journey [SEE **journey** noun], SEE **travel** verb.

joust noun, verb SEE **fight** noun, verb.

jovial adjective SEE **joyful**.

jowl noun PARTS OF YOUR HEAD: SEE **head** noun.

joy noun bliss, cheerfulness, delight, ecstasy, elation, euphoria, exaltation, exultation, felicity, gaiety, gladness, glee, happiness, hilarity, joyfulness, jubilation, mirth, pleasure, rapture, rejoicing, triumph.
OPPOSITES: SEE **sorrow** noun.

joyful adjective *a joyful occasion, a joyful welcome.* cheerful, delighted, ecstatic, elated, enraptured, euphoric, exultant, gay, glad, gleeful, happy, jocund, jolly, jovial, joyous, jubilant, merry, overjoyed, pleased, rapturous, rejoicing, triumphant.
OPPOSITES: SEE **sad**.

joyless adjective SEE **sad**.

joyous, jubilant adjectives SEE **joyful**.

jubilee noun anniversary, celebration, commemoration, festival.

judge noun **1** *a judge at a sporting event.* adjudicator, arbiter, arbitrator, referee, umpire.
2 *a judge in a lawcourt.* SEE **law**.
3 *a good judge of wines.* connoisseur, critic, expert.

judge verb **1** *to judge someone in a lawcourt.* condemn, convict, examine, pronounce judgement on [SEE **judgement**], punish, sentence, try.
2 *The umpire judged that the ball was out.* adjudicate, conclude, decide, decree, deem, determine, pass judgement, rule.
3 *to judge others. to judge a work of art.* appraise, assess, criticize, evaluate, give your opinion of, rebuke, scold, sit in judgement on.
4 *I judged that the eggs would be cooked.* believe, consider, estimate, gauge, guess, reckon, suppose.

judgement noun **1** *The court pronounced its judgement.* arbitration, award, conclusion, conviction, decision, decree, [*old-fashioned*] doom, finding, outcome, penalty, punishment, result, ruling, verdict.
2 *Use your judgement.* acumen, common sense, discernment, discretion, discrimination, expertise, good sense, SEE **intelligence**, reason, wisdom.

3 *In my judgement, he was driving too fast.* assessment, belief, estimation, evaluation, idea, impression, mind, notion, opinion, point of view, valuation.

judicial adjective [Do not confuse with *judicious.*] *a judicial decision.* legal, official.

judicious adjective [Do not confuse with *judicial.*] *a judicious change of policy.* appropriate, astute, SEE **clever,** diplomatic, expedient, politic, prudent, sensible, shrewd, thoughtful, well judged, wise.

judo noun SEE **martial (martial arts).**

jug noun carafe, SEE **container,** ewer, flagon, jar, pitcher, vessel.

juggle verb *He juggled the figures to make it seem that he'd made a profit.* alter, [*informal*] cook, [*informal*] doctor, falsify, [*informal*] fix, manipulate, move about, rearrange.

juice noun *the juice of an orange.* SEE **drink** noun, fluid, liquid, sap.

juicy adjective *juicy fruit.* full of juice, lush, moist, soft, [*informal*] squelchy, succulent, wet.
OPPOSITES: SEE **dry** adjective.

jumble noun *a jumble of odds and ends.* chaos, clutter, confusion, disorder, farrago, hotchpotch, mess, muddle.
jumble sale SEE **sale.**

jumble verb *Don't jumble the papers I've just sorted.* confuse, disarrange, [*informal*] mess up, mix up, muddle, shuffle, tangle.
OPPOSITES: SEE **organize.**

jumbo noun VARIOUS AIRCRAFT: SEE **aircraft.**

jump noun **1** *a jump in the air.* bounce, bound, hop, leap, pounce, skip, spring, vault.
JUMPS IN ATHLETICS: high jump, long jump, pole vault, triple jump.
2 *The horse easily cleared the last jump.* ditch, fence, gap, gate, hurdle, obstacle.
3 *a jump in prices.* SEE **rise** noun.

jump verb **1** *to jump in the air.* bounce, bound, hop, leap, skip, spring.
2 *to jump a fence.* clear, hurdle, vault.
3 *to jump about.* caper, dance, frisk, frolic, gambol, prance.
4 *The cat jumped on the mouse.* SEE **attack** verb, pounce.
5 *I jumped the boring chapters.* SEE **omit.**
6 *The bang made me jump.* SEE **flinch.**
7 *Prices jumped.* SEE **rise** verb.

jumpy adjective SEE **nervous.**

junction noun *a road junction. a junction between two routes.* confluence (*of two rivers*), corner, crossroads, interchange, intersection, joining, meeting, T-junction.

juncture noun SEE **moment.**

jungle noun *a jungle of vegetation.* forest, tangle, undergrowth, woods.

junior adjective *junior rank.* inferior, lesser, lower, minor, secondary, subordinate, subsidiary, younger.
OPPOSITES: SEE **senior.**

junk noun *a lot of old junk.* clutter, debris, flotsam-and-jetsam, garbage, litter, lumber, oddments, odds and ends, refuse, rubbish, rummage, scrap, trash, waste.

junketing noun SEE **merrymaking.**

junkie noun SEE **addict.**

junta noun SEE **government.**

jurisdiction noun SEE **authority.**

jurisprudence noun law.
LEGAL TERMS: SEE **law.**

just adjective *a just punishment. a just decision.* apt, deserved, equitable, ethical, even-handed, fair, fair-minded, honest, impartial, justified, lawful, legal, legitimate, merited, proper, reasonable, rightful, right-minded, unbiased, unprejudiced, upright.
OPPOSITES: SEE **unjust.**

justice noun **1** *Justice demands that women and men should be paid the same.* equity, fairness, honesty, impartiality, integrity, legality, right.
OPPOSITES: SEE **injustice.**
2 *Lawcourts exist to administer justice.* the law, legal proceedings, punishment, retribution, vengeance.

justifiable adjective *a justifiable course of action.* acceptable, allowable, defensible, excusable, forgivable, justified, lawful, legitimate, pardonable, permissible, reasonable, understandable, warranted.
OPPOSITES: SEE **unjustifiable.**

justify verb *Don't try to justify his wickedness.* condone, defend, [*informal*] exculpate, excuse, exonerate, explain, explain away, forgive, pardon, support, uphold, vindicate, warrant (*Nothing can warrant such cruelty*).

jut verb *The mantelpiece juts over the fireplace.* extend, overhand, poke out, project, protrude, stick out.

juvenile adjective **1** [*uncomplimentary*] *juvenile behaviour.* babyish, childish, immature, infantile, puerile.
OPPOSITES: SEE **mature.**
2 *juvenile novels.* adolescent, young, youthful.

juxtapose verb *When you juxtapose the two, you can see the difference.* SEE **compare**.

K

kaleidoscopic adjective *a kaleidoscopic effect.* brightly coloured, changing, fluctuating, multicoloured, shifting, variegated.

karate noun SEE **martial (martial arts)**.

karma noun SEE **fate**.

kayak noun canoe.

keel verb **to keel over** SEE **capsize**, collapse, lean, tilt.

keen adjective **1** *a keen cutting-edge.* piercing, pointed, razor-sharp, sharp, sharpened.
OPPOSITES: SEE **blunt** adjective.
2 *a keen wit.* biting, cutting, incisive, lively, mordant, satirical, scathing, shrewd, sophisticated.
OPPOSITES: SEE **dull** adjective.
3 *keen eyesight.* acute, clear, perceptive, sensitive.
OPPOSITES: SEE **dim** adjective.
4 *a keen wind.* bitter, cold, extreme, icy, intense, penetrating, severe.
OPPOSITES: SEE **mild**.
5 *keen prices.* competitive, low, rock-bottom.
OPPOSITES: SEE **exorbitant**.
6 *a keen pupil.* ambitious, anxious, assiduous, avid, bright, clever, committed, diligent, eager, enthusiastic, fervent, industrious, intelligent, intent, interested, motivated, quick, zealous.
OPPOSITES: SEE **apathetic**.

keep noun *the keep of a castle.* SEE **castle**.

keep verb **1** *to keep something safe. to keep it for later.* conserve, guard, hang on to, hold, preserve, protect, put aside, put away, retain, safeguard, save, store, stow away, withhold.
OPPOSITES: SEE **lose**, **use** verb.
2 *to keep looking for something.* carry on, continue, do again and again, do for a long time, keep on, persevere in, persist in.
OPPOSITES: SEE **abandon**.
3 *to keep a pet. to keep a shop.* be responsible for, care for, cherish, foster, guard, have, have charge of, look after, manage, mind, own, tend, watch over.
4 *to keep a family.* feed, maintain, pay for, provide for, support.

5 *to keep your birthday.* celebrate, commemorate, mark, observe, [*formal*] solemnize.
6 *How long does milk keep?* be preserved, be usable, last, stay good.
7 *I won't keep you.* block, check, curb, delay, detain, deter, get in the way of, hamper, hinder, hold up, impede, obstruct, prevent, restrain, retard.
to keep an eye open SEE **watch** verb.
to keep still linger, remain, stay.
to keep to *Keep to the rules!* abide by, adhere to, be ruled by, conform to, honour, obey, recognize, submit to.

keeper noun *the keeper of a museum.* curator, custodian, gaoler, guard, guardian, warden, warder.

keepsake noun memento, souvenir.

keg noun SEE **barrel**.

kerb noun SEE **edge** noun.

kerfuffle noun SEE **commotion**.

kernel noun core, heart, middle, nut.

ketchup noun relish, sauce.

kettle noun VARIOUS CONTAINERS: SEE **container**.

kettledrums noun timpani.
OTHER DRUMS: SEE **drum**.

key noun **1** *the key to a problem.* answer, clue, indicator, pointer, secret, solution.
2 *a key to a map.* explanation, glossary, guide, index.

keyboard noun KEYBOARD INSTRUMENTS: accordion, celesta, clavichord, clavier, harmonium, harpsichord, organ, piano, spinet, virginals.
OTHER MUSICAL TERMS: SEE **music**.

keynote noun *the keynote of a speech.* core, emphasis, gist, heart, message, theme.

kibbutz noun SEE **settlement**.

kick noun **1** *a kick at the ball.* SEE **hit** noun.
2 *It gave me a kick to see my story in print.* SEE **thrill** noun.

kick verb **1** *to kick a ball.* boot, heel, SEE **hit** verb, punt.
2 [*informal*] *to kick a habit.* SEE **cease**.

kid verb [*informal*] *Don't try to kid me!* bluff, SEE **deceive**, fool, hoodwink, lie to.

kidnap verb abduct, carry off, run away with, seize, snatch.

kidney noun RELATED ADJECTIVE: renal.

kill verb annihilate, assassinate, be guilty of the killing of [SEE **killing** noun], be the killer of [SEE **killer**], [*informal*] bump off, butcher, cull [= *kill animals* selectively], decimate [see note under *decimate*], destroy, [*informal*] dispatch, [*informal*] do away with, execute, exterminate, [*informal*] finish off, [*informal*] knock off, liquidate, martyr, massacre, murder, put down, put to death, slaughter, slay, take life.

WAYS TO KILL: behead, brain, choke, crucify, decapitate, disembowel, drown, electrocute, eviscerate, garrotte, gas, guillotine, hang, knife, lynch, poison, pole-axe, shoot, smother, stab, starve, stifle, stone, strangle, suffocate, throttle.

---

killer noun assassin, butcher, cut-throat, destroyer, executioner, exterminator, gunman, murderer, slayer.

killing adjective [*informal*] *a killing joke.* SEE **funny**.

killing noun annihilation, assassination, bloodshed, butchery, carnage, decimation [see note under *decimate*], destruction, elimination, eradication, euthanasia, execution, extermination, extinction, fratricide, genocide, homicide, infanticide, liquidation, manslaughter, martyrdom, massacre, matricide, murder, parricide, patricide, pogrom, regicide, slaughter, suicide.

kiln noun SEE **fire** noun.

kin noun SEE **family**.

kind adjective *a kind action. a kind person. a kind remark.* accommodating, affectionate, agreeable, altruistic, amenable, amiable, attentive, avuncular, beneficent, benevolent, benign, bountiful, brotherly, caring, charitable, comforting, compassionate, considerate, cordial, courteous, encouraging, fatherly, favourable, friendly, generous, genial, gentle, good-natured, good-tempered, gracious, helpful, hospitable, humane, indulgent, kind-hearted, kindly, lenient, loving, merciful, mild, motherly, neighbourly, nice, obliging, patient, philanthropic, pleasant, polite, public-spirited, sensitive, sisterly, softhearted, sweet, sympathetic, tactful, tender, thoughtful, understanding, unselfish, warm-hearted, well-intentioned, well-meaning, well-meant. OPPOSITES: SEE **unkind**.

kind noun *a kind of dog. a kind of food. a kind of book.* brand, breed, category, class, description, family, form, genre, genus, make, nature, race, set, sort, species, style, type, variety.

kindle verb 1 *to kindle a fire.* burn, fire, ignite, light, set fire to.

2 *to kindle strong emotions.* SEE **arouse**.

kindling noun firewood.

kindly adjective SEE **kind** adjective.

kindred noun SEE **family**.

king noun SEE **ruler**.

kingdom noun SEE **country**, monarchy, realm.

kingly adjective SEE **regal**.

kink noun *a kink in a rope.* bend, coil, knot, loop, tangle, twist.

kinsman, kinswoman nouns SEE **family**.

kiosk noun 1 *a newspaper kiosk.* bookstall, booth, news-stand, stall.
2 *a telephone kiosk.* telephone box.

kip verb SEE **sleep** verb.

kismet noun SEE **fate**.

kiss verb caress, embrace, SEE **touch** verb.

kit noun *games kit. a wine-making kit. a soldier's kit.* apparatus, baggage, effects, equipment, gear, [*informal*] impedimenta, luggage, outfit, paraphernalia, rig, tackle, tools.

kitchen, kitchenette nouns OTHER ROOMS: SEE **room**.

SOME KITCHEN EQUIPMENT: blender, cooker, SEE **crockery**, SEE **cutlery**, deep-freeze, dish rack, dishwasher, draining-board, extractor-fan, food-processor, freezer, fridge, grill, kettle, liquidizer, microwave-oven, mincer, mixer, oven, pantry, percolator, range, refrigerator, scales, sink, stove, thermos, toaster, tray, vacuum flask.

COOKING UTENSILS: SEE **cook**.

---

kith noun *kith and kin* SEE **family**.

kitsch adjective SEE **tasteless**.

kitten noun SEE **cat**.

kitty noun SEE **fund**.

knack noun *a knack for making friends. a knack for mending machines.* ability, adroitness, art, bent, dexterity, expertise, flair, genius, gift, skill, talent, trick.

knackered adjective SEE **exhausted**.

knapsack noun backpack, haversack, rucksack.

knave noun SEE **scoundrel**.

knead verb *to knead dough.* manipulate, massage, pound, press, pummel, squeeze, work.

kneel verb bend, bow, crouch, fall to your knees, genuflect, stoop.

knell noun SEE **bell**.

knickerbockers noun SEE **trousers**.

knickers noun [old-fashioned] bloomers, boxer-shorts, briefs, drawers, panties, pants, shorts, trunks, underpants.

knife noun KINDS OF KNIFE: butter-knife, carving-knife, clasp-knife, cleaver, dagger, flick-knife, machete, penknife, pocket-knife, scalpel, sheathknife. OTHER CUTLERY: SEE **cutlery**.

knife verb to knife someone. SEE **kill**, slash, stab, wound.

knight noun SEE **fighter**, horseman, warrior.

knit verb 1 to knit a pullover. crochet, weave.
2 to knit together. bind, combine, connect, fasten, interweave, knot, mend, tie, unite.
to knit your brow SEE **frown** verb.

knob noun 1 a door knob. handle.
2 boss, bulge, bump, lump, projection, protuberance, swelling.

knock verb 1 to knock against something. [informal] bash, buffet, bump, SEE **hit** verb, rap, smack, [old-fashioned] smite, strike, tap, thump.
2 to knock someone's work. SEE **criticize**.
to knock off to knock off work. SEE **cease**.
to knock out to knock someone out. make unconscious [SEE **unconscious**].

knock-out noun SEE **victory**.

knoll noun SEE **hill**.

knot noun 1 a knot in a rope. VARIOUS KNOTS: bow, bowline, clovehitch, grannyknot, hitch, noose, reef-knot, sheephank, slipknot.
2 a knot of people. SEE **group** noun.

knot verb to knot ropes together. bind, do up (do up your shoelace), entangle, entwine, SEE **fasten**, join, knit, lash, link, tie, unite. OPPOSITES: SEE **untie**.

know verb 1 to know facts. to know how to do something. comprehend, have experience of, have in mind, remember, understand.
2 to know that you are right. be certain, have confidence.
3 to know what something is. to know who someone is. discern, distinguish, identify, make out, perceive, realize, recognize, see.
4 to know a person. be acquainted with, be familiar with, be a friend of.

know-all noun expert, pundit, [informal] show-off, wiseacre.

know-how noun SEE **knowledge**.

knowing adjective Her knowing smile showed that she understood. artful, astute, aware, clever, crafty, cunning, discerning, experienced, expressive, intelligent, meaningful, perceptive, shrewd, sly, well-informed, wily. OPPOSITES: SEE **innocent**.

knowledge noun 1 An encyclopaedia contains a lot of knowledge. data, facts, information, learning, scholarship, science.
2 She's got enough knowledge to do the job. ability, awareness, background, competence, education, experience, familiarity, grasp, [informal] know-how, learning, lore, skill, talent, technique, training, understanding, wisdom. OPPOSITES: SEE **ignorance**.

knowledgeable adjective knowledgeable about antiques. aware, conversant, educated, erudite, experienced, familiar (with), informed, learned, scholarly, versed (in), well-informed. OPPOSITES: SEE **ignorant**.

knuckleduster noun cosh. OTHER WEAPONS: SEE **weapon**.

kowtow verb SEE **grovel**.

kung fu noun SEE **martial** (martial arts).

L

label noun a label on a parcel. docket, marker, sticker, tag, ticket.

label verb We labelled him as a troublemaker. brand, call, categorize, class, classify, define, describe, identify, mark, name, stamp.

laborious adjective a laborious climb. laborious effort. arduous, back-breaking, difficult, exhausting, fatiguing, gruelling, hard, heavy, onerous, stiff, strenuous, tiresome, tough, uphill, wearisome. OPPOSITES: SEE **easy**.

labour noun 1 You deserve a reward for your labour. [informal] donkey-work, drudgery, effort, exertion, industry, [informal] pains, toil, SEE **work** noun.
2 Because of increased orders, the firm took on extra labour. employees, [old-fashioned] hands, workers, workforce.
3 [= giving birth to a baby] childbirth, contractions, delivery, labour pains, [old-fashioned] travail.
the **Labour Party** POLITICAL TERMS: SEE **politics**.

labour verb drudge, exert yourself, [*informal*] slave away, [*informal*] sweat, toil, SEE **work** verb, work hard.

labourer noun SEE **worker**.

labour-saving adjective *labour-saving tools.* convenient, handy, helpful, time-saving.

labyrinth noun *a labyrinth of corridors.* complex, jungle, maze, network, tangle.

lace noun 1 *lace curtains.* filigree, net, tatting.
VARIOUS FABRICS: SEE **cloth**.
2 *a lace for your shoe.* cord, string, thong.

lace verb SEE **fasten**.

lacerate verb *to lacerate your skin.* claw, graze, mangle, rip, scrape, scratch, tear, SEE **wound** verb.

lachrymose adjective SEE **tearful**.

lack noun *a lack of food. a lack of self-confidence.* absence, dearth, deprivation, famine, need, paucity, privation, scarcity, shortage, want.
OPPOSITES: SEE **plenty**.

lack verb *The game lacked excitement.* be deficient in, be short of, be without, miss, need, require, want.

lackadaisical adjective SEE **apathetic**.

lackey noun SEE **servant**.

lacking adjective 1 *lacking in courage.* defective, deficient, inadequate, short, unsatisfactory, wanting, weak.
2 [*informal*] *He's a bit lacking.* SEE **stupid**.

laconic adjective SEE **terse**.

lacquer noun SEE **paint** noun.

lad noun SEE **boy**.

ladder noun fire-escape, step-ladder, steps.

laden adjective *laden with shopping.* burdened, fraught, full, hampered, loaded, oppressed, weighed down.

lading noun SEE **cargo**.

lady noun SEE **woman**.

ladylike adjective *ladylike behaviour.* dainty, genteel, modest, SEE **polite**, posh, prim and proper, [*uncomplimentary*] prissy, refined, respectable, well-bred.

lag verb 1 *to lag behind.* [*informal*] bring up the rear, come last, dally, dawdle, drop behind, fall behind, go too slow, hang about, idle, linger, loiter, saunter, straggle, trail.
2 *to lag water-pipes.* insulate, wrap up.

lager noun ale, beer.

lagoon noun SEE **lake**.

laid-back adjective SEE **easygoing**.

lair noun *an animal's lair.* den, hide-out, hiding-place, refuge, retreat, shelter.

lake noun boating-lake, lagoon, lido, (*Scottish*) loch, mere, pond, pool, reservoir, sea, tarn, water.

lam verb SEE **hit** verb.

lamb noun SEE **sheep**.

lama noun SEE **priest**.

lambast, lambaste verb SEE **hit** verb.

lame adjective 1 *a lame person.* crippled, disabled, SEE **handicapped**, incapacitated, maimed.
2 *a lame leg.* dragging, game (*a game leg*), [*informal*] gammy, injured, limping, stiff.
3 *a lame excuse.* feeble, flimsy, inadequate, poor, tame, thin, unconvincing, weak.
to be lame SEE **limp** verb.

lame verb *The accident temporarily lamed him.* cripple, disable, incapacitate, make limp [SEE **limp** verb], maim.

lament noun *a lament for the dead.* dirge, elegy, lamentation, monody, requiem, threnody.

lament verb *to lament the passing of someone or something.* bemoan, bewail, complain about, deplore, express your sorrow about, grieve about, mourn, regret, shed tears for, wail, weep.

lamentable adjective SEE **regrettable**.

lamentation noun *the lamentation of mourners at a funeral.* complaints, grief, SEE **lament** noun, mourning, regrets, tears, wailing, weeping.

laminated adjective *laminated chipboard.* coated, covered, layered, veneered.

lamp noun SEE **light** noun.

lampoon verb SEE **ridicule** verb.

lance noun javelin, spear, SEE **weapon**.

land noun 1 *Surveyors mapped out the lie of the land.* geography, landscape, terrain, topography.
2 *your native land.* country, nation, region, state, territory.
3 *land to grow things on.* farmland, earth, ground, soil.
4 *land belonging to a person.* estate, grounds, property.
5 *The sailors came to land.* coast, landfall, shore, [*joking*] terra firma.

land verb *to land from an aircraft, ship, or vehicle.* alight, arrive, berth, come ashore, disembark, dock, end a journey, get down, reach landfall, touch down.

landing noun 1 *the landing of an aircraft or spacecraft.* re-entry, return, touchdown.

2 *the landing of passengers.* SEE **arrival,** disembarkation.

landing-stage noun berth, dock, harbour, jetty, landing, quay, wharf.

landing-strip noun SEE **airfield.**

landlady, landlord nouns **1** *the landlady or landlord of a pub.* hotelier, [*oldfashioned*] innkeeper, licensee, publican.
2 *the landlady or landlord of rented property.* landowner, letter, owner, proprietor.

landmark noun **1** *a landmark in the countryside.* feature, high point, visible feature.
2 *a landmark in history.* milestone, new era, turning point.

landscape noun *a painting of a landscape.* countryside, outlook, panorama, prospect, rural scene, scene, scenery, view, vista.

landslide adjective *a landslide victory.* SEE **overwhelming.**

landslide noun avalanche, landslip.

lane noun SEE **road.**

language noun **1** *the language we speak. foreign languages.* [*informal*] lingo, speech, tongue.
2 *language of particular people or of particular situations.* argot, cant, colloquialism, dialect, formal language, idiolect, idiom, informal language, jargon, journalese, lingua franca, patois, register, slang, vernacular.
3 *a computer language.* code, system of signs.

EVERYDAY LINGUISTIC TERMS: accent, active verb or voice, adjective, adverb, clause, conjunction, consonant, grammar, indicative mood, noun, paragraph, passive verb or voice, phrase, plural, predicate, prefix, preposition, pronoun, SEE **punctuation,** sentence, singular, subject, subjunctive mood, suffix, syllable, synonym, syntax, tense, verb, vocabulary, vowel, word.

ASPECTS OF THE STUDY OF LANGUAGE: etymology, lexicography, linguistics, orthography, philology, phonetics, psycholinguistics, semantics, semiotics, sociolinguistics.

languid adjective [*uncomplimentary*] *His languid manner annoys me when there's work to be done.* apathetic, [*informal*] droopy, feeble, inactive, inert, lackadaisical, lazy, lethargic, slow, sluggish, torpid, unenthusiastic, weak.
OPPOSITES: SEE **energetic.**

languish verb *He languished after his dog died. Our project languished during the holidays.* become languid [SEE **languid**], decline, flag, lose momentum, mope, pine, slow down, stagnate, suffer, sulk, waste away, weaken, wither.
OPPOSITES: SEE **flourish** verb.

lank adjective **1** [*uncomplimentary*] *lank hair.* drooping, lifeless, limp, long, straight, thin.
2 *a lank figure.* SEE **lanky.**

lanky adjective [*uncomplimentary*] *a lanky figure.* angular, awkward, bony, gangling, gaunt, lank, lean, long, scraggy, scrawny, skinny, tall, thin, ungraceful, weedy.
OPPOSITES: SEE **graceful, sturdy.**

lantern noun SEE **light** noun.

lap noun **1** *Sit on my lap.* knees, thighs.
2 *a lap of a racetrack.* circle, circuit, course, orbit.

lap verb SEE **drink** verb.

lapse noun **1** *a lapse of memory. a lapse in behaviour.* backsliding, error, fault, flaw, mistake, relapse, shortcoming, slip, temporary failure, weakness.
2 *a lapse in a training programme.* break, gap, interruption, interval, lull, pause.

lapse verb **1** *to lapse from your normal standard of work.* decline, deteriorate, drop, fall, slide, slip.
2 *My membership has lapsed.* become invalid [SEE **invalid** adjective], expire, finish, run out, stop.

larceny noun SEE **stealing.**

larder noun food cupboard, pantry.

large adjective [The meaning of *large* is relative. You can speak of *a large ant* and *a small elephant,* but you are not really confused about which is larger in size! The words listed here are just some of the many words which can mean *larger than average for its kind.*] above average, abundant, ample, big, bold (*bold handwriting*), broad, bulky, capacious, colossal, commodious, considerable, copious, elephantine, enormous, extensive, [*informal*] fat (*a fat increase*), formidable, gargantuan, generous, giant, gigantic, grand, great, heavy, hefty, high, huge, [*informal*] hulking, immeasurable, immense, impressive, incalculable, infinite, [*informal*] jumbo, [*informal*] kingsized, large, largish, lofty, long, mammoth, massive, mighty, [*informal*] monstrous, monumental, mountainous, outsize, overgrown, oversized, prodigious, [*informal*] roomy, sizeable, spacious, substantial, swingeing (*a swingeing increase*), tall, thick, [*informal*] thumping,

[*informal*] tidy (*a tidy sum*), titanic, towering, tremendous, vast, voluminous, weighty, [*informal*] whacking, [*informal*] whopping, wide.
OPPOSITES: SEE **small**.

largess noun SEE **generosity**.

lariat noun lasso, SEE **rope** noun.

larva noun caterpillar, grub, maggot.

larynx noun throat, vocal cords.

lasagne noun SEE **pasta**.

lascivious adjective SEE **lustful**.

laser noun SEE **light** noun.

lash noun SEE **whip** noun.

lash verb 1 *to lash with a whip*. SEE **whip** verb.
2 *to lash with your tongue*. SEE **criticize**.
3 *to lash with rope*. SEE **fasten**.

lass noun SEE **girl**.

lassitude noun SEE **tiredness**.

lasso noun lariat, SEE **rope** noun.

last adjective 1 *last in the queue*. furthest, hindmost.
OPPOSITES: SEE **first**.
2 *Z is the last letter of the alphabet*. closing, concluding, final, terminal, terminating, ultimate.
OPPOSITES: SEE **initial**.
3 *What was his last record called?* latest, most recent.
OPPOSITES: SEE **next**.

last verb *I hope the fine weather lasts*. carry on, continue, endure, hold, hold out, keep on, linger, live, persist, remain, stay, survive, wear (*These jeans have worn well*).

lasting adjective *a lasting friendship*. abiding, continuing, durable, enduring, indestructible, indissoluble, lifelong, long-lasting, long-lived, long-standing, permament, stable, unchanging, undying, unending.
OPPOSITES: SEE **temporary**.

last-minute adjective *a last-minute dash for the bus*. belated, eleventh-hour, late.
OPPOSITES: SEE **early**.

latch noun *the latch on a door*. bolt, catch, SEE **fastener**, lock.

late adjective 1 *The bus is late*. behindhand, belated, delayed, dilatory, overdue, slow, tardy, unpunctual.
OPPOSITES: SEE **early**.
2 *the late king*. dead, deceased, departed, former.

lately adverb latterly, recently.

latent adjective *latent talent*. dormant, hidden, invisible, potential, undeveloped, undiscovered.

later adjective SEE **following**.

lateral adjective *lateral shoots on a plant*. side, sideways.

lather noun *soapy lather*. bubbles, foam, froth, suds.

latitude noun *He gives his students latitude to express themselves*. [*informal*] elbow-room, freedom, leeway, liberty, room, scope, space.

latrine noun SEE **lavatory**.

latter adjective *The latter part of the speech became tedious*. closing, concluding, last, later, recent, second.
OPPOSITES: SEE **former**.

lattice noun *honeysuckle growing over a lattice*. criss-cross, framework, grid, mesh, trellis.

laud verb SEE **praise** verb.

laudable adjective SEE **praiseworthy**.

laudanum noun opium.

laudatory adjective SEE **complimentary**.

laugh verb WAYS TO EXPRESS AMUSEMENT: beam, burst into laughter [SEE **laughter**], chortle, chuckle, giggle, grin, guffaw, simper, smile, smirk, sneer, snigger, titter.
to laugh at SEE **ridicule** verb.

laughable adjective *The play was a tragedy, but the acting was laughable*. absurd, derisory, SEE **funny**, ludicrous, preposterous, ridiculous.

laughing-stock noun *His eccentric ways made him a laughing-stock*. butt, figure of fun, victim.

laughter noun *Their performance caused a lot of laughter*. chuckling, giggling, guffaws, hilarity, [*informal*] hysterics, laughing, laughs, merriment, mirth, sniggering, tittering.

launch noun 1 *a seagoing launch*. VARIOUS VESSELS: SEE **vessel**.
2 *the launch of a rocket*. blast-off, launching.

launch verb 1 *to launch a ship*. float.
2 *to launch a rocket*. blast off, fire, propel, send off, set off.
3 *to launch a new business*. begin, embark on, establish, found, inaugurate, initiate, open, set up, start.

launder verb *to launder clothes*. clean, wash.

laundry noun *to do the laundry*. washing.

lavatory noun cloakroom, convenience, latrine, [*informal*] loo, [*childish*] potty, [*old-fashioned*] privy, public convenience, toilet, urinal, water-closet, WC.

lavish adjective *a lavish supply of food*. abundant, bountiful, copious, extravagant, exuberant, generous, liberal, luxuriant, luxurious, munificent, opulent,

plentiful, prodigal, sumptuous, unstinting, wasteful.
OPPOSITES: SEE **economical**.

law noun 1 *the laws of the land.* act, bill [=*draft of a proposed law*], commandment, decree, edict, order, pronouncement, statute.
2 *the laws of a game.* code, principle, regulation, rule.
3 *a court of law.* justice, litigation.
RELATED ADJECTIVES: legal, litigious.

EVENTS IN A COURT OF LAW: action, case, court martial, hearing, inquest, lawsuit, litigation, proceedings, suit, trial.

PEOPLE INVOLVED IN LEGAL AFFAIRS: accused, advocate, attorney, bailiff, barrister, clerk, coroner, counsel for the defence, counsel for the prosecution, defendant, judge, juror, lawyer, magistrate, plaintiff, police, prosecutor, solicitor, usher, witness.

SOME EVERYDAY LEGAL TERMS: accusation, arrest, bail, the bar, the bench, charge, court, dock, evidence, judgement, jurisprudence, lawcourt, litigant, notary public, plea, probate, SEE **punishment**, remand, sentence, statute, sue, summons, testimony, tort, verdict.

law-abiding adjective *law-abiding citizens.* compliant, decent, disciplined, good, honest, obedient, orderly, peaceable, peaceful, respectable, well-behaved.
OPPOSITES: SEE **lawless**.

lawful adjective 1 *It isn't lawful to steal.* allowable, allowed, authorized, just, permissible, permitted, right.
2 *Who's the lawful owner of this car?* documented, legal, legitimate, prescribed, proper, recognized, regular, rightful, valid.
OPPOSITES: SEE **illegal**.

lawless adjective *a lawless mob.* anarchic, anarchical, badly behaved, chaotic, disobedient, disorderly, ill-disciplined, insubordinate, mutinous, rebellious, riotous, rowdy, seditious, turbulent, uncontrolled, undisciplined, ungoverned, unrestrained, unruly, wild.
OPPOSITES: SEE **law-abiding**.

lawlessness noun *lawlessness in the streets.* anarchy, chaos, disobedience, disorder, mob-rule, rebellion, rioting.
OPPOSITES: SEE **order** noun.

lawn noun green, mown grass.

lawsuit, lawyer nouns SEE **law**.

lax adjective *lax morals. lax discipline.* careless, casual, SEE **easygoing**, lenient, loose, neglectful, negligent, permissive, remiss, slack, unreliable, vague.
OPPOSITES: SEE **strict**.

laxative noun aperient, enema, purgative.

lay verb 1 *Lay your work on the table. Lay the paint on thickly.* apply, arrange, deposit, leave, place, position, put down, rest, set down, set out, spread.
2 *Don't lay all the blame on her.* ascribe, assign, burden, impose, plant, [*informal*] saddle.
3 *We laid secret plans.* concoct, create, design, establish, organize, plan, set up. [*Lay* is also past tense of the verb *to lie: I lay down yesterday evening for a rest.* It is often used wrongly as present tense. Do NOT say *Let's lay down and have a rest* but *Let's lie* . . .]
to lay bare SEE **reveal**.
to lay down the law SEE **dictate**.
to lay into someone SEE **attack** verb.
to lay someone low SEE **defeat** verb.
to lay someone off SEE **dismiss**.
to lay off something SEE **cease**.
to lay to rest SEE **bury**.
to lay up SEE **store** verb.
to lay waste SEE **destroy**.

layabout noun SEE **loafer**.

layer noun 1 *a layer of paint.* coat, coating, covering, film, sheet, skin, surface, thickness.
2 *a layer of rock.* seam, stratum, substratum.
in layers laminated, layered, sandwiched, stratified.

layer verb *to layer plants.* SEE **propagate**.

layman noun 1 *A layman shouldn't do electrical work.* amateur, untrained person.
OPPOSITES: SEE **professional**.
2 *laymen of the church.* layperson, member of the congregation, parishioner, unordained person.
OPPOSITES: SEE **clergyman**.

layout noun SEE **arrangement**.

laze verb *to laze in the sun.* be lazy [SEE **lazy**], do nothing, lie about, loaf, lounge, relax, sit about, unwind.

laziness noun dilatoriness, idleness, inactivity, indolence, lethargy, loafing, lounging about, sloth, slowness, sluggishness.
OPPOSITES: SEE **industry**.

lazy adjective 1 *a lazy worker.* easily pleased, idle, inactive, indolent, languid, lethargic, listless, shiftless, [*informal*] skiving, slack, slothful, slow, sluggish, torpid, unenterprising, work-shy.
OPPOSITES: SEE **industrious**.

2 *a lazy holiday.* peaceful, quiet, relaxing.
OPPOSITES: SEE **energetic**.
to be lazy idle, laze, loaf, malinger, shirk, [*informal*] skive.
a lazy person [*informal*] good-for-nothing, malingerer, [*informal*] skiver, slacker, sluggard.

lead noun 1 [pronounced *led*] *lead pipes.* METALS: SEE **metal**.
2 [pronounced *leed*] *We looked to the captain for a lead.* direction, example, guidance, leadership.
3 [*informal*] *The police hoped for a lead on the crime.* clue, hint, line, tip, tip-off.
4 *She was in the lead from the start.* first place, front position, spearhead, vanguard.
5 *the lead in a play or film.* chief part, starring role, title role.
6 *an electrical lead.* cable, flex, wire.
7 *a dog's lead.* chain, leash, strap.

lead verb 1 *to lead someone in a certain direction.* conduct, draw, escort, guide, influence, pilot, steer, usher.
OPPOSITES: SEE **follow**.
2 *to lead an expedition.* be in charge of, command, direct, govern, head, manage, preside over, rule, supervise.
3 *to lead in a race.* be in front, be in the lead, head the field.

leaden adjective *leaden skies.* SEE **grey**.

leader noun 1 LEADERS IN VARIOUS SITUATIONS: ayatollah, boss, captain, chief, chieftain, commander, conductor, courier, demagogue, director, figure-head, godfather, guide, head, patriarch, premier, prime minister, principal, ringleader, SEE **ruler**, superior, [*informal*] supremo.
2 *a leader in a newspaper.* editorial, leading article.

leading adjective *a leading figure in politics.* SEE **chief** adjective, dominant, foremost, important, inspiring, outstanding, prominent, well-known.

leaf noun 1 *leaves of a plant.* blade (*of grass*), foliage, frond, greenery.
2 *leaves in a book.* folio, page, sheet.

leaflet noun *an advertising leaflet.* booklet, brochure, circular, handout, pamphlet.

league noun *a football league.* SEE **group** noun.
to be in league with SEE **conspire**.

leak noun *a leak in a bucket.* crack, drip, hole, opening, perforation, puncture.

leak verb 1 *to leak water or oil.* drip, escape, exude, ooze, percolate, seep, spill, trickle.

2 *to leak secrets.* disclose, divulge, give away, let out, make known, pass on, reveal.

leaky adjective cracked, dripping, holed, perforated, punctured.
OPPOSITES: SEE **watertight**.

lean adjective 1 *a lean figure.* bony, emaciated, gaunt, lanky, skinny, slender, slim, spare, thin, wiry.
OPPOSITES: SEE **fat** adjective.
2 *lean meat.* OPPOSITE: fatty.

lean verb 1 *to lean to one side.* bank, heel over, incline, list, loll, slant, slope, tilt, tip.
2 *to lean against the fence.* prop yourself up, recline, rest, support yourself.

leaning noun *a leaning towards science. a leaning towards vegetarianism.* bent, bias, inclination, instinct, liking, partiality, penchant, predilection, preference, propensity, readiness, taste, tendency, trend.

leap verb 1 *to leap in the air.* bound, clear (*clear a fence*), jump, leap-frog, spring, vault.
2 *to leap on someone.* ambush, attack, pounce.
3 *to leap for joy.* caper, cavort, dance, frisk, gambol, hop, prance.

learn verb *At school, you learn facts and skills.* acquire, assimilate, become aware of, be taught [SEE **teach**], discover, find out, gain, gain understanding of, gather, grasp, master, memorize, [*informal*] mug up, pick up, remember, study, [*informal*] swot up.

learned adjective *a learned professor.* academic, clever, cultured, educated, erudite, highbrow, intellectual, SEE **knowledgeable**, scholarly.

learner noun apprentice, beginner, cadet, L-driver, novice, pupil, scholar, starter, student, trainee, tiro.

learning noun *a person of great learning.* culture, education, erudition, information, knowledge, scholarship, wisdom.

lease noun SEE **contract** noun.

lease verb SEE **rent** verb.

leash noun *a dog's leash.* chain, lead, strap.

least adjective *the least amount. least in importance. least in number.* fewest, lowest, minimum, negligible, poorest, slightest, smallest, tiniest.

leather noun chamois, hide, skin, suede.

leathery adjective SEE **tough**.

leave noun 1 *Will you give me leave to speak?* authorization, liberty, permission.

2 *leave from the army.* absence, free time, holiday, sabbatical, time off, vacation.
to take your leave SEE **leave** verb.

leave verb **1** *I have to leave.* depart, go away, go out, [*informal*] pull out, run away, say goodbye, set off, take your leave, withdraw.
OPPOSITES: SEE **arrive, enter.**
2 *The rats left the sinking ship.* abandon, desert, evacuate, forsake, vacate.
3 *I left my job.* [*informal*] chuck in, give up, quit, relinquish, resign from, retire from, [*informal*] walk out of.
4 *Leave it where it is.* allow (it) to stay, let (it) alone, [*informal*] let (it) be.
5 *She left me some money in her will.* bequeath, hand down, will.
6 *Leave the milk bottles by the front door.* deposit, place, position, put down, set down.
7 *Leave the arrangements to me.* consign, entrust, refer.
8 *to leave the stage.* exeunt [= *they go out*], exit [= *she or he goes out*].
to leave off SEE **stop** verb.
to leave out SEE **omit** verb.

leaven verb SEE **lighten.**

lecherous adjective SEE **lustful.**

lectern noun reading-desk.

lecture noun **1** *a lecture on science.* address, discourse, lesson, speech, talk.
2 *a lecture on bad manners.* SEE **reprimand** noun.

lecture verb **1** *I lecture at a polytechnic.* be a lecturer [SEE **lecturer**], teach.
2 *He lectured on an interesting topic.* discourse, give a lecture, [*informal*] hold forth, speak, talk formally.
3 *She lectured us on our bad manners.* SEE **reprimand** verb.

lecturer noun *a college lecturer.* don, fellow, instructor, professor, speaker, teacher, tutor.

ledge noun projection, ridge, shelf, sill, step, window-sill.

lee noun SEE **shelter** noun.

leer noun, verb FACIAL EXPRESSIONS: SEE **expression.**

lees noun SEE **sediment.**

leeward adjective SEE **sheltered.**

leeway noun SEE **latitude.**

left adjective, noun **1** *on the left side.* left-hand, port [= *left side of a ship when you face the bow*].
2 *the left in politics.* communist, Labour, leftist, left-wing, liberal, Marxist, progressive, radical, revolutionary, socialist.
OPPOSITES: SEE **right** adjective, noun.

leg noun **1** lower limb, [*informal*] pin (*unsteady on his pins*), shank.
PARTS OF YOUR LEG: ankle, calf, foot, hock, knee, shin, thigh.
WORDS TO DESCRIBE PEOPLE'S LEGS: bandy, bandy-legged, bow-legged, knock-kneed.
2 *a leg of a table.* prop, support, upright.
3 *a leg of a journey.* lap, part, section, stage.
to pull someone's leg SEE **hoax** verb.

legacy noun *a legacy bequeathed in a will.* bequest, endowment, estate, inheritance.

legal adjective **1** *legal proceedings.* judicial.
2 *I'm the legal owner of my car.* aboveboard, allowable, allowed, authorized, constitutional, lawful, legalized, legitimate, licensed, permissible, permitted, regular, rightful, valid.
OPPOSITES: SEE **illegal.**

legalize verb *They won't ever legalize the drugs trade.* allow, legitimize, license, make legal [SEE **legal**], normalize, permit, regularize.
OPPOSITES: SEE **ban** verb.

legate noun SEE **ambassador.**

legend noun SEE **story.**

CREATURES YOU READ ABOUT IN LEGENDS: brownie, centaur, chimera, dragon, dwarf, elf, fairy, faun, giant, gnome, goblin, griffin, imp, leprechaun, leviathan, mermaid, monster, nymph, ogre, phoenix, pixie, troll, unicorn, vampire, werewolf, witch, wizard.

legendary adjective **1** *Unicorns are legendary beasts.* apocryphal, fabled, fabulous, fictional, fictitious, invented, made-up, mythical, non-existent, story-book.
OPPOSITES: SEE **real.**
2 *Presley is a legendary name in the pop world.* SEE **famous.**

legible adjective *legible handwriting.* clear, decipherable, distinct, intelligible, neat, plain, readable.
OPPOSITES: SEE **illegible.**

legitimate adjective **1** *The solicitor said it was legitimate to sell the house.* SEE **legal.**
OPPOSITES: SEE **illegal.**
2 *Do you believe it's legitimate to copy his ideas?* ethical, just, justifiable, moral, proper, reasonable, right.
OPPOSITES: SEE **immoral.**
3 *a legitimate child* = *a child born within a legal marriage.*
OPPOSITES: SEE **illegitimate.**

legitimize verb SEE **legalize**.

leg-pull noun SEE **hoax** noun.

leisure noun *Most people enjoy their leisure.* ease, holiday time, liberty, recreation, relaxation, rest, spare time, time off.

leisurely adjective *a leisurely walk.* easy, gentle, lingering, peaceful, relaxed, relaxing, restful, SEE **slow** adjective, unhurried.
OPPOSITES: SEE **brisk**.

lend verb *to lend money.* advance, loan.
OPPOSITES: SEE **borrow**.

length noun 1 *the length of a piece of string.* distance, extent, measurement, stretch.
2 *the length of a piece of music.* duration, period, time.

lengthen verb *The days lengthen in spring. You can lengthen the ladder if you need to.* draw out, enlarge, elongate, expand, extend, get longer, increase, make longer, prolong, pull out, stretch.
OPPOSITES: SEE **shorten**.

lengthy adjective SEE **long** adjective.

lenient adjective *a lenient teacher.* easy-going, forgiving, indulgent, kind, merciful, mild, soft, soft-hearted, tolerant.
OPPOSITES: SEE **strict**.

lens adjective SEE **optical instruments**.

lesbian adjective, noun SEE **homosexual**.

lesion noun SEE **wound** noun.

lessen verb 1 *The ointment will lessen the pain.* assuage, cut, deaden, decrease, lower, make less, minimize, mitigate, reduce, tone down.
2 *The pain lessened.* abate, become less, decline, decrease, die away, diminish, dwindle, ease off, moderate, slacken, subside, tail off, weaken.
OPPOSITES: SEE **increase** verb.

less adjective fewer, smaller.
OPPOSITES: SEE **more**.

lesson noun 1 *Pupils are expected to attend lessons.* class, lecture, seminar, tutorial.
2 *Let that be a lesson to you!* example, moral, SEE **reprimand** noun, warning.
to teach someone a lesson SEE **reprimand** verb.

let verb 1 *You let it happen. Let him have it.* agree to, allow, consent to, give permission to, permit.
OPPOSITES: SEE **forbid, object** verb.
2 *a house to let.* hire, lease, rent.
to let alone, to let be *Let the poor creature alone!* allow to stay, leave, leave untouched.
to let go, to let loose *to let prisoners go. to let animals loose.* free, liberate, release.

to let off *to let off fireworks.* detonate, discharge, explode, fire, set off.
to let someone off *to let an accused person off.* acquit, excuse, exonerate.

let-down noun *After all the publicity, the film was a bit of a let-down.* anti-climax, disappointment, [*informal*] wash-out.

lethal adjective *a lethal dose of a drug.* deadly, fatal, mortal, poisonous.

lethargic adjective *The fumes made us feel lethargic.* apathetic, inactive, languid, lazy, listless, SEE **sleepy**, slow, sluggish, torpid.
OPPOSITES: SEE **energetic**.

lethargy noun apathy, laziness, listlessness, slowness, sluggishness, torpor.

letter noun 1 *the letters of the alphabet.* character, consonant, vowel.
2 *a letter to a friend.* [*old-fashioned*] billet-doux, card, SEE **communication**, [*formal*] dispatch, [*formal or joking*] epistle, message, [*joking*] missive, note, postcard.
letters correspondence, mail, post.

letter-box noun pillar-box, post-box.

level adjective 1 *a level surface.* even, flat, flush, horizontal, plane, regular, smooth, uniform.
OPPOSITES: SEE **uneven**.
2 *level scores.* balanced, equal, even, matching, [*informal*] neck-and-neck, the same.

level noun 1 *floods at a dangerous level. prices at a high level.* altitude, depth, height, value.
2 *the first level of an exam.* grade, stage, standard.
3 *promotion to a higher level.* degree, echelon, plane, position, rank, [*informal*] rung on the ladder, standing, status.
4 *rooms on the ground level.* floor, storey.

level verb 1 *We levelled the ground to make a lawn.* bulldoze, even out, flatten, rake, smooth.
2 *An earthquake levelled the town.* demolish, destroy, devastate, knock down, lay low, raze.

level-headed adjective SEE **sensible**.

lever verb *to lever open a box.* force, prise, wrench.

levitate verb SEE **rise** verb.

levity noun SEE **frivolity**.

levy noun SEE **tax** noun.

lewd adjective SEE **obscene**.

lexicon noun dictionary, glossary, vocabulary.

liable adjective 1 *The drunken driver was held to be liable for the accident.* accountable, answerable, responsible.
2 *I'm liable to fall asleep in the evenings.* disposed, inclined, likely, predisposed, prone, ready, willing.
OPPOSITES: SEE **unlikely**.

liaise verb SEE **mediate**.

liaison noun 1 *liaison between business interests.* communication, co-operation, liaising, links, mediation.
2 *a liaison between a man and a woman.* SEE **love** noun (**love affair**).

liar noun deceiver, [*informal*] fibber, [*formal*] perjurer, [*informal*] story-teller.

libel noun, verb SEE **slander** noun, verb.
[A *libel* is a slander published in a book, newspaper, etc.]

libellous adjective SEE **slanderous**.

liberal adjective 1 *a liberal supply of food.* abundant, ample, bounteous, bountiful, copious, generous, lavish, munificent, plentiful, unstinting.
OPPOSITES: SEE **mean** adjective.
2 *liberal attitudes.* broad-minded, charitable, easygoing, enlightened, fair-minded, humanitarian, indulgent, lenient, magnanimous, permissive, tolerant, unbiased, unprejudiced.
OPPOSITES: SEE **narrow-minded**.
3 *liberal political views.* progressive, radical.
OPPOSITES: SEE **conservative** adjective.
The Liberal Party POLITICAL TERMS: SEE **politics**.

liberalize verb *to liberalize the laws on drinking.* make more liberal, relax, soften.

liberate verb *to liberate prisoners.* discharge, emancipate, free, let out, loose, ransom, release, rescue, save, set free, untie.
OPPOSITES: SEE **enslave, imprison**.

libertine noun SEE **immoral** (**immoral person**).

liberty noun *liberty from slavery. liberty to do what you want.* emancipation, freedom, independence, liberation, release.
at liberty SEE **free** adjective.
civil liberties privileges, rights.

libido noun SEE **lust**.

licence noun 1 *a TV licence.* certificate, document, permit, warrant.
2 *licence to do as you please.* SEE **permission**.

license verb 1 *The authorities license certain shops to sell tobacco.* allow, authorize, empower, entitle, give a licence to, permit.

2 *to license a car.* buy a licence for, make legal.

licentious adjective SEE **lustful**.

lick verb 1 *to lick a lollipop.* suck.
2 [*informal*] *to lick the opposition.* SEE **defeat** verb.

lid noun *the lid of a container.* cap, cover, covering, top.

lie noun *His lies didn't fool us.* deceit, dishonesty, disinformation, fabrication, falsehood, falsification, [*informal*] fib, fiction, invention, untruth.
OPPOSITES: SEE **truth**.

lie verb 1 *to lie in order to deceive.* be economical with the truth, bluff, SEE **deceive**, falsify the facts, [*informal*] fib, perjure yourself.
2 *to lie on a bed.* be horizontal, be prone [= *lie face downwards*], be supine [= *lie face upwards*], lean back, lounge, recline, repose, rest, sprawl, stretch out.
3 *The house lies in a valley.* be, be found, be located, be situated, exist.
to lie low SEE **hide** verb.

life noun 1 *life on earth.* being, existence.
2 *full of life.* activity, animation, energy, [*informal*] go, liveliness, spirit, sprightliness, verve, vigour, vitality, vivacity, zest.
3 *a life of Elvis Presley.* autobiography, biography, story.

lifeless adjective 1 *a lifeless body.* comatose, dead, deceased, inanimate, inert, killed, motionless, unconscious.
OPPOSITES: SEE **living** adjective.
2 *lifeless desert.* arid, bare, barren, sterile.
OPPOSITES: SEE **fertile**.
3 *a lifeless performance.* apathetic, boring, flat, lack-lustre, lethargic, slow, unexciting.
OPPOSITES: SEE **animated**.

lifelike adjective *a lifelike image.* authentic, convincing, natural, photographic, realistic, true-to-life.
OPPOSITES: SEE **unrealistic**.

lifelong adjective SEE **lasting**.

lift noun elevator, escalator, hoist.

lift verb 1 *to lift into the air.* buoy up, carry, elevate, hoist, jack up, pick up, pull up, raise, rear.
2 *The plane lifted off the ground.* ascend, rise, soar.
3 [*informal*] *to lift someone else's property.* SEE **steal**.

light adjective 1 *light to carry.* lightweight, SEE **portable**, underweight, weightless.
OPPOSITES: SEE **heavy**.

2 *a light and airy room.* SEE **bright**, illuminated, lit-up, well-lit.
OPPOSITES; SEE **dark**.
[The adjective *light* has many other senses. We refer you to entries where you can find synonyms for some of the common ones.]
3 *light work.* SEE **easy**.
4 *light wind.* SEE **gentle**.
5 *a light touch.* SEE **delicate**.
6 *light colours.* SEE **pale** adjective.
7 *a light heart.* SEE **cheerful**.
8 *light traffic.* SEE **sparse**.

light noun *a shining light.* beam, blaze, brightness, brilliance, effulgence, flare, flash, fluorescence, glare, gleam, glint, glitter, glow, halo, illumination, incandescence, luminosity, lustre, phosphorescence, radiance, ray, reflection, shine, sparkle, twinkle.
to give light, to reflect light be bright, be luminous, be phosphorescent, blaze, blink, burn, coruscate, dazzle, flash, flicker, glare, gleam, glimmer, glint, glisten, glitter, glow, radiate, reflect, scintillate, shimmer, shine, spark, sparkle, twinkle.

KINDS OF LIGHT: daylight, electric light, firelight, floodlight, half-light, moonlight, starlight, sunlight, torchlight, twilight.

THINGS WHICH GIVE LIGHT: arc light, beacon, bulb, candelabra, candle, chandelier, fire, fluorescent lamp, headlamp, headlight, illuminations, lamp, lantern, laser, lighter, lighthouse, lightship, match, moon, neon light, pilot light, searchlight, spotlight, standard lamp, star, street light, strobe or stroboscope, sun, torch, traffic lights.

---

light verb **1** *to light a fire.* begin to burn, fire, ignite, kindle, set alight, set fire to, put a match to, switch on.
OPPOSITES: SEE **quench**.
2 *The bonfire lit the sky.* brighten, cast light on, floodlight, illuminate, irradiate, lighten, light up, shed light on, shine on.
OPPOSITES: SEE **obscure** verb.

lighten verb **1** *The bonfire lightened the sky.* SEE **light** verb.
2 *to lighten someone's burden.* SEE **ease** verb.

light-fingered adjective SEE **thieving** adjective.

light-headed adjective SEE **dizzy**.

light-hearted adjective SEE **cheerful**.

lighthouse noun beacon, light, lightship, warning-light.

lightweight adjective SEE **insignificant**.

like adjective SEE **similar**.

like verb *to like a person. to like food.* admire, appreciate, approve of, be interested in, be fond of, be partial to, be pleased by, delight in, enjoy, find pleasant, [*informal*] go in for, have a high regard for, SEE **love** verb, prefer, relish, [*informal*] take to, welcome.
I (you, she, etc.) would like fancy, SEE **want** verb, wish for.
OPPOSITES: SEE **dislike** verb.

likeable adjective *a likeable person.* attractive, charming, congenial, endearing, SEE **friendly**, lovable, nice, personable, pleasant, pleasing.
OPPOSITES: SEE **hateful**.

likelihood noun *Is there any likelihood of a change in the weather?* chance, hope, possibility, probability, prospect.

likely adjective **1** *a likely result.* anticipated, expected, feasible, foreseeable, plausible, possible, predictable, probable, reasonable, unsurprising.
2 *a likely candidate for election.* appropriate, convincing, credible, favourite, fitting, hopeful, qualified, suitable, [*informal*] tipped to win.
3 *He's likely to be late.* apt, disposed, inclined, liable, prone, willing.
OPPOSITES: SEE **unlikely**.

like-minded adjective SEE **compatible**.

liken verb SEE **compare**.

likeness noun **1** *The photo is a good likeness of her.* copy, depiction, image, picture, portrait, replica, representation, reproduction, study.
2 *There's a strong likeness between the two sisters.* affinity, compatibility, congruity, correspondence, resemblance, similarity.
OPPOSITES: SEE **difference**.

liking noun *a liking for classical music. a liking for sweet things.* affection, fondness, inclination, love, partiality, penchant, predilection, preference, propensity, [*informal*] soft spot, taste, weakness (*Chocolate is one of my weaknesses*).
OPPOSITES: SEE **dislike** noun.

lilliputian adjective SEE **small**.

lilting adjective *lilting music.* attractive, dance-like, light, pleasant, song-like, tuneful.

limb noun *limbs of an animal. a limb of a tree.* appendage, member, offshoot, projection.
VARIOUS LIMBS: arm, bough, branch, flipper, foreleg, forelimb, leg, wing.

limber adjective SEE **lithe**.

limber verb to limber up exercise, get ready, loosen up, prepare, warm up.

limbo noun in limbo *Neither party accepted her, so she was in limbo.* abandoned, forgotten, left out, neglected, neither one thing nor the other, unattached.
limbo dancing SEE **dance** noun.

limelight noun SEE **publicity**.

limit noun 1 *the limit of a territory.* border, boundary, bounds, brink, confines, edge, end, extent, extreme point, frontier, perimeter.
2 *a speed-limit. a limit on numbers.* ceiling, curb, cut-off point, deadline [= *a time-limit*], limitation, maximum, restraint, restriction, threshold.

limit verb to limit someone's freedom. to limit numbers. check, circumscribe, confine, control, curb, fix, put a limit on, ration, restrain, restrict.

limitation noun 1 *a limitation on numbers.* SEE **limit** noun.
2 *I know my limitations.* defect, deficiency, inadequacy, weakness.

limited adjective *limited funds. limited space.* circumscribed, controlled, cramped, defined, determinate, finite, fixed, inadequate, insufficient, narrow, rationed, reduced, restricted, short, small, unsatisfactory.
OPPOSITES: SEE **limitless**.

limitless adjective *limitless funds. limitless opportunities.* boundless, countless, endless, incalculable, inexhaustible, infinite, never-ending, renewable, unbounded, unending, unimaginable, unlimited, vast.
OPPOSITES: SEE **limited**.

limousine noun SEE **car**.

limp adjective *limp lettuce.* [*informal*] bendy, drooping, flabby, flexible, [*informal*] floppy, pliable, sagging, slack, soft, weak, wilting, yielding.
OPPOSITES: SEE **rigid**.

limp verb be lame, falter, hobble, hop, SEE **walk** verb.

limpid adjective SEE **transparent**.

linctus noun cough mixture, expectorant.

line noun 1 *a dirty line round the bath. a line drawn on paper.* band, borderline, boundary, contour, contour line, dash, mark, streak, striation, strip, stripe, stroke, trail.
2 *lines on a person's face.* crease, furrow, groove, score, wrinkle.
3 *Hold the end of this line.* cable, cord, flex, hawser, lead, rope, string, thread, wire.

4 *a line of cars. a line of police.* chain, column, cordon, crocodile, file, procession, queue, rank, row, series.
5 *a railway line.* branch, mainline, route, service, track.

line verb to line a garment with fabric. to line a dish with pastry. cover the inside, encase, insert a lining [SEE **lining**], reinforce.
to line up *They lined up in rows.* [*military command*] fall in, form a line, queue.

lineage noun SEE **ancestry**.

lineaments noun SEE **feature** noun.

liner noun VARIOUS SHIPS: SEE **vessel**.

linger verb 1 *The smell of burning lingered.* continue, endure, hang about, last, persist, remain, stay, survive.
OPPOSITES: SEE **disappear**.
2 *Don't linger outside in this cold weather.* dally, dawdle, delay, hang about, hover, idle, lag, loiter, stay behind, wait about.
OPPOSITES: SEE **hurry** verb.

lingerie noun SEE **underclothes**.

linguist noun interpreter, translator.

linguistic adjective LINGUISTIC TERMS: SEE **language**.

liniment noun cream, embrocation, lotion, ointment, salve.

lining noun *the lining of a garment. a lining of a container.* inner coat, inner layer, interfacing, liner, padding.

link noun 1 *a link between two things.* bond, connection, connector, coupling, SEE **fastener**, join, joint, linkage, tie, yoke.
2 *links between nations. a link between two groups.* alliance, association, communication, liaison, partnership, relationship, [*informal*] tie-up, twinning, union.

link verb 1 *to link one object with another.* amalgamate, attach, connect, couple, SEE **fasten**, interlink, join, merge, network (*networked microcomputers*), twin (*an English town twinned with a French town*), unite, yoke.
OPPOSITES: SEE **isolate**, **separate** verb.
2 *to link one idea with another.* associate, compare, make a link, relate, see a link.

linkage noun SEE **link** noun.

lion noun king of beasts, lioness.
RELATED ADJECTIVE: leonine.
OTHER ANIMALS: SEE **animal** noun.

lionize verb SEE **worship** verb.

lip noun *the lip of a cup.* brim, brink, edge, rim.

liquefy verb *Ice liquefies at 0°C.* become liquid, dissolve, SEE **liquidize**, melt, run, thaw.
OPPOSITES: SEE **solidify**.

liqueur noun DRINKS: SEE **drink** noun.

liquid adjective *a liquid substance.* aqueous, flowing, fluid, molten, running, [*informal*] runny, sloppy, [*informal*] sloshy, thin, watery, wet.
OPPOSITES: SEE **solid**.

liquid noun *He can only consume liquids.* fluid, liquid substance [SEE **liquid** adjective].

liquidate verb [Do not confuse with *liquidize*.] *to liquidate your enemy.* annihilate, destroy, [*informal*] do away with, [*informal*] get rid of, SEE **kill**, remove, silence, wipe out.

liquidize verb [Do not confuse with *liquidate*.] *to liquidize vegetables to make soup.* SEE **liquefy**, make into liquid, pulp.

liquor noun alcohol, spirits, strong drink.
DRINKS: SEE **drink** noun.

lisp verb SEE **speak**.

lissom adjective SEE **lithe**.

list noun *a list of names.* catalogue, column, directory, file, index, inventory, listing, register, roll, shopping-list, table.

list verb 1 *to list your possessions.* catalogue, file, index, itemize, make a list of [SEE **list** noun], record, register, tabulate, write down.
2 *to list to one side.* heel, incline, lean, slope, tilt, tip.

listen verb *Did you listen to what I said?* attend, concentrate on, [*old-fashioned*] hark, hear, heed, eavesdrop, lend an ear to, overhear, pay attention to, take notice of.

listless adjective *listless in the heat.* apathetic, enervated, feeble, heavy, lackadaisical, languid, lazy, lethargic, lifeless, sluggish, tired, torpid, unenthusiastic, uninterested, weak, weary.
OPPOSITES: SEE **lively**.

litany noun SEE **prayer**.

literal adjective [Do not confuse with *literary*.] *the literal meaning of something.* close, plain, prosaic, strict, unimaginative, word for word.

literary adjective 1 *literary writing.* highly regarded, imaginative, ornate, polished, recognized as literature, [*uncomplimentary*] self-conscious, sophisticated, stylish.
2 *literary tastes.* cultured, educated, erudite, literate, refined, well-read, widely read.
a literary person [*informal*] bookworm, critic, reader, scholar, SEE **writer**.

literate adjective 1 *a literate person.* able to read and write, SEE **educated**.
2 *literate writing.* accurate, correct, properly spelt, readable, well-written.

literature noun 1 *literature about local tourist attractions.* brochures, handouts, leaflets, pamphlets, papers.
2 *English literature.* books, writings.

KINDS OF LITERATURE: autobiography, biography, children's literature, comedy, crime fiction, criticism, drama, epic, essay, fantasy, fiction, folk-tale, journalism, myth and legend, novels, parody, poetry, prose, romance, satire, science fiction, tragedy, tragi-comedy.
OTHER KINDS OF WRITING: SEE **writing**.

lithe adjective *a lithe gymnast.* agile, flexible, limber, lissom, loose-jointed, pliant, supple.

litigation noun LEGAL TERMS: SEE **law**.

litter noun 1 *Clear up the litter.* bits and pieces, clutter, debris, garbage, jumble, junk, mess, odds and ends, refuse, rubbish, trash, waste.
2 *a litter of puppies.* SEE **family**.

litter verb *to litter a room with papers.* clutter, fill with litter [SEE **litter** noun], make untidy, [*informal*] mess up, scatter, strew.

little adjective SEE **small**.

liturgy noun SEE **service** noun.

live adjective 1 *live animals.* SEE **living**.
2 *a live fire.* SEE **burning**.
3 *a live volcano.* active, functioning.
4 *a live issue.* contemporary, current, important, pressing, relevant, topical, vital.

live verb 1 *Will these plants live through the winter?* continue, exist, flourish, last, remain, stay alive, survive.
OPPOSITES: SEE **die**.
2 *I can live on £20 a week.* [*informal*] get along, keep going, make a living, pay the bills, subsist.
to live in *I live in a flat.* dwell in, inhabit, occupy, reside in.
to live on *What do polar bears live on?* eat, feed on.

livelihood noun SEE **living** noun, **work** noun.

liveliness noun activity, animation, boisterousness, bustle, dynamism, energy, enthusiasm, exuberance, [*informal*] go, gusto, high spirits, spirit, sprightliness, verve, vigour, vitality, vivacity, zeal.
OPPOSITES: SEE **inertia**, **tiredness**.

lively adjective *lively kittens. a lively party. a lively expression.* active, agile, alert, animated, boisterous, bubbly, bustling, busy, cheerful, colourful, dashing, energetic, enthusiastic, exciting, expressive, exuberant, frisky, gay, SEE **happy**, high-spirited, irrepressible, jaunty, jolly, merry, nimble, [*informal*] perky, playful, quick, spirited, sprightly, stimulating, vigorous, vital, vivacious, [*informal*] zippy.
OPPOSITES: SEE **apathetic, tired**.

liven verb SEE **animate** verb.

livery noun uniform.

livestock noun cattle, farm animals.

livid adjective **1** *a livid colour.* bluish-grey.
2 *livid with anger.* SEE **angry**.

living adjective *living creatures.* SEE **active**, alive, animate, breathing, existing, live, sentient, surviving, vigorous, vital.
OPPOSITES: SEE **dead, extinct**.

living noun *She makes a living from painting.* income, livelihood, occupation, subsistence, way of life.

living-room drawing-room, lounge, sitting-room.
OTHER ROOMS: SEE **room**.

lizard noun RELATED ADJECTIVE: saurian.

load noun **1** *a load of goods.* cargo, consignment, freight, [*formal*] lading, lorry-load, shipment, van-load.
2 *a heavy load of responsibility.* burden, millstone, onus, weight.

load verb **1** *We loaded the luggage into the car.* fill, heap, pack, pile, ply, stow.
2 *They loaded me with their shopping.* burden, encumber, weigh down.

loaded adjective **1** *loaded with gifts.* burdened, inundated, laden, piled high, weighed down.
2 *a loaded argument.* biased, distorted, emotive, one-sided, partial, prejudiced, unfair.
3 [*informal*] *He can afford it—he's loaded!* SEE **wealthy**.

loaf noun SEE **bread**.

loaf verb *to loaf about.* SEE **lounge** verb.

loafer noun idler, [*informal*] good-for-nothing, layabout, [*informal*] lazybones, lounger, shirker, [*informal*] skiver, wastrel.

loam noun *Plant the seeds in good loam.* SEE **soil** noun.

loan noun *I need a loan to buy a car.* advance, credit, mortgage.

loan verb *Can you loan me 50p?* SEE **lend**.

loath adjective SEE **unwilling**.

loathe verb *Our dog loathes cats.* SEE **hate** verb.

loathing noun SEE **hatred**.

loathsome adjective SEE **hateful**.

lob verb *to lob a ball in the air.* bowl, cast, chuck, fling, loft, pitch, shy, sling, throw, toss.

lobby noun **1** *Wait for me in the lobby.* ante-room, entrance hall, foyer, hall, hallway, porch, vestibule.
2 *the environmental lobby. the road-users lobby.* campaign, campaigners, pressure-group, supporters.

lobby verb *to lobby your MP.* persuade, petition, pressurize, try to influence, urge.

local adjective **1** *local amenities.* nearby, neighbourhood, neighbouring, serving the locality [SEE **locality**].
2 *a matter of local interest.* community, limited, narrow, parochial, particular, provincial, regional.
OPPOSITES: SEE **general, national**.

local noun **1** [*informal*] *the local.* SEE **pub**.
2 *If you want to know the way, ask one of the locals.* inhabitant, person from the locality [SEE **locality**], resident.

locality noun *There are good shops in our locality.* area, catchment area, community, district, location, neighbourhood, parish, region, residential area, town, vicinity, zone.

localize verb *The authorities tried to localize the epidemic.* concentrate, confine, contain, enclose, keep within bounds, limit, narrow down, pin down, restrict.
OPPOSITES: SEE **spread** verb.

locate verb **1** *I located the book I wanted in the library.* detect, discover, find, identify, [*informal*] run to earth, search out, track down, unearth.
OPPOSITES: SEE **lose**.
2 *They located the new offices in the middle of town.* build, establish, find a place for, found, place, position, put, set up, site, situate, station.

location noun **1** *Can you find the location on the map?* locale, SEE **locality**, place, point, position, site, situation, spot, venue, whereabouts.
2 *The film was shot in real locations.* background, scene, setting.

loch noun SEE **lake**.

lock noun **1** *a lock on a door.* bolt, catch, clasp, SEE **fastening**, latch, padlock.
2 *a lock of hair.* SEE **hair**.

lock verb *to lock a door.* bolt, close, SEE **fasten**, seal, secure, shut.
to lock in, to lock up SEE **imprison**.
to lock out SEE **exclude**.

locker noun SEE **cupboard**.

locomotive noun engine.

locum noun SEE **deputy** noun.

locus noun SEE **position** noun.

lodestar noun SEE **star**.

lodge noun SEE **house** noun.

lodge verb **1** *to lodge homeless families in a hostel.* accommodate, billet, board, SEE **house** verb, put up.
2 *to lodge in a motel.* reside, stay.
3 *to lodge a complaint.* file, make formally, put on record, register, submit.

lodger noun *a lodger in a guest-house.* boarder, guest, inmate, paying guest, resident, tenant.

lodgings noun accommodation, apartments, billet, boarding-house, [*informal*] digs, lodging-house, [*informal*] pad, quarters, rooms, [*informal*] squat, temporary home.

loft noun attic.

lofty adjective *a lofty spire.* SEE **high**.

log noun **1** *logs to burn.* timber, wood.
2 *the log of a voyage.* account, diary, journal, record.

loggerheads adjective **to be at loggerheads** SEE **quarrel** verb.

logic noun *I admired the logic of his argument.* clarity, logical thinking [SEE **logical**], rationality, reasoning, sense, validity.

logical adjective *a logical argument.* clear, cogent, coherent, consistent, intelligent, methodical, rational, reasonable, sensible, sound, systematic, valid.
OPPOSITES: SEE **illogical**.

logistics noun SEE **organization**.

logo noun SEE **symbol**.

loiter verb *We'll be left behind if we loiter.* be slow, dally, dawdle, hang back, linger, [*informal*] loaf about, [*informal*] mess about, skulk, [*informal*] stand about, straggle.

loll verb SEE **lean** verb.

lone adjective *a lone walker on the hills. a lone voice.* isolated, SEE **lonely**, separate, single, solitary, solo, unaccompanied.

lonely adjective **1** *I was lonely while my friends were away.* alone, forlorn, friendless, lonesome, neglected, SEE **sad**, solitary.
2 *a lonely farmhouse. a lonely road.* abandoned, desolate, distant, far-away, forsaken, isolated, [*informal*] off the beaten track, out of the way, remote, secluded, unfrequented, uninhabited.

loner noun hermit, outsider, recluse.

lonesome adjective SEE **lonely**.

long adjective *a long piece of rope. a long wait.* drawn out, elongated, endless, extended, extensive, interminable, lasting, lengthy, longish, prolonged, protracted, slow, stretched, time-consuming, unending.
a long face SEE **expression**.

long verb **to long for** [*informal*] be dying for (*I'm dying for a drink*), desire, fancy, hanker after, have a longing for [SEE **longing**], hunger after, [*informal*] itch for, lust after, pine for, thirst for, want, wish for, yearn for.

longevity noun long life, old age.

longing noun appetite, craving, desire, hunger, [*informal*] itch, need, thirst, urge, wish, yearning, [*informal*] yen.

longitudinal adjective lengthwise, longways.

long-lasting, **long-lived** adjectives SEE **lasting**.

long-playing record noun album, LP, SEE **record** noun.

long-standing adjective SEE **lasting**.

long-suffering adjective SEE **patient** adjective.

long-winded adjective *a long-winded speaker.* boring, diffuse, dreary, dry, garrulous, lengthy, long, rambling, tedious, uninteresting, verbose, wordy.

loo noun SEE **lavatory**.

look noun **1** *Give me a look. Take a look.* glance, glimpse, observation, peek, peep, sight, [*informal*] squint, view.
2 *She has a friendly look.* [*often plural*] *He's vain about his looks.* air, appearance, aspect, bearing, complexion, countenance, demeanour, expression, face, manner, mien.

look verb **1 to look at** behold, [*informal*] cast your eye over, consider, contemplate, examine, eye, gape at, [*informal*] gawp at, gaze at, glance at, glimpse, goggle at, inspect, observe, ogle, peek at, peep at, peer at, read, regard, scan, scrutinize, see, skim through (*I'll just skim through the book*), squint at, stare at, study, survey, take a look at, take note of, view, watch.
2 *Our house looks south.* face, overlook.
3 *You look pleased.* appear, seem.
to look after SEE **care** verb (**to care for**).
to look down on SEE **despise**.
to look for SEE **seek**.
to look into SEE **investigate**.
to look out *If you don't look out, you'll get wet.* be vigilant, beware, keep an eye open, keep an eye out, pay attention, watch out.
to look up to SEE **admire**.

looking-glass noun mirror.

look-out noun guard, sentinel, sentry, watchman.

loom verb *A castle loomed on the skyline.* appear, arise, dominate, emerge, materialize, rise, stand out, stick up, threaten, tower.

loony adjective SEE **mad.**

loop noun *a loop in a rope.* bend, circle, coil, curl, hoop, kink, noose, ring, turn, twist.

loop verb *Loop the rope round the post.* bend, coil, curl, entwine, make a loop [SEE **loop** noun], turn, twist, wind.

loophole noun *a loophole in the law.* escape, [*informal*] get-out, [*informal*] let-out.

loose adjective 1 *loose stones. loose wires.* detachable, detached, disconnected, insecure, loosened, movable, shaky, unattached, unfastened, unsteady, untied, wobbly.
2 *loose animals.* at large, free, roaming, uncaged, unconfined, unrestricted.
OPPOSITES: SEE **secure** adjective.
3 *loose clothing.* baggy, [*informal*] floppy, loose-fitting, slack, unbuttoned.
OPPOSITES: SEE **tight.**
4 *a loose agreement. a loose translation.* diffuse, general, ill-defined, imprecise, inexact, informal, vague.
OPPOSITES: SEE **precise.**
5 *loose behaviour.* SEE **immoral.**

loose verb *to loose an animal from its cage.* SEE **free** verb.

loosen verb 1 *Loosen the knots.* ease off, free, let go, loose, make loose, relax, release, slacken, undo, unfasten, unloose, untie.
2 *Check that the knots haven't loosened.* become loose, come adrift, open up.
OPPOSITES: SEE **tighten.**

loot noun *thieves' loot.* booty, contraband, haul, [*informal*] ill-gotten gains, plunder, prize, spoils, [*informal*] swag, takings.

loot verb *Rioters looted the shops.* pillage, plunder, raid, ransack, rifle, rob, steal from.

lop verb *to lop off a branch.* SEE **cut** verb.

lope verb SEE **walk** verb.

lopsided adjective *The lopsided load on the lorry looked dangerous.* askew, asymmetrical, [*informal*] cock-eyed, crooked, tilting, unbalanced, uneven.

Several English words, including *colloquial, eloquent,* and *loquacious,* are related to Latin *loqui = to speak.*

---

loquacious adjective SEE **talkative.**

lord noun noble, peer, [*old-fashioned*] thane.
VARIOUS TITLES: SEE **title** noun.

lordly adjective SEE **bossy.**

lore noun SEE **knowledge.**

lorry noun VARIOUS VEHICLES: SEE **vehicle.**

lose verb 1 *to lose something or someone.* be deprived of, be unable to find, cease to have, drop, find yourself without, forfeit, forget, leave behind, mislay, misplace, miss, stray from, suffer the loss of [SEE **loss**].
OPPOSITES: SEE **find, gain** verb.
2 *to lose in a game or race.* be defeated, capitulate, [*informal*] come to grief, fail, get beaten, [*informal*] get thrashed, suffer defeat.
OPPOSITES: SEE **win.**

loser noun the defeated, runner-up, the vanquished.
OPPOSITES: SEE **winner.**

losing adjective *the losing side.* bottom, defeated, last, unsuccessful, vanquished.
OPPOSITES: SEE **winning.**

loss noun bereavement, damage, defeat, deficit, deprivation, destruction, disappearance, failure, forfeiture, impairment, privation.
OPPOSITES: SEE **gain** noun.

losses *losses in battle.* casualties, deaths, death toll, fatalities.

lost adjective 1 *lost property. lost animals.* abandoned, disappeared, gone, irrecoverable, left behind, mislaid, misplaced, strayed, untraceable, vanished.
2 *lost in thought.* absorbed, day-dreaming, dreamy, distracted, engrossed, preoccupied, rapt.
3 *lost souls.* corrupt, damned, SEE **wicked.**

lot noun 1 *a lot of, lots of a lot of food. lots of money.* SEE **plenty.**
2 *the lot Give her the lot.* all, everything.
3 *a lot in an auction sale.* SEE **item.**
to draw lots SEE **choose, gamble** verb.

lotion noun balm, cream, embrocation, liniment, ointment, salve.

lottery noun gamble.

loud adjective 1 *loud noise.* audible, blaring, booming, clamorous, clarion (*a clarion call*), deafening, ear-splitting, echoing, fortissimo, high, noisy, penetrating, piercing, raucous, resounding, reverberating, rowdy, shrieking, shrill,

stentorian, strident, thundering, thunderous, uproarious, vociferous.
OPPOSITES: SEE **quiet**.
2 *loud colours*. SEE **gaudy**.

lounge noun drawing-room, living-room, sitting-room.
OTHER ROOMS: SEE **room**.

lounge verb *to lounge about. to lounge in a chair*. be idle, be lazy, dawdle, hang about, idle, [*informal*] kill time, laze, loaf, lie around, loiter, [*informal*] loll about, [*informal*] mess about, [*informal*] mooch about, relax, [*informal*] skive, slouch, slump, sprawl, stand about, take it easy, waste time.

lour verb SEE **frown** verb.

lousy adjective [*slang*] *What lousy weather!* SEE **nasty**.

lout noun *ill-mannered lout*. boor, churl, rude person [SEE **rude**], oaf, [*informal*] yob.

loutish adjective *loutish behaviour*. SEE **rude**.

lovable adjective *Teddy bears are lovable toys*. adorable, appealing, attractive, charming, cuddly, enchanting, endearing, engaging, likeable, lovely, pleasing, taking, winning.
OPPOSITES: SEE **hateful**.

love noun **1** *Giving flowers is one way to show your love*. admiration, adoration, affection, ardour, desire, devotion, fondness, friendship, infatuation, liking, passion.
2 *My dearest love*. beloved, darling, dear, dearest, loved one, SEE **lover**.
in love with devoted to, enamoured with, fond of, infatuated with.
to make love court, flirt, have sexual intercourse [SEE **sex**], philander, woo.
love affair affair, courtship, intrigue, liaison, relationship, romance.
RELATED ADJECTIVES: amatory, erotic.

love verb **1** *to love someone*. admire, adore, be charmed by, be in love with [SEE **love** noun (**in love with**)], care for, cherish, desire, dote on, fancy, feel love for [SEE **love** noun], have a passion for, idolize, lust after, treasure, value, want, worship.
OPPOSITES: SEE **hate** verb.
2 *I love fish and chips*. SEE **like** verb.

loved adjective *loved ones*. adored, beloved, darling, dear, idolized, valued.

loveless adjective *a loveless relationship*. cold, frigid, heartless, passionless, undemonstrative, unfeeling, unloving, unresponsive.
OPPOSITES: SEE **loving**.

lovely adjective *a lovely day. lovely flowers*. appealing, attractive, SEE **beautiful**, charming, delightful, enjoyable, fine, nice, pleasant, pretty, sweet.
OPPOSITES: SEE **nasty**.

love-making noun courting, courtship, kissing, petting, SEE **sex**, wooing.

lover noun [*old-fashioned*] admirer, boyfriend, companion, concubine, [*male*] fiancé, [*female*] fiancée, [*old-fashioned*] follower, friend, gigolo, girlfriend, mistress, [*old-fashioned*] paramour, suitor, sweetheart, valentine, wooer.

lovesick adjective frustrated, languishing, lovelorn, pining.

loving adjective *loving kisses. a loving nature*. affectionate, amorous, ardent, demonstrative, devoted, doting, fatherly, fond, SEE **friendly**, kind, maternal, motherly, passionate, paternal, tender, warm.
OPPOSITES: SEE **loveless**.

low adjective **1** *low land*. flat, low-lying, sunken.
OPPOSITES: SEE **high**.
2 *a low position*. abject, base, degraded, humble, inferior, junior, lower, lowly, menial, modest, servile.
OPPOSITES: SEE **superior**.
3 *low behaviour*. churlish, coarse, common, cowardly, crude, [*old-fashioned*] dastardly, disreputable, ignoble, SEE **immoral**, mean, nasty, vulgar, wicked.
OPPOSITES: SEE **noble**.
4 *low whispers*. muffled, muted, pianissimo, quiet, soft, subdued.
OPPOSITES: SEE **loud**.
5 *a low note*. bass, deep.
OPPOSITES: SEE **high**.
a low point nadir, trough.
in low spirits SEE **sad**.

low verb *Cows were lowing*. VARIOUS SOUNDS: SEE **sound** noun.

lowbrow adjective **1** *lowbrow literature*. easy, popular, [*uncomplimentary*] rubbish, simple, straightforward, [*uncomplimentary*] trashy, undemanding.
2 *lowbrow music*. pop, popular.
3 *a lowbrow person*. ordinary, simple, [*uncomplimentary*] uncultured, unpretentious, unsophisticated.
OPPOSITES: SEE **highbrow**.

lower verb **1** *to lower a flag*. dip, drop, haul down, let down, take down.
2 *to lower prices*. bring down, cut, decrease, lessen, reduce, [*informal*] slash.
3 *to lower the volume*. abate, quieten, tone down, turn down.
OPPOSITES: SEE **raise**.
4 *He's too high-and-mighty to lower himself by coming out with us*. degrade, demean, discredit, disgrace, humiliate, stoop.

lowly adjective *a lowly position in life*. base, humble, insignificant, low, low-born, meek, modest.

loyal adjective *a loyal supporter.* constant, dependable, devoted, dutiful, faithful, honest, patriotic, reliable, sincere, staunch, steadfast, true, trustworthy, trusty, unswerving.
OPPOSITES: SEE **disloyal**.

loyalty noun allegiance, constancy, dependability, devotion, faithfulness, fealty, fidelity, honesty, patriotism, reliability, staunchness, steadfastness, trustworthiness.
OPPOSITES: SEE **disloyalty**.

lozenge noun 1 *a lozenge to suck.* cough sweet, pastille.
2 *in the shape of a lozenge.* diamond, rhombus.

LP SEE **long-playing record**.

lubricate verb grease, oil.

lucid adjective *a lucid explanation.* SEE **clear** adjective.

luck noun 1 *I found my watch by luck.* accident, [*informal*] break (*a lucky break*), chance, coincidence, destiny, fate, [*informal*] fluke, fortune.
2 *I had a bit of luck today.* good fortune, happiness, prosperity, success.

luckless adjective SEE **unlucky**.

lucky adjective 1 *a lucky discovery.* accidental, chance, [*informal*] fluky, fortuitous, providential, timely, unintended, unintentional, unplanned, welcome.
OPPOSITES: SEE **intentional**.
2 *a lucky person.* favoured, fortunate, SEE **happy**, successful.
3 *3 is my lucky number.* auspicious.
OPPOSITES: SEE **unlucky**.

lucrative adjective SEE **profitable**.

lucre noun SEE **money**.

ludicrous adjective SEE **ridiculous**.

lug verb SEE **carry**.

luggage noun baggage, bags, belongings, boxes, cases, impedimenta, paraphernalia, things.

ITEMS OF LUGGAGE: bag, basket, box, briefcase, case, chest, hamper, handbag, hand luggage, haversack, holdall, knapsack, pannier, [*old-fashioned*] portmanteau, purse, rucksack, satchel, suitcase, trunk, wallet.

---

lugubrious adjective SEE **mournful**.

lukewarm adjective 1 *lukewarm water.* tepid, warm.
2 *a lukewarm response.* apathetic, cool, half-hearted, unenthusiastic.

lull noun *a lull in a storm.* break, calm, gap, interval, [*informal*] let-up, pause, respite, rest, silence.

lull verb *to lull someone to sleep.* calm, hush, pacify, quell, quieten, soothe, subdue, tranquillize.

lumber noun 1 *cutting lumber in the forest.* timber, wood.
2 *We cleared the lumber out of the garage.* bits and pieces, clutter, jumble, junk, odds and ends, rubbish, trash.

lumber verb 1 [*informal*] *They lumbered me with the clearing up.* SEE **burden** verb.
2 *A rhinoceros lumbered towards them.* blunder, move clumsily, shamble, trudge.

luminous adjective *a luminous dial.* glowing, luminescent, lustrous, phosphorescent, shining.

lump noun 1 *a lump of chocolate. a lump of soap.* ball, bar, bit, block, cake, chunk, clod, clot, [*informal*] dollop, gobbet, hunk, ingot, mass, nugget, piece, slab, [*informal*] wodge.
2 *a lump on the head.* bulge, bump, hump, knob, node, nodule, protrusion, protuberance, spot, swelling, tumour.

lump verb to lump together SEE **combine**.
to lump it SEE **tolerate**.

lunacy noun SEE **madness**.

lunatic adjective SEE **mad**.

lunatic noun SEE **madman**.

lunch, luncheon nouns OTHER MEALS: SEE **meal**.

lung noun RELATED ADJECTIVE: pulmonary.

lunge verb 1 *to lunge with a sword.* jab, stab, strike, thrust.
2 *to lunge after someone.* charge, dash, dive, lurch, pounce, rush, throw yourself.

lurch noun to leave in the lurch SEE **abandon**.

lurch verb *to lurch from side to side.* heave, lean, list, lunge, pitch, plunge, reel, roll, stagger, stumble, sway, totter, wallow.

lure verb *to lure someone into a trap.* allure, attract, bait, coax, decoy, draw, entice, inveigle, invite, lead on, persuade, seduce, tempt.

lurid adjective 1 *lurid colours.* SEE **gaudy**.
2 *lurid details.* SEE **sensational**.

lurk verb *to lurk in wait for prey.* crouch, hide, lie in wait, lie low, skulk, wait.

luscious adjective *luscious peaches.* appetizing, delicious, juicy, succulent, sweet, tasty.

lush adjective 1 *lush grass*. SEE **luxuriant**.
2 *lush surroundings*. SEE **luxurious**.

lust noun 1 *sexual lust*. carnality, lasciviousness, lechery, libido, licentiousness, passion, sensuality.
2 *a lust for power*. appetite, craving, desire, greed, itch, hunger, longing.

lustful adjective carnal, lascivious, lecherous, libidinous, licentious, passionate, [*informal*] randy, sensual, SEE **sexy**.

lustrous adjective SEE **bright**.

lusty adjective SEE **vigorous**.

luxuriant adjective *luxuriant growth*. abundant, ample, copious, dense, exuberant, fertile, flourishing, green, lush, opulent, plenteous, plentiful, profuse, prolific, rich, teeming, thick, thriving, verdant.
OPPOSITES: SEE **barren**, **sparse**.

luxuriate verb to luxuriate in SEE **enjoy**.

luxurious adjective *luxurious surroundings*. comfortable, costly, expensive, grand, hedonistic, lavish, lush, magnificent, [*informal*] plush, rich, self-indulgent, splendid, sumptuous, voluptuous.
OPPOSITES: SEE **spartan**.

luxury noun *a life of luxury*. affluence, comfort, ease, enjoyment, extravagance, hedonism, high living, indulgence, pleasure, relaxation, self-indulgence, splendour, sumptuousness, voluptuousness.

lying adjective *a lying witness*. crooked, deceitful, dishonest, double-dealing, false, inaccurate, insincere, mendacious, perfidious, unreliable, untrustworthy, untruthful.
OPPOSITES: SEE **truthful**.

lying noun deceit, dishonesty, falsehood, mendacity, [*formal*] perjury.

lynch verb SEE **kill**.

lyric noun *the lyric of a song*. SEE **poem**, words.

lyrical adjective *a lyrical tune*. *a lyrical description*. emotional, expressive, inspired, poetic, song-like.

M

mac noun SEE **mackintosh**.

macabre adjective *He takes a macabre interest in graveyards*. eerie, ghoulish, SEE **gruesome**, morbid, sick, unhealthy, weird.

macaroni noun SEE **pasta**.

machiavellian adjective SEE **crafty**, **wicked**.

machinations noun SEE **scheme** noun.

machine noun apparatus, appliance, contraption, contrivance, device, engine, gadget, instrument, SEE **machinery**, mechanism, robot, tool.

machinery noun 1 *machinery in a factory*. equipment, gear, machines [SEE **machine**], plant.
2 *machinery for electing a new leader*. constitution, method, organization, procedure, structure, system.

macho noun SEE **manly**.

mackintosh noun anorak, cape, mac, raincoat, sou'wester, waterproof.
OTHER COATS: SEE **coat** noun.

mad adjective 1 [Many of these words are used informally. Though they may be used jokingly, they are often offensive.] *a mad person*. *mad behaviour*. batty, berserk, bonkers, certified, crackers, crazed, crazy, daft, delirious, demented, deranged, disordered, dotty, eccentric, fanatical, frantic, frenzied, hysterical, insane, irrational, loony, lunatic, maniacal, manic, mental, mentally unstable, moonstruck, [*Latin*] non compos mentis, nutty, off your head, off your rocker, out of your mind, possessed, potty, [*formal*] psychotic, queer in the head, round the bend, round the twist, screwy, touched, unbalanced, unhinged, unstable, up the pole, wild.
OPPOSITES: SEE **sane**.
2 *a mad sense of humour*. SEE **absurd**.
3 *mad with rage*. SEE **angry**.
4 *mad about snooker*. SEE **enthusiastic**.
a mad person SEE **madman**, **madwoman**.
to be mad [*informal*] have a screw loose, rave.

madam, **madame** nouns SEE **title** noun, **woman**.

madcap adjective SEE **impulsive**.

madden verb *The noise maddened me*. anger, craze, derange, enrage, exasperate, incense, inflame, infuriate, irritate, make mad [SEE **mad**], provoke, [*informal*] send round the bend, unhinge, vex.

madhouse noun SEE **asylum**.

madman, madwoman nouns [Though these words may be used jokingly, they are often offensive.] [*informal*] crackpot, [*informal*] crank, eccentric, lunatic, mad person [SEE **mad**], maniac, [*informal*] mental case, [*informal*] nutcase, [*informal*] nutter, [*formal*] psychopath, [*formal*] psychotic.

madness noun delirium, derangement, eccentricity, frenzy, hysteria, insanity, lunacy, mania, mental illness, psychosis.

maelstrom noun SEE **confusion**, vortex, whirlpool.

maestro noun VARIOUS MUSICIANS: SEE **music**.

magazine noun 1 *a magazine to read.* comic, journal, monthly, newspaper, pamphlet, paper, periodical, publication, quarterly, weekly.
2 *a magazine of weapons.* ammunition dump, arsenal, storehouse.

maggot noun caterpillar, grub, larva.

magic adjective *a magic trick.* conjuring, magical, miraculous, supernatural.

magic noun 1 *magic performed by witches.* black magic, charms, enchantment, hocus-pocus, incantation, [*informal*] mumbo-jumbo, necromancy, occultism, sorcery, spell, voodoo, witchcraft, witchery, wizardry.
2 *magic performed by a conjuror.* conjuring, illusion, legerdemain, sleight of hand, trick, trickery.
to do magic bewitch, cast spells, charm, conjure, enchant, work miracles.

magician noun conjuror, enchanter, enchantress, SEE **entertainer**, illusionist, sorcerer, [*old-fashioned*] warlock, witch, witch-doctor, wizard.

magisterial adjective SEE **bossy**.

magistrate noun LEGAL TERMS: SEE **law**.

magnanimous adjective SEE **generous**.

magnate noun SEE **businessman**.

magnetic adjective *a magnetic personality.* alluring, SEE **attractive**, captivating, charismatic, charming, compelling, fascinating, hypnotic, irresistible, seductive.
OPPOSITES: SEE **repulsive**.

magnetism noun *personal magnetism.* allure, appeal, attractiveness, charisma, charm, fascination, lure, power, seductiveness.

magnetize verb SEE **attract**.

magnificent adjective *a magnificent palace. magnificent mountain scenery.* SEE beautiful, excellent, glorious, gorgeous, grand, grandiose, imposing, impressive, majestic, marvellous, noble, opulent, [*informal*] posh, regal, spectacular, splendid, stately, sumptuous, superb, wonderful.
OPPOSITES: SEE **ordinary, paltry**.

magnify verb 1 *to magnify an image.* amplify, augment, [*informal*] blow up, enlarge, expand, increase, intensify, make larger.
OPPOSITES: SEE **reduce**.
2 *to magnify difficulties.* [*informal*] blow up out of all proportion, dramatize, exaggerate, inflate, make too much of, maximize, overdo, overestimate, overstate.
OPPOSITES: SEE **minimize**.

magnifying glass SEE **optical** (optical instruments).

magnitude noun SEE **size**.

maid noun SEE **girl, servant**.

maiden noun SEE **girl**.

mail noun 1 *The postman brings the mail.* correspondence, letters, parcels, post.
2 *chain-mail.* armour, protection.

mail verb *The shop mailed the book to me.* dispatch, forward, post, send.

maim verb *He was maimed in an accident.* cripple, disable, handicap, injure, mutilate, SEE **wound** verb.

main adjective *the main ingredients. the main point of a story.* basic, biggest, cardinal, central, chief, crucial, dominant, essential, foremost, fundamental, greatest, important, largest, leading, major, outstanding, predominant, preeminent, prevailing, primary, prime, principal, special, supreme, top (*the top attraction*).
OPPOSITES: SEE **unimportant**.

mainly adverb chiefly, especially, generally, in the main, largely, mostly, normally, on the whole, predominantly, primarily, principally, usually.

mainstream adjective SEE **conventional, orthodox**.

maintain verb 1 *to maintain a constant speed.* carry on, continue, hold to, keep up, retain, stick to.
2 *to maintain a car in good order.* keep in good condition, look after, preserve, service, take care of.
3 *to maintain a family.* feed, keep, pay for, provide for, support.
4 *to maintain that you are innocent.* affirm, allege, argue, assert, aver, claim, contend, declare, insist, proclaim, profess, state, uphold.

maintenance noun 1 *the maintenance of a house or a car.* care, conservation, looking after, preservation, repairs, servicing, upkeep.
2 *He pays maintenance to his ex-wife.* alimony, allowance, subsistence.

maisonette noun SEE **house** noun.

maize noun corn on the cob, sweetcorn. OTHER CEREALS: SEE **cereal**.

majestic adjective *a majestic palace.* august, awe-inspiring, awesome, dignified, distinguished, grand, imperial, imposing, impressive, kingly, lordly, magnificent, monumental, noble, pompous, princely, regal, royal, SEE **splendid**, stately.

majesty noun 1 *the majesty of the mountains.* SEE **splendour**.
2 *His Majesty the King.* SEE **royalty**.

major adjective *major roadworks. a major city, a major operation.* bigger, chief, considerable, extensive, great, greater, important, key, large, larger, leading, outstanding, principal, serious, significant.
OPPOSITES: SEE **minor**.

majority noun 1 *The majority voted to go back to work.* bulk, greater number, preponderance.
2 *the age of majority.* adulthood, coming of age, manhood, maturity, womanhood.
OPPOSITES: SEE **minority**.
to be in the majority be greater, dominate, outnumber, predominate, preponderate, prevail.

make noun *What make is your car?* brand, kind, model, sort, type, variety.

make verb 1 *to make furniture. to make a success of something.* assemble, beget, bring about, build, compose, constitute, construct, create, do, engender, erect, execute, fabricate, fashion, forge, form, generate, invent, make up, manufacture, mass-produce, originate, produce, think up.
[*Make* is used in many other senses. We give only a selection of them here.]
2 *to make a cake.* SEE **cook** verb.
3 *to make clothes.* knit, [*informal*] run up, sew, weave.
4 *to make a sculpture.* carve, cast, model, mould, shape.
5 *to make a speech.* deliver, pronounce, speak, utter.
6 *to make someone captain.* appoint, elect, nominate, ordain.
7 *to make a P into a B.* alter, change, convert, modify, transform, turn.

8 *to make a fortune.* earn, gain, get, obtain, receive.
9 *to make a good games player.* become, change into, grow into, turn into.
10 *to make your objective.* accomplish, achieve, arrive at, attain, catch, get to, reach, win.
11 *2 and 2 make 4.* add up to, amount to, come to, total.
12 *to make rules.* agree, arrange, codify, establish, decide on, draw up, fix, write.
13 *to make someone happy.* cause to become, render.
14 *to make trouble.* bring about, carry out, cause, give rise to, provoke, result in.
15 *to make someone do something.* coerce, compel, constrain, force, induce, oblige, order, pressurize, prevail on, require.
to make amends SEE **compensate**.
to make believe SEE **imagine**.
to make fun of, to make jokes about SEE **ridicule**.
to make good SEE **prosper**.
to make love SEE **love** noun (make love).
to make off SEE **depart**.
to make off with SEE **steal**.
to make out, to make sense of SEE **understand**.
to make up SEE **invent**.
to make up for SEE **compensate**.
to make up your mind SEE **decide**.

make-believe adjective *a make-believe story.* fanciful, fantasy, feigned, imaginary, made-up, mock, [*childish*] pretend, pretended, sham, simulated, unreal.

maker noun architect, author, builder, creator, manufacturer, originator, producer.

makeshift adjective SEE **temporary**.

make-up noun SEE **cosmetics**.

A number of English words, including *maladjusted, malefactor, malevolent, malnutrition,* etc., are related to Latin *male-* = *badly, evilly, ill.* Contrast words beginning *bene-,* such as *benefactor, benevolent,* etc.

maladjusted adjective *a maladjusted child.* disturbed, muddled, neurotic, unbalanced.

maladroit adjective SEE **clumsy**.

malady, malaise nouns SEE **illness**.

malcontent noun SEE **rebel** noun.

male adjective *male characteristics.* SEE **manly, masculine**.
OPPOSITES: SEE **female**.
MALE HUMAN BEINGS: SEE **boy, man**.
MALE CREATURES: SEE **animal** noun.

malediction noun SEE **curse** noun.

malefactor noun SEE **wrongdoer**.

malevolent adjective SEE **malicious**.

malformation noun SEE **deformity**.

malfunction noun SEE **fault** noun.

malice noun animosity, [*informal*] bitchiness, bitterness, [*informal*] cattiness, enmity, hatred, hostility, ill-will, malevolence, maliciousness, malignity, nastiness, rancour, spite, spitefulness, vengefulness, venom, viciousness, vindictiveness.

malicious adjective *malicious remarks*. [*informal*] bitchy, bitter, [*informal*] catty, evil, evil-minded, hateful, ill-natured, malevolent, malignant, mischievous, nasty, rancorous, revengeful, sly, spiteful, vengeful, venomous, vicious, villainous, vindictive, wicked. OPPOSITES: SEE **benevolent**, **kind** adjective.

malignant adjective 1 *a malignant disease*. dangerous, destructive, harmful, injurious, poisonous, spreading, [*informal*] terminal, uncontrollable, virulent. OPPOSITE: benign.
2 *malignant intentions*. SEE **malicious**.

malinger verb SEE **shirk**.

malleable adjective *a malleable substance*. ductile, plastic, pliable, soft, tractable, workable. OPPOSITES: SEE **brittle**.

mallet noun hammer.

malnutrition noun famine, hunger, starvation, under-nourishment.

malpractice noun SEE **wrongdoing**.

maltreat verb SEE **harm** verb.

mammal noun VARIOUS ANIMALS: SEE **animal**.

mammoth adjective SEE **large**.

man noun 1 = *human beings of either sex*. SEE **mankind**.
2 = *male human being*. bachelor, boy, [informal] bloke, boyfriend, [*informal*] bridegroom, chap, [*informal*] codger, father, fellow, gentleman, groom, [*informal*] guy, husband, lad, lover, male, son, [*joking*] squire, widower.

man verb *to man an undertaking*. *to man a ship*. provide men for, provide staff for, staff.

manacle noun, verb SEE **chain** noun, verb.

manage verb 1 *to manage a business. to manage a crowd*. administer, be in charge of, be the manager of [SEE **manager**], command, conduct, control, cope with, deal with, direct, dominate, govern, handle, lead, look after, manipulate, mastermind, operate, oversee, preside over, regulate, rule, run, superintend, supervise, take control of, take over.
2 *How much work can you manage before dinner?* accomplish, achieve, bring about, carry out, contrive, do, finish, perform, succeed in, undertake.
3 *If you can't pay it all, pay what you can manage*. afford, spare.

manageable adjective 1 *a manageable size. a manageable quantity*. acceptable, convenient, easy to manage [SEE **manage**], governable, handy, neat, reasonable. OPPOSITES: SEE **awkward**.
2 *a manageable horse. a manageable crowd*. amenable, disciplined, docile, SEE **obedient**, tractable. OPPOSITES: SEE **disobedient**.

manager noun administrator, boss, SEE **chief**, controller, director, executive, governor, head, organizer, overseer, proprietor, ruler, superintendent, supervisor.

mandarin noun SEE **official** noun.

mandate noun SEE **authority**.

mandatory adjective SEE **compulsory**.

mangle verb *He was off work because he'd mangled his hand in a machine*. crush, cut, damage, disfigure, injure, lacerate, maim, maul, mutilate, squash, tear, SEE **wound** verb.

mangy adjective *a mangy animal*. dirty, scabby, scruffy, [*informal*] tatty, unkempt.

manhandle verb 1 *We manhandled the piano up the stairs*. carry, haul, heave, hump, lift, manoeuvre, move, pull, push.
2 *The muggers manhandled him*. [*informal*] beat up, knock about, maltreat, mistreat, misuse, [*informal*] rough up, treat roughly.

mania noun *a mania for collecting things*. craze, enthusiasm, fad, fetish, frenzy, hysteria, infatuation, insanity, lunacy, madness, obsession, passion, preoccupation.

maniac noun *a raving maniac*. SEE **madman**.

maniacal, manic adjectives SEE **mad**.

manifest adjective SEE **clear** adjective.

manifesto noun *a party manifesto*. declaration, policy, statement.

manipulate verb 1 *to manipulate a crowd. to manipulate election results*. control,

engineer, guide, handle, influence, manage, steer.
2 *to manipulate an injured person's leg.* feel, massage, rub.

mankind noun human beings, humanity, the human race, man, men and women, people [SEE **person**].
RELATED ADJECTIVE: anthropological.

manly adjective [*Manly* as a term of approval may have sexist overtones.] SEE **brave**, heroic, [*uncomplimentary*] macho, male, mannish, masculine, strong, swashbuckling, vigorous, virile. OPPOSITES: SEE **effeminate**.

man-made adjective *man-made substances.* artificial, imitation, manufactured, simulated, synthetic, unnatural. OPPOSITES: SEE **natural**.

mannequin noun SEE **model** noun.

manner noun **1** *She does things in a professional manner.* fashion, means, method, mode, procedure, process, style, way.
2 *I don't like his cheeky manner.* air, attitude, bearing, behaviour, character, conduct, demeanour, disposition, look, mien.
3 *We've tried all manner of things.* genre, kind, sort, type, variety.
good manners good behaviour, breeding, civility, conduct, courtesy, etiquette, gentility, politeness, refinement.

mannerism noun *an annoying mannerism.* characteristic, habit, idiosyncrasy, peculiarity, quirk, trait.

manœuvre noun **1** *Getting the car into the drive is a tricky manœuvre.* move, operation.
2 *It was a clever manœuvre to take his bishop.* dodge, gambit, move, plan, plot, ploy, ruse, scheme, stratagem, strategy, tactics, trick.
manœuvres *army manœuvres,* exercise, movement, operation, training.

manœuvre verb *to manœuvre something into position.* engineer, guide, jockey, manipulate, move, navigate, negotiate, pilot, steer.

manor, manor-house nouns SEE **mansion**.

manservant noun VARIOUS SERVANTS: SEE **servant**.

mansion noun castle, château, manor, manor-house, palace, stately home, villa.
OTHER HOUSES: SEE **house** noun.

manslaughter noun SEE **killing** noun.

mantle noun cape, cloak, hood, shroud, wrap.

mantrap noun SEE **trap** noun.

manual adjective *manual work.* by hand, physical.

manual noun KINDS OF BOOK: SEE **book** noun.

manufacture verb *to manufacture goods in a factory.* assemble, build, fabricate, make, mass-produce, prefabricate, process, [*informal*] turn out.

manufactured adjective **1** *manufactured goods.* factory-made, mass-produced.
OPPOSITES: SEE **home-made**.
2 *manufactured substances.* artificial, man-made, synthetic.
OPPOSITES: SEE **natural**.

manufacturer noun factory-owner, industrialist, producer.

manure noun compost, dung, fertilizer, [*informal*] muck.

manuscript noun SEE **book** noun, document, papers, script.

many adjective abundant, copious, countless, frequent, innumerable, multifarious, numberless, numerous, profuse, [*informal*] umpteen, untold, various.
OPPOSITES: SEE **few**.

map noun chart, diagram, plan.
a book of maps atlas, roadbook.
the drawing of maps cartography.

map verb *to map an area.* chart, survey.
to map out *to map out your future.* SEE **plan** verb.

mar verb SEE **spoil**.

marauder noun bandit, buccaneer, invader, pirate, plunderer, raider.

march noun **1** *The band played a march.* MUSICAL COMPOSITIONS: SEE **music**.
2 *the march of time.* SEE **progress** noun.

march verb *Soldiers marched into town.* file, parade, stride, troop, SEE **walk** verb.

mare noun SEE **horse**.

margin noun *the margin of a piece of paper. the margin of a lake.* border, boundary, SEE **edge** noun, frieze, perimeter, side, verge.

marginal adjective *of marginal importance.* borderline, doubtful, minimal, negligible, peripheral, small, unimportant.

marina noun SEE **harbour** noun.

marine adjective SEE **sea** adjective.

marine noun SEE **soldier**.

mariner noun sailor, seafarer, seaman.

marionette noun SEE **doll**.

mark noun **1** *dirty marks. marks on your skin.* blemish, blot, blotch, dot, fingermark, [*plural*] graffiti, marking, print, scar, scratch, scribble, smear, smudge, smut, [*informal*] splotch, SEE **spot** noun, stain, [*formal*] stigma (*plural* stigmata), streak, trace, vestige.

2 *a mark of respect. a mark of good breeding.* characteristic, emblem, feature, hallmark, indication, sign, symbol, token.

3 *a manufacturer's mark.* badge, brand, device, label, seal, stamp, standard.

mark verb **1** *to mark a surface.* blemish, blot, brand, bruise, damage, deface, dirty, disfigure, draw on, make a mark on [SEE **mark** noun], mar, scar, scratch, scrawl over, scribble on, smudge, spot, stain, stamp, streak, tattoo, write on.

2 *to mark students' work.* appraise, assess, correct, evaluate, grade.

3 *Mark what I say.* attend to, heed, listen to, mind, note, notice, observe, take note of, [*informal*] take to heart, watch.

marked adjective SEE **noticeable**.

market noun auction, bazaar, fair, sale.

market verb *His firm markets furniture.* SEE **advertise**, retail, sell, [*informal*] tout, trade, trade in.

marketable adjective *marketable goods.* in demand, merchantable, saleable, sellable.

marking noun SEE **mark** noun.

marksman noun [*informal*] crack shot, gunman, sharpshooter, sniper.

marl noun SEE **soil** noun.

maroon verb *to maroon someone on an island.* abandon, cast away, desert, forsake, isolate, leave, put ashore, strand.
a marooned person castaway.

marquee noun SEE **tent**.

marriage noun **1** *They celebrated 25 years of marriage.* matrimony, partnership, union, wedlock.
2 *Today is the anniversary of their marriage.* [*old-fashioned*] espousal, match, nuptials, wedding.
VARIOUS STATES OF MARRIAGE: bigamy, monogamy, polyandry, polygamy.
COMPARE: bachelorhood, celibacy, divorce, separation, spinsterhood, widowhood.
RELATED ADJECTIVES: conjugal, marital, matrimonial, nuptial.

marriageable adjective adult, mature, nubile.

marry verb **1** *to marry a husband or wife.* espouse, [*informal*] get hitched, join in matrimony, [*informal*] tie the knot, wed.
2 *to marry two things together.* SEE **unite**.

marsh noun bog, fen, marshland, mire, morass, mud, mudflats, quagmire, quicksands, saltings, saltmarsh, [*old-fashioned*] slough, swamp, wetland.

marshal noun SEE **official** noun, **rank** noun.

marshal verb *to marshal troops. to marshal your thoughts.* arrange, assemble, collect, deploy, draw up, gather, group, line up, muster, organize, set out.

marshy adjective SEE **swampy**.

martial adjective **1** *a martial figure.* aggressive, bellicose, belligerent, militant, pugnacious, warlike.
OPPOSITES: SEE **peaceable**.
2 *martial law.* military.
OPPOSITE: civil.
martial arts judo, karate, kung fu, taekwondo.

martinet noun SEE **disciplinarian**.

martyr verb SEE **kill**.

martyrdom noun SEE **killing** noun.

marvel noun *the marvel of space travel.* miracle, wonder.

marvel verb **to marvel at** *We marvelled at their skill.* admire, applaud, be amazed by, be astonished by, be surprised by, gape at, SEE **praise** verb, wonder at.

marvellous adjective **1** *a marvellous scientific discovery. marvellous works of art.* admirable, amazing, astonishing, excellent, extraordinary, [*informal*] fabulous, [*informal*] fantastic, glorious, incredible, magnificent, miraculous, phenomenal, praiseworthy, remarkable, sensational, spectacular, splendid, [*informal*] super, superb, surprising, unbelievable, wonderful, wondrous.
OPPOSITES; SEE **ordinary**.
2 [*informal*] *We had a marvellous time.* SEE **good**.

Marxism noun POLITICAL TERMS: SEE **politics**.

masculine adjective [*Masculine* and its synonyms may have sexist overtones, and therefore should be used with care.] *a masculine appearance. masculine behaviour.* boyish, [*informal*] butch, dynamic, gentlemanly, heroic, [*uncomplimentary*] macho, male, manly, mannish, muscular, powerful, strong, vigorous, virile.
OPPOSITES: SEE **feminine**.

mash verb *to mash something to a pulp.* beat, crush, grind, mangle, pound, pulp, pulverize, smash, squash.

mask noun *a mask to cover your face.* camouflage, cover, disguise, façade, front, screen, shield, veil, visor.

mask verb *We planted a tree to mask the ugly building.* blot out, camouflage, cloak, conceal, cover, disguise, hide, obscure, screen, shield, shroud, veil.

masonry noun bricks, brickwork, stone, stonework.

masquerade noun SEE **pretence**.

mass adjective *a mass revolt*. comprehensive, general, large-scale, popular, universal, wholesale, widespread.
the mass media SEE **communication**.

mass noun 1 *a mass of rubbish*. accumulation, body, bulk, [*informal*] chunk, concretion, conglomeration, [*informal*] dollop, heap, [*informal*] hunk, [*informal*] load, lot, lump, mound, pile, quantity, stack.
2 *a mass of people*. SEE **group** noun.
3 *We go to Mass on Sundays*. SEE **service** noun.

mass verb *to mass together*. SEE **gather**.

massacre noun SEE **killing** noun.

massacre verb SEE **kill**.

massage verb *The trainer massaged my injured leg*. knead, manipulate, rub.

massive adjective SEE **huge**.

mast noun aerial, flagpole, maypole, pylon, transmitter.

master noun 1 *the master of a dog*. keeper, owner, person in charge, proprietor.
2 *a schoolmaster*. SEE **teacher**.
3 *the master of a ship*. captain.
4 *a master at chess*. [*informal*] ace, expert, genius, mastermind, virtuoso.

master verb [Some people regard the verb *master* as sexist.] 1 *to master the rules*. acquire, [*informal*] get off by heart, [*informal*] get the hang of, grasp, learn, understand.
2 *to master a wild horse*. break in, bridle, conquer, control, curb, defeat, dominate, [*informal*] get the better of, govern, manage, overcome, overpower, quell, regulate, rule, subdue, subjugate, suppress, tame, triumph over, vanquish.

masterful adjective [Do not confuse with *masterly*.] *a masterful personality*. SEE **bossy**.

masterly adjective [Do not confuse with *masterful*.] *masterly control of the ball*. SEE **expert** adjective.

mastermind noun 1 *the mastermind behind an undertaking*. architect, brains, creator, engineer, inventor, manager, originator, planner, prime mover.
2 [*informal*] *Ask the mastermind!* [*informal*] egghead, expert, genius, intellectual, master.

mastermind verb *She masterminded the whole operation*. be the mastermind behind [SEE **mastermind** noun], carry through, direct, execute, SEE **manage**, organize, plan.

masterpiece noun *This piece of music is the composer's masterpiece*. best work, chef-d'œuvre, classic, [*informal*] hit, pièce de résistance.

mastery noun 1 *mastery over other people*. SEE **control** noun.
2 *Her mastery in several foreign languages amazed us*. SEE **cleverness**.

masticate verb SEE **chew**.

mat noun carpet, floor-covering, matting, rug.

match noun 1 *It was an exciting match on Saturday*. competition, contest, game, test match, tie, tournament.
2 *The jacket and tie are a good match*. combination, complement, counterpart, double, equivalent, fit, pair, similarity, tally, twin.
3 *a love match*. friendship, marriage, partnership, relationship, union.

match verb 1 *The tie matches my shirt*. agree with, be compatible with, be the same colour (style, etc.) as, be similar to, blend with, coincide with, combine with, compare with, correspond to, fit with, go with, harmonize with, marry with, tally with, tone in with.
OPPOSITES: SEE **contrast** verb.
2 *We'll match you with a suitable partner*. ally, combine, couple, fit, join, link up, mate, put together, team.

matching adjective *a blue shirt with matching tie*. alike, appropriate, comparable, compatible, co-ordinating, corresponding, equal, equivalent, harmonizing, identical, similar, toning, twin.
OPPOSITES: SEE **incongruous**.

matchless adjective SEE **unequalled**.

mate noun 1 *a plumber's mate*. assistant, collaborator, colleague, helper, partner.
2 *a mate for life*. husband, spouse, wife.
3 [*informal*] *He's a mate of mine*. SEE **friend**.

mate verb *Many birds mate in the springtime*. become partners, copulate, couple, have intercourse, [*informal*] have sex [SEE **sex**], marry, unite, wed.

material noun 1 *material to make a shirt*. SEE **cloth**, fabric, textile.
2 *material for a story*. content, data, facts, ideas, information, matter, notes, subject matter.
3 *material to make a patio*. building materials, stuff, substances, things.
VARIOUS BUILDING MATERIALS: SEE **building**.

materialize verb *A shape materialized out of the fog*. SEE **appear**.

maternal adjective *maternal love.* motherly.

maternity noun motherhood, pregnancy.

matey adjective SEE **friendly**.

mathematics noun [*informal*] maths, number work.

BRANCHES OF MATHEMATICS: algebra, arithmetic, calculus, geometry, statistics, trigonometry.

EVERYDAY MATHEMATICAL TERMS: addition, angle, area, binary system, concentric, congruence, cosine, decimal, fraction, decimal point, diagonal, diameter, division, equation, equilateral, exponent, factor, fraction, function, graph, index (*plural* indices), locus, logarithm, matrix, mensuration, minus, multiplication, negative number, parallel, percentage, perpendicular, plus, positive number, radius, ratio, right angle, SEE **shape** noun, sine, subtraction, sum, symmetry, tangent, tessellation, theorem.

MATHEMATICAL INSTRUMENTS: compasses, dividers, protractor, ruler, set-square.

matriarch noun SEE **woman**.

matrimony noun SEE **marriage**.

matron noun SEE **woman**.

matt adjective SEE **dull** adjective.

matted adjective *matted hair.* knotted, tangled, uncombed, unkempt.

matter noun 1 *mind over matter. colouring matter.* body, material, stuff, substance. 2 *poisonous matter in a wound.* discharge, pus, suppuration.
3 *The manager will deal with this matter.* affair, business, concern, incident, issue, situation, subject, thing, topic.
4 *What's the matter with the car?* difficulty, problem, trouble, upset, worry, wrong (*What's wrong?*).

matter verb *Will it matter if I'm late?* be important, count, make a difference, signify.

matter-of-fact adjective *a matter-of-fact description.* [*informal*] dead-pan, down to earth, SEE **factual**, mechanical, prosaic, to the point, unadorned, unemotional, unimaginative.
OPPOSITES: SEE **emotional, imaginative**.

matting noun SEE **mat**.

mature adjective 1 *mature for her age.* adult, advanced, full-grown, grown-up, nubile, well-developed.
OPPOSITES: SEE **immature**.

2 *mature fruit.* mellow, ready, ripe.
OPPOSITES: SEE **unripe**.

maudlin adjective SEE **sentimental**.

maul verb *The lion mauled the keeper.* claw, injure, [*informal*] knock about, lacerate, mangle, manhandle, mutilate, paw, treat roughly, SEE **wound** verb.

maunder verb *to maunder on boringly.* SEE **talk** verb.

mausoleum noun SEE **tomb**.

maverick noun SEE **rebel** noun.

mawkish adjective SEE **sentimental**.

maxim noun SEE **saying**.

maximize verb 1 *to maximize your profits.* SEE **increase** verb.
2 *to maximize your problems.* SEE **exaggerate**.
OPPOSITE: **minimize**.

maximum adjective *maximum size. maximum speed.* biggest, full, fullest, greatest, highest, largest, most, supreme, top.
OPPOSITES: SEE **minimum** adjective.

maximum noun *Temperatures usually reach their maximum after noon.* ceiling, highest point, peak, top, upper limit, zenith.
OPPOSITES: SEE **minimum** noun.

maybe adverb conceivably, perhaps, possibly.
OPPOSITES: SEE **definitely**.

mayhem noun SEE **confusion**.

mayor, mayoress nouns SEE **official** noun.

maze noun *a maze of corridors.* confusion, labyrinth, network, tangle, web.

meadow noun field, [*poetic*] mead, paddock, pasture.

meagre adjective SEE **scanty**.

meal noun [*informal*] blow-out, repast, [*informal*] spread.

VARIOUS MEALS: banquet, barbecue, breakfast, buffet, dinner, [*informal*] elevenses, feast, high tea, lunch, luncheon, picnic, snack, supper, take-away, tea, tea-break, [*old-fashioned*] tiffin.

COURSES OF A MEAL: [*informal*] afters, dessert, [*formal*] entrée, hors-d'œuvres, main course, pudding, starter, sweet.

mealy-mouthed adjective SEE **flattering**.

mean adjective 1 *too mean to give a donation.* beggarly, [*informal*] cheese-paring, close, close-fisted, [*informal*] mingy, miserly, niggardly, parsimonious, [*informal*] penny-pinching, selfish, sparing, [*informal*] stingy, [*informal*] tight, tight-fisted.
OPPOSITES: SEE **generous**.
2 *a mean trick.* base, callous, churlish, contemptible, cruel, despicable, hard-hearted, malicious, nasty, shabby, shameful, [*informal*] sneaky, spiteful, unkind, vicious.
OPPOSITES: SEE **kind** adjective.
3 [*old-fashioned*] *a mean dwelling.* humble, inferior, insignificant, lowly, SEE **poor**, squalid, wretched.
OPPOSITES: SEE **superior**.
4 *mean temperature.* SEE **average** adjective.

mean verb 1 *What does that sign mean?* betoken, communicate, connote, convey, denote, express, hint at, imply, indicate, portend, presage, say, signify, spell out, stand for, suggest, symbolize.
2 *I mean to work harder.* aim, desire, intend, plan, propose, purpose, want, wish.
3 *The job means working long hours.* entail, involve, necessitate.

meander verb SEE **wander**.

meandering adjective SEE **roundabout** adjective.

meaning adjective *a meaning glance.* SEE **meaningful**.

meaning noun 1 *the meaning of a word.* connotation, definition, denotation, force, sense, signification.
2 *the meaning of a poem. the meaning of someone's behaviour.* explanation, gist, implication, interpretation, message, point, purport, purpose, significance, thrust.

meaningful adjective *a meaningful glance. meaningful discussions.* eloquent, expressive, meaning, pointed, positive, pregnant, significant, suggestive, warning, worthwhile.
OPPOSITES: SEE **meaningless**.

meaningless adjective 1 *meaningless compliments.* empty, flattering, hollow, insincere, sycophantic, worthless.
2 *a meaningless message.* absurd, coded, incoherent, incomprehensible, inconsequential, nonsensical, pointless, senseless.
OPPOSITES: SEE **meaningful**.

means noun 1 *the means to do something. a means to an end.* ability, capacity, channel, course, fashion, machinery, manner, medium, method, mode, process, way.

2 *the means to pay for something. private means.* affluence, capital, finances, funds, income, money, resources, riches, wealth, [*informal*] wherewithal.

measly adjective [*slang*] *a measly spoonful of pudding.* SEE **scanty**.

measurable adjective *a measurable amount.* appreciable, considerable, perceptible, quantifiable, reasonable, significant.
OPPOSITES: SEE **negligible**.

measure noun 1 *full measure.* amount, capacity, distance, extent, length, magnitude, measurement, quantity, ration, size, unit, way.
2 *a measure of someone's ability.* criterion, standard, test, touchstone, yardstick.
3 *measures to curb crime.* act, action, bill, expedient, law, means, procedure, step.

UNITS USED IN MEASURING:
BREADTH, DEPTH, DISTANCE, GAUGE, HEIGHT, LENGTH, WIDTH: centimetre, cubit, fathom, foot, furlong, inch, kilometre, light-year, metre, millimetre, parsec, yard.
AREA: acre, hectare, square centimetres (metres, etc.).
TIME: century, day, decade, hour, microsecond, millennium, minute, month, second, week, year.
CAPACITY, VOLUME: bushel, cubic centimetres (inches, etc.), gallon, hogshead, litre, millilitre, pint, quart.
WEIGHT: carat, drachm, gram, hundredweight, kilo or kilogram, megaton, megatonne, milligram, ounce, pound, stone, ton, tonne.
SPEED, VELOCITY: kilometres per hour, knot, Mach number, miles per hour, [*informal*] ton.
QUANTITY: century [= *100*], dozen, gross, score.
TEMPERATURE: degree Celsius, degree centigrade, degree Fahrenheit.
INFORMAL MEASUREMENTS: armful, cupful, handful, mouthful, pinch, plateful, spoonful.

---

measure verb *He measured its size.* assess, calculate, calibrate, compute, determine, gauge, judge, mark-out, plumb (*to plumb the depths of water*), quantify, survey, take measurements of, weigh.
to measure out *She measured out their daily ration.* allot, apportion, deal out, dispense, distribute, [*informal*] dole out, ration out, share out.

measured adjective *a measured rhythm.* SEE **regular**.

measurement noun 1 *the measurements of a room.* dimensions, extent, SEE **measure** noun, size.
2 *The children did some work on measurement in maths.* mensuration.

meat noun flesh.

KINDS OF MEAT: bacon, beef, chicken, game, gammon, ham, lamb, mutton, offal, oxtail, pork, poultry, tripe, turkey, veal, venison.

VARIOUS CUTS OR JOINTS OF MEAT: breast, brisket, chine, chops, chuck, cutlet, fillet, flank, leg, loin, oxtail, rib, rump, scrag, shoulder, silverside, sirloin, spare-rib, steak, topside, trotter.

KINDS OF PROCESSED MEAT: brawn, burger, corned beef, hamburger, mince, pasty, pâté, pie, potted meat, rissole, salted meat, sausage.

mechanic noun *a motor mechanic.* engineer, technician.

mechanical adjective 1 *a mechanical process.* automated, automatic, machine-driven, technological.
OPPOSITE: manual.
2 *a mechanical response.* cold, inhuman, lifeless, matter-of-fact, perfunctory, routine, soulless, unconscious, unemotional, unfeeling, unimaginative, unthinking.
OPPOSITES: SEE **thoughtful**.

mechanism noun SEE **machine**.

mechanize verb *to mechanize a production line.* automate, bring up to date, equip with machines, modernize.

medal noun award, decoration, honour, medallion, prize, reward, trophy.

medallist noun champion, victor, winner.

meddle verb SEE **interfere**.

meddlesome adjective SEE **interfering**.

media noun SEE **communication**.

medial, median adjectives SEE **middle** adjective.

mediate verb *to mediate in a dispute.* act as mediator [SEE **mediator**], arbitrate, intercede, liaise, negotiate.

mediator noun arbitrator, broker, go-between, intermediary, negotiator, peacemaker, referee, umpire.

medicinal adjective *a medicinal ointment.* healing, medical, restorative, therapeutic.

medicine noun 1 *the study of medicine.* healing, surgery, therapeutics, treatment of diseases.
2 *medicine from the chemist's.* cure, dose, drug, medicament, medication, [*uncomplimentary*] nostrum, prescription, remedy, treatment.

SOME BRANCHES OF MEDICAL PRACTICE: anaesthesiology (*anaesthetics*), audiometrics (*hearing*), chiropody (*feet*), dentistry (*teeth*), dermatology (*skin*), dietetics (*diet*), family practice, general practice, geriatrics (*old age*), gynaecology (*women's illnesses*), homeopathy, immunology (*resistance to infection*), neurology (*nerves*), neurosurgery, obstetrics (*childbirth*), ophthalmology (*eyes*), orthopaedics (*bones & muscles*), osteopathy, paediatrics (*children*), pathology, plastic surgery, preventive or preventative medicine, psychiatry (*mind*), radiology (*X-rays*), surgery, SEE **therapy**.

PEOPLE WHO LOOK AFTER OUR HEALTH: acupuncturist, anaesthetist, audiometrician, chiropodist, chiropractor, dentist, dermatologist, dietician, doctor, general practitioner, gynaecologist, homeopath, hygienist, hypnotherapist, [*male*] masseur, [*female*] masseuse, medical practitioner, midwife, neurologist, nurse, obstetrician, oculist, optician, osteopath, paediatrician, physician, physiotherapist, plastic surgeon, psychiatrist, radiographer, sister, surgeon.

PLACES WHERE YOU GET MEDICAL TREATMENT: clinic, dispensary, health centre, health farm, hospital, infirmary, intensive-care unit, nursing home, operating theatre, outpatients' department, sickbay, surgery, ward.

VARIOUS MEDICINES, ETC.: anaesthetic, antibiotic, antidote, antiseptic, aspirin, capsule, embrocation, gargle, herbs, inhaler, iodine, linctus, lotion, lozenge, manipulation, massage, morphia, narcotic, ointment, pastille, penicillin, [*informal*] the pill, sedative, suppository, tablet, tonic, tranquillizer.

OTHER MEDICAL TERMS: bandage, biopsy, dressing, first aid, forceps, hypodermic syringe, immunization, injection, inoculation, lint, plaster, poultice, scalpel, sling, splint, stethoscope, stretcher, syringe, thermometer, transfusion, transplant, tweezers, X-ray.

WORDS TO DO WITH ILLNESS: SEE **ill**, **illness**.

mediocre adjective *mediocre work.* amateurish, average, commonplace, fair, indifferent, inferior, middling, moderate, [*informal*] neither one thing nor the other, [*informal*] nothing special, ordinary, passable, pedestrian, poorish, second-rate, [*informal*] so-so, undistinguished, unexciting, uninspired, unremarkable, weakish.

meditation noun contemplation, prayer, reflection, yoga.

meditate verb *to meditate in silence.* brood, cogitate, consider, contemplate, deliberate, mull things over, muse, ponder, pray, reflect, ruminate, think.

meditative adjective SEE **thoughtful**.

medium adjective average, intermediate, mean, middle, middling, midway, moderate, normal, ordinary, usual.

medium noun 1 *a happy medium.* average, compromise, mean, middle, midpoint,
2 *This artist's favourite medium is watercolour.* form, means, method, vehicle, way.
3 *a medium who claims to communicate with the dead.* clairvoyant, seer, spiritualist.
the media [*Media* is plural, so we should speak not of *a media*, but of *the media*.] SEE **communication**.
mass media broadcasting, magazines, newspapers, the press, radio, television.

medley noun SEE **mixture**.

meek adjective *meek acceptance of defeat.* acquiescent, compliant, docile, forbearing, gentle, humble, long-suffering, lowly, mild, modest, obedient, patient, quiet, resigned, soft, spineless, tame, unassuming, unprotesting, weak.
OPPOSITES: SEE **aggressive**.

meet verb 1 *I met my friend in town.* [*informal*] bump into, chance upon, come across, confront, contact, encounter, face, happen on, have a meeting with [SEE **meeting**], [*informal*] run across, [*informal*] run into, see.
2 *I'll meet you at the station.* come and fetch, greet, [*informal*] pick up, welcome.
3 *We all met in the hall.* assemble, collect, come together, congregate, convene, forgather, gather, have a meeting [SEE **meeting**], muster, rally.
4 *Two roads meet here.* come together, connect, converge, cross, intersect, join, link up, merge, unite.

5 *We met their demands.* acquiesce in, agree to, comply with, fulfil, [*informal*] measure up to, satisfy.

meeting noun 1 *a business meeting.* assembly, audience (*an audience with the king*), board meeting, briefing, cabinet meeting, committee, conclave, conference, congregation, congress, convention, council, discussion group, forum, gathering, [*informal*] powwow, prayer meeting, rally, seminar, service (*in church*), synod (*of the church*).
2 *a chance meeting.* confrontation, contact, encounter.
3 *an arranged meeting with someone.* appointment, assignation, date, engagement, [*informal*] get-together, rendezvous, [*old-fashioned*] tryst.
4 *the meeting of two routes.* confluence (*of rivers*), convergence, crossing, crossroads, intersection, junction.

The prefix *mega-* is related to Greek *megas = great, large.*

---

megalomania noun SEE **pride**.

megaphone noun amplifier, loudhailer.

melancholia noun depression.

melancholy adjective *a melancholy look on her face. a melancholy scene.* cheerless, dejected, depressed, depressing, despondent, dispirited, dispiriting, [*informal*] down, down-hearted, gloomy, joyless, lifeless, low, lugubrious, melancholic, miserable, moody, mournful, sad, sombre, sorrowful, unhappy, woebegone, woeful.
OPPOSITES: SEE **cheerful**.

mélange noun SEE **mixture**.

mêlée noun SEE **confusion, fight** noun.

mellifluous adjective SEE **tuneful**.

mellow adjective 1 *a mellow taste.* mature, mild, pleasant, rich, ripe, smooth, sweet.
2 *mellow light. mellow sounds. mellow surroundings.* agreeable, comforting, genial, gentle, happy, kindly, peaceful, reassuring, soft, subdued, warm.
OPPOSITES: SEE **harsh**.

melodious adjective SEE **tuneful**.

melody noun air, strain, theme, tune.

melt verb *The sun's warmth melts the snow.* deliquesce, liquefy, soften, thaw, unfreeze.
to melt away *The crowd melted away.* dematerialize, disappear, disperse, dissolve, dwindle, evaporate, fade, pass away, vanish.

member noun 1 *a member of a club.* associate, fellow.
2 *the members of your body.* SEE **limb**.
to be a member SEE **belong**.

membrane noun SEE **skin** noun.

memento noun SEE **souvenir**.

memo noun SEE **communication**.

memoir, memoirs nouns autobiography, SEE **biography**, recollections.

memorable adjective 1 *a memorable occasion.* distinguished, SEE **extraordinary**, impressive, indelible, ineradicable, outstanding, remarkable, striking, unforgettable.
2 *a memorable tune.* [*informal*] catchy, haunting.
OPPOSITES: SEE **commonplace**.

memorandum noun SEE **communication**.

memorial noun cairn, cenotaph, gravestone, headstone, monument, plaque, tablet, SEE **tomb**.

memorize noun *to memorize facts.* commit to memory, [*informal*] get off by heart, SEE **learn**, learn by rote, learn parrot-fashion, remember.

memory noun 1 *a bad memory.* ability to remember, recall, retention.
2 *happy memories of our holiday.* impression, recollection, remembrance, reminder, reminiscence, souvenir.
3 *The memory of people we loved is always with us.* fame, name, reputation.

menace noun *a menace to society.* SEE **threat**.

menace verb SEE **threaten**.

menacing adjective SEE **threatening**.

ménage noun [*informal*] domestic set-up, family, household.

menagerie noun zoo.
VARIOUS ANIMALS: SEE **animal** noun.

mend verb 1 *to mend the car. to mend clothes.* fix, put right, rectify, renew, renovate, repair, restore.
WAYS TO MEND THINGS: beat out (*to beat out dents*), darn, patch, replace parts, sew up, solder, stitch up, touch up, weld.
2 *to mend your ways.* amend, correct, cure, improve, make better, reform, revise.
3 *The wound mended quickly.* get better, heal, recover, recuperate.

mendacious adjective SEE **lying**.

mendicant noun SEE **beggar**.

menial adjective *menial jobs.* base, boring, degrading, demeaning, humble, lowly, mean, servile, slavish, subservient, unskilled, unworthy.

menial noun SEE **servant**.

menstruate verb have a period.

mensuration noun measuring, measurement.

mental adjective 1 *mental arithmetic. mental effort.* abstract, cerebral, intellectual, rational, theoretical.
2 *a mental condition.* emotional, psychological, subjective, temperamental.
3 [*informal*] *He must be mental.* SEE **mad**.

mentality noun *a criminal mentality.* attitude, character, disposition, frame of mind, [*informal*] make-up, outlook, personality, predisposition, propensity, psychology, way of thinking.

mention verb 1 *to mention something casually.* allude to, comment on, disclose, hint at, [*informal*] let drop, let out, refer to, reveal, speak about, touch on.
2 *The speaker mentioned all the prize-winners.* acknowledge, cite, draw attention to, enumerate, make known, name, point out.
3 *I mentioned that I might go out.* observe, remark, say.

mentor noun SEE **adviser**.

menu noun bill of fare, tariff.

mercenary noun SEE **fighter**, **soldier**.

merchandise noun commodities, goods, things for sale.

merchandise verb SEE **advertise**, **sell**.

merchant noun *a timber merchant,* dealer, retailer, salesman, shopkeeper, stockist, supplier, trader, tradesman, wholesaler.

merciful adjective *a merciful judge. merciful treatment.* benevolent, charitable, clement, compassionate, forbearing, forgiving, generous, gracious, humane, humanitarian, kind, lenient, liberal, mild, pitying, [*uncomplimentary*] soft, sympathetic, tender-hearted, tolerant.
OPPOSITES: SEE **merciless**.

merciless adjective *a merciless judge. merciless punishment.* barbaric, callous, cruel, cut-throat, hard, hard-hearted, harsh, heartless, inexorable, inhuman, inhumane, intolerant, pitiless, relentless, remorseless, ruthless, savage, severe, stern, strict, unfeeling, unforgiving, unkind, unrelenting, unremitting, vicious.
OPPOSITES: SEE **merciful**.

mercurial adjective SEE **changeable**.

mercury noun quicksilver.

mercy noun *The attackers showed no mercy.* charity, clemency, compassion, feeling, forbearance, forgiveness,

grace, humanity, kindness, leniency, love, pity, sympathy, understanding.
OPPOSITES: SEE **cruelty**.

merge verb 1 *to merge two schools*. amalgamate, blend, combine, come together, confederate, fuse, integrate, join together, link up, mingle, mix, put together, unite.
2 *motorways merge*. converge, join, meet.
OPPOSITES: SEE **separate** verb.

merit noun 1 *Your work has some merit*. asset, excellence, goodness, importance, quality, strength, talent, value, virtue, worth.
2 *a certificate of merit*. credit, distinction.

merit verb *Her performance merited first prize*. be entitled to, deserve, earn, incur, justify, rate, warrant.

meritorious adjective SEE **praiseworthy**.

merriment noun *What's all the merriment about?* amusement, gaiety, hilarity, jocularity, joking, jollity, joviality, laughter, levity, light-heartedness, liveliness, SEE **merrymaking**, mirth, vivacity.

merry adjective *a merry tune*. bright, carefree, cheerful, [*informal*] chirpy, festive, fun-loving, gay, glad, SEE **happy**, hilarious, jocular, jolly, jovial, joyful, joyous, light-hearted, lively, rollicking, spirited, vivacious.
OPPOSITES: SEE **serious**.

merry-go-round noun carousel, roundabout.

merrymaking noun *Come and join in the merrymaking*. carousing, celebration, conviviality, festivity, frolic, fun, [*informal*] fun and games, [*joking*] jollification, [*informal*] junketing, merriment, SEE **party**, revelry, roistering, sociability, [*old-fashioned*] wassailing.

mesh noun *a mesh of intersecting lines*. lattice, net, netting, network, tangle, tracery, web.

mesmerize verb SEE **hypnotize**.

mess noun 1 *Clear up this mess*. chaos, clutter, SEE **confusion**, SEE **dirt**, disorder, jumble, litter, muddle, [*informal*] shambles, untidiness.
2 *I made a mess of it!* [*informal*] botch, failure, [*informal*] hash, [*informal*] mix-up.
3 *I got into a mess*. difficulty, dilemma, [*informal*] fix, [*informal*] jam, plight, predicament, problem.
to make a mess of SEE **bungle**, **muddle** verb.

mess verb **to mess about** [*informal*] *Stop messing about and start work!* amuse

yourself, loaf, loiter, lounge about [SEE **lounge** verb], [*informal*] monkey about, [*informal*] muck about, play about.
to mess up SEE **muddle** verb.
to mess up a job SEE **bungle**.

message noun announcement, bulletin, cable, SEE **communication**, communiqué, dispatch, letter, memo, memorandum, note, notice, report, statement.

messenger noun bearer, carrier, courier, dispatch-rider, [*formal*] emissary, [*formal*] envoy, go-between, [*poetic*] harbinger, herald, postman, runner.

messy adjective *a messy appearance*. blowzy, careless, chaotic, cluttered, dirty, dishevelled, disorderly, filthy, grubby, mucky, muddled, [*informal*] shambolic, slapdash, sloppy, slovenly, unkempt, untidy.
OPPOSITES: SEE **neat**.

metal noun *a lump of metal* ingot, nugget.

METALLIC ELEMENTS: aluminium, barium, beryllium, bismuth, cadmium, calcium, chromium, cobalt, copper, gold, iridium, iron, lead, lithium, magnesium, manganese, mercury, molybdenum, nickel, platinum, potassium, silver, sodium, strontium, tin, titanium, tungsten, uranium, zinc.

SOME METAL ALLOYS: brass, bronze, gunmetal, pewter, solder, steel.

metallic adjective 1 *a metallic sheen*. gleaming, lustrous, shiny.
2 *a metallic sound*. clanking, clinking, ringing.

metamorphose verb SEE **change** verb.

metamorphosis noun SEE **change** noun.

metaphor noun SEE **figure** noun (figures of speech).

metaphysics noun SEE **philosophy**.

mete verb **to mete out** SEE **distribute**.

meteor, meteorite nouns ASTRONOMICAL TERMS: SEE **astronomy**.

meter verb SEE **measure** verb.

method noun 1 *a method of doing something*. fashion, [*informal*] knack, manner, means, mode, plan, procedure, process, recipe, scheme, style, technique, trick, way.
2 *method behind the chaos*. arrangement, design, order, orderliness, organization, pattern, routine, system.

methodical adjective *a methodical worker*. businesslike, careful, deliberate, disciplined, logical, meticulous,

neat, orderly, organized, painstaking, precise, rational, regular, structured, systematic, tidy.
OPPOSITES: SEE **arbitrary, careless.**

meticulous adjective SEE **scrupulous.**

metric adjective *the metric system of weights and measures.* decimal.
OPPOSITE: imperial.

metrical adjective SEE **rhythmic.**

metricate verb decimalize, make metric.

metropolis noun SEE **city.**

mettle noun SEE **courage.**

mezzanine noun landing.

miasma noun fog, reek, smell, stench, vapour.

The prefix *micro-* is related to Greek *mikros = small.*

---

micro noun SEE **computer.**

microbe noun SEE **micro-organism.**

microlight noun SEE **aircraft.**

micro-organism noun bacillus, [*plural*] bacteria, [*informal*] bug, germ, microbe, virus.

microphone noun SEE **audio equipment.**

microscope noun SEE **optical (optical instruments).**

microscopic adjective SEE **tiny.**

microwave-oven noun KITCHEN EQUIPMENT: SEE **kitchen.**

midday noun lunchtime, noon.
OTHER TIMES OF DAY: SEE **time** noun.

midden noun dung-heap, dunghill, manure-heap.

middle adjective *the middle stump.* central, half-way, inner, inside, intermediate, intervening, mean, medial, median, middle-of-the-road, midway, neutral.

middle noun *the middle of the earth. the middle of the road.* centre, core, crown (*of the road*), focus, heart, hub, inside, middle position [SEE **middle** adjective], midpoint, midst (*in the midst of the confusion*), nucleus.

middleman noun *the middleman in business.* agent, broker, distributor.

middle-of-the-road adjective SEE **moderate** adjective.

middling adjective *a middling performance.* average, fair, [*informal*] fair to middling, indifferent, mediocre, moderate, modest, [*informal*] nothing to write home about, ordinary, passable, run-of-

the-mill, [*informal*] so-so, unremarkable.
OPPOSITES: SEE **outstanding.**

midge noun SEE **insect.**

midget adjective SEE **small.**

midget noun dwarf, pygmy.

midshipman noun SEE **sailor.**

midst noun SEE **middle** noun.

midwife noun obstetrician.

mien noun SEE **look** noun.

miffed adjective SEE **annoyed.**

might noun *I banged at the door with all my might.* energy, force, power, strength, vigour.

mighty adjective *a mighty blow. a mighty figure.* big, enormous, forceful, great, hefty, SEE **huge**, muscular, powerful, strong, vigorous.
OPPOSITES: SEE **weak.**

migraine noun headache.

migrate verb SEE **travel** verb.

migration noun SEE **travel** noun.

mild adjective 1 *a mild person.* amiable, docile, easygoing, forbearing, gentle, good-tempered, harmless, indulgent, kind, lenient, SEE **merciful**, placid, [*uncomplimentary*] soft, soft-hearted, understanding.
2 *mild weather.* balmy, calm, clement, peaceful, pleasant, temperate, warm.
OPPOSITES: SEE **severe.**
3 *a mild flavour.* bland, delicate, faint, mellow, subtle.
OPPOSITES: SEE **strong.**

mildew noun fungus, mould.

mildness noun *the mildness of someone's manner. the mildness of a punishment.* amiability, clemency, docility, forbearance, gentleness, kindness, leniency, moderation, softness, tenderness.
OPPOSITES: SEE **asperity.**

milieu noun SEE **surroundings.**

militant adjective [Do not confuse with *militaristic* or *military*.] *militant political views.* active, aggressive, assertive, attacking, positive.

militant noun *a political militant.* activist, extremist, [*informal*] hawk, partisan.

militaristic adjective [Do not confuse with *militant*.] belligerent, combative, fond of fighting, hostile, pugnacious, warlike.
OPPOSITES: SEE **peaceable.**

military adjective 1 *military might. military personnel.* armed, belligerent, enlisted, uniformed, warlike.
OPPOSITE: civilian.

2 *military law.* martial.
OPPOSITE: civil.

militate verb **to militate against** SEE **counteract.**

militia noun SEE **armed forces.**

milk noun KINDS OF MILK: condensed, dried, evaporated, long-life, pasteurized, skimmed, UHT.

FOODS MADE FROM MILK: butter, cheese, cream, curds, custard, dairy products, junket, milk pudding, yoghurt.

---

milk verb *to milk someone of all they have.* SEE **exploit** verb.

milksop noun SEE **weakling.**

milky adjective *a milky liquid.* chalky, cloudy, misty, opaque, whitish.
OPPOSITES: SEE **clear** adjective.

mill noun **1** *a steel mill.* factory, processing plant, works, workshop.
2 *a mill for grinding corn.* water-mill, windmill.
3 *a pepper-mill.* grinder.

mill verb *to mill corn.* SEE **grind.**
to mill about move aimlessly, swarm, throng.

millionaire noun SEE **rich (rich person).**

millstone noun *a millstone round my neck.* SEE **burden** noun.

mime noun SEE **theatre.**

mimic noun impersonator, impressionist.

mimic verb *Children often mimic their teachers.* ape, caricature, copy, do impressions of, echo, imitate, impersonate, look like, parody, parrot, pretend to be, simulate, sound like, [*informal*] take off.

minatory adjective SEE **threatening.**

mince verb **1** *to mince food.* SEE **cut** verb.
2 *to mince along the street.* SEE **walk** verb.

mincer noun blender, food-processor, mincing machine.

mind noun **1** *Use your mind!* brain, cleverness, [*informal*] grey matter, head, intellect, intelligence, judgement, memory, mental power, psyche, rationality, reasoning, remembrance, sense, thinking, understanding, wits.
RELATED ADJECTIVES: mental, psychological.
2 *He's changed his mind.* belief, intention, opinion, outlook, point of view, view, way of thinking, wishes.

mind verb **1** *Mind my things while I'm swimming.* attend to, care for, guard, keep an eye on, look after, watch.

2 *Mind the step.* be careful about, beware of, heed, look out for, note, remember, take notice of, watch out for.
3 *We won't mind if you're late.* be resentful, bother, care, complain, disapprove, grumble, object, take offence, worry.

mindful adjective SEE **careful.**

mindless adjective SEE **stupid.**

mine noun **1** *a coal-mine.* colliery, excavation, pit, quarry, shaft, tunnel, working.
2 *a land-mine.* WEAPONS: SEE **weapons.**

mine verb *to mine gold.* dig for, excavate, extract, quarry, remove.

miner noun coal-miner, collier.

mineral noun *minerals quarried out of the ground.* metal, ore, rock.

mingle verb *People mingled happily at the carnival.* associate, blend, circulate, combine, get together, intermingle, merge, mix, move about, [*informal*] rub shoulders, socialize.

mingy adjective SEE **mean** adjective.

The prefix *mini-* and words like *miniature, minimize, minimum,* etc. are related to Latin *minimus = least, smallest.*

---

miniature adjective SEE **tiny.**

miniature noun SEE **painting.**

minibus, minicab nouns VEHICLES: SEE **vehicle.**

minimal adjective *Modern cars require minimal servicing.* SEE **minimum** adjective, negligible, slightest.

minimize verb **1** *They banned smoking to minimize the danger of fire.* SEE **reduce.**
2 *He always minimizes the difficulties.* gloss over, make light of, play down, SEE **underestimate.**
OPPOSITES: SEE **maximize.**

minimum adjective *minimum wages. minimum temperature.* bottom, least, littlest, lowest, minimal, [*informal*] rock bottom, slightest, smallest.
OPPOSITES: SEE **maximum** adjective.

minimum noun *Keep expenses to the minimum.* lowest level, minimum amount (quantity, etc.) [SEE **minimum** adjective], nadir.
OPPOSITES: SEE **maximum** noun.

minion noun SEE **assistant.**

minister noun **1** *a government minister.* SEE **government.**
2 *a minister of the church.* SEE **clergyman.**

minister verb *to minister to the sick.* SEE **attend (attend to).**

minor adjective *a minor accident. a minor official.* inconsequential, inferior, insignificant, lesser, little, petty, secondary, SEE **small**, subordinate, trivial, unimportant.
OPPOSITES: SEE **major** adjective.

minority noun *Only a minority voted to strike.* lesser number, smaller number.
to be in a minority be outnumbered, lose.

minster noun SEE **church**.

minstrel noun bard, entertainer, musician, singer, troubadour.

mint adjective *in mint condition.* brand-new, first-class, fresh, immaculate, new, perfect, unblemished, unmarked, unused.

mint noun 1 *a mint of money.* fortune, heap, [*informal*] packet, pile, stack, unlimited supply, vast amount.
2 *strong-smelling mint.* SEE **herb**.

mint verb *to mint coins.* cast, coin, forge, make, manufacture, stamp out, strike.

minuscule, minute adjectives SEE **tiny**.

minute noun *minutes of a meeting.* SEE **record** noun.

minutiae noun SEE **detail** noun.

miracle noun *the miracle of birth.* marvel, miraculous event [SEE **miraculous**], mystery, wonder.

miraculous adjective *a miraculous cure.* amazing, astonishing, extraordinary, incredible, inexplicable, magic, marvellous, mysterious, preternatural, supernatural, unaccountable, unbelievable, wonderful.

mirage noun *a mirage in the desert.* delusion, hallucination, illusion, vision.

mire noun *sinking in the mire.* bog, SEE **dirt**, marsh, morass, mud, ooze, quagmire, quicksand, slime, swamp.

mirror noun looking-glass, reflector.

mirror verb SEE **reflect**.

mirth noun SEE **merriment**.

The prefix *mis-* usually gives the sense of *bad, wrong* or *badly, wrongly*.

---

misadventure noun *death by misadventure.* accident, calamity, catastrophe, disaster, ill fortune, mischance, misfortune, mishap.

misanthropic adjective *a misanthropic attitude towards your fellow human beings.* cynical, mean, nasty, surly, unfriendly, unpleasant, unsociable.
OPPOSITES: SEE **philanthropic**.

misappropriate verb SEE **misuse** verb.

misbehave verb behave badly, be mischievous [SEE **mischievous**], be a nuisance, [*informal*] blot your copybook, [*informal*] carry on, commit an offence, default, disobey, do wrong, err, fool about, make mischief, [*informal*] mess about, [*informal*] muck about, offend, [*informal*] play up, sin, transgress.

misbehaviour noun delinquency, disobedience, horseplay, indiscipline, insubordination, mischief, mischief-making, misconduct, naughtiness, rudeness, sin, vandalism, wrongdoing.

miscalculate verb [*informal*] boob, err, [*informal*] get it wrong, go wrong, make a mistake [SEE **mistake** noun], misjudge, [*informal*] slip up.

miscalculation noun SEE **mistake** noun.

miscarriage noun 1 *miscarriage of a baby.* abortion, premature birth, termination of pregnancy.
2 *a miscarriage of justice.* breakdown, error, failure, SEE **mistake** noun, perversion.

miscarry verb 1 *to miscarry in pregnancy.* [*informal*] lose the baby, suffer a miscarriage [SEE **miscarriage**].
2 *The project miscarried.* break down, come to nothing, fail, fall through, go wrong, misfire.
OPPOSITES: SEE **succeed**.

miscellaneous adjective *miscellaneous odds and ends.* assorted, different, diverse, heterogeneous, mixed, motley (*a motley crowd*), multifarious, sundry, varied, various.
OPPOSITES: SEE **identical**.

miscellany noun SEE **mixture**.

mischief noun 1 *Don't get into mischief.* devilment, [*joking*] devilry, escapade, misbehaviour, misconduct, [*informal*] monkey business, naughtiness, prank, scrape, trouble.
2 *Did you come to any mischief?* damage, harm, hurt, injury, misfortune.
to make mischief SEE **misbehave**.

mischievous adjective *mischievous children.* annoying, badly behaved, boisterous, disobedient, fractious, full of mischief [SEE **mischief**], impish, lively, naughty, playful, [*informal*] puckish, roguish, uncontrollable, [*informal*] up to no good, wicked.
a mischievous person imp, rascal, rogue, scamp.

misconception noun SEE **misunderstanding**.

misconduct noun SEE **misbehaviour**.

miscreant noun SEE **wrongdoer.**

miser noun hoarder, miserly person [SEE miserly], [*informal*] skinflint.
OPPOSITES: SEE **spendthrift.**

miserable adjective 1 *miserable after hearing bad news.* broken-hearted, dejected, depressed, desolate, despondent, disconsolate, distressed, doleful, [*informal*] down, downcast, down-hearted, forlorn, gloomy, glum, grief-stricken, heartbroken, joyless, lonely, melancholy, moping, mournful, SEE **sad,** tearful, uneasy, unfortunate, unhappy, unlucky, woebegone, wretched.
OPPOSITES: SEE **happy.**
2 *miserable living conditions.* abject, destitute, disgraceful, distressing, heartbreaking, hopeless, impoverished, inhuman, pathetic, pitiable, pitiful, SEE **poor,** sordid, soul-destroying, squalid, uncivilized, uncomfortable, vile, worthless, wretched.
OPPOSITES: SEE **affluent.**
3 *miserable weather.* SEE **bad,** cheerless, depressing, dismal, dreary, grey.
OPPOSITES: SEE **bright.**
4 *He's a miserable old so-and-so!* churlish, cross, disagreeable, discontented, [*informal*] grumpy, ill-natured, mean, miserly, morose, sulky, sullen, surly, unfriendly, unhelpful.
OPPOSITES: SEE **cheerful.**

miserly adjective avaricious, [*informal*] close, [*informal*] close-fisted, covetous, economical, grasping, mean, mercenary, mingy, niggardly, parsimonious, penny-pinching, stingy, [*informal*] tight, [*informal*] tight-fisted.
OPPOSITES: SEE **generous.**

misery noun 1 *You could see the misery on their faces.* anguish, bitterness, depression, despair, distress, gloom, grief, heartache, heartbreak, melancholy, sadness, sorrow, suffering, unhappiness, wretchedness.
2 *a life of misery.* adversity, affliction, deprivation, destitution, hardship, misfortune, need, oppression, penury, poverty, privation, squalor, tribulation, want.

misfire verb *The plan misfired.* abort, fail, fall through, [*informal*] flop, founder, go wrong, miscarry.
OPPOSITES: SEE **succeed.**

misfortune noun *We had the misfortune of breaking down.* accident, adversity, affliction, bad luck, bane (*the bane of my life*), calamity, catastrophe, disappointment, disaster, hardship, misadventure, mischance, mishap, reverse, setback, tragedy, trouble, vicissitude.
OPPOSITES: SEE **luck.**

misgiving noun SEE **anxiety.**

misguided adjective SEE **mistaken.**

mishap noun SEE **accident.**

misinform verb SEE **mislead.**

misjudge verb *to misjudge a situation.* get wrong, guess wrongly, [*informal*] jump to the wrong conclusion about, make a mistake about, miscalculate, misinterpret, SEE **misunderstand,** overestimate, underestimate, undervalue.

mislay verb *I mislaid my purse.* SEE **lose.**

mislead verb *Don't try to mislead us!* bluff, confuse, deceive, delude, fool, give misleading information to [SEE **misleading**], give a wrong impression to, hoax, hoodwink, [*informal*] kid, [*informal*] lead up the garden path, lie to, misinform, [*informal*] take for a ride, take in, trick.

misleading adjective *misleading directions.* ambiguous, confusing, deceptive, dishonest, distorted, equivocal, evasive, fallacious, false, SEE **lying,** muddling, puzzling, specious, spurious, unreliable, unsound, wrong.

mismanage verb SEE **bungle.**

misplace verb SEE **lose,** put in the wrong place.

misprint noun SEE **mistake** noun.

misrepresent verb SEE **falsify.**

miss verb 1 *to miss a bus.* be too late for, let go, lose.
2 *to miss a target.* be wide of, fail to hit, fall short of.
3 *to miss an appointment.* avoid, be absent from, forget, play truant from, [*informal*] skip, [*informal*] skive off.
4 *to miss someone who is absent.* grieve for, lament, long for, need, pine for, want, yearn for.
to miss something out SEE **omit.**

missal noun prayer-book.

misshapen adjective *a misshapen tree-trunk.* crooked, deformed, disfigured, distorted, grotesque, malformed, monstrous, twisted, ugly, warped.
OPPOSITE: SEE **perfect** adjective.

missile noun VARIOUS MISSILES: arrow, bomb, brickbat, bullet, dart, grenade, projectile, rocket, shell, shot, torpedo.
VARIOUS WEAPONS: SEE **weapons.**

missing adjective *missing children.* absent, disappeared, lost, mislaid, straying, unaccounted for.

mission noun 1 *a mission into the unknown.* expedition, exploration, journey, sortie, voyage.
2 *a mission to help the starving.* SEE **campaign.**

missionary noun SEE **preacher**.

missive noun SEE **letter**.

mist noun 1 *mist in the air.* cloud, drizzle, fog, haze, vapour.
2 *mist on the windows.* condensation, film, steam.

mistake noun [*informal*] bloomer, blunder, [*informal*] boob, [*informal*] clanger, error, faux pas, gaffe, [*informal*] howler, inaccuracy, indiscretion, lapse, miscalculation, miscarriage (*of justice*), misjudgement, misprint, misspelling, misunderstanding, omission, oversight, slip, slip-up, [*formal*] solecism.

mistake verb *I mistook your message.* confuse, get wrong, [*informal*] get the wrong end of the stick, misconstrue, misinterpret, misjudge, misread, misunderstand, mix up.

mistaken adjective *a mistaken decision.* erroneous, ill-judged, inappropriate, incorrect, inexact, misguided, misinformed, unfounded, unjust, unsound, SEE **wrong** adjective.

mistimed adjective *mistimed publicity. a mistimed visit.* badly timed, early, inconvenient, inopportune, late, unseasonable, untimely.

mistreat verb *to mistreat animals.* abuse, batter, harm, hurt, ill-treat, ill-use, [*informal*] knock about, misuse.

mistress noun 1 *the mistress of a dog.* keeper, owner, person in charge, proprietor.
2 [*mostly old-fashioned*] *a man's mistress.* SEE **lover**.

mistrust verb *I mistrust his judgement.* be sceptical about, be wary of, disbelieve, distrust, doubt, fear, have misgivings about, question, suspect.
OPPOSITES: SEE **trust** verb.

misty adjective *misty windows. a misty view.* bleary, blurred, blurry, clouded, cloudy, dim, faint, foggy, fuzzy, hazy, indistinct, opaque, shadowy, smoky, steamy, unclear, vague.
OPPOSITES: SEE **clear** adjective.

misunderstand verb *to misunderstand a message.* get wrong, [*informal*] get the wrong end of the stick, have a misunderstanding about [SEE **misunderstanding**], misconstrue, mishear, misinterpret, SEE **misjudge**, misread, miss the point, mistake, mistranslate.
OPPOSITES: SEE **understand**.

misunderstanding noun 1 *a misunderstanding of the problem.* error, failure of understanding, misapprehension, misconception, misinterpretation, misjudgement, mistake, [*informal*] mix-up.

2 *a misunderstanding with someone.* argument, [*informal*] contretemps, difference of opinion, disagreement, dispute, SEE **quarrel** noun.

misuse noun *You won't get your money back if it's damaged through misuse.* abuse, careless use, ill-treatment, illuse, maltreatment, mishandling, mistreatment.

misuse verb 1 *Someone misused my tape-recorder.* damage, harm, mishandle, treat carelessly.
2 *He misused his dog shamefully.* abuse, batter, hurt, ill-treat, injure, [*informal*] knock about, mistreat, treat badly.
3 *She misused the club funds.* fritter away, misappropriate, squander, use wrongly, waste.

mitigate verb *to mitigate the effect of something.* SEE **lessen**.

mitigating adjective *mitigating circumstances.* extenuating, justifying, qualifying.

mix verb 1 *Mix the ingredients together. Oil and water won't mix.* amalgamate, blend, coalesce, combine, compound, confuse, diffuse, emulsify, fuse, homogenize, integrate, intermingle, join, jumble up, make a mixture [SEE **mixture**], meld, merge, mingle, mix up, muddle, put together, shuffle (*cards or papers*), unite.
OPPOSITES: SEE **separate** verb.
2 *He mixed with the wrong crowd.* SEE **socialize**.

mixed adjective 1 *mixed biscuits.* assorted, different, diverse, heterogeneous, miscellaneous, muddled, varied, various.
2 *a mixed team.* amalgamated, combined, composite, integrated, hybrid, joint, united.
3 *mixed feelings.* ambiguous, ambivalent, confused, equivocal, uncertain.

mixture noun *a mixture of ingredients.* alloy (*of metals*), amalgam, association, assortment, blend, collection, combination, composite, compound, concoction, conglomeration, emulsion (*of a solid in a liquid*), fusion, [*informal*] hotchpotch, hybrid [= *a mixture of species or varieties*], jumble, medley, mélange, miscellany, mix, mongrel [= *a mixture of breeds*], pot-pourri, suspension (*of a solid in a liquid*), variety.

mnemonic noun SEE **reminder**.

moan verb 1 VARIOUS SOUNDS: SEE **sound** noun.
2 *We moaned about the food.* SEE **complain**.

moat noun SEE **ditch** noun.

mob noun *an angry mob.* [*informal*] bunch, crowd, gang, SEE **group** noun, herd, horde, pack, rabble, riot, [*informal*] shower, swarm, throng.

mob verb *to mob a pop idol.* besiege, crowd round, hem in, jostle, surround, swarm round, throng round.

mobile adjective **1** *a mobile caravan.* itinerant, movable, portable, travelling.
2 *It didn't take me long to get mobile after my accident.* able to move, active, agile, independent, moving about, [*informal*] on the go, [*informal*] up and about.
3 *mobile features.* changeable, changing, expressive, flexible, fluid, shifting.
OPPOSITES: SEE **immobile, static.**

mobilize verb *to mobilize support.* activate, assemble, call up, enlist, gather, get together, levy, marshal, muster, organize, rally, stir up, summon.

mock adjective *mock cream.* SEE **imitation** adjective.

mock verb *They mocked my pathetic attempts.* deride, disparage, insult, jeer at, lampoon, laugh at, make fun of, parody, poke fun at, ridicule, satirize, scoff at, scorn, [*informal*] send up, sneer at, taunt, tease, travesty.

mockery noun *a mockery of the truth.* lampoon, parody, satire, [*informal*] send-up, travesty.

mocking adjective *mocking insults.* contemptuous, derisive, disparaging, disrespectful, insulting, irreverent, rude, sarcastic, satirical, scornful, taunting, teasing, uncomplimentary, unkind.
OPPOSITES: SEE **respectful.**

mock-up noun SEE **model** noun.

mode noun SEE **method.**

model adjective **1** *a model railway.* SEE **imitation** adjective, **toy** adjective.
2 *a model pupil.* SEE **ideal** adjective.

model noun **1** *scale models.* copy, dummy, effigy, image, imitation, miniature, replica, representation, toy.
2 *a model of a futuristic car.* archetype, [*informal*] mock-up, paradigm, pattern, prototype.
3 *a model of good behaviour.* byword, example, ideal, paragon, yardstick.
4 *an out-of-date model.* design, mark, type, version.
5 *a fashion model.* mannequin.

model verb **1** *to model something in clay.* SEE **sculpture** verb.
2 *I modelled the characters on my own family.* base.

moderate adjective **1** *moderate prices. moderate opinions. a moderate drinker.* average, cautious, deliberate, fair, medium, middle, [*informal*] middle-of-the-road, middling, modest, normal,

ordinary, rational, reasonable, respectable, sensible, sober, steady, temperate, usual.
2 *a moderate wind.* gentle, light, mild.
OPPOSITES: SEE **excessive, extreme** adjective.

moderate verb **1** *The storm moderated.* abate, become less extreme, decline, decrease, die down, ease off, subside.
2 *Please moderate the noise.* check, curb, keep down, lessen, make less extreme, mitigate, modify, modulate, regulate, restrain, subdue, temper, tone down.

moderately adverb *moderately good.* fairly, passably, [*informal*] pretty, quite, rather, reasonably, somewhat, to some extent.

moderation noun *He always showed moderation in his drinking.* caution, reasonableness, sobriety, temperance.

modern adjective *modern music. modern architecture.* advanced, avant-garde, contemporary, current, fashionable, forward-looking, futuristic, the latest, new, [*uncomplimentary*] newfangled, novel, present, present-day, progressive, recent, stylish, [*informal*] trendy, up-to-date, up-to-the-minute, [*informal*] with it.
OPPOSITES: SEE **old.**

modernize verb *to modernize an old house.* [*informal*] do up, improve, make modern [SEE **modern**], rebuild, refurbish, regenerate, renovate, update.

modest adjective **1** *modest about your success.* humble, lowly, meek, quiet, reserved, reticent, unassuming, unpretentious.
OPPOSITES: SEE **conceited.**
2 *modest about getting undressed.* bashful, coy, demure, shamefaced, shy.
3 *a modest dress.* chaste, decent, discreet, plain, proper, seemly, simple.
OPPOSITES: SEE **indecent.**
4 *a modest sum of money.* SEE **moderate** adjective.

modesty noun **1** *modesty about your success.* humbleness, humility, reserve, reticence, self-effacement.
2 *modesty about getting undressed.* bashfulness, coyness, demureness, shyness.

modicum noun SEE **small (small amount).**

modify verb *to modify the design of something.* adapt, adjust, alter, change, convert, improve, SEE **moderate** verb, re-design, re-organize, revise, transform, vary.

modish adjective SEE **fashionable.**

modulate verb *to modulate your voice.* adjust, change, change the tone of, SEE **moderate** verb, regulate, tone down.

module noun SEE **unit.**

mogul noun SEE **important (important person).**

moist adjective affected by moisture [SEE **moisture**], clammy, damp, dank, dewy, humid [*informal*] muggy, rainy, [*informal*] runny, steamy, watery, SEE **wet** adjective.
OPPOSITES: SEE **dry** adjective.

moisten verb damp, dampen, humidify, make moist [SEE **moist**], moisturize, soak, wet.
OPPOSITES: SEE **dry** verb.

moisture noun condensation, damp, dampness, dankness, dew, humidity, liquid, [*formal*] precipitation, steam, vapour, water, wet, wetness.

moisturize verb SEE **moisten.**

molar noun SEE **tooth.**

mole noun 1 *a mole on the skin.* SEE **spot** noun.
2 *a mole built into the sea.* SEE **breakwater.**
3 [*informal*] *a mole working for the government.* agent, secret agent, spy.

molecule noun SEE **particle.**

molest verb *Hooligans molested the bystanders.* abuse, annoy, assault, attack, badger, bother, harass, harry, hassle, interfere with, irritate, manhandle, mistreat, persecute, pester, set on, tease, torment, vex, worry.

mollify verb SEE **soothe.**

mollycoddle verb SEE **pamper.**

molten adjective *molten metal.* liquefied, liquid, melted.

moment noun 1 *over in a moment.* flash, instant, [*informal*] jiffy, minute, second, split second, [*informal*] tick, [*informal*] trice, [*informal*] twinkling of an eye.
2 *an important moment.* juncture, occasion, opportunity, point in time, time.

momentary adjective *a momentary lapse of memory.* brief, ephemeral, fleeting, passing, quick, short, temporary, transient, transitory.
OPPOSITES: SEE **permanent.**

momentous adjective *a momentous decision.* critical, crucial, decisive, epoch-making, fateful, historic, SEE **important,** significant.
OPPOSITES: SEE **unimportant.**

momentum noun SEE **impetus.**

monarch noun SEE **ruler.**

monarchy noun kingdom, realm.
FORMS OF GOVERNMENT: SEE **government.**

monastery noun SEE **church.**

monaural adjective SEE **monophonic.**

money noun [*informal*] bread, currency, [*informal*] dough, finances, [*informal*] lolly, [*old-fashioned*] lucre, riches, wealth, [*informal*] the wherewithal.
RELATED ADJECTIVES: financial, monetary, pecuniary.

FORMS IN WHICH YOU CAN SPEND MONEY: bank-notes, cash, change, cheque, coins, coppers, credit card, credit transfer, notes, pennies, silver, sterling, traveller's cheque.

EVERYDAY TERMS FOR MONEY YOU OWE, OWN, PAY, OR RECEIVE: arrears, assets, capital, damages, debt, dividend, dowry, dues, duty, earnings, endowment, estate, expenditure, fortune, funds, grant, income, interest, investments, loan, mortgage, [*informal*] nest-egg, outgoings, patrimony, pay, pension, pocket-money, proceeds, profits, remittance, resources, revenue, salary, savings, takings, tax, wages, winnings.

money-box noun cash-box, coffer, piggy-bank, safe, till.

moneyed adjective SEE **wealthy.**

money-grubbing adjective SEE **greedy.**

mongolism noun Down's syndrome.

mongrel noun cross-breed, hybrid.

monitor noun *a TV monitor.* screen, set, television, TV, VDU [= *visual display unit*].

monk noun brother, friar, hermit.

monkey noun SOME KINDS OF MONKEY: ape, baboon, chimpanzee, gibbon, gorilla, marmoset, orang-utan.
RELATED ADJECTIVE: simian.
OTHER ANIMALS: SEE **animal** noun.

monkey verb to **monkey about** SEE **mess** verb (**to mess about**).

The prefix *mono-* or *mon-* in words such as *monarchy, monaural, monogamy,* etc. is related to Greek *monos = alone, single.*

mono adjective SEE **monophonic.**

monochrome adjective *monochrome pictures.* black and white.
OPPOSITES: coloured, in colour.

monocle noun SEE **glass (glasses).**

monogamy noun SEE **marriage.**

monogram noun SEE **symbol.**

monograph noun SEE **writing.**

monolith noun SEE **stone** noun.

monologue noun SEE **speech.**

monophonic adjective monaural, [*informal*] mono.
OPPOSITES: stereo, stereophonic.

monopolize verb *to monopolize a conversation.* control, [*informal*] corner, have a monopoly of, [*informal*] hog, keep for yourself, shut others out of, take over.
OPPOSITES: SEE **share** verb.

monotonous adjective *a monotonous voice. a monotonous landscape.* boring, dreary, dull, featureless, flat, level, repetitive, tedious, toneless, unchanging, uneventful, unexciting, uniform, uninteresting, unvarying, wearisome.
OPPOSITES: SEE **interesting**.

monsoon noun SEE **wind** noun.

monster adjective *a monster birthday cake.* SEE **huge**.

monster noun *a frightening monster.* abortion, beast, brute, freak, giant, monstrosity, monstrous creature or thing [SEE **monstrous**], mutant, ogre.
OTHER LEGENDARY CREATURES: SEE **legend**.

monstrosity noun SEE **monster** noun.

monstrous adjective **1** *a creature of monstrous size.* SEE **big**, colossal, elephantine, enormous, gargantuan, giant, gigantic, great, huge, hulking, immense, mammoth, mighty, titanic, towering, vast.
2 *a monstrous crime.* abhorrent, atrocious, cruel, dreadful, evil, gross, gruesome, heinous, hideous, [*informal*] horrendous, horrible, horrifying, inhuman, obscene, outrageous, repulsive, shocking, terrible, villainous, wicked.

montage noun SEE **picture** noun.

monument noun *a monument to the dead. an ancient monument.* cairn, cenotaph, cross, gravestone, headstone, mausoleum, memorial, obelisk, pillar, prehistoric remains [SEE **prehistoric**], relic, reminder, shrine, tomb, tombstone.

monumental adjective **1** *a monumental plaque.* commemorative, memorial.
2 *of monumental size.* awe-inspiring, awesome, grand, SEE **huge**, impressive.

moo verb VARIOUS SOUNDS: SEE **sound** noun.

mooch verb SEE **walk** verb.

mood noun **1** *in a good mood. in a bad mood.* disposition, humour, spirit, state of mind, temper, vein.
2 *the mood of a piece of music.* atmosphere, feeling, tone.
WORDS TO DESCRIBE VARIOUS MOODS: SEE angry, happy, sad, etc.

moody adjective bad-tempered, capricious, changeable, cross, depressed, depressive, disgruntled, erratic, gloomy, grumpy, irritable, melancholy, miserable, morose, peevish, short-tempered, snappy, sulky, sullen, temperamental, [*informal*] touchy, unpredictable, unstable, volatile.

moon noun ASTRONOMICAL TERMS: SEE **astronomy**.
RELATED ADJECTIVE: lunar.

moon verb *to moon about.* SEE **mope**.

moonlight noun SEE **light** noun.

moor noun *a windswept moor.* fell, heath, moorland.

moor verb *to moor a boat.* anchor, berth, SEE **fasten**, secure, tie up.

moot adjective *a moot point.* SEE **debatable**.

moot verb *to moot an idea.* SEE **suggest**.

mop verb *to mop up.* SEE **clean** verb.

mope verb *He moped about because he wasn't invited to the party.* be sad [SEE **sad**], brood, despair, grieve, languish, [*informal*] moon, pine, sulk.

moral adjective **1** *a moral person. moral principles.* blameless, chaste, decent, ethical, good, high-minded, honest, honourable, incorruptible, innocent, irreproachable, just, law-abiding, noble, principled, pure, responsible, right, righteous, sinless, trustworthy, truthful, upright, virtuous.
2 *a moral tale.* cautionary, didactic, moralistic, moralizing.
OPPOSITES: SEE **immoral**.
a moral tale cautionary tale, fable, parable.

moral noun *What's the moral of the story?* lesson, meaning, message, precept, principle.
morals SEE **morality**.

morale noun *The team's morale is high.* cheerfulness, confidence, [*informal*] heart, mood, self-confidence, self-esteem, spirit, state of mind.

morality noun *I question the morality of some kinds of advertising.* conduct, decency, ethics, ethos, goodness, honesty, ideals, integrity, morals, principles, scruples, standards, uprightness, virtue.
OPPOSITES: SEE **immorality**.

moralize verb lecture, philosophize, pontificate, preach, sermonize.

morass noun SEE **marsh**.

moratorium noun SEE **ban** noun, **delay** noun.

morbid adjective *a morbid account of her death.* brooding, ghoulish, gloomy, grim, macabre, melancholy, morose, pessimistic, [*informal*] sick, unhappy, unhealthy, unpleasant, unwholesome. OPPOSITES: SEE **cheerful**.

mordant adjective *mordant criticism*. SEE **sharp**.

more adjective added, additional, extra, further, increased, new, other, renewed, supplementary.
OPPOSITES: SEE **less**.

moreover adverb also, besides, further, furthermore, too.

morgue noun mortuary.

moribund adjective SEE **dying**.

morning noun TIMES OF THE DAY: SEE **day**.
RELATED ADJECTIVE: matutinal.

moron noun SEE **idiot**.

moronic adjective SEE **stupid**.

morose adjective *a morose expression*. bad-tempered, churlish, depressed, gloomy, glum, grim, humourless, ill-natured, melancholy, moody, mournful, pessimistic, SEE **sad**, saturnine, sour, sulky, sullen, surly, taciturn, unhappy, unsociable.
OPPOSITES: SEE **cheerful**.

morsel noun *a morsel of food*. bite, crumb, fragment, mouthful, nibble, piece, scrap, small amount [SEE **small**], taste, titbit.

mortal adjective 1 *mortal beings*. earthly, ephemeral, human, passing, transient.
OPPOSITES: SEE **immortal**.
2 *a mortal sickness*. deadly, fatal, lethal, terminal.
3 *mortal enemies*. deadly, implacable, irreconcilable, remorseless, sworn (*sworn enemy*), unrelenting.

mortal noun *We are mortals, not gods*. human being, mortal creature [SEE **mortal** adjective], SEE **person**.

mortality noun 1 *We aren't gods: we must accept our mortality*. corruptibility, humanity, impermanence, transience.
OPPOSITES: SEE **immortality**.
2 *There is high mortality among young birds*. death-rate, dying, fatalities, loss of life.
OPPOSITES: SEE **survival**.

mortgage noun SEE **loan**.

mortify verb SEE **humiliate**.

mortuary noun morgue.

mosaic noun VARIOUS PICTURES: SEE **picture** noun.

mostly adverb chiefly, commonly, generally, largely, mainly, normally, predominantly, primarily, principally, typically, usually.

motel noun SEE **accommodation**.

moth-eaten adjective *a moth-eaten appearance*. antiquated, decrepit, mangy, SEE **old**, ragged, shabby, [*informal*] tatty.

mother noun 1 [*informal*] ma or mamma, [*old-fashioned*] mater, [*informal*] mum or mummy, parent.

mother verb *He likes to mother the toddlers*. care for, cherish, comfort, cuddle, fuss over, love, nurse, pamper, protect.

motherly adjective *a motherly person*. caring, kind, SEE **loving**, maternal, protective.

motif noun *a floral motif on the curtains*. design, device, ornament, pattern, SEE **symbol**, theme.

motion noun SEE **movement**.

motion verb *She motioned him to sit down*. SEE **gesture** verb.

motionless adjective *motionless statues*. *motionless waters*. at rest, calm, frozen, immobile, inanimate, inert, lifeless, paralysed, peaceful, resting, stagnant, static, stationary, still, stock-still, unmoving.
OPPOSITES: SEE **moving**.

motivate verb *What motivated her to do such a thing?* arouse, be the motivation of [SEE **motivation**], encourage, incite, induce, inspire, move, persuade, prompt, provoke, push, spur, stimulate, stir, urge.

motivation noun *the motivation behind someone's achievement*. drive, encouragement, impulse, incentive, inducement, inspiration, instigation, SEE **motive**, provocation, push, spur, stimulus.

motive noun *the motive for a crime*. aim, cause, grounds, intention, SEE **motivation**, object, purpose, rationale, reason, thinking.

motley adjective SEE **miscellaneous**.

motor noun *an electric motor*. engine.
a motor boat BOATS: SEE **vessel**.
a motor car VEHICLES: SEE **vehicle**.

motor verb *We motored into town*. drive, go by car, SEE **travel** verb.

motorist noun SEE **traveller**.

motorway noun VARIOUS ROADS: SEE **road**.

mottled adjective SEE **dappled**.

motto noun SEE **saying**.

mould noun *mould on cheese*. fungus, growth, mildew.

mould verb *to mould clay.* cast, fashion, form, model, [*informal*] sculpt, shape.

moulder verb SEE **decay.**

mouldy adjective *a mouldy smell.* damp, decaying, fusty, mildewed, musty, rotten, stale.

mound noun *a mound of rubbish.* SEE **pile** noun.

mount noun SEE **mountain.**

mount verb 1 *to mount the stairs. to mount into the air.* ascend, climb, go up, rise, soar.
OPPOSITES: SEE **descend.**
2 *to mount a horse.* get astride, get on, jump onto.
OPPOSITES: SEE **dismount.**
3 *My savings mounted. The excitement mounted.* accumulate, get bigger, grow, increase, intensify, multiply, pile up, swell.
OPPOSITES: SEE **decrease** verb.
4 *to mount a picture. to mount an exhibition.* display, frame, install, put in place, set up.

mountain noun 1 [*poetic*] alp, arête, [*Scottish*] ben, eminence, height, hill, mound, mount, peak, range, ridge, sierra, summit, volcano.
2 [*informal*] *a mountain of business to get through.* SEE **pile** noun.

mountaineer noun climber.

mountaineering noun climbing, rock-climbing.

mountainous adjective 1 *mountainous slopes.* alpine, daunting, high, hilly, precipitous, rocky, rugged, steep, towering.
2 *mountainous waves.* SEE **huge.**

mountebank noun SEE **swindler.**

mourn verb *He mourned for his dead dog.* bewail, fret, go into mourning, grieve, lament, mope, pine, wail, weep.
OPPOSITES: SEE **rejoice.**

mourner noun WORDS TO DO WITH FUNERALS: SEE **funeral.**

mournful adjective *a mournful cry. a mournful occasion.* dismal, distressed, distressing, doleful, funereal, gloomy, grief-stricken, grieving, heartbreaking, heartbroken, lamenting, lugubrious, melancholy, plaintive, plangent, SEE **sad,** sorrowful, tearful, tragic, unhappy, woeful.
OPPOSITES: SEE **cheerful.**

moustache noun whiskers.

mousy adjective SEE **timid.**

mouth noun 1 [*slang*] gob, jaws, lips, palate.
RELATED ADJECTIVE: oral.

2 *the mouth of a cave. the mouth of a bottle.* aperture, doorway, entrance, exit, gateway, opening, orifice, outlet.
3 *the mouth of a river.* estuary, outlet.

mouth verb *to mouth curses.* articulate, form, pronounce, SEE **say.**

mouthful noun *a mouthful of food.* bite, gobbet, gulp, morsel, spoonful, swallow, taste.

mouth-organ noun harmonica.

movable adjective *movable furniture.* adjustable, detachable, mobile, portable, transferable, transportable.
OPPOSITES: SEE **immobile.**

move noun 1 *What will the criminal's next move be?* act, action, deed, gambit, manœuvre, measure, movement, ploy, [*informal*] shift, step, stratagem, [*informal*] tack, tactic.
2 *It's your move next.* chance, go, opportunity, turn.

move verb [Many words can be used as synonyms of *move.* We give some of the commoner ones.]
1 *to move about.* be agitated, be astir, budge, change places, change position, fidget, flap, roll, shake, shift, stir, swing, toss, tremble, turn, twist, twitch, wag, [*informal*] waggle, wave, [*informal*] wiggle.
2 *to move along.* cruise, fly, jog, journey, make headway, make progress, march, pass, proceed, SEE **travel** verb, **walk** verb.
3 *to move along quickly.* bolt, canter, career, dart, dash, flit, flounce, fly, gallop, hasten, hurry, hurtle, hustle, [*informal*] nip, race, run, rush, shoot, speed, stampede, streak, tear (*We tore home*), [*informal*] zip, [*informal*] zoom.
4 *to move along slowly.* amble, crawl, dawdle, drift, stroll.
5 *to move along gracefully.* dance, flow, glide, skate, skim, slide, slip, sweep.
6 *to move along awkwardly.* dodder, falter, flounder, lumber, lurch, pitch, shuffle, stagger, stumble, sway, totter, trip, trundle.
7 *to move along stealthily.* crawl, creep, edge, slink, slither.
8 *to move things from one place to another.* carry, export, import, shift, ship, relocate, transfer, transplant, transport, transpose.
9 *to move someone to do something.* encourage, impel, influence, inspire, persuade, prompt, stimulate, urge.
10 *to move someone's feelings.* affect, arouse, enrage, fire, impassion, rouse, stir, touch.
11 *I wonder when they will move on our application.* act, do something, make a move [SEE **move** noun], take action.

to move away budge, depart, go, leave, migrate, quit, start.

to move back back off, retreat, reverse, withdraw.

to move down descend, drop, fall, lower, sink, swoop.

to move in enter, penetrate.

to move round circulate, revolve, roll, rotate, spin, tour, turn, twirl, twist, wheel, whirl.

to move towards advance, approach, come, proceed, progress.

to move up arise, ascend, climb, mount, rise.

movement noun 1 *Animals are capable of movement.* action, activity, SEE **gesture** noun, motion, SEE **move** noun.
2 *Has there been any movement in their attitude?* change, development, evolution, progress, shift, trend.
3 *a political movement.* campaign, crusade, group, organization, party.
4 *military movements.* exercise, operation.

movie noun SEE **film**.

moving adjective 1 *a moving object.* active, alive, astir, dynamic, mobile, movable, on the move, travelling, under way.
OPPOSITES: SEE **motionless**.
2 *a moving story.* affecting, emotional, emotive, heart-warming, inspiring, pathetic, poignant, [*uncomplimentary*] sentimental, stirring, [*informal*] tearjerking, touching.
OPPOSITES: SEE **unemotional**.

mow verb *to mow the grass.* clip, SEE **cut** verb, trim.

Mr, Mrs, Ms VARIOUS TITLES: SEE **title** noun.

muck noun dirt, dung, filth, grime, manure, mire, mud, ooze, rubbish, sewage, slime, sludge.

mucky adjective dirty, filthy, foul, grimy, grubby, messy, muddy, soiled, sordid, squalid.
OPPOSITES: SEE **clean** adjective.

mucus noun phlegm, slime.

mud noun clay, dirt, mire, muck, ooze, silt, slime, sludge, slurry, soil.

muddle noun 1 *There was a muddle over the arrangements.* bewilderment, confusion, misunderstanding, [*informal*] mix-up.
2 *My room is in a muddle.* clutter, disorder, jumble, mess, [*informal*] shambles, tangle, untidiness.

muddle verb 1 *You muddle me when you talk fast.* bewilder, confuse, disorientate, mislead, perplex, puzzle.
OPPOSITES: SEE **clarify**.

2 *Don't muddle the clothes in the drawer.* disarrange, disorder, disorganize, [*informal*] foul up, jumble, make a mess of, [*informal*] mess up, mix up, shuffle, tangle.
OPPOSITES: SEE **tidy** verb.

muddled, muddle-headed adjectives SEE **confused**.

muddy adjective 1 *muddy shoes.* caked, dirty, filthy, messy, mucky, soiled.
OPPOSITES: SEE **clean** adjective.
2 *muddy ground.* boggy, marshy, sloppy, sodden, soft, spongy, waterlogged, SEE **wet** adjective.
OPPOSITES: SEE **firm** adjective, **dry** adjective.
3 *muddy water.* cloudy, impure, misty, opaque.
OPPOSITES: SEE **clear** adjective.

muff verb SEE **bungle**.

muffle verb 1 *to muffle yourself up in cold weather.* cover, enclose, envelop, swathe, wrap up.
2 *to muffle a noise.* dampen, deaden, disguise, dull, make muffled [SEE **muffled**], mask, mute, quieten, silence, soften, stifle, suppress.

muffled adjective *a muffled sound.* deadened, dull, fuzzy, indistinct, muted, unclear, woolly.
OPPOSITE: SEE **clear** adjective.

muffler noun scarf.

mug noun 1 *a mug to drink from.* beaker, cup, [*old-fashioned*] flagon, tankard.
2 [*slang*] *a mug who is easily fooled.* SEE **fool** noun.

mug verb assault, attack, beat up, jump on, molest, rob, set on, steal from.
to mug up SEE **learn**.

mugger noun attacker, SEE **criminal** noun, hooligan, robber, ruffian, thief, thug.

mugging noun attack, robbery, street crime.
OTHER CRIMES: SEE **crime**.

muggins noun SEE **fool** noun.

muggy adjective *muggy weather.* clammy, close, damp, humid, moist, oppressive, steamy, sticky, stuffy, sultry, warm.

mulct verb SEE **rob**.

mule noun SEE **horse**.

mulish adjective SEE **stubborn**.

mull verb to mull over SEE **think**.

The prefix *multi-* and words such as *multifarious, multiply,* and *multitude* are related to Latin *multus = much, many.*

---

multifarious adjective SEE **various**.

multiple adjective *a multiple crash on the motorway. multiple injuries.* complex, compound, double [= × 2], involving many, numerous, plural, quadruple [= × 4], quintuple [= × 5], triple [= × 3].

multiplicity noun *The accident was due to a multiplicity of causes.* abundance, array, complex, diversity, number, plurality, profusion, variety.

multiply verb **1** double [= *multiply by 2*], quadruple [× 4], quintuple [× 5], triple [× 3], [*informal*] times.
MATHEMATICAL TERMS: SEE **mathematics**.
2 *Mice multiply quickly.* become numerous, breed, increase, proliferate, propagate, reproduce, spread.

multitude noun *a multitude of people. a multitude of things to do.* SEE **crowd** noun, host, large number, legion, lots, mass, myriad, swarm, throng.

multitudinous adjective SEE **numerous**.

mum adjective *Keep mum!* SEE **silent**.

mum noun SEE **mother** noun.

mumble verb SEE **talk** verb.

mumbo-jumbo noun SEE **magic** noun.

mummify verb embalm, SEE **preserve** verb.

mummy noun **1** SEE **mother** noun.
2 *an Egyptian mummy.* SEE **body**.

munch verb bite, chew, chomp, crunch, SEE **eat**, gnaw.

mundane adjective *It was hard to return to mundane matters after such excitement.* banal, common, commonplace, down-to-earth, dull, everyday, familiar, human, material, SEE **ordinary**, physical, practical, quotidian, routine, worldly.
OPPOSITES: SEE **extraordinary, spiritual**.

municipal adjective *municipal government. municipal affairs.* borough, city, civic, community, district, local, public, urban.
OPPOSITES: SEE **national**.

munificent adjective SEE **generous**.

munitions noun SEE **weapons**.

mural noun fresco, wall-painting.
VARIOUS PICTURES: SEE **picture** noun.

murder noun assassination, fratricide, homicide, infanticide, SEE **killing** noun, matricide, parricide, patricide, regicide.

murder verb assassinate, SEE **kill**.

murderer noun assassin, SEE **killer**.

murderous adjective *murderous bandits.* barbarous, bloodthirsty, brutal, cruel, dangerous, deadly, ferocious, fierce, homicidal, pitiless, ruthless, savage, vicious, violent.

murky adjective *murky water. murky light.* cloudy, dark, dim, dull, foggy, gloomy, grey, misty, muddy, obscure, sombre.
OPPOSITES: SEE **clear** adjective.

murmur noun, verb SEE **sound** noun, **talk** verb.

muscle noun PARTS OF YOUR BODY: SEE **body**.

muscular adjective *a muscular wrestler.* athletic, [*informal*] beefy, brawny, burly, hefty, [*informal*] hulking, husky, powerful, robust, sinewy, [*informal*] strapping, strong, sturdy, tough, well-built, well-developed, wiry.
OPPOSITES: SEE **feeble**.

muse verb SEE **think**.

mush noun SEE **pulp** noun.

mushroom noun SEE **fungus**.

mushroom verb SEE **grow**.

mushy adjective SEE **soft**.

music noun harmony, pleasant sound.

KINDS OF MUSIC: chamber music, choral music, classical music, dance music, disco music, folk-music, instrumental music, jazz, orchestral music, plainsong, pop music, ragtime, reggae, rock, soul, swing.

VARIOUS MUSICAL COMPOSITIONS: anthem, ballad, blues, cadenza, calypso, canon, cantata, canticle, carol, chant, concerto, SEE **dance** noun, dirge, duet, étude, fanfare, fugue, hymn, improvisation, intermezzo, lullaby, march, musical, nocturne, nonet, octet, opera, operetta, oratorio, overture, prelude, quartet, quintet, rhapsody, rondo, scherzo, sea shanty, septet, sextet, sonata, SEE **song**, spiritual, symphony, toccata, trio.

FAMILIES OF MUSICAL INSTRUMENTS: brass, keyboard, percussion, strings, woodwind.

MUSICAL INSTRUMENTS: accordion, bagpipes, banjo, barrel organ, bassoon, bugle, castanets, cello, clarinet, clavichord, concertina, cor anglais, cornet, cymbals, double-bass, drum, dulcimer, euphonium, fiddle, fife, flute, French horn, glockenspiel, gong, guitar.

harmonica, harmonium, harp, harpsichord, horn, hurdy-gurdy, kettledrum, keyboard, lute, lyre, mouth-organ, oboe, organ, piano, piccolo, pipes, recorder, saxophone, sitar, spinet, synthesizer, tambourine, timpani, tomtom, triangle, trombone, trumpet, tuba, tubular bells, ukulele, viol, viola, violin, virginals, xylophone, zither.

VARIOUS MUSICIANS: accompanist, bass, bugler, cellist, clarinettist, composer, conductor, contralto, drummer, fiddler, flautist, guitarist, harpist, instrumentalist, maestro, minstrel, oboist, organist, percussionist, pianist, piper, singer, soloist, soprano, tenor, timpanist, treble, trombonist, trumpeter, violinist, virtuoso, vocalist.

GROUPS OF MUSICIANS: band, choir, chorus, consort, duet, duo, ensemble, group, nonet, octet, orchestra, quartet, quintet, septet, sextet, trio.

OTHER EVERYDAY MUSICAL TERMS: baton, chord, chromatic scale, clef, counterpoint (adjective contrapuntal), crotchet, diatonic scale, discord, flat, harmony, key, melody, metronome marking, minim, natural, note, octave, pentatonic scale, pitch, polyphony, quaver, rhythm, scale, semibreve, semiquaver, semitone, sharp, stave, tempo, theme, time signature, tone, tune, unison.

---

musical adjective *musical sounds.* euphonious, harmonious, lyrical, melodious, pleasant, sweet-sounding, tuneful. OPPOSITES: SEE **cacophonous**.

musician noun performer, player. VARIOUS MUSICIANS: SEE ABOVE.

musky adjective SEE **smelling**.

muster verb *Can we muster a team for Saturday?* assemble, call together, collect, convene, gather, get together, group, marshal, mobilize, rally, round up, summon.

musty adjective *a musty smell.* airless, damp, dank, fusty, mildewed, mouldy, smelly, stale, stuffy, unventilated.

mutable adjective SEE **changeable**.

mutant noun abortion, deviant, freak, monster, monstrosity, sport.

mutate verb SEE **change** verb, undergo mutation (SEE **mutation**).

mutation noun *a genetic mutation.* alteration, change, deviance, evolution, metamorphosis, modification, transformation, variation.

mute adjective dumb, silent, speechless, tongue-tied, voiceless.

mutilate verb *The soldier was horribly mutilated in the explosion.* cripple, damage, disable, disfigure, injure, lame, maim, mangle, SEE **wound** verb.

mutineer noun SEE **rebel** noun.

mutinous adjective *a mutinous crew.* SEE **rebellious**.

mutiny noun *a mutiny on board ship.* SEE **rebellion**.

mutiny verb SEE **rebel** verb.

mutt noun SEE **fool** noun.

mutter verb SEE **talk** verb.

mutual adjective *friends with mutual interests.* common, joint, reciprocal, reciprocated, shared.

muzzle noun *an animal's muzzle.* jaws, mouth, nose, snout.

muzzle verb *to muzzle someone.* censor, gag, restrain, silence, stifle, suppress.

muzzy adjective *muzzy in the head.* blurred, SEE **confused**, dazed, hazy, muddled.

myopic adjective short-sighted.

myriad noun SEE **multitude**.

mysterious adjective *a mysterious illness. mysterious powers.* arcane, baffling, curious, enigmatic, incomprehensible, inexplicable, insoluble, magical, miraculous, SEE **mystical**, mystifying, obscure, perplexing, puzzling, secret, strange, uncanny, unexplained, unfathomable, unknown, weird. OPPOSITES: SEE **straightforward**.

mystery noun 1 *an insoluble mystery.* enigma, miracle, mysterious happening [SEE **mysterious**], problem, puzzle, riddle, secret. 2 *I like reading a good mystery.* SEE **thriller**.

mystic noun SEE **visionary** noun.

mystical adjective *a mystical experience.* abnormal, metaphysical, SEE **mysterious**, occult, religious, spiritual, supernatural. OPPOSITES: SEE **mundane**.

mystify verb baffle, bamboozle, bewilder, perplex, SEE **puzzle** verb.

mythical adjective *mythical monsters.* fabled, fabulous, fanciful, fictional, imaginary, invented, legendary, make-believe, mythological, non-existent, unreal. OPPOSITES: SEE **real**.

mythological adjective SEE **mythical**.

N

nab verb SEE **capture**.

nadir noun bottom, lowest point.
OPPOSITES: SEE **zenith**.

naevus noun birthmark, mole, SEE **spot** noun.

nag noun SEE **horse**.

nag verb *to nag about jobs to be done.* badger, [*informal*] go on (*Stop going on about it!*), [*informal*] henpeck, keep complaining, pester, [*informal*] plague, scold.

nail noun *an iron nail.* pin, stud, tack.

nail verb OTHER WAYS TO FASTEN THINGS: SEE **fasten**.

naïve adjective *too naïve to succeed in politics.* artless, childlike, credulous, [*informal*] green, guileless, gullible, inexperienced, ingenuous, innocent, open, simple, simple-minded, [*uncomplimentary*] stupid, unsophisticated, unwary.
OPPOSITES: SEE **knowing**.

naked adjective bare, denuded, disrobed, exposed, nude, stark naked, stripped, unclothed, uncovered, undressed.
OPPOSITES: SEE **clothed**.

namby-pamby adjective SEE **feeble**.

name noun 1 *a person's name.* alias [= assumed name], [*formal*] appellation, Christian name, first name, forename, given name, [*informal*] handle, identity, nickname, nom de plume, pen name, personal name, pseudonym, sobriquet, surname.
2 *the name of a book.* title.
to call someone names SEE **insult** verb.

name verb 1 *His parents named him Antony.* baptize, call, christen, dub, style.
2 *What did you name your story?* entitle, label.
3 *They named me as captain.* appoint, choose, designate, elect, nominate, select, single out, specify.

named adjective *named varieties of flowers.* identified, known, specific, specified.

nameless adjective 1 *nameless heroes.* anonymous, unheard of, unidentified, unnamed.
2 *nameless horrors.* SEE **unspeakable**.

nanny noun governess, nurse.

nanny-goat noun SEE **goat**.

nap noun SEE **sleep** noun.
to take a nap SEE **sleep** verb.

napkin noun *a table-napkin.* serviette.

nappy noun *a baby's nappy.* diaper.

narrate verb *to narrate a story.* chronicle, describe, recount, relate, report, tell.

narration noun *Whose voice was doing the narration?* account, commentary, description, reading, relation, story-telling, voice-over.

narrative noun *a narrative of events.* account, chronicle, history, story, tale, [*informal*] yarn.

narrow adjective 1 *a narrow line.* fine, slender, slim, thin.
2 *a narrow space.* close, confined, constricting, cramped, enclosed, limited, [*old-fashioned*] strait.
OPPOSITES: SEE **wide**.
3 *a narrow outlook.* SEE **narrow-minded**.

narrow-minded adjective *a narrow-minded outlook.* biased, bigoted, conservative, hidebound, illiberal, inflexible, insular, intolerant, narrow, old-fashioned, parochial, petty, prejudiced, prim, prudish, rigid, small-minded, straight, straight-laced.
OPPOSITES: SEE **broad-minded**.

nasty adjective [The meaning of *nasty* is vague: it can refer to almost anything you don't like. The number of synonyms is virtually limitless, so we give just some of the commoner ones here, and refer you to some of the places where you may find more.] SEE **bad** (*a nasty person*), beastly, SEE **dangerous** (*a nasty weapon*), SEE **difficult** (*a nasty problem*), SEE **dirty** (*a nasty mess*), disagreeable, disgusting, distasteful, foul, hateful, horrible, loathsome, [*slang*] lousy, SEE **objectionable** (*a nasty smell*), obnoxious, SEE **obscene** (*a nasty film*), [*informal*] off-putting, repulsive, revolting, SEE **severe** (*a nasty illness*), sickening, SEE **unkind** (*nasty to animals*), SEE **unpleasant**.
OPPOSITES: SEE **nice**.

Several words, including *nation, native, nativity, post-natal,* etc., are related to Latin *natus = born.*

nation noun 1 *The nation mourned when the king died.* community, people, population, society.
2 *the nations of the world.* civilization, country, land, power, race, state, superpower.

national adjective 1 *national customs.* ethnic, popular, racial.
2 *a national emergency.* countrywide, general, nationwide, state, widespread.
OPPOSITES: SEE **local** adjective.

national noun *British nationals.* citizen, native, resident, subject.

nationalism noun [uncomplimentary] chauvinism, [uncomplimentary] jingoism, patriotism, [uncomplimentary] xenophobia.

nationalistic adjective nationalistic feelings. [uncomplimentary] chauvinist or chauvinistic, [uncomplimentary] jingoistic, loyal, patriotic, [uncomplimentary] xenophobic.

native adjective 1 native inhabitants. aboriginal, indigenous, local, original.
2 native wit. congenital, hereditary, inborn, inbred, inherent, inherited, innate, natural.

native noun 1 a native of the USA. citizen, life-long resident.
2 The early invaders fought the natives. aborigine, native inhabitant [SEE **native** adjective]. [Do not use savage or uncivilized person as synonyms for native.]

nativity noun birth.
The Nativity birth of Christ, Christmas.

natter noun, verb SEE **talk** noun, verb.

natty adjective SEE **smart** adjective.

natural adjective 1 the natural world. normal, ordinary, predictable, regular, usual.
2 natural feelings. healthy, hereditary, human, inborn, inherited, innate, instinctive, intuitive, kind, maternal, native, paternal, proper, right.
3 natural behaviour. artless, authentic, genuine, sincere, spontaneous, unaffected, uncorrupted, unselfconscious, unsurprising.
4 natural resources. crude (crude oil), found in nature, raw, unadulterated, unprocessed, unrefined.
5 a natural leader. born, congenital, untaught.
OPPOSITES: SEE **unnatural**.
natural history biology, nature study.

nature noun 1 A naturalist loves nature. countryside, natural environment, natural history, wildlife.
2 He has a kind nature. character, disposition, make-up, manner, personality, temperament.
3 I collect coins, medals, and things of that nature. description, kind, sort, species, type, variety.

naturist noun nudist.

naught noun SEE **nothing**.

naughty adjective 1 naughty children. SEE **bad**, badly-behaved, bad-mannered, boisterous, contrary, delinquent, disobedient, fractious, headstrong, impish, impolite, incorrigible, insubordinate, intractable, mischievous, obstinate, perverse, playful, rascally, rebellious, rude, self-willed, stubborn, troublesome, uncontrollable, ungovernable, unmanageable, unruly, wayward, wicked, wilful.
OPPOSITES: SEE **well-behaved**.
2 [childish] naughty words. naughty jokes. cheeky, improper, SEE **obscene**, ribald, risqué, shocking, [informal] smutty, vulgar.
OPPOSITES: SEE **proper**.
to be naughty SEE **misbehave**.

nausea noun SEE **sickness**.

nauseate verb SEE **sicken**.

nauseating, nauseous adjectives SEE **sickening**.

nautical adjective nautical dress. marine, maritime, naval, of sailors, seafaring, seagoing.

naval adjective naval warfare. marine, maritime, nautical, of the navy.

navel noun [informal] tummy-button, [formal] umbilicus.

navigate verb 1 to navigate a ship. captain, direct, drive, guide, handle, manœuvre, pilot, sail, steer.
2 [informal] Who's going to navigate? map-read.

navvy noun SEE **worker**.

navy noun armada, convoy, fleet, flotilla.
navy blue SEE **blue** adjective.
RANKS IN THE NAVY: SEE **rank** noun.

near adjective 1 near neighbours. adjacent, adjoining, bordering, close, connected, nearby, neighbouring, next-door.
2 My birthday is near. approaching, coming, forthcoming, imminent, impending, [informal] round the corner.
3 near friends. close, dear, familiar, intimate, related.
OPPOSITES: SEE **distant**.

nearby adjective SEE **near**.

nearly adverb It's nearly dinner time. about, almost, approaching, approximately, around, not quite, practically, roughly, virtually.

neat adjective 1 a neat room. clean, orderly, [informal] shipshape, [informal] spick and span, straight, tidy, uncluttered, well-kept.
2 neat clothes. dainty, elegant, pretty, smart, spruce, trim.
3 a neat person. a neat job. accurate, adroit, deft, expert, houseproud (a houseproud person), methodical, meticulous, precise, skilful.
OPPOSITES: SEE **untidy**.

neaten verb SEE **tidy** verb.

neatness noun SEE **tidiness**.

nebulous adjective SEE **vague**.

necessary adjective *necessary repairs.* compulsory, essential, imperative, important, indispensable, inescapable, inevitable, mandatory, needed, needful, obligatory, required, requisite, unavoidable, vital.
OPPOSITES: SEE **unnecessary**.

necessitate verb SEE **compel**.

necessity noun 1 *Is it a necessity, or can we do without it?* compulsion, essential, inevitability, [*informal*] must (*It's a must!*), need, obligation, requirement, [*Latin*] sine qua non.
2 *Necessity compelled them to steal.* beggary, destitution, hardship, need, penury, poverty, privation, shortage, suffering, want.

neck noun cervix, nape, throat.
RELATED ADJECTIVE: cervical.

necktie noun cravat, tie.

need noun 1 SEE **necessity**.
2 *There's a great need for more shops in our area.* call, demand, requirement.

need verb 1 *We need £10.* be short of, lack, miss, require, want.
2 *We need your support.* crave, depend on, rely on.

needful adjective SEE **necessary**.

needle noun *injection with a needle.* hypodermic, syringe.

needle verb SEE **annoy**.

needless adjective SEE **unnecessary**.

needlework noun SEE **sewing**.

needy adjective SEE **poor**.

ne'er-do-well noun SEE **rascal**.

nefarious adjective SEE **wicked**.

negate verb SEE **nullify**.

negative adjective *a negative attitude.* antagonistic, contradictory, destructive, dissenting, grudging, nullifying, obstructive, opposing, pessimistic, rejecting, saying "no", uncooperative, unenthusiastic, unwilling.
OPPOSITES: SEE **positive**.
a negative reply SEE **refusal**.

neglect noun *guilty of neglect.* carelessness, dereliction of duty, inattention, indifference, negligence, slackness.

neglect verb *Don't neglect your work.* disregard, forget, ignore, leave alone, let slide, miss, omit, overlook, pay no attention to, shirk, skip.

neglected adjective 1 *neglected by friends. feeling neglected.* abandoned, disregarded, forlorn, [*informal*] in limbo, overlooked, unappreciated, unloved.

2 *a neglected garden.* derelict, overgrown, uncared for, untended, unweeded.

négligé noun dressing-gown.

negligent adjective *negligent work. a negligent attitude.* careless, forgetful, inattentive, inconsiderate, indifferent, irresponsible, lax, offhand, reckless, remiss, slack, sloppy, slovenly, thoughtless, uncaring, unthinking.
OPPOSITE: SEE **careful**.

negligible adjective *a negligible amount.* imperceptible, inconsiderable, insignificant, slight, small, SEE **tiny**, trifling, trivial, unimportant.
OPPOSITES: SEE **considerable**.

negotiate verb *to negotiate a price, to negotiate with an enemy.* arbitrate, bargain, confer, discuss terms, enter into negotiation [SEE **negotiation**], haggle, make arrangements, mediate, parley.

negotiation noun arbitration, bargaining, conciliation, debate, diplomacy, discussion, mediation, transaction.

negotiator noun ambassador, arbitrator, broker, conciliator, diplomat, go-between, intermediary, mediator.

neigh verb whinny.

neighbourhood noun *Are there many shops in your neighbourhood?* area, community, district, environs, locality, place, region, surroundings, vicinity, zone.

neighbouring adjective *The cats from the neighbouring houses come to our garden.* adjacent, adjoining, attached, bordering, close, closest, connecting, near, nearby, nearest, next-door.

neighbourly adjective SEE **friendly**.

nemesis noun SEE **fate**.

nephew noun FAMILY RELATIONSHIPS: SEE **family**.

nepotism noun SEE **bias** noun.

nerve noun 1 *the nerves in your body.*
RELATED ADJECTIVE: neural.
2 [*informal*] *That steeplejack has some nerve!* SEE **courage**.
3 [*informal*] *She's got a nerve, taking my pen!* SEE **cheek**.

nervous adjective *I get nervous before an exam.* afraid, agitated, anxious, apprehensive, edgy, excitable, fearful, fidgety, flustered, highly-strung, insecure, [*informal*] jittery, jumpy, [*informal*] nervy, neurotic, on edge, restless, shaky, shy, strained, tense, timid, [*informal*] touchy, [*informal*] twitchy, uneasy, [*informal*] uptight, worried.
OPPOSITES: SEE **calm** adjective.

to be nervous fret, [*informal*] have the collywobbles, [*informal*] have the willies, worry.

nervy adjective SEE **nervous**.

nest-egg noun SEE **money**.

nestle verb *to nestle up against someone.* cuddle, curl up, huddle, lie comfortably, nuzzle, snuggle.

nestling noun chick, fledgeling, young bird.

net noun *a fish net.* mesh, netting, SEE **network**.

net verb **1** *to net a fish.* SEE **catch** verb, enmesh, trammel.
2 *to net a big salary.* accumulate, bring in, clear, earn, get, make, receive.

nether adjective inferior, lower.

netting noun SEE **network**.

nettle verb SEE **annoy**.

network noun **1** *a network of lines.* crisscross pattern, grid, labyrinth, lattice, maze, mesh, net, netting, tracery, web.
2 *a railway network.* complex, organization, system.

neurosis noun abnormality, anxiety, depression, mental condition, obsession, phobia.

neurotic adjective *Don't get neurotic about things that worry you.* anxious, distraught, disturbed, maladjusted, mentally unbalanced, nervous, obsessive, overwrought, unstable.

neuter adjective *neuter gender.* ambiguous, ambivalent, indeterminate, neither one thing nor the other, uncertain.
COMPARE: feminine, hermaphrodite, masculine.

neuter verb *to neuter an animal.* castrate, [*informal*] doctor, geld, spay, sterilize.

neutral adjective **1** *a neutral referee.* detached, disinterested, dispassionate, fair, impartial, indifferent, non-aligned, non-partisan, objective, unbiased, uninvolved, unprejudiced.
OPPOSITES: SEE **prejudiced**.
2 *neutral colours.* characterless, colourless, dull, indefinite, indeterminate, intermediate, middle.
OPPOSITES: SEE **distinctive**.

neutralize verb *Alkalis neutralize acids.* cancel out, counteract, counterbalance, invalidate, make ineffective, negate, nullify, offset.

never-ending adjective SEE **continual**.

new adjective **1** *a new banknote.* brand-new, clean, fresh, mint, unused.
2 *a new invention. new music.* advanced, contemporary, current, latest, modern, modernistic, [*uncomplimentary*] new-fangled, novel, original, recent, revolutionary, [*informal*] trendy, up-to-date.
3 *new evidence. a new problem.* added, additional, changed, different, extra, just arrived, more, supplementary, unaccustomed, unexpected, unfamiliar, unknown.
OPPOSITES: SEE **old**.

newcomer noun *Get to know the newcomers.* arrival, beginner, immigrant, new boy, new girl, outsider, settler, stranger.

newfangled adjective SEE **new**.

news noun *news from abroad. news of a special event.* advice, announcement, bulletin, communiqué, dispatch, headlines, information, intelligence, [*informal*] latest (*What's the latest?*), message, newscast, newsletter, notice, press-release, proclamation, report, rumour, statement, [*old-fashioned*] tidings, word.

newsagent noun paper-shop.

newspaper noun [*informal*] daily, gazette, journal, paper, periodical, [*uncomplimentary*] rag, tabloid.
OTHER MEDIA: SEE **communication**.

newsworthy adjective SEE **significant**.

next adjective **1** *the next street.* adjacent, adjoining, closest, nearest, neighbouring.
OPPOSITES: SEE **distant**.
2 *the next bus.* following, soonest, subsequent, succeeding.
OPPOSITES: SEE **previous**.

next-door adjective SEE **neighbouring**.

next-of-kin noun SEE **relation**.

nibble verb SEE **eat**.

nice adjective **1** *nice food. a nice view. a nice person.* [In this sense, the meaning of *nice* is vague: it can refer to almost anything you like. The number of synonyms is virtually limitless, so we give just some of the commoner ones here, and refer you to some of the places where you may find more.] acceptable, agreeable, amiable, attractive, SEE **beautiful**, SEE **delicious**, delightful, SEE **friendly**, SEE **good**, gratifying, SEE **kind** adjective, likeable, SEE **pleasant**, pleasing, satisfactory, welcome.
OPPOSITES: SEE **nasty**.
2 *a nice calculation. a nice distinction.* accurate, careful, delicate, discriminating, exact, fine, meticulous, precise, punctilious, scrupulous.
OPPOSITES: SEE **careless**.
3 *nice table-manners.* dainty, elegant, fastidious, [*uncomplimentary*] fussy, particular, [*informal*] pernickety, polished, refined, well-mannered.
OPPOSITES: SEE **inelegant**.

niche noun SEE **recess**.

nick verb 1 *to nick your finger*. SEE **cut** verb.
2 [*informal*] *to nick money*. SEE **steal**.

nickname noun alias, SEE **name** noun, sobriquet.

niece noun FAMILY RELATIONSHIPS: SEE **family**.

night noun TIMES OF THE DAY: SEE **day**. RELATED ADJECTIVE: nocturnal.

night-cap noun DRINKS: SEE **drink** noun.

night-clothes noun night-dress, night-gown, [*informal*] nightie, [*old-fashioned*] night-shirt, pyjamas.

night-club noun VARIOUS ENTERTAINMENTS: SEE **entertainment**.

night-dress, night-gown nouns SEE **night-clothes**.

nightmare noun SEE **dream** noun.

night-shirt noun SEE **night-clothes**.

nil noun SEE **nothing**.

nimble adjective *nimble movements*. acrobatic, active, agile, brisk, deft, dextrous, lively, [*informal*] nippy, quick, quick-moving, sprightly, spry, swift.

nincompoop, ninny nouns SEE **idiot**.

nip noun SEE **drink** noun.

nip verb 1 *The teeth nipped my leg*. bite, clip, pinch, snag, snap at, squeeze.
2 [*informal*] *I nipped along to the shops*. SEE **go**.
to nip something in the bud SEE **stop** verb.

nipper noun SEE **child**.

nippy adjective 1 [*informal*] *a nippy car*. fast, SEE **nimble**, quick, rapid, speedy.
2 [*informal*] *nippy weather*. SEE **cold** adjective.

nirvana noun SEE **heaven**.

nit-picking adjective [*informal*] *nit-picking objections*. SEE **fussy**.

nitty-gritty noun SEE **reality**.

nitwit noun SEE **idiot**.

nobble verb 1 [*informal*] *to nobble a race-horse*. get at, hamper, incapacitate, interfere with, tamper with.
2 [*informal*] *to nobble a criminal*. SEE **catch** verb.

nobility noun 1 *nobility of character*. dignity, greatness, integrity, magnanimity, morality, nobleness, uprightness, virtue, worthiness.
2 *the nobility*. aristocracy, gentry, nobles [SEE **noble** noun], peerage.

noble adjective 1 *a noble family*. aristocratic, [*informal*] blue-blooded, courtly, élite, gentle, high-born, princely, royal, thoroughbred, titled, upper-class.
OPPOSITES: SEE **common** adjective.
2 *a noble deed*. brave, chivalrous, courageous, gallant, glorious, heroic, honourable, magnanimous, upright, virtuous, worthy.
OPPOSITES: SEE **ignoble**.
3 *a noble edifice*. dignified, distinguished, elegant, grand, great, imposing, impressive, magnificent, majestic, SEE **splendid**, stately.
OPPOSITES: SEE **insignificant**.

noble noun aristocrat, grandee, lady, lord, nobleman, noblewoman, peer, peeress.
VARIOUS NOBLE TITLES: SEE **title** noun.

nobody noun *He's a nobody*. nonentity.

nod verb *to nod your head*. bend, bob, bow, SEE **gesture** verb.
to nod off SEE **sleep** verb.

node, nodule nouns SEE **lump** noun.

noggin noun SEE **drink** noun.

noise noun *a dreadful noise*. babble, [*informal*] ballyhoo, [*informal*] bedlam, blare, cacophony, clamour, clatter, commotion, din, discord, fracas, hubbub, hullabaloo, outcry, pandemonium, racket, row, rumpus, screaming, screeching, shrieking, shouting, tumult, uproar, yelling.
OPPOSITES: SEE **silence** noun.
VARIOUS WAYS TO MAKE NOISE: SEE **sound** noun.

noiseless adjective SEE **silent**.

noisome adjective SEE **objectionable**.

noisy adjective *a noisy class of children. noisy traffic*. blaring, boisterous, booming, cacophonous, chattering, clamorous, deafening, ear-splitting, fortissimo, loud, raucous, resounding, reverberating, rowdy, screaming, screeching, shrieking, shrill, strident, talkative, thunderous, tumultuous, uproarious, vociferous.
OPPOSITES: SEE **silent**.

nomad noun *a wandering nomad*. SEE **traveller**.

nomadic adjective SEE **travelling**.

nom de plume *She writes under a nom de plume*. alias, assumed name, pen name, pseudonym.

nominal adjective 1 *He's the nominal head, but his deputy does the work*. formal, in name only, ostensible, supposed, theoretical.
2 *If we pay a nominal sum, the dog is ours*. minimal, small, token.

nominate verb *We nominated him as captain.* appoint, choose, elect, name, select.

non-aligned adjective SEE **neutral**.

nonchalant adjective SEE **casual**.

non-committal adjective SEE **cautious**.

nonconformist noun SEE **rebel** noun.
a **nonconformist** church SEE **church**.

nondescript adjective SEE **ordinary**.

nonentity noun nobody.

non-existent adjective *Unicorns are non-existent.* fictitious, hypothetical, imaginary, imagined, legendary, made-up, mythical, unreal.
OPPOSITES: SEE **existing**.

non-fiction noun SEE **writing**.

non-flammable adjective SEE **non-inflammable**.

non-inflammable adjective *non-inflammable material.* fireproof, fire-resistant, flameproof, incombustible, non-flammable.
OPPOSITES: SEE **inflammable**.

non-partisan adjective SEE **unbiased**.

nonplussed adjective SEE **amazed**.

non-resident adjective *non-resident guests.* casual, living out, passing, transient, visiting.
OPPOSITES: SEE **resident** adjective.

nonsense noun 1 *She's talking nonsense.* [Most of these synonyms are used *informally.*] balderdash, bilge, boloney, bosh, bunk, bunkum, claptrap, codswallop, double Dutch, drivel, fiddlesticks, gibberish, gobbledegook, piffle, poppycock, rot, rubbish, stuff and nonsense, tommy-rot, tripe, twaddle.
2 *I thought from the start that her plan was a nonsense.* absurdity, inanity, mistake, nonsensical idea [SEE **nonsensical**].

nonsensical adjective absurd, crazy, fatuous, foolish, inane, incomprehensible, illogical, impractical, irrational, laughable, ludicrous, meaningless, ridiculous, senseless, SEE **silly**, stupid, unreasonable.
OPPOSITES: SEE **sensible**.

non-stop adjective 1 *a non-stop train.* direct, express, fast.
OPPOSITE: stopping.
2 *non-stop chattering.* SEE **continual**.

noodles noun SEE **pasta**.

nook noun SEE **recess**.

noon noun midday.
OTHER TIMES OF THE DAY: SEE **day**.

noose noun *a noose in a rope.* collar, halter, loop.

norm noun SEE **standard** noun.

normal adjective 1 *normal temperature. a normal kind of day.* accepted, accustomed, average, common, commonplace, conventional, customary, established, everyday, familiar, habitual, natural, ordinary, predictable, prosaic, quotidian, regular, routine, [*informal*] run-of-the-mill, standard, typical, unsurprising, usual.
2 *a normal person.* balanced, healthy, rational, reasonable, sane, [*informal*] straight, well-adjusted.
OPPOSITES: SEE **abnormal**.

normalize verb *to normalize relationships after a quarrel.* legalize, regularize, return to normal.

north noun GEOGRAPHICAL TERMS: SEE **geography**.

nose noun 1 nostrils, [*formal*] proboscis, snout,
RELATED ADJECTIVE: nasal.
ADJECTIVES DESCRIBING TYPES OF NOSE: aquiline, retroussé, Roman, snub.
2 *the nose of a boat.* bow, front, prow.

nose verb *to nose into a space. to nose into the traffic.* enter cautiously, insinuate, yourself, intrude, nudge your way in, penetrate, probe, push, shove.
to **nose about** *He was nosing about in my room!* interfere, look, meddle, pry, search, snoop.

nosedive verb SEE **plunge**.

nostalgia noun *nostalgia for the past.* longing, memory, nostalgic feeling [SEE **nostalgic**], pining, regret, reminiscence, sentiment, sentimentality, yearning.

nostalgic adjective *nostalgic feelings about your childhood.* emotional, maudlin, regretful, romantic, sentimental, wistful, yearning.

nostrum noun SEE **remedy** noun.

nosy adjective SEE **inquisitive**.

notability noun SEE **celebrity**.

notable adjective *a notable example of something. a notable visitor.* celebrated, conspicuous, distinguished, eminent, evident, extraordinary, famous, important, impressive, memorable, noted, noteworthy, noticeable, obvious, outstanding, pre-eminent, prominent, rare, remarkable, renowned, striking, uncommon, unusual, well-known.
OPPOSITES: SEE **ordinary**.

notary public LEGAL TERMS: SEE **law**.

notation noun SEE **writing**.

notch noun, verb SEE **cut** noun, verb.

note noun 1 *I wrote her a note.* billet-doux, chit, communication, [*joking*] epistle, jotting, letter, [*informal*] memo, memorandum, message.

2 *a note in a textbook.* annotation, cross-reference, explanation, footnote, gloss. **3** *an angry note in her voice.* feeling, quality, sound, tone. **4** *a £5 note.* bill, banknote. OTHER FORMS OF MONEY: SEE **money**.
to take note of SEE **notice** verb.

note verb **1** *to note what is happening.* SEE **notice** verb.
2 *to note something on paper.* enter, jot down, record, scribble, write down.

notebook noun diary, exercise-book, jotter, writing-book.

notecase noun pocket-book, wallet.

noted adjective SEE **famous**.

notepaper noun SEE **paper** noun.

noteworthy adjective SEE **remarkable**.

nothing noun [*cricket*] duck, [*tennis*] love, [*football*] nil, [*old-fashioned*] naught, nought, zero.

notice noun **1** *Didn't you see the notice?* advertisement, announcement, handbill, handout, intimation, leaflet, message, note, placard, poster, sign, warning.
2 *She didn't take any notice of the signs.* cognizance, heed, note, regard, warning.
to give someone notice SEE **dismiss**.
to take notice SEE **notice** verb.

notice verb *to notice what is happening.* detect, discern, discover, feel, find, heed, mark, mind (*Mind what I say*), note, observe, pay attention to, register, remark, see, spy, take note of, take notice of [SEE **notice** noun].

noticeable adjective *a noticeable improvement in the weather. a noticeable foreign accent.* appreciable, audible, clear, conspicuous, detectable, discernible, distinct, important, manifest, marked, measurable, notable, obtrusive, obvious, perceptible, plain, prominent, pronounced, salient, significant, striking, unmistakable, visible.
OPPOSITES: SEE **imperceptible**.

notify verb *If you see anything suspicious, notify the police.* acquaint, advise, alert, inform, make known to, report to, tell, warn.

notion noun *I had a notion that you were on holiday. He has strange notions about religion.* apprehension, belief, concept, fancy, hypothesis, idea, impression, opinion, sentiment, theory, thought, understanding, view.

notional adjective SEE **theoretical**.

notorious adjective *a notorious criminal.* disreputable, famous, flagrant, known, infamous, obvious, outrageous, overt, patent, scandalous, shocking, talked about, undisguised, undisputed, well-known, wicked.

nought noun SEE **nothing**.

nourish verb *Food nourishes us.* feed, maintain, strengthen, support, sustain.

nourishing adjective *nourishing food.* beneficial, good for you, health-giving, nutritious, sustaining, wholesome.

nourishment noun diet, food, goodness, nutrient, nutriment, nutrition, sustenance.

nous noun SEE **sense** noun.

nouveau riche noun SEE **upstart**.

novel adjective *a novel way of doing something.* different, fresh, imaginative, innovative, new, odd, original, rare, singular, startling, strange, surprising, uncommon, unconventional, unfamiliar, unusual.
OPPOSITES: SEE **familiar**.

novel noun *I like to read a novel.* fiction, novelette, romance, story.
OTHER KINDS OF WRITING: SEE **writing**.

novelist noun author, story-teller.
OTHER WRITERS: SEE **writer**.

novelty noun **1** *The novelty will soon wear off.* freshness, newness, oddity, originality, strangeness, surprise, unfamiliarity.
2 *novelties sold in holiday resorts.* curiosity, gimmick, knick-knack, souvenir, trinket.

novice noun SEE **beginner**.

now adverb at present, here and now, immediately, nowadays, straight away.

noxious adjective *noxious fumes.* corrosive, foul, SEE **harmful**, nasty, noisome, objectionable, poisonous, polluting, sulphureous, sulphurous, unpleasant, unwholesome.

nozzle noun spout.

nuance noun SEE **difference**.

nub noun *the nub of the problem.* centre, core, crux, essence, gist, heart, kernel, nucleus, point.

nubile adjective [*often sexist*] *a nubile young woman.* attractive, buxom, marriageable, mature, [*informal*] sexy, voluptuous, well-developed.
OPPOSITES: SEE **immature**.

nucleus noun centre, core, heart, middle.

nude adjective SEE **naked**.

nudge verb *to nudge someone with your elbow.* bump, SEE **hit** verb, jog, jolt, poke, prod, shove, touch.

nudist noun naturist.

nugget noun *a nugget of gold.* ingot, SEE **lump** noun.

nuisance noun *That dog's a nuisance.* annoyance, bother, inconvenience, irritation, [*informal*] pain, pest, plague, trouble, vexation, worry.

nullify verb *to nullify an agreement.* abolish, annul, SEE **cancel**, do away with, invalidate, negate, neutralize, repeal, rescind, revoke, stultify.

numb adjective *My leg's gone numb.* anaesthetized, [*informal*] asleep, cold, dead, deadened, frozen, immobile, insensitive, paralysed, suffering from pins and needles.
OPPOSITES: SEE **sensitive**.

numb verb *The cold numbs my hands. The dentist's injection numbed my mouth.* anaesthetize, deaden, desensitize, freeze, immobilize, make numb, paralyse.

number noun 1 *numbers written on paper.* digit, figure, integer, numeral, unit.
RELATED ADJECTIVE: numerical.
2 *a large number.* aggregate, amount, collection, crowd, multitude, quantity, sum, total.
3 *a musical number.* item, piece, song.
4 *a special number of a magazine.* copy, edition, impression, issue, printing, publication.

number verb *The crowd numbered a thousand.* add up to, total, work out at.

numberless adjective SEE **numerous**.

numeral noun digit, figure, integer, number.

numerate adjective SEE **educated**.

numerous adjective *a numerous crowd. numerous people.* abundant, copious, countless, innumerable, many, multitudinous, numberless, plentiful, plenty of, several, uncountable, untold.
OPPOSITES: SEE **few, small**.

nun noun abbess, mother-superior, prioress, sister.

nunnery noun convent.
OTHER RELIGIOUS INSTITUTIONS: SEE **church**.

nuptials plural noun marriage, wedding.

nurse noun 1 *a medical nurse.* district-nurse, [*old-fashioned*] matron, sister.
2 *a child's nurse.* nanny, nursemaid.

nurse verb 1 *to nurse a sick person.* care for, look after, tend, treat.
2 *to nurse a baby.* breast-feed, feed, suckle.
3 *to nurse someone in your arms.* cherish, cradle, cuddle, dandle, hold, hug, mother.

nursery noun 1 *a nursery for young children.* crèche, kindergarten, nursery school.
2 *a nursery for growing plants.* garden centre, market garden.

nurseryman noun market gardener.

nursing home noun SEE **hospital**.

nurture verb *to nurture the young. to nurture tender plants.* bring up, cultivate, educate, feed, look after, nourish, nurse, rear, tend, train.

nut noun kernel.

KINDS OF NUT: almond, brazil, cashew, chestnut, cob-nut, coconut, filbert, hazel, peanut, pecan, pistachio, walnut.

nutrient noun *Provide plants with their proper nutrients.* fertilizer, SEE **nourishment**.

nutriment noun SEE **nourishment**.

nutritious adjective SEE **nourishing**.

nutty adjective SEE **mad**.

nuzzle verb SEE **touch** verb.

O

oaf noun SEE **lout**.

oafish adjective SEE **rude**.

oar noun paddle.

oarsman noun boatman, rower.

oasis noun 1 *an oasis in the desert.* spring, watering-hole, well.
2 *an oasis of peace.* haven, refuge, retreat.

oath noun 1 *to swear an oath.* assurance, guarantee, pledge, promise, undertaking, vow, word of honour.
2 *a terrible oath.* blasphemy, curse, exclamation, expletive, imprecation, profanity, swear-word.

obdurate adjective SEE **stubborn**.

obedient adjective *obedient servants. obedient animals.* acquiescent, amenable, biddable, compliant, deferential, disciplined, docile, dutiful, law-abiding, manageable, submissive, subservient, tamed, tractable, well-behaved, well-trained.
OPPOSITES: SEE **disobedient**.

obelisk noun SEE **monument**.

obese adjective SEE **fat** adjective.

obey verb 1 *Obey the rules.* abide by, adhere to, be ruled by, carry out, comply with, conform to, execute, follow, heed, implement, keep to, mind, observe, submit to.
2 *Soldiers are trained to obey.* acquiesce, be obedient [SEE **obedient**], conform, do what you are told, submit, take orders.
OPPOSITES: SEE **disobey**.

object noun 1 *What's that object you've found?* article, body, item, thing.
2 *What is the object of this exercise?* aim, end, goal, intent, intention, objective, point, purpose, target.

object verb *She objected to the smell. He objected against the plan.* argue, be opposed, carp, complain, demur, disapprove, dispute, dissent, expostulate, [*slang*] grouse, grumble, make an objection [SEE **objection**], mind, moan, protest, quibble, raise questions, remonstrate, take exception (to).
OPPOSITES: SEE **accept, agree**.

objection noun *The secretary noted our objection.* challenge, complaint, disapproval, opposition, outcry, protest, query, question, quibble, remonstration.

objectionable adjective *an objectionable smell.* abhorrent, detestable, disagreeable, disgusting, dislikeable, displeasing, distasteful, foul, hateful, insufferable, intolerable, loathsome, nasty, nauseating, noisome, obnoxious, odious, offensive, [*informal*] offputting, repellent, repugnant, revolting, sickening, unacceptable, undesirable, SEE **unpleasant**, unwanted.
OPPOSITES: SEE **acceptable**.

objective adjective *objective evidence. an objective account.* detached, disinterested, dispassionate, empirical, existing, factual, impartial, impersonal, observable, outward-looking, rational, real, scientific, unbiased, unemotional, unprejudiced.
OPPOSITES: SEE **subjective**.

objective noun *The objective is to get the ball into the net. Our objective was the top of the hill.* aim, ambition, aspiration, design, destination, end, goal, intent, intention, object, point, purpose, target.

objet d'art noun SEE **art (work of art)**.

obligation noun *an obligation to pay taxes.* commitment, compulsion, duty, liability, need, requirement, responsibility.
OPPOSITES: SEE **option**.

oblige verb *to oblige someone to do something.* coerce, compel, constrain, force, make, require.

obliged adjective 1 *He's obliged to come.* bound, certain, compelled, constrained, forced, required, sure.
2 *I'm obliged to you for your kindness.* appreciative, grateful, gratified, indebted, thankful.

obliging adjective *Thank you for being so obliging.* accommodating, agreeable, civil, considerate, co-operative, courteous, friendly, helpful, kind, neighbourly, polite, thoughtful, willing.
OPPOSITES: SEE **unhelpful**.

oblique adjective 1 *an oblique line.* angled, diagonal, inclined, slanting, sloping, tilted.
2 *an oblique insult.* backhanded, circumlocutory, SEE **evasive**, implicit, indirect, roundabout.
OPPOSITES: SEE **direct** adjective.

obliterate verb *to obliterate your tracks.* blot out, cancel, cover over, delete, destroy, efface, eradicate, erase, expunge, extirpate, leave no trace of, rub out, wipe out.

oblivion noun 1 *Most of this composer's music has fallen into oblivion.* disregard, extinction, neglect, obscurity.
2 *After the accident I was in a state of oblivion.* amnesia, coma, forgetfulness, ignorance, insensibility, obliviousness, unawareness, unconsciousness.

oblivious adjective *oblivious of what is going on.* forgetful, heedless, ignorant, insensible (to), insensitive (to), unacquainted (with), unaware, unconscious, uninformed (about), unmindful, unresponsive (to).
OPPOSITES: SEE **aware**.

oblong noun rectangle.
OTHER SHAPES: SEE **shape** noun.

obnoxious adjective SEE **objectionable**.

obscene adjective *obscene language. obscene books.* bawdy, [*informal*] blue, coarse, corrupting, crude, depraved, dirty, disgusting, filthy, foul, gross, immodest, immoral, improper, impure, indecent, indecorous, indelicate, [*informal*] kinky, lewd, nasty, SEE **objectionable**, offensive, outrageous, perverted, pornographic, prurient, repulsive, rude, salacious, scurrilous, shameless, shocking, [*informal*] sick, smutty, suggestive, vile, vulgar.
OPPOSITES: SEE **decent**.

obscenity noun 1 *the obscenity of war. the obscenity of pornography.* abomination, blasphemy, coarseness, dirtiness, evil, filth, foulness, immorality, impropriety, indecency, lewdness, licentiousness, offensiveness, outrage, pornography, profanity, vileness.

2 *His language was full of obscenities.* SEE **swearword.**

obscure adjective **1** *an obscure shape in the mist.* blurred, clouded, concealed, covered, dark, dim, hidden, inconspicuous, indefinable, indistinct, masked, misty, murky, shadowy, shady, shrouded, unclear, unlit, unrecognizable, vague, veiled.
OPPOSITES: SEE **clear** adjective.
2 *an obscure poet.* forgotten, minor, undistinguished, unheard of, unimportant, unknown.
OPPOSITES: SEE **famous.**
3 *an obscure joke.* arcane, complex, cryptic, enigmatic, esoteric, incomprehensible, puzzling, recherché, recondite.
OPPOSITES: SEE **obvious.**

obscure verb *Mist obscured the view. The complications obscured the main point.* block out, blur, cloud, conceal, cover, darken, disguise, eclipse, envelop, hide, make obscure [SEE **obscure** adjective], mask, screen, shade, shroud, veil.
OPPOSITES: SEE **clarify.**

obsequies noun SEE **funeral.**

obsequious adjective *obsequious flattery.* abject, cringing, deferential, fawning, flattering, [*informal*] greasy, grovelling, ingratiating, menial, [*informal*] oily, servile, [*informal*] smarmy, subservient, sycophantic, unctuous.
to be obsequious [*informal*] crawl, fawn, flatter, grovel, [*informal*] suck up (to), [*informal*] toady.

observant adjective *an observant sentry.* alert, astute, attentive, aware, careful, eagle-eyed, heedful, perceptive, percipient, quick, sharp-eyed, shrewd, vigilant, watchful.
OPPOSITES: SEE **inattentive.**

observation noun **1** *an astronomer's observation of the stars.* attention (to), examination, inspection, monitoring, scrutiny, study, surveillance, watching.
2 *Have you any observations?* comment, opinion, reaction, reflection, remark, response, statement, thought, utterance.

observe verb **1** *to observe an eclipse. to observe someone's behaviour.* contemplate, detect, discern, [*informal*] keep an eye on, look at, monitor, note, notice, perceive, regard, scrutinize, see, spot, spy, stare at, study, view, watch, witness.
2 *to observe the rules.* abide by, adhere to, comply with, conform to, follow, heed, honour, keep, obey, pay attention to, respect.

3 *to observe Christmas.* celebrate, commemorate, keep, remember, solemnize.
4 *I observed that it was a nice day.* comment, declare, explain, make an observation [SEE **observation**], mention, reflect, remark, say.

observer noun bystander, commentator, eye-witness, onlooker, spectator, viewer, watcher, witness.

obsess verb *His hobby obsessed him.* become an obsession with [SEE **obsession**], consume, dominate, grip, haunt, monopolize, plague, possess, rule, take hold of.

obsession noun *Don't let your hobby become an obsession.* addiction, [*informal*] bee in your bonnet, fetish, fixation, [*informal*] hobby-horse, infatuation, mania, passion, preoccupation.

obsessive adjective *an obsessive interest in something.* addictive, compulsive, consuming, dominating.

obsolescent adjective *an obsolescent design.* [*Obsolescent* does not mean *obsolete* but *becoming obsolete.*] ageing or aging, dying out, going out of use, losing popularity, moribund, [*informal*] on the way out, waning.

obsolete adjective *an obsolete design.* anachronistic, antiquated, antique, archaic, dated, dead, discarded, disused, extinct, old-fashioned, outdated, out-of-date, outmoded, primitive, superannuated, superseded, unfashionable.
OPPOSITES: SEE **current** adjective.

obstacle noun *an obstacle to be got over.* bar, barricade, barrier, block, blockage, check, difficulty, hindrance, hurdle, impediment, obstruction, problem, snag, [*informal*] stumbling-block.

obstetrician noun midwife.

obstinate adjective *an obstinate refusal to co-operate.* defiant, determined, dogged, firm, headstrong, inflexible, intractable, intransigent, [*informal*] mulish, obdurate, persistent, perverse, [*informal*] pig-headed, refractory, rigid, self-willed, [*informal*] stiff-necked, stubborn, tenacious, unreasonable, unyielding, wilful, wrong-headed.
OPPOSITES: SEE **amenable.**

obstreperous adjective *a class of obstreperous children.* awkward, boisterous, disorderly, irrepressible, noisy, SEE **noisy,** rough, rowdy, [*informal*] stroppy, unmanageable, unruly.
OPPOSITES: SEE **well-behaved.**

obstruct verb *to obstruct progress.* bar, block, check, curb, deter, frustrate, halt, hamper, hinder, hold up, impede, inhibit, interfere with, interrupt,

[*formal*] occlude, prevent, restrict, retard, slow down, [*informal*] stonewall, stop, [*informal*] stymie, thwart.
OPPOSITE: SEE **help** verb.

obstruction noun SEE **obstacle**.

obstructive adjective SEE **uncooperative**.

obtain verb 1 *to obtain what you want.* acquire, attain, be given, bring, buy, come by, come into possession of, earn, elicit, enlist (*She enlisted my help*), extort, extract, find, gain, get, get hold of, [*informal*] lay hands on, [*informal*] pick up, procure, purchase, receive, secure, win. 2 *The old rules still obtain.* be in force, be in use, be valid, exist, prevail, stand.

obtrude verb SEE **interfere**.

obtrusive adjective *The factory is an obtrusive eyesore.* blatant, conspicuous, inescapable, interfering, intrusive, SEE **obvious**, out of place, prominent, ugly, unwanted, unwelcome.
OPPOSITES: unobtrusive, SEE **inconspicuous**.

obtuse adjective SEE **stupid**.

obverse noun *the obverse of a coin.* face, front, head.
OPPOSITE: reverse.

obviate verb *to obviate the need for something.* avert, forestall, make unnecessary, preclude, prevent, remove, take away.

obvious adjective *an obvious accent. an obvious landmark. obvious favouritism.* blatant, clear, conspicuous, distinct, evident, eyecatching, flagrant, glaring, gross (*gross negligence*), inescapable, intrusive, notable, noticeable, obtrusive, open, patent, perceptible, plain, prominent, pronounced, recognizable, self-evident, unconcealed, undisguised, undisputed, unmistakable, visible.
OPPOSITES: SEE **hidden**.

occasion noun 1 *A party should be a happy occasion.* affair, celebration, ceremony, event, happening, incident, occurrence.
2 *If I can find the right occasion, I'll tell him.* chance, moment, opportunity, time.
3 *There was no occasion for rudeness.* cause, excuse, justification, need, reason.

occasional adjective *occasional showers. occasional moments of enthusiasm.* casual, desultory, fitful, infrequent, intermittent, irregular, odd, [*informal*] once in a while, periodic, rare, scattered, spasmodic, sporadic, uncommon, unpredictable.
OPPOSITES: SEE **frequent** adjective, **regular**.

occlude verb SEE **obstruct**.

occult adjective *occult powers.* SEE **supernatural**.

occult noun *the occult* black magic, diabolism, sorcery, the supernatural, witchcraft.

occupant noun 1 *the occupant of a house.* householder, inhabitant, occupier, resident, tenant.
2 *the occupant of a position.* incumbent.

occupation noun 1 *the occupation of a house.* lease, occupancy, possession, residency, tenancy, tenure, use.
2 *the occupation of a foreign country.* colonization, conquest, invasion, seizure, subjugation, [*informal*] take-over, usurpation.
3 *a full-time occupation.* business, calling, employment, job, [*informal*] line, post, profession, trade, vocation, work.
VARIOUS OCCUPATIONS: SEE **job**.
4 *a leisure occupation.* activity, hobby, pastime, pursuit.

occupied adjective 1 *occupied in your work.* absorbed, active, busy, engaged, engrossed, [*informal*] hard at it, involved.
2 *an occupied house.* inhabited, lived-in, tenanted.
3 *an occupied country.* conquered, defeated, overrun, subjugated.

occupy verb 1 *We occupy a council house.* dwell in, inhabit, live in, reside in.
2 *Troops occupied the town.* capture, conquer, garrison, invade, overrun, possess, take over, take possession of.
3 *The garden occupies her spare time.* absorb, engage, engross, fill, monopolize, preoccupy, take up, use, utilize.

occur verb *Earthquakes don't often occur in this part of the world.* appear, arise, befall, be found, come about, come into being, crop up, develop, exist, happen, manifest itself, materialize, [*informal*] show up, take place, [*informal*] turn up.

occurrence noun *an unusual occurrence.* affair, case, circumstance, development, event, happening, incident, manifestation, occasion, phenomenon, proceeding.

ocean noun SEE **sea**.

octogenarian noun SEE **old** (old person).

odd adjective 1 *odd numbers.* uneven.
OPPOSITE: even.
2 *an odd sock.* left over, remaining, single, spare, unmatched.
3 *odd jobs.* casual, irregular, miscellaneous, occasional, random, varied, various.

4 *odd behaviour.* abnormal, atypical, bizarre, [*informal*] cranky, curious, eccentric, freak, funny, incongruous, inexplicable, [*informal*] kinky, peculiar, puzzling, queer, singular, strange, uncharacteristic, uncommon, unconventional, unusual, weird.
OPPOSITES: SEE **normal**.

oddity noun **1** *I noticed the oddity of his behaviour.* SEE **strangeness**.
2 *From his weird behaviour, he seems a bit of an oddity.* SEE **eccentric** noun.

oddment noun *oddments left over from a jumble sale.* bit, [*plural*] bits and pieces, fragment, leftover, [*plural*] odds and ends, offcut, remnant, scrap, unwanted piece.

odious adjective SEE **hateful**.

odium noun SEE **hatred**.

odorous adjective SEE **smelling**.

odour noun SEE **smell** noun.

odourless adjective deodorized, unscented.

odyssey noun SEE **journey** noun.

off-beat adjective SEE **unconventional**.

off-colour adjective SEE **ill**.

offcut noun SEE **oddment**.

offence noun **1** *a criminal offence.* crime, fault, infringement, misdeed, misdemeanour, outrage, peccadillo, sin, transgression, trespass, wrong, wrongdoing.
2 *The bad language caused offence to our neighbours.* anger, annoyance, disgust, displeasure, hard feelings, indignation, irritation, resentment, [*informal*] upset.
to give offence SEE **offend**.

offend verb **1** *to offend someone.* affront, anger, annoy, cause offence [SEE **offence**], disgust, displease, give offence (to), insult, irritate, make angry, outrage, pain, provoke, rile, sicken, upset, vex.
to be offended be annoyed, [*informal*] take umbrage.
2 *to offend against the law.* do wrong, transgress, violate.

offender noun criminal, culprit, delinquent, guilty party, malefactor, miscreant, sinner, transgressor, wrongdoer.

offensive adjective *offensive behaviour. offensive language.* abusive, aggressive, annoying, antisocial, coarse, detestable, disagreeable, disgusting, displeasing, disrespectful, embarrassing, foul, impolite, improper, indecent, insulting, loathsome, nasty, nauseating, objectionable, obnoxious, SEE **obscene**, [*informal*] offputting, revolting, rude, sickening, unpleasant, vile, vulgar.

OPPOSITES: SEE **pleasant**.

offer noun *He made me an offer.* bid, proposal, proposition, suggestion, tender.

offer verb **1** *He offered me a cup of tea. The bank offered me a loan.* be willing to provide, extend, give the opportunity of, hold out, make available, make an offer of [SEE **offer** noun], proffer, put forward, suggest.
2 *She offered to come with me.* propose, [*informal*] show willing, volunteer.

offering noun *an offering in church.* contribution, donation, gift, offertory, sacrifice.

offhand adjective **1** *an offhand manner.* aloof, SEE **casual**, curt, offhanded, perfunctory, unceremonious, uncooperative, uninterested.
2 *I can't think of anything offhand.* SEE **impromptu**.

office noun **1** *the manager's office.* bureau, room, workroom.

OFFICE EQUIPMENT INCLUDES: answering machine, calculator, computer, copier, desk, diary, dictating machine, duplicator, file, filing cabinet, intercom, photocopier, stapler, stationery, switchboard, telephone, typewriter, word-processor.

OFFICE WORKERS INCLUDE: cashier, clerk, filing clerk, office-boy, office-girl, office junior, receptionist, secretary, shorthand-typist, stenographer, telephonist, typist, word-processor operator.

---

2 *The office of prime minister is a responsible one.* appointment, duty, function, occupation, place, position, post, responsibility, situation, work.

officer noun **1** *an officer in the armed services.* adjutant, aide-de-camp, CO, commandant, commanding officer.
VARIOUS RANKS: SEE **rank** noun.
2 *an officer of an organization.* SEE **official** noun.
3 *a police officer.* constable, policeman, policewoman.

official adjective *an official document. an official organization.* accredited, approved, authentic, authoritative, authorized, bona fide, certified, formal, legitimate, licensed, proper, trustworthy.

official noun *We spoke to an official of the organization.* agent, authorized person, [*uncomplimentary*] bureaucrat, SEE **chief** noun, executive, [*often uncomplimentary*] functionary, [*often uncomplimentary*] mandarin, officer, organizer, representative, responsible person.

TITLES OF VARIOUS OFFICIALS: bailiff, captain, clerk of the court, commander, commanding officer, commissioner, consul, customs officer, director, elder (*of the church*), equerry, governor, manager, managing director, marshal, mayor, mayoress, monitor, ombudsman, overseer, prefect, president, principal, proctor, proprietor, registrar, sheriff, steward, superintendent, supervisor, usher.

officiate verb *to officiate at a ceremony.* be in charge, be responsible, have official authority, manage, preside.

officious adjective *an officious car-park attendant.* SEE **bossy**, bumptious, [*informal*] cocky, impertinent, interfering, meddling, over-zealous, [*informal*] pushy, self-important.

offload verb SEE **unload**.

offputting adjective SEE **disconcerting**.

offset verb SEE **balance** verb.

offshoot noun *an unexpected offshoot of my research.* branch, by-product, [*informal*] development, spin-off, subsidiary product.

offspring noun [*Offspring* can refer either to one (*singular*) or to many (*plural*).]
Singular: baby, child, descendant, heir, successor.
Plural: brood, family, fry, issue, litter, progeny, seed, spawn, young.

often adverb again and again, constantly, frequently, generally, many times, regularly, repeatedly, time after time.

ogle verb SEE **look** verb.

ogre noun giant, monster.
LEGENDARY CREATURES: SEE **legend**.

oil noun SEE **fat** noun, **fuel** noun.

oil verb *to oil your bike.* grease, lubricate.

oily adjective 1 *oily food.* fat, fatty, greasy. 2 *an oily manner.* SEE **obsequious**.

ointment noun *an ointment for the skin.* balm, cream, embrocation, emollient, liniment, lotion, paste, salve, unguent.

old adjective 1 *old buildings. an old car.* ancient, [*joking*] antediluvian, antiquated, antique, crumbling, decayed, decaying, decrepit, dilapidated, early, historic, medieval, obsolete, prehistoric, primitive, quaint, ruined, [*joking*]

superannuated, venerable, veteran, vintage.
2 *old times.* bygone, forgotten, former, immemorial (*from time immemorial*), [*old-fashioned*] olden, past, prehistoric, previous, primeval, remote.
3 *old people.* aged, [*informal*] doddery, elderly, [*formal*] geriatric, grey-haired, hoary, [*informal*] in your dotage, oldish, [*informal*] past it, senile.
4 *old clothes.* moth-eaten, SEE **old-fashioned**, ragged, scruffy, shabby, worn, worn-out.
5 *old bread. old news.* dry, stale.
6 *old bus-tickets.* cancelled, expired, invalid, used.
7 *an old hand at the game.* experienced, expert, familiar, long-established, mature, practised, skilled, well-established.
OPPOSITES: SEE **new, recent, young**.
old age decrepitude [*informal*] dotage, senility.
an old person centenarian, [*uncomplimentary*] fogy or fogey, nonagenarian, octogenarian, pensioner, septuagenarian.
medical treatment of old people geriatrics.

old-fashioned adjective 1 *old-fashioned ways.* anachronistic, antiquated, archaic, backward-looking, conventional, dated, fusty, hackneyed, obsolete, old, outdated, out-of-date, out-of-touch, outmoded, passé, reactionary, time-honoured, traditional, unfashionable.
OPPOSITES: SEE **modern**.
old-fashioned person [*informal*] fogy or fogey, [*informal*] fuddy-duddy, [*informal*] square.
2 *old-fashioned morals.* narrow-minded, prim, proper, prudish.
OPPOSITES: SEE **advanced**.

ombudsman noun SEE **official** noun.

omen noun *an omen of disaster.* augury, auspice, foreboding, indication, portent, premonition, presage, prognostication, sign, warning.
to be an omen of SEE **foretell**.

ominous adjective *ominous signs of disaster.* baleful, dire, fateful, forbidding, grim, inauspicious, menacing, portentous, sinister, threatening, unlucky, unpropitious.
OPPOSITES: SEE **auspicious**.

omission noun *an unfortunate omission.* exclusion, gap, oversight.

omit verb 1 *to omit facts from a report.* cut, drop, edit out, eliminate, exclude, ignore, jump, leave out, miss out, overlook, pass over, reject, skip.

2 *to omit to do something.* fail, forget, neglect.

The prefix *omni-* is related to Latin *omnis = all.*

---

omnibus adjective *an omnibus edition.* compendious, eclectic, encyclopaedic, inclusive, varied, wide-ranging.

omnipotent adjective all-powerful, almighty, supreme.

oncoming adjective *oncoming traffic.* advancing, approaching, looming.

onerous adjective SEE **burdensome**.

one-sided adjective **1** *a one-sided referee.* SEE **prejudiced**.
2 *a one-sided match.* SEE **uneven**.

ongoing adjective SEE **continual**.

onlooker noun SEE **observer**.

onset noun SEE **beginning**.

onslaught noun SEE **attack** noun.

onus noun SEE **burden** noun.

oodles noun SEE **plenty**.

ooze noun SEE **mud**.

ooze verb SEE **seep**.

opaque adjective *The diver couldn't see through the opaque water.* cloudy, dark, dull, filmy, hazy, impenetrable, muddy, murky, obscure, turbid, unclear.
OPPOSITES: SEE **clear** adjective.

open adjective **1** *an open door. an open mouth.* ajar, gaping, unfastened, unlocked, wide, wide-open, yawning.
2 *open to the public.* accessible, available, exposed, public, revealed.
OPPOSITES: SEE **shut** adjective.
3 *open space. the open road.* broad, clear, empty, extensive, uncrowded, unfenced, unobstructed, unrestricted.
OPPOSITES: SEE **enclosed**.
4 *an open nature. an open face.* artless, communicative, frank, honest, SEE **open-minded**, sincere, straightforward.
OPPOSITES: SEE **deceitful**.
5 *open defiance.* barefaced, blatant, candid, conspicuous, evident, flagrant, obvious, outspoken, overt, plain, unconcealed, undisguised, visible.
OPPOSITE: SEE **concealed**.
6 *an open question.* arguable, debatable, unanswered, undecided, unresolved.

open verb **1** *to open a door, bottle, letter, etc.* unblock, unbolt, unclose, uncork, undo, unfasten, unfold, unfurl, unlock, unroll, unseal, unwrap.

2 *The door opened. Her mouth opened.* become open [SEE **open** adjective], gape, yawn.
3 *to open a campaign. to open a new shop.* begin, commence, establish, [*informal*] get going, inaugurate, initiate, launch, set up, start.
OPPOSITES: **close** verb.

open-air adjective SEE **outdoor**.

open-handed adjective SEE **generous**.

opening adjective *the opening item in a concert.* first, inaugural, initial, introductory.
OPPOSITES: SEE **final**.

opening noun **1** *an opening in a fence.* aperture, breach, break, chink, crack, cut, door, doorway, fissure, gap, gash, gate, gateway, hatch, hole, leak, mouth, orifice, outlet, rent, rift, slit, slot, space, split, tear, vent.
2 *the opening of a concert. the opening of a new era.* beginning, birth, commencement, dawn, inauguration, inception, initiation, launch, outset, start.
3 *The job provides a good opening for someone with initiative.* [*informal*] break, chance, opportunity.

open-minded adjective SEE **unbiased**.

opera noun grand opera, light opera, musical, operetta.

operable adjective *an operable illness.* curable, treatable.

opera-glasses noun SEE **optical** (optical instruments).

operate verb **1** *The device operates in all weathers.* act, function, go, perform, run, work.
2 *Can you operate this machine?* deal with, drive, handle, manage, use, work.
3 *The surgeon operated to remove her appendix.* do an operation, perform surgery.

operation noun **1** *a military operation. a business operation.* action, activity, campaign, effort, enterprise, exercise, manoeuvre, movement, procedure, proceeding, process, transaction, undertaking.
2 *a surgical operation.* biopsy, surgery, transplant.

operational adjective *Is the new machinery operational yet?* functioning, going, operating, usable, working.

operative adjective [*informal*] *When I say "come quickly", the operative word is "quickly".* crucial, effective, important, key, principal, relevant, significant.

operative, operator nouns SEE **worker**.

operetta noun SEE **opera**.

opiate noun drug, narcotic, sedative, tranquillizer.

opinion noun *I've got my own opinion.* assessment, attitude, belief, comment, conclusion, conjecture, conviction, estimate, feeling, guess, idea, impression, judgement, notion, perception, point of view, theory, thought, view.

opinionated adjective SEE **stubborn**.

opponent noun *an opponent in a debate.* adversary, antagonist, challenger, competitor, contestant, enemy, foe, opposer, opposition, rival.
OPPOSITES: SEE **ally** noun.

opportune adjective *an opportune moment.* advantageous, appropriate, auspicious, convenient, favourable, lucky, propitious, right, suitable, timely.
OPPOSITES: SEE **inconvenient**.

opportunity noun *The weekend is a good opportunity for shopping.* [*informal*] break, chance, moment, occasion, opening, time.

oppose verb *to oppose someone's ideas. to oppose an enemy.* argue with, attack, be opposed to [SEE **opposed**], challenge, combat, compete against, confront, contest, contradict, controvert, counter, counter-attack, defy, disapprove of, face, fight, obstruct, [*informal*] pit your wits against, quarrel with, resist, rival, stand up to, [*informal*] take a stand against, withstand.
OPPOSITES: SEE **support** verb.

opposed adjective *I'm opposed to the idea.* against, antagonistic, antipathetic, hostile, inimical, SEE **opposite** adjective, unsympathetic.

opposite adjective 1 *the opposite view. the opposite theory.* antithetical, conflicting, contradictory, contrary, contrasting, converse, different, incompatible, SEE **opposed**, opposing, reverse.
2 *the opposite side of the road. your opposite number.* corresponding, equivalent, facing, matching, similar.

opposite noun *She says one thing and does the opposite.* antithesis, contrary, converse, reverse.

opposition noun 1 *We didn't expect so much opposition.* antagonism, competition, disapproval, resistance, scepticism, unfriendliness.
OPPOSITES: SEE **support** noun.
2 *We underestimated the strength of the opposition.* SEE **opponent**.

oppress verb *The factory owners oppressed their workers.* abuse, afflict, crush, depress, enslave, exploit, grind down, [*informal*] keep under, persecute, subdue, subjugate, SEE **terrorize**, [*informal*] trample on, tyrannize.

oppressed adjective *oppressed sections of the community.* abused, browbeaten, crushed, disadvantaged, downtrodden, enslaved, exploited, maltreated, misused, persecuted, subjugated.
OPPOSITES: SEE **privileged**.

oppressive adjective 1 *an oppressive ruler.* brutal, cruel, despotic, harsh, repressive, severe, tyrannical, unjust.
2 *oppressive weather.* airless, close, heavy, hot, humid, muggy, stifling, stuffy, sultry.

opprobrium noun SEE **disgrace** noun.

opt verb SEE **choose**.

optical adjective VARIOUS OPTICAL INSTRUMENTS: bifocals, binoculars, field-glasses, glasses, lens, magnifier, magnifying glass, microscope, monocle, opera-glasses, periscope, spectacles, sun-glasses, telescope.

Several English words, including *optimism* and *optimum*, are related to Latin *optimus* = *best.* Compare *pessimism*, which is related to Latin *pessimus* = *worst.*

---

optimism noun cheerfulness, confidence, hope, positiveness.
OPPOSITES: SEE **pessimism**.

optimistic adjective *optimistic about our chances.* buoyant, cheerful, confident, expectant, hopeful, positive, sanguine.
OPPOSITES: SEE **pessimistic**.

optimum adjective *the optimum value of something.* best, highest, ideal, maximum, perfect, top.
OPPOSITE: worst.

option noun *You had the option of staying or leaving.* alternative, choice, possibility.
OPPOSITES: SEE **compulsion**.

optional adjective *optional extras.* discretionary, dispensable, elective, inessential, possible, unnecessary, voluntary.
OPPOSITES: SEE **compulsory**.

opulent adjective SEE **rich**.

oracle noun SEE **prophet**.

oral adjective *an oral report.* by mouth, said, spoken, unwritten, verbal.
OPPOSITE: written.

oration noun SEE **speech**.

orator noun SEE **speaker**.

oratory noun *I admire the oratory of some politicians.* eloquence, rhetoric, speaking, speechmaking.

orb noun SEE **sphere**.

orbit noun *the orbit of a spacecraft.* circuit, course, path, revolution, trajectory.

orbit verb *to orbit the earth.* circle, travel round.

orbital adjective *an orbital route.* circular, encircling.

orchestra noun GROUPS OF MUSICIANS: SEE **music**.

orchestrate verb 1 *to orchestrate music.* arrange, compose.
2 *to orchestrate a demonstration.* SEE **organize**.

ordain verb *to ordain that something shall happen.* SEE **command** verb.

ordeal noun *a painful ordeal.* difficulty, experience, [*informal*] nightmare, suffering, test, torture, trial, tribulation, trouble.

order noun 1 *alphabetical order. chronological order.* arrangement, array, classification, [*informal*] line-up, pattern, progression, sequence, series, succession.
2 *We restored order after the party.* neatness, system, tidiness.
3 *The army restored order after the riot.* calm, control, discipline, good behaviour, government, harmony, law and order, obedience, orderliness, organization, peace, quiet, rule.
OPPOSITES: SEE **disorder**.
4 *Keep your car in good order.* condition, state.
5 *The boss gives the orders.* command, decree, directive, edict, injunction, instruction.
6 *an order for a new carpet. an order for work to be done.* application, booking, commission, demand, mandate, request, requisition, reservation.
7 *an order of monks. a chivalric order.* brotherhood, community, fraternity, SEE **group** noun, society.
to put things in order SEE **arrange**.

order verb 1 *to order things properly.* SEE **arrange**.
2 *She ordered us to be quiet.* [*old-fashioned*] bid, charge, command, compel, decree, direct, enjoin, instruct, ordain, require.
3 *He ordered a new magazine.* apply for, book, requisition, reserve.

orderly adjective 1 *orderly work.* careful, methodical, neat, organized, systematic, tidy, well-arranged, well-organized, well-prepared.
2 *orderly behaviour. an orderly crowd.* civilized, controlled, decorous, disciplined, law-abiding, peaceable, restrained, well-behaved.
OPPOSITES: SEE **disorderly**.

ordinance noun SEE **decree** noun.

ordinary adjective *ordinary people. ordinary behaviour.* accustomed, average, common, commonplace, conventional, customary, established, everyday, familiar, habitual, humble, [*informal*] humdrum, indifferent, mediocre, medium, middling, moderate, modest, mundane, nondescript, normal, orthodox, pedestrian, plain, prosaic, quotidian, reasonable, regular, routine, [*informal*] run-of-the-mill, satisfactory, simple, standard, stock (*a stock reply*), typical, undistinguished, unexceptional, unexciting, unimpressive, uninteresting, unsurprising, usual, well-known, workaday.
OPPOSITES: SEE **exceptional**.

ordnance noun WEAPONS: SEE **weapons**.

ore noun SEE **rock** noun.

organ noun 1 *a church organ.* KEYBOARD INSTRUMENTS: SEE **keyboard**.
2 *organs of the body.* PARTS OF THE BODY: SEE **body**.

organic adjective 1 *an organic substance.* animate, biological, growing, live, living, natural.
OPPOSITES: SEE **inorganic**.
2 *an organic whole.* evolving, integrated, organized, structured, systematic.

organism noun *a living organism.* animal, cell, creature, living thing, plant.

organization noun 1 *Who was responsible for the organization of the outing?* arrangement, co-ordination, logistics, organizing, planning, regimentation, [*informal*] running.
2 *a business organization. a charitable organization.* alliance, association, body, business, club, company, concern, confederation, consortium, corporation, federation, firm, group, institute, institution, league, network, [*informal*] outfit, party, society, syndicate, union.

organize verb 1 *to organize into groups.* arrange, classify, group, put in order, rearrange, regiment, sort, sort out, structure, systematize, tidy up.
OPPOSITES: SEE **jumble** verb.
2 *to organize a party. to organize a demonstration.* co-ordinate, create, establish, make arrangements for, mobilize, orchestrate, plan, run, [*informal*] see to, set up.

organized adjective *an organized argument. organized effort.* careful, clear, efficient, logical, methodical, neat, orderly, planned, regimented, scientific, structured, systematic, tidy, well-arranged, well-presented, well-run.
OPPOSITES: SEE **disorganized**.

orgy noun Bacchanalia, [*informal*] binge, party, revelry, Saturnalia.

orient verb SEE **orientate**.

oriental adjective *oriental nations*. Asiatic, eastern, far-eastern.

orientate verb *to orientate yourself to a new situation*. acclimatize, accustom, adapt, adjust, familiarize, orient, position.

orifice noun hole, mouth, SEE **opening**.

origin noun 1 *the origin of life on earth. the origin of a rumour*. basis, beginning, birth, cause, commencement, creation, derivation, foundation, genesis, inauguration, inception, provenance, root, source, start.
OPPOSITES: SEE **end** noun.
2 *a millionaire of humble origin*. ancestry, background, descent, extraction, family, parentage, pedigree, start in life, stock.

original adjective 1 *the original inhabitants of a country*. aboriginal, archetypal, earliest, first, initial, native, primal, primitive, primordial.
OPPOSITES: SEE **recent**.
2 *an original idea. an original story*. creative, first-hand, fresh, imaginative, innovative, inspired, inventive, new, novel, resourceful, thoughtful, unconventional, unfamiliar, unique, unusual.
OPPOSITES: SEE **unoriginal**.
3 *an original work of art*. authentic, genuine, real, unique.
OPPOSITES: SEE **fake** adjective.

originate verb 1 *Where did the idea originate?* arise, be born, begin, commence, crop up, emanate, emerge, start.
2 *Who originated the idea?* be the inventor of, conceive, create, design, discover, give birth to, inaugurate, initiate, inspire, institute, introduce, invent, launch, pioneer.

ornament noun accessory, adornment, bauble, decoration, embellishment, filigree, frill, frippery, garnish, gewgaw, SEE **jewel**, tracery, trimming, trinket.

ornament verb adorn, beautify, deck, decorate, dress up, embellish, emblazon, emboss, embroider, festoon, garnish, [*uncomplimentary*] prettify, trim.

ornamental adjective attractive, decorative, fancy, [*uncomplimentary*] flashy, pretty, showy.

ornate adjective *ornate decorations*. [*formal*] baroque, decorated, elaborate, fancy, florid, flowery, fussy, ornamented, [*formal*] rococo.
OPPOSITES: SEE **plain** adjective.

ornithology noun bird-watching.

orphan noun foundling, stray, waif.
FAMILY RELATIONSHIPS: SEE **family**.

orthodox adjective *orthodox beliefs. the orthodox way to do something*. accepted, approved, conformist, conventional, customary, established, mainstream, normal, official, ordinary, regular, standard, traditional, usual, well-established.
OPPOSITES: unorthodox, SEE **unconventional**.

orthodoxy noun compliance, conformity, conventionality, submission.

oscillate verb fluctuate, move to and fro, [*informal*] see-saw, swing, vacillate, vary, vibrate.

ossify verb SEE **harden**.

ostensible adjective *The ostensible reason wasn't the real reason*. alleged, apparent, offered, outward, pretended, professed, [*informal*] put-on, reputed, specious, supposed, visible.
OPPOSITES: SEE **real**.

ostentation noun *I don't like the ostentation of their expensive life-style*. affectation, display, exhibitionism, flamboyance, [*informal*] flashiness, pretentiousness, self-advertisement, show, showing off, [*informal*] swank.
OPPOSITES: SEE **modesty**.

ostracize verb *to ostracize someone you don't like*. avoid, [*informal*] black, blackball, blacklist, boycott, cast out, cold-shoulder, [*informal*] cut, [*informal*] cut dead, [*formal*] excommunicate, exile, expel, reject, [*informal*] send to Coventry, shut out.
OPPOSITES: SEE **friend** (make friends with).

oust verb banish, eject, expel, [*informal*] kick out, remove, unseat.

out-and-out adjective SEE **complete** adjective.

outboard motor noun SEE **engine**.

outbreak noun *an outbreak of measles. an outbreak of vandalism*. epidemic, [*informal*] flare-up, SEE **outburst**, plague, rash, upsurge.

outburst noun *an outburst of laughter*. attack, eruption, explosion, fit, paroxysm, spasm, surge.

outcast noun *an outcast from society*. castaway, exile, outlaw, outsider, pariah, refugee, untouchable.

outclass verb SEE **beat** verb, **surpass**.

outcome noun SEE **result** noun.

outcry noun SEE **protest** noun.

outdated adjective SEE **obsolete**.

outdistance verb SEE **beat** verb.

outdo verb SEE **beat** verb, **surpass**.

outdoor adjective *an outdoor party.* alfresco, open-air, outside.

outer adjective 1 *outer clothing.* exterior, external, outside, outward, superficial, surface.
2 *outer regions.* distant, further, outlying, peripheral, remote.
OPPOSITES: SEE **inner**.

outfit noun 1 *a complete water-skiing outfit.* SEE **equipment**.
2 *a new outfit of clothes.* costume, ensemble, [*informal*] get-up, suit, [*informal*] turn-out.

outgoing adjective 1 *an outgoing personality.* SEE **sociable**.
2 *the outgoing president.* ex-, former, last, past, retiring.
3 *the outgoing tide.* ebbing, falling, retreating.
OPPOSITES: SEE **incoming**.

outgoings noun SEE **expense**.

outhouse noun shed.

outing noun *an outing to the seaside.* excursion, expedition, jaunt, picnic, tour, trip.

outlandish adjective SEE **strange**.

outlast verb SEE **survive**.

outlaw noun *outlaws hiding in the mountains.* bandit, brigand, criminal, deserter, desperado, fugitive, marauder, outcast, renegade, robber.

outlaw verb SEE **prohibit**.

outlay noun SEE **expense**.

outlet noun *an outlet for waste water.* channel, duct, exit, mouth, opening, orifice, vent, way out.

outline noun 1 *an outline of a scheme.* [*informal*] bare bones, diagram, framework, plan, rough idea, skeleton, sketch, summary.
2 *the outline of someone passing the window.* figure, form, profile, shadow, shape, silhouette.

outline verb *to outline your plans.* delineate, draft, give an outline of [SEE outline noun], rough out, sketch, summarize.

outlive verb SEE **survive**.

outlook noun 1 *the outlook from my window.* aspect, panorama, prospect, scene, sight, vantage-point, view, vista.
2 *a person's mental outlook.* attitude, frame of mind, point of view, standpoint, viewpoint.
3 *the weather outlook.* expectations, forecast, [*informal*] look-out, prediction, prognosis.

outlying adjective *outlying areas.* distant, far-flung, far-off, outer, remote.
OPPOSITES: SEE **central**.

outmoded adjective SEE **old-fashioned**.

outnumber verb SEE **exceed**.

out-of-date adjective SEE **old-fashioned**.

outpace verb SEE **beat** verb.

output noun *the output of a factory.* production, yield.

outrage noun 1 *The way he treats his pets is an outrage.* atrocity, crime, disgrace, outrageous act [SEE **outrageous**], scandal, sensation.
2 *You can imagine our outrage when we heard what he'd done.* anger, disgust, fury, horror, indignation, resentment, revulsion, sense of shock.

outrageous adjective *outrageous behaviour. outrageous prices.* abominable, atrocious, beastly, bestial, criminal, disgraceful, disgusting, excessive, execrable, extortionate, extravagant, immoderate, infamous, iniquitous, monstrous, nefarious, notorious, offensive, preposterous, revolting, scandalous, shocking, unreasonable, unspeakable, unthinkable, vile, villainous, wicked.
OPPOSITES: SEE **reasonable**.

outright adjective *an outright villain.* SEE **complete** adjective.

outrun verb SEE **beat** verb.

outset noun SEE **beginning**.

outshine verb SEE **surpass**.

outside adjective 1 *outside walls.* exterior, external, outer, outward, superficial, surface, visible.
2 *outside interference.* alien, extraneous, foreign.
OPPOSITES: SEE **inside** adjective.
3 *an outside chance.* SEE **remote**.

outside noun *the outside of a house.* exterior, façade, shell, skin, surface.
OPPOSITES: SEE **inside** noun.

outsider noun *Make outsiders feel welcome.* alien, foreigner, immigrant, interloper, intruder, newcomer, nonresident, outcast, stranger, visitor.
OPPOSITES: SEE **member**, **resident** noun.

outsize adjective SEE **large**, overgrown, oversized.

outskirts plural noun *the outskirts of the town.* edge, fringe, margin, outer areas, periphery, purlieus, suburbs.
OPPOSITES: SEE **centre**.

outspoken adjective SEE **frank**.

outspread adjective SEE **wide**.

outstanding adjective **1** *an outstanding player. an outstanding feature.* above the rest, celebrated, conspicuous, distinguished, dominant, eminent, excellent, exceptional, extraordinary, great, important, impressive, memorable, notable, noteworthy, noticeable, predominant, pre-eminent, prominent, remarkable, singular, special, striking, unrivalled, well-known.
OPPOSITES: SEE **ordinary.**
2 *outstanding bills.* due, overdue, owing, unpaid, unsettled.

outstrip verb SEE **surpass.**

outvote verb SEE **defeat** verb.

outward adjective *outward appearances.* apparent, evident, exterior, external, noticeable, obvious, ostensible, outer, outside, superficial, surface, visible.

outweigh verb SEE **cancel (cancel out).**

outwit verb *The fox outwitted the hounds.* cheat, SEE **deceive,** dupe, fool, hoax, hoodwink, [*informal*] outsmart, [*informal*] take in, trick.

oval adjective egg-shaped, elliptical, ovoid.
OTHER SHAPES: SEE **shape** noun.

ovation noun SEE **applause.**

oven noun cooker, stove.

overact verb SEE **exaggerate.**

overall adjective *the overall impression given by something.* SEE **total** adjective.

overbalance verb SEE **fall** verb.

overbearing adjective SEE **arrogant, tyrannical.**

overcast adjective *an overcast sky.* black, cloudy, dark, dismal, dull, gloomy, grey, leaden, lowering, stormy, threatening.

overcoat noun greatcoat, mackintosh, top-coat, trench-coat.
OTHER CLOTHES: SEE **clothes.**

overcome adjective *overcome by the heat.* beaten, [*informal*] done in, SEE **exhausted,** prostrate.

overcome verb **1** *to overcome an opponent.* SEE **defeat** verb.
2 *to overcome a problem.* SEE **deal** verb **(deal with).**

overcrowded adjective *an overcrowded room.* congested, crammed, filled to capacity, full, jammed, overloaded, packed.

overdo verb do excessively, SEE **exaggerate.**

overdue adjective **1** *The train is overdue.* belated, delayed, late, slow, tardy, unpunctual.
OPPOSITES: SEE **early.**

2 *The gas bill is overdue.* outstanding, owing, unpaid.

overeat verb be greedy [SEE **greedy**], eat too much, gorge yourself, gormandize, [*informal*] guzzle, indulge yourself, [*informal*] make a pig of yourself.

overeating noun excess, gluttony, self-indulgence.
OPPOSITES: SEE **starvation.**

overestimate verb SEE **exaggerate.**

overflow verb *The lavatory cistern overflowed.* brim over, flood, pour over, run over, spill, well up.

overgrown adjective **1** *an overgrown schoolboy.* SEE **large,** outsize, oversized.
2 *an overgrown garden.* rank, tangled, uncut, unkempt, untidy, untrimmed, unweeded, weedy, wild.

overhang verb SEE **jut.**

overhaul verb **1** *to overhaul an engine.* check over, examine, inspect, renovate, repair, restore, service.
2 *The express overhauled a goods train.* SEE **overtake.**

overhead adjective *an overhead walkway.* aerial, elevated, high, overhanging, raised.

overheads noun SEE **expense.**

overhear verb *to overhear a conversation.* eavesdrop on, listen in to.

overjoyed adjective SEE **pleased.**

overload verb SEE **burden** verb.

overlook verb **1** *to overlook someone's wrongdoing.* condone, disregard, excuse, forget, ignore, leave out, let pass, miss, neglect, omit, pardon, pass over, pay no attention to, [*informal*] turn a blind eye to.
2 *My window overlooks the pie factory.* face, front, have a view of, look at, look on to.

overpass noun SEE **bridge** noun.

overpower verb *to overpower an attacker.* SEE **subdue.**

overpowering adjective *an overpowering urge.* compelling, irrepressible, irresistible, overwhelming, powerful, uncontrollable.

override, overrule verbs SEE **cancel.**

overrun verb SEE **invade.**

overseas adjective *overseas travel.* foreign.

overseas adverb *to travel overseas.* abroad.

oversee verb SEE **supervise.**

overseer noun SEE **supervisor**

overshadow verb SEE **dominate.**

oversight noun *It wasn't deliberate—just an oversight.* SEE **error.**

oversimplify verb SEE **falsify.**

oversized adjective SEE **large,** outsize, overgrown.

overstate verb SEE **exaggerate.**

overt adjective *overt hostility.* blatant, SEE **obvious,** open, plain, unconcealed, undisguised.
OPPOSITES: SEE **secret** adjective.

overtake verb *Overtake the car in front.* catch up with, leave behind, outdistance, outpace, outstrip, overhaul, pass.

overthrow noun, verb SEE **defeat** noun, verb.

overtire verb SEE **tire.**

overtone noun *The word "witchcraft" has sinister overtones.* association, connotation, implication, reverberation, suggestion.

overturn verb 1 *The boat overturned.* capsize, keel over, tip over, turn over, turn turtle.
2 *The cat overturned the milk.* knock over, spill, tip over, topple, upset.

overweight adjective SEE **fat** adjective.

overwhelm verb 1 *to overwhelm the opposition.* SEE **defeat** verb.
2 *A tidal-wave overwhelmed the town.* SEE **submerge.**

overwhelming adjective *an overwhelming victory.* crushing, devastating, SEE **great,** landslide, overpowering.

overwrought adjective SEE **excited.**

ovoid adjective egg-shaped, elliptical, oval.

owe verb **to owe money** be in debt, have debts.

owing adjective *I'll pay whatever is owing.* due, outstanding, overdue, owed, payable, unpaid, unsettled.
owing to because of, caused by, thanks to.

own verb *We own our house.* be the owner of, have, hold, possess.
to own up acknowledge your guilt, admit, [*informal*] come clean, confess, [*informal*] make a clean breast of it, [*informal*] tell all.

owner noun *the owner of property.* freeholder, landlady, landlord, possessor, proprietor.

ox noun SEE **cattle.**
RELATED ADJECTIVE: bovine.

P

pace noun 1 *Move forward two paces.* step, stride.
2 *The front runner set a quick pace.* gait, [*informal*] lick, movement, quickness, rate, speed, velocity.

pace verb SEE **walk** verb.

pacific adjective SEE **peaceable.**

pacifism noun non-violence.
OPPOSITE: militarism.

pacify verb *to pacify an angry person. to pacify someone's anger.* appease, assuage, calm, conciliate, humour, mollify, placate, propitiate, quell, quieten, soothe, subdue, tame, tranquillize.
OPPOSITES: SEE **anger** verb.

pack noun 1 *a pack of goods.* bale, box, bundle, package, packet, parcel.
2 *a pack to carry on your back.* back-pack, haversack, kitbag, knapsack, rucksack.
3 *a pack of wolves.* SEE **group** noun.

pack verb 1 *to pack things in a box.* bundle, fill, load, package, put, put together, store, stow, wrap up.
2 *to pack things tightly. to pack people into a minibus.* compress, cram, crowd, huddle, jam, overcrowd, press, ram, squeeze, stuff, wedge.

package, packet nouns SEE **pack** noun.

pact noun *a pact with the enemy.* agreement, alliance, armistice, arrangement, bargain, compact, contract, covenant, deal, entente, league, peace, settlement, treaty, truce, understanding.

pad noun 1 *a pad to kneel on.* cushion, hassock, kneeler, padding, pillow, wad.
2 *a writing-pad.* jotter, notebook.

pad verb 1 *to pad something with soft material.* cover, fill, line, pack, protect, stuff, upholster.
2 *to pad along quietly.* SEE **walk** verb.

padding noun 1 *padding in an armchair.* filling, protection, upholstery, stuffing, wadding.
2 *padding in an essay.* prolixity, verbiage, verbosity, [*informal*] waffle, wordiness.

paddle noun oar, scull.

paddle verb 1 *to paddle a boat.* propel, row, scull.
2 *to paddle in the sea.* dabble, splash about, wade.

paddock noun enclosure, field, meadow, pasture.

paddy noun *to be in a paddy.* SEE **angry (be angry).**

padlock noun SEE **fastening,** lock.

padlock verb OTHER WAYS TO FASTEN THINGS: SEE **fasten.**

padre noun SEE **clergyman.**

pagan adjective *pagan tribes.* atheistic, godless, heathen, idolatrous, irreligious, unchristian.

pagan noun *Missionaries wished to convert the pagans.* atheist, heathen, infidel, savage, unbeliever.

page noun 1 *a page of a book.* folio, leaf, sheet, side.
2 *a page serving at court.* OTHER SERVANTS: SEE **servant.**

pageant noun *a historical pageant.* display, parade, procession, spectacle, tableau.

pageantry noun *the pageantry of a royal wedding.* ceremony, display, formality, grandeur, magnificence, pomp, ritual, show, spectacle, splendour.

pail noun bucket.
OTHER CONTAINERS: SEE **container.**

pain noun ache, affliction, agony, anguish, cramp, crick (*in the neck*), discomfort, distress, headache, hurt, irritation, ordeal, pang, smart, soreness, spasm, stab, sting, suffering, tenderness, throb, throes (*throes of childbirth*), toothache, torment, torture, twinge.
to suffer pain SEE **hurt** verb.

pain verb SEE **hurt** verb.

pained adjective *a pained expression.* distressed, grieved, hurt, offended.

painful adjective 1 *painful torture.* agonizing, cruel, excruciating, severe.
2 *a painful wound.* aching, [*informal*] achy, hurting, inflamed, raw, smarting, sore, [*informal*] splitting (*a splitting headache*), tender.
3 *a painful experience.* distressing, hard to bear, harrowing, hurtful, nasty, [*informal*] traumatic, trying, unpleasant, upsetting.
4 *a painful decision.* difficult, hard, laborious, troublesome.
OPPOSITES: SEE **painless.**
to be painful SEE **hurt** verb.

pain-killer noun anaesthetic, analgesic, anodyne, sedative.

painless adjective *a painless visit to the dentist. a painless decision.* comfortable, easy, effortless, pain-free, simple, trouble-free, undemanding.
OPPOSITES: SEE **painful.**

painstaking adjective SEE **careful.**

paint noun colour, colouring, pigment, tint.
KINDS OF PAINT: distemper, emulsion, enamel, gloss paint, lacquer, matt paint, oil-colour, oil-paint, pastel, primer, stain, tempera, undercoat, varnish, water-colour, whitewash.

paint verb 1 *to paint a wall. to paint a toy.* apply paint to, coat with paint, colour, cover with paint, decorate, enamel, gild, lacquer, redecorate, varnish, whitewash.
2 *to paint a picture.* delineate, depict, describe, portray, represent.

painter noun 1 *a house painter.* decorator.
2 *a painter of pictures.* SEE **artist.**

painting noun KINDS OF PAINTED PICTURE: fresco, landscape, miniature, mural, oil-painting, portrait, still-life, water-colour.
OTHER KINDS OF PICTURE: SEE **picture** noun.

pair noun *a pair of friends. working as a pair.* brace, couple, duet, duo, mates, partners, partnership, set of two, twins, twosome.

pair verb SEE **couple** verb.

pal noun SEE **friend.**

palace noun castle, château, mansion, official residence, stately home.
RELATED ADJECTIVE: palatial.

palatable adjective *palatable food.* acceptable, agreeable, appetizing, easy to take, eatable, edible, nice to eat, pleasant, tasty.
OPPOSITES: SEE **unpalatable.**

palatial adjective SEE **grand.**

palaver noun SEE **commotion.**

pale adjective 1 *a pale face.* anaemic, ashen, bloodless, colourless, drained, etiolated, ill-looking, pallid, pasty, [*informal*] peaky, sallow, sickly, unhealthy, wan, [*informal*] washed-out, [*informal*] whey-faced, white, whitish.
OPPOSITES: SEE **ruddy.**
2 *pale colours.* bleached, dim, faded, faint, light, pastel, subtle, weak.
OPPOSITES: SEE **bright.**

pale verb *He paled when he heard the bad news. Plants pale through lack of light.* become pale, blanch, etiolate, fade, lighten, lose colour, whiten.

palfrey noun SEE **horse.**

paling noun fence, fencing, palisade, railing, stockade.

palisade noun SEE **paling.**

pall noun 1 *a pall on a coffin.* mantle, shroud, veil.
2 *a pall of smoke.* SEE **covering.**

pall verb *The novelty soon began to pall.* become boring, become uninteresting, weary.

pallet, palliasse nouns SEE **bed.**

palliate verb SEE **alleviate**.

palliative adjective *a palliative treatment.* alleviating [SEE **alleviate**], calming, reassuring, sedative, soothing.

palliative noun *The medicine she took was only a palliative, not a real cure.* SEE **pain-killer**, sedative, tranquillizer.

pallid adjective SEE **pale** adjective.

pally adjective SEE **friendly**.

palm noun *the palm of your hand.* SEE **hand** noun.

palmer noun SEE **pilgrim**.

palmist noun SEE **fortune-teller**.

palpable adjective SEE **tangible**.

palpitate verb SEE **pulsate**.

palsied adjective SEE **paralysed**.

palsy noun SEE **paralysis**.

paltry adjective SEE **worthless**.

pamper verb *to pamper your pet.* coddle, cosset, humour, indulge, mollycoddle, over-indulge, pet, spoil, spoon-feed.

pamphlet noun *a pamphlet about road safety.* booklet, brochure, catalogue, folder, handout, leaflet, tract.

pan noun COOKING UTENSILS: SEE **cook** verb.

pan verb SEE **criticize**.

panacea noun SEE **remedy** noun.

panache noun *We were bowled over by the panache of her performance.* SEE **confidence**, enthusiasm, flourish, spirit, style, verve, zest.

pandemonium noun SEE **uproar**.

pander verb **to pander to** *to pander to low tastes.* cater for, fulfil, gratify, indulge, please, provide, satisfy.

pane noun glass, sheet of glass, window.

panegyric noun SEE **praise** noun.

panel noun **1** *a wooden panel.* insert, rectangle, rectangular piece.
panels panelling, wainscot.
2 *a panel of experts.* committee, group, jury, team.
member of a panel expert, panellist, pundit.

pang noun SEE **pain** noun.

panic noun *If a fire starts, we don't want any panic!* alarm, consternation, SEE **fear** noun, [*informal*] flap, horror, hysteria, stampede, terror.

panic verb *Don't panic!* become panic-stricken [SEE **panic-stricken**], [*informal*] flap, [*informal*] go to pieces, [*informal*] lose your head, over-react, stampede.

panicky adjective SEE **panic-stricken**.

panic-stricken adjective alarmed, disorientated, frantic, SEE **frightened**, horrified, hysterical, overexcited, panicky, terror-stricken, undisciplined, unnerved.
OPPOSITES: SEE **cool** adjective.

pannier noun basket.

panoply noun SEE **array** noun.

panorama noun *a beautiful panorama across the valley.* landscape, perspective, prospect, scene, view, vista.

panoramic adjective SEE **wide**.

pant verb *to pant because you've been running.* breathe quickly, gasp, puff, wheeze.

panting adjective *panting after running for the bus.* breathless, exhausted, gasping, out of breath, puffed, tired out, winded.

panties noun SEE **pants**.

pantry noun food cupboard, larder.

pants noun **1** briefs, knickers, panties, shorts, trunks, underpants.
OTHER UNDERCLOTHES: SEE **underclothes**.
2 SEE **trousers**.

pap noun SEE **pulp** noun.

paper noun **1** *a piece of paper.* folio, leaf, sheet.

KINDS OF PAPER: card, cardboard, cartridge paper, manila, notepaper, papyrus, parchment, postcard, stationery, tissue-paper, toilet-paper, tracing-paper, vellum, wallpaper, wrapping-paper, writing-paper.

PAPER SIZES: A4 (A1, A2, etc.), foolscap, quarto.

---

2 *I keep important papers in a file.* certificates, deeds, documents, forms, records.
3 *a daily paper.* SEE **newspaper**.
4 *a scientific paper.* article, dissertation, essay, monograph, thesis, treatise.

paper verb *to paper a room.* decorate.

paperback noun KINDS OF BOOK: SEE **book** noun.

papoose noun SEE **baby**.

papyrus noun SEE **paper** noun.

parable noun KINDS OF STORY: SEE **story**.

parade noun *a military parade. a fancy dress parade.* cavalcade, ceremony, column, display, march-past, motorcade, pageant, procession, review, show.

parade verb **1** *to parade in front of the judges.* assemble, file past, form up, line

up, make a procession, march past, present yourself, process.
2 *to parade up and down.* SEE **walk** verb.
3 *to parade your virtues.* SEE **display** verb.

paradigm noun SEE **model** noun.

paradise noun SEE **delight** noun, Eden, Elysium, heaven, nirvana, Utopia.

paradox noun absurdity, anomaly, contradiction, self-contradiction.

paradoxical adjective *It seems paradoxical to make weapons in order to maintain peace.* absurd, anomalous, conflicting, contradictory, illogical, incongruous, self-contradictory.

paragon noun SEE **model** noun.

paragraph noun LINGUISTIC TERMS: SEE **language**.

parakeet noun parrot.

parallel adjective **1** *parallel lines.* equidistant.
2 *a parallel example. parallel events.* analogous, corresponding, matching, SEE **similar**.

parallel noun *I saw a parallel between her situation and mine.* analogy, comparison, correspondence, likeness, match, resemblance, similarity.

paralyse verb *The shock paralysed him.* anaesthetize, cripple, deaden, desensitize, freeze, immobilize, incapacitate, lame, numb, petrify, stun.

paralysed adjective *a paralysed person. paralysed limbs.* crippled, desensitized, disabled, SEE **handicapped**, immobile, immovable, incapacitated, lame, numb, palsied, paralytic, paraplegic, rigid, unusable, useless.

paralysis noun immobility, palsy, paraplegia.

paralytic adjective **1** SEE **paralysed**.
2 SEE **drunk**.

paramount adjective SEE **supreme**.

paramour noun SEE **lover**.

parapet noun battlement, fortification, rampart.

paraphernalia noun *Can you move all your paraphernalia out of the way?* baggage, belongings, effects, equipment, gear, impedimenta, [*informal*] odds and ends, stuff, tackle, things.

paraphrase verb *to paraphrase something in simpler language.* interpret, rephrase, reword, rewrite, translate.

paraplegia noun SEE **paralysis**.

paraplegic adjective SEE **paralysed**.

parasol noun sunshade, umbrella.

paratroops noun SEE **armed services**.

parboil verb SEE **cook** verb.

parcel noun bale, bundle, carton, pack, package, packet.

parcel verb **to parcel out** SEE **divide**.

parch verb SEE **dry** verb.

parched adjective **1** *Plants won't grow in parched ground.* arid, baked, barren, dehydrated, dry, lifeless, scorched, sterile, waterless.
2 *I'm parched!* gasping, thirsty.

parchment noun SEE **paper** noun.

pardon noun *pardon for a condemned criminal.* absolution, amnesty, discharge, forgiveness, mercy, reprieve.

pardon verb *to pardon a condemned person.* absolve, condone, [*formal*] exculpate, excuse, exonerate, forgive, free, let off, overlook, release, reprieve, set free, spare.

pardonable adjective *a pardonable mistake.* allowable, excusable, forgivable, justifiable, minor, negligible, petty, understandable, venial (*a venial sin*).
OPPOSITES: SEE **unforgivable**.

pare verb **1** *to pare an apple.* peel, skin.
2 *to pare something down.* clip, SEE **cut** verb, prune, reduce, trim.

parent noun FAMILY RELATIONSHIPS: SEE **family**.

parentage noun SEE **ancestry**.

parenthesis noun aside, interpolation.

pariah noun SEE **outcast**.

parity noun SEE **equality**.

park noun KINDS OF PARK: amusement park, arboretum, botanical gardens, car-park, estate, nature reserve, parkland, public gardens, recreation ground, safari park, theme park.

park verb *to park a car.* leave, place, position, station.
to park yourself SEE **settle**.

parky adjective SEE **cold** adjective.

parlance noun SEE **phraseology**.

parley verb SEE **negotiate**.

parliament noun assembly, conclave, congress, convocation, council, SEE **government**, the Houses of Parliament, legislature, senate.

parliamentarian noun SEE **politician**.

parlour noun VARIOUS ROOMS: SEE **room**.

parochial adjective SEE **local** adjective.

parody noun caricature, SEE **imitation**, satire, [*informal*] send-up, [*informal*] take-off, travesty.
OTHER KINDS OF WRITING: SEE **writing**.

parody verb ape, caricature, guy, SEE **imitate**, satirize, [*informal*] send up, [*informal*] take off, travesty.

paroxysm noun SEE **spasm**.

parrot noun parakeet.

parry verb *to parry a blow*. avert, block, deflect, evade, fend off, push away, repel, repulse, stave off, ward off.

parsimonious adjective SEE **stingy**.

parson noun SEE **clergyman**.

parsonage noun rectory, vicarage.
OTHER HOUSES: SEE **house** noun.

part noun 1 *a part of a whole*. bit, branch, component, constituent, department, division, element, fraction, fragment, ingredient, particle, piece, portion, ramification, scrap, section, sector, segment, share, single item, subdivision, unit.
2 *a part of a book or TV programme*. chapter, episode.
3 *a part of a town or country*. area, district, neighbourhood, quarter, region, sector.
4 *parts of your body*. limb, member, organ.
PARTS OF THE BODY: SEE **body**.
5 *a part in a play*. cameo, character, role.

part verb 1 *to part a child from its parents. to part a branch from the trunk*. cut off, detach, disconnect, divide, separate, sever, split, sunder.
OPPOSITES: SEE **join** verb.
2 *to part from someone*. depart, go away, leave, quit, say goodbye, split up, take your leave, withdraw.
to part with SEE **relinquish**.

partake verb SEE **participate**.

partial adjective 1 *Our play was only a partial success*. imperfect, incomplete, limited, unfinished.
OPPOSITES: SEE **complete** adjective.
2 *a partial referee*. SEE **prejudiced**.
to be partial to *I'm partial to a drink at bedtime*. appreciate, be fond of, be keen on, enjoy, [*informal*] go for, like.

participate verb *to participate in a game*. assist, be active, be involved, co-operate, engage, help, join in, partake, share, take part.

participation noun *participation in sport. participation in a crime*. assistance, complicity, contribution, co-operation, involvement, partnership, sharing.

particle noun 1 *a particle of food*. bit, crumb, drop, fragment, grain, iota, jot, morsel, piece, scrap, shred, sliver, speck.
2 *a particle of matter*. atom, electron, molecule, neutron.

particoloured adjective SEE **dappled**.

particular adjective 1 *I recognized his particular way of talking*. distinct, individual, peculiar, personal, singular, specific, uncommon, unique, unmistakable.
OPPOSITES: SEE **general**.
2 *I made a particular effort*. exceptional, important, notable, outstanding, special, unusual.
OPPOSITES: SEE **ordinary**.
3 *The cat's particular about food*. choosy, discriminating, fastidious, finicky, fussy, meticulous, nice, pernickety, selective.
OPPOSITES: SEE **undiscriminating**.

particulars plural noun *Give me the particulars*. circumstances, details, facts, information, [*slang*] low-down.

particularize verb SEE **specify**.

parting noun *We were sad when it came to parting*. departure, going, leave-taking, leaving, saying goodbye [SEE **goodbye**], separation, splitting up.

partisan adjective SEE **prejudiced**.

partisan noun SEE **fighter**.

partition noun 1 *the partition of a country after a war*. division.
2 *a partition between two parts of a room*. barrier, panel, room-divider, screen, wall.

partition verb *to partition a country*. divide, parcel out, separate off, share out, split up, subdivide.

partner noun 1 *a business partner*. accomplice, ally, assistant, [*joking*] bedfellow, collaborator, colleague, companion, confederate, helper.
2 *a marriage partner*. consort, husband, mate, spouse, wife.

partnership noun 1 *a business partnership*. affiliation, alliance, combination, company, co-operative, syndicate.
2 *partnership in crime*. association, collaboration, complicity, co-operation.
3 *a marriage partnership*. marriage, relationship, union.

parturition noun SEE **birth**.

party noun 1 *a Christmas party*. celebration, [*informal*] do, festivity, function, gathering, [*informal*] get-together, [*joking*] jollification, merrymaking, [*informal*] rave-up.

VARIOUS KINDS OF PARTY: ball, banquet, barbecue, birthday party, ceilidh, Christmas party, dance, [*informal*] disco, discothèque, feast, [*informal*] hen-party, house-warming, orgy, picnic, reception, reunion, social, [*informal*] stag-party, tea-party, wedding.

2 *a political party.* alliance, association, cabal, [*informal*] camp (*He went over to their camp*), coalition, faction, SEE **group** noun, league.

pass noun **1** *a mountain pass.* canyon, defile, gap, gorge, ravine, valley, way through.
2 *a bus pass.* authority, authorization, licence, permission, permit, ticket, warrant.

pass verb **1** *We watched the traffic pass.* go by, move on, move past, proceed, progress, [*informal*] thread your way.
2 *Try to pass the car in front.* go beyond, outstrip, overhaul, overtake.
3 *The time passed slowly.* elapse, lapse, [*informal*] tick by.
4 *The pain passed.* disappear, fade, go away, vanish.
5 *Pass the books round.* circulate, deal out, deliver, give, hand over, offer, present, share, submit, supply, transfer.
6 *They passed a law. The judge passed sentence.* agree, approve, authorize, confirm, decree, enact, establish, ordain, pronounce, ratify, validate.
7 *I pass!* [*informal*] give in, opt out, say nothing, waive your rights.
to pass away SEE **die.**
to pass out SEE **faint** verb.
to pass over SEE **ignore.**

passable adjective **1** *a passable standard of work.* acceptable, adequate, all right, fair, mediocre, middling, moderate, ordinary, satisfactory, [*informal*] so-so, tolerable.
OPPOSITES: SEE **unacceptable.**
2 *The road is passable again.* clear, navigable, open, traversable, unblocked, usable.
OPPOSITES: SEE **impassable.**

passage noun **1** *the passage of time.* advance, moving on, passing, progress, progression.
2 *a sea passage.* crossing, SEE **journey** noun, voyage.
3 *a secret passage.* corridor, passageway, thoroughfare, tube, tunnel, way through.
4 *Wait in the passage!* entrance, hall, hallway, lobby, vestibule.
5 *a passage of a book.* episode, excerpt, extract, paragraph, piece, quotation, scene, section.

passé adjective SEE **old-fashioned.**

passenger noun commuter, rider, SEE **traveller.**

passer-by noun bystander, onlooker, witness.

passing adjective SEE **temporary.**

passion noun *a passion for adventure.* appetite, ardour, commitment, craving, desire, drive, eagerness, emotion, enthusiasm, fervour, frenzy, greed, [*informal*] heat (*in the heat of the moment*), infatuation, love, lust, obsession, strong feeling, thirst, urge, zeal, zest.

passionate adjective *passionate feelings.* ardent, avid, burning, committed, greedy, eager, emotional, enthusiastic, excited, fervent, fiery, frenzied, hot, impassioned, inflamed, intense, lustful, obsessive, sexy, strong, urgent, vehement, violent, zealous.
OPPOSITES: SEE **apathetic.**

passive adjective *a passive response.* compliant, docile, impassive, inactive, long-suffering, non-violent, patient, resigned, submissive, unresisting.
OPPOSITES: SEE **active.**

passport noun SEE **document**, pass, permit, visa.

past adjective *past events.* bygone, earlier, ended, finished, former, gone, [*informal*] over and done with, previous.
OPPOSITES: SEE **future** adjective.
past it SEE **old.**

past noun *In the past, things were different.* antiquity, days gone by, history, old days, olden days, past times [SEE **past** adjective].
OPPOSITES: SEE **future** noun.

pasta noun KINDS OF PASTA: cannelloni, lasagne, macaroni, noodles, ravioli, spaghetti, tagliatelle, vermicelli.
OTHER FOODS: SEE **food.**

paste noun **1** *adhesive paste.* adhesive, fixative, glue, gum.
2 *fish-paste.* pâté, spread.

paste verb *to paste wallpaper.* SEE **fasten**, glue, gum.

pastel adjective *pastel colours.* SEE **pale** adjective.

pastel noun SEE **paint** noun.

pasteurize verb SEE **sterilize.**

pastiche noun *a pastiche of various styles.* blend, composite, [*informal*] hodgepodge or hotchpotch, medley, mixture, motley collection, patchwork, selection.

pastille noun *a cough pastille.* lozenge.

pastime noun *What's your favourite pastime?* activity, amusement, diversion, entertainment, game, hobby, occupation, recreation, relaxation, sport.
VARIOUS SPORTS AND GAMES: SEE **game** noun, **sport.**

Several English words, including *pastor, pastoral,* and *pasture,* are related to Latin *pastor* = *shepherd.*

---

pastor noun SEE **clergyman**.

pastoral adjective 1 *a pastoral scene.* agrarian, bucolic, country, farming, idyllic, outdoor, peaceful, rural, rustic. OPPOSITES: SEE **urban**.
2 *a clergyman's pastoral duties.* caring, ecclesiastical, parochial, ministerial, priestly.

pasture noun *pasture for sheep or cattle.* field, grassland, grazing, [*old-fashioned, poetic*] mead, meadow, paddock, pasturage.

pasty adjective *a pasty complexion.* SEE **pale** adjective.

pasty noun *a meat pasty.* SEE **pie**.

pat verb *to pat with your hand.* caress, dab, slap, tap, SEE **touch** verb.

patch noun *a patch on your jeans.* mend, repair.

patch verb *to patch a hole.* cover, darn, fix, mend, reinforce, repair, sew up, stitch up.

patchy adjective 1 *patchy fog. patchy success.* [*informal*] bitty, changeable, changing, erratic, inconsistent, irregular, uneven, unpredictable, variable, varied, varying.
2 *patchy colours.* SEE **dappled**.
OPPOSITES: SEE **uniform** adjective.

patent adjective *a patent lie.* SEE **obvious**.

paternal adjective [Compare with *paternalistic.*] *paternal love.* fatherly.

paternalistic adjective [Compare with *paternal.*] *a paternalistic attitude.* SEE **patronizing**.

path noun alley, bridle-path, bridle-way, esplanade, footpath, footway, SEE **road**, route, pathway, pavement, [*American*] sidewalk, towpath, track, trail, walk, walkway, way.

pathetic adjective 1 *a pathetic farewell.* affecting, distressing, heartrending, lamentable, moving, piteous, pitiable, pitiful, poignant, SEE **sad**, touching, tragic.
2 [*informal*] *He's a pathetic goalkeeper.* SEE **inadequate**.

pathos noun *The pathos of the situation brought tears to our eyes.* emotion, feeling, pity, poignancy, sadness, tragedy.

patience noun *I waited with great patience.* calmness, composure, endurance, equanimity, forbearance, fortitude, long-suffering, perseverance, persistence, resignation, restraint, self-control, stoicism, toleration.

patient adjective 1 *patient suffering. a patient animal.* accommodating, calm, composed, docile, easygoing, even-tempered, forbearing, long-suffering, mild, philosophical, quiet, resigned, self-possessed, serene, stoical, submissive, tolerant, uncomplaining.
2 *patient effort. a patient worker.* determined, diligent, persevering, persistent, steady, unhurried, untiring.
OPPOSITES: SEE **impatient**.

patient noun *a hospital patient.* case, invalid, outpatient, sufferer.

patio noun courtyard, paved area, terrace.

patois noun SEE **dialect**.

patriarch noun *the patriarch of a tribe.* father, head, SEE **leader**.

patrician adjective SEE **aristocratic**.

patrimony noun SEE **money**.

patriot noun [*uncomplimentary*] chauvinist, loyalist, nationalist.

patriotic adjective *a patriotic person.* [*uncomplimentary*] chauvinistic, [*uncomplimentary*] jingoistic, loyal, nationalistic, [*uncomplimentary*] xenophobic.

patriotism noun [*uncomplimentary*] chauvinism, [*uncomplimentary*] jingoism, loyalty, nationalism, [*uncomplimentary*] xenophobia.

patrol noun 1 *on patrol.* guard, policing, sentry-duty, surveillance, watch.
2 *a night-patrol.* guard, look-out, sentinel, sentry, watchman.
patrol car panda car, police car.

patrol verb *Police patrolled the area all night.* be on patrol [SEE **patrol** noun], guard, inspect, keep a look-out, police, tour, walk the beat.

patron noun 1 *a patron of the arts.* [*informal*] angel, backer, benefactor, champion, defender, helper, sponsor, subscriber, supporter.
2 *a patron of a shop or restaurant.* client, customer, frequenter, [*informal*] regular, shopper.

patronage noun *We give our patronage to local shops.* backing, business, custom, help, sponsorship, SEE **support** noun, trade.

patronize verb 1 *I patronize the local shops.* back, be a patron of [SEE **patron**], encourage, frequent, give patronage to [SEE **patronage**], shop at, support.
2 *to patronize someone.* be patronizing towards [SEE **patronizing**], talk down to.

patronizing adjective *a patronizing attitude.* condescending, disdainful, haughty, lofty, paternalistic, snobbish, supercilious, superior.

patter noun *a comedian's patter.* WAYS OF TALKING: SEE **talk** verb.

patter verb VARIOUS SOUNDS: SEE **sound** noun.

pattern noun **1** *patterns on wallpaper.* arrangement, decoration, design, device, figuration, figure, motif, ornamentation, shape, tessellation.
2 *a pattern to copy.* archetype, criterion, example, guide, model, norm, original, precedent, prototype, sample, specimen, standard.

patty noun SEE **pie.**

paucity noun SEE **lack** noun.

paunch noun SEE **belly.**

pauper noun SEE **poor (poor person).**

pause noun *a pause to get our breath back.* break, [*informal*] breather, check, delay, gap, halt, interlude, intermission, interruption, interval, lull, respite, rest, stand-still, stop, stoppage, suspension, wait.

pause verb *She paused uncertainly. We'll pause for a rest.* break off, delay, halt, hang back, have a pause [SEE **pause** noun], hesitate, rest, stop, [*informal*] take a break, wait.

pave verb *to pave a path.* asphalt, concrete, cover with paving [SEE **paving**], flag, [*informal*] make up, surface, tile.

pavement noun SEE **path.**

paving noun VARIOUS KINDS OF PAVING: cobbles, concrete, crazy-paving, flagstones, paving-stones, setts, tiles.

paw noun *an animal's paw.* foot.

paw verb *to paw the ground.* SEE **touch** verb.

pay noun *How much pay do you get?* earnings, emoluments, fee, [*formal*] honorarium, income, SEE **payment**, reimbursement, salary, stipend, wages.

pay verb **1** *Did you pay a lot for your bike?* [*informal*] cough up, [*informal*] fork out, give, hand over, proffer, spend.
2 *They pay her a good wage.* grant, remunerate.
3 *I'll pay my debts.* clear, [*informal*] foot, meet, pay off, pay up, settle.
4 *He paid me for the glass he broke.* bear the cost of, compensate, indemnify, pay back, recompense, refund, reimburse, repay.
5 *Crime doesn't pay.* be profitable [SEE **profitable**].
6 *She'll pay for her mistake!* SEE **suffer.**
to pay back *to pay someone back for an insult, injury, etc.* SEE **retaliate.**
to pay the penalty for *to pay the penalty for wrongdoing.* SEE **atone.**

payment noun *monthly payments.* charge, cost, expenditure, figure, outgoings, outlay, price, rate, remittance.
OPPOSITES: SEE **income.**

KINDS OF PAYMENT: advance, alimony, allowance, commission, compensation, contribution, deposit, donation, fare, fee, fine, instalment, loan, SEE **pay** noun, pocket-money, premium, ransom, reward, royalty, [*informal*] sub, subscription, subsistence, supplement (*a supplement for first-class travel*), surcharge, tip, toll, wage.

peace noun **1** *After the war, there was a period of peace.* accord, agreement, amity, conciliation, concord, friendliness, harmony, order.
OPPOSITES: SEE **war.**
2 *The two sides signed a peace.* alliance, armistice, cease-fire, pact, treaty, truce.
OPPOSITE: declaration of war.
3 *the peace of the countryside. peace of mind.* calmness, peace and quiet, peacefulness, placidity, quiet, repose, serenity, silence, stillness, tranquillity.
OPPOSITES: SEE **activity, anxiety, noise.**

peaceable adjective *a peaceable community.* amicable, conciliatory, co-operative, friendly, gentle, harmonious, mild, non-violent, pacific, SEE **peaceful**, peace-loving, placid, understanding.
OPPOSITES: SEE **quarrelsome.**

peaceful adjective *a peaceful evening. peaceful music.* balmy, calm, easy, gentle, pacific, SEE **peaceable**, placid, pleasant, quiet, relaxing, restful, serene, slow-moving, soothing, still, tranquil, undisturbed, unruffled, untroubled.
OPPOSITES: SEE **noisy, troubled.**

peacemaker noun arbitrator, conciliator, intercessor, mediator,

peak noun **1** *the peak of a mountain.* apex, brow, cap, crest, crown, pinnacle, point, summit, tip, top.
2 *snowy peaks.* SEE **mountain.**
3 *the peak of her career.* acme, climax, crisis, culmination, height, highest point, zenith.

peaky adjective SEE **pale** adjective.

peal noun *a peal of bells.* carillon, chime, ringing.

peal verb *The bells pealed.* chime, ring, toll.
OTHER SOUNDS: SEE **sound** noun.

peasant noun **1** *Peasants working on the land.* SEE **worker.**
2 [*uncomplimentary*] bumpkin, churl, rustic, serf, yokel.

pebbles noun cobbles, gravel, stones.

peckish adjective SEE **hungry**.

peculiar adjective 1 *There's a peculiar person snooping around. That's a peculiar way to do it.* abnormal, bizarre, curious, eccentric, funny, odd, outlandish, out of the ordinary, quaint, queer, quirky, surprising, strange, uncommon, unconventional, unusual, weird.
OPPOSITES: SEE **ordinary**.
2 *I recognized her peculiar way of writing.* characteristic, different, distinctive, identifiable, idiosyncratic, individual, particular, personal, private, special, singular, unique.
OPPOSITES: SEE **common** adjective.

peculiarity noun *We all have our peculiarities.* abnormality, characteristic, eccentricity, foible, idiosyncrasy, mannerism, oddity, peculiar feature [SEE **peculiar**], quirk, singularity, speciality, trait, uniqueness.

pecuniary adjective SEE **financial**.

pedagogue noun SEE **teacher**.

A number of English words such as *pedal, pedestal, pedestrian* are related to Latin *pes, pedis = foot*.

---

pedal verb SEE **travel** verb.

pedantic adjective 1 *a pedantic use of long words.* academic, bookish, formal, humourless, learned, old-fashioned, pompous, scholarly, schoolmasterly, stilted.
OPPOSITES: SEE **informal**.
2 *pedantic observance of the rules.* inflexible, [*informal*] nit-picking, precise, strict, unimaginative.
OPPOSITES: SEE **flexible**.

peddle verb SEE **sell**.

pedestal noun SEE **base** noun.

pedestrian adjective 1 *a pedestrian precinct.* pedestrianized, traffic-free.
2 *a pedestrian performance.* SEE **ordinary**.

pedestrian noun foot-traveller, walker.

pedigree adjective *a pedigree animal.* pure-bred, thoroughbred.

pedigree noun *a dog's pedigree.* ancestry, descent, SEE **family**, family history, line.

pedlar noun *a pedlar of cheap goods.* [*oldfashioned*] chapman, door-to-door salesman, hawker, seller, street-trader, vendor.

peek noun, verb SEE **look** noun, verb.

peel noun *orange peel.* rind, skin.

peel verb *to peel an orange. to peel off a covering.* denude, pare, skin, strip.

peep noun, verb SEE **look** noun, verb.
peep of day SEE **dawn**.

peer verb SEE **look** verb.

peer, peeress nouns aristocrat, noble, nobleman, noblewoman, titled person.
OPPOSITE: commoner.

TITLES OF BRITISH PEERS: baron, baroness, duchess, duke, earl, lady, lord, marchioness, marquis or marquess, viscount, viscountess.

OTHER TITLES: SEE **title** noun.

---

peers 1 *the peers of the land.* the aristocracy, the nobility, the peerage.
OPPOSITE: the commons.
2 *She's quite at ease with her peers.* equals, fellows.

peerless adjective SEE **unequalled**.

peeved adjective SEE **annoyed**.

peevish adjective SEE **irritable**.

peewit noun lapwing, plover.

peg noun SEE **fastener**.

peg verb SEE **fasten**.

pejorative adjective SEE **uncomplimentary**.

pelargonium noun geranium.

pellet noun ball, pill.

pell-mell adjective, adverb SEE **hasty**.

pellucid adjective SEE **clear** adjective.

pelt noun SEE **skin** noun.

pelt verb *to pelt someone with missiles.* assail, bombard, shower, SEE **throw**.

pen noun 1 *a pen for animals.* SEE **enclosure**.
2 *a pen to write with.* ball-point, biro, felt-tipped pen, fountain pen.
OTHER WRITING IMPLEMENTS: SEE **write**.
pen-name SEE **pseudonym**.

pen verb SEE **write**.

penal adjective penal servitude SEE **punishment**.

penalize verb SEE **punish**.

penalty noun SEE **punishment**.
to pay the penalty for SEE **atone**.

penance noun to do penance for SEE **atone**.

penchant noun SEE **inclination**.

pendent adjective *the pendent branches of a willow.* dangling, hanging, loose, pendulous, suspended, swinging, trailing.

pending adjective *There's an inquiry pending.* about to happen, forthcoming imminent, impending, [*informal*] in the offing, undecided, waiting.

pendulous adjective SEE **pendent**.

pendulum noun SEE **clock**.

penetrate verb 1 *The drill can penetrate concrete*. bore through, make a hole in, pierce, puncture.
2 *We penetrated their defences*. enter, get through, infiltrate, probe.
3 *Damp had penetrated the brick-work*. impregnate, permeate, pervade, seep into.

penetrating adjective 1 *a penetrating analysis*. SEE **intelligent**.
2 *a penetrating scream*. SEE **loud**.

penitent adjective *penitent about his mistake*. apologetic, conscience-stricken, contrite, regretful, remorseful, repentant, sorry.
OPPOSITES: impenitent, SEE **unrepentant**.

pen-name noun SEE **pseudonym**.

pennant noun SEE **flag** noun.

penniless adjective SEE **poor**.

pennon noun SEE **flag** noun.

penny-pinching adjective SEE **stingy**.

pension noun SEE **money**.

pensioner noun SEE **old (old person)**.

pensive adjective SEE **thoughtful**.

A number of English words beginning *penta-* are related to Greek *pente = five*.

---

pentagon noun SEE **shape** noun.

pentagram noun SEE **star**.

pentathlon noun ATHLETIC SPORTS: SEE **athletics**.

penthouse noun SEE **house** noun.

penumbra noun SEE **shadow** noun.

penurious adjective SEE **poor**.

penury noun SEE **poverty**.

people noun 1 *Do you like being with other people?* folk, [*uncomplimentary*] hoi polloi, human beings, humanity, humans, individuals, mankind, mortals, persons.
2 *In an election, the people decide who will govern*. citizens, common people, community, electorate, nation, populace, population, the public, society.
3 *After living abroad for a time, he returned to his people*. clan, family, kith and kin, nation, race, relatives, tribe.

people verb *a strange world peopled by monsters*. colonize, fill, inhabit, occupy, overrun, populate, settle.

pep verb to pep up SEE **animate** verb.
pep talk SEE **exhortation**.

pepper verb SEE **sprinkle**.

peppery adjective *a peppery taste*. hot, spicy.

perambulate verb SEE **walk** verb.

perambulator noun baby-carriage, pram, push-chair.

perceive verb 1 *I perceived a shape on the horizon*. become aware of, catch sight of, detect, discern, distinguish, make out, notice, observe, recognize, see, spot.
2 *I began to perceive what she meant*. apprehend, comprehend, deduce, feel, gather, grasp, know, realize, sense, understand.

perceptible adjective *a perceptible drop in temperature. perceptible anger in his voice*. appreciable, audible, detectable, distinct, evident, marked, noticeable, observable, obvious, palpable, perceivable, recognizable, visible.
OPPOSITES: SEE **imperceptible**.

perception noun *What is your perception of the problem? Ears and eyes are organs of perception*. apprehension, awareness, cognition, comprehension, consciousness, discernment, insight, observation, recognition, sensation, sense, understanding, view.

perceptive adjective [Do not confuse with *perceptible*.] *a perceptive judge of character*. acute, alert, astute, aware, clever, discriminating, discerning, SEE **intelligent**, observant, penetrating, percipient, perspicacious, responsive, sensitive, sharp, sharp-eyed, shrewd, sympathetic, understanding.

perch noun *a bird's perch*. resting-place, roost.

perch verb *to perch on a fence*. balance, rest, roost, settle, sit.

percipient adjective SEE **perceptive**.

percolate verb SEE **filter** verb.

percussion noun [*uncomplimentary*] kitchen department.

PERCUSSION INSTRUMENTS INCLUDE: castanets, celesta or celeste, chime bars, cymbals, SEE **drum**, glockenspiel, gong, kettledrum, maracas, rattle, tambourine, [*plural*] timpani, triangle, tubular bells, vibraphone, wood block, xylophone.

OTHER MUSICAL INSTRUMENTS: SEE **music**.

---

perdition noun damnation, doom, hell, ruination.

peregrination noun SEE **journey** noun.

peremptory adjective SEE **bossy**.

perennial adjective SEE **continual**.

perfect adjective 1 *a perfect example of something.* complete, excellent, faultless, finished, flawless, ideal, mint (*in mint condition*), unbeatable, undamaged, unexceptionable, whole.
2 *Nobody is perfect.* blameless, irreproachable, pure, spotless.
3 *a perfect fit. a perfect copy.* accurate, correct, exact, faithful, immaculate, impeccable, precise, tailor-made.
OPPOSITES: SEE **imperfect**.
4 [*informal*] *perfect chaos.* SEE **absolute**.

perfect verb *to perfect your plans.* bring to fruition, carry through, complete, consummate, finish, fulfil, make perfect [SEE **perfect** adjective], [*informal*] see through (*When I've started a thing I like to see it through*).

perfection noun 1 *the perfection of a lovely jewel.* beauty, completeness, excellence, ideal, precision, wholeness.
2 *the perfection of our plans.* accomplishment, achievement, completion, consummation, end, fruition, fulfilment, realization.

perfectionist noun idealist, purist, [*informal*] stickler.

perfidious adjective SEE **treacherous**.

perforate verb *to perforate something with a pin.* bore through, drill, penetrate, pierce, prick, puncture.

perform verb 1 *to perform your duty.* accomplish, achieve, bring about, carry out, commit, complete, discharge, do, execute, finish, fulfil.
2 *to perform on the stage.* act, appear, dance, enact, play, present, produce, put on (*to put on a play*), render, represent, serenade, sing, take part.

performance noun 1 *a performance by actors or musicians.* acting, concert, début [= *a first performance*], impersonation, interpretation, matinée, play, playing, portrayal, première, presentation, preview, production, rendition, representation, show, sketch, turn.
MUSICAL TERMS: SEE **music**.
THEATRICAL TERMS: SEE **theatre**.
2 *a poor performance by our team.* achievement, behaviour, conduct, exhibition, exploit, feat.
3 *He put on a bit of a performance.* act, deception, play-acting, pretence.

performer noun actor, actress, artist, artiste, player, singer, star, [*informal*] superstar, trouper.
VARIOUS ENTERTAINERS: SEE **entertainer**.

perfume noun *the perfume of roses.* aroma, fragrance, odour, scent, SEE **smell** noun, whiff.
VARIOUS COSMETICS: SEE **cosmetics**.

perfunctory adjective *perfunctory applause.* apathetic, brief, cursory, dutiful, half-hearted, hurried, inattentive, indifferent, mechanical, offhand, routine, superficial, uncaring, unenthusiastic, uninterested, uninvolved.
OPPOSITES: SEE **enthusiastic**.

perhaps adverb conceivably, maybe, possibly.
OPPOSITES: SEE **definitely**.

peril noun SEE **danger**.

perilous adjective SEE **dangerous**.

The prefix *peri-* in words like *perimeter, peripatetic, periphery, periphrasis,* and *periscope* is from Greek *peri* = *around, about.*

---

perimeter noun *the perimeter of a field.* border, borderline, boundary, bounds, circumference, confines, edge, fringe, frontier, margin, periphery.

period noun *a period of history. a period spent doing something.* age, epoch, era, interval, phase, season, session, spell, stage, stint, stretch, term, SEE **time** noun, while.

periodic adjective SEE **occasional**.

periodical noun SEE **magazine**.

peripatetic adjective SEE **travelling**.

peripheral adjective 1 *peripheral areas of town.* distant, on the perimeter [SEE **perimeter**], outer, outermost, outlying.
2 *Don't waste time on peripheral details.* borderline, inessential, irrelevant, marginal, minor, secondary, unimportant, unnecessary.
OPPOSITES: SEE **central**.

periphery noun SEE **perimeter**.

periphrasis noun SEE **verbosity**.

perish verb 1 *Many birds perished in the cold weather.* be destroyed, be killed, die, expire, fall, pass away.
2 *There was a leak where the rubber hose had perished.* crumble away, decay, decompose, disintegrate, go bad, rot.

perishable adjective *perishable goods.* biodegradable (*biodegradable plastic*), destructible, liable to perish [SEE **perish**], unstable.
OPPOSITES: SEE **lasting**.

perjure verb *to perjure yourself* SEE **lie** verb.

perjury noun SEE **lying** noun.

perk noun [*informal*] *Are there any perks that go with your job?* SEE **perquisite.**

perky adjective SEE **lively.**

permanent adjective *a permanent job. a permanent relationship. a permanent problem.* abiding, chronic, constant, continual, continuous, durable, enduring, everlasting, fixed, immutable, incessant, incurable, indestructible, ineradicable, irreparable (*irreparable damage*), irreversible (*an irreversible decision*), lasting, lifelong, long-lasting, neverending, perennial, perpetual, persistent, stable, steady, unalterable, unchanging, unending.
OPPOSITES: SEE **temporary.**

permeable adjective SEE **porous.**

permeate verb *The smell permeated the house.* filter through, flow through, impregnate, penetrate, percolate, pervade, saturate, spread through.

permissible adjective *Is it permissible to smoke?* acceptable, admissible, allowable, allowed, lawful, legal, legitimate, permitted, proper, right, sanctioned, valid.
OPPOSITES: SEE **forbidden.**

permission noun *We had her permission to leave.* agreement, approval, assent, authority, authorization, consent, dispensation, [*informal*] go-ahead, [*informal*] green light, leave, licence, SEE **permit** noun, [*informal*] rubber stamp, sanction.

permissive adjective SEE **tolerant.**

permit noun *a permit to fish in the lake.* authorization, charter, licence, order, pass, passport, ticket, visa, warrant.

permit verb 1 *We don't permit smoking in the house.* agree to, allow, approve of, authorize, consent to, endorse, give permission for [SEE **permission**], license, [*old-fashioned*] suffer, tolerate.
2 *Will you permit me to speak?* give an opportunity, make it possible.

permutation noun SEE **variation.**

pernicious adjective SEE **harmful.**

pernickety adjective SEE **fussy.**

peroration noun SEE **conclusion.**

perpendicular adjective at right angles, upright, vertical.

perpetrate verb *to perpetrate a crime.* SEE **commit.**

perpetual adjective *the perpetual cycle of life and death. a baby's perpetual crying for attention.* abiding, ceaseless, chronic, constant, continual, continuous, endless, eternal, everlasting, frequent, immortal, incessant, interminable, lasting, long-lasting, neverending, non-stop, ongoing, perennial, permanent, persistent, protracted, recurrent, recurring, repeated, unceasing, unchanging, unending, unfailing, unremitting.
OPPOSITES: SEE **brief** adjective, **temporary.**

perpetuate verb SEE **preserve** verb.

perplex verb *The mystery perplexed us.* baffle, bewilder, confound, confuse, disconcert, muddle, mystify, puzzle, [*informal*] stump, [*informal*] throw, worry.

perquisite noun *She gets various perquisites in addition to her wages.* benefit, bonus, extra, fringe benefit, gratuity, [*informal*] perk, tip.

persecute verb *to persecute people for their religious beliefs.* badger, bother, bully, discriminate against, harass, hound, ill-treat, intimidate, maltreat, martyr, molest, oppress, pester, [*informal*] put the screws on, terrorize, torment, torture, tyrannize, victimize, worry.

persevere verb *If you persevere you'll succeed in the end.* be diligent, be steadfast [SEE **steadfast**], carry on, continue, endure, [*informal*] hang on, [*informal*] keep at it, keep going, persist, [*informal*] plug away, [*informal*] soldier on, stand firm, [*informal*] stick at it.
OPPOSITES: SEE **cease, falter.**

persiflage noun SEE **banter.**

persist verb 1 *If you persist, you'll succeed in the end.* SEE **persevere.**
2 *How long will this snow persist?* go on, keep on, last, linger, remain.
OPPOSITES: SEE **cease.**

persistent adjective 1 *a persistent cold. persistent rumours.* ceaseless, chronic, constant, continual, continuous, endless, eternal, everlasting, incessant, interminable, lasting, long-lasting, neverending, obstinate, permanent, perpetual, persisting, recurrent, recurring, repeated, unending, unrelenting, unrelieved, unremitting.
OPPOSITES: SEE **intermittent, short-lived.**
2 *a persistent worker.* assiduous, determined, dogged, hard-working, indefatigable, patient, persevering, pertinacious, relentless, resolute, steadfast, steady, stubborn, tenacious, tireless, unflagging, untiring, unwavering, zealous.
OPPOSITES: SEE **lazy.**

person noun adolescent, adult, baby, being, [*informal*] body, character, SEE **child**, [*joking*] customer (*a difficult customer*), figure, human, human being, individual, infant, SEE **man** noun, personage, soul, [*informal*] type, SEE **woman**. SEE ALSO **people**.

persona noun *On stage, the actor adopts a fictitious persona.* character, image, personality, role.

personable adjective SEE **good-looking**.

personal adjective 1 *personal characteristics.* distinct, distinctive, idiosyncratic, individual, inimitable, particular, peculiar, private, special, unique, your own.
OPPOSITES: SEE **general**.
2 *personal information.* confidential, intimate, private, secret.
OPPOSITES: SEE **public** adjective.
3 *personal remarks.* critical, derogatory, disparaging, insulting, offensive, pejorative, SEE **rude**, slighting.

personality noun 1 *She has an attractive personality.* character, disposition, identity, individuality, [*informal*] make-up, nature, [*formal*] psyche, temperament.
2 *She has great personality.* attractiveness, charisma, charm, magnetism.
3 *a show-business personality.* big name, celebrity, figure (*a well-known figure in show-business*), star, [*informal*] superstar.

personification noun *Santa Claus is the personification of Christmas.* allegorical representation, embodiment, epitome, human likeness, incarnation, living image, manifestation.

personify verb *Santa Claus personifies the spirit of Christmas.* allegorize, be the personification of [SEE **personification**], embody, epitomize, give a human shape to, incarnate, personalize, represent, symbolize.

personnel noun *the personnel who work in a factory.* employees, manpower, people, staff, work-force, workers.

perspective noun *Birds see a garden from a different perspective.* angle, outlook, point of view, slant, view, viewpoint.

perspicacious adjective *a perspicacious criticism.* SEE **perceptive**.

perspicuous adjective *a perspicuous explanation.* SEE **clear** adjective.

perspire verb sweat.

persuade verb *I persuaded him to accept my terms.* bring round, cajole, coax, convert, convince, entice, induce, influence, inveigle, prevail upon, talk into, tempt, urge, use persuasion [SEE **persuasion**], wheedle (into), win over.
OPPOSITES: SEE **dissuade**.

persuasion noun 1 *It took a lot of persuasion to convince him.* argument, blandishment, cajolery, brainwashing, conditioning, enticement, exhortation, persuading [SEE **persuade**], propaganda, reasoning.
2 *What is your religious persuasion?* SEE **belief**.

persuasive adjective *a persuasive argument.* cogent, compelling, convincing, credible, effective, eloquent, forceful, influential, logical, plausible, reasonable, sound, strong, telling, valid, watertight.
OPPOSITES: SEE **unconvincing**.

pert adjective SEE **cheeky**.

pertain verb *Will the same conditions pertain next year?* appertain, apply, be relevant [SEE **relevant**].

pertinacious adjective SEE **persistent**.

pertinent adjective SEE **relevant**.

perturb verb *The bad news perturbed us.* agitate, alarm, bother, disconcert, distress, disturb, frighten, make anxious [SEE **anxious**], scare, shake, trouble, unsettle, upset, vex, worry.
OPPOSITES: SEE **reassure**.

peruse verb SEE **read**.

pervade verb *The smell pervaded the whole building.* affect, diffuse, fill, filter through, flow through, impregnate, penetrate, percolate, permeate, saturate, spread through, suffuse.

pervasive adjective *a pervasive smell.* general, inescapable, insidious, permeating, pervading, prevalent, rife, ubiquitous, universal, widespread.

perverse adjective *It's perverse of him to buy hot dogs when we want ice-cream.* contradictory, contrary, disobedient, fractious, headstrong, illogical, inappropriate, intractable, intransigent, obdurate, obstinate, [*informal*] pigheaded, rebellious, refractory, stubborn, tiresome, uncooperative, unhelpful, unreasonable, wayward, wilful, wrong-headed.
OPPOSITES: SEE **helpful, reasonable**.

perversion noun 1 *perversion of the truth.* corruption, distortion, falsification, misrepresentation, misuse, twisting.
2 *sexual perversion.* abnormality, depravity, deviance, deviation, immorality, impropriety, [*informal*] kinkiness, unnaturalness, vice, wickedness.

pervert noun *a sexual pervert.* deviant, perverted person [SEE **perverted**].

pervert verb 1 *to pervert the course of justice.* bend, distort, divert, perjure, subvert, twist, undermine.
2 *to pervert a witness.* bribe, corrupt, lead astray.

perverted adjective *perverted behaviour.* *perverted sexual practices.* abnormal, corrupt, debauched, depraved, deviant, eccentric, immoral, improper, [*informal*] kinky, SEE **obscene**, sick, twisted, unnatural, warped, wicked, wrong.
OPPOSITES: SEE **natural**.

pessimism noun [See note preceding *optimism*.] *pessimism about the future.* cynicism, despair, despondency, fatalism, gloom, hopelessness, negativeness, resignation, unhappiness.
OPPOSITES: SEE **optimism**.

pessimistic adjective *pessimistic about our chances.* cynical, defeatist, despairing, despondent, fatalistic, gloomy, hopeless, melancholy, morbid, negative, resigned, unhappy.
OPPOSITES: SEE **optimistic**.

pest noun 1 *Don't be a pest!* annoyance, bother, curse, irritation, nuisance, [*informal*] pain in the neck, trial, vexation.
2 *garden pests.* [*informal*] bug, [*informal*] creepy-crawly, insect, parasite, [*plural*] vermin.

pester noun *Don't pester me while I'm busy!* annoy, badger, bait, besiege, bother, harass, harry, [*informal*] hassle, molest, nag, plague, torment, trouble, worry.

pesticide noun SEE **poison** noun.

pestiferous adjective SEE **troublesome**.

pestilence noun SEE **illness**.

pestilential adjective SEE **troublesome**.

pet noun 1 CREATURES COMMONLY KEPT AS PETS: budgerigar, canary, cat, dog, ferret, fish, gerbil, goldfish, guinea-pig, hamster, mouse, parrot, pigeon, rabbit, rat, tortoise.
OTHER ANIMALS: SEE **animal** noun.
2 [*informal*] *teacher's pet.* darling, favourite.

pet verb *Our dog loves you to pet him.* caress, cuddle, fondle, kiss, pat, stroke, SEE **touch** verb.

peter verb to peter out SEE **diminish**.

petite adjective SEE **small**.

petition noun *a petition to the government.* appeal, entreaty, list of signatures, plea, request, suit, supplication.

petitioner noun suppliant.

petrify verb SEE **terrify**.

petrol noun [*informal or American*] gas, gasoline.

pettifogging adjective SEE **trivial**.

petting noun SEE **love-making**.

pettish adjective SEE **irritable**.

petty adjective 1 *petty crime.* insignificant, minor, small, trifling, trivial, SEE **unimportant**.
OPPOSITES: SEE **important**.
2 *a petty attitude.* grudging, nit-picking, SEE **small-minded**, ungenerous.
OPPOSITES: SEE **open-minded**.

petulant adjective SEE **irritable**.

pew noun SEE **seat** noun.

phalanx noun SEE **group** noun.

phantasm, phantom nouns SEE **ghost**.

pharmacist noun dispensing chemist.

pharmacy noun *Get your medicine from the pharmacy.* chemists, dispensary, [*American*] drug-store.

phase noun *a phase of your life. a phase of an activity.* development, period, season, spell, stage, step, SEE **time** noun.

phenomenal adjective *The winner of the quiz had a phenomenal memory.* amazing, exceptional, extraordinary, [*informal*] fantastic, incredible, notable, outstanding, remarkable, [*informal*] sensational, singular, unbelievable, unusual, [*informal*] wonderful.
OPPOSITES: SEE **ordinary**.

phenomenon noun 1 *Snow is a common phenomenon in winter.* circumstance, event, fact, happening, incident, occurrence, sight.
2 *They said the six-year old pianist was quite a phenomenon.* curiosity, marvel, phenomenal person or thing [SEE **phenomenal**], prodigy, wonder.

phial noun SEE **bottle** noun.

A number of words like *philander, philanthropic, philosophy* are related to Greek *phileo = to love*. Compare words like *bibliophile* [= *a lover of books*], *Francophile* [= *a lover of French things*], etc.

---

philander verb SEE **love** noun (**to make love**).

philanthropic adjective *She's known for her philanthropic work in the community.* altruistic, beneficent, benevolent, bountiful, caring, charitable, generous, humane, humanitarian, SEE **kind** adjective, munificent.
OPPOSITES: SEE **misanthropic**.

philanthropist noun SEE **benefactor**.

philately noun stamp-collecting.

Philistine adjective *a Philistine attitude to the arts.* SEE **uncivilized**.

philology noun LINGUISTIC TERMS: SEE **language**.

philosopher noun sage, student of philosophy, thinker.

philosophical adjective **1** *a philosophical debate.* abstract, academic, analytical, ideological, intellectual, learned, logical, metaphysical, rational, reasoned, theoretical, thoughtful, wise.
2 *philosophical in defeat.* calm, collected, composed, patient, reasonable, resigned, stoical, unemotional, unruffled.
OPPOSITES: SEE **emotional**.

philosophize verb *He philosophizes instead of actually doing something.* analyse, be philosophical [SEE **philosophical**], moralize, pontificate, preach, rationalize, reason, sermonize, theorize, think things out.

philosophy noun *your philosophy of life.* convictions, ideology, metaphysics, set of beliefs, values, wisdom.

philtre noun SEE **potion**.

phlegm noun mucus, spittle.

phlegmatic adjective *a phlegmatic temperament.* apathetic, cold, cool, frigid, impassive, imperturbable, lethargic, placid, slow, sluggish, stolid, undemonstrative, unemotional, unresponsive.
OPPOSITES: SEE **excitable**.

phobia noun *a phobia about spiders.* anxiety, aversion, dislike, dread, SEE **fear** noun, [*informal*] hang-up, hatred, horror, neurosis, obsession, revulsion.

Phobia is related to Greek *phobos = fear.* There are a number of words for particular fears which end in *-phobia,* such as: acrophobia *(fear of heights),* agoraphobia *(open spaces),* anglophobia *(the English),* arachnephobia *(spiders),* claustrophobia *(enclosed spaces),* hydrophobia *(water),* nyctophobia *(the dark),* photophobia *(light),* xenophobia *(strangers),* zoophobia *(animals).*

---

phone verb *I phoned granny.* call, dial, [*informal*] give a buzz, ring, telephone.

Several English words, including *phone, phonetics, phonograph, telephone,* etc., are related to Greek *phone = sound, voice.*

---

phonetics noun LINGUISTIC TERMS: SEE **language**.

phoney adjective [*slang*] *a phoney Welsh accent.* affected, artificial, assumed, bogus, cheating, counterfeit, faked, false, fictitious, fraudulent, imitation, insincere, pretended, [*informal*] put-on, [*informal*] put-up (*a put-up job*), sham, synthetic, trick, unreal.
OPPOSITES: SEE **real**.

phosphorescent adjective SEE **glowing**.

A number of English words, including *photocopy, photograph, photosynthesis,* etc., are related to Greek *photos = light.*

---

photo noun, verb SEE **photograph** noun, verb.

photocopy verb copy, duplicate, photostat, print off, reproduce, [*informal*] run off.

photograph noun enlargement, exposure, negative, photo, plate, positive, print, shot, slide, [*informal*] snap, snapshot, transparency.
OTHER PICTURES: SEE **picture** noun.

photograph verb *to photograph an event.* shoot, snap, take a picture of [SEE **picture** noun].

photographic adjective **1** *a photographic description.* accurate, exact, faithful, graphic, lifelike, naturalistic, realistic, representational, true to life.
2 *a photographic memory.* pictorial, retentive, visual.

PHOTOGRAPHIC EQUIPMENT INCLUDES: box camera, ciné-camera, dark-room, developer, enlarger, exposure-meter, fixer, light-meter, Polaroid camera, reflex camera, SLR camera, telephoto lens, tripod, zoom lens.

---

photography noun taking photographs.

phrase noun SEE **expression**.

phrase verb SEE **express** verb.

phraseology noun *I liked her neat phraseology.* diction, SEE **expression**, idiom, language, parlance, phrasing, style, turn of phrase, wording.

physical adjective **1** *physical contact.* bodily, carnal, corporal, corporeal.
2 *Ghosts have no physical existence.* earthly, fleshly, material, mortal, palpable, physiological, real, solid, substantial, tangible.
OPPOSITES: SEE **incorporeal, spiritual**.

physician noun SEE **doctor**.

physics noun VARIOUS SCIENCES: SEE **science**.

physiognomy noun SEE **face** noun.

physiological adjective anatomical, bodily, physical.

physiology noun anatomy, the body.

physique noun *a person's physique.* body, build, figure, form, frame, muscles, physical condition, shape.

piazza noun concourse, market place, plaza, square.

pick noun 1 *Take your pick.* SEE **choice** noun, election, preference, selection.
2 *the pick of the bunch.* best, cream, élite, favourite, flower, pride.

pick verb 1 *Pick a partner. Pick your representative.* choose, decide on, elect, fix on, make a choice of, name, nominate, opt for, prefer, select, settle on, single out, vote for.
2 *to pick flowers.* collect, cull, cut, gather, harvest, pluck, pull off, take.

picket noun SEE **group** noun.

pickle verb *to pickle onions.* SEE **preserve** verb.

picnic noun SEE **meal**.

pictogram, pictograph nouns SEE **symbol**.

pictorial adjective *a pictorial representation of something.* diagrammatic, graphic, illustrated, representational.

picture noun *a recognizable picture.* delineation, depiction, image, likeness, outline, portrayal, profile, representation.
to take pictures of film, photograph, shoot (*to shoot a film*), video.

KINDS OF PICTURE: abstract, cameo, caricature, cartoon, collage, design, doodle, drawing, engraving, etching, film, fresco, [*plural*] graffiti, [*plural*] graphics, icon, identikit, illustration, landscape, montage, mosaic, mural, oil-painting, old master, painting, photofit, photograph, pin-up, plate (*photographic plate*), portrait, print, reproduction, self-portrait, sketch, slide, [*informal*] snapshot, still life, transfer, transparency, triptych, trompe l'œil, video, vignette.

---

picture verb 1 *Historical scenes were pictured on the wall.* delineate, depict, evoke, illustrate, outline, portray, represent, show.

WAYS TO MAKE A PICTURE: caricature, doodle, draw, engrave, etch, film, paint, photograph, print, sketch, video.

---

2 *Can you picture what the world will be like in 100 years?* conceive, describe, dream up, envisage, imagine, think up, visualize.

picturesque adjective 1 *picturesque scenery.* attractive, SEE **beautiful**, charming, pleasant, pretty, quaint, scenic.
OPPOSITES: SEE **ugly**.
2 *picturesque language.* colourful, descriptive, expressive, graphic, imaginative, poetic, vivid.
OPPOSITES: SEE **prosaic**.

pie noun flan, pasty, patty, quiche, tart, tartlet, turnover, vol-au-vent.

piebald adjective SEE **pied**.

piece noun 1 *a piece of cake. a piece of wood.* bar, bit, bite, block, chip, chunk, crumb, division, [*informal*] dollop, fraction, fragment, grain, helping, hunk, length, lump, morsel, part, particle, portion, quantity, sample, scrap, section, segment, share, shred, slab, slice, snippet, speck, stick, tablet, [*informal*] titbit.
2 *a piece of a machine.* component, constituent, element, spare part, unit.
3 *a piece of music. a piece of writing. a piece of clothing.* article, composition, example, instance, item, number, passage, specimen, work.

piecemeal adverb *to do something piecemeal.* a bit at a time, bit by bit, intermittently, little by little, piece by piece.

pied adjective dappled, flecked, mottled, particoloured, piebald, spotted, variegated.

pied-à-terre noun SEE **accommodation**.

pier noun 1 *Passengers disembark at the pier.* breakwater, SEE **dock** noun, jetty, landing-stage, quay, wharf.
2 *the piers of a bridge. a pier supporting a wall.* buttress, column, pile, pillar, support, upright.

pierce verb bore through, drill through, enter, go through, impale, make a hole in, penetrate, perforate, prick, punch (*punch a hole in a ticket*), puncture, skewer, spike, spit, stab, stick into, transfix, wound.

piercing adjective 1 *a piercing scream.* deafening, high-pitched, SEE **loud**, penetrating, sharp, shrill.
2 *a piercing wind.* SEE **cold** adjective.

piety noun *the piety of the martyrs.* devotion, devoutness, faith, godliness, holiness, piousness, religion, [*uncomplimentary*] religiosity, saintliness, sanctity.
OPPOSITES: SEE **impiety**.

piffle noun SEE **nonsense**.

piffling adjective SEE **trivial**.

pig noun boar, hog, [*childish*] piggy, piglet, runt [= *smallest piglet in a litter*], sow, swine.

pigeon-hole noun SEE **compartment**.

piggy-bank noun money-box.

pigment, pigmentation nouns SEE colouring.

pigmy dwarf, midget.

pigsty noun piggery, sty.

pike noun *armed with a pike*. lance, spear. OTHER WEAPONS: SEE weapons.

pikelet noun crumpet.

pile noun 1 *a pile of rubbish*. accumulation, heap, hoard, mass, mound, [*informal*] mountain, quantity, stack.
2 *piles driven into the ground*. column, pier, post, support, upright.
piles *suffering from piles*. haemorrhoids.

pile verb *Pile everything in the corner*. accumulate, amass, assemble, bring together, build up, collect, concentrate, gather, heap up, hoard, load, mass, stack up, store.

pilfer verb SEE steal.

pilgrim noun *pilgrims to a holy shrine*. [*old-fashioned*] palmer, SEE traveller.

pilgrimage noun SEE journey noun.

pill noun *Swallow the pills with a little water*. capsule, pellet, tablet.
the pill SEE contraceptive.

pillage noun *The invading troops were guilty of rape and pillage*. depredation, despoliation, devastation, looting, plundering, ransacking, robbing, stealing.

pillage verb SEE plunder verb.

pillar noun *supporting pillars*. baluster, column, pier, pilaster [= *ornamental pillar*], pile, post, prop, shaft, stanchion, support, upright.

pillar-box noun letter-box, post-box.

pillion noun SEE seat noun.

pillory verb SEE ridicule verb.

pillow noun bolster, cushion.
OTHER BEDDING: SEE bedclothes.

pilot adjective *a pilot scheme*. SEE experimental.

pilot noun 1 *the pilot of an aircraft*. airman, [*old-fashioned*] aviator, flier.
2 *the pilot of a boat*. coxswain, helmsman, navigator, steersman.

pilot verb *He piloted us back to safety*. conduct, convey, direct, drive, fly, guide, lead, navigate, steer.

pilot-light noun SEE light noun.

pimple noun boil, pustule, [*plural*] rash, spot, swelling, [*slang*] zit.

pin noun [*old-fashioned*] bodkin, brooch, clip, drawing-pin, SEE fastener, hat-pin, peg, safety-pin, tie-pin.

pin verb SEE fasten, pierce, transfix.

pinafore noun apron.

pince-nez noun SEE glass (glasses).

pincers noun VARIOUS TOOLS: SEE tool.

pinch verb 1 *to pinch something between your fingers*. crush, nip, squeeze, tweak.
2 [*informal*] *to pinch things from other people*. SEE steal.

pine verb *The dog pined when its master died*. mope, mourn, sicken, waste away.
to pine for *In winter I pine for warm sunshine!* crave, hanker after, long for, miss, SEE want verb, yearn for.

ping verb VARIOUS SOUNDS: SEE sound noun.

ping-pong noun table-tennis.

pinion noun [*poetic*] *gliding on outspread pinions*. wing.

pinion verb SEE restrain.

pink adjective OTHER COLOURS: SEE colour noun.

pinnacle noun 1 *the pinnacle of your career*. acme, apex, climax, height, highest point, peak, summit, top, zenith.
2 *a tower topped with ornate pinnacles*. spire, steeple, turret.

pin-up noun SEE picture noun.

pioneer noun 1 *pioneers who opened up new territories*. colonist, discoverer, explorer, settler.
2 *a pioneer of a new technique*. innovator, inventor, originator.

pioneer verb *to pioneer a new idea*. [*informal*]. bring out, develop, discover, experiment with, invent, launch, originate, set up, start.

pious adjective 1 [*complimentary*] *pious worshippers*. dedicated, devout, godfearing, godly, holy, moral, religious, reverent, saintly, sincere, spiritual.
OPPOSITES: SEE impious.
2 [*uncomplimentary*] *I hate their pious moralizing*. [*informal*] holier-than-thou, hypocritical, insincere, sanctimonious, self-righteous, self-satisfied, unctuous.
OPPOSITES: SEE sincere.

pip noun 1 *an orange pip*. seed, stone.
2 *a pip on a dice, officer's uniform, etc.* mark, spot, star.
3 *At the last pip it will be exactly six o'clock*. bleep, blip, stroke.
OTHER SOUNDS: SEE sound noun.

pipe noun *a water pipe*. conduit, duct, hose, hydrant, pipeline, piping, tube.
pipes bagpipes.

pipe verb 1 *to pipe something to another place*. carry along a pipe or wire, channel, convey, transmit.
2 *to pipe a tune*. blow, play, sound, whistle.
to pipe down SEE silent (be silent).
to pipe up SEE speak.

piping adjective *a piping voice*. SEE shrill.
piping hot SEE hot.

pippin noun apple.

piquant adjective 1 *a piquant taste.* pungent, salty, sharp, spicy, tangy, tart, tasty.
OPPOSITES: SEE **bland**.
2 *a piquant notion.* arresting, exciting, interesting, provocative, stimulating.
OPPOSITES: SEE **banal**.

pique noun SEE **annoyance**.

pirate noun *a pirate on the high seas.* buccaneer, [*old-fashioned*] corsair, marauder, SEE **thief**.

pirate verb *to pirate a video.* SEE **plagiarize**.

pirouette verb SEE **spin**.

pistol noun SEE **gun**.

pit noun 1 *a deep pit.* abyss, chasm, crater, depression, excavation, hole, hollow, pothole.
2 *Miners work in a pit.* coal-mine, colliery, mine, quarry, shaft, working.

pitch noun 1 *black as pitch.* tar.
2 *the pitch of a roof.* angle, gradient, incline, slope, steepness, tilt.
3 *the pitch of a musical note.* height, tuning.
4 *a football pitch.* arena, ground, playing-field, stadium.

pitch verb 1 *to pitch a tent.* erect, put up, raise, set up.
2 *to pitch a stone into a pond.* bowl, [*informal*] bung, cast, [*informal*] chuck, fling, heave, hurl, lob, sling, throw, toss.
3 *to pitch into the water.* dive, drop, fall heavily, plunge, topple.
4 *to pitch about in a storm.* dip up and down, lurch, rock, roll, toss.
to pitch in SEE **co-operate**.
to pitch into SEE **attack** verb.

pitch-black adjective SEE **black** adjective.

pitch-dark adjective SEE **dark**.

pitcher noun SEE **container**, jar, jug, urn.

pitchfork verb SEE **propel**.

Piteous means *deserving pity* (*We wept to hear their piteous cries*). *Pitiable* and *pitiful* may also mean *deserving pity*; but they often mean *deserving contempt* (*We laughed at their pitiful efforts*).

---

piteous adjective *piteous cries for help.* affecting, distressing, heartbreaking, heartrending, miserable, moving, pathetic, pitiable, pitiful, SEE **sad**, touching, wretched.

pitfall noun *I tried to avoid the obvious pitfalls.* catch, danger, difficulty, hazard, snag, trap.

pitiable adjective SEE **piteous**, **pitiful**.

pitiful adjective 1 *pitiful cries for help.* SEE **piteous**.
2 [*uncomplimentary*] *a pitiful attempt to stop the ball.* abject, contemptible, deplorable, hopeless, inadequate, incompetent, laughable, [*informal*] miserable, [*informal*] pathetic, pitiable, ridiculous, useless, worthless.
OPPOSITES: SEE **admirable**.

pitiless adjective *a pitiless attack.* bloodthirsty, callous, cruel, hard, heartless, inexorable, SEE **merciless**, relentless, ruthless, unfeeling, unrelenting, unrelieved, unremitting.
OPPOSITES: SEE **merciful**.

pittance noun SEE **money**.

pitted adjective *a pitted surface.* dented, holey, marked, pock-marked, rough, scarred, uneven.
OPPOSITES: SEE **smooth** adjective.

pity noun *The thugs showed no pity.* charity, clemency, compassion, feeling, forbearance, forgiveness, grace, humanity, kindness, leniency, love, mercy, regret, softness, sympathy, tenderness, understanding, warmth.
OPPOSITES: SEE **cruelty**.
to take pity on SEE **help** verb.

pity verb *I pitied anyone who was out in the storm.* [*informal*] bleed for (*My heart bleeds for them*), commiserate with, [*informal*] feel for, feel or show pity for [SEE **pity** noun], sympathize with, weep for.

pivot noun *turning on a pivot.* axis, axle, centre, fulcrum, hub, point of balance, swivel.

pivot verb SEE **turn** verb.

pivotal adjective SEE **central**.

placard noun *an advertising placard.* advert, advertisement, bill, notice, poster, sign.

placate verb SEE **pacify**.

place noun 1 *a place on a map.* location, point, position, site, situation, [*informal*] spot, [*informal*] whereabouts.
2 *a nice place for a holiday.* area, country, district, locale, locality, neighbourhood, region, SEE **town**, venue, vicinity.
3 *your place in society.* degree, function, grade, SEE **job**, office, position, rank, station, status.
4 *a place to live.* SEE **house** noun.
5 *a place to sit.* SEE **seat** noun.

place verb 1 *Place your things on the table.* arrange, deposit, dispose, [*informal*] dump, lay, leave, locate, plant, position, put down, rest, set down, settle, situate, stand, station, [*informal*] stick.

2 *The judges placed me third.* grade, position, put in order, rank.

3 *I've heard the tune before, but I can't place it.* identify, locate, put a name to, put into context, recognize.

placid adjective **1** *a placid temperament.* collected, composed, cool, equable, even-tempered, imperturbable, level-headed, mild, phlegmatic, restful, sensible, stable, steady, unexcitable.
OPPOSITES: SEE **excitable.**
2 *a placid sea.* calm, motionless, peaceful, quiet, tranquil, unruffled, untroubled.
OPPOSITES: SEE **stormy.**

plagiarize verb *to plagiarize someone else's ideas.* borrow, copy, [*informal*] crib, imitate, [*informal*] lift, pirate, reproduce, SEE **steal.**

plague noun **1** *bubonic plague.* blight, contagion, epidemic, SEE **illness,** infection, outbreak, pestilence.
2 *a plague of flies.* infestation, invasion, nuisance, scourge, swarm.

plague verb *The flies plagued us. Don't plague me with your questions.* afflict, annoy, be a nuisance to, be a plague to, bother, disturb, irritate, molest, [*informal*] nag, persecute, pester, torment, trouble, vex, worry.

plain adjective **1** *a plain signal.* apparent, audible, certain, clear, comprehensible, definite, distinct, evident, legible, manifest, obvious, unambiguous, unmistakable, visible, well-defined.
OPPOSITES: SEE **unclear.**
2 *plain speech. the plain truth.* basic, blunt, candid, direct, downright, explicit, forthright, frank, honest, informative, outspoken, plain-spoken, prosaic, sincere, straightforward, unadorned, unequivocal, unvarnished.
OPPOSITES: SEE **cryptic, evasive.**
3 *a plain appearance. plain cooking.* austere, everyday, frugal, homely, modest, ordinary, simple, unattractive, undecorated, unprepossessing, unpretentious, unremarkable, workaday.
OPPOSITES: SEE **attractive, elaborate** adjective.

plain noun *a wide plain.* prairie, savannah, steppe.

plain-spoken SEE **plain** adjective.

plaintiff noun *the plaintiff in a lawsuit.* accuser.
OPPOSITES: SEE **defendant.**
LEGAL TERMS: SEE **law.**

plaintive adjective *a plaintive tune.* doleful, melancholy, mournful, SEE **sad,** sorrowful, wistful.

plan noun **1** *a plan of the town.* [*informal*] bird's-eye view, chart, diagram, drawing, layout, map, representation, sketch-map.
2 *a carefully worked-out plan.* aim, blueprint, course of action, design, idea, intention, method, plot, policy, procedure, programme, project, proposal, proposition, scenario, scheme, strategy.

plan verb **1** *We planned our campaign.* arrange, concoct, contrive, design, devise, draw up a plan of [SEE **plan** noun], formulate, invent, map out, [*informal*] mastermind, organize, outline, plot, prepare, scheme, think out, work out.
2 *What do they plan to do next?* aim, conspire, contemplate, envisage, intend, mean, propose, think of.

plane adjective *a plane surface.* SEE **level** adjective.

plane noun **1** *raised to a higher plane.* SEE **level** noun.
2 [=*aircraft*] OTHER AIRCRAFT: SEE **aircraft.**
3 [=*carpenter's tool*] OTHER TOOLS: SEE **tool.**

planet noun globe, orb, satellite, sphere, world.

PLANETS OF THE SOLAR SYSTEM: Earth, Jupiter, Mars, Mercury, Neptune, Pluto, Saturn, Uranus, Venus.

OTHER ASTRONOMICAL TERMS: SEE **astronomy.**

plangent adjective *a plangent cry.* SEE **mournful.**

plank noun beam, board, planking, timber.

planned adjective *Was the meeting planned, or did it happen by chance?* arranged, contrived, SEE **deliberate** adjective, designed, masterminded, organized, premeditated, [*informal*] set up, thought out, worked out.
OPPOSITES: SEE **unplanned.**

planning noun *You should do the planning in advance.* arrangement, design, drafting, forethought, organization, preparation, setting up, thinking out.

plant noun **1** **plants** greenery, growth, undergrowth, vegetation.

KINDS OF PLANT: annual, SEE **bulb,** cactus, SEE **cereal,** climber, fern, SEE **flower** noun, SEE **fungus,** grass, SEE **herb,** lichen, moss, perennial, seedling, shrub, SEE **tree,** SEE **vegetable,** water-plant, weed.

PARTS OF A PLANT: bloom, blossom, branch, bud, bulb, corm, SEE **flower** noun, frond, fruit, [*formal*] inflorescence, leaf, [*formal*] panicle, petal, pod, [*formal*] raceme, root, seed, shoot, [*formal*] spadix, stalk, stem, trunk, tuber, twig.

---

2 *industrial plant*. SEE **equipment**.

plant verb *to plant flowers*. set out, sow, transplant.

plantation noun SEE **farm** noun.

plaque noun SEE **memorial**.

plasma noun SEE **fluid** noun.

plaster noun **1** *plaster on a wall*. mortar, stucco.
2 *a plaster to cover a wound*. dressing, sticking-plaster.

plaster verb *to plaster a wall*. coat, cover, daub.

plastic adjective SEE **pliable**.

plastic noun KINDS OF PLASTIC: bakelite, celluloid, polystyrene, polythene, polyurethane, polyvinyl, PVC, vinyl.

plate noun **1** *plates piled with food*. dinner-plate, dish, [*old-fashioned*] platter, side-plate, soup-plate.
OTHER ITEMS OF CROCKERY: SEE **crockery**.
2 *a steel plate. plates of rock*. layer, panel, sheet, slab, stratum.
3 *plates in a book*. illustration, [*informal*] photo, SEE **picture** noun.
4 *a dental plate*. dentures, false teeth.

plate verb *to plate one metal with a layer of another*. anodize, coat, cover, electroplate, galvanize (*with zinc*), gild (*with gold*).

platform **1** *The speakers sat on a platform*. dais, podium, rostrum, stage.
2 *a political platform*. SEE **policy**.

platinum noun OTHER METALS: SEE **metal**.

platitude noun SEE **commonplace** (**commonplace remark**).

platitudinous adjective SEE **commonplace**.

platoon noun SEE **armed services**.

platter noun SEE **plate** noun.

plaudits noun SEE **applause**.

plausible adjective *a plausible excuse*. acceptable, believable, conceivable, credible, likely, persuasive, possible, probable, reasonable, tenable.
OPPOSITES: SEE **implausible**.

play noun **1** *We all enjoy play*. amusement, diversion, fun, [*informal*] fun and games, joking, make-believe, playing, pretending, recreation, sport.

VARIOUS GAMES AND SPORTS: SEE **game** noun, **sport**.
2 *a play on TV*. drama, performance, production.
THEATRICAL ENTERTAINMENTS: SEE **theatre**.
3 *play in the moving parts of a machine*. freedom, freedom of movement, latitude, leeway, looseness, tolerance.

play verb **1** *The children went to play*. amuse yourself, caper, disport yourself, fool about, frisk, frolic, gambol, have fun, [*informal*] mess about, romp, sport.
2 *He won't play*. join in, participate, take part.
3 *I played him at snooker*. challenge, compete against, oppose, vie with.
4 *Who played Mary in the nativity play?* act, impersonate, perform, portray, pretend to be, represent, take the part of.
5 *to play the piano*. make music on, perform on, strum.
6 *to play records. to play a tape-recorder*. have on, listen to, operate, put on, switch on.
to play about SEE **fidget**.
to play ball SEE **co-operate**.
to play (it) by ear SEE **improvise**.
to play down SEE **minimize**.
to play for time SEE **delay** verb.
to play up SEE **misbehave**.
to play up to SEE **flatter**.

player noun **1** *the players in a game*. competitor, contestant, sportsman, sportswoman.
2 *players on stage*. actor, actress, entertainer, instrumentalist, musician, performer, soloist, [*joking*] Thespian.
VARIOUS PERFORMERS: SEE **music**, **theatre**.

playful adjective *a playful puppy. playful teasing*. active, cheerful, flirtatious, frisky, good-natured, humorous, impish, [*informal*] jokey, joking, light-hearted, lively, mischievous, puckish, roguish, skittish, spirited, sportive, sprightly, [*informal*] tongue-in-cheek, vivacious, waggish.
OPPOSITES: SEE **serious**.

playground noun play-area, recreation ground, school yard.

play-group noun SEE **school**.

playing-field noun arena, ground, pitch, recreation ground, sportsground.

playmate noun SEE **friend**.

plaything noun SEE **toy** noun.

playtime noun break.

playwright noun dramatist, scriptwriter.
OTHER WRITERS: SEE **writer**.

plaza noun SEE **piazza**.

plea noun *a plea for mercy*. appeal, entreaty, invocation, petition, prayer, request, supplication.
LEGAL TERMS: SEE **law**.

plead verb *He pleaded to be let off*. appeal, ask, beg, entreat, implore, importune, petition, request, solicit.

pleasant adjective [*Pleasant* can refer to anything which pleases you, and there are many possible synonyms. We give just some of the commoner ones here.] *pleasant food*. *pleasant weather*. *pleasant manners*. acceptable, affable, agreeable, amiable, attractive, balmy, beautiful, charming, cheerful, congenial, decent, delicious, delightful, enjoyable, entertaining, excellent, fine, friendly, genial, gentle, SEE **good**, gratifying, [*informal*] heavenly, hospitable, kind, likeable, lovely, mellow, mild, nice, palatable, peaceful, pleasing, pleasurable, pretty, relaxed, satisfying, soothing, sympathetic, warm, welcome, welcoming.
OPPOSITES: SEE **unpleasant**.

please verb 1 *I did it to please you*. amuse, content, delight, entertain, give pleasure to, gladden, gratify, make happy, satisfy.
2 *Do what you please*. SEE **want** verb.

pleased adjective *a pleased expression*. [*informal*] chuffed, [*uncomplimentary*] complacent, contented, delighted, elated, euphoric, glad, grateful, gratified, SEE **happy**, satisfied, thankful, thrilled.
OPPOSITES: SEE **annoyed**.

pleasing, pleasurable adjectives SEE **pleasant**.

pleasure noun 1 *I get pleasure from my garden*. bliss, comfort, contentment, delight, ecstasy, enjoyment, gladness, gratification, happiness, joy, rapture, satisfaction, solace.
2 *What are your favourite pleasures?* amusement, diversion, entertainment, fun, luxury, recreation, self-indulgence.

pleasure-loving adjective SEE **hedonistic**.

pleat noun *a pleat in a skirt*. crease, flute, fold, gather, tuck.

plebeian adjective SEE **common** adjective.

plebiscite noun ballot, poll, referendum, vote.

pledge noun 1 *a pledge left at a pawnbroker's*. bail, bond, deposit, security, surety.

2 *a pledge of good faith*. assurance, guarantee, oath, pact, promise, undertaking, vow, word.

pledge verb *She pledged to give her support*. agree, commit yourself, contract, give a pledge [SEE **pledge** noun], guarantee, promise, swear, undertake, vow.

plenary adjective *a plenary session of the conference*. full, general, open.

plenipotentiary noun SEE **ambassador**.

plentiful adjective *a plentiful supply of food*. abounding, abundant, ample, bounteous, bountiful, bristling, bumper (*a bumper crop*), copious, generous, inexhaustible, lavish, liberal, overflowing, plenteous, profuse, prolific.
OPPOSITES: SEE **scarce**.
to be plentiful *Fish are plentiful in this part of the river*. abound, flourish, proliferate, swarm, thrive.

plenty noun *plenty to do*. *plenty in the garden*. abundance, affluence, cornucopia, excess, fertility, flood, fruitfulness, glut, more than enough, [*informal*] oodles, plentifulness, plethora, profusion, prosperity, sufficiency, superabundance, surfeit, surplus, wealth.
OPPOSITES: SEE **scarcity**.
plenty of *plenty of food*. abundant, ample, heaps of, [*informal*] lashings of, [*informal*] loads of, a lot of, lots of, [*informal*] masses of, much, [*informal*] oodles of, piles of, SEE **plentiful**.

pliable adjective 1 *pliable wire*. bendable, [*informal*] bendy, ductile, flexible, plastic, pliant, springy, supple.
2 *a pliable character*. compliant, easily influenced, easily led, easily persuaded, impressionable, responsive, suggestible, tractable.

pliant adjective SEE **pliable**.

plight noun SEE **difficulty**.

plinth noun SEE **base** noun.

plod verb 1 *to plod through mud*. tramp, trudge, SEE **walk** verb.
2 *to plod through your work*. grind on, labour, persevere, SEE **work** verb.

plop noun, verb VARIOUS SOUNDS: SEE **sound** noun.

plot noun 1 *a plot of ground*. allotment, area, estate, garden, lot, parcel, patch, smallholding, tract.
2 *the plot of a novel*. narrative, organization, outline, scenario, story, thread.
3 *a plot against the government*. cabal, conspiracy, intrigue, machination, plan, scheme.

plot verb 1 *to plot a route*. chart, draw, map out, plan, project.

2 *They plotted to rob a bank.* collude, conspire, have designs, intrigue, scheme.
3 *What are you two plotting?* [*informal*] brew, [*informal*] cook up, design, hatch.

plough verb *to plough a field.* cultivate, till, turn over.

ploy noun SEE **trick** noun.

pluck noun SEE **courage**.

pluck verb **1** *to pluck fruit off a tree.* collect, gather, harvest, pick, pull off.
2 *to pluck a chicken.* denude, remove the feathers from, strip.
3 *to pluck something out of someone's hand.* grab, jerk, seize, snatch, tweak, yank.
4 *to pluck the strings of a violin.* play pizzicato, strum, twang.

lucky adjective SEE **brave**.

plug noun **1** *Put a plug in the hole.* bung, cork, stopper.
2 [*informal*] *a plug for a new record.* SEE **advertisement**.

plug verb **1** *to plug a leak.* block up, [*informal*] bung up, close, cork, fill, jam, seal, stop up, stuff up.
2 [*informal*] *to plug a record on radio.* advertise, mention frequently, promote.
to plug away SEE **work** verb.

plumage noun feathers, plumes.

plumb adverb *plumb in the middle.* [*informal*] dead, exactly, precisely, [*informal*] slap.

plumb verb *to plumb the depths.* measure, penetrate, probe, sound.

plumber noun heating-engineer.

plumbing noun pipes, water-supply.

plume noun feather, quill.

plummet verb SEE **plunge**.

plump adjective *a plump figure.* buxom, chubby, dumpy, SEE **fat** adjective, over-weight, podgy, portly, pudgy, rotund, round, squat, stout, tubby.
OPPOSITES: SEE **thin** adjective.

plump verb *to plump down.* SEE **drop** verb.
to plump for SEE **choose**.

plunder noun *The robbers escaped with their plunder.* booty, contraband, loot, pickings, prize, spoils, swag, takings.

plunder verb *Rioters plundered the shops.* despoil, loot, pillage, raid, ransack, ravage, rifle, rob, sack, steal from.

plunge verb **1** *She plunged into the water.* dive, drop, fall, hurtle, jump, leap, nose-dive, pitch, plummet, swoop, tumble.
2 *I plunged my hand in the water.* dip, lower, immerse, sink, submerge.

3 *He plunged his spear into the animal's side.* force, push, thrust.

plural adjective OPPOSITE: singular.

plush adjective SEE **luxurious**.

plutocrat noun SEE **wealthy (wealthy person)**.

pneumatic adjective *pneumatic tyres.* air-filled, pumped up.

poach verb **1** *to poach an egg.* SEE **cook** verb.
2 *to poach game.* hunt, steal.

pocket verb *Who'll pocket the profits?* SEE **take**.

pocket-knife noun VARIOUS KNIVES: SEE **knife** noun.

pocket-money noun allowance.

pod noun *a pea-pod.* case, hull, shell.

podgy adjective *a podgy figure.* SEE **plump** adjective.

podium noun SEE **platform**.

poem noun poetry, rhyme, verse.

KINDS OF POEM: ballad, ballade, [*informal*] ditty, doggerel, eclogue, elegy, epic, epithalamium, free-verse, haiku, idyll, [*informal*] jingle, lay, limerick, lyric, nursery-rhyme, pastoral, ode, sonnet.

VERSE FORMS: SEE **verse**.

OTHER KINDS OF WRITING: SEE **writing**.

---

poet noun bard, lyricist, minstrel, rhymer, sonneteer, versifier.
OTHER WRITERS: SEE **writer**.

poetic adjective *poetic language.* emotive, [*uncomplimentary*] flowery, imaginative, lyrical, metrical, poetical.
OPPOSITES: SEE **prosaic**.

poetry noun SEE **poem**.

pogrom noun SEE **killing** noun.

poignant adjective *a poignant moment of farewell.* affecting, distressing, heart-breaking, moving, painful, pathetic, piquant, SEE **sad**, tender, touching.

point noun **1** *the point of a spear.* prong, sharp end, spike, tine, tip.
2 *a point on a map.* location, place, position, site, situation.
3 *a point of time.* instant, juncture, moment, second, stage, time.
4 *a decimal point.* dot, full stop, spot.
5 *the point of a story.* aim, crux, drift, end, essence, gist, goal, idea, intention, meaning, motive, nub, object, objective, purpose, subject, theme, use, useful-ness.

6 *Honesty is one of his good points.* aspect, attribute, characteristic, facet, feature, peculiarity, quality, trait.
7 *a point jutting into the sea.* SEE **promontory.**
to the point SEE **relevant.**

point verb **1** *She pointed the way.* draw attention to, indicate, point out, show, signal.
2 *She pointed us in the right direction.* aim, direct, guide, lead, steer.

point-blank adjective **1** *at point-blank range.* SEE **close** adjective.
2 *a point-blank question.* SEE **direct** adjective.

pointed adjective **1** *a pointed stick.* SEE **sharp.**
2 *I didn't like her pointed remarks.* barbed, biting, edged, hinting, hurtful, insinuating, sarcastic, sharp, telling, trenchant. OPPOSITES: SEE **bland.**

pointless adjective SEE **futile.**

poise noun *She showed considerable poise on her first public appearance.* aplomb, assurance, balance, calmness, composure, coolness, dignity, equilibrium, presence, self-confidence, self-control, serenity, steadiness.

poise verb *He poised himself on a narrow ledge.* balance, be poised [SEE **poised**], keep in balance, support, suspend.

poised adjective **1** *poised on the edge.* balanced, hovering, in equilibrium, steady.
2 *poised to begin.* keyed up, ready, set, waiting.
3 *a poised performer.* assured, calm, composed, cool, dignified, self-confident, suave, urbane.

poison noun toxin, venom.

POISONS INCLUDE: arsenic, cyanide, DDT, digitalin, hemlock, herbicide, insecticide, Paraquat, pesticide, rat-poison, strychnine, weed-killer.

---

poison verb **1** *to poison someone.* SEE **kill.**
2 *Chemicals are poisoning the sea.* contaminate, infect, pollute, taint.
3 *Propaganda can poison people's minds.* corrupt, deprave, pervert, prejudice, subvert, warp.

poisoned adjective *a poisoned wound.* diseased, festering, infected, septic.

poisonous adjective *a poisonous snake-bite.* deadly, fatal, lethal, mortal, noxious, toxic, venomous, virulent.

poke verb *to poke with a finger or a stick.* dig, SEE **hit** verb, jab, nudge, prod, stab, stick, thrust.
to poke about SEE **search** verb.
to poke fun at SEE **ridicule** verb.
to poke out SEE **protrude.**

poker-face noun SEE **expression.**

poker-faced adjective SEE **expressionless.**

poky adjective *a poky little room.* confined, cramped, inconvenient, restrictive, SEE **small,** uncomfortable.
OPPOSITES: SEE **spacious.**

polar adjective *polar regions.* antarctic, arctic.

polarize verb *Opinions have polarized into two opposing sides.* diverge, divide, move to opposite positions, separate, split.

pole noun **1** *[plural] the poles of the earth.* extremes, opposite ends.
GEOGRAPHICAL TERMS: SEE **geography.**
2 *a long pole.* bar, column, flagpole, mast, post, rod, shaft, spar, staff, stake, stick, stilt.
poles apart SEE **different.**

pole-axe verb SEE **kill.**

polemic noun SEE **argument.**

polemical adjective SEE **controversial.**

police noun *[plural] Call the police.* constabulary, [informal] the law, police force, policemen [SEE **policeman**].

police verb *to police a football match.* control, keep in order, keep the peace at, monitor, patrol, provide a police presence at, supervise, watch over.

policeman, policewoman nouns [informal] bobby, constable, [informal] cop, [informal] copper, detective, inspector, officer.

policy noun **1** *the library's policy on lost books.* approach, code of conduct, guidelines, [informal] line, practice, procedure, protocol, rules, stance, strategy, tactics.
2 *the policy of a political party.* intentions, manifesto, plan of action, platform, programme, proposals.
3 *an insurance policy.* SEE **document.**

polish noun **1** *a lovely polish on the woodwork.* brightness, brilliance, finish, glaze, gloss, lustre, sheen, shine, smoothness, sparkle.
2 *I wish his manners had more polish.* [informal] class, elegance, finesse, grace, refinement, sophistication, style, suavity, urbanity.

polish verb *to polish the furniture. to polish the cutlery.* brush up, buff up

burnish, French-polish, rub down, rub up, shine, wax.
to polish off SEE **finish** verb.

SUBSTANCES USED TO SMOOTH AND POL-ISH THINGS: beeswax, Carborundum, emery, emery-paper, furniture polish, glasspaper, oil, sandpaper, shellac, varnish, wax.

---

polished adjective **1** *a polished surface.* bright, burnished, glassy, gleaming, glossy, lustrous, shining, shiny.
2 *polished manners.* cultured, elegant, gracious, perfected, SEE **polite**, [*sometimes uncomplimentary*] posh, refined, sophisticated, suave, urbane.
OPPOSITES: SEE **rough**.

polite adjective *polite behaviour. polite language.* acceptable, attentive, chivalrous, civil, considerate, correct, courteous, cultivated, deferential, diplomatic, discreet, euphemistic, gallant, genteel, gentlemanly, ladylike, obliging, SEE **polished**, respectful, tactful, thoughtful, well-bred, well-mannered, well-spoken.
OPPOSITES: SEE **rude**.

politic adjective SEE **prudent**.

politics noun *In a democracy, everyone should be involved in politics.* diplomacy, government, political affairs, political science, statesmanship.

VARIOUS POLITICAL POSITIONS: activist, anarchist, capitalist, communist, conservative, democrat, fascist, Labour, leftist, left-wing, liberal, Marxist, moderate, monarchist, nationalist, Nazi, parliamentarian, radical, republican, revolutionary, rightist, right-wing, socialist, Tory, [*old-fashioned*] Whig.

VARIOUS POLITICAL SYSTEMS: anarchy, capitalism, communism, democracy, dictatorship, martial law, monarchy, oligarchy, parliamentary democracy, republic.

---

poll noun **1** *to go to the polls.* ballot, election, vote.
2 *an opinion poll.* census, plebiscite, referendum, survey.

poll verb **1** *Our candidate polled few votes.* receive votes.
2 *to poll a tree.* SEE **pollard**.

pollard verb *to pollard a tree.* SEE **cut** verb, cut the top off, lop, poll, [*informal*] top.

pollinate verb SEE **fertilize**.

pollute verb *Chemicals pollute the rivers.* contaminate, defile, dirty, foul, infect, poison, soil, taint.

poltergeist noun SEE **ghost**.

The prefix *poly-* is related to Greek *polus = much, polloi = many.*

---

polyglot adjective multilingual.

polygon, polyhedron nouns VARIOUS SHAPES: SEE **shape** noun.

polyphonic adjective *polyphonic music.* contrapuntal.

polytechnic noun SEE **college**.

pomp noun *The coronation was conducted with great pomp.* ceremonial, ceremony, display, formality, grandeur, magnificence, ostentation, pageantry, ritual, show, solemnity, spectacle, splendour.

pompous adjective [*uncomplimentary*] *pompous language. a pompous manner.* affected, arrogant, bombastic, grandiose, haughty, [*informal*] high-faluting, long-winded, ostentatious, pontifical, posh, pretentious, self-important, sententious, showy, snobbish, [*informal*] stuck-up, supercilious.
OPPOSITES: SEE **modest**.

pond noun *a fish pond.* lake, pool, puddle.

ponder verb SEE **think**.

ponderous adjective **1** *a ponderous load.* bulky, burdensome, cumbersome, heavy, hefty, massive, unwieldy, weighty.
OPPOSITES: SEE **light** adjective.
2 *a ponderous style.* dull, heavy-handed, humourless, laboured, lifeless, long-winded, plodding, prolix, slow, stilted, stodgy, tedious, verbose.
OPPOSITES: SEE **lively**.

pong noun, verb SEE **smell** noun, verb.

pontifical adjective SEE **pompous**.

pontificate verb SEE **preach**.

pony noun SEE **horse**.

pooh-pooh verb SEE **dismiss**.

pool noun *a pool of water.* lake, mere, oasis, pond, puddle, swimming-pool, tarn.

pool verb *to pool resources.* SEE **combine**.

poor adjective **1** *Poor people can't afford luxuries.* badly off, bankrupt, beggarly, [*informal*] broke, deprived, destitute, hard up, homeless, impecunious, impoverished, in debt, indigent, needy, penniless, penurious, poverty-stricken, [*informal*] skint, underpaid, underprivileged.
OPPOSITES: SEE **rich**.

2 *poor soil* barren, exhausted, infertile, sterile, unproductive.
OPPOSITES: SEE **fertile**.
3 *a poor yield from the garden*. low, mean, SEE **scanty**, small, sparse, unprofitable, unrewarding.
OPPOSITES: SEE **plentiful**.
4 *goods of poor quality*. bad, cheap, deficient, faulty, imperfect, inadequate, inferior, low-grade, mediocre, paltry, second-rate, shoddy, substandard, unsatisfactory, useless, worthless.
OPPOSITES: SEE **superior**.
5 [*informal*] *The poor animals stood in the rain*. forlorn, hapless, luckless, miserable, pathetic, pitiable, sad, unfortunate, unhappy, unlucky, wretched.
OPPOSITES: SEE **lucky**.
a poor person beggar, down-and-out, pauper, tramp, vagrant, wretch.
poor people the destitute, the homeless.

poorly adjective *I felt poorly*. SEE **ill**.

pop verb *The cork popped*. VARIOUS SOUNDS: SEE **sound** noun.

poppycock noun SEE **nonsense**.

populace noun the masses, the people, the public.

popular adjective *a popular performer*. *popular styles*. accepted, celebrated, famous, fashionable, favoured, favourite, [*informal*] in (*It's the in thing*), liked, lionized, loved, renowned, sought after, well-known, well-liked.
OPPOSITES: SEE **unpopular**.
popular music pop.
OPPOSITE: classical music.

popularize verb **1** *to popularize a new product*. make popular [SEE **popular**], promote, spread.
2 *to popularize Shakespeare's plays*. make easy, present in a popular way, simplify, [*informal*] tart up.

populate verb *In summer the town is populated mainly by holidaymakers*. colonize, fill, inhabit, live in, occupy, overrun, settle.

population noun *the population of a country*. citizens, community, inhabitants, natives, occupants, SEE **populace**, residents.

populous adjective *a populous area*. crowded, full, overpopulated, packed, swarming, teeming.

porcelain noun SEE **crockery**.

porch noun doorway, entrance, lobby, portico.

pore verb **to pore over** SEE **study** verb.

pornographic adjective SEE **obscene**.

pornography noun SEE **obscenity**.

porous adjective *Porous substances will soak up liquid*. absorbent, cellular, holey, permeable, pervious, spongy.
OPPOSITES: SEE **impermeable**.

port adjective *the port side of a ship*. left-hand (when facing forward).
OPPOSITE: starboard.

port noun *The ship entered port*. anchorage, SEE **dock** noun, dockyard, harbour, haven, marina, sea-port.

portable adjective *a portable tool-box*. compact, convenient, easy to carry, handy, light, lightweight, manageable, mobile, movable, small, transportable.
OPPOSITES: SEE **unwieldy**.

portal noun SEE **door**.

The two meanings of *porter* relate to two different Latin words: *porta* = *door* [compare *portal*, *portico*]; and *portare* = *to carry* [compare *portable*].

---

porter noun **1** caretaker, door-keeper, doorman, gatekeeper, janitor, security guard.
2 baggage-handler, bearer, carrier.

portfolio noun cover, folder.

porthole noun window.

portico noun SEE **porch**.

portion noun *a small portion of pie*. allocation, allowance, bit, fraction, fragment, helping, measure, part, piece, quantity, quota, ration, section, segment, serving, share, slice.

portly adjective *a portly figure*. SEE **plump**.

portmanteau noun SEE **luggage**.

portrait noun *a portrait of a famous person*. depiction, image, likeness, SEE **picture** noun, portrayal, profile, representation, self-portrait.

portray verb *The book portrays what life was like 1000 years ago*. delineate, depict, describe, evoke, illustrate, SEE **picture** verb, represent, show.

pose noun **1** *The model adopted a suitable pose*. attitude, position.
2 *Don't take his behaviour seriously—it's only a pose*. act, affectation, façade, masquerade, posture, pretence.

pose verb **1** *to pose for a portrait*. model sit.
2 *to pose in front of your friends*. adopt a pose [SEE **pose** noun], be a poser [SEE **poser**], posture, show off.
3 *to pose a question*. ask, posit, present put forward, suggest.
to pose as *The burglar posed as the gas man*. impersonate, masquerade as, pass yourself off as, pretend to be.

poser noun 1 [*informal*] *The dilemma presented quite a poser.* SEE **puzzle** noun.
2 [*informal*] *I hate to see posers showing off.* exhibitionist, [*informal*] phoney, poseur, [*informal*] show-off.

posh adjective [*informal*] *a posh party.* [*informal*] classy, elegant, fashionable, formal, lavish, ostentatious, showy, smart, snobbish, stylish, [*informal*] swanky, [*informal*] swish.

position noun 1 *Mark our position on the map.* locality, location, locus, place, point, reference, site, situation, spot, whereabouts.
2 *Having lost my money, I was in an embarrassing position.* circumstances, condition, predicament, state.
3 *I'll get cramp if I don't shift my position.* angle, posture.
4 *A referee adopts a neutral position.* attitude, opinion, outlook, perspective, standpoint, view, viewpoint.
5 *a responsible position in the firm.* appointment, degree, employment, function, grade, job, level, niche, occupation, rank, role, standing, station, status, title.

position verb *The captain positioned her players where she wanted them.* arrange, deploy, dispose, locate, place, put, settle, situate, stand, station.

positive adjective 1 *He was positive that he was right.* affirmative, assured, certain, confident, convinced, decided, definite, emphatic, sure, unequivocal.
2 *I can show you positive evidence.* categorical, clear, conclusive, explicit, firm, incontestable, incontrovertible, irrefutable, real, undeniable.
2 *The counsellor gave me positive advice.* beneficial, constructive, helpful, optimistic, practical, useful, worthwhile.
OPPOSITES: SEE **negative**.

posse noun SEE **group** noun.

possess verb 1 *Do you possess a pen?* be in possession of, have, own.
2 *Foreign invaders possessed the country.* acquire, control, dominate, govern, occupy, rule, seize, take over.

possessions noun assets, belongings, chattels, effects, estate, fortune, goods, property, riches, wealth.

possessive adjective *a possessive nature.* clinging, domineering, jealous, proprietorial, protective, selfish.

possibility noun *a possibility of rain. the possibility of travelling to Mars.* capability, chance, danger, feasibility, likelihood, opportunity, potential, potentiality, practicality, probability, risk.
OPPOSITES: SEE **impossibility**.

possible adjective *a possible outcome. a possible explanation.* achievable, attainable, conceivable, credible, feasible, imaginable, likely, obtainable, plausible, potential, practicable, practical, probable, prospective, viable, workable.
OPPOSITES: SEE **impossible**.

possibly adverb [*informal*] hopefully, maybe, perhaps.

post noun 1 VARIOUS KINDS OF UPRIGHT POST: baluster, bollard, capstan, column, gate-post, leg, newel, pier, pile, pillar, pole, prop, shaft, stake, stanchion, starting-post, strut, support, upright, winning-post.
2 *a sentry's post.* location, place, point, position.
3 *a post in a local business.* appointment, employment, SEE **job**, occupation, office, place, position, situation, work.
4 *Was there any post today?* airmail, cards, delivery, letters, mail, packets, parcels, postcards.

post verb 1 *to post information.* advertise, announce, display, pin up, put up, stick up.
2 *to post a letter.* dispatch, mail, send, transmit.

post-box noun letter-box, pillar-box.

postcard noun SEE **letter**.

poster noun *We put up posters advertising sports day.* advertisement, announcement, bill, display, notice, placard, sign.

posterior adjective SEE **back** adjective.

posterior noun SEE **buttocks**.

posterity noun *What will posterity say about modern architecture?* descendants, future generations, heirs, offspring, successors.

postern noun SEE **door**.

The prefix *post-* in words like *postgraduate, posthumous, post-mortem, postpone*, etc., is from Latin *post = after*.

postgraduate noun SEE **student**.

post-haste adverb SEE **fast** adverb.

posthumous adjective SEE **belated**.

post-mortem noun 1 *a post-mortem on a dead body.* autopsy.
2 [*informal*] *a post-mortem on last week's disaster.* SEE **investigation**.

postpone verb *to postpone a meeting. to postpone a decision.* adjourn, defer, delay, extend, hold over, put back, put off, [*informal*] put on ice, [*informal*] shelve, stay (*to stay judgement*), suspend.

postscript noun *a postscript to a letter.* [*formal*] addendum, addition, afterthought, codicil (*to a will*), epilogue, [*informal*] PS.

postulate verb assume, hypothesize, posit, propose, suppose, theorize.

posture noun *your physical posture.* bearing, deportment, stance.
2 *a mental posture.* SEE **attitude**.

posy noun *a posy of flowers.* bouquet, bunch, buttonhole, corsage, nosegay, spray.

pot noun *a cooking pot. pots and pans.* basin, bowl, casserole, cauldron, container, crock, crucible, dish, jar, pan, saucepan, teapot, urn, vessel.

pot-bellied adjective SEE **fat** adjective.

potent adjective *a potent drug. a potent smell. a potent influence.* effective, forceful, formidable, influential, intoxicating (*potent drink*), overpowering, overwhelming, powerful, strong.
OPPOSITES: SEE **impotent, weak**.

potentate noun SEE **ruler**.

potential adjective 1 *a potential champion.* budding, embryonic, future, likely, possible, probable, promising, prospective.
OPPOSITES: SEE **established**.
2 *a potential disaster.* imminent, impending, latent, looming, threatening.

pot-hole noun 1 *exploring pot-holes.* SEE **cave** noun.
2 *pot-holes in the road.* SEE **hole**.

pot-holing noun caving.

potion noun *a health-giving potion.* brew, concoction, dose, draught, drug, elixir, liquid, medicine, mixture, philtre, tonic.

pot-pourri noun SEE **mixture**.

potted adjective *a potted version of a story.* SEE **abridged**.

potter noun ARTISTS AND CRAFTSMEN: SEE **artist**.

potter verb **to potter about** SEE **work** verb.

pottery noun ceramics, china, SEE crockery, crocks, earthenware, porcelain, stoneware.

potty adjective SEE **mad**.

pouch noun *a pouch to keep money in.* bag, SEE **container**, purse, sack, wallet.

poultry noun KINDS OF POULTRY: bantam, chicken, duck, fowl, goose, guineafowl, hen, pullet, turkey.

pounce verb **to pounce on** *The cat pounced on the mouse.* ambush, attack, drop on, jump on, leap on, seize, snatch, spring at, swoop down on.

pound noun 1 *a pound of jam.* SEE **measure** noun.
2 *Lend me a few pounds.* SEE **money**.
3 *a pound for animals.* SEE **enclosure**.

pound verb *I pounded the clay until it was soft.* batter, beat, crush, grind, SEE **hit** verb, knead, mash, pulp, smash.

pour verb 1 *Water poured through the hole.* cascade, course, disgorge, flow, gush, run, spew, spill, spout, stream.
2 *I poured the milk out of the bottle.* decant, serve, tip.

pout noun FACIAL EXPRESSIONS: SEE **expression**.

poverty noun *He was rich, but is now reduced to poverty.* bankruptcy, beggary, dearth, debt, destitution, hardship, indigence, lack, necessity, need, penury, privation, scarcity, shortage, want.
OPPOSITES: SEE **wealth**.

poverty-stricken adjective SEE **poor**.

powder noun dust, particles.

powder verb 1 *to powder a substance in a pestle and mortar.* atomize, crush, grind, pound, pulverize, reduce to powder.
2 *to powder a baby's bottom.* cover with powder, dust, sprinkle.

powdered adjective 1 *powdered coffee. powdered stone.* crushed, granulated, ground, pulverized.
2 *powdered milk.* dehydrated, dried.

powdery adjective *a powdery substance.* chalky, crumbly, disintegrating, dry, dusty, fine, friable, granular, loose, pulverized, sandy.
OPPOSITES: SEE **solid, wet** adjective.

power noun 1 *the power to do something.* ability, capability, competence, energy, faculty, force, might, muscle, skill, strength, talent, vigour.
2 *the power to arrest someone.* authority, privilege, right.
3 *the power of a tyrant.* [*informal*] clout, command, control, domination, influence, omnipotence, oppression, potency, rule, sovereignty, supremacy, sway.
OPPOSITES: SEE **impotence**.

powerful adjective *a powerful machine. a powerful ruler. a powerful argument.* authoritative, cogent, commanding, compelling, consuming, convincing, dominant, dynamic, effective, effectual, energetic, forceful, influential, invincible, irresistible, high-powered, mighty, muscular, omnipotent, overpowering,

overwhelming, persuasive, potent, sovereign, SEE **strong**, vigorous, weighty.
OPPOSITES: SEE **powerless, weak**.

powerless *powerless against the enemy's might.* defenceless, feeble, helpless, impotent, incapable, ineffective, ineffectual, unable, SEE **weak**.
OPPOSITES: SEE **powerful, strong**.

powwow noun SEE **meeting**.

practicable adjective *a practicable plan.* achievable, attainable, feasible, possible, practical, realistic, sensible, viable, workable.
OPPOSITES: impracticable, SEE **impractical**.

practical adjective 1 *practical science.* applied, empirical, experimental.
2 *a practical approach.* businesslike, efficient, down-to-earth, hard-headed, matter-of-fact, [*informal*] no-nonsense, pragmatic, realistic, sensible, utilitarian.
OPPOSITES: SEE **theoretical**.
3 *a practical worker.* accomplished, capable, competent, expert, proficient, skilled.
4 *a practical tool.* convenient, functional, handy, usable, useful.
OPPOSITES: SEE **impractical**.
5 *a practical plan* SEE **practicable**.
a practical joke hoax, prank, trick.

practically adverb *We're practically there.* almost, close to, just about, nearly, virtually.

practice noun 1 *What does the plan mean in practice?* action, actuality, application, effect, operation, reality, use.
2 *We need more practice.* [*informal*] dummy-run, exercise, preparation, rehearsal, [*informal*] run-through, training.
OPPOSITES: SEE **theory**.
3 *Smoking is still a common practice.* custom, habit, routine, tradition.
4 *a doctor's practice.* SEE **business**.

Notice the different spellings of *practice* (noun) and *practise* (verb).

---

practise verb 1 *Keep practising.* do exercises, drill, exercise, prepare, rehearse, train, warm up.
2 *Practise what you preach.* apply, carry out, do, engage in, follow, perform, put into practice.

practitioner noun **medical practitioner** SEE **doctor**.

pragmatic adjective SEE **practical**.

prairie noun grassland, plain.

praise noun 1 *Our praise embarrassed her.* acclamation, accolade, admiration, adulation, applause, approval, commendation, compliment, congratulation, [*formal*] encomium, eulogy, homage, honour, ovation, panegyric, plaudits, testimonial, thanks, tribute.
2 *Give praise to God.* adoration, worship.

praise verb 1 *to praise someone for an achievement. to praise a performance.* acclaim, admire, applaud, cheer, clap, commend, compliment, congratulate, [*informal*] crack up (*They cracked her up as one of our best actresses*), eulogize, exalt, extol, give a good review of, marvel at, offer praise to [SEE **praise** noun], pay tribute to, [*informal*] rave about, recommend, [*informal*] say nice things about, show approval of.
OPPOSITES: SEE **criticize**.
2 *to praise God.* adore, glorify, honour, [*formal*] laud, magnify, worship.
OPPOSITES: SEE **curse** verb.

praiseworthy adjective *a praiseworthy effort.* admirable, commendable, creditable, deserving, SEE **good**, laudable, meritorious, worthy.
OPPOSITES: SEE **deplorable**.

pram noun baby-carriage, [*old-fashioned*] perambulator, push-chair.

prance verb *to prance about.* caper, cavort, dance, frisk, frolic, gambol, jump, leap, play, romp, skip.

prank noun SEE **escapade**.

prattle verb babble, chatter, [*informal*] rattle on, SEE **talk** verb.

pray verb 1 *to pray to God.* call upon, invoke, say prayers, supplicate.
2 SEE **ask**.

prayer noun *a prayer to God.* collect, devotion, entreaty, invocation, litany, meditation, petition, supplication.

prayer-book noun breviary, missal.

preach verb 1 *to preach in church.* deliver a sermon, evangelize, expound, proselytize, spread the Gospel.
2 *He's a fine one to preach about turning up on time!* expatiate, give moral advice, [*informal*] lay down the law, lecture, moralize, pontificate, sermonize, tell others what to do.

preacher noun SEE **clergyman**, crusader, evangelist, minister, missionary, moralist, pastor, revivalist.

The prefix *pre-* is from Latin *prae* = *before*.

---

preamble noun SEE **preface**.

pre-arranged adjective *a pre-arranged meeting.* arranged beforehand, fixed, planned, predetermined, prepared.
OPPOSITES: SEE **unplanned**.

precarious adjective dangerous, insecure, perilous, risky, rocky, shaky, uncertain, unsafe, unstable, unsteady, vulnerable, wobbly.
OPPOSITES: SEE **safe**.

precaution noun *What precautions can you take against flu?* anticipation, defence, insurance, protection, provision, safeguard, safety measure.

precede verb 1 *A flag-bearer preceded the procession.* be in front of, come before, go before, lead.
2 *He preceded his speech with an announcement.* introduce, lead into, preface, prefix, start.
OPPOSITES: SEE **follow**.

precedent noun SEE **pattern**.

precept noun SEE **rule** noun.

preceptor noun SEE **teacher**.

precinct noun SEE **area**.

precious adjective SEE **valuable**.

precipice noun *The climber fell down a precipice.* cliff, crag, drop, escarpment, precipitous face [SEE **precipitous**], rock.

precipitate adjective *a precipitate departure.* SEE **hasty, premature**.

precipitate verb *to precipitate a crisis.* bring on, cause, encourage, expedite, further, hasten, induce, occasion, spark off, trigger off.

precipitation noun KINDS OF PRECIPITATION: dew, drizzle, hail, rain, sleet, snow.

precipitous adjective *a precipitous hillside.* abrupt, perpendicular, sharp, sheer, steep, vertical.

précis noun SEE **summary**.

précis verb SEE **summarize**.

precise adjective 1 *the precise time. precise instructions.* accurate, clear-cut, correct, defined, definite, distinct, exact, explicit, fixed, measured, right, specific, unambiguous, unequivocal.
OPPOSITES: SEE **imprecise**.
2 *precise workmanship.* careful, finicky, meticulous, punctilious, scrupulous.
OPPOSITES: SEE **careless**.

preclude verb *Does this agreement preclude changes later on?* debar, exclude, make impossible, pre-empt, prevent, rule out.

precocious adjective *a precocious child.* advanced, SEE **clever**, forward, mature, quick.
OPPOSITES: SEE **backward**.

preconception noun *I had no preconceptions about what to expect.* assumption, expectation, prejudice, presupposition.

precondition noun SEE **prerequisite** noun.

precursor noun SEE **predecessor**.

predator noun hunter.

predatory adjective *predatory animals. predatory bands of robbers.* acquisitive, covetous, greedy, hunting, marauding, pillaging, plundering, preying, rapacious, voracious.

predecessor noun ancestor, antecedent, forebear, forefather, forerunner, precursor.

predestination noun SEE **fate**.

predestined adjective SEE **fated**.

predetermined adjective 1 *Do you believe his death was predetermined?* SEE **fated**.
2 *a predetermined signal.* SEE **pre-arranged**.

predicament *How did you get out of that predicament?* crisis, difficulty, dilemma, embarrassment, emergency, jam, [*informal*] mess, [*informal*] pickle, plight, problem, quandary.

predict verb *to predict the future.* forebode, forecast, foresee, foretell, forewarn, prognosticate, prophesy, tell fortunes.

predictable adjective *a predictable disaster.* certain, expected, foreseeable, likely, probable.
OPPOSITES: SEE **unpredictable**.

predilection noun SEE **preference**.

predispose verb SEE **prejudice** verb.

predisposition noun SEE **inclination, prejudice** noun.

predominant adjective SEE **chief** adjective.

predominate verb *Women still predominate in the nursing profession.* be in the majority, dominate, hold sway, outnumber, outweigh, preponderate, prevail.

pre-eminent adjective SEE **outstanding**.

pre-empt verb *We pre-empted any criticism by admitting that we'd done a poor job.* anticipate, forestall.

preen verb *to preen yourself* SEE **groom** verb.

prefab noun SEE **house** noun.

prefabricate verb SEE **manufacture**.

preface noun *the preface to a book.* foreword, introduction, preamble, prelude, prologue.

preface verb *He prefaced his speech with an announcement.* introduce, lead into, precede, prefix, start.

prefatory adjective *prefatory remarks.* SEE **preliminary**.

prefect noun *a school prefect.* monitor. VARIOUS OFFICIALS: SEE **official** noun.

prefer verb *Which style do you prefer?* advocate, [*informal*] back, choose, fancy, favour, [*informal*] go for, incline towards, like, like better, pick out, [*informal*] plump for, recommend, single out, think preferable [SEE **preferable**], vote for, SEE **want** verb.

preferable adjective *Vote for whoever you think is preferable.* advantageous, better, better-liked, desirable, likely, nicer, preferred, recommended, wanted. OPPOSITES: SEE **objectionable**.

preference noun *a preference for sweet things. What's your preference?* choice, fancy, favouritism, inclination, liking, option, partiality, predilection, wish. **to show a preference for** SEE **choose**.

preferential adjective *preferential treatment.* better, biased, favoured, privileged, showing favouritism, special.

preferment noun SEE **promotion**.

prefix noun LINGUISTIC TERMS: SEE **language**. OPPOSITE: suffix.

prefix verb SEE **precede**.

pregnancy noun gestation.

pregnant adjective 1 *a pregnant woman.* carrying a child, expectant, [*informal*] expecting, [*old-fashioned*] with child. 2 *a pregnant remark.* SEE **meaningful**. **to be pregnant** expect a baby.

WORDS TO DO WITH PREGNANCY: abortion, SEE **birth**, conception, gestation, miscarriage, parturition, premature birth.

prehensile adjective able to grasp [SEE **grasp**].

prehistoric adjective SEE **old**. **prehistoric remains** barrow, dolmen, menhir, standing stones.

prejudice noun *racial prejudice. sexual prejudice.* bias, bigotry, chauvinism, discrimination, dogmatism, fanaticism, favouritism, intolerance, jingoism, narrow-mindedness, partisanship, predisposition, racialism, racism, sexism, unfairness, xenophobia. OPPOSITES: SEE **tolerance**.

prejudice verb 1 *His dirty appearance prejudiced me against him.* bias, incline, predispose, sway. 2 *Publicity might prejudice the result of the trial.* influence, interfere with, prejudge, sway. 3 *Will a criminal record prejudice your chances of a job?* damage, harm, injure, ruin, spoil, undermine.

prejudiced adjective *a prejudiced attitude. prejudiced remarks.* biased, bigoted, chauvinist, discriminatory, illiberal, intolerant, jingoistic, leading (*a leading question*), loaded, narrow-minded, one-sided, partial, partisan, racist, sexist, tendentious, unfair, xenophobic. OPPOSITES: SEE **impartial**. **a prejudiced person** bigot, chauvinist, fanatic, racist, sexist, zealot.

prejudicial adjective *The news-report was prejudicial to the defendant's case.* damaging, detrimental, harmful, injurious, unfavourable.

prelate noun SEE **clergyman**.

preliminary adjective *We'll go ahead if the preliminary survey is encouraging.* earliest, early, experimental, exploratory, first, inaugural, initial, introductory, opening, prefatory, preparatory, qualifying, (*qualifying rounds of a competition*), tentative, trial.

prelude noun *The first match was an exciting prelude to the series.* beginning, [*informal*] curtain-raiser, introduction, opener, opening, overture, preamble, precursor, preface, preliminary, preparation, prologue, start, starter, [*informal*] warm-up. OPPOSITES: SEE **epilogue**.

premature adverb *a premature birth. a premature decision.* abortive, before time, early, hasty, precipitate, [*informal*] previous (*You were a bit previous with your congratulations!*), too early, too soon, untimely. OPPOSITES: SEE **late**.

premeditated adjective *a premeditated crime.* calculated, conscious, considered, deliberate, intended, intentional, planned, pre-arranged, predetermined, pre-planned, wilful. OPPOSITES: unpremeditated, SEE **impulsive**.

premier noun prime minister.

première noun *the première of a play.* SEE **performance**.

premises noun SEE **building**, **property**.

premiss noun SEE **assumption**.

premium noun SEE **payment**.

premonition noun *I had a premonition that something nasty would happen.* anxiety, fear, foreboding, forewarning, indication, intuition, misgiving, omen, portent, presentiment, suspicion, warning, worry.

preoccupied adjective **1** *preoccupied in her work.* absorbed, engaged, engrossed, immersed, interested, involved, obsessed, sunk, taken up, wrapped up. **2** *You look preoccupied: what are you thinking of?* absent-minded, day-dreaming, faraway, inattentive, pensive, rapt, thoughtful.

prep noun SEE **homework**.
   prep school VARIOUS SCHOOLS: SEE **school**.

preparation noun [*often plural*] *preparations for Christmas.* arrangement(s), getting ready, groundwork, making provision, measure(s), organization.

preparatory adjective *a preparatory meeting to fix an agenda.* SEE **preliminary**.

prepare verb **1** *to prepare dinner. to prepare for visitors.* arrange, SEE **cook** verb, devise, [*informal*] do what's necessary, [*informal*] fix up, get ready, make arrangements for, organize, plan, process, set up.
2 *A teacher has to prepare pupils for exams.* brief, coach, educate, equip, instruct, rehearse, teach, train, tutor.
to prepare yourself *Prepare yourself for a shock.* be prepared, be ready, brace yourself, discipline yourself, steel yourself.

prepared adjective **1** *prepared to go anywhere.* able, equipped, fit, ready, set, trained, willing.
OPPOSITES: SEE **unwilling**.
2 *a prepared statement* SEE **pre-arranged**.

preponderance noun SEE **majority**.

preponderate verb SEE **majority (to be in a majority)**.

prepossessing adjective SEE **attractive**.

preposterous adjective SEE **absurd**.

prerequisite adjective *prerequisite qualifications for entry to college.* compulsory, indispensable, mandatory, necessary, prescribed, required, requisite, specified, stipulated.
OPPOSITES: SEE **optional**.

prerequisite noun *It is a prerequisite of entry to the profession that you pass the exams.* condition, essential, necessity, precondition, qualification, requirement, stipulation.

prerogative noun SEE **right** noun.

prescribe noun **1** *The doctor prescribed medicine.* advise, recommend, suggest.

2 *The boss prescribed our duties.* assign, dictate, fix, impose, lay down, ordain, specify, stipulate.

prescription noun SEE **medicine**.

presence noun **1** *The boss requires your presence.* attendance.
2 *I value the presence of friends when I'm sad.* closeness, companionship, company, nearness, propinquity, proximity.
3 *an actor with a commanding presence.* air, appearance, bearing, demeanour, impressiveness, personality.

present adjective **1** *Is everyone present?* at hand, here, in attendance.
2 *Who's the present champion?* contemporary, current, existing, extant.

present noun **1** *We live in the present, not in the past.* [*informal*] here and now, present time [SEE **present** adjective].
2 *She gave me a present.* contribution, donation, gift, gratuity, offering, tip.

present verb **1** *to present prizes.* award, confer, donate, give, hand over, offer.
2 *to present your work.* demonstrate, display, exhibit, reveal, show.
3 *to present a guest.* introduce, make known.
4 *to present a play.* act, bring out, perform, put on.
to present yourself *Present yourself at the office.* appear at, attend, go to, visit.

presentable adjective *a presentable appearance.* acceptable, clean, decent, neat, passable, proper, respectable, satisfactory, tidy, tolerable, worthy.

presentiment noun SEE **foreboding**.

presently adverb shortly, soon.

preservative noun VARIOUS PRESERVATIVES: alcohol, creosote, salt, sugar.

preserve noun **1** *strawberry preserve.* conserve, jam.
2 *a wildlife preserve.* SEE **reserve** noun.

preserve verb **1** *to preserve peace.* defend, guard, maintain, perpetuate, protect, retain, safeguard, secure, sustain, uphold.
2 *to preserve food. to preserve resources.* conserve, keep, lay up, look after, save, stockpile, store.

WAYS TO PRESERVE FOOD: bottle, can, chill, cure, dehydrate, dry, freeze, freeze-dry, irradiate, jam (*to jam fruit*), pickle, refrigerate, salt, tin.

---

3 *to preserve a dead body.* embalm, mummify.
OPPOSITES: SEE **destroy**.

preserved adjective *preserved food*. bottled, canned, chilled, dehydrated, desiccated, dried, freeze-dried, frozen, irradiated, pickled, refrigerated, salted, tinned.
OPPOSITES: SEE **fresh**.

preside verb *to preside at a meeting*. be in charge, officiate, take charge.
to preside over SEE **govern**.

president noun PEOPLE INVOLVED IN GOVERNMENT: SEE **government**.

press noun *the press*. newspapers, magazines, the media.
FORMS OF COMMUNICATION: SEE **communication**.

press verb 1 *to press things together*. compress, condense, cram, crowd, crush, force, gather, [*informal*] jam, shove, squash, squeeze.
2 *to press a pair of trousers*. flatten, iron, smooth.
3 *Press the bell*. apply pressure to [SEE **pressure**], depress, push.
4 *They pressed me to stay*. beg, bully, coerce, constrain, dragoon, entreat, exhort, implore, importune, [*informal*] lean on, persuade, pressure, pressurize, put pressure on, require, urge.

press-gang verb SEE **compel**.

pressing adjective *pressing business*. SEE **urgent**.

pressure noun 1 *the pressure of a load on your back*. burden, force, heaviness, load, might, power, stress, weight.
2 *air pressure in a tyre*. compression.
3 *the pressure of modern life*. adversity, constraint, difficulty, [*informal*] hassle, hurry, oppression, stress, urgency.

pressurize verb *They pressurized me to stay*. SEE **press** verb.

prestige noun *If we lose again, our prestige will suffer*. credit, esteem, fame, glory, good name, honour, importance, [*informal*] kudos, renown, reputation, standing.

prestigious adjective SEE **reputable**.

presume verb 1 *I presume you want something to eat*. assume, believe, conjecture, guess, hypothesize, imagine, infer, postulate, suppose, surmise, [*informal*] take it for granted, think.
2 *She presumed to tell us what to do*. be presumptuous enough [SEE **presumptuous**], dare, make bold, [*informal*] take the liberty, venture.

presumptuous adjective *It was presumptuous of him to take charge*. arrogant, bold, [*informal*] cheeky, conceited, forward, impertinent, impudent, insolent, over-confident, [*informal*] pushy, shameless, unauthorized, unwarranted.

presuppose verb SEE **assume**.

pretence noun *I saw through her pretence*. act, acting, affectation, charade, counterfeiting, deceit, deception, disguise, dissembling, dissimulation, façade, feigning, feint, guise, hoax, insincerity, invention, lying, make-believe, masquerade, pose, posing, posturing, ruse, sham, show, simulation, subterfuge, trickery, wile.

pretend verb 1 *Don't believe him—he was pretending. I pretended to be someone else*. act, affect, behave insincerely, bluff, counterfeit, deceive, disguise, dissemble, dissimulate, fake, feign, fool, hoax, hoodwink, imitate, impersonate, [*informal*] kid, lie, mislead, play a part, perform, pose, posture, profess, purport, put on an act, sham, simulate, take someone in, trick.
2 *Pretend you're on a desert island*. SEE **imagine**.
3 *I don't pretend that I play well*. SEE **claim** verb.

pretentious adjective *a pretentious show of knowledge*. affected, [*informal*] arty, conceited, grandiose, inflated, ostentatious, [*informal*] over the top, SEE **pompous**, showy.
OPPOSITES: SEE **modest**.

preternatural adjective SEE **supernatural**.

pretext noun SEE **excuse** noun.

prettify verb SEE **beautify**.

pretty adjective *pretty decorations*. appealing, attractive, SEE **beautiful**, charming, [*informal*] cute, dainty, delicate, good-looking, lovely, nice, pleasing, [*uncomplimentary*] pretty-pretty.
OPPOSITES: SEE **ugly**.

pretty adverb [*informal*] *That's pretty good!* fairly, moderately, quite, rather, somewhat, tolerably.
OPPOSITES: SEE **very**.

prevail verb 1 *to prevail over an enemy*. SEE **win**.
2 *After a long argument, common sense prevailed*. SEE **predominate**.

prevailing adjective *the prevailing fashion*. accepted, chief, common, current, dominant, familiar, fashionable, general, influential, main, mainstream, normal, ordinary, orthodox, popular, predominant, prevalent, principal, usual, widespread.
OPPOSITES: SEE **unusual**.

prevalent adjective SEE **prevailing**.

prevaricate verb *Stop prevaricating and say what you think.* [*informal*] beat about the bush, be evasive [SEE **evasive**], cavil, dither, equivocate, hedge, [*informal*] hesitate, hum and haw, quibble, [*informal*] shilly-shally, temporize, vacillate, waver.

prevent verb 1 *to prevent a mishap.* anticipate, avert, avoid, foil, forestall, frustrate, [*informal*] head off, [*informal*] help (*I can't help coughing*), inoculate against (*a disease*), intercept, [*informal*] nip in the bud, pre-empt, stave off, take precautions against, thwart, ward off.
OPPOSITES: SEE **encourage**.
2 *to prevent someone from doing something.* check, curb, deter, hamper, hinder, impede, obstruct, save, stop.
OPPOSITES: SEE **help** verb.

preventative, preventive adjectives *preventive measures.* deterrent, obstructive, precautionary, pre-emptive.

preview noun SEE **performance**.

previous adjective *looking back on previous events.* antecedent, earlier, foregoing, former, preceding, prior.
OPPOSITES: SEE **following**.

prey noun *The lion killed its prey.* quarry, victim.

prey verb *to prey on* *Owls prey on small animals.* eat, feed on, hunt, kill.

price noun 1 *a reasonable price to pay.* amount, charge, cost, [*informal*] damage (*What's the damage?*), expenditure, expense, fare, fee, figure, outlay, payment, rate, sum, terms, toll, valuation, value, worth.
to pay the price for *He paid the price for his crime.* SEE **atone**.

priceless adjective 1 *priceless jewels.* costly, dear, expensive, inestimable, invaluable, irreplaceable, precious, [*informal*] pricey, rare, valuable.
2 [*informal*] *a priceless joke.* SEE **funny**.

prick verb 1 *to prick with a pin.* bore into, jab, perforate, pierce, punch, puncture, stab, sting.
2 *to prick someone into action.* SEE **goad**.

prickle noun 1 *a bush with prickles on.* barb, needle, spike, spine, thorn.
2 *The scream sent a prickle down my spine.* itch, pricking sensation, prickling, tingle, tingling.

prickly adjective 1 *a prickly bush.* bristly, scratchy, sharp, spiky, spiny, thorny.
2 [*informal*] *He's in a prickly mood.* SEE **irritable**.

pride noun 1 *Display your work with pride.* delight, dignity, gratification, happiness, honour, pleasure, satisfaction, self-respect, self-satisfaction.

2 *The new car is her pride and joy.* jewel, treasured possession.
3 [*uncomplimentary*] *Pride goes before a fall.* arrogance, being proud [SEE **proud**], [*informal*] big-headedness, conceit, egotism, haughtiness, megalomania, presumption, self-esteem, self-importance, self-love, smugness, snobbery, vainglory, vanity.
OPPOSITES: SEE **humility**.
4 *a pride of lions.* SEE **group** noun.

priest noun SEE **clergyman**, Druid, lama.

prig noun SEE **self-righteous** (**self-righteous person**).

priggish adjective SEE **self-righteous**.

prim adjective *She's too prim to enjoy rude jokes!* demure, fastidious, SEE **narrow-minded**, [*informal*] prissy, proper, prudish, starchy, strait-laced.
OPPOSITES: SEE **broad-minded**.

A number of words, including *primal, primary, prime, primitive,* etc., are related to Latin *primus = first.*

---

primal adjective 1 *primal forms of life.* earliest, early, first, original, primeval, primitive, primordial.
2 *matters of primal importance.* central, chief, fundamental, major, paramount, principal.

primarily adverb basically, chiefly, especially, firstly, fundamentally, generally, mainly, mostly, predominantly, principally.

primary adjective *Our primary aim was to win.* basic, chief, dominant, first, foremost, fundamental, greatest, important, initial, leading, main, major, outstanding, paramount, prime, principal, supreme, top.
primary school OTHER SCHOOLS: SEE **school**.

prime adjective 1 *Our prime aim was to win.* SEE **primary**.
2 *prime beef. prime grade.* best, first-class, select, top.

prime verb *to prime a pump.* get ready, prepare.

primer noun 1 *primer paint.* SEE **paint** noun.
2 *a Latin primer.* textbook.
OTHER BOOKS: SEE **book** noun.

primeval adjective SEE **primal, primitive**.

primitive adjective 1 *primitive tribes.* ancient, barbarian, early, prehistoric, primeval, savage, uncivilized, uncultivated, unsophisticated.
OPPOSITES: SEE **civilized**.

2 *primitive technology.* backward, basic, [*informal*] behind the times, crude, elementary. SEE **obsolete**, rough, rudimentary, simple, undeveloped.
OPPOSITES: SEE **advanced**.

primordial adjective SEE **primal**.

prince, princess OTHER ROYAL RANKS: SEE **royal**.

principal adjective *What's your principal interest in life?* basic, chief, dominant, dominating, first, foremost, fundamental, greatest, highest, important, leading, main, major, outstanding, paramount, pre-eminent, primary, prime, supreme, top.

principal noun *the principal of a college.* SEE **chief** noun.

principality noun SEE **country**.

principle noun **1** *moral principles.* assumption, axiom, belief, doctrine, dogma, ethic, ideal, maxim, precept, proposition, rule, tenet, theory, values.
2 [*plural*] *the basic principles of a subject.* basics, elements, essentials, fundamentals, laws.
3 *a person of principle.* high-mindedness, honesty, honour, ideals, integrity, morality, probity, scruples, standards, uprightness, virtue.

print noun **1** *the print of feet in the sand.* impression, imprint, indentation, mark, stamp.
2 *I like a book with clear print.* characters, fount, lettering, letters, printing, type, typeface.
3 *It's a print, not an original painting.* copy, duplicate, engraving, lithograph, photograph, reproduction.

print verb **1** *to print a book.* issue, publish.
2 *Print your name clearly.* SEE **write**.

prior adjective SEE **previous**.

priority noun *Give priority to traffic on the main road.* greater importance, precedence, right-of-way, seniority.

priory noun abbey, SEE **church**, monastery.

prise, prize verb *to prise off a lid.* force, lever, wrench.

prism noun VARIOUS SHAPES: SEE **shape** noun.

prison noun *sentenced to six months in prison.* Borstal, cell, confinement, custody, detention centre, dungeon, gaol, house of correction, imprisonment, jail, [*American*] penitentiary, reformatory.

prisoner noun captive, convict, detainee, hostage, inmate, internee.

prissy adjective SEE **prim**.

privacy noun *I enjoy the privacy of my own room.* concealment, isolation, quietness, seclusion, secrecy, solitude.

private adjective **1** *private property.* individual, personal, privately owned.
2 *private information.* classified, confidential, intimate, secret.
OPPOSITES: SEE **public** adjective.
3 *a private meeting.* clandestine, closed, restricted.
OPPOSITES: SEE **open** adjective.
4 *a private hideaway.* concealed, hidden, SEE **isolated**, little-known, quiet, secluded, sequestered, solitary, unknown.
OPPOSITES: SEE **popular**.

privation noun SEE **poverty**.

privilege noun *Club members enjoy special privileges.* advantage, benefit, concession, entitlement, licence, right.

privileged adjective *The boss has a privileged position.* advantaged, élite, favoured, powerful, special, superior.
OPPOSITES: SEE **oppressed**.

prize noun *a prize for coming first.* award, jackpot, reward, trophy, winnings.

prize verb **1** *Which of your possessions do you prize most highly?* appreciate, approve of, cherish, esteem, hold dear, like, rate, regard, revere, treasure, value.
OPPOSITES: SEE **disregard**.
2 SEE **prise**.

probable adjective *the probable result.* believable, credible, expected, feasible, likely, plausible, possible, predictable, presumed.
OPPOSITES: SEE **improbable**.

probate noun LEGAL TERMS: SEE **law**.

probation noun **1** *New employees are on probation for three months.* apprenticeship, test, trial period.
2 *The magistrate put her on probation.*
VARIOUS PUNISHMENTS: SEE **punishment**.

probationer noun apprentice, beginner, inexperienced worker, learner, novice.

probe noun *a probe into a smuggling racket.* examination, inquiry, investigation, research, scrutiny, study.

probe verb **1** *to probe a wound.* poke, prod.
2 *to probe the depths of the sea.* SEE **explore**, penetrate, plumb (*the depths*).
3 *to probe a problem.* examine, go into, inquire into, investigate, look into, research into, scrutinize, study.

probity noun SEE **honesty**.

problem noun **1** *an intriguing problem to solve.* brainteaser, conundrum, enigma, mystery, poser, puzzle, question, riddle.

2 *a worrying problem to overcome.* burden, complication, difficulty, dilemma, dispute, [*informal*] headache, predicament, quandary, set-back, snag, trouble, worry.

problematic, problematical adjectives *There's no easy solution to such a problematical issue.* complicated, controversial, debatable, difficult, enigmatic, hard to deal with, intractable, puzzling, taxing, worrying.
OPPOSITES: SEE **straightforward**.

proboscis noun SEE **snout**.

procedure noun *What's the procedure for getting a licence?* course of action, formula, method, [*Latin*] modus operandi, plan of action, practice, process, routine, scheme, strategy, system, technique, way.

proceed verb **1** *After a rest, we proceeded.* advance, carry on, continue, follow, go ahead, go on, make progress, move forward, [*informal*] press on, progress.
2 *Great things proceed from small beginnings.* arise, originate, SEE **result** verb.

proceedings noun **1** *legal proceedings.* action, lawsuit.
2 *The secretary writes up the proceedings of the meeting.* [*informal*] doings, minutes, records, report, transactions.
3 [*informal*] *On sports day, a storm ended proceedings.* events, [*informal*] goings-on, happenings, matters, things.

proceeds *proceeds from an OXFAM collection.* earnings, income, SEE **money**, profit, receipts, revenue, takings.

process noun **1** *a manufacturing process.* method, operation, SEE **procedure**, system, technique.
2 *the process of growing up.* course, development, evolution, experience, progression.

process verb **1** *to process crude oil.* alter, change, convert, deal with, make usable, prepare, refine, transform, treat.
2 [*informal*] *A cavalcade processed through town.* SEE **parade** verb.

procession noun cavalcade, column, cortège, line, march, motorcade, pageant, parade.

proclaim verb **1** *to proclaim something publicly.* announce, assert, declare, give out, make known, profess, pronounce.
2 *to proclaim a public holiday.* SEE **decree** verb.

proclivity noun SEE **tendency**.

procrastinate verb *Stop procrastinating and do something.* be indecisive, defer a decision, delay, [*informal*] dilly-dally,

dither, [*informal*] drag your feet, [*informal*] hum and haw, [*informal*] play for time, postpone, prevaricate, put things off, [*informal*] shilly-shally, stall, temporize.

procreate verb SEE **reproduce**.

proctor noun SEE **official** noun.

procurable adjective SEE **available**.

procure verb SEE **obtain**.

prod verb *to prod with a stick.* dig, goad, SEE **hit** verb, jab, nudge, poke, push, urge on.

prodigal adjective SEE **wasteful**.

prodigious adjective SEE **amazing**.

prodigy noun *a child prodigy.* curiosity, freak, genius, marvel, phenomenon, rarity, sensation, talent, wonder.

produce noun *garden produce.* crop, harvest, output, products, yield.

produce verb **1** *Can you produce evidence?* advance, bring out, disclose, display, exhibit, furnish, offer, present, put forward, reveal, show, supply, throw up.
2 *A factory produces goods.* Farmers produce crops. cause, compose, conjure up, construct, create, cultivate, develop, fabricate, form, generate, give rise to, grow, invent, make, manufacture, originate, provoke, result in, think up, turn out, yield.
3 *to produce children.* bear, beget, breed, give birth to, raise, rear.
4 *to produce a play.* direct.

producer, production nouns SEE **theatre**.

product noun **1** *What kind of product does this factory make?* artefact, commodity, end-product, goods, merchandise, output, produce, production.
2 *Our plan was the product of much thought.* consequence, effect, fruit, outcome, result, upshot.

productive adjective **1** *productive work.* beneficial, busy, constructive, creative, effective, efficient, gainful (*gainful employment*), profitable, profitmaking, rewarding, useful, valuable, worthwhile.
2 *a productive garden.* fertile, fruitful, lush, prolific.
OPPOSITES: SEE **unproductive**.

profane adjective *profane language.* SEE **blasphemous**.

profess verb **1** *He professed to be the gas man.* allege, claim, make out, pretend, purport.
2 *to profess your faith.* SEE **declare**.

profession noun **1** *Nursing is a worthwhile profession.* business, calling, career, employment, job, line of work, occupation, trade, vocation, work.

2 *a profession of faith.* acknowledgement, confession, declaration, statement, testimony.

professional adjective **1** *professional advice.* competent, efficient, expert, paid, proficient, qualified, skilled, trained.
OPPOSITES: SEE **amateur**.
2 *a professional attitude.* conscientious, dutiful, responsible.
OPPOSITES: SEE **unprofessional**.

professor noun SEE **lecturer**.

proffer verb SEE **offer** verb.

proficient adjective *a proficient worker.* SEE **competent**.

profile noun **1** *the profile of a person's face.* outline, SEE **picture** noun, shape, side view, silhouette.
2 *a profile of a famous personality.* account, biography, [*Latin*] curriculum vitae, sketch, study.

profit noun *a profit on your investment.* advantage, benefit, excess, gain, interest, SEE **money**, return, surplus, yield.

profit verb **1** *It won't profit anyone to get angry.* benefit, further the interests of, SEE **help** verb, pay (*It doesn't pay to get angry*), serve.
2 *Did you profit from the sale?* earn money, gain, make money, receive a profit [SEE **profit** noun].
to profit by or **from** *You can sometimes profit from other people's mistakes.* capitalize on, [*informal*] cash in on, exploit, take advantage of, use.

profitable adjective *profitable employment.* advantageous, beneficial, commercial, fruitful, gainful, lucrative, moneymaking, paying, productive, profitmaking, remunerative, rewarding, useful, valuable, worthwhile.
OPPOSITES: SEE **unprofitable**.

profiteering noun *Profiteering in a time of shortage is wrong.* exploitation, extortion, overcharging.

profligate adjective SEE **wasteful**.

profound adjective **1** *profound sympathy.* deep, heartfelt, intense, sincere.
OPPOSITES: SEE **insincere**.
2 *a profound discussion.* abstruse, erudite, imponderable, intellectual, knowledgeable, learned, philosophical, serious, thoughtful, wise.
OPPOSITES: SEE **facile**.

profuse adjective SEE **plentiful**.

progenitor noun SEE **ancestor**.

progeny noun SEE **offspring**.

prognosis, prognostication nouns SEE **forecast** noun.

program noun COMPUTER TERMS: SEE **computer**.

programme noun **1** *a published programme of events.* agenda, [*informal*] line-up, listing, plan, schedule, timetable.
2 *a television programme.* broadcast, performance, production, transmission.

progress noun **1** *scientific progress.* advance, breakthrough, development, gain, headway, improvement, march (*the march of time*), movement, progression, [*informal*] step forward.
2 *I traced their progress on a map.* journey, route, travels, way.

progress verb *Our plans are progressing.* advance, [*informal*] come on, develop, [*informal*] forge ahead, improve, make progress [SEE **progress** noun], move forward, proceed, prosper.
OPPOSITES: SEE **regress**.

progression noun *a progression of events.* chain, row, sequence, series, string, succession.

progressive adjective **1** *a progressive increase in prices.* accelerating, continuing, continuous, escalating, growing, increasing, ongoing, steady.
OPPOSITES: SEE **erratic**.
2 *progressive ideas.* advanced, avant-garde, contemporary, enterprising, forward-looking, [*informal*] go-ahead, modernistic, radical, revolutionary, up-to-date.
OPPOSITES: SEE **conservative** adjective.

prohibit verb *to prohibit smoking. to prohibit non-members.* ban, bar, censor, [*informal*] cut out, debar, disallow, exclude, forbid, hinder, [*formal*] interdict, make illegal, outlaw, place an embargo on, preclude, prevent, proscribe, restrict, rule out, shut out, stop, veto.
OPPOSITES: SEE **allow**.

prohibitive adjective *prohibitive prices.* discouraging, excessive, SEE **exorbitant**, impossible, out of reach, unreasonable, unthinkable.

project noun **1** *a project to build a bypass.* design, enterprise, idea, plan, proposal, scheme, undertaking, venture.
2 *a history project.* activity, assignment, piece of research, piece of work, task.

project verb **1** *A narrow ledge projects from the cliff.* beetle, bulge, extend, jut out, overhang, protrude, stand out, stick out.
2 *The lighthouse projects a strong beam.* cast, flash, shine, throw out.
3 *Can you project what your profits will be next year?* SEE **estimate** verb.

projectile noun SEE **missile**.

projector noun AUDIO-VISUAL AIDS: SEE audio-visual.

proletariat noun working class.
OPPOSITE: bourgeoisie.
TERMS FOR SOCIAL CLASSES: SEE **class** noun.

proliferate verb SEE **multiply**.

prolific adjective *prolific crops. a prolific writer.* abundant, copious, fertile, fruitful, productive, profuse, rich.
OPPOSITES: SEE **unproductive**.

prologue noun SEE **prelude**.

prolong verb *The game was prolonged by injuries.* delay, draw out, extend, increase, lengthen, make longer, protract, [*informal*] spin out, stretch out.
OPPOSITES: SEE **shorten**.

prolonged adjective SEE **long** adjective.

promenade noun SEE **walk** noun.

prominent adjective 1 *prominent teeth.* bulging, jutting out, large, projecting, protruding, sticking out.
2 *a prominent landmark.* conspicuous, eye-catching, noticeable, obtrusive, obvious, pronounced, salient, significant.
OPPOSITES: SEE **inconspicuous**.
3 *a prominent politician.* celebrated, distinguished, eminent, familiar, famous, foremost, important, leading, major, much-publicized, noted, outstanding, recognizable, renowned, well-known.
OPPOSITES: SEE **unknown**.

promiscuous adjective *promiscuous sexual relationships.* casual, haphazard, SEE immoral, indiscriminate, random, undiscriminating.
OPPOSITES: SEE **moral** adjective.

promise noun 1 *We had promises of help from many people.* assurance, commitment, [*formal*] covenant, guarantee, oath, pledge, undertaking, vow, word, word of honour.
2 *The young actor shows promise.* latent ability, potential, promising qualities [SEE **promising**], talent.

promise verb 1 *You promised me that you'd pay. She promised to come.* agree, assure, consent, contract, engage, give a promise [SEE **promise** noun], give your word, guarantee, pledge, swear, take an oath, undertake, vow.
2 *The clouds promise rain.* augur, forebode, indicate, presage, prophesy, suggest.

promising adjective *a promising debut. a promising newcomer.* auspicious, budding, encouraging, hopeful, likely, propitious, talented, [*informal*] up-and-coming.

promontory noun cape, foreland, headland, peninsula, point, projection, ridge, spit, spur.

promote verb 1 *to promote someone to a higher rank.* advance, elevate, exalt, give promotion [SEE **promotion**], move up, prefer, raise, upgrade.
2 *A local firm promoted our festival.* back, boost, encourage, help, sponsor, support.
3 *to promote a new product.* advertise, make known, market, [*informal*] plug, popularize, publicize, [*informal*] push, sell.

promoter noun backer, sponsor.

promotion noun 1 *promotion to a higher rank.* advancement, elevation, preferment, rise, upgrading.
2 *the promotion of a new product.* advertising, backing, encouragement, marketing, publicity, selling.

prompt adjective *a prompt reply.* eager, efficient, immediate, instantaneous, on time, punctual, SEE **quick**, unhesitating, willing.
OPPOSITES: SEE **belated**.

prompt verb *If you forget what to say, I'll prompt you.* advise, egg on, encourage, help, incite, inspire, jog the memory, motivate, nudge, persuade, prod, provoke, remind, spur, stimulate, urge.

prone adjective 1 *lying prone on the floor.* face down, on your front, prostrate.
OPPOSITES: SEE **supine**.
2 *She's prone to exaggerate. I'm prone to colds.* apt, disposed, given, inclined, liable, likely, predisposed, susceptible, vulnerable.
OPPOSITES: SEE **immune**.

prong noun *the prong of a fork.* point, spike, spur, tine.

pronounce verb 1 *Try to pronounce the words clearly.* articulate, aspirate, enunciate, say, sound, speak, utter.
2 *The doctor pronounced me fit again.* announce, assert, declare, decree, judge, make known, proclaim.

pronounced adjective *a pronounced limp.* clear, conspicuous, decided, definite, distinct, evident, marked, noticeable, obvious, prominent, striking, unmistakable.

pronunciation noun *The announcer's pronunciation is very clear.* accent, articulation, diction, elocution, enunciation, inflection, intonation.

proof noun *proof of guilt.* confirmation, corroboration, demonstration, evidence, facts, grounds, testimony, verification.

prop noun *a prop to lean on.* buttress, crutch, post, strut, support.

prop verb *to prop a bike against a wall.* lean, rest, stand.
to prop up *to prop up a wall.* buttress, hold up, reinforce, shore up, support.

propaganda noun *government propaganda.* advertising, brain-washing, indoctrination, persuasion, publicity.

propagate verb 1 *to propagate lies.* disseminate, generate, multiply, pass on, produce, proliferate, spread, transmit.
2 *to propagate plants.* breed, grow from seed, increase, layer, reproduce, sow, take cuttings.

propel verb *The crowd propelled me forward. The spacecraft was propelled by a rocket.* drive, force, impel, launch, move, pitchfork (*They pitchforked me into it*), push, send, shoot, spur, thrust, urge.

propeller noun rotor, screw, vane.
PARTS OF AN AIRCRAFT: SEE **aircraft**.

propensity noun SEE **tendency**.

proper adjective 1 *proper language. proper manners.* acceptable, becoming, decent, decorous, delicate, dignified, fitting, formal, genteel, gentlemanly, grave, in good taste, ladylike, modest, orthodox, polite, respectable, sedate, seemly, serious, solemn, suitable, tactful, tasteful.
2 *the proper thing to do. a proper price.* advisable, appropriate, conventional, correct, deserved, fair, fitting, just, lawful, legal, right, usual, valid.
OPPOSITES: SEE **improper**.

property noun 1 *I don't own much property.* assets, belongings, [*formal*] chattels, effects, fortune, goods, patrimony, possessions, riches, wealth.
2 *Keep off! Private property.* buildings, estate, land, premises.
3 *This chemical has unusual properties.* attribute, characteristic, feature, idiosyncrasy, peculiarity, quality, trait.

Notice the difference in spelling between *prophecy* (noun) and *prophesy* (verb).

---

prophecy noun *a prophecy that came true.* augury, forecast, prediction, prognosis, prognostication.

prophesy verb *She prophesied the tragic outcome.* forecast, foresee, foretell, predict, prognosticate.

prophet noun clairvoyant, forecaster, fortune-teller, oracle, seer, soothsayer.

prophetic adjective *a prophetic warning.* apocalyptic, far-seeing, oracular, prophesying.

propinquity noun SEE **proximity**.

propitiate verb SEE **pacify**.

propitious adjective SEE **favourable**.

proportion noun 1 *the proportion of girls to boys in a class.* balance, ratio.
2 *A large proportion of the audience cheered.* fraction, part, piece, quota, section, share.
proportions *a gentleman of large proportions.* dimensions, measurements, size.

proportionate adjective *The cost of the ticket is proportionate to the distance you travel.* commensurate, comparable, corresponding, in proportion, proportional, relative.
OPPOSITES: SEE **disproportionate**.

proposal noun *a proposal to build a supermarket.* bid, motion [= *a proposal made at a meeting*], offer, plan, project, proposition, recommendation, scheme, suggestion.

propose verb 1 *I proposed a change in the rules.* ask for, present, put forward, recommend, submit, suggest.
2 *Our friends propose to visit us.* aim, have in mind, intend, mean, offer, plan, purpose.
3 *They proposed me as a candidate in the election.* nominate, put up.
to propose marriage [*old-fashioned*] ask for someone's hand, get engaged, [*informal*] pop the question.

proposition noun 1 *I don't accept the proposition that the moon is made of cheese.* SEE **statement**.
2 *I made a proposition that we should adjourn the meeting.* SEE **proposal**.

propound verb *to propound a theory.* SEE **suggest**.

proprietor noun *the proprietor of a shop.* boss, manager, owner.

propriety noun *The sensitive matter was handled with great propriety.* appropriateness, correctness, decency, decorum, delicacy, etiquette, good manners, politeness, seemliness, sensitivity, tact.
OPPOSITES: SEE **impropriety**.

prorogue verb SEE **adjourn**.

prosaic adjective *a prosaic statement.* clear, dry, dull, hackneyed, matter-of-fact, ordinary, pedestrian, plain, prosy, simple, straightforward, trite, unimaginative, uninspired, uninspiring, unvarnished.
OPPOSITES: SEE **poetic**.

proscenium noun SEE **stage** noun.

proscribe verb SEE **prohibit**.

prose noun KINDS OF WRITING: SEE **writing**.

prosecute verb *They prosecuted him for dangerous driving.* accuse, bring to trial, charge, institute legal proceedings against, prefer charges against, sue, take legal proceedings against.
LEGAL TERMS: SEE **law**.

prosecution, prosecutor nouns
LEGAL TERMS: SEE **law**.

proselytize verb SEE **preach**.

prosody noun *the prosody of a poem.* metre, rhythm, scansion, verse form.
VARIOUS VERSE FORMS: SEE **verse**.

prospect noun 1 *a lovely prospect from the top of the hill.* landscape, outlook, panorama, perspective, scene, sight, spectacle, view, vista.
2 *the prospect of a change in the weather.* chance, expectation, hope, likelihood, possibility, probability, promise.

prospect verb *to prospect for gold.* explore, quest, search, survey.

prospective adjective *prospective changes. a prospective employee.* anticipated, coming, expected, forthcoming, future, imminent, intended, likely, negotiable, possible, potential, probable.

prospectus noun *a college prospectus.* brochure, catalogue, leaflet, manifesto, pamphlet, programme, scheme, syllabus.

prosper verb *to prosper in business.* become prosperous [SEE **prosperous**], be successful, [*informal*] boom, burgeon, do well, flourish, [*informal*] get on, [*informal*] go from strength to strength, grow, make good, progress, strengthen, succeed, thrive.
OPPOSITES: SEE **fail**.

prosperity noun *Will this prosperity last?* affluence, [*informal*] bonanza, [*informal*] boom, growth, plenty, profitability, success, wealth.

prosperous adjective *a prosperous business.* affluent, [*informal*] booming, buoyant, flourishing, moneymaking, profitable, prospering, rich, successful, thriving, wealthy, well-off, well-to-do.
OPPOSITES: SEE **unsuccessful**.

prostitute noun [*old-fashioned*] bawd, call-girl, [*informal*] courtesan, [*old-fashioned*] harlot, [*old-fashioned*] strumpet, [*informal*] tart, whore.

prostitute verb *to prostitute your talents.* cheapen, debase, devalue, misuse.

prostrate adjective 1 *lying prostrate.* SEE **prone**.
2 *prostrate with grief.* SEE **overcome** adjective.

prostrate verb **to prostrate yourself** SEE **grovel**.

prosy adjective SEE **prosaic**.

protagonist noun *the protagonist of a play.* chief actor, contender, contestant, hero, heroine, leading figure, principal.

protect verb 1 *to protect someone from danger.* defend, escort, guard, harbour, insulate, keep safe, preserve, provide cover (for), safeguard, screen, secure, shield.
2 *Parents protect their young.* care for, cherish, look after, mind, support, watch over.
OPPOSITES: SEE **abandon**.

protection noun *protection from the weather. protection against enemies.* barrier, bulwark, cloak, cover, defence, guard, guardianship, insulation, preservation, safety, screen, security, shelter, shield, tutelage.

protective adjective 1 *a protective cover.* defensive, insulating, protecting, sheltering, shielding.
2 *protective parents.* careful, jealous, paternalistic, possessive, solicitous, watchful.

protector noun benefactor, bodyguard, champion, defender, guard, guardian, patron.

protectorate noun SEE **country**.

protégé noun *The professor took a keen interest in the work of her protégé.* discovery, pupil, student.

protest noun 1 *We made a protest against the referee's decision.* complaint, cry of disapproval, objection, outcry, protestation, remonstrance.
2 *They held a big protest in the square.* [*informal*] demo, demonstration, march, rally.

protest verb 1 *We protested against his decision.* argue, complain, cry out, expostulate, express disapproval, fulminate, grouse, grumble, make a protest [SEE **protest** noun], moan, object, remonstrate.
2 *A big crowd protested in the square.* demonstrate, [*informal*] hold a demo, march.
3 *He protested that he was innocent.* SEE **declare**.

protestation noun SEE **declaration**.

protocol noun 1 *We must observe the correct protocol.* SEE **etiquette**.
2 *The statesmen signed a protocol.* SEE **agreement**.

prototype noun SEE **model** noun.

protracted adjective SEE **long** adjective.

protrude verb *His stomach protrudes above his waistband.* be protruding [SEE **protruding**], bulge, jut out, poke out, project, stand out, stick out, swell.

protruding adjective *a protruding stomach.* bulbous, bulging, projecting, prominent, protuberant, swollen.

protuberant adjective SEE **protruding**.

proud adjective 1 *proud of his new car.* appreciative, delighted (with), happy (with), pleased (with), satisfied (with). 2 *a proud bearing.* dignified, honourable, independent, self-respecting. 3 *He's too proud to mix with the likes of us!* arrogant, boastful, bumptious, [*informal*] cocky, conceited, disdainful, egotistical, grand, haughty, [*informal*] high and mighty, lordly, self-important, snobbish, [*informal*] snooty, [*informal*] stuck-up, [*informal*] toffee-nosed, vain.
OPPOSITES: SEE **humble** adjective.

provable adjective demonstrable, verifiable.

prove verb *to prove a theory.* ascertain, attest, authenticate, [*informal*] bear out, confirm, corroborate, demonstrate, establish, explain, justify, show to be true, substantiate, test, verify.
OPPOSITES: SEE **disprove**.

proven adjective *a player of proven ability.* accepted, authenticated, certified, checked, confirmed, corroborated, demonstrated, established, proved, reliable, tested, tried, trustworthy, undoubted, unquestionable, valid, verified.
OPPOSITES: SEE **doubtful**.

provenance noun SEE **origin**.

provender noun SEE **food**.

proverb noun SEE **saying**.

proverbial adjective *a proverbial remark.* conventional, clichéd, customary, famous, legendary, traditional, well-known.

provide verb *We provide food and clothing for our families.* afford, allot, allow, arrange for, cater, contribute, donate, endow, equip, [*informal*] fork out, furnish, give, grant, lay on, lend, make provision, produce, spare, supply.

providence noun SEE **fate**.

provident adjective SEE **thrifty**.

providential adjective SEE **lucky**.

province noun SEE **district**.

provincial adjective *a provincial area. provincial government.* local, regional.
OPPOSITES: SEE **national** adjective.
2 [*uncomplimentary*] *City dwellers think country folk have provincial attitudes.*

bucolic, insular, narrow-minded, parochial, rural, rustic, small-minded, unsophisticated.
OPPOSITES: SEE **cosmopolitan**.

provisional adjective *a provisional agreement.* conditional, interim, stop-gap, temporary, tentative.
OPPOSITES: SEE **permanent**.

provisions noun food, foodstuff, groceries, rations, requirements, stores, subsistence, supplies.

proviso noun SEE **condition**.

provocation noun *The dog won't attack without provocation.* [*informal*] aggravation, cause, challenge, grievance, grounds, incitement, inducement, justification, motivation, reason, taunts, teasing.

provoke verb 1 *If you provoke the dog, it'll bite.* [*informal*] aggravate, anger, annoy, arouse, encourage, enrage, exasperate, goad, incense, incite, inflame, infuriate, insult, irk, irritate, offend, pique, rile, tease, torment, upset, urge on, vex, worry.
OPPOSITES: SEE **pacify**.
2 *His jokes provoked a lot of laughter.* arouse, bring about, cause, elicit, excite, generate, give rise to, induce, inspire, kindle, occasion, produce, promote, prompt, spark off, stimulate, stir up.

prow noun *the prow of a ship.* bow, front.

prowess noun 1 *prowess in battle.* bravery, courage, daring, heroism, spirit, valour.
2 *The dancers showed off their prowess.* ability, accomplishment, adroitness, aptitude, cleverness, competence, excellence, expertise, genius, skill, talent.

prowl verb *to prowl about in the dark.* creep, roam, slink, sneak, steal, SEE **walk** verb.

prowler noun intruder.

proximity noun 1 *We objected to the proximity of the pig-farm.* closeness, nearness, propinquity.
2 *There are several shops in the proximity.* neighbourhood.

prude noun SEE **puritan**.

prudent adjective *It's prudent to keep money in a bank.* advisable, careful, cautious, discreet, economical, far-sighted, politic, proper, sensible, shrewd, thoughtful, thrifty, wise.
OPPOSITES: SEE **unwise**.

prudish adjective *a prudish attitude to sex.* easily shocked, illiberal, intolerant, narrow-minded, old-fashioned, priggish, prim, [*informal*] prissy, proper,

puritanical, shockable, strait-laced, strict.
OPPOSITES: SEE **open-minded**.

prune verb SEE **cut** verb, trim.

pry verb *Don't pry into my affairs.* be curious, be inquisitive, delve, [*informal*] ferret, interfere, meddle, [*informal*] nose about, peer rudely, poke about, [*informal*] snoop, [*informal*] stick your nose in.

prying adjective *We pulled down the blind to keep out prying eyes.* curious, impertinent, inquisitive, interfering, meddlesome, [*informal*] nosy, [*informal*] snooping, spying.
OPPOSITES: SEE **discreet**.

The prefix *pseudo-* is related to Greek *pseudes* = *false*.

---

pseudonym noun alias, assumed name, false name, [*French*] nom de plume, penname, sobriquet.

A number of English words like *psyche, psychiatry, psychic, psychology* are related to Greek *psukhe* = *breath, life, soul.*

---

psyche noun SEE **mind** noun, **soul**.

psychiatrist noun OTHER MEDICAL PRACTITIONERS: SEE **medicine**.

psychic adjective *Some people are said to have psychic powers.* clairvoyant, extrasensory, mystic, occult, psychical, supernatural, telepathic.

psychological adjective *a psychological condition.* emotional, mental, subconscious, subjective.
OPPOSITES: SEE **physiological**.

psychopath noun SEE **madman**.

pub noun bar, [*old-fashioned*] hostelry, inn, [*informal*] local, public house, saloon, tavern.

puberty noun *You reach puberty in your teens.* adolescence, growing-up, sexual maturity.

public adjective *a public place.* public knowledge. accessible, common, communal, familiar, general, known, national, open, popular, shared, unconcealed, universal, unrestricted, well-known.
OPPOSITES: SEE **private**.
public house SEE **pub**.
public school VARIOUS SCHOOLS: SEE **school**.

public noun *the public.* citizens, the community, the country, the nation, people, the populace, society, voters.

publication noun 1 *the publication of a book.* appearance, issuing, printing, production.
2 *the publication of secret information.* announcement, broadcasting, disclosure, dissemination, promulgation, reporting.
3 *I bought his latest publication.* KINDS OF PUBLICATION: SEE **book** noun, **magazine**, **recording**.

publicity noun 1 *Did you see the publicity for our play?* SEE **advertisement**.
2 *Famous people don't always enjoy publicity.* attention, [*informal*] ballyhoo, fame, limelight, notoriety.

publicize verb SEE **advertise**.

public-spirited adjective SEE **unselfish**.

publish verb 1 *to publish a book or magazine.* bring out, circulate, issue, print, produce, release.
2 *to publish secrets.* announce, broadcast, communicate, declare, disclose, disseminate, divulge, [*informal*] leak, make known, make public, proclaim, promulgate, publicize, report, reveal, spread.

pucker verb *to pucker your lips.* compress, crease, purse, screw up, tighten, wrinkle.

puckish adjective SEE **mischievous**.

pudding noun [*informal*] afters, dessert, sweet.
VARIOUS FOODS: SEE **food**.

puddle noun pool.

pudenda plural noun SEE **genitals**.

pudgy adjective SEE **plump**.

puerile adjective SEE **childish**.

puff noun 1 *a puff of wind.* blast, breath, draught, flurry, gust.
2 *a puff of smoke.* cloud, whiff.

puff verb 1 *By the end of the race I was puffing.* blow, breathe heavily, gasp, pant, wheeze.
2 *The sails puffed out.* become inflated, billow, distend, rise, swell.

puffy adjective *puffy eyes.* SEE **swollen**.

pugilist noun SEE **fighter**.

pugnacious adjective *a pugnacious fighter.* aggressive, bellicose, belligerent, combative, excitable, hostile, hot-tempered, militant, quarrelsome, warlike.
OPPOSITES: SEE **placid**.

puke verb SEE **vomit**.

pull verb 1 *A locomotive pulls a train.* drag, draw, haul, lug, tow, trail.
OPPOSITES: SEE **push**.
2 *You nearly pulled my arm off!* jerk, tug, pluck, rip, wrench.
3 *The dentist pulled a tooth.* extract, pull out, remove, take out.
to pull someone's leg SEE **tease**.
to pull out SEE **withdraw**.
to pull round, to pull through SEE **recover**.
to pull together SEE **co-operate**.
to pull up SEE **halt** verb.

pulp noun *fruit pulp. squashed to a pulp.* mash, mush, paste, purée.

pulp verb *to pulp food.* crush, liquidize, mash, pound, pulverize, purée, smash, squash.

pulpit noun SEE **church**.

pulpy adjective SEE **soft**.

pulsar noun ASTRONOMICAL TERMS: SEE **astronomy**.

pulsate verb *A regular rhythm pulsated in our ears.* beat, drum, oscillate, palpitate, quiver, throb, tick, vibrate.

pulse noun *a regular pulse.* beat, drumming, oscillation, pulsation, rhythm, throb, ticking, vibration.

pulverize verb SEE **powder** verb.

pumice noun lava.
VARIOUS ROCKS: SEE **rock** noun.

pummel verb batter, beat, SEE **hit** verb, pound, thump.

pump verb *The fire brigade pumped water out of the cellar.* drain, draw off, empty, force, raise, siphon.

pun noun double meaning, SEE **joke** noun.

punch noun *hot punch.* VARIOUS DRINKS: SEE **drink** noun.

punch verb 1 *to punch someone on the nose.* beat, clout, cuff, SEE **hit** verb, jab, poke, prod, slog, strike, thump.
2 *to punch a hole.* SEE **pierce**.

punch-up noun SEE **fight** noun.

punctilious adjective SEE **conscientious**.

punctual adjective *The bus is punctual today.* in good time, [*informal*] on the dot, on time, prompt.
OPPOSITES: SEE **unpunctual**.

punctuate verb 1 *to punctuate a piece of writing.* insert punctuation [SEE **punctuation**].
2 *His speech was punctuated by cat-calls.* SEE **interrupt**.

punctuation noun PUNCTUATION MARKS: accent, apostrophe, asterisk, bracket, caret, cedilla, colon, comma, dash, exclamation mark, full stop, hyphen, question mark, quotation marks, semicolon, speech marks.

puncture noun 1 *a puncture in a tyre.* burst, hole, leak, pin-prick, rupture.
2 *We had a puncture on the way home.* blow-out, burst tyre, [*informal*] flat, flat tyre.

puncture verb *A nail punctured my tyre.* deflate, let down, SEE **pierce**, rupture.

pundit noun SEE **expert** noun.

pungent adjective SEE **smelling**.

punish verb *to punish someone for wrongdoing.* chasten, chastise, correct, discipline, exact retribution (from), impose or inflict punishment on [SEE **punishment**], [*informal*] make an example of, pay back, penalize, [*informal*] teach (someone) a lesson.

WAYS TO PUNISH PEOPLE: beat, cane, detain, SEE **execute**, exile, fine, flog, gaol or jail, give a hiding (to), imprison, [*old-fashioned*] keelhaul, pillory, put in the stocks, put on probation, scourge, send to prison, spank, torture, whip.

punishable adjective *a punishable offence.* actionable, criminal, illegal.

punishing adjective *a punishing session of training.* SEE **strenuous**.

punishment noun chastisement, correction, discipline, penalty, retribution, revenge.
RELATED ADJECTIVE: penal.

VARIOUS PUNISHMENTS: beating, Borstal, the cane, capital punishment, confiscation, corporal punishment, detention, execution [SEE **execute**], fine, flogging, forfeit, gaol or jail, [*informal*] a hiding, imposition, pillory, prison, probation, spanking, the stocks, torture, whipping.

punitive adjective *They took punitive measures against the whole gang.* penal, retaliatory, revengeful, vindictive.

punt verb *to punt a ball.* boot, SEE **hit** verb, kick.

punter noun better, gambler, speculator.

puny adjective *a puny child.* SEE **feeble**.

pup noun SEE **dog** noun.

pupa noun chrysalis.

pupil noun 1 *a teacher's pupil.* discipline, follower, learner, protégé, scholar, schoolboy, schoolchild, schoolgirl, student.

2 *the pupil of your eye.* PARTS OF THE EYE: SEE **eye** noun.

puppet noun doll, dummy, glove-puppet, marionette.

puppy noun SEE **dog** noun.

purchase noun **1** *I put my purchases in a bag.* acquisition, [*informal*] buy (*That was a good buy*), investment.
2 *I can't get enough purchase to prise this lid off.* grasp, hold, leverage.

purchase verb *What can you purchase for £1?* acquire, buy, get, invest in, obtain, pay for, procure, secure.

pure adjective **1** *pure alcohol. pure gold.* authentic, genuine, neat, real, straight, unadulterated, unalloyed, undiluted.
2 *pure food.* eatable, germ-free, hygienic, natural, pasteurized, uncontaminated, untainted, wholesome.
3 *pure water.* clean, clear, distilled, drinkable, fresh, potable, sterile, unpolluted.
OPPOSITES: SEE **impure**.
4 *a pure person.* chaste, good, innocent, irreproachable, modest, moral, sinless, stainless, virginal, virtuous.
OPPOSITES: SEE **immoral**.
5 *pure nonsense. pure genius.* absolute, complete, perfect, sheer, total, true, unmitigated, utter.
6 *pure science.* abstract, theoretical.
OPPOSITES: SEE **applied**.

purée noun, verb SEE **pulp** noun, verb.

purgative noun aperient, enema, laxative.

purgatory noun SEE **torment** noun.

purge verb **1** *to purge your bowels.* clean out, cleanse, empty, purify.
2 *to purge spies from the government.* eradicate, expel, get rid of, remove, root out.

purify verb *to purify water.* clarify, clean, disinfect, distil, filter, make pure [SEE **pure**], refine, sterilize.

puritan noun [*uncomplimentary*] killjoy, moralist, [*uncomplimentary*] prude, puritanical person [SEE **puritanical**], zealot.
OPPOSITES: SEE **hedonist**.

puritanical adjective *a puritanical dislike of self-indulgence.* ascetic, austere, moralistic, narrow-minded, prim, prudish, self-denying, self-disciplined, severe, strait-laced, strict, temperate, unbending.
OPPOSITES: SEE **hedonistic**.

purlieus noun SEE **outskirts**.

purloin verb SEE **steal**.

purport noun *the purport of a message.* SEE **meaning**.

purport verb *She purports to represent the whole group.* SEE **pretend**.

purpose noun **1** *a particular purpose in mind.* aim, ambition, aspiration, design, end, goal, hope, intention, motive, object, objective, outcome, plan, result, target, wish.
2 *a sense of purpose.* determination, devotion, firmness, persistence, resolution, resolve, steadfastness, zeal.
3 *What's the purpose of this gadget?* application, point, use, usefulness, value.

purpose verb SEE **intend**.

purposeful adjective *Her purposeful stare showed she meant business.* calculated, decided, decisive, deliberate, determined, firm, positive, resolute, steadfast, unwavering.
OPPOSITES: SEE **hesitant**.

purposeless adjective *purposeless vandalism.* aimless, gratuitous, pointless, senseless, unnecessary, useless, wanton.
OPPOSITES: SEE **useful**.

purposely adverb consciously, deliberately, intentionally, knowingly, on purpose, wilfully.

purr verb VARIOUS SOUNDS: SEE **sound** noun.

purse noun bag, handbag, pouch, wallet.

pursue verb **1** *Hounds pursue the fox.* chase, follow, go in pursuit of, harry, hound, hunt, run after, seek, shadow, tail, track down.
2 *She's pursuing a career in engineering.* aim for, aspire to, [*informal*] go for, strive for, try for.
3 *I pursue my hobbies at weekends.* carry on, conduct, continue, engage in, follow up, inquire into, investigate, keep up with, persevere in, proceed with.

pursuit noun **1** *The hounds were in pursuit of the fox.* chase, [*informal*] hue and cry, hunt, tracking down, trail.
2 *What are your favourite pursuits?* activity, hobby, interest, occupation, pastime, pleasure.

purvey verb SEE **supply** verb.

purveyor noun SEE **supplier**.

push verb **1** *to push something away from you.* advance, drive, force, hustle, impel, jostle, poke, press, prod, propel, shove, thrust.
OPPOSITES: SEE **pull**.
2 *I pushed my things into a bag.* compress, cram, crowd, crush, insert, jam, pack, put, ram, squash, squeeze.

3 *They pushed him to work even harder.* browbeat, bully, coerce, compel, constrain, dragoon, hurry, importune, [*informal*] lean on, persuade, put pressure on, pressurize, urge.
4 *The firm is pushing its new product hard.* advertise, make known, market, [*informal*] plug, promote, publicize.
to push (someone) around SEE **bully** verb.
to push off SEE **depart**.
push-chair noun SEE **pram**.
pushy adjective SEE **assertive**.
pusillanimous adjective SEE **timid**.
pustule noun SEE **pimple**.
put verb **1** *Put the books on the shelf.* arrange, assign, consign, deploy, deposit, dispose, fix, hang, lay, leave, locate, park, place, [*informal*] plonk, position, rest, set down, situate, stand, station.
2 *to put a question.* express, formulate, frame, phrase, say, state, suggest, utter, voice, word, write.
3 *to put the blame on someone else.* cast, impose, inflict, lay.
to put across *to put your ideas across.* SEE **communicate**.
to put by *to put food by for later.* SEE **save**.
to put down 1 *to put down a rebellion.* SEE **suppress**.
2 *to put down an animal.* SEE **kill**.
to put in *to put in new sparking-plugs.* SEE **insert** verb, **install**.
to put off *to put off a visit.* SEE **postpone**.
to put out *to put out a fire.* SEE **extinguish**.
to put right *to put damage right.* SEE **repair** verb.
to put up 1 *to put up a tent.* SEE **erect** verb.
2 *to put up prices.* SEE **raise**.
3 *to put up guests.* SEE **accommodate**.
to put your foot down SEE **insist**.
to put your foot in it SEE **blunder** verb.
putative adjective SEE **supposed**.
putrefy verb SEE **rot** verb.
putrid adjective SEE **rotten**.
putt verb SEE **hit** verb, strike, tap.
puzzle noun *Can you solve this puzzle?* brainteaser, difficulty, dilemma, enigma, mystery, [*informal*] poser, problem, quandary, question.
KINDS OF PUZZLE: acrostic, anagram, conundrum, crossword, maze, riddle.
puzzle verb **1** *His coded message puzzled us.* baffle, bewilder, confuse, [*informal*] floor, [*informal*] flummox, mystify, nonplus, perplex, set thinking, stump, worry.
2 *We puzzled over the problem for hours.* SEE **think**.

puzzling adjective *a puzzling problem.* baffling, bewildering, confusing, cryptic, enigmatic, impenetrable, inexplicable, insoluble, [*informal*] mindboggling, mysterious, mystifying, perplexing, strange, unaccountable, unanswerable, unfathomable.
OPPOSITES: SEE **straightforward**.
pygmy adjective SEE **small**.
pygmy noun dwarf, lilliputian, midget.
pyjamas noun night-clothes.
pyramid noun VARIOUS SHAPES: SEE **shape** noun.

Several English words, including *pyre, pyromaniac,* and *pyrotechnics,* are related to Greek *pur* = fire.

---

pyre noun *a funeral pyre.* SEE **fire** noun.
pyromaniac noun arsonist, fireraiser, incendiary.
pyrotechnics noun firework display, fireworks.

Q

quack noun **1** *That doctor's a quack!* SEE **cheat** noun.
2 *the quack of a duck.* VARIOUS SOUNDS: SEE **sound** noun.

The first syllable of words like *quadrilateral, quadrangle,* and *quadruped* is related to Latin *quattuor* = four.

---

quadrangle noun *a quadrangle surrounded by buildings.* cloisters, courtyard, enclosure, [*informal*] quad, yard.
quadrant, quadrilateral nouns SEE **shape** noun.
quadruped noun VARIOUS ANIMALS: SEE **animal** noun.
quadruple adjective SEE **multiple**.
quadruple verb *Prices quadrupled in ten years.* SEE **multiply**.
quaff verb SEE **drink** verb.
quagmire noun *My wellingtons got stuck in a quagmire.* bog, fen, marsh, mire, morass, mud, quicksand, [*old-fashioned*] slough, swamp.
quail verb *I quailed at the danger.* back away, blench, cower, cringe, falter, flinch, quake, recoil, show fear, shrink, tremble, wince.

quaint adjective *a quaint thatched cottage.* antiquated, antique, charming, curious, fanciful, fantastic, odd, old-fashioned, old-world, picturesque, [*informal*] twee, unusual, whimsical.

quake verb *The buildings quaked when the bomb went off.* convulse, heave, move, quaver, quiver, rock, shake, shiver, shudder, sway, tremble, vibrate, wobble.

qualification noun 1 *the proper qualifications for a job.* ability, certification, competence, eligibility, experience, fitness, [*informal*] know-how, knowledge, quality, skill, suitability, training.
2 *academic qualifications.* Bachelor's degree (*BA, BEd, BEng, BSc, LLB,* etc.), certificate, degree, diploma, doctorate, first degree, Master's degree (*MA, MEng, MPhil, MSc,* etc.), matriculation.
3 *I'd say without qualification that he's our best player.* condition, exception, limitation, proviso, reservation, restriction.

qualified adjective 1 *a qualified electrician.* certificated, chartered, competent, equipped, experienced, graduate, professional, skilled, trained.
OPPOSITES: SEE **amateur** adjective.
2 *qualified applicants for a job.* appropriate, eligible, suitable.
3 *qualified praise.* cautious, conditional, equivocal, guarded, half-hearted, limited, modified, reserved, restricted.
OPPOSITES: SEE **unconditional**.

qualify verb 1 *The driving test qualifies you to drive.* authorize, empower, entitle, equip, fit, permit, sanction.
2 *The first three runners qualify for the final.* become eligible, [*informal*] get through, pass.
3 *He qualified his praise with one criticism.* abate, lessen, limit, moderate, restrain, restrict, soften, temper, weaken.

quality noun 1 *top quality meat.* calibre, class, condition, excellence, grade, rank, sort, standard, value.
2 *She has many good qualities.* attribute, characteristic, feature, peculiarity, property, trait.

qualm noun SEE **anxiety**.

quandary noun *in a quandary.* confusion, SEE **dilemma**, perplexity, uncertainty.

quantify verb SEE **measure** verb.

quantity noun *a quantity of goods. a measurable quantity.* aggregate, amount, bulk, consignment, dosage, dose, expanse, extent, length, load, lot, magnitude, mass, SEE **measure** noun, measurement, number, part (*1 part of*

sugar to 2 parts of flour*), pinch (*a pinch of salt*), portion, proportion, quantum, sum, total, volume, weight.

An almost infinite number of words indicating *quantity* can be formed using suffixes *-ful* and *-load*: e.g., armful, barrowload, bucketful, busload, cupful, handful, lorryload, mouthful, plateful, pocketful, spadeful, spoonful.

UNITS OF MEASUREMENT: SEE **measure** noun.

quantum noun SEE **quantity**.

quarantine noun isolation, segregation.

quarrel noun *a quarrel between rivals.* altercation, argument, bickering, brawl, clash, conflict, confrontation, contention, controversy, difference, disagreement, discord, disharmony, dispute, dissension, division, feud, SEE **fight** noun, [*informal*] hassle, misunderstanding, row, [*informal*] ructions, rupture, [*informal*] scene, schism, [*informal*] slanging match, split, squabble, strife, [*informal*] tiff, vendetta, wrangle.

quarrel verb *Members of the rival teams often quarrel.* argue [*informal*] be at loggerheads, be at odds, bicker, clash, conflict, contend, [*informal*] cross swords, differ, disagree, dissent, fall out, SEE **fight** verb, haggle, have a quarrel [SEE **quarrel** noun], [*informal*] row, squabble, wrangle.
to quarrel with *I can't quarrel with your decision.* complain about, disagree with, dispute, fault, object to, SEE **oppose**, [*informal*] pick holes in, query, question, take exception to.

quarrelsome adjective *a quarrelsome customer.* aggressive, SEE **angry**, argumentative, bad-tempered, belligerent, cantankerous, contentious, cross, defiant, explosive, fractious, impatient, irascible, irritable, petulant, quick-tempered, [*informal*] stroppy, truculent.
OPPOSITES: SEE **peaceable**.

quarry noun 1 *a lion's quarry.* game, kill, prey, victim.
2 *a slate quarry.* excavation, mine, pit, working.

quarry verb *to quarry stone.* dig out, excavate, extract, mine.

quarter noun 1 *the commercial quarter of a city.* area, district, division, locality, neighbourhood, part, sector, vicinity, zone.
2 [*plural*] *soldiers' quarters.* SEE **accommodation**, barracks, billet, housing, living quarters, lodgings.

quarter verb *The troops were quartered in barracks.* accommodate, billet, board, house, lodge, [*informal*] put up, station.

quash verb 1 *to quash a court order.* SEE **abolish.**
2 *to quash a rebellion.* SEE **suppress.**

quatrain noun VERSE FORMS: SEE **verse.**

quaver verb 1 *I quavered when I heard him shout.* falter, quake, quiver, shake, shudder, tremble, waver.
2 *His voice quavered.* pulsate, vibrate.

quay noun *a quay where ships tie up.* berth, dock, harbour, jetty, landing-stage, pier, wharf.

queasy adjective bilious, SEE **ill,** nauseous, [*informal*] poorly, [*informal*] queer, sick, unwell.

queen noun ROYALTY: SEE **royal.**

queer adjective 1 *A queer thing happened.* aberrant, abnormal, anomalous, atypical bizarre, curious, eerie, [*informal*] fishy, SEE **funny,** inexplicable, irrational, mysterious, odd, off-beat, outlandish, peculiar, puzzling, quaint, remarkable, [*informal*] rum, singular, strange, unaccountable, uncanny, uncommon, unconventional, unexpected, unnatural, unorthodox, unusual, weird.
2 [*informal*] *a queer person.* [*informal*] cranky, deviant, eccentric, SEE **mad,** questionable, [*informal*] shady (*a shady customer*), [*informal*] shifty, suspect, suspicious.
3 *I felt queer after eating too much.* SEE **ill.**
4 [= *homosexual*] SEE **homosexual.**

quell verb *to quell a riot.* SEE **suppress.**

quench 1 *to quench a fire.* damp down, douse, extinguish, put out, smother, snuff out.
OPPOSITES: SEE **light** verb.
2 *to quench your thirst.* allay, cool, satisfy, slake.

querulous adjective SEE **irritable.**

query noun, verb SEE **question** noun, verb.

quest noun *a quest for treasure.* crusade, expedition, hunt, mission, search.

question noun 1 *Answer this question.* [*informal*] brainteaser, conundrum, demand, enquiry, inquiry, mystery, [*informal*] poser, problem, puzzle, query, riddle.
2 *There's some question about whether he can play.* argument, controversy, debate, dispute, doubt, misgiving, SEE **objection,** uncertainty.

question verb 1 *They questioned me about the accident.* ask, [*formal*] catechize, cross-examine, cross-question, debrief,

examine, [*informal*] grill, interrogate, interview, probe, [*informal*] pump, quiz.
2 *He questioned the referee's decision.* argue over, be sceptical about, challenge, dispute, doubt, enquire about, impugn, inquire about, object to [SEE **object** verb], oppose, quarrel with, query.

questionable adjective *questionable evidence.* arguable, borderline, debatable, disputable, doubtful, dubious, [*informal*] iffy, moot (*a moot point*), suspect, uncertain, unclear, unprovable, unreliable.

questionnaire noun [*formal*] catechism, opinion poll, question sheet, quiz, survey, test.

queue noun *a queue of cars.* column, file, line, line-up, procession, row, string, tail-back.

queue verb *Please queue at the door.* form a queue [SEE **queue** noun], line up, wait in a queue.

quibble noun *a quibble about the wording of a statement.* SEE **objection.**

quibble verb *He quibbled about the price.* carp, cavil, equivocate, SEE **object** verb, [*informal*] split hairs.

quiche noun SEE **pie.**

quick adjective 1 *a quick pace. a quick journey.* breakneck, brisk, expeditious, express (*an express train*), fast, [*old-fashioned*] fleet, hasty, headlong, high-speed, hurried, [*informal*] nippy, precipitate, rapid, [*informal*] smart (*a smart pace*), [*informal*] spanking, speedy, swift.
2 *quick movements.* adroit, agile, animated, brisk, deft, dextrous, lively, nimble, sudden.
OPPOSITES: SEE **slow** adjective.
3 *a quick rest.* brief, fleeting, momentary, passing, perfunctory, short, short-lived, temporary, transitory.
OPPOSITES: SEE **long** adjective.
4 *a quick reply.* abrupt, early, immediate, instant, instantaneous, prompt, punctual, ready, unhesitating.
OPPOSITES: SEE **belated.**
5 *a quick pupil.* acute, alert, apt, astute, bright, clever, intelligent, perceptive, quick-witted, sharp, shrewd, smart.
OPPOSITES: SEE **stupid.**
6 [*old-fashioned*] *the quick and the dead.* SEE **alive.**

quicken verb 1 *Our speed quickened.* accelerate, hasten, hurry, go faster, speed up.
2 *The appearance of a new character quickened our interest.* SEE **arouse.**

quicksand noun SEE **quagmire.**

quicksilver noun mercury.

quick-tempered adjective SEE **quarrelsome**.

quiescent adjective SEE **dormant**.

quiet adjective 1 *a quiet engine*. inaudible, noiseless, silent, soundless.
OPPOSITES: SEE **audible**.
2 *quiet music*. hushed, low, pianissimo, soft.
OPPOSITES: SEE **loud**.
3 *a quiet person. a quiet member of a group*. reserved, retiring, taciturn, uncommunicative, unforthcoming.
OPPOSITES: SEE **talkative**.
4 *a quiet personality. a quiet mood*. composed, contemplative, contented, gentle, introverted, meditative, meek, mild, modest, peaceable, shy, thoughtful.
OPPOSITES: SEE **extroverted**.
5 *quiet weather*. calm, motionless, placid, restful, serene, still, tranquil, untroubled.
OPPOSITES: SEE **turbulent**.
6 *a quiet road. a quiet place for a holiday*. isolated, lonely, peaceful, private, secluded, sequestered, undisturbed, unfrequented.
OPPOSITES: SEE **busy**.

quieten verb 1 *Please quieten the baby!* calm, compose, hush, pacify, soothe, subdue, tranquillize.
2 *A silencer quietens the noise of the engine*. deaden, dull, muffle, mute, reduce the volume of, silence, soften, stifle, suppress, tone down.

quill noun feather, plume.

quilt noun SEE **bedclothes**.

The first syllable of words like *quinquereme, quintet*, and *quintuplet* is related to Latin *quinque* = *five*.

---

quintessence noun SEE **essence**.

quintuple adjective SEE **multiple**.

quintuple verb SEE **multiply**.

quip noun SEE **joke** noun.

quirk noun SEE **peculiarity**.

quisling noun SEE **traitor**.

quit verb 1 *to quit the house. It's time to quit*. abandon, decamp, depart, desert, forsake, go away, leave, walk out, withdraw.
2 *to quit your job*. abdicate, discontinue, drop, give up, [*informal*] pack it in, relinquish, renounce, repudiate, resign from.
3 [*informal*] *Quit pushing!* cease, leave off, stop.

quite adverb [Take care how you use *quite*, as the two senses are almost opposite.] 1 *Yes, I have quite finished*. absolutely, altogether, completely, entirely, perfectly, totally, utterly, wholly.
2 *It was quite good, but far from perfect*. comparatively, fairly, moderately, [*informal*] pretty, rather, relatively, somewhat.

quits adjective *to be quits with someone*. equal, even, level, repaid, revenged, square.

quiver verb *The leaves quivered in the breeze*. flicker, flutter, oscillate, palpitate, pulsate, quake, quaver, shake, shiver, shudder, tremble, vibrate, wobble.

quixotic adjective *a quixotic act of chivalry*. fanciful, SEE **idealistic**. impractical, unrealistic, unselfish, Utopian.
OPPOSITES: SEE **realistic**.

quiz noun competition, examination, questioning, questionnaire, test.

quiz verb SEE **question** verb.

quizzical adjective *a quizzical smile*. SEE **amused**.

quorum noun *a quorum for a meeting*. minimum number.

quota noun *a daily quota of food*. allocation, allowance, assignment, portion, proportion, ration, share.

quotation noun 1 *a quotation from a book*. [*informal*] citation, [*informal*] clip (*a clip from a TV programme*), cutting (*a cutting from a newspaper*), excerpt, extract, passage, piece, reference.
2 *The garage gave us a quotation for repairing the car*. estimate, likely price, tender.

quotation marks inverted commas, speech marks.

quote verb 1 *to quote what someone has said or written*. cite, instance, mention, produce a quotation from [SEE **quotation**], refer to, repeat, reproduce.
2 *The builder quoted a figure of £10,000 for our extension*. estimate, tender.

R

rabble noun *a noisy rabble*. crowd, gang, SEE **group** noun, herd, horde, mob, swarm, throng.

rabid adjective 1 *a rabid attack*. SEE **frenzied**.
2 *a rabid extremist*. SEE **fanatical**.

rabies noun SEE **illness**.

race noun 1 *a race of people.* clan, ethnic group, nation, people, tribe.
RELATED ADJECTIVES: ethnic, racial.
the study of race ethnology.
2 *the human race.* breed, genus, kind, species, variety.
3 *a running race.* chase, competition, contest, heat, rivalry.

COMPETITIVE RACES: cross-country, horse-race, hurdles, marathon, motor-race, regatta, relay race, road-race, rowing, scramble, speedway, sprint, steeple-chase, stock-car race, swimming, track race.

OTHER SPORTS: SEE **sport**.

race verb 1 *I'll race you.* compete with, contest with, have a race with, try to beat.
2 *I raced home because I was late.* career, dash, fly, gallop, hasten, hurry, move fast, run, rush, sprint, tear, zoom.

racecourse, racetrack nouns cinder-track, circuit, dog-track, lap.

racial adjective *racial characteristics.* ethnic, national, tribal.

racialism, racism nouns anti-Semitism, apartheid, bias, bigotry, chauvinism, discrimination, intolerance, prejudice, racial hatred, xenophobia.

racialist, racist adjectives *racist attitudes.* anti-Semitic, biased, bigoted, chauvinist, discriminatory, intolerant, prejudiced.

rack noun *a plate rack. a luggage rack.* frame, framework, shelf, stand, support.

rack verb SEE **torture** verb.
to rack your brains SEE **think**.

racket noun 1 *a tennis racket.* bat, club.
2 [*informal*] *a noisy racket.* SEE **commotion**.
3 [*informal*] *a money-making racket.* SEE **swindle** noun.

racketeer noun SEE **swindler**.

raconteur noun SEE **storyteller**.

racy adjective 1 *a racy style.* SEE **spirited**.
2 *racy jokes.* SEE **bawdy**.

radiant adjective 1 *a radiant light.* SEE **bright**.
2 *a radiant smile.* SEE **beautiful, happy**.

radiate verb *The fire radiates heat.* diffuse, emit, give off, glow, send out, shed, shine, spread, transmit.

radiator noun KINDS OF HEATING: SEE **fire** noun.

radical adjective 1 *a radical inquiry.* basic, drastic, fundamental, thorough.
OPPOSITES: SEE **superficial**.
2 *radical political views.* extreme, extremist, far-reaching, revolutionary, [*uncomplimentary*] subversive.
OPPOSITES: SEE **moderate** adjective.

radio noun receiver, set, [*informal*] transistor, transmitter, [*old-fashioned*] wireless.
OTHER MODES OF COMMUNICATION: SEE **communication**.

radiogram noun SEE **audio equipment**.

radiotherapy noun MEDICAL TREATMENTS: SEE **medicine**.

raffish adjective *a raffish appearance.* SEE **disreputable, tawdry**.

raffle noun KINDS OF GAMBLING: SEE **gamble**.

raft noun KINDS OF BOAT: SEE **vessel**.

rafter noun *rafters in the roof.* beam, girder, joist.

rag noun SEE **rags**.

rage noun SEE **anger** noun.

rage verb SEE **angry (be angry)**.

ragged adjective 1 *ragged clothes.* frayed, in ribbons, old, patched, patchy, rent, ripped, shabby, shaggy, tattered, tatty, threadbare, torn, unkempt, worn out.
2 *a ragged line.* disorganized, erratic, irregular, uneven.

ragout noun SEE **stew** noun.

rags noun [*plural*] bits and pieces, cloths, old clothes, remnants, scraps, shreds, tatters.

raid noun *a raid on an enemy.* assault, attack, blitz, foray, incursion, inroad, invasion, onslaught, sortie, strike, swoop.

raid verb 1 *Police raided the gang's hideaway.* attack, descend on, invade, make a raid on [SEE **raid** noun], pounce on, rush, storm, swoop on.
2 *We raided the larder.* loot, pillage, plunder, ransack, rob, steal from.

raider noun *Raiders swooped down from the mountains.* attacker, brigand, invader, looter, marauder, pillager, pirate, plunderer, ransacker, robber, rustler, thief.

rail noun bar, rod.

railing noun barrier, fence, paling.

raillery noun SEE **teasing**.

railway noun line, permanent way, [*American*] railroad, rails, track.

KINDS OF RAILWAY: branch line, cable railway, funicular, light railway, main line, metro, mineral line, monorail, mountain railway, narrow gauge, rack-and-pinion railway, rapid transit system, siding, standard gauge, tramway, tube, underground railway.

TRAINS AND ROLLING-STOCK: buffet-car, cable-car, carriage, coach, container wagon, diesel, dining-car, DMU, electric train, engine, express, freight train, goods train, goods van, goods wagon, guard's van, Inter-city, locomotive, shunter, sleeper, sleeping-car, steam-engine, steam-train, stopping train, tender, truck, tube-train, underground train, wagon.

PEOPLE WHO WORK ON THE RAILWAY: announcer, booking-clerk, crossing-keeper, driver, engineer, fireman, guard, plate-layer, porter, signalman, station manager, [old-fashioned] station-master, steward.

SOME OTHER RAILWAY TERMS: bogie, booking-office, buffer, compartment, corridor, coupling, cutting, footplate, gauge, halt, left-luggage office, level-crossing, luggage, trolley, marshalling yard, platform, points, sidings, signals, signal-box, sleepers, station, terminus, ticket-office, timetable, track, waiting-room.

---

raiment noun SEE **clothes**.

rain noun *Take a mac to keep the rain off.* cloudburst, deluge, downpour, drizzle, [*formal*] precipitation, raindrops, rainfall, rainstorm, shower, squall.

rain verb *It always seems to rain when we go on holiday.* bucket, drizzle, pelt, pour, [*informal*] rain cats and dogs, spit, teem. METEOROLOGICAL TERMS: SEE **weather** noun.

rainfall noun *annual rainfall.* [*formal*] precipitation.

rainy adjective *a rainy day.* damp, drizzly, pouring, showery, wet.

raise verb 1 *to raise your hand. to raise your head.* hold up, lift, put up, rear.
2 *to raise something to a higher position.* elevate, heave up, hoist, jack up, lift, pick up.
3 *to raise prices. to raise the volume on a radio.* augment, boost, increase, inflate, put up, [*informal*] up.
OPPOSITES: SEE **lower**.
4 *to raise someone to a higher rank.* exalt, prefer, promote, upgrade.
OPPOSITES: SEE **demote**.
5 *to raise a monument.* build, construct, create, erect, set up.
6 *to raise someone's hopes.* activate, arouse, awaken, build up, cause, encourage, engender, enlarge, excite,

foment, foster, heighten, incite, kindle, motivate, provoke, rouse, stimulate, uplift.
OPPOSITES: SEE **destroy**.
7 *to raise animals and crops. to raise a family.* breed, bring up, care for, cultivate, educate, grow, look after, nurture, produce, propagate, rear.
8 *to raise money for charity.* collect, get, make, receive.
9 *to raise questions.* advance, broach, instigate, introduce, moot, originate, pose, present, put forward, suggest.
to raise from the dead SEE **resurrect**.
to raise the alarm SEE **warn**.

rake noun 1 *a garden rake.* SEE **tool**.
2 *the rake of a stage.* SEE **slope** noun.
3 [= *immoral person*] SEE **immoral** (immoral person).

rally noun 1 *a political rally.* [*informal*] demo, demonstration, march, meeting, protest.
2 *a motor rally.* SEE **competition**.

rally verb 1 *to rally your supporters.* SEE **assemble**.
2 *to rally after an illness.* SEE **recover**.

ram noun SEE **sheep**.

ram verb *Our car rammed the one in front.* bump, collide with, crash into, SEE **hit** verb, smash into, strike.

ramble noun *a ramble in the country.* hike, SEE **walk** noun.

ramble verb 1 *to ramble in the hills.* hike, roam, rove, stroll, SEE **walk** verb.
2 *to ramble off the point.* digress, drift, maunder, wander.

rambling adjective 1 *a rambling route.* circuitous, indirect, labyrinthine, meandering, roundabout, tortuous, twisting, wandering, winding, zigzag.
OPPOSITES: SEE **direct** adjective.
2 *a rambling speech. a rambling speaker.* aimless, SEE **confused**, disconnected, discursive, disjointed, incoherent, unstructured, verbose, wordy.
OPPOSITES: SEE **coherent**.
3 *a rambling old farmhouse.* asymmetrical, extensive, large, sprawling, straggling.
OPPOSITES: SEE **compact** adjective.

ramification noun *I don't understand all the ramifications of your plan.* branch, complication, consequence, extension, implication, offshoot, result, upshot.

ramp noun SEE **slope** noun.

rampage verb *Hooligans rampaged through the town.* behave violently, go berserk, go wild, race about, run amok, run riot, rush about.

rampant adjective unchecked, unrestrained, wild.

rampart noun PARTS OF A CASTLE: SEE castle.

ramshackle adjective *a ramshackle old hut.* broken down, decrepit, dilapidated, rickety, ruined, shaky, tumbledown, unsafe.
OPPOSITES: SEE solid.

ranch noun SEE farm noun.

rancour noun SEE animosity.

random adjective *a random choice.* accidental, aimless, arbitrary, casual, chance, fortuitous, haphazard, indiscriminate, irregular, unconsidered, unplanned, unpremeditated.
OPPOSITES: SEE deliberate adjective.

randy adjective SEE lustful.

range noun 1 *a range of mountains.* chain, file, line, row, series, string.
2 *a wide range of goods. your range of knowledge.* area, compass, extent, field, gamut, limits, scope, selection, spectrum, variety.
3 *the range of a gun.* distance, limit, reach.
4 [*old-fashioned*] *a kitchen range.* SEE stove.

range verb 1 *His trophies were ranged on the shelf.* SEE arrange.
2 *Prices range from £10 to £15.* differ, extend, fluctuate, reach, vary.
3 *Sheep range over the hills.* roam, rove, stray, travel, wander.

rangy adjective SEE thin adjective.

rank adjective 1 *a rank growth of weeds.* SEE abundant.
2 *a rank smell of garbage.* SEE smelling.
3 *rank injustice.* SEE complete adjective.

rank noun 1 *Line up in single rank.* column, file, formation, line, order, row, series, tier.
2 *a high rank. a low rank.* caste, class, condition, degree, estate, grade, level, position, standing, station, status, title.

RANKS IN THE ARMED SERVICES [within each group, these are listed in descending order of seniority]:

AIR FORCE: Marshal of the RAF, Air Chief Marshal, Air Marshal, Air Vice-Marshal, air commodore, group captain, wing-commander, squadron leader, flight-lieutenant, flying officer, pilot officer; warrant officer, flight sergeant, chief technician, sergeant, corporal, junior technician, senior aircraftman, leading aircraftman, aircraftman.

ARMY: Field Marshal, general, lieutenant general, major general, brigadier, colonel, lieutenant colonel, major, captain, lieutenant, second lieutenant or subaltern; warrant officer, staff sergeant, sergeant, corporal, lance-corporal, private.

NAVY: Admiral of the Fleet, admiral, vice-admiral, rear-admiral, commodore, captain, commander, lieutenant commander, lieutenant, sub-lieutenant; chief petty officer, petty officer, leading rating, able rating, ordinary rating.

rankle verb SEE annoy.

ransack verb 1 *I ransacked the house looking for my purse.* comb, rummage through, scour, search, [*informal*] turn upside down.
2 *Rioters ransacked the shops.* loot, pillage, plunder, raid, ravage, rob, wreck.

ransom noun SEE payment.

rant verb WAYS OF TALKING: SEE talk verb.

rap verb *to rap on a door.* SEE hit verb, knock, strike, tap.

rapacious adjective SEE greedy.

rape noun assault, SEE crime, sexual attack.

rape verb [*applied to the action of a man*] *to rape a woman.* assault, defile, force yourself on, [*old-fashioned*] ravish, SEE sex (**have sexual intercourse**).

rapid adjective *rapid progress.* breakneck, brisk, expeditious, express, fast, hasty, high-speed, headlong, hurried, [*informal*] nippy, precipitate, quick, smooth, speedy, swift, unchecked, uninterrupted.
OPPOSITES: SEE slow adjective.

rapids noun *swept along by the rapids.* cataract, current, waterfall, white water.

rapier noun SEE sword.

rapport noun SEE harmony.

rapscallion noun SEE rascal.

rapt adjective SEE absorbed.

rapture noun SEE delight noun.

rapturous SEE happy.

rare adjective 1 *a rare visitor. a rare example of something.* abnormal, curious, exceptional, infrequent, irreplaceable, occasional, odd, peculiar, scarce, singular, special, strange, surprising, uncommon, unusual.
OPPOSITES: SEE common adjective.
2 [*informal*] *We had a rare time.* SEE good.

rarefied adjective *a rarefied atmosphere.* thin.

raring adjective SEE enthusiastic.

rascal noun [*Rascal* and its synonyms are often used informally or jokingly.]

blackguard, SEE **criminal** noun, good-for-nothing, imp, knave, miscreant, ne'er-do-well, rapscallion, rogue, scallywag, scamp, scoundrel, trouble-maker, villain.

rascally adjective SEE **naughty**.

rash adjective *a rash decision.* careless, foolhardy, hare-brained, hasty, headstrong, heedless, hot-headed, hurried, ill-advised, ill-considered, impetuous, imprudent, impulsive, incautious, injudicious, precipitate, reckless, risky, thoughtless, unthinking.
OPPOSITES: SEE **careful**.

rash noun 1 *a rash on your skin.* eruption, spots.
2 [*informal*] *a rash of petty thefts.* SEE **outbreak**.

rasher noun *a rasher of bacon.* slice.

rasp noun file.

rasp verb *to rasp with a file.* SEE **scrape** verb.

rasping adjective *a rasping voice.* croaking, croaky, grating, gravelly, gruff, harsh, hoarse, husky, raucous, rough.

rat verb *to rat on a promise.* SEE **renege**.

rate noun 1 *We set out at a fast rate.* pace, speed, tempo, velocity.
2 *What's a reasonable rate for the job?* amount, charge, cost, fare, fee, figure, SEE **payment**, price, wage.

rate verb 1 *How do you rate our chance of winning?* appraise, assess, consider, estimate, evaluate, judge, measure, prize, put a price on, rank, regard, value, weigh.
2 *We rated him for his incompetence.* SEE **reprimand** verb.

rather adverb 1 *I was rather ill.* fairly, moderately, [*informal*] pretty, quite, relatively, slightly, somewhat.
2 *I'd rather have an apple than an orange.* preferably, sooner.

ratify verb *to ratify an agreement.* SEE **confirm**.

rating noun *Her performance would get a high rating from me.* SEE **class** noun, evaluation, grade, grading, mark, placing, ranking.

ratio noun *The ratio of boys to girls is about 50:50.* balance, correlation, fraction, percentage, proportion, relationship.

ration noun *You've had your ration of sweets!* allocation, allowance, helping, measure, portion, quota, share.
rations *The expedition carried rations to last a month.* food, necessaries, necessities, provisions, stores, supplies.

ration verb SEE *In time of war, the government may ration food supplies.* allocate, allot, apportion, conserve, control, distribute fairly, dole out, give out a ration [SEE **ration** noun], limit, restrict, share equally.

rational adjective *a rational discussion. a rational decision.* balanced, intelligent, judicious, logical, lucid, normal, reasonable, reasoned, sane, sensible, sound, thoughtful, wise.
OPPOSITES: SEE **irrational**.

rationale noun SEE **reason** noun.

rationalize verb 1 *I rationalized the silly arrangement of books in the library.* make rational [SEE **rational**], reorganize, [*informal*] sort out.
2 *I can't rationalize my absurd fear of insects.* be rational about [SEE **rational**], elucidate, explain, justify, think through.

rattle noun, verb VARIOUS SOUNDS: SEE **sound** noun.

ratty adjective SEE **angry**.

raucous adjective *raucous laughter.* harsh, grating, jarring, noisy, rough, shrill, strident.

ravage verb *The invaders ravaged the countryside.* damage, despoil, destroy, devastate, lay waste, loot, pillage, plunder, raid, ransack, ruin, sack, wreck.

rave verb 1 *The head raved about our bad behaviour.* be angry [SEE **angry**], fulminate, fume, rage, rant, roar, storm.
2 *The papers raved about her success.* be enthusiastic [SEE **enthusiastic**].

ravel verb SEE **tangle** verb.

ravenous adjective *The ravenous children ate everything on the table.* famished, gluttonous, greedy, hungry, insatiable, ravening, starved, starving, voracious.

ravine noun *a deep ravine.* SEE **valley**.

ravioli noun SEE **pasta**.

ravish verb 1 SEE **rape** verb.
2 *We were ravished by her beauty.* SEE **delight** verb.

ravishing adjective SEE **beautiful**.

raw adjective 1 *raw food.* fresh, rare (*rare steak*), uncooked, underdone, wet (*wet fish*).
OPPOSITE: cooked.
2 *raw materials.* crude, natural, unprocessed, unrefined, untreated.
OPPOSITE: processed.
3 *a raw place on your skin.* bloody, chafed, grazed, inflamed, painful, red, rough, scraped, scratched, sore, tender, vulnerable.
4 *a raw recruit.* ignorant, SEE **inexperienced**, innocent, new, untrained.

OPPOSITES: SEE **experienced**.

5 *a raw wind.* SEE **cold** adjective.

ray noun **1** *a ray of light.* bar, beam, laser, shaft, stream.

2 *a ray of hope.* gleam, glimmer, hint, indication, sign.

raze verb *Fire razed the building to the ground.* SEE **demolish**.

razor noun cut-throat razor, disposable razor, electric razor, safety razor.

reach noun *The shops are in easy reach.* compass, distance, range, scope.

reach verb **1** *I reached the end. We reached our target.* achieve, arrive at, attain, get to, go as far as, [*informal*] make.

2 *I can't reach the handle.* grasp, get hold of, take, touch.

3 *You can reach me by phone.* communicate with, contact, get in touch with.

to reach out *Reach out your hand.* extend, hold out, put out, raise, stick out, stretch.

The common English prefix *re-* comes from a Latin prefix meaning *again, back.*

---

react verb *How did she react when you asked for money?* act, answer, behave, reply, respond, retort.

reaction noun *a reaction to a question. a reaction to a stimulus.* answer, backlash, [*informal*] come-back, feedback, reflex, rejoinder, reply, response, retort, [*joking*] riposte.

reactionary adjective, noun SEE **conservative** adjective, noun.

read verb **1** *to read a story.* [*informal*] dip into, glance at, interpret, peruse, pore over, scan, skim, study.

2 *I can't read your handwriting.* decipher, decode, make out, understand.

readable adjective **1** *a readable story.* compulsive, enjoyable, entertaining, gripping, interesting, well-written.

OPPOSITES: SEE **boring**.

2 *readable handwriting.* clear, decipherable, legible, neat, plain, understandable.

OPPOSITES: SEE **illegible**.

readily adverb eagerly, easily, gladly, happily, voluntarily, willingly.

reading noun **1** *Take some reading for the train journey.* SEE **book** noun, **magazine**.

2 *What is your reading of her remarks?* SEE **interpretation**.

ready adjective **1** *Dinner is ready.* available, complete, convenient, done, finalized, finished, obtainable, prepared, set up, waiting.

OPPOSITE: unready.

2 *I'm ready to lend a hand.* disposed, eager, fit, [*informal*] game (*game for a laugh*), glad, inclined, keen, [*informal*] keyed up, liable, likely, minded, organized, pleased, poised, predisposed, primed, raring (*raring to go*), willing.

OPPOSITES: SEE **reluctant**.

3 *a ready reply. a ready wit.* acute, alert, facile, immediate, prompt, quick, quick-witted, rapid, sharp, smart, speedy.

OPPOSITES: SEE **slow** adjective.

real adjective **1** *real events. real people.* actual, certain, everyday, existing, factual, ordinary, palpable, SEE **realistic**, tangible, true, verifiable.

OPPOSITES: SEE **imaginary**.

2 *real wood. real gold.* authentic, genuine, natural, pure.

OPPOSITES: SEE **artificial**.

3 *a real work of art.* authenticated, bona fide, legitimate, unquestionable, valid.

OPPOSITES: SEE **imitation** adjective.

4 *a real friend.* dependable, positive, reliable, sound, trustworthy, worthy.

OPPOSITES: SEE **untrustworthy**.

5 *real grief.* heartfelt, honest, sincere, undoubted, unfeigned.

OPPOSITES: SEE **insincere**.

realism noun **1** *realism in a work of art.* authenticity, fidelity, truth to life, verisimilitude.

2 *realism in the way you deal with things.* clear-sightedness, common sense, objectivity, practicality, pragmatism.

realistic adjective **1** *a realistic portrait.* authentic, convincing, faithful, lifelike, natural, recognizable, representational, true to life, truthful.

2 *a realistic plan. a realistic assessment of the situation.* businesslike, clear-sighted, common-sense, down-to-earth, feasible, level-headed, logical, objective, possible, practicable, practical, pragmatic, rational, sensible, unemotional, viable, workable.

3 *realistic prices. realistic wages.* acceptable, adequate, fair, justifiable, moderate, reasonable.

OPPOSITES: SEE **unrealistic**.

reality noun *Stop day-dreaming and face reality.* actuality, certainty, fact, [*informal*] nitty-gritty, the real world [SEE **real**], truth, verity.

OPPOSITES: SEE **fantasy**.

realize verb **1** *I suddenly realized what you meant.* accept, appreciate, apprehend, be aware of, [*informal*] catch on to, comprehend, grasp, know, recognize, see, sense, [*informal*] twig, understand, [*informal*] wake up to.

2 *It'll take years to realize my ambition.* accomplish, achieve, complete, fulfil, implement, obtain, perform.

3 *My old car realized a good price.* [*informal*] bring in, [*informal*] clear, earn, fetch, make, net, obtain, produce.

realm noun SEE **country**, domain, empire, kingdom, monarchy.

reap verb **1** *to reap corn.* SEE **cut** verb, gather in, harvest, mow.
2 *to reap your reward.* collect, get, obtain, receive, win.

reappear verb SEE **return** verb.

reappraisal noun SEE **review** noun.

rear adjective *the rear legs of an animal.* back, end, hind, hinder, hindmost, last, rearmost.
OPPOSITES: SEE **front** adjective.

rear noun **1** *the rear of a train.* back, end, stern (*of a ship*), tail-end.
2 [*informal*] *Our dog nipped the intruder in the rear.* SEE **buttocks**.

rear verb **1** *Parents rear their families. Farmers rear cattle.* breed, bring up, care for, cultivate, feed, look after, nurture, produce, raise, train.
2 *The animal reared its head.* elevate, lift, raise.
3 *They reared a monument to the victims of the earthquake.* SEE **build**.

rearguard noun SEE **armed services**.
OPPOSITE: vanguard.

rearrange verb SEE **change** verb, regroup, reorganize, switch round, swop round, transpose.

rearrangement noun anagram [= *rearrangement of letters*], SEE **change** noun, reorganization, transposition.

reason noun **1** *He had a good reason for his behaviour.* apology, argument, case, cause, excuse, explanation, grounds, incentive, justification, motive, occasion, pretext, rationale, vindication.
2 *Show some reason!* brains, common sense, [*informal*] gumption, intelligence, judgement, mind, [*informal*] nous, rationality, SEE **reasoning**, understanding, wisdom, wit.
3 *She tried to make him see reason.* logic, reasonableness, sanity, sense.

reason verb **1** *I reasoned that it was cheaper to go by bus.* calculate, conclude, consider, deduce, infer, judge, resolve, think, work out.
2 *I reasoned with him, but I couldn't persuade him.* argue, debate, discuss, expostulate, intellectualize, remonstrate, use reason.

reasonable adjective **1** *a reasonable person. reasonable behaviour.* calm, honest, intelligent, rational, realistic, sane, sensible, sincere, sober, thoughtful, unemotional, wise.

OPPOSITES: SEE **irrational**.
2 *a reasonable argument.* believable, credible, defensible, justifiable, logical, plausible, practical, reasoned, sound, tenable, viable.
OPPOSITES: SEE **absurd**.
3 *a reasonable price.* acceptable, average, cheap, fair, inexpensive, moderate, ordinary, proper.
OPPOSITES: SEE **excessive**.

reasoning noun *I don't follow your reasoning.* analysis, argument, case, [*uncomplimentary*] casuistry, deduction, dialectic, hypothesis, line of thought, logic, proof, SEE **reason** noun, [*uncomplimentary*] sophistry, thinking.

reassemble verb SEE **return** verb.

reassure verb *to reassure someone who is worried.* assure, bolster (up), calm, comfort, encourage, give confidence to, hearten, support.
OPPOSITES: SEE **threaten**.

reassuring adjective *a reassuring smile. reassuring signs of success.* calming, caring, comforting, encouraging, favourable, hopeful, promising, supportive, sympathetic, understanding.
OPPOSITES: SEE **threatening**.

rebate noun SEE **refund** noun.

rebel adjective *rebel forces.* breakaway, insubordinate, insurgent, malcontent, mutinous, SEE **rebellious**, revolutionary.

rebel noun *a rebel against authority.* anarchist, apostate, dissenter, heretic, iconoclast, insurgent, malcontent, maverick, mutineer, nonconformist, revolutionary, schismatic.

rebel verb *to rebel against authority.* be a rebel [SEE **rebel** noun], disobey, dissent, fight, [*informal*] kick (against), [*informal*] kick over the traces, mutiny, refuse to obey, revolt, rise up, [*informal*] run riot, [*informal*] take a stand.
OPPOSITES: SEE **obey**.

rebellion noun *rebellion in the ranks.* disobedience, insubordination, insurgency, insurrection, mutiny, rebelliousness, resistance, revolt, revolution, rising, schism, sedition, uprising.

rebellious adjective *rebellious troops. a rebellious class of children.* [*informal*] bolshie, breakaway, defiant, difficult, disaffected, disloyal, disobedient, insubordinate, insurgent, intractable, malcontent, mutinous, quarrelsome, rebel, refractory, resistant, revolting, revolutionary, seditious, uncontrollable, ungovernable, unmanageable, unruly, wild.
OPPOSITES: SEE **obedient**.

rebirth noun SEE **renewal**.

rebound verb 1 *The dart rebounded off the wall.* SEE **bounce**, ricochet, spring back. 2 *His wily plan rebounded on him.* [*informal*] backfire, [*informal*] boomerang, misfire, recoil.

rebuff noun, verb SEE **snub** noun, verb.

rebuild noun *to rebuild a town.* build again, reconstruct, redevelop, regenerate. 2 *to rebuild an old car.* make good, overhaul, reassemble, recondition, recreate, refashion, remake, renew, renovate, repair, restore.

rebuke noun, verb SEE **reprimand** noun, verb.

rebut verb SEE **refute**.

recalcitrant adjective SEE **disobedient**.

recall verb 1 *The garage recalled the faulty cars.* bring back, call in, withdraw. 2 *Try to recall what happened.* SEE **remember**.

recant verb SEE **repudiate**.

recapitulate verb SEE **repeat**.

recapture verb SEE **retrieve**.

recede verb *The flood gradually receded.* decline, ebb, go back, regress, retire, retreat, return, shrink back, slacken, subside.

receipt noun *a receipt for goods bought.* account, acknowledgement, bill, proof of purchase, ticket.
receipts gains, gate (*at a football match*), income, proceeds, profits, takings.

receive verb 1 *to receive payment for something.* accept, acquire, be given, be sent, collect, earn, get, obtain, take.
OPPOSITES: SEE **give**.
2 *to receive an injury.* bear, experience, suffer, sustain, undergo.
OPPOSITES: SEE **inflict**.
3 *to receive visitors.* accommodate, entertain, greet, meet, welcome.

receiver noun *a radio receiver.* apparatus, radio, set, tuner, [*old-fashioned*] wireless.

recent adjective *recent events. recent innovations.* contemporary, current, fresh, modern, new, novel, present-day, up-to-date.
OPPOSITES: SEE **old**.

receptacle noun SEE **container**.

reception noun 1 *They gave us a friendly reception.* greeting, welcome.
2 *a wedding reception.* SEE **party**.

receptive adjective *receptive to new ideas.* amenable, favourable, interested, kindly disposed, open, open-minded, responsive, susceptible, sympathetic, welcoming.

recess noun 1 *a recess in a wall.* alcove, apse, bay, cavity, corner, hollow, indentation, niche, nook.
2 *a recess during a meeting.* adjournment, break, breathing-space, interlude, intermission, interval, respite, rest.

recession noun *an economic recession.* decline, depression, downturn, slump.

recherché adjective SEE **abstruse**.

recidivist noun SEE **criminal** noun.

recipe noun *a recipe for a cake.* directions, instructions, method, procedure.

recipient noun *the recipient of a gift or bequest.* beneficiary, legatee, receiver.
OPPOSITES: SEE **donor**.

reciprocal adjective *reciprocal affection.* corresponding, mutual, returned, shared.

reciprocate verb *Did she reciprocate his love?* exchange, give the same in return, match, requite, return.

recital noun 1 *a piano recital.* concert, performance, programme.
2 *a recital of events.* account, narration, narrative, SEE **recitation**, repetition, story, telling.

recitation noun *a recitation of a poem.* declaiming, delivery, narration, performance, [*old-fashioned*] rendition, speaking, telling.

recite verb *to recite a poem.* articulate, declaim, deliver, narrate, perform, recount, rehearse, relate, repeat, speak, tell.

reckless adjective 1 *reckless driving. reckless extravagance.* brash, careless, [*informal*] crazy, daredevil, foolhardy, [*informal*] harum-scarum, hasty, heedless, imprudent, impulsive, inattentive, incautious, irresponsible, [*informal*] mad, madcap, negligent, rash, thoughtless, unconsidered.
OPPOSITES: SEE **careful**.
2 *reckless criminals.* dangerous, desperate, violent, wild.

reckon verb 1 *I reckoned up how much she owed me.* add up, assess, calculate, compute, count, estimate, evaluate, figure out, gauge, number, total, work out.
2 [*informal*] *I reckon it's going to rain.* SEE **think**.

reckoning noun [*informal*] *The waiter gave me the reckoning.* addition, bill, score, sum, tally, total.

reclaim verb 1 *You can reclaim expenses after your interview.* get back, [*informal*] put in for, recover, regain.

2 *to reclaim derelict land.* make usable, regenerate, reinstate, restore, salvage, save.

recline verb *to recline on a sofa.* lean back, lie, loll, lounge, rest, sprawl, stretch out.

recluse noun *a recluse who never appears in public.* hermit, loner, solitary.

recognizable adjective *a recognizable figure.* distinctive, distinguishable, identifiable, known, undisguised, unmistakable.

recognize verb **1** *to recognize a person. to recognize a landmark.* discern, distinguish, identify, know, name, perceive, pick out, [*informal*] put a name to, recall, recollect, remember, see, spot.
2 *The doctor recognized the symptoms.* detect, diagnose, notice, perceive.
3 *I recognize my shortcomings.* accept, acknowledge, admit to, be aware of, concede, confess, grant, realize, understand.

recoil verb **1** *His wily plan recoiled on him.* SEE **rebound**.
2 *I recoiled when I saw blood.* blench, draw back, falter, flinch, jerk back, quail, shrink, wince.

recollect verb SEE **remember**.

recollection noun *I have no recollection of what happened.* SEE **memory**.

recommend verb **1** *The doctor recommends a complete rest.* advise, counsel, prescribe, propose, suggest, urge.
2 *The critics recommend this film.* advocate, applaud, approve of, commend, [*informal*] plug, praise, speak well of, vouch for.

recompose verb SEE **repay**.

reconcile verb *I managed to reconcile them after their quarrel.* bring together, conciliate, harmonize, placate, reunite.
to be reconciled to *I'm reconciled to doing without a holiday.* SEE **accept**.

recondite adjective SEE **obscure** adjective.

recondition verb SEE **rebuild**.

reconnaissance noun *The troops moved in after a reconnaissance of the area.* examination, exploration, inspection, investigation, observation, reconnoitring [SEE **reconnoitre**], spying, survey.

reconnoitre verb *The troops reconnoitred the area before moving in.* [*informal*] case, examine, explore, gather intelligence, inspect, investigate, patrol, scout, spy, survey.

reconsider verb SEE **review** verb.

reconstitute verb SEE **renew**.

reconstruct verb SEE **rebuild**.

record noun **1** *We kept a record of what we saw.* account, chronicle, diary, dossier, file, journal, log, minute (*minutes of a meeting*), narrative, note, register, report.
2 [*plural*] *historical records.* annals, archives, documents.
3 *a gramophone record.* album, disc, long-playing record, LP, SEE **recording**, single.
4 *Her time in the last race was a school record.* [*informal*] best, [*informal*] highest.

record verb **1** *I recorded what I saw in a notebook.* enter, inscribe, log, minute, note, put down, register, set down, write down.
2 *We recorded our performance on tape.* keep, preserve, tape, tape-record, video.

recorder noun *a tape recorder.* SEE **audio equipment**.

recording noun *Have you heard their latest recording?* performance, release.

KINDS OF RECORDING: audio-tape, cassette, compact disc, digital recording, mono recording, quadraphonic recording, SEE **record** noun, stereo recording, tape, tape-recording, tele-recording, video, video-cassette, video disc, videotape.

record-player noun SEE **audio equipment**.

recount verb *He recounted his adventures.* describe, detail, narrate, recite, relate, report, retail, tell.

recoup verb SEE **recover**, **refund** verb.

recover verb **1** *to recover after an illness.* come round, convalesce, get better, heal, improve, mend, [*informal*] pull round, [*informal*] pull through, rally, recuperate, revive.
2 *to recover something you have lost.* find, get back, make good, recapture, reclaim, recoup, regain, repossess, restore, retrieve, salvage, trace, track down.

recovery noun **1** *recovery from an illness.* convalescence, cure, healing, improvement, recuperation.
2 *the recovery of business after a recession.* revival, upturn.
3 *recovery of something you had lost.* recapture, reclamation, repossession, restoration, retrieval, salvaging.

recreate verb SEE **renew**.

recreation noun *We deserve some recreation after working hard.* amusement, diversion, enjoyment, entertainment, fun, games, hobby, leisure, pastime, play, pleasure, relaxation.

recreation ground park, playground, playing-field.

ecrimination noun *I don't want any recriminations if this goes wrong.* accusation, [*informal*] come-back, retaliation, retort.

ecrudescence noun SEE **return** noun.

ecruit noun *a recruit in the services. a new recruit to the firm.* apprentice, beginner, conscript, learner, [*informal*] new boy, [*informal*] new girl, new member, novice, tiro, trainee.
OPPOSITES: SEE **veteran** noun.

ecruit verb *to recruit new staff.* advertise for, engage, enlist, enrol, mobilize, sign on, take on.

ectangle noun oblong.
VARIOUS SHAPES: SEE **shape** noun.

ectify verb SEE **correct** verb.

ector noun SEE **clergyman**.

ecumbent adjective *a recumbent posture.* flat, horizontal, lying down, prone, reclining, supine.
OPPOSITES: SEE **upright**.

ecuperate verb SEE **recover**.

ecuperating adjective SEE **convalescent**.

ecur verb *Go to the dentist if the pain recurs.* come again, persist, reappear, repeat, return.

ecurrent adjective *a recurrent illness. recurrent problems.* chronic, SEE **continual**, cyclical, frequent, intermittent, periodic, persistent, recurring, regular, repeated.

ecycle verb *to recycle waste.* reclaim, recover, retrieve, re-use, salvage, use again.

ed adjective 1 *red in the face.* blushing, embarrassed, flaming, florid, flushed, glowing, inflamed, rosy, rubicund, ruddy.
2 *red eyes.* bloodshot.

VARIOUS SHADES OF RED: auburn, blood-red, brick-red, cardinal red, carmine, carroty, cerise, cherry, crimson, damask, flame-coloured, magenta, maroon, pink, rose, roseate, ruby, scarlet, vermilion, wine-coloured.
OTHER COLOURS: SEE **colour** noun.

red herring decoy, distraction, diversion, trick.

red-blooded adjective SEE **vigorous**.

redden verb *His face reddened with embarrassment.* blush, colour, flush, glow.

redecorate verb SEE **renew**.

redeem verb 1 *He redeemed his watch from the pawnbroker's.* buy back, reclaim, recover, re-purchase.
2 *I redeemed some Premium Bonds.* cash in, exchange for cash, trade in.
to redeem yourself *After playing badly for weeks, he redeemed himself by scoring a goal.* SEE **atone**.

redeemer noun SEE **saviour**.

re-deploy verb SEE **reorganize**.

redevelop verb SEE **rebuild, renew**.

red-hot adjective SEE **hot**.

redirect verb *to redirect a letter.* re-address, send on.

redo verb SEE **renew, repeat**.

redolent adjective 1 *redolent of onions.* SEE **smelling**.
2 *redolent of the past.* SEE **reminiscent**.

redouble verb SEE **intensify**.

redoubtable adjective *a redoubtable enemy.* SEE **formidable**.

redress verb SEE **correct** verb.

reduce verb 1 *to reduce the amount or intensity or effect of something.* commute (*to commute a prison sentence*), curtail, cut, cut back, decimate [see note under *decimate*], decrease, detract from, devalue, dilute, diminish, [*informal*] dock (*to dock someone's wages*), halve, impair, lessen, lower, make less, minimize, moderate, narrow, shorten, shrink, [*informal*] slash, slim down, trim, truncate, weaken, whittle.
2 *Our supplies gradually reduced.* become less, contract, dwindle, shrink.
OPPOSITES: SEE **increase** verb.
3 *to reduce liquid by boiling.* concentrate, condense, thicken.
OPPOSITES: SEE **dilute** verb.
4 *to reduce someone to a lower rank. to reduce someone to poverty.* degrade, demote, downgrade, humble, impoverish, move down, put down, ruin.
OPPOSITES: SEE **promote**.

reduction noun 1 *a reduction in amount or intensity or effect.* contraction, cutback, deceleration [= *reduction in speed*], decimation, decline, decrease, diminution, drop, impairment, lessening, limitation, loss, moderation, narrowing, remission, shortening, shrinkage, weakening.
2 *a reduction in price.* concession, cut, depreciation, devaluation, discount, rebate, refund.
OPPOSITES: SEE **increase** noun.

redundant adjective *redundant workers. Omit any redundant words in your essay.* excessive, superfluous, surplus, too many, unnecessary, unwanted.
OPPOSITES: SEE **necessary**.

reduplicate verb SEE **double** verb.

re-echo verb SEE **repeat**.

reek noun, verb SEE **smell** noun, verb.

reel noun *a reel of cotton.* bobbin, spool.

reel verb *I reeled after that knock on the head.* lurch, rock, roll, spin, stagger, stumble, sway, totter, whirl, wobble.

reeling adjective *My head was reeling.* SEE **dizzy**.

re-enter verb SEE **return** verb.

refectory noun cafeteria, dining-room.

refer verb 1 *I won't refer to your mistake.* allude to, cite, comment on, draw attention to, make reference to, mention, quote, speak of, touch on.
2 *They didn't have what I wanted, so they referred me to another shop.* direct, guide, recommend, send.
to refer to *If I can't spell a word, I refer to my dictionary.* consult, go to, look up, turn to.

referee noun adjudicator, arbitrator, judge, umpire.

reference noun 1 *Which book does this reference come from?* allusion, citation, example, illustration, instance, mention, quotation, remark.
2 *When you apply for jobs you need a reference.* recommendation, testimonial.

referendum noun SEE **poll** noun.

refill verb *Refill the tank.* refuel, renew, replenish, top up.

refine verb 1 *to refine raw materials.* clarify, distil, process, purify, treat.
2 *to refine your behaviour.* SEE **improve**.

refined adjective *refined tastes.* civilized, courteous, cultivated, cultured, delicate, dignified, discerning, discriminating, elegant, fastidious, genteel, gentlemanly, ladylike, nice, polished, polite, [*informal*] posh, [*uncomplimentary*] pretentious, [*uncomplimentary*] prissy, sophisticated, subtle, tasteful, [*informal*] upper crust, urbane, well-bred, well brought-up.
OPPOSITES: SEE **vulgar**.
2 *refined oil.* distilled, processed, purified, treated.
OPPOSITES: SEE **crude**.

refinement noun 1 *refinement of manners.* breeding, [*informal*] class (*She's got real class*), courtesy, cultivation, delicacy, discrimination, elegance, finesse, gentility, polish, [*uncomplimentary*] pretentiousness, sophistication, style, subtlety, taste, urbanity.
2 *They've made some refinements in the design of the new model.* alteration, change, improvement, modification.

refit verb SEE **renew**, **repair** verb.

reflect verb 1 *A mirror reflects your image. Cat's-eyes reflect headlights.* mirror, return, send back, shine back, throw back.
2 *Their success reflects their hard work.* bear witness to, correspond to, demonstrate, echo, exhibit, indicate, match, reveal, show.
to reflect on *to reflect on past events.* brood on, [*informal*] chew over, consider, contemplate, meditate on, ponder, remind yourself of, reminisce about, ruminate, talk over, think about.

reflection noun 1 *a reflection in a mirror.* image, likeness.
2 *Their success is a reflection of their hard work.* demonstration, echo, indication, manifestation, result.
3 *Your exam failure is no reflection on your intelligence.* censure, criticism, discredit, reproach, shame, slur.
4 *a quiet time for reflection.* contemplation, deliberation, meditation, pondering, rumination, study, thinking, thought.

reflective adjective 1 *reflective glass.* reflecting, SEE **shiny**.
2 *a reflective mood.* SEE **thoughtful**.

reflector noun Cat's-eyes, looking-glass, mirror, reflective glass, reflective patch.

reflex adjective *a reflex action.* SEE **involuntary**.

reform verb 1 *to reform your behaviour.* amend, become better, change, convert, correct, improve, make better, save.
2 *to reform a political system.* purge, reconstitute, regenerate, remodel, reorganize, revolutionize.

reformatory noun SEE **prison**.

refract verb *to refract light rays.* bend, distort.

refractory adjective SEE **stubborn**.

refrain noun *the refrain of a song.* chorus.

refrain verb **to refrain from** *Please refrain from smoking.* abstain from, avoid, desist from, do without, eschew, forbear, [*informal*] quit, stop.

refresh verb 1 *The drink refreshed us.* cool, freshen, invigorate, quench the thirst of, rejuvenate, renew, restore, revitalize, revive.

2 *Let me refresh your memory.* jog, remind, prod, prompt, stimulate.

refreshing adjective **1** *a refreshing drink. a refreshing shower.* bracing, cool, enlivening, invigorating, restorative, reviving, stimulating, thirst-quenching, tingling.
OPPOSITES: SEE **cloying, exhausting.**
2 *a refreshing change.* different, fresh, interesting, new, novel, original, unexpected, unfamiliar, unforeseen, unpredictable, welcome.
OPPOSITES: SEE **boring.**

refreshments noun drink, [*informal*] eats, food, snack.

refrigerate verb *to refrigerate food.* chill, cool, freeze, keep cold, SEE **preserve** verb.

refuel verb SEE **refill.**

refuge noun *The climbers found refuge from the blizzard.* asylum, [*informal*] bolt-hole, cover, haven, hideout, hiding-place, protection, retreat, safety, sanctuary, security, shelter.

refugee noun displaced person, exile, fugitive, outcast.

refund noun *If you are not satisfied, ask for a refund.* rebate, repayment.

refund verb *to refund expenses.* give back, pay back, recoup, reimburse, repay, return.

refurbish verb SEE **renew.**

refusal noun *Our request was met with a refusal.* [*informal*] brush-off, denial, negative reply, rebuff, rejection.
OPPOSITES: SEE **acceptance.**

refuse noun *Throw away the refuse.* SEE **rubbish.**

refuse verb **1** *to refuse an invitation.* baulk at, decline, give a negative reply to, [*informal*] jib at, reject, say no to, spurn, turn down.
OPPOSITES: SEE **accept.**
2 *to refuse someone their rights.* deny, deprive of, withhold.
OPPOSITES: SEE **grant** verb.

refute verb *to refute an argument.* counter, discredit, disprove, negate, prove wrong, rebut.

regain verb *to regain something you've lost.* be reunited with, find, get back, recapture, reclaim, recoup, recover, repossess, retake, retrieve, return to, win back.

Regal, regalia, regicide, and a number of similar words are related to Latin *rex = king* and *regina = queen.*

---

regal adjective *a regal figure.* kingly, majestic, noble, princely, queenly, royal, SEE **splendid,** stately.

regale verb SEE **entertain.**

regalia noun SEE **emblem.**

regard noun **1** *I quailed under his stern regard.* gaze, look, scrutiny, stare.
2 *Give due regard to the warnings.* attention, care, concern, consideration, deference, heed, notice, respect, thought.
3 *I have a high regard for her ability.* admiration, affection, esteem, honour, love, respect.

regard verb **1** *to regard something closely.* contemplate, eye, gaze at, look at, observe, scrutinize, stare at, view, watch.
2 *We regard her as our best swimmer.* account, consider, deem, esteem, judge, reckon, respect, think, value.

regardful adjective *under his regardful gaze.* SEE **attentive.**

regarding preposition about, concerning, connected with, involving, on the subject of, with reference to, with regard to.

regardless adjective *regardless of danger.* careless (about), heedless, indifferent (to), neglectful, uncaring (about), unconcerned (about), unmindful.

regenerate verb SEE **renew.**

regent noun VARIOUS RULERS: SEE **ruler.**

regime noun SEE **government, system.**

regiment noun SEE **armed services.**

regiment verb SEE **organize.**

regimented adjective SEE **organized.**

region noun *The Arctic is a cold region.* area, SEE **country,** district, expanse, land, locality, neighbourhood, place, province, quarter, territory, tract, vicinity, zone.

register noun *a register of names and addresses.* catalogue, directory, file, index, ledger, list, record, roll.

register verb **1** *to register as a voter. to register as a member of a club.* enlist, enrol, enter your name, join, sign on.
2 *to register a complaint.* make official, present, record, set down, write down.
3 *Did you register what she was wearing?* keep in mind, make a note of, mark, notice, take account of.
4 *His face registered pleasure.* express, indicate, reveal, show.

registrar noun VARIOUS OFFICIALS: SEE **official** noun.

regress verb *Business tends to regress during a holiday.* backslide, degenerate, deteriorate, fall back, go back, move backwards, retreat, retrogress, revert, slip back.
OPPOSITES: SEE **progress** verb.

regressive adjective SEE **backward**.

regret noun 1 *regret for doing wrong.* compunction, contrition, guilt, penitence, pricking of conscience, remorse, repentance, self-accusation, shame.
2 *regret about someone's loss.* grief, sadness, sorrow, sympathy.

regret verb 1 *I regret that I lost my temper.* be regretful [SEE **regretful**], feel regret [SEE **regret** noun], repent, reproach yourself.
2 *I deeply regret the death of your friend.* be sad about, feel regret about [SEE **regret** noun], grieve over, lament, mourn.

regretful adjective *a regretful smile.* apologetic, ashamed, conscience-stricken, contrite, disappointed, penitent, remorseful, repentant, SEE **sad**, sorry.
OPPOSITES: SEE **happy, unrepentant**.

regrettable adjective *a regrettable accident.* deplorable, disappointing, distressing, lamentable, reprehensible, sad, shameful, undesirable, unfortunate, unhappy, unlucky, unwanted.

regroup verb SEE **rearrange**.

regular adjective 1 *regular intervals. a regular pattern.* consistent, constant, daily, equal, even, fixed, hourly, measured, monthly, ordered, predictable, recurring, repeated, rhythmic, steady, symmetrical, systematic, uniform, unvarying, weekly, yearly.
2 *the regular procedure. our regular postman.* accustomed, common, commonplace, conventional, customary, established, everyday, familiar, frequent, habitual, known, normal, official, ordinary, orthodox, prevailing, proper, routine, scheduled, standard, traditional, typical, usual.
3 *a regular supporter.* dependable, faithful, reliable.
OPPOSITES: SEE **irregular**.

regular noun *She's one of the regulars here.* [*informal*] faithful, frequenter, habitué, regular customer [SEE **regular** adjective], patron.

regularize verb SEE **legalize**.

regulate verb 1 *to regulate the traffic.* control, direct, govern, manage, order, organize, restrict, supervise.
2 *to regulate the temperature.* adjust, alter, change, get right, moderate, vary.

regulation noun *Obey the regulations.* by-law, commandment, decree, directive, edict, law, order, requirement, restriction, rule, statute.

regurgitate verb 1 *to regurgitate food.* SEE **vomit**.
2 [*informal*] *to regurgitate what you have learned.* SEE **repeat**.

rehabilitate verb SEE **reinstate**.

rehash verb SEE **revise**.

rehearsal noun *a rehearsal for a play.* practice, preparation, [*informal*] run-through, [*informal*] try-out.
THEATRICAL TERMS: SEE **theatre**.

rehearse verb *to rehearse a play.* go over, practise, prepare, [*informal*] run over (*Just run over the last scene*), try out.

rehearsed adjective *I'm sure his remarks were rehearsed, not impromptu.* calculated, practised, pre-arranged, premeditated, prepared, thought out.
OPPOSITES: SEE **impromptu**.

reign verb *Which British monarch reigned the longest?* be king, be queen, be on the throne, govern, have power, rule.

rein verb SEE **check** verb.

reincarnation noun *the reincarnation of souls.* rebirth, return to life, [*formal*] transmigration.

reinforce verb 1 *to reinforce a wall.* back up, bolster, buttress, fortify, give strength to, hold up, prop up, stiffen, strengthen, support, toughen.
2 *to reinforce an army.* add to, assist, help, increase the size of, provide reinforcements for, supplement.

reinforcements noun additional troops, auxiliaries, back-up, help, reserves, support.

reinstate verb *The firm reinstated the man who was wrongly dismissed.* recall, rehabilitate, restore, take back, welcome back.
OPPOSITES: SEE **dismiss**.

reject verb 1 *Good shops reject sub-standard goods.* discard, eliminate, exclude, jettison, scrap, send back, throw away, throw out.
2 *It's not nice to reject your friends.* dismiss, disown, [*informal*] drop, jilt, rebuff, renounce, repel, repudiate, repulse, spurn.
3 *to reject an invitation.* decline, refuse, say no to, turn down, veto.
OPPOSITES: SEE **accept**.

rejoice verb *Everyone rejoiced in their team's success.* be happy [SEE **happy**], celebrate, delight, exult, glory, revel, triumph.
OPPOSITES: SEE **grieve**.

rejoin verb SEE **answer** verb.

rejoinder noun SEE **answer** noun.

rejuvenate verb SEE **renew**.

relapse noun *After making some progress, he suffered a relapse.* deterioration, recurrence, set-back.

relapse verb *to relapse after making progress.* degenerate, deteriorate, fall back, have a relapse, regress, revert, slip back, weaken.

relate verb 1 *to relate your adventures.* describe, detail, narrate, recite, recount, rehearse, report, tell.
2 *The police related the two crimes.* associate, compare, connect, consider together, join, link.
3 *I saw a TV programme which related to a book I'd just read.* be relevant [SEE **relevant**], concern, pertain, refer.
4 *The team members relate well to each other.* be friends, fraternize, have a relationship [SEE **relationship**], socialize.

related adjective *related crimes. related businesses. related facts.* affiliated, akin, allied, associated, cognate, comparable, connected, interconnected, joined, linked, parallel, SEE **relative** adjective, similar.
OPPOSITES: SEE **separate** adjective.
FAMILY RELATIONSHIPS: SEE **family**.

relation noun 1 *the relation between two people or things.* SEE **relationship**.
2 *All our relations came to the wedding.* SEE **relative** noun.
3 *the relation of a story.* SEE **narration**.

relationship 1 *the relationship between two people or things.* affinity, association, bond, connection, [*formal*] consanguinity, contrast, correlation, correspondence, kinship, link, parallel, ratio (= *relationship of one number to another*), similarity, tie.
2 *The twins have a close relationship.* attachment, closeness, SEE **friendship**, rapport, understanding.
3 [*informal*] *a sexual relationship.* affair, [*informal*] intrigue, [*informal*] liaison, love affair, romance, sexual relations.
FAMILY RELATIONSHIPS: SEE **family**.

relative adjective 1 *I've had relative good luck recently.* comparative.
2 *The police gathered evidence relative to the crime.* allied, appropriate, associated, cognate, connected, germane, pertinent, related, relevant.
OPPOSITES: SEE **unrelated**.

relative noun *All our relatives came to the wedding.* [*old-fashioned*] kinsman, [*old-fashioned*] kinswoman, [*plural*] kith and kin, member of the family, relation.
FAMILY RELATIONSHIPS: SEE **family**.

relax verb 1 *to relax your grip. to relax the pressure on something.* diminish, ease off, lessen, loosen, moderate, reduce, release, relieve, slacken, soften, unclench, unfasten, weaken.
OPPOSITES: SEE **increase, tighten**.
2 *to relax in front of the TV.* be easy, be relaxed [SEE **relaxed**], feel at home, rest, unbend, unwind.

relaxation noun informality, loosening up, SEE **recreation**, relaxing, rest, unwinding.
OPPOSITES: SEE **tension**.

relaxed adjective *a relaxed atmosphere. a relaxed conversation.* calm, carefree, casual, comfortable, contented, cosy, easygoing, friendly, good-humoured, happy, informal, [*informal*] laid-back, leisurely, light-hearted, nonchalant, reassuring, restful, serene, [*uncomplimentary*] SEE **slack** adjective, tranquil, unconcerned, unhurried, untroubled.
OPPOSITES: SEE **tense** adjective.

relay noun 1 *working in relays.* shift, turn.
2 *a live relay on TV.* broadcast, programme, transmission.
relay race VARIOUS RACES: SEE **race** noun.

relay verb *to relay information.* broadcast, communicate, pass on, send out, spread, transmit, televise.

release verb 1 *to release prisoners.* acquit, allow out, deliver, discharge, dismiss, emancipate, excuse, exonerate, free, let go, let loose, liberate, loose, pardon, rescue, save, set free, set loose, unleash, SEE **unfasten**, untie.
OPPOSITES: SEE **detain**.
2 *to release a missile.* fire off, launch, let fly, let off, send off.
3 *to release information.* circulate, disseminate, distribute, issue, make available, publish, send out.

relegate verb SEE **demote**.

relent verb *He was cross at first, but later he relented.* become more lenient, give in, show pity, soften, weaken, yield.

relentless adjective *a relentless attack. relentless nagging.* SEE **continual**, cruel, fierce, hard-hearted, implacable, incessant, inexorable, merciless, pitiless, remorseless, ruthless, unceasing, uncompromising, unfeeling, unforgiving, unmerciful, unrelieved, unremitting.
OPPOSITES: SEE **temporary**.

relevant adjective *Don't interrupt unless you have something relevant to say.* appertaining, applicable, apposite, appropriate, apropos, apt, connected, essential,

fitting, germane, linked, material, pertinent, related, relative, significant, suitable, to the point.
OPPOSITES: SEE **irrelevant**.

reliable adjective *reliable information. a reliable friend. a reliable car.* certain, consistent, constant, dependable, devoted, efficient, faithful, loyal, predictable, proven, regular, responsible, safe, solid, sound, stable, staunch, steady, sure, trustworthy, unchanging, unfailing.
OPPOSITES: SEE **unreliable**.

reliance noun *Don't put too much reliance on patent medicines.* confidence, dependence, faith, trust.

relic noun *a relic from the past.* memento, reminder, remnant, souvenir, survival, token, vestige.

relief noun *The pills gave some relief from the pain.* abatement, aid, alleviation, assistance, comfort, cure, diversion, ease, easement, help, [*informal*] let-up, mitigation, palliation, relaxation, release, remission, respite, rest.

relieve verb *to relieve pain. to relieve pressure on something.* alleviate, anaesthetize, assuage, bring relief [SEE **relief**], calm, comfort, console, cure, diminish, dull, ease, SEE **help** verb, lessen, lighten, make less, mitigate, moderate, palliate, reduce, relax, soothe.
OPPOSITES: SEE **intensify**.
to relieve your feelings [*informal*] let go, [*informal*] let off steam, show your feelings.

religion noun 1 *the religions of the world.* creed, cult, denomination, faith, sect.
2 *An evangelist preaches religion.* belief, doctrine, dogma, theology.
COMPARE: agnosticism, atheism, humanism.

SOME PRINCIPAL WORLD RELIGIONS: Buddhism, Christianity, Hinduism, Islam, Judaism, Sikhism, Taoism, Zen.
CHRISTIAN DENOMINATIONS: SEE **denomination**.
OTHER RELATED WORDS: SEE **church, clergyman, worship**.

religious adjective 1 *a religious service. religious writings.* devotional, divine, holy, sacramental, sacred, scriptural, theological.
OPPOSITES: SEE **secular**.
2 *a religious person.* committed, dedicated, devout, God-fearing, godly, pious, reverent, [*uncomplimentary*] religiose, righteous, [*uncomplimentary*] sanctimonious, spiritual.
OPPOSITES: SEE **irreligious**.

3 *a religious dispute. religious wars.* bigoted, doctrinal, fanatical, sectarian, schismatic.

relinquish verb SEE **surrender**.

relish noun 1 *We tucked into the food with relish.* appetite, delight, enjoyment, enthusiasm, gusto, zest.
2 *Spices add relish to a dish.* flavour, piquancy, savour, tang, taste.

relish verb *She relishes a challenge.* appreciate, delight in, enjoy, like, love, revel in.

relocate verb *They've relocated our bus-stop.* move, reposition.

reluctant adjective *I was reluctant to pay what they demanded.* disinclined, grudging, hesitant, loath, unenthusiastic, SEE **unwilling**.
OPPOSITES: SEE **eager**.

rely verb *You can rely on me to do my best.* [*informal*] bank on, count on, depend on, have confidence in, trust.

remain verb *Only half the audience remained at the end of the concert.* be left, carry on, continue, endure, keep on, linger, live on, persist, stay, survive.

remainder noun *Use what you can now, and keep the remainder for later.* balance, excess, extra, SEE **remains**, remnant, residue, rest, surplus.

remaining adjective abiding, continuing, left over, persisting, residual, surviving, unused.

remains noun 1 *the remains of something that has been used, damaged, or destroyed.* crumbs, debris, dregs, fragments, [*informal*] left-overs, [*informal*] odds and ends, SEE **remainder**, remnants, residue, rubble, ruins, scraps, traces, vestiges, wreckage.
2 *historic remains.* heritage, relics.
3 *the remains of a dead animal.* ashes, body, carcass, corpse.

remake verb SEE **renew**.

remand verb LEGAL TERMS: SEE **law**.

remark noun *The judge made a few remarks about our performance.* comment, mention, observation, opinion, reflection, statement, thought, utterance, word.

remark verb 1 *He remarked that it was a nice day.* comment, declare, mention, note, observe, reflect, say, state.
2 *Did you remark anything unusual?* heed, mark, notice, observe, perceive, see.

remarkable adjective *a remarkable achievement.* amazing, conspicuous, distinguished, exceptional, extraordinary,

important, impressive, notable, note-worthy, out of the ordinary, outstand-ing, phenomenal, prominent, singular, special, strange, striking, surprising, [*informal*] terrific, [*informal*] tremen-dous, uncommon, unusual, wonderful.
OPPOSITES: SEE **ordinary**.

emedy noun *a remedy for a cold. a remedy for a problem.* [*informal*] answer, anti-dote, corrective, cure, elixir, medicine, nostrum, palliative, panacea [= *a cure for everything*], prescription, relief, res-torative, solution, therapy, treatment.

emedy verb *I remedied the fault in the car.* alleviate, correct, counteract, cure, [*in-formal*] fix, heal, help, mend, mitigate, palliate, put right, rectify, redress, re-lieve, repair, solve, treat.

emember verb 1 *Do you remember Uncle George?* have a memory of, have in mind, recall, recognize, recollect, sum-mon up.
2 *Remember what I say!* keep in mind, learn, memorize, retain.
OPPOSITES: SEE **forget**.
3 *We sat for hours remembering old times.* be nostalgic about, hark back to, recall, reminisce about, review, tell stories about, think back to.
4 *They always go out for a meal to remem-ber their anniversary.* celebrate, com-memorate, observe.

emind verb *Remind me to buy potatoes.* give a reminder to [SEE **reminder**], jog the memory, prompt.

eminder noun 1 *a reminder of what you have to do or say.* aide-mémoire, cue, hint, [*informal*] memo, [*formal*] memor-andum, mnemonic, nudge, prompt, [*in-formal*] shopping list.
2 *a reminder of the past.* memento, relic, souvenir.

eminisce verb *to reminisce about the past.* be nostalgic, hark back, recall, remember, review, tell stories, think back.

eminiscence noun *reminiscences of childhood.* account, anecdote, memoir, memory, recollection, remembrance.

eminiscent adjective *scenes reminiscent of the past.* evocative, nostalgic, recal-ling, redolent, suggestive.

emiss adjective SEE **negligent**.

emission noun SEE **reduction**.

emit verb 1 *to remit a debt.* SEE **cancel**.
2 *to remit money in the post.* SEE **send**.

emittance noun SEE **money**.

emnants noun SEE **remains**.

emodel verb SEE **renew**.

emonstrate verb SEE **protest** verb.

remorse noun *remorse for wrongdoing.* compunction, contrition, grief, guilt, penitence, pricking of conscience, re-gret, repentance, sadness, self-accusa-tion, shame, sorrow.

remorseful adjective SEE **repentant**.

remorseless adjective SEE **relentless**.

remote adjective 1 *a remote corner of the world.* alien, cut off, desolate, distant, faraway, foreign, godforsaken, hard to find, inaccessible, isolated, lonely, out of reach, outlying, out of the way, secluded, solitary, unfamiliar, un-frequented, [*informal*] unget-at-able, unreachable.
OPPOSITES: SEE **accessible**.
2 *a remote chance of winning.* doubtful, implausible, improbable, negligible, outside, poor, slender, slight, small, unlikely.
OPPOSITES: SEE **likely**.
3 *a remote manner.* aloof, cold, cool, detached, haughty, preoccupied, re-served, standoffish, uninvolved, with-drawn.
OPPOSITES: SEE **friendly**.

removable adjective detachable, separ-able.
OPPOSITES: SEE **integral**.

removal noun 1 *the removal of furniture from a house.* relocation, taking away, transfer, transportation.
2 *the removal of a tooth.* drawing, extrac-tion, taking out, withdrawal.
3 *the removal of someone from a job or position.* dismissal, displacement, ejec-tion, elimination, eradication, exile, expulsion, ousting, purge, purging.

remove verb 1 *to remove unwanted people or things.* abolish, abstract, amputate (*amputate a limb*), clear away, cut out, delete, depose (*depose a monarch*), de-tach, disconnect, dismiss, dispense with, displace, eject, eliminate, eradi-cate, erase, evict (*evict a tenant*), excise, exile, expel, expunge, [*informal*] get rid of, [*informal*] kick out, kill, oust, purge, root out, rub out, send away, separate, strike out (*strike out words in a docu-ment*), take out, throw out, turn out, uproot, wash off, wipe (*wipe a recording from a tape*), wipe out.
2 *to remove furniture.* carry away, con-vey, move, take away, transfer, trans-port.
3 *to remove a tooth.* draw out, extract, pull out, take out.
4 *to remove clothes.* doff (*to doff a hat*), peel off, strip off, take off.

remunerate verb SEE **pay** verb.

remunerative adjective SEE **profitable**.

renaissance noun SEE **renewal**.

rend verb SEE **tear** verb.

render verb 1 *to render someone a service.* SEE **give**.
2 *to render a song.* SEE **perform**.
3 *to render someone speechless.* SEE **make**.

rendezvous noun *a secret rendezvous.* appointment, assignation, date, engagement, meeting, meeting-place.

rendition noun SEE **performance**.

renegade noun *Faithful supporters were bitter about the renegades.* apostate, backslider, defector, deserter, fugitive, mutineer, outlaw, rebel, runaway, traitor, turncoat.

renege verb **to renege on** *to renege on an agreement.* break, fail to keep, go back on, [*informal*] rat on, repudiate, [*informal*] welsh on (*to welsh on a bet*).

renew verb VARIOUS WAYS TO RENEW OLD THINGS: bring up to date, [*informal*] do up, [*informal*] give a face-lift to, improve, mend, modernize, overhaul, recondition, reconstitute, recreate, redecorate, redesign, redevelop, redo, refit, refresh (*refresh the paintwork*), refurbish, regenerate, reintroduce, rejuvenate, remake, remodel, renovate, repaint, repair, replace, replenish, restore, resume, revamp, revitalize, revive, touch up, transform, update.

renewal noun 1 *the renewal of life in the spring.* reawakening, rebirth, regeneration, renaissance, resumption, resurgence, resurrection, return, revival.
2 *renewal of the paintwork.* SEE **renovation**.
3 *renewal of your passport.* replacement, revalidation, updating.

renounce verb 1 *to renounce violence.* abandon, abjure, declare your opposition to, discard, disown, forsake, forswear, reject, repudiate, spurn.
2 *to renounce the throne.* abdicate, give up, quit, relinquish, resign.

renovation noun *the renovation of an old building.* improvement, modernization, overhaul, reconditioning, redevelopment, refit, refurbishment, renewal, repair, restoration, transformation, updating.

renovate verb SEE **renew**.

renown noun SEE **fame**.

renowned adjective SEE **famous**.

rent noun 1 *I forgot to pay the rent for the TV.* fee, hire, instalment, regular payment, rental.
2 *a rent in my jeans.* SEE **tear** noun.

rent verb *We rented a caravan for our holiday.* charter, hire, lease, let.

rental noun SEE **rent** noun.

reorganize verb *to reorganize a business. to reorganize your time.* rearrange, redeploy, reshuffle, restructure.

repair verb 1 *to repair a damaged car.* [*informal*] fix, mend, overhaul, patch up, put right, rectify, refit, SEE **renew**, service.
2 *to repair clothes.* darn, patch, sew up.

reparation noun **to make reparation** SEE **compensate**.

repartee noun SEE **wit**.

repast noun SEE **meal**.

repatriate verb SEE **return** verb.

repay verb 1 *They repaid my expenses.* compensate, pay back, recompense, refund, reimburse, remunerate, settle.
2 [*uncomplimentary*] *She repaid his insult with interest.* avenge, get even with, [*informal*] get your own back for, reciprocate, requite, retaliate, return, revenge.

repeal verb SEE **cancel**.

repeat verb *to repeat an action or an event or a saying.* do again, duplicate, echo, quote, recapitulate, redo, re-echo, regurgitate, rehearse, reiterate, replay, reproduce, re-run, restate, retell, say again, show again.

repeated adjective SEE **recurrent**.

repel verb 1 *to repel an attack.* check, drive away, fend off, fight off, hold off, parry, push away, rebuff, repulse, ward off.
2 *This oily material repels water.* be impermeable to, exclude, keep out, reject, resist.
OPPOSITES: SEE **attract**.
3 *Her callous attitude repels me.* be repellent to [SEE **repellent**], disgust, nauseate, offend, [*informal*] put off (*Her attitude puts me off*), revolt, sicken, [*informal*] turn off (*Her attitude turns me off*).
OPPOSITES: SEE **delight** verb.

repellent adjective 1 *Tents are made of material which is repellent to water.* impermeable, impervious, resistant, unsusceptible.
2 *a repellent smell.* SEE **repulsive**.

repent verb *to repent your sins.* be repentant about [SEE **repentant**], feel repentance for [SEE **repentance**], regret, reproach yourself for.

repentance noun contrition, guilt, penitence, regret, remorse, self-accusation, self-reproach, sorrow.

repentant adjective *He was repentant when he saw what he'd done.* apologetic, ashamed, conscience-stricken, contrite

grief-stricken, guilt-ridden, guilty, penitent, regretful, remorseful, sorry.
OPPOSITES: SEE **unrepentant.**

epercussion noun SEE **result** noun.

epertoire, repertory nouns *He has a vast repertoire of stories.* collection, reserve, stock, supply.

epetitive adjective *a repetitive job. a repetitive story.* boring, monotonous, recurrent, repeating, repetitious, tautological, tedious, unchanging, unvaried.

ephrase verb SEE **revise.**

eplace verb 1 *Replace the books on the shelf.* put back, reinstate, restore, return.
2 *Who will replace the present prime minister?* be a substitute for, come after, follow, oust, succeed, supersede, supplant, take over from, take the place of.
3 *It's time we replaced those tyres.* change, provide a substitute for, renew.

eplacement noun *a replacement for the regular teacher.* [*informal*] fill-in, proxy, stand-in, substitute, successor, understudy [= *replacement for an actor*].

eplay verb SEE **repeat.**

eplenish verb SEE **refill.**

eplete adjective SEE **full.**

eplica noun *a replica of a lunar-module. a replica of a document.* clone, copy, duplicate, facsimile, imitation, model, reconstruction, reproduction.

eply noun *a reply to a letter or a question.* acknowledgement, answer, [*informal*] come-back, reaction, rejoinder, response, retort, [*joking*] riposte.

eply verb **to reply to** *to reply to a letter or a question.* acknowledge, answer, counter, give a reply to [SEE **reply** noun], react to, respond to.

eport noun 1 *a report in a newspaper. a report on an investigation.* account, announcement, article, communication, communiqué, description, dispatch, narrative, news, record, statement, story, [*informal*] write-up.
2 *the report of a gun.* bang, blast, crack, detonation, explosion, noise.

eport verb 1 *I reported the results of my investigation.* announce, circulate, communicate, declare, describe, document, give an account of, notify, present a report on [SEE **report** noun], proclaim, publish, record, recount, reveal, state, tell.
2 *Report to reception when you arrive.* announce yourself, introduce yourself, make yourself known, present yourself.

3 *I reported him to the police.* complain about, SEE **denounce,** inform against, [*informal*] tell of.

reporter noun *a newspaper reporter.* correspondent, journalist.

repose noun *a moment of repose in the midst of activity.* calm, comfort, ease, inactivity, peace, peacefulness, poise, quiet, quietness, relaxation, respite, rest, serenity, stillness, tranquillity.

repository noun SEE **store** noun.

repossess verb SEE **retrieve.**

reprehend verb SEE **reprimand** verb.

reprehensible adjective *reprehensible behaviour.* SEE **bad,** blameworthy, culpable, deplorable, disgraceful, immoral, objectionable, regrettable, remiss, shameful, unworthy, wicked.

represent verb 1 *Our pageant represented scenes from history.* act out, delineate, depict, describe, draw, enact, exhibit, illustrate, paint, picture, portray, show.
2 *Santa Claus represents the spirit of Christmas.* embody, epitomize, exemplify, incarnate, personify, stand for, symbolize.
3 *Our spokesperson represents the views of us all.* be an example of, express, present, speak for.

representation noun *a representation of a goddess.* depiction, figure, icon, image, imitation, likeness, model, picture, portrait, portrayal, resemblance, statue.

representative adjective 1 *representative voters.* average, characteristic, illustrative, normal, typical.
OPPOSITES: SEE **abnormal.**
2 *representative government.* chosen, democratic, elected, elective, popular.
OPPOSITES: SEE **undemocratic.**

representative noun 1 *a representative who speaks for someone else.* delegate [= *a person representing a group*], deputy, proxy, stand-in, substitute.
2 *a sales representative.* agent, [*informal*] rep, salesman, salesperson, saleswoman, [*informal*] traveller.
3 *a government representative.* ambassador, consul, diplomat.

repress verb *to repress your feelings.* [*informal*] bottle up, control, crush, curb, inhibit, keep down, quell, restrain, stifle, suppress.

repressed adjective 1 *a repressed person.* cold, frigid, inhibited, neurotic, unbalanced.
2 *repressed emotions.* [*informal*] bottled up, hidden, latent, subconscious, suppressed, unconscious, unfulfilled.
OPPOSITES: SEE **uninhibited.**

repression noun **1** *political repression.* authoritarianism, censorship, coercion, control, despotism, dictatorship, oppression, subjugation, totalitarianism, tyranny.
OPPOSITES: SEE **freedom**.
2 *repression of a person's feelings.* [*informal*] bottling up, inhibition, suffocation.

repressive adjective *repressive laws.* authoritarian, autocratic, coercive, cruel, despotic, dictatorial, harsh, illiberal, oppressive, restricting, severe, totalitarian, tyrannical, undemocratic, unenlightened.
OPPOSITES: SEE **liberal**.

reprieve verb *to reprieve a condemned prisoner.* forgive, let off, pardon, set free, spare.

reprimand noun *The teacher gave the class a severe reprimand.* admonition, censure, [*informal*] dressing-down, [*informal*] going-over, lecture, lesson, rebuke, reproach, reproof, scolding, [*informal*] talking-to, [*informal*] telling-off, [*informal*] ticking-off, [*informal*] wigging.

reprimand verb *to reprimand a wrongdoer.* admonish, censure, chide, condemn, criticize, disapprove of, give a reprimand to [SEE **reprimand** noun], lecture, [*informal*] rap, rate, rebuke, reprehend, reproach, reprove, scold, [*informal*] slate, [*informal*] take to task, [*informal*] teach (someone) a lesson, [*informal*] tell off, [*informal*] tick off, upbraid.
OPPOSITES: SEE **congratulate**.

reprisal noun *a reprisal against the attackers.* counter-attack, retaliation, retribution, revenge, vengeance.

reproach noun *She gave the naughty child a look of reproach.* blame, disapproval, disgrace, SEE **reprimand** noun, scorn.

reproach verb *to reproach someone you disapprove of.* censure, criticize, SEE **reprimand** verb, show disapproval of, upbraid.
OPPOSITES: SEE **praise** verb.

reproachful adjective *a reproachful frown.* censorious, critical, disapproving, reproving, scornful, withering.

reprobate noun SEE **immoral** (immoral person).

reproduce verb **1** *to reproduce a document.* copy, counterfeit, duplicate, forge, imitate, mimic, photocopy, print, redo, reissue, SEE **repeat**, reprint, simulate.
2 *to reproduce your own kind.* breed, increase, multiply, procreate, produce offspring, propagate, spawn.

reproduction noun **1** *the reproduction of animals or plants.* breeding, increase, multiplying, procreation, propagation.
2 *a reproduction of an original picture.* copy, duplicate, facsimile, fake, forgery, imitation, likeness, print, replica.

reprographics noun REPROGRAPHIC MACHINES: cyclostyle, duplicator, heat copier, laser printer, photocopier, printer, printing press, spirit copier.
OTHER REPROGRAPHIC PROCESSES: desktop publishing, offset litho, Xerox.

reproof noun SEE **reprimand** noun.

reprove verb SEE **reprimand** verb.

reptile noun

SOME REPTILES: alligator, basilisk, chameleon, crocodile, lizard, salamander, snake, tortoise, turtle.
OTHER ANIMALS: SEE **animal** noun.

---

republic noun SEE **country**.

republican adjective, noun POLITICAL TERMS: SEE **politics**.

repudiate verb **1** *to repudiate an accusation.* deny, disagree with, dispute, rebuff, refute, reject, renounce.
2 *to repudiate an agreement.* disown, go back on, recant, rescind, retract, reverse, revoke.
OPPOSITES: SEE **acknowledge**.

repugnant adjective SEE **repulsive**.

repulse verb SEE **reject, repel**.

repulsive adjective *repulsive behaviour. a repulsive appearance.* abhorrent, disagreeable, disgusting, distasteful, foul, hateful, hideous, loathsome, nauseating, objectionable, obnoxious, odious, offensive, [*informal*] off-putting, repellent, repugnant, revolting, sickening, SEE **ugly**, unattractive, unpleasant, unsightly, vile.
OPPOSITES: SEE **attractive**.

reputable adjective *a reputable business.* dependable, esteemed, famous, highly regarded, honoured, prestigious, reliable, respectable, respected, trustworthy, unimpeachable, [*informal*] up-market, well thought of.
OPPOSITES: SEE **disreputable**.

reputation noun *a good reputation for reliability.* character, fame, name, prestige, recognition, renown, repute, standing.

repute noun SEE **reputation**.

reputed adjective *reputed to be of good quality.* alleged, believed, considered, famed, reckoned, regarded, rumoured, said, supposed, thought.

request noun *He didn't listen to our request.* appeal, application, call, demand, entreaty, petition, plea, prayer, question, requisition, [*formal*] suit, supplication.

request verb *We requested help. He requested to see my licence.* adjure, appeal (for), apply (for), ask, beg, call (for), claim, demand, desire, entreat, implore, importune, invite, [*formal*] petition, pray for, require, requisition, seek, solicit, [*formal*] supplicate.

requiem noun SEE **funeral**.

require verb 1 *We required 3 runs to win.* be short of, depend on, lack, need, want. 2 *The officer required me to show my licence.* command, compel, direct, force, instruct, make, oblige, order, SEE **request** verb.

required adjective *Have you got the required qualifications?* compulsory, essential, imperative, indispensable, mandatory, necessary, needed, obligatory, prescribed, requisite, set, stipulated.
OPPOSITES: SEE **optional**.

requisite adjective SEE **required**.

requisition noun *a requisition for goods.* application, demand, order, request.

requisition verb *to requisition vehicles to deal with an emergency.* appropriate, commandeer, occupy, seize, take over.

reroute verb SEE **divert**.

rescind verb SEE **repeal**.

rescue noun *the rescue of a prisoner. a heroic rescue at sea.* deliverance, liberation, recovery, release, relief, salvage.

rescue verb 1 *to rescue someone from captivity.* deliver, extricate, free, liberate, ransom, release, save, set free. 2 *I rescued my belongings from the flood.* bring away, recover, retrieve, salvage.

research noun *research into the causes of disease.* experimentation, exploration, inquiry, investigation, [*informal*] probe, searching, study.

researcher noun analyst, [*informal*] boffin, investigator, scientist, student.

resemblance noun *the resemblance of twins.* affinity, closeness, correspondence, likeness, similarity, similitude.

resemble verb *Twins usually resemble each other.* be similar to, look like, mirror, [*informal*] take after.

resent verb *to resent someone else's success.* begrudge, be resentful about [SEE

resentful], dislike, envy, grudge, grumble at, object to, [*informal*] take exception to, [*informal*] take umbrage at.

resentful adjective *resentful feelings about someone else's success.* aggrieved, SEE **angry**, annoyed, bitter, displeased, embittered, envious, grudging, hurt, indignant, jaundiced, jealous, malicious, offended, [*informal*] peeved, [*informal*] put out, spiteful, unfriendly, ungenerous, upset, vexed, vindictive.

resentment noun *feelings of resentment.* SEE **anger** noun, animosity, bitterness, discontent, grudge, hatred, hurt, illwill, indignation, malevolence, malice, pique, rancour, spite, unfriendliness, vexation, vindictiveness.

reservation noun 1 *a hotel reservation.* booking. 2 *I have reservations about our plan.* condition, doubt, hesitation, misgiving, proviso, qualification, scepticism, scruple. 3 *a wildlife reservation.* SEE **reserve** noun.

reserve noun 1 *a reserve of food.* fund, hoard, reservoir, savings, stock, stockpile, store, supply. 2 *reserves for a game of football.* deputy, [*plural*] reinforcements, replacement, stand-by, [*informal*] stand-in, substitute, understudy. 3 *a wildlife reserve.* enclave, game park, preserve, protected area, reservation, safari-park, sanctuary. 4 *Overcome your reserve and join in.* aloofness, caution, modesty, reluctance, reserved behaviour [SEE **reserved**], reticence, self-consciousness, self-effacement, shyness, timidity.

reserve verb 1 *Reserve some food to eat later.* earmark, hoard, hold back, keep, keep back, preserve, put aside, retain, save, set aside, stockpile, store up. 2 *We reserved seats on the train.* [*informal*] bag, book, order, pay for.

reserved adjective *too reserved to speak up for herself.* aloof, bashful, cautious, cool, demure, diffident, discreet, distant, modest, quiet, restrained, reticent, retiring, secretive, self-conscious, self-effacing, shy, silent, [*uncomplimentary*] standoffish, taciturn, timid, uncommunicative, undemonstrative, unforthcoming, withdrawn.
OPPOSITES: SEE **demonstrative**.

reservoir noun SEE **lake**.

reshuffle verb SEE **reorganize**.

reside verb *to reside in* dwell in, have as a home, inhabit, live in, lodge in, occupy, settle in.

residence noun *your permanent residence.* [*old-fashioned*] abode, address, [*formal*] domicile, dwelling, habitation, home, SEE **house** noun.

resident adjective *The hostel has its own resident staff.* in residence, living-in, permanent.
OPPOSITES: SEE **non-resident**.

resident noun *the residents of an area.* citizen, denizen, inhabitant, [*informal*] local, native.
a temporary resident guest, lodger, occupant, tenant, visitor.

residential adjective *a residential area.* built-up, suburban.
OPPOSITES: commercial, industrial, rural.

residual adjective SEE **remaining**.

residue noun SEE **remainder**.

resign verb *to resign your job.* abdicate, forsake, give up, leave, quit, relinquish, renounce, stand down from, surrender, vacate.
to resign yourself to SEE **accept**.

resigned adjective *resigned about your problems.* calm, [*uncomplimentary*] defeatist, long-suffering, patient, philosophical, reasonable, stoical, submissive.

resilient adjective 1 *Rubber is a resilient material.* bouncy, elastic, firm, plastic, pliable, rubbery, springy, supple.
OPPOSITES: SEE **brittle**.
2 *a resilient person.* adaptable, buoyant, irrepressible, strong, tough, unstoppable.
OPPOSITES: SEE **vulnerable**.

resist verb *to resist arrest. to resist temptation.* avoid, be resistant to [SEE **resistant**], counteract, defy, SEE **fight** verb, oppose, prevent, refuse, stand up to, withstand.

resistant adjective *resistant to heat. resistant to temptation.* hostile, impervious, invulnerable, opposed, repellent, unaffected (by), unresponsive, unsusceptible, unyielding.
OPPOSITES: SEE **susceptible**.

resolute adjective *resolute opposition. resolute courage.* adamant, bold, committed, constant, courageous, decided, decisive, determined, dogged, firm, immovable, [*uncomplimentary*] inflexible, [*uncomplimentary*] obstinate, relentless, resolved, staunch, steadfast, strong-minded, strong-willed, [*uncomplimentary*] stubborn, unbending, undaunted, unflinching, unswerving, unwavering.
OPPOSITES: SEE **irresolute**.

resolution noun 1 *resolution in the face of danger.* boldness, commitment, constancy, courage, devotion, firmness, fortitude, [*uncomplimentary*] obstinacy, perseverance, resolve, staunchness, steadfastness, [*uncomplimentary*] stubbornness, tenacity, will-power.
2 *a resolution passed at a meeting.* decision, motion, statement.
3 *a resolution of all our problems.* answer, settlement, solution.

resolve noun SEE **resolution**.

resolve verb *We resolved to start our own business.* agree, conclude, decide formally, determine, elect, make a firm decision, opt, pass a resolution, settle, undertake, vote.

resonant adjective *a resonant voice. the resonant sound of a gong.* booming, echoing, full, resounding, reverberant, reverberating, rich, ringing, sonorous, vibrant.

resonate verb SEE **resound**.

resort noun 1 *Use violence only as a last resort.* alternative, course of action, expedient, option, recourse, refuge.
2 *a seaside resort.* holiday town, retreat, spa, [*old-fashioned*] watering-place.

resort verb *I don't want to resort to violence.* adopt, [*informal*] fall back on, make use of, turn to, use.

resound verb *Our voices resounded in the cave.* boom, echo, resonate, reverberate, ring, vibrate.

resounding adjective 1 *a resounding clash of cymbals.* SEE **resonant**.
2 [*informal*] *a resounding success.* SEE **great**.

resourceful adjective *a resourceful inventor.* clever, creative, enterprising, imaginative, ingenious, innovative, inspired, inventive, original, talented.
OPPOSITES: SEE **unimaginative**.

resources noun 1 *financial resources.* assets, capital, funds, SEE **money**, reserves, riches, wealth.
2 *natural resources.* materials, raw materials.

respect noun 1 *We remained silent as a sign of respect.* admiration, awe, consideration, deference, esteem, homage, honour, liking, love, regard, reverence, tribute, veneration.
2 *My work isn't perfect in every respect.* aspect, characteristic, detail, facet, feature, particular, point, way.

respect verb *Everyone respects her for her courage.* admire, esteem, honour, pay

homage to, revere, reverence, show re-spect to [SEE **respect** noun], think well of, value, venerate.
OPPOSITES: SEE **scorn** verb.

respectable adjective 1 *respectable people.* decent, honest, honourable, law-abiding, respected, upright, worthy.
2 *respectable clothes.* clean, modest, pre-sentable, proper.
OPPOSITES: SEE **disreputable**.
3 *He gets a respectable income.* SEE **con-siderable**.

respectful adjective *a respectful greeting.* civil, courteous, deferential, dutiful, gracious, humble, polite, proper, rever-ent, reverential, [*uncomplimentary*] ser-vile, subservient.
OPPOSITES: disrespectful, SEE **rude**.

respective adjective *We all returned to our respective homes.* individual, own, particular, personal, several, specific.

respiration noun breathing.

respire verb SEE **breathe**.

respite noun *a respite from your labours.* break, [*informal*] breather, interval, [*in-formal*] let-up, lull, pause, recess, relax-ation, relief, remission, rest.

resplendent adjective *resplendent in her jewels.* bright, SEE **brilliant**, dazzling, glittering, shining, splendid.

respond verb **to respond to** *to respond to a question.* acknowledge, answer, coun-ter, give a response to [SEE **response**], react to, reply to.

response noun *a response to a question.* acknowledgement, answer, [*informal*] come-back, counterblast, feedback, reaction, rejoinder, reply, retort, [*jok-ing*] riposte.

responsible adjective 1 *A teacher is re-sponsible for her class.* accountable, an-swerable, in charge of.
2 *I was responsible for the damage.* culp-able, guilty, liable.
3 *We need a responsible person as treasurer.* concerned, conscientious, dependable, diligent, dutiful, ethical, honest, law-abiding, loyal, mature, moral, reliable, sensible, sober, steady, thinking, thoughtful, trustworthy, unselfish.
OPPOSITES: SEE **irresponsible**.
4 *a responsible job.* burdensome, execu-tive, important.

responsive adjective *a responsive audience. responsive pupils.* alert, alive, aware, impressionable, interested, open, perceptive, receptive, sympa-thetic, warm-hearted, willing.
OPPOSITES: SEE **uninterested**, **unsym-pathetic**.

rest noun 1 *a rest from work. a rest on the sofa.* break, [*informal*] breather, breathing-space, comfort, ease, holiday, idleness, inactivity, interlude, intermis-sion, interval, leisure, [*informal*] lie-down, lull, nap, pause, quiet, relaxa-tion, relief, repose, siesta, time off, vaca-tion.
2 *a rest for a telescope.* base, holder, prop, stand, support.
to come to rest SEE **halt** verb.
the rest SEE **remainder**.

rest verb 1 *to rest on the sofa. to rest from your labours.* be still, doze, have a rest [SEE **rest** noun], idle, laze, lie back, lie down, lounge, nod off, recline, relax, sleep, slumber, snooze, [*informal*] take a nap.
2 *Rest the ladder against the wall.* lean, place, prop, stand, support.
3 *Everything rests on the committee's de-cision.* depend, hang, hinge, rely, turn.

restaurant noun bistro, brasserie, buf-fet, café, cafeteria, canteen, carvery, diner, dining-room, eating-place, grill, snack-bar, steak-house.

restful adjective *a restful holiday.* calm, comfortable, leisurely, peaceful, quiet, relaxing, soothing, tranquil, undis-turbed, unhurried, untroubled.
OPPOSITES: SEE **exhausting**.

restitution noun *the restitution of someone's rights.* SEE **compensation**, restoration, return.

restive adjective SEE **restless**.

restless adjective 1 *restless animals.* agi-tated, anxious, edgy, excitable, fidgety, impatient, jittery, jumpy, nervous, res-tive, worried.
OPPOSITES: SEE **relaxed**.
2 *a restless night.* disturbed, interrupted, sleepless, troubled, uncomfortable, unsettled.
OPPOSITES: SEE **restful**.

restore verb 1 *to restore something you have borrowed.* give back, put back, re-place, return.
2 *to restore an old building.* clean, [*infor-mal*] do up, fix, [*informal*] make good, mend, rebuild, recondition, recon-struct, refurbish, renew, renovate, re-pair, touch up.
3 *to restore good relations with the neigh-bours.* bring back, re-establish, rehabili-tate, reinstate, reintroduce, revive.
4 *to restore someone to health.* cure, nurse, rejuvenate, revitalize.

restrain verb *Please restrain your dog. Restrain your laughter.* bridle, check, confine, control, curb, fetter, govern, handcuff, harness, hold back, inhibit, keep back, keep under control, muzzle, pinion, rein in, repress, restrict, stop, straitjacket, subdue, suppress, tie up.

restrained adjective *In spite of his anger, his remarks were restrained.* calm, controlled, discreet, low-key, mild, moderate, muted, quiet, repressed, reserved, reticent, soft, subdued, temperate, undemonstrative, understated, unemotional.
OPPOSITES: SEE **uninhibited**.

restrict verb 1 *to restrict someone's freedom.* circumscribe, control, cramp, inhibit, limit, regulate.
2 *The prisoners were restricted in their cells.* confine, enclose, imprison, keep, SEE **restrain**, shut.
OPPOSITES: SEE **free** verb.

restriction noun 1 *restrictions on your freedom.* check, constraint, control, curb, curfew, inhibition, limitation, restraint.
2 *a speed restriction.* ban, limit, regulation, rule, stipulation.

result noun 1 *The water shortage is a result of the hot weather.* consequence, effect, end-product, issue, outcome, product, repercussion, sequel, upshot.
2 *the result of a trial.* decision, judgement, verdict.
3 *the result of a game.* score.
4 *the result of a calculation.* answer.

result verb *What resulted from your interview?* arise, come about, culminate, develop, emanate, emerge, ensue, eventuate, follow, happen, issue, occur, proceed, spring, stem, take place, turn out.
to result in *I hope it doesn't result in tears!* achieve, bring about, cause, give rise to, lead to, provoke.

resume verb *to resume after a break.* begin again, carry on, continue, [*informal*] pick up the threads, proceed, recommence, reconvene, re-open, restart.

resumption noun *the resumption of work after a holiday.* continuation, recommencement, re-opening, restarting.

résumé noun SEE **summary** noun.

resurgence noun SEE **renewal**.

resurrect verb *to resurrect an old railway line.* bring back, SEE **renew**, restore, resuscitate, revitalize, revive.
2 *to resurrect from the dead.* bring back to life, raise.

resurrection noun SEE **renewal**.

resuscitate verb SEE **resurrect**.

retail verb 1 *to retail goods.* SEE **sell**.
2 *to retail your adventures.* SEE **recount**.

retain verb 1 *Please retain your ticket.* [*informal*] hang on to, hold, hold back, keep, reserve, save.
OPPOSITES: SEE **surrender**.
2 *Throughout the crisis he retained his composure.* keep control of, maintain, preserve.
OPPOSITES: SEE **lose**.
3 *He retains everything he reads.* keep in mind, learn, memorize, remember.
OPPOSITES: SEE **forget**.

retainer noun SEE **servant**.

retaliate verb *to retaliate against someone who hurt you.* [*informal*] get even (with), [*informal*] get your own back, hit back, make a counter-attack, pay back, repay, revenge yourself, seek retribution, strike back, take revenge.

retaliation noun counter-attack, reprisal, retribution, revenge, vengeance.

retard verb SEE **delay** verb.

retarded adjective *a retarded pupil.* backward, disadvantaged, handicapped, slow, undeveloped.

retch verb SEE **vomit**.

reticent adjective *a reticent person.* SEE **reserved**.

retinue noun attendants, entourage, followers, servants.
VARIOUS SERVANTS: SEE **servant**.

retire verb *to retire from work.* *to retire from a fight.* give up, leave, quit, resign SEE **withdraw**.

retiring adjective *a retiring personality* SEE **reserved**.

retort noun *a sharp retort.* answer, come back, quip, recrimination, rejoinder, reply, response, retaliation, [*joking*] riposte.

retort verb *He retorted rudely.* answer counter, react, reply, respond, retaliate return.

retrace verb *to retrace your steps* SEE return verb.

retract verb 1 *A snail can retract it horns.* draw in, pull back, pull in.
2 *to retract an accusation.* abandon, cancel, disclaim, disown, [*informal*] hav second thoughts about, recant renounce, repeal, repudiate, rescind reverse, revoke, withdraw.

retractable adjective SEE **collapsible**.

retreat noun 1 *We made a quick retrea.* departure, escape, evacuation, exit flight, withdrawal.
2 *a secluded retreat in the hills.* asylum den, haven, [*informal*] hide-away, hide

out, hiding-place, refuge, resort, sanctuary, shelter.

etreat verb 1 *The army retreated.* back away, back down, climb down, depart, fall back, go away, leave, move back, retire, [*informal*] run away, [*informal*] turn tail, withdraw.
2 *The floods retreated.* ebb, flow back, recede, shrink back.

etribution noun *The victim's family sought retribution.* compensation, recompense, redress, reprisal, retaliation, revenge, vengeance.
OPPOSITES: SEE **forgiveness**.

etrieve verb *to retrieve something you lost.* fetch back, find, get back, recapture, recoup, recover, regain, repossess, rescue, restore, return, salvage, save, trace, track down.

The prefix *retro-* is from Latin *retro* = *backwards.*

---

etrograde, retrogressive adjectives *a retrograde step.* SEE **backward**.

etrospective adjective *a retrospective glance.* backward-looking, looking behind.

eturn noun 1 *We look forward to your return.* arrival, re-entry, homecoming, reappearance.
2 *After the flood there was a slow return to normality.* re-establishment (of), regression, restoration (of), reversion.
3 *We must avoid a return of the problem.* recrudescence, recurrence.
4 *I want a good return on my investment.* gain, income, interest, profit.

eturn verb 1 *I'll see you when you return.* come back, reappear, reassemble, reconvene, re-enter, retrace your steps.
2 *to return someone or something to their place of origin.* convey, deliver, repatriate, replace, restore, send back.
3 *Things soon returned to their original state.* go back, regress, revert.
4 *The problem may return.* happen again, recur.
5 *Please return the money I lent you.* give back, refund, reimburse, repay.
6 *She returned a witty response.* SEE **answer** verb.

eunion noun VARIOUS KINDS OF PARTY: SEE **party**.

evamp verb SEE **renew**.

eveal verb *to reveal the truth.* announce, bare, betray, communicate, confess, declare, disclose, display, divulge, exhibit, expose, [*informal*] give the game away, lay bare, leak, make known, proclaim,

produce, publish, show, show up, [*informal*] spill the beans, tell, uncover, unfold, unmask, unveil.
OPPOSITES: SEE **hide** verb.

revel verb *We were revelling all night.* carouse, celebrate, [*informal*] have a spree, have fun, indulge in revelry [SEE **revelry**], make merry.
to revel in *I revel in the sunshine.* be happy in, delight in, enjoy, love, luxuriate in, rejoice in, relish, take pleasure in.

revelation noun *The revelation of what he'd done amazed me.* announcement, confession, disclosure, discovery, exposé, exposure, news, publication, revealing, unmasking.

revelry noun *The revelry continued all night.* carousing, celebration, conviviality, debauchery, festivity, fun, [*joking*] jollification, [*informal*] junketing, merrymaking, orgy, party, revelling, revels, roistering, [*informal*] spree.

revenge noun *His cruel heart was set on revenge.* reprisal, retaliation, retribution, vengeance, vindictiveness.
to take revenge SEE **revenge** verb.

revenge verb *to revenge a wrong.* avenge, [*informal*] get your own back for, repay, retaliate, take revenge for.
to be revenged be even, [*informal*] be quits.

revenue noun *the revenue from a business.* income, SEE **money**, proceeds, profits, receipts.

reverberate verb SEE **resound**.

reverberation noun *the reverberation of a gong.* echo, resonance, ringing, rumble, vibration.

revere verb *We revere our heroes.* admire, adore, feel reverence for [SEE **reverence**], honour, idolize, pay homage to, praise, respect, reverence, value, venerate, worship.
OPPOSITES: SEE **despise**.

reverence noun *reverence for our heroes.* admiration, adoration, awe, deference, devotion, esteem, homage, praise, respect, veneration, worship.

reverent adjective *reverent worshippers. a reverent silence.* adoring, awed, awestruck, deferential, devout, pious, respectful, reverential, solemn.
OPPOSITES: SEE **irreverent**.

reverie noun SEE **dream** noun.

reverse adjective *the reverse side.* back, contrary, opposite, rear.

reverse noun 1 *He says one thing and does the reverse.* antithesis, contrary, converse, opposite.

2 *We suffered a number of reverses last year.* defeat, failure, SEE **misfortune**, reversal, set-back, [*informal*] upset.

reverse verb **1** *to reverse a sequence.* change, invert, transpose, turn round.
2 *to reverse a car.* back, drive backwards, go backwards, go into reverse.
3 *to reverse a decision.* countermand, negate, overturn, repeal, rescind, retract, revoke, undo.

review noun **1** *a review of the year.* look back, reappraisal, recapitulation, reconsideration, re-examination, report, study, survey.
2 *a book or record review.* appreciation, criticism, critique, notice, [*informal*] write-up.

review verb **1** *to review the evidence.* appraise, assess, consider, evaluate, [*informal*] go over, inspect, recapitulate, reconsider, re-examine, scrutinize, study, survey, [*informal*] weigh up.
2 *to review a book or record.* criticize, write a review of [SEE **review** noun].

revile verb SEE **abuse** verb.

revise verb **1** *to revise your opinions. to revise a draft.* adapt, alter, change, correct, edit, emend, improve, modify, [*informal*] polish up, reconsider, [*informal*] redo, [*informal*] rehash, rephrase, revamp, reword, rewrite, update.
2 *to revise for an exam.* [*informal*] cram, learn, study, [*informal*] swot.

revival noun *a revival of interest in old crafts.* reawakening, rebirth, recovery, renaissance, renewal, restoration, resurgence, resurrection, return, revitalization, upsurge.

revivalist noun SEE **preacher**.

revive verb **1** *He soon revived after his black-out.* awaken, come back to life, [*informal*] come round, [*informal*] come to, rally, recover, rouse.
2 *A cold drink revived us.* bring back to life, [*informal*] cheer up, freshen up, invigorate, refresh, renew, restore, resuscitate, revitalize.
OPPOSITES: SEE **weaken, weary** verb.

revoke verb *to revoke a decree.* SEE **cancel**.

revolt verb **1** *to revolt against authority.* disobey, mutiny, rebel, riot, rise up.
2 *Cruelty to animals revolts us.* SEE **disgust** verb.

revolting adjective *a revolting mess.* SEE **disgusting**.

revolution noun **1** *a political revolution.* civil war, coup, coup d'état, mutiny, SEE **rebellion**, reformation, revolt, rising, uprising.

2 *a revolution of the earth.* circuit, orbit, rotation, turn.
3 *Computers have created an economic revolution.* change, reorganization, reorientation, shift, transformation, [*informal*] turn-about, upheaval, [*informal*] upset, [*informal*] U-turn.

revolutionary adjective *revolutionary ideas.* avant-garde, challenging, experimental, extremist, innovative, new, novel, progressive, radical, seditious, subversive, [*informal*] unheard of, upsetting.
OPPOSITES: SEE **conservative** adjective.

revolutionize verb SEE **transform**.

revolve verb *Wheels revolve. Planets revolve round the sun.* circle, gyrate, orbit, pirouette (*Dancers pirouette*), rotate, spin, swivel, turn, twirl, wheel, whirl.

revolver noun SEE **gun**.

revue noun KINDS OF ENTERTAINMENT: SEE **entertainment**.

revulsion noun *a revulsion against cruelty.* SEE **disgust** noun.

reward noun *a reward for bravery. a reward for hard work.* award, bonus, bounty, compensation, decoration, honour, medal, payment, prize, recompense, remuneration, return.
OPPOSITES: SEE **punishment**.

reward verb **1** *to reward someone for bravery.* decorate, honour.
2 *to reward someone for hard work.* compensate, give a reward to [SEE **reward** noun], recompense, remunerate, repay.
OPPOSITES: SEE **punish**.

rewarding adjective *Nursing is said to be a rewarding job.* fulfilling, gratifying, satisfying, worthwhile.
OPPOSITES: SEE **thankless**.

reword verb *to reword a statement.* paraphrase, rephrase, SEE **revise**.

rewrite verb SEE **revise**.

rhapsody noun MUSICAL TERMS: SEE **music**.

rhetoric noun *a politician's rhetoric.* eloquence, [*uncomplimentary*] grandiloquence, [*uncomplimentary*] magniloquence, oratory, rhetorical language [SEE **rhetorical**].

rhetorical adjective [*nowadays usually uncomplimentary*] *a rhetorical style.* artificial, bombastic, [*informal*] flowery, high-flown, insincere, oratorical, ornate, pretentious, verbose, wordy.
OPPOSITES: SEE **simple**.

rhyme noun SEE **poem**.

rhythm noun *a steady rhythm.* accent, beat, metre, movement, pattern, pulse, tempo, throb.

hythmic adjective *a rhythmic beat.* metrical, predictable, regular, repeated, steady, throbbing.
OPPOSITES: SEE **irregular**.

ia noun SEE **bay**.

ibald adjective *ribald laughter.* SEE **bawdy**, disrespectful, naughty, rude, vulgar.

ibbon noun 1 *a ribbon for her hair.* braid, head-band, tape.
2 *a ribbon of colour.* band, strip, stripe.
in ribbons SEE **ragged**.

ice noun VARIOUS CEREALS: SEE **cereal**.

ich adjective 1 *a rich industrialist.* affluent, [*informal*] flush, [*informal*] loaded, moneyed, opulent, [*joking*] plutocratic, prosperous, wealthy, [*informal*] well-heeled, well-off, well-to-do.
2 *rich furnishings.* costly, elaborate, expensive, lavish, luxurious, splendid, sumptuous, valuable.
3 *rich agricultural land.* fertile, fruitful, lush, productive.
4 *a rich harvest.* abundant, copious, plenteous, plentiful, prolific, teeming.
5 *rich colours.* deep, full, strong, vivid, warm.
OPPOSITES: SEE **poor**.
a rich person billionaire, capitalist, millionaire, plutocrat, tycoon.

iches noun SEE **wealth**.

ick noun hayrick, haystack.

ick verb *to rick your neck.* SEE **strain** verb.

ickety adjective *a rickety old building.* SEE **unsteady**.

icochet verb bounce, rebound.

id verb *to rid the town of rats.* clear, free, purge.
to get rid of dispense with, eject, evict, expel, remove, throw out.

iddle noun 1 *Can you solve this riddle?* conundrum, mystery, [*informal*] poser, problem, puzzle, question.
2 *She sifted the soil in a riddle.* sieve.

iddle verb 1 *to riddle out large bits with a sieve.* filter, screen, sieve, sift, strain.
2 *to riddle something with holes.* [*informal*] pepper, perforate, pierce, puncture.

ide noun *a ride in a car.* SEE **journey** noun.

ide verb 1 *to ride a horse.* control, handle, manage, sit on.
2 *to ride on a bike.* be carried, free-wheel, pedal, SEE **travel** verb.

idge noun *There's a good view from the ridge.* bank, edge, embankment, escarpment, SEE **hill**.

ridicule noun *We had to put up with the ridicule of local youths.* badinage, banter, derision, jeering, laughter, mockery, raillery, [*informal*] ribbing, sarcasm, satire, scorn, sneers, taunts, teasing.

ridicule verb *Don't ridicule them because of their appearance.* be sarcastic about, be satirical about, caricature, chaff, deride, guy, jeer at, joke about, lampoon, laugh at, make fun of, make jokes about, mock, parody, pillory, [*informal*] poke fun at, [*informal*] rib, scoff at, [*informal*] send up, sneer at, subject (someone) to ridicule [SEE **ridicule** noun], taunt, tease.

ridiculous adjective *a ridiculous comedy. ridiculous behaviour.* absurd, amusing, comic, [*informal*] crazy, [*informal*] daft, eccentric, farcical, foolish, funny, grotesque, hilarious, illogical, irrational, laughable, ludicrous, mad, nonsensical, preposterous, senseless, silly, stupid, unbelievable, unreasonable, weird, [*informal*] zany.
OPPOSITES: SEE **sensible**.

rife adjective *Disease is rife in the area.* abundant, common, endemic, prevalent, widespread.

rifle noun SEE **gun**.

rift noun *a rift in a rock. a rift in a friendship.* breach, break, chink, cleft, crack, division, fracture, gap, opening, separation, split.

rig noun 1 *a ship's rig.* SEE **rigging**.
2 *an oil rig.* platform.
3 [*informal*] *the rig you need for mountaineering.* apparatus, clothes, equipment, gear, kit, outfit, stuff, tackle.

rigging noun *a ship's rigging.* rig, tackle.
PARTS OF A SHIP'S RIGGING: halyard, pulley, rope, sail.

right adjective 1 *the right thing to do.* decent, ethical, fair, honest, honourable, just, law-abiding, lawful, moral, principled, responsible, righteous, upright, virtuous.
2 *the right answer. the right word.* accurate, apposite, appropriate, apt, correct, exact, factual, faultless, fitting, genuine, precise, proper, suitable, true.
3 *Have we come the right way?* best, convenient, good, normal, recommended, sensible, usual.
OPPOSITES: SEE **wrong** adjective.
4 *your right side.* right-hand, starboard [= *right side of a ship when you face the bow*].
5 *right in politics.* conservative, fascist, reactionary, right-wing, Tory.

right noun 1 *the right to free speech.* entitlement, facility, freedom, liberty, prerogative, privilege.

2 *a teacher's right to give orders. a chemist's right to sell medicines.* authority, commission, franchise, influence, licence, position, power.

right verb **1** *to right something which was overturned.* make perpendicular, pick up, set upright, stand upright, straighten.
OPPOSITES: SEE **overturn.**
2 *to right a wrong.* correct, make amends for, put right, rectify, redress, remedy, repair, set right.

righteous adjective *It is not only the righteous who go to church.* blameless, God-fearing, good, guiltless, just, law-abiding, moral, pure, [*uncomplimentary*] SEE **sanctimonious,** upright, virtuous.
OPPOSITES: unrighteous, SEE **sinful.**

rightful adjective *the rightful owner of a car.* authorized, just, lawful, legal, legitimate, licensed, proper, real, true, valid.
OPPOSITES: SEE **illegal.**

rigid adjective **1** *a rigid board. a rigid framework. a rigid expression.* adamant, firm, hard, inflexible, solid, stiff, unbending, wooden.
2 *a rigid disciplinarian.* harsh, intransigent, stern, strict, stubborn, uncompromising, unkind, unyielding.
OPPOSITES: SEE **flexible.**

rigorous adjective **1** *rigorous training.* conscientious, demanding, exacting, hard, painstaking, rigid, stringent, structured, thorough, tough, unsparing.
OPPOSITES: SEE **easygoing.**
2 *a rigorous climate.* extreme, harsh, inclement, inhospitable, severe, unfriendly, unpleasant.
OPPOSITES: SEE **mild.**

rile verb SEE **annoy.**

rill noun SEE **stream** noun.

rim noun *the rim of a cup.* brim, brink, circumference, edge, lip.

rind noun *cheese rind. the rind of an orange.* crust, outer layer, peel, skin.

ring noun **1** *in the shape of a ring.* band, circle, hoop, loop.
OTHER SHAPES: SEE **shape** noun.
2 *a boxing-ring.* arena.
3 *a smuggling ring.* association, band, gang, SEE **group** noun, mob, organization, syndicate.
ring road SEE **road.**

ring verb **1** *The police ringed the area.* circle, encircle, enclose, encompass, surround.
2 *The bell rang.* chime, clang, clink, jangle, peal, ping, resonate, resound, reverberate, sound the knell, tinkle, toll.

3 *Ring me tomorrow evening.* call, [*informal*] give a buzz, phone, ring up, telephone.

ring-leader noun SEE **leader.**

ringlet noun SEE **curl** noun.

ringmaster noun SEE **circus.**

rink noun *an ice-rink.* SEE **arena.**

rinse verb *to rinse in clean water.* bathe, clean, sluice, swill, wash.

riot noun *a riot in the streets.* anarchy, brawl, chaos, commotion, demonstration, disorder, disturbance, hubbub, insurrection, lawlessness, mass protest, mutiny, pandemonium, revolt, rioting, rising, [*informal*] rumpus, [*informal*] shindy, turmoil, unrest, uproar, violence.

riot verb *The discontented crowd rioted.* create a riot [SEE **riot** noun], [*informal*] go wild, mutiny, rampage, rebel, revolt, rise up, run riot.

rioting noun SEE **riot** noun.

riotous adjective *a riotous party.* anarchic, boisterous, disorderly, lawless, mutinous, noisy, rampageous, rebellious, rowdy, uncivilized, uncontrollable, undisciplined, ungovernable, unrestrained, unruly, violent, wild.
OPPOSITES: SEE **orderly.**

rip verb SEE **tear** verb.

ripe adjective *ripe fruit.* mature, mellow, ready to use.

ripen verb *These pears need to ripen.* age, become riper, develop, mature, mellow.

riposte noun SEE **reply** noun.

ripple noun SEE **wave** noun.

ripple verb *Wind rippled the surface of the water.* agitate, disturb, make waves on, ruffle, stir.

rise noun **1** *a rise in the ground.* ascent, bank, climb, elevation, SEE **hill,** incline, ramp, slope.
2 *a rise in wages, temperature, etc.* escalation, increase, increment, jump, leap, upsurge, upswing, upturn, upward movement.

rise verb **1** *to rise into the air.* arise, ascend, climb, fly up, go up, jump, leap, levitate, lift, lift off, mount, soar, spring, take off.
2 *to rise from bed.* get up, stand up.
3 *Prices have risen.* escalate, grow, increase.
4 *A cliff rose above us.* loom, stand out, stick up, tower.

rising noun SEE **revolution.**

risk noun **1** *a risk of frost.* chance, likelihood, possibility.

2 *Starting a business involves financial risk.* danger, gamble, hazard, peril, speculation, uncertainty, venture.

risk verb *He risked his capital starting the business.* chance, dare, gamble, hazard, jeopardize, speculate, venture.

risky adjective *It's risky to cycle on icy roads.* [*informal*] chancy, SEE **dangerous**, hazardous, perilous, precarious, unsafe.
OPPOSITES: SEE **safe**.

rite noun SEE **ritual**.

ritual noun *a religious ritual.* ceremonial, ceremony, formality, liturgy, practice, rite, sacrament, service, solemnity, tradition.

rival noun *sporting rivals.* adversary, challenger, competitor, contender, contestant, enemy, opponent, opposition.

rival verb *The new shop rivals the shop down the road.* be as good as, compare with, compete with, contend with, contest, emulate, equal, match, oppose, struggle with, vie with.
OPPOSITES: SEE **co-operate**.

rivalry noun *rivalry between two teams.* antagonism, competition, competitiveness, opposition.
OPPOSITES: SEE **co-operation**.

river noun rivulet, SEE **stream** noun, waterway.
PARTS OF A RIVER: channel, confluence, delta, estuary, lower reaches, mouth, source, tributary, upper reaches.
RELATED ADJECTIVE: fluvial.
GEOGRAPHICAL TERMS: SEE **geography**.

rivet verb SEE **fasten**.

rivulet noun SEE **stream** noun.

road noun roadway, route, way.

ROADS AND PATHWAYS: alley, arterial road, avenue, boulevard, bridle-path, bridle-way, bypass, by-road, byway, cart-track, causeway, clearway, crescent, cul-de-sac, drive, driveway, dual carriageway, esplanade, footpath, [*American*] freeway, highway, lane, motorway, one-way street, path, pathway, pavement, ring road, service road, side-road, side-street, slip-road, street, thoroughfare, tow-path, track, trail, trunk-road, [*old-fashioned*] turnpike, walk, walkway.

WORDS TO DO WITH ROADS: bridge, camber, flyover, footbridge, ford, hairpin bend, junction, lay-by, level crossing, roadworks, roundabout, service area, service station, signpost, traffic lights, underpass, viaduct, zebra crossing.

SURFACES FOR ROADS AND PATHS: asphalt, cobbles, concrete, crazy paving, flagstones, gravel, paving stones, Tarmac, tiles.

---

roadworthy adjective *a roadworthy vehicle.* safe, usable.

roam verb *Sheep roam over the hills.* meander, prowl, ramble, range, rove, stray, travel, SEE **walk** verb, wander.

roar noun, verb VARIOUS SOUNDS: SEE **sound** noun.

roast verb SEE **cook** verb.

roasting adjective SEE **hot**.

rob verb *to rob a shop. to rob someone in the street.* [*informal*] con, defraud, loot, [*informal*] mug, [*informal*] mulct, pick (someone's) pocket, pilfer from, pillage, plunder, ransack, steal from [SEE **steal**].

robber noun bandit, brigand, burglar, [*informal*] con-man, embezzler, fraud, highwayman, looter, mugger, pickpocket, pirate, shop-lifter, swindler, thief.
OTHER CRIMINALS: SEE **criminal** noun.

robbery noun burglary, confidence trick, embezzlement, fraud, [*informal*] hold-up, larceny, mugging, pillage, plunder, shop-lifting, stealing, [*informal*] stick-up, theft.
OTHER CRIMES: SEE **crime**.

robe noun bath-robe, dress, dressing-gown, frock, gown, habit (*a monk's habit*), house-coat.

robe verb SEE **dress** verb.

robot noun android, automated machine, automaton, bionic man, bionic woman, computerized machine.

robust adjective **1** *a robust physique.* athletic, brawny, hardy, healthy, muscular, powerful, rugged, sound, strong, vigorous.
2 *a robust machine.* durable, serviceable, sturdy, tough.
OPPOSITES: SEE **weak**.

rock noun **1** *a lorry-load of rock.* ore, stone.
2 *We clambered over the rocks.* boulder, crag, outcrop, scree.

PRINCIPAL TYPES OF ROCK: igneous, metamorphic, sedimentary.

SOME KINDS OF ROCK: basalt, chalk, clay, flint, gneiss, granite, gravel, lava, limestone, marble, obsidian, pumice, quartz, sandstone, schist, shale, slate, tufa, tuff.

---

rock verb 1 *to rock to and fro.* move gently, sway, swing.
2 *The ship rocked in the storm.* lurch, pitch, reel, roll, shake, toss, totter.
3 *The nation was rocked by the news.* SEE **amaze** verb, **amazed** adjective.

rockery noun alpine garden, rock-garden.

rocket noun SEE **firework, space** noun, **weapons.**

rocky adjective 1 *rocky terrain.* barren, inhospitable, pebbly, rough, rugged, stony.
2 *a rocky chair.* SEE **unsteady.**

rococo adjective SEE **ornate.**

rod noun bar, baton, cane, dowel, pole, rail, shaft, spoke, staff, stick, strut, wand.

rodent noun VARIOUS ANIMALS: SEE **animal** noun.

roe noun SEE **deer.**

rogue noun *rogues and criminals.* [old-fashioned] blackguard, charlatan, cheat, [informal] con-man, SEE **criminal** noun, fraud, [old-fashioned] knave, mischievous person [SEE **mischievous**], [informal] quack, rascal, ruffian, scoundrel, swindler, villain.

roguish adjective SEE **mischievous.**

roistering noun SEE **revelry.**

role noun 1 *an actor's role.* character, part, portrayal.
2 *What's her role in this business?* contribution, duty, function, job, position, post, task.

roll noun 1 *a roll of paper.* cylinder, drum, scroll.
2 *a roll of honour.* catalogue, index, inventory, list, record, register.

roll verb 1 *The wheels began to roll.* gyrate, move round, revolve, rotate, run, spin, turn, twirl, whirl.
2 *to roll up a carpet, a sail, etc.* coil, curl, furl, make into a roll, twist, wind, wrap.
3 *to roll a cricket pitch.* flatten, level out, smooth, use a roller on.
4 *The ship rolled in the storm. A drunk rolled along the street.* lumber, lurch, pitch, reel, rock, stagger, sway, toss, totter, wallow, welter.
to roll in, to roll up SEE **arrive.**

rollicking adjective SEE **boisterous.**

rolling adjective *a rolling sea. rolling hills.* heaving, undulating, up and down, wavy.

romance noun 1 *a historical romance.* KINDS OF WRITING: SEE **writing.**
2 *the romance of travel.* adventure, excitement, fascination, glamour.

3 *Are those two having a romance?* affair, attachment, intrigue, liaison, love affair, relationship.

romantic adjective 1 *a romantic setting for a love affair.* colourful, dream-like, exotic, glamorous, idyllic, picturesque.
2 *a romantic novel.* emotional, escapist, heart-warming, nostalgic, reassuring, sentimental, [uncomplimentary] sloppy, tender, unrealistic.
3 *romantic notions of changing the world.* [informal] head in the clouds, idealistic, impractical, improbable, quixotic, starry-eyed, unworkable, Utopian, visionary.
OPPOSITES: SEE **realistic.**

romp verb *The children romped in the playground.* caper, cavort, dance, frisk, frolic, leap about, play, prance, run about.

roof noun MATERIALS USED FOR ROOFS: asbestos, corrugated iron, slates, thatch, tiles.

rook verb SEE **swindle** verb.

room noun 1 *Give me more room.* [informal] elbow-room, freedom, latitude, leeway, scope, space, territory.
2 *a room in a house.* [old-fashioned] chamber.

VARIOUS ROOMS: ante-room, attic, audience chamber, bathroom, bedroom, boudoir, cell, cellar, chapel, classroom, cloakroom, conservatory, corridor, dining-room, dormitory, drawing-room, dressing-room, gallery, guest-room, hall, kitchen, kitchenette, laboratory, landing, larder, laundry, lavatory, library, living-room, loft, lounge, music-room, nursery, office, outhouse, pantry, parlour, passage, play-room, porch, salon, saloon, scullery, sick-room, sitting-room, spare-room, state-room, store-room, studio, study, toilet, utility room, waiting-room, ward, washroom, WC, work-room, workshop.

roomy adjective *a roomy car.* SEE **big,** capacious, commodious, large, sizeable, spacious, voluminous.
OPPOSITES: SEE **cramped.**

root noun 1 *the root of a plant.* radicle, rhizome, rootlet, tuber.
2 *the root of a problem.* basis, bottom (*I want to get to the bottom of this*), origin, seat, source, starting-point.

root verb **to root out** SEE **remove, up-root.**

rope noun cable, cord, halyard, hawser, lanyard, lariat, lasso, line, string.

rope verb [= *to fasten with a rope*] bind, hitch, moor, tie.
OTHER WAYS TO FASTEN THINGS: SEE **fasten**.

rosette noun SEE **badge**.

roster noun SEE **rota**.

rostrum noun SEE **platform**.

rot noun 1 *The damp has caused some rot.* corrosion, decay, decomposition, deterioration, disintegration, dry rot, mouldiness, wet rot.
2 [*informal*] *Don't talk rot.* SEE **nonsense**.

rot verb *Most substances eventually rot.* become rotten [SEE **rotten**], corrode, crumble, decay, decompose, degenerate, deteriorate, disintegrate, go bad, perish, putrefy, spoil.

rota noun *a duty rota.* list, roster, schedule, timetable.

rotary adjective *rotary movement.* gyrating, revolving, rotating, rotatory, spinning, turning, twirling, twisting, whirling.

rotate verb *to rotate on an axis.* gyrate, have a rotary movement, pirouette, pivot, reel, revolve, spin, swivel, turn, turn anticlockwise, turn clockwise, twiddle, twirl, twist, wheel, whirl.

rotor noun propeller, screw, vane.
PARTS OF AN AIRCRAFT: SEE **aircraft**.

rotten adjective 1 *rotten wood. rotten iron-work.* corroded, crumbling, decayed, decaying, decomposed, disintegrating, [*of iron, etc.*] rusty, unsound.
2 *rotten food.* foul, mouldering, mouldy, [*informal*] off (*The fish is off*), perished, putrid, smelly, tainted, unfit for consumption.
OPPOSITES: SEE **sound** adjective.
3 *a rotten thing to do.* SEE **bad**.

rough adjective 1 *a rough surface.* broken, bumpy, coarse, craggy, irregular, jagged, pitted, rocky, rugged, stony, uneven.
OPPOSITES: SEE **even** adjective.
2 *rough skin.* bristly, callused, chapped, coarse, hairy, harsh, leathery, scratchy, shaggy, unshaven, wrinkled.
OPPOSITES: SEE **smooth** adjective.
3 *a rough sea.* choppy, stormy, tempestuous, turbulent, violent, wild.
OPPOSITES: SEE **calm** adjective.
4 *a rough voice.* grating, gruff, harsh, hoarse, husky, rasping, raucous, unpleasant.
OPPOSITES: SEE **soft**.
5 *a rough crowd. rough manners.* badly behaved, bluff, blunt, brusque, churlish, ill-bred, impolite, loutish, SEE rowdy, rude, surly, [*informal*] ugly,

uncivil, uncivilized, undisciplined, unfriendly.
OPPOSITES: SEE **polite**.
6 *rough work.* amateurish, careless, clumsy, crude, hasty, imperfect, inept, [*informal*] rough and ready, unfinished, unpolished, unskilful.
OPPOSITES: SEE **skilful**.
7 *a rough estimate.* approximate, imprecise, inexact, vague.
OPPOSITES: SEE **exact** adjective.

roughage noun dietary fibre.

roughly adverb about, approximately, around, close to, nearly.

round adjective 1 *a round shape.* bulbous, circular, curved, cylindrical, globular, spherical.
2 *a round figure.* ample, SEE **fat** adjective, full, plump, rotund, rounded, well-padded.
round the bend SEE **mad**.
round the clock SEE **continual**.

round noun *a round in a competition.* bout, contest, game, heat, stage.

round verb *to round a corner.* skirt, travel round, turn.
to round off *We rounded the evening off with some songs.* SEE **complete** verb.
to round on *He rounded on me for not supporting his plan.* SEE **attack** verb.
to round up *The farmer rounded up his sheep.* SEE **assemble**.

roundabout adjective *a roundabout route.* circuitous, devious, indirect, long, meandering, rambling, tortuous, twisting, winding.
OPPOSITES: SEE **direct** adjective.

roundabout noun 1 merry-go-round.
2 traffic island.

round-shouldered adjective humpbacked, hunchbacked, stooping.

roundsman noun delivery man, tradesman.

rouse verb 1 *to rouse someone from sleep.* arouse, awaken, call, get up, wake up.
2 *to rouse someone to a frenzy.* agitate, animate, excite, incite, inflame, provoke, stimulate, stir up.

rousing adjective *rousing music.* SEE **exciting**.

rout verb *We routed the opposition.* conquer, crush, SEE **defeat** verb, overwhelm.

route noun *Which route shall we take?* course, direction, itinerary, journey, path, road, way.

routine noun 1 *a normal routine.* course of action, custom, [*informal*] drill (*Follow the usual drill*), habit, method, pattern, practice, procedure, system, way.
2 *The skaters performed their new routine.* act, performance, programme.

rove verb SEE **roam**.

row noun 1 [Rhymes with *crow*.] *Arrange them in a row*. chain, column, cordon, file, line, queue, rank, sequence, series, string.
2 [Rhymes with *cow*.] *I heard his row all down the street*. SEE **noise**, [*informal*] racket, rumpus, tumult, uproar.
3 [Rhymes with *cow*.] *They don't speak to each other since their row*. altercation, argument, controversy, disagreement, dispute, fight, SEE **quarrel** noun, [*informal*] ructions, [*informal*] slanging match, squabble.

row verb 1 [Rhymes with *crow*.] *to row a boat*. move, propel, scull.
2 [Rhymes with *cow*.] [*informal*] *They row about politics*. SEE **quarrel** verb.

rowdy adjective *a rowdy crowd*. badly behaved, boisterous, disorderly, ill-disciplined, irrepressible, lawless, SEE **noisy**, obstreperous, riotous, rough, turbulent, undisciplined, unruly, violent, wild.
OPPOSITES: SEE **quiet**.

rowing-boat noun dinghy, eight, skiff.
VARIOUS BOATS: SEE **vessel**.

royal adjective *a royal palace. by royal command*. imperial, kingly, majestic, princely, queenly, regal, stately.

royalty noun 1 = *royal family*.
2 = *payment to an author*. SEE **payment**.

MEMBERS OF ROYALTY: consort, Her or His Majesty, Her or His Royal Highness, king, monarch, prince, princess, queen, queen mother, regent, sovereign.
OTHER RULERS: SEE **ruler**.

---

rub verb 1 *to rub a sore place and make it better*. caress, knead, massage, smooth, stroke.
2 *to rub a place and damage it*. abrade, chafe, graze, scrape, wear away.
3 *to rub something clean*. polish, scour, scrub, wipe.
to rub out blot out, cancel, delete, erase, expunge, obliterate, remove, wipe out.
to rub up the wrong way SEE **annoy**.

rubber noun *a blackboard rubber*. cleaner, eraser.

rubbery adjective SEE **tough**.

rubbish noun 1 *Throw away that rubbish*. debris, dross, flotsam and jetsam, garbage, junk, leavings, [*informal*] left-overs, litter, lumber, muck, [*informal*] odds and ends, offcuts, refuse, rubble, scrap, trash, waste.
2 *Don't talk rubbish!* SEE **nonsense**.

rubble noun *The building collapsed into a pile of rubble*. broken bricks, debris, fragments, remains, ruins, wreckage.

rubicund adjective SEE **red**.

rubric noun SEE **explanation**.

ruck noun, verb SEE **crease** noun, verb.

rucksack noun bag, haversack, knapsack.

ructions noun SEE **row** noun.

ruddy adjective *a ruddy complexion*. fresh, flushed, glowing, healthy, SEE **red**, sunburnt.

rude noun *rude language. rude behaviour. a rude person*. abrupt, abusive, bad-mannered, bad-tempered, blasphemous, blunt, boorish, brusque, cheeky, churlish, coarse, common, condescending, contemptuous, crude, discourteous, disparaging, disrespectful, foul, graceless, gross, ignorant, ill-bred, ill-mannered, impertinent, impolite, improper, impudent, in bad taste, inconsiderate, indecent, insolent, insulting, loutish, mocking, naughty, oafish, SEE **obscene**, offensive, offhand, patronizing, peremptory, personal (*Don't make personal remarks*), saucy, scurrilous, shameless, tactless, unchivalrous, uncivil, uncomplimentary, uncouth, ungracious, [*old-fashioned*] unmannerly, unprintable, vulgar.
OPPOSITES: SEE **polite**.
to be rude to abuse, SEE **insult** verb, offend, sneer at, snub.

rudeness noun *I'm sick of her rudeness*. abuse, [*informal*] backchat, bad manners, boorishness, [*informal*] cheek, churlishness, condescension, contempt, discourtesy, disrespect, ill-breeding, impertinence, impudence, incivility, insolence, insults, oafishness, tactlessness, uncouthness, vulgarity.

rudiments noun *the rudiments of a subject*. basic principles, basics, elements, essentials, foundations, fundamentals, principles.

rudimentary adjective *He has only a rudimentary knowledge of the subject*. basic, crude, elementary, embryonic, immature, introductory, preliminary, primitive, provisional, undeveloped.
OPPOSITES: SEE **advanced**.

rueful adjective *a rueful expression*. SEE **sorrowful**.

ruffian noun [*informal*] brute, bully, desperado, gangster, hoodlum, hooligan, lout, mugger, SEE **rogue**, scoundrel, thug, [*informal*] tough, villain, [*informal*] yob.

ruffle verb 1 *A breeze ruffled the water*. agitate, disturb, ripple, stir.

2 *She ruffled his hair.* derange, dishevel, [*informal*] mess up, rumple, tousle.
OPPOSITES: SEE **smooth** verb.
3 *Their unexpected rudeness ruffled him.* annoy, disconcert, fluster, irritate, [*informal*] nettle, [*informal*] rattle, unsettle, upset, vex, worry.
OPPOSITES: SEE **calm** verb.

rug noun **1** *a rug to wrap yourself in.* blanket, coverlet.
2 *a rug to go on the floor.* mat, matting.

rugged adjective **1** *rugged mountains.* bumpy, craggy, irregular, jagged, rocky, rough, uneven.
2 *rugged good looks.* burly, husky, muscular, robust, rough, strong, sturdy, tough, unpolished, weather-beaten.

ruin noun **1** *the ruin of a business.* bankruptcy, breakdown, collapse, [*informal*] crash, destruction, downfall, end, failure, fall, ruination, undoing, wreck.
2 [*often plural*] *the ruins of a building.* debris, havoc, remains, rubble, ruined buildings [SEE **ruined**], wreckage.

ruin verb *The storm ruined the flowers.* damage, demolish, destroy, devastate, flatten, overthrow, shatter, spoil, wreck.

ruined adjective *a ruined castle.* crumbling, derelict, dilapidated, fallen down, in ruins, ramshackle, ruinous, tumbledown, uninhabitable, unsafe, wrecked.

ruinous adjective **1** *a ruinous disaster.* apocalyptic, cataclysmic, catastrophic, crushing, destructive, devastating, dire, disastrous, fatal, pernicious, shattering.
2 *The house was in a ruinous condition.* SEE **ruined**.

rule noun **1** *rules of conduct. the rules of a game.* code, convention, custom, law, practice, precept, principle, regulation, routine.
2 *under foreign rule.* administration, authority, command, control, domination, dominion, empire, government, influence, jurisdiction, management, mastery, power, regime, reign, sovereignty, supremacy, sway.

rule verb **1** *to rule a country.* administer, command, control, direct, dominate, govern, lead, manage, reign over, run.
2 *Elizabeth I ruled for many years.* be ruler [SEE **ruler**], reign.
3 *The umpire ruled that the batsman was out.* adjudicate, decide, decree, determine, find, judge, pronounce, resolve.
to rule out SEE **exclude**.

ruler noun VARIOUS RULERS: autocrat, caesar, SEE **chief** noun, demagogue, dictator, doge, emir, emperor, empress, governor, kaiser, king, lord, monarch, potentate, president, prince, princess, queen, rajah, regent, satrap, sovereign, sultan, suzerain, triumvirate [= *three people ruling jointly*], tyrant, tzar, viceroy.

rumble noun, verb VARIOUS SOUNDS: SEE **sound** noun.

ruminate verb SEE **meditate**.

rummage verb SEE **search** verb.

rumour noun *The scandalous story was only a rumour.* gossip, hearsay, prattle, scandal, whisper.

rump noun SEE **buttocks**.

rumple verb SEE **crumple**.

rumpus noun SEE **commotion**.

run noun **1** *a run across the park.* canter, dash, gallop, jog, marathon, race, sprint, trot.
2 *a run in the car.* drive, SEE **journey** noun, joyride, ride, [*informal*] spin.
3 *a run of bad luck.* chain, sequence, series, stretch.
4 *a chicken run.* compound, coop, enclosure, pen.

run verb **1** *We ran as fast as our legs could carry us.* bolt, canter, career, dash, gallop, hare, hurry, jog, race, rush, scamper, scoot, scurry, scuttle, speed, sprint, tear, trot.
2 *The buses don't run on Sundays.* go, operate, ply, provide a service, travel.
3 *The car runs well.* behave, function, perform, work.
4 *Water ran down the wall.* cascade, dribble, flow, gush, leak, pour, spill, stream, trickle.
5 *The government is supposed to run the country's affairs.* administer, conduct, control, direct, govern, look after, maintain, manage, rule, supervise.
to run across SEE **meet**.
to run after SEE **pursue**.
to run away abscond, [*informal*] beat it, bolt, depart, elope, SEE **escape** verb, [*informal*] take to your heels, [*informal*] turn tail.
to run into SEE **collide**.

runaway noun SEE **fugitive**.

runner noun **1** *a runner in a race.* athlete, competitor, entrant, jogger, participant, sprinter.
2 *The commanding officer sent a runner to headquarters.* courier, messenger.
3 *a runner of a plant.* offshoot, shoot, sprout.

running adjective **1** *three days running.* SEE **consecutive**.
2 *running water.* flowing, SEE **liquid** adjective.

runny adjective fluid, free-flowing, liquid, thin, watery.
OPPOSITES: SEE **viscous**.

runt noun SEE **small (small person)**.

runway noun air strip, landing-strip. SEE **airport**.

rupture verb SEE **burst**.

rural adjective *I like to get away from the town into rural surroundings*. agricultural, bucolic, countrified, pastoral, rustic, sylvan.

ruse noun SEE **trick** noun.

rush noun 1 *a rush to get things finished*. haste, hurry, pressure, race, scramble, urgency.
2 *a rush of water*. cataract, flood, gush, spate.
3 *a rush of people or animals*. charge, onslaught, panic, stampede.

rush verb *to rush home. to rush in with good news*. bolt, burst, canter, career, charge, dash, fly, gallop, hare, hasten, hurry, jog, move fast, race, run, scamper, scramble, scurry, scuttle, shoot, speed, sprint, stampede, [*informal*] tear, trot, [*informal*] zoom.

rust verb *Iron rusts*. become rusty [SEE **rusty**], corrode, crumble away, oxidize, rot.

rustic adjective 1 *rustic surroundings*. SEE **rural**.
2 *rustic fencing. rustic simplicity*. artless, clumsy, crude, rough, simple, unpolished, unsophisticated.

rustle verb VARIOUS SOUNDS: SEE **sound** noun.

rusty adjective 1 *rusty iron*. corroded, oxidized, rotten, tarnished.
2 [*informal*] *My French is a bit rusty*. dated, forgotten, unused.

rut noun *a rut in a path*. channel, furrow, groove, indentation, pothole, track, trough.

rutted adjective SEE **uneven**.

ruthless *a ruthless attack. ruthless criminals*. brutal, cruel, dangerous, ferocious, fierce, SEE **pitiless**, vicious, violent.

S

sabbatical noun SEE **holiday**.

sable adjective SEE **black** adjective.

sabotage noun *Terrorists were responsible for the sabotage*. deliberate destruction, disruption, treachery, vandalism, wilful damage, wrecking.

sabotage verb *to sabotage a machine*. cripple, damage, destroy, disable, put out of action, vandalize, wreck.

saboteur noun traitor, vandal, wrecker.

sabre noun SEE **sword**.

sachet noun SEE **container**.

sack noun bag, SEE **container**, pouch.
to get the sack be sacked [SEE **sack** verb], [*informal*] get your cards, lose your job.
to give someone the sack SEE **sack** verb.

sack verb 1 *to sack someone from a job*. [*informal*] axe, discharge, dismiss, [*informal*] fire, give (someone) notice, [*informal*] give (someone) the sack, lay off [= to discharge temporarily], make redundant.
2 *to sack a town*. SEE **plunder** verb.

sacred adjective *The Koran is a sacred book*. blessed, consecrated, dedicated, divine, godly, hallowed, holy, religious, revered, sacrosanct, venerated.
OPPOSITES: SEE **secular**.

sacrifice noun *a sacrifice to the gods*. [*formal*] oblation, offering, propitiation, votive offering.

sacrifice verb 1 *I sacrificed my weekend to finish the job*. abandon, forgo, give up, let go, lose, relinquish, surrender.
2 *to sacrifice an animal to the gods*. kill, offer up, slaughter.

sacrilege noun blasphemy, desecration, godlessness, impiety, irreverence, profanity, ungodliness.
OPPOSITES: SEE **piety**.

sacrilegious adjective SEE **blasphemous**.

sacrosanct adjective inviolate, protected, respected, SEE **sacred**, secure, untouchable.

sad adjective 1 *sad faces. sad emotions*. [*informal*] blue, broken-hearted, careworn, cheerless, crestfallen, dejected, depressed, desolate, despairing, desperate, despondent, disappointed, disconsolate, discontented, discouraged, disgruntled, dismal, dispirited, dissatisfied, distracted, distraught, distressed, doleful, dolorous, [*informal*] down, downcast, down-hearted, dreary, forlorn, gloomy, glum, grave, grief-stricken, grieving, grim, guilty, heartbroken, [*informal*] heavy, heavy-hearted, homesick, hopeless, in low spirits, [*informal*] in the doldrums, joyless, lachrymose, lonely, [*informal*] long-faced, [*informal*] low, lugubrious, melancholy, miserable, moody, moping, morose, mournful, pathetic, penitent, pessimistic, piteous, pitiable, pitiful, plaintive, poignant, regretful, rueful, serious, sober, sombre, sorrowful, sorry, tearful, troubled, unhappy upset, wistful, woebegone, woeful, wretched.

2 *sad news. a sad event.* calamitous, deplorable, depressing, disastrous, discouraging, distressing, grievous, heart-breaking, heart-rending, lamentable, morbid, moving, painful, regrettable, [*informal*] tear-jerking, touching, tragic, unfortunate, unsatisfactory, unwelcome, upsetting.
OPPOSITES: SEE **happy**.

sadden verb *Our friend's illness saddened us.* [*informal*] break (someone's) heart, depress, disappoint, discourage, dishearten, dismay, dispirit, distress, grieve, make sad [SEE **sad**], upset.
OPPOSITES: SEE **cheer** verb.

sadistic adjective SEE **cruel**.

sadness noun SEE **sorrow** noun.

safari noun SEE **holiday**.

safe adjective **1** *Is your house safe against burglars?* defended, foolproof, guarded, immune, impregnable, invulnerable, protected, secure.
OPPOSITES: SEE **vulnerable**.

2 *We got home safe in spite of the storm.* [*informal*] alive and well, [*informal*] all right, [*informal*] in one piece, intact, sound, undamaged, unharmed, unhurt, uninjured, unscathed.
OPPOSITES: SEE **damaged**.

3 *She's a safe driver.* cautious, circumspect, dependable, reliable, trustworthy.

4 *The dog's quite safe.* docile, friendly, harmless, innocuous, tame.

5 *The water's safe to drink. The food's safe to eat.* drinkable, eatable, good, non-poisonous, non-toxic, potable, pure, uncontaminated, wholesome.
OPPOSITES: SEE **dangerous**.

6 *a safe aircraft or ship.* airworthy. seaworthy.
to make safe defuse (*a bomb*), fasten down, fix, neutralize, secure, sterilize, tie down.

safeguard verb SEE **protect**.

safety noun **1** *The airline does all it can to ensure passengers' safety.* immunity, invulnerability, protection, security.
2 *The nurse assured me of the safety of the drug.* harmlessness, reliability.

safety-belt noun safety-harness, seat-belt.

sag verb *The rope sags in the middle.* be limp, dip, droop, fall, flop, hang down, sink, slump.

saga noun VARIOUS STORIES: SEE **story**.

sagacious, sage adjectives SEE **wise**.

sage noun SEE **wise** (**wise person**).

sail noun **1** *the sails of a ship.*
KINDS OF SAIL: foresail, gaffsail, jib, lateen sail, lugsail, mainsail, mizzen, spinnaker, spritsail, topsail.
2 *We went for a sail.* cruise, SEE **journey** noun, sea-passage, voyage.

sail verb **1** *to sail a boat.* captain, navigate, pilot, skipper, steer.
2 *to sail in a boat.* cruise, paddle, punt, row, steam, SEE **travel** verb.

sailor noun mariner, seaman.
VARIOUS SAILORS: able seaman, bargee, boatman, boatswain or bosun, captain, cox or coxswain, [*plural*] crew, helmsman, mate, midshipman, navigator, pilot, rating, rower, yachtsman
RANKS IN THE NAVY: SEE **rank** noun.

saint noun SEE **good** (**good person**).

saintly adjective angelic, blessed, SEE **good**, holy, innocent, pure, religious, sinless, virtuous.
OPPOSITES: SEE **devilish**.

sake noun *Do it for my sake.* advantage, behalf, benefit, gain, good, interest, welfare.

salacious adjective SEE **bawdy**.

salad noun

VEGETABLES OFTEN EATEN IN SALADS: beetroot, celery, chicory, cress, cucumber, lettuce, mustard and cress, onion, potato, radish, tomato, watercress.
OTHER VEGETABLES: SEE **vegetable**.

---

salary noun *a salary of £15,000 a year.* earnings, emolument, income, pay, payment, remuneration, stipend, wages.

sale noun KINDS OF SALE: auction, bazaar, closing-down sale, fair, jumble sale, market, winter sales.

salesman, salesperson, saleswoman nouns assistant, auctioneer, representative, shopkeeper.

salient adjective *salient features.* SEE **prominent**.

saline adjective SEE **salt** adjective.

saliva noun [*informal*] dribble, [*informal*] spit, spittle, [*formal*] sputum.

sallow adjective *a sallow complexion.* anaemic, bloodless, colourless, etiolated, pale, pallid, pasty, unhealthy, wan, yellowish.

salon noun SEE **room**.

saloon noun **1** SEE **room**.
2 [= *saloon car*] SEE **car**.

salt adjective *salt water.* brackish, briny, saline, salted, salty, savoury.
OPPOSITES: SEE **fresh**.
salt water brine, saline solution.

salting noun SEE **marsh**.

salty adjective SEE **salt** adjective.

salubrious adjective *The surroundings were not very salubrious.* health-giving, healthy, hygienic, invigorating, nice, pleasant, refreshing, sanitary, wholesome.
OPPOSITES: SEE **unhealthy**.

salutary adjective SEE **beneficial**.

salutation noun SEE **greeting**.

salute verb SEE **greet**.
WAYS TO GESTURE: SEE **gesture** verb.

salvage noun 1 *The salvage of the wreck will take weeks.* reclamation, recovery, rescue, retrieval, saving.
2 *We collect old newspapers and other salvage.* recyclable material, waste.

salvage verb *to salvage waste materials.* conserve, preserve, reclaim, recover, recycle, rescue, retrieve, re-use, save, use again.

salvation noun 1 [*theological*] *the salvation of souls.* redemption, saving.
OPPOSITE: damnation.
2 *When I lost my cash, my credit card was my salvation.* deliverance, escape, help, preservation, rescue, way out.

salve noun SEE **ointment**.

salve verb SEE **soothe**.

salver noun *a silver salver.* tray.

salvo noun *a salvo of guns.* SEE **gunfire**.

Samaritan noun SEE **good (good person)**.

same adjective 1 *That's the same person who came yesterday.* actual, identical, selfsame.
2 *Make it the same shape. Come on the same date next year.* analogous, comparable, consistent, corresponding, duplicate, equal, equivalent, indistinguishable, interchangeable, matching, parallel, similar, synonymous [= *having the same meaning*], twin, unaltered, unchanged, uniform, unvaried.
OPPOSITES: SEE **different**.

sample noun *a sample of your work.* demonstration, example, foretaste, free sample, illustration, indication, instance, model, pattern, representative piece, selection, specimen.

sample verb *We sampled the food.* inspect, take a sample of [SEE **sample** noun], taste, test, try.

sanatorium noun SEE **hospital**.

sanctify verb SEE **bless**.

sanctimonious adjective [*uncomplimentary*] *sanctimonious preaching.* holier-than-thou, hypocritical, insincere, moralizing, pious, SEE **righteous**, self-righteous, sententious, [*informal*] smarmy, smug, superior, unctuous.
OPPOSITES: SEE **modest**.

sanction noun SEE **permission**.

sanction verb SEE **authorize**.

sanctity adjective SEE **holiness**.

sanctuary noun *The hunted fox found sanctuary in a wood.* asylum, haven, protection, refuge, retreat, safety, shelter.

sanctum noun holy place, retreat.
PLACES OF WORSHIP: SEE **worship** noun.

sand noun grit.
sands beach, seaside, shore, [*poetic*] strand.

sandal noun VARIOUS SHOES: SEE **shoe**.

sand-dune noun sand-hill.

sandstone noun VARIOUS ROCKS: SEE **rock** noun.

sane adjective *a sane person. a sane decision.* balanced, [*informal*] compos mentis, level-headed, lucid, normal, rational, reasonable, sensible, sound, stable.
OPPOSITES: SEE **mad**.

sang-froid noun SEE **calmness**.

sanguine adjective SEE **optimistic**.

sanitary adjective *sanitary conditions in a hospital.* aseptic, clean, disinfected, germ-free, healthy, hygienic, pure, salubrious, sterilized, uncontaminated, unpolluted.
OPPOSITES: insanitary, SEE **unhealthy**.

sanitation noun *You need proper sanitation on a camp-site.* drainage, drains, lavatories, sanitary arrangements, sewage disposal, sewers.

sap noun *the sap of a tree.* moisture, vital juices.

sap verb *The climb sapped our energy.* SEE **exhaust**.

sapling noun SEE **tree**.

sapper noun SEE **soldier**.

sarcasm noun SEE **ridicule** noun.

sarcastic adjective *sarcastic jokes. a sarcastic manner.* SEE **comic** adjective, contemptuous, cutting, demeaning, derisive, disparaging, hurtful, ironical, mocking, SEE **sardonic**, satirical, scathing, sharp, sneering, taunting, vitriolic, withering.

sarcophagus noun coffin.

sardonic adjective *sardonic humour.* acid, biting, black (*black comedy*), SEE

comic adjective, cynical, heartless, malicious, mordant, SEE **sarcastic**, wry.

sash noun *a sash round the waist.* band, belt, cummerbund, girdle, waistband.

satanic adjective SEE **devilish**.

satchel noun bag, SEE **container**, schoolbag, shoulder-bag.

sate verb SEE **satisfy**.

satellite noun 1 moon, planet.
ASTRONOMICAL TERMS: SEE **astronomy**.
2 *a man-made satellite.* SEE **space** noun.

satiate verb SEE **satisfy**.

satire noun *a satire on human folly.* burlesque, caricature, invective, irony, lampoon, mockery, parody, SEE **ridicule** noun, satirical comedy [SEE **satirical**], [*informal*] send-up, [*informal*] spoof, [*informal*] take-off, travesty.
OTHER KINDS OF WRITING: SEE **writing**.

satirical adjective *a satirical comedy.* SEE **comic** adjective, critical, disparaging, disrespectful, ironic, irreverent, mocking, SEE **sarcastic**.

satirize verb *to satirize someone's faults.* be satirical about [SEE **satirical**], burlesque, caricature, SEE **criticize**, deride, lampoon, laugh at, make fun of, mock, parody, ridicule, [*informal*] send up, [*informal*] take off, travesty.

satisfaction noun *I get satisfaction from my hobby.* comfort, contentment, enjoyment, fulfilment, gratification, happiness, pleasure, pride, self-satisfaction, sense of achievement.
OPPOSITES: SEE **dissatisfaction**.

satisfactory adjective *satisfactory work.* acceptable, adequate, [*informal*] all right, competent, fair, [*informal*] good enough, passable, pleasing, satisfying, sufficient, suitable, tolerable, [*informal*] up to scratch.
OPPOSITES: SEE **unsatisfactory**.

satisfy verb *to satisfy a need. to satisfy someone's curiosity.* appease, assuage, content, fulfil, gratify, make happy, meet, pacify, please, put an end to, quench (*your thirst*), sate, satiate, settle, slake (*your thirst*), supply.
OPPOSITES: SEE **frustrate**.

saturate verb *to saturate a sponge with water.* drench, impregnate, permeate, soak, steep, suffuse, wet.

saturated adjective *saturated with water.* drenched, soaked, sodden, steeped (in), suffused, waterlogged, wringing.

saturnine adjective SEE **gloomy**.

sauce noun KINDS OF SAUCE: bread sauce, cranberry sauce, custard, gravy, horse-radish sauce, ketchup, mayonnaise, mint sauce, salad cream.

saucepan noun cauldron, pan, pot, skillet, stockpot.
OTHER CONTAINERS: SEE **container**.

saucer noun OTHER ITEMS OF CROCKERY: SEE **crockery**.

saucy adjective *saucy jokes.* SEE **impudent**.

sauna noun SEE **bath**.

saunter verb SEE **walk** verb.

sausage noun KINDS OF SAUSAGE: [*informal*] banger, chipolata, frankfurter, salami, saveloy.
OTHER KINDS OF MEAT: SEE **meat**.

sauté adjective *sauté potatoes.* fried.

savage adjective 1 *savage tribes.* barbarian, barbaric, cannibal, heathen, pagan, primitive, uncivilized, uncultivated, uneducated.
OPPOSITES: SEE **civilized**.
2 *savage beasts.* fierce, undomesticated, untamed, wild.
OPPOSITES: SEE **domesticated**.
3 *a savage attack.* angry, atrocious, barbarous, beastly, bestial, blistering, blood-thirsty, bloody, brutal, callous, cold-blooded, cruel, diabolical, ferocious, heartless, inhuman, merciless, murderous, pitiless, ruthless, sadistic, unfeeling, vicious, violent.
OPPOSITES: SEE **humane**.

savage noun *a violent savage.* barbarian, beast, brute, cannibal, fiend, savage person [SEE **savage** adjective].

savannah noun SEE **plain** noun.

save verb 1 *to save money.* collect, conserve, hold back, hold on to, hoard, invest, keep, [*informal*] put by, put in a safe place, reserve, retain, scrape together, set aside, [*informal*] stash away, store up, take care of.
OPPOSITES: SEE **squander**.
2 *to save fuel.* be sparing with, economize on, use wisely.
OPPOSITES: SEE **waste** verb.
3 *to save people or property from a wreck.* free, liberate, recover, release, rescue, retrieve, salvage, set free.
4 *to save someone from danger.* defend, guard, keep safe, preserve, protect, safe-guard, screen, shield.
5 *I saved him from making a fool of himself.* check, deter, prevent, stop.

saving noun *You can make a saving if you buy in a sale.* cut, discount, economy, reduction.
savings *I put my savings in the bank.*

nest-egg, reserves, resources, riches, wealth.

saviour noun **1** *the saviour of a cause.* champion, defender, guardian, rescuer. **2** [*theological*] *Our Saviour.* Christ, Our Lord, The Messiah, The Redeemer.

savoir-faire noun SEE **knowledge**.

savour noun SEE **taste** noun.

savoury adjective *We often follow the savoury course with a sweet course.* appetizing, piquant, salty, SEE **tasty**.
OPPOSITES: SEE **sweet** adjective.

saw noun chain-saw, hack-saw, jigsaw. VARIOUS TOOLS: SEE **tool**.

saw verb *to saw logs.* SEE **cut** verb.

say verb *Did you hear what I said?* affirm, allege, announce, answer, articulate, assert, [*informal*] come out with, comment, communicate, convey, declare, disclose, divulge, ejaculate, enunciate, exclaim, express, intimate, maintain, mention, mouth, pronounce, read aloud, recite, rejoin, remark, repeat, reply, report, respond, retort, reveal, speak, state, suggest, SEE **talk** verb, utter.

saying noun *an old Chinese saying.* adage, aphorism, apophthegm, axiom, [*informal*] catch-phrase, catchword, cliché, dictum, epigram, expression, formula, maxim, motto, phrase, precept, proverb, quotation, remark, [*old-fashioned*] saw, slogan, statement, tag, truism, watchword.

scab noun *a scab on a wound.* clot of blood, crust, sore.

scabbard noun *a scabbard for a sword.* sheath.

scaffold noun gallows.

scald verb SEE **heat** verb, **wound** verb.

scale noun **1** *scales on a fish.* flake, plate. **2** *scale in a kettle.* crust, deposit, encrustation, [*informal*] fur. **3** *a scale on a measuring instrument.* [*formal*] calibration, gradation. **4** *the social scale.* hierarchy, ladder, order, ranking, spectrum. **5** *a musical scale.* chromatic scale, diatonic scale, major scale, minor scale, sequence, series. **6** *the scale of a map.* proportion, ratio. **7** *We were amazed by the huge scale of the building.* SEE **size**.
scales *bathroom scales.* balance, weighing-machine.

scale verb *to scale a ladder.* ascend, climb, mount.

scallywag noun SEE **rascal**.

scalp noun SEE **head** noun.

scalpel noun SEE **knife** noun.

scamp noun SEE **rascal**.

scamper verb *to scamper home.* dash, hasten, hurry, run, rush, scuttle.
to scamper about frisk, frolic, gambol, play, romp, run about.

scampi plural noun prawns.

scan verb **1** *to scan the horizon.* examine, eye, gaze at, look at, scrutinize, search, stare at, study, survey, view, watch. **2** *to scan a newspaper.* glance at, read quickly, skim.

scandal noun **1** *It's a scandal when food is wasted.* disgrace, embarrassment, notoriety, outrage, reproach, sensation, shame. **2** *The newspapers shouldn't print such scandal.* calumny, gossip, libel, rumour, slander, [*informal*] tittle-tattle.

scandalize verb SEE **shock** verb.

scandalmonger noun SEE **gossip** noun.

scandalous adjective **1** *a scandalous waste of money.* disgraceful, improper, infamous, notorious, outrageous, shameful, shocking, wicked. **2** *a scandalous lie.* defamatory, libellous, scurrilous, slanderous, untrue.

scansion noun *the scansion of a line of verse.* metre, prosody, rhythm, SEE **verse**.

scanty adjective **1** *a scanty supply of food.* inadequate, insufficient, meagre, mean, [*slang*] measly, [*informal*] mingy, scant, scarce, [*informal*] skimpy, small, sparing, sparse, stingy.
OPPOSITES: SEE **plentiful**.
2 *scanty clothes.* barely adequate, indecent, revealing, [*informal*] see-through, thin.

scapegoat noun whipping-boy.

scar noun *The cut left a scar.* blemish, mark, scab, SEE **wound** noun.

scar verb *The wound scarred his face.* brand, damage, deface, disfigure, leave a scar on, mark, spoil.

scarce adjective *Water was scarce during the drought.* [*informal*] few and far between, [*informal*] hard to find, inadequate, infrequent, in short supply, insufficient, lacking, meagre, rare, scant, scanty, sparse, [*informal*] thin on the ground, uncommon, unusual.
OPPOSITES: SEE **plentiful**.

scarcely adverb barely, hardly, only just.

scarcity noun *a scarcity of water.* dearth, famine, inadequacy, insufficiency, lack, paucity, poverty, rarity, shortage, want.
OPPOSITES: SEE **plenty**.

scare noun *The bang gave us a nasty scare.* alarm, SEE **fright**, jolt, shock.

scare verb 1 *The bang scared us.* alarm, dismay, shake, shock, startle, unnerve. 2 *The ruffians tried to scare us.* bully, cow, daunt, dismay, SEE **frighten**, intimidate, make afraid, menace, panic, terrorize, threaten.
OPPOSITES: SEE **reassure**.

scaremonger noun alarmist.

scarf noun headscarf, muffler, shawl, stole.

scarify verb SEE **scratch** verb.

scarlet adjective SEE **red**.

scarp noun SEE **slope** noun.

scarper verb SEE **escape** verb.

scary adjective SEE **frightening**.

scathing adjective SEE **critical**.

scatter verb 1 *to scatter a crowd.* break up, disband, disintegrate, dispel, disperse, divide, send in all directions.
2 *to scatter seeds.* broadcast, disseminate, intersperse [= *scatter between other things*], shed, shower, sow, spread, sprinkle, strew, throw about.
OPPOSITES: SEE **gather**.

scatter-brained adjective absent-minded, careless, crazy, disorganized, forgetful, frivolous, inattentive, muddled, [*informal*] not with it, [*informal*] scatty, SEE **silly**, thoughtless, unreliable, unsystematic, vague.

scatty adjective SEE **scatter-brained**.

scavenge verb *to scavenge in a rubbish heap.* forage, rummage, scrounge, search.

scenario noun *the scenario of a film.* outline, plan, SEE **story**, summary.

scene noun 1 *the scene of a crime.* locale, locality, location, place, position, setting, site, situation, spot.
2 *a beautiful scene.* landscape, outlook, panorama, picture, prospect, scenery, sight, spectacle, view, vista.
3 *the scene for a play.* backdrop, scenery, set, stage.
4 *a scene from a play.* act, [*informal*] clip, episode, part, section, sequence.
5 *He made a scene because he didn't win.* argument, [*informal*] carry-on, commotion, disturbance, fuss, quarrel, row, [*informal*] to-do.

scenery noun SEE **scene**.

scenic adjective *a scenic journey.* attractive, beautiful, lovely, panoramic, picturesque, pretty, spectacular.

scent noun 1 *the scent of flowers.* fragrance, odour, perfume, redolence, SEE **smell** noun.
2 *a bottle of scent.* after-shave, eau de Cologne, lavender water, perfume.
OTHER COSMETICS: SEE **cosmetics**.
3 *The dog followed the scent.* trail.

scent verb SEE **smell** verb.

scented adjective SEE **smelling**.

sceptic noun agnostic, cynic, doubter, sceptical person [SEE **sceptical**].
OPPOSITES: SEE **believer**.

sceptical adjective *I was sceptical about the truth of his story.* cynical, disbelieving, distrustful, doubting, dubious, incredulous, mistrustful, questioning, suspicious, uncertain, unconvinced, unsure.
OPPOSITES: SEE **confident**.

scepticism noun agnosticism, cynicism, disbelief, distrust, doubt, incredulity, lack of confidence, suspicion.
OPPOSITES: SEE **faith**.

schedule noun *a schedule of events.* agenda, calendar, diary, itinerary, list, plan, programme, scheme, timetable.

schedule verb *When are we scheduled to arrive?* appoint, arrange, book, fix a time, organize, plan, programme, timetable.

scheme noun 1 *a proper scheme for running the business.* idea, method, plan, procedure, project, proposal, system.
2 *a dishonest scheme to make money.* conspiracy, [*informal*] dodge, intrigue, machinations, manœuvre, plot, [*informal*] ploy, [*informal*] racket, ruse, scheming, stratagem.
3 *a colour scheme.* arrangement, design.

scheme verb *Two boys schemed together.* collude, conspire, intrigue, plan, plot.

schism noun SEE **division**.

scholar noun 1 *a scholar of a school.* SEE **pupil**.
2 *The professor is a real scholar.* SEE **academic** noun.

scholarly adjective SEE **academic** adjective.

scholarship noun 1 *a scholarship to study at college.* award, bursary, exhibition, grant.
2 *a woman of great scholarship.* academic achievement, education, erudition, intellectual attainment, knowledge, learning, wisdom.

scholastic adjective SEE **academic** adjective.

school noun 1 See panel below.
2 *a school of whales.* SEE **group** noun, shoal.

KINDS OF SCHOOL: academy, boarding-school, coeducational school, college, comprehensive school, grammar school, high school, infant school, junior school, kindergarten, nursery school, play group, preparatory school, primary school, public school, secondary school.

PARTS OF A SCHOOL: assembly hall, cafeteria, common room, dormitory, classroom, cloakroom, foyer, gymnasium, hall, laboratory, library, office, playground, playing-field, reception, refectory, staff room, stock room.

PEOPLE WHO HELP RUN A SCHOOL: assistant, caretaker, groundsman, headmaster, headmistress, head teacher, librarian, monitor, peripatetic teacher, prefect, principal, secretary, [*plural*] staff, SEE **teacher**, technician, tutor.

schoolchild noun SEE **pupil**.
schooling noun SEE **education**.
schoolteacher noun SEE **teacher**.
science noun organized knowledge, systematic study.

SOME BRANCHES OF SCIENCE AND TECHNOLOGY: acoustics, aeronautics, agricultural science, anatomy, anthropology, artificial intelligence, astronomy, astrophysics, behavioural science, biochemistry, biology, biophysics, botany, chemistry, climatology, computer science, cybernetics, dietetics, domestic science, dynamics, earth science, ecology, economics, electronics, engineering, entomology, environmental science, food science, genetics, geographical science, geology, geophysics, hydraulics.

information technology, life science, linguistics, materials science, mathematics, mechanics, medical science [SEE **medicine**], metallurgy, meteorology, microbiology, mineralogy, ornithology, pathology, pharmacology, physics, physiology, political science, psychology, robotics, sociology, space technology, sports science, telecommunications, thermodynamics, toxicology, veterinary science, zoology.

scientific adjective *a scientific investigation.* analytical, methodical, organized, precise, systematic.

scientist noun [*informal*] boffin, researcher, scientific expert, technologist.
VARIOUS SCIENCES: SEE **science**.

scintillate verb SEE **light** noun (give light).

scion noun SEE **descendant**.

scissors noun SEE **cutter**.

scoff verb 1 *to scoff at someone.* SEE **jeer**.
2 [*informal*] *to scoff food.* SEE **eat**.

scold verb *to scold someone for wrongdoing.* admonish, berate, blame, castigate, censure, chide, criticize, find fault with, [*informal*] lecture, [*informal*] nag, rebuke, reprimand, reproach, reprove, [*informal*] tell off, [*informal*] tick off, upbraid.

scoop noun *an ice-cream scoop.* ladle, shovel, spoon.

scoop verb *to scoop out a hole.* dig, excavate, gouge, hollow, scrape, shovel.

scoot verb SEE **run** verb.

scope noun 1 *That kind of work is beyond my scope.* ambit, capacity, compass, competence, extent, limit, range, reach, sphere, terms of reference.
2 *scope for expansion.* chance, [*informal*] elbow-room, freedom, latitude, leeway, liberty, opportunity, outlet, room, space.

scorch verb SEE **burn** verb, **heat** verb.

scorching adjective SEE **hot**.

score noun 1 *the score in a game.* mark, number of points, reckoning, result, tally, total.
2 *a score to settle.* SEE **debt**.

score verb 1 *to score points in a game.* SEE **achieve**, add up, [*informal*] chalk up, earn, gain, [*informal*] knock up, make, win.
2 *to score a line on a surface.* cut, engrave, gouge, incise, mark, scrape, scratch, slash.
3 *to score a piece of music.* orchestrate, write out.

scorn noun *They viewed my cooking with scorn.* contempt, derision, detestation, disdain, disgust, dislike, disparagement, disrespect, mockery, ridicule.
OPPOSITES: SEE **admiration**.

scorn verb *They scorned my efforts.* be scornful about [SEE **scornful**], deride, despise, disapprove of, disdain, dislike, dismiss, hate, insult, jeer at, laugh at, look down on, make fun of, mock, reject, ridicule, [*informal*] scoff at, sneer at, spurn, taunt.
OPPOSITES: SEE **admire**.

scornful adjective *scornful laughter.* condescending, contemptuous, derisive, disdainful, dismissive, disrespectful, insulting, jeering, mocking, patronizing, sarcastic, satirical, scathing, sneering, [*informal*] snide, [*informal*] snooty, supercilious, taunting, withering (*a withering look*).
OPPOSITES: SEE **flattering**.

scotch verb SEE **end** verb.

scot-free adjective *He got off scot-free.* safe, unharmed, unhurt, unpunished, unscathed.

scoundrel noun [*Scoundrel* and synonyms are mostly used *informally.*] blackguard, blighter, good-for-nothing, heel, knave, miscreant, ne'er-do-well, rascal, rogue, ruffian, scallywag, scamp, villain.

scour verb 1 *to scour a saucepan.* buff up, burnish, clean, polish, rub, scrape, scrub, wash.
2 *I scoured the house looking for my purse.* comb, forage (through), hunt through, ransack, rummage through, search, [*informal*] turn upside down.

scourge noun, verb SEE **whip** noun, verb.

scout noun *They sent out scouts to get information.* lookout, spy.

scout verb *Wait here while I scout round.* explore, get information, investigate, look about, reconnoitre, search, [*informal*] snoop, spy.

scowl verb frown, glower.
FACIAL EXPRESSIONS: SEE **expression**.

scrabble verb *to scrabble about in the sand.* claw, dig, grope, scrape, scratch.

scraggy adjective *a weak, scraggy animal.* bony, emaciated, gaunt, lanky, lean, scrawny, skinny, starved, thin, underfed.
OPPOSITES: SEE **plump**.

scram verb SEE **depart**.

scramble noun SEE **race** noun.

scramble verb 1 *to scramble over rocks.* clamber, climb, crawl, move awkwardly.
2 *to scramble for food.* compete, contend, fight, jostle, push, scuffle, strive, struggle, tussle, vie.
3 *to scramble into your places.* dash, hasten, hurry, run, rush.
4 *to scramble eggs.* SEE **cook** verb.

scrap noun 1 *a scrap of food. a scrap of cloth.* bit, crumb, fraction, fragment, iota, mite, morsel, particle, piece, rag, shred, snippet, speck.
2 *a pile of scrap.* junk, litter, odds and ends, refuse, rubbish, salvage, waste.
3 *Two dogs had a scrap.* SEE **fight** noun.

scrap verb 1 *We scrapped our plan when we worked out the cost.* abandon, cancel, discard, [*informal*] ditch, drop, give up, jettison, throw away, write off.
2 *Those two are always scrapping.* SEE **fight** verb.

scrape noun *Don't get into any scrapes.* escapade, mischief, prank, trouble.

scrape verb 1 *to scrape your skin.* abrade, bark, graze, lacerate, scratch, scuff.
2 *to scrape something clean.* clean, file, rasp, rub, scour, scrub.
to scrape together *I scraped together enough for the bus fare.* SEE **collect**.

scrappy adjective *a scrappy programme which didn't hold my attention. scrappy work.* bitty, disjointed, fragmentary, hurriedly put together, imperfect, incomplete, inconclusive, sketchy, slipshod, unfinished, unpolished, unsatisfactory.
OPPOSITES: SEE **perfect** adjective.

scratch noun 1 *scratches on the furniture.* gash, groove, line, mark, scoring, scrape.
2 *a scratch on your skin.* graze, laceration, SEE **wound** noun.
up to scratch SEE **satisfactory**.

scratch verb *to scratch a car. to scratch your skin.* claw at, cut, damage the surface of, gouge, graze, incise, lacerate, mark, rub, scarify, score, scrape.

scrawl verb SEE **write**.

scrawny adjective SEE **scraggy**.

scream noun, verb bawl, cry, howl, roar, screech, shout, shriek, squeal, wail, yell.

scree noun stones.

screech noun, verb SEE **scream**.

screed noun SEE **writing**.

screen noun *a dividing screen.* blind, curtain, partition.

screen verb 1 *We planted a hedge to screen the manure heap.* camouflage, cloak, conceal, cover, disguise, guard, hide, mask, protect, safeguard, shade, shelter, shield, shroud, veil.
2 *All employees were screened before being appointed.* examine, investigate, vet.

screw noun 1 *a screw used in woodwork.*
OTHER FASTENERS: SEE **fastener**.
2 *the screws of a ship.* propeller.

screw verb 1 *to screw something down.* SEE **fasten**.
2 *to screw something into a spiral shape or with a spiral movement.* SEE **twist** verb.

screwy adjective SEE **mad**.

scribble verb SEE **write**.

scribe noun amanuensis, secretary, writer.

scrimmage noun SEE **fight** noun.

script noun 1 *cursive script.* handwriting.
2 *the script of a play.* screenplay, text, words.
VARIOUS KINDS OF WRITING: SEE **writing**.

scripture noun Bible, Koran, sacred writings, Word of God.

scroll noun SEE **book** noun.

scrounge verb *The stray cat scrounged scraps.* beg, cadge.

scrub verb 1 *to scrub the floor.* brush, clean, rub, scour, wash.
2 [*informal*] *to scrub your plans.* SEE **cancel**.

scruffy adjective *a scruffy appearance. scruffy clothes.* bedraggled, dirty, dishevelled, disordered, dowdy, messy, ragged, scrappy, shabby, slatternly, slovenly, tatty, ungroomed, unkempt, untidy, worn out.
OPPOSITES: SEE **smart** adjective.

scrumping noun SEE **stealing**.

scrumptious adjective SEE **delicious**.

scrunch verb SEE **crunch** verb.

scruples noun *Don't trust him—he has no scruples about cheating.* compunction, conscience, doubts, hesitation, misgivings, qualms.

scrupulous adjective 1 *a scrupulous worker. scrupulous attention to detail.* SEE **careful**, conscientious, diligent, fastidious, meticulous, minute, painstaking, precise, punctilious, rigorous, strict, systematic, thorough.
2 *a scrupulous businessman. scrupulous honesty.* ethical, fair-minded, honest, honourable, just, moral, proper, upright.
OPPOSITES: SEE **unscrupulous**.

scrutinize verb SEE **examine**.

scrutiny noun *She subjected my work to close scrutiny.* examination, inspection, investigation, search, study.

scuff verb SEE **scrape** verb.

scuffle noun, verb SEE **fight** noun, verb.

scull noun [Do not confuse with *skull.*] *the sculls of a rowing-boat.* oar, paddle.

scull verb *to scull a rowing-boat.* paddle, row.

sculpt verb SEE **sculpture** verb.

sculptor noun VARIOUS ARTISTS: SEE **artist**.

sculpture noun three-dimensional art.

KINDS OF SCULPTURE: bas-relief, bronze, bust, carving, caryatid, cast, effigy, figure, figurine, maquette, moulding, plaster cast, statue.
OTHER WORKS OF ART: SEE **art**.

sculpture verb *to sculpture a statue.* carve, cast, chisel, form, hew, model, mould, [*informal*] sculpt, shape.

scum noun *scum on dirty water.* film, foam, froth, impurities.

scupper verb SEE **sink** verb.

scurf noun *scurf in your hair.* dandruff, dry skin, flakes, scales.

scurrilous adjective 1 *a scurrilous attack on someone.* SEE **insulting**.
2 *scurrilous jokes.* SEE **obscene**.

scurry verb SEE **run** verb.

scuttle verb 1 *to scuttle a ship.* SEE **sink** verb.
2 *to scuttle away.* SEE **run** verb.

scythe noun billhook, sickle.

sea adjective *sea creatures. a sea voyage. a sea port.* aquatic, marine, maritime, nautical, naval, oceangoing, oceanic, saltwater, seafaring, seagoing.

sea noun [*joking*] the briny, [*poetic*] the deep, lake, ocean.

seal noun 1 sea-lion, walrus.
2 *the royal seal.* crest, emblem, impression, sign, stamp, symbol.

seal verb 1 *to seal a lid. to seal an envelope.* close, fasten, lock, secure, shut, stick down.
2 *to seal a leak.* make airtight, make waterproof, plug, stop up.
3 *to seal an agreement.* authenticate, [*informal*] clinch, conclude, confirm, decide, finalize, ratify, settle, sign, validate.

sealant noun SEE **glue** noun.

sea-lion noun seal, walrus.

seam noun 1 *the seam of a garment.* join, stitching.
2 *a seam of coal.* layer, stratum, thickness, vein.

seaman noun SEE **sailor**.

seamy adjective SEE **sordid**.

seaplane noun VARIOUS AIRCRAFT: SEE **aircraft**.

seaport noun SEE **port** noun.

sear verb SEE **burn** verb.

search noun *a search for the things we'd lost. a search for intruders.* check, examination, hunt, inspection, investigation, look, quest, scrutiny.

---

search verb 1 *I searched for the things we'd lost.* explore, ferret about, hunt, look, nose about, poke about, prospect, pry, seek.
2 *Security staff search all passengers.* check, examine, [*informal*] frisk, inspect, investigate, scrutinize.
3 *I searched the house for my purse.* comb, ransack, rifle, rummage through, scour.

searching adjective *searching questions.* deep, intimate, minute, penetrating, probing, sharp, thorough.
OPPOSITES: SEE **superficial**.

sea-shore noun SEE **seaside**.

seaside noun *a day at the seaside.* beach, coast, coastal resort, sands, sea-coast, sea-shore, shore.

season noun *the festive season. the holiday season.* period, phase, time.
SEASONS OF THE YEAR: autumn, spring, summer, winter.

season verb 1 *to season food.* add seasoning to, flavour, salt, spice.
2 *to season wood.* harden, mature.

seasonable adjective 1 *seasonable weather.* appropriate, normal, predictable, suitable.
2 *I'll wait for a seasonable moment to speak to her.* opportune, timely, well-timed.

seasoning noun *I don't add much seasoning to my food.* additives, condiments, flavouring.
KINDS OF SEASONING: dressing, herbs, mustard, pepper, relish, salt, SEE **sauce**, spice, vinegar.

seat noun KINDS OF SEAT: armchair, bench, chair, chaise longue, couch, deck-chair, pew, pillion, place, pouffe, reclining chair, rocking-chair, saddle, settee, settle, sofa, squab, stall, stool, throne, window seat.
ITEMS OF FURNITURE: SEE **furniture**.

seat verb to seat yourself SEE **sit**.

seat-belt noun safety-belt, safety-harness.

seaworthy adjective *a seaworthy ship.* safe, sound, watertight.

secateurs noun clippers, SEE **cutter**, pruning shears.

secede verb SEE **withdraw**.

secluded adjective *a secluded existence. a secluded beach.* cloistered, concealed, cut off, inaccessible, isolated, lonely, private, remote, screened, sequestered, sheltered, shut away, solitary, unfrequented, unvisited.
OPPOSITES: SEE **busy**.

seclusion noun *the seclusion of your own home. the seclusion of a hermit.* concealment, isolation, loneliness, privacy, retirement, shelter, solitariness.

second adjective *You won't get a second chance.* additional, alternative, another, duplicate, extra, further, repeated, SEE **secondary**, subsequent.

second noun 1 *The pain only lasted a second.* flash, instant, [*informal*] jiffy, moment, [*informal*] tick, [*informal*] twinkling.
2 *a second to a boxer in a fight.* assistant, helper, supporter.

second verb 1 *to second a proposal. to second someone in a fight.* assist, back, encourage, give approval to, help, promote, side with, support.
2 [pronounced se-*cond*] *to second someone to another job.* move, relocate, transfer.

secondary adjective 1 *of secondary importance.* inferior, lesser, lower, minor, second-rate, subordinate, subsidiary.
2 *a secondary line of attack.* auxiliary, extra, reinforcing, reserve, second, supplementary, supportive.
secondary school SEE **school**.

second-class adjective SEE **second-rate**.

second-hand adjective 1 *a second-hand car.* old, used.
OPPOSITES: SEE **new**.
2 *second-hand experience.* indirect, vicarious.
OPPOSITE: personal.

second-rate adjective *a second-rate performance.* commonplace, indifferent, inferior, low-grade, mediocre, middling, ordinary, poor, second-best, second-class, undistinguished, unexciting, uninspiring.

secret adjective *secret messages. secret meetings.* arcane, clandestine, classified, concealed, confidential, covert, cryptic, disguised, hidden, [*informal*] hushed up, [*informal*] hush-hush, inaccessible, intimate, invisible, occult, personal, private, secluded, SEE **secretive**, stealthy, undercover, underground, undisclosed, unknown, unpublished.
OPPOSITES: SEE **open** adjective.

secretary noun amanuensis, clerk, filing-clerk, personal assistant, scribe, shorthand-typist, stenographer, typist, word-processor operator.

secrete verb 1 *He secreted his winnings in a drawer.* SEE **hide** verb.
2 *The pores of your body secrete sweat.* SEE **discharge** verb.

secretion noun SEE **discharge** noun.

secretive adjective *secretive about his private life.* close-lipped, enigmatic, furtive, mysterious, quiet, reserved, reticent, shifty, tight-lipped, uncommunicative, unforthcoming, withdrawn.
OPPOSITES: SEE **communicative.**

sect noun *a religious sect.* cult, denomination, faction, SEE **group** noun, party.

sectarian adjective *sectarian beliefs.* bigoted, cliquish, dogmatic, exclusive, factional, fanatical, inflexible, narrow, narrow-minded, partisan, prejudiced, rigid, schismatic.

section noun *a section of a more complex whole.* bit, branch, chapter (*of a book*), compartment, component, department, division, fraction, fragment, instalment, part, passage (*from a book or piece of music*), portion, SEE **sector,** segment, slice, stage (*of a journey*), subdivision, subsection.

sector noun *a sector of a town.* area, district, division, part, quarter, region, SEE **section,** zone.

secular adjective *the secular authorities. secular music.* civil, earthly, lay, mundane, non-religious, [*formal*] temporal, worldly.
OPPOSITES: SEE **religious.**

secure adjective **1** *Is the house secure against burglars?* defended, foolproof, guarded, impregnable, invulnerable, protected, safe.
2 *During the storm we remained secure indoors.* snug, unharmed, unhurt, unscathed.
3 *Is that hook secure?* fast, firm, fixed, immovable, solid, steady, tight, unyielding.

secure verb SEE **fasten.**

security noun SEE **safety.**

sedate adjective *The procession moved at a sedate pace.* calm, collected, composed, cool, decorous, deliberate, dignified, grave, level-headed, quiet, sensible, serene, serious, slow, sober, solemn, staid, tranquil.
OPPOSITES: SEE **lively.**

sedate verb *The nurse sedated the patient.* calm, put to sleep, tranquillize, treat with sedatives.

sedative noun anodyne, barbiturate, narcotic, opiate, sleeping-pill, tranquillizer.

sedentary adjective *People in sedentary jobs need to take exercise.* immobile, inactive, seated, sitting down.
OPPOSITES: SEE **active.**

sediment noun *sediment at the bottom of a bottle.* deposit, dregs, lees, [*formal*] precipitate, remains, [*informal*] sludge.

sedition noun SEE **rebellion.**

seduce verb *to seduce someone into wicked ways.* allure, beguile, corrupt, debauch, decoy, deprave, entice, inveigle, lead astray, lure, mislead, tempt.

seduction noun **1** *the seductions of the big city.* SEE **temptation.**
2 *sexual seduction.* SEE **sex (sexual intercourse).**

seductive adjective *a seductive dress. seductive music.* alluring, appealing, SEE **attractive,** bewitching, captivating, enticing, irresistible, provocative, [*informal*] sexy, tempting.
OPPOSITES: SEE **repulsive.**

sedulous adjective SEE **diligent.**

see verb **1** *What did you see?* [*old-fashioned*] behold, discern, discover, distinguish, [*old-fashioned*] espy, glimpse, identify, look at, make out, mark, note, notice, observe, perceive, recognize, sight, spot, spy, view, witness.
2 *I can see what you mean.* appreciate, comprehend, fathom, follow, grasp, know, realize, take in, understand.
3 *I see problems ahead.* anticipate, conceive, envisage, foresee, foretell, imagine, picture, visualize.
4 *I'll have to see what I can do.* consider, decide, investigate, reflect on, think about, weigh up.
5 *Did you see the game on Saturday?* attend, be a spectator at, watch.
6 *She's going to see him again tonight.* go out with, have a date with, meet, visit.
7 *Shall I see you home?* accompany, conduct, escort.
8 *The homeless see much misery.* endure, experience, go through, suffer, undergo.
9 *Guess who I saw in town!* encounter, face, meet, run into, visit.
to see red SEE **angry (become angry).**
to see to SEE **attend (attend to).**

seed noun **1** *a seed from which something will grow.* egg, germ, ovule, ovum, semen, [*plural*] spawn, sperm, spore.
2 *a seed in a fruit.* pip, stone.

seed verb *to seed a lawn.* SEE **sow** verb.

seedy adjective **1** [*informal*] *a seedy appearance.* SEE **shabby.**
2 [*informal*] *feeling seedy.* SEE **ill.**

seek verb *to seek something you've lost. to seek revenge.* ask for, aspire to, beg for, desire, hunt for, inquire after, look for, pursue, search for, solicit, strive after, want, wish for.

seem verb *She isn't as well as she seems.* appear, feel, give an impression of being, look, pretend, sound.

seemly adjective SEE **proper.**

seep verb *Oil seeped through the crack.* dribble, drip, exude, flow, leak, ooze, percolate, run, soak, trickle.

seer noun SEE **prophet**.

see-saw verb SEE **alternate** verb.

seethe verb 1 *The water in the pan began to seethe.* be agitated, boil, bubble, foam, froth up, rise, simmer, surge.
2 *She seethed with anger.* SEE **angry (be angry)**.

segment noun SEE **section**.

segregate verb *They segregated visitors from the home supporters.* cut off, isolate, keep apart, put apart, separate, set apart.

segregation noun 1 *racial segregation.* apartheid, discrimination, separation.
2 *the segregation of sick animals.* isolation, quarantine.

seismic adjective SEE **earthquake**.

seize verb 1 *to seize something in your hands.* catch, clutch, grab, grasp, grip, hold, pluck, snatch, take.
2 *to seize a person by force.* abduct, apprehend, arrest, capture, [*informal*] collar, detain, [*informal*] nab, take prisoner.
3 *to seize a country.* annex, invade.
4 *to seize property.* appropriate, commandeer, confiscate, hijack, impound, steal, take away.
OPPOSITES: SEE **release** verb.

seizure noun *to suffer a seizure.* apoplexy, attack, convulsion, epileptic fit, fit, paroxysm, spasm, stroke.

seldom adverb infrequently, rarely.
OPPOSITES: SEE **often**.

select adjective *Only a select few were invited.* choice, chosen, élite, exclusive, first-class, [*informal*] hand-picked, preferred, privileged, rare, selected, special, top-quality.
OPPOSITES: SEE **ordinary**.

select verb *to select a representative. to select your purchases.* appoint, choose, decide on, elect, nominate, opt for, pick, prefer, settle on, single out, vote for.

selection noun 1 *There's a wide selection to choose from.* assortment, SEE **range** noun, variety.
2 *Make your selection.* choice, option, pick.

selective adjective *She's very selective in what she watches on TV.* careful, [*informal*] choosy, discerning, discriminating, particular, specialized.
OPPOSITES: SEE **undiscriminating**.

self-assured adjective SEE **self-evident**.

self-catering noun SEE **accommodation**.

self-centred adjective SEE **selfish**.

self-command noun SEE **self-control**.

self-confident adjective *Try to look self-confident at the interview.* assertive, assured, bold, collected, cool, fearless, poised, positive, self-assured, self-possessed, sure of yourself.
OPPOSITES: SEE **self-conscious**.

self-conscious adjective *self-conscious in front of an audience.* awkward, bashful, blushing, coy, diffident, embarrassed, ill at ease, insecure, nervous, reserved, self-effacing, sheepish, shy, uncomfortable, unnatural.
OPPOSITES: SEE **self-confident**.

self-contained adjective 1 *a self-contained flat.* complete, separate.
2 *a self-contained person.* aloof, cold, independent, reserved, self-reliant, undemonstrative, unemotional.
OPPOSITES: SEE **sociable**.

self-control noun *He showed great self-control when they were teasing him.* calmness, composure, coolness, patience, restraint, self-command, self-discipline, will-power.

self-denial noun *Lent is a time of self-denial.* abstemiousness, fasting, moderation, self-sacrifice, temperance.
OPPOSITES: SEE **self-indulgence**.

self-employed adjective *a self-employed journalist.* free-lance, independent.

self-esteem noun SEE **pride**.

self-evident, self-explanatory adjectives SEE **obvious**.

self-governing adjective *a self-governing country.* autonomous, independent, sovereign.

self-important adjective SEE **pompous**.

self-indulgent adjective *a self-indulgent pursuit of pleasure.* dissipated, epicurean, extravagant, greedy, hedonistic, intemperate, pleasure-loving, profligate, SEE **selfish**, sybaritic.
OPPOSITES: SEE **abstemious**.

self-indulgence noun extravagance, greed, hedonism, pleasure, self-gratification, SEE **selfishness**.
OPPOSITES: SEE **self-denial**.

self-interest noun SEE **selfishness**.

selfish adjective *It's selfish to keep it all to yourself.* demanding, egocentric, egotistic, grasping, greedy, mean, mercenary, miserly, self-centred, self-indulgent, self-seeking, [*informal*] stingy, thoughtless, worldly.
OPPOSITES: SEE **unselfish**.

selfishness noun egotism, greed, meanness, miserliness, self-indulgence, self-

interest, self-love, self-regard, [*informal*] stinginess, thoughtlessness.
OPPOSITES: SEE **unselfishness**.

selfless adjective SEE **unselfish**.

self-possessed adjective SEE **self-confident**.

self-reliant adjective SEE **self-supporting**.

self-respect noun SEE **pride**.

self-righteous adjective *Don't feel self-righteous just because you gave an odd coin to charity.* complacent, [*informal*] holier-than-thou, pious, pompous, priggish, proud, sanctimonious, self-important, self-satisfied, sleek, smug, vain.
a **self-righteous person** [*informal*] goody-goody, prig.

self-sacrifice noun SEE **unselfishness**.

self-satisfied adjective SEE **self-righteous**.

self-seeking adjective SEE **selfish**.

self-sufficient adjective SEE **self-supporting**.

self-supporting adjective *a self-supporting community.* independent, self-contained, self-reliant, self-sufficient.

self-willed adjective SEE **obstinate**.

sell verb 1 *What does this shop sell?* deal in, [*informal*] keep, offer for sale, retail, stock, trade in (*He trades in electrical goods*), traffic in, vend.

VARIOUS WAYS TO SELL THINGS: auction, barter, give in part-exchange, hawk, [*informal*] knock down, peddle, [*informal*] put under the hammer, sell off, tout, trade-in (*He traded-in his old car*).

2 *If business is slack, we must sell our product more attractively.* advertise, market, merchandise, package, promote, [*informal*] push.

seller noun vendor.

PEOPLE WHO SELL THINGS: agent, barrow-boy, costermonger, dealer, [*old-fashioned*] hawker, market-trader, merchant, pedlar, [*informal*] rep, representative, retailer, salesman, saleswoman, shopkeeper, stockist, storekeeper, street-trader, supplier, trader, tradesman, traveller, wholesaler.
PARTICULAR SHOPS: SEE **shop**.

selvage noun SEE **edge** noun.

semantic adjective SEE **meaning**.

semblance noun SEE **appearance**.

semester noun SEE **time** noun.

semi-detached noun VARIOUS HOUSES: SEE **house** noun.

seminal adjective *seminal ideas.* constructive, creative, fertile, imaginative, important, innovative, new, original, productive.

senate, senator nouns SEE **government**.

send verb 1 *to send a parcel. to send a cheque.* convey, dispatch, post, remit, transmit.
2 *to send a rocket to the moon.* direct, fire, launch, propel, shoot.
to send away banish, dismiss, exile, expel.
to send out belch, broadcast, discharge, emit, give off.
to send round circulate, distribute, issue, publish.
to send up SEE **parody** verb.

send-off noun SEE **farewell**.

send-up noun SEE **parody** noun.

senile adjective SEE **old**.

senior adjective *a senior position. a senior member of the team.* chief, higher, major, older, principal, revered, superior, well-established.
OPPOSITES: SEE **junior**.

sensation noun 1 *a tingling sensation in my fingers.* awareness, feeling, sense.
2 *The robbery caused a sensation.* SEE commotion, excitement, furore, outrage, scandal, surprise, thrill.

sensational adjective 1 *a sensational account of a murder. the sensational experience of hang-gliding.* blood-curdling, breathtaking, exciting, hair-raising, lurid, shocking, startling, stimulating, thrilling, violent.
2 [*informal*] *a sensational football result.* amazing, SEE **extraordinary**, fabulous, fantastic, great, marvellous, remarkable, spectacular, superb, surprising, unexpected, wonderful.

sense noun 1 *She has no sense of shame.* awareness, consciousness, faculty, feeling, intuition, perception, sensation.
YOUR FIVE SENSES ARE: hearing, sight, smell, taste, touch.
2 *If you had any sense you'd stay at home.* brains, cleverness, gumption, intellect, intelligence, judgement, logic, [*informal*] nous, reason, reasoning, understanding, wisdom, wit.
3 *Did you grasp the sense of her message?* denotation, [*informal*] drift, gist, import,

interpretation, meaning, point, significance.

to make sense of SEE **understand.**

sense verb *I sensed that he was bored. The machine senses any change of temperature.* be aware (of), detect, discern, feel, guess, notice, perceive, realize, respond to, suspect, understand.
WAYS IN WHICH WE SENSE THINGS: SEE **feel, hear, see, smell, taste** verbs.

senseless adjective 1 *a senseless thing to do.* SEE **stupid.**
2 *knocked senseless.* SEE **unconscious.**

sensibility noun *artistic sensibility.* SEE **feeling.**

sensible adjective 1 *a sensible person. a sensible decision.* calm, common-sense, cool, discriminating, intelligent, judicious, level-headed, logical, prudent, rational, realistic, reasonable, sane, serious-minded, sound, straightforward, thoughtful, wise.
OPPOSITES: SEE **stupid.**
2 *sensible clothes.* comfortable, functional, [*informal*] no-nonsense, practical, useful.
OPPOSITES: SEE **fashionable, impractical.**

sensitive adjective 1 *sensitive to light.* affected (by), responsive, susceptible.
2 *sensitive to someone's problems.* considerate, perceptive, sympathetic, tactful, thoughtful, understanding.
3 *Take care what you say—he's very sensitive.* emotional, hypersensitive, thin-skinned, touchy.
4 *a sensitive skin.* delicate, fine, fragile, painful, soft, tender.
5 *a sensitive subject.* confidential, controversial, secret.
OPPOSITES: SEE **insensitive.**

sensual adjective 1 *sensual pleasures.* animal, bodily, carnal, fleshly, physical, self-indulgent, SEE **sexual,** voluptuous, worldly.
2 *a sensual expression. sensual lips.* pleasure-loving, SEE **sexy.**
OPPOSITES: SEE **ascetic.**

Sensual often implies disapproval (especially when it has sexual connotations), whereas *sensuous* does not.

---

sensuous adjective *a sensuous description. sensuous music.* affecting, appealing, beautiful, emotional, lush, rich, richly embellished.
OPPOSITES: SEE **simple.**

sentence noun 1 LINGUISTIC TERMS: SEE **language.**
2 LEGAL TERMS: SEE **law.**

sentence verb *The judge sentenced the convicted man.* condemn, pass judgement on, pronounce sentence on.

sententious adjective SEE **pompous.**

sentient adjective SEE **conscious.**

sentiment noun 1 *What are your sentiments about experiments on animals?* attitude, belief, idea, judgement, opinion, thought, view.
2 *The reader communicated the sentiment of the poem most powerfully.* emotion, feeling, SEE **sentimentality.**

The noun *sentimentality* always implies disapproval (*I hate the sentimentality of animal stories*), whereas *sentiment* does not necessarily imply disapproval.

---

sentimental adjective 1 *Old family photographs make me sentimental.* emotional, nostalgic, romantic, soft-hearted, tearful, tender, [*informal*] weepy.
2 [*uncomplimentary*] *I hate sentimental words on birthday cards.* gushing, indulgent, insincere, maudlin, mawkish, [*informal*] mushy, overdone, over-emotional, [*informal*] sloppy, [*informal*] soppy, [*informal*] sugary, tear-jerking, [*informal*] treacly, unrealistic.
OPPOSITES: SEE **cynical, realistic.**

sentimentality noun emotionalism, insincerity, [*informal*] kitsch, mawkishness, nostalgia, [*informal*] slush.

sentinel, sentry nouns guard, look-out, picket, watchman.

separable adjective *separable components.* detachable, removable.

separate adjective 1 *They kept visiting supporters separate from ours.* apart, cut off, divided, divorced, fenced off, isolated, segregated.
2 *We all have separate jobs to do. We work in separate buildings.* detached, different, discrete, distinct, free-standing, unattached, unconnected, unrelated.
3 *The islanders have their own separate government.* autonomous, free, independent, particular.

separate verb 1 *to separate people or things or places from each other.* break up, cut off, detach, disconnect, disentangle, disjoin, dissociate, divide, fence off, hive off, isolate, keep apart, part, segregate, set apart, sever, split, sunder, take apart.
OPPOSITES: SEE **unite.**
2 *Our paths separated.* diverge, fork.
OPPOSITES: SEE **merge.**
3 *to separate grain from chaff.* abstract, filter out, remove, sift out, winnow.
OPPOSITES: SEE **mix.**

4 *to separate from your spouse.* become estranged, divorce, part company, [*informal*] split up.

separation noun **1** *the separation of one thing from another.* amputation, cutting off, detachment, disconnection, dissociation, division, parting, removal, segregation, severance, splitting.
OPPOSITES: SEE **connection.**
2 *the separation of a married couple.* [*informal*] break-up, divorce, estrangement, rift, split.

septic adjective *a septic wound.* festering, infected, inflamed, poisoned, purulent, putrefying, suppurating.

septuagenarian noun SEE **old (old person).**

sepulchral adjective SEE **funereal.**

sepulchre noun SEE **tomb.**

sequel noun *the sequel of an event or story.* consequence, continuation, [*informal*] follow-up, outcome, result, upshot.

sequence noun **1** *an unbroken sequence of events.* chain, concatenation, cycle, procession, progression, SEE **series,** succession, train.
2 *a sequence from a film.* episode, scene, section.

sequester verb SEE **confiscate.**

sequin noun decoration, spangle.

seraphic adjective SEE **angelic.**

serenade verb SEE **perform.**

serene adjective *a serene mood. serene music.* calm, contented, imperturbable, peaceful, placid, pleasing, quiet, tranquil, unclouded, unruffled, untroubled.
OPPOSITES: SEE **agitated.**

serial noun SEE **series.**

series noun **1** *a series of events.* arrangement, chain, concatenation, course, cycle, line, order, procession, programme, progression, range, row, run, sequence, set, string, succession, train.
2 *a television series.* mini-series, serial, [*informal*] soap, soap-opera.

serious adjective **1** *a serious expression.* dignified, grave, grim, humourless, long-faced, pensive, sedate, sober, solemn, staid, stern, thoughtful, unsmiling.
OPPOSITES: SEE **cheerful.**
2 *a serious discussion. serious literature.* deep, earnest, heavy, important, intellectual, profound, sincere, weighty.
OPPOSITES: SEE **frivolous.**
3 *a serious accident. a serious illness.* acute, appalling, awful, calamitous, critical, dangerous, dreadful, frightful, ghastly, grievous, hideous, horrible,

nasty, severe, shocking, terrible, unfortunate, unpleasant, violent.
OPPOSITES: SEE **trivial.**
4 *a serious worker.* careful, committed, conscientious, diligent, hard-working.
OPPOSITES: SEE **casual.**

sermon noun SEE **talk** noun.

sermonize verb SEE **preach.**

serpent noun snake.

serpentine adjective SEE **twisty.**

serrated adjective *a serrated edge.* jagged, notched, saw-like, toothed.
OPPOSITES: SEE **straight.**

servant noun assistant, attendant, [*informal*] dogsbody, drudge, [*joking*] factotum, [*joking*] flunkey, helper, hireling, menial, [*informal*] skivvy, slave, vassal.

VARIOUS SERVANTS: au pair, barmaid, barman, batman, butler, chamber-maid, [*informal*] char, charwoman, chauffeur, commissionaire, cook, [*informal*] daily, errand boy, footman, home help, housekeeper, housemaid, kitchenmaid, lackey, lady-in-waiting, maid, manservant, page, parlourmaid, retainer, [*plural*] retinue, scout, slave, steward, stewardess, valet, waiter, waitress.

---

serve verb **1** *to serve the community.* aid, assist, attend, further, help, look after, minister to, work for.
2 *to serve in the armed forces.* be employed, do your duty.
3 *to serve food. to serve at table.* [*informal*] dish up, distribute, give out, officiate, wait.
4 *to serve in a shop.* assist, be an assistant, sell goods.

service noun **1** *Would you do me a small service?* assistance, benefit, favour, help, kindness, office.
2 *He spent his life in the service of the same firm.* attendance (on), employment, ministering (to), work (for).
3 *a bus service.* business, organization, provision, system, timetable.
4 *a service for a car.* check-over, maintenance, overhaul, repair, servicing.
5 *a religious service.* ceremony, liturgy, meeting, rite, worship.

VARIOUS CHURCH SERVICES: baptism, christening, communion, compline, Eucharist, evensong, funeral, Lord's Supper, marriage, Mass, matins, Requiem Mass, vespers.

---

service verb *to service a car.* check, maintain, mend, overhaul, repair, tune.

serviceable adjective *a pair of strong serviceable shoes.* dependable, durable, functional, hard-wearing, lasting, practical, strong, tough, usable.
OPPOSITES: SEE **impractical**.

serviceman, servicewoman nouns SEE **armed services**.

serviette noun napkin, table-napkin.

servile adjective *servile self-abasement.* abject, [*informal*] boot-licking, craven, cringing, fawning, flattering, grovelling, humble, ingratiating, menial, obsequious, slavish, submissive, subservient, sycophantic, unctuous.
OPPOSITES: SEE **bossy**.
to be servile be at someone's beck and call, fawn, grovel, ingratiate yourself, [*informal*] kowtow, [*informal*] lick (someone's) boots, toady.

serving noun *a serving of food.* helping, plateful, portion, ration.

servitude noun SEE **slavery**.

session noun 1 *The court is in session.* assembly, conference, discussion, hearing, meeting, sitting.
2 *a session at the swimming-baths.* period, time.

set noun 1 *a set of people. a set of tools.* batch, bunch, category, class, clique, collection, SEE **group** noun, kind, series, sort.
2 *a TV set.* apparatus, receiver.
3 *a set for a play.* scene, scenery, setting, stage.

set verb 1 *to set something in place.* arrange, assign, deploy, deposit, dispose, lay, leave, locate, lodge, park, place, plant, [*informal*] plonk, position, put, rest, set down, set out, settle, situate, stand, station.
2 *to set a gate-post in concrete.* embed, fasten, fix.
3 *to set a watch.* adjust, correct, put right, rectify, regulate.
4 *to set a question in an exam.* ask, express, formulate, frame, phrase, put forward, suggest, write.
5 *Has the jelly set?* become firm, congeal, [*informal*] gel, harden, [*informal*] jell, stiffen, take shape.
6 *to set a target. to set a date.* allocate, allot, appoint, decide, designate, determine, establish, identify, name, ordain, prescribe, settle.
to set about 1 *I set about my work.* SEE **begin**.
2 *They set about us with their fists.* SEE **attack** verb.

to set free SEE **liberate**.
to set off 1 *We set off on a journey.* SEE **depart**.
2 *They set off a bomb.* SEE **explode**.
to set on *The dogs set on him.* SEE **attack** verb.
to set on fire SEE **ignite**.
to set to SEE **begin**.
to set up SEE **establish**.

set-back noun *We were delayed by a set-back.* [*informal*] blow, complication, difficulty, disappointment, [*informal*] hitch, misfortune, obstacle, problem, reverse, snag, upset.

settee noun chaise longue, couch, sofa.

setting noun 1 *a beautiful setting for a picnic.* background, context, environment, location, place, position, site, surroundings.
2 *a setting for a drama.* backcloth, backdrop, scene, scenery, set.

settle noun SEE **seat** noun.

settle verb 1 *to settle something in place.* SEE **set** verb.
2 *They plan to settle here.* become established, colonize, immigrate, make your home, move to, occupy, people, set up home, stay.
3 *We settled on the sofa. A bird settled on the fence.* alight, come to rest, land, light, [*informal*] make yourself comfortable, [*informal*] park yourself, pause, rest, sit down.
4 *Wait until the dust settles.* calm down, clear, compact, go down, sink, subside.
5 *We settled what to do.* agree, choose, decide, establish, fix.
6 *They settled their differences.* conclude, deal with, end, reconcile, resolve, square.
7 *I settled the bill.* pay.

settlement noun 1 *a business settlement.* SEE **arrangement**.
2 *a human settlement.* colony, community, encampment, kibbutz, SEE **town**, village.

settler noun colonist, immigrant, newcomer, pioneer, squatter.

sever verb *to sever a limb. to sever a relationship.* amputate, break, break off, SEE **cut** verb, cut off, disconnect, end, part, remove, separate, split, terminate.

several adjective assorted, different, a few, many, miscellaneous, a number of, sundry, various.

severe adjective 1 *a severe ruler. a severe look.* cold-hearted, cruel, disapproving, forbidding, grim, hard, harsh, oppressive, pitiless, relentless, stern, strict, unkind, unsmiling, unsympathetic.
OPPOSITES: SEE **kind** adjective.

2 *a severe frost. severe flu.* acute, bad, drastic, extreme, great, intense, keen, serious, sharp, troublesome, violent. OPPOSITES: SEE **mild**.
3 *severe conditions. a severe test of stamina.* arduous, dangerous, demanding, difficult, nasty, spartan, stringent, taxing, tough. OPPOSITES: SEE **easy**.
4 *a severe style of dress.* austere, chaste, plain, simple, unadorned. OPPOSITES: SEE **ornate**.

sew verb *to sew up a hole in your jeans.* darn, mend, repair, stitch, tack.

sewage noun effluent, waste.

sewers noun drainage, drains, sanitation, septic tank, soak-away.

sewing noun dressmaking, embroidery, mending, needlepoint, needlework, tapestry.

sex noun *a person's sex.* gender, sexuality.
to have sexual intercourse be intimate, consummate marriage, copulate, couple, fornicate, [*informal*] have sex, make love, mate, rape, unite.

KINDS OF SEXUALITY: bisexual, hermaphrodite, heterosexual, homosexual.

WORDS TO DESCRIBE SEXUAL ACTIVITY: [*old-fashioned*] carnal knowledge, coitus, consummation of marriage, copulation, coupling, fornication, incest, intercourse, intimacy, love-making, masturbation, mating, orgasm, perversion, rape, seduction, sexual intercourse, union.

---

sexism noun [*informal*] chauvinism (*male chauvinism*), SEE **prejudice** noun.

sexist adjective [*informal*] chauvinist, SEE **prejudiced**.

sexual adjective *sexual feelings.* carnal, erotic, physical, sensual, SEE **sexy**, venereal (*venereal diseases*).

sexuality noun SEE **sex**.

sexy adjective **1** *a sexy person.* attractive, desirable, [*informal*] dishy, flirtatious, seductive, sensual, [*informal*] sultry, voluptuous.
2 *sexy feelings.* amorous, erotic, lascivious, lecherous, libidinous, lustful, passionate, [*informal*] randy.
3 *sexy talk. sexy books.* aphrodisiac, erotic, SEE **obscene**, pornographic, provocative, [*informal*] raunchy, suggestive, titillating, [*informal*] torrid.

shabby adjective **1** *shabby clothes.* dingy, dirty, dowdy, drab, faded, frayed, grubby, [*informal*] moth-eaten, ragged, [*informal*] scruffy, seedy, tattered, [*informal*] tatty, threadbare, unattractive, worn, worn-out. OPPOSITES: SEE **smart** adjective.
2 *shabby behaviour. a shabby trick.* despicable, dishonest, dishonourable, disreputable, [*informal*] low-down, mean, nasty, shameful, unfair, unfriendly, unkind, unworthy. OPPOSITES: SEE **honourable**.

shack noun cabin, SEE **house** noun, hovel, hut, lean-to, shanty, shed.

shackle verb SEE **chain** verb.

shackles noun SEE **chain** noun.

shade noun **1** *the shade of a tree.* SEE **shadow** noun.
2 *a shade to keep the sun off.* blind, canopy, covering, parasol, screen, shelter, shield, umbrella.
3 *a pale shade of blue.* colour, hue, tinge, tint, tone.

shade verb **1** *I shaded my eyes from the sun.* conceal, hide, mask, protect, screen, shield, shroud, veil.
2 *I shaded the background with a pencil.* block in, cross-hatch, darken, fill in, make dark.

shadow noun **1** *I sat in the shadow of a tree.* darkness, dimness, gloom, [*formal*] penumbra, semi-darkness, shade, [*formal*] umbra.
2 *The sun casts shadows.* outline, shape.

shadow verb *The detective shadowed the suspect.* follow, hunt, [*informal*] keep tabs on, keep watch on, pursue, stalk, [*informal*] tag onto, tail, track, trail, watch.

shadowy adjective **1** *a shadowy figure.* dim, faint, ghostly, hazy, indistinct, nebulous, obscure, unrecognizable, vague.
2 *a shadowy path through the woods.* SEE **shady**.

shady adjective **1** *a shady spot under a tree.* cool, dark, dim, gloomy, shaded, shadowy, sheltered, sunless. OPPOSITES: SEE **sunny**.
2 *a shady character.* dishonest, disreputable, dubious, [*informal*] fishy, shifty, suspicious, untrustworthy. OPPOSITES: SEE **honest**.

shaft noun **1** *a wooden shaft.* arrow, column, handle, pillar, pole, post, rod, stem, stick.
2 *a shaft of light.* beam, ray.
3 *a mine-shaft.* mine, pit, working.

shaggy adjective *a shaggy beard. a shaggy texture.* bushy, fibrous, fleecy, hairy,

hirsute, rough, tousled, unkempt, untidy, woolly.
OPPOSITES: SEE **clean-shaven, smooth** adjective.

shake verb 1 *An explosion made the house shake.* convulse, heave, jump, quake, quiver, rattle, rock, shiver, shudder, sway, throb, totter, tremble, vibrate, waver, wobble.
2 *I shook my watch to get it going again.* agitate, brandish, flourish, jar, jerk, [*informal*] jiggle, [*informal*] joggle, jolt, twirl, twitch, wag, [*informal*] waggle, wave, [*informal*] wiggle.
3 *The terrible news shook us.* alarm, distress, disturb, frighten, perturb, shock, startle, unnerve, unsettle, upset.

shaky adjective 1 *shaky hands.* quivering, shaking, trembling.
2 *a shaky table.* flimsy, frail, ramshackle, rickety, rocky, unsteady, weak, wobbly.
3 *a shaky voice.* faltering, nervous, quavering, tremulous.
OPPOSITES: SEE **steady** adjective.
4 *a shaky start.* insecure, precarious, uncertain, under-confident, unimpressive, unpromising, unreliable, unsound.

shallow adjective 1 *shallow water.* [Surprisingly, there are no convenient synonyms for this common sense of *shallow*.]
2 *a shallow person, shallow arguments.* facile, foolish, frivolous, glib, insincere, puerile, silly, simple, slight, superficial, trivial, unconvincing, unscholarly, unthinkable.
OPPOSITES: SEE **deep.**

sham adjective *I saw through his sham surprise.* SEE **imitation** adjective.

sham noun *It was all a sham.* SEE **pretence.**

sham verb *He was shamming.* SEE **pretend.**

shamble verb SEE **walk** verb.

shambles noun 1 slaughter-house.
2 [*informal*] *My room is a shambles.* chaos, confusion, disorder, mess, muddle.

shame noun 1 *the shame of being found out.* degradation, discredit, disgrace, dishonour, embarrassment, guilt, humiliation, ignominy, mortification, opprobrium, remorse, stain, stigma.
2 [*informal*] *It's a shame to treat a dog so badly!* outrage, pity, scandal.

shame verb *They shamed him into admitting everything.* discomfit, disconcert, disgrace, embarrass, humble, humiliate, make ashamed [SEE **ashamed**], [*informal*] show up.

shamefaced adjective *a shamefaced expression.* abashed, SEE **ashamed,** embarrassed, [*informal*] hang-dog, mortified, penitent, repentant, self-conscious, sheepish, sorry.
OPPOSITES: SEE **shameless.**

shameful adjective *a shameful defeat. a shameful crime.* base, contemptible, degrading, discreditable, disgraceful, dishonourable, humiliating, ignominious, inglorious, outrageous, reprehensible, scandalous, unworthy, SEE **wicked.**
OPPOSITES: SEE **honourable.**

shameless adjective *He's shameless about his cheating and lying.* barefaced, bold, brazen, cheeky, cool, defiant, flagrant, hardened, impenitent, impudent, incorrigible, insolent, rude, unabashed, unashamed, unrepentant.
OPPOSITES: SEE **shamefaced.**

shampoo verb SEE **wash** verb.

shanghai verb SEE **compel.**

shanty noun *a shanty town.* SEE **shack.**

shape noun configuration, figure, form, format, model, mould, outline, pattern, silhouette.

FLAT SHAPES: circle, diamond, ellipse, heptagon, hexagon, lozenge, oblong, octagon, oval, parallelogram, pentagon, polygon, quadrant, quadrilateral, rectangle, rhomboid, rhombus, ring, semicircle, square, trapezium, trapezoid, triangle.

THREE-DIMENSIONAL SHAPES: cone, cube, cylinder, decahedron, hemisphere, hexahedron, octahedron, polyhedron, prism, pyramid, sphere.

---

shape verb *The sculptor shaped the stone.* carve, cast, cut, fashion, form, frame, give shape to, model, mould, [*informal*] sculpt, sculpture, whittle.

shapeless adjective 1 *a shapeless mass.* amorphous, formless, indeterminate, irregular, nebulous, undefined, unformed, vague.
OPPOSITE: defined.
2 *a shapeless figure.* [*informal*] dumpy, unattractive, unshapely.
OPPOSITES: SEE **shapely.**

shapely adjective *a shapely figure.* attractive, [*informal, sexist*] curvaceous, elegant, graceful, trim, [*informal, sexist*] voluptuous, well-proportioned.
OPPOSITES: SEE **shapeless.**

share noun *Everyone got a share of the cake.* allocation, allowance, bit, cut, division, fraction, helping, part, piece, portion, proportion, quota, ration, [*informal*] whack.

share verb 1 *We shared the food equally.* allocate, allot, apportion, deal out, distribute, divide, [*informal*] go halves or shares (with), halve, partake of, portion out, ration out, share out, split.
2 *If we share the work we'll finish quickly.* be involved, co-operate, join, participate, take part.

shared adjective *a shared responsibility.* collective, combined, common, co-operative, corporate, joint, united.
OPPOSITES: SEE **individual** adjective.

sharp adjective 1 *a sharp knife. a sharp point.* cutting, fine, jagged, keen, pointed, razor-sharp, sharpened, spiky.
OPPOSITES: SEE **blunt** adjective.
2 *a sharp corner. a sharp drop.* abrupt, acute, angular, hairpin (*a hairpin bend*), precipitous (*a precipitous drop*), steep, sudden, surprising, unexpected.
OPPOSITES: SEE **gradual**.
3 *a sharp picture.* clear, defined, distinct, focused, well-defined.
OPPOSITES: SEE **blurred**.
4 *a sharp frost.* extreme, heavy, intense, serious, severe, violent.
OPPOSITES: SEE **slight** adjective.
5 *a sharp pain.* acute, excruciating, painful, stabbing, stinging.
6 *a sharp tongue.* acerbic, acid, acidulous, barbed, biting, caustic, critical, hurtful, incisive, mocking, mordant, sarcastic, sardonic, scathing, trenchant, unkind, vitriolic.
OPPOSITES: SEE **kind** adjective.
7 *a sharp taste or smell.* acid, acrid, bitter, caustic, pungent, sour, tangy, tart.
OPPOSITES: SEE **bland**.
8 *a sharp mind.* acute, alert, astute, bright, clever, cute, discerning, incisive, intelligent, observant, perceptive, quick, quick-witted, shrewd, [*informal*] smart.
OPPOSITES: SEE **stupid**.
9 *a sharp sound.* clear, high, penetrating, piercing, shrill.
OPPOSITES: SEE **muffled**.

sharpen verb *to sharpen a knife.* file, grind, hone, make sharp, strop, whet.
OPPOSITE: blunt.

sharpener noun KINDS OF SHARPENER: file, grindstone, hone, pencil-sharpener, strop, whetstone.

sharp-eyed adjective SEE **observant**.

sharpshooter noun SEE **marksman**.

shatter verb *to shatter a window.* blast, break, break up, burst, crack, destroy, disintegrate, explode, pulverize, shiver, smash, splinter, split, wreck.

shattered adjective 1 *shattered by the bad news.* SEE **upset** adjective.
2 [*informal*] *shattered after all that effort.* SEE **exhausted**.

shave verb SEE **cut** verb.

shaven adjective SEE **clean-shaven**.

shawl noun scarf, stole.

sheaf noun *a sheaf of papers.* bunch, bundle.

shear verb *to shear sheep.* clip, SEE **cut** verb, strip, trim.

shears noun SEE **cutter**.

sheath noun *a sheath for a sword.* casing, covering, scabbard, sleeve.

sheathe verb *Sheathe your swords!* cocoon, cover, encase, SEE **enclose**, put away, put in a sheath.

sheath-knife noun SEE **knife** noun.

shed noun *a garden shed.* hut, lean-to, outhouse, potting-shed, shack, shelter, storehouse.
OTHER BUILDINGS: SEE **building**.

shed verb *A lorry shed its load. I shed a few tears.* cast off, discard, drop, let fall, scatter, shower, spill, throw off.

sheen noun *a nice sheen on the furniture.* brightness, burnish, gleam, gloss, lustre, patina, polish, shine.

sheep noun ewe, lamb, mutton [= *meat from sheep*], ram, wether.

sheep-fold noun SEE **enclosure**.

sheepish adjective *a sheepish look.* abashed, ashamed, bashful, coy, embarrassed, guilty, mortified, self-conscious, shamefaced, shy, timid.
OPPOSITES: SEE **shameless**.

sheer adjective 1 *sheer nonsense.* absolute, complete, out-and-out, pure, total, unmitigated, unqualified, utter.
2 *a sheer cliff.* abrupt, perpendicular, precipitous, vertical.
3 *sheer silk.* diaphanous, fine, flimsy, [*informal*] see-through, thin, transparent.

sheet noun 1 *sheets for a bed.* OTHER BEDCLOTHES: SEE **bedclothes**.
2 *a sheet of paper.* folio, leaf, page.
3 *a sheet of glass.* pane, panel, plate.
4 *a sheet of ice on a pond.* coating, covering, film, layer, skin.
5 *a sheet of water.* area, expanse, surface.

shelf noun ledge, shelving.

shell noun 1 *a hard outer shell.* carapace [= *shell of a tortoise*], case, casing, covering, crust, exterior, husk, outside, pod.
2 *a shell from a gun.* SEE **ammunition**.

shell verb *to shell the enemy.* attack, barrage, bomb, bombard, fire at, shoot at, strafe.

shellac noun, verb varnish.

shellfish noun bivalve, crustacean, mollusc.

VARIOUS SHELLFISH: barnacle, clam, cockle, conch, crab, crayfish, cuttlefish, limpet, lobster, mussel, oyster, prawn, scallop, shrimp, whelk, winkle.

---

shelter noun 1 *Where can we find shelter from the wind?* asylum, cover, haven, lee, protection, refuge, safety, sanctuary.
2 *a shelter against the wind.* barrier, cover, fence, hut, roof, screen, shield.
3 *an air-raid shelter.* bunker.

shelter verb 1 *The fence sheltered us from the wind.* defend, guard, protect, safeguard, screen, shade, shield.
2 *Is it wrong to shelter a criminal?* accommodate, give shelter to [SEE **shelter** noun], harbour, hide.

sheltered adjective 1 *a sheltered spot.* enclosed, on the leeward side, protected, quiet, screened, shielded, snug, windless.
OPPOSITE: exposed.
2 *a sheltered life.* cloistered, isolated, limited, lonely, unadventurous, unexciting, withdrawn.
OPPOSITES: SEE **adventurous**.

shelve verb 1 *They shelved their plan.* SEE **postpone**.
2 *The beach shelves gently.* SEE **slope** verb.

shemozzle noun SEE **commotion**.

shepherd noun FARM WORKERS: SEE **farm** noun.

sheriff noun SEE **official** noun.

shield noun 1 *a shield against the wind.* barrier, defence, guard, protection, safeguard, screen, shelter.
2 *a warrior's shield.* buckler, [in heraldry] escutcheon.

shield verb *to shield someone from danger.* cover, defend, guard, keep safe, protect, safeguard, screen, shade, shelter.

shift noun 1 *a shift in your position.* SEE **change** noun, **move** noun.
2 *working on a night shift.* group, period.
3 *a woman's shift.* SEE **dress** noun.

shift verb *to shift your position.* SEE **change** verb, **move** verb.

shiftless adjective SEE **ineffective**.

shifty adjective *I didn't trust his shifty expression.* crafty, deceitful, devious, dishonest, evasive, furtive, scheming,
secretive, [informal] shady, [informal] slippery, sly, tricky, untrustworthy, wily.
OPPOSITES: SEE **straightforward**.

shilly-shally verb SEE **prevaricate**.

shimmer verb SEE **light** noun (give light).

shine noun *a shine on the furniture.* SEE **polish** noun.

shine verb 1 SEE **light** noun (give light).
2 *What do you shine at?* be clever, do well, excel.
3 [informal] *to shine your shoes.* SEE **polish** verb.

shining adjective 1 *a shining light.* brilliant, glittering, glowing, luminous, radiant, SEE **shiny**, sparkling.
2 *a shining example.* conspicuous, eminent, glorious, outstanding, praiseworthy, resplendent, splendid.

shingle noun 1 *shingle on the beach.* gravel, pebbles, stones.
2 *shingles on the roof.* tile.

shiny adjective *a shiny surface.* bright, burnished, dazzling, gleaming, glistening, glossy, lustrous, polished, reflective, rubbed, shining, sleek.
OPPOSITES: SEE **dull** adjective, matt.

ship noun VARIOUS SHIPS: SEE **vessel**.

ship verb *to ship goods to a foreign country.* SEE **transport** verb.

shipment noun SEE **load** noun.

shipshape adjective SEE **tidy** adjective.

shipwreck noun SEE **disaster**.

shipwright noun shipbuilder.

shire noun county.

shirk verb *to shirk your duty.* avoid, dodge, duck, evade, get out of, neglect.
to shirk work be lazy, malinger, [informal] skive, slack.

shirty adjective SEE **annoyed**.

shiver verb *to shiver with cold.* quake, quaver, quiver, shake, shudder, tremble, twitch, vibrate.

shoal noun 1 *a shoal of fish.* SEE **group** noun.
2 *stranded on a shoal.* sand-bank, shallows.

shock noun 1 *the shock of an explosion.* blow, collision, concussion, impact, jolt.
2 *His sudden death was a great shock.* blow, bombshell, SEE **surprise** noun.
3 *in a state of shock.* dismay, distress, fright, [formal] trauma, upset.

shock verb 1 *The unexpected news shocked us.* alarm, amaze, astonish, astound, confound, daze, dismay, distress, frighten, [informal] give someone a turn, jolt, numb, paralyse, scare, shake, stagger,

startle, stun, stupefy, surprise, [*formal*] traumatize, unnerve.
2 *The bad language shocked us.* appal, disgust, horrify, offend, outrage, repel, revolt, scandalize.

shocking adjective **1** *a shocking experience.* alarming, distressing, frightening, SEE **painful**, staggering, traumatic, unnerving, upsetting.
2 *shocking bad language.* SEE **outrageous**.

shoddy adjective **1** *shoddy goods.* cheap, flimsy, gimcrack, inferior, jerry-built, nasty, poor quality, rubbishy, tawdry, trashy.
OPPOSITES: SEE **superior**.
2 *shoddy work.* careless, messy, negligent, slipshod, sloppy, slovenly, untidy.
OPPOSITES: SEE **careful**.

shoe noun [*plural*] footwear.

KINDS OF SHOE: boot, bootee, brogue, clog, espadrille, [*plural*] galoshes, gumboot, [*informal*] lace-up, moccasin, plimsoll, pump, sabot, sandal, [*informal*] slip-on, slipper, trainer, wader, wellington.

---

shoemaker noun bootmaker, cobbler.

shoot noun *shoots of a plant.* branch, bud, new growth, offshoot, sprout, twig.

shoot verb **1** *to shoot a gun.* aim, discharge, fire.
2 *to shoot animals. to shoot someone in the street.* aim at, bombard, fire at, gun down, hit, SEE **hunt** verb, SEE **kill** verb, open fire on, [*informal*] pick off, shell, snipe at, strafe, [*informal*] take pot-shots at.
3 *He shot out of his chair.* dart, dash, hurtle, leap, move quickly, rush, streak.
4 *Plants shoot in the spring.* bud, grow, put out shoots, spring up, sprout.

shooting-range noun butts, rifle-range.

shooting star meteor.
ASTRONOMICAL TERMS: SEE **astronomy**.

shop noun boutique, cash-and-carry, department store, [*old-fashioned*] emporium, establishment, market, retailer, seller, store, wholesaler.

VARIOUS SHOPS AND BUSINESSES: antique shop, baker, bank, barber, betting shop, bookmaker, bookshop, building society, butcher, café, chandler, chemist, clothes shop, confectioner, creamery, dairy, delicatessen, DIY, draper.

electrician, estate agent, fish and chip shop, fishmonger, florist, furniture store, garden-centre, greengrocer, grocer, haberdasher, hairdresser, hardware store, health-food shop, herbalist, hypermarket, insurance brokers, ironmonger, jeweller.

launderette, market, newsagent, off-licence, outfitters, pawnbroker, pharmacy, post office, poulterer, radio and TV shop, shoemaker, stationer, supermarket, tailor, take-away, tobacconist, toyshop, video-shop, vintner, watchmaker.

---

shopkeeper noun dealer, merchant, retailer, salesgirl, salesman, saleswoman, stockist, storekeeper, supplier, trader, tradesman.

shop-lifter noun SEE **thief**.

shopper noun buyer, customer.

shopping noun **1** *Christmas shopping.* buying, [*informal*] spending-spree.
2 *Put the shopping in a carrier-bag.* goods, purchases.

shopping-bag noun SEE **bag** noun.

shopping-centre noun *an indoor shopping-centre.* arcade, complex, mall, precinct.

shore noun *the shore of a lake or the sea.* bank, beach, coast, edge, foreshore, sands, seashore, seaside, shingle, [*old-fashioned*] strand.

shore verb to shore up SEE **support** verb.

short adjective **1** *a short piece of string.* [There is no obvious synonym for *short* in this sense.] OPPOSITES: SEE **long** adjective.
2 *a short person.* diminutive, dumpy, dwarfish, little, [*of a woman*] petite, small, squat, stubby, stumpy, tiny, [*informal*] wee, undergrown.
OPPOSITES: SEE **tall**.
3 *a short visit.* brief, cursory, curtailed, ephemeral, fleeting, momentary, passing, quick, temporary, transient, transitory.
OPPOSITES: SEE **long** adjective.
4 *a short book.* abbreviated, abridged, compact, concise, shortened, succinct, terse.
OPPOSITES: SEE **long** adjective.
5 *During the drought water was in short supply.* deficient, inadequate, insufficient, lacking, limited, meagre, scanty, scarce, sparse, wanting.
OPPOSITES: SEE **plentiful**.
6 *He was short with me when I asked for a loan.* abrupt, bad-tempered, blunt, brusque, cross, curt, gruff, grumpy, impolite, irritable, laconic, sharp, snappy,

testy, unfriendly, unkind, unsympathetic.
OPPOSITES: SEE **friendly**.

shortage noun *a shortage of water during drought.* absence, dearth, deficiency, insufficiency, lack, paucity, poverty, scarcity, shortfall, want.
OPPOSITES: SEE **plenty**.

short-change verb SEE **cheat** verb.

shortcoming noun *Bad language is one of his shortcomings.* defect, failing, fault, foible, imperfection, vice, weakness.

shorten verb *I shortened my story because it was too long.* abbreviate, abridge, compress, condense, curtail, cut down, cut short, précis, prune, reduce, summarize, telescope, trim, truncate.
OPPOSITES: SEE **lengthen**.

shorthand noun stenography.

short-lived adjective SEE **temporary**.

shortly adverb *The post will arrive shortly.* directly, presently, soon.

shorts noun SEE **trousers**.

short-tempered adjective SEE **cross** adjective.

short-term adjective *a short-term solution.* SEE **temporary**.

shot noun 1 *a shot from a gun.* ball, bang, blast, bullet, crack, discharge, pellet, round, [*informal*] slug.
2 *He's a good shot.* SEE **marksman**.
3 *a shot at goal.* attempt, effort, endeavour, [*informal*] go (*Have a go!*), hit, kick, stroke, try.
4 *The photographer took some unusual shots.* angle, photograph, picture, scene, sequence, snap.
a shot in the arm SEE **encouragement**.
a shot in the dark SEE **guess** noun.

shotgun noun SEE **gun**.

shoulder verb SEE **carry**.

shout verb bawl, bellow, [*informal*] belt (*Belt it out!*), call, cheer, clamour, cry out, exclaim, rant, roar, scream, screech, shriek, talk loudly, vociferate, yell, yelp.
OPPOSITES: SEE **whisper** verb.
OTHER WAYS TO USE YOUR VOICE: SEE **talk** verb.

shouting noun SEE **clamour** noun.

shove verb *They shoved me out of the way.* barge, crowd, drive, elbow, hustle, jostle, SEE **push**, shoulder.

shovel verb *I shovelled the snow off the path.* clear, dig, scoop, shift.

show noun 1 *a show at the theatre.* SEE **entertainment**, performance, production.

2 *an art show. a dog show.* competition, display, exhibition, presentation.
3 *a show of strength.* appearance, demonstration, façade, illusion, impression, pose, pretence, threat.
4 *He does it all for show.* exhibitionism, flamboyance, ostentation, showing off.

show verb 1 *We showed our work in public.* display, exhibit, open up, present, produce, reveal.
2 *My knee showed through a hole in my jeans.* appear, be seen, be visible, emerge, materialize, stand out.
3 *She showed me the way.* conduct, direct, guide, indicate, point out.
4 *He showed me great kindness.* bestow (upon), confer (upon), treat with.
5 *The photo shows us at work.* depict, give a picture of, illustrate, picture, portray, represent.
6 *She showed me how to do it.* describe, explain, instruct, make clear, teach, tell.
7 *The tests showed that I was right.* attest, demonstrate, evince, exemplify, manifest, prove, witness (to).
to show off SEE **boast**.
to show up SEE **appear, reveal**.

show-down noun *a show-down between two rivals.* confrontation, crisis, [*informal*] decider, decisive encounter.

shower noun 1 SEE **rain** noun.
2 douche.

shower verb *A passing bus showered mud over us.* deluge, rain, spatter, splash, spray, sprinkle.

showery adjective WORDS TO DESCRIBE WEATHER: SEE **weather** noun.

show-off noun [*informal*] big-head, boaster, braggart, conceited person [SEE **conceited**], egotist, exhibitionist, [*informal*] poser, poseur, [*informal*] showman.

showy adjective *showy clothes.* bright, conspicuous, flamboyant, flashy, garish, gaudy, [*informal*] loud, lurid, ostentatious, pretentious, striking, trumpery.
OPPOSITES: SEE **restrained**.

shred noun *not a shred of evidence.* bit, iota, jot, piece, scrap, snippet, trace.
shreds *torn to shreds.* rags, ribbons, strips, tatters.

shred verb cut to shreds, grate, tear.

shrewd adjective *a shrewd politician.* artful, astute, [*informal*] canny, clever, crafty, cunning, discerning, discriminating, ingenious, intelligent, knowing, observant, perceptive, quick-witted, sharp, sly, smart, wily, wise.
OPPOSITES: SEE **stupid**.

shrewish adjective SEE **bad-tempered**.

shriek noun, verb SEE **scream**.

shrill adjective *a shrill voice*. ear-splitting, high, high-pitched, penetrating, piercing, piping, screaming, sharp, strident, treble.
OPPOSITES: SEE **gentle, sonorous**.

shrine noun holy place.
PLACES OF WORSHIP: SEE **worship** noun.

shrink verb 1 *The pond shrank during the drought. The laundry has shrunk my jumper.* become smaller, contract, decrease, diminish, dwindle, lessen, make smaller, narrow, reduce, shorten, SEE **shrivel**.
OPPOSITES: SEE **expand**.
2 *The dog shrank when the cat spat at him.* back off, cower, cringe, flinch, hang back, quail, recoil, retire, wince, withdraw.

shrivel verb *The plants shrivelled in the heat.* become parched, dehydrate, droop, dry out, dry up, SEE **shrink**, wilt, wither, wrinkle.

shrivelled adjective SEE **wrinkled**.

shroud noun *a shroud of mist*. blanket, cover, mantle, pall, veil.

shroud verb *Mist shrouded the top of the mountain.* cloak, conceal, cover, enshroud, envelop, hide, mask, screen, swathe, veil, wrap up.

shrub noun bush, tree.

COMMON SHRUBS: azalea, berberis, blackthorn, broom, bryony, buddleia, camellia, daphne, forsythia, gorse, heather, hydrangea, japonica, jasmine, lavender, lilac, myrtle, privet, rhododendron, rosemary, rue, viburnum.

---

shrubbery noun SEE **garden**.

shrug noun, verb SEE **gesture** noun, verb.

shudder verb *I shuddered when I heard the gory details.* be horrified, convulse, quake, quiver, shake, shiver, squirm, tremble.

shuffle verb 1 *I shuffled upstairs in my slippers.* SEE **walk** verb.
2 *to shuffle cards.* jumble, mix, mix up, rearrange, reorganize.

shun verb SEE **avoid**.

shunt verb SEE **divert**.

shut verb *Shut the door.* bolt, close, fasten, latch, lock, push to, replace, seal, secure, slam.
to shut in, to shut up confine, detain, enclose, imprison, incarcerate, keep in.
to shut off cut off, isolate, segregate, separate, stop.

to shut out ban, bar, exclude, keep out, prohibit.
Shut up! Be quiet! Be silent! [*informal*] Hold your tongue! Hush! Keep quiet! [*informal*] Pipe down! Silence! Stop talking!

shutter noun *Close the shutter.* blind, louvre, screen.

shuttle verb SEE **travel** verb.

shy adjective *I was too shy to call out.* backward, bashful, cautious, chary, coy, diffident, hesitant, inhibited, modest, [*informal*] mousy, nervous, reserved, reticent, retiring, self-conscious, self-effacing, timid, timorous, wary.
OPPOSITES: SEE **assertive**.

shy verb SEE **throw**.

sibilant adjective hissing.

sibling noun brother, sister, twin.
FAMILY RELATIONSHIPS: SEE **family**.

sibyl noun SEE **prophet**.

sibylline adjective SEE **prophetic**.

sick adjective 1 *unable to work because she was sick.* ailing, bedridden, diseased, SEE **ill**, indisposed, infirm, [*informal*] laid up, [*informal*] poorly, [*informal*] queer, sickly, unwell.
2 *He feels sick.* bilious, likely to vomit, nauseous, queasy.
3 *We're sick of their rude behaviour.* annoyed (by), disgusted (by), distressed (by), nauseated (by), sickened (by), upset (by).
4 *I'm sick of that tune.* bored (with), [*informal*] fed up (with), glutted (with), sated (with), tired, weary.
to be sick SEE **vomit**.

sicken verb *The sight of people fighting sickens me.* disgust, nauseate, repel, revolt, [*informal*] turn off.

sickening adjective *sickening cruelty.* bestial, disgusting, distressing, foul, hateful, inhuman, loathsome, nasty, nauseating, nauseous, offensive, repulsive, revolting, SEE **unpleasant**, vile.

sickle verb billhook, scythe.

sickly adjective 1 *a sickly child.* ailing, delicate, feeble, frail, SEE **ill**, pallid, [*informal*] peaky, unhealthy, weak.
OPPOSITES: SEE **healthy**.
2 *sickly sweetness. sickly sentiment.* cloying, nasty, nauseating, obnoxious, syrupy, treacly, unpleasant.
OPPOSITES: SEE **refreshing**.

sickness noun 1 *a bout of sickness.* biliousness, nausea, queasiness, vomiting.
2 VARIOUS ILLNESSES: SEE **illness**.

side noun 1 *the sides of a cube.* face, facet, elevation, flank, surface.
2 *the side of a road, pool, etc.* border, boundary, brim, brink, edge, fringe, limit, margin, perimeter, rim, verge.
3 *I saw both sides of the problem.* angle, aspect, perspective, slant, standpoint, view, viewpoint.
4 *The two sides attacked each other.* army, camp, faction, team.
RELATED ADJECTIVE: lateral.

side verb *Who do you side with?* SEE **ally** verb.

side-effect noun SEE **by-product.**

sideline noun *He does decorating as a sideline.* additional activity, extra.

sidelong adjective SEE **sideways.**

side-show noun SEE **fun-fair.**

side-step verb SEE **avoid.**

side-street noun SEE **road.**

sideways adjective 1 *sideways movement.* indirect, lateral, oblique.
2 *a sideways glance.* covert, sidelong, sly, [*informal*] sneaky, unobtrusive.

sidle verb SEE **edge** verb.

siege noun blockade.

siesta noun SEE **sleep** noun.

sieve noun colander, riddle, screen, strainer.

sieve verb *Sieve out the lumps.* filter, riddle, separate, sift, strain.

sift verb 1 *to sift flour.* SEE **sieve** verb.
2 *to sift the evidence.* analyse, examine, investigate, review, scrutinize, sort out, winnow.

sigh noun, verb VARIOUS SOUNDS: SEE **sound** noun.

sight noun 1 *the power of sight.* eyesight, seeing, vision, visual perception.
2 *We live within sight of the power-station.* field of vision, range, view, visibility.
3 *The sight of home brought tears to his eyes.* appearance, glimpse, look.
4 *The procession was an impressive sight.* display, exhibition, scene, show, show-piece, spectacle.

sight verb *The look-out sighted a ship.* behold, discern, distinguish, glimpse, make out, notice, observe, perceive, recognize, see, spot.

sightless adjective SEE **blind** adjective.

sightseer noun *The castle was full of sightseers.* holiday-maker, tourist, tripper, visitor.

sign noun 1 *signs of a change in the weather.* augury, forewarning, hint, indication, intimation, omen, pointer, portent, presage, warning.

2 *a sign to begin.* cue, SEE **gesture** noun, signal, [*informal*] tip-off.
3 *a sign that someone was here.* clue, [*informal*] giveaway, proof, reminder, spoor (*of an animal*), trace, vestige.
4 *The flowers are a sign of our love.* manifestation, marker, symptom, token.
5 *We painted a sign for our sweet-stall.* advertisement, notice, placard, poster, publicity, signboard.
6 *Do you recognize the British Rail sign?* badge, cipher, device, emblem, insignia, logo, mark, symbol, trademark.

sign verb 1 *Sign your name.* autograph, endorse, inscribe, write.
2 *I signed that I was turning left.* SEE **signal** verb.
to **sign off** *The DJ signed off with his catch-phrase.* conclude, end, finish, say goodbye, take your leave.
to **sign on** *He signed on in the army.* enlist, join up, volunteer.
to **sign up** *They signed up several new workers.* engage, enrol, recruit, register, take on.

signal noun 1 *I gave a clear signal.* communication, cue, SEE **gesture** noun, [*informal*] go-ahead, indication, sign, [*informal*] tip-off, token, warning.

VARIOUS SIGNALS: alarm-bell, beacon, bell, burglar-alarm, buzzer, flag, flare, gong, green light, indicator, light, lights, password, red light, reveille, rocket, semaphore signal, siren, smoke-signal, [*old-fashioned*] tocsin, traffic-ator, traffic-lights, warning-light, whistle, winker.

2 *They sent a signal to say all was well.* cable, telegram, transmission.

signal verb *I signalled that I was ready.* beckon, communicate, flag, gesticulate, SEE **gesture** verb, give or send a signal [SEE **signal** noun], indicate, motion, sign, wave.

signature noun *a signature on a cheque.* autograph, endorsement, mark, name.

signboard noun SEE **sign** noun.

signet noun seal, stamp.

significance noun *the significance of wearing a red poppy.* force, implication, importance, meaning, message, point, purport, relevance, sense, signification, usefulness.

significant adjective 1 *a significant remark.* eloquent, expressive, indicative, knowing, meaningful, pregnant, revealing, symbolic, [*informal*] tell-tale.

2 *a significant moment in history.* big, considerable, SEE **important**, influential, newsworthy, noteworthy, salient, serious, sizeable, valuable, vital, worthwhile.
OPPOSITES: SEE **insignificant**.

signify verb **1** *A green light signifies "all clear".* be a sign of [SEE **sign** noun], betoken, bode, connote, denote, imply, mean, portend, presage, represent, say, spell, stand for, symbolize.
2 *Signify your agreement by raising your hand.* announce, communicate, convey, express, indicate, intimate, make known, signal, tell, transmit.

signpost noun pointer, sign.

silage noun fodder.

silence noun **1** *the silence of the night.* calm, hush, peace, quiet, quietness, stillness.
OPPOSITES: SEE **noise**.
2 *We couldn't understand her silence.* dumbness, muteness, reticence, taciturnity, uncommunicativeness.
OPPOSITES: SEE **verbosity**.

silence verb **1** *The gang silenced witnesses by intimidation.* gag, keep quiet, make silent, muzzle, shut up, suppress.
2 *The silencer is supposed to silence the engine noise.* deaden, muffle, mute, quieten.

silent adjective **1** *a silent engine.* inaudible, muffled, muted, noiseless, soundless.
2 *a silent audience.* attentive, hushed, quiet, rapt, restrained, still.
OPPOSITES: SEE **noisy**.
3 *a silent person.* dumb, laconic, [*informal*] mum (*Keep mum!*), mute, reserved, reticent, speechless, taciturn, tongue-tied, uncommunicative, unforthcoming, voiceless.
OPPOSITES: SEE **talkative**.
to be silent [*informal*] pipe down, [*informal*] shut up.

silhouette noun SEE **outline** noun.

silky adjective *A cat has silky fur.* fine, satiny, sleek, smooth, soft, velvety.

silly adjective *silly behaviour. a silly plan.* absurd, asinine, brainless, childish, crazy, daft, [*informal*] dopey, [*informal*] dotty, fatuous, feather-brained, feeble-minded, flighty, foolish, [*old-fashioned*] fond (*fond hopes*), frivolous, grotesque, [*informal*] half-baked, hare-brained, idiotic, illogical, immature, inane, infantile, irrational, [*informal*] jokey, laughable, ludicrous, mad, meaningless, mindless, misguided, naïve, nonsensical, playful, pointless, preposterous, ridiculous, scatter-brained,

[*informal*] scatty, senseless, shallow, simple (*He's a bit simple*), simple-minded, simplistic, [*informal*] soppy, stupid, thoughtless, unintelligent, unreasonable, unsound, unwise, wild, witless.
OPPOSITES: SEE **serious, wise**.
a silly person halfwit, SEE **idiot**, joker, madcap, scatter-brain, simpleton, [*informal*] twerp.

silt noun *silt at the bottom of an estuary.* [*formal*] alluvium, deposit, mud, sediment, slime, sludge.

silvan adjective *a silvan landscape.* arboreal, leafy, tree-covered, wooded.

silvery adjective *a silvery sound.* SEE **clear** adjective.

simian adjective monkey-like.

similar adjective *similar in appearance.* akin, alike, analogous, comparable, compatible, congruous, corresponding, equal, equivalent, homogeneous, identical, indistinguishable, like, matching, parallel, related, resembling, the same, uniform, well-matched.
OPPOSITES: SEE **dissimilar**.

similarity noun *the similarity of twins.* affinity, closeness, congruity, correspondence, likeness, resemblance, sameness, similitude, uniformity.
OPPOSITES: SEE **difference**.

simile noun SEE **figure** noun (**figure of speech**).

simmer verb boil, SEE **cook** verb, seethe, stew.

simper verb SEE **smile** verb.

simple adjective **1** *a simple person. a simple life-style.* artless, guileless, homely, honest, humble, innocent, lowly, modest, [*uncomplimentary*] naïve, natural, sincere, straightforward, unaffected, uncomplicated, unpretentious, unsophisticated.
OPPOSITES: SEE **sophisticated**.
2 *a simple explanation.* basic, clear, direct, easy, elementary, foolproof, intelligible, lucid, understandable.
OPPOSITES: SEE **complicated**.
3 *a simple dress.* austere, classical, plain, stark, unadorned.
OPPOSITES: SEE **ornate**.
4 [*uncomplimentary*] *He's a bit simple.* SEE **silly**.

simple-minded adjective SEE **silly, unsophisticated**.

simpleton noun SEE **silly** (**silly person**).

simplify verb *They simplified the way we pay taxes.* clarify, make simple, prune, streamline.
OPPOSITES: SEE **complicate**.

simplistic adjective *a simplistic view of things.* facile, inadequate, naïve, over-simple, shallow, silly, superficial.
OPPOSITES: SEE **sophisticated**.

simulate verb 1 *to simulate a crash-landing.* SEE **reproduce**.
2 *to simulate drunkenness.* SEE **pretend**.

simulated adjective SEE **artificial**.

simultaneous adjective *I can't attend two simultaneous events.* coinciding, concurrent, contemporaneous, parallel, synchronized, synchronous.

sin noun *sin against God.* blasphemy, depravity, error, evil, guilt, immorality, impiety, iniquity, offence, sacrilege, sinfulness, transgression, [*formal*] trespass, ungodliness, unrighteousness, vice, wickedness, wrong, wrongdoing.

sin verb *to sin against God.* be guilty of sin [SEE **sin** noun], blaspheme, do wrong, err, go astray, misbehave, offend, transgress.

sincere adjective *sincere beliefs.* candid, earnest, frank, genuine, guileless, heartfelt, honest, open, real, serious, simple, straightforward, true, truthful, unaffected, wholehearted.
OPPOSITES: SEE **insincere**.

sincerity noun *I trust her sincerity.* candour, directness, frankness, genuineness, honesty, honour, integrity, openness, straightforwardness, trustworthiness, truthfulness.

sinecure noun SEE **job**.

sinewy adjective SEE **muscular**.

sinful adjective *sinful behaviour.* bad, blasphemous, corrupt, damnable, depraved, erring, evil, fallen, guilty, immoral, impious, iniquitous, irreligious, sacrilegious, ungodly, unholy, unrighteous, wicked, wrong.
OPPOSITES: SEE **righteous**.

sing verb chant, croon, descant, hum, intone, serenade, trill, warble, yodel.
MUSIC FOR SINGING: SEE **song**.

singe verb blacken, SEE **burn** verb, char, scorch.

singer noun songster, vocalist.

VARIOUS SINGERS: alto, baritone, bass, [*plural*] choir, choirboy, choirgirl, chorister, [*plural*] chorus, coloratura, contralto, crooner, folk singer, minstrel, precentor, opera singer, pop star, prima donna, soloist, soprano, tenor, treble, troubadour.

---

single adjective 1 *I got all my things into a single suitcase.* exclusive, individual, isolated, one, only, personal, separate, sole, solitary, unique.
OPPOSITE: plural.
2 *a single person.* celibate, [*informal*] free, unattached, unmarried.
OPPOSITES: SEE **married**.
a single person bachelor, spinster.

single verb **to single out** SEE **choose**.

single-handed adjective *I can't shift the piano single-handed.* alone, independently, unaided, without help.

single-minded adjective SEE **determined**.

singlet noun T-shirt, vest.

singular adjective 1 [*as grammatical term*] SEE **language**.
OPPOSITE: plural.
2 *a singular happening.* abnormal, curious, extraordinary, odd, peculiar, remarkable, uncommon, unusual.

sinister 1 *a sinister leer. a sinister groan.* disquieting, disturbing, evil, forbidding, frightening, menacing, ominous, threatening, villainous, upsetting.
2 *sinister motives.* bad, corrupt, criminal, dishonest, illegal, questionable, [*informal*] shady, suspect.

sink noun *the kitchen sink.* basin.

sink verb 1 *The sun sinks in the west.* decline, descend, disappear, drop, fall, go down, go lower, set, slip down, subside.
2 *Our spirits sank.* diminish, droop, dwindle, ebb, fail, fall, weaken.
3 *The ship sank.* become submerged, founder, go down.
4 *The attackers sank the ship.* scupper, scuttle.

sinless adjective SEE **innocent**.

sinner noun offender, reprobate, transgressor, wrongdoer.

sinuous adjective SEE **curved**.

sip noun, verb SEE **drink** noun, verb.

siphon verb SEE **pump** verb.

sir, sire nouns SEE **title** noun.

siren noun *a fire siren.* SEE **warning**.

sissy noun SEE **effeminate** (**effeminate man**).

sister noun sibling.
FAMILY RELATIONSHIPS: SEE **family**.

sit verb 1 *to sit on a chair.* be seated, perch, rest, seat yourself, settle, squat.
2 *to sit for your portrait.* pose.
3 *to sit an exam.* be a candidate in, [*informal*] go in for, take, write.
4 *Parliament does not sit over Christmas.* assemble, be in session [SEE **session**], convene, meet.

site noun *a site for a new building.* campus, ground, location, place, plot, position, setting, situation, spot.

site verb SEE **situate**.

sitting noun *a sitting of Parliament.* SEE **session**.

sitting-room noun drawing-room, living-room, lounge.
OTHER ROOMS: SEE **room**.

situate verb *The house is situated in the park.* build, establish, found, locate, place, position, put, set up, site, station.

situation noun 1 *The house is in a pleasant situation.* locality, location, place, position, setting, site, spot.
2 *I was in an awkward situation when I lost my money.* circumstances, condition, plight, position, predicament.
3 *She applied for a situation in the new firm.* employment, job, position, post.

size noun amount, area, breadth, bulk, capacity, depth, dimensions, extent, gauge, height, immensity, largeness, length, magnitude, measurement, proportions, scale, volume, width.
UNITS OF SIZE: SEE **measure** noun.

sizeable adjective *sizeable helpings.* SEE **big**, considerable, decent, generous, largish, significant, worthwhile.

sizzle verb VARIOUS SOUNDS: SEE **sound** noun.

skate verb roller-skate, SEE **slide** verb.

skeleton noun bones, frame, framework, structure.

PRINCIPAL BONES IN YOUR BODY: backbone, carpus, coccyx, cranium, digit, femur, fibula, humerus, jaw, metacarpus, patella, pelvis, radius, rib, sacrum, scapula, skull, tarsal, tibia, ulna, vertebra.
SEE ALSO: **joint** noun.
OTHER PARTS OF YOUR BODY: SEE **body**.

---

sketch noun 1 *a quick sketch of someone.* description, design, diagram, draft, drawing, outline, SEE **picture** noun, plan, skeleton, vignette.
2 *a comic sketch on TV.* SEE **performance**, playlet, scene, skit, turn.

sketch verb *to sketch with crayons.* depict, draw, portray, represent.
to sketch out *I sketched out my plan.* draft, give the gist of, outline, rough out.

sketchy adjective *a sketchy essay.* bitty, imperfect, incomplete, perfunctory, rough, scrappy, undeveloped, unfinished.
OPPOSITES: SEE **perfect** adjective.

skewer verb SEE **pierce**.

skid verb *to skid on a slippery road.* aquaplane, glide, go out of control, slide, slip.

skiff noun rowing-boat.

skilful adjective *a skilful carpenter. skilful work.* able, accomplished, adept, adroit, apt, artful, brilliant, [*informal*] canny, capable, clever, competent, consummate, crafty, cunning, deft, dextrous, experienced, expert, gifted, handy, ingenious, masterly, practised, professional, proficient, shrewd, smart, talented, versatile.
OPPOSITES: SEE **unskilful**.

skill noun *the skill of a carpenter.* ability, accomplishment, adroitness, aptitude, art, capability, cleverness, competence, craft, cunning, deftness, dexterity, experience, expertise, gift, handicraft, ingenuity, knack, mastery, professionalism, proficiency, prowess, shrewdness, talent, technique, training, versatility, workmanship.

skilled adjective experienced, qualified, SEE **skilful**, trained, versed.

skim verb 1 *to skim across ice or water.* aquaplane, coast, glide, move lightly, plane, skate, ski, skid, slide, slip.
2 *to skim through a book.* look through, read quickly, scan, skip.

skimp verb SEE **economize**.

skimpy adjective SEE **scanty**.

skin noun 1 *the skin of an animal, fruit, etc.* casing, coat, coating, covering, [*formal*] epidermis, exterior, film, fur, hide, husk, membrane, outside, peel, pelt, rind, shell, surface.
2 *a person's skin.* SEE **complexion**.

skin verb *to skin an orange. to skin an animal.* flay, pare, peel, strip.

skin-deep adjective SEE **superficial**.

skinflint noun SEE **miser**.

skinny adjective *a skinny figure.* emaciated, lanky, scraggy, SEE **thin** adjective.

skip noun SEE **container**.

skip verb 1 *to skip and play.* bound, caper, cavort, dance, frisk, gambol, hop, jump, leap, prance, spring.
2 *to skip the boring bits.* forget, ignore, leave out, miss out, neglect, overlook, pass over, skim through.
3 *to skip lessons.* be absent from, cut, miss, play truant from.

skipper noun captain.

skirl noun VARIOUS SOUNDS: SEE **sound** noun.

skirmish noun, verb SEE **fight** noun, verb.

skirt noun OTHER CLOTHES: SEE **clothes**.

skirt verb *The path skirts the playing-field.* avoid, border, bypass, circle, encircle, go round, pass round, [*informal*] steer clear of, surround.

skit noun burlesque, parody, satire, sketch, spoof, [*informal*] take-off.

skittish adjective SEE **playful**.

skive verb SEE **lazy (be lazy)**.

skiver noun SEE **lazy (lazy person)**.

skivvy noun SEE **servant**.

skulduggery noun SEE **trickery**.

skulk verb SEE **loiter**.

skull noun head.
PARTS OF YOUR SKELETON: SEE **skeleton**.

sky noun *The rocket rose into the sky.* air, atmosphere, [*poetic*] blue, [*poetic*] firmament, [*poetic*] heavens, space, stratosphere, [*poetic*] welkin.

skylight noun SEE **window**.

skyline noun horizon.

skyscraper noun OTHER BUILDINGS: SEE **building**.

slab noun *a slab of rock, cake, etc.* block, chunk, hunk, lump, piece, slice, wedge.

slack adjective 1 *slack ropes.* limp, loose.
OPPOSITES: SEE **tight**.
2 *a slack attitude.* disorganized, easygoing, flaccid, idle, lax, lazy, listless, negligent, permissive, relaxed, unbusinesslike, uncaring, undisciplined.
OPPOSITES: SEE **businesslike**.
3 *slack trade.* inactive, quiet, slow, slow-moving, sluggish.
OPPOSITES: SEE **busy**.

slack verb SEE **lazy (be lazy)**.

slacken verb 1 *to slacken the tension in ropes.* ease off, loosen, relax, release.
2 *The pace slackened in the second half.* abate, decrease, ease, lessen, lower, moderate, reduce, slow down.

slacker noun SEE **lazy (lazy person)**.

slacks noun SEE **trousers**.

slake verb *to slake your thirst.* allay, cool, quench, satisfy.

slam verb 1 *to slam a door.* bang, shut.
2 [*informal*] *to slam someone's work.* SEE **criticize**.

slander noun *The slander in the papers ruined his reputation.* backbiting, calumny, defamation, denigration, insult, libel, lie, misrepresentation, obloquy, scandal, slur, smear.

slander verb *to slander someone.* blacken the name of, defame, denigrate, disparage, libel, malign, misrepresent, smear, spread tales about, tell lies about, traduce, vilify.

slanderous adjective *slanderous rumours.* abusive, cruel, damaging, defamatory, disparaging, false, hurtful, insulting, libellous, malicious, scurrilous, untrue, vicious.

slang noun argot, cant, jargon.
LINGUISTIC TERMS: SEE **language**.

slang verb SEE **insult** verb.
slanging match SEE **quarrel** noun.

slant noun 1 *Rest the ladder at a slant.* angle, diagonal, gradient, incline, list, rake, ramp, slope, tilt.
2 *I didn't like the slant they gave to the news.* bias, distortion, emphasis, imbalance, perspective, prejudice, viewpoint.

slant verb 1 *Her handwriting slants backwards.* be at an angle, be skewed, incline, lean, shelve, slope, tilt.
2 *He slanted the evidence in her favour.* bias, distort, prejudice, twist, weight.

slanting adjective *a slanting line.* angled, askew, diagonal, inclined, listing, oblique, raked, skewed, slantwise, sloping, tilted.
OPPOSITES: SEE **level** adjective, **perpendicular**.

slap verb SEE **hit** verb.

slapdash adjective SEE **careless**.

slap-happy adjective SEE **casual**.

slapstick noun SEE **comedy**.

slash verb SEE **cut** verb.

slat noun SEE **strip** noun.

slate verb [*informal*] *to slate someone's work.* SEE **criticize**.

slatternly adjective SEE **slovenly**.

slaughter noun bloodshed, butchery, carnage, SEE **killing**, massacre, murder.

slaughter verb *to slaughter men on a battlefield.* annihilate, butcher, SEE **kill**, massacre, murder, slay.

slaughter-house noun abattoir, [*old-fashioned*] shambles.

slave noun drudge, serf, SEE **servant**, thrall, vassal.

slave verb *We slaved away all day.* drudge, exert yourself, labour, [*informal*] sweat, toil, SEE **work** verb.

slave-driver noun despot, hard taskmaster, tyrant.

slaver verb dribble, drool, foam at the mouth, salivate, slobber.

slavery noun bondage, captivity, enslavement, serfdom, servitude.
OPPOSITES: SEE **freedom**.

slavish adjective 1 *slavish submission.* abject, cringing, fawning, grovelling, humiliating, menial, obsequious, servile, submissive.
OPPOSITES: SEE **proud**.

2 *a slavish imitation.* close, flattering, strict, sycophantic, unimaginative, unoriginal.
OPPOSITES: SEE **independent**.

slay verb assassinate, bump off, butcher, destroy, dispatch, execute, exterminate, [*informal*] finish off, SEE **kill**, martyr, massacre, murder, put down, put to death, slaughter.

sleazy adjective *a sleazy night-club.* dirty, disreputable, mucky, seedy, slovenly, sordid, squalid, unprepossessing.

sledge noun bob-sleigh, sled, sleigh, toboggan.

sleek adjective **1** *The cat had a sleek coat.* brushed, glossy, shiny, silky, smooth, soft, velvety, well-groomed.
OPPOSITES: SEE **unkempt**.
2 *The cat had a sleek look.* complacent, contented, self-satisfied, smug, thriving, well-fed.

sleep noun cat-nap, coma, dormancy, doze, [*informal*] forty winks, hibernation, [*informal*] kip, [*informal*] nap, rest, [*informal*] shut-eye, siesta, slumber, snooze.

sleep verb cat-nap, [*informal*] doss down, doze, [*informal*] drop off, drowse, hibernate, [*informal*] nod off, rest, slumber, snooze, [*informal*] take a nap.

sleepiness noun drowsiness, lethargy, somnolence, torpor.

sleeping adjective asleep, comatose, dormant, hibernating, [*informal*] in the land of Nod, [*informal*] off, [*informal*] out like a light, resting, slumbering, unconscious.

sleeping-car noun sleeper.

sleepless adjective *sleepless through the night.* awake, disturbed, insomniac, restless, wakeful, watchful, wide awake.

sleeplessness noun insomnia.

sleep-walker noun somnambulist.

sleepy adjective **1** *sleepy after a big meal.* comatose, [*informal*] dopey, drowsy, heavy, lethargic, ready to sleep, sluggish, somnolent, soporific, tired, torpid, weary.
2 *a sleepy little village.* inactive, quiet, restful, unexciting.
OPPOSITES: SEE **lively**.

sleigh noun SEE **sledge**.

slender adjective **1** *a slender figure.* graceful, slight, SEE **slim** adjective, svelte, thin.
OPPOSITES: SEE **fat** adjective.
2 *a slender thread.* feeble, fine, fragile, tenuous.
OPPOSITES: SEE **strong**.

3 *slender means.* inadequate, meagre, scanty.
OPPOSITES: SEE **adequate**.

sleuth noun SEE **detective**.

slice noun *a slice of bread.* SEE **piece**.

slice verb carve, SEE **cut** verb.

slick adjective *a slick bit of deception.* adroit, artful, clever, cunning, deft, dextrous, glib, plausible, quick, smart, smooth, [*informal*] tricky, wily.
OPPOSITES: SEE **clumsy**.

slide noun **1** *The children play on the slide.* chute.
2 *I take slides with my camera.* transparency.

slide verb *to slide over a slippery surface.* aquaplane, coast, glide, glissade, skate, skid, ski, skim, slip, slither, toboggan.

slight adjective **1** *a slight improvement.* imperceptible, insignificant, minor, negligible, slim (*a slim chance*), superficial, tiny, trifling, trivial, unimportant.
2 *a slight figure.* delicate, feeble, flimsy, fragile, frail, sickly, slender, SEE **slim** adjective, thin, weak.
OPPOSITES: SEE **big**.

slight noun, verb SEE **insult** noun, verb.

slightly adverb *slightly warm.* hardly, moderately, only just, scarcely.
OPPOSITES: SEE **very**.

slim adjective **1** *a slim figure.* fine, graceful, lean, narrow, slender, slight, svelte, sylphlike, SEE **thin** adjective, trim.
2 *a slim chance of winning.* SEE **slight** adjective.

slim verb become slimmer, diet, lose weight, reduce.

slime noun muck, mucus, mud, ooze, sludge.

sling verb *I slung the rubbish on the tip.* cast, chuck, fling, heave, hurl, lob, pelt, pitch, shy, throw, toss.

slink verb *He slunk away in disgrace.* creep, edge, move guiltily, slither, sneak, steal.

slinky adjective [*informal*] *a slinky dress.* clinging, close-fitting, sexy, sleek.

slip noun *I made a silly slip.* accident, [*informal*] bloomer, blunder, error, fault, inaccuracy, indiscretion, lapse, miscalculation, mistake, oversight, [*informal*] slip of the pen/tongue, [*informal*] slip-up.
to give someone the slip SEE **escape** verb.

slip verb **1** *I slipped on the wet floor.* aquaplane, coast, glide, glissade, move out of control, skate, skid, ski, skim, slide, slip, slither.

2 *She slipped into the room without being noticed.* creep, edge, move quietly, slink, sneak, steal.

to slip away SEE **escape** verb.

to slip up SEE **blunder** verb.

slipper noun VARIOUS SHOES: SEE **shoe**.

slippery adjective **1** *Take care: the floor is slippery.* glassy, greasy, icy, lubricated, oily, [*informal*] slippy, slithery, smooth.

2 [*informal*] *a slippery customer.* SEE **devious**.

slippy adjective SEE **slippery**.

slipshod adjective SEE **careless**.

slit noun *a slit in a fence. a slit made with a knife.* breach, break, chink, crack, cut, fissure, gap, gash, hole, incision, opening, rift, slot, split, tear, vent.

slit verb *to slit with a knife.* SEE **cut** verb.

slither verb *The snake slithered away.* creep, glide, slide, slink, SEE **slip** verb, snake, worm.

sliver noun SEE **strip** noun.

slobber verb dribble, drool, salivate, slaver.

slog verb SEE **hit** verb.

slogan noun *an advertising slogan.* catchphrase, catchword, jingle, motto, SEE **saying**.

slop verb *I slopped tea in the saucer.* SEE **splash** verb.

slope noun *an upwards slope. a downwards slope.* ascent, bank, camber, cant, declivity, descent, dip, fall, gradient, hill, incline, rake, ramp, rise, scarp, slant, tilt.

slope verb **1** *The beach slopes gently.* bank, fall, rise, shelve.

2 *The leaning tower slopes to one side.* incline, lean, slant, tilt, tip.

sloppy adjective **1** *a sloppy mixture.* liquid, messy, runny, slushy, splashing about, watery, wet.

2 *sloppy work.* SEE **slovenly**.

3 *a sloppy love-story.* SEE **sentimental**.

slosh verb **1** *to slosh someone.* SEE **hit** verb.

2 *to slosh water about.* SEE **splash** verb.

slot noun **1** *Put a coin in the slot.* break, chink, crack, cut, fissure, gap, gash, groove, hole, incision, opening, rift, slit, split.

2 *TV has a weekly slot for viewers' comments.* place, space, time.

sloth noun SEE **laziness**.

slothful adjective SEE **lazy**.

slouch verb *Don't slouch in that slovenly way!* droop, loaf, lounge, shamble, slump, stoop.

slough noun SEE **bog**.

slovenly adjective *slovenly work. a slovenly appearance.* careless, disorganized, hasty, messy, shoddy, slapdash, slatternly, sloppy, thoughtless, untidy.

OPPOSITES: SEE **careful**.

slow adjective **1** *slow progress.* careful, cautious, dawdling, delayed, deliberate, dilatory, gradual, leisurely, lingering, loitering, measured, moderate, painstaking, plodding, protracted, sluggish, steady, tardy, unhurried.

OPPOSITES: SEE **fast** adjective.

2 *a slow learner.* backward, dense, dim, dull, obtuse, stupid, [*informal*] thick.

3 *a slow worker.* idle, lazy, sluggish.

to be slow dally, dawdle, delay, [*informal*] hang about, idle, lag behind, linger, loiter, move slowly, straggle, [*informal*] take your time, trail behind.

slow verb **to slow down** brake, decelerate, go slower, reduce speed.

sludge noun mud, ooze, silt, slime, slurry, slush.

slug verb SEE **hit** verb.

sluggard noun SEE **lazy** (lazy person).

sluggish adjective *a sluggish response.* dull, idle, lazy, lethargic, lifeless, listless, phlegmatic, slothful, SEE **slow** adjective, torpid, unresponsive.

OPPOSITES: SEE **lively**.

sluice verb *I sluiced the dirt down the drain.* flush, rinse, swill, wash.

slumber noun, verb SEE **sleep** noun, verb.

slump noun *a slump in trade.* collapse, crash, decline, depression, downturn, drop, fall, recession, trough.

OPPOSITES: SEE **boom** noun.

slump verb **1** *Trade slumped after Christmas.* collapse, decline, drop, fall off, plummet, plunge, sink, worsen.

OPPOSITES: SEE **prosper**.

2 *He slumped across his desk.* be limp, collapse, droop, flop, loll, sag, slouch.

slur noun *a slur on his reputation.* SEE **slander** noun.

slur verb *to slur your words.* WAYS OF TALKING: SEE **talk** verb.

slurp verb VARIOUS SOUNDS: SEE **sound** noun.

slurry noun SEE **mud**, ooze, slime.

sly adjective *a sly trick.* artful, [*informal*] catty, conniving, crafty, cunning, deceitful, devious, [*informal*] foxy, furtive, guileful, knowing, scheming, secretive,

[*informal*] shifty, [*informal*] sneaky, [*informal*] snide, stealthy, surreptitious, tricky, underhand, wily.
OPPOSITES: SEE **straightforward**.

smack verb *to smack someone on the wrist.* SEE **hit** verb, pat, slap, spank.

small adjective **1** *a small person. small things.* [*informal*] baby, compact, concise, diminutive, [*informal*] dinky, dwarf, exiguous, fractional, infinitesimal, lilliputian, little, microscopic, midget, [*informal*] mini, miniature, minuscule, minute, petite (*a petite woman*), [*informal*] pint-sized, [*informal*] poky (*a poky room*), portable, pygmy, short, [*informal*] teeny, tiny, toy, undersized, [*informal*] wee, [*informal*] weeny.
2 *small helpings.* inadequate, insufficient, meagre, mean, measly, scanty, stingy.
3 *a small problem.* SEE **trivial**.
OPPOSITES: SEE **big**.
a small amount, a small thing bagatelle, [*informal*] chicken-feed, fragment, modicum, morsel, particle, scrap, [*informal*] smattering, snippet, soupçon, spot, trifle.
a small animal, a small person dwarf, midget, pygmy, runt, [*informal*] titch.
small arms SEE **weapons**.

smallholding noun SEE **farm** noun.

small-minded adjective *small-minded objections.* bigoted, grudging, hidebound, illiberal, intolerant, mean, narrow-minded, old-fashioned, parochial, petty, prejudiced, selfish, trivial.
OPPOSITES: SEE **broad-minded**.

smarmy adjective [*uncomplimentary*] *I hate his smarmy compliments.* SEE **obsequious**.

smart adjective **1** *a smart pace.* brisk, [*informal*] cracking, fast, forceful, quick, rapid, [*informal*] rattling, speedy, swift.
OPPOSITES: SEE **slow** adjective.
2 *a smart idea.* acute, artful, astute, bright, clever, crafty, [*informal*] cute, ingenious, intelligent, shrewd.
OPPOSITES: SEE **stupid**.
3 *a smart appearance.* chic, clean, dapper, [*informal*] dashing, elegant, fashionable, modish, [*informal*] natty, neat, [*informal*] posh, [*informal*] snazzy, spruce, stylish, tidy, trim, well-dressed.
OPPOSITES: SEE **dowdy**.

smart verb *The sting smarts.* SEE **hurt** verb.

smarten verb SEE **tidy** verb.

smash verb **1** *to smash an egg.* SEE **break** verb, crumple, crush, demolish, destroy, shatter, squash, wreck.

2 *to smash into a wall.* bang, bash, batter, bump, collide, crash, hammer, SEE **hit** verb, knock, pound, ram, slam, strike, thump, wallop.

smashing adjective SEE **excellent**.

smattering noun *a smattering of French.* SEE **small** (small amount).

smear noun **1** *a smear of grease.* mark, smudge, streak.
2 *a smear on his good name.* SEE **slander** noun.

smear verb **1** *He smeared paint over the canvas.* dab, daub, plaster, rub, smudge, spread, wipe.
2 *The papers smeared his reputation.* attack, malign, SEE **slander** verb, vilify.

smeary adjective SEE **dirty** adjective.

smell noun aroma, bouquet, fragrance, incense, nose, odour, perfume, [*informal*] pong, redolence, reek, scent, stench, stink, whiff.
RELATED ADJECTIVE: olfactory.

smell verb **1** *Smell these roses.* scent, sniff.
2 *Those onions smell.* [*informal*] pong, reek, stink, whiff.

smelling adjective [*Smelling* is usually used not on its own but in combination with other words: *strong-smelling, sweet-smelling,* etc.] **1** *pleasant-smelling.* aromatic, fragrant, musky, odorous, perfumed, redolent, scented.
2 *strong- or unpleasant-smelling.* fetid, foul, [*informal*] high, malodorous, musty, noisome, [*informal*] off, pongy, pungent, putrid, rank, reeking, rotten, smelly, stinking, [*informal*] whiffy.
OPPOSITES: SEE **odourless**.

smelly adjective SEE **smelling**.

smile noun, verb beam, grin, SEE **laugh**, leer, simper, smirk, sneer.
FACIAL EXPRESSIONS: SEE **expression**.

smirk noun, verb SEE **smile**.

smite verb SEE **hit** verb.

smith noun blacksmith.
ARTISTS AND CRAFTSMEN: SEE **artist**.

smithereens noun SEE **fragment** noun.

smog noun SEE **fog**.

smoke noun **1** *clouds of smoke.* air pollution, exhaust, fog, fumes, gas, smog, steam, vapour.
2 *She offered me a smoke.* cheroot, cigar, cigarette, [*informal*] fag, pipe, tobacco.

smoke verb **1** *The fire was smoking.* emit smoke, fume, reek, smoulder.
2 *He smokes cigars.* inhale, puff at.

smokeless adjective clean, smoke-free.

smoke-screen noun SEE **disguise** noun.

moky adjective *a smoky atmosphere.* clouded, dirty, foggy, grimy, hazy, sooty.
OPPOSITES: SEE **clear** adjective.

mooth adjective 1 *a smooth lawn.* even, flat, horizontal, level.
2 *a smooth sea.* calm, glassy, peaceful, placid, quiet, restful, unruffled.
3 *a cat's smooth coat. a smooth finish on the car.* glossy, polished, shiny, silken, silky, sleek, soft, velvety.
4 *a smooth ride. smooth progress.* comfortable, easy, steady, uneventful, uninterrupted.
5 *a smooth taste.* agreeable, bland, mellow, mild, pleasant.
6 *a smooth mixture.* creamy, flowing, runny.
OPPOSITE: lumpy.
7 *a smooth manner. a smooth talker.* convincing, facile, glib, insincere, plausible, polite, self-assured, self-satisfied, smug, sophisticated, suave, untrustworthy, urbane.
OPPOSITES: SEE **rough**.

mooth verb *to smooth a rough surface.* even out, file, flatten, iron, level, level off, plane, polish, press, roll out, sand down, sandpaper.

mother verb *to smother a fire. to smother someone with a pillow.* choke, cover, SEE **kill**, snuff out, stifle, strangle, suffocate, throttle.

moulder verb SEE **burn** verb, smoke.

mudge noun *a smudge on the paper.* SEE **mark** noun.

mudge verb 1 *I smudged the ink.* blur, smear, streak.
2 *I smudged the paper.* blot, dirty, mark, stain.

mug adjective *a smug expression.* complacent, conceited, pleased, priggish, self-righteous, self-satisfied, sleek, superior.
OPPOSITES: SEE **humble** adjective.

muggling noun VARIOUS CRIMES: SEE **crime**.

mut noun *a smut on your nose.* SEE **mark** noun.

mutty adjective *smutty jokes.* SEE **obscene**.

nack noun bite, [*informal*] elevenses, [*informal*] nibble, refreshments.
VARIOUS MEALS: SEE **meal**.

nack-bar noun buffet, café, cafeteria, fast-food restaurant.

nag noun *An unexpected snag delayed our plan.* complication, difficulty, hindrance, hitch, obstacle, problem, setback, [*informal*] stumbling-block.

nag verb SEE **tear** verb.

snake noun serpent.

VARIOUS SNAKES: adder, anaconda, boa constrictor, cobra, copperhead, flying-snake, grass snake, mamba, python, rattlesnake, sand snake, sea snake, sidewinder, tree snake, viper.

---

snap adjective *a snap decision.* SEE **sudden**.

snap verb 1 *A twig snapped.* SEE **break** verb, crack.
2 *The dog snapped at me.* bite, nip, snatch.
3 *She snapped at us.* SEE **angry (be angry)**.

snappy adjective [*informal*] *a snappy answer.* SEE **brisk**.

snapshot noun KINDS OF PHOTOGRAPH: SEE **photograph** noun.

snare noun ambush, booby-trap, [*old-fashioned*] gin, noose, trap.

snare verb *to snare animals.* catch, decoy, ensnare, net, trap.

snarl verb 1 *The dog snarled.* bare the teeth, growl.
WAYS PEOPLE SPEAK: SEE **talk** verb.
2 *The rope got snarled up in the wheels.* SEE **tangle** verb.

snatch verb *The muggers snatched her handbag.* catch, clutch, grab, grasp, pluck, seize, take, wrench away, wrest away.

snazzy adjective SEE **stylish**.

sneak verb 1 *I sneaked in without anyone seeing.* creep, move stealthily, prowl, slink, stalk, steal.
2 [*informal*] *She sneaked on me.* [*informal*] grass, inform (against), report, [*informal*] tell tales (about).

sneaking adjective 1 *a sneaking suspicion.* half-formed, intuitive, nagging, niggling, persistent, private, uncomfortable, unproved, worrying.
2 SEE **sneaky**.

sneaky adjective [*informal*] *a sneaky way of getting an advantage.* cheating, contemptible, crafty, deceitful, despicable, devious, dishonest, furtive, [*informal*] low-down, mean, nasty, shady, [*informal*] shifty, sly, sneaking, treacherous, underhand, unorthodox, untrustworthy.
OPPOSITES: SEE **straightforward**.

sneer verb boo, hiss, hoot, jeer, SEE **laugh**, scoff.
to sneer at be contemptuous of, be scornful of [SEE **scornful**], denigrate, mock, ridicule, [*informal*] sniff at, taunt.
FACIAL EXPRESSIONS: SEE **expression**.

sneering adjective SEE **scornful**.

snick noun, verb SEE **cut** noun, verb.

snicker verb SEE **snigger**.

snide adjective SEE **scornful**.

sniff verb 1 *to sniff the roses*. SEE **smell** verb.
2 *to sniff because you have a cold*. [*informal*] sniffle, snivel, snuffle.
to sniff at SEE **sneer (sneer at)**.

snigger verb *to snigger at a rude joke*. chuckle, giggle, SEE **laugh**, snicker, titter.

snip noun, verb SEE **cut** noun, verb.

snipe verb *A gunman sniped at them from the roof*. fire, SEE **shoot** verb, [*informal*] take pot-shots.

snippet noun *snippets of information*. fragment, morsel, particle, piece, scrap, shred, snatch (*a snatch of a song*).

snitch verb SEE **steal**.

snivel verb *He began to snivel when he heard his punishment*. blubber, cry, grizzle, grovel, sniff, sob, weep, whimper, whine, [*informal*] whinge.

snob noun élitist, snobbish person [SEE **snobbish**].

snobbish adjective *too snobbish to eat convenience foods. a snobbish attitude to art*. condescending, disdainful, élitist, haughty, patronizing, pompous, [*informal*] posh, presumptuous, pretentious, [*informal*] snooty, [*informal*] stuck-up, superior, [*informal*] toffee-nosed.
OPPOSITES: SEE **unpretentious**.

snoop verb *Don't snoop into my affairs!* be inquisitive [SEE **inquisitive**], interfere, intrude, meddle, [*informal*] nose about, pry, sneak, spy, [*informal*] stick your nose (into).

snooper noun SEE **busybody**.

snooty adjective SEE **snobbish**.

snooze noun, verb SEE **sleep** noun, verb.

snore noun, verb VARIOUS SOUNDS: SEE **sound** noun.

snorkelling noun SEE **diving**.

snort noun, verb VARIOUS SOUNDS: SEE **sound** noun.

snout noun *an animal's snout*. face, muzzle, nose, proboscis, trunk.

snowy adjective WORDS TO DESCRIBE WEATHER: SEE **weather** noun.

snub verb *She snubbed him by ignoring his question*. be rude to, brush off, cold-shoulder, disdain, humiliate, insult, offend, [*informal*] put (someone) down, rebuff, reject, scorn, [*informal*] squash.

snuff noun SEE **tobacco**.

snuff verb *to snuff a candle*. extinguish, put out.
to snuff it SEE **die**.

snuffle verb SEE **sniff**.

snug adjective 1 *snug in bed*. comfortable, [*informal*] comfy, cosy, relaxed, safe, secure, soft, warm.
2 *The jacket was a snug fit*. close-fitting, exact, well-tailored.

snuggle verb SEE **cuddle**.

soak verb 1 *to soak something in liquid*. bathe, drench, [*informal*] dunk, immerse, [*in cooking*] marinate, pickle, souse, steep, submerge, wet thoroughly.
2 *Rain soaked the pitch*. make soaked [SEE **soaked**], penetrate, permeate, saturate.
3 *A sponge soaks up water*. absorb, take up.

soaked, soaking adjectives drenched, dripping, sodden, soggy, sopping, waterlogged, SEE **wet** adjective, wet through.
OPPOSITES: SEE **dry** adjective.

soap noun detergent.

soar verb *An eagle soared overhead*. ascend, climb, float, fly, glide, hover, rise, tower.

sob verb SEE **weep**.

sober adjective 1 *He got drunk, but you stayed sober. I spent time in sober reflection*. calm, clear-headed, composed, in control, lucid, rational, sensible, steady.
OPPOSITES: SEE **drunk, irrational**.
2 *a sober life-style*. abstemious, moderate, plain, restrained, self-controlled, staid, temperate, unexciting.
OPPOSITES: SEE **self-indulgent**.
3 *a sober occasion. sober colours*. dignified, dull, grave, peaceful, quiet, sedate, serene, serious, solemn, sombre, subdued.
OPPOSITES: SEE **frivolous**.

sobriquet noun SEE **nickname**.

soccer noun Association football.

sociable adjective *a sociable crowd of people*. affable, approachable, [*old-fashioned*] clubbable, companionable, convivial, extroverted, friendly, gregarious, hospitable, neighbourly, outgoing, SEE **social** adjective, warm, welcoming.
OPPOSITES: SEE **unfriendly**.

social adjective 1 *Humans are supposed to be social creatures*. civilized, collaborative, friendly, gregarious, organized, SEE **sociable**.
OPPOSITES: SEE **solitary**.
2 *We organized some social events*. communal, community, group, public.
OPPOSITES: SEE **individual** adjective.

ocial noun *a Christmas social.* dance, disco, [*informal*] do, gathering, [*informal*] get-together, SEE **party**, reception, reunion, soirée.

ocialism noun POLITICAL TERMS: SEE **politics**.

ocialize verb *She's got lots of friends: she likes to socialize.* associate, be sociable [SEE **sociable**], entertain, fraternize, get together, join in, mix, relate.

ociety noun 1 *We are part of human society.* civilization, community, nation, the public.
2 *We enjoy the society of our friends.* camaraderie, companionship, company, fellowship, friendship.
3 *a secret society.* association, brotherhood, club, fraternity, group, league, organization, sisterhood, union.

ock verb SEE **hit** verb.

odden adjective SEE **soaked**.

ofa noun chaise longue, couch, SEE **seat** noun, settee.
OTHER FURNITURE: SEE **furniture**.

oft adjective 1 *soft rubber. soft sponge-cake. soft clay.* crumbly, cushiony, elastic, flabby, flexible, floppy, limp, malleable, mushy, plastic, pliable, pulpy, spongy, springy, squashy, supple, tender, yielding.
2 *a soft bed.* comfortable, cosy.
OPPOSITES: SEE **hard**.
3 *a soft texture.* downy, feathery, fleecy, furry, silky, sleek, smooth, velvety.
OPPOSITES: SEE **rough**.
4 *a soft voice. soft music. soft lighting.* faint, dim, low, mellifluous, muted, peaceful, soothing, subdued.
OPPOSITES: SEE **bright, loud**.
5 [*informal*] *a soft teacher.* compassionate, easygoing, indulgent, kind, lenient, permissive, sympathetic, tender-hearted, understanding.
OPPOSITES: SEE **severe**.
6 *a soft breeze. a soft touch.* delicate, gentle, light, mild.
OPPOSITES: SEE **violent**.
7 [*informal*] *a soft job. a soft option.* easy, undemanding.
OPPOSITES: SEE **difficult**.

often verb 1 *to soften your tone.* deaden, decrease, lower, make quieter, moderate, muffle, quieten, subdue, tone down.
2 *to soften a blow.* alleviate, buffer, cushion, deflect, reduce the impact of, temper.
OPPOSITES: SEE **intensify**.
3 *to soften ingredients before mixing a cake.* dissolve, fluff up, lighten, liquefy, make softer, melt.
OPPOSITES: SEE **harden**.

soft-hearted adjective SEE **kind** adjective.

soft-pedal verb SEE **understate**.

soggy adjective 1 *a soggy towel.* drenched, saturated, soaked, sodden, sopping, wet through.
OPPOSITES: SEE **dry** adjective.
2 *soggy cake.* heavy, moist, stodgy.
OPPOSITE: light.

soil noun *the soil in the garden.* earth, ground, humus, land, loam, marl, topsoil.

soil verb *Don't soil your hands with that filthy stuff.* contaminate, defile, dirty, make dirty, pollute, stain, tarnish.

soiled adjective SEE **dirty** adjective.

soirée noun SEE **social** noun.

sojourn noun, verb SEE **stay** noun, verb.

solace noun, verb SEE **comfort** noun, verb.

solder verb SEE **fasten**, weld.

soldier noun cavalryman, centurion, commando, conscript, SEE **fighter**, guardsman, gunner, infantryman, lancer, marine, mercenary, NCO, officer, paratrooper, private, regular, rifleman, sapper, sentry, serviceman, trooper, [*plural*] troops, warrior.
RANKS IN THE ARMY: SEE **rank** noun.

sole adjective *the sole survivor.* exclusive, individual, lone, one, only, single, solitary, unique.

solecism noun SEE **mistake** noun.

solemn adjective 1 *a solemn expression.* earnest, glum, grave, grim, sedate, serious, sober, sombre, staid, thoughtful, unsmiling.
OPPOSITES: SEE **cheerful**.
2 *a solemn occasion.* awe-inspiring, ceremonious, dignified, formal, grand, holy, important, imposing, impressive, pompous, religious, stately.
OPPOSITES: SEE **frivolous**.

solemnize verb SEE **celebrate**.

solicit verb *to solicit help.* SEE **seek**.

solicitor noun lawyer.
LEGAL TERMS: SEE **law**.

solicitous adjective SEE **concerned**.

solicitude noun SEE **concern** noun.

solid adjective 1 *solid rock. frozen solid.* compact, dense, firm, fixed, hard, rigid, stable, unbending, unyielding.
OPPOSITES: SEE **fluid, powdery, soft**.
2 *solid gold.* pure, unalloyed, unmixed.
OPPOSITE: alloyed.
3 *three solid hours.* SEE **continual**, continuous, unbroken, uninterrupted.
OPPOSITES: SEE **intermittent**.

4 *a solid piece of furniture.* robust, sound, steady, SEE **strong**, sturdy, well-made.
OPPOSITES: SEE **flimsy**.
5 *a solid shape.* cubic, rounded, spherical, thick, three-dimensional.
OPPOSITE: two-dimensional.
6 *solid evidence.* concrete, genuine, physical, proven, real, tangible, weighty.
OPPOSITES: SEE **hypothetical**.
7 *solid support from friends.* complete, dependable, like-minded, reliable, trustworthy, unanimous, undivided, united.
OPPOSITES: SEE **unreliable**.

solidarity noun *We can depend on the solidarity of our team.* cohesion, harmony, like-mindedness, unanimity, unity.
OPPOSITES: SEE **disunity**.

solidify verb *The liquid solidifies as it cools down.* cake, clot, coagulate, congeal, SEE **harden**, set.
OPPOSITES: SEE **liquefy**.

Some words beginning *sol-*, including *soliloquy, solitary,* and *solo,* are related to Latin *solus = alone.* Others, including *solar, solarium,* and *solstice,* are related to Latin *sol = sun.*

---

soliloquize verb SEE **speak**.

soliloquy noun monologue, SEE **speech**.

solitary adjective **1** *a solitary existence.* alone, anti-social, cloistered, companionless, friendless, isolated, lonely, unsociable.
OPPOSITES: SEE **social** adjective.
2 *a solitary survivor.* one, only, single, sole.
3 *a solitary place.* desolate, hidden, isolated, out-of-the-way, remote, secluded, sequestered, unfrequented.
a solitary person hermit, [*informal*] loner, recluse.

solitude noun *the solitude of the wilderness.* isolation, loneliness, privacy, remoteness, retirement, seclusion.

solo adverb *to perform solo.* alone, unaccompanied.

soloist noun MUSICAL PERFORMERS: SEE **music**.

solstice noun OPPOSITE: equinox.

soluble adjective **1** *soluble in water.* dispersing, dissolving.
2 *a soluble problem.* explicable, manageable, solvable, tractable, understandable.
OPPOSITES: SEE **insoluble**.

solution noun **1** *a solution of salt in water.* blend, compound, mixture.
2 *the solution to a problem.* answer, elucidation, explanation, key, resolution, solving.

solvable adjective *a solvable problem.* SEE **soluble**.

solve verb *to solve a riddle.* answer, [*informal*] crack, decipher, elucidate, explain, find the solution to, interpret, work out.

solvent adjective *Accountants confirmed that the firm was solvent.* in credit, self-supporting, sound, viable.
OPPOSITES: SEE **bankrupt**.

sombre adjective *sombre colours. a sombre expression.* cheerless, dark, dim, dismal, doleful, drab, dull, gloomy, grave, lugubrious, melancholy, mournful, SEE **sad**, serious, sober.
OPPOSITES: SEE **cheerful**.

somersault noun forward roll.

somewhat adverb *somewhat annoyed.* fairly, moderately, [*informal*] pretty, quite, rather, [*informal*] sort of.

somnambulist noun sleep-walker.

son noun FAMILY RELATIONSHIPS: SEE **family**.

song noun lyric.

MUSIC FOR SINGING: air, anthem, aria, ballad, blues, calypso, cantata, canticle, carol, chant, chorus, descant, ditty, folk-song, hymn, jingle, lied, lullaby, madrigal, musical, number, nursery rhyme, opera, oratorio, pop song, psalm, reggae, rock, serenade, shanty, soul, spiritual, wassail.
OTHER MUSICAL TERMS: SEE **music**.

---

songster noun SEE **singer**.

sonorous adjective *a sonorous voice* deep, full, loud, powerful, resonant, resounding, rich, ringing.
OPPOSITES: SEE **quiet**, **shrill**.

soon adverb [*old-fashioned*] anon, presently, quickly, shortly.

sooner adverb **1** *I wish you'd come sooner* before, earlier.
2 *I'd sooner have an apple than sweets* preferably, rather.

soot noun dirt, grime.

soothe verb *Quiet music soothes my nerves.* allay, appease, assuage, calm, comfort, compose, ease, mollify, pacify, quiet, relieve, salve, settle, still, tranquillize.

oothing adjective 1 *soothing ointment.* balmy, comforting, emollient, healing, mild, palliative.
2 *soothing music.* calming, gentle, peaceful, pleasant, relaxing, restful.

ooty adjective SEE **dirty** adjective.

ophisticated adjective 1 *sophisticated behaviour. sophisticated clothes.* adult, cosmopolitan, cultivated, cultured, fashionable, [*informal*] grown-up, mature, [*informal*] posh, [*uncomplimentary*] pretentious, refined, stylish, urbane, worldly.
OPPOSITES: SEE **naïve, simple.**
2 *sophisticated ideas. sophisticated machinery.* advanced, clever, complex, complicated, elaborate, hard to understand, ingenious, intricate, involved, subtle.
OPPOSITES: SEE **primitive, simple.**

ophistry noun *I wasn't taken in by his sophistry.* SEE **casuistry.**

oporific adjective *I dozed off during the soporific music.* boring, hypnotic, sedative, sleep-inducing, sleepy, somnolent.
OPPOSITES: SEE **lively, stimulating.**

opping adjective SEE **soaked.**

oppy adjective SEE **sentimental, silly.**

oprano noun SEE **singer.**

orbet noun fruit-ice, ice, water-ice.

orcerer noun conjuror, enchanter, magician, necromancer, sorceress, [*old-fashioned*] warlock, witch, witch-doctor, wizard.

orcery noun black magic, charms, conjuring, incantations, magic, necromancy, the occult, spells, voodoo, witchcraft, wizardry.

ordid adjective 1 *sordid surroundings. sordid details.* dirty, disreputable, filthy, foul, mucky, nasty, seamy, [*informal*] sleazy, [*informal*] slummy, squalid, ugly, undignified, SEE **unpleasant,** wretched.
OPPOSITES: SEE **elegant.**
2 *sordid dealings on the stock-exchange.* avaricious, corrupt, covetous, degenerate, dishonourable, immoral, mercenary, rapacious, selfish, [*informal*] shabby, shameful, unethical.
OPPOSITES: SEE **honourable.**

ore adjective 1 *a sore wound. a sore place on your skin.* aching, chafing, hurting, inflamed, painful, raw, red, sensitive, smarting, tender.
2 *She was sore about the way she'd been treated.* SEE **annoyed.**
to make sore *The continual rubbing made my skin sore.* chafe, chap, gall, hurt, inflame, redden.

sore noun *I put ointment on the sores.* abscess, boil, carbuncle, gall, gathering, graze, inflammation, laceration, pimple, rawness, spot, ulcer, SEE **wound** noun.

sorrow noun 1 *the sorrow of parting.* affliction, anguish, dejection, depression, desolation, despair, desperation, despondency, disappointment, discontent, disgruntlement, dissatisfaction, distress, [*poetic*] dolour, gloom, glumness, grief, heartache, heartbreak, heaviness, homesickness, hopelessness, loneliness, melancholy, misery, misfortune, mourning, sad feelings [SEE **sad**], sadness, suffering, tearfulness, tribulation, trouble, unhappiness, wistfulness, woe, wretchedness.
OPPOSITES: SEE **happiness.**
2 *She expressed her sorrow for what she had done.* apologies, feeling of guilt, penitence, regret, remorse, repentance.
OPPOSITE: impenitence.

sorrow verb *to sorrow at someone's misfortune.* be sorrowful [SEE **sorrowful**], be sympathetic [SEE **sympathetic**], grieve, lament, mourn, weep.
OPPOSITES: SEE **rejoice.**

sorrowful adjective *sorrowful feelings. a sorrowful expression.* broken-hearted, concerned, dejected, disconsolate, distressed, doleful, grief-stricken, heartbroken, long-faced, lugubrious, melancholy, miserable, mournful, regretful, rueful, SEE **sad,** saddened, sombre, SEE **sorry,** sympathetic, tearful, unhappy, upset, woebegone, woeful, wretched.
OPPOSITES: SEE **happy.**

sorry adjective 1 *I'm sorry for what I did.* apologetic, ashamed, conscience-stricken, contrite, guilt-ridden, penitent, regretful, remorseful, repentant, shamefaced.
2 *We are sorry for the girl who came last.* compassionate, merciful, pitying, sympathetic, understanding.
3 [*informal*] *Things were in a sorry state.* SEE **bad.**

sort noun 1 *Pop is my sort of music. The club welcomes all sorts of people.* brand, category, class, description, form, genre, group, kind, make, set, quality, type, variety.
2 *a sort of dog. a sort of wild flower.* breed, class, family, genus, race, species.
sort of [*informal*] *I feel sort of anxious.* SEE **somewhat.**

sort verb *to sort things into sets.* arrange, assort, catalogue, categorize, classify, divide, file, grade, group, organize, put in order, tidy.
OPPOSITES: SEE **mix.**

to sort out 1 *Sort out the things you need.* choose, [*informal*] put on one side, segregate, select, separate, set aside.
2 *I sorted out their problem.* attend to, clear up, cope with, deal with, find an answer to, grapple with, handle, manage, resolve, solve, tackle.

sortie noun SEE **attack** noun.

sot noun SEE **drunkard**.

sought-after adjective SEE **attractive**.

soul noun **1** *your immortal soul.* psyche, spirit.
2 [*informal*] *The poor souls had to wait ages for a bus.* SEE **person**.

soulful adjective *a soulful expression. a soulful performance.* deeply felt, eloquent, emotional, expressive, heartfelt, inspiring, moving, passionate, profound, sincere, spiritual, stirring, uplifting.
OPPOSITES: SEE **soulless**.

soulless adjective *a soulless performance.* cold, insincere, mechanical, perfunctory, routine, spiritless, superficial, trite, unemotional, unfeeling, uninspiring, unsympathetic.
OPPOSITES: SEE **soulful**.

sound adjective **1** *in a sound condition.* fit, healthy, hearty, robust, secure, solid, strong, sturdy, undamaged, well, whole.
OPPOSITES: SEE **damaged, ill**.
2 *sound advice.* coherent, convincing, correct, logical, prudent, rational, reasonable, reasoned, sensible, wise.
OPPOSITES: SEE **silly**.
3 *a sound business.* dependable, established, recognized, reliable, reputable, safe, trustworthy, viable.
OPPOSITES: SEE **disreputable**.

sound noun noise, timbre.
the science of sound acoustics.
RELATED ADJECTIVES [= *to do with sound*]: acoustic, sonic.

VARIOUS SOUNDS [Most of these words can be used either as nouns or as verbs]: bang, bark, bawl, bay, bellow, blare, bleat, bleep, boo, boom, bray, buzz, cackle, caw, chime, chink, chirp, chirrup, chug, clack, clamour, clang, clank, clap, clash, clatter, click, clink, cluck, coo, crack, crackle, crash, creak, croak, croon, crow, crunch, cry.

drone, echo, fizz, grate, grizzle, groan, growl, grunt, gurgle, hiccup, hiss, honk, hoot, howl, hum, jabber, jangle, jeer, jingle, lisp, low, miaow, moan, moo, murmur, neigh, patter, peal, ping, pip,

plop, pop, purr, quack, rattle, reverberation, ring, roar, rumble, rustle.

scream, screech, shout, shriek, sigh, sizzle, skirl, slam, slurp, snap, snarl, sniff, snore, snort, sob, splutter, squawk, squeak, squeal, squelch, swish, throb, thud, thunder, tick, ting, tinkle, toot, trumpet, twang, tweet, twitter, wail, warble, whimper, whine, whinny, whir, whistle, whiz, whoop, woof, yap, yell, yelp, yodel, yowl.
SEE ALSO: **music, noise, talk** verb.

---

sound verb **1** *The signal sounded.* become audible, be heard, make a noise, resound, reverberate.
2 *They sounded the signal.* cause, create, make, make audible, produce, pronounce, utter.
3 *to sound the depth of a river. to sound out public opinion.* examine, investigate, measure, plumb, probe, test, try.

soundless adjective SEE **silent**.

soup noun KINDS OF SOUP: broth, consommé, minestrone, mulligatawny, Scotch broth, stock. [There are many other kinds of soup. Often they are named after the principal ingredient *chicken soup, tomato soup,* etc.]

soupçon noun SEE **small** (**small amount**).

sour adjective **1** *sour fruit.* acid, bitter, pungent, sharp, tangy, tart, unripe, vinegary.
OPPOSITES: SEE **sweet** adjective.
OTHER WORDS DESCRIBING TASTE: SEE **taste** verb.
2 *a sour temper. sour comments.* acerbic, bad-tempered, bitter, cynical, disagreeable, grudging, grumpy, ill-natured, irritable, jaundiced, peevish, snappy, testy, unpleasant.
OPPOSITES: SEE **kind** adjective.

source noun **1** *the source of a rumour.* author, cause, derivation, initiator, originator, starting-point.
2 *the source of a river.* beginning, head, origin, spring, start.

sourpuss noun SEE **angry** (**angry person**).

souse verb SEE **soak**.

south noun GEOGRAPHICAL TERMS: SEE **geography**.

souvenir noun *a souvenir of a holiday* keepsake, memento, reminder.

sovereign adjective **1** *sovereign power* absolute, dominant, supreme.
2 *a sovereign state.* autonomous, independent, self-governing.

vereign noun emperor, empress, ing, monarch, queen, SEE **ruler**.

w noun SEE **pig**.

w verb *to sow seeds*. broadcast, plant, catter, seed, spread.

a noun SEE **spring** noun.

ace adjective *space exploration*. extraterrestrial, interplanetary, interstellar, rbiting.
pace travel astronautics.

WORDS TO DO WITH TRAVEL IN SPACE: stronaut, blast-off, booster rocket, capule, cosmonaut, count-down, heathield, module, orbit, probe, re-entry, etro-rocket, rocket, satellite, spaceraft, spaceship, space-shuttle, spacetation, spacesuit, splash-down, sputik.

---

ace noun 1 *interstellar space*. emptiness, endlessness, ionosphere, infinity, tratosphere, the universe.
STRONOMICAL TERMS: SEE **astronomy**.
space to move about. [*informal*] elbowoom, freedom, leeway, room, scope.
an empty space. area, blank, break, hasm, concourse, distance, gap, hitus, hole, interval, lacuna, opening, lace, vacuum.

ace verb *to space things out*. SEE arange.

acious adjective *a spacious house*. mple, SEE **big**, capacious, commodious, xtensive, large, open, roomy, sizeable.
PPOSITES: SEE **poky, small**.

adework noun SEE **work** noun.

aghetti noun SEE **pasta**.

an noun *a span of time*. *We could look long the whole span of the lake*. breadth, ompass, distance, duration, extent, ength, reach, scope, stretch, width.

an verb *to span a river*. arch over, ridge, cross, extend across, pass over, each over, straddle, stretch over, traerse.

ank verb SEE **hit** verb, slap, smack.

anking adjective *a spanking pace*. SEE risk.

anking noun SEE **punishment**.

ar noun SEE **pole**.

ar verb box, SEE **fight** verb.

are adjective 1 *spare players*. *spare food*. dditional, extra, inessential, leftover, dd, remaining, superfluous, surplus, nnecessary, unneeded, unused, nwanted.
PPOSITES: SEE **necessary**.

2 *a spare figure*. SEE **thin** adjective.

spare verb 1 *The judge did not spare the guilty man*. be merciful to, forgive, free, [*informal*] let off, pardon, release, reprieve, save.
2 *Can you spare something for charity?* afford, allow, give, give up, manage (*£10 is all I can manage*), part with, provide, sacrifice.

sparing adjective *sparing with his money*. careful, [*informal*] close, economical, frugal, mean, miserly, prudent, stingy, thrifty.
OPPOSITES: SEE **generous, wasteful**.

spark noun *a spark of light*. flash, flicker, gleam, glint, sparkle.

spark verb SEE **light** noun (**give light**).
to spark off *He sparked off an argument*. SEE **provoke**.

sparkle verb SEE **light** noun (**give light**).

sparkling adjective 1 *sparkling jewels*. brilliant, flashing, glinting, glittering, scintillating, shining, shiny, twinkling.
OPPOSITES: SEE **dull** adjective.
2 *sparkling drinks*. aerated, bubbling, bubbly, carbonated, effervescent, fizzy, foaming.
OPPOSITES: flat, still.

sparse adjective *sparse vegetation*. inadequate, light (*light traffic*), meagre, scanty, scarce, scattered, thin, [*informal*] thin on the ground.
OPPOSITES: SEE **dense**.

spartan adjective *spartan conditions*. abstemious, ascetic, austere, bare, bleak, frugal, hard, harsh, plain, rigorous, severe, simple, stern, strict.
OPPOSITES: SEE **luxurious**, pampered.

spasm noun *a spasm of coughing*. *a muscular spasm*. attack, contraction, convulsion, fit, jerk, paroxysm, seizure, [*plural*] throes, twitch.

spasmodic adjective *a spasmodic fault on our TV*. erratic, fitful, intermittent, irregular, occasional, [*informal*] on and off, sporadic.
OPPOSITES: SEE **continual, regular**.

spat noun gaiter.

spate noun *a spate of water*. cataract, flood, gush, rush, torrent.
OPPOSITES: SEE **trickle** noun.

spatter verb *The bus spattered water over us*. pepper, scatter, shower, slop, splash, spray, sprinkle.

speak verb articulate, communicate, converse, deliver a speech, discourse, enunciate, express yourself, hold a conversation, [*informal*] pipe up, pronounce words, say something,

soliloquize, talk, tell, use your voice, utter, verbalize, vocalize.
FOR A LONGER LIST OF SYNONYMS: SEE **talk** verb.
to speak about allude to, comment on, discuss, mention, refer to, relate.
to speak to address, harangue, lecture.
to speak your mind be honest [SEE honest], say what you think, speak honestly, speak out, state your opinion, voice your thoughts.

speaker noun *a speaker at a meeting.* lecturer, mouthpiece (*She can be our mouthpiece*), orator, spokesperson.

spear noun assegai, harpoon, javelin, lance, pike.

spearhead verb SEE **lead** verb.

special adjective 1 *a special occasion. a special visitor.* distinguished, exceptional, extraordinary, important, infrequent, momentous, notable, [*informal*] out-of-the-ordinary, rare, red-letter (*a red-letter day*), significant, uncommon, unusual.
OPPOSITES: SEE **ordinary**.
2 *Petrol has a special smell.* characteristic, distinctive, memorable, unique, unmistakable.
OPPOSITES: SEE **common** adjective.
3 *my special chair.* especial, individual, particular, personal.
4 *a special tool for cutting glass.* proper, specific, specialized, tailor-made.

specialist noun 1 *a science specialist. a specialist in antiques.* authority, connoisseur, expert, fancier (*a pigeon fancier*), professional, researcher.
2 *a medical specialist.* consultant.
MEDICAL SPECIALISTS: SEE **medicine**.

speciality noun *What's your speciality?* expertise, forte, [*informal*] line (*What's your line?*), special knowledge or skill, strength, strong point.

specialize verb **to specialize in** be a specialist in [SEE **specialist**], be best at, concentrate on, have a reputation for.

specialized adjective *specialized knowledge.* esoteric, expert, specialist, unfamiliar.
OPPOSITES: SEE **general**.

species noun *a species of animal.* breed, class, genus, kind, race, sort, type, variety.

specific adjective *I need specific information, not rumours.* clear-cut, definite, detailed, exact, explicit, particular, precise, special.
OPPOSITES: SEE **general**.

specify verb *Specify your requirements.* be specific about [SEE **specific**], define, detail, enumerate, identify, itemize, list,

name, particularize, [*informal*] spe out, stipulate.

specimen noun *a specimen of your han writing.* example, illustration, instanc model, pattern, representative, sampl

specious adjective *specious argument* SEE **misleading**.

speck noun *a speck of dirt.* bit, dot, flec grain, mark, mite, particle, speckl spot, trace.

speckled adjective *speckled with patch of colour.* blotchy, brindled, dapple dotted, flecked, freckled, mottle patchy, spotted, spotty, stippled.

spectacle noun *a colourful spectacle. th spectacle of a coronation.* ceremonia ceremony, colourfulness, displa' exhibition, extravaganza, grandeu magnificence, ostentation, pageantr parade, pomp, show, spectacular effec [SEE **spectacular**], splendour.
spectacles SEE **glass (glasses)**.

spectacular adjective *a spectaculc display.* SEE **beautiful**, breathtakin colourful, dramatic, elaborate, ey catching, impressive, magnificen [*uncomplimentary*] ostentatious, sens tional, showy, splendid, stunning.

spectator noun [*plural*] audience, b stander, [*plural*] crowd, eye-witnes looker-on, observer, onlooker, passe by, viewer, watcher, witness.

spectral adjective SEE **ghostly**.

spectre noun SEE **ghost**.

spectrum noun SEE **range** noun.

speculate verb 1 *We speculated as whether they would marry.* conjectur hypothesize, make guesses, reflect, su mise, theorize, wonder.
2 *He speculates on the stock exchang* gamble, hope to make profit, inve speculatively.

speculative adjective 1 *speculati rumours.* based on guesswork, conje tural, [*informal*] gossipy, hypothetica suppositional, theoretical, unfounde uninformed.
OPPOSITES: SEE **knowledgeable**.
2 *speculative investments.* chancy, [*formal*] dicey, [*informal*] dodgy, haza dous, [*informal*] iffy, risky, uncertai unpredictable, unsafe.
OPPOSITES: SEE **safe**.

speech noun 1 *clear speech.* articulatio communication, declamation, deliver elocution, enunciation, pronunciatio speaking, talking, using words, utte ance.
2 *a speech to an audience.* address, d course, disquisition, harangue, homil

ecture, oration, paper (*to give a paper*), resentation, sermon, [*informal*] spiel, alk.

3 *a speech in a play.* dialogue, lines, nonologue, soliloquy.

OTHER RELEVANT ENTRIES: **language, ay, speak, talk** noun, verb.

peechless adjective *speechless with age.* dumb, dumbfounded, dumbstruck, inarticulate, [*informal*] mum, nute, nonplussed, silent, thunder-truck, tongue-tied.

OPPOSITES: SEE **talkative**.

peed noun 1 *What speed were you going?*)ace, rate, tempo (*the tempo of a piece of nusic*), velocity.

2 *I was amazed by her speed.* alacrity, celerity, fleetness, haste, hurry, quickness, rapidity, swiftness.

peed verb 1 *We sped along.* [*informal*])elt, [*informal*] bolt, canter, career, dart, lash, flash, flit, fly, gallop, hasten, nurry, hurtle, move quickly, [*informal*] nip, [*informal*] put your foot down, race, run, rush, shoot, sprint, stampede, streak, tear, [*informal*] zoom.

2 *She was speeding when the police stopped ner.* break the speed limit, go too fast.

to speed up accelerate, go faster, increase speed, quicken, spurt.

peedway noun VARIOUS RACES: SEE **race** noun.

peedy adjective SEE **fast** adjective.

pell noun 1 *a magic spell.* bewitchment, charm, conjuration, conjuring, enchantment, incantation, magic formula, sorcery, witchcraft.

2 *the spell of the theatre.* allure, charm, fascination, glamour, magic.

3 *a spell of fine weather.* interval, period, ohase, season, session, stint, stretch, cerm, time, turn.

pell verb *The rain spelt disaster for the garden-party.* foretell, indicate, mean, signal, signify, suggest.

to spell out SEE **explain**.

pellbound adjective *spellbound by the music.* bewitched, captivated, charmed, enchanted, enthralled, entranced, fascinated, hypnotized, mesmerized, transported.

pend verb 1 *I spent all my money.* [*informal*] blue, consume, [*informal*] cough up, exhaust, [*informal*] fork out, fritter, [*informal*] get through, invest, [*informal*] lash out, pay out, [*informal*] shell out, [*informal*] splurge, squander.

2 *We spent all our time talking.* fill, occupy, pass, use up, waste.

pending noun *I must cut back on my spending.* SEE **expense**.

spendthrift noun big spender, prodigal, profligate, wasteful person [SEE **wasteful**], wastrel.
OPPOSITES: SEE **miser**.

spew verb SEE **vomit**.

sphere noun 1 ball, globe, orb, spheroid.
OTHER SHAPES: SEE **shape** noun.
2 *He's an expert in his own limited sphere.* area, department, domain, field, milieu, province, range, scope, subject, territory.

spherical adjective *a spherical object.* ball-shaped, globular, rotund, round, spheroidal.

spice noun 1 *spices used in cooking.* flavouring, piquancy, seasoning.

SOME COMMON SPICES: allspice, bayleaf, capsicum, cardamom, cassia, cayenne, chilli, cinnamon, cloves, coriander, curry powder, ginger, grains of paradise, juniper, mace, nutmeg, paprika, pepper, pimento, poppy seed, saffron, sesame, turmeric.

2 *Seeing exotic places adds spice to a holiday.* colour, excitement, interest, zest.

spicy adjective *a spicy smell. spicy food.* highly flavoured, hot, piquant, pungent, seasoned.

spiel noun SEE **speech**.

spike noun *He tore his jeans on a spike.* barb, nail, point, projection, prong, tine (*the tines of a fork*).

spike verb *to spike something with a pin.* SEE **pierce**.

spiky adjective SEE **prickly**.

spill verb 1 *to spill milk.* overturn, slop, splash about, tip over, upset.
2 *Milk spilled out of the bottle.* brim, flow, overflow, run, pour.
3 *The lorry spilled its load.* discharge, drop, scatter, shed, tip.

spin verb 1 *A wheel spins on an axle.* gyrate, pirouette, revolve, rotate, swirl, turn, twirl, twist, wheel, whirl.
2 *Alcohol makes my head spin.* reel, swim.

spindle noun axle, rod, shaft.

spindly adjective SEE **thin** adjective.

spine noun 1 backbone, spinal column, vertebrae.
OTHER BONES OF YOUR BODY: SEE **skeleton**.
2 *A hedgehog has sharp spines.* bristle, needle, point, quill, spike.

spine-chilling adjective SEE **frightening**.

spineless adjective *a spineless coward.* cowardly, faint-hearted, feeble, helpless, irresolute, [*informal*] soft, timid, unheroic, weak, weedy.
OPPOSITES: SEE **brave**.

spinnaker noun SEE **sail** noun.

spinney noun SEE **wood**.

spin-off noun SEE **by-product**.

spinster noun SEE **unmarried**.

spiny adjective SEE **prickly**.

spiral adjective coiled, turning.
OTHER CURVING SHAPES: SEE **curved**.

spiral noun coil, screw, whorl.

spiral verb SEE **twist** verb.

spire noun *a church spire.* pinnacle, steeple.
OTHER PARTS OF A CHURCH: SEE **church**.

spirit noun 1 *a person's spirit.* mind, psyche, soul.
OPPOSITES: SEE **body**.
2 *supernatural spirits.* apparition, [*informal*] bogy, demon, devil, genie, ghost, ghoul, gremlin, hobgoblin, imp, incubus, nymph, phantasm, phantom, poltergeist, [*poetic*] shade, shadow, spectre, [*informal*] spook, sprite, sylph, vision, visitant, wraith, zombie.
3 *It took some time to get into the spirit of the party.* atmosphere, essence, feeling, mood.
4 *The athletes had great spirit.* animation, bravery, cheerfulness, confidence, courage, daring, determination, energy, enthusiasm, fortitude, [*informal*] go, [*informal*] guts, heroism, morale, motivation, optimism, pluck, valour, verve, will-power.
5 *strong spirits.* SEE **alcohol**.

spirited adjective *a spirited performance. spirited opposition.* active, animated, assertive, brave, courageous, daring, energetic, frisky, gallant, intrepid, lively, plucky, positive, sparkling, sprightly, vigorous.
OPPOSITES: SEE **spiritless**.

spiritless adjective *a spiritless performance.* apathetic, cowardly, defeatist, despondent, dispirited, dull, lacklustre, languid, lifeless, listless, melancholy, negative, unenthusiastic.
OPPOSITES: SEE **spirited**.

spiritual adjective *Are spiritual or worldly values more important?* devotional, eternal, heavenly, holy, incorporeal, other-worldly, religious, sacred, unworldly.
OPPOSITES: SEE **physical**.

spirituous adjective SEE **alcoholic**.

spit noun 1 *spit dribbling down his face.* dribble, saliva, spittle, [*formal*] sputum.

2 *a spit of land.* SEE **promontory**.

spit verb *to spit something out.* eject, spew.

spite noun *They showed their spite by not co-operating.* animosity, animus, [*informal*] bitchiness, bitterness, [*informal*] cattiness, grudge, hate, hostility, ill-feeling, malevolence, malice, malignity, rancour, resentment, spleen, vindictiveness.

spiteful adjective *spiteful remarks.* acid, [*informal*] bitchy, bitter, [*informal*] catty, cruel, cutting, hateful, hostile, hurtful, ill-natured, malevolent, malicious, nasty, poisonous, rancorous, resentful, revengeful, sharp, [*informal*] snide, sour, venomous, vicious, vindictive.

spitfire noun SEE **angry (angry person)**.

spittle noun SEE **spit** noun.

splash verb 1 *The bus splashed water over us.* shower, slop, [*informal*] slosh, spatter, spill, splatter, spray, sprinkle, squirt, wash.
2 *We splashed about in the water.* bathe, dabble, paddle, wade.
3 *The news was splashed across the front page.* display, exhibit, flaunt, [*informal*] plaster, publicize, show.
to splash out SEE **spend**.

splash-down noun SEE **landing**.

splatter verb SEE **splash**.

splay verb *to splay your feet.* make a V shape, slant, spread.

spleen noun *He gave vent to his spleen.* SEE **spite**.

splendid adjective 1 *a splendid banquet. splendid clothes. splendid surroundings.* beautiful, brilliant, costly, dazzling, elegant, glittering, glorious, gorgeous, grand, great, handsome, imposing, impressive, lavish, luxurious, magnificent, majestic, marvellous, noble, ornate, palatial, [*informal*] posh, regal, resplendent, rich, royal, stately, sublime, sumptuous, [*informal*] super, superb, supreme, wonderful.
2 *splendid work.* admirable, excellent, first-class, SEE **good**.

splendour noun *Tourists love the splendour of a royal occasion.* brilliance, ceremony, display, glory, grandeur, magnificence, majesty, ostentation, pomp, richness, show, spectacle, stateliness, sumptuousness.

splice verb SEE **join** verb.

splinter noun *a splinter of wood.* chip, flake, fragment, shaving, [*plural*] shivers, sliver.

splinter verb *He splintered the door when he kicked it.* SEE **break** verb, chip, crack.

racture, shatter, shiver, smash, split.

lit noun 1 *a split in a tree. a split in my eans.* break, cleavage, cleft, crack, fissure. SEE **opening** noun, rent, rift, rupure, slash, slit, tear.
a split in a political party. a split in a narriage. breach, difference, dissension, divergence of opinion, division, livorce, estrangement, SEE **quarrel** noun, schism, separation.

lit verb 1 *We split into two teams.* break up, divide, separate.
The axe split the log. I split my jeans. urst, chop, cleave, crack, SEE **cut** verb, rend, rip open, slice, splinter, tear.
We split the profits. allocate, allot, apportion, distribute, divide, halve, share.
The roads split here. branch, diverge, ork.
[*informal*] *to split on your friends.* SEE nform (**inform against**).

litting adjective *a splitting headache.* SEE **painful**.

lotch noun SEE **mark** noun.

lurge verb SEE **spend**.

lutter verb VARIOUS SOUNDS: SEE sound noun.

oil verb 1 *Don't spoil that neat work. She spoilt her reputation.* blight, blot, blotch, oungle, damage, deface, destroy, disfigure, [*informal*] dish, harm, injure, [*informal*] make a mess of, mar, [*informal*] ness up, ruin, stain, undermine, undo, upset, vitiate, worsen, wreck.
OPPOSITES: SEE **improve**.
Soft fruit spoils quickly. become useless, decompose, go bad, go off, perish, outrefy, rot.
Grandad spoils the little ones. coddle, cosset, indulge, make a fuss of, mollycoddle, over-indulge, pamper.

oils noun *the spoils of war.* SEE **booty**.

oken adjective *Her spoken French is excellent.* oral, unwritten, verbal.
OPPOSITES: SEE **written**.

okesperson noun mouthpiece, representative, spokesman, spokeswoman.

onge verb 1 *to sponge down the car.* clean, mop, rinse, swill, wash, wipe.
2 [*informal*] *to sponge on your friends.* cadge (from), scrounge (from).

ongy adjective *spongy rubber.* absorbent, porous, soft, springy.
OPPOSITES: SEE **solid**.

onsor noun *Our team's sponsor donated the new equipment.* backer, benefactor, donor, patron, promoter.

onsor verb *to sponsor someone in a race. to sponsor an arts festival.* back, be a

sponsor of, finance, fund, help, promote, subsidize, support.

sponsorship noun *We were able to go ahead under the sponsorship of a local firm.* aegis, [*plural*] auspices, backing, benefaction, guarantee, patronage, promotion, support.

spontaneous adjective 1 *a spontaneous display of affection.* extempore, impromptu, impulsive, unconstrained, unforced, unplanned, unpremeditated, unprepared, unrehearsed, voluntary.
2 *a spontaneous reaction.* automatic, instinctive, involuntary, natural, reflex.
OPPOSITES: SEE **premeditated**.

spoof noun SEE **satire**.

spook noun SEE **ghost**.

spooky adjective [*informal*] *a spooky big house.* creepy, eerie, frightening, ghostly, haunted, mysterious, scary, uncanny, unearthly, weird.

spool noun *a spool of cotton.* bobbin, reel.

spoon noun dessert-spoon, ladle, tablespoon, teaspoon.
OTHER ITEMS OF CUTLERY: SEE **cutlery**.

spoon-feed verb cosset, help, indulge, mollycoddle, pamper, spoil.

spoor noun *an animal's spoor.* footprints, scent, traces, track.

sport noun 1 *Sport can help you keep healthy.* exercise, games, pastime, play, recreation.
2 *They were having a bit of sport at my expense.* amusement, diversion, entertainment, fun, joking, merriment, raillery, teasing.
blood sports beagling, fishing, hunting, shooting.

VARIOUS SPORTS: aerobics, American football, angling, archery, Association football, SEE **athletics**, badminton, baseball, basketball, billiards, bobsleigh, bowls, boxing, bullfighting, canoeing, climbing, cricket, croquet, crosscountry, curling.

darts, decathlon, discus, fishing, football, gliding, golf, gymnastics, hockey, hurdling, ice-hockey, javelin, jogging, keep-fit, lacrosse, marathon, SEE **martial (martial arts)**, mountaineering, netball, orienteering, pentathlon, [*informal*] ping-pong, polo, pool, pot-holing, quoits.

racing [SEE **race** noun], rock-climbing, roller-skating, rounders, rowing, Rugby, running, sailing, shot, showjumping, skating, skiing, skin-diving, sky-diving, snooker, soccer, sprinting, squash, street-hockey, surfing or surf-riding, SEE **swimming**, table-tennis, tennis, tobogganing, trampolining, volleyball, water-polo, water-skiing, windsurfing, SEE **winter sports**, wrestling, yachting.

PLACES WHERE SPORTS TAKE PLACE: arena, boxing-ring, circuit, course, court, field, golf-course, ground, gymnasium, ice-rink, links, pitch, playing-field, race-course, race-track, stadium.

sporting adjective *a sporting gesture.* considerate, fair, generous, honourable, sportsmanlike.

sportive adjective SEE **playful**.

sportsperson noun contestant, participant, player, sportsman, sportswoman.

sporty adjective SEE **athletic**.

spot noun 1 *a dirty spot on your clothing.* blemish, blot, blotch, discoloration, dot, fleck, mark, smudge, speck, speckle, stain.
2 *a spot on the skin.* birthmark, boil, freckle, impetigo [= *skin disease causing spots*], mole, naevus, pimple, rash [= *spots*], sty, whitlow.
3 *a spot of rain.* bead, blob, drop.
4 *a nice spot for a picnic.* locality, location, place, point, position, site, situation.
5 [*informal*] *I'd love a spot of tea.* SEE **small** (**small quantity**).
6 [*informal*] *I was in a bit of a spot.* SEE **difficulty**.

spot verb 1 *My overalls were spotted with paint.* blot, discolour, fleck, mark, mottle, smudge, spatter, speckle, stain.
2 *I spotted a rare bird.* SEE **see**.

spotless adjective 1 *spotless laundry.* SEE **clean** adjective, unmarked.
2 *a spotless reputation.* blameless, immaculate, innocent, irreproachable, pure, unblemished, unsullied, untarnished, [*informal*] whiter than white.

spotlight noun SEE **light** noun.

spotty adjective *a spotty face.* blotchy, freckled, mottled, pimply, speckled, spotted.

to **be spotty** erupt in spots, have a rash.

spouse noun [*joking*] better half, [*old-fashioned*] helpmate, husband, partner, wife.

spout noun *Water poured from the spout.* fountain, gargoyle, geyser, jet, lip (*of a jug*), nozzle, outlet, rose (*of a watering-can*), spray.

spout verb 1 *Water spouted through the hole.* discharge, erupt, flow, gush, jet, pour, shoot, spurt, squirt, stream.
2 [*informal*] *The lecturer spouted for hours.* SEE **talk** verb.

sprain verb *to sprain your ankle.* SE **wound** verb.

sprawl verb 1 *We sprawled on the law* flop, lean back, lie, loll, lounge, reclin relax, slouch, slump, spread out, stretc out.
2 *The village sprawled across the valley.* b scattered, spread, straggle.

spray noun 1 *a spray of water.* droplet: fountain, mist, shower, splash, sprinl ling.
2 *a spray of flowers.* arrangement, bo quet, branch, bunch, corsage, posy sprig.
3 *a paint spray.* aerosol, atomizer, spray gun, sprinkler.

spray verb *The bus sprayed mud over u* scatter, shower, spatter, splash, sprea in droplets, sprinkle.

spray-gun noun SEE **spray** noun.

spread noun [*informal*] *an appetizin spread.* SEE **meal**.

spread verb 1 *to spread things on a tabl* to spread out a map. arrange, display, la out, open out, unfold, unroll.
2 *The epidemic spread. The stain sprea* broaden, enlarge, expand, extend, ge bigger or longer or wider, lengther [*informal*] mushroom, proliferat widen.
3 *to spread butter.* apply, cover a surfac with.
4 *to spread news.* advertise, broadcas circulate, diffuse, disperse, dissemi ate, distribute, divulge, give out, mak known, pass on, pass round, proclain promulgate, publicize, publish, scatte transmit.

to **spread out** *to spread out in a line.* fa out, scatter, SEE **straggle**.

spree noun *to go out on a spree.* [*informa* binge, [*informal*] fling, [*informal*] org outing, SEE **revelry**.

sprightly adjective *a sprightly 90-yea old.* active, agile, animated, brisk, ene getic, lively, nimble, [*informal*] perk playful, quickmoving, spirited, spr vivacious.

OPPOSITES: SEE **lethargic**.

spring noun 1 *a clock's spring.* coil, mai spring.
2 *a spring in your step.* bounc buoyancy, elasticity, give, liveliness.
3 *a spring of water.* fount, fountai geyser, source (*of a river*), spa, well.

spring verb 1 *He sprang over the ga* bounce, bound, hop, jump, leap, pounc vault.
2 *Weeds sprang up.* appear, develo emerge, germinate, grow, shoot u sprout.

---

springy adjective bendy, elastic, flexible, pliable, resilient, spongy, stretchy, supple.
OPPOSITES: SEE **rigid**.

sprinkle verb *to sprinkle salt on food. to sprinkle water about.* drip, dust, pepper, scatter, shower, spatter, splash, spray, strew.

sprint verb SEE **run** verb.

sprite noun SEE **spirit**.

sprout noun *a sprout growing from a seed.* bud, shoot.

sprout verb *The seeds began to sprout.* bud, develop, emerge, germinate, grow, shoot up, spring up.

spruce adjective *He looked spruce in his best clothes.* clean, dapper, elegant, groomed, [*informal*] natty, neat, [*informal*] posh, smart, tidy, trim, well-dressed.
OPPOSITES: SEE **scruffy**.

spruce verb *to spruce yourself up.* SEE **tidy** verb.

spry adjective SEE **sprightly**.

spume noun SEE **froth** noun.

spunk noun SEE **courage**.

spur noun *Applause is a spur to greater effort.* encouragement, impetus, incentive, inducement, motive, prompting, stimulus.

spur verb *The applause spurred us to greater efforts.* egg on, encourage, incite, prick, prod, prompt, provide a spur [SEE **spur** noun], stimulate, urge.

spurious adjective SEE **false**.

spurn verb SEE **reject**.

spurt verb 1 *Water spurted from the hole.* SEE **squirt**.
2 *She spurted ahead.* SEE **speed** verb (**speed up**).

sputum noun dribble, saliva, spit, spittle.

spy noun *a spy working for the enemy.* contact, double agent, infiltrator, informer, mole, private detective, secret agent, snooper, undercover agent.

spy verb 1 *to spy for the enemy.* be a spy [SEE **spy** noun], be engaged in spying [SEE **spying**], eavesdrop, gather intelligence, inform, snoop.
2 *I spy with my little eye.* SEE **see**.

spying noun counter-espionage, detective work, eavesdropping, espionage, intelligence, snooping.

squab noun SEE **seat** noun.

squabble verb SEE **quarrel** verb.

squad, squadron nouns SEE **group** noun.

squalid adjective 1 *squalid surroundings.* dingy, dirty, disgusting, filthy, foul, mucky, nasty, poverty-stricken, repulsive, run-down, [*informal*] sleazy, slummy, sordid, ugly, uncared for, unpleasant, unsalubrious.
OPPOSITES: SEE **clean** adjective.
2 *squalid behaviour.* corrupt, degrading, dishonest, dishonourable, disreputable, immoral, scandalous, [*informal*] shabby, shameful, unethical.
OPPOSITES: SEE **honourable**.

squall noun SEE **storm** noun.

squally adjective SEE **stormy**.

squander verb *to squander your money.* [*informal*] blow, [*informal*] blue, dissipate, [*informal*] fritter, misuse, spend unwisely, [*informal*] splurge, use up, waste.
OPPOSITES: SEE **save**.

square adjective 1 *square corners.* right-angled.
2 *a square deal.* SEE **honest**.

square noun 1 SEE **shape** noun.
2 *a market square.* piazza, plaza.
3 [*informal*] *Don't be a square!* conformist, conservative, conventional person, die-hard, [*informal*] old fogy, [*informal*] stick-in-the-mud, traditionalist.
marked in squares chequered, crisscrossed.

square verb *to square an account.* SEE **settle** verb.

squash verb 1 *Don't squash the strawberries.* compress, crumple, crush, flatten, mangle, mash, pound, press, pulp, smash, stamp on, tread on.
2 *We all squashed into the room.* crowd, pack, squeeze.
3 *They squashed the uprising.* control, put down, quell, repress, suppress.
4 *She squashed him with a withering look.* humiliate, [*informal*] put down, silence, snub.

squashy adjective *squashy fruit.* mashed up, mushy, pulpy, shapeless, soft, spongy, squelchy, yielding.
OPPOSITES: SEE **firm** adjective.

squat adjective *a squat figure.* burly, dumpy, plump, podgy, short, stocky, thick, thickset.
OPPOSITES: SEE **slender**.

squat verb *to squat on the ground.* crouch, sit.

squawk, squeak, squeal nouns, verbs
VARIOUS SOUNDS: SEE **sound** noun.

squeamish adjective *squeamish about dirty things.* [*informal*] choosy, fastidious, finicky, particular, prim, [*informal*] prissy, scrupulous.

squeeze verb 1 *He squeezed my hand.* clasp, compress, crush, embrace, enfold, exert pressure on, grip, hug, pinch, press, squash, wring.
2 *They squeezed us into a little room.* cram, crowd, push, ram, shove, stuff, thrust, wedge.
to squeeze out *Squeeze out the last of the toothpaste.* expel, extrude, force out.

squelch verb VARIOUS SOUNDS: SEE **sound** noun.

squint verb 1 be cross-eyed, have a squint.
2 *I squinted through the keyhole.* SEE **look** verb.

squirm verb *The worm squirmed.* twist, wriggle, writhe.

squirt verb *Water squirted out. They squirted water at us.* ejaculate, gush, jet, send out, shoot, spit, spout, spray, spurt.

stab noun 1 *a stab with a dagger.* blow, jab, prick, thrust, wound, wounding.
2 *a stab of pain.* SEE **pain** noun, pang, sting, throb, twinge.
3 [*informal*] *Have a stab at it.* SEE **try** noun.

stab verb *to stab with a dagger.* bayonet, cut, injure, jab, SEE **pierce**, stick, thrust, wound.

stability noun balance, equilibrium, firmness, permanence, solidity, soundness, steadiness, strength.
OPPOSITES: SEE **instability**.

stabilize verb *to stabilize a ship. to stabilize a political regime.* balance, give stability to [SEE **stability**], keep upright, make stable [SEE **stable**], settle.
OPPOSITES: SEE **upset**.

stable adjective 1 *Make sure the tripod is stable.* balanced, firm, fixed, solid, sound, steady, strong.
2 *a stable relationship.* constant, continuing, durable, established, lasting, permanent, predictable, steadfast, unchanging, unwavering.
OPPOSITES: SEE **changeable**, unstable.

stack noun 1 *a stack of books.* heap, mound, mountain, pile, quantity.
2 *a stack of hay.* [*old-fashioned*] cock, haycock, rick, stook.
3 *a tall stack.* chimney, pillar.

stack verb *Stack the books on the table.* accumulate, assemble, build up, collect, gather, heap, load, mass, pile.

stadium noun arena, sports-ground.

staff noun 1 *She carried a staff as a sign of her authority.* cane, crosier, pole, rod, sceptre, stave, stick.

2 *the staff of a business.* assistants, crew, employees, personnel, officers, team, workers, workforce.

staff verb *The business is staffed by volunteers.* [*sexist*] man, provide with staff, run.

stag noun SEE **deer**.

stage noun 1 *the stage in a theatre.* apron, dais, performing area, platform, proscenium.
2 *a stage of a journey. a stage in your life.* juncture, leg, period, phase, point, time.

stage verb *to stage a play. to stage a demonstration.* arrange, [*informal*] get up, mount, organize, perform, present, produce, put on, set up, stage-manage.

stage-manage verb SEE **stage** verb.

stagger verb 1 *He staggered under the heavy load.* falter, lurch, reel, stumble, sway, totter, walk unsteadily, waver, wobble.
2 *The price staggered us.* alarm, amaze, astonish, astound, confuse, dismay, dumbfound, flabbergast, shake, shock, startle, stun, stupefy, surprise, worry.

stagnant adjective *stagnant water.* motionless, stale, standing, static, still.
OPPOSITE: flowing.

stagnate verb *to stagnate in the same job for years.* achieve nothing, become stale, deteriorate, idle, languish, stand still, stay still, vegetate.
OPPOSITES: SEE **progress** verb.

stagy adjective SEE **theatrical**.

staid adjective SEE **sedate** adjective.

stain noun 1 *What's that stain on your shirt?* blemish, blot, blotch, discoloration, mark, smear, spot.
2 *a wood stain.* colouring, paint, pigment, tint, varnish.

stain verb 1 *to stain something with dirty marks.* blacken, blemish, blot, contaminate, defile, dirty, discolour, make dirty, mark, smudge, soil, sully, taint, tarnish.
2 *to stain wood.* colour, dye, paint, tinge, tint, varnish.

stainless adjective 1 *a stainless reputation.* SEE **pure**.
2 *stainless steel.* rust-free.

stair noun *one stair at a time.* riser, step, tread.
stairs escalator, flight of stairs, staircase, stairway, steps.

stake noun 1 *a wooden stake.* paling, pile, pole, post, spike, stave, stick.
2 *the stake you risk when you gamble.* bet, pledge, wager.

stale adjective **1** *stale bread.* dry, hard, mouldy, old, tasteless.
2 *stale ideas.* hackneyed, out-of-date, overused, uninteresting, unoriginal, worn out.
OPPOSITES: SEE **fresh**.

stalemate noun *stalemate in negotiations.* deadlock, impasse, SEE **standstill**.

stalk noun *the stalk of a plant.* branch, shoot, stem, trunk, twig.

stalk verb **1** *The lion stalked its prey.* follow, hound, hunt, pursue, shadow, tail, track, trail.
2 *I stalked up and down.* prowl, rove, stride, strut, SEE **walk** verb.

stall noun **1** *a market stall.* booth, kiosk, stand.
2 *We sat in the stalls.* SEE **theatre**.

stall verb *Stop stalling!* delay, hang back, hesitate, pause, [*informal*] play for time, postpone, prevaricate, put off, stop, temporize.

stallion noun SEE **horse**.

stalwart adjective *stalwart supporters.* dependable, faithful, reliable, robust, staunch, strong, sturdy, tough, trustworthy, valiant.
OPPOSITES: SEE **feeble**.

stamina noun *I don't have the stamina to run long distances.* energy, resilience, staying-power.

stammer verb falter, splutter, stumble, stutter, SEE **talk** verb.

stamp noun **1** *an official stamp.* brand, hallmark, impression, imprint, mark, print, seal.
2 *a stamp on a letter.* franking, postage stamp.

stamp verb **1** *to stamp your foot.* bring down, strike, thump.
2 *to stamp a mark on something.* brand, engrave, impress, imprint, mark, print.
to stamp on *to stamp on a cigarette stub.* crush, trample, tread on.
to stamp out *to stamp out crime.* eliminate, end, eradicate, extinguish, put an end to, [*informal*] scotch, suppress.

stamp-collecting noun philately.

stampede noun *a stampede towards the exit.* charge, dash, rout, rush, sprint.

stampede verb *The cattle stampeded.* bolt, career, charge, dash, gallop, panic, run, rush, sprint, tear.

stance noun SEE **posture**.

stanch verb SEE **stop** verb.

stanchion noun SEE **pillar**.

stand noun **1** *a stand to put something on.* base, pedestal, rack, support, tripod, trivet.
2 *a newspaper stand.* booth, kiosk, stall.
3 *a stand for spectators.* grandstand, terraces.

stand verb **1** *Stand when the visitor comes.* get to your feet, get up, rise.
2 *A tree stands by our gate.* be, be situated, exist.
3 *They stood the monument on a hill.* erect, locate, position, put up, set up, situate, station.
4 *I stood my books on a shelf.* arrange, deposit, place, set upright.
5 *My offer still stands.* be unchanged, continue, remain valid, stay.
6 *I can't stand smoking in the house.* abide, bear, endure, put up with, suffer, tolerate, [*informal*] wear.
to stand by *She stood by her friends.* adhere to, be faithful to, stay with, stick to, support.
to stand for *What do your initials stand for?* be a sign for, denote, indicate, mean, represent, signify, symbolize.
to stand in for *She stood in for the regular teacher.* be a substitute for [SEE **substitute** noun], cover for, deputize for, replace, substitute for, take over from, understudy.
to stand out *He stands out in a crowd.* be obvious, be prominent, catch the eye, show, stick out.
to stand up for *Stand up for yourself.* champion, defend, fight for, help, look after, protect, shield, side with, speak up for, support.
to stand up to *They bravely stood up to the attack.* clash with, confront, defy, face up to, oppose, resist, withstand.

standard adjective *a standard procedure. a standard size.* accepted, accustomed, approved, average, basic, common, conventional, customary, established, everyday, familiar, habitual, normal, official, ordinary, orthodox, popular, recognized, regular, routine, set, staple (*a staple diet*), typical, usual.
OPPOSITES: SEE **abnormal**.

standard noun **1** *a high standard.* achievement, benchmark, criterion, example, gauge, grade, guideline, ideal, level, measure, measurement, model, norm, pattern, rule, sample, specification, touchstone, yardstick.
2 *the standard of a regiment.* banner, colours, ensign, flag, pennant.
standards *Have you no standards?* SEE **morality**.

standardize verb *Standardize your results. Standardize the presentation of your work.* average out, conform to a standard, equalize, normalize, regiment, stereotype.

stand-in noun SEE **substitute** noun.

standing noun SEE **status**.

standoffish adjective SEE **unfriendly**.

standpoint noun *Can you understand my standpoint?* angle, attitude, belief, opinion, perspective, point of view, position, stance, vantage-point, view, viewpoint.

standstill noun *We came to a standstill.* [*informal*] dead end, deadlock, halt, [*informal*] hold-up, impasse, stalemate, stop, stoppage.

stanza noun SEE **verse**.

staple adjective *our staple diet.* chief, main, principal, SEE **standard** adjective.

staple noun, verb SEE **fasten, fastener**.

star noun 1 asteroid, lodestar, nova, shooting star, sun, supernova.
RELATED ADJECTIVES: astral, stellar.
OTHER ASTRONOMICAL TERMS: SEE astronomy.
2 *the shape of a star.* asterisk, pentagram.
3 *a TV star.* attraction, big name, celebrity, [*informal*] draw, idol, SEE performer, starlet, superstar.

starboard adjective *starboard side of a ship.* right-hand (when facing forward).
OPPOSITE: port.

starch noun *starch in food.* carbohydrate.

starchy adjective [*informal*], *Don't be so starchy.* aloof, conventional, formal, prim, stiff, SEE **unfriendly**.

stare verb *Why are you staring?* gape, gaze, glare, goggle, look fixedly, peer.
to stare at contemplate, examine, eye, scrutinize, study, watch.

stark adjective 1 *a stark prospect.* SEE **grim**.
2 *a stark contrast.* SEE **absolute**.

starlight noun SEE **light** noun.

starry adjective *a starry sky.* clear, glittering, star-filled, twinkling.
OPPOSITE: starless.

starry-eyed adjective SEE **romantic**.

start noun 1 *the start of something new.* beginning, birth, commencement, creation, dawn, establishment, inauguration, inception, initiation, institution, introduction, launch, onset, opening.
OPPOSITES: SEE **finish** noun.
2 *the start of a journey.* point of departure, setting out.
3 *Having a rich mother gave her a start in life.* advantage, opportunity.
4 *The explosion gave me a nasty start.* jump, shock, surprise.
to give someone a start SEE **startle**.

start verb 1 *to start something new.* activate, begin, commence, create, embark on, engender, establish, found, [*informal*] get cracking on, give birth to, inaugurate, initiate, instigate, institute, introduce, launch, open, originate, pioneer, set up.
OPPOSITES: SEE **finish** verb.
2 *The train is ready to start.* depart, [*informal*] get going, leave, move off, set off, set out.
OPPOSITES: SEE **stop** verb.
3 *I started when the gun went off.* blench, flinch, jerk, jump, recoil, spring up, twitch, wince.
to make someone start SEE **startle**.

startle verb *The explosion startled us.* agitate, alarm, catch unawares, frighten, give you a start, jolt, make you start, scare, shake, shock, surprise, take by surprise, upset.
OPPOSITES: SEE **calm** verb.

startling adjective SEE **surprising**.

starvation noun *dying of starvation.* deprivation, famine, hunger, malnutrition, undernourishment, want.
OPPOSITES: SEE **overeating, plenty**.

starve verb *Many starved in the drought.* die of starvation [SEE **starvation**], go hungry, go without, perish.
to starve yourself diet, fast, go on hunger strike, refuse food.
OPPOSITES: SEE **overeat**.

starving adjective *starving refugees.* emaciated, famished, hungry, ravenous, starved, underfed, undernourished.

state noun 1 *in an excellent state.* [*plural*] circumstances, condition, fitness, health, mood, situation.
2 [*informal*] *He was in such a state!* agitation, excitement, [*informal*] flap, panic, plight, predicament, [*informal*] tizzy.
3 *a sovereign state.* SEE **country**, nation.

state verb *to state the obvious.* affirm, announce, assert, communicate, declare, express, formulate, proclaim, put into words, report, say, SEE **speak**, submit, voice.

stately adjective *a stately ceremony.* dignified, elegant, formal, grand, imposing, impressive, majestic, noble, pompous, regal, royal, solemn, splendid.
OPPOSITES: SEE **informal**.
a stately home SEE **palace**.

statement noun *an official statement.* account, announcement, assertion, bulletin, comment, communication, communiqué, declaration, explanation, message, notice, proclamation, proposition, report, testament, testimony, utterance.

stateroom noun VARIOUS ROOMS: SEE room.

statesman noun diplomat, politician.

static adjective **1** *a static caravan.* fixed, immobile, motionless, SEE **stationary**, still, unmoving.
OPPOSITES: SEE **mobile**.
2 *static sales figures.* constant, invariable, stable, stagnant, steady, unchanging.
OPPOSITES: SEE **variable**.

station noun **1** *your station in life.* calling, class, employment, occupation, place, position, post, rank, situation, standing, status.
2 *a fire station. a police station.* base, depot, headquarters, office.
3 *a radio station.* channel, company, transmitter, wavelength.
4 *a railway station.* halt, platform, stopping-place, terminus.

station verb *We stationed a look-out on the roof.* assign, garrison, locate, place, position, put, situate, stand.

stationary adjective *stationary cars.* at a standstill, at rest, halted, immobile, immovable, motionless, parked, standing, static, still, stock-still, unmoving.
OPPOSITES: SEE **moving**.

Notice the difference in spelling between *stationary* and *stationery*.

stationery noun paper, writing materials.
WRITING MATERIALS: SEE **write**.

statistics noun data, figures, information, numbers.

statue noun SEE **sculpture** noun.

statuesque adjective *a statuesque figure.* dignified, elegant, poised, stately, upright.

stature noun **1** *a woman of average stature.* build, height, size, tallness.
2 *a politician of international stature.* esteem, greatness, importance, prominence, recognition, significance, SEE **status**.

status noun *your status in society or in your job.* class, degree, eminence, grade, importance, level, position, prestige, rank, standing, title.

statute noun SEE **law**.

staunch adjective *a staunch supporter.* constant, dependable, faithful, firm, loyal, reliable, sound, stalwart, steadfast, strong, true, trustworthy, unswerving.
OPPOSITES: SEE **unreliable**.

stave verb to stave off SEE **avert**.

stay noun **1** *a stay in a hotel.* holiday, [old-fashioned] sojourn, stop, visit.
2 [= *a support*] SEE **support** noun.

stay verb **1** *to stay in one place.* [old-fashioned] abide, carry on, continue, endure, [informal] hang about, hold out, keep on, last, linger, live on, loiter, persist, remain, survive, [old-fashioned] tarry, wait.
OPPOSITES: SEE **depart**.
2 *to stay in a hotel.* be accommodated, be a guest, be housed, board, dwell, live, lodge, reside, settle, [old-fashioned] sojourn, stop, visit.
3 *to stay judgement.* SEE **postpone**.

steadfast adjective *steadfast support.* committed, constant, dedicated, dependable, faithful, firm, loyal, patient, persevering, reliable, resolute, staunch, steady, unchanging, unfaltering, unflinching, unswerving, unwavering.
OPPOSITES: SEE **unreliable**.

steady adjective **1** *Is the ladder steady? Baby isn't steady on her feet yet.* balanced, confident, fast, firm, immovable, poised, safe, secure, settled, solid, stable.
2 *a steady supply of water.* ceaseless, consistent, constant, continuous, dependable, incessant, non-stop, regular, reliable, uninterrupted.
3 *a steady rhythm.* even, invariable, regular, repeated, rhythmic, smooth, unbroken, unchanging, uniform, unhurried, unremitting, unvarying.
4 *a steady friend.* devoted, faithful, loyal, serious, SEE **steadfast**.
OPPOSITES: SEE **unsteady**.

steady verb *to steady a rocking boat.* balance, hold, secure, stabilize.

steal verb **1** *to steal someone's property.* appropriate, burgle, embezzle, [informal] filch, hijack, [informal] knock off, [informal] lift, loot, [informal] make off with, misappropriate, [informal] nick, pick someone's pocket, pilfer, pillage, [informal] pinch, pirate, plagiarize [= *to steal someone else's ideas*], plunder, poach, purloin, [informal] rip someone off, rob, shop-lift, [informal] sneak, [informal] snitch, [informal] swipe, take, thieve, walk off with.
SEE ALSO: **stealing**.
2 *I stole quietly upstairs.* creep, move stealthily, slink, sneak, tiptoe, SEE **walk** verb.

stealing noun VARIOUS KINDS OF STEALING: burglary, embezzlement, fraud,

hijacking, housebreaking, larceny, looting, misappropriation, mugging, [*formal*] peculation, pilfering, pillage, piracy, plagiarism [= *stealing someone else's ideas*], plundering, purloining, robbery, scrumping, shop-lifting, theft, thieving.
OTHER CRIMES: SEE **crime**.

stealthy adjective *stealthy movements*. concealed, covert, disguised, furtive, inconspicuous, quiet, secret, secretive, [*informal*] shifty, sly, sneaky, surreptitious, underhand, unobtrusive.
OPPOSITES: SEE **blatant**.

steam noun condensation, haze, mist, smoke, vapour.

steamy adjective 1 *steamy windows*. cloudy, hazy, misty.
2 *a steamy atmosphere*. close, damp, humid, moist, muggy, sultry, sweaty.

steed noun SEE **horse**.

steel noun OTHER METALS: SEE **metal**.

steep adjective 1 *a steep cliff. a steep rise.* abrupt, headlong, precipitous, sharp, sheer, sudden, vertical.
OPPOSITES: SEE **gradual**.
2 *steep prices*. SEE **exorbitant**.

steep verb *to steep in liquid*. SEE **soak**.

steeple noun spire.
OTHER PARTS OF A CHURCH: SEE **church**.

steeple-chase noun OTHER RACES: SEE **race** noun.

steer noun SEE **cattle**.

steer verb *to steer a vehicle*. be at the wheel of, control, direct, drive, guide, navigate, pilot.
to steer clear of SEE **avoid**.

steersman noun SEE **helmsman**.

stem noun *the stem of a plant*. shoot, stalk, trunk, twig.

stem verb *to stem the flow of blood from a wound*. SEE **check**.

stench noun SEE **smell** noun.

stencil noun print.

stenographer noun SEE **secretary**.

stentorian adjective SEE **loud**.

step noun 1 *I took a step forward*. footstep, pace, stride.
2 *a step into the unknown*. advance, movement, progress, progression.
3 *She explained the next step in the process*. action, manœuvre, measure, phase, stage.
4 *I stood on the step*. doorstep, rung, stair, tread (*the treads of a staircase*).
steps ladder, staircase, stairs, stepladder.

step verb *Don't step in the mud!* put your foot, stamp, trample, tread, SEE **walk** verb.
to step in *The boss stepped in to sort things out*. SEE **intervene**.
to step on it SEE **hurry** verb.
to step up *They stepped up the pressure*. SEE **increase** verb.

stepchild, step-parent FAMILY RELATIONSHIPS: SEE **family**.

step-ladder noun steps.

steppe noun SEE **plain** noun.

stepping-stone noun SEE **crossing**.

stereo adjective stereophonic.
OPPOSITES: mono, monophonic.

stereo noun SEE **audio equipment**.

stereoscopic adjective solid-looking, three-dimensional, [*informal*] 3-D.
OPPOSITE: two-dimensional.

stereotype noun *He's my stereotype of a schoolteacher*. formula, model, pattern, stereotyped idea [SEE **stereotyped**].

stereotyped adjective *a stereotyped character in a play*. clichéd, conventional, hackneyed, predictable, standard, standardized, stock, typecast, unoriginal.
OPPOSITES: SEE **individual** adjective.

sterile adjective 1 *sterile soil*. arid, barren, dry, infertile, lifeless, unproductive.
OPPOSITES: SEE **fertile**.
2 *sterile bandages*. antiseptic, aseptic, clean, disinfected, germ-free, hygienic, sterilized, uninfected.
OPPOSITES: SEE **infected**, unsterilized.
3 *a sterile attempt to reach agreement*. abortive, fruitless, hopeless, pointless, unfruitful, unprofitable, useless.
OPPOSITES: SEE **fruitful**.

sterilize verb 1 *to sterilize medical equipment. to sterilize food*. clean, decontaminate, disinfect, fumigate, make sterile [SEE **sterile**], pasteurize, purify.
OPPOSITES: SEE **infect**.
2 *to sterilize animals so that they cannot reproduce*. castrate, geld, neuter, perform a vasectomy, spay.

sterilized adjective *sterilized bandages*. SEE **sterile**.

sterling adjective 1 *sterling silver*. SEE **genuine**.
2 *sterling qualities*. SEE **excellent**.

sterling noun SEE **money**.

stern adjective *a stern rebuke. a stern disciplinarian*. austere, authoritarian, dour, forbidding, grim, hard, harsh, inflexible, rigid, rigorous, severe, strict, unbending, unrelenting.
OPPOSITES: SEE **lenient**.

stern noun *the stern of a ship.* aft, back, rear end.

stertorous adjective SEE **harsh**.

stevedore noun docker.

stew noun *stew for dinner.* casserole, goulash, hash, hot-pot, ragout.

stew verb *to stew meat.* boil, braise, casserole, simmer.
OTHER WAYS TO COOK: SEE **cook** verb.

steward, stewardess nouns 1 *a steward on a ship.* attendant, SEE **servant**, waiter.
2 *a steward at a racecourse.* marshal, officer, official.

stick noun *dry sticks used for firewood.* branch, stalk, twig.
VARIOUS KINDS OF STICK: bar, baton, cane, club, hockey-stick, pole, rod, staff, walking-stick, wand.

stick verb 1 *to stick a pin in. to stick someone in the ribs.* dig, jab, poke, prod, punch, puncture, stab, thrust.
2 *to stick something with glue. to stick together.* adhere, affix, agglutinate, bind, bond, cement, cling, coagulate, SEE **fasten**, fuse together, glue, weld.
3 *His head stuck between the railings.* become trapped, jam, wedge.
4 [*informal*] *I can't stick snobs.* SEE **tolerate**.
to stick at [*informal*] *Stick at it!* SEE **persevere**.
to stick in *The pin won't stick in.* go in, pass through, penetrate, pierce.
to stick out *A shelf stuck out above my head.* jut, overhang, project, protrude.
to stick up *The spire sticks up above the trees.* loom, rise, stand out, tower.
to stick up for SEE **defend**.

sticker noun SEE **label** noun.

sticky adjective 1 *sticky tape.* adhesive, glued, gummed, self-adhesive.
OPPOSITE: non-adhesive.
2 *sticky fingers.* gluey, [*informal*] gooey, gummy, tacky.
OPPOSITES: SEE **clean** adjective.
3 *a sticky atmosphere.* clammy, damp, dank, humid, moist, muggy, steamy, sultry, sweaty.
OPPOSITES: SEE **dry** adjective.

stiff adjective 1 *stiff cardboard. stiff clay.* firm, hard, heavy, inflexible, rigid, solid, solidified, thick, unbending, unyielding, viscous.
OPPOSITES: SEE **soft**.
2 *stiff joints.* arthritic, immovable, painful, paralysed, rheumatic, taut, tight.
OPPOSITES: SEE **supple**.
3 *a stiff task. stiff opposition.* arduous, difficult, exacting, hard, laborious,

powerful, severe, strong, stubborn, tiring, tough, uphill.
OPPOSITES: SEE **easy**.
4 *a stiff manner.* awkward, clumsy, cold, formal, graceless, inelegant, starchy, stilted, tense, ungainly, unnatural, wooden.
OPPOSITES: SEE **relaxed**.
5 *a stiff penalty.* excessive, harsh, merciless, pitiless, relentless, rigorous, strict.
OPPOSITES: SEE **lenient**.
6 *a stiff breeze.* brisk, fresh, strong.
OPPOSITES: SEE **gentle**.

stiffen verb become stiff [SEE **stiff**], congeal, harden, set, solidify, thicken, tighten.

stiff-necked adjective SEE **obstinate**.

stifle verb 1 *The heat stifled us.* asphyxiate, choke, smother, strangle, suffocate, throttle.
2 *We stifled our laughter.* check, curb, dampen, deaden, muffle, repress, restrain, silence, stop, suppress.

stifling adjective SEE **stuffy**.

stigma noun *the stigma of prison.* blot, disgrace, dishonour, reproach, shame, slur, stain.

stigmata plural noun SEE **mark** noun.

stigmatize verb *He was stigmatized as an ex-convict.* brand, condemn, label, mark, pillory, vilify.

stiletto noun SEE **dagger**.

still adjective 1 *a still evening.* calm, hushed, noiseless, peaceful, placid, quiet, restful, serene, silent, tranquil, untroubled, windless.
OPPOSITES: SEE **stormy, troubled**.
2 *Keep still!* immobile, inert, lifeless, motionless, stagnant (*stagnant water*), static, stationary, unmoving.
OPPOSITES: SEE **moving**.
3 *still drinks.* flat.
OPPOSITES: SEE **fizzy**.

still verb *She stilled my fears. He stilled the audience by raising his hand.* allay, appease, calm, lull, make still [SEE **still** adjective], pacify, quieten, settle, silence, soothe, subdue, tranquillize.
OPPOSITES: SEE **agitate**.

stillborn adjective SEE **abortive**.

stilt noun SEE **pole**.

stilted adjective *stilted language.* SEE **formal**.

stimulant noun VARIOUS DRUGS: SEE **drug** noun.

stimulate verb *to stimulate interest. to stimulate people to greater effort.* activate, arouse, encourage, excite, fan, fire, foment, galvanize, goad, incite, inflame, inspire, invigorate, prompt, provoke,

quicken, rouse, spur, stir up, titillate, urge, whet.
OPPOSITES: SEE **discourage**.

stimulating adjective *a stimulating discussion. stimulating company.* challenging, exciting, exhilarating, inspiring, interesting, intoxicating, invigorating, provoking, rousing, stirring, thought-provoking.
OPPOSITES: SEE **boring**.

stimulus noun *a stimulus to greater effort.* encouragement, fillip, goad, incentive, inducement, inspiration, prompting, provocation, spur.
OPPOSITES: SEE **discouragement**.

sting noun 1 *a wasp sting.* SEE **wound** noun.
2 *the sting of acid in a wound.* SEE **pain** noun.

sting verb 1 *Some insects can sting you.* bite, nip, SEE **wound** verb.
2 *The salt water stings.* SEE **hurt** verb, smart, tingle.

stingy adjective 1 *a stingy miser.* avaricious, cheese-paring, close, close-fisted, covetous, mean, mingy, miserly, niggardly, parsimonious, penny-pinching, tight-fisted, ungenerous.
OPPOSITES: SEE **generous**.
2 *stingy helpings.* inadequate, insufficient, meagre, [*informal*] measly, scanty, SEE **small**.
OPPOSITES: SEE **big**.

stink noun, verb SEE **smell** noun, verb.

stipulate verb SEE **insist (insist on)**.

stipulation noun SEE **condition**.

stir noun *The news caused quite a stir.* SEE **commotion**.

stir verb 1 *Stir yourself!* SEE **move** verb.
2 *Stir the ingredients thoroughly.* agitate, beat, blend, mix, whisk.
3 *The music stirred us.* affect, arouse, challenge, electrify, excite, exhilarate, fire, impress, inspire, move, rouse, stimulate, touch.
to stir up *Don't stir up any trouble!* awaken, cause, incite, instigate, kindle, provoke, set off.

stirring adjective *stirring music. a stirring speech.* affecting, dramatic, emotional, exciting, heady, impassioned, moving, rousing, spirited, stimulating, thrilling.
OPPOSITES: SEE **boring**.

stitch verb *to stitch a hole in your jeans.* darn, mend, repair, sew, tack.

stoat noun ermine.

stock adjective *a stock response.* accustomed, common, conventional, customary, expected, ordinary, predictable, regular, set, standard, staple, stereotyped, traditional, unoriginal, usual.
OPPOSITES: SEE **unexpected**.

stock noun 1 *a stock of provisions.* hoard, reserve, reservoir, stockpile, store, supply.
2 *the stock in a shop.* commodities, goods, merchandise, wares.
3 *the stock on a cattle farm.* animals, beasts, cattle, flocks, herds, livestock.
4 *descended from ancient stock.* ancestry, blood, breed, descent, extraction, family, forebears, line, lineage, parentage.
5 *We boiled bones to make stock.* broth, soup.
out of stock sold out, unavailable.

stock verb *The local shop stocks most things.* deal in, handle, [*informal*] keep, keep in stock, provide, sell, supply, trade in.

stockade noun fence, paling, palisade, wall.

stockings noun nylons, panti-hose, socks, tights.

stockist noun merchant, retailer, shopkeeper, supplier.

stockpile noun, verb SEE **store** noun, verb.

stock-pot noun SEE **saucepan**.

stockroom noun SEE **storehouse**.

stock-still adjective SEE **motionless**.

stocky adjective *a stocky figure.* compact, dumpy, short, solid, squat, stubby, sturdy, thickset.
OPPOSITES: SEE **thin** adjective.

stodgy adjective 1 *stodgy food.* filling, heavy, indigestible, lumpy, soggy, solid, starchy.
OPPOSITES: SEE **appetizing**.
2 *a stodgy lecture.* boring, dull, [*informal*] stuffy, tedious, turgid, unexciting, unimaginative, uninteresting.
OPPOSITES: SEE **lively**.

stoical adjective *a stoical response to pain.* calm, impassive, imperturbable, long-suffering, patient, philosophical, phlegmatic, resigned, stolid, uncomplaining.
OPPOSITES: SEE **excitable**.

stoke verb *to stoke a fire.* fuel, keep burning, mend, put fuel on, tend.

stole noun cape, shawl, wrap.

stolid adjective *a dependable, stolid member of the team.* heavy, impassive, SEE **stoical**, unemotional, unexciting, unimaginative, wooden.
OPPOSITES: SEE **lively**.

stomach noun abdomen, belly, [*informal*] guts, [*informal*] insides, [*uncomplimentary*] paunch, [*informal*] tummy.
OTHER PARTS OF YOUR BODY: SEE **body**.

stomach verb *I can't stomach any more of this drivel.* SEE **tolerate**.

stomach-ache noun colic, [*informal*] colly-wobbles, [*childish*] tummy-ache.

stomp verb SEE **walk** verb.

stone noun 1 *stones on the beach.* boulder, cobble, [*plural*] gravel, pebble, rock, [*plural*] scree.
KINDS OF STONE: SEE **rock** noun.
2 *stones used by builders.* block, flagstone, sett, slab.
3 *a stone to commemorate the fallen.* memorial, monolith, obelisk.
4 *a precious stone.* gem, SEE **jewel**.
5 *a plum stone.* pip, seed.

stone verb *to stone someone.* SEE **execute**.

stonewall verb SEE **obstruct**.

stony adjective 1 *a stony beach.* pebbly, rocky, rough, shingly.
2 *a stony silence. a stony response.* cold, expressionless, frigid, hard, heartless, hostile, icy, indifferent, pitiless, steely, stony-hearted, uncaring, unemotional, unfeeling, unforgiving, unfriendly, unresponsive.
OPPOSITES: SEE **emotional**.

stooge noun butt, dupe, [*informal*] fall-guy, lackey, puppet.

stook noun SEE **stack** noun.

stool noun SEE **seat** noun.

stool-pigeon noun SEE **decoy** noun.

stoop verb 1 *I stooped to go under the barrier.* bend, bow, crouch, duck, hunch your shoulders, kneel, lean, squat.
2 *She wouldn't stoop to be seen with the likes of us.* condescend, deign, lower yourself, sink.

stop noun 1 *Everything came to a stop.* cessation, conclusion, end, finish, halt, shut-down, standstill, stoppage, termination.
2 *a stop on a journey.* break, destination, pause, resting-place, station, stopover, terminus.
3 *a stop at a hotel.* [*old-fashioned*] sojourn, stay, visit.

stop verb 1 *to stop what you are doing.* break off, call a halt to, cease, conclude, cut off, desist from, discontinue, ·end, finish, [*informal*] knock off, leave· off, [*informal*] pack in, pause, quit, refrain from, rest from, suspend, terminate.
OPPOSITES: SEE **start** verb.
2 *to stop traffic. to stop something happening.* bar, block, check, curb, delay, frustrate, halt, hamper, hinder, immobilize,

impede, intercept, interrupt, [*informal*] nip in the bud, obstruct, put a stop to, stanch or staunch, stem.
3 *to stop in a hotel.* be a guest, have a holiday, [*old-fashioned*] sojourn, spend time, stay, visit.
4 *to stop a gap.* [*informal*] bung up, close, fill in, plug, seal.
5 *Wait for the bus to stop.* come to rest, draw up, halt, pull up.
6 *Stop the thief!* arrest, capture, catch, detain, hold, seize.

stop-cock noun SEE **tap** noun.

stopgap noun SEE **substitute** noun.

stoppage noun SEE **stop** noun.

stopper noun *a stopper in a bottle.* bung, cork, plug.

stopping noun *a stopping in a tooth.* filling.

storage noun SEE **storehouse**.

store noun 1 *a store of supplies.* accumulation, cache, fund, hoard, quantity, reserve, reservoir, stock, stockpile, SEE **storehouse**, supply.
2 *a grocery store.* outlet, retail business, retailers, SEE **shop**, supermarket.

store verb *to store food for future use.* accumulate, deposit, hoard, keep, lay by, lay up, preserve, put away, reserve, save, set aside, [*informal*] stash away, stockpile, stock up, stow away.

storehouse noun PLACES TO STORE THINGS: armoury, arsenal, barn, cellar, cold-storage, depot, granary, larder, pantry, repository, safe, silo, stock-room, storage, store-room, strong-room, treasury, vault, warehouse.

storey noun [Don't confuse with *story.*] *a building with six storeys.* deck, floor, level, stage, tier.

storm noun 1 *The forecast predicts a storm.* disturbance, onslaught, outbreak, stormy weather [SEE **stormy**], tempest, tumult, turbulence.
OPPOSITES: SEE **calm** noun.
2 *a storm of protest.* SEE **clamour** noun.

KINDS OF STORM: blizzard, cyclone, deluge, dust-storm, gale, hurricane, rainstorm, sandstorm, squall, thunderstorm, tornado, typhoon, whirlwind.

METEOROLOGICAL TERMS: SEE **weather** noun.

---

storm verb *The army stormed the castle.* SEE **attack** verb.

stormy adjective *stormy seas. stormy weather.* angry, blustery, choppy, gusty, raging, rough, squally, tempestuous,

thundery, tumultuous, turbulent, violent, wild, windy.
OPPOSITES: SEE **calm** adjective.

story noun 1 *the story of my life. Tell me a story.* account, chronicle, fiction, history, narration, narrative, plot, scenario, tale, yarn.
2 *a story in a newspaper.* article, [*informal*] exclusive, feature, news item, report.
3 [*informal*] *Don't tell stories.* falsehood, [*informal*] fib, lie, untruth.

VARIOUS KINDS OF STORY: anecdote, children's story, crime story, detective story, fable, fairy-tale, fantasy, folktale, legend, mystery, myth, novel, parable, romance, saga, science fiction or SF, thriller, [*informal*] whodunit.

OTHER KINDS OF WRITING: SEE **writing**.

---

storyteller noun author, narrator, raconteur, teller.

stoup noun SEE **basin**.

stout adjective 1 *stout rope.* reliable, robust, sound, strong, sturdy, substantial, thick, tough.
OPPOSITES: SEE **weak**.
2 *a stout person.* [*informal*] beefy, [*informal*] chubby, SEE **fat** adjective, heavy, overweight, plump, portly, solid, stocky, tubby, well-built.
OPPOSITES: SEE **thin** adjective.
3 *a stout fighter.* bold, brave, courageous, fearless, gallant, heroic, intrepid, plucky, resolute, spirited, valiant.
OPPOSITES: SEE **cowardly**.

stove noun boiler, cooker, fire, furnace, heater, oven, range.

stow verb 1 *I stow unwanted things in the attic.* SEE **store** verb.
2 *Stow the luggage in the car.* SEE **load** verb.

stowaway noun SEE **traveller**.

straddle verb *The bridge straddles the river.* SEE **span** verb.

strafe verb SEE **bombard**.

straggle verb *Some of the runners straggled behind.* dawdle, fall behind, lag, loiter, ramble, scatter, spread out, stray, string out, trail, wander.

straggling adjective *a straggling village.* disorganized, rambling, scattered, spread out.
OPPOSITES: SEE **compact** adjective.

straight adjective [Do not confuse with *strait.*] 1 *a straight line. a straight road.* aligned, direct, smooth, undeviating, unswerving.
OPPOSITES: SEE **crooked**.

2 *Put the room straight.* neat, orderly, organized, right, [*informal*] shipshape, tidy.
OPPOSITES: SEE **untidy**.
3 *a straight sequence.* consecutive, continuous, non-stop, perfect, sustained, unbroken, uninterrupted, unrelieved.
4 *straight talking.* SEE **straightforward**.
straight away at once, directly, immediately, instantly, now, without delay.

straighten verb **to straighten out** disentangle, make straight, sort out, SEE **tidy** verb, unbend, untwist.

straightforward adjective *straightforward talk. a straightforward person.* blunt, candid, direct, easy, forthright, frank, genuine, honest, intelligible, lucid, open, plain, simple, sincere, straight, truthful, uncomplicated.
OPPOSITES: SEE **devious**.

strain noun *He's been under great strain.* anxiety, difficulty, hardship, pressure, stress, tension, worry.

strain verb 1 *We strained at the ropes.* haul, pull, stretch, tighten, tug.
2 *I strained to hear what he said.* attempt, endeavour, exert yourself, make an effort, strive, struggle, try.
3 *Don't strain yourself.* exhaust, tire out, weaken, wear out, weary.
4 *I strained my neck.* damage, hurt, injure, rick, sprain, twist, wrench.
5 *to strain solids out of a liquid.* filter, percolate, riddle, separate, sieve, sift.

strained adjective *a strained expression. strained good humour.* artificial, drawn, embarrassed, false, forced, self-conscious, stiff, tense, tired, uncomfortable, uneasy, unnatural.
OPPOSITES: SEE **relaxed**.

strainer noun colander, filter, riddle, sieve.

strait adjective [Do not confuse with *straight.*] [*old-fashioned*] *the strait way.* SEE **narrow**.

strait noun *the Strait of Gibraltar.* channel, sound.
GEOGRAPHICAL TERMS: SEE **geography**.

strait-jacket verb SEE **restrain**.

strait-laced adjective SEE **prim**.

strand noun 1 *one strand of a rope.* fibre, filament, string, thread, wire.
2 [*old-fashioned*] *The tide covered the strand.* SEE **shore** noun.

strand verb 1 *to strand a ship.* beach, ground, run aground.
2 *to strand someone on an island.* abandon, desert, forsake, leave stranded [SEE **stranded**], maroon.

stranded adjective **1** *a stranded ship.* aground, beached, grounded, [*informal*] high and dry, shipwrecked, stuck.
2 *stranded in London without any money.* abandoned, alone, deserted, forsaken, helpless, in difficulties, left, lost, marooned, without help.

strange adjective **1** *a strange event. strange goings-on.* abnormal, astonishing, atypical, bizarre, curious, eerie, exceptional, extraordinary, [*informal*] funny, irregular, odd, out of the ordinary, peculiar, queer, rare, remarkable, singular, surprising, uncommon, unexpected, unheard of, unique, unnatural, untypical, unusual.
2 *We have strange neighbours.* [*informal*] cranky, eccentric, sinister, unconventional, weird, [*informal*] zany.
3 *The experts agreed it was a strange problem.* baffling, bewildering, inexplicable, insoluble, mysterious, mystifying, perplexing, puzzling, unaccountable.
4 *We travelled to some strange places.* alien, exotic, foreign, little-known, off the beaten track, outlandish, remote, unexplored, unmapped.
5 *Eating the local food was a strange experience.* different, fresh, new, novel, unaccustomed, unfamiliar.
OPPOSITES: SEE **familiar, ordinary**.

strangeness noun abnormality, bizarreness, eccentricity, eeriness, extraordinariness, irregularity, mysteriousness, novelty, oddity, oddness, outlandishness, peculiarity, queerness, rarity, singularity, unconventionality, unfamiliarity.

stranger noun *I'm a stranger here.* alien, foreigner, guest, newcomer, outsider, visitor.

strangle verb asphyxiate, choke, garotte, smother, stifle, SEE **strangulate**, suffocate, throttle.

stranglehold noun SEE **grip** noun.

strangulate verb compress, constrict, squeeze, SEE **strangle**.

strangulation noun asphyxiation, garotting, suffocation.
METHODS OF KILLING: SEE **killing**.

strap noun band, belt, strop, tawse, thong, webbing.

strap verb *to strap things together.* SEE **fasten**.

strapping adjective SEE **sturdy**.

stratagem noun SEE **trick** noun.

strategic adjective **1** *the strategic deployment of troops.* advantageous, deliberate, planned, politic, tactical.

2 [*informal*] *the strategic moment.* SEE **important**.

strategy noun *a strategy to beat the opposition.* approach, manœuvre, method, plan, plot, policy, procedure, programme, scheme, tactics.

stratosphere noun SEE **space** noun.

stratum noun *a stratum of rock.* layer, seam, thickness, vein.

straw noun corn, stalks, stubble.

strawberry noun SEE **fruit**.

stray verb **1** *Don't stray in the hills.* get lost, go astray, meander, move about aimlessly, ramble, range, roam, rove, straggle, wander.
2 *Don't stray from the point.* deviate, digress, diverge, drift.

streak noun **1** *a streak of dirt on the window.* band, line, smear, stain, strip, stripe, vein.
2 *a streak of selfishness in her character.* component, element, trace.

streak verb **1** *Rain streaked the new paint.* mark with streaks, smear, smudge, stain.
2 [*informal*] *Cars streaked past.* dash, flash, fly, gallop, hurtle, move at speed, rush, speed, sprint, tear, zoom.

streaky adjective lined, smeary, smudged, streaked, striated, stripy, veined.

stream noun **1** *a rippling stream.* beck, brook, burn, SEE **channel** noun, [*poetic*] rill, river, rivulet, streamlet, watercourse.
2 *A stream of water poured through the hole.* cataract, current, flood, flow, gush, jet, outpouring, rush, spate, surge, tide, torrent.

stream verb *Water streamed through the hole.* cascade, course, flood, flow, gush, issue, pour, run, spill, spout, spurt, squirt, surge, well.

streamer noun banner, SEE **flag** noun, pennant, pennon, ribbon.

streamlined adjective *a car with a streamlined body.* aerodynamic, efficient, graceful, sleek, smooth.
OPPOSITE: air-resistant.

street noun SEE **road**.

strength noun **1** *physical strength.* brawn, capacity, condition, energy, fitness, force, health, might, muscle, power, robustness, stamina, sturdiness, toughness, vigour.
2 *strength of purpose.* commitment, courage, firmness, resolution, spirit.
OPPOSITES: SEE **weakness**.

strengthen verb **1** *to strengthen your muscles.* build up, fortify, harden, increase, make stronger, tone up, toughen.

2 *to strengthen a fence.* bolster, brace, buttress, prop up, reinforce, support.

3 *We need more evidence to strengthen our case.* back up, consolidate, corroborate, enhance, justify, substantiate.

OPPOSITES: SEE **weaken**.

strenuous adjective **1** *strenuous efforts.* active, committed, determined, dynamic, energetic, herculean, laborious, resolute, spirited, strong, tireless, unremitting, vigorous.

OPPOSITES: SEE **apathetic, casual**.

2 *strenuous work.* arduous, demanding, difficult, exhausting, gruelling, hard, punishing, stiff, taxing, tough, uphill.

OPPOSITES: SEE **easy**.

stress noun **1** *a time of stress.* anxiety, difficulty, hardship, pressure, strain, tension, trauma, worry.

2 *Put a stress on the important words.* accent, beat, emphasis, importance, weight.

stress verb *He stressed the importance of keeping fit.* accentuate, assert, emphasize, insist on, lay stress on, put the stress on, repeat, underline.

stressful adjective *a stressful period in my life.* anxious, difficult, tense, traumatic, worrying.

OPPOSITES: SEE **easy**.

stretch noun **1** *a stretch in prison.* period, spell, stint, term, time.

2 *a stretch of road.* distance, length.

3 *a stretch of countryside.* area, expanse, sweep, tract.

stretch verb **1** *to stretch something to make it longer or bigger or wider.* crane (*to crane your neck*), distend, draw out, elongate, expand, extend, flatten out, inflate, lengthen, open out, pull out, spread out, swell, tauten, tighten.

2 *The lake stretches into the distance.* be unbroken, continue, disappear, extend, go, spread.

stretchy adjective SEE **elastic** adjective.

strew verb SEE **scatter**.

striated adjective SEE **streaky**.

striation noun SEE **line** noun.

stricken adjective SEE **troubled**.

strict adjective **1** *strict rules.* absolute, binding, [*informal*] hard and fast, inflexible, invariable, rigid, stringent, tight, unchangeable.

OPPOSITES: SEE **flexible**.

2 *strict discipline. a strict teacher.* austere, authoritarian, autocratic, firm, harsh, merciless, [*informal*] no-nonsense,

rigorous, severe, stern, stringent, tyrannical, uncompromising.

OPPOSITES: SEE **lax, lenient**.

3 *the strict truth.* accurate, complete, correct, exact, perfect, precise, right, scrupulous, true.

OPPOSITES: SEE **approximate** adjective.

stricture noun SEE **criticism**.

stride noun *Take two strides forward.* pace, step.

stride verb SEE **walk** verb.

strident adjective *a strident cry. strident voices.* clamorous, grating, harsh, jarring, loud, noisy, raucous, screeching, shrill.

OPPOSITES: SEE **soft**.

strife noun SEE **conflict** noun.

strike noun *an industrial strike.* industrial action, stoppage, withdrawal of labour.

strike verb **1** *I struck my head.* SEE **hit** verb.

2 *The invaders struck without warning.* SEE **attack** verb.

3 *The clock struck one.* chime, ring.

4 *The workforce threatened to strike.* [*informal*] come out, [*informal*] down tools, stop work, take industrial action, withdraw your labour.

5 *to strike a flag or tent.* lower, take down.

striking adjective *a striking contrast. a striking hair-do.* arresting, conspicuous, distinctive, impressive, memorable, noticeable, obvious, outstanding, prominent, showy, stunning, telling, unmistakable, unusual.

OPPOSITES: SEE **inconspicuous**.

string noun **1** *a length of string.* cord, line, rope, twine.

2 *a string of cars waiting at the lights.* file, line, procession, queue, row, succession.

3 *a string of coincidences.* chain, progression, sequence, series.

MUSICAL INSTRUMENTS WITH STRINGS: banjo, cello, clavichord, double-bass, [*informal*] fiddle, guitar, harp, harpsichord, lute, lyre, piano, sitar, spinet, ukulele, viola, violin, zither.

OTHER INSTRUMENTS: SEE **music**.

---

string verb *to string things together.* connect, join, line up, link, thread.

stringent adjective SEE **strict**.

stringy adjective *stringy meat.* chewy, fibrous, gristly, sinewy, tough.

OPPOSITES: SEE **tender**.

strip noun *a strip of carpet. a strip of wood. a strip of land.* band, belt, lath, line, narrow piece, ribbon, shred, slat, sliver, stripe, swathe.

strip verb 1 *to strip clothes, vegetation, paint, etc., off something*. clear, defoliate, denude, divest, [*old-fashioned*] doff, flay [=*strip skin off*], peel, remove, skin, take.
OPPOSITES: SEE **cover** verb.
2 *to strip to the waist*. bare yourself, expose yourself, lay yourself bare, uncover yourself.
OPPOSITES: SEE **dress** verb.
to strip down *to strip a machine down*. dismantle, take apart.
OPPOSITES: SEE **assemble**.
to strip off disrobe, get undressed, peel off, undress.
OPPOSITES: SEE **dress** verb.

stripe noun *football shirts with red and white stripes*. band, bar, line, [*formal*] striation, strip.

striped adjective banded, barred, lined, streaky, striated, stripy.

stripling noun SEE **youth**.

strive verb SEE **try** verb.

strobe, stroboscope nouns SEE **light** noun.

stroke noun 1 *a stroke with a cricket bat*. SEE **hit** noun.
2 *You can't change the world at a single stroke*. action, blow, effort, move.
3 *a stroke of the pen*. flourish, line, mark, movement, sweep.
4 [=*medical condition*] apoplexy, seizure.

stroke verb *to stroke the cat*. caress, fondle, pass your hand over, pat, pet, rub, touch.

stroll noun, verb SEE **walk** noun, verb.

strong adjective 1 *a strong person*. athletic, [*informal*] beefy, [*informal*] brawny, burly, fit, [*informal*] hale and hearty, hardy, hefty, mighty, muscular, powerful, [*informal*] strapping, sturdy, tough, well-built, wiry.
2 *a strong structure. strong materials*. durable, hard, hardwearing, heavy-duty, impregnable (*an impregnable fortress*), indestructible, permanent, reinforced, resilient, robust, sound, stout, substantial, thick, unbreakable, well-made.
3 *strong government. strong efforts*. aggressive, assertive, decisive, dependable, determined, [*uncomplimentary*] SEE **dictatorial**, domineering, fearless, firm, forceful, herculean, loyal, reliable, resolute, stalwart, staunch, steadfast, [*informal*] stout, strong-minded, strong-willed, true, unflinching, unswerving, vehement, vigorous, violent.

4 *a strong army*. formidable, invincible, large, numerous, unconquerable, well-armed, well-equipped, well-trained.
5 *a strong light*. bright, brilliant, clear, dazzling, glaring.
6 *a strong taste or smell*. highly-flavoured, hot, noticeable, obvious, overpowering, prominent, pronounced, pungent, spicy, unmistakable.
7 *strong drink*. alcoholic, concentrated, intoxicating, potent, undiluted.
8 *strong evidence*. clear-cut, cogent, compelling, convincing, evident, persuasive, plain, solid, undisputed.
9 *strong convictions*. committed, deep-rooted, deep-seated, eager, earnest, enthusiastic, fervent, fierce, genuine, intense, keen, zealous.
OPPOSITES: SEE **weak**.

stronghold noun bastion, bulwark, castle, citadel, fort, fortress, garrison.

strong-minded adjective SEE **determined**.

strongroom noun SEE **storehouse**.

strop noun SEE **strap** noun.

stroppy adjective SEE **bad-tempered**.

structure noun 1 *the structure of a poem. the structure of a living cell*. arrangement, composition, constitution, design, [*informal*] make-up, organization, plan, shape.
2 *a structure of steel and stone*. SEE **building**, construction, edifice, erection, fabric, framework, pile, superstructure.

structure verb SEE **organize**.

struggle noun 1 *a struggle to get things finished*. challenge, difficulty, effort, endeavour, exertion, labour, problem.
2 *a struggle against an enemy or opponent*. SEE **fight** noun.

struggle verb 1 *to struggle to get free*. endeavour, exert yourself, labour, make an effort, move violently, strain, strive, toil, try, work hard, wrestle, wriggle about, writhe about.
2 *to struggle with an enemy*. SEE **fight** verb.
3 *to struggle through mud*. flail, flounder, stumble, wallow.

strut noun *a wooden strut*. SEE **bar** noun.

strut verb SEE **walk** verb.

stub noun *a cigarette stub. the stub of a tree*. butt, end, remains, remnant, stump.

stub verb *to stub your toe*. SEE **hit** verb.

stubble noun 1 *stubble of corn*. stalks, straw.
2 *stubble on a man's chin*. beard, bristles, [*informal*] five-o'clock shadow, hair, roughness.

stubbly adjective *a man with a stubbly chin*. bristly, prickly, rough, unshaven.

stubborn adjective *a stubborn donkey.* *stubborn opposition.* defiant, difficult, disobedient, dogged, headstrong, inflexible, intractable, intransigent, mulish, obdurate, obstinate, opinionated, persistent, [*informal*] pig-headed, recalcitrant, refractory, rigid, self-willed, uncontrollable, uncooperative, unmanageable, unreasonable, unyielding, wilful.
OPPOSITES: SEE **obedient**.

stubby adjective SEE **short**.

stucco noun *stucco on the walls.* cement, mortar, plaster.

stuck adjective 1 *stuck in the mud.* bogged down, fast, fastened, fixed, immovable.
2 *stuck on a problem.* baffled, beaten, held up, [*informal*] stumped.

stuck-up adjective [*informal*] *a stuck-up snob.* arrogant, [*informal*] big-headed, bumptious, [*informal*] cocky, conceited, condescending, [*informal*] high-and-mighty, patronizing, proud, self-important, snobbish, [*informal*] snooty, supercilious, [*informal*] toffee-nosed.
OPPOSITES: SEE **modest**.

stud noun SEE **nail** noun.

student noun learner, pupil, postgraduate, scholar, undergraduate.

studied adjective *studied carelessness.* SEE **deliberate** adjective.

studio noun *an artist's studio.* workroom, workshop.

studious adjective *a studious pupil.* academic, bookish, brainy, earnest, hard-working, intellectual, scholarly, serious-minded, thoughtful.

study noun OTHER ROOMS: SEE **room**.

study verb 1 *We studied the evidence.* analyse, consider, contemplate, enquire into, examine, give attention to, investigate, learn about, look closely at, peruse, pore over, read carefully, research, scrutinize, survey, think about.
2 *to study for an examination.* [*informal*] cram, learn, [*informal*] mug up, read, [*informal*] swot, work.

stuff noun 1 *What's this stuff in the jar?* matter, substance.
2 *stuff to make a skirt.* cloth, fabric, material, textile.
3 [*informal*] *That's my stuff in the drawer.* articles, belongings, [*informal*] clobber, [*formal*] effects, [*informal*] gear, junk, objects, [*informal*] paraphernalia, possessions, [*informal*] tackle, things.

stuff verb 1 *I stuffed everything into a suitcase.* compress, cram, crowd, force, jam, pack, push, ram, shove, squeeze, stow, tuck.

2 *to stuff a cushion.* fill, pad.
to stuff yourself SEE **eat**.

stuffing noun 1 *stuffing in a cushion.* filling, padding, quilting, wadding.
2 *stuffing in a roast chicken.* forcemeat, seasoning.

stuffy adjective 1 *a stuffy room.* airless, close, fetid, fuggy, fusty, heavy, humid, muggy, musty, oppressive, stale, steamy, stifling, suffocating, sultry, unventilated, warm.
OPPOSITES: SEE **airy**.
2 [*informal*] *a stuffy old bore.* boring, conventional, dreary, dull, formal, humourless, narrow-minded, old-fashioned, pompous, prim, staid, [*informal*] stodgy, strait-laced.
OPPOSITES: SEE **informal**.

stultify verb SEE **nullify**.

stumble verb 1 *to stumble as you walk.* blunder, flounder, lurch, reel, stagger, totter, trip, tumble, SEE **walk** verb.
2 *to stumble in your speech.* falter, hesitate, stammer, stutter, SEE **talk** verb.

stumbling-block noun SEE **difficulty**.

stump verb *The riddle stumped us.* baffle, bewilder, [*informal*] catch out, confound, confuse, defeat, [*informal*] flummox, mystify, outwit, perplex, puzzle.

stumpy adjective SEE **short**.

stun verb 1 *The blow stunned him.* daze, knock out, knock senseless, make unconscious.
2 *The terrible news stunned us.* amaze, astonish, astound, bewilder, confound, confuse, dumbfound, flabbergast, numb, shock, stagger, stupefy.

stunning adjective SEE **beautiful**, **stupendous**.

stunt noun exploit, feat, trick.
stunt man daredevil, SEE **entertainer**.

stunt verb *to stunt someone's growth.* SEE **check** verb.

stupefy verb SEE **stun**.

stupendous adjective *stupendous strength.* *a stupendous achievement.* amazing, colossal, enormous, exceptional, extraordinary, huge, incredible, marvellous, miraculous, notable, phenomenal, prodigious, remarkable, [*informal*] sensational, singular, special, staggering, stunning, tremendous, unbelievable, wonderful.
OPPOSITES: SEE **ordinary**.

stupid adjective 1 [Note that all these words can be insulting, and some will be more insulting than others. Many are used only *informally*.] *a stupid person.* brainless, clueless, cretinous, dense, dim, dopey, drippy, dull, dumb, feeble-minded, foolish, gormless, half-witted, idiotic, ignorant, imbecilic, ineducable, irrational, irresponsible, lacking, mindless, moronic, naïve, obtuse, puerile, senseless, silly, simple, slow, slow in the uptake, slow-witted, subnormal, thick, thick-headed, thick-skulled, thick-witted, unintelligent, unthinking, unwise, vacuous, witless.

2 *a stupid thing to do.* absurd, asinine, crack-brained, crass, crazy, fatuous, [*informal*] feeble, futile, [*informal*] half-baked, ill-advised, inane, irrelevant, laughable, ludicrous, [*informal*] lunatic, [*informal*] mad, nonsensical, pointless, rash, reckless, ridiculous, thoughtless, unjustifiable.
OPPOSITES: SEE **intelligent**.

3 *stupid after a knock on the head.* dazed, in a stupor [SEE **stupor**], semi-conscious, sluggish, stunned, stupefied.
a stupid person SEE **fool** noun.

stupidity noun *I could hardly believe her stupidity.* absurdity, crassness, denseness, dullness, [*informal*] dumbness, fatuousness, folly, foolishness, idiocy, imbecility, inanity, lack of intelligence, lunacy, madness, naïvety, silliness, slowness.
OPPOSITES: SEE **intelligence**.

stupor noun coma, daze, lethargy, shock, state of insensibility, torpor, trance, unconsciousness.

sturdy adjective 1 *a sturdy person.* athletic, brawny, burly, hardy, healthy, hefty, husky, muscular, powerful, robust, stalwart, stocky, [*informal*] strapping, strong, vigorous, well-built.
OPPOSITES: SEE **weak**.

2 *a sturdy pair of shoes.* durable, solid, sound, substantial, tough, well-made.
OPPOSITES: SEE **flimsy**.

stutter verb stammer, stumble, SEE **talk** verb.

sty noun 1 pigsty.
2 *a sty on your eyelid.* SEE **spot** noun.

style noun 1 *a style of writing.* custom, habit, idiosyncrasy, manner, method, phraseology, register, tone, way, wording.
2 *the latest style in clothes.* cut, design, fashion, mode, pattern, taste, type, vogue.
3 *She dresses with great style.* chic, dress-sense, elegance, flair, flamboyance, panache, refinement, smartness, sophistication, stylishness, taste.

stylish adjective *stylish clothes.* chic, [*informal*] classy, contemporary, [*informal*] dapper, elegant, fashionable, modern, modish, [*informal*] natty, [*informal*] posh, smart, [*informal*] snazzy,

sophisticated, [*informal*] trendy, up-to-date.
OPPOSITES: SEE **dowdy**.

stylus noun *the stylus of a record-player.* needle.

stymie verb SEE **obstruct**.

suave adjective SEE **smooth** adjective.

The prefix *sub-* is related to the Latin preposition *sub = under.*

sub-aqua adjective underwater.

subconscious adjective *subconscious awareness.* intuitive, repressed, subliminal, unacknowledged, unconscious.
OPPOSITES: SEE **conscious**.

subdivide verb SEE **divide**.

subdue verb 1 *to subdue the opposition.* beat, conquer, control, crush, defeat, master, overcome, overpower, overrun, quell, subject (*to subject a country*), subjugate, vanquish.
2 *to subdue your excitement.* check, curb, hold back, keep under, quieten, repress, restrain, suppress.

subdued adjective 1 *a subdued mood.* depressed, downcast, grave, reflective, repressed, restrained, serious, silent, sober, solemn, thoughtful.
OPPOSITES: SEE **excitable**.

2 *subdued music.* hushed, muted, peaceful, placid, quiet, soft, soothing, toned down, unobtrusive.
OPPOSITES: SEE **loud**.

subhuman adjective bestial, brutal, brutish, inhuman.
OPPOSITES: SEE **superhuman**.

subject adjective *subject nations within an empire.* captive, dependent, enslaved, oppressed, ruled, subjugated.
OPPOSITES: SEE **independent**.

subject noun 1 *a British subject.* citizen, dependant, national, passport-holder.
2 *a subject for discussion.* affair, business, issue, matter, point, question, theme, topic.

SUBJECTS WHICH STUDENTS STUDY: anatomy, archaeology, architecture, art, astronomy, biology, business, chemistry, classics, computing, craft, design, divinity, domestic science, drama, economics, education, electronics, engineering, English, environmental science, ethnology, etymology.
geography, geology, heraldry, history, languages, Latin, law, linguistics, literature, mathematics, mechanics, SEE **medicine**, metallurgy, metaphysics,

meteorology, music, natural history, oceanography, ornithology.

penology, pharmacology, pharmacy, philology, philosophy, photography, physics, physiology, politics, psychology, religious studies, SEE **science**, scripture, social work, sociology, sport, surveying, technology, theology, topology, zoology.

---

subject verb 1 *to subject a country to your control.* SEE **subdue**.
2 *to subject something to close examination.* expose, submit.

subjective adjective *a subjective reaction to something.* biased, emotional, [*informal*] gut (*a gut reaction*), idiosyncratic, instinctive, intuitive, personal, prejudiced.
OPPOSITES: SEE **objective** adjective.

subjugate verb SEE **subdue**.

sublimate verb *to sublimate your emotions.* divert, purify, redirect, refine.

sublime adjective *a sublime religious experience.* ecstatic, elated, elevated, exalted, lofty, noble, spiritual, transcendent.
OPPOSITES: SEE **base** adjective.

submarine noun VARIOUS VESSELS: SEE **vessel**.

submerge verb 1 *The flood submerged the village.* cover, drown, engulf, flood, immerse, inundate, overwhelm, swamp.
2 *The submarine submerged.* dive, go under, subside.

submission noun 1 *the submission of a wrestler.* capitulation, giving in, surrender.
2 *The judge accepted counsel's submission.* argument, claim, contention, idea, presentation, proposal, suggestion, theory.
3 *cowardly submission.* SEE **submissiveness**.

submissive adjective *submissive acceptance of someone else's authority.* acquiescent, compliant, deferential, docile, humble, meek, obedient, passive, resigned, [*uncomplimentary*] SEE **servile**, supine, tame, tractable, unassertive, uncomplaining, [*uncomplimentary*] weak.
OPPOSITES: SEE **assertive**.

submissiveness noun *submissiveness to someone else's authority.* acquiescence, assent, compliance, deference, docility, meekness, obedience, passivity, resignation, submission, subservience.

submit verb 1 *to submit to an opponent.* accede, capitulate, give in, [*informal*] knuckle under, surrender, yield.

2 *to submit work to a teacher.* give in, hand in, present.
3 *to submit your views.* advance, offer, put forward, propound, SEE **state** verb, suggest.
to submit to *to submit to authority.* bow to, comply with, conform to, defer to, keep to, obey.

subnormal adjective 1 *subnormal temperatures.* low.
2 *educationally subnormal.* SEE **backward**.

subordinate adjective *subordinate rank.* inferior, junior, lesser, lower, menial, minor, secondary, subservient, subsidiary.

subordinate noun *He likes ordering subordinates about.* assistant, dependant, employee, inferior, junior, menial, servant, [*informal*] underling.

suborn verb SEE **bribe** verb.

subpoena verb SEE **summon**.

subscribe verb **to subscribe to** 1 *to subscribe to a good cause.* contribute to, donate to, give to, support.
2 *to subscribe to a magazine.* be a subscriber to, buy regularly, pay a subscription to.
3 *to subscribe to a theory or a course of action.* advocate, agree with, approve of, believe in, condone, endorse, [*informal*] give your blessing to.

subscriber noun patron, regular customer, sponsor, supporter.

subscription noun *a club subscription.* fee, SEE **payment**, regular contribution.

subsequent adjective *I made a guess, but subsequent events proved me wrong.* consequent, ensuing, following, later, next, resulting, succeeding.
OPPOSITES: SEE **previous**.

subservient adjective SEE **servile**.

subside verb 1 *The flood subsided. The pain subsided.* abate, decline, decrease, diminish, dwindle, ebb, fall, go down, lessen, melt away, moderate, recede, shrink, slacken, wear off.
2 *I subsided into a comfortable chair.* collapse, settle, sink.
OPPOSITES: SEE **rise** verb.

subsidiary adjective *of subsidiary importance.* ancillary, auxiliary, contributory, lesser, minor, secondary, SEE **subordinate** adjective.

subsidize verb *Their parents subsidized their trip abroad.* aid, back, finance, fund, promote, sponsor, support, underwrite.

subsidy noun *Public transport needs a subsidy from taxes.* backing, financial help, grant, sponsorship, support.

subsist verb SEE **exist**.

subsistence noun SEE **payment, provisions**.

substance noun 1 *What is this substance?* chemical, material, matter, stuff.
2 *the substance of an argument.* essence, gist, meaning, subject-matter, theme.
3 [*old-fashioned*] *a woman of substance.* SEE **wealth**.

substandard adjective *substandard workmanship.* [*informal*] below par, disappointing, inadequate, inferior, poor, shoddy, unworthy.

substantial adjective 1 *a substantial door.* durable, hefty, solid, sound, strong, sturdy, well-made.
OPPOSITES: SEE **flimsy**.
2 *a substantial amount of money.* big, considerable, generous, large, significant, sizeable, worthwhile.
OPPOSITES: SEE **small**.

substantiate verb SEE **confirm**.

substitute adjective 1 *a substitute player.* acting, deputy, relief, reserve, standby, surrogate, temporary.
2 *a substitute ingredient.* alternative, ersatz, imitation.

substitute noun deputy, locum [= *substitute doctor*], proxy [= *substitute voter*], relief, replacement, reserve, stand-in, stopgap, supply [= *substitute teacher*], surrogate, understudy.

substitute verb 1 *to substitute one thing for another.* change, exchange, interchange, replace, [*informal*] swop, [*informal*] switch.
2 [*informal*] *to substitute for an absent colleague.* act as a substitute [SEE **substitute** noun], deputize, stand in, understudy.

substratum noun SEE **layer**.

substructure noun SEE **base** noun.

subsume verb SEE **include**.

subterfuge noun SEE **trick** noun.

subterranean adjective *subterranean passageways.* underground.

subtitle noun *a film with subtitles.* caption.

subtle adjective 1 *subtle flavours.* delicate, elusive, faint, mild, slight, unobtrusive.
2 *a subtle hint.* gentle, indirect, tactful, understated.

3 *a subtle argument.* clever, SEE **cunning**, ingenious, refined, shrewd, sophisticated.
OPPOSITES: SEE **obvious**.

subtract verb *to subtract one number from another.* debit, deduct, remove, take away.
OPPOSITES: SEE **add**.

subtropical adjective SEE **warm** adjective.

suburban adjective *the suburban areas of a town.* residential, outer, outlying.

suburbs noun *the suburbs of a city.* fringes, outer areas, outskirts, residential areas, suburbia.

subversive adjective *subversive ideas. subversive propaganda.* challenging, disruptive, questioning, revolutionary, seditious, undermining, unsettling.
OPPOSITES: SEE **orthodox**.

subvert verb *to subvert justice.* challenge, corrupt, destroy, disrupt, overthrow, pervert, undermine.

subway noun tunnel, underpass.

succeed verb 1 *If you work hard you will succeed.* accomplish your objective, be successful, do well, flourish, [*informal*] make it, prosper, thrive.
2 *The plan succeeded.* be effective, [*informal*] catch on, produce results, work.
OPPOSITES: SEE **fail**.
3 *Elizabeth II succeeded George VI.* come after, follow, replace, take over from.

succeeding adjective *We didn't guess what would happen in the succeeding days.* coming, ensuing, following, later, next, subsequent, successive.

success noun 1 *How do you measure success?* accomplishment, achievement, attainment, fame, prosperity.
2 *The success of the plan depends on your co-operation.* completion, effectiveness, successful outcome.
3 *The plan was a success.* [*informal*] hit, [*informal*] sensation, triumph, victory, [*informal*] winner.
OPPOSITES: SEE **failure**.

successful adjective 1 *a successful business.* effective, flourishing, fruitful, lucrative, productive, profitable, profit-making, prosperous, rewarding, thriving, well-off.
2 *a successful team.* unbeaten, victorious, winning.
OPPOSITES: SEE **unsuccessful**.

succession noun *a succession of disasters.* chain, line, procession, progression, run, sequence, series, string.

successive adjective *We had rain on seven successive days.* consecutive, in succession, uninterrupted.

successor noun *the successor to the throne.* heir, inheritor, replacement.

succinct adjective SEE **concise**.

succour noun, verb SEE **help** noun, verb.

succulent adjective *succulent fruit.* fleshy, juicy, luscious, moist, rich.

succumb verb SEE **surrender**.

suck verb **to suck up** *to suck up liquid.* absorb, draw up, pull up, soak up.
to suck up to SEE **flatter**.

suckle verb SEE **feed**.

sucrose noun SEE **sugar** noun.

suction noun sucking.

sudden adjective 1 *a sudden decision.* abrupt, hasty, hurried, impetuous, impulsive, quick, rash, [*informal*] snap, swift, unconsidered.
OPPOSITES: SEE **slow** adjective.
3 *a sudden happening.* acute (*an acute illness*), sharp, startling, surprising, unexpected, unforeseen, unlooked for.
OPPOSITES: SEE **expected**.

suds noun bubbles, foam, froth, lather, soapsuds.

sue verb indict, prosecute.
LEGAL TERMS: SEE **law**.

suede noun SEE **leather**.

suffer verb 1 *to suffer pain.* bear, cope with, endure, experience, feel, go through, put up with, stand, tolerate, undergo.
2 *Did you suffer when you were ill?* experience pain [SEE **pain** noun], hurt.
3 *He suffered for his crime.* be punished, make amends, pay.
4 [*old-fashioned*] *Suffer the children to come to me.* SEE **permit** verb.

suffering noun SEE **torment** noun.

suffice verb *A cup of water sufficed to keep him alive.* be sufficient [SEE **sufficient**], [*informal*] do (*Will this do?*), serve.

sufficient adjective *sufficient money to live on.* adequate, enough, satisfactory.
OPPOSITES: SEE **insufficient**.

suffix noun OPPOSITE: **prefix**.

suffocate verb asphyxiate, choke, SEE **kill**, smother, stifle, strangle, throttle.

sugar noun FORMS OF SUGAR: brown sugar, cane sugar, caster sugar, demerara, glucose, granulated sugar, icing sugar, lump sugar, molasses, sucrose, SEE **sweets**, syrup, treacle.

sugar verb SEE **sweeten**.

sugary adjective 1 *a sugary taste.* SEE **sweet** adjective.
2 *sugary sentiments.* cloying, SEE **sentimental**, sickly.

suggest verb 1 *I suggest we go home.* advise, advocate, moot, move, propose, propound, put forward, raise, recommend.
2 *Her face suggests that she's bored.* communicate, hint, imply, indicate, insinuate, intimate, mean, signal.

suggestible adjective SEE **impressionable**.

suggestion noun 1 *I made a suggestion.* offer, plan, proposal, recommendation.
2 *a suggestion of cheating.* hint, suspicion, trace.

suggestive adjective 1 *suggestive images in a poem.* evocative, expressive, thought-provoking.
2 *suggestive jokes.* SEE **indecent**.

suicidal adjective 1 *a suicidal mood.* SEE **depressed**.
2 *a suicidal mission.* hopeless, [*informal*] kamikaze, self-destructive.

suicide noun SEE **killing**.

suit noun 1 *a suit to wear.* VARIOUS ITEMS OF CLOTHING: SEE **clothes**.
2 *a suit of cards.* set.
SUITS IN A PACK OF CARDS: clubs, diamonds, hearts, spades.
3 *a suit in a court of law.* LEGAL TERMS: SEE **law**.

suit verb 1 *What you suggest suits me.* be suitable for [SEE **suitable**], gratify, please, satisfy.
OPPOSITES: SEE **displease**.
2 *Their offer suits our requirements.* accommodate, conform to, fit in with, harmonize with, match, tally with.
3 *That colour suits you.* become, fit, look good on.

suitable adjective *a suitable present for granny.* acceptable, applicable, apposite, appropriate, apt, becoming, congenial, convenient, fit, fitting, handy, pertinent, proper, relevant, satisfactory, seemly, timely, well-chosen, well-judged, well-timed.
OPPOSITES: SEE **unsuitable**.

suitcase noun SEE **luggage**.

suite noun *a suite of rooms.* SEE **group** noun.

suitor noun SEE **lover**.

sulk verb *to sulk after a defeat.* be sullen [SEE **sullen**], brood, mope.

sulky adjective *a sulky look.* SEE **sullen**.

sullen adjective 1 *a sullen expression.* bad-tempered, churlish, cross, disgruntled, grudging, moody, morose, petulant, resentful, sad, silent, sour, stubborn, sulky, surly, uncommunicative, unfriendly, unhappy, unsociable.
OPPOSITES: SEE **cheerful**.

2 *a sullen sky.* brooding, cheerless, dark, dismal, dull, gloomy, grey, sombre.
OPPOSITES: SEE **bright**.

sully verb SEE **stain** verb.

sulphureous, sulphurous adjectives SEE **noxious**.

sultry adjective **1** *sultry weather.* close, hot, humid, [*informal*] muggy, oppressive, steamy, stifling, stuffy, warm.
OPPOSITES: SEE **cool** adjective.
2 *a sultry beauty.* dark, mysterious, sensual, SEE **sexy**, voluptuous.

sum noun *Add up the sum.* aggregate, amount, number, quantity, reckoning, result, score, tally, total, whole.
MATHEMATICAL TERMS: SEE **mathematics**.

sum verb **to sum up** SEE **summarize**.

summarize verb **1** *to summarize evidence.* make a summary of [SEE **summary** noun], outline, [*informal*] recap, recapitulate, review, sum up.
2 *to summarize a story.* abridge, condense, précis, reduce, shorten.
OPPOSITES: SEE **elaborate** verb.

summary adjective **1** *a summary account.* SEE **brief** adjective.
2 *summary justice.* SEE **hasty**.

summary noun **1** *a summary of the main points.* abstract, digest, outline, recapitulation, resumé, review, summation, summing-up.
2 *a summary of a story.* abridgement, condensation, précis, reduction, synopsis.

summation noun SEE **summary**.

summer-house noun gazebo, pavilion.

summery adjective *summery weather.* bright, SEE **hot**, sunny, tropical, warm.
OPPOSITES: SEE **wintry**.

summit noun **1** *the summit of a mountain.* apex, crown, head, height, peak, pinnacle, point, top.
OPPOSITES: SEE **foot**.
2 *the summit of your success.* acme, apogee, high point, zenith.
OPPOSITES: SEE **nadir**.

summon verb **1** *to summon someone to attend.* command, demand, invite, order, send for, [*formal*] subpoena.
2 *to summon a meeting.* assemble, call, convene, convoke, gather together, muster, rally.

summons noun LEGAL TERMS: SEE **law**.

sumptuous *a sumptuous banquet.* costly, dear, expensive, extravagant, grand, lavish, luxurious, magnificent, opulent, [*informal*] posh, rich, splendid, superb.
OPPOSITES: SEE **mean** adjective.

sun noun sunlight, sunshine.
RELATED ADJECTIVE: solar.
ASTRONOMICAL TERMS: SEE **astronomy**.

sunbathe verb bask, [*informal*] get a tan, sun yourself.

sunburn noun sunstroke, suntan, tanning.

sunburnt adjective blistered, bronzed, brown, peeling, tanned, weatherbeaten.

sunder verb SEE **part** verb.

sundown noun SEE **sunset**.

sundry adjective SEE **various**.

sun-glasses noun SEE **glass (glasses)**.

sunken adjective *a sunken area.* concave, depressed, hollow, hollowed, low.

sunless adjective *a sunless day.* cheerless, cloudy, dark, dismal, dreary, dull, gloomy, grey, overcast.
OPPOSITES: SEE **sunny**.

sunlight noun daylight, sun, sunbeams, sunshine.

sunlit adjective SEE **sunny**.

sunny adjective **1** *a sunny day.* bright, clear, cloudless, fine, summery, sunlit.
OPPOSITES: SEE **sunless**.
WORDS TO DESCRIBE WEATHER: SEE **weather** noun.
2 *a sunny smile.* SEE **cheerful**.

sunrise noun dawn, daybreak.
OTHER TIMES OF DAY: SEE **day**.

sunset noun dusk, evening, [*poetic*] gloaming, nightfall, sundown, twilight.
OTHER TIMES OF DAY: SEE **day**.

sunshade noun awning, canopy, parasol.

sunshine noun SEE **sunlight**.

suntan noun sunburn, tan.

super adjective SEE **good**.

The prefix *super-* is related to the Latin preposition *super = above, over*.

---

superabundance noun SEE **excess**.

superannuated adjective **1** *a superannuated employee.* discharged, [*informal*] pensioned off, [*informal*] put out to grass, old, retired.
2 [*informal*] *superannuated possessions,* discarded, disused, obsolete, thrown out, worn out.

superannuation noun annuity, pension.

superb adjective SEE **splendid**.

supercilious adjective SEE **superior**.

superficial adjective 1 *a superficial wound.* exterior, on the surface, shallow, skin-deep, slight, surface, unimportant.
OPPOSITE: deep.
2 *a superficial examination.* careless, casual, cursory, desultory, hasty, hurried, inattentive, [*informal*] nodding (*a nodding acquaintance*), passing, perfunctory.
OPPOSITE: SEE **thorough**.
3 *superficial arguments.* facile, frivolous, lightweight, simple-minded, simplistic, sweeping (*sweeping generalizations*), trivial, unconvincing, uncritical, unscholarly, unsophisticated.
OPPOSITES: SEE **analytical**.

superfluity noun SEE **excess**.

superfluous adjective *superfluous possessions.* excess, excessive, needless, redundant, spare, surplus, unnecessary, unwanted.
OPPOSITES: SEE **necessary**.

superhuman adjective 1 *superhuman efforts.* herculean, heroic, phenomenal, prodigious.
2 *superhuman powers.* divine, higher, metaphysical, supernatural.
OPPOSITES: SEE **subhuman**.

superimpose verb *to superimpose one thing on another.* overlay, place on top of.

superintend verb SEE **supervise**.

superintendent noun SEE **supervisor**.

superior adjective 1 *superior in rank.* greater, higher, more important, senior.
2 *superior quality.* better, choice, exclusive, fine, first-class, first-rate, select, top, unrivalled.
3 *a superior attitude.* arrogant, condescending, disdainful, haughty, [*informal*] high-and-mighty, lofty, patronizing, self-important, smug, snobbish, [*informal*] snooty, stuck-up, supercilious.
OPPOSITES: SEE **inferior**.

superlative adjective SEE **excellent**, **supreme**.

superman noun SEE **hero**.

supermarket noun SEE **shop**.

supernatural adjective *supernatural powers, supernatural manifestations.* abnormal, ghostly, inexplicable, magical, metaphysical, miraculous, mysterious, mystic, occult, paranormal, preternatural, psychic, spiritual, uncanny, unearthly, unnatural, weird.
SUPERNATURAL BEINGS: SEE **spirit**.

supernumerary adjective SEE **extra**.

superpower noun SEE **nation**.

superscription noun SEE **inscription**.

supersede verb SEE **replace**.

supersonic adjective SEE **fast** adjective.

superstar noun big name, celebrity, idol, SEE **performer**, star.

superstition noun *My fear of Friday 13th is just superstition.* delusion, illusion, myth, [*informal*] old wives' tale, superstitious belief [SEE **superstitious**].

superstitious adjective *superstitious beliefs.* groundless, illusory, irrational, mythical, traditional, unfounded, unprovable.
OPPOSITES: SEE **scientific**.

superstructure noun SEE **structure**.

supervise verb *to supervise a task.* administer, be in charge (of), be the supervisor (of) [SEE **supervisor**], conduct, control, direct, invigilate [= *supervise an exam*]. lead, look after, manage, organize, oversee, preside over, run, superintend, watch over.

supervision noun *the supervision of a production line. the supervision of an exam.* administration, conduct, control, invigilation, management, organization, oversight, surveillance.

supervisor noun administrator, SEE **chief** noun, controller, director, foreman, [*informal*] gaffer, head, inspector, invigilator, leader, manager, organizer, overseer, superintendent, timekeeper.

supine adjective *lying supine on the floor.* face upwards, on your back.
OPPOSITES: SEE **prone**.

supper noun VARIOUS MEALS: SEE **meal**.

supplant verb *to supplant a leader.* displace, oust, replace, [*informal*] step into the shoes of, [*informal*] topple, unseat.

supple adjective *supple leather. supple limbs.* bending, [*informal*] bendy, elastic, flexible, graceful, limber, lithe, plastic, pliable, pliant, soft.
OPPOSITES: SEE **brittle**, **rigid**.

supplement noun 1 *a supplement to travel first class.* additional payment, excess, surcharge.
2 *a newspaper supplement.* addendum, addition, SEE **appendix**, **extra**, **insert**.

supplement verb *I do odd jobs to supplement my income.* add to, augment, boost, complement, reinforce, [*informal*] top up.

supplementary adjective *a supplementary fare. supplementary information.* accompanying, additional, auxiliary, complementary, extra.

suppliant noun petitioner.

supplicate verb SEE **request** verb.

supplication noun SEE **request** noun.

supplier noun dealer, provider, purveyor, retailer, seller, shopkeeper, vendor, wholesaler.

supply noun *a supply of sweets.* quantity, reserve, reservoir, stock, stockpile, store.

supplies *supplies for the weekend.* equipment, food, necessities, provisions, rations, shopping.

supply verb *to supply goods.* contribute, donate, equip, feed, furnish, give, hand-over, pass on, produce, provide, purvey, sell, stock.

support noun 1 *Thank you for your support.* aid, approval, assistance, backing, contribution, co-operation, donation, encouragement, friendship, help, interest, loyalty, patronage, protection, reassurance, reinforcement, sponsorship, succour.

2 *a support to lean or rest on.* bracket, buttress, crutch, foundation, pillar, post, prop, sling, stanchion, stay, strut, trestle, truss.

support verb 1 *to support a weight.* bear, bolster, buttress, carry, give strength to, hold up, prop up, provide a support for, reinforce, shore up, strengthen, underlie, underpin.

2 *to support someone in trouble.* aid, assist, back, champion, comfort, defend, encourage, give support to [SEE **support** noun], rally round, reassure, speak up for, stand by, stand up for, take (someone's) part.

3 *to support a family.* bring up, feed, finance, fund, keep, maintain, nourish, provide for, sustain.

4 *to support a charity.* be a supporter of [SEE **supporter**], be interested in, contribute to, espouse (*to espouse a cause*), follow, give to, patronize, pay money to, sponsor, subsidize, work for.

5 *to support a point of view.* advocate, agree with, argue for, confirm, corroborate, defend, endorse, explain, justify, promote, substantiate, uphold, verify.

OPPOSITES: SEE **undermine**.

to support yourself *She supported herself on her arms.* lean, rest.

supporter noun 1 *a football supporter.* enthusiast, [*informal*] fan, fanatic, follower.

2 *a supporter of an idea. a supporter of a political party.* adherent, advocate, apologist (for), champion, defender, seconder, upholder, voter.

3 *a supporter of someone in a job or in a contest.* ally, collaborate, helper, [*old-fashioned*] henchman, second.

supportive adjective *a supportive group of friends.* caring, concerned, encouraging, helpful, interested, kind, loyal, positive, reassuring, sympathetic, understanding.

OPPOSITES: SEE **subversive**.

suppose verb 1 *I suppose you want some food.* accept, assume, believe, conclude, conjecture, expect, guess, infer, judge, postulate, presume, speculate, surmise, think.

2 *Just suppose you had lots of money.* fancy, fantasize, imagine, hypothesize, maintain, pretend.

supposed adjective *No one has ever seen the supposed monster.* alleged, assumed, conjectural, hypothetical, imagined, presumed, putative, reported, reputed, rumoured.

to be supposed to *I'm supposed to start work at 8.30.* be due to, be expected to, be meant to, be required to, have a duty to, need to, ought to.

supposition noun *a supposition, not a known fact.* assumption, conjecture, guess, [*informal*] guesstimate, hypothesis, inference, notion, opinion, presumption, speculation, surmise, theory, thought.

suppress verb 1 *to suppress a rebellion.* conquer, crush, overcome, overthrow, put an end to, put down, quash, quell, stamp out, stop, subdue.

2 *to suppress the truth. to suppress your feelings.* bottle up, censor, conceal, cover up, SEE **hide** verb, [*informal*] keep quiet about, repress, restrain, silence, smother.

suppurate verb SEE **fester**.

supremacy noun *No one could challenge her supremacy in gymnastics.* dominance, domination, lead, predominance, pre-eminence, sovereignty.

supreme adjective *Her supreme moment was winning a gold medal.* best, consummate, crowning, culminating, greatest, highest, incomparable, matchless, outstanding, paramount, predominant, pre-eminent, prime, principal, superlative, surpassing, top, ultimate, unbeatable, unbeaten, unparalleled, unrivalled, unsurpassable, unsurpassed.

surcharge noun SEE **supplement** noun.

sure adjective 1 *I'm sure that I'm right.* assured, confident, convinced, decided, definite, persuaded, positive, resolute.

2 *He's sure to come.* bound, certain, compelled, obliged, required.

3 *a sure fact.* accurate, clear, convincing, guaranteed, indisputable, inescapable, inevitable, precise, proven, true,

unchallenged, undeniable, undisputed, undoubted, verifiable.

4 *a sure ally.* dependable, effective, faithful, firm, infallible, loyal, reliable, safe, secure, solid, steadfast, steady, trustworthy, trusty, unerring, unfailing, unswerving.

OPPOSITES: SEE **uncertain**.

surety noun SEE **guarantee** noun.

surf noun SEE **wave** noun.

surface noun **1** *the outer surface.* coat, covering, crust, exterior, façade, outside, shell, skin, veneer.

OPPOSITES: SEE **centre**.

2 *A cube has six surfaces.* face, facet, plane, side.

3 *a working surface.* top, worktop.

surface verb **1** *I surfaced the wood with plastic.* coat, cover, veneer.

2 *The submarine surfaced. A problem surfaced.* appear, [*informal*] come to light, come up, emerge, materialize, rise, [*informal*] pop up.

surf-boarding noun SEE **surfing**.

surfeit noun *a surfeit of rich food.* excess, glut, over-indulgence, superfluity.

surfing noun surf-boarding, surf-riding.

surge noun **1** *a surge of water.* SEE **wave** noun.

2 *a surge of enthusiasm.* gush, increase, onrush, outpouring, rush, upsurge.

surge verb **1** *Water surged around them.* billow, eddy, gush, heave, make waves, roll, swirl.

2 *The crowd surged forward.* move irresistibly, push, rush, stampede, sweep.

surgeon noun MEDICAL PRACTITIONERS: SEE **medicine**.

surgery noun **1** *She underwent surgery.* biopsy, operation.

2 *I visited the doctor's surgery.* clinic, consulting room, health centre, infirmary, medical centre, sick-bay.

surly adjective *a surly mood, a surly answer.* bad-tempered, churlish, cross, [*informal*] crusty, gruff, [*informal*] grumpy, ill-natured, irascible, miserable, morose, peevish, rude, sulky, sullen, testy, uncivil, unfriendly, ungracious.

OPPOSITES: SEE **friendly**.

surmise noun, verb SEE **guess** noun, verb.

surmount verb SEE **deal** verb (**deal with**).

surname noun SEE **name** noun.

surpass verb *The success of the sale surpassed our expectations.* beat, better, do better than, eclipse, exceed, excel, outclass, outdo, outshine, outstrip, overshadow, top, transcend.

surpassing adjective SEE **excellent**.

surplus noun *If you've had all you want, give the surplus to others.* balance, excess, extra, remainder, residue, superfluity, surfeit.

surprise noun **1** *Imagine our surprise when she walked in.* alarm, amazement, astonishment, consternation, dismay, incredulity, wonder.

2 *Her arrival was a complete surprise.* [*informal*] bolt from the blue, [*informal*] bombshell, [*informal*] eye-opener, shock.

surprise verb **1** *The news surprised us.* alarm, amaze, astonish, astound, disconcert, dismay, shock, stagger, startle, stun, [*informal*] take aback, take by surprise, [*informal*] throw (*The unexpected news threw me*).

2 *The security officer surprised him opening the safe.* capture, catch out, [*informal*] catch red-handed, come upon, detect, discover, take unawares.

surprised adjective *I admit that I was surprised.* alarmed, amazed, astonished, astounded, disconcerted, dumbfounded, flabbergasted, incredulous, nonplussed, shocked, speechless, staggered, startled, stunned, taken aback, taken by surprise, thunderstruck.

surprising adjective *a surprising turn of events.* alarming, amazing, astonishing, astounding, disconcerting, extraordinary, incredible, [*informal*] offputting, shocking, staggering, startling, stunning, sudden, unexpected, unforeseen, unlooked for, unplanned.

OPPOSITES: SEE **predictable**.

surrender verb **1** *to surrender to an enemy.* capitulate, [*informal*] cave in, collapse, concede, fall, [*informal*] give in, resign, submit, succumb, [*informal*] throw in the towel, [*informal*] throw up the sponge, yield.

2 *to surrender your ticket.* give, hand over, relinquish.

3 *to surrender your rights.* abandon, cede, give up, renounce, waive.

surreptitious adjective *a surreptitious look at the answers.* concealed, covert, crafty, disguised, furtive, hidden, secretive, shifty, sly, [*informal*] sneaky, stealthy, underhand.

OPPOSITES: SEE **blatant**.

surrogate noun SEE **substitute** noun.

surround verb *The park is surrounded by houses.* besiege, beset, encircle, encompass, engulf, girdle, hedge in, hem in, ring, skirt.

surroundings noun *You work more happily in pleasant surroundings.* ambience, area, background, context, environment, location, milieu, neighbourhood, setting, vicinity.

surveillance noun *Police maintained a 24-hour surveillance on the building.* check, observation, scrutiny, supervision, vigilance, watch.

survey noun *a traffic survey, a land survey.* appraisal, assessment, census, count, evaluation, examination, inspection, investigation, scrutiny, study, [*formal*] triangulation.

survey verb 1 *to survey the damage after an accident.* appraise, assess, estimate, evaluate, examine, inspect, investigate, look over, scrutinize, study, view, weigh up.
2 *to survey building land.* do a survey of, map out, measure, plan out, plot, reconnoitre, [*formal*] triangulate.

survival noun *Commercial exploitation of resources threatens our survival.* continuance, continued existence.

survive verb 1 *You can't survive without water.* carry on, continue, endure, keep going, last, live, persist, remain.
OPPOSITES: SEE **die**.
2 *He survived the disasters which plagued him.* come through, live through, outlast, outlive, weather, withstand.
OPPOSITE: succumb to.

sus verb **to sus out** SEE **investigate**.

susceptible adjective *susceptible to colds.* disposed, given, inclined, liable, predisposed, prone, sensitive, vulnerable.
OPPOSITES: SEE **resistant**.

suspect adjective 1 *His evidence was suspect.* doubtful, inadequate, questionable, unconvincing, unreliable, unsatisfactory.
OPPOSITES: SEE **satisfactory**.
2 *a suspect character.* dubious, suspected, SEE **suspicious**.

suspect verb 1 *I suspect his motives.* call into question, distrust, doubt, mistrust.
2 *I suspect that he's lying.* believe, conjecture, consider, guess, imagine, infer, presume, speculate, suppose, surmise, think.

suspend verb 1 *to suspend something from a hook, etc.* dangle, hang, swing.
2 *to suspend a meeting.* adjourn, break off, defer, delay, discontinue, interrupt, postpone, put off.
3 *to suspend someone from school or from a job.* debar, dismiss, expel, send down.

suspended adjective *a suspended sentence. a suspended meeting.* adjourned, deferred, frozen, in abeyance, pending,

postponed, [*informal*] put on ice, shelved.

suspense noun *The suspense was unbearable.* anticipation, anxiety, drama, excitement, expectancy, expectation, tension, uncertainty, waiting.

suspicion noun 1 *a suspicion that she was lying.* apprehension, distrust, doubt, feeling, guess, [*informal*] hunch, impression, misgiving, presentiment, qualm, uncertainty, wariness.
2 *a suspicion of a smile on his face.* hint, shadow, suggestion, tinge, touch, trace.

suspicious adjective 1 *suspicious of the evidence.* [*informal*] chary, disbelieving, distrustful, doubtful, incredulous, mistrustful, sceptical, unconvinced, uneasy, wary.
OPPOSITES: SEE **credulous**.
2 *a suspicious character.* disreputable, dubious, [*informal*] fishy, peculiar, questionable, shady, suspect, suspected, unreliable, untrustworthy.
OPPOSITES: SEE **straightforward**.

sustain verb SEE **support** verb.

sustenance noun SEE **food**.

suzerain noun SEE **ruler**.

svelte adjective SEE **slender**.

swab verb SEE **clean** verb.

swaddle verb **wrap** verb.

swag noun [*informal*] *robbers' swag.* booty, loot, plunder, takings.

swagger verb SEE **walk** verb.

swallow verb consume, SEE **drink** verb, eat.
to swallow up *Fog swallowed them up.* absorb, enclose, enfold, envelop, SEE **swamp** verb.

swamp noun bog, fen, marsh, marshland, mire, morass, mud, mudflats, quagmire, quicksand, saltmarsh, [*old-fashioned*] slough, wetlands.

swamp verb *A hugh wave swamped the ship.* deluge, drench, engulf, flood, inundate, overwhelm, sink, submerge, swallow up.

swampy adjective *swampy ground.* boggy, marshy, miry, muddy, soft, soggy, unstable, waterlogged, wet.
OPPOSITES: SEE **dry** adjective.

swan noun cob [= *male swan*], cygnet [= *young swan*].

swank verb see **boast**.

swanky adjective SEE **ostentatious**.

swap verb SEE **exchange** verb.

swarm noun *a swarm of bees.* SEE **group** noun.

swarm verb *People swarm to watch an accident.* cluster, congregate, crowd, flock, mass, move in a swarm, throng.
to swarm up *to swarm up a tree.* SEE **climb** verb.
to swarm with *The kitchen swarmed with ants.* abound, be alive with, be infested with, be invaded by, be overrun with, crawl, teem.

swarthy adjective *a swarthy complexion.* brown, dark, dusky, tanned.

swashbuckling adjective *a swashbuckling hero.* adventurous, aggressive, bold, daredevil, dashing, [*informal*] macho, SEE **manly**, **swaggering**.

swat verb *to swat a fly.* SEE **hit** verb.

swathe verb SEE **wrap** verb.

sway verb 1 *to sway in the breeze.* bend, lean from side to side, rock, roll, swing, wave.
2 *Nothing I can say will sway them.* affect, change the mind of, govern, influence, persuade.
3 *She swayed from her chosen path.* divert, go off course, swerve, veer, waver.

swear verb 1 *He swore that he would tell the truth.* affirm, attest, declare, give your word, pledge, promise, state on oath, take an oath, testify, vow.
2 *She swore when she hit her finger.* blaspheme, curse, use swearwords [SEE **swearword**].

swearword noun blasphemy, curse, expletive, [*informal*] four-letter word, oath, obscenity, profanity.
swearwords bad language, foul language, swearing.

sweat verb perspire, swelter.

sweaty adjective *sweaty hands.* clammy, damp, moist, perspiring, sticky, sweating.

sweep verb 1 *Sweep the floor.* brush, clean, clear, dust.
2 *The bus swept past.* SEE **move** verb.

sweeping adjective 1 *sweeping changes.* comprehensive, extensive, far-reaching, indiscriminate, radical, wholesale.
OPPOSITES: SEE **specific**.
2 *a sweeping statement* broad, general, oversimplified, simplistic, superficial, uncritical, undiscriminating, unqualified, unscholarly.
OPPOSITES: SEE **analytical**.

sweepstake noun SEE **gambling**.

sweet adjective 1 *a sweet taste. a sweet smell.* cloying, fragrant, luscious, mellow, perfumed, sickly, sugary, sweetened, syrupy.
OPPOSITES: SEE **acid**, **acrid**, **bitter**, **savoury**.

2 *sweet sounds.* [*often joking*] dulcet (*dulcet tones*), euphonious, harmonious, heavenly, melodious, musical, pleasant, silvery, soothing, tuneful.
OPPOSITES: SEE **discordant**.
3 *a sweet nature.* affectionate, attractive, charming, dear, endearing, engaging, gentle, gracious, lovable, lovely, nice, pretty, unselfish, winning.
OPPOSITES: SEE **selfish**, **ugly**.
sweetcorn corn on the cob, maize.

sweet noun [= *the sweet course of a meal*] [*informal*] afters, dessert, pudding.
sweets [*old-fashioned*] bon-bons, [*American*] candy, confectionery, [*childish*] sweeties, [*old-fashioned*] sweetmeats.

VARIOUS SWEETS: acid drop, barley sugar, boiled sweet, bull's-eye, butterscotch, candy, candyfloss, caramel, chewing-gum, chocolate, fondant, fruit pastille, fudge, humbug, liquorice, lollipop, marshmallow, marzipan, mint, nougat, peppermint, rock, toffee, Turkish delight.

sweeten verb 1 *to sweeten your coffee.* make sweeter, sugar.
2 *to sweeten someone's temper.* appease, calm, mellow, mollify, pacify, soothe.

sweetener noun VARIOUS SWEETENERS: artificial sweetener, honey, saccharine, SEE **sugar** noun, sweetening.

sweetheart noun SEE **lover**.

swell noun *an ocean swell.* SEE **wave** noun.

swell verb 1 *The balloon swelled as it filled with air.* balloon, become bigger, billow, blow up, bulge, dilate, distend, enlarge, expand, fatten, grow, inflate, puff up, rise.
2 *We invited friends to swell the numbers in the audience.* augment, boost, build up, extend, increase, make bigger.
OPPOSITES: SEE **shrink**.

swelling noun *a painful swelling.* blister, bulge, bump, hump, inflammation, knob, lump, protuberance, tumescence, tumour.

sweltering adjective SEE **hot**.

swerve verb *The car swerved to avoid a hedgehog.* change direction, deviate, dodge about, swing, take avoiding action, turn aside, veer, wheel.

swift adjective *a swift journey. a swift reaction.* agile, brisk, fast, [*old-fashioned*] fleet, fleet-footed, hasty, hurried, nimble, [*informal*] nippy, prompt, SEE **quick**, rapid, speedy, sudden.
OPPOSITES: SEE **slow** adjective.

swig verb SEE **drink** verb.

swill verb 1 *Swill the car with clear water.* bathe, clean, rinse, sponge down, wash. 2 [*informal*] *They sat there swilling champagne.* SEE **drink** verb.

swim verb *to swim in the sea.* bathe, dive in, float, go swimming, [*informal*] take a dip.
VARIOUS SWIMMING STROKES: backstroke, breaststroke, butterfly, crawl.

swimming-bath noun baths, leisure-pool, lido, swimming-pool.

swim-suit noun bathing-costume, bathing-dress, bathing-suit, bikini, swim-wear, trunks.

swindle noun *I don't want to get involved in a swindle.* cheat, chicanery, [*informal*] con, deception, double-dealing, fraud, [*informal*] racket, [*informal*] rip-off, [*informal*] sharp practice, [*informal*] swizz, trickery.

swindle verb *He swindled us out of a lot of money.* [*informal*] bamboozle, cheat, [*informal*] con, deceive, defraud, [*informal*] do, double-cross, dupe, [*informal*] fiddle, [*informal*] fleece, fool, hoax, hoodwink, [*informal*] rook, trick, [*informal*] welsh (*to welsh on a bet*).

swindler noun charlatan, cheat, cheater, [*informal*] con-man, counterfeiter, double-cross, extortioner, forger, fraud, hoaxer, impostor, mountebank, quack, racketeer, [*informal*] shark, trickster, [*informal*] twister.

swine noun SEE **pig**.

swineherd noun SEE **farmer**.

swing noun *a swing in public opinion.* change, fluctuation, movement, oscillation, shift, variation.

swing verb 1 *He swung from the end of a rope.* be suspended, dangle, flap, hang loose, rock, sway, swivel, turn, twirl, wave about.
2 *The car swung from one side of the road to the other.* SEE **swerve**.
3 *During the election, support swung to the opposition.* change, fluctuate, move across, oscillate, shift, transfer, vary.

swingeing adjective 1 *a swingeing blow.* SEE **violent**.
2 *a swingeing increase in price.* SEE **exorbitant**.

swinish adjective SEE **beastly**.

swipe verb 1 *to swipe with a bat.* SEE **hit** verb.
2 [*informal*] *She swiped my pen.* SEE **steal**.

swirl verb *The water swirled round.* boil, churn, eddy, move in circles, spin, surge, twirl, twist, whirl.

swish adjective SEE **posh**.

swish noun, verb VARIOUS SOUNDS: SEE **sound** noun.

switch noun 1 *an electric switch.* circuit-breaker, light-switch, power-point.
2 [= *whip*] SEE **whip** noun.

switch verb *to switch places.* change, exchange, replace, shift, substitute, [*informal*] swap.

swivel verb *to swivel round.* gyrate, pirouette, pivot, revolve, rotate, spin, swing, turn, twirl, wheel.

swizz noun SEE **swindle** noun.

swollen adjective big, bulging, distended, enlarged, fat, full, inflated, puffy, tumescent.

swoon verb SEE **faint** verb.

swoop verb *The owl swooped down.* descend, dive, drop, fall, fly down, lunge, plunge, pounce.
to swoop on [*informal*] *The police swooped on the club.* SEE **raid** verb.

swop verb SEE **exchange** verb.

sword noun blade, broadsword, cutlass, foil, rapier, sabre, scimitar.
OTHER WEAPONS: SEE **weapons**.

swordsman noun SEE **fighter**.

sworn adjective SEE **determined**.

swot verb SEE **study** verb.

sybarite noun SEE **hedonist**.

sybaritic adjective SEE **hedonistic**.

sycophant noun flatterer, today.

sycophantic adjective SEE **flattering**.

syllabus noun course, curriculum, outline, programme of study.

symbol noun 1 *A crown is a symbol of royal power.* badge, emblem, figure, ideogram, ideograph, image, insignia, logo, monogram, motif, pictogram, pictograph, sign.
2 *symbols used in writing.* character, letter.

symbolic adjective *a symbolic image. a symbolic gesture.* allegorical, emblematic, figurative, meaningful, metaphorical, representative, significant, suggestive, token (*a token gesture*).

symbolize verb *Easter eggs symbolize the renewal of life.* be a sign of, betoken, communicate, connote, denote, indicate, mean, represent, signify, stand for, suggest.

symmetrical adjective *a symmetrical design.* balanced, even, regular.
OPPOSITES: SEE **asymmetrical**.

sympathetic adjective *sympathetic about someone's problems.* benevolent,

caring, charitable, comforting, compassionate, concerned, consoling, friendly, humane, interested, kind, merciful, pitying, soft-hearted, sorry, supportive, tender, tolerant, understanding, warm.
OPPOSITES: SEE **unsympathetic**.

sympathize verb **to sympathize with** *to sympathize with someone in trouble.* be sorry for, be sympathetic towards [SEE **sympathetic**], comfort, commiserate with, console, empathize with, feel for, identify with, pity, show sympathy for [SEE **sympathy**], understand.

sympathy noun *She showed no sympathy when I described my problem.* affinity, commiseration, compassion, condolences, consideration, empathy, feeling, fellow-feeling, kindness, mercy, pity, tenderness, understanding.

symposium noun SEE **discussion**.

symptom noun *A rash is one of the symptoms of measles.* feature, indication, manifestation, mark, sign, warning.

symptomatic adjective *Do you think violence is symptomatic of our times?* characteristic, indicative, suggestive, typical.

synagogue noun SEE **worship** noun (place of worship).

synchronize verb *Synchronize your watches.* match up, set to the same time.

synchronous adjective SEE **contemporary**.

synonym noun OPPOSITE: antonym.

synthesis noun SEE **combination**.

synthesize verb SEE **combine**.

synthetic adjective *Nylon is a synthetic material.* artificial, concocted, ersatz, fabricated, fake [*informal*] made-up, man-made, manufactured, mock, simulated, unnatural.
OPPOSITES: SEE **authentic, natural**.

syringe noun hypodermic, needle.

syrup noun SEE **sugar** noun.

system noun 1 *a railway system.* network, organization, [*informal*] setup.
2 *a system for getting your work done.* arrangement, logic, method, methodology, order, plan, practice, procedure, process, routine, rules, scheme, structure, technique, theory.
3 *a system of government.* constitution, philosophy, principles, regime, science.

systematic adjective *a systematic worker. systematic organization.* businesslike, logical, methodical, ordered, orderly, organized, planned, scientific, structured.
OPPOSITES: SEE **unsystematic**.

systematize verb *You need to systematize your work routine.* arrange, classify, codify, make systematic [SEE **systematic**], organize, rationalize, standardize.

T

tab noun SEE **tag** noun.

tabernacle noun SEE **worship** noun (place of worship).

table noun 1 coffee-table, dining-table, gate-leg table, kitchen table.
OTHER ITEMS OF FURNITURE: SEE **furniture**.
2 *a table of information.* catalogue, chart, diagram, graph, index, list, register, schedule, tabulation, timetable.
table tennis [*informal*] ping-pong.

tableau noun picture, representation, scene.

tablespoon noun serving spoon.
OTHER CUTLERY: SEE **cutlery**.

tablet noun 1 *a tablet of soap.* bar, block, chunk, piece, slab.
2 *The doctor prescribed some tablets.* capsule, medicine, pellet, pill.

tabloid noun SEE **newspaper**.

taboo adjective *a taboo subject.* banned, disapproved of, forbidden, prohibited, proscribed, unacceptable, unmentionable, unnameable.

taboo noun *a religious taboo.* ban, curse, prohibition, taboo subject [SEE **taboo** adjective].

tabulate verb *to tabulate information.* arrange as a table, catalogue, list, set out in columns.

tacit adjective *tacit agreement.* implicit, implied, silent, understood, unspoken, unvoiced.

taciturn adjective SEE **silent**.

tack noun 1 drawing-pin, nail, pin, tin-tack.
OTHER FASTENERS: SEE **fastener**.
2 *a tack in a garment.* stitch.
3 *You're on the wrong tack.* approach, SEE **direction**, policy, procedure.

tack verb 1 *to tack down a carpet.* nail, pin.
OTHER WAYS TO FASTEN THINGS: SEE **fasten**.
2 *to tack up a hem.* sew, stitch.
3 *to tack in a sailing-boat.* beat against the wind.
to tack on SEE **add**.

tackle noun **1** *fishing tackle*. apparatus, equipment, gear, implements, kit, outfit, [*joking*] paraphernalia, rig, tools.
2 *a football tackle*. attack, block, challenge, interception, intervention.

tackle verb **1** *to tackle a problem*. address yourself to, attempt, attend to, combat, confront, cope with, deal with, face up to, grapple with, handle, manage, set about, sort out, undertake.
2 *to tackle an opposing player*. attack, challenge, intercept, stop, take on.

tacky adjective *tacky paint*. gluey, sticky, wet.
OPPOSITES: SEE **dry** adjective.

tact noun *He showed tact in dealing with their embarrassment*. consideration, delicacy, diplomacy, discretion, sensitivity, tactfulness, thoughtfulness, understanding.
OPPOSITES: SEE **tactlessness**.

tactful adjective *a tactful reminder*. appropriate, considerate, delicate, diplomatic, discreet, judicious, polite, sensitive, thoughtful.
OPPOSITES: SEE **tactless**.

tactical adjective *a tactical manœuvre*. calculated, deliberate, planned, politic, prudent, shrewd, skilful, strategic.

tactics noun *The manager explained the tactics for the next game*. approach, campaign, course of action, manœuvring, plan, ploy, policy, procedure, scheme, strategy.

tactile adjective SEE **touch** noun.

tactless adjective *a tactless reference to her illness*. blundering, boorish, clumsy, gauche, heavy-handed, hurtful, impolite, inappropriate, inconsiderate, indelicate, indiscreet, inept, insensitive, misjudged, SEE **rude**, thoughtless, uncouth, undiplomatic, unkind.
OPPOSITES: SEE **tactful**.

tactlessness noun *I'm surprised by his tactlessness in discussing her illness*. gaucherie, indelicacy, indiscretion, ineptitude, insensitivity, SEE **rudeness**, thoughtlessness.
OPPOSITES: SEE **tact**.

tag noun **1** *a price tag*. docket, label, marker, slip, sticker, tab, ticket.
2 *a Latin tag*. SEE **saying**.

tag verb *to tag items in a database. to tag goods with price-labels*. identify, label, mark, ticket.
to tag on *I tagged on a PS at the end of the letter*. add, append, attach, tack on.

to tag along *We tagged along at the end of the queue*. SEE **follow**, join, [*informal*] latch on, trail, unite.

tagliatelle noun SEE **pasta**.

tail noun **1** *an animal's tail. the tail of a queue*. back, end, extremity, rear, tail-end.
2 [*informal*] *a person's tail*. SEE **bottom** noun.

tail verb *to tail a car*. follow, pursue, shadow, stalk, track, trail.
to tail off *Our enthusiasm tailed off when we got tired*. decline, decrease, dwindle, lessen, peter out, reduce, slacken, subside, wane.

tailcoat noun evening dress, [*informal*] tails.

tailor-made adjective SEE **perfect** adjective.

taint verb **1** *to taint food or water*. adulterate, contaminate, dirty, infect, poison, pollute, soil.
2 *to taint someone's reputation*. blacken, dishonour, ruin, slander, smear, stain.

take verb [*Take* has many meanings and uses. We give just the commoner ones here.]
1 *Take my hand*. clutch, grab, grasp, hold, pluck, seize, snatch.
2 *They took prisoners*. abduct, arrest, capture, catch, corner, detain, ensnare, entrap, secure.
3 *Someone took my pen*. appropriate, move, pick up, pocket, remove, SEE **steal**.
4 *Take 2 from 4*. deduct, eliminate, subtract, take away.
5 *My car takes four people*. accommodate, carry, contain, have room for, hold.
6 *We took him home*. accompany, bring, [*informal*] cart, conduct, convey, escort, ferry, fetch, guide, lead, transport.
7 *We took a taxi*. catch, engage, hire, make use of, travel by, use.
8 *She took science at college*. have lessons in, learn about, read, study.
9 *I can't take rich food. I won't take any more insults*. abide, accept, bear, brook, consume, drink, eat, endure, have, receive, [*informal*] stand, [*informal*] stomach, suffer, swallow, tolerate, undergo, withstand.
10 *It took a lot of courage to own up*. necessitate, need, require, use up.
11 *She took a new name*. adopt, assume, choose, select.
to take aback *The news took me aback*. SEE **surprise** verb.
to take after *She takes after her mother*. SEE **resemble**.
to take against *He took against me from the start*. SEE **dislike** verb.

to take back *He took back all he'd said.* SEE **withdraw**.

to take in 1 *The trick took me in.* SEE **deceive**.

2 *He takes in lodgers.* SEE **accommodate**.

3 *I hope you took in all I said.* SEE **understand**.

to take life SEE **kill**.

to take off 1 *Take off your clothes.* SEE **remove**.

2 *The mimic took off the prime minister.* SEE **imitate**.

to take on *I took on a new job.* SEE **undertake**.

to take over *I was angry when she took over my job.* SEE **usurp**.

to take part *We took part in the organization.* SEE **participate**.

to take place *The incident took place last week.* SEE **happen**.

to take to task *She took me to task for my lateness.* SEE **reprimand** verb.

to take up 1 *She's taken up a new hobby.* SEE **begin**.

2 *Studying takes up a lot of my time.* SEE **occupy**.

take-away noun OTHER MEALS: SEE **meal**.

SHOPS AND BUSINESSES: SEE **shop**.

take-off noun 1 *the take-off of an aircraft.* lift-off.

2 *a take-off of the prime minister.* SEE **imitation**.

take-over noun *a business take-over.* amalgamation, combination, incorporation, merger.

taking adjective SEE **attractive**.

takings noun *the takings of a shop.* earnings, gains, gate [= *takings at a football match*], income, proceeds, profits, receipts, revenue.

talcum noun OTHER COSMETICS: SEE **cosmetics**.

tale noun *She told us her tale.* account, anecdote, narration, narrative, relation, report, [*slang*] spiel, story, yarn.
VARIOUS KINDS OF STORY: SEE **story**.

to tell tales SEE **inform** (inform against).

talent noun *musical talent. sporting talent.* ability, accomplishment, aptitude, brilliance, capacity, expertise, flair, genius, gift, knack, [*informal*] know-how, prowess, skill.

talented adjective *a talented player.* able, accomplished, artistic, brilliant, SEE **clever**, distinguished, expert, gifted, inspired, skilful, skilled, versatile.
OPPOSITES: SEE **unskilful**.

talisman noun *a good-luck talisman.* amulet, charm, mascot.

talk noun 1 *talk between two or more people.* chat, confabulation, conference, conversation, dialogue, discussion, gossip, intercourse, palaver, words.

2 *a talk to an audience.* address, discourse, harangue, lecture, oration, presentation, sermon, speech.

talk verb 1 *As far as we know, animals can't talk.* address each other, articulate ideas, commune, communicate, confer, converse, deliver a speech, discourse, enunciate, exchange views, have a conversation, negotiate, [*informal*] pipe up, pronounce words, say something [SEE **say**], speak, tell, use language, use your voice, utter, verbalize, vocalize.

2 *Can you talk French?* communicate in, express yourself in, pronounce, speak.

3 *The police tried to get him to talk.* confess, give information, [*informal*] grass, inform, [*informal*] let on, [*informal*] spill the beans, [*informal*] squeal, [*informal*] tell tales.

to talk about allude to, comment on, discuss, mention, refer to, relate.

to talk to address, harangue, lecture.

VERBS EXPRESSING DIFFERENT MODES OF TALKING: SEE **answer**, argue, SEE **ask**, assert, complain, declaim, declare, ejaculate, exclaim, fulminate, harangue, object, plead, read aloud, recite, soliloquize, [*informal*] speechify.

WORDS EXPRESSING DIFFERENT WAYS OF TALKING [many of these words are used both as nouns and as verbs; many are used *informally*]: babble, baby-talk, bawl, bellow, blab, blarney, blether, blurt out, breathe (*Don't breathe a word!*), burble, call out, chat, chatter, chin-wag, chit-chat, clamour, croak, cry, drawl, drone, gabble, gas, gibber, gossip, grunt, harp, howl, intone, jabber, jaw, jeer, lisp, maunder, moan, mumble, murmur, mutter, natter, patter, prattle, pray, preach, rabbit, rant, rasp, rave, roar, scream, screech, shout, shriek, slur, snap, snarl, speak in an undertone, splutter, spout, squeal, stammer, stutter, tattle, tittle-tattle, utter, vociferate, wail, whimper, whine, whinge, whisper, witter, yell.

---

talkative adjective *a talkative person.* articulate, [*informal*] chatty, communicative, effusive, eloquent, expansive, garrulous, glib, gossipy, long-winded, loquacious, prolix, unstoppable, verbose, vocal, voluble, wordy.

a talkative person chatter-box, [*informal*] gas-bag, gossip, [*informal*] windbag.

tall adjective *a tall skyscraper.* SEE **big**, giant, high, lofty, towering.
OPPOSITE: SEE **short**.

tally noun SEE **reckoning**.

tally verb SEE **correspond**.

talon noun claw.

tame adjective 1 *tame animals.* amenable, biddable, compliant, disciplined, docile, domesticated, gentle, manageable, meek, obedient, safe, subdued, submissive, tractable.
OPPOSITE: SEE **wild**.
2 *a tame story.* bland, boring, dull, feeble, flat, lifeless, tedious, unadventurous, unexciting, uninspiring, uninteresting.
OPPOSITE: SEE **exciting**.

tame verb 1 *to tame a wild animal.* break in, discipline, domesticate, house-train, make tame [SEE **tame** adjective], master, train.
2 *to tame your passions.* conquer, curb, humble, keep under, quell, repress, subdue, subjugate, suppress, temper.

tamper verb *to tamper with* alter, [*informal*] fiddle about with, interfere with, make adjustments to, meddle with, tinker with.

tan adjective SEE **brown** adjective.

tan noun *I got a tan on holiday.* sunburn, suntan.

tan verb *to tan in the sun.* burn, bronze, brown, colour, darken, get tanned [SEE **tanned**].

tang noun *The flavour has quite a tang to it.* acidity, [*informal*] bite, piquancy, pungency, savour, sharpness.

tangent noun **to go off at a tangent** SEE **diverge**.

tangible adjective *tangible evidence.* actual, concrete, definite, material, palpable, physical, positive, provable, real, solid, substantial, touchable.
OPPOSITES: SEE **intangible**.

tangle noun *a tangle of string.* coil, confusion, jumble, jungle, knot, mass, muddle, twist, web.

tangle verb 1 *to tangle string or ropes.* confuse, entangle, entwine, [*informal*] foul up, interweave, muddle, ravel, [*informal*] snarl up, twist.
OPPOSITES: SEE **disentangle**.
2 *A fish was tangled in the net.* catch, enmesh, ensnare, entrap, trap.
3 *Don't tangle with those criminals.* become involved with, confront, cross.

tangled adjective 1 *a tangled situation.* complicated, confused, convoluted, entangled, intricate, involved, knotty, messy.
OPPOSITES: SEE **straightforward**.

2 *tangled hair.* dishevelled, knotted, matted, tousled, uncombed, unkempt, untidy.
OPPOSITES: SEE **tidy** adjective.

tangy adjective *a tangy taste.* acid, appetizing, bitter, fresh, piquant, pungent, refreshing, sharp, spicy, strong, tart.
OPPOSITES: SEE **bland**.

tank noun 1 *a water tank.* basin, cistern, reservoir.
OTHER CONTAINERS: SEE **container**.
2 *a fish tank.* aquarium.
3 *an army tank.* armoured vehicle.

tankard noun SEE **cup**.

tanned adjective brown, sunburnt, suntanned, weather-beaten.

tantalize verb *The delicious smell tantalized us.* entice, frustrate, [*informal*] keep on tenterhooks, lead on, provoke, taunt, tease, tempt, titillate, torment.

tantamount adjective SEE **equivalent**.

tantrum noun SEE **temper** noun.

tap noun 1 *a water tap.* [*American*] faucet, stop-cock, valve.
2 *a tap on the door.* SEE **hit** noun.

tap verb *I tapped on the door.* SEE **hit** verb, knock, rap, strike.

tape noun 1 *I tied the parcel with tape.* band, binding, braid, ribbon, strip.
2 *recording tape.* SEE **record** noun.
tape deck, **tape recorder** SEE **audio equipment**.

tape verb *to tape up a parcel.* SEE **fasten**.

taper noun candle, lighter, spill.

taper verb *to taper to a point.* attenuate, become narrower, narrow, thin.
to taper off *The conversation tapered off.* SEE **decrease** verb.

tape-record verb SEE **record** verb.

tar noun pitch.

tardy adjective SEE **late**, **slow** adjective.

target noun 1 *Our target was to raise £100.* aim, ambition, end, goal, hope, intention, objective, purpose.
2 *Who was the target of their criticism?* butt, object, quarry, victim.

tariff noun 1 *a hotel's tariff.* charges, menu, price-list, schedule.
2 *a tariff on imports.* customs, duty, excise, levy, tax, toll.

tarn noun SEE **lake**.

tarnish verb 1 *Acid rain tarnished the metal.* blacken, corrode, discolour.
2 *The slander tarnished his reputation.* blemish, blot, dishonour, mar, spoil, stain, sully.

tarpaulin noun SEE **covering**.

tarry verb SEE **delay** verb.

tart adjective *the tart taste of lemons*. acid, biting, piquant, pungent, sharp, sour, tangy.
OPPOSITES: SEE **bland, sweet** adjective.

tart noun flan, pastry, pie, quiche, tartlet.

task noun *We were given several tasks to do*. activity, assignment, burden, business, chore, duty, employment, enterprise, errand, imposition, job, mission, requirement, undertaking, work.
to take to task SEE **reprimand** verb.

task-force noun SEE **armed services**.

taskmaster noun SEE **employer**.

taste noun **1** *the taste of strawberries*. character, flavour, savour.
2 *I gave her a taste of my apple*. bit, bite, morsel, mouthful, nibble, piece, sample, titbit.
3 *We share the same tastes in music*. appreciation, choice, inclination, judgement, liking, preference.
4 *She is a person of taste*. breeding, culture, discernment, discretion, discrimination, education, elegance, fashion sense, finesse, good judgement, perception, polish, refinement, sensitivity, style.
in bad taste SEE **tasteless**.
in good taste SEE **tasteful**.

taste verb *Taste a bit of this!* nibble, relish, sample, savour, sip, test, try.

WORDS TO DESCRIBE HOW THINGS TASTE: acid, bitter, creamy, fresh, fruity, hot, luscious, meaty, mellow, peppery, piquant, pungent, rancid, refreshing, salty, savoury, sharp, sour, spicy, stale, strong, sugary, sweet, tangy, tart, SEE **tasteless**, SEE **tasty**, unpalatable.

---

tasteful adjective *tasteful clothes. a tasteful choice of colours*. artistic, attractive, cultivated, dignified, discerning, discreet, discriminating, elegant, fashionable, in good taste, judicious, proper, refined, restrained, sensitive, smart, stylish, well-judged.
OPPOSITES: SEE **tasteless**.

tasteless adjective **1** *tasteless food*. bland, characterless, flavourless, insipid, mild, uninteresting, watered down, watery, weak.
OPPOSITES: SEE **tasty**.
2 *a tasteless choice of colours. a tasteless joke*. crude, garish, gaudy, graceless, improper, inartistic, in bad taste, indelicate, inelegant, injudicious, [*informal*]

kitsch, ugly, unattractive, undiscriminating, unfashionable, unimaginative, unpleasant, unseemly, unstylish, SEE **vulgar**.
OPPOSITES: SEE **tasteful**.

tasty adjective *tasty food*. appetizing, delicious, flavoursome, [*informal*] mouthwatering, [*informal*] nice, piquant, savoury, [*informal*] scrumptious.
OTHER WORDS TO DESCRIBE HOW THINGS TASTE: SEE **taste** verb.
OPPOSITES: SEE **tasteless**.

tattered adjective *tattered clothes*. frayed, ragged, ripped, tatty, threadbare, torn, worn out.
OPPOSITES: SEE **smart** adjective.

tatters noun *Her clothes were in tatters*. rags, ribbons, shreds, torn pieces.

tattle verb SEE **talk** verb.

tattoo noun **1** *a drum tattoo*. SEE **signal** noun.
2 *a military tattoo*. SEE **entertainment**.
3 *a tattoo on the skin*. SEE **mark** noun.

tatty adjective **1** *tatty clothes*. frayed, old, patched, ragged, ripped, scruffy, shabby, tattered, torn, threadbare, untidy, worn out.
OIPPOSITES: SEE **new**.
2 *tatty ornaments*. SEE **tawdry**.

taunt verb SEE **ridicule** verb.

taut adjective *Make sure the rope is taut*. firm, stretched, tense, tight.
OPPOSITES: SEE **slack** adjective.

tauten verb SEE **tighten**.

tautological adjective *a tautological use of words*. otiose, pleonastic, redundant, repetitious, repetitive, superfluous, tautologous, SEE **wordy**.
OPPOSITES: SEE **concise**.

tautology noun duplication, pleonasm, repetition.

tavern noun (*old-fashioned*) *They had a drink at the tavern*. [*old-fashioned*] alehouse, bar, (*joking*) hostelry, inn, [*informal*] local, pub, public house.

tawdry adjective *tawdry ornaments. a tawdry imitation*. cheap, common, eye-catching, fancy, [*informal*] flashy, garish, gaudy, inferior, meretricious, poor quality, raffish, showy, tasteless, tatty, vulgar, worthless.
OPPOSITES: SEE **superior**.

tawny adjective SEE **brown** adjective, **yellow**.

tawse noun SEE **strap** noun.

tax noun charge, imposition, levy, tariff.

VARIOUS TAXES: airport tax, community charge, customs, duty, excise, income tax, poll-tax, rates, [*old-fashioned*] tithe, toll, value-added tax.

---

tax verb 1 *to tax income, goods, etc.* impose a tax on, levy a tax on.
2 *The problem taxed me severely.* burden, exhaust, make heavy demands on, overwork, SEE **tire**.
to tax with *They taxed me with inefficiency.* accuse of, blame for, censure for, charge with, reproach for, reprove for.

taxi noun cab, [*old-fashioned*] hackney carriage, minicab.

taxonomy noun SEE **classification**.

taxpayer noun SEE **citizen**.

tea noun 1 *a cup of tea.* OTHER DRINKS: SEE **drink** noun.
2 *She invited me to tea.* OTHER MEALS: SEE **meal**.

tea-break noun SEE **break** noun.

teach verb VARIOUS WAYS TO TEACH THINGS TO OTHERS: advise, brainwash, coach, counsel, demonstrate to, discipline, drill, educate, enlighten, familiarize with, ground (someone) in, impart knowledge to, implant knowledge in, inculcate habits in, indoctrinate, inform, instruct, lecture, school, train, tutor.

teacher noun VARIOUS TEACHERS: adviser, coach, counsellor, demonstrator, don, educator, governess, guide, guru, headteacher, housemaster, housemistress, instructor, lecturer, maharishi, master, mentor, mistress, pedagogue, preacher, preceptor, professor, pundit, schoolmaster, schoolmistress, schoolteacher, trainer, tutor.

tea-chest noun SEE **box**.

teaching noun 1 VARIOUS KINDS OF TEACHING: advice, brainwashing, briefing, coaching, computer-aided learning, counselling, demonstration, distance learning, grounding, guidance, indoctrination, instruction, lecture, lesson, practical (*a science practical*), preaching, rote learning, schooling, seminar, training, tuition, tutorial, work experience, workshop (*a writing workshop*).
2 *the teachings of holy scripture.* doctrine, dogma, gospel, precept, principle, tenet.

tea-cloth noun SEE **towel** noun.

team noun 1 *a football team.* club, [*informal*] line-up, side.
2 *working as a team.* SEE **group** noun.

team verb **to team up** SEE **group** verb.

tea-party noun SEE **party**.

teapot noun ITEMS OF CROCKERY: SEE **crockery**.

tear noun 1 [rhymes with *fear*] *tears in his eyes.* droplet, tear-drop.
tears [*informal*] blubbering, crying, sobs, weeping.
to shed tears SEE **weep**.
2 [rhymes with *bear*] *a tear in my jeans.* cut, gap, gash, hole, opening, rent, rip, slit, split.

tear verb 1 *The barbed wire tore my jeans.* claw, gash, lacerate, mangle, pierce, rend, rip, rupture, scratch, shred, slit, snag, split.
2 [*informal*] *We tore to the station.* SEE **rush** verb.

tearaway noun SEE **hooligan**.

tearful adjective *tearful children. a tearful farewell.* [*informal*] blubbering, crying, emotional, lachrymose, SEE **sad**, sobbing, weeping, [*informal*] weepy.

tearing adjective [*informal*] *a tearing hurry.* SEE **impetuous**.

tea-room, tea-shop nouns SEE **café**.

tea-towel noun SEE **towel** noun.

tease verb *The cat scratches if you tease her.* [*informal*] aggravate, annoy, bait, chaff, goad, irritate, laugh at, make fun of, mock, [*informal*] needle, pester, plague, provoke, [*informal*] pull someone's leg, [*informal*] rib, SEE **ridicule** verb, tantalize, taunt, torment, vex, worry.

teasing noun *I was annoyed by their teasing.* badinage, banter, joking, mockery, provocation, raillery, [*informal*] ribbing, ridicule, taunts.

teaser noun SEE **problem**.

teat noun nipple.

technical adjective 1 *technical data. technical details.* esoteric, expert, professional, specialized.
2 *technical skill.* engineering, mechanical, scientific.

technician noun engineer, mechanic, skilled worker, [*plural*] technical staff.

technique noun *the technique you need to do a task.* art, craft, craftsmanship, dodge, expertise, facility, knack, [*informal*] know-how, manner, means, method, mode, procedure, proficiency, routine, skill, system, trick, way, workmanship.

technological adjective *technological equipment.* advanced, automated, computerized, electronic, scientific.

technology noun BRANCHES OF SCIENCE AND TECHNOLOGY: SEE **science**.

tedious adjective *a tedious journey. a tedious lecture.* boring, dreary, dull, [*informal*] humdrum, irksome, laborious,

long-winded, monotonous, slow, tiresome, tiring, unexciting, uninteresting, wearisome.
OPPOSITES: SEE **interesting**.

tedium noun *We played games to relieve the tedium of the journey.* boredom, dreariness, dullness, long-windedness, monotony, slowness, tediousness.

teem verb *The pond teemed with tadpoles.* abound (in), be full (of), be infested, be overrun (by), [*informal*] crawl, seethe, swarm.

teenager noun adolescent, boy, girl, juvenile, minor, youngster, youth.

teeny adjective SEE **small**.

teeter verb *to teeter on the brink.* SEE **waver**.

teetotal adjective *He won't drink because he's teetotal.* abstemious, abstinent, restrained, self-denying, self-disciplined, temperate.
OPPOSITES: SEE **drunken**.

teetotaller noun abstainer, nondrinker.
OPPOSITES: SEE **drunkard**.

The prefix *tele-* is from Greek *tele = far off.*

---

telecommunications noun SEE **communication**.

telegram noun cable, fax, telex, wire.

telegraph, telegraphy nouns SEE **communication**.

telepathic adjective *If you know what I'm thinking, you must be telepathic.* clairvoyant, psychic.

telephone noun [*informal*] blower, car-phone, handset, phone.

telephone verb *Telephone us if you can't come.* [*informal*] buzz, call, dial, [*informal*] give (someone) a call, phone, ring.
OTHER WAYS OF COMMUNICATING: SEE **communication**.

telephonist noun switchboard operator.

telerecording noun SEE **recording**.

telescope noun SEE **optical (optical instruments)**.

telescope verb *to telescope things together.* SEE **shorten**.

telescopic adjective *a tripod with telescopic legs.* adjustable, collapsible, expanding, extending, retractable.

televise verb *They televise a lot of snooker these days.* broadcast, relay, send out, transmit.

television noun monitor, receiver, [*informal*] telly, [*informal*] the box, [*informal*] the small screen, video.
OTHER WAYS OF COMMUNICATING: SEE **communication**.

TELEVISION PROGRAMMES: cartoon, chat show, comedy, commercial, documentary, drama, SEE **entertainment**, film, interview, mini series, movie, news, panel game, play, quiz, serial, series, [*informal*] sitcom, situation comedy, [*informal*] soap, soap opera, sport.

telex noun SEE **telegram**.

tell verb 1 *Tell the whole story.* announce, communicate, describe, disclose, divulge, explain, impart, make known, narrate, portray, recite, recount, rehearse, relate, reveal, speak, utter.
2 *Tell me the time.* acquaint (someone) with, advise, inform, notify.
3 *Can you tell the difference?* calculate, comprehend, decide, discover, discriminate, distinguish, identify, notice, recognize, see.
4 *He told me I could trust him.* assure, promise.
5 *Tell them to stop.* command, direct, instruct, order.
to tell someone off SEE **reprimand** verb.

teller noun 1 *a teller of tales.* SEE **storyteller**.
2 *a teller in a bank.* bank clerk, cashier.

telling adjective SEE **effective, striking**.

telling-off noun SEE **reprimand** noun.

tell-tale adjective *tell-tale signs.* SEE **significant**.

temerity noun SEE **audacity**.

temper noun 1 *in a good temper. in a bad temper.* attitude, disposition, humour, mood, state of mind, temperament.
2 *He sometimes flies into a temper.* fit (of anger), fury, [*informal*] paddy, passion, rage, tantrum.
3 *Try to keep your temper.* calmness, composure, coolness, sang-froid, self-control.
4 *Beware of his temper.* anger, irascibility, irritability, peevishness, petulance, surliness, unpredictability, volatility, wrath.

temper verb *to temper your opposition to something.* SEE **moderate** verb.

temperament noun *a melancholy temperament.* character, [*old-fashioned*] complexion, disposition, [*old-fashioned*] humour, nature, personality, spirit, temper.

temperamental adjective **1** *a temperamental aversion to work.* characteristic, congenital, constitutional, inherent, innate, natural.
2 *temperamental moods.* capricious, changeable, emotional, erratic, excitable, fickle, highly strung, impatient, inconsistent, inconstant, irritable, mercurial, moody, neurotic, passionate, touchy, unpredictable, unreliable, [*informal*] up and down, variable, volatile.

temperance noun SEE **moderation.**

temperate adjective SEE **moderate** adjective.

temperature noun SCALES FOR MEASURING TEMPERATURE: Celsius, centigrade, Fahrenheit.
to have a temperature be feverish, have a fever.

tempest noun SEE **storm** noun.

tempestuous adjective SEE **stormy.**

temple noun *a temple of the gods.* SEE **worship** noun (place of worship).

tempo noun *the tempo of a piece of music.* pace, rhythm, speed.

temporal adjective *temporal affairs.* earthly, impermanent, materialistic, mortal, mundane, passing, secular, sublunary, terrestrial, transient, transitory, worldly.
OPPOSITES: SEE **spiritual.**

temporary adjective **1** *a temporary building. a temporary arrangement.* brief, ephemeral, evanescent, fleeting, impermanent, interim, makeshift, momentary, passing, provisional, short, short-lived, short-term, stop-gap, transient, transitory.
OPPOSITES: SEE **permanent.**
2 *temporary captain.* acting.

temporize verb SEE **delay** verb.

tempt verb *I tempted the mouse with a bit of cheese.* allure, attract, bait, bribe, coax, decoy, entice, fascinate, inveigle, lure, persuade, seduce, tantalize, woo.

temptation noun *He succumbed to the temptations of the big city.* allurement, appeal, attraction, draw, enticement, fascination, lure, pull, seduction.

tempting adjective SEE **attractive.**

tenable adjective *a tenable theory.* arguable, credible, defensible, feasible, justifiable, legitimate, logical, plausible, rational, reasonable, sensible, sound, understandable, viable.
OPPOSITES: SEE **untenable.**

tenacious adjective *a tenacious hold on something.* determined, dogged, firm, intransigent, obdurate, obstinate, pertinacious, resolute, single-minded, strong, stubborn, tight, unshakeable, unswerving, unwavering, unyielding.
OPPOSITES: SEE **weak.**

tenant noun *the tenant of a rented flat.* inhabitant, leaseholder, lessee, lodger, occupant, resident.

tend verb **1** *A shepherd tends sheep.* attend to, care for, cherish, cultivate, guard, keep, look after, manage, mind, protect, watch.
2 *Doctors tend the sick.* nurse, treat.
3 *I tend to fall asleep in the evening.* be disposed to, be inclined to, be liable to, have a tendency to [SEE **tendency**], incline.

tendency noun *a tendency to be lazy.* bias, disposition, inclination, instinct, leaning, liability, partiality, penchant, predilection, predisposition, proclivity, propensity, readiness, susceptibility, trend.

tendentious adjective SEE **prejudiced.**

tender adjective **1** *tender meat.* eatable, edible.
OPPOSITES: SEE **tough.**
2 *tender plants.* dainty, delicate, fleshy, fragile, frail, soft, succulent, vulnerable, weak.
OPPOSITES: SEE **hardy.**
3 *a tender wound.* aching, painful, sensitive, smarting, sore.
4 *a tender love-song.* emotional, moving, poignant, romantic, sentimental, touching.
OPPOSITES: SEE **cynical.**
5 *tender care.* affectionate, caring, compassionate, concerned, considerate, fond, gentle, humane, kind, loving, merciful, pitying, soft-hearted, sympathetic, tender-hearted, warm-hearted.
OPPOSITES: SEE **callous.**

tenet noun SEE **principle.**

tense adjective **1** *tense muscles.* strained, stretched, taut, tight.
2 *a tense atmosphere.* anxious, apprehensive, edgy, excited, exciting, fidgety, highly strung, jittery, jumpy, [*informal*] nail-biting, nerve-racking, nervous, restless, stressed, [*informal*] strung up, touchy, uneasy, [*informal*] uptight, worried, worrying.
OPPOSITES: SEE **relaxed.**

tense noun TENSES OF A VERB: future, imperfect, past, perfect, pluperfect, present.
LINGUISTIC TERMS: SEE **language.**

tension noun **1** *the tension of guy ropes.* strain, stretching, tautness, tightness.
OPPOSITE: SEE **slackness.**
2 *the tension of waiting for an answer.* anxiety, apprehension, excitement,

nervousness, stress, suspense, unease, worry.
OPPOSITES: SEE **relaxation**.

tent noun KINDS OF TENT: bell tent, big-top, frame tent, marquee, ridge tent, tepee, trailer tent, wigwam.

tentacle noun *the tentacles of an octopus.* feeler, limb.

tentative adjective 1 *a tentative attempt.* cautious, diffident, doubtful, half-hearted, hesitant, indecisive, indefinite, nervous, timid, uncertain, [*informal*] wishy-washy.
2 *a tentative enquiry.* experimental, preliminary, provisional, speculative, uncommitted.
OPPOSITES: SEE **decisive**.

tenuous adjective *a tenuous connection. a tenuous line of argument.* fine, flimsy, insubstantial, slight, SEE **thin** adjective, weak.
OPPOSITES: SEE **strong**.

tepid adjective 1 *tepid bath-water.* lukewarm, warm.
2 *a tepid response.* SEE **apathetic**.

term noun 1 *a term in prison.* duration, period, season, span, spell, stretch, time.
2 *a school term.* [*American*] semester, session.
3 *a technical term. a foreign term.* epithet, expression, phrase, saying, title, word.
terms 1 *the terms of an agreement.* conditions, particulars, provisions, specifications, stipulations.
2 *a hotel's terms.* charges, fees, prices, rates, tariff.

termagant noun SEE **woman**.

terminal adjective *a terminal illness.* deadly, fatal, final, incurable, killing, lethal, mortal.

terminal noun 1 *a computer terminal.* VDU, work-station.
2 *a passenger terminal.* SEE **airport**, destination, terminus.
3 *an electrical terminal.* connection, connector.

terminate verb SEE **end** verb.

termination noun SEE **end** noun.

terminology noun *I didn't understand her terminology.* choice of words, jargon, language, phraseology, special terms, technical language, vocabulary.

terminus noun destination, terminal, termination.

termite noun SEE **insect**.

terrace noun *a terrace in the garden.* patio, paved area.

A number of English words, including *extraterrestrial, Mediterranean, terrain,* and *territory,* are related to Latin *terra* = *earth*.

terra firma noun SEE **land** noun.

terrain noun *They made slow progress across difficult terrain.* country, ground, land, landscape, SEE **territory**, topography.

terrestrial adjective *terrestrial beings.* earthly, mundane, ordinary.
OPPOSITE: extraterrestrial.

terrible adjective 1 *a terrible accident. terrible living-conditions.* appalling, distressing, dreadful, fearful, frightful, ghastly, hideous, horrible, horrific, horrifying, insupportable, intolerable, loathsome, nasty, outrageous, revolting, shocking, unbearable, unpleasant, vile.
2 [*informal*] *This coffee is terrible!* SEE **bad**.

terrific adjective [Like *terrible, terrific* is related to Latin *terrere* meaning *to frighten* and to our English word *terror.* However, the meaning of *terrific* is now vague. It is used informally to describe anything which is extreme in its own way, e.g. *We faced a terrific problem.* SEE **extreme**; *My fish was a terrific size.* SEE **big**; *We had a terrific time.* SEE **excellent**; *There was a terrific storm.* SEE **violent**.]

terrified adjective afraid, appalled, dismayed, SEE **frightened**, horrified, horror-struck, panicky, petrified, terror-stricken, unnerved.
OPPOSITES: SEE **calm** adjective.

terrify verb appal, dismay, SEE **frighten**, horrify, petrify, scare, shock, terrorize, unnerve.

terrifying adjective blood-curdling, dreadful, SEE **frightening**, hair-raising, horrifying, petrifying, [*informal*] scary, spine-chilling, traumatic, unnerving.

territory noun *enemy territory.* area, colony, SEE **country**, [*old-fashioned*] demesne, district, dominion, enclave, jurisdiction, land, preserve, province, region, sector, sphere [*sphere of influence*], state, terrain, tract, zone.

terror noun alarm, consternation, dread, SEE **fear** noun, [*informal*] funk, fright, horror, panic, shock, trepidation.

terrorist noun assassin, SEE **criminal** noun, gunman, hijacker.

terrorize verb *A criminal gang terrorized the neighbourhood.* browbeat, bully, coerce, cow, SEE **frighten**, intimidate, menace, persecute, terrify, threaten, torment, tyrannize.

terror-stricken adjective SEE **terrified.**

terse adjective *a terse comment.* SEE **brief** adjective, brusque, concise, crisp, curt, epigrammatic, incisive, laconic, pithy, short, [*informal*] snappy, succinct, to the point.
OPPOSITES: SEE **verbose.**

tessellation noun SEE **pattern.**

test noun *You have to pass a test before you get the job.* appraisal, assessment, audition, [*informal*] check-over, evaluation, examination, interrogation, investigation, probation, quiz, trial.

test verb *to test the quality of a product or a substance. to test a candidate.* analyse, appraise, assay, assess, audition, check, evaluate, examine, experiment with, inspect, interrogate, investigate, [*informal*] put someone through their paces, put to the test, screen, question, try out.

testament noun SEE **statement.**

testify verb *to testify in a court of law.* affirm, attest, bear witness, declare, give evidence, state on oath, swear, vouch, witness.

testimonial noun *a testimonial for an applicant for a job.* character reference, commendation, recommendation, reference.

testimony noun *testimony given in court.* affidavit, declaration, deposition, evidence, statement, submission, witness.
LEGAL TERMS: SEE **law.**

test-tube noun SEE **container.**

testy, tetchy adjectives SEE **irritable.**

tête-à-tête noun SEE **conversation.**

tether noun *an animal's tether.* chain, cord, halter, lead, leash, rope.

tether verb *to tether an animal.* chain up, SEE **fasten,** keep on a tether, restrain, rope, secure, tie up.

text noun 1 *the text of a document.* argument, contents, matter, wording.
2 *a literary text.* book, textbook, work, SEE **writing.**
3 *the text of a sermon. a text from the Bible.* motif, passage of scripture, sentence, theme, topic, verse.

textbook noun VARIOUS KINDS OF BOOK: SEE **book** noun.

textiles noun SEE **cloth,** fabric, material, stuff.

texture noun *the soft texture of velvet.* composition, consistency, feel, quality, touch.

thane noun SEE **lord.**

thank verb *to thank someone for a kindness.* acknowledge, express thanks [SEE **thanks**].

thankful adjective *thankful to be home.* appreciative, contented, grateful, happy, pleased, relieved.
OPPOSITES: SEE **ungrateful.**

thankless adjective *a thankless task.* unappreciated, unrecognized, unrewarded, unrewarding.
OPPOSITES: SEE **rewarding.**

thanks noun acknowledgement, appreciation, gratefulness, gratitude, recognition, thanksgiving.

thanksgiving noun SEE **thanks.**

thatch noun SEE **roof.**

thaw verb *The snow thawed.* become liquid, defrost, melt, soften, uncongeal, unfreeze, unthaw, warm up.
OPPOSITES: SEE **freeze.**

theatre noun auditorium, drama studio, hall, opera-house, playhouse.

THEATRICAL ENTERTAINMENTS: ballet, comedy, drama, farce, masque, melodrama, mime, music-hall, nativity play, opera, operetta, pantomime, play, tragedy.

OTHER ENTERTAINMENTS: SEE **entertainment.**

KINDS OF PERFORMANCE: command performance, dress rehearsal, first night, last night, matinée, première, preview, production, rehearsal, show.

THEATRE PEOPLE: actor, actress, backstage staff, ballerina, dancer, director, dresser, make-up artist, performer, player, producer, prompter, stage-manager, understudy, usher or usherette.

PARTS OF A THEATRE: back-stage, balcony, box-office, circle, dressing-room, foyer, front of house, gallery, [*informal*] the gods, [*old-fashioned*] pit, stage, stalls.

---

theatrical adjective 1 *I made my first theatrical appearance in a Shakespeare play.* dramatic, histrionic.
2 *He made the announcement in a theatrical manner.* demonstrative, exaggerated, melodramatic, ostentatious, pompous, self-important, showy, stagy, stilted, unnatural.
OPPOSITES: SEE **natural.**

theft noun SEE **stealing.**

theme noun 1 *the theme of a talk.* argument, idea, issue, keynote, matter, subject, text, thesis, topic.

2 *a musical theme.* air, melody, motif, [*formal*] subject, tune.

theology noun divinity, religion.

theoretical adjective *theoretical knowledge.* abstract, academic, conjectural, doctrinaire, hypothetical, ideal, notional, pure (*pure science*), speculative, unproven, untested.
OPPOSITES: SEE **applied, empirical.**

theorize verb *to theorize about a problem.* conjecture, form a theory, hypothesize, speculate.

theory noun 1 *My theory would explain what happened.* argument, assumption, belief, conjecture, explanation, guess, hypothesis, idea, notion, speculation, supposition, surmise, thesis, view.
2 *the theory of musical composition.* laws, principles, rules, science.
OPPOSITES: SEE **practice.**

Several English words like *therapeutic* and *therapy* are related to Greek *therapeia = healing.*

---

therapeutic adjective *When I was sad, music had a therapeutic effect.* beneficial, corrective, curative, healing, helpful, restorative.
OPPOSITES: SEE **harmful.**

therapist noun healer, physiotherapist, psychotherapist.

therapy noun cure, healing, remedy, tonic, treatment.

SOME KINDS OF THERAPY: chemotherapy, group therapy, hydrotherapy, hypnotherapy, occupational therapy, physiotherapy, psychotherapy, radiotherapy.
OTHER MEDICAL TREATMENT: SEE **medicine.**

---

therefore adverb accordingly, consequently, hence, so, thus.

Several English words like *thermal, thermometer,* and *Thermos* are related to Greek *therm = heat.*

---

thermal adjective SEE **hot.**

Thermos noun vacuum flask.

thesaurus noun OTHER KINDS OF BOOK: SEE **book** noun.

thesis noun 1 *She argued a convincing thesis.* argument, hypothesis, idea, premise or premiss, proposition, theory, view.

2 *He wrote a thesis about his research.* disquisition, dissertation, essay, monograph, paper, tract, treatise.

thick adjective 1 *a thick book. thick rope. a thick line.* broad, [*informal*] bulky, chunky, fat, stout, sturdy, substantial, wide.
2 *thick snow. thick cloth.* deep, heavy.
3 *a thick crowd.* dense, impenetrable, numerous, packed, solid.
4 *The place was thick with photographers.* covered, filled, swarming, teeming.
5 *thick mud. thick cream.* clotted, coagulated, concentrated, condensed, heavy, stiff, viscous.
OPPOSITES: SEE **thin** adjective.
6 [*informal*] *a thick pupil.* SEE **stupid.**

thicken verb *to thicken a sauce.* concentrate, condense, reduce, stiffen.

thicket noun SEE **wood.**

thick-headed adjective SEE **stupid.**

thickness noun 1 *a thickness of paint.* coating, layer.
2 *a thickness of rock.* seam, stratum.

thickset adjective SEE **stocky.**

thick-skinned adjective SEE **insensitive.**

thick-witted adjective SEE **stupid.**

thief noun bandit, burglar, SEE **criminal** noun, embezzler, highwayman, housebreaker, looter, mugger, pickpocket, pirate, plagiarist [=*person who steals other people's ideas*], poacher, robber, shop-lifter, stealer, swindler.

thieve verb SEE **steal.**

thieving adjective *The thieving rogue!* SEE **dishonest,** light-fingered, rapacious.

thieving noun SEE **stealing.**

thigh noun SEE **leg.**

thin adjective 1 *a thin figure.* anorexic, attenuated, bony, emaciated, flatchested, gaunt, lanky, lean, narrow, rangy, scraggy, scrawny, skeletal, skinny, slender, slight, slim, small, spare, spindly, underweight, wiry.
OPPOSITES: SEE **fat** adjective.
2 *thin cloth.* delicate, diaphanous, filmy, fine, flimsy, insubstantial, light, sheer (*sheer silk*), wispy.
3 *thin gravy.* dilute, flowing, fluid, runny, watery.
4 *a thin crowd.* meagre, scanty, scarce, scattered, sparse.
OPPOSITES: SEE **thick.**
5 *a thin atmosphere.* rarefied.
OPPOSITES: SEE **dense.**
6 *a thin excuse.* feeble, implausible, tenuous, unconvincing.
OPPOSITES: SEE **convincing.**

thin verb *to thin paint.* dilute, water down, weaken.
to thin out 1 *The crowd thinned out.* become less dense, diminish, disperse. **2** *to thin out seedlings. to thin out a hedge.* make less dense, prune, trim, weed out.

thing noun **1** *a thing you can touch or hold.* artefact, article, body, device, entity, implement, item, object. **2** *a thing that happens.* affair, circumstance, deed, event, eventuality, happening, incident, occurrence, phenomenon. **3** *a thing on your mind. things you want to say.* concept, detail, fact, factor, idea, point, statement, thought. **4** *a thing you have to do.* act, action, job, task. **5** [*informal*] *He's got a thing about snakes.* [*informal*] hang-up, obsession, phobia, preoccupation.
things 1 *Put your things in the back of the car.* baggage, belongings, clothing, equipment, [*informal*] gear, luggage, possessions, [*informal*] stuff. **2** *Things improved when I found a place to live.* circumstances, conditions, life.

think verb **1** *I thought about my mistakes.* attend, brood, cogitate, concentrate, consider, contemplate, deliberate, give thought (to), meditate, [*informal*] mull over, muse, ponder, [*informal*] rack your brains, reason, reflect, ruminate, use your intelligence, work things out, worry. **2** *He thinks that science can explain everything.* accept, admit, be convinced, believe, conclude, deem, have faith, judge. **3** *I think she's angry.* assume, believe, be under the impression, estimate, feel, guess, imagine, presume, reckon, suppose, surmise.
to think better of *When I saw the rain, I thought better of going out.* change your mind about, reconsider, revise your opinion of.
to think out *She thought out how to do it.* analyse, answer, calculate, puzzle out, work out.
to think twice about *I'd think twice about taking a cut in wages.* be cautious, think carefully.
to think up *We thought up a plan.* conceive, concoct, create, design, devise, [*informal*] dream up, imagine, improvise, invent, make up.

thinker noun *Plato was one of the world's great thinkers.* [*informal*] brain, innovator, intellect, philosopher.

thinking adjective *She said that all thinking people would agree with her.* educated,

intelligent, rational, reasonable, sensible, thoughtful.
OPPOSITES: SEE **stupid**.

thin-skinned adjective SEE **sensitive**.

thirst noun **1** *a thirst for water.* drought, dryness, thirstiness. **2** *a thirst for knowledge.* appetite, craving, desire, eagerness, hunger, itch, longing, love (of), lust, passion, urge, wish, yearning.
to have a thirst SEE **thirst** verb.

thirst verb *to thirst after* be thirsty for [SEE **thirsty**], crave, have a thirst for, hunger after, long for, need, strive after, want, wish for, yearn for.

thirsty adjective **1** *thirsty after a long walk.* dehydrated, dry, [*informal*] gasping (for a drink), panting, parched. **2** *thirsty for adventure.* avid, eager, greedy, itching, longing, yearning.

thong noun SEE **lace** noun.

thorax noun chest.

thorn noun *thorns on a rose-bush.* barb, needle, prickle, spike, spine.

thorny adjective **1** *a thorny bush.* barbed, bristly, prickly, scratchy, sharp, spiky, spiny.
OPPOSITE: thornless. **2** [*informal*] *a thorny problem.* SEE **difficult**.

thorough adjective **1** *a thorough piece of work.* assiduous, attentive, careful, comprehensive, conscientious, diligent, efficient, exhaustive, full, [*informal*] in-depth, methodical, meticulous, observant, orderly, organized, painstaking, scrupulous, systematic, thoughtful, watchful.
OPPOSITES: SEE **superficial**. **2** [*informal*] *He's a thorough rascal!* absolute, arrant, complete, downright, out-and-out, perfect, thoroughgoing, total, unmitigated, unqualified, utter.
OPPOSITES: SEE **incomplete**.

thoroughfare noun SEE **road**.

thoroughgoing adjective SEE **thorough**.

thought noun **1** *deep in thought.* [*informal*] brainwork, brooding, [*informal*] brown study (*in a brown study*), cogitation, concentration, consideration, contemplation, day-dreaming, deliberation, introspection, meditation, musing, pensiveness, reasoning, reflection, reverie, rumination, study, thinking, worrying. **2** *a clever thought.* belief, concept, conception, conclusion, conjecture, conviction, idea, notion, opinion.

3 *We had no thought of staying so long.* aim, design, expectation, intention, objective, plan, purpose.

4 *It was a nice thought to give them flowers.* attention, concern, kindness, solicitude, thoughtfulness.

thoughtful adjective **1** *a thoughtful expression.* absorbed, abstracted, anxious, attentive, brooding, contemplative, dreamy, grave, introspective, meditative, pensive, philosophical, rapt, reflective, serious, solemn, studious, wary, watchful, worried.

2 *a thoughtful piece of work.* careful, conscientious, diligent, exhaustive, methodical, meticulous, observant, orderly, organized, painstaking, scrupulous, systematic, thorough.

3 *a thoughtful kindness.* attentive, caring, concerned, considerate, friendly, good-natured, helpful, SEE **kind** adjective, obliging, public-spirited, solicitous, unselfish.

OPPOSITES: SEE **thoughtless**.

thoughtless adjective **1** *thoughtless stupidity.* absent-minded, careless, forgetful, hasty, heedless, ill-considered, impetuous, inadvertent, inattentive, injudicious, irresponsible, mindless, negligent, rash, reckless, [*informal*] scatterbrained, SEE **stupid**, unobservant, unthinking.

2 *a thoughtless insult.* cruel, heartless, impolite, inconsiderate, insensitive, rude, selfish, tactless, uncaring, undiplomatic, unfeeling, SEE **unkind**.

OPPOSITES: SEE **thoughtful**.

thrall noun SEE **slave** noun.

thrash verb **1** *to thrash with a stick.* SEE **whip** verb.

2 [*informal*] *to thrash your opponents.* SEE **defeat** verb.

thread noun **1** *threads in a piece of cloth.* fibre, filament, hair, strand.

KINDS OF THREAD: cotton, silk, thong, twine, wool, yarn.

2 *the thread of a story.* argument, continuity, course, direction, line of thought, story-line, theme.

thread verb *to thread beads.* put on a thread, string together.

to thread your way SEE **pass** verb.

threadbare adjective *threadbare clothes.* frayed, old, ragged, shabby, tattered, tatty, worn, worn-out.

threat noun **1** *threats against his life.* menace, warning.

2 *a threat of snow.* danger, forewarning, omen, portent, presage, risk, warning.

threaten verb **1** *A gang of hooligans threatened us.* browbeat, bully, SEE frighten, intimidate, make threats against, menace, pressurize, terrorize.

2 *The forecast threatened rain.* forebode, foreshadow, forewarn of, give warning of, portend, presage, warn of.

3 *An avalanche threatened the town.* endanger, imperil, jeopardize.

OPPOSITES: SEE **reassure**.

threatening adjective *threatening storm clouds.* forbidding, grim, menacing, minatory, ominous, sinister, stern, unfriendly, worrying.

OPPOSITES: SEE **reassuring**.

three noun [= *a group of three*]. triad, trio, triplet, triumvirate.

RELATED ADJECTIVES: SEE **triple**.

three-cornered adjective triangular.

three-dimensional adjective rounded, solid, stereoscopic.

thresh verb **to thresh about** SEE **writhe**

threshold noun **1** *the threshold of a house.* doorstep, doorway, entrance, sill.

2 *the threshold of a new era.* SEE **beginning**.

thrifty adjective *thrifty with your money.* careful, economical, frugal, parsimonious, provident, prudent, sparing.

OPPOSITES: SEE **extravagant**.

thrill noun *the thrill of a fun-fair.* adventure, [*informal*] buzz, excitement, [*informal*] kick, pleasure, sensation, suspense, tingle, tremor.

thrill verb *The music thrilled us.* delight, electrify, excite, rouse, stimulate, stir, titillate.

OPPOSITES: SEE **bore** verb.

thriller noun crime story, detective story, mystery, [*informal*] whodunit.

VARIOUS KINDS OF WRITING: SEE **writing**.

thrilling adjective *thrilling feats.* electrifying, exciting, extraordinary, gripping, [*informal*] hair-raising, rousing, sensational, spectacular, stimulating, stirring.

OPPOSITES: SEE **boring**.

thrive verb *Tomato plants thrive in my greenhouse.* be vigorous, burgeon, develop strongly, do well, flourish, grow, prosper, succeed.

OPPOSITES: SEE **die**.

thriving adjective *a thriving business.* affluent, alive, booming, burgeoning, developing, expanding, flourishing, growing, healthy, profitable, prosperous, successful, vigorous.

OPPOSITES: SEE **dying**.

throat noun gullet, neck, oesophagus, uvula, wind pipe.

RELATED ADJECTIVE: guttural.

OTHER PARTS OF YOUR BODY: SEE **body**.

throaty adjective *a throaty voice.* deep, gravelly, gruff, guttural, hoarse, husky, rasping, rough, thick.

throb noun 1 *a throb of toothache.* SEE **pain** noun.
2 *the throb of music.* SEE **rhythm**.

throb verb *Blood throbs through our veins.* beat, palpitate, pound, pulsate, pulse.

throes plural noun *the throes of childbirth.* convulsions, effort, labour, labour-pains, pangs, spasms.

thrombosis noun blood-clot, embolism.

throne noun OTHER SEATS: SEE **seat** noun.

throng noun, verb SEE **crowd** noun, verb.

throttle noun SEE **valve**.

throttle verb asphyxiate, choke, SEE **kill**, smother, stifle, strangle, suffocate.

throw verb 1 *to throw a ball. to throw stones at something.* bowl, [*informal*] bung, cast, [*informal*] chuck, fling, heave, hurl, launch, lob, pelt, pitch, project, propel, put (*to put the shot*), [*informal*] shy, [*informal*] sling, toss.
2 *The horse threw the rider.* dislodge, shake off, throw off, unseat.
3 [*informal*] *The unexpected question threw me.* SEE **disconcert**.
to throw away *I threw away some old clothes.* SEE **discard**.
to throw out *He threw out a gatecrasher.* SEE **expel**.
to throw up 1 *The enquiry threw up new evidence.* SEE **produce**.
2 [*informal*] SEE **vomit**.
to throw in the towel, to throw up the sponge SEE **surrender**.

throwaway adjective 1 *throwaway plastic cups.* cheap, disposable.
2 *a throwaway remark.* casual, offhand, passing, unimportant.

thrust verb 1 *to thrust someone or something forward.* drive, force, press, propel, push, send, shove, urge.
2 *to thrust with a dagger.* jab, lunge, plunge, poke, prod, stab, stick.

thud noun, verb VARIOUS SOUNDS: SEE **sound** noun.

thug noun [*informal*] bully-boy, SEE **criminal** noun, delinquent, gangster, hooligan, killer, mugger, ruffian, [*informal*] tough, trouble-maker, vandal, [*informal*] yob.

thumb verb *to thumb through a book.* SEE **browse**.
to thumb your nose at SEE **insult** verb.

thump noun, verb SEE **hit** noun, verb.

thumping adjective SEE **large**.

thunder noun, verb WORDS FOR THE SOUND OF THUNDER: clap, crack, peal, roll, rumble.

thunderous adjective SEE **loud**.

thunderstorm noun SEE **storm** noun.

thunderstruck adjective SEE **amazed**.

thus adverb accordingly, consequently, hence, so, therefore.

thwack noun, verb SEE **hit** noun, verb.

thwart verb *to thwart someone's wishes.* foil, frustrate, hinder, impede, obstruct, prevent, stand in the way of, stop.

tiara noun diadem, crown.

tic noun *a nervous tic.* SEE **twitch** noun.

tick noun, verb *the tick of a clock.* VARIOUS SOUNDS: SEE **sound** noun.
to tick someone off SEE **reprimand** verb.

ticket noun 1 *an entry ticket.* coupon, pass, permit, token, voucher.
2 *a price ticket.* docket, label, marker, tab, tag.

ticking noun SEE **cloth**.

tickle verb 1 *to tickle someone with your fingertips.* SEE **touch** verb.
2 *My foot tickles.* SEE **itch** verb.
3 [*informal*] *His antics tickled us.* SEE **amuse**.

ticklish adjective 1 *Are you ticklish?* [*informal*] giggly, responsive to tickling, sensitive.
2 *a ticklish problem.* awkward, delicate, difficult, risky, [*informal*] thorny, touchy, tricky.

tidal adjective *tidal waters.* ebbing and flowing.
OPPOSITE: tideless.
tidal wave SEE **wave** noun.

tide noun *the tides of the sea.* current, drift, ebb and flow, movement, rise and fall.

tidiness noun *I admire her tidiness.* meticulousness, neatness, order, orderliness, organization, system.
OPPOSITES: SEE **disorder**.

tidings noun [*old-fashioned*] *good tidings.* SEE **news**.

tidy adjective 1 *tidy in appearance.* neat, orderly, presentable, shipshape, smart, spick and span, spruce, straight, trim, uncluttered, well-groomed.
2 *tidy in your habits.* businesslike, careful, house-proud, methodical, meticulous, organized, systematic.
OPPOSITES: SEE **untidy**.

tidy verb *Please tidy your room.* arrange, clean up, groom (*your hair*), make tidy [SEE **tidy** adjective], neaten, put in order, set straight, smarten, spruce up, straighten, titivate.
OPPOSITES: SEE **muddle** verb.

tie verb 1 *to tie something with string.* bind, SEE **fasten**, hitch, interlace, join, knot, lash, truss up.
OPPOSITES: SEE **untie**.
2 *to tie with an opponent in a game.* be equal, be level, draw.
to tie up *to tie up a boat or an animal.* anchor, moor, secure, tether.

tier noun *seats arranged in tiers.* level, line, rank, row, stage, storey, terrace.

tiff noun SEE **quarrel** noun.

tiffin noun SEE **meal**.

tight adjective 1 *a tight fit.* close, close-fitting, fast, firm, fixed, immovable, secure, snug.
2 *a jar with a tight lid.* airtight, hermetic, impervious, sealed, watertight.
3 *tight controls.* inflexible, precise, rigorous, severe, strict, stringent.
4 *tight ropes.* rigid, stiff, stretched, taut, tense.
5 *a tight space.* compact, constricted, crammed, cramped, crowded, dense, packed.
OPPOSITES: SEE **loose**.
6 [*informal*] *tight after drinking a few beers.* SEE **drunk**.
7 [*informal*] *tight with her money.* SEE **miserly**.

tighten verb 1 *to tighten your grip.* clamp down, constrict, hold tighter, squeeze, tense.
2 *to tighten a rope.* pull tighter, stretch, tauten.
3 *to tighten a screw.* give another turn to, make tighter, screw up.
OPPOSITES: SEE **loosen**.

tight-fisted adjective SEE **miserly**.

tights noun panti-hose.

tile noun OTHER ROOFING MATERIALS: SEE **roof**.

tile verb *to tile a floor.* SEE **cover** verb.

till noun *money in the till.* cash-register.

till verb *to till the land.* SEE **cultivate**.

tiller noun *the tiller of a boat.* helm.

tilt verb 1 *to tilt to one side.* careen, incline, keel over, lean, list, slant, slope, tip.
2 *to tilt with lances.* SEE **fight** verb, joust, thrust.
at full tilt SEE **fast** adjective.

timber noun *a house built of timber.* beams, boarding, boards, deal, lath, logs, lumber, planking, planks, posts, softwood, trees, tree trunks, SEE **wood**.

timbre noun SEE **sound** noun.

time noun 1 [= *a moment in time*] date, hour, instant, juncture, moment, occasion, opportunity.

2 [= *a length of time*] duration, period, phase, season, semester, session, spell, stretch, term, while.
3 *the time of Elizabeth I.* age, days, epoch, era, period.
4 *Keep time with the music.* beat, rhythm, tempo.
RELATED ADJECTIVE: chronological.
in no time SEE **fast** adjective.
on time SEE **punctual**.

UNITS OF TIME: aeon, century, day, decade, eternity, fortnight, hour, instant, leap year, lifetime, minute, month, second, week, weekend, year.

DEVICES FOR MEASURING TIME: calendar, chronometer, clock, digital clock, digital watch, hour-glass, stop-watch, sundial, timepiece, timer, watch, wristwatch.

SPECIAL TIMES OF THE YEAR: Advent, autumn, Christmas, Easter, equinox, Hallowe'en, hogmanay, Lent, midsummer, midwinter, New Year, Passover, Ramadan, solstice, spring, summer, Whitsun, winter, Yom Kippur, yuletide.

TIMES OF THE DAY: SEE **day**.

time verb 1 *I timed my arrival to coincide with hers.* choose a time for, estimate, fix a time for, judge, schedule, timetable.
2 *You use a stop-watch to time a race.* clock, measure the time (of).

time-consuming adjective SEE **long** adjective.

time-honoured adjective SEE **traditional**.

timekeeper noun SEE **supervisor**.

time-lag noun SEE **interval**.

timeless adjective SEE **immortal**.

timely adjective appropriate, apt, fitting, suitable.

timepiece, timer nouns DEVICES FOR MEASURING TIME: SEE **time** noun.

time-share adjective SEE **accommodation**.

timetable noun *a timetable of events.* agenda, calendar, diary, list, programme, roster, rota, schedule.

timid adjective *Don't be timid—dive in at the deep end!* afraid, apprehensive, bashful, cowardly, coy, diffident, faint hearted, fearful, [*informal*] mousy, nervous, pusillanimous, reserved, retiring, sheepish, shrinking, shy, spineless, tentative, timorous, unadventurous unheroic.
OPPOSITES: SEE **bold**.

imorous adjective SEE **timid**.

impani plural noun kettledrums.
OTHER DRUMS: SEE **drum**.

impanist noun drummer, kettledrummer.

in noun 1 OTHER METALS: SEE **metal**.
2 *a tin of beans*. can.
OTHER CONTAINERS: SEE **container**.

in verb *to tin food*. can.
OTHER WAYS TO PRESERVE FOOD: SEE **preserve** verb.

ine noun SEE **prong**.

ing noun, verb VARIOUS SOUNDS: SEE **sound** noun.

inge noun, verb SEE **colour** noun, verb.

ingle noun 1 *a tingle under the skin*. itch, itching, pins and needles, prickling, stinging, tickle, tickling.
2 *a tingle of excitement*. quiver, sensation, shiver, thrill.

ingle verb *I tingle where I sat in the nettles*. itch, prickle, sting, tickle.

inker verb *Don't tinker with the TV*. fiddle, interfere, meddle, [*informal*] mess about, [*informal*] play about, tamper, try to mend, work amateurishly.

inkle noun, verb VARIOUS SOUNDS: SEE **sound** noun.

inny adjective [*informal*] *a tinny old car*. cheap, inferior, poor-quality.
OPPOSITES: SEE **solid**.

insel noun *decorated with tinsel*. glitter, sparkle, tin foil.

int noun, verb SEE **colour** noun, verb.

iny adjective *a tiny insect, a tiny amount*. diminutive, imperceptible, infinitesimal, insignificant, microscopic, midget, [*informal*] mini, miniature, minuscule, minute, negligible, pygmy, SEE **small**, [*informal*] teeny, unimportant, [*informal*] wee, [*informal*] weeny.
OPPOSITES: SEE **big**.

ip noun 1 *the tip of a pen or pencil*. end, extremity, nib, point, sharp end.
2 *the tip of a mountain or iceberg*. apex, cap, crown, head, peak, pinnacle, summit, top.
3 *a tip for the waiter*. gift, gratuity, money, [*informal*] perk, present, reward, service-charge.
4 *useful tips on how to do it*. advice, clue, hint, information, suggestion, warning.
5 *a rubbish tip*. dump, rubbish-heap.

ip verb 1 *to tip to one side*. careen, incline, keel over, lean, list, slant, slope, tilt.
2 *to tip something from a container*. dump, empty, pour out, spill, unload.
3 *to tip a waiter*. give a tip to, remunerate, reward.

to tip over *A wave tipped the boat over*. capsize, knock over, overturn, topple, turn over, upset.

tip-off noun SEE **information**.

tipple noun, verb SEE **drink** noun, verb.

tipsy adjective SEE **drunk**.

tiptoe verb SEE **walk** verb.

tiptop adjective SEE **excellent**.

tirade noun SEE **attack** noun.

tire verb *The long game tired us*. drain, enervate, exhaust, fatigue, [*informal*] finish, make tired [SEE **tired**], overtire, tax, wear out, weary.
OPPOSITES: SEE **refresh**.

tired adjective [*informal*] dead beat, [*informal*] dog-tired, [*informal*] done in, drawn [= *looking tired*], drained, drowsy, exhausted, [*informal*] fagged, fatigued, flagging, footsore, jaded, [*informal*] jet-lagged, [*slang*] knackered, listless, [*informal*] shattered, sleepy, spent, travel-weary, wearied, weary, [*informal*] whacked, worn out.
tired of *I'm tired of all this noise*. bored with, [*informal*] fed up with, impatient with, sick of, [*informal*] sick and tired.

tiredness noun drowsiness, exhaustion, fatigue, inertia, jet-lag, lassitude, lethargy, listlessness, sleepiness, weariness.

tireless adjective *a tireless worker*. determined, diligent, energetic, indefatigable, persistent, sedulous, unceasing, unflagging, untiring.
OPPOSITES: SEE **lazy**.

tiresome adjective *tiresome interruptions*. annoying, bothersome, distracting, exasperating, irksome, irritating, petty, troublesome, unwelcome, vexing, wearisome.
OPPOSITES: SEE **welcome** adjective.

tiring adjective *tiring work*. demanding, difficult, exhausting, fatiguing, hard, laborious, taxing, wearying.
OPPOSITES: SEE **refreshing**.

tiro noun SEE **inexperienced** (**inexperienced person**).

tissue noun 1 *bodily tissue*. material, structure, stuff, substance.
2 *paper tissue*. tissue-paper, tracing-paper.
3 *a box of tissues*. handkerchief, napkin, serviette.

titanic adjective SEE **huge**.

titbit noun SEE **piece**.

titillate verb SEE **excite**.

titivate verb SEE **tidy** verb.

title noun 1 *the title of a picture or story.* caption, heading, name.
2 *a person's title.* appellation, designation, form of address, office, position, rank, status.
3 *the title to an inheritance.* claim, entitlement, ownership, prerogative, right.

TITLES YOU USE BEFORE SOMEONE'S NAME: Baron, Baroness, Count, Countess, Dame, Dr or Doctor, Duchess, Duke, Earl, Lady, Lord, Marchioness, Marquis, Master, Miss, Mr, Mrs, Ms, Professor, Rev or Reverend, Sir, Viscount, Viscountess.

OTHER TITLES: SEE **rank** noun, **royalty**.

TITLES YOU USE WHEN ADDRESSING PEOPLE: madam or madame, my lady, my lord, sir, sire, your grace, your honour, your majesty.

---

title verb *to title a story.* entitle, give a title to, name.

titled adjective *a titled family.* aristocratic, noble.
a titled person SEE **peer** noun.

titter verb chuckle, giggle, SEE **laugh**, snigger.

tittle-tattle verb SEE **gossip** verb.

titular adjective *the titular head of state.* formal, nominal, official, theoretical, token.
OPPOSITES: SEE **actual**.

tizzy noun [*informal*] in a tizzy SEE **confused**.

T-junction noun SEE **junction**.

toady noun SEE **flatterer**.

toady verb SEE **flatter**.

toast verb 1 *to toast bread.* brown, grill.
OTHER WAYS TO COOK THINGS: SEE **cook** verb.
2 *to toast a guest at a banquet.* drink a toast to, drink the health of, raise your glass to.

tobacco noun FORMS IN WHICH PEOPLE USE TOBACCO: cigar, cigarette, pipe-tobacco, plug, snuff.

toboggan noun SEE **sledge**.

tocsin noun SEE **signal** noun.

toddle verb SEE **walk** verb.

to-do noun SEE **commotion**.

toe noun digit.

toe verb to toe the line SEE **conform**.

tog verb to tog yourself up SEE **dress** verb.

together adverb all at once, at the same time, collectively, concurrently, consecutively, continuously, co-operatively, hand in hand, in chorus, in unison, jointly, shoulder to shoulder, side by side, simultaneously.
OPPOSITES: independently, separately.

toil noun [*informal*] donkey work, drudgery, effort, exertion, industry, labour, SEE **work** noun.

toil verb drudge, exert yourself, [*informal*] keep at it, labour, [*informal*] plug away, [*informal*] slave away, struggle, [*informal*] sweat, SEE **work** verb.

toilet noun 1 SEE **lavatory**.
2 SEE **washing**.

toiletries plural noun THINGS USED IN PERFORMING YOUR TOILET: SEE **cosmetics**, hair conditioner, lotion, moisturizer, rinse, shampoo, soap, talcum powder.

token noun 1 *a token of our affection.* evidence, expression, indication, mark, proof, reminder, sign, symbol, testimony.
2 *a bus-token.* counter, coupon, voucher.

tolerable adjective 1 *tolerable noise. tolerable pain.* acceptable, bearable, endurable, sufferable, supportable.
OPPOSITES: SEE **intolerable**.
2 *tolerable food. a tolerable performance.* adequate, all right, fair, mediocre, middling, [*informal*] OK, ordinary, passable, satisfactory.

tolerance noun 1 *tolerance towards those who do wrong.* broad-mindedness, charity, fairness, forbearance, forgiveness, lenience, openness, permissiveness.
2 *tolerance of others' opinions.* acceptance, sufferance, sympathy (towards), toleration, understanding.
OPPOSITES: intolerance, SEE **prejudice** noun.

tolerant adjective *tolerant of people's mistakes.* charitable, easygoing, fair, forbearing, forgiving, generous, indulgent, [*uncomplimentary*] lax, lenient, liberal, magnanimous, open-minded, patient, permissive, [*uncomplimentary*] soft, sympathetic, understanding, unprejudiced, willing to forgive.
OPPOSITES: SEE **intolerant**.

tolerate verb 1 *I can't tolerate this toothache!* abide, bear, endure, [*informal*] lump (*You'll have to lump it!*), [*informal*] put up with, [*informal*] stand, [*informal*] stick, [*informal*] stomach, suffer, [*informal*] take (*I can't take any more*), undergo.
2 *They don't tolerate smoking in the house.* accept, admit, brook, condone, countenance, make allowances for, permit

sanction, [*informal*] wear (*You can ask, but I'm sure they won't wear it*).

toll noun *a toll to cross the bridge.* charge, duty, fee, levy, payment, tax.

toll verb *to toll a bell.* SEE **ring** verb.

tomahawk noun SEE **axe** noun.

tomb noun burial-place, catacomb, crypt, grave, gravestone, mausoleum, SEE **memorial**, sepulchre, tombstone, vault.

tomboy noun SEE **girl**.

tombstone noun SEE **tomb**.

tom-cat noun SEE **cat**.

tome noun SEE **book** noun.

tommy-gun noun OTHER GUNS: SEE **gun**.

tommy-rot noun SEE **nonsense**.

tom-tom noun OTHER DRUMS: SEE **drum**.

tonality noun *the tonality of a piece of music.* key, tonal centre.

tone noun 1 *an angry tone in her voice.* accent, expression, feel, inflection, intonation, manner, modulation, note, quality, sound, timbre.
2 *eerie music to create the right tone for a mystery.* atmosphere, character, effect, feeling, mood, spirit, style, vein.
3 *paint with a pink tone.* SEE **colour** noun.

tone verb **to tone down** *to tone down the noise.* SEE **soften**.
to tone in *to tone in with something else.* SEE **harmonize**.
to tone up *to tone up your muscles.* SEE **strengthen**.

toneless adjective *a toneless voice.* SEE **monotonous**.

tongue noun 1 PARTS OF YOUR HEAD: SEE **head** noun.
2 *a foreign tongue.* SEE **language**.

tongue-tied adjective *He can't explain because he gets tongue-tied.* dumb, inarticulate, mute, silent, speechless.

tonic noun *You need a tonic after being ill.* boost, cordial, [*formal*] dietary supplement, fillip, [*informal*] pick-me-up, restorative.

tonsure noun VARIOUS HAIR-STYLES: SEE **hair-style**.

tool noun *a tool for every job.* apparatus, appliance, contraption, contrivance, device, gadget, hardware, implement, instrument, invention, machine, utensil, weapon.

CARPENTER'S TOOLS: auger, awl, brace and bit, bradawl, chisel, clamp, cramp, drill, file, fretsaw, gimlet, glass-paper, hack-saw, hammer, jigsaw, mallet, pincers, plane, pliers, power-drill, rasp, sander, sandpaper, saw, spokeshave, T-square, vice, wrench.

GARDENING TOOLS: billhook, dibber, fork, grass-rake, hoe, lawn mower, mattock, rake, roller, scythe, secateurs, shears, sickle, spade, strimmer, trowel.

COOKING UTENSILS: SEE **cook** verb.

VARIOUS OTHER TOOLS: axe, bellows, chain-saw, chopper, clippers, crowbar, cutter, hatchet, jack, ladder, lever, penknife, pick, pickaxe, pitchfork, pocket-knife, scissors, screw-driver, shovel, sledge-hammer, spanner, tape-measure, tongs, tweezers.

---

toot noun, verb VARIOUS SOUNDS: SEE **sound** noun.

tooth noun VARIOUS TEETH: canine, eye-tooth, fang, incisor, molar, tusk, wisdom tooth.
false teeth bridge, denture, dentures, plate.
RELATED ADJECTIVE: dental.
DENTAL PROBLEMS: caries, cavity, decay, plaque, toothache.

toothache noun SEE **pain** noun.

toothed adjective *a toothed edge.* cogged, indented, jagged.

top adjective *top marks. top speed. the top performance.* best, first, foremost, greatest, highest, leading, maximum, most, topmost, winning.
OPPOSITES: SEE **bottom** adjective.
top hat [*informal*] topper.

top noun 1 *the top of a mountain.* apex, crest, crown, head, peak, pinnacle, summit, tip, vertex.
2 *the top of the table.* surface.
3 *the top of her fame.* acme, apogee, culmination, height, zenith.
4 *the top of a jar.* cap, cover, covering, lid.
OPPOSITES: SEE **bottom** noun.

top verb 1 *I topped the cake with chopped nuts.* cover, decorate, finish off, garnish.
2 *Our charity collection topped last year's record.* beat, be higher than, better, cap, exceed, excel, outdo, surpass.

topcoat noun 1 *a topcoat to wear in winter.* SEE **overcoat**.
2 *a topcoat of paint.* final coat, finish, gloss, outer coat.

toper noun SEE **drunkard**.

topic noun *a topic for discussion.* issue, matter, question, subject, talking-point, theme, [*formal*] thesis.

topical adjective *topical news.* contemporary, current, recent, up-to-date.

topmost adjective SEE **top** adjective.

topography noun *the topography of an area.* features, geography, [*informal*] lie of the land.

topper noun top hat.

topple verb 1 *The gale toppled our TV aerial.* knock down, overturn, throw down, tip over, upset.
2 *He toppled off the wall.* fall, overbalance, tumble.
3 *The opposition eventually toppled the prime minister.* oust, overthrow, unseat.

topsoil noun SEE **soil** noun.

topsy-turvy adjective SEE **untidy**.

tor noun SEE **hill**.

torch noun bicycle lamp, [*old-fashioned*] brand, electric lamp, flashlight, [*old-fashioned*] link.

torchlight noun SEE **light** noun.

toreador noun bullfighter, matador.

torment noun *the torment of toothache.* affliction, agony, anguish, distress, misery, SEE **pain** noun, persecution, plague, purgatory, scourge, suffering, torture.

torment verb *My bad tooth was tormenting me. We were tormented by flies.* afflict, annoy, bait, be a torment to, bedevil, bother, bully, distress, harass, hurt, inflict pain on, intimidate, [*informal*] nag, pain, persecute, pester, plague, tease, torture, vex, victimize, worry.

tornado noun SEE **storm** noun.

torpid adjective SEE **lethargic**.

torpor noun SEE **lethargy**.

torrent noun *a torrent of water.* cascade, cataract, deluge, downpour, flood, flow, gush, rush, spate, stream, tide.

torrential adjective *a torrential downpour.* heavy, soaking, violent.
torrential rain cloudburst, deluge, rainstorm.

torrid adjective 1 *a torrid climate.* SEE **hot**.
2 [*informal*] *a torrid love-scene.* SEE **sexy**.

torso noun *a human torso.* body, trunk.

tortuous adjective *a tortuous route. a tortuous explanation.* circuitous, complicated, convoluted, crooked, devious, indirect, involved, meandering, roundabout, twisted, twisting, winding, zigzag.
OPPOSITES: SEE **straightforward**.

torture noun 1 *Many political prisoners experience torture in prison.* cruelty, degradation, humiliation, inquisition, persecution, torment.

2 *the torture of toothache.* affliction, agony, anguish, distress, misery, plague, scourge, suffering.

torture verb 1 *to torture a prisoner.* be cruel to, brainwash, bully, cause pain to, degrade, dehumanize, humiliate, hurt, inflict pain on, intimidate, persecute, rack, torment, victimize.
2 *I was tortured by doubts.* afflict, agonize, annoy, bedevil, bother, distress, harass, [*informal*] nag, pester, plague, tease, vex, worry.

Tory noun POLITICAL TERMS: SEE **politics**.

toss verb 1 *to toss something into the air.* bowl, cast, [*informal*] chuck, fling, flip (*to flip a coin*), heave, hurl, lob, pitch, shy, sling, throw.
2 *to toss about in a storm. to toss about in bed.* bob, lurch, move restlessly, pitch, reel, rock, roll, shake, twist and turn, wallow, welter, writhe.

tot noun 1 *tiny tots.* SEE **child**.
2 *a tot of rum.* SEE **drink** noun.

tot verb to tot up SEE **total** verb.

total adjective 1 *The bill shows the total amount.* complete, comprehensive, entire, full, gross (*gross income*), overall, whole.
2 *Our play was a total disaster.* absolute, downright, perfect, sheer, thorough, unmitigated, unqualified, utter.

total noun *Add up the figures and tell me the total.* aggregate, amount, answer, lot, sum, totality, whole.

total verb 1 *Our shopping totalled £37.* add up to, amount to, come to, make.
2 *to total a list of figures.* add up, calculate, count, find the total of, reckon up, totalize, [*informal*] tot up, work out.

totalitarian adjective *a totalitarian regime.* authoritarian, dictatorial, one party, oppressive, tyrannous, undemocratic, unrepresentative.
OPPOSITES: SEE **democratic**.

totality noun SEE **total** noun.

totalize verb SEE **total** verb.

totter verb *We tottered unsteadily off the ship.* dodder, falter, reel, stagger, SEE **walk** verb.

touch noun 1 *the sense of touch.* feeling, touching.
2 *I felt a touch on the arm.* caress, contact, dab, pat, stroke, tap.
3 *Working with animals requires a special touch.* ability, feel, flair, knack, manner, sensitivity, skill, style, technique, understanding, way.
4 *There's a touch of frost in the air.* hint, suggestion, suspicion, tinge, trace.
RELATED ADJECTIVE: tactile.

touch verb 1 *to touch physically.* brush, caress, contact, cuddle, dab, embrace, feel, finger, fondle, graze, handle, SEE **hit** verb, kiss, manipulate, massage, nuzzle, pat, paw, pet, push, rub, stroke, tap, tickle.
2 *to touch someone emotionally.* affect, concern, disturb, influence, inspire, move, stir, upset.
3 *Our speed touched 100 m.p.h.* attain, reach, rise to.
4 *No one could touch her performance.* [*informal*] come up to, compare with, equal, match, parallel, rival.
to touch off SEE **begin.**
to touch up SEE **improve.**

touched adjective 1 *I was touched by her kindness.* affected, moved, responsive (to), stirred, sympathetic (towards).
2 [*informal*] *He's a bit touched.* SEE **mad.**

touching adjective *a touching scene.* affecting, SEE **emotional,** moving, tender.

touchstone noun SEE **criterion.**

touchy adjective *Be careful what you say because he's touchy.* edgy, irascible, irritable, jittery, jumpy, nervous, quick-tempered, sensitive, snappy, temperamental, thin-skinned.

tough adjective 1 *tough shoes.* durable, hard-wearing, indestructible, lasting, stout, unbreakable, well-made.
OPPOSITES: SEE **delicate.**
2 *a tough physique.* [*informal*] beefy, brawny, burly, hardy, muscular, robust, stalwart, strong, sturdy.
3 *tough opposition.* invulnerable, merciless, obstinate, resilient, resistant, resolute, ruthless, stiff, stubborn, tenacious, unyielding.
OPPOSITES: SEE **weak.**
4 *tough meat.* chewy, hard, gristly, leathery, rubbery, uneatable.
OPPOSITES: SEE **tender.**
5 *a tough climb.* arduous, difficult, exacting, exhausting, gruelling, hard, laborious, stiff, strenuous.
6 *a tough problem.* baffling, intractable, [*informal*] knotty, puzzling, [*informal*] thorny.
OPPOSITES: SEE **easy.**

tough noun SEE **ruffian.**

toughen verb harden, make tougher, reinforce, strengthen.

toupee noun hair-piece, wig.

tour noun *a sight-seeing tour.* circular tour, drive, excursion, expedition, jaunt, journey, outing, ride, trip.

tour verb *to tour the beauty spots.* do the rounds of, explore, go round, make a tour of, SEE **travel** verb, visit.

tourist noun *The cathedral was full of tourists.* holiday-maker, sightseer, traveller, tripper, visitor.

tournament noun *a tennis tournament.* championship, competition, contest, match, meeting, series.

tousle verb *to tousle someone's hair.* SEE **ruffle.**

tout verb SEE **sell.**

tow verb *to tow a trailer.* drag, draw, haul, pull, trail, tug.

towel noun bath-towel, hand-towel, tea-cloth, tea-towel.

towel verb SEE **dry** verb.

tower noun KINDS OF TOWER: belfry, castle, fort, fortress, keep, minaret, skyscraper, steeple, turret.

tower verb *The castle towers above the village.* dominate, loom, rear, rise, stand out, stick up.

towering adjective 1 *a towering figure.* colossal, gigantic, high, imposing, lofty, mighty, soaring, SEE **tall.**
2 *a towering rage.* extreme, fiery, SEE **intense,** overpowering, passionate, violent.

town noun borough, city, conurbation, municipality, SEE **settlement.**

PLACES IN A TOWN: bank, SEE **building,** café, car-park, cinema, college, concert-hall, council-house, factory, filling-station, flats, garage, ghetto, hotel, SEE **house** noun, housing estate, industrial estate, leisure-centre, library, museum, office block, park, police station, post office, [*informal*] pub, recreation ground, residential area, restaurant, SEE **road,** school, SEE **shop,** shopping-centre, snack-bar, sports-centre, square, station, suburb, supermarket, theatre, warehouse.

---

townsfolk, townspeople nouns SEE **inhabitant.**

toxic adjective *toxic fumes.* dangerous, deadly, harmful, lethal, noxious, poisonous.
OPPOSITES: SEE **harmless.**

toy adjective *a toy car.* imitation, model, [*informal*] pretend, scaled down, SEE **small,** small-scale.

toy noun game, model, plaything, puzzle.

trace noun 1 *traces left by an animal.* evidence, footprint, [*informal*] give-away, hint, indication, mark, remains, sign, spoor, track, trail, vestige.

2 *a trace of jam left in the jar.* SEE **amount** noun (**small amount**).

to kick over the traces SEE **rebel** verb.

trace verb **1** *I traced my lost relatives.* detect, discover, find, get back, recover, retrieve, seek out.
2 *The hounds traced the fox across the field.* SEE **track** verb.
3 *to trace a picture.* copy, draw, go over, make a copy of, mark out, sketch.

tracery noun SEE **decoration**.

trachea noun windpipe.

tracing noun SEE **copy** noun.

track noun **1** *an animal's tracks.* footmark, footprint, mark, scent, spoor, trace, trail.
2 *a cross-country track.* bridle-path, bridle-way, cart-track, footpath, path, SEE **road**, way.
3 *a racing track.* circuit, course, dirt-track, race-track.
4 *a railway track.* SEE **railway**.

to make tracks SEE **depart**.

track verb *The hunters tracked the deer.* chase, dog, follow, hound, hunt, pursue, shadow, stalk, tail, trace, trail.

to track down discover, find, get back, recover, retrieve, trace.

tract noun **1** *a tract of land.* SEE **area**.
2 *a religious tract.* SEE 4TREATISE.

tractable adjective SEE **obedient**.

tractor noun VEHICLES: SEE **vehicle**.

trade noun **1** *international trade.* barter, business, buying and selling, commerce, dealing, exchange, industry, market, trading, traffic, transactions.
2 *trained in a trade.* calling, craft, employment, SEE **job**, [*informal*] line (*What's your line?*), occupation, profession, pursuit, work.

trade verb be involved in trade (SEE **trade** noun], do business, market goods, retail, sell, traffic (in).

to trade in *to trade in your old car.* exchange, offer in part exchange, swop.

to trade on *to trade on someone's good nature.* SEE **exploit** verb.

trader, tradesman nouns *market traders. local tradesmen.* dealer, merchant, retailer, roundsman, salesman, seller, shopkeeper, stockist, supplier, trafficker [= *trader in something illegal or suspect*], vendor.
SHOPS AND BUSINESSES: SEE **shop**.

trading noun SEE **trade** noun.

tradition noun **1** *It's a tradition to give gifts at Christmas.* convention, custom, habit, institution, practice, routine.
2 *Popular tradition portrays Richard III as a hunchback.* belief, folklore.

traditional adjective **1** *a traditional Christmas dinner.* accustomed, conventional, customary, established, familiar, habitual, historic, normal, orthodox, regular, time-honoured, typical, usual.
OPPOSITES: SEE **unconventional**.
2 *traditional stories.* folk, handed down, oral, popular, unwritten.
OPPOSITES: SEE **literary**.

traditionalist noun SEE **conservative** noun.

traduce verb SEE **denigrate**.

traffic noun **1** *road traffic.* movement, transport, transportation.
VARIOUS VEHICLES: SEE **vehicle**.
2 *traffic in drugs.* SEE **trade** noun.

traffic verb SEE **trade** verb.

trafficker noun SEE **trader**.

traffic-lights noun SEE **signal** noun.

tragedy noun **1** *"Romeo and Juliet" is a tragedy by Shakespeare.* KINDS OF WRITING: SEE **writing**.
2 *It was a tragedy when their dog was killed.* affliction, blow, calamity, catastrophe, disaster, misfortune.
OPPOSITES: SEE **comedy**.

tragic adjective **1** *a tragic accident.* appalling, awful, calamitous, catastrophic, depressing, dire, disastrous, dreadful, fatal, fearful, ill-fated, lamentable, terrible, unfortunate, unlucky.
2 *a tragic expression on her face.* bereft, distressed, grief-stricken, hurt, pathetic, piteous, pitiful, SEE **sad**, sorrowful, woeful, wretched.
OPPOSITES: SEE **comic**. adjective.

trail noun **1** *The hounds followed the fox's trail.* evidence, footprints, mark, scent, signs, spoor, traces.
2 *a nature trail.* path, pathway, SEE **road**, route, track.

trail verb **1** *to trail something behind you.* dangle, drag, draw, haul, pull, tow.
2 *to trail someone.* chase, follow, hunt, pursue, shadow, stalk, tail, trace, track down.
3 *to trail behind.* SEE **dawdle**.

train noun **1** *a railway train.* SEE **railway**.
2 *a train of events.* SEE **sequence**.

train verb **1** *to train a football team.* coach, educate, instruct, prepare, teach, tutor.
2 *to train hard.* do exercises, exercise, [*informal*] get fit, practise, prepare yourself, rehearse, [*informal*] work out.
3 *to train your sights on a target.* SEE **aim** verb.

trainee noun apprentice, beginner, cadet, learner, [*informal*] L-driver, novice, pupil, starter, student, tiro, unqualified person.

trainer noun **1** coach, instructor, teacher, tutor.
2 [= *light shoe*] SEE **shoe**.

traipse verb SEE **tramp** verb.

trait noun SEE **characteristic** noun.

traitor noun *a traitor to a cause.* apostate, betrayer, blackleg, collaborator, defector, deserter, double-crosser, informer, [*informal*] Judas, quisling, renegade, treacherous person [SEE **treacherous**], turncoat.

traitorous adjective SEE **treacherous**.

trajectory noun SEE **flight**.

tram noun tram-car.

trammel verb SEE **hamper**.

tramp noun **1** *a long tramp across country.* SEE **walk** noun.
2 *a homeless tramp.* beggar, [*informal*] destitute person, [*informal*] dosser, [*informal*] down and out, homeless person, traveller, vagabond, vagrant, wanderer.

tramp verb *We tramped across the hills.* [*informal*] foot-slog, hike, march, plod, stride, toil, traipse, trek, trudge, SEE **walk** verb, [*slang*] yomp.

trample verb *Don't trample on the flowers.* crush, flatten, squash, stamp on, tread on, walk over.

tramway noun SEE **railway**.

trance noun *lost in a trance.* day-dream, daze, dream, ecstasy, hypnotic state, reverie, spell, stupor, unconsciousness.

tranquil adjective **1** *a tranquil lake.* calm, peaceful, placid, quiet, restful, serene, still, undisturbed, unruffled.
OPPOSITES: SEE **stormy**.
2 *a tranquil mood.* collected, composed, dispassionate, [*informal*] laid-back, sedate, sober, unemotional, unexcited, untroubled.
OPPOSITES: SEE **excited**.

tranquillize verb SEE **calm** verb.

tranquillizer noun barbiturate, narcotic, opiate, sedative.

The prefix *trans-* is related to Latin *trans = across.*

---

transact verb SEE **perform**.

transaction noun *a business transaction.* SEE **deal** noun.

transcend verb SEE **surpass**.

transcendental adjective SEE **visionary** adjective.

transcribe verb *to transcribe a tape-recording.* copy out [SEE **copy** verb], take down, transliterate, write out.

transcript noun SEE **writing**.

transfer verb *to transfer from one place to another.* carry, change, convey, displace, ferry, hand over, move, relocate, remove, second (*seconded to another job*), take, transplant, transport, transpose.

transfigure verb SEE **transform**.

transfix verb SEE **pierce**.

transform verb *We transformed the attic into a games room.* adapt, alter, SEE **change** verb, convert, metamorphose, modify, rebuild, reconstruct, remodel, revolutionize, transfigure, translate, [*joking*] transmogrify, transmute, turn.

transformation noun *a transformation in her appearance.* alteration, SEE **change** noun, conversion, improvement, metamorphosis, revolution, transfiguration, transition, [*informal*] turn-about.

transfusion noun *a blood transfusion.*
OTHER MEDICAL TERMS: SEE **medicine**.

transgress verb SEE **sin** verb.

transgression noun SEE **sin** noun.

transgressor noun SEE **sinner**.

transient adjective *transient visitors. a transient glimpse.* brief, evanescent, fleeting, impermanent, momentary, passing, [*informal*] quick, short, temporary, transitory.
OPPOSITES: SEE **permanent**.

transistor noun SEE **radio**.

transit noun *goods damaged in transit.* journey, movement, passage, shipment, transportation, travel.

transition noun *the transition from childhood to adulthood.* alteration, SEE **change** noun, change-over, evolution, movement, progress, progression, shift, transformation, transit.

transitory adjective SEE **transient**.

translate verb *to translate words into English.* SEE **change** verb, convert, decode, express, interpret, make a translation, paraphrase, render, transcribe.

translation noun gloss, interpretation, paraphrase, rendering, transcription, version.

translator noun interpreter, linguist.

transliterate verb SEE **transcribe**.

translucent adjective SEE **transparent**.

transmigration noun *the transmigration of souls.* reincarnation.

transmission noun 1 *the transmission of a TV programme.* broadcast, diffusion, dissemination, relaying, sending out. 2 *the transmission of goods.* carriage, conveyance, dispatch, shipment, transportation.

transmit verb *to transmit a message. to transmit radio signals.* broadcast, communicate, convey, dispatch, disseminate, emit, pass on, relay, send.
OPPOSITES: SEE **receive**.

transmogrify, transmute verbs SEE **transform**.

transparency noun slide.
OTHER PHOTOGRAPHS: SEE **photograph** noun.

transparent adjective *transparent material.* clear, crystalline, diaphanous, filmy, gauzy, limpid, pellucid, [*informal*] see-through, sheer, translucent.

transpire verb SEE **happen**.

transplant noun *a heart transplant.* operation, surgery.

transplant verb *to transplant seedlings.* move, relocate, reposition, shift, transfer, uproot.

transport noun *public transport.* conveyance, haulage, shipping, transportation.

KINDS OF TRANSPORT: SEE **aircraft**, barge, boat [SEE **vessel**], bus, cable-car, cable railway, canal, car, chair-lift, coach, cycle, ferry, horse, lorry, Metro, minibus, [*old-fashioned*] omnibus, SEE **railway**, road transport [SEE **vehicle**], sea, ship [SEE **vessel**], space-shuttle, taxi, train, tram, van, waterways.

WAYS TO TRAVEL: SEE **travel** noun.

---

transport verb *to transport goods.* bring, carry, convey, fetch, haul, move, shift, ship, take, transfer.

transportable adjective SEE **movable**.

transpose verb *to transpose letters in a word.* change, exchange, move round, rearrange, reverse, substitute, swap, switch, transfer.

transverse adjective crosswise, diagonal, oblique.

trap noun *a trap to catch someone or something.* ambush, booby-trap, gin, mantrap, net, noose, snare.

trap verb *to trap an animal. to trap a criminal.* ambush, arrest, capture, catch, corner, ensnare, entrap, snare.

trapper noun hunter.

trappings noun *The judge wore a wig and all the trappings of his position.* accessories, accompaniments, accoutrements, adornments, decorations, equipment, finery, fittings, [*informal*] gear, ornaments, [*joking*] paraphernalia, [*informal*] things, trimmings.

trash noun garbage, junk, litter, refuse, rubbish, waste.

trashy adjective SEE **worthless**.

trauma noun SEE **shock** noun.

traumatic adjective *a traumatic experience.* SEE **shocking**.

travail noun SEE **effort**.

travel noun *They say that travel broadens the mind.* globe-trotting, moving around, [*joking*] peregrination, travelling.

KINDS OF TRAVEL: cruise, drive, excursion, expedition, exploration, flight, hike, holiday, journey, march, migration, mission, outing, pilgrimage, ramble, ride, safari, sail, sea-passage, tour, trek, trip, visit, voyage, walk.

WAYS TO TRAVEL: aviate, circumnavigate the world, commute, cruise, cycle, drive, emigrate, fly, free-wheel, [*informal*] gad about, [*informal*] gallivant, hike, hitch-hike, march, migrate, motor, navigate, paddle (*paddle a canoe*), pedal, pilot, punt, ramble, ride, roam, [*poetic*] rove, row, sail, shuttle, steam, tour, trek, voyage, walk, wander.

---

travel verb *to travel to work. to travel to foreign lands.* go, journey, move, proceed, progress, [*old-fashioned*] wend.

traveller noun 1 astronaut, aviator, cosmonaut, cyclist, driver, flyer, migrant, motor-cyclist, motorist, passenger, pedestrian, sailor, voyager, walker. 2 [= *person travelling on business or work*] commuter, [*informal*] rep, representative, salesman, saleswoman. 3 [= *person travelling for adventure or pleasure*] explorer, globe-trotter, hiker, hitch-hiker, holiday-maker, pilgrim, rambler, stowaway, tourist, tripper, wanderer, wayfarer. 4 [= *person for whom travelling is a way of life*] gypsy, itinerant, nomad, tinker, tramp, vagabond.

travelling adjective *travelling tribes.* itinerant, migrant, migratory, mobile, nomadic, peripatetic, roaming, roving, touring, vagrant, wandering.

travel-stained adjective SEE **dirty** adjective.

travel-weary adjective SEE **tired**.

traverse verb SEE **cross** verb.

travesty noun SEE **imitation**.

travesty verb SEE **imitate**.

trawl verb SEE **fish** verb.

trawler noun fishing-boat.

tray noun salver.

treacherous adjective 1 *a treacherous ally*. deceitful, disloyal, double-crossing, double-dealing, duplicitous, faithless, false, perfidious, sneaky, unfaithful, untrustworthy.
OPPOSITES: SEE **loyal**.
treacherous person SEE **traitor**.
2 *treacherous weather conditions*. dangerous, deceptive, hazardous, misleading, perilous, risky, shifting, unpredictable, unreliable, unsafe, unstable.
OPPOSITES: SEE **reliable**.

treachery noun *treachery against an ally*. betrayal, dishonesty, disloyalty, double-dealing, duplicity, faithlessness, infidelity, perfidy, SEE **treason**, untrustworthiness.
OPPOSITES: SEE **loyalty**.

treacle noun SEE **sugar** noun.

tread noun 1 *the tread of approaching feet*. footstep.
2 *the treads of a staircase*. step.

tread verb *to tread carefully*. OTHER WAYS TO WALK: SEE **walk** verb.
to tread on *She trod on my foot*. crush, squash underfoot, stamp on, step on, trample, walk on.

treason noun *treason against your country*. betrayal, mutiny, rebellion, sedition, SEE **treachery**.
OPPOSITES: SEE **loyalty**.

treasure noun *hidden treasure*. fortune, gold, hoard, jewels, riches, treasure trove, valuables, wealth.

treasure verb *She treasures the brooch granny gave her*. adore, appreciate, cherish, esteem, guard, keep safe, love, prize, value, venerate, worship.

treasury noun hoard, repository, storeroom, treasure-house, vault.

treat noun *a birthday treat*. entertainment, gift, outing, pleasure, surprise.

treat verb 1 *to treat someone kindly*. attend to, behave towards, care for, look after, use.
2 *to treat a subject thoroughly*. consider, deal with, discuss, tackle.
3 *to treat a patient. to treat a wound*. cure, dress, give treatment to [SEE **treatment**], heal, medicate, nurse, prescribe medicine for, tend.

4 *to treat food to kill germs*. process.
5 *I didn't have any money, but they were kind enough to treat me*. entertain, give (someone) a treat, pay for, provide for.

treatise noun disquisition, dissertation, essay, monograph, pamphlet, paper, thesis, tract.
OTHER KINDS OF WRITING: SEE **writing**.

treatment noun 1 *the treatment of prisoners. the treatment of a problem*. care, conduct, dealing (with), handling, management, organization, use.
2 *the treatment of illness*. cure, first aid, healing, nursing, remedy, therapy.
VARIOUS KINDS OF MEDICAL TREATMENT: SEE **medicine, therapy**.

treaty noun *a peace treaty*. agreement, alliance, armistice, compact, concordat, contract, convention, covenant, [*informal*] deal, entente, pact, peace, [*formal*] protocol, settlement, truce, understanding.

tree noun SOME TYPES OF TREE: bonsai, conifer, cordon, deciduous, espalier, evergreen, pollard, standard.
small tree bush, half-standard, shrub.
young tree sapling.
RELATED ADJECTIVE: arboreal.

VARIOUS TREES: ash, banian, bay, baobab, beech, birch, cacao, cedar, chestnut, cypress, elder, elm, eucalyptus, fir, fruit-tree [SEE **fruit**], gum-tree, hawthorn, hazel, holly, horse-chestnut, larch, lime, maple, oak, olive, palm, pine, plane, poplar, redwood, rowan, sequoia, spruce, sycamore, tamarisk, tulip tree, willow, yew.

treeless adjective *a treeless landscape*. SEE **bare** adjective.

trefoil noun clover, shamrock.

trek noun, verb SEE **travel** noun, verb.

trellis noun SEE **framework**.

tremble verb *to tremble with cold*. quake, quaver, quiver, shake, shiver, shudder, vibrate, waver.

Tremendous (like *tremble, tremor, tremulous*, etc.) is related to Latin *tremere* = *to tremble*. Sometimes *tremendous* still means *fearful*, but more often we use it informally and rather vaguely to describe things which are impressive in some way.

tremendous adjective 1 *a tremendous explosion*. alarming, appalling, awful,

fearful, fearsome, frightening, frightful, horrifying, shocking, terrible, terrific.
2 [*informal*] *a tremendous helping of potatoes.* SEE **big**.
3 [*informal*] *a tremendous piece of music.* SEE **excellent**.
4 [*informal*] *a tremendous achievement.* SEE **remarkable**.

tremor noun *a tremor in someone's voice.* agitation, hesitation, quavering, quiver, shaking, trembling, vibration.
an earth tremor SEE **earthquake**.

tremulous adjective 1 *We waited in tremulous anticipation.* agitated, anxious, excited, frightened, jittery, jumpy, nervous, timid, uncertain.
OPPOSITES: SEE **calm** adjective.
2 *I opened the important letter with tremulous fingers.* quivering, shaking, shivering, trembling, [*informal*] trembly, vibrating.
OPPOSITES: SEE **steady** adjective.

trench noun SEE **ditch** noun.

trench verb SEE **dig**.
trench coat SEE **overcoat**.

trenchant adjective *trenchant criticisms.* SEE **sharp**, **intelligent**.

trend noun 1 *an upward trend in prices.* bias, direction, inclination, leaning, movement, shift, tendency.
2 *the latest trend in clothes.* [*informal*] fad, fashion, mode, style, [*informal*] thing (*It's the latest thing*), way.

trendy adjective [*informal*] *trendy clothes.* contemporary, fashionable, [*informal*] in (*the in fashion*), latest, modern, stylish, up-to-date.
OPPOSITES: SEE **old-fashioned**.

trepidation noun SEE **fear** noun.

trespass noun [*old-fashioned*] *Forgive us our trespasses.* SEE **sin** noun.

trespass verb *to trespass on someone's property.* encroach, enter illegally, intrude, invade.

tress noun SEE **hair**.

trestle noun SEE **support** noun.

trestle-table noun SEE **table**.

trews noun SEE **trousers**.

trial noun 1 *a legal trial.* case, court martial, examination, hearing, tribunal.
LEGAL TERMS: SEE **law**.
2 *a trial of a new product.* attempt, experiment, test, testing, [*informal*] try-out.
3 *Appearing in public can be a trial for shy people.* affliction, burden, difficulty, hardship, ordeal, problem, tribulation, trouble, worry.

The prefix *tri-* in words like *triangle, tricycle, tripod,* etc. is related to Latin *tres = three*.

---

triangle noun VARIOUS SHAPES: SEE **shape** noun.

triangular adjective three-cornered, three-sided.

tribe noun *a close-knit tribe.* clan, dynasty, family, group, horde, nation, people, race, stock.

tribulation noun SEE **trouble** noun.

tribunal noun SEE **trial**.

tributary noun SEE **river**.

tribute noun *Her friends read moving tributes to her courage.* accolade, appreciation, commendation, compliment, eulogy, panegyric, testimony.
to pay tribute to *They paid tribute to her courage.* applaud, celebrate, commend, SEE **honour** verb, pay homage to, praise, respect.

trick noun 1 *a conjuring trick.* illusion, legerdemain, magic, sleight of hand.
2 *a deceitful trick.* cheat, [*informal*] con, deceit, deception, fraud, hoax, imposture, manœuvre, ploy, pretence, ruse, scheme, stratagem, stunt, subterfuge, swindle, trap, SEE **trickery**, wile.
3 *I never learned the trick of standing on my head.* art, craft, device, dodge, expertise, gimmick, knack, [*informal*] know-how, secret, skill, technique.
4 *He has a trick of repeating himself.* characteristic, habit, idiosyncrasy, mannerism, peculiarity, way.
5 *She played a trick on me.* joke, [*informal*] leg-pull, practical joke, prank.

trick verb *He tricked me into buying rubbish.* [*informal*] bamboozle, bluff, catch out, cheat, [*informal*] con, deceive, defraud, [*informal*] diddle, dupe, fool, hoax, hoodwink, [*informal*] kid, mislead, outwit, [*informal*] pull (someone's) leg, swindle.

trickery noun bluffing, cheating, chicanery, deceit, deception, dishonesty, fraud, [*informal*] hocus-pocus, [*informal*] jiggery-pokery, [*informal*] skulduggery, swindling, SEE **trick** noun.

trickle verb *Water trickled from a crack.* dribble, drip, flow slowly, leak, ooze, percolate, run, seep.
OPPOSITES: SEE **gush** verb.

trickster noun SEE **cheat** noun.

tricky adjective 1 *a tricky customer.* SEE **deceitful**.
2 *a tricky manœuvre.* SEE **complicated**.

tricycle noun SEE **cycle** noun.

trifle noun *It cost only a trifle.* SEE **small** (small amount).

trifle verb *Don't trifle with me!* behave frivolously, dabble, fool about, play about.

trifling adjective *a trifling amount.* SEE **trivial.**

trigger verb **to trigger off** SEE **activate.**

trilby noun SEE **hat.**

trill verb *birds trilling in the garden.* SEE sing, twitter, warble, whistle.

trim adjective *a trim garden. a trim figure.* compact, neat, orderly, [*informal*] ship-shape, smart, spruce, tidy, well-groomed, well-kept.
OPPOSITES: SEE **untidy.**

trim verb *to trim a hedge.* clip, crop, SEE cut verb, shape, shear, tidy.

trip noun *a trip to the seaside.* excursion, expedition, jaunt, journey, outing, tour, visit, voyage.
to make a trip SEE **travel** verb.

trip verb 1 *to trip along lightly.* run, skip, SEE **walk** verb.
2 *to trip over something.* catch your foot, fall, stagger, stumble, totter, tumble.

tripartite adjective SEE **triple.**

tripe noun 1 *tripe and onions.* SEE **meat.**
2 [*informal*] *She's talking tripe!* SEE **nonsense.**

triple adjective threefold, tripartite, triplicate (*Complete the form in triplicate*).

tripod noun *a camera tripod.* SEE **stand** noun, support.

tripper noun SEE **traveller.**

trite adjective *a trite remark.* SEE **commonplace.**

triumph noun 1 *a triumph over our opponents.* conquest, knock-out, victory, [*informal*] walk-over, win.
2 *The pudding I made was a triumph.* accomplishment, achievement, [*informal*] hit, master-stroke, [*informal*] smash hit, success.

triumph verb *We triumphed in the end.* be victorious, prevail, succeed, win.
to triumph over SEE **defeat** verb.

triumphant adjective 1 *We cheered the triumphant team.* conquering, dominant, successful, victorious, winning.
OPPOSITES: SEE **unsuccessful.**
2 *The losers didn't like our triumphant laughter.* boastful, [*informal*] cocky, elated, exultant, gleeful, gloating, immodest, joyful, jubilant, proud.
OPPOSITES: SEE **modest.**

trivet noun SEE **stand** noun.

trivial adjective *trivial details.* [*informal*] fiddling, [*informal*] footling, frivolous, inconsequential, inconsiderable, insignificant, little, minor, negligible, paltry, pettifogging, petty, [*informal*] piffling, silly, slight, small, superficial, trifling, trite, unimportant, worthless.
OPPOSITES: SEE **important.**

troglodyte noun cave-dweller, caveman.

trombone noun OTHER BRASS INSTRUMENTS: SEE **brass.**

troop noun SEE **group** noun.
troops *armed troops.* SEE **armed services.**

troop verb *We trooped along the road.* march, parade, SEE **walk** verb.

trooper noun SEE **soldier.**

trophy noun 1 [*plural*] *trophies of war.* booty, loot, mementoes, rewards, souvenirs, spoils.
2 *a sporting trophy.* award, cup, medal, prize.

tropical adjective *a tropical climate.* equatorial, SEE **hot.**
OPPOSITES: arctic, SEE **cold** adjective.

trot noun, verb SEE **run** noun, verb.

trotter noun SEE **foot.**

trouble noun 1 *personal troubles.* adversity, affliction, anxiety, burden, difficulty, distress, grief, hardship, SEE **illness**, inconvenience, misery, misfortune, pain, problem, sadness, sorrow, suffering, trial, tribulation, unhappiness, vexation, worry.
2 *trouble in the crowd.* bother, commotion, conflict, discontent, discord, disorder, dissatisfaction, disturbance, fighting, fuss, misbehaviour, misconduct, naughtiness, row, strife, turmoil, unpleasantness, unrest, violence.
3 *engine trouble.* break-down, defect, failure, fault, malfunction.
4 *I took a lot of trouble to get it right.* care, concern, effort, exertion, labour, pains, struggle, thought.

trouble verb *You look sad—is something troubling you?* afflict, annoy, bother, cause trouble to, concern, distress, disturb, grieve, hurt, inconvenience, interfere with, molest, pain, perturb, pester, plague, threaten, torment, upset, vex, worry.
OPPOSITES: SEE **reassure.**

troubled adjective *a troubled conscience. troubled times.* anxious, disturbed, fearful, [*informal*] fraught, guilt-ridden, insecure, perturbed, restless, stricken, uncertain, uneasy, unhappy, vexed, worried.
OPPOSITES: SEE **peaceful.**

trouble-maker noun agitator, SEE **criminal** noun, culprit, delinquent, hooligan, mischief-maker, offender, rabble-rouser, rascal, ring-leader, ruffian, vandal, wrongdoer.

troublesome adjective *troublesome insects. troublesome neighbours.* annoying, badly behaved, bothersome, disobedient, disorderly, distressing, inconvenient, irksome, irritating, naughty, [*informal*] pestiferous, pestilential, rowdy, tiresome, trying, uncooperative, unruly, upsetting, vexing, wearisome, worrisome, worrying.
OPPOSITES: SEE **helpful**.

trounce verb SEE **defeat** verb.

troupe noun SEE **group** noun.

trouper noun SEE **entertainer**.

trousers noun

KINDS OF TROUSERS: [*informal*] bags, breeches, corduroys, culottes, denims, dungarees, jeans, jodhpurs, [*old-fashioned*] knickerbockers, [*informal*] Levis, overalls, [*American*] pants, plus fours, shorts, ski-pants, slacks, [*Scottish*] trews, trunks.

OTHER GARMENTS: SEE **clothes**.

---

truancy noun absenteeism, malingering, shirking, [*informal*] skiving.

truant noun *a truant from school or work.* absentee, deserter (*from the army*), dodger, malingerer, runaway, shirker, [*informal*] skiver.
to play truant be absent, desert, malinger, [*informal*] skive, stay away.

truce noun *a truce between two warring sides.* armistice, cease-fire, moratorium, pact, peace, suspension of hostilities, treaty.

truck noun SEE **railway, vehicle**.

truculent adjective SEE **quarrelsome**.

trudge noun, verb SEE **walk** noun, verb.

true adjective 1 *a true happening. true facts. a true copy.* accurate, actual, authentic, confirmed, correct, exact, factual, faithful, genuine, proper, real, right, veracious, veritable.
2 *a true friend. true love.* constant, dependable, devoted, faithful, firm, honest, honourable, loyal, reliable, responsible, sincere, steady, trustworthy, trusty.
OPPOSITES: SEE **false**.
3 *Are you the true owner of this car?* authorized, legal, legitimate, rightful, valid.

4 *the true aim of a marksman. a true alignment.* accurate, exact, perfect, precise, [*informal*] spot-on, unerring, unswerving.
OPPOSITES: SEE **inaccurate**.

trug noun SEE **basket**.

truism noun SEE **saying**.

trump verb **to trump up** *They trumped up charges against him.* SEE **invent**.

trumpery adjective SEE **showy, worthless**.

trumpet noun OTHER BRASS INSTRUMENTS: SEE **brass**.

trumpet verb VARIOUS SOUNDS: SEE **sound** noun.

truncate verb SEE **shorten**.

truncheon noun *a policeman's truncheon.* baton, club, cudgel, staff, stick.

trundle verb *A wagon trundled up the road.* lumber, lurch, SEE **move** verb.

trunk noun 1 *a tree trunk.* bole, shaft, stalk, stem.
2 *a person's trunk.* body, frame, torso.
3 *an elephant's trunk.* nose, proboscis.
4 *a clothes' trunk.* box, case, chest, coffer, crate, suitcase.
trunks *swimming trunks.* briefs, shorts, SEE **trousers**.

truss noun 1 *a truss of hay.* SEE **bundle** noun.
2 *a truss supporting a bridge.* SEE **support** noun.

truss verb SEE **tie**.

trust noun 1 *The dog has trust in his owner.* belief, certainty, confidence, credence, faith, reliance.
2 *a position of trust.* responsibility, trusteeship.

trust verb 1 *We trust you to do your duty.* bank on, believe in, be sure of, count on, depend on, have confidence in, have faith in, rely on.
2 *I trust you are well.* assume, expect, hope, imagine, presume, suppose, surmise.
OPPOSITES: SEE **doubt** verb.

trustee noun SEE **agent**.

trustful adjective *Small children are often very trustful.* credulous, gullible, innocent, trusting, unquestioning, unsuspecting, unwary.
OPPOSITES: SEE **suspicious**.

trustworthy adjective *a trustworthy friend.* constant, dependable, faithful, honest, honourable, [*informal*] on the level, loyal, reliable, responsible, [*informal*] safe, sensible, steadfast, steady, straightforward, true, [*old-fashioned*] trusty, truthful, upright.
OPPOSITES: SEE **deceitful**.

truth noun 1 *Tell the truth.* facts, reality.

2 *I doubt the truth of her story.* accuracy, authenticity, correctness, exactness, factuality, integrity, reliability, truthfulness, validity, veracity, verity.
3 *an accepted truth.* axiom, fact, maxim, truism.
OPPOSITES: SEE **lie** noun.

ruthful adjective **1** *a truthful person.* candid, credible, forthright, frank, honest, reliable, sincere, [*informal*] straight, straightforward, trustworthy, veracious.
2 *a truthful answer.* accurate, correct, proper, right, true, valid.
OPPOSITES: SEE **dishonest**.

ry noun *Have a try!* attempt, [*informal*] bash, [*informal*] crack, effort, endeavour, experiment, [*informal*] go, [*informal*] shot, [*informal*] stab, test, trial.

ry verb **1** *Try to do your best.* aim, attempt, endeavour, essay, exert yourself, make an effort, strain, strive, struggle, venture.
2 *We tried a new method.* [*informal*] check out, evaluate, examine, experiment with, investigate, test, try out, undertake.
3 *She tries us with her chattering.* SEE **annoy**.

rying adjective SEE **annoying**.

ub noun barrel, bath, butt, cask, drum, keg, pot, vat.
OTHER CONTAINERS: SEE **container**.

ubby adjective [*informal*] *a tubby figure.* SEE **fat** adjective.

ube noun *tubes to carry liquids.* capillary, conduit, cylinder, duct, hose, main, pipe, spout, tubing.

uber noun SEE **root**.

uberculosis noun consumption.

ubing noun SEE **tube**.

uck verb *Tuck your shirt into your jeans.* cram, gather, insert, push, put away, shove, stuff.
to tuck in SEE **eat**.

ufa, tuff nouns SEE **rock** noun.

uft noun *a tuft of grass.* bunch, clump, cluster, tuffet, tussock.

ug verb **1** *We tugged the cart behind us.* drag, draw, haul, heave, lug, pull, tow.
2 *I tugged at the rope.* jerk, pluck, twitch, wrench, yank.

uition noun SEE **teaching**.

umble verb **1** *I tumbled into the water.* collapse, drop, fall, flop, pitch, stumble, topple, trip up.
2 *I tumbled everything into a heap.* disarrange, jumble, mix up, roll, rumple, shove, spill, throw carelessly, toss.

tumbledown adjective *a tumbledown cottage.* badly maintained, broken down, crumbling, decrepit, derelict, dilapidated, ramshackle, rickety, ruined, shaky.

tummy noun SEE **stomach** noun.

tummy-button noun navel, umbilicus.

tumour noun SEE **growth**.

tumult noun SEE **uproar**.

tumultuous adjective *tumultuous applause.* agitated, boisterous, confused, excited, hectic, passionate, tempestuous, turbulent, unrestrained, unruly, uproarious, violent, wild.
OPPOSITES: SEE **calm** adjective.

tun noun SEE **barrel**.

tuna noun tunny.

tune noun air, melody, song, strain, theme.
MUSICAL TERMS: SEE **music**.
in tune SEE **harmonious**.

tune verb *to tune a violin. to tune an engine.* adjust, regulate, set, temper.

tuneful adjective *tuneful music.* [*informal*] catchy, mellifluous, melodious, musical, pleasant, singable.
OPPOSITES: SEE **tuneless**.

tuneless adjective *tuneless music.* atonal, boring, cacophonous, discordant, dissonant, harsh, monotonous, unmusical.
OPPOSITES: SEE **tuneful**.

tunic noun SEE **coat** noun.

tunnel noun burrow, gallery, hole, mine, passage, passageway, shaft, subway, underpass.

tunnel verb *A rabbit tunnelled under the fence.* burrow, dig, excavate, mine.

turbid adjective **1** *turbid waters.* clouded, cloudy, hazy, muddy, murky, opaque, unclear, unsettled.
OPPOSITES: SEE **clear** adjective.
2 *a turbid state of mind.* SEE **turbulent**.

turbine noun SEE **engine**.

turbulence noun SEE **turmoil**.

turbulent adjective **1** *turbulent emotions.* agitated, boisterous, confused, disordered, excited, hectic, passionate, restless, seething, turbid, unrestrained, violent, volatile, wild.
2 *a turbulent crowd.* badly behaved, disorderly, lawless, obstreperous, riotous, rowdy, undisciplined, unruly.
3 *turbulent weather.* blustery, bumpy (*a bumpy flight*), choppy (*choppy seas*), rough, stormy, tempestuous, violent, wild, windy.
OPPOSITES: SEE **calm** adjective.

tureen noun *a soup tureen.* SEE **dish** noun.

turf noun grass, lawn, [*poetic*] sward.
  turf accountant [*informal*] bookie, bookmaker.

turgid adjective *a turgid style of writing.* affected, bombastic, flowery, fulsome, grandiose, high-flown, over-blown, pompous, pretentious, stilted, wordy.
  OPPOSITES: SEE **lucid**.

turmoil noun *The place was in turmoil until we organized ourselves.* [*informal*] bedlam, chaos, commotion, confusion, disorder, disturbance, ferment, [*informal*] hubbub, [*informal*] hullabaloo, pandemonium, riot, row, rumpus, tumult, turbulence, unrest, upheaval, uproar, welter.
  OPPOSITES: SEE **calm** noun.

turn noun 1 *a turn of a wheel.* circle, cycle, revolution, rotation, spin, twirl, whirl.
  2 *a turn in the road.* angle, bend, corner, curve, deviation, hairpin bend, junction, loop, twist.
  3 *a turn in someone's fortunes.* change of direction, reversal, shift, turning-point, [*informal*] U-turn.
  4 *a player's turn in a game.* chance, [*informal*] go, innings, opportunity, shot.
  5 *a comic turn in a concert.* SEE **performance**.
  6 [*informal*] *He had a bad turn and had to go to hospital.* SEE **illness**.
  to give someone a turn SEE **shock** verb.

turn verb 1 *to turn round a central point as a wheel does.* circle, gyrate, hinge, move in a circle, orbit, pivot, revolve, roll, rotate, spin, spiral, swivel, twirl, twist, whirl, yaw.
  2 *to turn left or right.* change direction, corner, deviate, divert, go round a corner, negotiate a corner, steer, swerve, veer, wheel.
  3 *to turn a wire round a stick.* bend, coil, curl, loop, twist, wind.
  4 *We turned the attic into a games room.* adapt, alter, change, convert, make, modify, remake, remodel, transfigure, transform.
  5 *The snake turned this way and that.* squirm, twist, wriggle, writhe.
  to turn away *They turned uninvited guests away.* decline, dismiss, exclude, send away, [*informal*] send packing.
  to turn down 1 *I turned the invitation down.* decline, refuse, reject, spurn.
  2 *Turn down the heat.* decrease, lessen, reduce.
  to turn into *Tadpoles turn into frogs.* become, be transformed into, change into, metamorphose into.
  to turn off 1 *We turned off the main road.* branch off, deviate from, leave.

2 *Turn off the water. Turn off the light.* cut off, disconnect, put off, shut off, stop, switch off, turn out.
  3 [*informal*] *She turned me off with her bossy manner.* alienate, irritate, put off, repel.
  4 [*informal*] *He was so boring that I turned off.* lose interest, stop listening.
  to turn on 1 *Turn on the water. Turn on the light.* connect, start, put on, switch on.
  2 [*informal*] *He quite turned her on with his flattering grin.* attract, excite, [*informal*] get going, stimulate.
  to turn out 1 *How did your party turn out?* befall, emerge, happen, result.
  2 *We had to turn out an intruder.* eject, evict, expel, [*informal*] kick out, remove, throw out.
  3 *The factory turns out hundreds of items each day.* make, manufacture, produce.
  4 *Turn out the light.* SEE **turn off**.
  to turn over 1 *The boat turned over.* capsize, flip, invert, keel over, overturn, turn turtle, turn upside down.
  2 *I turned the problem over.* consider, contemplate, deliberate, mull over, ponder, reflect on, think about, weigh up.
  to turn tail abscond, [*informal*] beat it, [*informal*] bolt, [*informal*] do a bunk, escape, flee, run away, [*informal*] take to your heels.
  to turn up 1 *I turned up some interesting facts.* [*informal*] dig up, disclose, discover, expose, find, reveal, show up, unearth.
  2 *Some friends turned up unexpectedly.* appear, arrive, come, [*informal*] drop in, materialize, [*informal*] pop up, visit.
  3 *Turn up the volume.* amplify, increase, raise.

turncoat noun SEE **renegade**.

turning noun *a turning in the road.* SEE **corner** noun.

turning-point noun *a turning-point in your life.* crisis, crossroads, new direction, revolution, watershed.

turnover noun 1 *the turnover of a business.* cash-flow, efficiency, output, production, productivity, profits, throughput, yield.
  2 *an apple turnover.* SEE **pie**.

turnstile noun entrance, exit, SEE **gate**.

turpitude noun SEE **wickedness**.

turret noun SEE **tower** noun.

tusk noun SEE **tooth**.

tussle noun, verb SEE **struggle** noun, verb.

tussock noun *a tussock of grass.* bunch, clump, cluster, tuffet, tuft.

tutelage noun SEE **protection**.

tutor noun SEE **teacher**.

tutorial noun SEE **teaching**.

tutu noun ballet-skirt.

twaddle noun SEE **nonsense**.

twang noun, verb VARIOUS SOUNDS: SEE **sound** noun.

tweak verb SEE **pinch** verb.

twee adjective SEE **quaint**.

tweet noun, verb VARIOUS SOUNDS: SEE **sound** noun.

twerp noun SEE **idiot**.

twiddle verb *to twiddle your thumbs.* fiddle with, fidget with, twirl, twist.

twig noun branch, offshoot, shoot, spray, stalk, stem, stick.

twig verb [*informal*] *I soon twigged what was happening.* SEE **realize**.

twilight noun dusk, evening, [*poetic*] eventide, [*poetic*] gloaming, gloom, half-light, nightfall, sundown, sunset. OTHER TIMES OF DAY: SEE **day**.

twin adjective *twin statuettes on the mantelpiece.* balancing, corresponding, duplicate, identical, indistinguishable, matching, paired, similar, symmetrical. OPPOSITES: SEE **contrasting**.

twin noun *This statue is a twin of the one in the antique shop.* clone, double, duplicate, [*informal*] lookalike, match, pair. FAMILY RELATIONSHIPS: SEE **family**.

twine noun SEE **string** noun.

twinge noun *a twinge in your tooth.* SEE **pain** noun.

twinkle verb SEE **light** noun (give light).

twirl verb 1 *The dancers twirled faster and faster.* gyrate, pirouette, revolve, rotate, spin, turn, twist, wheel, whirl. 2 *I twirled my umbrella.* brandish, twiddle, wave.

twist noun 1 *a twist in a rope. a twist in the road.* bend, coil, curl, kink, knot, loop, tangle, turn, zigzag. 2 *an unexpected twist to a story.* revelation, surprise ending.

twist verb 1 *to twist and turn.* bend, coil, corkscrew, curl, curve, loop, revolve, rotate, screw, spin, spiral, turn, weave, wind, wreathe, wriggle, writhe, zigzag. 2 *The ropes became twisted.* entangle, entwine, intertwine, interweave, tangle. 3 *to twist the lid off a jar.* jerk, wrench, wrest. 4 *to twist something out of shape.* buckle, contort, crinkle, crumple, distort, warp, wrinkle. 5 *to twist the meaning of something.* alter, change, falsify, misquote, misrepresent.

twisted adjective 1 *a twisted rope. a twisted shape.* bent, coiled, contorted, corkscrew, crumpled, deformed, distorted, knotted, looped, misshapen, screwed up, tangled, warped. 2 *a twisted message.* garbled, misreported, misrepresented, misunderstood. 3 *a twisted mind.* SEE **perverted**.

twister noun SEE **swindler**.

twisty adjective [*informal*] *a twisty road.* bendy, crooked, curving, indirect, serpentine, tortuous, twisting, winding, zigzag. OPPOSITES: SEE **straight**.

twit noun SEE **idiot**.

twitch noun *a nervous twitch.* blink, convulsion, flutter, jerk, jump, spasm, tic, tremor.

twitch verb 1 *Our dog's legs twitch while he's asleep.* fidget, flutter, jerk, jump, start, tremble. 2 *to twitch at a rope.* SEE **tug** verb.

twitter noun, verb VARIOUS SOUNDS: SEE **sound** noun.

two noun couple, duet, duo, pair, twosome. RELATED ADJECTIVES: binary, bipartite, double, dual, duple, paired, SEE **twin** adjective, twofold.

two-dimensional adjective flat. OPPOSITES: SEE **three-dimensional**.

two-faced adjective SEE **insincere**.

twosome noun SEE **two** noun.

tycoon noun SEE **businessman**.

type noun 1 *Things of the same type are classed together.* category, class, classification, description, designation, form, genre, group, kind, mark, set, sort, species, variety. 2 *Job is often quoted as a type of patient suffering.* embodiment, epitome, example, model, pattern, personification, standard. 3 *a book printed in large type.* characters, [*formal*] font or fount, letters, lettering, print, printing, type-face.

type verb *to type business letters.* SEE **write**.

typecast verb *to typecast an actor.* stereotype.

typescript noun SEE **document**.

typewriter noun WRITING IMPLEMENTS: SEE **write**.

typhoon noun SEE **storm** noun.

typical adjective 1 *a typical Chinese dinner.* characteristic, distinctive, particular, representative, special. OPPOSITES: SEE **atypical**.

2 *a typical day.* average, conventional, normal, ordinary, orthodox, predictable, standard, stock, unsurprising, usual.
OPPOSITES: SEE **unusual**.

typify verb SEE **characterize**.

tyrannical adjective *a tyrannical ruler.* absolute, authoritarian, autocratic, [*informal*] bossy, cruel, despotic, dictatorial, domineering, harsh, high-handed, imperious, oppressive, overbearing, ruthless, severe, tyrannous, unjust.
OPPOSITES: SEE **liberal**.

tyrannize verb SEE **oppress**.

tyrannous adjective SEE **tyrannical**.

tyrant noun autocrat, despot, dictator, [*informal*] hard taskmaster, oppressor, SEE **ruler**, slave-driver.

tyre noun pneumatic tyre.

U

ubiquitous adjective [*Ubiquitous* is related to Latin *ubique = everywhere.*] common, commonplace, pervasive, SEE **universal**.

ugliness noun deformity, hideousness, repulsiveness, unsightliness.
OPPOSITES: SEE **beauty**.

ugly adjective **1** *ugly monsters.* deformed, disfigured, disgusting, frightful, ghastly, grisly, grotesque, gruesome, hideous, [*informal*] horrid, ill-favoured, misshapen, monstrous, nasty, objectionable, SEE **repulsive**, revolting.
2 *an ugly room. an ugly piece of furniture.* displeasing, inartistic, inelegant, plain, tasteless, unattractive, unpleasant, unsightly.
OPPOSITES: SEE **beautiful**.
3 *ugly storm clouds. in an ugly mood.* SEE **angry**, dangerous, forbidding, hostile, menacing, ominous, sinister, threatening, unfriendly.

A number of English words like *ulterior*, *ultimate*, and words with the prefix *ultra-* are related to Latin *ultra = beyond*.

ulterior adjective *ulterior motives.* concealed, covert, hidden, personal, private, secondary, secret, undeclared, undisclosed.
OPPOSITES: SEE **overt**.

ultimate adjective **1** *We scored in the ultimate minutes of the game.* closing, concluding, eventual, extreme, final, last, terminal.
2 *The ultimate cause of the fire was an electrical fault.* basic, fundamental, primary, root.

ultimatum noun *The enemy issued an ultimatum.* final demand.

umbra noun SEE **shadow** noun.

umbrage noun **to take umbrage** be annoyed [SEE **annoyed**], be offended.

umpire noun adjudicator, arbiter, arbitrator, judge, linesman, moderator, [*informal*] ref, referee.

umpteen adjective SEE **many**.

un- The prefix *un-* can be attached to a vast number of words. Sometimes it simply signifies *not* (*happy/unhappy*; *safe/unsafe*); sometimes it has the effect of reversing the action indicated by a verb (*do/undo*; *lock/unlock*). The number of words beginning with *un-* is almost unlimited: we don't have space to include all of them.

unabridged adjective SEE **whole**.

unacceptable adjective *unacceptable work. an unacceptable level of pollution.* inadequate, inadmissible, inappropriate, insupportable, intolerable, unsatisfactory, unsuitable.
OPPOSITE: SEE **acceptable**.

unaccompanied adjective *an unaccompanied traveller.* alone, lone, sole, solo (*a solo performer*), unescorted.

unaccountable adjective SEE **inexplicable**.

unaccustomed adjective SEE **strange**.

unadulterated adjective SEE **pure**.

unadventurous adjective **1** *an unadventurous spirit.* cautious, cowardly, spiritless, SEE **timid**, unimaginative.
2 *an unadventurous life.* cloistered, limited, protected, sheltered, unexciting.
OPPOSITES: SEE **adventurous, enterprising**.

unaided adjective single-handed, solo.

unalloyed adjective SEE **pure**.

unalterable adjective SEE **immutable**.

unambiguous adjective SEE **definite**.

unanimous adjective SEE **united**.

unanswerable adjective **1** *an unanswerable riddle.* SEE **insoluble**.
2 *an unanswerable argument.* SEE **indisputable**.

unapproachable adjective SEE **aloof**.

unarguable adjective SEE **indisputable**.

unarmed adjective SEE **undefended**.

unashamed adjective SEE **unrepentant**.

unasked adjective, adverb *It's not often someone does you a favour unasked*. spontaneous(ly), unbidden, uninvited, unprompted, unsolicited, voluntary (voluntarily).

unassuming adjective SEE **modest**.

unattached adjective [*informal*] available, free, independent, single, uncommitted, unmarried, [*informal*] unspoken for.
OPPOSITES: SEE **engaged, married**.

unattractive adjective repulsive, SEE ugly, uninviting, unprepossessing.
OPPOSITES: SEE **attractive**.

unauthorized adjective *The train made an unauthorized stop*. abnormal, illegal, irregular, unlawful, unusual.

unavoidable adjective **1** *an unavoidable accident*. certain, destined, fated, inescapable, inevitable, sure.
2 *an unavoidable payment*. compulsory, mandatory, necessary, obligatory, required.
OPPOSITES: SEE **unnecessary**.

unaware adjective SEE **ignorant**.

unbalanced adjective **1** *an unbalanced shape*. asymmetrical, irregular, lopsided, off-centre, uneven.
2 *an unbalanced argument*. biased, bigoted, one-sided, partial, partisan, prejudiced, unfair, unjust.
3 *an unbalanced mind*. SEE **mad**.
OPPOSITES: SEE **balanced**.

unbearable adjective *unbearable pain. an unbearable snob*. insufferable, insupportable, intolerable, unacceptable, unendurable.
OPPOSITES: SEE **tolerable**.

unbeatable adjective SEE **invincible**.

unbecoming adjective *unbecoming behaviour*. dishonourable, ill-mannered, improper, inappropriate, indecorous, indelicate, offensive, tasteless, unattractive, unbefitting, unseemly, unsuitable.
OPPOSITES: SEE **decorous**.

unbelievable adjective SEE **incredible**.

unbend verb **1** *to unbend something that has been bent*. straighten, uncurl, untwist.
OPPOSITES: SEE **bend** verb.
2 [*informal*] *to unbend in front of the TV in the evening*. loosen up, relax, rest, unwind.

unbending adjective SEE **inflexible**.

unbiased adjective *an unbiased opinion*. disinterested, enlightened, even-handed, fair, impartial, independent, just, neutral, non-partisan, objective, open-minded, reasonable, [*informal*] straight, unbigoted, undogmatic, unprejudiced.
OPPOSITES: SEE **biased**.

unbidden adjective SEE **uninvited**.

unbind verb SEE **unfasten**.

unblemished adjective SEE **spotless**.

unblock, unbolt verbs SEE **open** verb.

unblushing adjective SEE **unrepentant**.

unbosom verb to unbosom yourself SEE **confess**.

unbounded adjective SEE **boundless**.

unbreakable adjective SEE **indestructible**.

unbridled adjective SEE **unrestrained**.

unbroken adjective SEE **continuous, whole**.

unburden verb to unburden yourself SEE **confess**.

uncalled for adjective SEE **unnecessary**.

uncanny adjective SEE **eerie**.

uncared for adjective SEE **neglected**.

uncaring adjective SEE **callous**.

unceasing adjective SEE **continual**.

unceremonious adjective SEE **informal**.

uncertain adjective **1** *The outcome of the trial is uncertain*. ambiguous, arguable, conjectural, imprecise, incalculable, inconclusive, indefinite, indeterminate, speculative, unclear, unconvincing, undecided, undetermined, unforeseeable, unknown, unresolved.
2 *I'm uncertain what to believe*. agnostic, ambivalent, doubtful, dubious, [*informal*] hazy, insecure, [*informal*] in two minds, self-questioning, unconvinced, undecided, unsure, vague, wavering.
3 *My chance of success is uncertain*. [*informal*] chancy, hazardous, [*informal*] iffy, problematical, questionable, risky, [*informal*] touch and go.
4 *Our climate is uncertain*. changeable, erratic, fitful, inconstant, irregular, precarious, unpredictable, unreliable, variable.
OPPOSITES: SEE **certain**.

unchangeable adjective SEE **invariable**.

unchanging adjective SEE **constant**.

uncharitable, unchristian adjectives SEE **unkind**.

uncivil adjective SEE **rude**.

uncivilized adjective *uncivilized behaviour*. anarchic, antisocial, badly

behaved, barbarian, barbaric, barbarous, disorganized, illiterate, Philistine, primitive, savage, uncultured, uneducated, unenlightened, unsophisticated, wild.
OPPOSITES: SEE **civilized**.

uncle noun FAMILY RELATIONSHIPS: SEE **family**.
RELATED ADJECTIVE: avuncular.

unclean adjective SEE **dirty** adjective.

unclear adjective *unclear evidence. unclear meaning.* ambiguous, cryptic, doubtful, dubious, hazy, imprecise, obscure, puzzling, SEE **uncertain**, vague.
OPPOSITES: SEE **clear** adjective.

unclose verb SEE **open** verb.

unclothed adjective SEE **naked**.

uncomfortable adjective 1 *uncomfortable surroundings. an uncomfortable bed.* SEE bleak, comfortless, cramped, hard, inconvenient, lumpy, painful.
OPPOSITES: SEE **comfortable**.
2 *uncomfortable clothes.* formal, restrictive, stiff, tight, tight-fitting.
3 *an uncomfortable silence.* awkward, distressing, SEE **embarrassing**, nervous, restless, troubled, uneasy, worried.

uncommon adjective SEE **unusual**.

uncommunicative adjective SEE **silent**.

uncomplimentary adjective *uncomplimentary remarks.* censorious, critical, deprecatory, depreciatory, derogatory, disapproving, disparaging, pejorative, SEE **rude**, scathing, slighting, unfavourable, unflattering.
OPPOSITES: SEE **complimentary**.

uncompromising adjective SEE **inflexible**.

unconcealed adjective SEE **obvious**.

unconcerned adjective SEE **callous**.

unconditional adjective *unconditional surrender.* absolute, categorical, complete, full, outright, total, unequivocal, unlimited, unqualified, unreserved, unrestricted, whole-hearted, [*informal*] with no strings attached.
OPPOSITES: SEE **conditional**.

uncongenial adjective *I can't work in uncongenial surroundings.* alien, antipathetic, disagreeable, incompatible, unattractive, unfriendly, unpleasant, unsympathetic.
OPPOSITES: SEE **congenial**.

unconnected adjective SEE **irrelevant**, **separate** adjective.

unconquerable adjective SEE **invincible**.

unconscionable adjective 1 *an unconscionable rogue.* SEE **unscrupulous**.

2 *He kept me waiting an unconscionable time.* SEE **unjustifiable**.

unconscious adjective 1 *unconscious after a knock on the head.* anaesthetized, comatose, concussed, [*informal*] dead to the world, insensible, [*informal*] knocked out, oblivious, [*informal*] out for the count, senseless, sleeping.
2 *unconscious of her effect on others.* blind (to), oblivious, unaware, unwitting.
3 *unconscious humour.* accidental, inadvertent, unintended, unintentional.
4 *an unconscious reaction.* automatic, impulsive, instinctive, involuntary, reflex, spontaneous, unthinking.
5 *your unconscious desires.* repressed, subconscious, subliminal, suppressed.
OPPOSITES: SEE **conscious**.

unconsciousness noun coma, faint, oblivion, sleep.

uncontrollable adjective SEE **rebellious**.

unconventional adjective *unconventional ideas. an unconventional appearance.* abnormal, atypical, [*informal*] cranky, eccentric, exotic, futuristic, idiosyncratic, inventive, non-conforming, non-standard, odd, off-beat, original, peculiar, progressive, revolutionary, strange, surprising, unaccustomed, unorthodox, [*informal*] way-out, wayward, weird, zany.
OPPOSITES: SEE **conventional**.

unconvincing adjective SEE **incredible**.

uncooked adjective SEE **raw**.

uncooperative adjective *an uncooperative partner.* lazy, obstructive, recalcitrant, selfish, unhelpful, unwilling.
OPPOSITES: SEE **co-operative**.

uncoordinated adjective SEE **clumsy**.

uncouple verb SEE **disconnect**.

uncouth adjective SEE **rude**.

uncover verb 1 *to uncover something which has been concealed.* bare, disclose, disrobe, expose, reveal, show, strip, take the wraps off, undress, unmask, unveil, unwrap.
2 *to uncover something which was lost.* come across, detect, dig up, discover, exhume, locate, unearth.
OPPOSITES: SEE **cover** verb.

uncritical adjective SEE **undiscriminating**.

unctuous adjective SEE **obsequious**.

uncultivated adjective SEE **wild**.

undamaged adjective *The goods survived the journey undamaged.* faultless, [*informal*] in one piece, intact, mint (*in mint condition*), perfect, safe, sound,

unharmed, unhurt, unimpaired, uninjured, unscathed, whole, [informal] without a scratch.
OPPOSITES: SEE damaged.

undaunted adjective SEE brave.

undeceive verb SEE disillusion.

undecided adjective 1 *The outcome is still undecided.* SEE uncertain.
2 *an undecided manner.* SEE hesitant.

undefended adjective *The army withdrew and left the post undefended.* defenceless, exposed, helpless, insecure, unarmed, unfortified, unguarded, unprotected, vulnerable, weaponless.
OPPOSITES: SEE secure adjective.

undefiled adjective SEE chaste.

undefined adjective SEE imprecise.

undemanding adjective *undemanding work.* SEE easy.

undemocratic adjective *an undemocratic political system.* SEE totalitarian.

undemonstrative adjective SEE aloof.

undeniable adjective SEE indisputable.

Often, the prefix *under-* simply adds the notion *below, beneath, lower* to the word it is attached to (e.g. *underground, underclothes, undertone*). It can also mean *less than might be expected* (e.g. *underprivileged, understaffed*).

---

underclothes noun lingerie, underclothing, undergarments, underwear, [informal] undies.

VARIOUS UNDERGARMENTS: bra, braces, brassière, briefs, camiknickers, corset, drawers, garter, girdle, knickers, panties, panti-hose, pants, petticoat, slip, suspenders, tights, trunks, underpants, underskirt, vest.

OTHER GARMENTS: SEE clothes.

---

undercover adjective SEE secret adjective.

undercurrent noun *an undercurrent of hostility.* atmosphere, feeling, hint, sense, suggestion, trace, undertone.

undercut verb SEE compete (compete against).

underdeveloped adjective SEE backward.

underdog noun SEE subordinate noun.

underdone adjective SEE raw.

underestimate verb *to underestimate difficulties.* belittle, dismiss, disparage,

minimize, misjudge, underrate, undervalue.
OPPOSITES: SEE exaggerate.

underfed adjective SEE hungry.

undergarment noun SEE underclothes.

undergo verb *to undergo an operation.* bear, be subjected to, endure, experience, go through, put up with, submit yourself to, suffer, withstand.

undergraduate noun SEE student.

underground adjective 1 *an underground store.* subterranean.
2 *an underground society.* SEE secret adjective.
underground railway metro, tube.

undergrowth noun *undergrowth in the woods.* brush, bushes, ground cover, plants, vegetation.

underhand adjective SEE sly.

underlie verb SEE support verb.

underline verb SEE emphasize.

underling noun SEE subordinate noun.

undermine verb 1 *to undermine a wall.* burrow under, dig under, erode, excavate, mine under, sabotage, tunnel under, undercut.
OPPOSITES: underpin, SEE support verb.
2 *to undermine someone's confidence.* destroy, ruin, sap, weaken, wear away.
OPPOSITES: SEE boost verb.

underpants noun SEE underclothes.

underpaid adjective SEE poor.

underpass noun subway.

underpin verb SEE support verb.

underprivileged adjective deprived, destitute, disadvantaged, impoverished, needy, SEE poor.

underrate verb SEE underestimate.

undersea adjective subaquatic, submarine, underwater.

undersized adjective SEE small.

understand verb 1 *to understand what something means.* appreciate, apprehend, comprehend, [informal] cotton on to, decipher, decode, fathom, follow, gather, [informal] get, [informal] get to the bottom of, grasp, interpret, know, learn, make out, make sense of, master, perceive, realize, recognize, see, take in, [informal] twig.
2 *She understands animals.* empathize with, sympathize with.

understanding noun 1 *a person of quick understanding.* ability, acumen, brains, cleverness, discernment, insight, intellect, intelligence, judgement, penetration, perceptiveness, sense, wisdom.

2 *an understanding of a problem*. appreciation, apprehension, awareness, cognition, comprehension, grasp, knowledge.
3 *friendly understanding between two people*. accord, agreement, consensus, consent, consideration, empathy, fellow feeling, harmony, kindness, mutuality, sympathy, tolerance.
4 *a formal understanding between two parties*. arrangement, bargain, compact, contract, deal, entente, pact, settlement, treaty.

understate verb *to understate a problem*. belittle, [*informal*] make light of, minimize, [*informal*] play down, [*informal*] soft-pedal.
OPPOSITES: SEE **exaggerate**.

understudy noun SEE **deputy**.

understudy verb SEE **deputize**.

undertake verb **1** *to undertake to do something*. agree, consent, guarantee, pledge, promise.
2 *to undertake a task*. accept responsibility for, address, approach, attempt, attend to, begin, commence, commit yourself to, cope with, deal with, embark on, grapple with, handle, manage, tackle, take on, take up, try.

undertaker noun funeral director, [*American*] mortician.

undertaking noun SEE **enterprise**.

undertone noun SEE **undercurrent**.

undertow noun SEE **current** noun.

undervalue verb SEE **underestimate**.

underwater adjective *underwater exploration*. subaquatic, submarine, undersea.

underwear noun SEE **underclothes**.

underweight adjective SEE **light** adjective.

underworld noun SEE **hell**.

underwrite verb *to underwrite a business enterprise*. SEE **finance** verb.

undeserved adjective *undeserved punishment*. unearned, unfair, unjustified, unmerited, unwarranted.

undesirable adjective SEE **objectionable**.

undeveloped adjective SEE **backward**.

undignified adjective *an undignified rush to be first*. indecorous, inelegant, ridiculous, scrambled, unbecoming, unseemly.
OPPOSITES: SEE **dignified**.

undisciplined adjective *an undisciplined rabble*. anarchic, chaotic, disobedient,

disorderly, disorganized, intractable, rebellious, uncontrolled, unruly, unsystematic, untrained, wild, wilful.
OPPOSITES: SEE **disciplined**.

undiscriminating adjective *an undiscriminating audience*. easily pleased, imperceptive, superficial, thoughtless, uncritical, undiscerning, unselective.
OPPOSITES: SEE **discriminating**.

undisguised adjective SEE **blatant**.

undisputed adjective SEE **indisputable**.

undistinguished adjective SEE **ordinary**.

undo verb **1** *to undo a fastening*. *to undo a parcel*. detach, disconnect, disengage, loose, loosen, open, part, separate, unbind, unbuckle, unbutton, unchain, unclasp, unclip, uncouple, unfasten, unfetter, unhook, unleash, unlock, unpick, unpin, unscrew, unseal, unshackle, unstick, untether, untie, unwrap, unzip.
2 *to undo someone's good work*. annul, cancel out, destroy, mar, nullify, quash (*to quash a decision*), reverse, ruin, spoil, undermine, vitiate, wipe out, wreck.

undoing noun SEE **ruin** noun.

undoubted adjective SEE **indisputable**.

undoubtedly adverb certainly, definitely, doubtless, indubitably, of course, surely, undeniably, unquestionably.

undreamed of adjective SEE **inconceivable**.

undress verb disrobe, divest yourself, [*informal*] peel off, shed your clothes, strip, take off your clothes, uncover yourself.
OPPOSITES: SEE **dress** verb.

undressed adjective SEE **naked**.

undue adjective SEE **excessive**.

undulating adjective SEE **wavy**.

undying adjective SEE **eternal**.

unearth verb SEE **uncover**.

unearthly adjective SEE **eerie**.

uneasy adjective **1** *an uneasy night*. disturbed, restive, restless, uncomfortable, unsettled.
OPPOSITES: SEE **comfortable**.
2 *an uneasy feeling*. anxious, apprehensive, awkward, concerned, distressing, edgy, fearful, insecure, jittery, nervous, tense, troubled, upsetting, worried.
OPPOSITES: SEE **secure** adjective.

uneconomic adjective SEE **unprofitable**.

uneducated adjective SEE **ignorant**.

unemotional adjective **1** *a doctor's unemotional approach to illness*. clinical, cool, dispassionate, impassive, objective.

2 *an unemotional reaction to a tragedy.* apathetic, cold, frigid, hard-hearted, heartless, indifferent, unfeeling, unmoved, unresponsive.
OPPOSITES: SEE **emotional.**

unemployed adjective jobless, on the dole, out of work, redundant.
OPPOSITES: SEE **working.**

unending adjective SEE **endless.**

unendurable adjective SEE **unbearable.**

unenthusiastic adjective SEE **apathetic.**

unequal adjective **1** *unequal contributions from two participants.* different, differing, disparate, dissimilar, uneven, varying.
OPPOSITES: SEE **equal.**

2 *unequal treatment of contestants by the referee.* biased, prejudiced, unjust.

3 *an unequal contest.* ill-matched, one-sided, unbalanced, uneven, unfair.
OPPOSITES: SEE **fair** adjective.

unequalled adjective *an unequalled reputation.* incomparable, inimitable, matchless, peerless, supreme, surpassing, unmatched, unparalleled, unrivalled, unsurpassed.

unequivocal adjective SEE **definite.**

unerring adjective SEE **accurate.**

unethical adjective SEE **immoral.**

uneven adjective **1** *an uneven surface.* bent, broken, bumpy, crooked, irregular, jagged, jerky, pitted, rough, rutted, undulating, wavy.
OPPOSITES: SEE **smooth** adjective.

2 *an uneven rhythm.* erratic, fitful, fluctuating, inconsistent, spasmodic, unpredictable, variable, varying.
OPPOSITES: SEE **consistent.**

3 *an uneven load.* asymmetrical, lopsided, unsteady.

4 *an uneven contest.* ill-matched, one-sided, unbalanced, unequal, unfair.
OPPOSITES: SEE **balanced.**

unexceptionable adjective SEE **perfect** adjective.

unexceptional, unexciting adjectives SEE **ordinary.**

unexpected adjective *an unexpected meeting.* accidental, chance, fortuitous, sudden, surprising, unforeseen, unhoped for, unlooked for, unplanned, unpredictable, unusual.
OPPOSITES: SEE **expected.**

unfailing adjective SEE **dependable.**

unfair adjective SEE **unjust.**

unfaithful adjective deceitful, disloyal, double-dealing, duplicitous, faithless, false, fickle, inconstant, perfidious, traitorous, treacherous, treasonable, unreliable, untrue, untrustworthy.
OPPOSITES: SEE **faithful.**

unfaithfulness noun **1** *unfaithfulness to your country or your party.* duplicity, perfidy, treachery, treason.
2 *unfaithfulness to a husband or wife.* adultery, infidelity.

unfamiliar adjective SEE **strange.**

unfashionable adjective dated, obsolete, old-fashioned, [*informal*] out (*Bright colours are out this year*), outmoded, passé, superseded, unstylish.
OPPOSITES: SEE **fashionable.**

unfasten verb SEE **undo.**

unfavourable adjective **1** *unfavourable criticism. unfavourable winds.* adverse, attacking, contrary, critical, disapproving, discouraging, hostile, ill-disposed, inauspicious, negative, opposing, uncomplimentary, unfriendly, unhelpful, unkind, unpromising, unpropitious, unsympathetic.
2 *an unfavourable reputation.* bad, undesirable, unenviable, unsatisfactory.
OPPOSITES: SEE **favourable.**

unfeeling adjective SEE **callous.**

unfinished adjective imperfect, incomplete, rough, sketchy, uncompleted, unpolished.
OPPOSITES: SEE **perfect** adjective.

unfit adjective **1** *A drunkard is unfit to drive. A slum is unfit to live in.* ill-equipped, inadequate, incapable, incompetent, unsatisfactory, useless.
2 *The film was unfit for children's viewing.* improper, inappropriate, unbecoming, unsuitable, unsuited.
3 *You won't play well if you're unfit.* feeble, flabby, SEE **ill,** out of condition, unhealthy.
OPPOSITES: SEE **fit** adjective.

unflagging adjective SEE **tireless.**

unflappable adjective SEE **calm** adjective.

unflattering adjective SEE **candid.**

unflinching adjective SEE **resolute.**

unfold verb SEE **open** verb.

unforeseen adjective SEE **unexpected.**

unforgettable adjective SEE **memorable.**

unforgivable adjective *an unforgivable mistake.* inexcusable, mortal (*a mortal sin*), reprehensible, shameful, unjustifiable, unpardonable, unwarrantable.
OPPOSITES: SEE **forgivable.**

unfortunate adjective SEE **unlucky**.

unfounded adjective SEE **groundless**.

unfreeze verb SEE **thaw**.

unfrequented adjective SEE **inaccessible**.

unfriendly adjective *an unfriendly welcome. unfriendly people.* aggressive, aloof, antagonistic, antisocial, cold, cool, detached, disagreeable, distant, forbidding, hostile, ill-disposed, impersonal, indifferent, inhospitable, menacing, nasty, obnoxious, offensive, reserved, rude, sour, stand-offish, [*informal*] starchy, stern, threatening, uncivil, uncongenial, unenthusiastic, unkind, unneighbourly, unsociable, unsympathetic, unwelcoming.
OPPOSITES: SEE **friendly**.

unfruitful adjective SEE **unproductive**.

unfurl verb SEE **open** verb.

ungainly adjective SEE **awkward**.

ungentlemanly adjective SEE **vulgar**.

unget-at-able adjective SEE **inaccessible**.

ungodly adjective SEE **irreligious**.

ungovernable adjective SEE **rebellious**.

ungrateful adjective *I won't give her any more if she's ungrateful.* displeased, ill-mannered, selfish, unappreciative, unthankful.
OPPOSITES: SEE **grateful**.

unguarded adjective SEE **careless**.

unguent noun SEE **ointment**.

unhappy adjective **1** *unhappy because things are not going well.* SEE **sad**.
2 *an unhappy accident.* SEE **unlucky**.
3 *an unhappy arrangement.* SEE **unsatisfactory**.

unhealthy adjective **1** *unhealthy animals.* ailing, delicate, diseased, SEE **ill**, infected, [*informal*] poorly, sick, sickly, suffering, unwell, weak.
2 *unhealthy conditions.* deleterious, dirty, harmful, insalubrious, insanitary, polluted, unhygienic, unwholesome.
OPPOSITES: SEE **healthy**.

unheard of adjective SEE **exceptional**.

unhelpful adjective *an unhelpful shop-assistant.* disobliging, inconsiderate, negative, slow, uncivil, uncooperative, unwilling.
OPPOSITES: SEE **obliging**.

unhinged adjective SEE **mad**.

unhoped for adjective SEE **unexpected**.

unhurried adjective SEE **leisurely**.

unhygienic adjective SEE **unhealthy**.

unidentifiable adjective camouflaged, disguised, hidden, SEE **unidentified**, unrecognizable.
OPPOSITES: SEE **identifiable**.

unidentified adjective *an unidentified benefactor.* anonymous, incognito, nameless, unfamiliar, unknown, unnamed, unrecognized, unspecified.
OPPOSITES: SEE **named**.

The prefix *uni-* in words like *unicorn, uniform, unisex,* etc., is related to Latin *unus = one.* (Do not confuse with words like *unidentified* and *unimaginable,* which are formed by attaching prefix *un-* to words beginning with *i-!*)

uniform adjective *a uniform appearance.* consistent, homogeneous, identical, indistinguishable, regular, the same, similar, single, unvarying.
OPPOSITES: SEE **different**.

uniform noun livery.

unify verb *unified by a common purpose.* amalgamate, bring together, combine, consolidate, fuse, harmonize, integrate, join, merge, unite, weld together.
OPPOSITES: SEE **separate** verb.

unilateral adjective *a unilateral decision.* one-sided.
OPPOSITE: multilateral.

unimaginable adjective SEE **inconceivable**.

unimaginative adjective *an unimaginative story.* banal, boring, derivative, dull, hackneyed, inartistic, obvious, ordinary, pedestrian, prosaic, stale, trite, uninspired, uninteresting, unoriginal.
OPPOSITES: SEE **imaginative**.

unimpeachable adjective SEE **indisputable**.

unimportant adjective *unimportant news. an unimportant mistake.* ephemeral, immaterial, inconsequential, inessential, insignificant, irrelevant, lightweight, minor, negligible, peripheral, petty, secondary, slight, SEE **small**, trifling, trivial, uninteresting, unremarkable, worthless.
OPPOSITES: SEE **important**.

unimpressive adjective SEE **ordinary**.

uninhabited adjective *an uninhabited island.* abandoned, deserted, empty, uncolonized, unoccupied, unpeopled, vacant.
OPPOSITES: SEE **inhabited**.

uninhibited adjective *uninhibited language.* abandoned, casual, frank, informal, natural, open, relaxed, spontaneous, unrepressed, unreserved, unrestrained, unselfconscious.
OPPOSITES: SEE **inhibited**.

uninspired adjective SEE **unimaginative**.

unintelligent adjective SEE **stupid**.

unintelligible adjective SEE **incomprehensible**.

unintentional adjective *an unintentional insult.* accidental, fortuitous, inadvertent, involuntary, unconscious, unintended, unplanned, unwitting.
OPPOSITES: SEE **intentional**.

uninterested adjective *uninterested pupils.* apathetic, bored, incurious, indifferent, lethargic, passive, phlegmatic, unconcerned, unenthusiastic, uninvolved, unresponsive.
OPPOSITES: SEE **interested**.

uninteresting adjective *an uninteresting book. an uninteresting voice.* boring, dreary, dry, dull, flat, monotonous, obvious, SEE **ordinary**, predictable, tedious, unexciting, uninspiring, vapid, wearisome.
OPPOSITE: SEE **interesting**.

uninterrupted adjective SEE **continuous**.

uninvited adjective *uninvited guests.* unasked, unbidden, unwelcome.

uninviting adjective SEE **unattractive**.

uninvolved adjective SEE **detached**.

union noun 1 *a union of two organizations or parties.* SEE **alliance**, amalgamation, association, coalition, conjunction, integration, joining together, merger, unification, unity.
2 *a union of two substances.* amalgam, blend, combination, compound, fusion, mixture, synthesis.
3 *a union of two people.* marriage, matrimony, partnership, wedlock.
4 *sexual union.* SEE **sex**.

unique adjective [Many people consider that *unique* correctly means *being the only one of its kind*, and that sense 2 is incorrect.] 1 [= *being the only one of its kind*] *She's proud of her ring because of its unique design.* distinctive, lone, [*informal*] one-off, peculiar, single, singular, unparalleled.
2 [*informal* = *rare, unusual*] SEE **unusual**.

unit noun 1 UNITS OF MEASUREMENT: SEE **measure** noun.
2 *a complete unit.* entity, item, whole.

3 *You can buy extra units to add on when you can afford them.* component, constituent, element, module, part, piece, portion, section, segment.

unite verb 1 *The manager decided to unite two departments.* amalgamate, blend, bring together, coalesce, combine, confederate, consolidate, couple, federate, fuse, harmonize, incorporate, integrate, join, link, marry, merge, unify, weld together.
OPPOSITES: SEE **separate** verb.
2 *Everyone united to support the appeal for charity.* ally, associate, collaborate, conspire, co-operate, go into partnership, join forces.
OPPOSITES: SEE **compete**.
3 *to unite in marriage* SEE **marry**.

united adjective *a united decision. a united effort.* agreed, common, collective, concerted, corporate, harmonious, joint, unanimous, undivided.
OPPOSITES: SEE **disunited**.
to be united SEE **agree**.

unity noun SEE **agreement**.

universal adjective *universal peace.* all-round, common, general, global, international, total, ubiquitous, widespread, worldwide.

universe noun cosmos, the heavens.
ASTRONOMICAL TERMS: SEE **astronomy**.

university noun SEE **college**.

unjust adjective *an unjust decision.* biased, bigoted, indefensible, inequitable, one-sided, partial, partisan, prejudiced, undeserved, unfair, unjustified, unlawful, unmerited, unreasonable, unwarranted, wrong, wrongful.
OPPOSITES: SEE **just**.

unjustifiable adjective *unjustifiable severity.* excessive, immoderate, indefensible, inexcusable, unacceptable, unconscionable, unforgivable, SEE **unjust**, unreasonable, unwarrantable.
OPPOSITES: SEE **justifiable**.

unkempt adjective SEE **untidy**.

unkind adjective [There are many other words you can use in addition to those listed here: SEE **angry, critical, cruel**, etc.] *unkind criticism. unkind treatment of animals.* [*informal*] beastly, callous, cold-blooded, cruel, discourteous, disobliging, hard, hard-hearted, harsh, heartless, hurtful, ill-natured, impolite, inconsiderate, inhumane, insensitive, malevolent, malicious, mean, merciless, nasty, pitiless, relentless, ruthless, sadistic, savage, selfish, severe, spiteful, stern, tactless, thoughtless, uncaring, uncharitable, unchristian,

unfeeling, unfriendly, unpleasant, unsympathetic, vicious.
OPPOSITES: SEE **kind** adjective.

unknown adjective **1** *unknown intruders*. anonymous, disguised, incognito, mysterious, nameless, strange, unidentified, unnamed, unrecognized, unspecified.
OPPOSITES: SEE **named**.
2 *unknown territory*. alien, foreign, uncharted, undiscovered, unexplored, unfamiliar, unmapped.
OPPOSITES: SEE **familiar**.
3 *an unknown actor*. humble, insignificant, little-known, lowly, obscure, undistinguished, unheard of, unimportant.
OPPOSITES: SEE **famous**.

unladen adjective SEE **empty**.

unladylike adjective SEE **vulgar**.

unlawful adjective SEE **illegal**.

unlearn verb SEE **forget**.

unleash verb SEE **release** verb.

unlettered adjective SEE **ignorant**.

unlike adjective SEE **dissimilar**.

unlikely adjective **1** *an unlikely story*. dubious, far-fetched, implausible, improbable, incredible, suspect, suspicious, [*informal*] tall (*a tall story*), unbelievable, unconvincing.
2 *an unlikely possibility*. distant, doubtful, faint, [*informal*] outside, remote, slight.
OPPOSITES: SEE **likely**.

unlimited adjective SEE **boundless**.

unload verb *We unloaded the cases at the station*. discharge, drop off, [*informal*] dump, empty, offload, take off, unpack.
OPPOSITES: SEE **load** verb.

unlock verb SEE **open** verb.

unlooked for adjective SEE **unexpected**.

unloved adjective abandoned, forsaken, SEE **hated**, lovelorn, neglected, rejected, spurned, uncared for, unvalued, unwanted.
OPPOSITE: loved [SEE **love** verb].

unlucky adjective **1** *an unlucky mistake*. accidental, calamitous, chance, disastrous, dreadful, tragic, unfortunate, untimely, unwelcome.
2 *an unlucky person*. [*informal*] accident-prone, hapless, luckless, unhappy, unsuccessful, wretched.
3 *13 is supposed to be an unlucky number*. cursed, ill-fated, ill-omened, ill-starred, inauspicious, jinxed, ominous, unfavourable.
OPPOSITES: SEE **lucky**.

unmanageable adjective SEE **rebellious**.

unmanly adjective SEE **effeminate**.

unmannerly adjective SEE **rude**.

unmarried adjective [*informal*] available, celibate, single, unwed.
an unmarried person [*male*] bachelor, [*female*] spinster.

unmask verb SEE **reveal**.

unmentionable adjective SEE **taboo** adjective.

unmindful adjective SEE **oblivious**.

unmistakable adjective SEE **obvious**.

unmitigated, unmixed adjectives SEE **absolute**.

unmoved adjective SEE **unemotional**.

unnamed adjective SEE **unidentified**.

unnatural adjective **1** *unnatural happenings*. abnormal, bizarre, eerie, extraordinary, fantastic, freak, inexplicable, magic, magical, odd, queer, strange, supernatural, unaccountable, uncanny, unusual, weird.
2 *unnatural feelings*. callous, cold-blooded, cruel, hard-hearted, heartless, inhuman, inhumane, monstrous, perverse, perverted, sadistic, savage, stony-hearted, unfeeling, unkind.
3 *unnatural behaviour. an unnatural accent*. actorish, affected, bogus, fake, feigned, insincere, mannered, [*informal*] phoney, pretended, [*informal*] pseudo, [*informal*] put on, self-conscious, stagey, stiff, stilted, theatrical, unspontaneous.
4 *unnatural materials*. artificial, fabricated, imitation, man-made, manufactured, simulated, synthetic.
OPPOSITES: SEE **natural**.

unnecessary adjective *Let's get rid of all the unnecessary things lying around*. dispensable, excessive, expendable, extra, inessential, needless, non-essential, redundant, superfluous, surplus, uncalled for, unjustified, unneeded, unwanted, useless.
OPPOSITES: SEE **necessary**.

unnerve verb SEE **discourage**.

unobtrusive adjective SEE **inconspicuous**.

unoccupied adjective SEE **uninhabited**.

unofficial adjective *an unofficial warning*. friendly, informal, [*informal*] off the record, private, unauthorized, unconfirmed, unlicensed.
OPPOSITES: SEE **official** adjective.

unoriginal adjective *an unoriginal joke*. banal, borrowed, conventional, copied, [*informal*] corny, derivative, hackneyed, old, orthodox, second-hand,

stale, traditional, unimaginative, uninspired, uninventive.
OPPOSITES: SEE original.

unorthodox adjective SEE unconventional.

unpaid adjective 1 *unpaid bills.* due, outstanding, owing.
2 *unpaid work.* unremunerative, voluntary.

unpalatable adjective *unpalatable food.* disgusting, inedible, nauseating, sickening, tasteless, unappetizing, SEE unpleasant.
OPPOSITES: SEE palatable.
WORDS DESCRIBING TASTE: SEE taste verb.

unparalleled adjective SEE unequalled.

unpardonable adjective SEE unforgivable.

unperturbed adjective SEE untroubled.

unpick verb SEE undo.

unplanned adjective SEE spontaneous.

unpleasant adjective [*Unpleasant* can refer to anything which displeases you: there are far more synonyms than we can give here.] abhorrent, abominable, antisocial, appalling, awful, SEE bad, bad-tempered, bitter, coarse, crude, detestable, diabolical, dirty, disagreeable, disgusting, displeasing, distasteful, dreadful, evil, fearful, fearsome, filthy, foul, frightful, ghastly, grim, grisly, gruesome, harsh, hateful, [*informal*] hellish, hideous, horrible, horrid, horrifying, improper, indecent, irksome, loathsome, [*informal*] lousy, malevolent, malicious, mucky, nasty, nauseating, objectionable, obnoxious, odious, offensive, repellent, repugnant, repulsive, revolting, rude, shocking, sickening, sickly, sordid, sour, spiteful, squalid, terrible, ugly, unattractive, uncouth, undesirable, unfriendly, unkind, unpalatable, unsavoury, unwelcome, upsetting, vexing, vicious, vile, vulgar.
OPPOSITES: SEE pleasant.

unpolished adjective SEE rough.

unpopular adjective *an unpopular choice. an unpopular government.* despised, disliked, hated, minority (*minority interests*), rejected, shunned, unfashionable, unloved, unwanted.
OPPOSITES: SEE popular.

unprecedented adjective SEE exceptional.

unpredictable adjective *unpredictable weather.* changeable, uncertain, unexpected, unforeseeable, SEE variable.
OPPOSITES: SEE predictable.

unprejudiced adjective SEE unbiased.

unpremeditated adjective SEE spontaneous.

unprepared adjective 1 *unprepared for bad weather.* [*informal*] caught napping, ill-equipped, unready.
2 *an unprepared speech.* SEE spontaneous.

unprepossessing adjective SEE unattractive.

unpretentious adjective *Although she was wealthy, she lived in an unpretentious house.* humble, modest, plain, simple, straightforward, unaffected, unassuming, unostentatious, unsophisticated.
OPPOSITES: SEE pretentious.

unprincipled adjective SEE unscrupulous.

unprintable adjective SEE rude.

unproductive adjective 1 *unproductive work.* ineffective, fruitless, futile, pointless, unprofitable, unrewarding, useless, valueless, worthless.
2 *an unproductive garden.* arid, barren, infertile, sterile, unfruitful.
OPPOSITES: SEE productive.

unprofessional adjective *an unprofessional attitude towards your work.* amateurish, SEE casual, incompetent, inefficient, irresponsible, lax, negligent, unethical, unseemly, unskilled, unworthy.
OPPOSITES: SEE professional.

unprofitable adjective *an unprofitable business.* loss-making, uncommercial, uneconomic, unproductive, unremunerative, unrewarding.
OPPOSITES: SEE profitable.

unpromising adjective SEE unfavourable.

unprotected adjective SEE helpless.

unprovable adjective SEE questionable, undemonstrable, unsubstantiated, unverifiable.
OPPOSITES: SEE provable.

unpunctual adjective behind-hand, delayed, late, overdue, tardy, unreliable.
OPPOSITES: SEE punctual.

unqualified adjective 1 *an unqualified worker.* SEE amateur adjective.
2 *an unqualified refusal.* SEE absolute.

unquestionable adjective SEE indisputable.

unravel verb SEE disentangle.

unreal adjective SEE imaginary.

unrealistic adjective 1 *an unrealistic portrait.* non-representational, unconvincing, unlifelike, unnatural, unrecognizable.

2 *an unrealistic suggestion.* fanciful, idealistic, impossible, impracticable, impractical, over-ambitious, quixotic, romantic, silly, unworkable.
3 *unrealistic prices.* SEE **exorbitant**.
OPPOSITES: SEE **realistic**.

unreasonable adjective **1** *an unreasonable person.* SEE **irrational**.
2 *an unreasonable argument.* SEE **absurd**.
3 *unreasonable prices.* SEE **excessive**.

unrecognizable adjective SEE **unidentifiable**.

unrefined adjective SEE **crude**.

unreformable, unregenerate adjectives SEE **unrepentant**.

unrelated adjective SEE **irrelevant, separate** adjective.

unrelenting adjective SEE **persistent, pitiless**.

unreliable adjective **1** *unreliable evidence.* deceptive, false, implausible, inaccurate, misleading, suspect, unconvincing.
2 *an unreliable friend.* changeable, fallible, fickle, inconsistent, irresponsible, undependable, unpredictable, unsound, unstable, untrustworthy.
OPPOSITES: SEE **reliable**.

unrelieved, unremitting adjectives SEE **persistent, pitiless**.

unrepentant adjective *an unrepentant criminal.* brazen, confirmed, hardened, impenitent, incorrigible, incurable, inveterate, SEE **irredeemable**, shameless, unashamed, unblushing, unreformable, unregenerate.
OPPOSITES: SEE **repentant**.

unreserved adjective *unreserved apologies.* SEE **absolute**.

unresisting adjective SEE **passive**.

unresolved adjective SEE **uncertain**.

unrest noun SEE **riot** noun.

unrestrained adjective SEE **wild**.

unrestricted adjective SEE **absolute**.

unripe adjective *unripe fruit.* immature, sour, unready.
OPPOSITES: SEE **ripe**.

unrivalled adjective SEE **unequalled**.

unroll verb SEE **open** verb.

unruffled adjective SEE **calm** adjective.

unruly adjective SEE **disobedient**.

unsafe adjective SEE **dangerous**.

unsaid adjective *It was what she left unsaid that worried me.* SEE **implicit**.

unsatisfactory adjective *an unsatisfactory result.* disappointing, displeasing, dissatisfying, frustrating, inadequate, incompetent, inefficient, insufficient, [*informal*] not good enough, poor, unacceptable, unhappy, unsatisfying, [*informal*] wretched.
OPPOSITES: SEE **satisfactory**.

unsavoury adjective SEE **unpleasant**.

unscathed adjective SEE **safe**.

unscrupulous adjective *unscrupulous cheating.* dishonest, dishonourable, SEE **immoral**, improper, self-interested, shameless, unconscionable.
OPPOSITES: SEE **moral** adjective.

unscrew verb SEE **unfasten**.

unscripted adjective SEE **impromptu**.

unseal verb SEE **open** verb.

unseat verb SEE **oust**.

unseemly adjective SEE **unbecoming**.

unseen adjective SEE **invisible**.

unselfish adjective altruistic, caring, charitable, considerate, disinterested, generous, humanitarian, kind, magnanimous, philanthropic, public-spirited, self-effacing, selfless, self-sacrificing, thoughtful, ungrudging, unstinting.
OPPOSITES: SEE **selfish**.

unselfishness noun altruism, consideration, generosity, kindness, magnanimity, philanthropy, self-denial, selflessness, thoughtfulness.
OPPOSITES: SEE **selfishness**.

unsettle verb SEE **disturb**.

unshakeable adjective SEE **firm** adjective.

unsightly adjective SEE **ugly**.

unskilful adjective *unskilful work.* amateurish, bungled, clumsy, crude, incompetent, inept, inexpert, maladroit, [*informal*] rough and ready, shoddy, unprofessional.
OPPOSITES: SEE **skilful**.

unskilled adjective *an unskilled worker.* inexperienced, SEE **unskilful**, unqualified, untrained.
OPPOSITES: SEE **skilled**.

unsociable adjective SEE **unfriendly**.

unsolicited adjective SEE **unasked**.

unsophisticated adjective *unsophisticated tastes.* [*uncomplimentary*] childish, childlike, ingenuous, innocent, low-brow, naïve, plain, provincial, simple, simple-minded, straightforward, unaffected, uncomplicated, unostentatious, unpretentious, unrefined, unworldly.
OPPOSITES: SEE **sophisticated**.

unsound adjective SEE **weak**.

unsparing adjective SEE **generous**.

unspeakable adjective *unspeakable horrors.* SEE **dreadful**, indescribable, inexpressible, nameless, unutterable.

unspecified adjective SEE **unidentified**.

unstable adjective SEE **changeable, unsteady**.

unsteady adjective **1** *unsteady on your legs. an unsteady structure.* flimsy, frail, insecure, precarious, rickety, [*informal*] rocky, shaky, tottering, unbalanced, unsafe, unstable, wobbly.
2 *an unsteady trickle of water.* changeable, erratic, inconstant, intermittent, irregular, variable.
3 *the unsteady light of a candle.* flickering, fluctuating, quavering, quivering, trembling, tremulous, wavering.
OPPOSITES: SEE **steady** adjective.

unstinting adjective SEE **generous**.

unsubstantial adjective SEE **flimsy**.

unsubstantiated adjective SEE **unproved**.

unsuccessful adjective **1** *an unsuccessful attempt.* abortive, failed, fruitless, futile, ill-fated, ineffective, ineffectual, loss-making, sterile, unavailing, unlucky, unproductive, unprofitable, unsatisfactory, useless, vain.
2 *unsuccessful contestants in a race.* beaten, defeated, losing.
OPPOSITES: SEE **successful**.

unsuitable adjective *an unsuitable choice.* ill-chosen, ill-judged, ill-timed, inapposite, inappropriate, incongruous, inept, irrelevant, mistaken, unbefitting, unfitting, unhappy, unsatisfactory, unseasonable, unseemly, untimely.
OPPOSITES: SEE **suitable**.

unsullied adjective SEE **spotless**.

unsung adjective SEE **anonymous**.

unsure adjective SEE **uncertain**.

unsurpassed adjective SEE **unequalled**.

unsuspecting adjective SEE **credulous**.

unswerving adjective SEE **resolute**.

unsympathetic adjective *an unsympathetic response.* apathetic, cold, cool, dispassionate, hard-hearted, heartless, impassive, indifferent, insensitive, neutral, reserved, uncaring, uncharitable, unconcerned, unfeeling, uninterested, unkind, unmoved, unpitying, unresponsive.
OPPOSITES: SEE **sympathetic**.

unsystematic adjective *an unsystematic worker. unsystematic work.* anarchic, chaotic, confused, disorderly, disorganized, haphazard, illogical, jumbled, muddled, [*informal*] shambolic, [*informal*] sloppy, unmethodical, unplanned, unstructured, untidy.
OPPOSITES: SEE **systematic**.

untamed adjective SEE **wild**.

untangle verb SEE **disentangle**.

untarnished adjective SEE **spotless**.

untenable adjective SEE **indefensible**.

unthinkable adjective SEE **incredible**.

unthinking adjective SEE **thoughtless**.

untidy adjective **1** *untidy work. an untidy room.* careless, chaotic, cluttered, confused, disorderly, disorganized, haphazard, [*informal*] higgledy-piggledy, in disarray, jumbled, littered, [*informal*] messy, muddled, [*informal*] shambolic, slapdash, [*informal*] sloppy, slovenly, [*informal*] topsy-turvy, unsystematic, upside-down.
2 *untidy hair. an untidy appearance.* bedraggled, blowzy, dishevelled, disordered, rumpled, scruffy, shabby, tangled, tousled, uncared for, uncombed, ungroomed, unkempt.
OPPOSITES: SEE **tidy** adjective.

untie verb *to untie a rope.* cast off [= *to untie a boat*], disentangle, free, loosen, release, unbind, undo, unfasten, unknot, untether.

untimely adjective SEE **unsuitable**.

untiring adjective SEE **persistent**.

untold adjective SEE **boundless, numerous**.

untoward adjective SEE **inconvenient**.

untraceable adjective SEE **lost**.

untrained adjective SEE **unskilled**.

untrammelled adjective SEE **free** adjective.

untried adjective *an untried formula.* experimental, innovatory, new, novel, unproved, untested.
OPPOSITES: SEE **established**.

untroubled adjective *untroubled progress.* carefree, SEE **peaceful**, straightforward, undisturbed, uninterrupted, unruffled.

untrue adjective SEE **false**.

untrustworthy adjective SEE **dishonest**.

untruth noun SEE **lie** noun.

untruthful adjective SEE **lying**.

untwist verb SEE **disentangle**.

unused adjective *The shop may take back any unused items.* blank, clean, fresh, intact, mint (*in mint condition*), new, pristine, unopened, untouched, unworn.
OPPOSITES: SEE **used**.

unusual adjective *unusual events. unusual things.* abnormal, atypical, curious, [*informal*] different, exceptional,

extraordinary, [*informal*] funny, irregular, odd, out of the ordinary, peculiar, queer, rare, remarkable, singular, SEE **strange**, surprising, uncommon, unconventional, unexpected, unfamiliar, [*informal*] unheard of, [*informal*] unique, unnatural, untypical, unwonted.
OPPOSITES: SEE **usual**.

unutterable adjective SEE **indescribable**.

unveil verb SEE **uncover**.

unwanted adjective SEE **unnecessary**.

unwarrantable adjective SEE **unforgivable**.

unwarranted adjective SEE **unjustified**.

unwary adjective SEE **careless**.

unwavering adjective SEE **resolute**.

unwelcome adjective *unwelcome guests.* disagreeable, unacceptable, undesirable, unwanted.
OPPOSITES: SEE **welcome** adjective.

unwell adjective SEE **ill**.

unwholesome adjective SEE **unhealthy**.

unwieldy adjective SEE **awkward**.

unwilling adjective *unwilling helpers.* averse, backward, disinclined, grudging, half-hearted, hesitant, ill-disposed, indisposed, lazy, loath, opposed, reluctant, resistant, slow, uncooperative, unenthusiastic, unhelpful.
OPPOSITES: SEE **willing**.

unwind verb SEE **unbend**.

unwise adjective *unwise advice. an unwise thing to do.* [*informal*] daft, foolhardy, foolish, ill-advised, ill-judged, illogical, imperceptive, impolitic, imprudent, inadvisable, indiscreet, inexperienced, injudicious, irrational, irresponsible, mistaken, obtuse, perverse, rash, reckless, senseless, short-sighted, silly, SEE **stupid**, thoughtless, unintelligent, unreasonable.
OPPOSITES: SEE **wise**.

unwitting adjective SEE **unintentional**.

unwonted adjective SEE **unusual**.

unworkable adjective SEE **impractical**.

unworldly adjective SEE **spiritual**.

unworn adjective SEE **unused**.

unworthy adjective *A person who cheats is an unworthy winner.* despicable, discreditable, dishonourable, disreputable, ignoble, inappropriate, shameful, undeserving, unsuitable.
OPPOSITES: SEE **worthy**.

unwrap verb SEE **open** verb.

unwritten adjective *an unwritten message.* oral, spoken, verbal, [*informal*] word-of-mouth.
OPPOSITES: SEE **written**.

unyielding adjective SEE **firm** adjective.

unzip verb SEE **undo**.

upbraid verb SEE **reproach** verb.

upbringing noun *the upbringing of children.* breeding, bringing up, care, education, instruction, nurture, raising, rearing, teaching, training.

update verb *to update information. to update a design.* amend, bring up to date, correct, modernize, review, revise.

upgrade verb *to upgrade a computer system.* enhance, expand, improve, make better.

upheaval noun SEE **commotion**.

uphill adjective *an uphill struggle.* arduous, difficult, exhausting, gruelling, hard, laborious, stiff, strenuous, taxing, tough.

uphold verb SEE **support** verb.

upholster verb *to upholster a chair.* SEE **pad** verb.

upholstery noun SEE **padding**.

upkeep noun *The upkeep of a car is expensive.* care, keep, maintenance, running, preservation.

uplift verb SEE **raise**.

uplifting adjective *an uplifting experience.* civilizing, edifying, educational, enlightening, ennobling, enriching, good, humanizing, improving, spiritual.
OPPOSITES: SEE **degrading**.

upper adjective *an upper floor.* elevated, higher, raised, superior, upstairs.

uppermost adjective *the uppermost level.* SEE **dominant**, highest, supreme, top, topmost.

upright adjective **1** *an upright position.* erect, perpendicular, vertical.
OPPOSITES: SEE **flat** adjective.
2 *an upright judge.* conscientious, fair, good, high-minded, honest, honourable, incorruptible, just, moral, principled, righteous, [*informal*] straight, true, trustworthy, upstanding, virtuous.
OPPOSITES: SEE **corrupt** adjective.

uproar noun *There was uproar when the referee gave his controversial decision.* [*informal*] bedlam, brawling, chaos, clamour, commotion, confusion, din, disorder, disturbance, furore, [*informal*] hubbub, [*informal*] hullabaloo, [*informal*] a madhouse, noise, outburst, outcry, pandemonium, [*informal*] racket, riot, row, [*informal*] ructions, [*informal*] rumpus, tumult, turbulence, turmoil.

uproarious adjective *an uproarious comedy.* SEE **funny**.

uproot verb *to uproot plants.* destroy, eliminate, eradicate, extirpate, get rid of, [*informal*] grub up, pull up, remove, root out, weed out.

upset verb 1 *to upset a cup. to upset a boat.* capsize, destabilize, overturn, spill, tip over, topple.
OPPOSITES: SEE **stabilize**.
2 *to upset someone's plans.* affect, alter, change, confuse, defeat, disorganize, disrupt, hinder, interfere with, interrupt, jeopardize, overthrow, spoil.
OPPOSITES: SEE **assist**.
3 *to upset someone's feelings.* agitate, alarm, SEE **annoy**, disconcert, dismay, distress, disturb, excite, fluster, frighten, grieve, irritate, offend, perturb, [*informal*] rub up the wrong way, ruffle, scare, unnerve, worry.
OPPOSITES: SEE **calm** verb.

upshot noun SEE **result** noun.

upside-down adjective 1 *I can't read it if it's upside-down.* inverted, [*informal*] topsy-turvy, upturned, wrong way up.
2 *They left the room upside-down.* SEE **chaotic**.

upstanding adjective 1 *a fine upstanding youth.* SEE **well-built**.
2 *an upstanding judge.* SEE **upright**.

upstart noun nouveau riche, social climber, [*informal*] yuppie.

upsurge noun SEE **rise** noun.

uptight adjective SEE **tense** adjective.

up-to-date adjective 1 *up-to-date technology.* advanced, current, latest, modern, new, present-day, recent.
2 *up-to-date clothes.* contemporary, fashionable, [*informal*] in, modish, stylish, [*informal*] trendy.
OPPOSITES: SEE **old-fashioned**.

upturn noun SEE **rise** noun.

upward adjective *an upward path.* ascending, rising, SEE **uphill**.

urban adjective *an urban area.* built-up, densely populated, metropolitan.

urbane adjective SEE **polite, sophisticated**.

urchin noun SEE **child**.

urge noun *an urge to giggle.* compulsion, desire, eagerness, impulse, inclination, instinct, [*informal*] itch, longing, wish, yearning, [*informal*] yen.

urge verb 1 *to urge a horse over a fence.* compel, drive, force, impel, press, propel, push, spur.

2 *I urge you to make a decision.* advise, advocate, appeal to, beg, beseech, [*informal*] chivvy, counsel, [*informal*] egg on, encourage, entreat, exhort, implore, incite, induce, invite, nag, persuade, plead with, prompt, recommend, solicit, stimulate.
OPPOSITES: SEE **deter**.

urgent adjective 1 *business needing urgent attention. an urgent problem.* acute, dire (*in dire need*), essential, exigent, immediate, important, inescapable, instant, necessary, pressing, top-priority, unavoidable.
2 *urgent cries for help.* eager, earnest, importunate, insistent, persistent, persuasive.

urinal noun SEE **lavatory**.

urn noun VARIOUS CONTAINERS: SEE **container**.

usable adjective 1 *Is the lift usable today?* fit for use, functional, functioning, operating, operational, serviceable, working.
OPPOSITE: unusable.
2 *My ticket is usable only on certain trains.* acceptable, current, valid.
OPPOSITES: SEE **invalid** adjective.

use noun *What's the use of this?* advantage, application, necessity, need, [*informal*] point, profit, purpose, usefulness, utility, value, worth.

use verb 1 *to use something for a particular purpose.* administer, apply, employ, exercise, exploit, make use of, utilize, wield.
2 *to use a tool or machine.* deal with, handle, manage, operate, work.
3 *How much money did you use?* consume, exhaust, expend, spend, use up, waste.
to use up SEE **consume**.

used adjective *used cars.* second-hand.

useful adjective 1 *useful advice.* advantageous, beneficial, constructive, good, helpful, invaluable, positive, profitable, salutary, valuable, worthwhile.
2 *a useful tool.* convenient, effective, efficient, handy, powerful, practical, productive, utilitarian.
3 *a useful player.* capable, competent, effectual, proficient, skilful, successful, talented.
OPPOSITES: SEE **useless**.

useless adjective 1 *a useless search. useless advice.* fruitless, futile, hopeless, pointless, unavailing, unprofitable, unsuccessful, vain, worthless.
2 *a useless machine.* [*informal*] broken down, [*informal*] clapped out, dead, dud, ineffective, inefficient, impractical, unusable.

3 *a useless player.* incapable, incompetent, ineffectual, lazy, unhelpful, unskilful, unsuccessful, untalented.
OPPOSITES: SEE **useful.**

usher, usherette nouns attendant, sidesman.

usual adjective *our usual route home. the usual price.* accepted, accustomed, average, common, conventional, customary, everyday, expected, familiar, general, habitual, natural, normal, official, ordinary, orthodox, predictable, prevalent, recognized, regular, routine, standard, stock, traditional, typical, unexceptional, unsurprising, well-known, widespread, wonted.
OPPOSITES: SEE **unusual.**

usurer noun money-lender.

usurp verb *to usurp someone's position or rights.* appropriate, assume, commandeer, seize, steal, take, take over.

utensil noun *kitchen utensils.* appliance, device, gadget, implement, instrument, machine, tool.
VARIOUS TOOLS: SEE **tool.**

uterus noun womb.

utilitarian adjective SEE **functional.**

utilize verb SEE **use** verb.

utmost adjective SEE **extreme** adjective.

Utopian adjective SEE **ideal** adjective.

utter adjective *utter exhaustion.* SEE **absolute.**

utter verb *I didn't utter a word!* SEE **speak.**

U-turn noun SEE **about-turn.**

V

vacancy noun *a job vacancy.* opening, place, position, post, situation.

vacant adjective **1** *a vacant space.* available, bare, blank, clear, empty, free, open, unfilled, unused, usable, void.
2 *a vacant house.* deserted, uninhabited, unoccupied, untenanted.
OPPOSITES: SEE **occupied.**
3 *a vacant look.* absent-minded, abstracted, blank, dreamy, expressionless, far away, inattentive, SEE **vacuous.**
OPPOSITES: SEE **alert** adjective.

vacate verb *to vacate a room.* abandon, depart from, evacuate, give up, leave, quit, withdraw from.

vacation noun holiday, leave, time off.

vaccinate verb SEE **immunize.**

vacillate verb SEE **waver.**

vacuous adjective *a vacuous expression on his face.* apathetic, blank, empty-headed, expressionless, inane, mindless, SEE **stupid,** uncomprehending, unintelligent, vacant.
OPPOSITES: SEE **alert** adjective.

vacuum noun emptiness, space, void.
vacuum cleaner noun Hoover, [*informal*] vacuum.
vacuum flask noun Thermos.

vagabond noun SEE **vagrant.**

vagary noun *the vagaries of fortune.* caprice, fancy, fluctuation, quirk, uncertainty, unpredictability, [*informal, plural*] ups and downs, whim.
OPPOSITES: SEE **certainty.**

vagrant noun beggar, destitute person, [*informal*] down-and-out, homeless person, itinerant, tramp, traveller, vagabond, wanderer, wayfarer.

vague adjective **1** *vague remarks. a vague plan.* ambiguous, ambivalent, broad (*broad generalizations*), confused, equivocal, evasive, general, generalized, imprecise, indefinite, inexact, loose, nebulous, uncertain, unclear, undefined, unspecific, unsure, [*informal*] woolly.
2 *a vague shape in the mist.* amorphous, blurred, dim, hazy, ill-defined, indistinct, misty, shadowy, unrecognizable.
3 *a vague person.* absent-minded, careless, disorganized, forgetful, inattentive, scatter-brained, thoughtless.
OPPOSITES: SEE **definite.**

vain adjective **1** *vain about your appearance.* arrogant, boastful, [*informal*] cocky, conceited, egotistical, haughty, narcissistic, proud, self-important, self-satisfied, [*informal*] stuck-up, vainglorious.
OPPOSITES: SEE **modest.**
2 *a vain attempt.* abortive, fruitless, futile, ineffective, pointless, senseless, unavailing, unproductive, unrewarding, unsuccessful, useless, worthless.
OPPOSITES: SEE **successful.**

vainglorious noun SEE **vain.**

valediction noun SEE **farewell** noun.

valedictory adjective SEE **farewell** adjective.

valentine noun SEE **lover.**

valet noun SEE **servant.**

valetudinarian noun hypochondriac, invalid, worrier.

valiant adjective SEE **brave.**

valid adjective *a valid excuse. a valid ticket.* acceptable, allowed, approved, authentic, authorized, bona fide, convincing, current, genuine, lawful, legal, legitimate, official, permissible, permitted, proper, ratified, reasonable, rightful, sound, suitable, usable.
OPPOSITES: SEE **invalid** adjective.

validate verb *You need an official signature to validate the order.* authenticate, authorize, certify, endorse, legalize, legitimize, make valid, ratify.

valley noun canyon, chasm, coomb, dale, defile, dell, dingle, glen, gorge, gulch, gully, hollow, pass, ravine, vale.

valorous adjective SEE **brave**.

valour noun SEE **bravery**.

valuable adjective 1 *valuable jewellery.* costly, dear, expensive, generous (*a generous gift*), precious, priceless.
2 *valuable advice.* advantageous, beneficial, constructive, esteemed, good, helpful, invaluable [NB *invaluable* is not used as an opposite of *valuable*], positive, prized, profitable, treasured, useful, valued, worthwhile.
OPPOSITES: SEE **worthless**.

value noun 1 *the value of an antique.* cost, price, worth.
2 *the value of keeping fit.* advantage, benefit, importance, merit, significance, use, usefulness.
values *moral values.* SEE **principles**.

value verb 1 *The jeweller valued my watch.* assess, estimate the value of, evaluate, price, [*informal*] put a figure on.
2 *I value your advice.* appreciate, care for, cherish, esteem, [*informal*] have a high regard for, [*informal*] hold dear, love, prize, respect, treasure.

valueless adjective SEE **worthless**.

valve noun SEE **tap** noun.

vamp verb SEE **improvise**.

vandal noun barbarian, delinquent, hooligan, looter, marauder, Philistine, raider, ruffian, savage, thug, troublemaker.

vane noun weather-cock, weather-vane.

vanguard noun SEE **armed services**.
OPPOSITE: rearguard.

vanish verb *The crowd vanished.* clear, clear off, disappear, disperse, dissolve, dwindle, evaporate, fade, go away, melt away, pass.
OPPOSITES: SEE **appear**.

vanity noun SEE **pride**.

vanquish verb SEE **conquer**.

vapid adjective SEE **uninteresting**.

vaporize verb *Petrol vaporizes quickly.* dry up, evaporate, turn to vapour [SEE **vapour**].
OPPOSITES: SEE **condense**.

vapour noun fog, fumes, gas, haze, miasma, mist, smoke, steam.

variable adjective *variable moods.* capricious, changeable, erratic, fickle, fitful, fluctuating, fluid, inconsistent, inconstant, mercurial, mutable, shifting, temperamental, uncertain, unpredictable, unreliable, unstable, unsteady, [*informal*] up-and-down, vacillating, varying, volatile, wavering.
OPPOSITES: SEE **constant**.

variance noun **to be at variance** SEE **disagree**.

variant noun SEE **variation**.

variation noun *a variation from the usual.* alteration, change, deviation, difference, discrepancy, diversification, elaboration, modification, permutation, variant.

varied adjective SEE **various**.

variegated adjective SEE **dappled**.

variety noun 1 *Variety is the spice of life.* alteration, change, difference, diversity, unpredictability, variation.
2 *a variety of things.* array, assortment, blend, collection, combination, jumble, medley, miscellany, mixture, multiplicity.
3 *a variety of baked beans. a variety of dog.* brand, breed, category, class, form, kind, make, sort, species, strain, type.
a variety show SEE **entertainment**.

various adjective *balloons of various colours.* assorted, contrasting, different, differing, dissimilar, diverse, heterogeneous, miscellaneous, mixed, [*informal*] motley (*a motley crowd*), multifarious, several, sundry, varied, varying.
OPPOSITES: SEE **similar, unchanging**.

varnish noun SEE **paint** noun.

vary verb 1 *The temperature varies during the day.* change, differ, fluctuate, go up and down.
2 *You can vary the temperature by turning the knob.* adapt, adjust, alter, convert, modify, reset, transform, upset.
OPPOSITES: SEE **stabilize**.

vast adjective *a vast desert. vast amounts of money.* SEE **big**, boundless, broad, enormous, extensive, great, huge, immeasurable, immense, large, limitless, massive, measureless, never-ending, unbounded, unlimited, wide.
OPPOSITES: SEE **small**.

vat noun VARIOUS CONTAINERS: SEE **container**.

vault noun *a wine vault. the vaults of a bank.* basement, cavern, cellar, crypt, repository, strongroom, undercroft.

vault verb *to vault a fence.* bound over, clear, hurdle, jump, leap, leap-frog, spring over.

VDU noun [= *visual display unit*] display, monitor, screen.
OTHER PARTS OF COMPUTER SYSTEM: SEE **computer**.

veer verb *The car veered across the road.* change direction, dodge, swerve, tack, turn, wheel.

vegetable adjective *vegetable matter.* growing, organic.

vegetable noun

VARIOUS VEGETABLES: asparagus, bean, beet, beetroot, broad bean, broccoli, Brussels sprout, butter bean, cabbage, carrot, cauliflower, celeriac, celery, courgette, kale, kohlrabi, leek, marrow, onion, parsnip, pea, potato, pumpkin, runner bean, shallot, spinach, sugar beet, swede, tomato, turnip, zucchini.

SALAD VEGETABLES: SEE **salad**.

---

vegetarian adjective graminivorous, herbivorous, vegan.
COMPARE: carnivorous, omnivorous.

vegetate verb be inactive, do nothing, [*informal*] go to seed, idle, lose interest, stagnate.

vegetation noun foliage, greenery, growing things, growth, plants, undergrowth, weeds.

vehement adjective *a vehement denial.* animated, ardent, eager, enthusiastic, excited, fervent, fierce, forceful, heated, impassioned, intense, passionate, powerful, strong, urgent, vigorous, violent.
OPPOSITES: SEE **apathetic**.

vehicle noun conveyance.

VARIOUS VEHICLES: ambulance, armoured car, articulated lorry, breakdown vehicle, [*informal*] buggy, bulldozer, bus, cab, camper, SEE **car**, caravan, carriage, cart, [*old-fashioned*] charabanc, chariot, coach, container lorry, SEE **cycle**, double-decker bus, dump truck, dustcart, estate car, fire-engine, float, gig, go-kart, [*old-fashioned*] hackney carriage, hearse, horse-box, jeep, juggernaut, lorry, milk float, minibus, minicab, moped, motor car, [*old-fashioned*] omnibus, panda car, pantechnicon, patrol-car, [*old-fashioned*] phaeton, pick-up, removal van, rickshaw, scooter, sedan-chair, side-car, single-decker bus, sledge, snowplough, stagecoach, steam-roller, tank, tanker (*oil tanker*), taxi, traction-engine, tractor, trailer, tram, transporter, trap, trolley-bus, truck, [*old-fashioned*] tumbrel, van, wagon.

PARTS OF A MOTOR VEHICLE: accelerator, accumulator, air-filter, axle, battery, big-end, bodywork, bonnet, boot, brake, bumper, carburettor, chassis, choke, clutch, cockpit, cylinder, dashboard, diesel engine, dipstick, distributor, engine, exhaust, fascia, fog-light, fuel tank, gear, gearbox, headlight, ignition, indicator, mileometer, mudguard, oil filter, piston, plug, radiator, rev counter, safety belt or seat-belt, shock-absorber, sidelight, silencer, spare wheel, sparking-plug or spark plug, speedometer, starter, steering-wheel, stop-light, tachograph, tachometer, tail-light, throttle, transmission, tyre, wheel, windscreen, windscreen-wiper, wing.

---

veil noun, verb SEE **cover** noun, verb.

vein noun **1** artery, blood vessel, capillary.
2 *in a sentimental vein.* SEE **mood**.

vellum noun SEE **paper** noun.

velocity noun SEE **speed** noun.

venal adjective SEE **corrupt** adjective.

vend verb SEE **sell**.

vendetta noun SEE **feud** noun.

vendor noun SEE **seller**.

veneer noun coating, covering, layer, surface.

veneer verb SEE **cover** verb.

venerable adjective *The cathedral is a venerable building.* aged, ancient, august, dignified, esteemed, honoured, old, respected, revered, reverenced, venerated, worthy of respect.

venerate verb SEE **respect** verb.

veneration noun SEE **respect** noun.

venereal adjective SEE **sexual**.

vengeance noun *vengeance for an injury or insult.* reprisal, retaliation, retribution, revenge, [*informal*] tit for tat.

vengeful adjective avenging, bitter, rancorous, revengeful, spiteful, unforgiving, vindictive.
OPPOSITES: SEE **forgiving**.

venial adjective *a venial sin.* SEE **forgivable.**

venom noun poison, toxin.

venomous adjective SEE **poisonous.**

vent noun *a vent in a garment. a fresh-air vent.* aperture, cut, duct, gap, hole, opening, outlet, passage, slit, split.
to give vent to SEE **vent** verb.

vent verb *to vent your anger.* SEE **express** verb, give vent to, let go, release.

ventilate verb 1 *to ventilate a room.* aerate, air, freshen.
2 *to ventilate your feelings.* SEE **express** verb.

venture noun SEE **enterprise.**

venture verb 1 *to venture a small wager. to venture an opinion.* chance, dare, gamble, put forward, risk, speculate, stake, wager.
2 *to venture out.* dare to go, risk going.

venturesome adjective SEE **adventurous.**

venue noun *a venue for a sporting event.* meeting-place, location, rendezvous.

veracious adjective SEE **true, truthful.**

verbal adjective 1 *verbal communication.* lexical, linguistic.
OPPOSITE: non-verbal.
2 *a verbal message.* oral, spoken, unwritten, word-of-mouth.
OPPOSITES: SEE **written.**

verbalize verb SEE **speak.**

verbatim adjective *a verbatim account of what was said.* exact, literal, precise, word for word.
OPPOSITE: paraphrased [SEE **paraphrase**].

verbiage noun SEE **verbosity.**

verbose adjective *a verbose speaker.* diffuse, garrulous, long-winded, loquacious, pleonastic, prolix, rambling, repetitious, talkative, tautological, unstoppable, wordy.
OPPOSITES: SEE **concise.**

verbosity noun *We became bored with his verbosity.* [informal] beating about the bush, circumlocution, diffuseness, garrulity, long-windedness, loquacity, periphrasis, pleonasm, prolixity, repetition, tautology, verbiage, wordiness.

verdant adjective SEE **green.**

verdict noun *the verdict of the jury.* adjudication, assessment, conclusion, decision, finding, judgement, opinion, sentence.
LEGAL TERMS: SEE **law.**

verge noun 1 *the verge of the road.* bank, edge, hard shoulder, kerb, margin, roadside, shoulder, side, wayside.

2 *on the verge of a discovery.* brink.

verifiable adjective demonstrable, provable.
OPPOSITE: unverifiable.

verify verb *to verify someone's story.* ascertain, authenticate, check out, confirm, corroborate, demonstrate the truth of, establish, prove, show the truth of, substantiate, support, uphold, validate.
OPPOSITES: SEE **discredit.**

verisimilitude noun authenticity, realism, truth to life.

veritable adjective SEE **true.**

vermilion adjective SEE **red.**

vermin noun parasites, pests.

verminous adjective SEE **infested.**

vernal adjective spring-like.

versatile adjective *a versatile player.* adaptable, all-round, gifted, resourceful, skilful, talented.

verse noun *a story in verse.* lines, metre, rhyme, stanza.

VARIOUS VERSE FORMS: blank verse, Chaucerian stanza, clerihew, couplet, free verse, haiku, hexameter, limerick, ottava rima, pentameter, quatrain, rhyme royal, sestina, sonnet, Spenserian stanza, terza rima, triolet, triplet, vers libre, villanelle.

VARIOUS METRICAL FEET: anapaest, dactyl, iamb, spondee, trochee.

VARIOUS KINDS OF POEM: SEE **poem.**

---

versed adjective **versed in** SEE **skilled.**

version noun 1 *an unbiased version of what happened.* account, description, portrayal, report, story.
2 *a modern version of the Bible.* adaptation, interpretation, paraphrase, rendering, translation.
3 *The car is an up-dated version of our old one.* design, form, kind, [formal] mark, model, type, variant.

vertebra noun [plural] **vertebrae** backbone, spine.

vertex noun SEE **top** noun.

vertical adjective 1 *a vertical position.* erect, perpendicular, upright.
2 *a vertical drop.* precipitous, sheer.
OPPOSITES: SEE **horizontal.**

vertigo noun dizziness, giddiness.

verve noun SEE **liveliness.**

very adverb acutely, enormously, especially, exceedingly, extremely,

greatly, highly, [*informal*] jolly, most, noticeably, outstandingly, particularly, really, remarkably, [*informal*] terribly, truly, uncommonly, unusually.
OPPOSITES: SEE **slightly**.

vessel noun 1 [=*container*] SEE **container**.
2 *vessels in the harbour*. boat, craft, ship.

VARIOUS VESSELS: aircraft-carrier, barge, bathysphere, battleship, brigantine, cabin cruiser, canoe, catamaran, clipper, coaster, collier, coracle, corvette, cruise-liner, cruiser, cutter, destroyer, dhow, dinghy, dredger, dugout, ferry, freighter, frigate, galleon, galley, gondola, gunboat.

houseboat, hovercraft, hydrofoil, hydroplane, ice-breaker, junk, kayak, ketch, landing-craft, launch, lifeboat, lighter, light-ship, liner, longboat, lugger, man-of-war, merchant ship, minesweeper, motor boat, narrow-boat, oil-tanker, [*old-fashioned*] packet-ship, paddle-steamer, pedalo, pontoon, power-boat, pram, privateer, punt.

quinquereme, raft, rowing-boat, sailing-boat, sampan, schooner, skiff, sloop, smack, speed-boat, steamer, steamship, sub or submarine, super-tanker, tanker, tender, torpedo boat, tramp steamer, trawler, trireme, troop ship, tug, warship, whaler, wind-jammer, yacht, yawl.

PARTS OF A VESSEL: aft, amidships, anchor, binnacle, boom, bow, bridge, bulwark, conning-tower, crow's nest, deck, fo'c'sle or forecastle, funnel, galley, gunwale, helm, hull, keel, mast, oar, paddle, poop, port, porthole, propeller, prow, quarterdeck, rigging, rudder, sail, scull, starboard, stern, tiller.

---

vestibule noun SEE **entrance** noun.

vet noun veterinary surgeon.

vet verb *to vet a person's credentials*. SEE **examine**.

veteran adjective *a veteran car*. SEE **old**.

veteran noun *a veteran of a war*. experienced soldier, old soldier, survivor.
OPPOSITES: SEE **recruit** noun.

veto noun *We couldn't act because of the boss's veto on new schemes*. ban, embargo, prohibition, refusal, rejection, [*informal*] thumbs down.
OPPOSITES: SEE **approval**.

veto verb *The boss vetoed our proposal*. ban, bar, blackball, disallow, dismiss,

forbid, prohibit, refuse, reject, rule out, say no to, turn down, vote against.
OPPOSITES: SEE **approve**.

vex verb SEE **annoy**.

vexation noun SEE **annoyance**.

vexatious adjective SEE **annoying**.

vexed adjective SEE **annoyed**.

viable adjective *a viable plan*. achievable, feasible, operable, possible, practicable, practical, realistic, usable, workable.
OPPOSITES: SEE **impractical**.

viaduct noun SEE **bridge** noun.

vial noun SEE **bottle** noun.

viands plural noun SEE **food**.

vibrant adjective *vibrant with energy*. alert, alive, dynamic, electric, energetic, living, pulsating, quivering, resonant, thrilling, throbbing, trembling, vibrating, vivacious.
OPPOSITES: SEE **lifeless**.

vibrate verb *The machine vibrated as the engine turned faster*. judder, oscillate, pulsate, quake, quiver, rattle, reverberate, shake, shiver, shudder, throb, tremble, wobble.

vibration noun juddering, oscillation, pulsation, quivering, rattling, reverberation, shaking, shivering, shuddering, throbbing, trembling, tremor, wobbling.

vicar noun SEE **clergyman**.

vicarious adjective *vicarious experiences*. indirect, second-hand.

vice noun 1 *The police wage war on crime and vice*. corruption, depravity, evil, evil-doing, immorality, iniquity, sin, venality, wickedness, wrongdoing.
2 *His worst vice is his continual chattering*. bad habit, blemish, defect, failing, fault, imperfection, shortcoming, weakness.

The prefix *vice-* is related to a Latin word meaning *change*. In words like *vice-captain*, *vice-president*, and *vice-principal* it means either *person acting on behalf of* or *person next in importance to*. SEE **deputy**.

---

viceroy noun SEE **ruler**.

vicinity noun *A taxi-driver ought to know the vicinity*. area, district, environs, locality, neighbourhood, outskirts, precincts, proximity, purlieus, region, sector, territory, zone.

vicious adjective 1 *a vicious attack*. atrocious, barbaric, barbarous, beastly,

blood-thirsty, brutal, callous, cruel, diabolical, fiendish, heinous, hurtful, inhuman, merciless, monstrous, murderous, pitiless, ruthless, sadistic, savage, unfeeling, vile, violent.
2 *a vicious character.* SEE **bad**, [*informal*] bitchy, [*informal*] catty, depraved, evil, heartless, immoral, malicious, mean, perverted, rancorous, sinful, spiteful, venomous, villainous, vindictive, vitriolic, wicked.
3 *a vicious animal.* aggressive, bad-tempered, dangerous, ferocious, fierce, snappy, untamed, wild.
4 *a vicious wind.* cutting, nasty, severe, sharp, unpleasant.
OPPOSITES: SEE **gentle**.

vicissitude noun *the vicissitudes of life.* alteration, SEE **change** noun, instability, mutability, shift, uncertainty.

victim noun **1** *a victim of an accident.* casualty, fatality, injured person, patient, sufferer, wounded person.
2 *a sacrificial victim.* martyr, offering, prey, sacrifice.

victimize verb *Don't victimize the weak.* bully, cheat, discriminate against, exploit, intimidate, oppress, persecute, [*informal*] pick on, terrorize, torment, treat unfairly, [*informal*] use (*She was just using him*).

victor noun SEE **winner**.

victorious adjective *the victorious team.* champion, conquering, first, leading, prevailing, successful, top, top-scoring, triumphant, unbeaten, undefeated, winning.
OPPOSITES: SEE **defeated**.

victory noun *We celebrated our team's victory.* achievement, conquest, knock-out, mastery, success, superiority, triumph, [*informal*] walk-over, win.
OPPOSITES: SEE **defeat** noun.

victuals noun SEE **food**.

video noun, verb SEE **recording** noun, **record** verb.

vie verb SEE **compete**.

view noun **1** *the view from the top of the hill.* aspect, landscape, outlook, panorama, perspective, picture, prospect, scene, scenery, spectacle, vista.
2 *I had a good view of what happened.* look, sight, vision.
3 *My view is that we should ban smoking.* attitude, belief, conviction, idea, notion, opinion, perception, thought.

view verb **1** *to view a scene.* behold, consider, contemplate, examine, eye, gaze at, inspect, observe, perceive, regard, scan, stare at, survey, witness.
2 *to view TV.* look at, see, watch.

viewer noun [*plural*] audience, observer, onlooker, spectator, watcher, witness.

viewpoint noun *Our visitor saw the problem from a foreign viewpoint.* angle, perspective, point of view, position, slant, standpoint.

vigil noun *an all-night vigil.* watch.

vigilant adjective *Be vigilant!* alert, attentive, awake, careful, observant, on the watch, on your guard, [*informal*] on your toes, wakeful, watchful, wide-awake.
OPPOSITES: SEE **negligent**.

vignette noun SEE **picture** noun.

vigorous adjective *a vigorous game. a vigorous player.* active, animated, brisk, dynamic, energetic, flourishing, forceful, full-blooded, healthy, lively, lusty, potent, red-blooded, robust, spirited, strenuous, strong, virile, vital, zestful.
OPPOSITES: SEE **feeble**.

vigour noun animation, dynamism, energy, force, forcefulness, gusto, health, life, liveliness, might, potency, power, robustness, spirit, stamina, strength, verve, [*informal*] vim, virility, vitality, zeal, zest.

vile adjective *a vile crime.* contemptible, degenerate, depraved, despicable, disgusting, evil, filthy, foul, horrible, loathsome, low, nasty, nauseating, obnoxious, offensive, odious, perverted, repellent, repugnant, repulsive, revolting, sickening, ugly, vicious, wicked.

vilify verb SEE **slander** verb.

villa noun SEE **house** noun.

village noun hamlet.
OTHER SETTLEMENTS: SEE **settlement**.

villain noun SEE **wicked** (wicked person).

villainous adjective SEE **wicked**.

vim noun SEE **vigour**.

vindicate verb SEE **excuse** verb, **justify**.

vindictive adjective *vindictive retaliation.* malicious, nasty, punitive, rancorous, revengeful, spiteful, unforgiving, vengeful, vicious.
OPPOSITES: SEE **forgiving**.

vinegary adjective SEE **sour**.

vineyard noun SEE **plantation**.

vintage adjective *a vintage wine. a vintage Presley record.* choice, classic, fine, good, high-quality, mature, old, venerable.

vintner noun wine-merchant.

violate verb **1** *to violate a rule.* break, contravene, defy, disobey, disregard, flout, ignore, infringe, transgress.

2 *to violate someone's privacy.* abuse, disturb, invade.

3 [*of a man*] *to violate a woman.* assault, dishonour, force yourself on, rape, ravish.

violation noun *the violation of a rule.* breach, contravention, defiance, flouting, infringement, offence (against), transgression.

violent adjective **1** *a violent explosion. a violent reaction.* acute, damaging, dangerous, destructive, devastating, explosive, ferocious, fierce, forceful, furious, hard, harmful, intense, powerful, rough, savage, severe, strong, swingeing, tempestuous, turbulent, uncontrollable, vehement, wild.
2 *violent criminals. violent behaviour.* barbaric, berserk, blood-thirsty, brutal, cruel, desperate, headstrong, homicidal, murderous, riotous, rowdy, ruthless, unruly, vehement, vicious, wild.
OPPOSITES: SEE **gentle**.

violin noun fiddle.
OTHER STRINGED INSTRUMENTS: SEE **string** noun.

VIP celebrity, dignitary, important person.

virago noun SEE **woman**.

virgin noun SEE **girl**, **woman**.

virginal adjective SEE **chaste**.

virile adjective *a virile man* [*uncomplimentary*] macho, manly, masculine, potent, vigorous.

virtue noun **1** *We respect virtue and hate vice.* decency, goodness, high-mindedness, honesty, honour, integrity, morality, nobility, principle, rectitude, righteousness, sincerity, uprightness, worthiness.
2 *sexual virtue.* abstinence, chastity, innocence, purity, virginity.
3 *This car's main virtue is that it's cheap to run.* advantage, asset, good point, merit, [*informal*] redeeming feature, strength.
OPPOSITES: SEE **vice**.

virtuoso noun expert, prodigy.
VARIOUS MUSICIANS: SEE **music**.

virtuous adjective *virtuous behaviour.* blameless, chaste, ethical, exemplary, God-fearing, good, [*uncomplimentary*] goody-goody, high-principled, honest, honourable, innocent, irreproachable, just, law-abiding, moral, praiseworthy, pure, right, righteous, [*uncomplimentary*] smug, spotless, trustworthy, unimpeachable, upright, worthy.
OPPOSITES: SEE **wicked**.

virulent adjective **1** *a virulent infection.* deadly, lethal, noxious, poisonous, toxic, venomous.

2 *virulent abuse.* acrimonious, bitter, hostile, malicious, nasty, spiteful, vicious, vitriolic.

virus noun SEE **micro-organism**.

visa noun SEE **document**.

visage noun SEE **face** noun.

viscera noun SEE **entrails**.

viscid adjective SEE **viscous**.

viscous adjective *a viscous liquid.* gluey, sticky, syrupy, thick, viscid.
OPPOSITES: SEE **runny**.

visible adjective *visible signs of weakness.* apparent, clear, conspicuous, detectable, discernible, distinct, evident, manifest, noticeable, obvious, perceptible, plain, recognizable, unconcealed, undisguised, unmistakable.
OPPOSITES: SEE **invisible**.

vision noun **1** *The optician said I had good vision.* eyesight, sight.
2 *He claims to have seen a vision.* apparition, day-dream, delusion, fantasy, ghost, hallucination, illusion, mirage, phantasm, phantom, spectre, spirit.
3 *Statesmen need to be people of vision.* farsightedness, foresight, imagination, insight, spirituality, understanding.

visionary adjective *a visionary scheme for the future.* fanciful, farsighted, futuristic, idealistic, imaginative, impractical, prophetic, quixotic, romantic, speculative, transcendental, unrealistic, Utopian.

visionary noun *The ideas of a visionary may seem impractical to us.* dreamer, idealist, mystic, poet, prophet, romantic, seer.

visit noun **1** *a visit to friends.* call, stay.
2 *an official visit.* visitation.
3 *a visit to London.* day out (in), excursion, outing, trip.

visit verb *to visit friends.* call on, come to see, [*informal*] descend on, [*informal*] drop in on, go to see, [*informal*] look up, make a visit to, pay a call on, stay with.
to visit repeatedly frequent, haunt.

visitant noun SEE **visitor**.

visitation noun **1** *an official visitation.* SEE **visit** noun.
2 *a visitation from God.* SEE **punishment**.

visitor noun **1** *We had visitors to dinner.* caller, [*plural*] company, guest.
2 *The town is full of visitors.* holidaymaker, sightseer, tourist, tripper.
3 *a visitor from another land.* alien, foreigner, migrant, traveller, visitant.

visor noun protector, shield, sun-shield.

vista noun landscape, outlook, panorama, prospect, scene, scenery, view.

visual adjective *visual effects.* eye-catching, optical.

visualize verb *I can't visualize what heaven is like.* conceive, dream up, envisage, imagine, picture.

vital adjective 1 *the vital spark of life.* alive, animate, dynamic, life-giving, live, living.
OPPOSITES: SEE **dead**.
2 *vital information.* current, crucial, essential, fundamental, imperative, important, indispensable, necessary, relevant.
OPPOSITES: SEE **inessential**.
3 *a vital sort of person.* animated, energetic, exuberant, lively, sparkling, spirited, sprightly, vigorous, vivacious, zestful.
OPPOSITES: SEE **lifeless**.

vitality noun *full of vitality.* animation, dynamism, energy, exuberance, [*informal*] go, life, liveliness, [*informal*] sparkle, spirit, sprightliness, vigour, [*informal*] vim, vivacity, zest.

vitalize verb SEE **animate** verb.

vitiate verb SEE **spoil**.

vitreous adjective SEE **glassy**.

vitriol noun sulphuric acid.

vitriolic adjective *vitriolic criticism.* abusive, acid, biting, bitter, caustic, cruel, destructive, hostile, hurtful, malicious, savage, scathing, vicious, vindictive, virulent.

vituperate verb SEE **abuse** verb.

viva noun SEE **examination**, oral, viva voce.

vivacious adjective SEE **lively**.

vivid adjective 1 *vivid colours.* bright, brilliant, colourful, [*uncomplimentary*] gaudy, gay, gleaming, glowing, intense, shiny, showy, striking, strong, vibrant.
2 *a vivid description.* clear, graphic, imaginative, lifelike, lively, memorable, powerful, realistic.
OPPOSITES: SEE **lifeless**.

vocabulary noun 1 *I speak French, but my vocabulary is limited.* diction, lexis, words.
2 *The vocabulary in your French book gives the meanings of words.* dictionary, glossary, lexicon, word-list.

vocal adjective 1 *vocal sounds.* oral, said, spoken, sung, voiced.
2 *Usually she's quiet, but today she was quite vocal.* outspoken, SEE **talkative**, vociferous.

vocalist noun SEE **singer**.

vocalize verb SEE **speak**.

vocation noun SEE **calling**.

vociferate verb SEE **shout** verb.

vogue noun *the latest vogue in clothes.* craze, fashion, rage, style, taste, trend.
in vogue SEE **fashionable**.

voice noun *I recognized her voice.* accent, inflexion, singing, sound, speaking, speech, tone.

voice verb *to voice your thoughts.* SEE **speak**.

void adjective SEE **empty** adjective.

volatile adjective 1 *Petrol is a volatile liquid.* explosive, unstable.
2 *Beware of his volatile moods!* changeable, fickle, inconstant, lively, SEE **temperamental**, unpredictable, [*informal*] up and down, variable.
OPPOSITES: SEE **stable**.

volcano noun eruption, SEE **mountain**.

volition noun SEE **will** noun.

volley noun *a volley of missiles.* SEE **bombardment**.

volte-face noun SEE **about-turn**.

voluble adjective SEE **talkative**.

volume 1 *an encyclopaedia in ten volumes.* book, [*old-fashioned*] tome.
KINDS OF BOOK: SEE **book** noun.
2 *the volume of a container.* amount, bulk, capacity, dimensions, mass, quantity, size.

voluminous adjective SEE **large**.

voluntary adjective 1 *voluntary work.* optional, unpaid, willing.
OPPOSITES: SEE **compulsory**.
2 *a voluntary act.* conscious, deliberate, intended, intentional.
OPPOSITES: SEE **involuntary**.

volunteer verb 1 *to volunteer to clear up.* be willing, offer, propose, put yourself forward.
2 *to volunteer for military service.* SEE **enlist**.

voluptuous adjective 1 *voluptuous living.* SEE **hedonistic**.
2 [*informal*] *a voluptuous figure.* [*informal*] curvaceous, erotic, sensual, [*informal*] sexy, shapely.

voodoo noun SEE **magic** noun.

vomit verb be sick, [*informal*] bring up, disgorge, [*informal*] heave up, [*informal*] puke, regurgitate, retch, [*informal*] sick up, [*informal*] spew up, [*informal*] throw up.

voracious adjective 1 *a voracious appetite.* SEE **greedy**.
2 *a voracious reader.* SEE **eager**.

vortex noun eddy, spiral, whirlpool, whirlwind.

vote noun *a democratic vote.* ballot, election, plebiscite, poll, referendum, show of hands.

vote verb *to vote in an election.* ballot, cast your vote.

to vote for choose, elect, nominate, opt for, pick, return, select, settle on.

vouch verb **to vouch for** SEE **guarantee** verb.

voucher noun *a voucher to be exchanged for goods.* coupon, ticket, token.

vouchsafe verb SEE **grant** verb.

vow noun *a solemn vow.* assurance, guarantee, oath, pledge, promise, undertaking, word of honour.

vow verb *She vowed to be good.* give an assurance, give your word, guarantee, pledge, promise, swear, take an oath.

voyage noun, verb SEE **travel** noun, verb.

vulgar adjective 1 *vulgar language.* churlish, coarse, foul, gross, ill-bred, impolite, improper, indecent, indecorous, low, SEE **obscene**, offensive, rude, uncouth, ungentlemanly, unladylike.
OPPOSITES: SEE **polite**.
2 *a vulgar colour scheme.* common, crude, gaudy, inartistic, in bad taste, inelegant, insensitive, lowbrow, plebeian, tasteless, tawdry, unrefined, unsophisticated.
OPPOSITES: SEE **tasteful**.

vulgarize verb SEE **debase**.

vulnerable adjective 1 *The defenders were in a vulnerable position.* at risk, defenceless, exposed, unguarded, unprotected, weak, wide open.
OPPOSITES: SEE **invulnerable**.
2 *He has a vulnerable nature.* easily hurt, sensitive, thin-skinned.
OPPOSITES: SEE **resilient**.

W

wad noun *a wad of bank-notes.* bundle, lump, mass, pad, roll.

wadding noun *protective wadding.* filling, lining, packing, padding, stuffing.

waddle verb SEE **walk** verb.

wade verb *to wade through water.* paddle, SEE **walk** verb.

wafer noun SEE **biscuit**.

waffle noun [*informal*] *Cut the waffle and get to the point.* evasiveness, padding, prevarication, SEE **verbosity**, wordiness.

waffle verb *Stop waffling and get to the point.* [*informal*] beat about the bush, hedge, prevaricate.

waft verb 1 *The scent wafted on the breeze.* drift, float, travel.
2 *A breeze wafted the scent towards us.* carry, convey, transmit, transport.

wag noun [*informal*] *a bit of a wag.* SEE **comedian**.

wag verb *A dog wags its tail.* move to and fro, shake, [*informal*] waggle, wave, [*informal*] wiggle.

wage noun *weekly wages.* earnings, income, SEE **pay** noun, pay packet.

wage verb *to wage war.* carry on, conduct, engage in, fight, undertake.

wager noun, verb SEE **bet** noun, verb.

waggle verb SEE **wag** verb.

wagon noun VARIOUS VEHICLES: SEE **vehicle**.

waif noun foundling, orphan, stray.

wail verb caterwaul, complain, cry, howl, lament, moan, shriek, waul, weep, [*informal*] yowl.

waist noun *a belt round the waist.* middle, waistline.

waistband noun belt, cummerbund, girdle.

waistcoat noun VARIOUS COATS: SEE **coat** noun.

wait noun *a long wait for the bus.* a wait before taking action. SEE **delay** noun, halt, hesitation, hiatus, [*informal*] hold-up, interval, pause, postponement, rest, stay.

wait verb 1 *We waited for a signal.* [*old-fashioned*] bide, SEE **delay** verb, halt, [*informal*] hang about, hesitate, hold back, keep still, linger, mark time, pause, remain, rest, stay, stop, [*old-fashioned*] tarry.
2 *to wait at table.* serve.

waiter, waitress nouns SERVANTS: SEE **servant**.

waive verb *to waive your right to something.* abandon, disclaim, dispense with, forgo, give up, relinquish, renounce, surrender.
OPPOSITES: SEE **enforce**.

wake noun 1 [=*funeral*] SEE **funeral**.
2 *the wake of a ship.* path, track, trail, turbulence, wash.

wake verb 1 *A loud noise woke me.* arouse, awaken, call, disturb, rouse, waken.
2 *I usually wake at about 7.* become conscious, [*informal*] come to life, get up, rise, [*informal*] stir, wake up.

to wake up to *I woke up to what she was really saying.* SEE **realize**.

wakeful adjective SEE **sleepless**.

waken verb SEE **wake** verb.

waking adjective *your waking hours.* active, alert, aware, conscious, daytime. OPPOSITE: sleeping.

walk noun 1 *He had a characteristic walk.* gait.
2 *a walk in the country.* [*joking*] constitutional, hike, [*old-fashioned*] promenade, ramble, saunter, stroll, traipse, tramp, trek, trudge, [*informal*] turn (*I'll take a turn in the garden*).
3 *I made a paved walk in the garden.* aisle, alley, path, pathway, pavement.

walk verb 1 *I walk to work.* be a pedestrian, travel on foot.
SEE PANEL BELOW.
2 *Don't walk on the flowers.* stamp, step, trample, tread.
to walk away with SEE **win**.
to walk off with SEE **steal**.
to walk out SEE **quit**.
to walk out on SEE **desert** verb.

VARIOUS WAYS TO WALK: amble, crawl, creep, dodder, [*informal*] foot-slog, hike, hobble, limp, lope, lurch, march, mince, [*slang*] mooch, pace, pad, paddle, parade, [*old-fashioned*] perambulate, plod, promenade, prowl, ramble, saunter, scuttle, shamble, shuffle, slink, stagger, stalk, steal, step, [*informal*] stomp, stride, stroll, strut, stumble, swagger, tiptoe, [*informal*] toddle, totter, traipse, tramp, trample, trek, troop, trot, trudge, waddle, wade.

---

walker noun hiker, pedestrian, rambler.

walk-over noun SEE **victory**.

wall noun KINDS OF WALL: barricade, barrier, bulkhead, bulwark, dam, dike, divider, embankment, fence, fortification, hedge, obstacle, paling, palisade, parapet, partition, rampart, screen, seawall, stockade.

wall verb SEE **enclose**.

wallet noun notecase, pocket-book, pouch, purse.

wallop verb SEE **hit** verb.

wallow verb 1 *to wallow in mud.* flounder, lie, roll about, stagger about, wade, welter.
2 *to wallow in luxury.* glory, indulge yourself, luxuriate, revel, take delight.

wallpaper noun SEE **paper** noun.

wan adjective SEE **pale** adjective.

wand noun SEE **stick** noun.

wander verb 1 *to wander about the hills.* go aimlessly, meander, ramble, range, roam, rove, stray, travel about, walk, wind.
2 *to wander off course.* curve, deviate, digress, drift, err, stray, swerve, turn, twist, veer, zigzag.

wanderer noun SEE **traveller**.

wandering adjective 1 *wandering tribes.* homeless, itinerant, nomadic, peripatetic, rootless, roving, strolling, travelling, vagrant, wayfaring.
2 *wandering thoughts.* drifting, inattentive, rambling, straying.

wane verb *The evening light waned. My enthusiasm waned after a while.* decline, decrease, dim, diminish, dwindle, ebb, fade, fail, [*informal*] fall off, lessen, shrink, subside, taper off, weaken.
OPPOSITES: SEE **strengthen**.

want noun 1 *The hotel staff try to satisfy all your wants.* demand, desire, need, requirement, wish.
2 *We had to abandon our project for want of a few pounds.* absence, lack, need.
3 *Why do we tolerate want when so many are rich?* dearth, famine, hunger, insufficiency, penury, poverty, privation, scarcity, shortage.

want verb 1 *We can't always have what we want.* covet, crave, demand, desire, fancy, hanker (after), [*informal*] have a yen (for), hunger (for), [*informal*] itch (for), like [often *would like* (*I would like a drink*)], long (for), pine (for), please (*You can take what you please*), prefer, [*informal*] set your heart on, wish (for), yearn (for).
2 *That rude man wants good manners!* be short of, lack, need, require.

war noun 1 *wars between nations.* conflict, fighting, hostilities, military action, strife, warfare.
2 *a war against crime.* campaign, crusade.
to wage war SEE **fight** verb.

VARIOUS KINDS OF ACTION IN WAR: ambush, assault, attack, battle, blitz, blockade, bombardment, campaign, counterattack, espionage, guerrilla warfare, hostilities, invasion, manœuvre, negotiation, operation, resistance, retreat, siege, skirmish, surrender, withdrawal.

---

warble verb SEE **sing**.

ward noun 1 *a hospital ward.* SEE **room**.

2 *the ward of a guardian.* charge, dependant, minor.

ward verb **to ward off** *to ward off an attack.* avert, beat off, block, check, deflect, fend off, forestall, parry, push away, repel, repulse, stave off, thwart, turn aside.

warden noun SEE **official** noun.

warder noun *a prison warder.* gaoler, guard, jailer, keeper, prison officer.

wardrobe noun SEE **cupboard**.

warehouse noun depository, depot, store, storehouse.

wares plural noun *wares for sale.* commodities, goods, merchandise, produce, stock.

warhead noun VARIOUS WEAPONS: SEE **weapon**.

warlike adjective SEE **belligerent**.

warm adjective **1** *warm weather.* close, SEE **hot**, subtropical, sultry, summery, temperate, warmish.
OPPOSITES: SEE **cold** adjective.
2 *warm water.* lukewarm, tepid.
3 *warm clothes.* cosy, thermal, thick, winter, woolly.
4 *a warm welcome.* affable, affectionate, cordial, enthusiastic, fervent, friendly, genial, kind, loving, sympathetic, warm-hearted.
OPPOSITES: SEE **unfriendly**.

warm verb SEE **heat** verb, make warmer, melt, raise the temperaure (of), thaw, thaw out.
OPPOSITES: SEE **chill** verb.

warm-hearted adjective SEE **friendly**.

warmongering adjective SEE **belligerent**.

warn verb *to warn someone of danger.* advise, alert, caution, forewarn, give a warning [SEE **warning**], inform, notify, raise the alarm, remind, [*informal*] tip off.

warning noun **1** *warning of impending trouble. She just turned up without warning.* advance notice, augury, forewarning, hint, indication, notice, omen, premonition, presage, sign, signal, threat, [*informal*] tip-off.
2 *They let him off with a warning.* admonition, advice, caveat, caution, reprimand.

VARIOUS WARNING SIGNALS: alarm, alarm-bell, beacon, bell, fire-alarm, flashing lights, fog-horn, gong, hooter, red light, siren, traffic-lights, whistle.

warp verb *warped floor-boards.* become deformed, bend, buckle, contort, curl, curve, distort, kink, twist.

warrant noun *a search-warrant.* authority, authorization, SEE **document**, licence, permit, voucher.

warrant verb *His crime didn't warrant such a stiff punishment.* SEE **justify**.

warranty noun SEE **guarantee** noun.

warren noun *a rabbit warren.* burrow.

warring adjective SEE **belligerent**.

warrior noun SEE **fighter**.

warship noun VARIOUS VESSELS: SEE **vessel**.

wart noun SEE **spot** noun.

wary adjective *wary of possible dangers. a wary approach.* alert, apprehensive, attentive, careful, cautious, chary, circumspect, distrustful, heedful, observant, on the look-out (for), suspicious, vigilant, watchful.
OPPOSITES: SEE **reckless**.

wash noun *I have a wash as soon as I get up.* [*joking*] ablutions, bath, rinse, shampoo, shower.

wash verb **1** *to wash the car. to wash clothes.* SEE **clean** verb, cleanse, launder, mop, rinse, scrub, shampoo, sluice, soap down, sponge down, swab down, swill, wipe.
2 *to wash yourself.* bath, bathe, [*old-fashioned*] make your toilet, [*joking*] perform your ablutions, shower.
3 *The sea washes against the cliff.* flow, splash.
to wash your hands of SEE **abandon**.

washing noun dirty clothes, laundry, [*informal*] the wash.

wash-out noun SEE **failure**.

waspish adjective SEE **irritable**.

wassailing noun SEE **merrymaking**.

wastage noun SEE **waste** noun.

waste adjective **1** *waste materials.* discarded, extra, superfluous, unused, unwanted.
2 *waste land.* bare, barren, derelict, empty, overgrown, run-down, uncared for, uncultivated, undeveloped, wild.

waste noun **1** *The disposal of waste is a problem in big cities.* debris, effluent, garbage, junk, litter, refuse, rubbish, scraps, trash.
2 *waste left after you've finished something.* dregs, excess, leavings, [*informal*] left-overs, offcuts, remnants, scrap, unusable material, unwanted material, wastage.

waste verb *to waste resources.* be prodigal with, dissipate, fritter, misspend, misuse, squander, use wastefully [SEE **wasteful**], use up.
OPPOSITES: SEE **conserve** verb.
to waste away *He wasted away when he was ill.* become emaciated, become thin, become weaker, mope, pine, weaken.

wasteful adjective *a wasteful use of resources.* excessive, expensive, extravagant, improvident, imprudent, lavish, needless, prodigal, profligate, reckless, thriftless, uneconomical.
OPPOSITES: SEE **economical**.
a wasteful person SEE **spendthrift**.

wasteland noun = waste land [SEE **waste** adjective].

watch noun chronometer, clock, digital watch, stop-watch, timepiece, timer, wrist-watch.
on the watch SEE **alert** adjective.
to keep watch SEE **guard** verb.

watch verb **1** *to watch what someone does. to watch TV.* attend to, concentrate on, contemplate, eye, gaze at, heed, keep your eyes on, look at, mark, note, observe, pay attention to, regard, see, stare at, take notice of, view.
2 *Watch the baby while I pop out for a minute.* care for, defend, guard, keep an eye on, keep watch on, look after, mind, protect, safeguard, shield, supervise, tend.
to watch out, to watch your step = to be careful [SEE **careful**].

watcher noun [*plural*] audience, [*informal*] looker-on, observer, onlooker, spectator, viewer, witness.

watchful adjective SEE **observant**.

watchman noun caretaker, custodian, guard, look-out, night-watchman, security guard, sentinel, sentry.

watchword noun SEE **saying**.

water noun VARIOUS KINDS OF WATER: bath-water, brine, distilled water, drinking water, rainwater, sea-water, spa water, spring water, tap water.
VARIOUS STRETCHES OF WATER: brook, lake, lido, ocean, pond, pool, river, sea, SEE **stream** noun.
RELATED ADJECTIVES: aquatic, hydraulic.

Many English words connected with the idea of *water* are related to Latin and Greek words for water. Related to Latin *aqua* are words like *aquarium, aquatic,* and *aqueduct;* related to Greek *hudor* are words like *hydraulic, hydrofoil,* and *hydrometer.*

---

water verb *to water the garden.* dampen, douse, drench, flood, hose, irrigate, moisten, soak, souse, sprinkle, wet.
to water something down dilute, thin, weaken.

water-closet noun SEE **lavatory**.

water-colour noun SEE **paint** noun.

watercourse noun SEE **channel** noun.

waterfall noun cascade, cataract, chute, rapids, torrent, white water.

waterless adjective SEE **dry** adjective.

waterlogged adjecive *a waterlogged pitch.* full of water, saturated, soaked.

waterproof adjective *waterproof material.* damp-proof, impermeable, impervious, water-repellent, water-resistant, watertight, weatherproof.

waterproof noun *Take a waterproof— it's going to be wet.* cape, groundsheet, mackintosh, [*informal*] mac, raincoat, sou'wester.

watershed noun SEE **turning-point**.

water-splash noun ford.

watertight adjective *a watertight container.* hermetic, sealed, sound, SEE **waterproof** adjective.
OPPOSITES: SEE **leaky**.

waterway noun SEE **channel** noun.

watery adjective **1** *a watery liquid. watery gravy.* aqueous, characterless, dilute, fluid, liquid, [*informal*] runny, [*informal*] sloppy, tasteless, thin, watered down, weak.
2 *watery eyes.* damp, moist, tear-filled, tearful, [*informal*] weepy, wet.

waul verb SEE **wail**.

wave noun **1** *waves on the sea.* billow, breaker, crest, ridge, ripple, roller, surf, swell, tidal wave, undulation, wavelet, [*informal*] white horse.
2 *a wave of enthusiasm.* flood, outbreak, surge, upsurge.
3 *a new wave in the world of fashion.* advance, tendency, trend.
4 *a wave of the hand.* flourish, gesticulation, gesture, shake, signal.
5 *radio waves.* pulse, vibration.

wave verb *to wave your arms about.* brandish, flail about, flap, flourish, flutter, move to and fro, shake, sway, swing, twirl, undulate, waft, wag, waggle, wiggle.
VARIOUS WAYS TO GESTURE: SEE **gesture** verb.
to wave something aside SEE **dismiss**.

wavelength noun *Tune your radio to the right wavelength.* channel, station, waveband.

waver verb 1 *to waver when confronted by danger. to waver on the brink.* become unsteady, change, falter, SEE **hesitate**, quake, quaver, quiver, shake, shiver, shudder, sway, teeter, totter, tremble, vacillate, wobble.
2 *The light from a candle wavers.* SEE **flicker**.

wavering adjective SEE **hesitant**.

wavy adjective *a wavy line.* curling, curly, curving, rippling, sinuous, undulating, winding, zigzag.
OPPOSITES: SEE **straight**.

wax verb SEE **increase** verb.

way noun 1 *the way home.* direction, journey, SEE **road**, route.
2 *a long way.* distance, length, measurement.
3 *the way to do something.* approach, avenue, course, knack, manner, means, method, mode, path, procedure, process, system, technique.
4 *I was not used to American ways.* custom, fashion, habit, practice, routine, style, tradition.
5 *Her funny ways take some getting used to.* characteristic, eccentricity, idiosyncrasy, oddity, peculiarity.
6 *It's all right in some ways.* aspect, circumstances, detail, feature, particular, respect.

wayfarer noun SEE **traveller**.

waylay verb *He waylaid me on my way to the meeting.* accost, ambush, attack, buttonhole, detain, intercept, lie in wait for, surprise.

way-out adjective SEE **unconventional**.

wayside noun *flowers growing on the wayside.* SEE **verge**.

wayward adjective *a wayward child.* disobedient, headstrong, SEE **naughty**, obstinate, self-willed, stubborn, uncontrollable, uncooperative, wilful.
OPPOSITES: SEE **co-operative**.

WC SEE **lavatory**.

weak adjective 1 *weak materials. a weak structure.* brittle, decrepit, delicate, feeble, flawed, flimsy, fragile, frail, inadequate, insubstantial, rickety, shaky, slight, substandard, tender, thin, unsafe, unsound, unsteady.
2 *a weak constitution.* anaemic, debilitated, delicate, enervated, exhausted, feeble, flabby, frail, helpless, ill, infirm, listless, low (*feeling low today*), [*informal*] poorly, puny, sickly, slight, thin,

wasted, weakly, [*uncomplimentary*] weedy.
3 *a weak leader.* cowardly, fearful, impotent, indecisive, ineffective, ineffectual, irresolute, poor, powerless, pusillanimous, spineless, timid, timorous, weak-minded.
4 *a weak position.* defenceless, exposed, unguarded, unprotected, vulnerable.
5 *a weak excuse.* feeble, lame, unconvincing, unsatisfactory.
6 *weak tea.* dilute, diluted, tasteless, thin, watery.
OPPOSITES: SEE **strong**.

weaken verb 1 *to weaken the strength of someone or something.* debilitate, destroy, diminish, emasculate, enervate, enfeeble, erode, impair, lessen, lower, make weaker, reduce, ruin, sap, soften, undermine, [*informal*] water down.
2 *Our resolve weakened.* abate, become weaker, decline, decrease, dwindle, ebb, fade, flag, give way, wane.
OPPOSITES: SEE **strengthen**.

weakling noun coward, [*informal*] milksop, [*informal*] runt, [*informal*] softie, weak person [SEE **weak**], [*informal*] weed.

weakness noun 1 *a weakness in the design of something.* blemish, defect, error, failing, fault, flaw, imperfection, mistake, shortcoming.
2 *a weakness in the foundations.* flimsiness, fragility, frailty, inadequacy, softness.
3 *a feeling of weakness.* debility, feebleness, SEE **illness**, impotence, infirmity, lassitude, vulnerability.
OPPOSITES: SEE **strength**.
4 *a weakness for chocolates.* fondness, inclination, liking, penchant, predilection, [*informal*] soft spot.

weal noun SEE **wound** noun.

wealth noun 1 *Most of his wealth is in stocks and shares.* affluence, assets, capital, fortune, [*old-fashioned*] lucre, SEE **money**, opulence, possessions, property, prosperity, riches, [*old-fashioned*] substance (*a man of substance*).
OPPOSITES: SEE **poverty**.
2 *a wealth of information.* abundance, SEE **plenty**, profusion, store.

wealthy adjective affluent, [*informal*] flush, [*informal*] loaded, moneyed, opulent, [*joking*] plutocratic, prosperous, rich, [*informal*] well-heeled, well-off, well-to-do.
OPPOSITES: SEE **poor**.
a wealthy person billionaire, capitalist, millionaire, plutocrat, tycoon.

weapons plural noun armaments, munitions, ordnance, weaponry.

TYPES OF WEAPON: artillery, automatic weapons, biological weapons, chemical weapons, firearms, missiles, nuclear weapons, small arms, strategic weapons, tactical weapons.

VARIOUS WEAPONS: airgun, arrow, atom bomb, ballistic missile, battering-ram, battleaxe, bayonet, bazooka, blowpipe, blunderbuss, bomb, boomerang, bow and arrow, bren-gun, cannon, carbine, catapult, claymore, cosh, crossbow, CS gas, cudgel, cutlass.

dagger, depth-charge, dirk, flame-thrower, foils, grenade, [old-fashioned] halberd, harpoon, H-bomb, howitzer, incendiary bomb, javelin, knuckledus-ter, lance, land-mine, laser beam, long-bow, machete, machine-gun, mine, mis-sile, mortar, musket, mustard gas, napalm bomb, pike, pistol, pole-axe.

rapier, revolver, rifle, rocket, sabre, scimitar, shotgun, [informal] six-shooter, sling, spear, sten-gun, stiletto, sub-machine-gun, sword, tank, tear-gas, time-bomb, tomahawk, tommy-gun, torpedo, truncheon, warhead, water-cannon.

PLACES WHERE WEAPONS ARE STORED: armoury, arsenal, depot, magazine.

---

wear verb 1 *to wear clothes.* be dressed in, clothe yourself in, dress in, have on, present yourself in, put on, wrap up in. **2** *Constant tramping in and out wears the carpet.* damage, fray, injure, mark, scuff, wear away, weaken. **3** *This carpet has worn well.* endure, last, [informal] stand the test of time, sur-vive.
to wear away abrade, corrode, eat away, erode, grind down, rub away.
to wear off *The effects soon wore off.* SEE subside.
to wear out *The effort wore me out.* SEE weary verb.

weariness noun SEE tiredness.

wearisome adjective *wearisome busi-ness.* boring, dreary, exhausting, mono-tonous, repetitive, tedious, tiring, SEE troublesome.
OPPOSITES: SEE stimulating.

weary adjective SEE tired.

weary verb SEE tire.

wearying adjective SEE tiring.

weather noun climate, the elements, meteorological conditions.
RELATED ADJECTIVE: meteorological.

FEATURES OF WEATHER: blizzard, breeze, cloud, cyclone, deluge, dew, downpour, drizzle, drought, fog, frost, gale, hail, haze, heatwave, hoar-frost, hurricane, ice, lightning, mist, rain, rainbow, shower, sleet, slush, snow, snowstorm, squall, storm, sunshine, tempest, thaw, thunder, tornado, typhoon, whirlwind, wind.

WORDS USED TO DESCRIBE WEATHER: autumnal, blustery, breezy, bright, bril-liant, chilly, clear, close, cloudless, cloudy, SEE cold, drizzly, dry, dull, fair, fine, foggy, foul, freezing, frosty, grey, hazy, SEE hot, humid, icy, inclement, misty, overcast, pouring, rainy, rough, showery, slushy, snowy, spring-like, squally, stormy, sultry, summery, sun-less, sunny, sweltering, teeming, thun-dery, torrential, turbulent, wet, wild, windy, wintry.

SOME METEOROLOGICAL TERMS: anti-cyclone, depression, front, isobar, iso-therm, temperature.

---

weather verb *to weather a storm.* SEE survive.

weather-beaten adjective SEE sun-burnt.

weathercock noun weather-vane.

weatherman noun forecaster, meteor-ologist.

weatherproof adjective SEE water-proof.

weave verb 1 *to weave threads.* braid, criss-cross, entwine, interlace, inter-twine, interweave, knit, plait, sew.
2 *to weave a story.* compose, create, make, plot, put together.
3 *to weave your way through a crowd.* tack, [informal] twist and turn, wind, zigzag.

weaver noun VARIOUS CRAFTSMEN: SEE artist.

weaving noun VARIOUS CRAFTS: SEE art.

web noun *a web of intersecting lines.* criss-cross, lattice, mesh, net, network.

webbing noun band, belt, strap.

wed verb SEE marry.

wedding noun marriage, matrimony, [joking] nuptials.

PEOPLE AT A WEDDING: best man, bride, bridegroom, bridesmaid, groom, page, registrar, usher, wedding guests.

OTHER WORDS TO DO WITH WEDDINGS: confetti, honeymoon, reception, regis-try office, service, trousseau, wedding-ring.

wedge verb *Wedge the door open.* SEE **fasten**, jam, stick.

wedlock noun SEE **marriage**.

wee adjective SEE **small**.

weed noun wild flower, wild plant, unwanted plant.

weedy adjective 1 *a weedy garden.* overgrown, rank, unkempt, untidy, unweeded, wild.
2 [*uncomplimentary*] *a weedy child.* SEE **weak**.

weeny adjective SEE **small**.

weep verb blubber, cry, [*informal*] grizzle, moan, shed tears, snivel, sob, wail, whimper.

weepy adjective SEE **tearful**.

weigh verb 1 *to weigh something on scales.* measure the weight of.
2 *We weighed the evidence.* consider, evaluate, SEE **weigh up**.
3 *His evidence weighed with the jury.* be important, count, have weight.
to weigh down *weighed down with troubles. weighed down with shopping.* afflict, burden, depress, load, make heavy, overload, weight.
to weigh up *We weighed up the pros and cons.* assess, consider, evaluate, examine, give thought to, meditate on, mull over, ponder, study, think about.

weighing-machine noun balance, scales, spring-balance, weighbridge.

weight noun 1 *a great weight to bear.* burden, heaviness, load, mass, pressure, strain.
UNITS OF WEIGHT: SEE **measure** noun.
2 *The boss's support lent weight to our campaign.* authority, emphasis, gravity, importance, seriousness, significance, substance.

weight verb *The end of the line is weighted with a lump of lead.* ballast, hold down, keep down, load, make heavy, weigh down.

weightless adjective SEE **light** adjective.

weighty adjective 1 *a weighty load.* SEE **heavy**.
2 *a weighty problem.* SEE **serious**.

weir noun dam.

weird adjective 1 *a weird atmosphere in the dungeon.* creepy, eerie, ghostly, mysterious, scary, [*informal*] spooky, supernatural, unaccountable, uncanny, unearthly, unnatural.
OPPOSITES: SEE **natural**.
2 *a weird style of dress.* abnormal, bizarre, [*informal*] cranky, curious, eccentric, [*informal*] funny, grotesque, odd, outlandish, peculiar, queer, quirky, strange, unconventional, unusual, [*informal*] way-out, [*informal*] zany.
OPPOSITES: SEE **conventional**.

weirdie, weirdo nouns SEE **eccentric** noun.

welcome adjective *a welcome rest.* acceptable, agreeable, gratifying, much-needed, [*informal*] nice, pleasant, pleasing, pleasurable.
OPPOSITES: SEE **unwelcome**.

welcome noun *a friendly welcome.* greeting, hospitality, reception.

welcome verb 1 *She welcomed us at the door.* greet, receive.
WORDS USED TO WELCOME PEOPLE: SEE **greeting**.
2 *We welcome constructive criticism.* accept, appreciate, approve of, delight in, like, want.

welcoming adjective SEE **friendly**.

weld verb bond, cement, SEE **fasten**, fuse, join, solder, unite.

welfare noun *Nurses look after the welfare of patients.* good, happiness, health, interests, prosperity, well-being.

welkin noun SEE **sky**.

well adjective *You look well.* fit, healthy, hearty, lively, robust, sound, strong, thriving, vigorous.

well noun 1 *water from a well.* artesian well, borehole, oasis, shaft, spring, waterhole, wishing-well.
2 *oil from a well.* gusher, oil well.

well verb SEE **flow** verb.

well-behaved adjective *a well-behaved class.* co-operative, disciplined, docile, dutiful, good, hard-working, law-abiding, manageable, [*informal*] nice, SEE **obedient**, polite, quiet, well-trained.
OPPOSITES: SEE **naughty**.

well-being noun SEE **happiness, health**.

well-bred adjective SEE **polite**.

well-built adjective *a well-built young person.* athletic, big, brawny, burly, hefty, muscular, powerful, stocky, [*informal*] strapping, strong, sturdy, upstanding.
OPPOSITES: undersized, SEE **small**.

well-disposed adjective SEE **friendly, kind** adjective.

well-dressed adjective SEE **smart** adjective.

well-groomed adjective SEE **tidy** adjective.

well-heeled adjective SEE **wealthy**.

wellington noun SEE **shoe**.

well-known adjective 1 *a well-known person.* SEE **famous**.
2 *a well-known fact. a well-known beauty spot.* SEE **public** adjective.

well-mannered adjective SEE **polite**.

well-meaning adjective [usually implies *kind but misguided*] *His well-meaning remarks misfired.* good-natured, SEE **kind** adjective, obliging, sincere, well-intentioned, well-meant.
OPPOSITES: SEE **malicious**.

well-off adjective SEE **wealthy**.

well-read adjective SEE **educated**.

well-spoken adjective SEE **polite**.

well-to-do adjective SEE **wealthy**.

welsh verb SEE **swindle** verb.

welt noun SEE **wound** noun.

welter verb SEE **wallow**.

wench noun SEE **girl**.

wend verb SEE **go**.

west noun GEOGRAPHICAL TERMS: SEE **geography**.

western noun *I watched a western on TV.* SEE **film**.

wet adjective 1 *wet clothes. wet grass.* awash, bedraggled, clammy, damp, dank, dewy, drenched, dripping, moist, muddy, saturated, sloppy, soaked, soaking, sodden, soggy, sopping, soused, spongy, submerged, waterlogged, watery, wringing.
2 *wet weather.* drizzly, humid, misty, pouring, rainy, showery.
WORDS TO DESCRIBE WEATHER: SEE **weather** noun.
3 *wet paint.* runny, sticky, tacky.
OPPOSITES: SEE **dry** adjective.

wet noun *Come in out of the wet.* dampness, drizzle, rain.

wet verb *Wet the soil before you plant the seeds.* dampen, douse, drench, irrigate, moisten, saturate, soak, spray, sprinkle, steep, water.
OPPOSITES: SEE **dry** verb.

wether noun SEE **sheep**.

whack noun, verb SEE **hit** noun, verb.

whacked adjective SEE **tired**.

whacking adjective SEE **large**.

wharf noun SEE **landing-stage**.

wheat noun corn.
OTHER CEREALS: SEE **cereal**.

wheedle verb SEE **coax**.

wheel noun KINDS OF WHEEL: bogie, castor, cog-wheel, spinning-wheel, steering-wheel.
PARTS OF A WHEEL: axle, hub, rim, spoke, tyre.

wheel verb *Gulls wheeled overhead.* SEE **circle** verb, gyrate, move in circles.
to wheel round *He wheeled round when he heard her voice.* change direction, swerve, swing round, turn, veer.

wheeze verb breathe noisily, cough, gasp, pant, puff.

whelp noun SEE **dog** noun.

whereabouts noun SEE **location**.

wherewithal noun SEE **money**.

whet verb 1 *to whet a knife.* SEE **sharpen**.
2 *to whet someone's appetite.* SEE **stimulate**.

whetstone noun SEE **sharpener**.

whiff noun *a whiff of cigar smoke.* breath, hint, puff, SEE **smell** noun.

while noun *I saw her a short while ago.* SEE **time** noun.

whim noun *an unaccountable whim.* caprice, desire, fancy, impulse, quirk, urge.

whimper, whine verbs complain, cry, [*informal*] grizzle, groan, moan, snivel, wail, weep, whimper, [*informal*] whinge.
OTHER SOUNDS: SEE **sound** noun.

whinge verb SEE **whine**.

whinny verb neigh.
OTHER SOUNDS: SEE **sound** noun.

whip noun VARIOUS INSTRUMENTS USED FOR WHIPPING: birch, cane, cat, cat-o'-nine-tails, crop, horsewhip, lash, riding-crop, scourge, switch.

whip verb 1 *to whip someone as a punishment.* beat, birch, cane, flagellate, flog, SEE **hit** verb, lash, scourge, [*informal*] tan, thrash.
2 *to whip cream.* beat, stir vigorously, whisk.

whippet noun SEE **dog** noun.

whipping-boy noun scapegoat.

whippy adjective SEE **flexible**.

whirl noun *My mind was in a whirl.* SEE **confusion**.

whirl verb *The dancers whirled round.* SEE **circle** verb, gyrate, pirouette, reel, revolve, rotate, spin, swivel, turn, twirl, twist, wheel.

whirlpool noun eddy, vortex.

whirlwind noun cyclone, tornado, vortex.

whirr noun, verb VARIOUS SOUNDS: SEE **sound** noun.

whisk noun *an egg-whisk.* beater, mixer.

whisk verb *to whisk eggs for an omelette.* beat, mix, stir, whip.

whiskers noun *whiskers on a man's face.* bristles, hairs, moustache.

whisper noun 1 *She spoke in a whisper.* murmur, undertone.
2 *I heard a whisper that they were engaged.* gossip, hearsay, rumour.

whisper verb *Keep quiet—don't even whisper.* breathe, murmur, SEE **talk** verb.

whistle noun *the sound of a whistle.* hooter, pipe, pipes, siren.

whistle verb *to whistle a tune.* blow, pipe.
OTHER SOUNDS: SEE **sound** noun.

white adjective 1 *white sheets.* clean, spotless.
2 *shades of white.* cream, ivory, SEE **pale** adjective, snow-white, snowy, whitish.
white horses SEE **wave** noun.

whiten verb blanch, bleach, etiolate, fade, lighten, pale.

whitewash noun, verb SEE **paint** noun, verb.

whitlow noun SEE **spot** noun.

whittle verb *to whittle a piece of wood.* SEE **shape** verb.
to whittle down SEE **reduce**.

whodunit noun SEE **thriller**.

whole adjective 1 *She told us the whole story.* complete, entire, full, total, unabbreviated, unabridged, uncut, unedited, unexpurgated.
OPPOSITES: SEE **incomplete**.
2 *When we unpacked it, the clock was still whole.* in one piece, intact, integral, perfect, sound, unbroken, undamaged, undivided, unharmed, unhurt.
OPPOSITES: SEE **fragmentary**.

wholesale adjective 1 *wholesale trade.* OPPOSITE: retail.
2 *wholesale destruction.* comprehensive, extensive, general, global, indiscriminate, mass, total, universal, widespread.

wholesome adjective *wholesome food. a wholesome atmosphere.* good, health-giving, healthy, hygienic, nourishing, nutritious, salubrious, sanitary.
OPPOSITES: SEE **unhealthy**.

whoop noun, verb VARIOUS SOUNDS: SEE **sound** noun.

whopper noun SEE **giant** noun.

whopping adjective SEE **large**.

whore noun SEE **prostitute** noun.

whorl noun coil, spiral, turn, twist.

wicked adjective *a wicked deed. a wicked person.* [*informal*] awful, bad, base, dissolute, SEE **evil** adjective, guilty, incorrigible, indefensible, insupportable, intolerable, irresponsible, lost (*a lost soul*), machiavellian, mischievous, naughty, nefarious, offensive, rascally, scandalous, shameful, sinful, sinister, spiteful, [*informal*] terrible, ungodly, unprincipled, unrighteous, vicious, vile, villainous, wrong.
OPPOSITES: SEE **moral** adjective.
a wicked person criminal, mischief-maker, sinner, villain, wretch.

wickedness noun enormity, SEE **evil** noun, guilt, heinousness, immorality, infamy, irresponsibility, [*old-fashioned*] knavery, misconduct, naughtiness, sinfulness, spite, turpitude, unrighteousness, vileness, villainy, wrong, wrongdoing.

wickerwork noun basket-work.

wicket, wicket-gate nouns SEE **gate**.

wide adjective 1 *a wide river. a wide area.* broad, expansive, extensive, large, panoramic (*a panoramic view*), spacious, vast, yawning.
2 *wide sympathies.* all-embracing, broad-minded, catholic, comprehensive, eclectic, encyclopaedic, inclusive, wide-ranging.
3 *wide trousers.* baggy, flared.
OPPOSITES: SEE **narrow**.
4 *I welcomed her with arms open wide.* extended, open, outspread, outstretched.
5 *The shot was wide.* off-course, off target.

widen verb 1 *to widen an opening* broaden, dilate, distend, make wider, open out, spread, stretch.
2 *to widen the scope of a business.* enlarge, expand, extend, increase.

widespread adjective *Disease was widespread.* common, endemic, extensive, far-reaching, general, global, pervasive, prevalent, rife, universal, wholesale.
OPPOSITES: SEE **uncommon**.

widow, widower nouns FAMILY RELATIONSHIPS: SEE **family**.

width noun beam (*of a ship*), breadth diameter (*of a circle*), distance across girth (*of a horse*), span (*of a bridge*), thickness.

wield verb 1 *to wield a tool or weapon* brandish, flourish, handle, hold, manage, ply, use.
2 *to wield influence.* employ, exercise, have, possess.

wife noun spouse.
FAMILY RELATIONSHIPS: SEE **family**.

wig noun toupee.

wigging noun SEE **reprimand** noun.

wiggle verb SEE **wriggle**.

wigwam noun SEE **tent**.

wild adjective 1 *wild animals. wild flowers.* free, natural, uncultivated, undomesticated, untamed.
OPPOSITES: cultivated, SEE **domestic**.

2 *wild tribes.* barbaric, barbarous, savage, uncivilized.
OPPOSITES: SEE **civilized**.
3 *wild country.* deserted, desolate, [*informal*] godforsaken, overgrown, remote, rough, rugged, uncultivated, unenclosed, unfarmed, uninhabited, waste.
OPPOSITES: SEE **cultivated**.
4 *wild behaviour.* aggressive, berserk, boisterous, disorderly, ferocious, fierce, frantic, hysterical, lawless, mad, noisy, obstreperous, out of control, rabid, rampant, rash, reckless, riotous, rowdy, savage, uncontrollable, uncontrolled, undisciplined, ungovernable, unmanageable, unrestrained, unruly, uproarious, violent.
OPPOSITES: SEE **restrained**.
5 *wild weather.* blustery, stormy, tempestuous, turbulent, violent, windy.
OPPOSITES: SEE **calm** adjective.
6 *wild enthusiasm.* eager, excited, extravagant, uninhibited, unrestrained.
7 *wild notions.* crazy, fantastic, impetuous, irrational, SEE **silly**, unreasonable.
8 *a wild guess.* inaccurate, random, unthinking.

wildebeest noun gnu.

wilderness noun *an uncultivated wilderness.* desert, jungle, waste, wasteland, wilds (*out in the wilds*).

wildlife noun ANIMALS: SEE **animal** noun.

vile noun SEE **trick** noun.

wilful adjective **1** *wilful disobedience.* [*informal*] bloody-minded, calculated, conscious, deliberate, intended, intentional, premeditated, voluntary.
OPPOSITES: SEE **accidental**.
2 *a wilful character.* determined, dogged, headstrong, intransigent, obdurate, obstinate, perverse, self-willed, stubborn, uncompromising.
OPPOSITES: SEE **amenable**.

will noun **1** *the will to succeed.* aim, desire, determination, inclination, intention, purpose, resolution, resolve, volition, will-power, wish.
2 *a last will and testament.* SEE **document**.

will verb **1** *We willed her to keep going.* encourage, influence, inspire, wish.
2 *He willed his fortune to his housekeeper.* bequeath, leave, pass on.

willing adjective **1** *willing to help.* content, disposed, eager, [*informal*] game (*I'm game for anything*), inclined, pleased, prepared, ready.
2 *willing workers.* amenable, compliant, consenting, co-operative, enthusiastic, helpful, obliging.
OPPOSITES: SEE **unwilling**.

willowy adjective *a willowy figure.* SEE **graceful**.

wilt verb *The plants wilted in the heat.* become limp, droop, fade, fail, flag, flop, languish, sag, shrivel, weaken, wither.
OPPOSITES: SEE **flourish** verb.

wily adjective *Foxes are supposed to be wily creatures.* artful, astute, clever, crafty, cunning, deceptive, designing, devious, furtive, guileful, ingenious, knowing, scheming, shifty, shrewd, skilful, sly, tricky, underhand.
OPPOSITES: SEE **straightforward**.

win verb **1** *to win in a game or battle.* be victorious, be the winner [SEE **winner**], come first, SEE **conquer**, overcome, prevail, succeed, triumph.
OPPOSITES: SEE **lose**.
2 *to win a prize. to win someone's admiration.* achieve, acquire, [*informal*] carry off, [*informal*] come away with, deserve, earn, gain, get, obtain, [*informal*] pick up, receive, secure, [*informal*] walk away with.

wince noun, verb FACIAL EXPRESSIONS: SEE **expression**.

winch noun, verb SEE **hoist** noun, verb.

wind noun **1** *a blustery wind. a gentle wind.* air-current, blast, breath, breeze, cyclone, draught, gale, gust, hurricane, monsoon, puff, squall, tornado, whirlwind, [*poetic*] zephyr.
2 *wind in the stomach.* flatulence, gas.
wind instruments SEE **brass**, **woodwind**.

wind verb **1** *to wind thread on to a reel.* coil, curl, curve, furl, loop, roll, turn, twine.
2 *The road winds up the hill.* bend, curve, meander, ramble, snake, twist, [*informal*] twist and turn, zigzag.
to wind up SEE **finish** verb.

windbag noun SEE **talkative** (**talkative person**).

wind-cheater noun anorak.
OTHER COATS: SEE **coat** noun.

winding adjective *a winding road.* bending, [*informal*] bendy, circuitous, curving, [*informal*] in and out, indirect, meandering, rambling, roundabout, serpentine, sinuous, snaking, tortuous, [*informal*] twisting and turning, zigzag.
OPPOSITES: SEE **straight**.

windlass noun SEE **hoist** noun.

windless adjective SEE **calm** adjective.

window noun KINDS OF WINDOW: casement, dormer, double-glazed window, embrasure, fanlight, French window, light, oriel, pane, sash window, sky-light, shop window, stained-glass window, windscreen.

window-seat noun SEE **seat** noun.

windscreen noun SEE **window**.

windswept adjective *a windswept moor.* bare, bleak, desolate, exposed, unprotected, windy.
OPPOSITES: SEE **sheltered**.

windy adjective **1** *windy weather.* blowy, blustery, boisterous, breezy, draughty, gusty, squally, stormy.
OPPOSITES: SEE **calm** adjective.
2 *a windy corner.* SEE **windswept**.

wine noun SOME KINDS OF WINE: beaujolais, Burgundy, champagne, chianti, claret, dry wine, hock, Madeira, malmsey, [*informal*] plonk, port, red wine, rosé, sherry, sweet wine, vintage, white wine.
OTHER DRINKS: SEE **drink** noun.

wing noun **1** PARTS OF AIRCRAFT: SEE **aircraft**.
2 *the wing of a car.* mudguard.
PARTS OF A VEHICLE: SEE **vehicle**.
3 *a new wing of a hospital.* annexe, end, extension.
to take wing SEE **fly** verb.

wink verb **1** *to wink an eye.* bat (*didn't bat an eyelid*), blink, flutter.
OTHER GESTURES: SEE **gesture** verb.
2 *The lights winked on and off.* flash, flicker, sparkle, twinkle.

winker noun [*informal*] *the winkers on a car.* indicator, signal, [*old-fashioned*] trafficator.

winner noun [*informal*] champ, champion, conqueror, first, medallist, victor.
OPPOSITES: SEE **loser**.

winning adjective **1** *the winning team.* champion, conquering, first, leading, prevailing, successful, top, top-scoring, triumphant, unbeaten, undefeated, victorious.
OPPOSITES: SEE **losing**.
2 *a winning smile.* SEE **charming**.

winnings noun SEE **money**.

winnow verb SEE **sift**.

winsome adjective SEE **charming**.

winter noun WINTER SPORTS: bob-sleigh, ice-hockey, skating, skiing, sledging, tobogganing.

wintry adjective *wintry weather.* SEE **cold** adjective.
OPPOSITE: summery.

wipe verb *to wipe things clean.* brush, clean, dry, dust, mop, polish, rub, scour, sponge, swab, wash.
to wipe out *to wipe out an ants' nest.* SEE **destroy**.

wire noun **1** *a length of wire.* cable, co-axial cable, flex, lead, [*plural*] wiring.
2 *She sent a wire to say she couldn't come.* cable, telegram.

wireless noun SEE **radio**.

wiry adjective *a wiry figure.* lean, sinewy, strong, thin, tough.

wisdom noun astuteness, common sense, discernment, discrimination, good sense, insight, SEE **intelligence**, judgement, penetration, prudence, reason, sagacity, sense, understanding.
wisdom tooth SEE **tooth**.

wise adjective **1** *a wise judge.* astute, discerning, enlightened, erudite, informed, SEE **intelligent**, judicious, knowledgeable, penetrating, perceptive, perspicacious, philosophical, prudent, rational, reasonable, sagacious, sage, sensible, shrewd, thoughtful, understanding, well-informed.
2 *a wise decision.* advisable, appropriate, fair, just, proper, right, sound.
OPPOSITES: SEE **unwise**.
a wise person philosopher, pundit, sage.
the three wise men magi.

wiseacre noun SEE **expert** noun, know-all.

wisecrack noun, verb SEE **joke** noun, verb.

wish noun *What's your dearest wish?* aim, ambition, aspiration, craving, desire, fancy, hankering, hope, longing, objective, request, want, yearning, [*informal*] yen.

wish verb *I wish that they'd be quiet.* ask, hope.
to wish for *What do you most wish for?* aspire to, covet, crave, desire, fancy, hanker after, long for, want, yearn for

wishy-washy adjective SEE **feeble**.

wisp noun *a wisp of hair. a wisp of cloud.* shred, strand, streak.

wispy adjective *wispy material. wispy clouds.* flimsy, fragile, gossamer, insubstantial, light, streaky, thin.

wistful adjective SEE **sad**.

wit noun **1** *a comedian's wit.* banter, cleverness, comedy, facetiousness, humour, ingenuity, jokes, puns, quickness, quips, repartee, witticisms, word play.
2 *She is quite a wit.* comedian, comic, humorist, jester, joker, [*informal*] wag.
3 *I didn't have the wit to understand.* SEE **intelligence**.

witch noun SEE **magician**.

witchcraft noun SEE **magic** noun.

witch-doctor noun SEE **magician**.

witchery noun SEE **magic** noun.

withdraw verb 1 *to withdraw an objection. to withdraw your troops.* call back, cancel, recall, remove, rescind, take away, take back.
2 *The attackers withdrew.* back away, draw back, fall back, leave, move back, retire, retreat, run away.
OPPOSITES: SEE **advance** verb.
3 *Some competitors withdrew at the last minute.* back out, [*informal*] chicken out, [*informal*] cry off, drop out, pull out, secede.
OPPOSITES: SEE **enter**.

withdrawn adjective SEE **reserved**.

wither verb *Plants withered in the drought.* become dry, become limp, dehydrate, desiccate, droop, dry out, dry up, fail, flag, flop, sag, shrink, shrivel, waste away, wilt.
OPPOSITES: SEE **thrive**.

withhold verb *to withhold information.* conceal, hide, hold back, keep back, keep secret, repress, retain, suppress.

withstand verb *to withstand an attack.* bear, brave, cope with, defy, endure, hold out against, last out against, oppose, [*informal*] put up with, resist, stand up to, survive, tolerate, weather (*to weather a storm*).
OPPOSITES: SEE **surrender**.

witless adjective SEE **silly**.

witness noun 1 *a witness of an accident.* bystander, eye-witness, looker-on, observer, onlooker, spectator, watcher.
2 *a witness in a legal case.* LEGAL TERMS: SEE **law**.
to bear witness SEE **testify**.

witness verb *to witness an accident.* attend, behold, be present at, look on, observe, see, view, watch.
2 *to witness in a lawcourt.* SEE **testify**.

witticism noun SEE **joke** noun.

witty adjective *a witty storyteller.* amusing, clever, comic, facetious, funny, humorous, ingenious, intelligent, quick-witted, sharp-witted, waggish.
OPPOSITES: SEE **dull** adjective.

wizard noun 1 SEE **magician**, sorcerer, [*old-fashioned*] warlock.
2 *a wizard with engines.* SEE **expert** noun.

wizardry noun SEE **magic** noun.

wizened adjective SEE **wrinkled**.

woad noun SEE **colouring**.

wobble verb be unsteady, heave, move unsteadily, oscillate, quake, quiver, rock, shake, sway, teeter, totter, tremble, vacillate, vibrate, waver.

wobbly adjective *a wobbly stone.* insecure, loose, rickety, rocky, shaky, teetering, tottering, unbalanced, unsafe, unstable, unsteady.
OPPOSITES: SEE **steady** adjective.

wodge noun SEE **lump** noun.

woe noun SEE **sorrow** noun.

woebegone, woeful SEE **sad**.

wok noun COOKING UTENSILS: SEE **cook** verb.

wold noun SEE **hill**.

wolf verb *to wolf your food.* SEE **eat**.

woman noun bride, [*old-fashioned*] dame, [*old-fashioned*] damsel, daughter, dowager, female, girl, girlfriend, [*uncomplimentary*] hag, [*uncomplimentary*] harridan, housewife, hoyden, [*uncomplimentary, old-fashioned*] hussy, lady, lass, [*formal*] madam or Madame, maid, [*old-fashioned*] maiden, matriarch, matron, mistress, mother, [*uncomplimentary*] termagant, [*uncomplimentary*] virago, virgin, widow, wife.
FAMILY RELATIONSHIPS: SEE **family**.

Some words connected with the concept *woman* are related to Greek *gune* = *woman*, e.g. *gynaecology, misogynist.*

womanly adjective SEE **feminine**.

womb noun uterus.

wonder noun 1 *We gasped with wonder.* admiration, amazement, astonishment, awe, bewilderment, curiosity, fascination, respect, reverence, surprise, wonderment.
2 *It was a wonder that she recovered.* marvel, miracle.

wonder verb *I wonder if dinner is ready?* ask yourself, be curious about, conjecture, ponder, question yourself, speculate, think.
to wonder at *We wondered at their skill.* admire, be amazed by, feel wonder at [SEE **wonder** noun], gape at, marvel at.

wonderful adjective 1 *She made a wonderful recovery.* amazing, astonishing, astounding, extraordinary, incredible, marvellous, miraculous, phenomenal, remarkable, surprising, unexpected, [*old-fashioned*] wondrous.
OPPOSITES: SEE **normal**.
2 [*informal*] *The food was wonderful.* SEE **excellent**.

wonderment noun SEE **wonder** noun.

wondrous adjective SEE **wonderful**.

wonted adjective SEE **usual**.

woo verb 1 [*old-fashioned*] *to woo a girlfriend or boyfriend.* court, make love to.

2 *The shop is wooing new customers.* attract, bring in, coax, cultivate, persuade, pursue, seek, try to get.

Some words connected with the concept *wood* are related to Latin words *arbor* = *tree*, *lignum* = *wood*, and *silva* = *a wood*, and to Greek *xulon* = *wood*. e.g. *arboreal*, *arboretum*; *ligneous*, *lignite*; *silvan*, *silviculture*; *xylophone*.

wood noun **1** *We went for a walk in the wood.* afforestation, coppice, copse, forest, grove, jungle, orchard, plantation, spinney, thicket, trees, woodland, woods.
2 *A carpenter works with wood.* blockboard, chipboard, deal, planks, plywood, timber.

KINDS OF WOOD OFTEN USED TO MAKE THINGS: balsa, beech, cedar, chestnut, ebony, elm, mahogany, oak, pine, rosewood, sandalwood, sapele, teak, walnut.

woodbine noun honeysuckle.

wooded adjective *a wooded hillside.* afforested, silvan, timbered, tree-covered, woody.

wooden adjective **1** *wooden furniture.* timber, wood.
2 *a wooden performance.* emotionless, expressionless, hard, inflexible, lifeless, rigid, stiff, unbending, unemotional, unnatural.
OPPOSITES: SEE **lively**.

woodland noun SEE **wood**.

woodman noun forester.

woodwind noun WOODWIND INSTRUMENTS: bassoon, clarinet, cor anglais, flute, oboe, piccolo, recorder.
OTHER INSTRUMENTS: SEE **music**.

woodwork noun carpentry, joinery.

woody adjective **1** *a woody substance. a woody plant.* fibrous, hard, ligneous, tough, wooden.
2 *a woody hillside.* afforested, silvan, timbered, tree-covered, wooded.

woof noun, verb VARIOUS SOUNDS: SEE **sound** noun.

woolly adjective **1** *a woolly jumper.* wool, woollen.
2 *a woolly teddybear.* cuddly, downy, fleecy, furry, fuzzy, hairy, shaggy, soft.
3 *woolly ideas.* ambiguous, blurry, confused, hazy, ill-defined, indefinite, indistinct, uncertain, unclear, unfocused, vague.

word noun **1** *A thesaurus is a book of words.* expression, term.
LINGUISTIC TERMS: SEE **language**.
2 *Have you had any word from granny?* SEE **news**.
3 *You gave me your word.* SEE **promise** noun.
word for word SEE **verbatim**.

Some English words connected with the concept *word* are related to Latin *verba* = *word* [e.g. *verbal*, *verbatim*]; or to Greek *lexis* = *word* [e.g. *lexical*, *lexicography*]; or to Greek *logos* = *word* [e.g. *dialogue*, *philology*].

word verb *I spent ages thinking how to word my letter.* SEE **express** verb.

wording noun *the wording of a letter.* choice of words, diction, expression, language, phraseology, phrasing, style, terminology.

word-processor noun OTHER TOOLS TO WRITE WITH: SEE **write**.

wordy adjective *a wordy lecture. a wordy speaker.* diffuse, garrulous, long-winded, loquacious, pleonastic, prolix, rambling, repetitious, talkative, tautological, unstoppable, verbose.
OPPOSITES: SEE **brief** adjective.

work noun **1** *He hates hard work.* [informal] donkey-work, drudgery, effort, exertion, [informal] fag, [informal] graft, [informal] grind, industry, labour, [informal] plod (*It was sheer plod*), slavery, [informal] slog, [informal] spadework, [informal] sweat, toil.
2 *He set me work to do.* assignment, chore, commission, homework, housework, job, project, task, undertaking.
3 *What work do you do?* business, employment, job, livelihood, living, occupation, profession, trade.
VARIOUS KINDS OF WORK: SEE **job**.

work verb **1** [informal] beaver away, be busy, drudge, exert yourself, [informal] fag, [informal] grind away, [informal] to keep your nose to the grindstone, labour, make efforts, [informal] peg away, [informal] plug away, [informal] potter about, slave, sweat, toil.
2 *She works her staff hard.* drive, exploit.
3 *Does your watch work? I hope my plan works.* act, be effective, function, go, operate, perform, run, succeed, thrive.
to work out *to work out answers.* SEE **calculate**.
to work up *to work up an appetite.* SEE **develop**.
worked up SEE **excited**.

workable adjective SEE **practicable**.

workaday adjective SEE **ordinary**.

worker noun [In British society, *worker* is usually seen as being opposite to *manager* or *owner*.] artisan, coolie, craftsman, employee, [*old-fashioned*] hand, labourer, member of staff, member of the working class, navvy, operative, operator, peasant, practitioner, servant, slave, tradesman, working man, working woman, workman.
WORKERS IN SPECIFIC JOBS: SEE **job**.

work-force noun employees, staff, workers [SEE **worker**].

working adjective **1** *a working woman.* employed, in work, practising.
OPPOSITES: SEE **unemployed**.
2 *Is the machine working?* functioning, going, in use, in working order, operational, running, usable.
OPPOSITES: SEE **defective**.

workman noun SEE **worker**.

workmanlike adjective *a workmanlike job.* SEE **competent**.

workmanship noun *We admired the blacksmith's workmanship.* art, artistry, competence, craft, craftsmanship, expertise, handicraft, handiwork, skill, technique.

workshop noun factory, mill, smithy, studio, workroom.

work-shy adjective SEE **lazy**.

world noun earth, globe, planet.
GEOGRAPHICAL TERMS: SEE **geography**.

world-famous adjective SEE **famous**.

worldly adjective *worldly things. a worldly outlook.* avaricious, earthly, greedy, material, materialistic, mundane, physical, selfish, temporal.
OPPOSITES: SEE **spiritual**.

worm verb *I wormed my way through the undergrowth.* crawl, creep, slither, squirm, wriggle, writhe.

worn adjective *worn at the elbows.* frayed, moth-eaten, SEE **old**, ragged, [*informal*] scruffy, shabby, tattered, [*informal*] tatty, thin, threadbare, worn-out.

worried adjective *worried about your work. worried about a sick relative.* afraid, agitated, anxious, apprehensive, bothered, concerned, distressed, disturbed, edgy, fearful, nervous, nervy, neurotic, obsessed (by), overwrought, perplexed, perturbed, solicitous, tense, troubled, uneasy, unhappy, upset, vexed.

worrisome adjective SEE **troublesome**.

worry noun **1** *She's in a constant state of worry.* agitation, anxiety, apprehension, distress, fear, neurosis, tension, uneasiness, vexation.

2 *She has a lot of worries.* burden, care, concern, misgiving, problem, [*informal, plural*] trials and tribulations, trouble.

worry verb **1** *Don't worry me while I'm busy.* agitate, annoy, [*informal*] badger, bother, distress, disturb, [*informal*] hassle, irritate, molest, nag, perplex, perturb, pester, plague, tease, torment, trouble, upset, vex.
2 *He worries about money.* agonize, be worried [SEE **worried**], brood, exercise yourself, feel uneasy, fret.

worrying adjective *worrying symptoms.* disquieting, distressing, disturbing, perturbing, SEE **troublesome**.
OPPOSITES: SEE **reassuring**.

worsen verb **1** *to worsen a situation.* aggravate, exacerbate, make worse.
2 *My temper worsened as the day went on.* become worse, decline, degenerate, deteriorate, get worse.
OPPOSITES: SEE **improve**.

worship noun *the worship of an idol.* adoration, adulation, deification, devotion, glorification, idolatry, love, praise, reverence (for), veneration.

PLACES OF WORSHIP: abbey, basilica, cathedral, chapel, church, meeting house, minster, mosque, oratory, pagoda, sanctuary, synagogue, tabernacle, temple.

---

worship verb **1** *She worships her grandad.* adore, be devoted to, deify, dote on, hero-worship, idolize, lionize, look up to, love, revere, reverence, venerate.
2 *to worship God.* glorify, laud, [*old-fashioned*] magnify, praise, pray to.

worth noun *What's the worth of this?* cost, importance, merit, price, quality, significance, use, usefulness, utility, value.
to be worth be priced at, cost, have a value of.

worthless adjective *worthless junk. worthless advice.* frivolous, futile, [*informal*] good-for-nothing, hollow, insignificant, meaningless, meretricious, paltry, pointless, poor, [*informal*] rubbishy, [*informal*] trashy, trifling, trivial, trumpery, unimportant, unusable, useless, valueless.
OPPOSITES: SEE **valuable, worthwhile**.

worthwhile adjective *a worthwhile sum of money. a worthwhile effort.* advantageous, beneficial, biggish, considerable, good, helpful, important, invaluable, meaningful, noticeable, productive, profitable, rewarding, significant, sizeable, substantial, useful, valuable, SEE **worthy**.
OPPOSITES: SEE **worthless**.

worthy adjective *a worthy cause. a worthy winner.* admirable, commendable, creditable, decent, deserving, good, honest, honourable, laudable, meritorious, praiseworthy, reputable, respectable, worthwhile.
OPPOSITES: SEE **unworthy**.

would-be adjective SEE **aspiring**.

wound noun disfigurement, hurt, injury, scar.

wound verb *Several were wounded in the accident.* cause pain to, damage, disfigure, harm, hurt, injure.

KINDS OF WOUND: amputation, bite, bruise, burn, cut, fracture, gash, graze, laceration, lesion, mutilation, scab, scald, scar, scratch, sore, sprain, stab, sting, strain, weal, welt.

WAYS TO WOUND: bite, blow up, bruise, burn, claw, cut, fracture, gash, gore, graze, SEE **hit** verb, impale, knife, lacerate, maim, make sore, mangle, maul, mutilate, scald, scratch, shoot, sprain, stab, sting, strain, torture.

wraith noun SEE **ghost**.

wrangle noun, verb SEE **quarrel** noun, verb.

wrap noun *a warm wrap round her shoulders.* cape, cloak, mantle, shawl, stole.

wrap verb *We wrapped it in brown paper.* bind, bundle up, cloak, cocoon, conceal, cover, encase, enclose, enfold, envelop, hide, insulate, lag, muffle, pack, package, shroud, surround, swaddle, swathe, wind.
OPPOSITES: SEE **open** verb.

wrapper noun SEE **cover** noun.

wrath noun SEE **anger** noun.

wrathful adjective SEE **angry**.

wreak verb *to wreak vengeance.* SEE **inflict**.

wreathe verb *wreathed in flowers.* adorn, decorate, encircle, festoon, intertwine, interweave, twist, weave.

wreck noun 1 *a broken wreck.* shipwreck, SEE **wreckage**.
2 *the wreck of all our hopes.* demolition, destruction, devastation, overthrow, ruin, termination, undoing.

wreck verb 1 *The ship was wrecked on the rocks. He wrecked his car.* break up, crumple, crush, demolish, destroy, shatter, shipwreck, smash, [*informal*] write off.

2 *The storm wrecked our picnic.* ruin, spoil.

wreckage noun bits, debris, [*informal*] flotsam and jetsam, fragments, pieces, remains, rubble, ruins.

wrench noun *The handle turns if you give it a wrench.* jerk, pull, tug, twist, [*informal*] yank.

wrench verb *to wrench a lid off. to wrench something out of shape.* force, jerk, lever, prize, pull, strain, tug, twist, wrest, wring, [*informal*] yank.

wrest verb SEE **wring**.

wrestle verb SEE **fight** verb, grapple, struggle, tussle.

wrestler noun SEE **fighter**.

wretch noun 1 *homeless wretches.* beggar, down and out, miserable person, pauper.
2 [*uncomplimentary*] *a villainous wretch* SEE **wicked** (wicked person).

wretched adjective 1 *a wretched look on his face.* SEE **miserable**.
2 [*informal*] *The wretched car won't start* SEE **unsatisfactory**.

wriggle verb *The snake wriggled away* snake, squirm, twist, waggle, wiggle, worm, writhe, zigzag.

wring verb 1 *to wring someone's hand* clasp, grip, shake.
2 *to wring water out of wet clothes.* compress, crush, press, squeeze, twist.
3 *to wring a promise out of someone* coerce, exact, extort, extract, force, wrench, wrest.

wringer noun SEE **drier**.

wringing adjective SEE **wet** adjective.

wrinkle noun *wrinkles in cloth. wrinkle in your face.* corrugation, crease, crinkle, [*informal*] crow's feet [= *wrinkles at the side of your eyes*], dimple, fold, furrow, gather, line, pleat, pucker, ridge.

wrinkle verb *Don't wrinkle the carpet* crease, crinkle, crumple, fold, furrow, make wrinkles (in), pucker up, ridge, ruck up, rumple.
OPPOSITES: SEE **smooth** verb.

wrinkled adjective *a wrinkled face. wrinkled surface.* corrugated, creased, crinkly, crumpled, furrowed, lined, pleated, ridged, rumpled, shrivelled, wavy, wizened, wrinkly.

wrist noun SEE **arm** noun.

wristlet noun bracelet.

writ noun SEE **command** noun.

write verb *to write a shopping list. to write your thoughts. to write a book.* compile compose, copy, correspond [= to write letters], doodle, draft, draw up, engrave, inscribe, jot down, note, pen, print, record, scrawl, scribble, set down, take down, transcribe, type.

TOOLS YOU WRITE WITH: ballpoint, Biro, chalk, crayon, felt-tip, fountain-pen, ink, pen, pencil, typewriter, word-processor.
THINGS YOU WRITE ON: blackboard, card, exercise book, form, jotter, notepaper, pad, paper, papyrus, parchment, postcard, stationery, writing-paper.

writer noun 1 [= person who writes things down] amanuensis, clerk, copyist, [uncomplimentary] pen-pusher, scribe, secretary, typist.
2 [= person who creates literature or music] author, [joking] bard, composer, [uncomplimentary] hack, poet.

VARIOUS WRITERS: biographer, columnist, copy-writer, correspondent, diarist, dramatist, essayist, ghost-writer, journalist, leader-writer, librettist, novelist, playwright, poet, reporter, scriptwriter.

writhe verb to writhe in agony. coil, contort, jerk, squirm, struggle, thrash about, thresh about, twist, wriggle.

writing noun 1 Can you read this writing? calligraphy, characters, copperplate, cuneiform, handwriting, hieroglyphics, inscription, italics, letters, longhand, notation, penmanship, printing, runes, scrawl, screed, scribble, script, shorthand.
2 The children were busy at their writing. authorship, composition.
writings the writings of Shakespeare. literary texts, literature, texts, works.

KINDS OF WRITING: article, autobiography, biography, children's literature, comedy, copy-writing, correspondence, crime story, criticism, detective story, diary, documentary, drama, editorial, epic, epistle, essay, fable, fairy story or fairy-tale, fantasy, fiction, folk-tale.
history, journalism, legal document, legend, letter, libretto, lyric, monograph, mystery, myth, newspaper column, non-fiction, novel, parable, parody, philosophy, play, SEE **poem**, propaganda, prose, reportage, romance.

saga, satire, science fiction, scientific writing, scriptwriting, SF, sketch, story, tale, thriller, tragi-comedy, tragedy, travel writing, treatise, trilogy, TV script, verse, [informal] whodunit, yarn.

written adjective written evidence. documentary, [informal] in black and white, inscribed, in writing, set down, transcribed, typewritten.
OPPOSITES: SEE **unwritten**.

wrong adjective 1 He was wrong to steal. Cruelty to animals is wrong. SEE **bad**, base, blameworthy, corrupt, criminal, crooked, deceitful, dishonest, dishonourable, evil, felonious, illegal, illicit, immoral, iniquitous, irresponsible, naughty, reprehensible, sinful, unethical, unlawful, unprincipled, unscrupulous, vicious, villainous, wicked.
2 a wrong answer. a wrong decision. erroneous, fallacious, false, imprecise, improper, inaccurate, incorrect, inexact, misinformed, mistaken, unacceptable, unfair, unjust, untrue, wrongful.
3 I put on the wrong coat. He came the wrong way. abnormal, inappropriate, incongruous, inconvenient, unconventional, unsuitable, worst.
4 What's wrong with the car? There's something wrong here. amiss, broken down, defective, faulty, out of order, unusable.
OPPOSITES: SEE **right** adjective.

wrong noun SEE **wrongdoing**.
to do wrong default, err, go astray, SEE **misbehave**, **sin** verb.

wrong verb I wronged him when I accused him without evidence. abuse, be unfair to, cheat, do an injustice to, harm, hurt, maltreat, misrepresent, mistreat, traduce, treat unfairly.

wrongdoer noun convict, criminal, crook, culprit, delinquent, evildoer, law-breaker, malefactor, mischief-maker, miscreant, offender, sinner, transgressor.

wrongdoing noun crime, delinquency, disobedience, evil, immorality, indiscipline, iniquity, malpractice, misbehaviour, mischief, naughtiness, offence, sin, sinfulness, wickedness.

wrongful adjective wrongful dismissal. SEE **unjust**.

wrongheaded adjective SEE **obstinate**.

wry adjective 1 a wry smile. askew, awry, bent, crooked, distorted, twisted, uneven.
2 a wry sense of humour. droll, dry, ironic, mocking, sardonic.

X

xenophobia noun SEE **patriotism**.
Xerox noun, verb SEE **copy** noun, verb.
xylophone noun PERCUSSION INSTRUMENTS: SEE **percussion**.

Y

yacht noun VARIOUS BOATS: SEE **vessel**.
yachtsman noun SEE **sailor**.
yam noun sweet potato.
yank verb SEE **tug** verb.
yap noun, verb VARIOUS SOUNDS: SEE **sound** noun.
yard noun 1 OTHER UNITS OF MEASUREMENT: SEE **measure** noun.
2 *a back yard.* court, courtyard, enclosure, garden, [*informal*] quad, quadrangle.
yardstick noun SEE **standard** noun.
yarn noun 1 *yarn woven into cloth.* SEE **thread** noun.
2 [*informal*] *a sailor's yarn.* anecdote, narrative, story, tale.
yashmak noun veil.
yaw verb SEE **turn** verb.
yawn noun OTHER FACIAL EXPRESSIONS: SEE **expression**.
yawning adjective *a yawning hole.* gaping, open, wide.
year noun OTHER UNITS OF TIME: SEE **time** noun.
yearly adjective *a yearly payment.* annual.
yearn verb SEE **long** verb.
yearning noun SEE **longing**.
yell noun, verb SEE **shout** noun, verb.
yellow adjective SHADES OF YELLOW: amber, chrome yellow, cream, gold, golden, orange, tawny.
OTHER COLOURS: SEE **colour** noun.
yelp noun, verb VARIOUS SOUNDS: SEE **sound** noun.
yen noun [*informal*] *a yen for sweets.* SEE **longing**.
yeoman noun SEE **farmer**.
yeti noun abominable snowman.
yield noun 1 *a good yield from our fruit-trees.* crop, harvest, produce, product.
2 *a good yield from my investment.* earnings, income, interest, profit, return.

yield verb 1 *to yield to your opponent.* acquiesce, bow, capitulate, [*informal*] cave in, cede, concede, defer, give in, give way, submit, succumb, surrender, [*informal*] throw in the towel, [*informal*] throw up the sponge.
2 *Our fruit-trees yield a big crop.* bear, grow, produce, supply.
3 *This investment yields a high interest.* earn, generate, pay out, provide, return.

yielding adjective SEE **soft**.

yob noun SEE **hooligan**.

yodel verb VARIOUS SOUNDS: SEE **sound** noun.

yoga noun SEE **meditation**.

yoke noun SEE **burden** noun, **link** noun.

yoke verb *to yoke things together.* SEE **link** verb.

young adjective 1 *young plants. young animals, young birds.* baby, early, growing, immature, newborn, undeveloped, unfledged, youngish, youthful.
2 *They're young for their age.* babyish, boyish, childish, girlish, immature, infantile, juvenile, puerile.

YOUNG PEOPLE: adolescent, baby, boy, [*uncomplimentary*] brat, child, girl, infant, juvenile, [*informal*] kid, lad, lass, [*informal*] nipper, teenager, toddler, [*uncomplimentary*] urchin, youngster, youth.

YOUNG ANIMALS: bullock, calf, colt, cub, fawn, foal, heifer, kid, kitten, lamb, leveret, piglet, puppy, whelp, yearling.

YOUNG BIRDS: chick, cygnet, duckling, fledgeling, gosling, nestling, pullet.

YOUNG FISH: elver [= *young eel*], [*plural*] fry, grilse [= *young salmon*].

YOUNG PLANTS: cutting, sapling, seedling.

young noun *Parents have an instinct to protect their young.* brood, family, issue, litter, offspring, progeny.

youngster noun SEE **youth**.

youth noun 1 *Grown-ups look back on their youth.* adolescence, babyhood, boyhood, childhood, girlhood, growing up, immaturity, infancy, [*informal*] teens.
2 [*often uncomplimentary*] *a noisy crowd of youths.* adolescent, boy, juvenile, [*informal*] kid, [*informal*] lad, stripling, teenager, youngster.
youth hostel SEE **accommodation**.

youthful adjective 1 *a youthful audience*
SEE **young** adjective.
2 [*complimentary*] *youthful in appearance*,
fresh, lively, sprightly, vigorous, well-
preserved, young-looking.
3 [*uncomplimentary*] *youthful behaviour*.
babyish, boyish, childish, girlish, immature, inexperienced, infantile, juvenile, puerile.

yowl noun, verb SEE **cry** noun, verb.
OTHER SOUNDS: SEE **sound** noun.

yule, yuletide nouns Christmas.

Z

zany adjective SEE **absurd, eccentric**.

zeal noun SEE **enthusiasm**.

zealot noun SEE **fanatic**.

zealous adjective *a zealous official*.
conscientious, diligent, eager, earnest,
enthusiastic, fanatical, fervent, keen,
passionate.
OPPOSITES: SEE **apathetic**.

zebra noun VARIOUS ANIMALS: SEE **animal** noun.
zebra crossing pedestrian crossing.

zenith noun 1 *The sun was at its zenith*.
highest point, meridian.
2 *He's at the zenith of his career*. acme,
apex, climax, height, peak, pinnacle,
top.
OPPOSITES: SEE **nadir**.

zephyr noun SEE **wind** noun.

zero noun SEE **nothing**.

zero verb **to zero in on** SEE **aim** verb.

zest noun *We tucked into the food with zest*.
eagerness, energy, enjoyment, enthusiasm, liveliness, pleasure, zeal.

zigzag adjective *a zigzag route*. bendy,
crooked, [*informal*] in and out, indirect,
meandering,   serpentine,   twisting,
winding.

zigzag verb *The road zigzags up the hill*.
bend, curve, meander, snake, tack (*to
tack against the wind*), twist, wind.

zip noun zip-fastener, [*informal*] zipper.
OTHER FASTENERS: SEE **fastener**.

zip verb 1 *Zip up your bag*. SEE **fasten**.
2 [*informal*] *She zipped along the road*.
SEE **zoom**.

zippy adjective SEE **lively**.

zodiac noun astrological signs.

SIGNS OF THE ZODIAC: Aquarius [*Water-
Carrier*], Aries [*Ram*], Cancer [*Crab*],
Capricorn [*Goat*], Gemini [*Twins*], Leo
[*Lion*], Libra [*Scales*], Pisces [*Fish*],
Sagittarius [*Archer*], Scorpio [*Scorpion*],
Taurus [*Bull*], Virgo [*Virgin*].

zombie noun SEE **spirit**.

zone noun *No one may enter the forbidden
zone*. area, district, locality, neighbourhood, region, sector, sphere, territory,
tract, vicinity.

zoo noun menagerie, safari-park, zoolo-
gical gardens.
VARIOUS ANIMALS: SEE **animal** noun.

zoom verb [*informal*] *She zoomed home
with her good news*. dash, hurry, hurtle,
SEE **move** verb, race, rush, speed, [*informal*] whiz, [*informal*] zip.
zoom lens PHOTOGRAPHIC EQUIPMENT:
SEE **photography**.

Notes

Notes

Notes

Notes

Notes

Notes

Notes